Praise for Brandon Sanderson and
The Way of Kings

"I *loved* this book. What else is there to say?"
—Patrick Rothfuss,
New York Times bestselling author of
The Name of the Wind and *The Wise Man's Fear*

"Sanderson, the author of *Elantris* and the Mistborn trilogy, once again creates an interesting world with a novel system of magic, but the best part of this series launch is the compelling, complex story of Dalinar, Kaladin, and Shallan as they struggle through emotional, physical, and moral challenges. Verdict: Sanderson is a master of hooking the reader in the first few pages, and once again he doesn't disappoint. Fans and lovers of epic fantasy will find the ending satisfying, yet will eagerly await the next volume."
—*Library Journal*

"It's rare for a fiction writer to have much understanding of how leadership works and how love really takes root in the human heart. Sanderson is astonishingly wise."
—Orson Scott Card

"Sanderson's skill and pure narrative power did not lose me at all over the course of time it took me to read the book or [over] the great page count he took to tell the story. Though it is a long novel . . . I can't say that it felt like a long tale. It felt epic and powerful, a story and world I was pleased to be immersed in during the entire reading experience of the novel.

"Sanderson has proved with his past novels he is a voice to be heard and recognized in the fantasy genre. With *The Way of Kings*, he stakes his claim as one of the preeminent purveyors of the fantasy genre—he will be spoken in the same breath as Tolkien, Leiber, Moorcock, Jordan (on his own merits and not just because he is completing The Wheel of Time), and George R. R. Martin. I have extremely high anticipation for future volumes in this series, and despite this being the first of a multivolume series, it ends with closure.

"I give this book my highest recommendation and think *The Way of Kings* will be one of those landmark novels of epic fantasy against which future novels will always be measured." —Rob H. Bedford, *SFFworld.com*

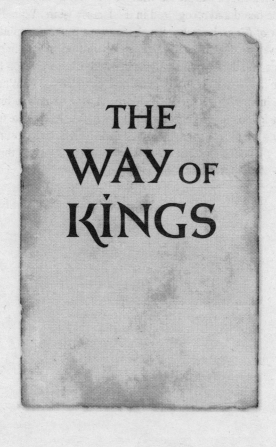

THE
WAY OF
KINGS

BY BRANDON SANDERSON®

THE STORMLIGHT ARCHIVE®
The Way of Kings
Words of Radiance
Oathbringer
Rhythm of War

THE MISTBORN® SAGA

THE ORIGINAL TRILOGY
Mistborn
The Well of Ascension
The Hero of Ages

THE WAX AND WAYNE SERIES
The Alloy of Law
Shadows of Self
The Bands of Mourning

Elantris
Warbreaker
Arcanum Unbounded: The Cosmere® Collection
Legion: The Many Lives of Stephen Leeds

ALCATRAZ VS. THE EVIL LIBRARIANS
Alcatraz vs. the Evil Librarians
The Scrivener's Bones
The Knights of Crystallia
The Shattered Lens
The Dark Talent

THE RECKONERS
Steelheart
Firefight
Calamity

SKYWARD
Skyward
Starsight

The Rithmatist

THE
WAY OF
KINGS

Book One of
THE STORMLIGHT ARCHIVE®

BRANDON
SANDERSON

TOR®
fantasy

A TOM DOHERTY ASSOCIATES BOOK • NEW YORK

This is a work of fiction. All of the characters, organizations, and events portrayed in this novel are either products of the author's imagination or are used fictitiously.

THE WAY OF KINGS

Copyright © 2010 by Dragonsteel Entertainment, LLC

Mistborn®, The Stormlight Archive®, Reckoners®, Cosmere®, and Brandon Sanderson® are registered trademarks of Dragonsteel Entertainment, LLC

All rights reserved.

Interior illustrations by Isaac Stewart, Ben McSweeney, and Greg Call

Edited by Moshe Feder

A Tor Book
Published by Tom Doherty Associates
120 Broadway
New York, NY 10271

www.tor-forge.com

Tor® is a registered trademark of Macmillan Publishing Group, LLC.

ISBN 978-0-7653-6527-9

Our books may be purchased in bulk for promotional, educational, or business use. Please contact your local bookseller or the Macmillan Corporate and Premium Sales Department at 1-800-221-7945, extension 5442, or by email at MacmillanSpecialMarkets@macmillan.com.

First Edition: August 2010
First Mass Market Edition: June 2011

Printed in the United States of America

20 19 18 17

For Emily,
    Who is too patient
        Too kindly
            And too wonderful
    For words.
    But I try anyway.

ACKNOWLEDGMENTS

I finished the first draft of *The Way of Kings* in 2003, but I started working on pieces of the book back in the late '90s. Threads of this novel go back even further in my brain. No book of mine has spent longer simmering; I've spent more than a decade building this novel. And so it should be no surprise that a lot of people have helped me with it. It's going to be impossible to mention them all; my memory simply isn't that good. However, there are some major players that I would like to thank most deeply.

First comes my wife, Emily, to whom this book is dedicated. She gave greatly of herself to see the novel come to pass. That included not only reading and giving advice on the manuscript, but giving up her husband during long stretches of writing time. If you readers get a chance to meet her, some thanks might be in order. (She likes chocolate.)

As always, my excellent editor and agent—Moshe Feder and Joshua Bilmes—worked quite hard on this novel. Moshe, by special note, doesn't get paid more when his authors turn in 400k-word monstrosities. But he edited the novel without a word of complaint; his help was invaluable in turning it into the novel you now hold. He also got F. Paul Wilson to check over the medical scenes, to their great benefit.

Special thanks also go to Harriet McDougal, one of the greatest editors of our time, who gave us a read and line edit on this novel out of the goodness of her heart. Wheel of Time fans will know her as the person who discovered, edited, and then married Robert Jordan. She doesn't do much editing these days outside of the Wheel of Time, and so I feel very honored and humbled to have her input and help here. Alan

Romanczuk, working with her, should also be thanked for facilitating this edit.

At Tor Books, Paul Stevens has been a huge help. He's been our in-house liaison for my books, and he's done an amazing job. Moshe and I are lucky to have his aid. Likewise, Irene Gallo—the art director—has been wonderfully helpful and patient in dealing with an intrusive author who wanted to do some crazy things with the artwork in his book. Many thanks to Irene, Justin Golenbock, Greg Collins, Karl Gold, Nathan Weaver, Heather Saunders, Meryl Gross, and the entire team at Tor Books. Dot Lin, who was my publicist up until this book's release (and who is now working to put a few extra letters after her name), was a wonderful help not just in publicity, but in giving me advice and a cheering section over in New York. Thank you all.

And speaking of artwork, you may notice that the interior art for this book is far more extensive than what you normally find in an epic fantasy. This is due to the extraordinary efforts of Greg Call, Isaac Stewart, and Ben McSweeney. They worked hard, drafting artwork numerous times to get things right. Ben's work on Shallan's sketchbook pages is simply beautiful, a melding of my best imaginings and his artistic interpretations. Isaac, who also did the interior artwork for the Mistborn novels, went far above and beyond what should reasonably have been expected of him. Late nights and demanding deadlines were the norm for this novel. He is to be commended. (The chapter icons, maps, colored endpages, and Navani notebook pages came from him, if you are wondering.)

As always, my writing group has been an amazing help. The members of it are joined by a few alpha and beta readers. In no particular order, these are: Karen Ahlstrom, Geoff and Rachel Biesinger, Ethan Skarstedt, Nathan Hatfield, Dan Wells, Kaylynn ZoBell, Alan and Jeanette Layton, Janci Olds, Kristina Kugler, Steve Diamond, Brian Delambre, Jason Denzel, Mi'chelle Trammel, Josh Walker, Chris King, Austin and Adam Hussey, Brian T. Hill, and that Ben guy whose name I can't spell right. I'm sure I'm forgetting some of you. You are all wonderful people, and I'd give you Shardblades if I could.

Whew. This is turning into an epic acknowledgments. But there are still a few more people that need notice. The writing of these words is happening right around the one year anniversary of my hiring the Inevitable Peter Ahlstrom as my personal assistant, editorial aid, and extra brain. If you go through previous acknowledgments pages, you'll always find him there. He's been a dear friend of mine, and an advocate of my work, for years. I'm lucky to now have him working for me full time. He got up at three a.m. today to get the last proofread of the book done. When you next see him at a convention, buy him a block of cheese.

I would also be remiss if I didn't thank Tom Doherty for letting me get away with writing this book. It's because of Tom's belief in this project that we were able to get away with the novel being so long, and a personal call from Tom was what managed to get Michael Whelan to do the cover. Tom has given me more here than I probably deserve; this novel (at the length it boasts, with the number of illustrations and artwork it contains) is the type that would make many publishers run away at full speed. This man is the reason Tor consistently releases such awesome books.

Finally, a moment on Michael Whelan's wonderful cover. For those who haven't heard the story, I started reading fantasy novels (indeed, I became a reader in the first place) back as a teenager because of a beautiful Michael Whelan cover painting. He has a unique ability to capture the true soul of a book in a painting—I always knew I could trust a novel with one of his covers. I've dreamed of someday having a painting of his on one of my books. It seemed something I was unlikely ever to receive.

To finally have it happen—and on the novel of my heart that I've been working on for so long—is an amazing honor.

CONTENTS

ILLUSTRATIONS

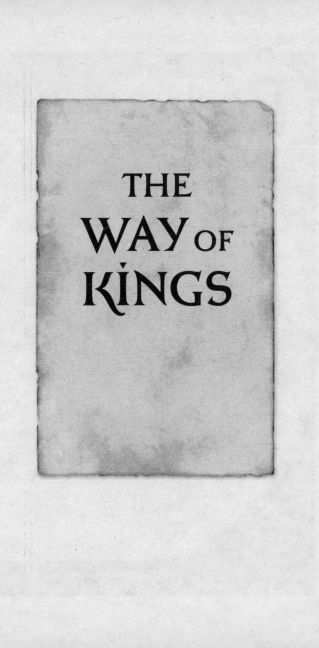

THE
WAY OF
KINGS

STEAMWATER OCEAN

ISLES

Northgrip   HERDAZ   Mourn's
Vault

u Parat   Varikev

Elanar   JAH KEVED   Kholinar

Valath   Shulin   UNCLAIMED HILLS

THAYLEN   BAVLAND   ALETHKAR   Rathalas   Dawn's
Shadow

TRIAX   Silnasen   Vedenar   Dumadari

Karanak   Shattered
Plains

Kharbranth   FROSTLANDS   New Natanan

THAYLENAH   The Shallow Crypts

OCEAN OF ORIGINS

THE STORMLIGHT ARCHIVE

Kalak rounded a rocky stone ridge and stumbled to a stop before the body of a dying thunderclast. The enormous stone beast lay on its side, riblike protrusions from its chest broken and cracked. The monstrosity was vaguely skeletal in shape, with unnaturally long limbs that sprouted from granite shoulders. The eyes were deep red spots on the arrowhead face, as if created by a fire burning deep within the stone. They faded.

Even after all these centuries, seeing a thunderclast up close made Kalak shiver. The beast's hand was as long as a man was tall. He'd been killed by hands like those before, and it hadn't been pleasant.

Of course, dying rarely was.

He rounded the creature, picking his way more carefully across the battlefield. The plain was a place of misshapen rock and stone, natural pillars rising around him, bodies littering the ground. Few plants lived here.

The stone ridges and mounds bore numerous scars. Some were shattered, blasted-out sections where Surgebinders had fought. Less frequently, he passed cracked, oddly shaped hollows where thunderclasts had ripped themselves free of the stone to join the fray.

Many of the bodies around him were human; many were not. Blood mixed. Red. Orange. Violet. Though none of the bodies around him stirred, an indistinct haze of sounds hung in the air. Moans of pain, cries of grief. They did not seem like the sounds of victory. Smoke curled from the occasional patches of growth or heaps of burning corpses. Even some sections of rock smoldered. The Dustbringers had done their work well.

But I survived, Kalak thought, hand to breast as he hastened to the meeting place. *I actually survived this time.*

That was dangerous. When he died, he was sent back, no choice. When he survived the Desolation, he was supposed to go back as well. Back to that place that he dreaded. Back to that place of pain and fire. What if he just decided . . . not to go?

Perilous thoughts, perhaps traitorous thoughts. He hastened on his way.

The place of meeting was in the shadow of a large rock formation, a spire rising into the sky. As always, the ten of them had decided upon it before the battle. The survivors would make their way here. Oddly, only one of the others was waiting for him. Jezrien. Had the other eight all died? It was possible. The battle had been so furious this time, one of the worst. The enemy was growing increasingly tenacious.

But no. Kalak frowned as he stepped up to the base of the spire. Seven magnificent swords stood proudly here, driven point-first into the stone ground. Each was a masterly work of art, flowing in design, inscribed with glyphs and patterns. He recognized each one. If their masters had died, the Blades would have vanished.

These Blades were weapons of power beyond even Shardblades. These were unique. Precious. Jezrien stood outside the ring of swords, looking eastward.

"Jezrien?"

The figure in white and blue glanced toward him. Even after all these centuries, Jezrien looked young, like a man barely into his thirtieth year. His short black beard was neatly trimmed, though his once-fine clothing was scorched and stained with blood. He folded his arms behind his back as he turned to Kalak.

"What is this, Jezrien?" Kalak asked. "Where are the others?"

"Departed." Jezrien's voice was calm, deep, regal. Though he hadn't worn a crown in centuries, his royal manner lingered. He always seemed to know what to do. "You might call it a miracle. Only one of us died this time."

"Talenel," Kalak said. His was the only Blade unaccounted for.

"Yes. He died holding that passage by the northern waterway."

Kalak nodded. Taln had a tendency to choose seemingly hopeless fights and win them. He also had a tendency to die in the process. He would be back now, in the place where they went between Desolations. The place of nightmares.

Kalak found himself shaking. When had he become so weak? "Jezrien, I can't return this time." Kalak whispered the words, stepping up and gripping the other man's arm. "I *can't.*"

Kalak felt something within him break at the admission. How long had it been? Centuries, perhaps millennia, of torture. It was so hard to keep track. Those fires, those hooks, digging into his flesh anew each day. Searing the skin off his arm, then burning the fat, then driving to the bone. He could smell it. Almighty, he could *smell* it!

"Leave your sword," Jezrien said.

"What?"

Jezrien nodded to the ring of weapons. "I was chosen to wait for you. We weren't certain if you had survived. A . . . a decision has been made. It is time for the Oathpact to end."

Kalak felt a sharp stab of horror. "What will that do?"

"Ishar believes that so long as there is one of us still bound to the Oathpact, it may be enough. There is a chance we might end the cycle of Desolations."

Kalak looked into the immortal king's eyes. Black smoke rose from a small patch to their left. Groans of the dying haunted them from behind. There, in Jezrien's eyes, Kalak saw anguish and grief. Perhaps even cowardice. This was a man hanging from a cliff by a thread.

Almighty above, Kalak thought. *You're broken too, aren't you?* They all were.

Kalak turned and walked to the side, where a low ridge overlooked part of the battlefield.

There were so many corpses, and among them walked the living. Men in primitive wraps, carrying spears topped by bronze heads. Juxtaposed between them were others in gleaming plate armor. One group walked past, four men in their ragged tanned skins or shoddy leather joining a powerful figure in beautiful silver plate, amazingly intricate. Such a contrast.

Jezrien stepped up beside him.

"They see us as divinities," Kalak whispered. "They rely upon us, Jezrien. We're all that they have."

"They have the Radiants. That will be enough."

Kalak shook his head. "He will not remain bound by this. The enemy. He will find a way around it. You know he will."

"Perhaps." The king of Heralds offered no further explanation.

"And Taln?" Kalak asked. *The flesh burning. The fires. The pain over and over and over . . .*

"Better that one man should suffer than ten," Jezrien whispered. He seemed so cold. Like a shadow caused by heat and light falling on someone honorable and true, casting this black imitation behind.

Jezrien walked back to the ring of swords. His own Blade formed in his hands, appearing from mist, wet with condensation. "It has been decided, Kalak. We will go our ways, and we will not seek out one another. Our Blades must be left. The Oathpact ends now." He lifted his sword and rammed it into the stone with the other seven.

Jezrien hesitated, looking at the sword, then bowed his head and turned away. As if ashamed. "We chose this burden willingly. Well, we can choose to drop it if we wish."

"What do we tell the people, Jezrien?" Kalak asked. "What will they say of this day?"

"It's simple," Jezrien said, walking away. "We tell them that they finally won. It's an easy enough lie. Who knows? Maybe it will turn out to be true."

Kalak watched Jezrien depart across the burned landscape. Finally, he summoned his own Blade and slammed it into the stone beside the other eight. He turned and walked in the direction opposite from Jezrien.

And yet, he could not help glancing back at the ring of

swords and the single open spot. The place where the tenth sword should have gone.

The one of them who was lost. The one they had abandoned.

Forgive us, Kalak thought, then left.

BOOK
ONE

❖

THE WAY OF KINGS

4,500 Years Later

Map of Alethkar and surroundings, created by His Majesty Gavilar Kholin's royal surveyors, circa 1167.

"The love of men is a frigid thing, a mountain stream only three steps from the ice. We are his. Oh Stormfather . . . we are his. It is but a thousand days, and the Everstorm comes."

—Collected on the first day of the week Palah of the month Shash of the year 1171, thirty-one seconds before death. Subject was a darkeyed pregnant woman of middle years. The child did not survive.

Szeth-son-son-Vallano, Truthless of Shinovar, wore white on the day he was to kill a king. The white clothing was a Parshendi tradition, foreign to him. But he did as his masters required and did not ask for an explanation.

He sat in a large stone room, baked by enormous firepits that cast a garish light upon the revelers, causing beads of sweat to form on their skin as they danced, and drank, and yelled, and sang, and clapped. Some fell to the ground red-faced, the revelry too much for them, their stomachs proving to be inferior wineskins. They looked as if they were dead, at least until their friends carried them out of the feast hall to waiting beds.

Szeth did not sway to the drums, drink the sapphire wine, or stand to dance. He sat on a bench at the back, a still servant in white robes. Few at the treaty-signing celebration noticed him. He was just a servant, and Shin were easy to ignore. Most out here in the East thought Szeth's kind were docile and harmless. They were generally right.

The drummers began a new rhythm. The beats shook Szeth like a quartet of thumping hearts, pumping waves of invisible blood through the room. Szeth's masters—who were dismissed as savages by those in more civilized kingdoms—sat at their own tables. They were men with skin of black marbled with red. Parshendi, they were named—cousins to the more docile servant peoples known as parshmen in most of the world. An oddity. They did not call themselves Parshendi; this was the Alethi name for them. It meant, roughly, "parshmen who can think." Neither side seemed to see that as an insult.

The Parshendi had brought the musicians. At first, the Alethi lighteyes had been hesitant. To them, drums were base instruments of the common, darkeyed people. But wine was the great assassin of both tradition and propriety, and now the Alethi elite danced with abandon.

Szeth stood and began to pick his way through the room. The revelry had lasted long; even the king had retired hours ago. But many still celebrated. As he walked, Szeth was forced to step around Dalinar Kholin—the king's own brother—who slumped drunken at a small table. The aging but powerfully built man kept waving away those who tried to encourage him to bed. Where was Jasnah, the king's daughter? Elhokar, the king's son and heir, sat at the high table, ruling the feast in his father's absence. He was in conversation with two men, a dark-skinned Azish man who had an odd patch of pale skin on his cheek and a thinner, Alethi-looking man who kept glancing over his shoulder.

The heir's feasting companions were unimportant. Szeth stayed far from the heir, skirting the sides of the room, passing the drummers. Musicspren zipped through the air around them, the tiny spirits taking the form of spinning translucent ribbons. As Szeth passed the drummers, they noted him. They would withdraw soon, along with all of the other Parshendi.

They did not seem offended. They did not seem angry. And yet they were going to break their treaty of only a few hours. It made no sense. But Szeth did not ask questions.

At the edge of the room, he passed rows of unwavering azure lights that bulged out where wall met floor. They held sapphires infused with Stormlight. Profane. How could the men of these lands use something so sacred for mere illumination? Worse, the Alethi scholars were said to be close to creating new Shardblades. Szeth hoped that was just wishful boasting. For if it *did* happen, the world would be changed. Likely in a way that ended with people in all countries—from distant Thaylenah to towering Jah Keved—speaking Alethi to their children.

They were a grand people, these Alethi. Even drunk, there was a natural nobility to them. Tall and well made, the men dressed in dark silk coats that buttoned down the sides of the chest and were elaborately embroidered in silver or gold. Each one looked a general on the field.

The women were even more splendid. They wore grand silk dresses, tightly fitted, the bright colors a contrast to the dark tones favored by the men. The left sleeve of each dress was longer than the right one, covering the hand. Alethi had an odd sense of propriety.

Their pure black hair was pinned up atop their heads, either in intricate weavings of braids or in loose piles. It was often woven with gold ribbons or ornaments, along with gems that glowed with Stormlight. Beautiful. Profane, but beautiful.

Szeth left the feasting chamber behind. Just outside, he passed the doorway into the Beggars' Feast. It was an Alethi tradition, a room where some of the poorest men and women in the city were given a feast complementing that of the king and his guests. A man with a long grey and black beard slumped in the doorway, smiling foolishly—though whether from wine or a weak mind, Szeth could not tell.

"Have you seen me?" the man asked with slurred speech. He laughed, then began to speak in gibberish, reaching for a wineskin. So it was drink after all. Szeth brushed by, continuing past a line of statues depicting the Ten Heralds from ancient Vorin theology. Jezerezeh, Ishi, Kelek, Talenelat. He counted off each one, and realized there were only nine here. One was conspicuously missing. Why had Shalash's statue been removed? King Gavilar was said to be very devout in his Vorin worship. Too devout, by some people's standards.

The hallway here curved to the right, running around the perimeter of the domed palace. They were on the king's floor, two levels up, surrounded by rock walls, ceiling, and floor. That was profane. Stone was not to be trod upon. But what was he to do? He was Truthless. He did as his masters demanded.

Today, that included wearing white. Loose white trousers tied at the waist with a rope, and over them a filmy shirt with long sleeves, open at the front. White clothing for a killer was a tradition among the Parshendi. Although Szeth had not asked, his masters had explained why.

White to be bold. White to not blend into the night. White to give warning.

For if you were going to assassinate a man, he was entitled to see you coming.

Szeth turned right, taking the hallway directly toward the king's chambers. Torches burned on the walls, their light unsatisfying to him, a meal of thin broth after a long fast. Flamespren danced around them, like large insects made solely of congealed light. The torches were useless to him. He reached for his pouch and the spheres it contained, but then hesitated when he saw more of the blue lights ahead: a pair of Stormlight lamps hanging on the wall, brilliant sapphires glowing at their hearts. Szeth walked up to one of these, holding out his hand to cup it around the glass-shrouded gemstone.

"You there!" a voice called in Alethi. There were two guards at the intersection. Double guard, for there were savages abroad in Kholinar this night. True, those savages were supposed to be allies now. But alliances could be shallow things indeed.

This one wouldn't last the hour.

Szeth looked as the two guards approached. They carried spears; they weren't lighteyes, and were therefore forbidden the sword. Their painted blue breastplates were ornate, however, as were their helms. They might be darkeyed, but they were high-ranking citizens with honored positions in the royal guard.

Stopping a few feet away, the guard at the front gestured with his spear. "Go on, now. This is no place for you." He had tan Alethi skin and a thin mustache that ran all the way around his mouth, becoming a beard at the bottom.

Szeth didn't move.

"Well?" the guard said. "What are you waiting for?"

Szeth breathed in deeply, drawing forth the Stormlight. It streamed into him, siphoned from the twin sapphire lamps on the walls, sucked in as if by his deep inhalation. The Stormlight raged inside of him, and the hallway suddenly grew darker, falling into shade like a hilltop cut off from the sun by a transient cloud.

Szeth could feel the Light's warmth, its fury, like a tempest that had been injected directly into his veins. The power of it was invigorating but dangerous. It pushed him to act. To move. To strike.

Holding his breath, he clung to the Stormlight. He could still feel it leaking out. Stormlight could be held for only a short time, a few minutes at most. It leaked away, the human body too porous a container. He had heard that the Voidbringers could hold it in perfectly. But, then, did they even exist? His punishment declared that they didn't. His honor demanded that they did.

Afire with holy energy, Szeth turned to the guards. They could see that he was leaking Stormlight, wisps of it curling from his skin like luminescent smoke. The lead guard squinted, frowning. Szeth was sure the man had never seen anything like it before. As far as he knew, Szeth had killed every stonewalker who had ever seen what he could do.

"What . . . what are you?" The guard's voice had lost its certainty. "Spirit or man?"

"What am I?" Szeth whispered, a bit of Light leaking from his lips as he looked past the man down the long hallway. "I'm . . . sorry."

Szeth blinked, Lashing himself to that distant point down the hallway. Stormlight raged from him in a flash, chilling his skin, and the ground immediately stopped pulling him downward. Instead, he was pulled toward that distant point—it was as if, to him, that direction had suddenly become *down*.

This was a Basic Lashing, first of his three kinds of Lashings. It gave him the ability to manipulate whatever force, spren, or god it was that held men to the ground. With this Lashing, he could bind people or objects to different surfaces or in different directions.

From Szeth's perspective, the hallway was now a deep shaft down which he was falling, and the two guards stood on one of the sides. They were shocked when Szeth's feet hit them, one for each face, throwing them over. Szeth shifted his view and Lashed himself to the floor. Light leaked from him. The floor of the hallway again became *down*, and he landed between the two guards, clothes crackling and dropping flakes of frost. He rose, beginning the process of summoning his Shardblade.

One of the guards fumbled for his spear. Szeth reached down, touching the soldier's shoulder while looking up. He focused on a point above him while willing the Light out of his body and into the guard, Lashing the poor man to the ceiling.

The guard yelped in shock as *up* became *down* for him. Light trailing from his form, he crashed into the ceiling and dropped his spear. It was not Lashed directly, and clattered back down to the floor near Szeth.

To kill. It was the greatest of sins. And yet here Szeth stood, Truthless, profanely walking on stones used for building. And it would not end. As Truthless, there was only one life he was forbidden to take.

And that was his own.

At the tenth beat of his heart, his Shardblade dropped into his waiting hand. It formed as if condensing from mist, water beading along the metal length. His Shardblade was long and thin, edged on both sides, smaller than most others. Szeth swept it out, carving a line in the stone floor and passing through the second guard's neck.

As always, the Shardblade killed oddly; though it cut easily through stone, steel, or anything inanimate, the metal fuzzed when it touched living skin. It traveled through the guard's neck without leaving a mark, but once it did, the man's eyes smoked and burned. They blackened, shriveling up in his head, and he slumped forward, dead. A Shardblade did not cut living flesh; it severed the soul itself.

Above, the first guard gasped. He'd managed to get to his feet, even though they were planted on the ceiling of the hallway. "Shardbearer!" he shouted. "A Shardbearer assaults the king's hall! To arms!"

Finally, Szeth thought. Szeth's use of Stormlight was unfamiliar to the guards, but they knew a Shardblade when they saw one.

Szeth bent down and picked up the spear that had fallen from above. As he did so, he released the breath he'd been holding since drawing in the Stormlight. It sustained him while he held it, but those two lanterns hadn't contained much of it, so he would need to breathe again soon. The Light began to leak away more quickly, now that he wasn't holding his breath.

Szeth set the spear's butt against the stone floor, then looked upward. The guard above stopped shouting, eyes opening wide as the tails of his shirt began to slip downward, the earth below reasserting its dominance. The Light steaming off his body dwindled.

He looked down at Szeth. Down at the spear tip pointing directly at his heart. Violet fearspren crawled out of the stone ceiling around him.

The Light ran out. The guard fell.

He screamed as he hit, the spear impaling him through the chest. Szeth let the spear fall away, carried to the ground with a muffled thump by the body twitching on its end. Shardblade in hand, he turned down a side corridor, following the map he'd memorized. He ducked around a corner and flattened himself against the wall just as a troop of guards reached the dead men. The newcomers began shouting immediately, continuing the alarm.

His instructions were clear. Kill the king, but be seen doing it. Let the Alethi know he was coming and what he was doing. Why? Why did the Parshendi agree to this treaty, only to send an assassin the very night of its signing?

More gemstones glowed on the walls of the hallway here. King Gavilar liked lavish display, and he couldn't know that he was leaving sources of power for Szeth to use in his Lashings. The things Szeth did hadn't been seen for millennia. Histories from those times were all but nonexistent, and the legends were horribly inaccurate.

Szeth peeked back out into the corridor. One of the guards at the intersection saw him, pointing and yelling. Szeth made sure they got a good look, then ducked away. He took a deep breath as he ran, drawing in Stormlight from the lanterns. His body came alive with it, and his speed increased, his muscles bursting with energy. Light became a storm inside of him; his blood thundered in his ears. It was terrible and wonderful at the same time.

Two corridors down, one to the side. He threw open the door of a storage room, then hesitated a moment—just long enough for a guard to round the corner and see him—before dashing into the room. Preparing for a Full Lashing, he raised his arm and commanded the Stormlight to pool there, causing the skin to burst alight with radiance. Then he flung his hand out toward the doorframe, spraying white luminescence across it like paint. He slammed the door just as the guards arrived.

The Stormlight held the door in the frame with the strength of a hundred arms. A Full Lashing bound objects together, holding them fast until the Stormlight ran out. It took longer to create—and drained Stormlight far more quickly—than a Basic Lashing. The door handle shook, and then the wood began to crack as the guards threw their weight against it, one man calling for an axe.

Szeth crossed the room in rapid strides, weaving around the shrouded furniture that had been stored here. It was of red cloth and deep expensive woods. He reached the far wall and—preparing himself for yet another blasphemy—he raised his Shardblade and slashed horizontally through the dark grey stone. The rock sliced easily; a Shardblade could cut any inanimate object. Two vertical slashes followed, then one across the bottom, cutting a large square block. He pressed his hand against it, willing Stormlight into the stone.

Behind him the room's door began to crack. He looked over his shoulder and focused on the shaking door, Lashing the block in that direction. Frost crystallized on his clothing— Lashing something so large required a great deal of Stormlight. The tempest within him stilled, like a storm reduced to a drizzle.

He stepped aside. The large stone block shuddered, sliding into the room. Normally, moving the block would have been impossible. Its own weight would have held it against the stones below. Yet now, that same weight pulled it free; for the block, the direction of the room's door was *down*. With a deep grinding sound, the block slid free of the wall and tumbled through the air, smashing furniture.

The soldiers finally broke through the door, staggering into the room just as the enormous block crashed into them.

Szeth turned his back on the terrible sound of the screams, the splintering of wood, the breaking of bones. He ducked and stepped through his new hole, entering the hallway outside.

He walked slowly, drawing Stormlight from the lamps he passed, siphoning it to him and stoking anew the tempest within. As the lamps dimmed, the corridor darkened. A thick wooden door stood at the end, and as he approached, small fearspren—shaped like globs of purple goo—began to wriggle from the masonry, pointing toward the doorway. They were drawn by the terror being felt on the other side.

Szeth pushed the door open, entering the last corridor leading to the king's chambers. Tall, red ceramic vases lined the pathway, and they were interspersed with nervous soldiers. They flanked a long, narrow rug. It was red, like a river of blood.

The spearmen in front didn't wait for him to get close. They broke into a trot, lifting their short throwing spears. Szeth slammed his hand to the side, pushing Stormlight into the doorframe, using the third and final type of Lashing, a Reverse Lashing. This one worked differently from the other two. It did not make the doorframe emit Stormlight; indeed, it seemed to pull nearby light *into* it, giving it a strange penumbra.

The spearmen threw, and Szeth stood still, hand on the doorframe. A Reverse Lashing required his constant touch, but took comparatively little Stormlight. During one, anything that approached him—particularly lighter objects—was instead pulled toward the Lashing itself.

The spears veered in the air, splitting around him and slamming into the wooden frame. As he felt them hit, Szeth leaped into the air and Lashed himself to the right wall, his feet hitting the stone with a slap.

He immediately reoriented his perspective. To his eyes, he wasn't standing on the wall, the soldiers were, the blood-red carpet streaming between them like a long tapestry. Szeth bolted down the hallway, striking with his Shardblade, shearing through the necks of two men who had thrown spears at him. Their eyes burned, and they collapsed.

The other guards in the hallway began to panic. Some tried to attack him, others yelled for more help, still others cringed away from him. The attackers had trouble—they were disoriented by the oddity of striking at someone who hung on the wall. Szeth cut down a few, then flipped into the air, tucking into a roll, and Lashed himself back to the floor.

He hit the ground in the midst of the soldiers. Completely surrounded, but holding a Shardblade.

According to legend, the Shardblades were first carried by the Knights Radiant uncounted ages ago. Gifts of their god, granted to allow them to fight horrors of rock and flame, dozens of feet tall, foes whose eyes burned with hatred. The

Voidbringers. When your foe had skin as hard as stone itself, steel was useless. Something supernal was required.

Szeth rose from his crouch, loose white clothes rippling, jaw clenched against his sins. He struck out, his weapon flashing with reflected torchlight. Elegant, wide swings. Three of them, one after another. He could neither close his ears to the screams that followed nor avoid seeing the men fall. They dropped round him like toys knocked over by a child's careless kick. If the Blade touched a man's spine, he died, eyes burning. If it cut through the core of a limb, it killed that limb. One soldier stumbled away from Szeth, arm flopping uselessly on his shoulder. He would never be able to feel it or use it again.

Szeth lowered his Shardblade, standing among the cinder-eyed corpses. Here, in Alethkar, men often spoke of the legends—of mankind's hard-won victory over the Voidbringers. But when weapons created to fight nightmares were turned against common soldiers, the lives of men became cheap things indeed.

Szeth turned and continued on his way, slippered feet falling on the soft red rug. The Shardblade, as always, glistened silver and clean. When one killed with a Blade, there was no blood. That seemed like a sign. The Shardblade was just a tool; it could not be blamed for the murders.

The door at the end of the hallway burst open. Szeth froze as a small group of soldiers rushed out, ushering a man in regal robes, his head ducked as if to avoid arrows. The soldiers wore deep blue, the color of the King's Guard, and the corpses didn't make them stop and gawk. They were prepared for what a Shardbearer could do. They opened a side door and shoved their ward through, several leveling spears at Szeth as they backed out.

Another figure stepped from the king's quarters; he wore glistening blue armor made of smoothly interlocking plates. Unlike common plate armor, however, this armor had no leather or mail visible at the joints—just smaller plates, fitting together with intricate precision. The armor was beautiful, the blue inlaid with golden bands around the edges of each piece of plate, the helm ornamented with three waves of small, hornlike wings.

Shardplate, the customary complement to a Shardblade. The newcomer carried a sword as well, an enormous Shardblade six feet long with a design along the blade like burning flames, a weapon of silvery metal that gleamed and almost seemed to glow. A weapon designed to slay dark gods, a larger counterpart to the one Szeth carried.

Szeth hesitated. He didn't recognize the armor; he had not been warned that he would be set at this task, and hadn't been given proper time to memorize the various suits of Plate or Blades owned by the Alethi. But a Shardbearer would have to be dealt with before he chased the king; he could not leave such a foe behind.

Besides, perhaps a Shardbearer could defeat him, kill him and end his miserable life. His Lashings wouldn't work directly on someone in Shardplate, and the armor would enhance the man, strengthen him. Szeth's honor would not allow him to betray his mission or seek death. But if that death occurred, he *would* welcome it.

The Shardbearer struck, and Szeth Lashed himself to the side of the hallway, leaping with a twist and landing on the wall. He danced backward, Blade held at the ready. The Shardbearer fell into an aggressive posture, using one of the swordplay stances favored here in the East. He moved far more nimbly than one would expect for a man in such bulky armor. Shardplate was special, as ancient and magical as the Blades it complemented.

The Shardbearer struck. Szeth skipped to the side and Lashed himself to the ceiling as the Shardbearer's Blade sliced into the wall. Feeling a thrill at the contest, Szeth dashed forward and attacked downward with an overhand blow, trying to hit the Shardbearer's helm. The man ducked, going down on one knee, letting Szeth's Blade cleave empty air.

Szeth leaped backward as the Shardbearer swung upward with his Blade, slicing into the ceiling. Szeth didn't own a set of Plate himself, and didn't care to. His Lashings interfered with the gemstones that powered Shardplate, and he had to choose one or the other.

As the Shardbearer turned, Szeth sprinted forward across the ceiling. As expected, the Shardbearer swung again, and Szeth leaped to the side, rolling. He came up from his roll and flipped, Lashing himself to the floor again. He spun to land on the ground behind the Shardbearer. He slammed his Blade into his opponent's open back.

Unfortunately, there was one major advantage Plate offered: It could block a Shardblade. Szeth's weapon hit solidly, causing a web of glowing lines to spread out across the back of the armor, and Stormlight began to leak free from them. Shardplate didn't dent or bend like common metal. Szeth would have to hit the Shardbearer in the same location at least once more to break through.

Szeth danced out of range as the Shardbearer swung in anger, trying to cut at Szeth's knees. The tempest within Szeth gave him many advantages—including the ability to quickly recover from small wounds. But it would not restore limbs killed by a Shardblade.

He rounded the Shardbearer, then picked a moment and dashed forward. The Shardbearer swung again, but Szeth briefly Lashed himself to the ceiling for lift. He shot into the air, cresting over the swing, then immediately Lashed himself back to the floor. He struck as he landed, but the Shardbearer recovered quickly and executed a perfect follow-through stroke, coming within a finger of hitting Szeth.

The man was dangerously skilled with that Blade. Many Shardbearers depended too much on the power of their weapon and armor. This man was different.

Szeth jumped to the wall and struck at the Shardbearer with quick, terse attacks, like a snapping eel. The Shardbearer fended him off with wide, sweeping counters. His Blade's length kept Szeth at bay.

This is taking too long! Szeth thought. If the king slipped away into hiding, Szeth would fail in his mission no matter how many people he killed. He ducked in for another strike, but the Shardbearer forced him back. Each second this fight lasted was another for the king's escape.

It was time to be reckless. Szeth launched into the air, Lashing himself to the other end of the hallway and falling feet-first toward his adversary. The Shardbearer didn't hesitate to swing, but Szeth Lashed himself down at an angle, dropping immediately. The Shardblade swished through the air above him.

He landed in a crouch, using his momentum to throw himself forward, and swung at the Shardbearer's side, where the Plate had cracked. He hit with a powerful blow. That piece of the Plate shattered, bits of molten metal streaking away. The Shardbearer grunted, dropping to one knee, raising a hand to his side. Szeth raised a foot to the man's side and shoved him backward with a Stormlight-enhanced kick.

The heavy Shardbearer crashed into the door of the king's quarters, smashing it and falling partway into the room beyond. Szeth left him, ducking instead through the doorway to the right, following the way the king had gone. The hallway here had the same red carpet, and Stormlight lamps on the walls gave Szeth a chance to recharge the tempest within.

Energy blazed within him again, and he sped up. If he could get far enough ahead, he could deal with the king, then turn back to fight off the Shardbearer. It wouldn't be easy. A Full Lashing on a doorway wouldn't stop a Shardbearer, and that Plate would let the man run supernaturally fast. Szeth glanced over his shoulder.

The Shardbearer wasn't following. The man sat up in his armor, looking dazed. Szeth could just barely see him, sitting in the doorway, surrounded by broken bits of wood. Perhaps Szeth had wounded him more than he'd thought.

Or maybe . . .

Szeth froze. He thought of the ducked head of the man who'd been rushed out, face obscured. The Shardbearer *still* wasn't following. He was so skilled. It was said that few men could rival Gavilar Kholin's swordsmanship. Could it be?

Szeth turned and dashed back, trusting his instincts. As soon as the Shardbearer saw him, he climbed to his feet with alacrity. Szeth ran faster. What was the safest place for your king? In the hands of some guards, fleeing? Or protected in a suit of Shardplate, left behind, dismissed as a bodyguard?

Clever, Szeth thought as the formerly sluggish Shard-bearer fell into another battle stance. Szeth attacked with re-newed vigor, swinging his Blade in a flurry of strikes. The Shardbearer—the king—aggressively struck out with broad, sweeping blows. Szeth pulled away from one of these, feel-ing the wind of the weapon passing just inches before him. He timed his next move, then dashed forward, ducking un-derneath the king's follow-through.

The king, expecting another strike at his side, twisted with his arm held protectively to block the hole in his Plate. That gave Szeth the room to run past him and into the king's cham-bers.

The king spun around to follow, but Szeth ran through the lavishly furnished chamber, flinging out his hand, touching pieces of furniture he passed. He infused them with Storm-light, Lashing them to a point behind the king. The furniture tumbled as if the room had been turned on its side, couches, chairs, and tables dropping toward the surprised king. Gavi-lar made the mistake of chopping at them with his Shard-blade. The weapon easily sheared through a large couch, but the pieces still crashed into him, making him stumble. A foot-stool hit him next, throwing him to the ground.

Gavilar rolled out of the way of the furniture and charged forward, Plate leaking streams of Light from the cracked sec-tions. Szeth gathered himself, then leaped into the air, Lash-ing himself backward and to the right as the king arrived. He zipped out of the way of the king's blow, then Lashed himself forward with two Basic Lashings in a row. Stormlight flashed out of him, clothing freezing, as he was pulled toward the king at twice the speed of a normal fall.

The king's posture indicated surprise as Szeth lurched in midair, then spun toward him, swinging. He slammed his Blade into the king's helm, then immediately Lashed himself to the ceiling and fell upward, slamming into the stone roof above. He'd Lashed himself in too many directions too quickly, and his body had lost track, making it difficult to land gracefully. He stumbled back to his feet.

Below, the king stepped back, trying to get into position to swing up at Szeth. The man's helm was cracked, leaking Stormlight, and he stood protectively, defending the side with the broken plate. The king used a one-handed swing, reaching for the ceiling. Szeth immediately Lashed himself downward, judging that the king's attack would leave him unable to get his sword back in time.

Szeth underestimated his opponent. The king stepped into Szeth's attack, trusting his helm to absorb the blow. Just as Szeth hit the helm a second time—shattering it—Gavilar punched with his off hand, slamming his gauntleted fist into Szeth's face.

Blinding light flashed in Szeth's eyes, a counterpoint to the sudden agony that crashed across his face. Everything blurred, his vision fading.

Pain. So much *pain*!

He screamed, Stormlight leaving him in a rush, and he slammed back into something hard. The balcony doors. More pain broke out across his shoulders, as if someone had stabbed him with a hundred daggers, and he hit the ground and rolled to a stop, muscles trembling. The blow would have killed an ordinary man.

No time for pain. No time for pain. No time for pain!

He blinked, shaking his head, the world blurry and dark. Was he blind? No. It was dark outside. He was on the wooden balcony; the force of the blow had thrown him through the doors. Something was thumping. Heavy footfalls. The Shardbearer!

Szeth stumbled to his feet, vision swimming. Blood streamed from the side of his face, and Stormlight rose from his skin, blinding his left eye. The Light. It would heal him, if it could. His jaw felt unhinged. Broken? He'd dropped his Shardblade.

A lumbering shadow moved in front of him; the Shardbearer's armor had leaked enough Stormlight that the king was having trouble walking. But he was coming.

Szeth screamed, kneeling, infusing Stormlight into the wooden balcony, Lashing it downward. The air frosted around him. The tempest roared, traveling down his arms into the wood. He Lashed it downward, then did it again. He Lashed a fourth time as Gavilar stepped onto the balcony. It lurched under the extra weight. The wood cracked, straining.

The Shardbearer hesitated.

Szeth Lashed the balcony downward a fifth time. The balcony supports shattered and the entire structure broke free from the building. Szeth screamed through a broken jaw and used his final bit of Stormlight to Lash himself to the side of the building. He fell to the side, passing the shocked Shardbearer, then hit the wall and rolled.

The balcony dropped away, the king looking up with shock as he lost his footing. The fall was brief. In the moonlight, Szeth watched solemnly—vision still fuzzy, blinded in one eye—as the structure crashed to the stone ground below. The wall of the palace trembled, and the crash of broken wood echoed from the nearby buildings.

Still lying on the side of the wall, Szeth groaned, climbing to his feet. He felt weak; he'd used up his Stormlight too quickly, straining his body. He stumbled down the side of the building, approaching the wreckage, barely able to remain standing.

The king was still moving. Shardplate would protect a man from such a fall, but a large length of bloodied wood stuck up through Gavilar's side, piercing him where Szeth had broken the Plate earlier. Szeth knelt down, inspecting the man's pain-wracked face. Strong features, square chin, black beard flecked with white, striking pale green eyes. Gavilar Kholin.

"I . . . expected you . . . to come," the king said between gasps.

Szeth reached underneath the front of the man's breast-plate, tapping the straps there. They unfastened, and he pulled the front of the breastplate free, exposing the gemstones on its interior. Two had been cracked and burned out. Three still glowed. Numb, Szeth breathed in sharply, absorbing the Light.

The storm began to rage again. More Light rose from the side of his face, repairing his damaged skin and bones. The pain was still great; Stormlight healing was far from instantaneous. It would be hours before he recovered.

The king coughed. "You can tell . . . Thaidakar . . . that he's too late. . . ."

"I don't know who that is," Szeth said, standing, his words slurring from his broken jaw. He held his hand to the side, resummoning his Shardblade.

The king frowned. "Then who . . . ? Restares? Sadeas? I never thought . . ."

"My masters are the Parshendi," Szeth said. Ten heartbeats passed, and his Blade dropped into his hand, wet with condensation.

"The Parshendi? That makes no sense." Gavilar coughed, hand quivering, reaching toward his chest and fumbling at a pocket. He pulled out a small crystalline sphere tied to a chain. "You must take this. They must not get it." He seemed dazed. "Tell . . . tell my brother . . . he must find the most important words a man can say. . . ."

Gavilar fell still.

Szeth hesitated, then knelt down and took the sphere. It was odd, unlike any he'd seen before. Though it was completely dark, it seemed to glow somehow. With a light that was black.

The Parshendi? Gavilar had said. *That makes no sense.*

"Nothing makes sense anymore," Szeth whispered, tucking the strange sphere away. "It's all unraveling. I am sorry, King of the Alethi. I doubt that you care. Not anymore, at least." He stood up. "At least you won't have to watch the world ending with the rest of us."

Beside the king's body, his Shardblade materialized from mist, clattering to the stones now that its master was dead. It was worth a fortune; kingdoms had fallen as men vied to possess a single Shardblade.

Shouts of alarm came from inside the palace. Szeth needed to go. But . . .

Tell my brother . . .

To Szeth's people, a dying request was sacred. He took the king's hand, dipping it in the man's own blood, then used it to scrawl on the wood, *Brother. You must find the most important words a man can say.*

With that, Szeth escaped into the night. He left the king's Shardblade; he had no use for it. The Blade Szeth already carried was curse enough.

PART

ONE

Above Silence

KALADIN • SHALLAN

"You've killed me. Bastards, you've killed me! While the sun is still hot, I die!"

—Collected on the fifth day of the week Chach of the month Betab of the year 1171, ten seconds before death. Subject was a darkeyed soldier thirty-one years of age. Sample is considered questionable.

FIVE YEARS LATER

I'm going to die, aren't I?" Cenn asked.

The weathered veteran beside Cenn turned and inspected him. The veteran wore a full beard, cut short. At the sides, the black hairs were starting to give way to grey.

I'm going to die, Cenn thought, clutching his spear—the shaft slick with sweat. *I'm going to die. Oh, Stormfather. I'm going to die. . . .*

"How old are you, son?" the veteran asked. Cenn didn't remember the man's name. It was hard to recall anything while watching that other army form lines across the rocky battlefield. That lining up seemed so civil. Neat, organized. Shortspears in the front ranks, longspears and javelins next, archers at the sides. The darkeyed spearmen wore equipment like Cenn's: leather jerkin and knee-length skirt with a simple steel cap and a matching breastplate.

Many of the lighteyes had full suits of armor. They sat astride horses, their honor guards clustering around them with breastplates that gleamed burgundy and deep forest green. Were there Shardbearers among them? Brightlord Amaram wasn't a Shardbearer. Were any of his men? What if Cenn had to fight one? Ordinary men didn't kill Shardbearers. It had happened so infrequently that each occurrence was now legendary.

It's really happening, he thought with mounting terror. This wasn't a drill in the camp. This wasn't training out in the fields, swinging sticks. This was *real.* Facing that fact—his heart pounding like a frightened animal in his chest, his legs unsteady—Cenn suddenly realized that he was a coward. He shouldn't have left the herds! He should never have—

"Son?" the veteran said, voice firm. "How old are you?"

"Fifteen, sir."

"And what's your name?"

"Cenn, sir."

The mountainous, bearded man nodded. "I'm Dallet."

"Dallet," Cenn repeated, still staring out at the other army. There were so many of them! Thousands. "I'm going to die, aren't I?"

"*No.*" Dallet had a gruff voice, but somehow that was comforting. "You're going to be just fine. Keep your head on straight. Stay with the squad."

"But I've barely had three months' training!" He swore he could hear faint clangs from the enemy's armor or shields. "I can barely hold this spear! Stormfather, I'm *dead.* I can't—"

"Son," Dallet interrupted, soft but firm. He raised a hand and placed it on Cenn's shoulder. The rim of Dallet's large round shield reflected the light from where it hung on his back. "You are *going* to be *fine.*"

"How can you know?" It came out as a plea.

"Because, lad. You're in Kaladin Stormblessed's squad." The other soldiers nearby nodded in agreement.

Behind them, waves and waves of soldiers were lining up—thousands of them. Cenn was right at the front, with Kaladin's squad of about thirty other men. Why had Cenn been moved to a new squad at the last moment? It had something to do with camp politics.

Why was this squad at the very front, where casualties were bound to be the greatest? Small fearspren—like globs of purplish goo—began to climb up out of the ground and gather around his feet. In a moment of sheer panic, he nearly dropped his spear and scrambled away. Dallet's hand tightened on his shoulder. Looking up into Dallet's confident black eyes, Cenn hesitated.

"Did you piss before we formed ranks?" Dallet asked.

"I didn't have time to—"

"Go now."

"Here?"

"If you don't, you'll end up with it running down your leg in battle, distracting you, maybe killing you. Do it."

Embarrassed, Cenn handed Dallet his spear and relieved himself onto the stones. When he finished, he shot glances at those next to him. None of Kaladin's soldiers smirked. They stood steady, spears to their sides, shields on their backs.

The enemy army was almost finished. The field between the two forces was bare, flat slickrock, remarkably even and smooth, broken only by occasional rockbuds. It would have made a good pasture. The warm wind blew in Cenn's face, thick with the watery scents of last night's highstorm.

"Dallet!" a voice said.

A man walked up through the ranks, carrying a shortspear that had two leather knife sheaths strapped to the haft. The newcomer was a young man—perhaps four years older than Cenn's fifteen—but he was taller by several fingers than even Dallet. He wore the common leathers of a spearman, but under them was a pair of dark trousers. That wasn't supposed to be allowed.

His black Alethi hair was shoulder-length and wavy, his eyes a dark brown. He also had knots of white cord on the shoulders of his jerkin, marking him as a squadleader.

The thirty men around Cenn snapped to attention, raising their spears in salute. *This is Kaladin Stormblessed?* Cenn thought incredulously. *This youth?*

"Dallet, we're soon going to have a new recruit," Kaladin said. He had a strong voice. "I need you to . . ." He trailed off as he noticed Cenn.

"He found his way here just a few minutes ago, sir," Dallet said with a smile. "I've been gettin' him ready."

"Well done," Kaladin said. "I paid good money to get that boy away from Gare. That man's so incompetent he might as well be fighting for the other side."

What? Cenn thought. *Why would anyone pay to get me?*

"What do you think about the field?" Kaladin asked. Several of the other spearmen nearby raised hands to shade from the sun, scanning the rocks.

"That dip next to the two boulders on the far right?" Dallet asked.

Kaladin shook his head. "Footing's too rough."

"Aye. Perhaps it is. What about the short hill over there? Far enough to avoid the first fall, close enough to not get too far ahead."

Kaladin nodded, though Cenn couldn't see what they were looking at. "Looks good."

"The rest of you louts hear that?" Dallet shouted.

The men raised their spears high.

"Keep an eye on the new boy, Dallet," Kaladin said. "He won't know the signs."

"Of course," Dallet said, smiling. Smiling! How could the man smile? The enemy army was blowing horns. Did that mean they were ready? Even though Cenn had just relieved himself, he felt a trickle of urine run down his leg.

"Stay firm," Kaladin said, then trotted down the front line to talk to the next squadleader over. Behind Cenn and the others, the dozens of ranks were still growing. The archers on the sides prepared to fire.

"Don't worry, son," Dallet said. "We'll be fine. Squadleader Kaladin is lucky."

The soldier on the other side of Cenn nodded. He was a

lanky, red-haired Veden, with darker tan skin than the Alethi. Why was he fighting in an Alethi army? "That's right. Kaladin, he's stormblessed, right sure he is. We only lost . . . what, one man last battle?"

"But someone *did* die," Cenn said.

Dallet shrugged. "People always die. Our squad loses the fewest. You'll see."

Kaladin finished conferring with the other squadleader, then jogged back to his team. Though he carried a shortspear—meant to be wielded one-handed with a shield in the other hand—his was a hand longer than those held by the other men.

"At the ready, men!" Dallet called. Unlike the other squadleaders, Kaladin didn't fall into rank, but stood out in front of his squad.

The men around Cenn shuffled, excited. The sounds were repeated through the vast army, the stillness giving way before eagerness. Hundreds of feet shuffling, shields slapping, clasps clanking. Kaladin remained motionless, staring down the other army. "Steady, men," he said without turning.

Behind, a lighteyed officer passed on horseback. "Be ready to fight! I want their blood, men. Fight and kill!"

"Steady," Kaladin said again, after the man passed.

"Be ready to run," Dallet said to Cenn.

"Run? But we've been trained to march in formation! To stay in our line!"

"Sure," Dallet said. "But most of the men don't have much more training than you. Those who can fight well end up getting sent to the Shattered Plains to battle the Parshendi. Kaladin's trying to get us into shape to go there, to fight for the king." Dallet nodded down the line. "Most of these here will break and charge; the lighteyes aren't good enough commanders to keep them in formation. So stay with us and run."

"Should I have my shield out?" Around Kaladin's team, the other ranks were unhooking their shields. But Kaladin's squad left their shields on their backs.

Before Dallet could answer, a horn blew from behind.

"Go!" Dallet said.

Cenn didn't have much choice. The entire army started moving in a clamor of marching boots. As Dallet had predicted, the steady march didn't last long. Some men began yelling, the roar taken up by others. Lighteyes called for them to go, run, fight. The line disintegrated.

As soon as that happened, Kaladin's squad broke into a dash, running out into the front at full speed. Cenn scrambled to keep up, panicked and terrified. The ground wasn't as smooth as it had seemed, and he nearly tripped on a hidden rockbud, vines withdrawn into its shell.

He righted himself and kept going, holding his spear in one hand, his shield clapping against his back. The distant army was in motion as well, their soldiers charging down the field. There was no semblance of a battle formation or a careful line. This wasn't anything like the training had claimed it would be.

Cenn didn't even know who the enemy was. A landlord was encroaching on Brightlord Amaram's territory—the land owned, ultimately, by Highprince Sadeas. It was a border skirmish, and Cenn thought it was with another Alethi princedom. Why were they fighting each other? Perhaps the king would have put a stop to it, but he was on the Shattered Plains, seeking vengeance for the murder of King Gavilar five years before.

The enemy had a lot of archers. Cenn's panic climbed to a peak as the first wave of arrows flew into the air. He stumbled again, itching to take out his shield. But Dallet grabbed his arm and yanked him forward.

Hundreds of arrows split the sky, dimming the sun. They arced and fell, dropping like skyeels upon their prey. Amaram's soldiers raised shields. But not Kaladin's squad. No shields for them.

Cenn screamed.

And the arrows slammed into the middle ranks of Amaram's army, behind him. Cenn glanced over his shoulder, still running. The arrows fell *behind* him. Soldiers screamed, arrows broke against shields; only a few straggling arrows landed anywhere near the front ranks.

"Why?" he yelled at Dallet. "How did you know?"

"They want the arrows to hit where the men are most crowded," the large man replied. "Where they'll have the greatest chance of finding a body."

Several other groups in the van left their shields lowered, but most ran awkwardly with their shields angled up to the sky, worried about arrows that wouldn't hit them. That slowed them, and they risked getting trampled by the men behind who *were* getting hit. Cenn itched to raise his shield anyway; it felt so wrong to run without it.

The second volley hit, and men screamed in pain. Kaladin's squad barreled toward the enemy soldiers, some of whom were dying to arrows from Amaram's archers. Cenn could hear the enemy soldiers bellowing war cries, could make out individual faces. Suddenly, Kaladin's squad pulled to a halt, forming a tight group. They'd reached the small incline that Kaladin and Dallet had chosen earlier.

Dallet grabbed Cenn and shoved him to the very center of the formation. Kaladin's men lowered spears, pulling out shields as the enemy bore down on them. The charging foe used no careful formation; they didn't keep the ranks of long-spears in back and shortspears in front. They all just ran forward, yelling in a frenzy.

Cenn scrambled to get his shield unlatched from his back. Clashing spears rang in the air as squads engaged one another. A group of enemy spearmen rushed up to Kaladin's squad, perhaps coveting the higher ground. The three dozen attackers had some cohesion, though they weren't in as tight a formation as Kaladin's squad was.

The enemy seemed determined to make up for it in passion; they bellowed and screamed in fury, rushing Kaladin's line. Kaladin's team held rank, defending Cenn as if he were some lighteyes and they were his honor guard. The two forces met with a crash of metal on wood, shields slamming together. Cenn cringed back.

It was over in a few eyeblinks. The enemy squad pulled back, leaving two dead on the stone. Kaladin's team hadn't lost anyone. They held their bristling V formation, though one man stepped back and pulled out a bandage to wrap a thigh wound. The rest of the men closed in to fill the spot. The wounded man was hulking and thick-armed; he cursed, but the wound didn't look bad. He was on his feet in a moment, but didn't return to the place where he'd been. Instead, he moved down to one end of the V formation, a more protected spot.

The battlefield was chaos. The two armies mingled indistinguishably; sounds of clanging, crunching, and screaming churned in the air. Many of the squads broke apart, members rushing from one encounter to another. They moved like hunters, groups of three or four seeking lone individuals, then brutally falling on them.

Kaladin's team held its ground, engaging only enemy squads that got too close. Was this what a battle really was? Cenn's practice had trained him for long ranks of men, shoulder to shoulder. Not this frenzied intermixing, this brutal pandemonium. Why didn't more hold formation?

The real soldiers are all gone, Cenn thought. *Off fighting in a real battle at the Shattered Plains. No wonder Kaladin wants to get his squad there.*

Spears flashed on all sides; it was difficult to tell friend from foe, despite the emblems on breastplates and colored paint on shields. The battlefield broke down into hundreds of small groups, like a thousand different wars happening at the same time.

After the first few exchanges, Dallet took Cenn by the shoulder and placed him in the rank at the very bottom of the V pattern. Cenn, however, was worthless. When Kaladin's team engaged enemy squads, all of his training fled him. It took everything he had to just remain there, holding his spear outward and trying to look threatening.

For the better part of an hour, Kaladin's squad held their small hill, working as a team, shoulder to shoulder. Kaladin often left his position at the front, rushing this way and that, banging his spear on his shield in a strange rhythm.

Those are signals, Cenn realized as Kaladin's squad moved

from the V shape into a ring. With the screams of the dying and the thousands of men calling to others, it was nearly impossible to hear a single person's voice. But the sharp clang of the spear against the metal plate on Kaladin's shield was clear. Each time they changed formations, Dallet grabbed Cenn by the shoulder and steered him.

Kaladin's team didn't chase down stragglers. They remained on the defensive. And, while several of the men in Kaladin's team took wounds, none of them fell. Their squad was too intimidating for the smaller groups, and larger enemy units retreated after a few exchanges, seeking easier foes.

Eventually something changed. Kaladin turned, watching the tides of the battle with discerning brown eyes. He raised his spear and smacked his shield in a quick rhythm he hadn't used before. Dallet grabbed Cenn by the arm and pulled him away from the small hill. Why abandon it now?

Just then, the larger body of Amaram's force broke, the men scattering. Cenn hadn't realized how poorly the battle in this quarter had been going for his side. As Kaladin's team retreated, they passed many wounded and dying, and Cenn grew nauseated. Soldiers were sliced open, their insides spilling out.

He didn't have time for horror; the retreat quickly turned into a rout. Dallet cursed, and Kaladin beat his shield again. The squad changed direction, heading eastward. There, Cenn saw, a larger group of Amaram's soldiers was holding.

But the enemy had seen the ranks break, and that made them bold. They rushed forward in clusters, like wild axe-hounds hunting stray hogs. Before Kaladin's team was halfway across the field of dead and dying, a large group of enemy soldiers intercepted them. Kaladin reluctantly banged his shield; his squad slowed.

Cenn felt his heart begin to thump faster and faster. Nearby, a squad of Amaram's soldiers was consumed; men stumbled and fell, screaming, trying to get away. The enemies used their spears like skewers, killing men on the ground like cremlings.

Kaladin's men met the enemy in a crash of spears and

shields. Bodies shoved on all sides, and Cenn was spun about. In the jumble of friend and foe, dying and killing, Cenn grew overwhelmed. So many men running in so many directions!

He panicked, scrambling for safety. A group of soldiers nearby wore Alethi uniforms. Kaladin's squad. Cenn ran for them, but when some turned toward him, Cenn was terrified to realize he didn't recognize them. This *wasn't* Kaladin's squad, but a small group of unfamiliar soldiers holding an uneven, broken line. Wounded and terrified, they scattered as soon as an enemy squad got close.

Cenn froze, holding his spear in a sweaty hand. The enemy soldiers charged right for him. His instincts urged him to flee, yet he had seen so many men picked off one at a time. He had to stand! He had to face them! He couldn't run, he couldn't—

He yelled, stabbing his spear at the lead soldier. The man casually knocked the weapon aside with his shield, then drove his shortspear into Cenn's thigh. The pain was hot, so hot that the blood squirting out on his leg felt cold by comparison. Cenn gasped.

The soldier yanked the weapon free. Cenn stumbled backward, dropping his spear and shield. He fell to the rocky ground, splashing in someone else's blood. His foe raised a spear high, a looming silhouette against the stark blue sky, ready to ram it into Cenn's heart.

And then *he* was there.

Squadleader. Stormblessed. Kaladin's spear came as if out of nowhere, narrowly deflecting the blow that was to have killed Cenn. Kaladin set himself in front of Cenn, alone, facing down six spearmen. He didn't flinch. He *charged*.

It happened so quickly. Kaladin swept the feet from beneath the man who had stabbed Cenn. Even as that man fell, Kaladin reached up and flipped a knife from one of the sheaths tied about his spear. His hand snapped, knife flashing and hitting the thigh of a second foe. That man fell to one knee, screaming.

A third man froze, looking at his fallen allies. Kaladin shoved past a wounded enemy and slammed his spear into the gut of the third man. A fourth man fell with a knife to the eye. When had Kaladin grabbed that knife? He spun between the last two, his spear a blur, wielding it like a quarterstaff. For a moment, Cenn thought he could see something surrounding the squadleader. A warping of the air, like the wind itself become visible.

I've lost a lot of blood. It's flowing out so quickly. . . .

Kaladin spun, knocking aside attacks, and the last two spearmen fell with gurgles that Cenn thought sounded surprised. Foes all down, Kaladin turned and knelt beside Cenn. The squadleader set aside his spear and whipped a white strip of cloth from his pocket, then efficiently wrapped it tight around Cenn's leg. Kaladin worked with the ease of one who had bound wounds dozens of times before.

"Kaladin, sir!" Cenn said, pointing at one of the soldiers Kaladin had wounded. The enemy man held his leg as he stumbled to his feet. In a second, however, mountainous Dallet was there, shoving the foe with his shield. Dallet didn't kill the wounded man, but let him stumble away, unarmed.

The rest of the squad arrived and formed a ring around Kaladin, Dallet, and Cenn. Kaladin stood up, raising his spear to his shoulder; Dallet handed him back his knives, retrieved from the fallen foes.

"Had me worried there, sir," Dallet said. "Running off like that."

"I knew you'd follow," Kaladin said. "Raise the red banner. Cyn, Korater, you're going back with the boy. Dallet, hold here. Amaram's line is bulging in this direction. We should be safe soon."

"And you, sir?" Dallet asked.

Kaladin looked across the field. A pocket had opened in the enemy forces, and a man rode there on a white horse, swinging about him with a wicked mace. He wore full plate armor, polished and gleaming silver.

"A Shardbearer," Cenn said.

Dallet snorted. "No, thank the Stormfather. Just a light-eyed officer. Shardbearers are far too valuable to waste on a minor border dispute."

Kaladin watched the lighteyes with a seething hatred. It was the same hatred Cenn's father had shown when he'd spoken of chull rustlers, or the hatred Cenn's mother would display when someone mentioned Kusiri, who had run off with the cobbler's son.

"Sir?" Dallet said hesitantly.

"Subsquads Two and Three, pincer pattern," Kaladin said, his voice hard. "We're taking a brightlord off his throne."

"You sure that's wise, sir? We've got wounded."

Kaladin turned toward Dallet. "That's one of Hallaw's officers. He might be the one."

"You don't know that, sir."

"Regardless, he's a battalionlord. If we kill an officer that high, we're all but guaranteed to be in the next group sent to the Shattered Plains. We're taking him." His eyes grew distant. "Imagine it, Dallet. Real soldiers. A warcamp with discipline and lighteyes with integrity. A place where our fighting will *mean* something."

Dallet sighed, but nodded. Kaladin waved to a group of his soldiers; then they raced across the field. A smaller group of soldiers, including Dallet, waited behind with the wounded. One of those—a thin man with black Alethi hair speckled with a handful of blond hairs, marking some foreign blood—pulled a long red ribbon from his pocket and attached it to his spear. He held the spear aloft, letting the ribbon flap in the wind.

"It's a call for runners to carry our wounded off the field," Dallet said to Cenn. "We'll have you out of here soon. You were brave, standing against those six."

"Fleeing seemed stupid," Cenn said, trying to take his mind off his throbbing leg. "With so many wounded on the field, how can we think that the runners'll come for us?"

"Squadleader Kaladin bribes them," Dallet said. "They usually only carry off lighteyes, but there are more runners than there are wounded lighteyes. The squadleader puts most of his pay into the bribes."

"This squad *is* different," Cenn said, feeling light-headed.

"Told you."

"Not because of luck. Because of training."

"That's part of it. Part of it is because we know if we get hurt, Kaladin will get us off the battlefield." He paused, looking over his shoulder. As Kaladin had predicted, Amaram's line was surging back, recovering.

The mounted enemy lighteyes from before was energetically laying about with his mace. A group of his honor guard moved to one side, engaging Kaladin's subsquads. The lighteyes turned his horse. He wore an open-fronted helm that had sloping sides and a large set of plumes on the top. Cenn couldn't make out his eye color, but he knew it would be blue or green, maybe yellow or light grey. He was a brightlord, chosen at birth by the Heralds, marked for rule.

He impassively regarded those who fought nearby. Then one of Kaladin's knives took him in the right eye.

The brightlord screamed, falling back off the saddle as Kaladin somehow slipped through the lines and leaped upon him, spear raised.

"Aye, it's part training," Dallet said, shaking his head. "But it's mostly him. He fights like a storm, that one, and thinks twice as fast as other men. The way he moves sometimes . . ."

"He bound my leg," Cenn said, realizing he was beginning to speak nonsense due to the blood loss. Why point out the bound leg? It was a simple thing.

Dallet just nodded. "He knows a lot about wounds. He can read glyphs too. He's a strange man, for a lowly darkeyed spearman, our squadleader is." He turned to Cenn. "But you should save your strength, son. The squadleader won't be pleased if we lose you, not after what he paid to get you."

"Why?" Cenn asked. The battlefield was growing quieter, as if many of the dying men had already yelled themselves hoarse. Almost everyone around them was an ally, but Dallet still watched to make sure no enemy soldiers tried to strike at Kaladin's wounded.

"Why, Dallet?" Cenn repeated, feeling urgent. "Why bring me into his squad? Why *me*?"

Dallet shook his head. "It's just how he is. Hates the thought of young kids like you, barely trained, going to battle.

Every now and again, he grabs one and brings him into his squad. A good half dozen of our men were once like you." Dallet's eyes got a far-off look. "I think you all remind him of someone."

Cenn glanced at his leg. Painspren—like small orange hands with overly long fingers—were crawling around him, reacting to his agony. They began turning away, scurrying in other directions, seeking other wounded. His pain was fading, his leg—his whole body—feeling numb.

He leaned back, staring up at the sky. He could hear faint thunder. That was odd. The sky was cloudless.

Dallet cursed.

Cenn turned, shocked out of his stupor. Galloping directly toward them was a massive black horse bearing a rider in gleaming armor that seemed to radiate light. That armor was seamless—no chain underneath, just smaller plates, incredibly intricate. The figure wore an unornamented full helm, and the plate was gilded. He carried a massive sword in one hand, fully as long as a man was tall. It wasn't a simple, straight sword—it was curved, and the side that wasn't sharp was ridged, like flowing waves. Etchings covered its length.

It was beautiful. Like a work of art. Cenn had never seen a Shardbearer, but he knew immediately what this was. How could he ever have mistaken a simple armored lighteyes for one of *these* majestic creatures?

Hadn't Dallet claimed there would be no Shardbearers on this battlefield? Dallet scrambled to his feet, calling for the subsquad to form up. Cenn just sat where he was. He couldn't have stood, not with that leg wound.

He felt so light-headed. How much blood had he lost? He could barely think.

Either way, he couldn't fight. You didn't fight something like this. Sun gleamed against that plate armor. And that gorgeous, intricate, sinuous sword. It was like . . . like the Almighty himself had taken form to walk the battlefield.

And why would you want to fight the Almighty?

Cenn closed his eyes.

HONOR IS DEAD

"Ten orders. We were loved, once. Why have you forsaken us, Almighty! Shard of my soul, where have you gone?"

—Collected on the second day of Kakash, year 1171, five seconds before death. Subject was a lighteyed woman in her third decade.

EIGHT MONTHS LATER

Kaladin's stomach growled as he reached through the bars and accepted the bowl of slop. He pulled the small bowl—more a cup—between the bars, sniffed it, then grimaced as the caged wagon began to roll again. The sludgy grey slop was made from overcooked tallew grain, and this batch was flecked with crusted bits of yesterday's meal.

Revolting though it was, it was all he would get. He began to eat, legs hanging out between the bars, watching the scenery pass. The other slaves in his cage clutched their bowls protectively, afraid that someone might steal from them. One of them tried to steal Kaladin's food on the first day. He'd nearly broken the man's arm. Now everyone left him alone.

Suited him just fine.

He ate with his fingers, careless of the dirt. He'd stopped noticing dirt months ago. He hated that he felt some of that same paranoia that the others showed. How could he not, after eight months of beatings, deprivation, and brutality?

He fought down the paranoia. He *wouldn't* become like them. Even if he'd given up everything else—even if all had been taken from him, even if there was no longer hope of escape. This one thing he would retain. He was a slave. But he didn't need to think like one.

He finished the slop quickly. Nearby, one of the other slaves began to cough weakly. There were ten slaves in the wagon, all men, scraggly-bearded and dirty. It was one of three wagons in their caravan through the Unclaimed Hills.

The sun blazed reddish white on the horizon, like the hottest part of a smith's fire. It lit the framing clouds with a spray of color, paint thrown carelessly on a canvas. Covered in tall, monotonously green grass, the hills seemed endless. On a nearby mound, a small figure flitted around the plants, dancing like a fluttering insect. The figure was amorphous, vaguely translucent. Windspren were devious spirits who had a penchant for staying where they weren't wanted. He'd hoped that this one had gotten bored and left, but as Kaladin tried to toss his wooden bowl aside, he found that it stuck to his fingers.

The windspren laughed, zipping by, nothing more than a ribbon of light without form. He cursed, tugging on the bowl. Windspren often played pranks like that. He pried at the bowl, and it eventually came free. Grumbling, he tossed it to one of the other slaves. The man quickly began to lick at the remnants of the slop.

"Hey," a voice whispered.

Kaladin looked to the side. A slave with dark skin and matted hair was crawling up to him, timid, as if expecting Kaladin to be angry. "You're not like the others." The slave's black eyes glanced upward, toward Kaladin's forehead, which bore three brands. The first two made a glyphpair, given to him eight months ago, on his last day in Amaram's army.

The third was fresh, given to him by his most recent master. *Shash*, the last glyph read. Dangerous.

The slave had his hand hidden behind his rags. A knife? No, that was ridiculous. None of these slaves could have hidden a weapon; the leaves hidden in Kaladin's belt were as close as one could get. But old instincts could not be banished easily, so Kaladin watched that hand.

"I heard the guards talking," the slave continued, shuffling a little closer. He had a twitch that made him blink too frequently. "You've tried to escape before, they said. You *have* escaped before."

Kaladin made no reply.

"Look," the slave said, moving his hand out from behind his rags and revealing his bowl of slop. It was half full. "Take me with you next time," he whispered. "I'll give you this. Half my food from now until we get away. Please." As he spoke, he attracted a few hungerspren. They looked like brown flies that flitted around the man's head, almost too small to see.

Kaladin turned away, looking out at the endless hills and their shifting, moving grasses. He rested one arm across the bars and placed his head against it, legs still hanging out.

"Well?" the slave asked.

"You're an idiot. If you gave me half your food, you'd be too weak to escape if I *were* to flee. Which I won't. It doesn't work."

"But—"

"Ten times," Kaladin whispered. "Ten escape attempts in eight months, fleeing from five different masters. And how many of them worked?"

"Well . . . I mean . . . you're still here. . . ."

Eight months. Eight months as a slave, eight months of slop and beatings. It might as well have been an eternity. He barely remembered the army anymore. "You can't hide as a slave," Kaladin said. "Not with that brand on your forehead. Oh, I got away a few times. But they always found me. And then back I went."

Once, men had called him lucky. Stormblessed. Those had been lies—if anything, Kaladin had *bad* luck. Soldiers were a superstitious sort, and though he'd initially resisted that way of thinking, it was growing harder and harder. Every person he had ever tried to protect had ended up dead. Time and time again. And now, here he was, in an even worse situation than where he'd begun. It was better not to resist. This was his lot, and he was resigned to it.

There was a certain power in that, a freedom. The freedom of not having to care.

The slave eventually realized Kaladin wasn't going to say anything further, and so he retreated, eating his slop. The wagons continued to roll, fields of green extending in all directions. The area around the rattling wagons was bare, however. When they approached, the grass pulled away, each individual stalk withdrawing into a pinprick hole in the stone. After the wagons moved on, the grass timidly poked back out and stretched its blades toward the air. And so, the cages moved along what appeared to be an open rock highway, cleared just for them.

This far into the Unclaimed Hills, the highstorms were incredibly powerful. The plants had learned to survive. That's what you had to do, learn to survive. Brace yourself, weather the storm.

Kaladin caught a whiff of another sweaty, unwashed body and heard the sound of shuffling feet. He looked suspiciously to the side, expecting that same slave to be back.

It was a different man this time, though. He had a long black beard stuck with bits of food and snarled with dirt. Kaladin kept his own beard shorter, allowing Tvlakv's mercenaries to hack it down periodically. Like Kaladin, the slave wore the remains of a brown sack tied with a rag, and he was darkeyed, of course—perhaps a deep dark green, though with darkeyes it was hard to tell. They all looked brown or black unless you caught them in the right light.

The newcomer cringed away, raising his hands. He had a rash on one hand, the skin just faintly discolored. He'd likely approached because he'd seen Kaladin respond to that other man. The slaves had been frightened of him since the first day, but they were also obviously curious.

Kaladin sighed and turned away. The slave hesitantly sat down. "Mind if I ask how you became a slave, friend? Can't help wondering. We're all wondering."

Judging by the accent and the dark hair, the man was Alethi, like Kaladin. Most of the slaves were. Kaladin didn't reply to the question.

"Me, I stole a herd of chull," the man said. He had a raspy voice, like sheets of paper rubbing together. "If I'd taken one chull, they might have just beaten me. But a whole herd. Seventeen head . . ." He chuckled to himself, admiring his own audacity.

In the far corner of the wagon, someone coughed again. They were a sorry lot, even for slaves. Weak, sickly, underfed. Some, like Kaladin, were repeat runaways—though Kaladin was the only one with a *shash* brand. They were the most worthless of a worthless caste, purchased at a steep discount. They were probably being taken for resale in a remote place where men were desperate for labor. There were plenty of small, independent cities along the coast of the Unclaimed Hills, places where Vorin rules governing the use of slaves were just a distant rumor.

Coming this way was dangerous. These lands were ruled by nobody, and by cutting across open land and staying away from established trade routes, Tvlakv could easily run afoul of unemployed mercenaries. Men who had no honor and no fear of slaughtering a slavemaster and his slaves in order to steal a few chulls and wagons.

Men who had no honor. Were there men who *had* honor?

No, Kaladin thought. *Honor died eight months ago.*

"So?" asked the scraggly-bearded man. "What did you do to get made a slave?"

Kaladin raised his arm against the bars again. "How did you get caught?"

"Odd thing, that," the man said. Kaladin hadn't answered his question, but he *had* replied. That seemed enough. "It was a woman, of course. Should have known she'd sell me."

"Shouldn't have stolen chulls. Too slow. Horses would have been better."

The man laughed riotously. "Horses? What do you think me, a madman? If I'd been caught stealing *those,* I'd have been hanged. Chulls, at least, only earned me a slave's brand."

Kaladin glanced to the side. This man's forehead brand was older than Kaladin's, the skin around the scar faded to white. What was that glyphpair? "*Sas morom,*" Kaladin said. It was the highlord's district where the man had originally been branded.

The man looked up with shock. "Hey! You know glyphs?" Several of the slaves nearby stirred at this oddity. "You must have an even better story than I thought, friend."

Kaladin stared out over those grasses blowing in the mild breeze. Whenever the wind picked up, the more sensitive of the grass stalks shrank down into their burrows, leaving the landscape patchy, like the coat of a sickly horse. That windspren was still there, moving between patches of grass. How long had it been following him? At least a couple of months now. That was downright odd. Maybe it wasn't the same one. They were impossible to tell apart.

"Well?" the man prodded. "Why are you here?"

"There are many reasons why I'm here," Kaladin said. "Failures. Crimes. Betrayals. Probably the same for most every one of us."

Around him, several of the men grunted in agreement; one of those grunts then degenerated into a hacking cough. *Persistent coughing,* a part of Kaladin's mind thought, *accompanied by an excess of phlegm and fevered mumbling at night. Sounds like the grindings.*

"Well," the talkative man said, "perhaps I should ask a different question. Be more specific, that's what my mother always said. Say what you mean and ask for what you want. What's the story of you getting that first brand of yours?"

Kaladin sat, feeling the wagon thump and roll beneath him. "I killed a lighteyes."

His unnamed companion whistled again, this time even more appreciative than before. "I'm surprised they let you live."

"Killing the lighteyes isn't why I was made a slave," Kaladin said. "It's the one I *didn't* kill that's the problem."

"How's that?"

Kaladin shook his head, then stopped answering the talkative man's questions. The man eventually wandered to the front of the wagon's cage and sat down, staring at his bare feet.

.&.

Hours later, Kaladin still sat in his place, idly fingering the glyphs on his forehead. This was his life, day in and day out, riding in these cursed wagons.

His first brands had healed long ago, but the skin around the *shash* brand was red, irritated, and crusted with scabs. It throbbed, almost like a second heart. It hurt even worse than the burn had when he grabbed the heated handle of a cooking pot as a child.

Lessons drilled into Kaladin by his father whispered in the back of his brain, giving the proper way to care for a burn. Apply a salve to prevent infection, wash once daily. Those memories weren't a comfort; they were an annoyance. He didn't *have* fourleaf sap or lister's oil; he didn't even have water for the washing.

The parts of the wound that had scabbed over pulled at his skin, making his forehead feel tight. He could barely pass a few minutes without scrunching up his brow and irritating the wound. He'd grown accustomed to reaching up and wiping away the streaks of blood that trickled from the cracks; his right forearm was smeared with it. If he'd had a mirror, he could probably have spotted tiny red rotspren gathering around the wound.

The sun set in the west, but the wagons kept rolling. Violet Salas peeked over the horizon to the east, seeming hesitant at first, as if making sure the sun had vanished. It was a clear night, and the stars shivered high above. Taln's Scar—a swath of deep red stars that stood out vibrantly from the twinkling white ones—was high in the sky this season.

That slave who'd been coughing earlier was at it again. A

ragged, wet cough. Once, Kaladin would have been quick to go help, but something within him had changed. So many people he'd tried to help were now dead. It seemed to him—irrationally—that the man would be better off without his interference. After failing Tien, then Dallet and his team, then ten successive groups of slaves, it was hard to find the will to try again.

Two hours past First Moon, Tvlakv finally called a halt. His two brutish mercenaries climbed from their places atop their wagons, then moved to build a small fire. Lanky Taran—the serving boy—tended the chulls. The large crustaceans were nearly as big as wagons themselves. They settled down, pulling into their shells for the night with clawfuls of grain. Soon they were nothing more than three lumps in the darkness, barely distinguishable from boulders. Finally, Tvlakv began checking on the slaves one at a time, giving each a ladle of water, making certain his investments were healthy. Or, at least, as healthy as could be expected for this poor lot.

Tvlakv started with the first wagon, and Kaladin—still sitting—pushed his fingers into his makeshift belt, checking on the leaves he'd hidden there. They crackled satisfactorily, the stiff, dried husks rough against his skin. He still wasn't certain what he was going to do with them. He'd grabbed them on a whim during one of the sessions when he'd been allowed out of the wagon to stretch his legs. He doubted anyone else in the caravan knew how to recognize blackbane—narrow leaves on a trefoil prong—so it hadn't been too much of a risk.

Absently, he took the leaves out and rubbed them between forefinger and palm. They had to dry before reaching their potency. Why did he carry them? Did he mean to give them to Tvlakv and get revenge? Or were they a contingency, to be retained in case things got too bad, too unbearable?

Surely I haven't fallen that far, he thought. It was just more likely his instinct of securing a weapon when he saw one, no matter how unusual. The landscape was dark. Salas was the smallest and dimmest of the moons, and while her violet coloring had inspired countless poets, she didn't do much to help you see your hand in front of your face.

"Oh!" a soft, feminine voice said. "What's that?"

A translucent figure—just a handspan tall—peeked up from over the edge of the floor near Kaladin. She climbed up and into the wagon, as if scaling some high plateau. The windspren had taken the shape of a young woman—larger spren could change shapes and sizes—with an angular face and long, flowing hair that faded into mist behind her head. She—Kaladin couldn't help but think of the windspren as a she—was formed of pale blues and whites and wore a simple, flowing white dress of a girlish cut that came down to midcalf. Like the hair, it faded to mist at the very bottom. Her feet, hands, and face were crisply distinct, and she had the hips and bust of a slender woman.

Kaladin frowned at the spirit. Spren were all around; you just ignored them most of the time. But this one was an oddity. The windspren walked upward, as if climbing an invisible staircase. She reached a height where she could stare at Kaladin's hand, so he closed his fingers around the black leaves. She walked around his fist in a circle. Although she glowed like an afterimage from looking at the sun, her form provided no real illumination.

She bent down, looking at his hand from different angles, like a child expecting to find a hidden piece of candy. "What is it?" Her voice was like a whisper. "You can show me. I won't tell anyone. Is it a treasure? Have you cut off a piece of the night's cloak and tucked it away? Is it the heart of a beetle, so tiny yet powerful?"

He said nothing, causing the spren to pout. She floated up, hovering though she had no wings, and looked him in the eyes. "Kaladin, why must you ignore me?"

Kaladin started. "What did you say?"

She smiled mischievously, then sprang away, her figure blurring into a long white ribbon of blue-white light. She shot between the bars—twisting and warping in the air, like a strip of cloth caught in the wind—and darted beneath the wagon.

"Storm you!" Kaladin said, leaping to his feet. "Spirit! What did you say? Repeat that!" Spren didn't use people's names. Spren weren't intelligent. The larger ones—like windspren or riverspren—could mimic voices and expressions, but they didn't actually think. They didn't . . .

"Did any of you hear that?" Kaladin asked, turning to the cage's other occupants. The roof was just high enough to let Kaladin stand. The others were lying back, waiting to get their ladle of water. He got no response beyond a few mutters to be quiet and some coughs from the sick man in the corner. Even Kaladin's "friend" from earlier ignored him. The man had fallen into a stupor, staring at his feet, wiggling his toes periodically.

Maybe they hadn't seen the spren. Many of the larger ones were invisible except to the person they were tormenting. Kaladin sat back down on the floor of the wagon, hanging his legs outside. The windspren *had* said his name, but undoubtedly she'd just repeated what she'd heard before. But . . . none of the men in the cage knew his name.

Maybe I'm going mad, Kaladin thought. *Seeing things that aren't there. Hearing voices.*

He took a deep breath, then opened his hand. His grip had cracked and broken the leaves. He'd need to tuck them away to prevent further—

"Those leaves look interesting," said that same feminine voice. "You like them a lot, don't you?"

Kaladin jumped, twisting to the side. The windspren stood in the air just beside his head, white dress rippling in a wind Kaladin couldn't feel.

"How do you know my name?" he demanded.

The windspren didn't answer. She walked on air over to the bars, then poked her head out, watching Tvlakv the slaver administer drinks to the last few slaves in the first wagon. She looked back at Kaladin. "Why don't you fight? You did before. Now you've stopped."

"Why do you care, spirit?"

She cocked her head. "I don't know," she said, as if surprised at herself. "But I do. Isn't that odd?"

It was more than odd. What did he make of a spren that not only used his name, but seemed to *remember* things he had done weeks ago?

"People don't eat leaves, you know, Kaladin," she said, folding translucent arms. Then she cocked her head. "Or do you? I can't remember. You're so strange, stuffing some things into your mouths, leaking out other things when you don't think anyone is looking."

"How do you know my name?" he whispered.

"How do *you* know it?"

"I know it because . . . because it's mine. My parents told it to me. I don't know."

"Well I don't either," she said, nodding as if she'd just won some grand argument.

"Fine," he said. "But why are you *using* my name?"

"Because it's polite. And you are *im*polite."

"Spren don't know what that means!"

"See, there," she said, pointing at him. "Impolite."

Kaladin blinked. Well, he was far from where he'd grown up, walking foreign stone and eating foreign food. Perhaps the spren who lived here were different from those back home.

"So why don't you fight?" she asked, flitting down to rest on his legs, looking up at his face. She had no weight that he could feel.

"I can't fight," he said softly.

"You did before."

He closed his eyes and rested his head forward against the bars. "I'm so tired." He didn't mean the physical fatigue, though eight months eating leftovers had stolen much of the lean strength he'd cultivated while at war. He *felt* tired. Even when he got enough sleep. Even on those rare days when he wasn't hungry, cold, or stiff from a beating. So tired . . .

"You have been tired before."

"I've failed, spirit," he replied, squeezing his eyes shut. "Must you torment me so?"

They were all dead. Cenn and Dallet, and before that Tukks and the Takers. Before that, Tien. Before that, blood on his hands and the corpse of a young girl with pale skin.

Some of the slaves nearby muttered, likely thinking he was mad. Anyone could end up drawing a spren, but you learned early that talking to one was pointless. *Was* he mad? Perhaps he should wish for that—madness was an escape from the pain. Instead, it terrified him.

He opened his eyes. Tvlakv was finally waddling up to Kaladin's wagon with his bucket of water. The portly, brown-eyed man walked with a very faint limp; the result of a broken leg, perhaps. He was Thaylen, and all Thaylen men had the same stark white beards—regardless of their age or the color of the hair on their heads—and white eyebrows. Those eyebrows grew very long, and the Thaylen wore them pushed back over the ears. That made him appear to have two white streaks in his otherwise black hair.

His clothing—striped trousers of black and red with a dark blue sweater that matched the color of his knit cap—had once been fine, but it was now growing ragged. Had he once been something other than a slaver? This life—the casual buying and selling of human flesh—seemed to have an effect on men. It wearied the soul, even if it did fill one's money pouch.

Tvlakv kept his distance from Kaladin, carrying his oil lantern over to inspect the coughing slave at the front of the cage. Tvlakv called to his mercenaries. Bluth—Kaladin didn't know why he'd bothered to learn their names—wandered over. Tvlakv spoke quietly, pointing at the slave. Bluth nodded, slablike face shadowed in the lanternlight, and pulled the cudgel free from his belt.

The windspren took the form of a white ribbon, then zipped over toward the sick man. She spun and twisted a few times before landing on the floor, becoming a girl again. She leaned in to inspect the man. Like a curious child.

Kaladin turned away and closed his eyes, but he could still hear the coughing. Inside his mind, his father's voice responded. *To cure the grinding coughs,* said the careful, precise tone, *administer two handfuls of bloodivy, crushed to a powder, each day. If you don't have that, be certain to give the patient plenty of liquids, preferably with sugar stirred in. As long as the patient stays hydrated, he will most likely survive. The disease sounds far worse than it is.*

Most likely survive . . .

Those coughs continued. Someone unlatched the cage door. Would they know how to help the man? Such an easy solution. Give him water, and he would live.

It didn't matter. Best not to get involved.

Men dying on the battlefield. A youthful face, so familiar and dear, looking to Kaladin for salvation. A sword wound slicing open the side of a neck. A Shardbearer charging through Amaram's ranks.

Blood. Death. Failure. Pain.

And his father's voice. *Can you really leave him, son? Let him die when you could have helped?*

Storm it!

"Stop!" Kaladin yelled, standing.

The other slaves scrambled back. Bluth jumped up, slamming the cage door closed and holding up his cudgel. Tvlakv shied behind the mercenary, using him as cover.

Kaladin took a deep breath, closing his hand around the leaves and then raising the other to his head, wiping away a smear of blood. He crossed the small cage, bare feet thumping on the wood. Bluth glared as Kaladin knelt beside the sick man. The flickering light illuminated a long, drawn face and nearly bloodless lips. The man had coughed up phlegm; it was greenish and solid. Kaladin felt the man's neck for swelling, then checked his dark brown eyes.

"It's called the grinding coughs," Kaladin said. "He will live, if you give him an extra ladle of water every two hours for five days or so. You'll have to force it down his throat. Mix in sugar, if you have any."

Bluth scratched at his ample chin, then glanced at the shorter slaver.

"Pull him out," Tvlakv said.

The wounded slave awoke as Bluth unlocked the cage. The mercenary waved Kaladin back with his cudgel, and Kaladin reluctantly withdrew. After putting away his cudgel, Bluth grabbed the slave under the arms and dragged him out, all the while trying to keep a nervous eye on Kaladin. Kaladin's last failed escape attempt had involved twenty armed slaves.

His master should have executed him for that, but he had claimed Kaladin was "intriguing" and branded him with *shash*, then sold him for a pittance.

There always seemed to be a reason Kaladin survived when those he'd tried to help died. Some men might have seen that as a blessing, but he saw it as an ironic kind of torment. He'd spent some time under his previous master speaking with a slave from the West, a Selay man who had spoken of the Old Magic from their legends and its ability to curse people. Could that be what was happening to Kaladin?

Don't be foolish, he told himself.

The cage door snapped back in place, locking. The cages were necessary—Tvlakv had to protect his fragile investment from the highstorms. The cages had wooden sides that could be pulled up and locked into place during the furious gales.

Bluth dragged the slave over to the fire, beside the unpacked water barrel. Kaladin felt himself relax. *There,* he told himself. *Perhaps you can still help. Perhaps there's a reason to care.*

Kaladin opened his hand and looked down at the crumbled black leaves in his palm. He didn't need these. Sneaking them into Tvlakv's drink would not only be difficult, but pointless. Did he really want the slaver dead? What would that accomplish?

A low crack rang in the air, followed by a second one, duller, like someone dropping a bag of grain. Kaladin snapped his head up, looking to where Bluth had deposited the sick slave. The mercenary raised his cudgel one more time, then snapped it down, the weapon making a cracking sound as it hit the slave's skull.

The slave hadn't uttered a cry of pain or protest. His corpse slumped over in the darkness; Bluth casually picked it up and slung it over his shoulder.

"No!" Kaladin yelled, leaping across the cage and slamming his hands against the bars.

Tvlakv stood warming himself by the fire.

"Storm you!" Kaladin screamed. "He could have lived, you bastard!"

[58]

Tvlakv glanced at him. Then, leisurely, the slaver walked over, straightening his deep blue knit cap. "He would have gotten you all sick, you see." His voice was lightly accented, smashing words together, not giving the proper syllables emphasis. Thaylens always sounded to Kaladin like they were mumbling. "I would not lose an entire wagon for one man."

"He's past the spreading stage!" Kaladin said, slamming his hands against the bars again. "If any of us were going to catch it, we'd have done so by now."

"Hope that you don't. I think he was past saving."

"I told you otherwise!"

"And I should believe you, deserter?" Tvlakv said, amused. "A man with eyes that smolder and hate? You would kill me." He shrugged. "I care not. So long as you are strong when it is time for sales. You should bless me for saving from that man's sickness."

"I'll bless your cairn when I pile it up myself," Kaladin replied.

Tvlakv smiled, walking back toward the fire. "Keep that fury, deserter, and that strength. It will pay me well on our arrival."

Not if you don't live that long, Kaladin thought. Tvlakv always warmed the last of the water from the bucket he used for the slaves. He'd make himself tea from it, hanging it over the fire. If Kaladin made sure he was watered last, then powdered the leaves and dropped them into the—

Kaladin froze, then looked down at his hands. In his haste, he'd forgotten that he'd been holding the blackbane. He'd dropped the flakes as he slammed his hands against the bars. Only a few bits stuck to his palms, not enough to be potent.

He spun to look backward; the floor of the cage was dirty and covered with grime. If the flakes had fallen there, there was no way to collect them. The wind gathered suddenly, blowing dust, crumbs, and dirt out of the wagon and into the night.

Even in this, Kaladin failed.

He sank down, his back to the bars, and bowed his head. Defeated. That cursed windspren kept darting around him, looking confused.

Skyeels

Skyeels are common near most coastal cities we pass. I had read of them often, and was excited to see them. Most are between 4 and 8 feet long, though I spotted one monster that must have been 7 feet from snout to tail.

They are so graceful and fluid in the air, often accompanied by thousands of tiny spren, flying around them in a swarm as if reliving their wakes. The sailors call them "luckspren". I doubt it is their true name.

How does the creature stay in the air? I noticed some sort of pouch under each wing that deflates as it dives.

They seek fish just below the waters surface, or crabs and rats on the docks, and aren't nearly as graceful when on land.

*"A man stood on a cliffside and watched his homeland fall
into dust. The waters surged beneath, so far beneath. And
he heard a child crying. They were his own tears."*

—Collected on the 4th of Tanates, year 1171, thirty seconds
before death. Subject was a cobbler of some renown.

Kharbranth, City of Bells, was not a place that Shallan had
ever imagined she would visit. Though she'd often
dreamed of traveling, she'd expected to spend her early life
sequestered in her family's manor, only escaping through the
books of her father's library. She'd expected to marry one of
her father's allies, then spend the rest of her life sequestered
in *his* manor.

But expectations were like fine pottery. The harder you
held them, the more likely they were to crack.

She found herself breathless, clutching her leather-bound
drawing pad to her chest as longshoremen pulled the ship
into the dock. Kharbranth was enormous. Built up the side of
a steep incline, the city was wedge-shaped, as if it were built
into a wide crack, with the open side toward the ocean. The
buildings were blocky, with square windows, and appeared
to have been constructed of some kind of mud or daub. Crem,

perhaps? They were painted bright colors, reds and oranges most often, but occasional blues and yellows too.

She could hear the bells already, tinkling in the wind, ringing with pure voices. She had to strain her neck to look up toward the city's loftiest rim; Kharbranth was like a mountain towering over her. How many people lived in a place like this? Thousands? Tens of thousands? She shivered again—daunted yet excited—then blinked pointedly, fixing the image of the city in her memory.

Sailors rushed about. The *Wind's Pleasure* was a narrow, single-masted vessel, barely large enough for her, the captain, his wife, and the half-dozen crew. It had seemed so small at first, but Captain Tozbek was a calm and cautious man, an excellent sailor, even if he was a pagan. He'd guided the ship with care along the coast, always finding a sheltered cove to ride out highstorms.

The captain oversaw the work as the men secured the mooring. Tozbek was a short man, even-shouldered with Shallan, and he wore his long white Thaylen eyebrows up in a curious spiked pattern. It was like he had two waving fans above his eyes, a foot long each. He wore a simple knit cap and a silver-buttoned black coat. She'd imagined him getting that scar on his jaw in a furious sea battle with pirates. The day before, she'd been disappointed to hear it had been caused by loose tackle during rough weather.

His wife, Ashlv, was already walking down the gangplank to register their vessel. The captain saw Shallan inspecting him, and so walked over. He was a business connection of her family's, long trusted by her father. That was good, since the plan she and her brothers had concocted had contained no place for her bringing along a lady-in-waiting or nurse.

That plan made Shallan nervous. Very, *very* nervous. She hated being duplicitous. But the financial state of her house . . . They either needed a spectacular infusion of wealth or some other edge in local Veden house politics. Otherwise, they wouldn't last the year.

First things first, Shallan thought, forcing herself to be calm. *Find Jasnah Kholin. Assuming she hasn't moved off without you again.*

"I've sent a lad on your behalf, Brightness," Tozbek said. "If the princess is still here, we shall soon know."

Shallan nodded gratefully, still clutching her drawing pad. Out in the city, there were people *everywhere*. Some wore familiar clothing—trousers and shirts that laced up the front for the men, skirts and colorful blouses for the women. Those could have been from her homeland, Jah Keved. But Kharbranth was a free city. A small, politically fragile city-state, it held little territory but had docks open to all ships that passed, and it asked no questions about nationality or status. People flowed to it.

That meant many of the people she saw were exotic. Those single-sheet wraps would mark a man or woman from Tashikk, far to the west. The long coats, enveloping down to the ankles, but open in the front like cloaks . . . where were those from? She'd rarely seen so many parshmen as she noted working the docks, carrying cargo on their backs. Like the parshmen her father had owned, these were stout and thick of limb, with their odd marbled skin—some parts pale or black, others a deep crimson. The mottled pattern was unique to each individual.

After chasing Jasnah Kholin from town to town for the better part of six months, Shallan was beginning to think she'd never catch the woman. Was the princess avoiding her? No, that didn't seem likely—Shallan just wasn't important enough to wait for. Brightness Jasnah Kholin was one of the most powerful women in the world. And one of the most infamous. She was the only member of a faithful royal house who was a professed heretic.

Shallan tried not to grow anxious. Most likely, they'd discover that Jasnah had moved on again. The *Wind's Pleasure* would dock for the night, and Shallan would negotiate a price with the captain—steeply discounted, because of her family's investments in Tozbek's shipping business—to take her to the next port.

Already, they were months past the time when Tozbek had expected to be rid of her. She'd never sensed resentment from him; his honor and loyalty kept him agreeing to her requests. However, his patience wouldn't last forever, and neither would her money. She'd already used over half the spheres she'd brought with her. He wouldn't abandon her in an unfamiliar city, of course, but he might regretfully insist on taking her back to Vedenar.

"Captain!" a sailor said, rushing up the gangplank. He wore only a vest and loose, baggy trousers, and had the darkly tanned skin of one who worked in the sun. "No message, sir. Dock registrar says that Jasnah hasn't left yet."

"Ha!" the captain said, turning to Shallan. "The hunt is over!"

"Bless the Heralds," Shallan said softly.

The captain smiled, flamboyant eyebrows looking like streaks of light coming from his eyes. "It must be your beautiful face that brought us this favorable wind! The windspren themselves were entranced by you, Brightness Shallan, and led us here!"

Shallan blushed, considering a response that wasn't particularly proper.

"Ah!" the captain said, pointing at her. "I can see you have a reply—I see it in your eyes, young miss! Spit it out. Words aren't meant to be kept inside, you see. They are free creatures, and if locked away will unsettle the stomach."

"It's not polite," Shallan protested.

Tozbek bellowed a laugh. "Months of travel, and still you claim that! I keep telling you that we're sailors! We forgot how to be polite the moment we set first foot on a ship; we're far beyond redemption now."

She smiled. She'd been trained by stern nurses and tutors to hold her tongue—unfortunately, her brothers had been even more determined in encouraging her to do the opposite. She'd made a habit of entertaining them with witty comments when nobody else was near. She thought fondly of hours spent by the crackling greatroom hearth, the younger three of her four brothers huddled around her, listening as she made sport of their father's newest sycophant or a traveling ardent. She'd often fabricated silly versions of conversations to fill the mouths of people they could see, but not hear.

That had established in her what her nurses had referred to as an "insolent streak." And the sailors were even more appreciative of a witty comment than her brothers had been.

"Well," Shallan said to the captain, blushing but still eager to speak, "I was just thinking this: You say that my beauty coaxed the winds to deliver us to Kharbranth with haste. But wouldn't that imply that on other trips, my lack of beauty was to blame for us arriving late?"

"Well . . . er . . ."

"So in reality," Shallan said, "you're telling me I'm beautiful precisely one-sixth of the time."

"Nonsense! Young miss, you're like a morning sunrise, you are!"

"Like a sunrise? By that you mean entirely too crimson"—she pulled at her long red hair—"and prone to making men grouchy when they see me?"

He laughed, and several of the sailors nearby joined in. "All right then," Captain Tozbek said, "you're like a flower."

She grimaced. "I'm allergic to flowers."

He raised an eyebrow.

"No, really," she admitted. "I think they're quite captivating. But if you were to give me a bouquet, you'd soon find me in a fit so energetic that it would have you searching the walls for stray freckles I might have blown free with the force of my sneezes."

"Well, be that true, I still say you're as *pretty* as a flower."

"If I am, then young men my age must be afflicted with the same allergy—for they keep their distance from me noticeably." She winced. "Now, see, I told you this wasn't polite. Young women should not act in such an irritable way."

"Ah, young miss," the captain said, tipping his knit cap toward her. "The lads and I will miss your clever tongue. I'm not sure what we'll do without you."

"Sail, likely," she said. "And eat, and sing, and watch the waves. All the things you do now, only you shall have rather *more* time to accomplish all of it, as you won't be stumbling across a youthful girl as she sits on your deck sketching and mumbling to herself. But you have my thanks, Captain, for a trip that was wonderful—if somewhat exaggerated in length."

He tipped his cap to her in acknowledgment.

Shallan grinned—she hadn't expected being out on her own to be so liberating. Her brothers had worried that she'd be frightened. They saw her as timid because she didn't like to argue and remained quiet when large groups were talking. And perhaps she *was* timid—being away from Jah Keved was daunting. But it was also wonderful. She'd filled three sketchbooks with pictures of the creatures and people she'd seen, and while her worry over her house's finances was a perpetual cloud, it was balanced by the sheer delight of experience.

Tozbek began making dock arrangements for his ship. He was a good man. As for his praise of her supposed beauty, she took that for what it was. A kind, if overstated, mark of affection. She was pale-skinned in an era when Alethi tan was seen as the mark of true beauty, and though she had light blue eyes, her impure family line was manifest in her auburn-red hair. Not a single lock of proper black. Her freckles had faded as she reached young womanhood—Heralds be blessed—but there were still some visible, dusting her cheeks and nose.

"Young miss," the captain said to her after conferring with his men, "Your Brightness Jasnah, she'll undoubtedly be at the Conclave, you see."

"Oh, where the Palanaeum is?"

"Yes, yes. And the king lives there too. It's the center of the city, so to speak. Except it's on the top." He scratched his chin. "Well, anyway, Brightness Jasnah Kholin is sister to a king; she will stay nowhere else, not in Kharbranth. Yalb here will show you the way. We can deliver your trunk later."

"Many thanks, Captain," she said. "*Shaylor mkabat nour.*" *The winds have brought us safely.* A phrase of thanks in the Thaylen language.

The captain smiled broadly. "*Mkai bade fortenthis!*"

She had no idea what that meant. Her Thaylen was quite

good when she was reading, but hearing it spoken was something else entirely. She smiled at him, which seemed the proper response, for he laughed, gesturing to one of his sailors.

"We'll wait here in this dock for two days," he told her. "There is a highstorm coming tomorrow, you see, so we cannot leave. If the situation with the Brightness Jasnah does not proceed as hoped, we'll take you back to Jah Keved."

"Thank you again."

"'Tis nothing, young miss," he said. "Nothing but what we'd be doing anyway. We can take on goods here and all. Besides, that's a right nice likeness of my wife you gave me for my cabin. Right nice."

He strode over to Yalb, giving him instructions. Shallan waited, putting her drawing pad back into her leather portfolio. Yalb. The name was difficult for her Veden tongue to pronounce. Why were the Thaylens so fond of mashing letters together, without proper vowels?

Yalb waved for her. She moved to follow.

"Be careful with yourself, lass," the captain warned as she passed. "Even a safe city like Kharbranth hides dangers. Keep your wits about you."

"I should think I'd prefer my wits inside my skull, Captain," she replied, carefully stepping onto the gangplank. "If I keep them 'about me' instead, then someone has gotten entirely too close to my head with a cudgel."

The captain laughed, waving her farewell as she made her way down the gangplank, holding the railing with her freehand. Like all Vorin women, she kept her left hand—her safehand—covered, exposing only her freehand. Common darkeyed women would wear a glove, but a woman of her rank was expected to show more modesty than that. In her case, she kept her safehand covered by the oversized cuff of her left sleeve, which was buttoned closed.

The dress was of a traditional Vorin cut, formfitting through the bust, shoulders, and waist, with a flowing skirt below. It was blue silk with chull-shell buttons up the sides, and she carried her satchel by pressing it to her chest with her safehand while holding the railing with her freehand.

She stepped off the gangplank into the furious activity of the docks, messengers running this way and that, women in red coats tracking cargos on ledgers. Kharbranth was a Vorin kingdom, like Alethkar and like Shallan's own Jah Keved. They weren't pagans here, and writing was a feminine art; men learned only glyphs, leaving letters and reading to their wives and sisters.

She hadn't asked, but she was certain Captain Tozbek could read. She'd seen him holding books; it had made her uncomfortable. Reading was an unseemly trait in a man. At least, men who weren't ardents.

"You wanna ride?" Yalb asked her, his rural Thaylen dialect so thick she could barely make out the words.

"Yes, please."

He nodded and rushed off, leaving her on the docks, surrounded by a group of parshmen who were laboriously moving wooden crates from one pier to another. Parshmen were thick-witted, but they made excellent workers. Never complaining, always doing as they were told. Her father had preferred them to ordinary slaves.

Were the Alethi really fighting *parshmen* out on the Shattered Plains? That seemed so odd to Shallan. Parshmen didn't fight. They were docile and practically mute. Of course, from what she'd heard, the ones out on the Shattered Plains—the Parshendi, they were called—were physically different from normal parshmen. Stronger, taller, keener of mind. Perhaps they weren't really parshmen at all, but distant relatives of some kind.

To her surprise, she could see signs of animal life all around the docks. A few skyeels undulated through the air, searching for rats or fish. Tiny crabs hid between cracks in the dock's boards, and a cluster of haspers clung to the dock's thick logs. In a street inland of the docks, a prowling mink skulked in the shadows, watching for morsels that might be dropped.

She couldn't resist pulling open her portfolio and beginning a sketch of a pouncing skyeel. Wasn't it afraid of all the people? She held her sketchpad with her safehand, hidden fingers wrapping around the top as she used a charcoal pencil to draw. Before she was finished, her guide returned with a man pulling a curious contraption with two large wheels and a canopy-covered seat. She hesitantly lowered her sketchpad. She'd expected a palanquin.

The man pulling the machine was short and dark-skinned, with a wide smile and full lips. He gestured for Shallan to sit, and she did so with the modest grace her nurses had drilled into her. The driver asked her a question in a clipped, terse-sounding language she didn't recognize.

"What was that?" she asked Yalb.

"He wants to know if you'd like to be pulled the long way or the short way." Yalb scratched his head. "I'm not right sure what the difference is."

"I suspect one takes longer," Shallan said.

"Oh, you *are* a clever one." Yalb said something to the porter in that same clipped language, and the man responded.

"The long way gives a good view of the city," Yalb said. "The short way goes straight up to the Conclave. Not many good views, he says. I guess he noticed you were new to the city."

"Do I stand out that much?" Shallan asked, flushing.

"Eh, no, of course not, Brightness."

"And by that you mean that I'm as obvious as a wart on a queen's nose."

Yalb laughed. "Afraid so. But you can't go someplace a second time until you been there a first time, I reckon. Everyone has to stand out sometime, so you might as well do it in a pretty way like yourself!"

She'd had to get used to gentle flirtation from the sailors. They were never too forward, and she suspected the captain's wife had spoken to them sternly when she'd noticed how it made Shallan blush. Back at her father's manor, servants—even those who had been full citizens—had been afraid to step out of their places.

The porter was still waiting for an answer. "The short way, please," she told Yalb, though she longed to take the scenic path. She was finally in a *real* city and she took the direct route? But Brightness Jasnah had proven to be as elusive as a wild songling. Best to be quick.

The main roadway cut up the hillside in switchbacks, and so even the short way gave her time to see much of the city. It proved intoxicatingly rich with strange people, sights, and ringing bells. Shallan sat back and took it all in. Buildings were grouped by color, and that color seemed to indicate purpose. Shops selling the same items would be painted the same shades—violet for clothing, green for foods. Homes had their own pattern, though Shallan couldn't interpret it. The colors were soft, with a washed-out, subdued tonality.

Yalb walked alongside her cart, and the porter began to talk back toward her. Yalb translated, hands in the pockets of his vest. "He says that the city is special because of the lait here."

Shallan nodded. Many cities were built in laits—areas protected from the highstorms by nearby rock formations.

"Kharbranth is one of the most sheltered major cities in the world," Yalb continued, translating, "and the bells are a symbol of that. It's said they were first erected to warn that a highstorm was blowing, since the winds were so soft that people didn't always notice." Yalb hesitated. "He's just saying things because he wants a big tip, Brightness. I've heard that story, but I think it's blustering ridiculous. If the winds blew strong enough to move bells, then people'd notice. Besides, people didn't notice it was *raining* on their blustering heads?"

Shallan smiled. "It's all right. He can continue."

The porter chatted on in his clipped voice—what language *was* that, anyway? Shallan listened to Yalb's translation, drinking in the sights, sounds, and—unfortunately—scents. She'd grown up accustomed to the crisp smell of freshly dusted furniture and flatbread baking in the kitchens. Her ocean journey had taught her new scents, of brine and clean sea air.

There was nothing clean in what she smelled here. Each passing alleyway had its own unique array of revolting stenches. These alternated with the spicy scents of street vendors and their foods, and the juxtaposition was even more nauseating. Fortunately, her porter moved into the central part of the roadway, and the stenches abated, though it did slow them as they had to contend with thicker traffic. She gawked at those they passed. Those men with gloved hands and faintly bluish skin were from Natanatan. But who were those tall, stately people dressed in robes of black? And the men with their beards bound in cords, making them rodlike?

The sounds put Shallan in mind of the competing choruses of wild songlings near her home, only multiplied in variety and volume. A hundred voices called to one another, mingling with doors slamming, wheels rolling on stone, occasional skyeels crying. The ever-present bells tinkled in the background, louder when the wind blew. They were displayed in the windows of shops, hung from rafters. Each lantern pole along the street had a bell hung under the lamp, and her cart had a small silvery one at the very tip of its canopy. When she was about halfway up the hillside, a rolling wave of loud clock bells rang the hour. The varied, unsynchronized chimes made a clangorous din.

The crowds thinned as they reached the upper quarter of the city, and eventually her porter pulled her to a massive building at the very apex of the city. Painted white, it was carved from the rock face itself, rather than built of bricks or clay. The pillars out front grew seamlessly from the stone, and the back side of the building melded smoothly into the cliff. The outcroppings of roof had squat domes atop them, and were painted in metallic colors. Lighteyed women passed in and out, carrying scribing utensils and wearing dresses like Shallan's, their left hands properly cuffed. The men entering or leaving the building wore military-style Vorin coats and stiff trousers, buttons up the sides and ending in a stiff collar that wrapped the entire neck. Many carried swords at their waists, the belts wrapping around the knee-length coats.

The porter stopped and made a comment to Yalb. The sailor began arguing with him, hands on hips. Shallan smiled at his stern expression, and she blinked pointedly, affixing the scene in her memory for later sketching.

"He's offering to split the difference with me if I let him

inflate the price of the trip," Yalb said, shaking his head and offering a hand to help Shallan from the cart. She stepped down, looking at the porter, who shrugged, smiling like a child who had been caught sneaking sweets.

She clutched her satchel with her cuffed arm, searching through it with her freehand for her money pouch. "How much should I actually give him?"

"Two clearchips should be more than enough. I'd have offered one. The thief wanted to ask for *five*."

Before this trip, she'd never used money; she'd just admired the spheres for their beauty. Each one was composed of a glass bead a little larger than a person's thumbnail with a much smaller gemstone set at the center. The gemstones could absorb Stormlight, and that made the spheres glow. When she opened the money pouch, shards of ruby, emerald, diamond, and sapphire shone out on her face. She fished out three diamond chips, the smallest denomination. Emeralds were the most valuable, for they could be used by Soulcasters to create food.

The glass part of most spheres was the same size; the size of the gemstone at the center determined the denomination. The three chips, for instance, each had only a tiny splinter of diamond inside. Even that was enough to glow with Stormlight, far fainter than a lamp, but still visible. A mark—the medium denomination of sphere—was a little less bright than a candle, and it took five chips to make a mark.

She'd brought only infused spheres, as she'd heard that dun ones were considered suspect, and sometimes a moneylender would have to be brought in to judge the authenticity of the gemstone. She kept the most valuable spheres she had in her safepouch, of course, which was buttoned to the inside of her left sleeve.

She handed the three chips to Yalb, who cocked his head. She nodded at the porter, blushing, realizing that she'd reflexively used Yalb like a master-servant intermediary. Would he be offended?

He laughed and stood up stiffly, as if imitating a master-servant, paying the porter with a mock stern expression. The porter laughed, bowed to Shallan, then pulled his cart away.

"This is for you," Shallan said, taking out a ruby mark and handing it to Yalb.

"Brightness, this is too much!"

"It's partially out of thanks," she said, "but is also to pay you to stay here and wait for a few hours, in case I return."

"Wait a few hours for a firemark? That's wages for a week's sailing!"

"Then it should be enough to make certain you don't wander off."

"I'll be right here!" Yalb said, giving her an elaborate bow that was surprisingly well-executed.

Shallan took a deep breath and strode up the steps toward the Conclave's imposing entrance. The carved rock really was remarkable—the artist in her wanted to linger and study it, but she didn't dare. Entering the large building was like being swallowed. The hallway inside was lined with Stormlight lamps that shone with white light. Diamond broams were probably set inside them; most buildings of fine construction used Stormlight to provide illumination. A broam—the highest denomination of sphere—glowed with about the same light as several candles.

Their light shone evenly and softly on the many attendants, scribes, and lighteyes moving through the hallway. The building appeared to be constructed as one broad, high, and long tunnel, burrowed into the rock. Grand chambers lined the sides, and subsidiary corridors branched off the central grand promenade. She felt far more comfortable than she had outdoors. This place—with its bustling servants, its lesser brightlords and brightladies—was familiar.

She raised her freehand in a sign of need, and sure enough, a master-servant in a crisp white shirt and black trousers hurried over to her. "Brightness?" he asked, speaking her native Veden, likely because of the color of her hair.

"I seek Jasnah Kholin," Shallan said. "I have word that she is within these walls."

The master-servant bowed crisply. Most master-servants prided themselves on their refined service—the very same air that Yalb had been mocking moments ago. "I shall return, Brightness." He would be of the second nahn, a darkeyed citizen of very high rank. In Vorin belief, one's Calling—the task to which one dedicated one's life—was of vital importance. Choosing a good profession and working hard at it was the best way to ensure good placement in the afterlife. The specific devotary that one visited for worship often had to do with the nature of one's chosen Calling.

Shallan folded her arms, waiting. She had thought long about her own Calling. The obvious choice was her art, and she did so love sketching. But it was more than just the drawing that attracted her—it was the *study*, the questions raised by observation. Why weren't the skyeels afraid of people? What did haspers feed on? Why did a rat population thrive in one area, but fail in another? So she'd chosen natural history instead.

She longed to be a true scholar, to receive real instruction, to spend time on deep research and study. Was that part of why she'd suggested this daring plan of seeking out Jasnah and becoming her ward? Perhaps. However, she needed to remain focused. Becoming Jasnah's ward—and therefore student—was only one step.

She considered this as she idly walked up to a pillar, using her freehand to feel the polished stone. Like much of Roshar—save for certain coastal regions—Kharbranth was built on raw, unbroken stone. The buildings outside had been set directly on the rock, and this one sliced into it. The pillar was granite, she guessed, though her geological knowledge was sketchy.

The floor was covered with long, burnt-orange rugs. The material was dense, designed to look rich but bear heavy traffic. The broad, rectangular hallway had an *old* feel to it. One book she'd read claimed that Kharbranth had been founded way back into the shadowdays, years before the Last Desolation. That would make it old indeed. Thousands of years old, created before the terrors of the Hierocracy, long before—

even—the Recreance. Back when Voidbringers with bodies of stone were said to have stalked the land.

"Brightness?" a voice asked.

Shallan turned to find that the servant had returned.

"This way, Brightness."

She nodded to the servant, and he led her quickly down the busy hallway. She went over how to present herself to Jasnah. The woman was a legend. Even Shallan—living in the remote estates of Jah Keved—had heard of the Alethi king's brilliant, heretic sister. Jasnah was only thirty-four years old, yet many felt she would already have obtained the cap of a master scholar if it weren't for her vocal denunciations of religion. Most specifically, she denounced the devotaries, the various religious congregations that proper Vorin people joined.

Improper quips would not serve Shallan well here. She would have to be proper. Wardship to a woman of great renown was the best way to be schooled in the feminine arts: music, painting, writing, logic, and science. It was much like how a young man would train in the honor guard of a brightlord he respected.

Shallan had originally written to Jasnah requesting a wardship in desperation; she hadn't actually expected the woman to reply in the affirmative. When she had—via a letter commanding Shallan to attend her in Dumadari in two weeks—Shallan had been shocked. She'd been chasing the woman ever since.

Jasnah was a heretic. Would she demand that Shallan renounce her faith? She doubted she could do such a thing. Vorin teachings regarding one's Glory and Calling had been one of her few refuges during the difficult days, when her father had been at his worst.

They turned into a narrower hallway, entering corridors increasingly far from the main cavern. Finally, the master-servant stopped at a corner and gestured for Shallan to continue. There were voices coming from the corridor to the right.

Shallan hesitated. Sometimes, she wondered how it had come to this. She was the quiet one, the timid one, the youngest of five siblings and the only girl. Sheltered, protected all her life. And now the hopes of her entire house rested on her shoulders.

Their father was dead. And it was vital that remain a secret.

She didn't like to think of that day—she all but blocked it from her mind, and trained herself to think of other things. But the effects of his loss could not be ignored. He had made many promises—some business deals, some bribes, some of the latter disguised as the former. House Davar owed great amounts of money to a great number of people, and without her father to keep them all appeased, the creditors would soon begin making demands.

There was nobody to turn to. Her family, mostly because of her father, was loathed even by its allies. Highprince Valam—the brightlord to whom her family gave fealty—was ailing, and no longer offered them the protection he once had. When it became known that her father was dead and her family bankrupt, that would be the end of House Davar. They'd be consumed and subjugated to another house.

They'd be worked to the bone as punishment—in fact, they might even face assassination by disgruntled creditors. Preventing that depended on Shallan, and the first step came with Jasnah Kholin.

Shallan took a deep breath, then strode around the corner.

*"I'm dying, aren't I? Healer, why do you take my blood?
Who is that beside you, with his head of lines? I can see a
distant sun, dark and cold, shining in a black sky."*

—Collected on the 3rd of Jesnan, 1172, 11 seconds pre-death.
Subject was a Reshi chull trainer. Sample is of particular note.

Why don't you cry?" the windspren asked.

Kaladin sat with his back to the corner of the cage,
looking down. The floor planks in front of him were splintered, as if someone had dug at them with nothing but his
fingernails. The splintered section was stained dark where
the dry grey wood had soaked up blood. A futile, delusional
attempt at escape.

The wagon continued to roll. The same routine each day.
Wake up sore and aching from a fitful night spent without
mattress or blanket. One wagon at a time, the slaves were let
out and hobbled with leg irons and given time to shuffle
around and relieve themselves. Then they were packed away
and given morning slop, and the wagons rolled until afternoon slop. More rolling. Evening slop, then a ladle of water
before sleep.

Kaladin's *shash* brand was still cracked and bleeding. At
least the cage's top gave shade from the sun.

The windspren shifted to mist, floating like a tiny cloud. She moved in close to Kaladin, the motion outlining her face at the front of the cloud, as if blowing back the fog and revealing something more substantial underneath. Vaporous, feminine, and angular. With such curious eyes. Like no other spren he'd seen.

"The others cry at night," she said. "But you don't."

"Why cry?" he said, leaning his head back against the bars. "What would it change?"

"I don't know. Why *do* men cry?"

He smiled, closing his eyes. "Ask the Almighty why men cry, little spren. Not me." His forehead dripped with sweat from the Eastern summer humidity, and it stung as it seeped into his wound. Hopefully, they'd have some weeks of spring again soon. Weather and seasons were unpredictable. You never knew how long they would go on, though typically each would last a few weeks.

The wagon rolled on. After a time, he felt sunlight on his face. He opened his eyes. The sun shone in through the upper side of the cage. Two or three hours past noon, then. What of afternoon slop? Kaladin stood, pulling himself up with one hand on the steel bars. He couldn't make out Tvlakv driving the wagon up ahead, only flat-faced Bluth behind. The mercenary had on a dirty shirt that laced up the front and wore a wide-brimmed hat against the sun, his spear and cudgel riding on the wagon bench beside him. He didn't carry a sword—not even Tvlakv did that, not near Alethi land.

The grass continued to part for the wagons, vanishing just in front, then creeping out after the wagons passed. The landscape here was dotted with strange shrubs that Kaladin didn't recognize. They had thick stalks and stems and spiny green needles. Whenever the wagons grew too close, the needles pulled into the stalks, leaving behind twisted, wormlike trunks with knotted branches. They dotted the hilly landscape, rising from the grass-covered rocks like diminutive sentries.

The wagons just kept on going, well past noon. *Why aren't we stopping for slop?*

The lead wagon finally pulled to a stop. The other two

lurched to a halt behind it, the red-carapaced chulls fidgeted, their antennae waving back and forth. The box-shaped animals had bulging, stony shells and thick, trunklike red legs. From what Kaladin had heard, their claws could snap a man's arm. But chulls were docile, particularly domesticated ones, and he'd never known anyone in the army to get more than a halfhearted pinch from one.

Bluth and Tag climbed down from their wagons and walked up to meet Tvlakv. The slavemaster stood on his wagon's seat, shading his eyes against the white sunlight and holding a sheet of paper in his hand. An argument ensued. Tvlakv kept waving in the direction they had been going, then pointing at his sheet of paper.

"Lost, Tvlakv?" Kaladin called. "Perhaps you should pray to the Almighty for guidance. I hear he has a fondness for slavers. Keeps a special room in Damnation just for you."

To Kaladin's left, one of the slaves—the long-bearded man who had talked to him a few days back—sidled away, not wanting to stand close to a person who was provoking the slaver.

Tvlakv hesitated, then waved curtly to his mercenaries, silencing them. The portly man hopped down from his wagon and walked over to Kaladin. "You," he said. "Deserter. Alethi armies travel these lands for their war. Do you know anything of the area?"

"Let me see the map," Kaladin said. Tvlakv hesitated, then held it up for Kaladin.

Kaladin reached through the bars and snatched the paper. Then, without reading it, Kaladin ripped it in two. In seconds he'd shredded it into a hundred pieces in front of Tvlakv's horrified eyes.

Tvlakv called for the mercenaries, but by the time they arrived, Kaladin had a double handful of confetti to toss out at them. "Happy Middlefest, you bastards," Kaladin said as the flakes of paper fluttered around them. He turned and walked to the other side of the cage and sat down, facing them.

Tvlakv stood, speechless. Then, red-faced, he pointed at Kaladin and hissed something at the mercenaries. Bluth took a step toward the cage, but then thought better of it. He glanced at Tvlakv, then shrugged and walked away. Tvlakv turned to Tag, but the other mercenary just shook his head, saying something soft.

After a few minutes of stewing at the cowardly mercenaries, Tvlakv rounded the cage and approached where Kaladin was sitting. Surprisingly, when he spoke, his voice was calm. "I see you are clever, deserter. You have made yourself invaluable. My other slaves, they aren't from this area, and I have never come this way. You can bargain. What is it you wish in exchange for leading us? I can promise you an extra meal each day, should you please me."

"You want me to lead the caravan?"

"Instructions will be acceptable."

"All right. First, find a cliff."

"That, it will give you a vantage to see the area?"

"No," Kaladin said. "It will give me something to throw you off of."

Tvlakv adjusted his cap in annoyance, brushing back one of his long white eyebrows. "You hate me. That is good. Hatred will keep you strong, make you sell for much. But you will not find vengeance on me unless I have a chance to take you to market. I will not let you escape. But perhaps someone else would. You want to be sold, you see?"

"I don't want vengeance," Kaladin said. The windspren came back—she'd darted off for a time to inspect one of the strange shrubs. She landed in the air and began walking around Tvlakv's face, inspecting him. He didn't seem to be able to see her.

Tvlakv frowned. "No vengeance?"

"It doesn't work," Kaladin said. "I learned that lesson long ago."

"Long ago? You cannot be older than eighteen years, deserter."

It was a good guess. He was nineteen. Had it really only been four years since he'd joined Amaram's army? Kaladin felt as if he'd aged a dozen.

"You are young," Tvlakv continued. "You could escape

this fate of yours. Men have been known to live beyond the slave's brand—you could pay off your slave price, you see? Or convince one of your masters to give you your freedom. You could become a free man again. It is not so unlikely."

Kaladin snorted. "I'll never be free of these brands, Tvlakv. You must know that I've tried—and failed—to escape ten times over. It's more than these glyphs on my head that makes your mercenaries wary."

"Past failure does not prove that there is not chance in the future, yes?"

"I'm finished. I don't care." He eyed the slaver. "Besides, you don't actually believe what you're saying. I doubt a man like you would be able to sleep at night if he thought the slaves he sold would be free to seek him out one day."

Tvlakv laughed. "Perhaps, deserter. Perhaps you are right. Or perhaps I simply think that if you *were* to get free, you would hunt down the first man who sold you to slavery, you see? Highlord Amaram, was it not? His death would give me warning so I can run."

How had he known? How had he heard about Amaram? *I'll find him,* Kaladin thought. *I'll gut him with my own hands. I'll twist his head right off his neck, I'll—*

"Yes," Tvlakv said, studying Kaladin's face, "so you were not so honest when you said you do not thirst for vengeance. I see."

"How do you know about Amaram?" Kaladin said, scowling. "I've changed hands a half-dozen times since then."

"Men talk. Slavers more than most. We must be friends with one another, you see, for nobody else will stomach us."

"Then you know that I didn't get this brand for deserting."

"Ah, but it is what we must pretend, you see? Men guilty of high crimes, they do not sell so well. With that *shash* glyph on your head, it will be difficult enough to get a good price for you. If I cannot sell you, then you . . . well, you will not wish for that status. So we will play a game together. I will say you are a deserter. And you will say nothing. It is an easy game, I think."

"It's illegal."

"We are not in Alethkar," Tvlakv said, "so there is no law. Besides, desertion was the official reason for your sale. Claim otherwise, and you will gain nothing but a reputation for dishonesty."

"Nothing besides a headache for you."

"But you just said you have no desire for vengeance against me."

"I could learn."

Tvlakv laughed. "Ah, if you have not learned that already, then you probably never will! Besides, did you not threaten to throw me off a cliff? I think you have learned already. But now, we *must* discuss how to proceed. My map has met with an untimely demise, you see."

Kaladin hesitated, then sighed. "I don't know," he said honestly. "I've never been this way either."

Tvlakv frowned. He leaned closer to the cage, inspecting Kaladin, though he still kept his distance. After a moment, Tvlakv shook his head. "I believe you, deserter. A pity. Well, I shall trust my memory. The map was poorly rendered anyway. I am almost glad you ripped it, for I was tempted to do the same myself. If I should happen across any portraits of my former wives, I shall see that they cross your path and take advantage of your unique talents." He strolled away.

Kaladin watched him go, then cursed to himself.

"What was that for?" the windspren said, walking up to him, head cocked.

"I almost find myself liking him," Kaladin said, pounding his head back against the cage.

"But . . . after what he did . . ."

Kaladin shrugged. "I didn't say Tvlakv isn't a bastard. He's just a likable bastard." He hesitated, then grimaced. "Those are the worst kind. When you kill them, you end up feeling guilty for it."

⁂

The wagon leaked during highstorms. That wasn't surprising; Kaladin suspected that Tvlakv had been driven to slaving by ill fortune. He would rather be trading other goods, but something—lack of funds, a need to leave his previous environs with haste—had forced him to pick up this least reputable of careers.

Men like him couldn't afford luxury, or even quality. They could barely stay ahead of their debts. In this case, that meant wagons which leaked. The boarded sides were strong enough to withstand highstorm winds, but they weren't comfortable.

Tvlakv had almost missed getting ready for this highstorm. Apparently, the map Kaladin had torn up had also included a list of highstorm dates purchased from a roving stormwarden. The storms could be predicted mathematically; Kaladin's father had made a hobby of it. He'd been able to pick the right day eight times out of ten.

The boards rattled against the cage's bars as wind buffeted the vehicle, shaking it, making it lurch like a clumsy giant's plaything. The wood groaned and spurts of icy rainwater sprayed through cracks. Flashes of lightning leaked through as well, accompanied by thunder. That was the only light they got.

Occasionally, light would flash without the thunder. The slaves would groan in terror at this, thinking about the Stormfather, the shades of the Lost Radiants, or the Voidbringers—all of which were said to haunt the most violent highstorms. They huddled together on the far side of the wagon, sharing warmth. Kaladin left them to it, sitting alone with his back to the bars.

Kaladin didn't fear stories of things that walked the storms. In the army, he'd been forced to weather a highstorm or two beneath the lip of a protective stone overhang or other bit of impromptu shelter. Nobody liked to be out during a storm, but sometimes you couldn't avoid it. The things that walked the storms—perhaps even the Stormfather himself—weren't nearly so deadly as the rocks and branches cast up into the air. In fact, the storm's initial tempest of water and wind—the stormwall—was the most dangerous part. The longer one endured after that, the weaker the storm grew, until the trailing edge was nothing more than sprinkling rain.

No, he wasn't worried about Voidbringers looking for

flesh to feast upon. He was worried that something would happen to Tvlakv. The slavemaster waited out the storm in a cramped wooden enclosure built into the bottom of his wagon. That was ostensibly the safest place in the caravan, but an unlucky twist of fate—a tempest-thrown boulder, the collapse of the wagon—could leave him dead. In that case, Kaladin could see Bluth and Tag running off, leaving everyone in their cages, wooden sides locked up. The slaves would die a slow death by starvation and dehydration, baking under the sun in these boxes.

The storm continued to blow, shaking the wagon. Those winds felt like live things at times. And who was to say they weren't? Were windspren attracted *to* gusts of wind, or *were* they the gusts of wind? The souls of the force that now wanted so badly to destroy Kaladin's wagon?

That force—sentient or not—failed. The wagons were chained to nearby boulders with their wheels locked. The blasts of wind grew more lethargic. Lightning stopped flashing, and the maddening drumming of rain became a quiet tapping instead. Only once during their journey had a wagon toppled during a highstorm. Both it and the slaves inside had survived with a few dents and bruises.

The wooden side to Kaladin's right shook suddenly, then fell open as Bluth undid its clasps. The mercenary wore his leather coat against the wet, streams of water falling from the brim of his hat as he exposed the bars—and the occupants—to the rain. It was cold, though not as piercingly so as during the height of the storm. It sprayed across Kaladin and the huddled slaves. Tvlakv always ordered the wagons uncovered before the rain stopped; he said it was the only way to wash away the slaves' stink.

Bluth slid the wooden side into place beneath the wagon, then opened the other two sides. Only the wall at the front of the wagon—just behind the driver's seat—couldn't be brought down.

"Little early to be taking down the sides, Bluth," Kaladin said. It wasn't quite the riddens yet—the period near the end of a highstorm when the rain sprinkled softly. This rain was still heavy, the wind still gusting on occasion.

"The master wants you plenty clean today."

"Why?" Kaladin asked, rising, water streaming from his ragged brown clothing.

Bluth ignored him. *Perhaps we're nearing our destination*, Kaladin thought as he scanned the landscape.

Over the last few days, the hills had given way to uneven rock formations—places where weathering winds had left behind crumbling cliffs and jagged shapes. Grass grew up the rocky sides that saw the most sun, and other plants were plentiful in the shade. The time right after a highstorm was when the land was most alive. Rockbud polyps split and sent out their vines. Other kinds of vine crept from crevices, licking up water. Leaves unfolded from shrubs and trees. Cremlings of all kinds slithered through puddles, enjoying the banquet. Insects buzzed into the air; larger crustaceans—crabs and leggers—left their hiding places. The very rocks seemed to come to life.

Kaladin noted a half-dozen windspren flitting overhead, their translucent forms chasing after—or perhaps cruising along with—the highstorm's last gusts. Tiny lights rose around the plants. Lifespren. They looked like motes of glowing green dust or swarms of tiny translucent insects.

A legger—its hairlike spines lifted to the air to give warning of changes in the wind—climbed along the side of the cart, its long body lined with dozens of pairs of legs. That was familiar enough, but he'd never seen a legger with such a deep purple carapace. Where was Tvlakv taking the caravan? Those uncultivated hillsides were perfect for farming. You could spread stumpweight sap on them—mixed with lavis seeds—during seasons of weaker storms following the Weeping. In four months, you'd have polyps larger than a man's head growing all along the hill, ready to break open for the grain inside.

The chulls lumbered about, feasting on rockbuds, slugs, and smaller crustaceans that had appeared after the storm.

Tag and Bluth quietly hitched the beasts to their harnesses as a grumpy-looking Tvlakv crawled out of his waterproof refuge. The slavemaster pulled on a cap and deep black cloak against the rain. He rarely came out until the storm had passed completely; he was *very* eager to get to their destination. Were they that close to the coast? That was one of the only places where they'd find cities in the Unclaimed Hills.

Within minutes, the wagons were rolling again across the uneven ground. Kaladin settled back as the sky cleared, the highstorm a smudge of blackness on the western horizon. The sun brought welcome warmth, and the slaves basked in the light, streams of water dripping from their clothing and running out the back of the rocking wagon.

Presently, a translucent ribbon of light zipped up to Kaladin. He was coming to take the windspren's presence for granted. She had gone out during the storm, but she'd come back. As always.

"I saw others of your kind," Kaladin said idly.

"Others?" she asked, taking the form of a young woman. She began to step around him in the air, spinning occasionally, dancing to some unheard beat.

"Windspren," Kaladin said. "Chasing after the storm. Are you certain you don't want to go with them?"

She glanced westward, longingly. "No," she finally said, continuing her dance. "I like it here."

Kaladin shrugged. She'd ceased playing as many pranks as she once had, and so he'd stopped letting her presence annoy him.

"There are others near," she said. "Others like you."

"Slaves?"

"I don't know. People. Not the ones here. Other ones."

"Where?"

She turned a translucent white finger, pointing eastward. "There. Many of them. Lots and lots."

Kaladin stood up. He couldn't imagine that a spren had a good handle on how to measure distance and numbers. *Yes . . .* Kaladin squinted, studying the horizon. *That's smoke. From chimneys?* He caught a gust of it on the wind; if not for the rain, he'd probably have smelled it sooner.

Should he care? It didn't matter where he was a slave; he'd still be a slave. He'd accepted this life. That was his way now. Don't care, don't bother.

Still, he watched with curiosity as his wagon climbed the side of a hill and gave the slaves inside a good vantage of what was ahead. It wasn't a city. It was something grander, something larger. An enormous army encampment.

"Great Father of Storms . . ." Kaladin whispered.

Ten masses of troops bivouacked in familiar Alethi patterns—circular, by company rank, with camp followers on the outskirts, mercenaries in a ring just inside them, citizen soldiers near the middle, lighteyed officers at the very center. They were camped in a series of enormous craterlike rock formations, only the sides were more irregular, more jagged. Like broken eggshells.

Kaladin had left an army much like this eight months ago, though Amaram's force had been much smaller. This one covered miles of stone, stretching far both north and south. A thousand banners bearing a thousand different family glyph-pairs flapped proudly in the air. There were some tents—mainly on the outside of the armies—but most of the troops were housed in large stone barracks. That meant Soulcasters.

That encampment directly ahead of them flew a banner Kaladin had seen in books. Deep blue with white glyphs—*khokh* and *linil*, stylized and painted as a sword standing before a crown. House Kholin. The king's house.

Daunted, Kaladin looked beyond the armies. The landscape to the east was as he'd heard it described in a dozen different stories detailing the king's campaign against the Parshendi betrayers. It was an enormous riven plain of rock—so wide he couldn't see the other side—that was split and cut by sheer chasms, crevasses twenty or thirty feet wide. They were so deep that they disappeared into darkness and formed a jagged mosaic of uneven plateaus. Some large, others tiny. The expansive plain looked like a platter that had been broken, its pieces then reassembled with small gaps between the fragments.

"The Shattered Plains," Kaladin whispered.

"What?" the windspren asked. "What's wrong?"

Kaladin shook his head, bemused. "I spent years trying to get to this place. It's what Tien wanted, in the end at least. To come here, fight in the king's army . . ."

And now Kaladin was here. Finally. *Accidentally.* He felt like laughing at the absurdity. *I should have realized,* he thought. *I should have known. We weren't ever heading toward the coast and its cities. We were heading here. To war.*

This place would be subject to Alethi law and rules. He'd expected that Tvlakv would want to avoid such things. But here, he'd probably also find the best prices.

"The Shattered Plains?" one of the slaves said. "Really?"

Others crowded around, peering out. In their sudden excitement, they seemed to forget their fear of Kaladin.

"It *is* the Shattered Plains!" another man said. "That's the king's army!"

"Perhaps we'll find justice here," another said.

"I hear the king's household servants live as well as the finest merchants," said another. "His slaves have to be better off too. We'll be in Vorin lands; we'll even make wages!"

That much was true. When worked, slaves had to be paid a small wage—half what a nonslave would be paid, which was already often less than a full citizen would make for the same work. But it was something, and Alethi law required it. Only ardents—who couldn't own anything anyway—didn't have to be paid. Well, them and parshmen. But parshmen were more animal than anything else.

A slave could apply his earnings to his slave debt and, after years of labor, earn his freedom. Theoretically. The others continued to chatter as the wagons rolled down the incline, but Kaladin withdrew to the back of the wagon. He suspected that the option to pay off a slave's price was a sham, intended to keep slaves docile. The debt was enormous, far more than a slave sold for, and virtually impossible to earn out.

Under previous masters, he'd demanded his wages be given

to him. They had always found ways to cheat him—charging him for his housing, his food. That's how lighteyes were. Roshone, Amaram, Katarotam . . . Each lighteyes Kaladin had known, whether as a slave or a free man, had shown himself to be corrupt to the core, for all his outward poise and beauty. They were like rotting corpses clothed in beautiful silk.

The other slaves kept talking about the king's army, and about justice. *Justice?* Kaladin thought, resting back against the bars. *I'm not convinced there* is *such a thing as justice.* Still, he found himself wondering. That was the king's army—the armies of all ten highprinces—come to fulfill the Vengeance Pact.

If there was one thing he still let himself long for, it was the chance to hold a spear. To fight again, to try and find his way back to the man he had been. A man who had cared.

If he would find that anywhere, he'd find it here.

"I have seen the end, and have heard it named. The Night of Sorrows, the True Desolation. The Everstorm."

—Collected on the 1st of Nanes, 1172, 15 seconds pre-death. Subject was a darkeyed youth of unknown origin.

Shallan had not expected Jasnah Kholin to be so beautiful. It was a stately, mature beauty—as one might find in the portrait of some historical scholar. Shallan realized that she'd naively been expecting Jasnah to be an ugly spinster, like the stern matrons who had tutored her years ago. How else could one picture a heretic well into her mid-thirties and still unmarried?

Jasnah was nothing like that. She was tall and slender, with clear skin, narrow black eyebrows, and thick, deep onyx hair. She wore part of it up, wrapped around a small, scroll-shaped golden ornament with two long hairpins holding it in place. The rest tumbled down behind her neck in small, tight curls. Even twisted and curled as it was, it came down to Jasnah's shoulders—if left unbound, it would be as long as Shallan's hair, reaching past the middle of her back.

She had a squarish face and discriminating pale violet eyes. She was listening to a man dressed in robes of burnt orange and white, the Kharbranthian royal colors. Brightness

Kholin was several fingers taller than the man—apparently, the Alethi reputation for height was no exaggeration. Jasnah glanced at Shallan, noting her, then returned to her conversation.

Stormfather! This woman *was* the sister of a king. Reserved, statuesque, dressed immaculately in blue and silver. Like Shallan's dress, Jasnah's buttoned up the sides and had a high collar, though Jasnah had a much fuller chest than Shallan. The skirts were loose below the waist, falling generously to the floor. Her sleeves were long and stately, and the left one was buttoned up to hide her safehand.

On her freehand was a distinctive piece of jewelry: two rings and a bracelet connected by several chains, holding a triangular group of gemstones across the back of the hand. A Soulcaster—the word was used for both the people who performed the process and the fabrial that made it possible.

Shallan edged into the room, trying to get a better look at the large, glowing gemstones. Her heart began to beat a little faster. The Soulcaster looked identical to the one she and her brothers had found in the inside pocket of her father's coat.

Jasnah and the man in robes began walking in Shallan's direction, still talking. How would Jasnah react, now that her ward had finally caught up to her? Would she be angry because of Shallan's tardiness? Shallan couldn't be blamed for that, but people often expect irrational things from their inferiors.

Like the grand cavern outside, this hallway was cut from the rock, but it was more richly furbished, with ornate hanging chandeliers made with Stormlit gemstones. Most were deep violet garnets, which were among the less valuable stones. Even so, the sheer number hanging there glistening with violet light would make the chandelier worth a small fortune. More than that, however, Shallan was impressed with the symmetry of the design and the beauty of the pattern of crystals hanging at the sides of the chandelier.

As Jasnah grew near, Shallan could hear some of what she was saying.

". . . realize that this action might prompt an unfavorable

reaction from the devotaries?" the woman said, speaking in Alethi. It was very near to Shallan's native Veden, and she'd been taught to speak it well during her childhood.

"Yes, Brightness," said the robed man. He was elderly, with a wispy white beard, and had pale grey eyes. His open, kindly face seemed very concerned, and he wore a squat, cylindrical hat that matched the orange and white of his robes. Rich robes. Was this some kind of royal steward, perhaps?

No. Those gemstones on his fingers, the way he carried himself, the way other lighteyed attendants deferred to him . . . *Stormfather!* Shallan thought. *This has to be the king himself!* Not Jasnah's brother, Elhokar, but the king of Kharbranth. Taravangian.

Shallan hastily performed an appropriate curtsy, which Jasnah noted.

"The ardents have much sway here, Your Majesty," Jasnah said with a smooth voice.

"As do I," the king said. "You needn't worry about me."

"Very well," Jasnah said. "Your terms are agreeable. Lead me to the location, and I shall see what can be done. If you will excuse me as we walk, however, I have someone to attend to." Jasnah made a curt motion toward Shallan, waving her to join them.

"Of course, Brightness," the king said. He seemed to defer to Jasnah. Kharbranth was a very small kingdom—just a single city—while Alethkar was one of the world's most powerful. An Alethi princess might well outrank a Kharbranthian king in real terms, however protocol would have it.

Shallan hurried to catch up to Jasnah, who walked a little behind the king as he began to speak to his attendants. "Brightness," Shallan said. "I am Shallan Davar, whom you asked to meet you. I deeply regret not being able to get to you in Dumadari."

"The fault was not yours," Jasnah said with a wave of the fingers. "I didn't expect that you would make it in time. I wasn't certain where I would be going after Dumadari when I sent you that note, however."

Jasnah wasn't angry; that was a good sign. Shallan felt some of her anxiety recede.

"I am impressed by your tenacity, child," Jasnah continued. "I honestly didn't expect you to follow me this far. After Kharbranth, I was going to forgo leaving you notes, as I'd presumed that you'd have given up. Most do so after the first few stops."

Most? Then it was a *test* of some sort? And Shallan had passed?

"Yes indeed," Jasnah continued, voice musing. "Perhaps I will actually allow you to petition me for a place as my ward."

Shallan almost stumbled in shock. *Petition* her? Wasn't that what she'd already done? "Brightness," Shallan said, "I thought that . . . Well, your letter . . ."

Jasnah eyed her. "I gave you leave to *meet* me, Miss Davar. I did not promise to take you on. The training and care of a ward is a distraction for which I have little tolerance or time at the present. But you have traveled far. I will entertain your request, though understand that my requirements are strict."

Shallan covered a grimace.

"No tantrum," Jasnah noted. "That is a good sign."

"Tantrum, Brightness? From a lighteyed woman?"

"You'd be surprised," Jasnah said dryly. "But attitude alone will not earn your place. Tell me, how extensive is your education?"

"Extensive in some areas," Shallan said. Then she hesitantly added, "Extensively lacking in others."

"Very well," Jasnah said. Ahead, the king seemed to be in a hurry, but he was old enough that even an urgent walk was still slow. "Then we shall do an evaluation. Answer truthfully and do not exaggerate, as I will soon discover your lies. Feign no false modesty, either. I haven't the patience for a simperer."

"Yes, Brightness."

"We shall begin with music. How would you judge your skill?"

"I have a good ear, Brightness," Shallan said honestly. "I'm best with voice, though I have been trained on the zither and the pipes. I would be far from the best you'd heard, but I'd also be far from the worst. I know most historical ballads by heart."

"Give me the refrain from 'Lilting Adrene.' "

"Here?"

"I'm not fond of repeating myself, child."

Shallan blushed, but began to sing. It wasn't her finest performance, but her tone was pure and she didn't stumble over any of the words.

"Good," Jasnah said as Shallan paused for a breath. "Languages?"

Shallan fumbled for a moment, bringing her attention away from frantically trying to remember the next verse. Languages? "I can speak your native Alethi, obviously," Shallan said. "I have a passable reading knowledge of Thaylen and good spoken Azish. I can make myself understood in Selay, but not read it."

Jasnah made no comment either way. Shallan began to grow nervous.

"Writing?" Jasnah asked.

"I know all of the major, minor, and topical glyphs and can paint them calligraphically."

"So can most children."

"The glyphwards that I paint are regarded by those who know me as quite impressive."

"Glyphwards?" Jasnah said. "I had reason to believe you wanted to be a scholar, not a purveyor of superstitious nonsense."

"I have kept a journal since I was a child," Shallan continued, "in order to practice my writing skills."

"Congratulations," Jasnah said. "Should I need someone to write a treatise on their stuffed pony or give an account of an interesting pebble they discovered, I shall send for you. Is there nothing you can offer that shows you have true skill?"

Shallan blushed. "With all due respect, Brightness, you have a letter from me yourself, and it was persuasive enough to make you grant me this audience."

"A valid point," Jasnah said, nodding. "It took you long

enough to make it. How is your training in logic and its related arts?"

"I am accomplished in basic mathematics," Shallan said, still flustered, "and I often helped with minor accounts for my father. I have read through the complete works of Tormas, Nashan, Niali the Just, and—of course—Nohadon."

"Placini?"

Who? "No."

"Gabrathin, Yustara, Manaline, Syasikk, Shauka-daughter-Hasweth?"

Shallan cringed and shook her head again. That last name was obviously Shin. Did the Shin people even *have* logicmasters? Did Jasnah really expect her wards to have studied such obscure texts?

"I see," Jasnah said. "Well, what of history?"

History. Shallan shrank down even further. "I . . . This is one of the areas where I'm obviously deficient, Brightness. My father was never able to find a suitable tutor for me. I read the history books he owned. . . ."

"Which were?"

"The entire set of Barlesha Lhan's *Topics*, mostly."

Jasnah waved her freehand dismissively. "Barely worth the time spent scribing them. A popular survey of historical events at best."

"I apologize, Brightness."

"This is an embarrassing hole. History is *the* most important of the literary subarts. One would think that your parents would have taken specific care in this area, if they'd hoped to submit you to study under a historian like myself."

"My circumstances are unusual, Brightness."

"Ignorance is hardly unusual, Miss Davar. The longer I live, the more I come to realize that it is the natural state of the human mind. There are many who will strive to defend its sanctity and then expect you to be impressed with their efforts."

Shallan blushed again. She'd realized she had some deficiencies, but Jasnah had unreasonable expectations. She said nothing, continuing to walk beside the taller woman. How long was this hallway, anyway? She was so flustered she didn't even look at the paintings they passed. They turned a corner, walking deeper into the mountainside.

"Well, let us move on to science, then," Jasnah said, tone displeased. "What can you say of yourself there?"

"I have the reasonable foundation in the sciences you might expect of a young woman my age," Shallan said, more stiffly than she would have liked.

"Which means?"

"I can speak with skill about geography, geology, physics, and chemistry. I've made particular study of biology and botany, as I was able to pursue them with a reasonable level of independence on my father's estates. But if you expect me to be able to solve Fabrisan's Conundrum with a wave of my hand, I suspect you shall be disappointed."

"Have I not a right to make reasonable demands of my potential students, Miss Davar?"

"Reasonable? Your demands are about as *reasonable* as the ones made of the Ten Heralds on Proving Day! With all due respect, Brightness, you seem to want potential wards to be master scholars already. I may be able to find a pair of eighty-year-old ardents in the city who *might* fit your requirements. They could interview for the position, though they may have trouble hearing well enough to answer your questions."

"I see," Jasnah replied. "And do you speak with such pique to your parents as well?"

Shallan winced. Her time spent with the sailors had loosened her tongue far too much. Had she traveled all this way only to offend Jasnah? She thought of her brothers, destitute, keeping up a tenuous facade back home. Would she have to return to them in defeat, having squandered this opportunity? "I did not speak to them this way, Brightness. Nor should I to you. I apologize."

"Well, at least you are humble enough to admit fault. Still, I am disappointed. How is it that your mother considered you ready for a wardship?"

"My mother passed away when I was just a child, Brightness."

"And your father soon remarried. Malise Gevelmar, I believe."

Shallan started at her knowledge. House Davar was ancient, but only of middling power and importance. The fact that Jasnah knew the name of Shallan's stepmother said a lot about her. "My stepmother passed away recently. She didn't send me to be your ward. I took this initiative upon myself."

"My condolences," Jasnah said. "Perhaps you should be with your father, seeing to his estates and comforting him, rather than wasting my time."

The men walking ahead turned down another side passage. Jasnah and Shallan followed, entering a smaller corridor with an ornate red and yellow rug, mirrors hanging on the walls.

Shallan turned to Jasnah. "My father has no need of me." Well, that was true. "But I have great need of you, as this interview itself has proven. If ignorance galls you so much, can you in good conscience pass up the opportunity to rid me of mine?"

"I've done so before, Miss Davar. You are the twelfth young woman to ask me for a wardship this year."

Twelve? Shallan thought. *In one year?* And she'd assumed that women would stay away from Jasnah because of her antagonism toward the devotaries.

The group reached the end of the narrow hallway, turning a corner to find—to Shallan's surprise—a place where a large chunk of rock had fallen from the ceiling. A dozen or so attendants stood here, some looking anxious. What was going on?

Much of the rubble had evidently been cleared away, though the gouge in the ceiling gaped ominously. It didn't look out on the sky; they had been progressing downward, and were probably far underground. A massive stone, taller than a man, had fallen into a doorway on the left. There was no getting past it into the room beyond. Shallan thought she heard sounds on the other side. The king stepped up to the stone, speaking in a comforting voice. He pulled a handkerchief out of his pocket and wiped his aged brow.

"The dangers of living in a building cut directly into the rock," Jasnah said, striding forward. "When did this happen?" Apparently she hadn't been summoned to the city specifically for this purpose; the king was simply taking advantage of her presence.

"During the recent highstorm, Brightness," the king said. He shook his head, making his drooping, thin white mustache tremble. "The palace architects might be able to cut a way into the room, but it would take time, and the next highstorm is scheduled to hit in just a few days. Beyond that, breaking in might bring down more of the ceiling."

"I thought Kharbranth was protected from the highstorms, Your Majesty," Shallan said, causing Jasnah to shoot her a glance.

"The city is sheltered, young woman," the king said. "But the stone mountain behind us is buffeted quite strongly. Sometimes it causes avalanches on that side, and that can cause the entire mountainside to shake." He glanced at the ceiling. "Cave-ins are very rare, and we thought this area was quite safe, but . . ."

"But it is rock," Jasnah said, "and there is no telling if a weak vein lurks just beyond the surface." She inspected the monolith that had fallen from the ceiling. "This will be difficult. I will probably lose a very valuable focal stone."

"I—" the king began, wiping his brow again. "If only we had a Shardblade—"

Jasnah cut him off with a wave of the hand. "I was not seeking to renegotiate our bargain, Your Majesty. Access to the Palanaeum is worth the cost. You will want to send someone for wet rags. Have the majority of the servants move down to the other end of the hallway. You may wish to wait there yourself."

"I will stay here," the king said, causing his attendants to object, including a large man wearing a black leather cuirass, probably his bodyguard. The king silenced them by raising his wrinkled hand. "I will not hide like a coward when my granddaughter is trapped."

No wonder he was so anxious. Jasnah didn't argue further, and Shallan could see from her eyes that it was of no consequence to her if the king risked his life. The same apparently went for Shallan, for Jasnah didn't order her away. Servants approached with wetted cloths and distributed them. Jasnah refused hers. The king and his bodyguard raised theirs to their faces, covering mouth and nose.

Shallan took hers. What was the point of it? A couple of servants passed some wet cloths through a space between the rock and the wall to those inside. Then all of the servants rushed away down the hallway.

Jasnah picked and prodded at the boulder. "Miss Davar," she said, "what method would you use to ascertain the mass of this stone?"

Shallan blinked. "Well, I suppose I'd ask His Majesty. His architects probably calculated it."

Jasnah cocked her head. "An elegant response. Did they do that, Your Majesty?"

"Yes, Brightness Kholin," the king said. "It's roughly fifteen thousand kavals."

Jasnah eyed Shallan. "A point in your favor, Miss Davar. A scholar knows not to waste time rediscovering information already known. It's a lesson I sometimes forget."

Shallan felt herself swell at the words. She already had an inkling that Jasnah did not give such praise lightly. Did this mean that the woman was still considering her as a ward?

Jasnah held up her freehand, Soulcaster glistening against the skin. Shallan felt her heartbeat speed up. She'd never seen Soulcasting done in person. The ardents were very secretive in using their fabrials, and she hadn't even known that her father had one until they'd found it on him. Of course, his no longer worked. That was one of the main reasons she was here.

The gemstones set into Jasnah's Soulcaster were enormous, some of the largest that Shallan had ever seen, worth many spheres each. One was smokestone, a pure glassy black gemstone. The second was a diamond. The third was a ruby. All three were cut—a cut stone could hold more Stormlight—into glistening, many-faceted oval shapes.

Jasnah closed her eyes, pressing her hand against the fallen boulder. She raised her head, inhaling slowly. The stones on the back of her hand began to glow more fiercely, the smokestone in particular growing so bright it was difficult to look at.

Shallan held her breath. The only thing she dared do was blink, committing the scene to memory. For a long, extended moment, nothing happened.

And then, briefly, Shallan heard a sound. A low thrumming, like a distant group of voices, humming together a single, pure note.

Jasnah's hand *sank* into the rock.

The stone vanished.

A burst of dense black smoke exploded into the hallway. Enough to blind Shallan; it seemed the output of a thousand fires, and smelled of burned wood. Shallan hastily raised the wet rag to her face, dropping to her knees. Oddly, her ears felt stopped up, as if she'd climbed down from a great height. She had to swallow to pop them.

She shut her eyes tightly as they began to water, and she held her breath. Her ears filled with a rushing sound.

It passed. She blinked open her eyes to find the king and his bodyguard huddled against the wall beside her. Smoke still pooled at the ceiling; the hallway smelled strongly of it. Jasnah stood, eyes still closed, oblivious of the smoke—though grime now dusted her face and clothing. It had left marks on the walls too.

Shallan had read of this, but she was still in awe. Jasnah had transformed the boulder into smoke, and since smoke was far less dense than stone, the change had pushed the smoke away in an explosive outburst.

It was true; Jasnah really *did* have a functioning Soulcaster. And a powerful one too. Nine out of ten Soulcasters were capable of a few limited transformations: creating water or grain from stone; forming bland, single-roomed rock buildings out of air or cloth. A greater one, like Jasnah's, could effectuate any transformation. Literally turn any substance into any other one. How it must grate on the ardents that such a powerful, holy relic was in the hands of someone outside the ardentia. And a heretic no less!

Shallan stumbled to her feet, leaving the cloth at her mouth, breathing humid but dust-free air. She swallowed, her ears popping again as the hall's pressure returned to normal. A moment later, the king rushed into the now-accessible room. A small girl—along with several nursemaids and other palace servants—sat on the other side, coughing. The king pulled the girl into his arms. She was too young to have a modesty sleeve.

Jasnah opened her eyes, blinking, as if momentarily confused by her location. She took a deep breath, and didn't cough. Indeed, she actually *smiled*, as if enjoying the scent of the smoke.

Jasnah turned to Shallan, focusing on her. "You are still waiting for a response. I'm afraid you will not like what I say."

"But you haven't finished your testing of me yet," Shallan said, forcing herself to be bold. "Surely you won't give judgment until you have."

"I haven't finished?" Jasnah asked, frowning.

"You didn't ask me about all of the feminine arts. You left out painting and drawing."

"I have never had much use for them."

"But *they* are of the arts," Shallan said, feeling desperate. This was where she was most accomplished! "Many consider the visual arts the most refined of them all. I brought my portfolio. I would show you what I can do."

Jasnah pursed her lips. "The visual arts are frivolity. I have weighed the facts, child, and I cannot accept you. I'm sorry."

Shallan's heart sank.

"Your Majesty," Jasnah said to the king, "I would like to go to the Palanaeum."

"Now?" the king said, cradling his granddaughter. "But we are going to have a feast—"

"I appreciate the offer," Jasnah said, "but I find myself with an abundance of everything *but* time."

"Of course," the king said. "I will take you personally. Thank you for what you've done. When I heard that you had requested entrance . . ." He continued to babble at Jasnah, who followed him wordlessly down the hallway, leaving Shallan behind.

She clutched her satchel to her chest, lowering the cloth from her mouth. Six months of chasing, for this. She gripped the rag in frustration, squeezing sooty water between her fingers. She wanted to cry. That was what she probably would have done if she'd been that same child she had been six months ago.

But things had changed. *She* had changed. If she failed, House Davar would fall. Shallan felt her determination redouble, though she wasn't able to stop a few tears of frustration from squeezing out of the corners of her eyes. She was not going to give up until Jasnah was forced to truss her up in chains and have the authorities drag her away.

Her step surprisingly firm, she walked in the direction Jasnah had gone. Six months ago, she had explained a desperate plan to her brothers. She would apprentice herself to Jasnah Kholin, scholar, heretic. Not for the education. Not for the prestige. But in order to learn where she kept her Soulcaster.

And then Shallan would steal it.

Charcoal rubbing of a map of Sadeas's warcamp as used by a common spearman. It was scratched on the back of a palm-size cremling shell. Rubbing labeled in ink by an anonymous Alethi scholar, circa 1173.

6

BRIDGE FOUR

"I'm cold. Mother, I'm cold. Mother? Why can I still hear the rain? Will it stop?"

—Collected on Vevishes, 1172, 32 seconds pre-death. Subject was a lighteyed female child, approximately six years old.

Tvlakv released all of the slaves from their cages at once. This time, he didn't fear runaways or a slave rebellion— not with nothing but wilderness behind them and over a hundred thousand armed soldiers just ahead.

Kaladin stepped down from the wagon. They were inside one of the craterlike formations, its jagged stone wall rising just to the east. The ground had been cleared of plant life, and the rock was slick beneath his unshod feet. Pools of rainwater had gathered in depressions. The air was crisp and clean, and the sun strong overhead, though with this Eastern humidity, he always felt damp.

Around them spread the signs of an army long settled; this war had been going on since the old king's death, nearly six years ago. Everyone told stories of that night, the night when Parshendi tribesmen had murdered King Gavilar.

Squads of soldiers marched by, following directions indicated by painted circles at each intersection. The camp was packed with long stone bunkers, and there were more tents than Kaladin had discerned from above. Soulcasters couldn't be used to create every shelter. After the stink of the slave caravan, the place smelled good, brimming with familiar scents like treated leather and oiled weapons. However, many of the soldiers had a disorderly look. They weren't dirty, but they didn't seem particularly disciplined either. They roamed the camp in packs with coats undone. Some pointed and jeered at the slaves. This was the army of a highprince? The elite force that fought for Alethkar's honor? This was what Kaladin had aspired to join?

Bluth and Tag watched carefully as Kaladin lined up with the other slaves, but he didn't try anything. Now was not the time to provoke them—Kaladin had seen how mercenaries acted when around commissioned troops. Bluth and Tag played their part, walking with their chests out and hands on their weapons. They shoved a few of the slaves into place, ramming a cudgel into one man's belly and cursing him gruffly.

They stayed clear of Kaladin.

"The king's army," said the slave next to him. It was the dark-skinned man who had talked to Kaladin about escaping. "I thought we were meant for mine work. Why, this won't be so bad at all. We'll be cleaning latrines or maintaining roads."

Odd, to look forward to latrine work or labor in the hot sun. Kaladin hoped for something else. Hoped. Yes, he'd discovered that he could still hope. A spear in his hands. An enemy to face. He could live like that.

Tvlakv spoke with an important-looking lighteyed woman. She wore her dark hair up in a complex weave, sparkling with infused amethysts, and her dress was a deep crimson. She looked much as Laral had, at the end. She was probably of the fourth or fifth dahn, wife and scribe to one of the camp's officers.

Tvlakv began to brag about his wares, but the woman raised a delicate hand. "I can see what I am purchasing, slaver," she said in a smooth, aristocratic accent. "I will inspect them myself."

She began to walk down the line, accompanied by several soldiers. Her dress was cut in the Alethi noble fashion—a solid swath of silk, tight and formfitting through the top with sleek skirts below. It buttoned up the sides of the torso from waist to neck, where it was topped by a small, gold-embroidered collar. The longer left cuff hid her safehand. Kaladin's mother had always just worn a glove, which seemed far more practical to him.

Judging by her face, she was not particularly impressed with what she saw. "These men are half-starved and sickly," she said, taking a thin rod from a young female attendant. She used it to lift the hair from one man's forehead, inspecting his brand. "You are asking two emerald broams a head?"

Tvlakv began to sweat. "Perhaps one and a half?"

"And what would I use them for? I wouldn't trust men this filthy near food, and we have parshmen to do most other work."

"If Your Ladyship is not pleased, I could approach other highprinces. . . ."

"No," she said, smacking the slave she'd been regarding as he shied away from her. "One and a quarter. They can help cut timber for us in the northern forests. . . ." She trailed off as she noticed Kaladin. "Here now. This is far better stock than the others."

"I thought that you might like this one," Tvlakv said, stepping up to her. "He *is* quite—"

She raised the rod and silenced Tvlakv. She had a small sore on one lip. Some ground cussweed root could help with that.

"Remove your top, slave," she commanded.

Kaladin stared her right in her blue eyes and felt an almost irresistible urge to spit at her. No. No, he couldn't afford that. Not when there was a chance. He pulled his arms out of the sacklike clothing, letting it fall to his waist, exposing his chest.

Despite eight months as a slave, he was far better muscled than the others. "A large number of scars for one so young," the noblewoman said thoughtfully. "You are a military man?"

"Yes." His windspren zipped up to the woman, inspecting her face.

"Mercenary?"

"Amaram's army," Kaladin said. "A citizen, second nahn."

"*Once* a citizen," Tvlakv put in quickly. "He was—"

She silenced Tvlakv again with her rod, glaring at him. Then she used the rod to push aside Kaladin's hair and inspect his forehead.

"*Shash* glyph," she said, clicking her tongue. Several of the soldiers nearby stepped closer, hands on their swords. "Where I come from, slaves who deserve these are simply executed."

"They are fortunate," Kaladin said.

"And how did you end up here?"

"I killed someone," Kaladin said, preparing his lies carefully. *Please,* he thought to the Heralds. *Please.* It had been a long time since he had prayed for anything.

The woman raised an eyebrow.

"I'm a murderer, Brightness," Kaladin said. "Got drunk, made some mistakes. But I can use a spear as well as any man. Put me in your brightlord's army. Let me fight again." It was a strange lie to make, but the woman would never let Kaladin fight if she thought he was a deserter. In this case, better to be known as an accidental murderer.

Please . . . he thought. To be a soldier again. It seemed, in one moment, the most glorious thing he could ever have wanted. How much better it would be to die on the battlefield than waste away emptying chamber pots.

To the side, Tvlakv stepped up beside the lighteyed woman. He glanced at Kaladin, then sighed. "He's a deserter, Brightness. Don't listen to him."

No! Kaladin felt a blazing burst of anger consume his hope. He raised hands toward Tvlakv. He'd strangle the rat, and—

Something cracked him across the back. He grunted, stumbling and falling to one knee. The noblewoman stepped back, raising her safehand to her breast in alarm. One of the army soldiers grabbed Kaladin and towed him back to his feet.

"Well," she finally said. "That is unfortunate."

"I *can* fight," Kaladin growled against the pain. "Give me a spear. Let me—"

She raised her rod, cutting him off.

"Brightness," Tvlakv said, not meeting Kaladin's eyes. "I would not trust him with a weapon. It is true that he is a murderer, but he is also known to disobey and lead rebellions against his masters. I couldn't sell him to you as a bonded soldier. My conscience, it would not allow it." He hesitated. "The men in his wagon, he might have corrupted them all with talk of escape. My honor demands that I tell you this."

Kaladin gritted his teeth. He was tempted to try to take down the soldier behind him, grab that spear and spend his last moments ramming it through Tvlakv's portly gut. Why? What did it matter to Tvlakv how Kaladin was treated by this army?

I should never have ripped up the map, Kaladin thought. *Bitterness is repaid more often than kindness.* One of his father's sayings.

The woman nodded, moving on. "Show me which ones," she said. "I'll still take them, because of your honesty. We need some new bridgemen."

Tvlakv nodded eagerly. Before moving on, he paused and leaned in to Kaladin. "I cannot trust that you will behave. The people in this army, they will blame a merchant for not revealing all he knew. I . . . am sorry." With that, the merchant scuttled away.

Kaladin growled in the back of his throat, and then pulled himself free of the soldiers, but remained in line. So be it. Cutting down trees, building bridges, fighting in the army. None of it mattered. He would just keep living. They'd taken his freedom, his family, his friends, and—most dear of all—his dreams. They could do nothing more to him.

After her inspection, the noblewoman took a writing board from her assistant and made a few quick notations on its paper. Tvlakv gave her a ledger detailing how much each slave had paid down on their slave debt. Kaladin caught a glimpse; it said that not a single one of the men had paid anything. Perhaps Tvlakv lied about the figures. Not unlikely.

Kaladin would probably just let all of his wages go to his debt this time. Let them squirm as they saw him actually call their bluff. What would they do if he got close to earning out his debt? He'd probably never find out—depending on what these bridgemen earned, it could take anything from ten to fifty years to get there.

The lighteyed woman assigned most of the slaves to forest duty. A half-dozen of the more spindly ones were sent to work the mess halls, despite what she'd said before. "Those ten," the noblewoman said, raising her rod to point at Kaladin and the others from his wagon. "Take them to the bridge crews. Tell Lamaril and Gaz that the tall one is to be given special treatment."

The soldiers laughed, and one began shoving Kaladin's group along the pathway. Kaladin endured it; these men had no reason to be gentle, and he wouldn't give them a reason to be rougher. If there was a group citizen soldiers hated more than mercenaries, it was deserters.

As he walked, he couldn't help noticing the banner flying above the camp. It bore the same symbol emblazoned on the soldiers' uniform coats: a yellow glyphpair in the shape of a tower and a hammer on a field of deep green. That was the banner of Highprince Sadeas, ultimate ruler of Kaladin's own home district. Was it irony or fate that had landed Kaladin here?

Soldiers lounged idly, even those who appeared to be on duty, and the camp streets were littered with refuse. Camp followers were plentiful: whores, worker women, coopers, chandlers, and wranglers. There were even children running through the streets of what was half city, half warcamp.

There were also parshmen. Carrying water, working on trenches, lifting sacks. That surprised him. Weren't they fighting parshmen? Weren't they worried that these would rise up? Apparently not. The parshmen here worked with the same docility as the ones back in Hearthstone. Perhaps it made sense. Alethi had fought against Alethi back in his armies at home, so why shouldn't there be parshmen on both sides of this conflict?

The soldiers took Kaladin all the way around to the northeastern quarter of the camp, a hike that took some time. Though the Soulcast stone barracks each looked exactly the same, the rim of the camp was broken distinctively, like ragged mountains. Old habits made him memorize the route. Here, the towering circular wall had been worn away by countless highstorms, giving a clear view eastward. That open patch of ground would make a good staging area for an army to gather on before marching down the incline to the Shattered Plains themselves.

The northern edge of the field contained a subcamp filled with several dozen barracks, and at their center a lumberyard filled with carpenters. They were breaking down some of the stout trees Kaladin had seen on the plains outside: stripping off their stringy bark, sawing them into planks. Another group of carpenters assembled the planks into large contraptions.

"We're to be woodworkers?" Kaladin asked.

One of the soldiers laughed roughly. "You're joining the bridge crews." He pointed to where a group of sorry-looking men sat on the stones in the shade of a barrack, scooping food out of wooden bowls with their fingers. It looked depressingly similar to the slop that Tvlakv had fed them.

One of the soldiers shoved Kaladin forward again, and he stumbled down the shallow incline and crossed the grounds. The other nine slaves followed, herded by the soldiers. None of the men sitting around the barracks so much as glanced at them. They wore leather vests and simple trousers, some with dirty laced shirts, others bare-chested. The grim, sorry lot weren't much better than the slaves, though they did look to be in slightly better physical condition.

"New recruits, Gaz," one of the soldiers called.

A man lounged in the shade a distance from the eating men. He turned, revealing a face that was so scarred his beard grew in patches. He was missing one eye—the other was brown—and didn't bother with an eye patch. White knots at his shoulders marked him as a sergeant, and he had the lean toughness Kaladin had learned to associate with someone who knew his way around a battlefield.

"These spindly things?" Gaz said, chewing on something as he walked over. "They'll barely stop an arrow."

The soldier beside Kaladin shrugged, shoving him forward once more for good measure. "Brightness Hashal said to do something special with this one. The rest are up to you." The soldier nodded to his companions, and they began to trot away.

Gaz looked the slaves over. He focused on Kaladin last.

"I have military training," Kaladin said. "In the army of Highlord Amaram."

"I don't really care," Gaz cut in, spitting something dark to the side.

Kaladin hesitated. "When Amaram—"

"You keep mentioning that name," Gaz snapped. "Served under some unimportant landlord, did you? Expect me to be impressed?"

Kaladin sighed. He'd met this kind of man before, a lesser sergeant with no hope of advancement. His only pleasure in life came from his authority over those even sorrier than himself. Well, so be it.

"You have a slave's mark," Gaz said, snorting. "I doubt you ever held a spear. Either way, you'll have to condescend to join us now, Lordship."

Kaladin's windspren flitted down and inspected Gaz, then closed one of her eyes, imitating him. For some reason, seeing her made Kaladin smile. Gaz misinterpreted the smile. The man scowled and stepped forward, pointing.

At that moment, a loud chorus of horns echoed through the camp. Carpenters glanced up, and the soldiers who had guided Kaladin dashed back toward the center of camp. The slaves behind Kaladin looked around anxiously.

"Stormfather!" Gaz cursed. "Bridgemen! Up, up, you louts!" He began kicking at some of the men who were eating. They scattered their bowls, scrambling to their feet. They wore simple sandals instead of proper boots.

"You, Lordship," Gaz said, pointing at Kaladin.

"I didn't say—"

"I don't care what in Damnation you said! You're in Bridge

Four." He pointed at a group of departing bridgemen. "The rest of you, go wait over there. I'll divide you up later. Get moving, or I'll see you strung up by your heels."

Kaladin shrugged and jogged after the group of bridgemen. It was one of many teams of such men pouring out of barracks or picking themselves up out of alleys. There seemed to be quite a lot of them. Around fifty barracks, with—perhaps—twenty or thirty men in each . . . that would make nearly as many bridgemen in this army as there had been soldiers in Amaram's entire force.

Kaladin's team crossed the grounds, weaving between boards and piles of sawdust, approaching a large wooden contraption. It had obviously weathered a few highstorms and some battles. The dents and holes scattered along its length looked like places where arrows had struck. The bridge in bridgeman, perhaps?

Yes, Kaladin thought. It was a wooden bridge, over thirty feet long, eight feet wide. It sloped down at the front and back, and had no railings. The wood was thick, with the largest boards for support through the center. There were some forty or fifty bridges lined up here. Perhaps one for each barrack, making one crew for each bridge? About twenty bridge crews were gathering at this point.

Gaz had found himself a wooden shield and a gleaming mace, but there were none for anyone else. He quickly inspected each team. He stopped beside Bridge Four and hesitated. "Where's your bridgeleader?" he demanded.

"Dead," one of the bridgemen said. "Tossed himself down the Honor Chasm last night."

Gaz cursed. "Can't you keep a bridgeleader for even a week? Storm it! Line up; I'll run near you. Listen for my commands. We'll sort out another bridgeleader after we see who survives." Gaz pointed at Kaladin. "You're at the back, lordling. The rest of you, get moving! Storm you, I won't suffer another reprimand because of you fools! Move, move!"

The others were lifting. Kaladin had no choice but to go to the open slot at the tail of the bridge. He'd been a little low in his assessment; looked like about thirty-five to forty men per bridge. There was room for five men across—three under the bridge and one on each side—and eight deep, though this crew didn't have a man for each position.

He helped lift the bridge into the air. They were probably using a very light wood for the bridges, but the thing was still storms-cursed heavy. Kaladin grunted as he struggled with the weight, hoisting the bridge up high and then stepping underneath. Men dashed in to fill the middle slots down the length of the structure, and slowly they all set the bridge down on their shoulders. At least there were rods on the bottom to use as handholds.

The other men had pads on the shoulders of their vests to cushion the weight and adjust their height to fit the supports. Kaladin hadn't been given a vest, so the wooden supports dug directly into his skin. He couldn't see a thing; there was an indentation for his head, but wood cut off his view to all sides. The men at the edges had better views; he suspected those spots were more coveted.

The wood smelled of oil and sweat.

"Go!" Gaz said from outside, voice muffled.

Kaladin grunted as the crew broke into a jog. He couldn't see where he was going, and struggled to keep from tripping as the bridge crew marched down the eastern slope to the Shattered Plains. Soon, Kaladin was sweating and cursing under his breath, the wood rubbing and digging into the skin on his shoulders. He was already starting to bleed.

"Poor fool," a voice said from the side.

Kaladin glanced to the right, but the wooden handholds obstructed his view. "Are you . . ." Kaladin puffed. "Are you talking to me?"

"You shouldn't have insulted Gaz," the man said. His voice sounded hollow. "He sometimes lets new men run in an outside row. Sometimes."

Kaladin tried to respond, but he was already gasping for breath. He'd thought himself in better shape than this, but he'd spent eight months being fed slop, being beaten, and waiting out highstorms in leaking cellars, muddy barns, or cages. He was hardly the same man anymore.

"Breathe in and out deeply," said the muffled voice. "Focus on the steps. Count them. It helps."

Kaladin followed the advice. He could hear other bridge crews running nearby. Behind them came the familiar sounds of men marching and hoofbeats on the stone. They were being followed by an army.

Below, rockbuds and small shalebark ridges grew from the stone, tripping him. The landscape of the Shattered Plains appeared to be broken, uneven, and rent, covered with outcroppings and shelves of rock. That explained why they didn't use wheels on the bridges—porters were probably much faster over such rough terrain.

Soon, his feet were ragged and battered. Couldn't they have given him shoes? He set his jaw against the agony and kept on going. Just another job. He would continue, and he would survive.

A thumping sound. His feet fell on wood. A bridge, a permanent one, crossing a chasm between plateaus on the Shattered Plains. In seconds the bridge crew was across it, and his feet fell on stone again.

"Move, move!" Gaz bellowed. "Storm you, keep going!"

They continued jogging as the army crossed the bridge behind them, hundreds of boots resounding on the wood. Before too long, blood ran down Kaladin's shoulders. His breathing was torturous, his side aching painfully. He could hear others gasping, the sounds carrying through the confined space beneath the bridge. So he wasn't the only one. Hopefully, they would arrive at their destination quickly.

He hoped in vain.

The next hour was torture. It was worse than any beating he'd suffered as a slave, worse than any wound on the battlefield. There seemed to be no end to the march. Kaladin vaguely remembered seeing the permanent bridges, back when he'd looked down on the plains from the slave cart. They connected the plateaus where the chasms were easiest to span, not where it would be most efficient for those traveling. That often meant detours north or south before they could continue eastward.

The bridgemen grumbled, cursed, groaned, then fell silent.

They crossed bridge after bridge, plateau after plateau. Kaladin never got a good look at one of the chasms. He just kept running. And running. He couldn't feel his feet any longer. He kept running. He knew, somehow, that if he stopped, he'd be beaten. He felt as if his shoulders had been rubbed to the bone. He tried counting steps, but was too exhausted even for that.

But he didn't stop running.

Finally, mercifully, Gaz called for them to halt. Kaladin blinked, stumbling to a stop and nearly collapsing.

"Lift!" Gaz bellowed.

The men lifted, Kaladin's arms straining at the motion after so much time holding the bridge in one place.

"Drop!"

They stepped aside, the bridgemen underneath taking handholds at the sides. It was awkward and difficult, but these men had practice, apparently. They kept the bridge from toppling as they set it on the ground.

"Push!"

Kaladin stumbled back in confusion as the men pushed at their handholds on the side or back of the bridge. They were at the edge of a chasm lacking a permanent bridge. To the sides, the other bridge crews were pushing their own bridges forward.

Kaladin glanced over his shoulder. The army was two thousand men in forest green and pure white. Twelve hundred darkeyed spearmen, several hundred cavalry atop rare, precious horses. Behind them, a large group of heavy foot, light-eyed men in thick armor and carrying large maces and square steel shields.

It seemed that they'd intentionally chosen a point where the chasm was narrow and the first plateau was a little higher than the second. The bridge was twice as long as the chasm's width here. Gaz cursed at him, so Kaladin joined the others, shoving the bridge across the rough ground with a scraping sound. When the bridge thumped into place on the other side of the chasm, the bridge crew drew back to let the cavalry trot across.

He was too exhausted to watch. He collapsed to the stones and lay back, listening to sounds of foot soldiers tromping across the bridge. He rolled his head to the side. The other bridgemen had lain down as well. Gaz walked among the various crews, shaking his head, his shield on his back as he muttered about their worthlessness.

Kaladin longed to lie there, staring at the sky, oblivious of the world. His training, however, warned that might cause him to cramp up. That would make the return trip even worse. That training . . . it belonged to another man, from another time. Almost from the shadowdays. But while Kaladin might not *be* him any longer, he could still *heed* him.

And so, with a groan, Kaladin forced himself to sit up and begin rubbing his muscles. Soldiers crossed the bridge four across, spears held high, shields forward. Gaz watched them with obvious envy, and Kaladin's windspren danced around the man's head. Despite his fatigue, Kaladin felt a moment of jealousy. Why was she bothering that blowhard instead of Kaladin?

After a few minutes, Gaz noticed Kaladin and scowled at him.

"He's wondering why you aren't lying down," said a familiar voice. The man who had been running beside Kaladin lay on the ground a short distance away, staring up at the sky. He was older, with greying hair, and he had a long, leathery face to complement his kindly voice. He looked as exhausted as Kaladin felt.

Kaladin kept rubbing his legs, pointedly ignoring Gaz. Then he ripped off some portions of his sacklike clothing and bound his feet and shoulders. Fortunately, he was accustomed to walking barefoot as a slave, so the damage wasn't too bad.

As he finished, the last of the foot soldiers passed over the bridge. They were followed by several mounted lighteyes in gleaming armor. At their center rode a man in majestic, burnished red Shardplate. It was distinct from the one other Kaladin had seen—each suit was said to be an individual work of art—but it had the same *feel*. Ornate, interlocking, topped by a beautiful helm with an open visor.

The armor felt *alien* somehow. It had been crafted in another epoch, a time when gods had walked Roshar.

"Is that the king?" Kaladin asked.

The leathery bridgeman laughed tiredly. "We could only wish."

Kaladin turned toward him, frowning.

"If that were the king," the bridgeman said, "then that would mean we were in Brightlord Dalinar's army."

The name was vaguely familiar to Kaladin. "He's a highprince, right? The king's uncle?"

"Aye. The best of men, the most honorable Shardbearer in the king's army. They say he's never broken his word."

Kaladin sniffed in disdain. Much the same had been said about Amaram.

"You should wish to be in Highprince Dalinar's force, lad," the older man said. "He doesn't use bridge crews. Not like these, at least."

"All right, you cremlings!" Gaz bellowed. "On your feet!"

The bridgemen groaned, stumbling upright. Kaladin sighed. The brief rest had been just enough to show how exhausted he was. "I'll be glad to get back," he muttered.

"Back?" the leathery bridgeman said.

"We aren't turning around?"

His friend chuckled wryly. "Lad, we aren't *nearly* there yet. Be glad we aren't. Arriving is the worst part."

And so the nightmare began its second phase. They crossed the bridge, pulled it over behind them, then lifted it up on sore shoulders once more. They jogged across the plateau. At the other side, they lowered the bridge again to span another chasm. The army crossed, then it was back to carrying the bridge again.

They repeated this a good dozen times. They did get to rest between carries, but Kaladin was so sore and overworked that the brief respites weren't enough. He barely caught his breath each time before being forced to pick up the bridge again.

They were expected to be quick about it. The bridgemen got to rest while the army crossed, but they had to make up the time by jogging across the plateaus—passing the ranks of soldiers—so that they could arrive at the next chasm before the army. At one point, his leathery-faced friend warned him that if they didn't have their bridge in place quickly enough, they'd be punished with whippings when they returned to camp.

Gaz gave orders, cursing the bridgemen, kicking them when they moved too slowly, never doing any real work. It didn't take long for Kaladin to nurture a seething hatred of the scrawny, scar-faced man. That was odd; he hadn't felt hatred for his other sergeants. It was their *job* to curse at the men and keep them motivated.

That wasn't what burned Kaladin. Gaz had sent him on this trip without sandals or a vest. Despite his bandages, Kaladin would bear scars from his work this day. He'd be so bruised and stiff in the morning that he'd be unable to walk.

What Gaz had done was the mark of a petty bully. He risked the mission by losing a carrier, all because of a hasty grudge.

Storming man, Kaladin thought, using his hatred of Gaz to sustain him through the ordeal. Several times after pushing the bridge into place, Kaladin collapsed, feeling sure he'd never be able to stand again. But when Gaz called for them to rise, Kaladin somehow struggled to his feet. It was either that or let Gaz win.

Why were they going through all of this? What was the point? Why were they running so much? They had to protect their bridge, the precious weight, the cargo. They had to hold up the sky and run, they had to . . .

He was growing delirious. Feet, running. One, two, one, two, one, two.

"Stop!"

He stopped.

"Lift!"

He raised his hands up.

"Drop!"

He stepped back, then lowered the bridge.

"Push!"

He pushed the bridge.

Die.

That last command was his own, added each time. He fell back to the stone, a rockbud hastily withdrawing its vines as he touched them. He closed his eyes, no longer able to care about cramps. He entered a trance, a kind of half sleep, for what seemed like one heartbeat.

"Rise!"

He stood, stumbling on bloody feet.

"Cross!"

He crossed, not bothering to look at the deadly drop on either side.

"Pull!"

He grabbed a handhold and pulled the bridge across the chasm after him.

"Switch!"

Kaladin stood up dumbly. He didn't understand that command; Gaz had never given it before. The troops were forming ranks, moving with that mixture of skittishness and forced relaxation that men often went through before a battle. A few anticipationspren—like red streamers, growing from the ground and whipping in the wind—began to sprout from the rock and wave among the soldiers.

A battle?

Gaz grabbed Kaladin's shoulder and shoved him to the front of the bridge. "Newcomers get to go first at this part, Your Lordship." The sergeant smiled wickedly.

Kaladin dumbly picked up the bridge with the others, raising it over his head. The handholds were the same here, but this front row had a notched opening before his face, allowing him to see out. All of the bridgemen had changed positions; the men who had been running in the front moved to the back, and those at the back—including Kaladin and the leathery-faced bridgeman—moved to the front.

Kaladin didn't ask the point of it. He didn't care. He liked the front, though; jogging was easier now that he could see ahead of him.

The landscape on the plateaus was that of rough storm-lands; there were scattered patches of grass, but the stone here was too hard for their seeds to fully burrow into. Rockbuds were more common, growing like bubbles across the entire plateau, imitating rocks about the size of a man's head. Many of the buds were split, trailing out their vines like thick green tongues. A few were even in bloom.

After so many hours breathing in the stuffy confines beneath the bridge, running in the front was almost relaxing. Why had they given such a wonderful position to a newcomer?

"Talenelat'Elin, bearer of all agonies," said the man to his right, voice horrified. "It's going to be a bad one. They're already lined up! It's going to be a bad one!"

Kaladin blinked, focusing on the approaching chasm. On the other side of the rift stood a rank of men with marbled crimson and black skin. They were wearing a strange rusty orange armor that covered their forearms, chests, heads, and legs. It took his numbed mind a moment to understand.

The Parshendi.

They weren't like common parshman workers. They were far more muscular, far more *solid*. They had the bulky build of soldiers, and each one carried a weapon strapped to his back. Some wore dark red and black beards tied with bits of rock, while others were clean-shaven.

As Kaladin watched, the front row of Parshendi knelt down. They held shortbows, arrows nocked. Not longbows intended to launch arrows high and far. Short, recurve bows to fire straight and quick and strong. An excellent bow to use for killing a group of bridgemen before they could lay their bridge.

Arriving is the worst part. . . .

Now, finally, the *real* nightmare began.

Gaz hung back, bellowing at the bridge crews to keep going. Kaladin's instincts screamed at him to get out of the line of fire, but the momentum of the bridge forced him forward. Forced him down the throat of the beast itself, its teeth poised to snap closed.

Kaladin's exhaustion and pain fled. He was shocked alert. The bridges charged forward, the men beneath them screaming as they ran. Ran toward death.

The archers released.

The first wave killed Kaladin's leathery-faced friend, dropping him with three separate arrows. The man to Kaladin's left fell as well—Kaladin hadn't even seen his face. That man cried out as he dropped, not dead immediately, but the bridge crew trampled him. The bridge got noticeably heavier as men died.

The Parshendi calmly drew a second volley and launched. To the side, Kaladin barely noticed another of the bridge crews floundering. The Parshendi seemed to focus their fire on certain crews. That one got a full wave of arrows from dozens of archers, and the first three rows of bridgemen dropped and tripped those behind them. Their bridge lurched, skidding on the ground and making a sickening crunch as the mass of bodies fell over one another.

Arrows zipped past Kaladin, killing the other two men in the front line with him. Several other arrows smacked into the wood around him, one slicing open the skin of his cheek.

He screamed. In horror, in shock, in pain, in sheer bewilderment. Never before had he felt so powerless in a battle. He'd charged enemy fortifications, he'd run beneath waves of arrows, but he'd always felt a measure of control. He'd had his spear, he'd had his shield, he could fight back.

Not this time. The bridge crews were like hogs running to the slaughter.

A third volley flew, and another of the twenty bridge crews fell. Waves of arrows came from the Alethi side as well, falling and striking the Parshendi. Kaladin's bridge was almost to the chasm. He could see the black eyes of the Parshendi on the other side, could make out the features of their lean marbled faces. All around him, bridgemen were screaming in pain, arrows cutting them out from underneath their bridges.

There was a crashing sound as another bridge dropped, its bridgemen slaughtered.

Behind, Gaz called out. "Lift and down, you fools!"

The bridge crew lurched to a stop as the Parshendi launched another volley. Men behind Kaladin screamed. The Parshendi firing was interrupted by a return volley from the Alethi army. Though he was shocked senseless, Kaladin's reflexes knew what do to. Drop the bridge, get into position to push.

This exposed the bridgemen who had been safe in the back ranks. The Parshendi archers obviously knew this was coming; they prepared and launched one final volley. Arrows struck the bridge in a wave, dropping a half-dozen men, spraying blood across the dark wood. Fearspren—wiggling and violet—sprang up through the wood and wriggled in the air. The bridge lurched, growing much harder to push as they suddenly lost those men.

Kaladin stumbled, hands slipping. He fell to his knees and pitched out, leaning over the chasm. He barely managed to catch himself.

He teetered, one hand dangling above the void, the other gripping the edge. His overextended mind wavered with vertigo as he stared down that sheer cliff, down into darkness. The height was beautiful; he'd always loved climbing high rock formations with Tien.

By reflex, he shoved himself back onto the plateau, scrambling backward. A group of foot soldiers, protected by shields, had taken up positions pushing the bridge. The army's archers exchanged arrows with the Parshendi as the soldiers pushed the bridge into place and heavy cavalry thundered across, smashing into the Parshendi. Four bridges had fallen, but sixteen had been placed in a row, allowing for an effective charge.

Kaladin tried to move, tried to crawl away from the bridge. But he just collapsed where he was, his body refusing to obey. He couldn't even roll over onto his stomach.

I should go . . . he thought in exhaustion. *See if that leathery-faced man is still alive. . . . Bind his wounds. . . . Save. . . .*

But he couldn't. He couldn't move. Couldn't think. To his shame, he just let himself close his eyes and gave himself over to unconsciousness.

* * *

"Kaladin."

He didn't want to open his eyes. To wake meant returning to that awful world of pain. A world where defenseless, exhausted men were made to charge lines of archers.

That world was the nightmare.

"Kaladin!" The feminine voice was soft, like a whisper, yet still urgent. "They're going to leave you. Get up! You'll die!"

I can't . . . I can't go back. . . .

Let me go.

Something snapped against his face, a slight *slap* of energy with a sting to it. He cringed. It was nothing compared with his other pains, but somehow it was far more demanding. He raised a hand, swatting. The motion was enough to drive away the last vestiges of stupor.

He tried to open his eyes. One refused, blood from a cut on his cheek having run down and crusted around the eyelid. The sun had moved. Hours had passed. He groaned—sitting up, rubbing the dried blood from his eye. The ground near him was littered with bodies. The air smelled of blood and worse.

A pair of sorry bridgemen were shaking each man in turn, checking for life, then pulling the vests and sandals off their bodies, shooing away the cremlings feeding on the bodies. The men would never have checked on Kaladin. He didn't have anything for them to take. They'd have left him with the corpses, stranded on the plateau.

Kaladin's windspren flitted through the air above him, moving anxiously. He rubbed his jaw where she'd struck him. Large spren like her could move small objects and give little pinches of energy. That made them all the more annoying.

This time, it had probably saved Kaladin's life. He groaned

at all the places where he hurt. "Do you have a name, spirit?" he asked, forcing himself to his battered feet.

On the plateau the army had crossed to, soldiers were picking through the corpses of the dead Parshendi, looking for something. Harvesting equipment, maybe? It appeared that Sadeas's force had won. At least, there didn't seem to be any Parshendi still alive. They'd either been killed or had fled.

The plateau they'd fought on seemed exactly like the others they'd crossed. The only thing that was different here was that there was a large lump of . . . something in the center of the plateau. It looked like an enormous rockbud, perhaps some kind of chrysalis or shell, a good twenty feet tall. One side had been hacked open, exposing slimy innards. He hadn't noticed it on the initial charge; the archers had demanded all of his attention.

"A name," the windspren said, her voice distant. "Yes. I *do* have a name." She seemed surprised as she looked at Kaladin. "Why do I have a name?"

"How should I know?" Kaladin said, forcing himself to move. His feet blazed with pain. He could barely limp.

The nearby bridgemen looked to him with surprise, but he ignored them, limping across the plateau until he found the corpse of a bridgeman who still had his vest and shoes. It was the leathery-faced man who had been so kind to him, dead with an arrow through the neck. Kaladin ignored those shocked eyes, staring blankly into the sky, and harvested the man's clothing—leather vest, leather sandals, lacing shirt stained red with blood. Kaladin felt disgusted with himself, but he wasn't going to count on Gaz giving him clothing.

Kaladin sat down and used the cleaner parts of the shirt to change his improvised bandages, then put on the vest and sandals, trying to keep from moving too much. A breeze now blew, carrying away the scents of blood and the sounds of soldiers calling to one another. The cavalry was already forming up, as if eager to return.

"A name," the windspren said, walking through the air to

stand beside his face. She was in the shape of a young woman, complete with flowing skirt and delicate feet. "Sylphrena."

"Sylphrena," Kaladin repeated, tying on the sandals.

"Syl," the spirit said. She cocked her head. "That's amusing. It appears that I have a nickname."

"Congratulations." Kaladin stood up again, wobbling.

To the side, Gaz stood with hands on hips, shield tied to his back. "You," he said, pointing at Kaladin. He then gestured to the bridge.

"You've got to be kidding," Kaladin said, looking as the remnants of the bridge crew—fewer than half of their previous number remained—gathered around the bridge.

"Either carry or stay behind," Gaz said. He seemed angry about something.

I was supposed to die, Kaladin realized. *That's why he didn't care if I had a vest or sandals. I was at the front.* Kaladin was the only one on the first row who had lived.

Kaladin nearly sat down and let them leave him. But dying of thirst on a lonely plateau was not the way he'd choose to go. He stumbled over to the bridge.

"Don't worry," said one of the other bridgemen. "They'll let us go slow this time, take lots of breaks. And we'll have a few soldiers to help—takes at least twenty-five men to lift a bridge."

Kaladin sighed, getting into place as some unfortunate soldiers joined them. Together, they heaved the bridge into the air. It was terribly heavy, but they managed it, somehow.

Kaladin walked, feeling numb. He'd thought that there was nothing more life could do to him, nothing worse than the slave's brand with a *shash*, nothing worse than losing all he had to the war, nothing more terrible than failing those he'd sworn to protect.

It appeared that he'd been wrong. There *had* been something more they could do to him. One final torment the world had reserved just for Kaladin.

And it was called Bridge Four.

7

ANYTHING REASONABLE

*"They are aflame. They burn. They bring the darkness
when they come, and so all you can see is that their skin is
aflame. Burn, burn, burn. . . ."*

—Collected on Palahishev, 1172, 21 seconds pre-death. Subject
was a baker's apprentice.

Shallan hurried down the hallway with its burnt-orange
colorings, the ceiling and upper walls now stained by the
passing of black smoke from Jasnah's Soulcasting. Hopefully, the paintings on the walls hadn't been ruined.

Ahead, a small group of parshmen arrived, bearing rags,
buckets, and stepladders to use in wiping off the soot. They
bowed to her as she passed, uttering no words. Parshmen
could speak, but they rarely did so. Many seemed mute. As a
child, she'd found the patterns of their marbled skin beautiful. That had been before her father forbade her to spend any
time with the parshmen.

She turned her mind to her task. How was she going to
convince Jasnah Kholin, one of the most powerful women in
the world, to change her mind about taking Shallan as a ward?
The woman was obviously stubborn; she had spent years resisting the devotaries' attempts at reconciliation.

She reentered the broad main cavern, with its lofty stone

ceiling and bustling, well-dressed occupants. She felt daunted, but that brief glimpse of the Soulcaster seduced her. Her family, House Davar, had prospered in recent years, coming out of obscurity. This had primarily been because of her father's skill in politics—he had been hated by many, but his ruthlessness had carried him far. So had the wealth lent by the discovery of several important new marble deposits on Davar lands.

Shallan had never known enough to be suspicious of that wealth's origins. Every time the family had exhausted one of its quarries, her father had gone out with his surveyor and discovered a new one. Only after interrogating the surveyor had Shallan and her brothers discovered the truth: Her father, using his forbidden Soulcaster, had been *creating* new deposits at a careful rate. Not enough to be suspicious. Just enough to give him the money he needed to further his political goals.

Nobody knew where he'd gotten the fabrial, which she now carried in her safepouch. It was unusable, damaged on the same disastrous evening that her father had died. *Don't think about that,* she told herself forcefully.

They'd had a jeweler repair the broken Soulcaster, but it no longer worked. Their house steward—one of her father's close confidants, an advisor named Luesh—had been trained to use the device, and he could no longer make it function.

Her father's debts and promises were outrageous. Their choices were limited. Her family had some time—perhaps as long as a year—before the missed payments became egregious, and before her father's absence became obvious. For once, her family's isolated, backcountry estates were an advantage, providing a reason that communications were being delayed. Her brothers were scrambling, writing letters in her father's name, making a few appearances and spreading rumors that Brightlord Davar was planning something big.

All to give her time to make good on her bold plan. Find Jasnah Kholin. Become her ward. Learn where she kept her Soulcaster. Then replace it with the nonfunctional one.

With the fabrial, they'd be able to make new quarries and restore their wealth. They'd be able to make food to feed their house soldiers. With enough wealth in hand to pay off debts and make bribes, they could announce their father's death and not suffer destruction.

Shallan hesitated in the main hallway, considering her next move. What she planned to do was very risky. She'd have to escape without implicating herself in the theft. Though she'd devoted much thought to that, she still didn't know how she'd manage it. But Jasnah was known to have many enemies. There had to be a way to pin the fabrial's "breaking" on them instead.

That step would come later. For now, Shallan *had* to convince Jasnah to accept her as a ward. All other results were unacceptable.

Nervously, Shallan held her arms in the sign of need, covered safehand bent across her chest and touching the elbow of her freehand, which was raised with fingers outspread. A woman approached, wearing the well-starched white laced shirt and black skirt that were the universal sign of a master-servant.

The stout woman curtsied. "Brightness?"

"The Palanaeum," Shallan said.

The woman bowed and led Shallan farther into the depths of the long hallway. Most of the women here—servants included—wore their hair bound, and Shallan felt conspicuous with hers loose. The deep red color made her stand out even more.

Soon, the grand hallway began to slope down steeply. But when the half-hour arrived, she could still hear distant bells ring behind her. Perhaps that was why the people here liked them so much; even in the depths of the Conclave, one could hear the outside world.

The servant led Shallan to a pair of grand steel doors. The servant bowed and Shallan dismissed her with a nod.

Shallan couldn't help but admire the beauty of the doors; their exterior was carved in an intricate geometric pattern with circles and lines and glyphs. It was some kind of chart, half on each door. There was no time to study the details, unfortunately, and she passed them by.

Beyond the doors was a breathtakingly large room. The sides were of smooth rock and they stretched high; the dim illumination made it impossible to tell just how high, but she saw flickers of distant light. Set into the walls were dozens of small balconies, much like the private box seats of a theater. Soft light shone from many of these. The only sounds were turning pages and faint whispers. Shallan raised her safehand to her breast, feeling dwarfed by the magnificent chamber.

"Brightness?" a young male master-servant said, approaching. "What do you need?"

"A new sense of perspective, apparently," Shallan said absently. "How . . ."

"This room is called the Veil," the servant explained softly. "That which comes before the Palanaeum itself. Both were here when the city was founded. Some think these chambers might have been cut by the Dawnsingers themselves."

"Where are the books?"

"The Palanaeum proper is this way." The servant gestured, leading her to a set of doors on the other side of the room. Through them, she entered a smaller chamber that was partitioned with walls of thick crystal. Shallan approached the nearest one, feeling it. The crystal's surface was rough like hewn rock.

"Soulcast?" she asked.

The servant nodded. Behind him, another servant passed leading an elderly ardent. Like most ardents, the aged man had a shaved head and a long beard. His simple grey robes were tied with a brown sash. The servant led him around a corner, and Shallan could vaguely make out their shapes on the other side, shadows swimming through the crystal.

She took a step forward, but her servant cleared his throat. "I will need your chit of admittance, Brightness."

"How much does one cost?" Shallan asked hesitantly.

"A thousand sapphire broams."

"So much?"

"The king's many hospitals require much upkeep," the man said apologetically. "The only things Kharbranth has to sell are fish, bells, and information. The first two are hardly unique to us. But the third . . . well, the Palanaeum has the finest collection of tomes and scrolls on Roshar. More, even, than the Holy Enclave in Valath. At last count, there were over seven hundred thousand separate texts in our archive."

Her father had owned exactly eighty-seven books. Shallan had read them all several times over. How much could be contained in *seven hundred thousand* books? The weight of that much information dazzled her. She found herself hungering to look through those hidden shelves. She could spend months just reading their titles.

But no. Perhaps once she'd made certain her brothers were safe—once her house's finances were restored—she could return. Perhaps.

She felt like she was starving, yet leaving a warm fruit pie uneaten. "Where might I wait?" she asked. "If someone I know is inside."

"You may use one of the reading alcoves," the servant said, relaxing. Perhaps he'd feared that she would make a scene. "No chit is required to sit in one. There are parshman porters who will raise you to the higher levels, if that is what you wish."

"Thank you," Shallan said, turning her back on the Palanaeum. She felt like a child again, locked in her room, not allowed to run through the gardens because of her father's paranoid fears. "Does Brightness Jasnah have an alcove yet?"

"I can ask," the servant said, leading the way back into the Veil, with its distant, unseen ceiling. He hurried off to speak with some others, leaving Shallan standing beside the doorway to the Palanaeum.

She could run in. Sneak through—

No. Her brothers teased her for being too timid, but it was not timidity that held her back. There would undoubtedly be guards; bursting in would not only be futile, it would ruin any chance she had of changing Jasnah's mind.

Change Jasnah's mind, prove herself. Considering it made her sick. She *hated* confrontation. During her youth, she'd felt like a piece of delicate crystalware, locked in a cabinet to be displayed but never touched. The only daughter, the last memory of Brightlord Davar's beloved wife. It still felt odd to her that *she* been the one to take charge after . . . After the incident . . . After . . .

Memories attacked her. Nan Balat bruised, his coat torn. A long, silvery sword in her hand, sharp enough to cut stones as if they were water.

No, Shallan thought, her back to the stone wall, clutching her satchel. *No. Don't think of the past.*

She sought solace in drawing, raising fingers to her satchel and reaching for her paper and pencils. The servant came back before she had a chance to get them out, however. "Brightness Jasnah Kholin has indeed asked that a reading alcove be set aside for her," he said. "You may wait there for her, if you wish it."

"I do," Shallan said. "Thank you."

The servant led her to a shadowed enclosure, inside of which four parshmen stood upon a sturdy wooden platform. The servant and Shallan stepped onto the platform, and the parshmen pulled ropes that were strung into a pulley above, raising the platform up the stone shaft. The only lights were broam spheres set at each corner of the lift's ceiling. Amethysts, which had a soft violet light.

She needed a plan. Jasnah Kholin did not seem the type to change her mind easily. Shallan would have to surprise her, impress her.

They reached a level about forty feet or so off the ground, and the servant waved for the porters to stop. Shallan followed the master-servant down a dark hallway to one of the small balconies that extended out over the Veil. It was round, like a turret, and had a waist-high stone rim with a wooden railing above that. Other occupied alcoves glowed with different colors from the spheres being used to light them; the darkness of the huge space made them seem to hover in the air.

This alcove had a long, curving stone desk joined directly into the rim of the balcony. There was a single chair and a gobletlike crystal bowl. Shallan nodded in thanks to the servant, who withdrew, then she pulled out a handful of spheres and dropped them into the bowl, lighting the alcove.

She sighed, sitting down in the chair and laying her satchel on the desk. She undid the laces on her satchel, busying herself as she tried to think of something—anything—that would persuade Jasnah.

First, she decided, *I need to clear my mind.*

From her satchel she removed a sheaf of thick drawing paper, a set of charcoal pencils of different widths, some brushes and steel pens, ink, and watercolors. Finally, she took out her smaller notebook, bound in codex form, which contained the nature sketches she'd done during her weeks aboard the *Wind's Pleasure.*

These were simple things, really, but worth more to her than a chest full of spheres. She took a sheet off the stack, then selected a fine-pointed charcoal pencil, rolling it between her fingers. She closed her eyes and fixed an image in her mind: Kharbranth as she'd memorized it in that moment soon after landing on the docks. Waves surging against the wooden posts, a salty scent to the air, men climbing rigging calling one another with excitement. And the city itself, rising up the hillside, homes stacked atop homes, not a speck of land wasted. Bells, distant, tinkling softly in the air.

She opened her eyes and began to draw. Her fingers moved on their own, sketching broad lines first. The cracklike valley the city was situated in. The port. Here, squares to be homes, there a slash to mark a switchback of the grand roadway that led up to the Conclave. Slowly, bit by bit, she added detail. Shadows as windows. Lines to fill out the roadways. Hints of people and carts to show the chaos of the thoroughfares.

She had read of how sculptors worked. Many would take a blank stone block and work it into a vague shape first. Then, they'd work it over again, carving more detail with each pass. It was the same for her in drawing. Broad lines first, then some details, then more, then down to the finest of lines. She had no formal training in pencils; she simply did what felt right.

The city took shape beneath her fingers. She coaxed it free, line by line, scratch by scratch. What would she do without this? Tension bled from her body, as if released from her fingertips into the pencil.

She lost track of time as she worked. Sometimes she felt like she was entering a trance, everything else fading. Her fingers almost seemed to draw of their own accord. It was so much easier to think while drawing.

Before too long, she had copied her Memory onto the page. She held up the sheet, satisfied, relaxed, her mind clear. The memorized image of Kharbranth was gone from her head; she'd released it into her sketch. There was a sense of relaxation to that too. As if her mind was put under tension holding Memories until they could be used.

She did Yalb next, standing shirtless in his vest and gesturing to the short porter who had pulled her up to the Conclave. She smiled as she worked, remembering Yalb's affable voice. He'd likely returned to the *Wind's Pleasure* by now. Had it been two hours? Probably.

She was always more excited by drawing animals and people than she was by drawing things. There was something energizing about putting a living creature onto the page. A city was lines and boxes, but a person was circles and curves. Could she get that smirk on Yalb's face right? Could she show his lazy contentedness, the way he would flirt with a woman far above his station? And the porter, with his thin fingers and sandaled feet, his long coat and baggy pants. His strange language, his keen eyes, his plan to increase his tip by offering not just a ride, but a tour.

When she drew, she didn't feel as if she worked with only charcoal and paper. In drawing a portrait, her medium was the soul itself. There were plants from which one could remove a tiny cutting—a leaf, or a bit of stem—then plant it and grow a duplicate. When she collected a Memory of a person, she was snipping free a bud of their soul, and she cultivated and grew it on the page. Charcoal for sinew, paper pulp for bone, ink for blood, the paper's texture for skin. She fell into a rhythm, a cadence, the scratching of her pencil like the sound of breathing from those she depicted.

Creationspren began to gather around her pad, looking at her work. Like other spren, they were said to always be around, but usually invisible. Sometimes you attracted them. Sometimes you didn't. With drawing, skill seemed to make a difference.

Creationspren were of medium size, as tall as one of her fingers, and they glowed with a faint silvery light. They transformed perpetually, taking new shapes. Usually the shapes were things they had seen recently. An urn, a person, a table, a wheel, a nail. Always of the same silvery color, always the same diminutive height. They imitated shapes exactly, but moved them in strange ways. A table would roll like a wheel, an urn would shatter and repair itself.

Her drawing gathered about a half-dozen of them, pulling them by her act of creation just as a bright fire would draw flamespren. She'd learned to ignore them. They weren't substantial—if she moved her arm through one, its figure would smear like scattered sand, then re-form. She never felt a thing when touching one.

Eventually, she held up the page, satisfied. It depicted Yalb and the porter in detail, with hints of the busy city behind. She'd gotten their eyes right. That was the most important. Each of the Ten Essences had an analogous part of the human body—blood for liquid, hair for wood, and so forth. The eyes were associated with crystal and glass. The windows into a person's mind and spirit.

She set the page aside. Some men collected trophies. Others collected weapons or shields. Many collected spheres.

Shallan collected people. People, and interesting creatures. Perhaps it was because she'd spent so much of her youth in a virtual prison. She'd developed the habit of memorizing faces, then drawing them later, after her father had discovered her sketching the gardeners. His daughter? Drawing pictures of darkeyes? He'd been furious with her—one of the infrequent times he'd directed his infamous temper at his daughter.

After that, she'd done drawings of people only when in private, instead using her open drawing times to sketch the insects, crustaceans, and plants of the manor gardens. Her father hadn't minded this—zoology and botany were proper feminine pursuits—and had encouraged her to choose natural history as her Calling.

She took out a third blank sheet. It seemed to beg her to fill it. A blank page was nothing but potential, pointless until it was used. Like a fully infused sphere cloistered inside a pouch, prevented from making its light useful.

Fill me.

The creationspren gathered around the page. They were still, as if curious, anticipatory. Shallan closed her eyes and imagined Jasnah Kholin, standing before the blocked door, the Soulcaster glowing on her hand. The hallway hushed, save for a child's sniffles. Attendants holding their breath. An anxious king. A still reverence.

Shallan opened her eyes and began to draw with vigor, intentionally losing herself. The less she was in the *now* and the more she was in the *then*, the better the sketch would be. The other two pictures had been warm-ups; this was the day's masterpiece. With the paper bound onto the board—safehand holding that—her freehand flew across the page, occasionally switching to other pencils. Soft charcoal for deep, thick blackness, like Jasnah's beautiful hair. Hard charcoal for light greys, like the powerful waves of light coming from the Soulcaster's gems.

For a few extended moments, Shallan was back in that hallway again, watching something that should not be: a heretic wielding one of the most sacred powers in all the world. The power of change itself, the power by which the Almighty had created Roshar. He had another name, allowed to pass only the lips of ardents. *Elithanathile.* He Who Transforms.

Shallan could smell the musty hallway. She could hear the child whimpering. She could feel her own heart beating in anticipation. The boulder would soon change. Sucking away the Stormlight in Jasnah's gemstone, it would give up its essence, becoming something new. Shallan's breath caught in her throat.

And then the memory faded, returning her to the quiet, dim alcove. The page now held a perfect rendition of the scene, worked in blacks and greys. The princess's proud figure regarded the fallen stone, demanding that it give way before her will. It *was* her. Shallan knew, with the intuitive certainty of an artist, that this was one of the finest pieces she had ever done. In a very small way, she had captured Jasnah Kholin, something the devotaries had never managed. That gave her a euphoric thrill. Even if this woman rejected Shallan again, one fact would not change. Jasnah Kholin had joined Shallan's collection.

Shallan wiped her fingers on her cleaning cloth, then lifted the paper. She noted absently that she'd attracted some two dozen creationspren now. She would have to lacquer the page with plytree sap to set the charcoal and protect it from smudges. She had some in her satchel. First she wanted to study the page and the figure it contained. Who *was* Jasnah Kholin? Not one to be cowed, certainly. She was a woman to the bone, master of the feminine arts, but not by any means delicate.

Such a woman would appreciate Shallan's determination. She *would* listen to another request for wardship, assuming it was presented properly.

Jasnah was also a rationalist, a woman with the audacity to deny the existence of the Almighty himself based on her own reasoning. Jasnah would appreciate strength, but only if it was shaped by logic.

Shallan nodded to herself, taking out a fourth sheet of paper and a fine-tipped brushpen, then shaking and opening her jar of ink. Jasnah had demanded proof of Shallan's logical and writing skills. Well, what better way to do that than to supplicate the woman with words?

Brightness Jasnah Kholin, Shallan wrote, painting the letters as neatly and beautifully as she could. She could have used a reed instead, but a brushpen was for works of art. She intended this page to be just that. *You have rejected my petition. I accept that. Yet, as anyone trained in formal inquiry knows, no supposition should be treated as axiomatic.* The actual argument usually read "no supposition— save for the existence of the Almighty himself—should be held as axiomatic." But this wording would appeal to Jasnah.

A scientist must be willing to change her theories if experiment disproves them. I hold to the hope that you treat decisions in a like manner: as preliminary results pending further information.

From our brief interaction, I can see that you appreciate tenacity. You complimented me on continuing to seek you out. Therefore, I presume that you will not find this letter a breach of good taste. Take it as proof of my ardor to be your ward, and not as disdain for your expressed decision.

Shallan raised the end of her brushpen to her lips as she considered her next step. The creationspren slowly faded away, vanishing. There were said to be logicspren—in the form of tiny stormclouds—who were attracted to great arguments, but Shallan had never seen them.

You expect proof of my worthiness, Shallan continued. *I wish I could demonstrate that my schooling is more complete than our interview revealed. Unfortunately, I haven't the grounds for such an argument. I have weaknesses in my understanding. That is plain and not subject to reasonable dispute.*

But the lives of men and women are more than logical puzzles; the context of their experiences is invaluable in making good decisions. My study in logic does not rise to your standards, but even I know that the rationalists have a rule: One cannot apply logic as an absolute where human beings are concerned. We are not beings of thought only.

Therefore, the soul of my argument here is to give perspective on my ignorance. Not by way of excuse, but of explanation. You expressed displeasure that one such as I should be trained so inadequately. What of my stepmother? What of my tutors? Why was my education handled so poorly?

The facts are embarrassing. I have had few tutors and virtually no education. My stepmother tried, but she had no education herself. It is a carefully guarded secret, but many of the rural Veden houses ignore the proper training of their women.

I had three different tutors when I was very young, but each left after a few months, citing my father's temper or rudeness as her reason. I was left to my own devices in education. I have learned what I could through reading, filling in the gaps by taking advantage of my own curious nature. But I will not be capable of matching knowledge with someone who has been given the benefit of a formal—and expensive—education.

Why is this an argument that you should accept me? Because everything I have learned has come by way of great personal struggle. What others were handed, I had to hunt. I believe that because of this, my education—limited though it is—has extra worth and merit. I respect your decisions, but I do ask you to reconsider. Which would you rather have? A ward who is able to repeat the correct answers because an overpriced tutor drilled them into her, or a ward who had to struggle and fight for everything she has learned?

I assure you that one of those two will prize your teachings far more than the other.

She raised her brush. Her arguments seemed imperfect now that she considered them. She exposed her ignorance, then expected Jasnah to welcome her? Still, it seemed the right thing to do, for all the fact that this letter was a lie. A lie built of truths. She hadn't truly come to partake of Jasnah's knowledge. She had come as a thief.

That made her conscience itch, and she nearly reached out and crumpled the page. Steps in the hallway outside made her freeze. She leaped to her feet, spinning, safehand held to her breast. She fumbled for words to explain her presence to Jasnah Kholin.

Light and shadows flickered in the hallway, then a figure hesitantly looked into the alcove, a single white sphere cupped in one hand for light. It was *not* Jasnah. It was a man in his early twenties wearing simple grey robes. An ardent. Shallan relaxed.

The young man noticed her. His face was narrow, his blue eyes keen. His beard was trimmed short and square, his head shaved. When he spoke, his voice had a cultured tone. "Ah, excuse me, Brightness. I thought this was the alcove of Jasnah Kholin."

"It is," Shallan said.

"Oh. You're waiting for her too?"

"Yes."

"Would you mind terribly if I waited with you?" He had a faint Herdazian accent.

"Of course not, Ardent." She nodded her head in respect, then gathered up her things in haste, preparing the seat for him.

"I can't take your seat, Brightness! I'll fetch another for myself."

She raised a hand in protest, but he had already retreated. He returned a few moments later, carrying a chair from another alcove. He was tall and lean, and—she decided with slight discomfort—rather handsome. Her father had owned only three ardents, all elderly men. They had traveled his lands and visited the villages, ministering to the people, helping them reach Points in their Glories and Callings. She had their faces in her collection of portraits.

The ardent set down his chair. He hesitated before sitting, glancing at the table. "My, my," he said in surprise.

For a moment, Shallan thought he was reading her letter, and she felt an irrational surge of panic. The ardent, however, was regarding the three drawings that lay at the head of the table, awaiting lacquer.

"You did these, Brightness?" he said.

"Yes, Ardent," Shallan said, lowering her eyes.

"No need to be so formal!" the ardent said, leaning down and adjusting his spectacles as he studied her work. "Please, I am Brother Kabsal, or just Kabsal. Really, it's fine. And you are?"

"Shallan Davar."

"By Vedeledev's golden keys, Brightness!" Brother Kabsal said, seating himself. "Did Jasnah Kholin teach you this skill with the pencil?"

"No, Ardent," she said, still standing.

"Still so formal," he said, smiling at her. "Tell me, am I so intimidating as that?"

"I have been brought up to show respect to ardents."

"Well, I myself find that respect is like manure. Use it where needed, and growth will flourish. Spread it on too thick, and things just start to smell." His eyes twinkled.

Had an *ardent*—a servant of the Almighty—just spoken of *manure*? "An ardent is a representative of the Almighty himself," she said. "To show you lack of respect would be to show it to the Almighty."

"I see. And this is how you'd respond if the Almighty himself appeared to you here? All of this formality and bowing?"

She hesitated. "Well, no."

"Ah, and how *would* you react?"

"I suspect with screams of pain," she said, letting her thought slip out too easily. "As it is written that the Almighty's glory is such that any who look upon him would immediately be burned to ash."

The ardent laughed at that. "Wisely spoken indeed. Please, do sit, though."

She did so, hesitant.

"You still appear conflicted," he said, holding up her portrait of Jasnah. "What must I do to put you at ease? Shall I step up onto this desk here and do a jig?"

She blinked in surprise.

"No objection?" Brother Kabsal said. "Well, then . . ." He set down the portrait and began to climb up on his chair.

"No, please!" Shallan said, holding out her freehand.

"Are you certain?" he glanced at the desk appraisingly.

"Yes," Shallan said, imagining the ardent teetering and making a misstep, then falling off the balcony and plunging dozens of feet to the ground below. "Please, I promise not to respect you any longer!"

He chuckled, hopping down and seating himself. He leaned closer to her, as if conspiratorially. "The table jig threat almost always works. I've only ever had to go through with it once, due to a lost bet against Brother Lhanin. The master ardent of our monastery nearly keeled over in shock."

Shallan found herself smiling. "You're an ardent; you're forbidden to have possessions. What did you bet?"

"Two deep breaths of a winter rose's fragrance," said Brother Kabsal, "and the sunlight's warmth on your skin." He smiled. "We can be rather creative at times. Years spent marinating in a monastery can do that to a man. Now, you were about to explain to me where you learned such skill with a pencil."

"Practice," Shallan said. "I should suspect that is how everyone learns, eventually."

"Wise words again. I am beginning to wonder which of us is the ardent. But surely you had a master to teach you."

"Dandos the Oilsworn."

"Ah, a true master of pencils if there ever was one. Now, not that I doubt your word, Brightness, but I'm rather intrigued how Dandos Heraldin could have trained you in arts, as—last I checked—he's suffering a rather terminal and perpetual ailment. Namely, that of being *dead*. For three hundred years."

Shallan blushed. "My father had a book of his instruction."

"You learned this," Kabsal said, lifting up her drawing of Jasnah, "from a *book*."

"Er . . . yes?"

He looked back at the picture. "I need to read more."

Shallan found herself laughing at the ardent's expression, and she took a Memory of him sitting there, admiration and perplexity blending on his face as he studied the picture, rubbing his bearded chin with one finger.

He smiled pleasantly, setting down the picture. "You have lacquer?"

"I do," she said, getting it out of her satchel. It was contained in a bulb sprayer of the type often used for perfume.

He accepted the small jar and twisted the clasp on the

front, then gave the bottle a shake and tested the lacquer on the back of his hand. He nodded in satisfaction and reached for the drawing. "A piece such as this should not be allowed to risk smudging."

"I can lacquer it," Shallan said. "No need to trouble yourself."

"It is no trouble; it's an honor. Besides, I am an ardent. We don't know what to do with ourselves when we aren't busying about, doing things others could do for themselves. It is best just to humor me." He began to apply the lacquer, dusting the page with careful puffs.

She had trouble keeping herself from reaching to snatch the sketch away. Fortunately, his hands were careful, and the lacquer went on evenly. He'd obviously done this before.

"You are from Jah Keved, I presume?" he asked.

"From the hair?" she asked, raising a hand to her red locks. "Or from the accent?"

"From the way you treat ardents. The Veden Church is by far the most traditional. I have visited your lovely country on two occasions; while your food sits well in my stomach, the amount of bowing and scraping you show ardents made me uncomfortable."

"Perhaps you should have danced on a few tables."

"I considered it," he said, "but my brother and sister ardents from your country would likely have dropped dead of embarrassment. I would hate to have that on my conscience. The Almighty is not kind toward those who kill his priests."

"I should think that killing in general would be frowned upon," she responded, still watching him apply the lacquer. It felt odd to let someone else work on her art.

"What does Brightness Jasnah think of your skill?" he asked as he worked.

"I don't think she cares," Shallan said, grimacing and remembering her conversation with the woman. "She doesn't seem terribly appreciative of the visual arts."

"So I have heard. It's one of her few faults, unfortunately."

"Another being that little matter of her heresy?"

"Indeed," Kabsal said, smiling. "I must admit, I stepped

in here expecting indifference, not deference. How did you come to be part of her entourage?"

Shallan started, realizing for the first time that Brother Kabsal must have assumed her to be one of the Brightlady Kholin's attendants. Perhaps a ward.

"Bother," she said to herself.

"Hum?"

"It appears I've inadvertently misled you, Brother Kabsal. I'm not associated with Brightness Jasnah. Not yet, anyway. I've been trying to get her to take me on as a ward."

"Ah," he said, finishing his lacquering.

"I'm sorry."

"For what? You did nothing wrong." He blew on the picture, then turned it for her to see. It was perfectly lacquered, without any smears. "If you would do me a favor, child?" he said, setting the page aside.

"Anything."

He raised an eyebrow at that.

"Anything reasonable," she corrected.

"By whose reason?"

"Mine, I guess."

"Pity," he said, standing. "Then I will limit myself. If you would kindly let Brightness Jasnah know that I called upon her?"

"She knows you?" What business had a Herdazian ardent with Jasnah, a confirmed atheist?

"Oh, I wouldn't say that," he replied. "I'd hope she's heard my name, though, since I've requested an audience with her several times."

Shallan nodded, rising. "You want to try to convert her, I presume?"

"She presents a unique challenge. I don't think I could live with myself if I didn't at least *try* to persuade her."

"And we wouldn't want you to be unable to live with yourself," Shallan noted, "as the alternative harks back to your nasty habit of almost killing ardents."

"Exactly. Anyway, I think a personal message from you might help where written requests have been ignored."

"I . . . doubt that."

"Well, if she refuses, it only means that I'll be back." He smiled. "That would mean—hopefully—that we shall meet each other again. So I look forward to it."

"I as well. And I'm sorry again about the misunderstanding."

"Brightness! Please. Don't take responsibility for *my* assumptions."

She smiled. "I should hesitate to take responsibility for you in *any* manner or regard, Brother Kabsal. But I still feel bad."

"It will pass," he noted, blue eyes twinkling. "But I'll do my best to make you feel well again. Is there anything you're fond of? Other than respecting ardents and drawing amazing pictures, that is?"

"Jam."

He cocked his head.

"I like it," she said, shrugging. "You asked what I was fond of. Jam."

"So it shall be." He withdrew into the dark corridor, fishing in his robe pocket for his sphere to give him light. In moments, he was gone.

Why didn't he wait for Jasnah to return himself? Shallan shook her head, then lacquered her other two pictures. She had just finished letting them dry—packing them in her satchel—when she heard footsteps in the hallway again and recognized Jasnah's voice speaking.

Shallan hurriedly gathered her things, leaving the letter on the desk, then stepped up to the side of the alcove to wait. Jasnah Kholin entered a moment later, accompanied by a small group of servants.

She did not look pleased.

"Victory! We stand atop the mount! We scatter them before us! Their homes become our dens, their lands are now our farms! And they shall burn, as we once did, in a place that is hollow and forlorn."

—Collected on Ishashan, 1172, 18 seconds pre-death. Subject was a lighteyed spinster of the eighth dahn.

Shallan's fears were confirmed as Jasnah looked straight at her, then lowered her safehand to her side in a mark of frustration. "So you *are* here."

Shallan cringed. "The servants told you, then?"

"You didn't think that they would leave someone in my alcove and not warn me?" Behind Jasnah, a small group of parshmen hesitated in the hallway, each carrying an armload of books.

"Brightness Kholin," Shallan said. "I just—"

"I have wasted enough time on you already," Jasnah said, eyes furious. "You will withdraw, Miss Davar. And I will not see you again during my time here. Am I *understood*?"

Shallan's hopes crumbled. She shrank back. There was a gravity to Jasnah Kholin. One did not disobey her. One need only look into those eyes to understand.

"I'm sorry to have bothered you," Shallan whispered,

clutching her satchel and leaving with as much dignity as she could manage. She barely kept the tears of embarrassment and disappointment from her eyes as she hastened down the hallway, feeling like a complete fool.

She reached the porter's shaft, though they had already returned below after bringing up Jasnah. Shallan didn't pull the bell to summon them. Instead she placed her back to the wall and sank down to the floor, knees up against her chest, satchel in her lap. She wrapped her arms around her legs, free-hand clasping her safehand through the fabric of her cuff, breathing quietly.

Angry people unsettled her. She couldn't help but think of her father in one of his tirades, couldn't help but hear screams, bellows, and whimpers. Was she weak because confrontation unsettled her so? She felt that she was.

Foolish, idiot girl, she thought, a few painspren crawling out of the wall near her head. *What made you think you could do this? You've only set foot off your family grounds a half-dozen times during your life. Idiot, idiot,* idiot!

She had persuaded her brothers to trust her, to put hope in her ridiculous plan. And now what had she done? Wasted six months during which their enemies circled closer.

"Brightness Davar?" asked a hesitant voice.

Shallan looked up, realizing she'd been so wrapped in her misery that she hadn't seen the servant approach. He was a younger man, wearing an all black uniform, no emblem on the breast. Not a master-servant, but perhaps one in training.

"Brightness Kholin would like to speak with you." The young man gestured back down the hallway.

To berate me further? Shallan thought with a grimace. But a highlady like Jasnah got what she wanted. Shallan forced herself to stop shaking, then stood. At least she'd been able to keep the tears away; she hadn't ruined her makeup. She followed the servant back to the lit alcove, satchel clutched before her like a shield on the battlefield.

Jasnah Kholin sat in the chair Shallan had been using, stacks of books on the table. Jasnah was rubbing her forehead with her freehand. The Soulcaster rested against the back of her skin, the smokestone dark and cracked. Though Jasnah looked fatigued, she sat with perfect posture, her fine silk dress covering her feet, her safehand held across her lap.

Jasnah focused on Shallan, lowering her freehand. "I should not have treated you with such anger, Miss Davar," she said in a tired voice. "You were simply showing persistence, a trait I normally encourage. Storms alight, I've oft been guilty of stubbornness myself. Sometimes we find it hardest to accept in others that which we cling to in ourselves. My only excuse can be that I have put myself under an unusual amount of strain lately."

Shallan nodded in gratitude, though she felt terribly awkward.

Jasnah turned to look out of the balcony into the dark space of the Veil. "I know what people say of me. I should hope that I am not as harsh as some say, though a woman could have far worse than a reputation for sternness. It can serve one well."

Shallan had to forcibly keep herself from fidgeting. Should she withdraw?

Jasnah shook her head to herself, though Shallan could not guess what thoughts had caused the unconscious gesture. Finally, she turned back to Shallan and waved toward the large, gobletlike bowl on the desk. It held a dozen of Shallan's spheres.

Shallan raised her freehand to her lips in shock. She'd completely forgotten the money. She bowed to Jasnah in thanks, then hurriedly collected the spheres. "Brightness, lest I forget, I should mention that an ardent—Brother Kabsal—came to see you while I waited here. He wished me to pass on his desire to speak with you."

"Not surprising," Jasnah said. "You seem surprised about the spheres, Miss Davar. I assumed that you were waiting outside to recover them. Is that not why you were so close?"

"No, Brightness. I was just settling my nerves."

"Ah."

Shallan bit her lip. The princess appeared to have gotten

past her initial tirade. Perhaps . . . "Brightness," Shallan said, cringing at her brashness, "what did you think of my letter?"

"Letter?"

"I . . ." Shallan glanced at the desk. "Beneath that stack of books, Brightness."

A servant quickly moved aside the stack of books; the parshman must have set it on the paper without noticing. Jasnah picked up the letter, raising an eyebrow, and Shallan hurriedly undid her satchel and placed the spheres in her money pouch. Then she cursed herself for being so quick, as now she had nothing to do but stand and wait for Jasnah to finish reading.

"This is true?" Jasnah looking up from the paper. "You are self-trained?"

"Yes, Brightness."

"That is remarkable."

"Thank you, Brightness."

"And this letter was a clever maneuver. You correctly assumed that I would respond to a written plea. This shows me your skill with words, and the rhetoric of the letter gives proof that you can think logically and make a good argument."

"Thank you, Brightness," Shallan said, feeling another surge of hope, mixed with fatigue. Her emotions had been jerked back and forth like a rope being used for a tugging contest.

"You should have left the note for me, and withdrawn before I returned."

"But then the note would have been lost beneath that stack of books."

Jasnah raised an eyebrow at her, as if to show that she did not appreciate being corrected. "Very well. The context of a person's life *is* important. Your circumstances do not excuse your lack of education in history and philosophy, but leniency is in order. I will allow you to petition me again at a later date, a privilege I have never given any aspiring ward. Once you have a sufficient groundwork in those two subjects, come to me again. If you have improved suitably, I will accept you."

Shallan's emotions sank. Jasnah's offer *was* kindly, but it would take years of study to accomplish what she asked. House Davar would have fallen by then, her family's lands divided among its creditors, her brothers and herself stripped of title and perhaps enslaved.

"Thank you, Brightness," Shallan said, bowing her head.

Jasnah nodded, as if considering the matter closed. Shallan withdrew, walking quietly down the hallway and pulling the cord to ring for the porters.

Jasnah had all but promised to accept her at a later date. For most, that would be a great victory. Being trained by Jasnah Kholin—thought by some to be the finest living scholar—would have ensured a bright future. Shallan would have married extremely well, likely to the son of a highprince, and would have found new social circles open to her. Indeed, if Shallan had possessed the time to train under Jasnah, the sheer prestige of a Kholin affiliation might have been enough to save her house.

If only.

Eventually, Shallan made her way out of the Conclave; there were no gates on the front, just pillars set before the open maw. She was surprised to discover how dim it was outside. She trailed down the large steps, then took a smaller, more cultivated side path where she would be out of the way. Small shelves of ornamental shalebark had been grown along this walkway, and several species had let out fanlike tendrils to wave in the evening breeze. A few lazy lifespren—like specks of glowing green dust—flitted from one frond to the next.

Shallan leaned back against the stonelike plant, the tendrils pulling in and hiding. From this vantage, she could look down at Kharbranth, lights glowing beneath her like a cascade of fire streaming down the cliff face. The only other option for her and her brothers was to run. To abandon the family estates in Jah Keved and seek asylum. But where? Were there old allies her father *hadn't* alienated?

There was that matter of the strange collection of maps they'd found in his study. What did they mean? He'd rarely spoken of his plans to his children. Even her father's advisors knew very little. Helaran—her eldest brother—had known more, but he had vanished over a year ago, and her father had proclaimed him dead.

As always, thinking of her father made her feel ill, and the pain started to constrict her chest. She raised her freehand to her head, suddenly overwhelmed by the weight of House Davar's situation, her part in it, and the secret she now carried, hidden ten heartbeats away.

"Ho, young miss!" a voice called. She turned, shocked to see Yalb standing up on a rocky shelf a short distance from the Conclave entrance. A group of men in guard uniforms sat on the rock around him.

"Yalb?" she said, aghast. He should have returned to his ship hours ago. She hurried over to stand below the short stone outcropping. "Why are you still here?"

"Oh," he said, grinning, "I found myself a game of kabers here with these fine, upstanding gentlemen of the city guard. Figured officers of the law were right unlikely to cheat me, so we entered into a friendly-type game while I waited."

"But you didn't *need* to wait."

"Didn't need to win eighty chips off these fellows neither," Yalb said with a laugh. "But I did both!"

The men sitting around him looked far less enthusiastic. Their uniforms were orange tabards tied about the middle with white sashes.

"Well, I suppose I should be leading you back to the ship, then," Yalb said, reluctantly gathering up the spheres in the pile at his feet. They glowed with a variety of hues. Their light was small—each was only a chip—but it was impressive winnings.

Shallan stepped back as Yalb hopped off the rock shelf. His companions protested his departure, but he gestured to Shallan. "You'd have me leave a lighteyed woman of her stature to walk back to the ship on her own? I figured you for men of honor!"

That quieted their protests.

Yalb chuckled to himself, bowing to Shallan and leading

her away down the path. He had a twinkle to his eyes. "Stormfather, but it's fun to win against lawmen. I'll have free drinks at the docks once this gets around."

"You shouldn't gamble," Shallan said. "You shouldn't try to guess the future. I didn't give you that sphere so you could waste it on such practices."

Yalb laughed. "It ain't gambling if you know you're going to win, young miss."

"You *cheated*?" she hissed, horrified. She glanced back at the guardsmen, who had settled down to continue their game, lit by the spheres on the stones before them.

"Not so loud!" Yalb said in a low voice. However, he seemed very pleased with himself. "Cheating four guardsmen, now that's a trick. Hardly believe I managed it!"

"I'm disappointed in you. This is *not* proper behavior."

"It is if you're a sailor, young miss." He shrugged. "It's what they right expected from me. Watched me like handlers of poisonous skyeels, they did. The game wasn't about the cards—it was about them trying to figure how I was cheating and me trying to figure how to keep them from hauling me off. I think I might not have managed to walk away with my skin if you hadn't arrived!" That didn't seem to worry him much.

The roadway down to the docks was not nearly as busy as it had been earlier, but there were still a surprisingly large number of people about. The street was lit by oil lanterns—spheres would just have ended up in someone's pouch—but many of the people about carried sphere lanterns, casting a rainbow of colored light on the roadway. The people were almost like spren, each a different hue, moving this way or that.

"So, young miss," Yalb said, leading her carefully through the traffic. "You really want to go back? I just said what I did so I could extract myself from that game there."

"Yes, I do want to go back, please."

"And your princess?"

Shallan grimaced. "The meeting was . . . unproductive."

"She didn't take you? What's wrong with her?"

"Chronic competence, I should guess. She's been so successful in life that she has unrealistic expectations of others."

Yalb frowned, guiding Shallan around a group of revelers stumbling drunkenly up the roadway. Wasn't it a little early for that sort of thing? Yalb got a few steps ahead, turning and walking backward, looking at her. "That doesn't make sense, young miss. What more could she want than you?"

"Much more, apparently."

"But you're perfect! Pardon my forwardness."

"You're walking backward."

"Pardon my backwardness, then. You look good from any side, young miss, that you do."

She found herself smiling. Tozbek's sailors had far too high an opinion of her.

"You'd make an ideal ward," he continued. "Genteel, pretty, refined and such. Don't much like your opinion on gambling, but that's to be expected. Wouldn't be right for a proper woman not to scold a fellow for gambling. It'd be like the sun refusing to rise or the sea turning white."

"Or Jasnah Kholin smiling."

"Exactly! Anyway, you're perfect."

"It's kind of you to say so."

"Well, it's true," he said, putting hands on hips, stopping. "So that's it? You're going to give up?"

She gave him a perplexed stare. He stood there on the busy roadway, lit from above by a lantern burning yellow-orange, hands on his hips, white Thaylen eyebrows drooping along the sides of his face, bare-chested under his open vest. That was a posture no citizen, no matter how high ranked, had ever taken at her father's mansion.

"I *did* try to persuade her," Shallan said, blushing. "I went to her a second time, and she rejected me again."

"Two times, eh? In cards, you always got to try a third hand. It wins the most often."

Shallan frowned. "But that's not really true. The laws of probability and statistics—"

"Don't know much blustering math," Yalb said, folding his arms. "But I do know the Passions. You win when you need it most, you see."

The Passions. Pagan superstition. Of course, Jasnah had

referred to glyphwards as superstition too, so perhaps it all came down to perspective.

Try a third time . . . Shallan shivered to consider Jasnah's wrath if Shallan bothered her yet again. She'd surely withdraw the offer to come study with her in the future.

But Shallan would never get to take that offer. It was like a glass sphere with no gemstone at the center. Pretty, but worthless. Was it not better to take one last chance at getting the position she needed *now*?

It wouldn't work. Jasnah had made it quite clear that Shallan was not yet educated enough.

Not yet educated enough . . .

An idea sparked in Shallan's head. She raised her safehand to her breast, standing on that roadway, considering the audacity of it. She'd likely get herself thrown from the city at Jasnah's demand.

Yet if she returned home without trying every avenue, could she face her brothers? They depended on her. For once in her life, someone *needed* Shallan. That responsibility excited her. And terrified her.

"I need a book merchant," she found herself saying, voice wavering slightly.

Yalb raised an eyebrow at her.

"Third hand wins the most. Do you think you can find me a book merchant who is open at this hour?"

"Kharbranth is a major port, young miss," he said with a laugh. "Stores stay open late. Just wait here." He dashed off into the evening crowd, leaving her with an anxious protest on her lips.

She sighed, then seated herself in a demure posture on the stone base of a lantern pole. It should be safe. She saw other lighteyed women passing on the street, though they were often carried in palanquins or those small, hand-pulled vehicles. She even saw the occasional real carriage, though only the very wealthy could afford to keep horses.

A few minutes later, Yalb popped out of the crowd as if from nowhere and waved for her to follow. She rose and hurried to him.

"Should we get a porter?" she asked as he led her to a large side street that ran laterally across the city's hill. She stepped carefully; her skirt was long enough that she worried about tearing the hem on the stone. The strip at the bottom was designed to be easily replaced, but Shallan could hardly afford to waste spheres on such things.

"Nah," Yalb said. "It's right here." He pointed along another cross street. This one had a row of shops climbing up the steep slope, each with a sign hanging out front bearing the glyphpair for *book*, and those glyphs were often styled into the shape of a book. Illiterate servants who might be sent to a shop had to be able to recognize them.

"Merchants of the same type like to clump together," Yalb said, rubbing his chin. "Seems dumb to me, but I guess merchants are like fish. Where you find one, you'll find others."

"The same could be said of ideas," Shallan said, counting. Six different shops. All were lit with Stormlight in the windows, cool and even.

"Third one on the left," Yalb said, pointing. "Merchant's name is Artmyrn. My sources say he's the best." It was a Thaylen name. Likely Yalb had asked others from his homeland, and they had pointed him here.

She nodded to Yalb and they climbed up the steep stone street to the shop. Yalb didn't enter with her; she'd noticed that many men were uncomfortable around books and reading, even those who weren't Vorin.

She pushed through the door—stout wood set with two crystal panels—and stepped into a warm room, uncertain what to expect. She'd never gone into a store to purchase anything; she'd either sent servants, or the merchants had come to her.

The room inside looked very inviting, with large, comfortable easy chairs beside a hearth. Flamespren danced on burning logs there, and the floor was wood. Seamless wood; it had probably been Soulcast that way directly from the stone beneath. Lavish indeed.

A woman stood behind a counter at the back of the room. She wore an embroidered skirt and blouse, rather than the sleek, silk, one-piece havah that Shallan wore. She was dark-eyed, but she was obviously affluent. In Vorin kingdoms, she'd likely be of the first or second nahn. Thaylens had their own system of ranks. At least they weren't completely pagan—they respected eye color, and the woman wore a glove on her safehand.

There weren't many books in the place. A few on the counter, one on a stand beside the chairs. A clock ticked on the wall, its underside hung with a dozen shimmering silver bells. This looked more like a person's home than a shop.

The woman slid a marker into her book, smiling at Shallan. It was a smooth, eager smile. Almost predatory. "Please, Brightness, sit," she said, waving toward the chairs. The woman had curled her long, white Thaylen eyebrows so they hung down the sides of her face like locks from her bangs.

Shallan sat hesitantly as the woman rang a bell on the underside of the counter. Soon, a portly man waddled into the room wearing a vest that seemed ready to burst from the stress of holding in his girth. His hair was greying, and he kept his eyebrows combed back, over his ears.

"Ah," he said, clapping ample hands, "dear young woman. Are you in the market for a nice novel? Some leisure reading to pass the cruel hours while you are separated from a lost love? Or perhaps a book on geography, with details of exotic locations?" He had a slightly condescending tone and spoke in her native Veden.

"I— No, thank you. I need an extensive set of books on history and three on philosophy." She thought back, trying to recall the names Jasnah had used. "Something by Placini, Gabrathin, Yustara, Manaline, or Shauka-daughter-Hasweth."

"Heavy reading for one so young," the man said, nodding to the woman, who was probably his wife. She ducked into the back room. He'd use her for reading; even if he could read himself, he wouldn't want to offend customers by doing so in their presence. He would handle the money; commerce was a masculine art in most situations.

"Now, why is a young flower like yourself bothering herself with such topics?" the merchant said, easing himself down into the chair across from her. "Can't I interest you in a nice romantic novel? They are my specialty, you see. Young women from across the city come to me, and I always carry the best."

His tone set her on edge. It was galling enough to *know* she was a sheltered child. Was it really necessary to remind her of it? "A romantic novel," she said, holding her satchel close to her chest. "Yes, perhaps that would be nice. Do you by chance have a copy of *Nearer the Flame*?"

The merchant blinked. *Nearer the Flame* was written from the viewpoint of a man who slowly descended into madness after watching his children starve.

"Are you certain you want something so, er, ambitious?" the man asked.

"Is ambition such an unseemly attribute in a young woman?"

"Well, no, I suppose not." He smiled again—the thick, toothy smile of a merchant trying to put someone at ease. "I can see you are a woman of discriminating taste."

"I am," Shallan said, voice firm though her heart fluttered. Was she destined to get into an argument with everyone she met? "I *do* like my meals prepared very carefully, as my palate is quite delicate."

"Pardon. I meant that you have discriminating taste *in books.*"

"I've never eaten one, actually."

"Brightness, I believe you are having sport with me."

"Not yet I'm not. I haven't even really begun."

"I—"

"Now," she said, "you were right to compare the mind and the stomach."

"But—"

"Too many of us," she said, "take great pains with what we ingest through our mouths, and far less with what we partake of through our ears and eyes. Wouldn't you say?"

He nodded, perhaps not trusting her to let him speak

without interrupting. Shallan knew, somewhere in the back of her mind, that she was letting herself go too far—that she was tense and frustrated after her interactions with Jasnah.

She didn't care at the moment. "Discriminating," she said, testing the world. "I'm not certain I agree with your choice of words. To discriminate is to maintain prejudice against. To be exclusive. Can a person afford to be exclusive with what they ingest? Whether we speak of food or of thoughts?"

"I think they must be," the merchant said. "Isn't that what you just said?"

"I said we should take thought for what we read or eat. Not that we should be exclusive. Tell me, what do you think would happen to a person who ate only sweets?"

"I know well," the man said. "I have a sister-in-law who periodically upsets her stomach by doing that."

"See, she was *too* discriminating. The body needs many different foods to remain healthy. And the mind needs many different ideas to remain sharp. Wouldn't you agree? And so if I were to read only these silly romances you presume that my ambition can handle, my mind would grow sick as surely as your sister-in-law's stomach. Yes, I should think that the metaphor is a solid one. You are quite clever, Master Artmyrn."

His smile returned.

"Of course," she noted, not smiling back, "being talked down to upsets both the mind *and* the stomach. So nice of you to give a poignant object lesson to accompany your brilliant metaphor. Do you treat all of your customers this way?"

"Brightness . . . I believe you stray into sarcasm."

"Funny. I thought I'd run straight into it, screaming at the top of my lungs."

He blushed and stood. "I'll go help my wife." He hurriedly withdrew.

She sat back, and realized she was annoyed at herself for letting her frustration boil out. It was just what her nurses had warned her about. A young woman had to mind her words. Her father's intemperate tongue had earned their house a regrettable reputation; would she add to it?

She calmed herself, enjoying the warmth and watching the dancing flamespren until the merchant and his wife returned, bearing several stacks of books. The merchant took his seat again, and his wife pulled over a stool, setting the tomes on the floor and then showing them one at a time as her husband spoke.

"For history, we have two choices," the merchant said, condescension—and friendliness—gone. "*Times and Passage,* by Rencalt, is a single volume survey of Rosharan history since the Hierocracy." His wife held up a red, cloth-bound volume. "I told my wife that you would likely be insulted by such a shallow option, but she insisted."

"Thank you," Shallan said. "I am not insulted, but I do require something more detailed."

"Then perhaps *Eternathis* will serve you," he said as his wife held up a blue-grey set of four volumes. "It is a philosophical work which examines the same time period by focusing only on the interactions of the five Vorin kingdoms. As you can see, the treatment is exhaustive."

The four volumes were thick. The *five* Vorin kingdoms? She'd thought there were four. Jah Keved, Alethkar, Kharbranth, and Natanatan. United by religion, they had been strong allies during the years following the Recreance. What was the fifth kingdom?

The volumes intrigued her. "I will take them."

"Excellent," the merchant said, a bit of the gleam returning to his eye. "Of the philosophical works you listed, we didn't have anything by Yustara. We have one each of works by Placini and Manaline; both are collections of excerpts from their most famous writings. I've had the Placini book read to me; it's quite good."

Shallan nodded.

"As for Gabrathin," he said, "we have four different volumes. My, but he was a prolific one! Oh, and we have a single book by Shauka-daughter-Hasweth." The wife held up a thin green volume. "I have to admit, I've never had any of her work read to me. I didn't realize that there were any Shin philosophers of note."

Shallan looked at the four books by Gabrathin. She had no idea which one she should take, so she avoided the question, pointing at the two collections he had mentioned first and the single volume by Shauka-daughter-Hasweth. A philosopher from distant Shin, where people lived in mud and worshipped rocks? The man who had killed Jasnah's father nearly six years before—prompting the war against the Parshendi in Natanatan—had been Shin. The Assassin in White, they called him.

"I will take those three," Shallan said, "along with the histories."

"Excellent!" the merchant repeated. "For buying so many, I will give you a fair discount. Let us say, ten emerald broams?"

Shallan nearly choked. An emerald broam was the largest denomination of sphere, worth a thousand diamond chips. Ten of them was more than her trip to Kharbranth had cost by several magnitudes!

She opened her satchel, looking in at her money pouch. She had around eight emerald broams left. She'd have to take fewer of the books, obviously, but which ones?

Suddenly, the door slammed open. Shallan jumped and was surprised to see Yalb standing there, holding his cap in his hands, nervous. He rushed to her chair, going down on one knee. She was too stunned to say anything. Why was he so worried?

"Brightness," he said, bowing his head. "My master bids you return. He's reconsidered his offer. Truly, we can take the price you offered."

Shallan opened her mouth, but found herself stupefied.

Yalb glanced at the merchant. "Brightness, don't buy from this man. He's a liar and a cheat. My master will sell you much finer books at a better price."

"Now, what's this?" Artmyrn said, standing. "How dare you! Who is your master?"

"Barmest," Yalb said defensively.

"That rat. He sends a boy into *my* shop trying to steal *my* customer? Outrageous!"

"She came to our shop first!" Yalb said.

Shallan finally recovered her wits. *Stormfather! He's quite the actor.* "You had your chance," she said to Yalb. "Run along and tell your master that I refuse to be swindled. I will visit every bookshop in the city if that is what it takes to find someone reasonable."

"Artmyrn isn't reasonable," Yalb said, spitting to the side. The merchant's eyes opened wide with rage.

"We shall see," Shallan said.

"Brightness," Artmyrn said, red-faced. "Surely you don't believe these allegations!"

"And how much were you going to charge her?" Yalb asked.

"Ten emerald broams," Shallan said. "For those seven books."

Yalb laughed. "And you didn't stand up and walk right out! You practically had my master's ears, and he offered you a better deal than that! Please, Brightness, return with me. We're ready to—"

"Ten was just an opening figure," Artmyrn said. "I didn't expect her to take them." He looked at Shallan. "Of course, *eight. . . .*"

Yalb laughed again. "I'm sure we have those same books, Brightness. I'll bet my master gives them to you for two."

Artmyrn grew more red-faced, muttering. "Brightness, surely you wouldn't patronize someone so *crass* as to send a servant into someone else's shop to steal his customers!"

"Perhaps I would," Shallan said. "At least he didn't insult my intelligence."

Artmyrn's wife glared at her husband, and the man grew even more red in the face. "Two emerald, three sapphire. That is as low as I can go. If you want cheaper than that, then buy from that scoundrel Barmest. The books will probably be missing pages, though."

Shallan hesitated, glancing at Yalb; he was caught up in his role, bowing and scraping. She caught his eyes, and he just kind of gave a shrug.

"I'll do it," she said to Artmyrn, prompting a groan from Yalb. He slunk away with a curse from Artmyrn's wife. Shallan rose and counted out the spheres; the emerald broams she retrieved from her safepouch.

Soon, she walked from the shop bearing a heavy canvas bag. She walked down the steep street, and found Yalb lounging beside a lamppost. She smiled as he took the bag from her. "How did you know what a fair price for a book was?" she asked.

"Fair price?" he said, slinging the bag over his shoulder. "For a book? I've no idea. I just figured he'd be trying to take you for as much as he could. That's why I asked around for who his biggest rival was and came back to help get him to be more reasonable."

"It was that obvious I'd let myself be swindled?" she asked with a blush, the two of them walking out of the side street.

Yalb chuckled. "Just a little. Anyway, conning men like him is almost as much fun as cheating guards. You probably could have gotten him down further by actually leaving with me, then coming back later to give him another chance."

"That sounds complicated."

"Merchants is like mercenaries, my gammer always said. Only difference is that merchants will take your head off, then pretend to be your friend all the same."

This from a man who had just spent the evening cheating a group of guards at cards. "Well, you have my thanks, anyway."

"Wasn't nothing. It was fun, though I can't believe you paid what you did. It's just a bunch of wood. I could find some driftwood and put some funny marks on it. Would you pay me pure spheres for that too?"

"I can't offer that," she said, fishing in her satchel. She took out the picture she'd drawn of Yalb and the porter. "But please, take this, with my thanks."

Yalb took the picture and stepped up beneath a nearby lantern to get a look. He laughed, cocking his head, smiling broadly. "Stormfather! Ain't that something? Looks like I'm seeing myself in a polished plate, it does. I can't take this, Brightness!"

"Please. I insist." She did, however, blink her eyes, taking a Memory of him standing there, one hand on his chin as he studied the picture of himself. She'd redraw him later. After what he'd done for her, she dearly wanted him in her collection.

Yalb carefully tucked the picture between the pages of a book, then hefted the bag and continued. They stepped back onto the main roadway. Nomon—the middle moon—had begun to rise, bathing the city in pale blue light. Staying up this late had been a rare privilege for her in her father's house, but these city people around them barely seemed to notice the late hour. What a strange place this city was.

"Back to the ship now?" Yalb asked.

"No," Shallan said, taking a deep breath. "Back to the Conclave."

He raised an eyebrow, but led her back. Once there, she bid Yalb farewell, reminding him to take his picture. He did so, wishing her luck before hastening from the Conclave, probably worried about meeting the guardsmen he'd cheated earlier.

Shallan had a servant carry her books, and made her way down the hallway back to the Veil. Just inside the ornate iron doors, she caught the attention of a master-servant.

"Yes, Brightness?" the man asked. Most of the alcoves were now dim, and patient servants were returning tomes to their safe place beyond the crystal walls.

Shaking off her fatigue, Shallan counted up the rows. There was still a light in Jasnah's alcove. "I'd like to use the alcove there," she said, pointing to the next balcony over.

"Do you have a chit of admittance?"

"I'm afraid not."

"Then you'll have to rent the space if you wish to use it regularly. Two skymarks."

Wincing at the price, Shallan dug out the proper spheres and paid. Her money pouches were looking depressingly flat. She let the parshman porters haul her up to the appropriate level, then she quietly walked to her alcove. There, she used all her remaining spheres to fill the oversized goblet lamp. To get enough light, she was forced to use spheres of all nine colors and all three sizes, so the illumination was patchy and varied.

Shallan peeked over the side of her alcove, out at the next balcony over. Jasnah sat studying, heedless of the hour, her goblet filled to the brim with pure diamond broams. They were best for light, but less useful in Soulcasting, so weren't as valuable.

Shallan ducked back around. There was a place at the very edge of the alcove's table where she could sit, hidden by the wall from Jasnah, so she sat there. Perhaps she should have chosen an alcove on another level, but she wanted to keep an eye on the woman. Hopefully Jasnah would spend weeks here studying. Enough time for Shallan to dedicate herself to some fierce cramming. Her ability to memorize pictures and scenes didn't work as well on text, but she could learn lists and facts at a rate that her tutors had found remarkable.

She settled herself in the chair, pulling out the books and arranging them. She rubbed her eyes. It was really quite late, but there wasn't time to waste. Jasnah had said that Shallan could make another petition when the gaps in her knowledge were filled. Well, Shallan intended to fill those gaps in record time, then present herself again. She'd do it when Jasnah was ready to leave Kharbranth.

It was a last, desperate hope, so frail that a strong gust of circumstance seemed likely to topple it. Taking a deep breath, Shallan opened the first of the history books.

"I'm never going to be rid of you, am I?" a soft, feminine voice asked.

Shallan jumped up, nearly knocking over her books as she spun toward the doorway. Jasnah Kholin stood there, deep blue dress embroidered in silver, its silken sheen reflecting the light of Shallan's spheres. The Soulcaster was covered by a fingerless black glove to block the bright gemstones.

"Brightness," Shallan said, rising and curtsying in an awkward rush. "I didn't mean to disturb you. I—"

Jasnah quieted her with a wave of the hand. She stepped aside as a parshman entered Shallan's alcove, carrying a chair. He placed it beside Shallan's desk, and Jasnah glided over and sat.

Shallan tried to judge Jasnah's mood, but the older woman's emotions were impossible to read. "I honestly didn't want to disturb you."

"I bribed the servants to tell me if you returned to the Veil," Jasnah said idly, picking up one of Shallan's tomes, reading the title. "I didn't want to be interrupted again."

"I—" Shallan looked down, blushing furiously.

"Don't bother apologizing," Jasnah said. She looked tired; more tired than Shallan felt. Jasnah picked through the books. "A fine selection. You chose well."

"It wasn't really much of a choice," Shallan said. "It was just about all the merchant had."

"You intended to study their contents quickly, I assume?" Jasnah said musingly. "Try to impress me one last time before I left Kharbranth?"

Shallan hesitated, then nodded.

"A clever ploy. I should have put a time restriction on your reapplication." She looked at Shallan, glancing her over. "You are very determined. That is good. And I know why you wish so desperately to be my ward."

Shallan started. She *knew*?

"Your house has many enemies," Jasnah continued, "and your father is reclusive. It will be difficult for you to marry well without a tactically sound alliance."

Shallan relaxed, though she tried to keep it from showing.

"Let me see your satchel," Jasnah said.

Shallan frowned, resisting the urge to pull it close. "Brightness?"

Jasnah held out her hand. "You recall what I said about repeating myself?"

Reluctantly, Shallan handed it over. Jasnah carefully removed its contents, neatly lining up the brushes, pencils, pens, jar of lacquer, ink, and solvent. She placed the stacks of paper, the notebooks, and the finished pictures in a line.

Then she got out Shallan's money pouches, noting their emptiness. She glanced at the goblet lamp, counting its contents. She raised an eyebrow.

Next, she began to look through Shallan's pictures. First the loose-leaf ones, where she lingered on Shallan's picture of Jasnah herself. Shallan watched the woman's face. Was she pleased? Surprised? Displeased at how much time Shallan spent sketching sailors and serving women?

Finally, Jasnah moved on to the sketchbook filled with drawings of plants and animals Shallan had observed during her trip. Jasnah spent the longest on this, reading through each notation. "Why have you made these sketches?" Jasnah asked at the end.

"Why, Brightness? Well, because I wanted to." She grimaced. Should she have said something profound instead?

Jasnah nodded slowly. Then she rose. "I have rooms in the Conclave, granted to me by the king. Gather your things and go there. You look exhausted."

"Brightness?" Shallan asked, rising, a thrill of excitement running through her.

Jasnah hesitated at the doorway. "At first meeting, I took you for a rural opportunist, seeking only to ride my name to greater wealth."

"You've changed your mind?"

"No," Jasnah said, "there is undoubtedly some of that in you. But we are each many different people, and you can tell much about a person by what they carry with them. If that notebook is any indication, you pursue scholarship in your free time for its own sake. That is encouraging. It is, perhaps, the best argument you could make on your own behalf.

"If I cannot be rid of you, then I might as well make use of you. Go and sleep. Tomorrow we will begin early, and you will divide your time between your education and helping me with my studies."

With that, Jasnah withdrew.

Shallan sat, bemused, blinking tired eyes. She got out a sheet of paper and wrote a quick prayer of thanks, which she'd burn later. Then she hurriedly gathered up her books and went looking for a servant to send to the *Wind's Pleasure* for her trunk.

It had been a very, *very* long day. But she'd won. The first step had been completed.

Now her real task began.

Chulls

Chulls are everywhere, of course, and they come in a variety of shapes and sizes. There must be far more breeds of the animals than I'd originally assumed. I've seen them pulling carts, towing boxes, carrying jugs of water in racks on their sides.

I even saw a man riding one for transportation, though it seems that walking would be far faster.

Apparently, the beasts aren't hurt if the shell is cracked, or even shaped. Some people want flat places on top to ride, and many carts are hooked to fittings drilled directly into the shell.

The shells aren't nearly as heavy as they look.

In the wild, plants grow in the crevices, and a sleeping chull looks much like a boulder.

Many of the drivers here on the coast direct the animals by tapping on their antennae with a long pole, rather than using a complex leather bridle like the workers on my father's estate.

DAMNATION

"Ten people, with Shardblades alight, standing before a wall of black and white and red."

—Collected: Jesachev, 1173, 12 seconds pre-death. Subject: one of our own ardents, overheard during his last moments.

Kaladin had not been assigned to Bridge Four by chance. Out of all the bridge crews, Bridge Four had the highest casualty rate. That was particularly notable, considering that average bridge crews often lost one-third to one-half of their number on a single run.

Kaladin sat outside, back to the barrack wall, a sprinkle of rain falling on him. It wasn't a highstorm. Just an ordinary spring rain. Soft. A timid cousin to the great storms.

Syl sat on Kaladin's shoulder. Or hovered on it. Whatever. She didn't seem to have any weight. Kaladin sat slumped, chin against his chest, staring at a dip in the stone, which was slowly collecting rainwater.

He should have moved inside Bridge Four's barrack. It was cold and unfurnished, but it would keep off the rain. But he just . . . couldn't care. How long had he been with Bridge Four now? Two weeks? Three? An eternity?

Of the twenty-five men who had survived his first bridge deployment, twenty-three were now dead. Two had been moved to other bridge crews because they'd done something to please Gaz, but they'd died there. Only one other man and Kaladin remained. Two out of nearly forty.

The bridge crew's numbers had been replenished with more unfortunates, and most of those had died too. They had been replaced. Many of those had died. Bridgeleader after bridgeleader had been chosen. It was supposed to be a favored position on a bridge crew, always getting to run in the best places. It didn't matter for Bridge Four.

Some bridge runs weren't as bad. If the Alethi arrived before the Parshendi, no bridgemen died. And if they arrived too late, sometimes another highprince was already there. Sadeas wouldn't help in that case; he'd take his army and go back to camp. Even in a bad run, the Parshendi would often choose to focus their arrows on certain crews, trying to bring them down one at a time. Sometimes, dozens of bridgemen would fall, but not a single one from Bridge Four.

That was rare. For some reason, Bridge Four always seemed to get targeted. Kaladin didn't bother to learn the names of his companions. None of the bridgemen did. What was the point? Learn a man's name, and one of you would be dead before the week was out. Odds were, you'd both be dead. Maybe he *should* learn names. Then he'd have someone to talk to in Damnation. They could reminisce about how terrible Bridge Four had been, and agree that eternal fires were much more pleasant.

He smirked dully, still staring at the rock in front of him. Gaz would come for them soon, send them to work. Scrubbing latrines, cleaning streets, mucking stables, gathering rocks. Something to keep their minds off their fate.

He still didn't know why they fought on those blustering plateaus. Something about those large chrysalises. They had gemstones at their hearts, apparently. But what did that have to do with the Vengeance Pact?

Another bridgeman—a youthful Veden with reddish-blond hair—lay nearby, staring up into the spitting sky. Rainwater pooled in the corners of his brown eyes, then ran down his face. He didn't blink.

They couldn't run. The warcamp might as well have been

a prison. The bridgemen could go to the merchants and spend their meager earnings on cheap wine or whores, but they couldn't leave the warcamp. The perimeter was secure. Partially, this was to keep out soldiers from the other camps—there was always rivalry where armies met. But mostly it was so bridgemen and slaves could not flee.

Why? Why did this all have to be so horrible? None of it made *sense*. Why not let a few bridgemen run out in front of the bridges with shields to block arrows? He'd asked, and had been told that would slow them down too much. He'd asked again, and had been told he'd be strung up if he didn't shut his mouth.

The lighteyes acted as if this entire mess were some kind of grand game. If it was, the rules were hidden from bridgemen, just as pieces on a board had no inkling what the player's strategy might be.

"Kaladin?" Syl asked, floating down and landing on his leg, holding the girlish form with the long dress flowing into mist. "Kaladin? You haven't spoken in days."

He kept staring, slumped. There *was* a way out. Bridgemen could visit the chasm nearest the camp. There were rules forbidding it, but the sentries ignored them. It was seen as the one mercy that could be given the bridgemen.

Bridgemen who took that path never returned.

"Kaladin?" Syl said, voice soft, worried.

"My father used to say that there are two kinds of people in the world," Kaladin whispered, voice raspy. "He said there are those who take lives. And there are those who save lives."

Syl frowned, cocking her head. This kind of conversation confused her; she wasn't good with abstractions.

"I used to think he was wrong. I thought there was a third group. People who killed in order to save." He shook his head. "I was a fool. There *is* a third group, a big one, but it isn't what I thought."

"What group?" she said, sitting down on his knee, brow scrunched up.

"The people who exist to be saved or to be killed. The group in the middle. The ones who can't do anything but die or be protected. The victims. That's all I am."

He looked up across the wet lumberyard. The carpenters had retreated, throwing tarps over untreated wood and bearing away tools that could rust. The bridgeman barracks ran around the west and north sides of the yard. Bridge Four's was set off a little from the others, as if bad luck were a disease that could be caught. Contagious by proximity, as Kaladin's father would say.

"We exist to be killed," Kaladin said. He blinked, glancing at the other few members of Bridge Four sitting apathetically in the rain. "If we're not dead already."

⁖

"I hate seeing you like this," Syl said, buzzing about Kaladin's head as his team of bridgemen dragged a log down into the lumberyard. The Parshendi often set fire to the outermost permanent bridges, so Highprince Sadeas's engineers and carpenters were always busy.

The old Kaladin might have wondered why the armies didn't work harder to defend the bridges. *There's something wrong here!* a voice inside him said. *You're missing part of the puzzle. They waste resources and bridgeman lives. They don't seem to care about pushing inward and assaulting the Parshendi. They just fight pitched battles on plateaus, then come back to the camps and celebrate. Why? WHY?*

He ignored that voice. It belonged to the man he had been.

"You used to be vibrant," Syl said. "So many looked up to you, Kaladin. Your squad of soldiers. The enemies you fought. The other slaves. Even some lighteyes."

Lunch would come soon. Then he could sleep until their bridgeleader kicked him awake for afternoon duty.

"I used to watch you fight," Syl said. "I can barely remember it. My memories of then are fuzzy. Like looking at you through a rainstorm."

Wait. That was odd. Syl hadn't started following him until after his fall from the army. And she'd acted just like an ordinary windspren back then. He hesitated, earning a curse and a lash on his back from a taskmaster's whip.

He started pulling again. Bridgemen who were laggard in

work were whipped, and bridgemen who were laggard on runs were executed. The army was very serious about that. Refuse to charge the Parshendi, try to lag behind the other bridges, and you'd be beheaded. They reserved that fate for that specific crime, in fact.

There were lots of ways to get punished as a bridgeman. You could earn extra work detail, get whipped, have your pay docked. If you did something really bad, they'd string you up for the Stormfather's judgment, leaving you tied to a post or a wall to face a highstorm. But the only thing you could do to be executed directly was refuse to run at the Parshendi.

The message was clear. Charging with your bridge *might* get you killed, but refusing to do so *would* get you killed.

Kaladin and his crew lifted their log into a pile with others, then unhooked their dragging lines. They walked back toward the edge of the lumberyard, where more logs waited.

"Gaz!" a voice called. A tall, yellow-and-black-haired soldier stood at the edge of the bridge grounds, a group of miserable men huddled behind him. That was Laresh, one of the soldiers who worked the duty tent. He brought new bridgemen to replace those who'd been killed.

The day was bright, without a hint of clouds, and the sun was hot on Kaladin's back. Gaz hustled up to meet the new recruits, and Kaladin and the others happened to be walking in that direction to pick up a log.

"What a sorry lot," Gaz said, looking over the recruits. "Of course, if they weren't, they wouldn't be sent *here*."

"That's the truth," Laresh said. "These ten at the front were caught smuggling. You know what to do."

New bridgemen were constantly needed, but there were always enough bodies. Slaves were common, but so were thieves or other lawbreakers from among the camp followers. Never parshmen. They were too valuable, and besides, the Parshendi were some kind of cousins to the parshmen. Better not to give the parshman workers in camp the sight of their kind fighting.

Sometimes a soldier would be thrown into a bridge crew. That only happened if he'd done something extremely bad, like striking an officer. Acts that would earn a hanging in many armies meant being sent to the bridge crews here. Supposedly, if you survived a hundred bridge runs, you'd be released. It had happened once or twice, the stories said. It was probably just a myth, intended to give the bridgemen some tiny hope for survival.

Kaladin and the others walked past the newcomers, gazes down, and began hooking their ropes to the next log.

"Bridge Four needs some men," Gaz said, rubbing his chin.

"Four always needs men," Laresh said. "Don't worry. I brought a special batch for it." He nodded toward a second group of recruits, much more ragtag, walking up behind.

Kaladin slowly stood upright. One of the prisoners in that group was a boy of barely fourteen or fifteen. Short, spindly, with a round face. "Tien?" he whispered, taking a step forward.

He stopped, shaking himself. Tien was dead. But this newcomer looked so familiar, with those frightened black eyes. It made Kaladin want to shelter the boy. Protect him.

But . . . he'd failed. Everyone he'd tried to protect—from Tien to Cenn—had ended up dead. What was the point?

He turned back to dragging the log.

"Kaladin," Syl said, landing on the log, "I'm going to leave."

He blinked in shock. Syl. Leave? But . . . she was the last thing he had left. "No," he whispered. It came out as a croak.

"I'll try to come back," she said. "But I don't know what will happen when I leave you. Things are strange. I have odd memories. No, most of them aren't even memories. Instincts. One of those tells me that if I leave you, I might lose myself."

"Then don't go," he said, growing terrified.

"I have to," she said, cringing. "I can't watch this anymore. I'll try to return." She looked sorrowful. "Goodbye." And with that, she zipped away into the air, adopting the form of a tiny group of tumbling, translucent leaves.

Kaladin watched her go, numb.

Then he turned back to hauling the log. What else could he do?

The youth, the one that reminded him of Tien, died during the very next bridge run.

It was a bad one. The Parshendi were in position, waiting for Sadeas. Kaladin charged the chasm, not even flinching as men were slaughtered around him. It wasn't bravery that drove him; it wasn't even a wish that those arrows would take him and end it all. He ran. That was what he did. Like a boulder rolled down a hill, or like rain fell from the sky. They didn't have a choice. Neither did he. He wasn't a man; he was a thing, and things just did what they did.

The bridgemen laid their bridges in a tight line. Four crews had fallen. Kaladin's own team had lost nearly enough to stop them.

Bridge placed, Kaladin turned away, the army charging across the wood to start the real battle. He stumbled back across the plateau. After a few moments, he found what he was looking for. The boy's body.

Kaladin stood, wind whipping at his hair, looking down at the corpse. It lay faceup in a small hollow in the stone. Kaladin remembered lying in a similar hollow, holding a similar corpse.

Another bridgeman had fallen nearby, bristling with arrows. It was the man who'd lived through Kaladin's first bridge run all those weeks back. His body slumped to the side, lying on a stone outcropping a foot or so above the corpse of the boy. Blood dripped from the tip of an arrow sticking out his back. It fell, one ruby drop at a time, splattering on the boy's open, lifeless eye. A little trail of red ran from the eye down the side of his face. Like crimson tears.

That night, Kaladin huddled in the barrack, listening to a highstorm buffet the wall. He curled against the cold stone. Thunder shattered the sky outside.

I can't keep going like this, he thought. *I'm dead inside, as sure as if I'd taken a spear through the neck.*

The storm continued its tirade. And for the first time in over eight months, Kaladin found himself crying.

NINE YEARS AGO

K al stumbled into the surgery room, the open door letting in bright white sunlight. At ten years old, he was already showing signs that he would be tall and lanky. He'd always preferred Kal to his full name, Kaladin. The shorter name made him fit in better. Kaladin sounded like a lighteyes's name.

"I'm sorry, Father," he said.

Kal's father, Lirin, carefully tightened the strap around the arm of the young woman who was tied onto the narrow operating table. Her eyes were closed; Kal had missed the administration of the drug. "We will discuss your tardiness later," Lirin said, securing the woman's other hand. "Close the door."

Kal cringed and closed the door. The windows were dark, shutters firmly in place, and so the only light was that of the Stormlight shining from a large globe filled with spheres. Each of those spheres was a broam, in total an incredible sum that was on permanent loan from Hearthstone's landlord. Lanterns flickered, but Stormlight was always true. That could save lives, Kal's father said.

Kal approached the table, anxious. The young woman,

Sani, had sleek black hair, not tinged with even a single strand of brown or blond. She was fifteen, and her freehand was wrapped with a bloody, ragged bandage. Kal grimaced at the clumsy bandaging job—it looked like the cloth had been ripped from someone's shirt and tied in haste.

Sani's head rolled to the side, and she mumbled, drugged. She wore only a white cotton shift, her safehand exposed. Older boys in the town sniggered about the chances they'd had—or *claimed* to have had—at seeing girls in their shifts, but Kal didn't understand what the excitement was all about. He *was* worried about Sani, though. He always worried when someone was wounded.

Fortunately, the wound didn't look terrible. If it had been life-threatening, his father would have already begun working on it, using Kal's mother—Hesina—as an assistant.

Lirin walked to the side of the room and gathered up a few small, clear bottles. He was a short man, balding despite his relative youth. He wore his spectacles, which he called the most precious gift he'd ever been given. He rarely got them out except for surgery, as they were too valuable to risk just wearing about. What if they were scratched or broken? Hearthstone was a large town, but its remote location in northern Alethkar would make replacing the spectacles difficult.

The room was kept neat, the shelves and table washed clean each morning, everything in its place. Lirin said you could tell a lot about a man from how he kept his workspace. Was it sloppy or orderly? Did he respect his tools or did he leave them casually about? The town's only fabrial clock sat here on the counter. The small device bore a single dial at the center and a glowing Smokestone at its heart; it had to be infused to keep the time. Nobody else in the town cared about minutes and hours as Lirin did.

Kal pulled over a stool to get a better vantage. Soon he wouldn't need the stool; he was growing taller by the day. He inspected Sani's hand. *She'll be all right,* he told himself, as his father had trained him. *A surgeon needs to be calm. Worry just wastes time.*

It was hard advice to follow.

"Hands," Lirin said, not turning away from gathering his tools.

Kal sighed, hopping off his stool and hurrying over to the basin of warm, soapy water by the door. "Why does it matter?" He wanted to be at work, helping Sani.

"Wisdom of the Heralds," Lirin said absently, repeating a lecture he'd given many times before. "Deathspren and rotspren hate water. It will keep them away."

"Hammie says that's silly," Kal said. "He says deathspren are mighty good at killing folk, so why should they be afraid of a little water?"

"The Heralds were wise beyond our understanding."

Kal grimaced. "But they're *demons*, father. I heard it off that ardent who came teaching last spring."

"That's the Radiants he spoke of," Lirin said sharply. "You're mixing them again."

Kal sighed.

"The Heralds were sent to teach mankind," Lirin said. "They led us against the Voidbringers after we were cast from heaven. The Radiants were the orders of knights they founded."

"Who were demons."

"Who betrayed us," Lirin said, "once the Heralds left." Lirin raised a finger. "They were not demons, they were just men who had too much power and not enough sense. Either way, you are *always* to wash your hands. You can see the effect it has on rotspren with your own eyes, even if deathspren cannot be seen."

Kal sighed again, but did as he was told. Lirin walked over to the table again, bearing a tray lined with knives and little glass bottles. His ways were odd—though Lirin made certain that his son didn't mix up the Heralds and the Lost Radiants, Kal had heard his father say that he thought the Voidbringers weren't real. Ridiculous. Who else could be blamed when things went missing in the night, or when a crop got infected with diggerworms?

The others in town thought Lirin spent too much time with books and sick people, and that made him strange. They were uncomfortable around him, and with Kal by association. Kal was only just beginning to realize how painful it could feel to be different.

Hands washed, he hopped back up onto the stool. He began to feel nervous again, hoping that nothing would go wrong. His father used a mirror to focus the spheres' light onto Sani's hand. Gingerly, he cut off the makeshift bandage with a surgeon's knife. The wound wasn't life-threatening, but the hand *was* pretty badly mangled. When his father had started training Kal two years before, sights like this had sickened him. Now he was used to torn flesh.

That was good. Kal figured this would be useful when he went to war someday, to fight for his highprince and the lighteyes.

Sani had three broken fingers and the skin on her hand was scraped and gouged, the wound cluttered with sticks and dirt. The third finger was the worst, shattered and twisted nastily, splinters of bone protruding through the skin. Kal felt its length, noting the fractured bones, the blackness on the skin. He carefully wiped away dried blood and dirt with a wet cloth, picking out rocks and sticks as his father cut thread for sewing.

"The third finger will have to go, won't it?" Kal said, tying a bandage around the base of the finger to keep it from bleeding.

His father nodded, a hint of a smile on his face. He'd hoped Kal would discern that. Lirin often said that a wise surgeon must know what to remove and what to save. If that third finger had been set properly at first . . . but no, it was beyond recovery. Sewing it back together would mean leaving it to fester and die.

His father did the actual amputation. He had such careful, precise hands. Training as a surgeon took over ten years, and it would be some time yet before Lirin let Kal hold the knife. Instead, Kal wiped away blood, handed his father knives, and held the sinew to keep it from tangling as his father sewed. They repaired the hand so far as they could, working with deliberate speed.

Kal's father finished the final suture, obviously pleased at having been able to save four of the fingers. That wasn't how Sani's parents would see it. They'd be disappointed that their beautiful daughter would now have a disfigured hand. It almost always happened that way—terror at the initial wound, then anger at Lirin's inability to work wonders. Lirin said it was because the townsfolk had grown accustomed to having a surgeon. To them, the healing had become an expectation, rather than a privilege.

But Sani's parents were good people. They'd make a small donation, and Kal's family—his parents, him, and his younger brother Tien—would continue to be able to eat. Odd, how they survived because of others' misfortune. Maybe that was part of what made the townsfolk resent them.

Lirin finished by using a small heated rod to cauterize where he felt the stitches wouldn't be enough. Finally, he spread pungent lister's oil across the hand to prevent infection—the oil frightened away rotspren even better than soap and water. Kal wrapped on clean bandages, careful not to disturb the splints.

Lirin disposed of the finger, and Kal began to relax. She'd be all right.

"You still need to work on those nerves of yours, son," Lirin said softly, washing blood from his hands.

Kal looked down.

"It is good to care," Lirin said. "But caring—like anything else—can be a problem if it interferes with your ability to perform surgery."

Caring too much can be a problem? Kal thought back at his father. *And what about being so selfless that you never charge for your work?* He didn't dare say the words.

Cleaning the room came next. It seemed like half of Kal's life was spent cleaning, but Lirin wouldn't let him go until they were done with it. At least he opened the shutters, letting sunlight stream in. Sani continued to doze; the winterwort would keep her unconscious for hours yet.

"So where were you?" Lirin asked, bottles of oil and alcohol clinking as he returned them to their places.

"With Jam."

"Jam is two years your senior," Lirin said. "I doubt he has much fondness for spending his time with those much younger than he."

"His father started training him in the quarterstaff," Kal said in a rush. "Tien and I went to see what he's learned." Kal cringed, waiting for the lecture.

His father just continued, wiping down each of his surgeon's knives with alcohol, then oil, as the old traditions dictated. He didn't turn toward Kal.

"Jam's father was a soldier in Brightlord Amaram's army," Kal said tentatively. Brightlord Amaram! The noble lighteyed general who watched over northern Alethkar. Kal wanted so much to see a *real* lighteyes, not stuffy old Wistiow. A soldier, like everyone talked about, like the stories were about.

"I know about Jam's father," Lirin said. "I've had to operate on that lame leg of his three times now. A gift of his glorious time as a soldier."

"We *need* soldiers, father. You'd have our borders violated by the Thaylens?"

"Thaylenah is an island kingdom," Lirin said calmly. "They don't share a border with us."

"Well, then, they could attack from the sea!"

"They're mostly tradesmen and merchants. Every one I've met has tried to swindle me, but that's hardly the same thing as invading."

All the boys liked to tell stories about far-off places. It was hard to remember that Kal's father—the only man of second nahn in the town—had traveled all the way to Kharbranth during his youth.

"Well, we fight with *someone*," Kal continued, moving to scrub the floor.

"Yes," his father said after a pause. "King Gavilar always finds people for us to fight. That much is true."

"So we need soldiers, like I said."

"We need surgeons more." Lirin sighed audibly, turning away from his cabinet. "Son, you nearly cry each time someone is brought to us; you grind your teeth anxiously during even simple procedures. What makes you think you could actually *hurt* someone?"

"I'll get stronger."

"That's foolishness. Who's put these ideas in your head? *Why* would you want to learn to hit other boys with a stick?"

"For honor, Father," Kal said. "Who tells stories about *surgeons*, for the Heralds' sake!"

"The children of the men and women whose lives we save," Lirin said evenly, meeting Kal's gaze. "That's who tell stories of surgeons."

Kal blushed and shrank back, then finally returned to his scrubbing.

"There are two kinds of people in this world, son," his father said sternly. "Those who save lives. And those who take lives."

"And what of those who protect and defend? The ones who save lives *by* taking lives?"

His father snorted. "That's like trying to stop a storm by blowing harder. Ridiculous. You can't protect by killing."

Kal kept scrubbing.

Finally, his father sighed, walking over and kneeling down beside him, helping with the scrubbing. "What are the properties of winterwort?"

"Bitter taste," Kal said immediately, "which makes it safer to keep, since people won't eat it by accident. Crush it to powder, mix it with oil, use one spoonful per ten brickweight of the person you're drugging. Induces a deep sleep for about five hours."

"And how can you tell if someone has the fiddlepox?"

"Nervous energy," Kal said, "thirst, trouble sleeping, and swelling on the undersides of the arms."

"You've got such a good mind, son," Lirin said softly. "It took me years to learn what you've done in months. I've been saving. I'd like to send you to Kharbranth when you turn sixteen, to train with real surgeons."

Kal felt a spike of excitement. Kharbranth? That was in an entirely different kingdom! Kal's father had traveled there as a courier, but he hadn't trained there as a surgeon. He'd learned from old Vathe in Shorsebroon, the nearest town of any size.

"You have a gift from the Heralds themselves," Lirin said, resting a hand on Kal's shoulder. "You could be ten times the surgeon I am. Don't dream the small dreams of other men. Our grandfathers bought and worked us to the second nahn so that we could have full citizenship and the right of travel. Don't waste that on killing."

Kal hesitated, but soon found himself nodding.

DROPLETS

"Three of sixteen ruled, but now the Broken One reigns."

—Collected: Chachanan, 1173, 84 seconds pre-death. Subject: a cutpurse with the wasting sickness, of partial Iriali descent.

The highstorm eventually subsided. It was the dusk of the day the boy had died, the day Syl had left him. Kaladin slid on his sandals—the same ones he'd taken from the leathery-faced man on that first day—and stood up. He walked through the crowded barrack.

There were no beds, just one thin blanket per bridgeman. One had to choose whether to use it for cushioning or warmth. You could freeze or you could ache. Those were a bridgeman's options, though several of the bridgemen had found a third use for the blankets. They wrapped them around their heads, as if to block out sight, sound, and smell. To hide from the world.

The world would find them anyway. It was good at these kinds of games.

Rain fell in sheets outside, the wind still stiff. Flashes lit the western horizon, where the center of the storm flew onward. This was an hour or so before the riddens, and was as early as one would want to go out in a highstorm.

Well, one never *wanted* to go out in a highstorm. But this was about as early as it was *safe* to go out. The lightning had passed; the winds were manageable.

He passed through the dim lumberyard, hunched against the wind. Branches lay scattered about like bones in a white-spine's lair. Leaves were plastered by rainwater to the rough sides of barracks. Kaladin splashed through puddles that chilled and numbed his feet. That felt good; they were still sore from the bridge run earlier.

Waves of icy rain blew across him, wetting his hair, dripping down his face and into his scruffy beard. He hated having a beard, particularly the way the whiskers itched at the corners of his mouth. Beards were like axehound pups. Boys dreamed of the day they'd get one, never realizing how annoying they could be.

"Out for a stroll, Your Lordship?" a voice said.

Kaladin looked up to find Gaz huddled in a nearby hollow between two of the barracks. Why was he out in the rain?

Ah. Gaz had fastened a small metal basket on the leeward wall of one of the barracks, and a soft glowing light came from within. He left his spheres out in the storm, then had come out early to retrieve them.

It was a risk. Even a sheltered basket could get torn free. Some people believed that the shades of the Lost Radiants haunted the storms, stealing spheres. Perhaps that was true. But during his time in the army, Kaladin had known more than one man who had been wounded sneaking around during full storm, looking for spheres. No doubt the superstition was due to more worldly thieves.

There were safer ways to infuse spheres. Moneychangers would exchange dun spheres for infused ones, or you could pay them to infuse yours in one of their safely guarded nests.

"What are you doing?" Gaz demanded. The short, one-eyed man clutched the basket to his chest. "I'll have you strung up if you've stolen anyone's spheres."

Kaladin turned away from him.

"Storm you! I'll have you strung up anyway! Don't think you can run away; there are still sentries. You—"

"I'm going to the Honor Chasm," Kaladin said quietly. His voice would barely be audible over the storm.

Gaz shut up. The Honor Chasm. He lowered his metal basket and made no further objections. There was a certain deference given to men who took that road.

Kaladin continued to cross the courtyard.

"Lordling," Gaz called.

Kaladin turned.

"Leave the sandals and vest," Gaz said. "I don't want to have to send someone down to fetch them."

Kaladin pulled the leather vest over his head and dropped it to the ground with a splash, then left the sandals in a puddle. That left him in a dirty shirt and stiff brown trousers, both taken off a dead man.

Kaladin walked through the storm to the east side of the lumberyard. A low thundering rumbled from the west. The pathway down to the Shattered Plains was familiar to him now. He'd run this way a dozen times with the bridge crews. There wasn't a battle every day—perhaps one in every two or three—and not every bridge crew had to go on every run. But many of the runs were so draining, so horrific, that they left the bridgemen stunned, almost unresponsive, for the days between.

Many bridgemen had trouble making decisions. The same happened to men who were shocked by battle. Kaladin felt those effects in himself. Even deciding to come to the chasm had been difficult.

But the bleeding eyes of that unnamed boy haunted him. He wouldn't make himself go through something like that again. He *couldn't*.

He reached the base of the slope, wind-driven rain pelting his face as if trying to shove him back toward the camp. He kept on, walking up to the nearest chasm. The Honor Chasm, the bridgemen called it, for it was the place where they could make the one decision left to them. The "honorable" decision. Death.

They weren't natural, these chasms. This one started narrow, but as it ran toward the east, it grew wider—and deeper—

incredibly quickly. At only ten feet long, the crack was already wide enough that it would be difficult to jump. A group of six rope ladders with wooden rungs hung here, affixed to spikes in the rock, used by bridgemen sent down to salvage from corpses that had fallen into the chasms during bridge runs.

Kaladin looked out over the plains. He couldn't see much through the darkness and rain. No, this place wasn't natural. The land had been broken. And now it broke the people who came to it. Kaladin walked past the ladders, a little farther along the edge of the chasm. Then he sat down, legs over the side, looking down as the rain fell around him, the droplets plunging into the dark depths.

To his sides, the more adventurous cremlings had already left their lairs, scuttling about, feeding on plants that lapped up the rainwater. Lirin had once explained that highstorm rains were rich with nutrients. Stormwardens in Kholinar and Vedenar had proven that plants given storm water did better than those given lake or river water. Why was it that scientists were so excited to discover facts that farmers had known for generations and generations?

Kaladin watched the drops of water streaking down toward oblivion in the crevasse. Little suicidal jumpers. Thousands upon thousands of them. Millions upon millions. Who knew what awaited them in that darkness? You couldn't see it, couldn't know it, until you joined them. Leaping off into the void and letting the wind bear you down . . .

"You were right, Father," Kaladin whispered. "You can't stop a storm by blowing harder. You can't save men by killing others. We should all become surgeons. Every last one of us. . . ."

He was rambling. But, oddly, his mind felt clearer now than it had in weeks. Perhaps it was the clarity of perspective. Most men spent their entire lives wondering about the future. Well, his future was empty now. So he turned backward, thinking about his father, about Tien, about decisions.

Once, his life had seemed simple. That was before he'd lost his brother, before he'd been betrayed in Amaram's army.

Would Kaladin go back to those innocent days, if he could? Would he prefer to pretend everything was simple?

No. He'd had no easy fall, like those drops. He'd earned his scars. He'd bounced off walls, bashed his face and hands. He'd killed innocent men by accident. He'd walked beside those with hearts like blackened coals, adoring them. He'd scrambled and climbed and fallen and stumbled.

And now here he was. At the end of it all. Understanding so much more, but somehow feeling no wiser. He climbed to his feet on the lip of that chasm, and could feel his father's disappointment looming over him, like the thunderheads above.

He put one foot out over the void.

"Kaladin!"

He froze at the soft but piercing voice. A translucent form bobbed in the air, approaching through the weakening rain. The figure lunged forward, then sank, then surged higher again, like it was bearing something heavy. Kaladin brought his foot back and held out his hand. Syl unceremoniously alighted upon it, shaped like a skyeel clutching something dark in its mouth.

She switched to the familiar form of a young woman, dress fluttering around her legs. She held in her hands a narrow, dark green leaf with a point divided in three. Blackbane.

"What is this?" Kaladin asked.

She looked exhausted. "These things are heavy!" She lifted the leaf. "I brought it for you!"

He took the leaf between two fingers. Blackbane. Poison. "Why did you bring this to me?" he said harshly.

"I thought . . ." Syl said, shying back. "Well, you kept those other leaves so carefully. Then you lost them when you tried to help that man in the slave cages. I thought it would make you happy to have another one."

Kaladin almost laughed. She had no concept of what she'd done, fetching him a leaf of one of Roshar's most deadly natural poisons because she'd wanted to make him happy. It was ridiculous. And sweet.

"Everything seemed to go wrong when you lost that leaf," Syl said in a soft voice. "Before that, you fought."

"I failed."

She cowered down, kneeling on his palm, misty skirt around her legs, drops of rainwater passing through her and rippling her form. "You don't like it then? I flew so far . . . I almost forgot myself. But I came back. I came *back*, Kaladin."

"Why?" he pled. "Why do you care?"

"Because I do," she said, cocking her head. "I watched you, you know. Back in that army. You'd always find the young, untrained men and protect them, even though it put you into danger. I can remember. Just barely, but I do."

"I failed them. They're dead now."

"They would have died more quickly without you. You made it so they had a family in the army. I remember their gratitude. It's what drew me in the first place. You helped them."

"No," he said, clutching the blackbane in his fingers. "Everything I touch withers and dies." He teetered on the ledge. Thunder rumbled in the distance.

"Those men in the bridge crew," Syl whispered. "You could help them."

"Too late." He closed his eyes, thinking of the dead boy earlier in the day. "It's too late. I've failed. They're dead. They're all going to die, and there's no way out."

"What is one more try, then?" Her voice was soft, yet somehow stronger than the storm. "What could it hurt?"

He paused.

"You can't fail this time, Kaladin. You've said it. They're all going to die anyway."

He thought of Tien, and his dead eyes staring upward.

"I don't know what you mean most of the time when you speak," she said. "My mind is so cloudy. But it seems that if you're worried about hurting people, you shouldn't be afraid to help the bridgemen. What more could you do to them?"

"I . . ."

"One more try, Kaladin," Syl whispered. "Please."

One more try. . . .

The men huddled in the barrack with barely a blanket to

call their own. Frightened of the storm. Frightened of each other. Frightened of what the next day would bring.

One more try. . . .

He thought of himself, crying at the death of a boy he hadn't known. A boy he hadn't even tried to help.

One more try.

Kaladin opened his eyes. He was cold and wet, but he felt a tiny, warm candle flame of determination come alight inside him. He clenched his hand, crushing the blackbane leaf inside, then dropped it over the side of the chasm. He lowered the other hand, which had been holding Syl.

She zipped up into the air, anxious. "Kaladin?"

He stalked away from the chasm, bare feet splashing in puddles and stepping heedlessly on rockbud vines. The incline he'd come down was covered with flat, slatelike plants that had opened like books to the rain, ruffled lacy red and green leaves connecting the two halves. Lifespren—little green blips of light, brighter than Syl but small as spores— danced among the plants, dodging raindrops.

Kaladin strode up, water streaming past him in tiny rivers. At the top, he returned to the bridge yard. It was still empty save for Gaz, who was tying a ripped tarp back into place.

Kaladin had crossed most of the distance to the man before Gaz noticed him. The wiry sergeant scowled. "Too cowardly to go through with it, Your Lordship? Well, if you think I'm giving back—"

He cut off with a gagging noise as Kaladin lunged forward, grabbing Gaz by the neck. Gaz lifted an arm in surprise, but Kaladin batted it away and swept the man's legs out from under him, slamming him down to the rocky ground, throwing up a splash of water. Gaz's eye opened wide with shock and pain, and he began to strangle under the pressure of Kaladin's grip on his throat.

"The world just changed, Gaz," Kaladin said, leaning in close. "I died down at that chasm. Now you've got my vengeful spirit to deal with."

Squirming, Gaz looked about frantically for help that wasn't there. Kaladin didn't have trouble holding him down.

There was one thing about running bridges: If you survived long enough, it built up the muscles.

Kaladin let up slightly on Gaz's neck, allowing him a gasping breath. Then Kaladin leaned down further. "We're going to start over new, you and I. Clean. And I want you to understand something from the start. I'm *already* dead. You can't hurt me. Understand?"

Gaz nodded slowly and Kaladin gave him another breath of frigid, humid air.

"Bridge Four is mine," Kaladin said. "You can assign us tasks, but I'm bridgeleader. The other one died today, so you have to pick a new leader anyway. Understand?"

Gaz nodded again.

"You learn quickly," Kaladin said, letting the man breathe freely. He stepped back, and Gaz hesitantly got to his feet. There was hatred in his eyes, but it was veiled. He seemed worried about something—something more than Kaladin's threats.

"I want to stop paying down my slave debt," Kaladin said. "How much do bridgemen make?"

"Two clearmarks a day," Gaz said, scowling at him and rubbing his neck.

So a slave would make half that. One diamond mark. A pittance, but Kaladin would need it. He'd also need to keep Gaz in line. "I'll start taking my wages," Kaladin said, "but you get to keep one mark in five."

Gaz started, glancing at him in the dim, overcast light.

"For your efforts," Kaladin said.

"For what efforts?"

Kaladin stepped up to him. "Your efforts in staying the *Damnation* out of my way. Understood?"

Gaz nodded again. Kaladin walked away. He hated to waste money on a bribe, but Gaz needed a consistent, repetitive reminder of why he should avoid getting Kaladin killed. One mark every five days wasn't much of a reminder—but for a man who was willing to risk going out in the middle of a highstorm to protect his spheres, it might be enough.

Kaladin walked back to Bridge Four's small barrack, pulling open the thick wooden door. The men huddled inside, just as he'd left them. But something had changed. Had they always looked that pathetic?

Yes. They had. Kaladin was the one who had changed, not they. He felt a strange dislocation, as if he'd allowed himself to forget—if only in part—the last nine months. He reached back across time, studying the man he had been. The man who'd still fought, and fought well.

He couldn't be that man again—he couldn't erase the scars—but he could *learn* from that man, as a new squad-leader learned from the victorious generals of the past. Kaladin Stormblessed was dead, but Kaladin Bridgeman was of the same blood. A descendant with potential.

Kaladin walked to the first huddled figure. The man wasn't sleeping—who could sleep through a highstorm? The man cringed as Kaladin knelt beside him.

"What's your name?" Kaladin asked, Syl flitting down and studying the man's face. He wouldn't be able to see her.

The man was older, with drooping cheeks, brown eyes, and close-cropped, white-salted hair. His beard was short and he didn't have a slave mark.

"Your name?" Kaladin repeated firmly.

"Storm off," the man said, rolling over.

Kaladin hesitated, then leaned in, speaking in a low voice. "Look, friend. You can either tell me your name, or I'll keep pestering you. Continue refusing, and I'll tow you out into that storm and hang you over the chasm by one leg until you tell me."

The man glanced back over his shoulder. Kaladin nodded slowly, holding the man's gaze.

"Teft," the man finally said. "My name's Teft."

"That wasn't so hard," Kaladin said, holding out his hand. "I'm Kaladin. Your bridgeleader."

The man hesitated, then took Kaladin's hand, wrinkling his brow in confusion. Kaladin vaguely remembered the man. He'd been in the crew for a while, a few weeks at least. Before that, he'd been on another bridge crew. One of the punishments for bridgemen who committed camp infractions was a transfer to Bridge Four.

"Get some rest," Kaladin said, releasing Teft's hand. "We're going to have a hard day tomorrow."

"How do you know?" Teft asked, rubbing his bearded chin.

"Because we're bridgemen," Kaladin said, standing. "*Every* day is hard."

Teft hesitated, then smiled faintly. "Kelek knows that's true."

Kaladin left him, moving down the line of huddled figures. He visited each man, prodding or threatening until the man gave his name. They each resisted. It was as if their names were the last things they owned, and wouldn't be given up cheaply, though they seemed surprised—perhaps even encouraged—that someone cared to ask.

He clutched to these names, repeating each one in his head, holding them like precious gemstones. The names mattered. The men mattered. Perhaps Kaladin would die in the next bridge run, or perhaps he would break under the strain, and give Amaram one final victory. But as he settled down on the ground to plan, he felt that tiny warmth burning steadily within him.

It was the warmth of decisions made and purpose seized. It was responsibility.

Syl alighted on his leg as he sat, whispering the names of the men to himself. She looked encouraged. Bright. Happy. He didn't feel any of that. He felt grim, tired, and wet. But he wrapped himself in the responsibility he had taken, the responsibility for these men. He held to it like a climber clung to his last handhold as he dangled from a cliff side.

He *would* find a way to protect them.

THE END OF

Part One

INTERLUDES

❖

ISHIKK • NAN BALAT • SZETH

ISHIKK

Ishikk splashed toward the meeting with the strange for-eigners, whistling softly to himself, his pole with buckets on each end resting on his shoulders. He wore lake sandals on his submerged feet and a pair of knee-length breeches. No shirt. Nu Ralik forbid! A good Purelaker never covered his shoulders when the sun was shining. A man could get sick that way, not getting enough sunlight.

He whistled, but not because he was having a pleasant day. In point of fact, the day Nu Ralik had provided was close to horrible. Only five fish swam in Ishikk's buckets, and four were of the dullest, most common variety. The tides had been irregular, as if the Purelake itself was in a foul mood. Bad days were coming; sure as the sun and the tide, they were.

The Purelake extended in all directions, hundreds of miles wide, its glassy surface perfectly transparent. At its deepest, it was never more than six feet from shimmering surface to the bottom—and in most places, the warm, slow-moving water came up only to about midcalf. It was filled with tiny fish, colorful cremlings, and eel-like riverspren.

The Purelake was life itself. Once, this land had been claimed by a king. Sela Tales, the nation had been called, one of the Epoch Kingdoms. Well, they could name it what they wanted, but Nu Ralik knew that the boundaries of nature were far more important than the boundaries of nations.

Ishikk was a Purelaker. First and foremost. By tide and sun he was.

He walked confidently through the water, though the footing could sometimes be precarious. The pleasantly warm water lapped at his legs just below the knees, and he made very few splashes. He knew to move slowly, careful not to put his weight down before he was sure he wasn't stepping on a spikemane or a sharp lip of rock.

Ahead, the village of Fu Abra broke the glassy perfection, a cluster of buildings perched on blocks beneath the water. Their domed roofs made them look like the rockbuds that sprouted from the ground, and they were the only things for miles around that broke the surface of the Purelake.

Other people walked about here, moving with the same slow gait. It was possible to run through the water, but there was rarely a reason. What could be so important that you had to go and make a splash and ruckus getting to it?

Ishikk shook his head at that. Only foreigners were so hasty. He nodded to Thaspic, a dark-skinned man who passed him pulling a small raft. It was stacked with a few piles of cloth; he'd probably taken them out for washing.

"Ho, Ishikk," the scrawny man said. "How's fishing?"

"Terrible," he called. "Vun Makak has blighted me right good today. And you?"

"Lost a shirt while washing," Thaspic replied, his voice pleasant.

"Ah, that's the way of things. Are my foreigners here?"

"Sure are. Over at Maib's place."

"Vun Makak send they don't eat her out of home," Ishikk said, continuing on his way. "Or infect her with their constant worries."

"Sun and tides send it!" Thaspic said with a chuckle, continuing on.

Maib's house was near the center of the village. Ishikk wasn't sure what made her want to live inside the building. Most nights he did just fine sleeping on his raft. It never got cold in the Purelake, except during highstorms, and you could last through those right well, Nu Ralik send the way.

The Purelake drained into pits and holes when the storms came, and so you just shoved your raft into a crevice between two ridges of stone and huddled up next to it, using it to break the fury of the tempest. The storms weren't so bad out here as they were in the East, where they flung boulders and blew down buildings. Oh, he'd heard stories about that sort of life. Nu Ralik send he never had to go to such a terrible place.

Besides, it was probably cold there. Ishikk pitied those who had to live in the cold. Why didn't they just come to the Purelake?

Nu Ralik send that they don't, he thought, walking up to Maib's place. If everyone knew how nice the Purelake was, surely they'd all want to live here, and there wouldn't be a place to walk without stumbling over some foreigner!

He stepped up into the building, exposing his calves to the air. The floor was low enough that a few inches of water still covered it; Purelakers liked it that way. It was natural, though if the tide dropped, sometimes buildings would drain.

Minnows shot out around his toes. Common types, not worth anything. Maib stood inside, fixing a pot of fish soup, and she nodded to him. She was a stout woman and had been chasing Ishikk for years, trying to bait him to wed her on account of her fine cooking. He just might let her catch him someday.

His foreigners were in the corner, at a table only they would choose—the one that was raised up an extra bit, with footrests so that the outsiders wouldn't have to get their toes wet. *Nu Ralik, what fools!* he thought with amusement. *Inside out of the sun, wearing shirts against its warmth, feet out of the tide. No wonder their thoughts are so odd.*

He set his buckets down, nodding to Maib.

She eyed him. "Good fishing?"

"Terrible."

"Ah well, your soup is free today, Ishikk. To make up for Vun Makak's cursing."

"Thanks much kindly," he said, taking a steaming bowl from her. She smiled. Now he owed her. Enough bowls, and he'd be forced to wed her.

"There's a kolgril in the bucket for you," he noted. "Caught it early this morning."

Her stout face grew uncertain. A kolgril was a *very* lucky fish. Cured aching joints for a good month after you ate it, and sometimes let you see when friends were going to visit by letting you read the shapes of the clouds. Maib had quite a fondness for them, on account of the finger aches Nu Ralik had sent her. One kolgril would be two weeks of soup, and would put *her* in debt to *him*.

"Vun Makak eye you," she muttered in annoyance walking over to check. "That's one all right. How am I ever going to catch you, man?"

"I'm a fisher, Maib," he said, taking a slurp of his soup—the bowl was shaped for easy slurping. "Hard to catch a fisher. You know that." He chuckled to himself, walking up to his foreigners as she plucked out the kolgril.

There were three of them. Two were dark-skinned Makabaki, though they were the strangest Makabaki he'd ever seen. One was thick limbed where most of his kind were small and fine-boned, and he had a completely bald head. The other was taller, with short dark hair, lean muscles, and broad shoulders. In his head, Ishikk called them Grump and Blunt, on account of their personalities.

The third man had light tan skin, like an Alethi. He didn't seem quite right either, though. The eyes were the wrong shape, and his accent was certainly *not* Alethi. He spoke the Selay language worse than the other two, and usually stayed quiet. He seemed thoughtful, though. Ishikk called him Thinker.

Wonder how he earned that scar across his scalp, Ishikk thought. Life outside the Purelake was very dangerous. Lots of wars, particularly to the east.

"You are late, traveler," said tall, stiff Blunt. He had the build and air of a soldier, though none of the three carried weapons.

Ishikk frowned, sitting and reluctantly pulling his feet out of the water. "Isn't it warli-day?"

"The day is right, friend," Grump said. "But we were to

meet at noon. Understand?" He generally did most of the talking.

"We're close to that," Ishikk said. Honestly. Who paid attention to what *hour* it was? Foreigners. Always so busy.

Grump just shook his head as Maib brought them some soup. Her place was the closest thing the village had to an inn. She left Ishikk a soft cloth napkin and nice cup of sweet wine, trying to balance that fish as quickly as possible.

"Very well," Grump said. "Let us have your report, friend."

"I've been by Fu Ralis, Fu Namir, Fu Albast, and Fu Moorin this month," Ishikk said, taking a slurp of soup. "Nobody has seen this man you search for."

"You asked right questions?" Blunt said. "You are certain?"

"Of course I'm certain," Ishikk said. "I have been doing this for ages now."

"Five months," Blunt corrected. "And no results."

Ishikk shrugged. "You wish me to make up stories? Vun Makak would like me to do that."

"No, no stories, friend," Grump said. "We want only the truth."

"Well, I've given it to you."

"You swear it by Nu Ralik, that god of yours?"

"Hush!" Ishikk said. "Don't say his name. Are you idiots?"

Grump frowned. "But he is your god. Understand? Is his name holy? Not to be spoken?"

Foreigners were so stupid. Of course Nu Ralik was their god, but you always *pretended* that he wasn't. Vun Makak—his younger, spiteful brother—had to be tricked into thinking you worshipped him, otherwise he'd get jealous. It was only safe to speak of these things in a holy grotto.

"I swear it by Vun Makak," Ishikk said pointedly. "May he watch over me and curse me as he pleases. I have looked diligently. No foreigner like this one you mention—with his white hair, clever tongue, and arrowlike face—has been seen."

"He dyes his hair sometimes," Grump said. "And wears disguises."

"I've asked, using the names you gave me," Ishikk said. "Nobody has seen him. Now, perhaps I could find you a *fish* that could locate him." Ishikk rubbed his stubbly chin. "I'll bet a stumpy cort could do it. Might take me a while to find one, though."

The three looked at him. "There may be something to these fish, you know," Blunt said.

"Superstition," Grump replied. "You always look for superstition, Vao."

Vao wasn't the man's real name; Ishikk was sure they used fake names. That was why he used his own names for them. If they were going to give him fake names, he'd give them fake names back.

"And you, Temoo?" Blunt snapped. "We can't pontificate our way to—"

"Gentlemen," Thinker said. He nodded to Ishikk, who was still slurping his soup. All three of them switched to another language and continued their argument.

Ishikk listened with half an ear, trying to determine what language it was. He never had been good with other kinds of languages. Why did he need them? Didn't help with fishing or selling fish.

He *had* searched for their man. He got around a lot, visited a lot of places around the Purelake. It was one of the reasons why he didn't want to be caught by Maib. He'd have to settle down, and that wasn't good for catching fish. Not the rare ones, at least.

He didn't bother wondering why they were looking for this Hoid, whoever he was. Foreigners were always looking for things they couldn't have. Ishikk sat back, dangling his toes in the water. That felt good. Eventually, they finished their argument. They gave him some more instructions, handed him a pouch of spheres, and stepped down into the water.

Like most foreigners, they wore thick boots that came all the way up to their knees. They splashed in the water as they walked to the entrance. Ishikk followed, waving to Maib and picking up his buckets. He'd be back later in the day for an evening meal.

Maybe I should *let her catch me,* he thought, stepping back out into the sunlight and sighing in relief. *Nu Ralik knows I'm getting old. Might be nice to relax.*

His foreigners splashed down into the Purelake. Grump was last. He seemed very dissatisfied. "Where are you, Roamer? What a fool's quest this is." Then, he added in his own tongue, *"Alavanta kamaloo kayana."*

He splashed after his companions.

"Well, you've got the 'fool' part right," Ishikk said with a chuckle, turning his own direction and heading off to check on his traps.

Nan Balat liked killing things.

Not people. Never people. But animals, those he could kill. Particularly the little ones. He wasn't sure why it made him feel better; it simply did.

He sat on the porch of his mansion, pulling the legs off a small crab one at a time. There was a satisfying rip to each one—he pulled on it lightly at first, and the animal grew stiff. Then he pulled harder, and it started to squirm. The ligament resisted, then started ripping, followed by a quick pop. The crab squirmed some more, and Nan Balat held up the leg, pinching the beast with two fingers on his other hand.

He sighed in satisfaction. Ripping a leg free soothed him, made the aches in his body retreat. He tossed the leg over his shoulder and moved on to the next one.

He didn't like to talk about his habit. He didn't even speak of it to Eylita. It was just something he did. You had to keep your sanity somehow.

He finished with the legs, then stood up, leaning on his cane, looking out over the Davar gardens, which were made up of stonework walls covered with different kinds of vines. They were beautiful, though Shallan had been the only one who truly appreciated them. This area of Jah Keved—to the west and south of Alethkar, of higher elevation and broken by mountains such as the Horneater Peaks—had a profusion of vines. They grew on everything, covering the mansion, growing over the steps. Out in the wilds, they hung from trees, grew over rocky expanses, as ubiquitous as grass was in other areas of Roshar.

Balat walked to the edge of the porch. Some wild songlings began to sing in the distance, scraping their ridged shells. They each played a different beat and notes, though they couldn't really be called melodies. Melodies were things of humans, not animals. But each one *was* a song, and at times they seemed to sing back and forth to one another.

Balat walked down the steps one at a time, the vines shaking and pulling away before his feet fell. It had been nearly six months since Shallan's departure. This morning, they'd had word from her via spanreed that she'd succeeded in the first part of her plan, becoming Jasnah Kholin's ward. And so, his baby sister—who before this had never left their estates—was preparing to rob the most important woman in the world.

Walking down the steps was depressingly hard work for him. *Twenty-three years old,* he thought, *and already a cripple.* He still felt a constant, latent ache. The break had been bad, and the surgeon had nearly decided to cut off the entire leg. Perhaps he could be thankful that hadn't proven necessary, though he would always walk with a cane.

Scrak was playing with something in the sitting green, a place where cultivated grass was grown and kept free of vines. The large axehound rolled about, gnawing at the object, antennae pulled back flat against her skull.

"Scrak," Balat said, hobbling forward, "what have you got there, girl?"

The axehound looked up at her master, antennae cocking upward. The hound trumped with two echoing voices overlapping one another, then went back to playing.

Blasted creature, Balat thought fondly, *never would obey properly.* He'd been breeding axehounds since his youth, and had discovered—as had many before him—that the smarter an animal was, the more likely it was to disobey. Oh, Scrak was loyal, but she'd ignore you on the little things. Like a young child trying to prove her independence.

As he got closer, he saw that Scrak had managed to catch a songling. The fist-size creature was shaped like a peaked disc with four arms that reached out from the sides and scraped rhythms along the top. Four squat legs underneath normally held it to a rock wall, though Scrak had chewed those off. She had two of the arms off too, and had managed to crack the shell. Balat almost took it away to pull the other two arms off, but decided it was best to let Scrak have her fun.

Scrak set the songling down and looked up at Balat, her antennae rising inquisitively. She was sleek and lean, six legs extending before her as she sat on her haunches. Axehounds didn't have shells or skin; instead, their body was covered with some fusion of the two, smooth to the touch and more pliable than true carapace, but harder than skin and made of interlocking sections. The axehound's angular face seemed curious, her deep black eyes regarding Balat. She trumped softly.

Balat smiled, reaching down and scratching behind the axehound's ear holes. The animal leaned against him—she probably weighed as much as he did. The bigger axehounds came up to a man's waist, though Scrak was of a smaller, quicker breed.

The songling quivered and Scrak pounced on it eagerly, crunching at its shell with her strong outer mandibles.

"Am I a coward, Scrak?" Balat asked, sitting down on a bench. He set his cane aside and snatched a small crab that had been hiding on the side of the bench, its shell having turned white to match the stone.

He held up the squirming animal. The green's grass had been bred to be less timid, and it poked out of its holes only a few moments after he passed. Other exotic plants bloomed, poking out of shells or holes in the ground, and soon patches of red, orange, and blue waved in the wind around him. The area around the axehound remained bare, of course. Scrak was having far too much fun with her prey, and she kept even the cultivated plants hidden in their burrows.

"I couldn't have gone to chase Jasnah," Balat said, starting to pull the crab's legs off. "Only a woman could get close enough to her to steal the Soulcaster. We decided that. Besides, someone needs to stay back and care for the needs of the house."

The excuses were hollow. He *did* feel like a coward. He pulled off a few more legs, but it was unsatisfying. The crab was too small, and the legs came off too easily.

"This plan probably won't even work," he said, taking off the last of the legs. Odd, looking at a creature like this when it had no legs. The crab was still alive. Yet how could you know it? Without the legs to wiggle, the creature seemed as dead as a stone.

The arms, he thought, *we wave them about to make us seem alive. That's what they're good for.* He put his fingers between the halves of the crab's shell and began to pry them apart. This, at least, had a nice feeling of resistance to it.

They were a broken family. Years of suffering their father's brutal temper had driven Asha Jushu to vice and Tet Wikim to despair. Only Balat had escaped unscathed. Balat and Shallan. She'd been left alone, never touched. At times, Balat had hated her for that, but how could you truly hate someone like Shallan? Shy, quiet, delicate.

I should never have let her go, he thought. *There should have been another way.* She'd never manage on her own; she was probably terrified. It was a wonder she'd done as much as she had.

He tossed the pieces of crab over his shoulder. *If only Helaran had survived.* Their eldest brother—then known as Nan Helaran, as he'd been the first son—had stood up to their father repeatedly. Well, he was dead now, and so was their father. They'd left behind a family of cripples.

"Balat!" a voice cried. Wikim appeared on the porch. The younger man was past his recent bout of melancholy, it appeared.

"What?" Balat said, standing.

Wikim rushed down the steps, hurrying up to him, vines—then grass—pulling back before him. "We have a problem."

"How large a problem?"

"Pretty big, I'd say. Come on."

THE GLORY OF IGNORANCE

Szeth-son-son-Vallano, Truthless of Shinovar, sat on the wooden tavern floor, lavis beer slowly soaking through his brown trousers. Grimy, worn, and fraying, his clothing was far different from the simple—yet elegant—whites he had worn over five years before when he'd assassinated the king of Alethkar.

Head bowed, hands in his lap, he carried no weapons. He hadn't summoned his Shardblade in years, and it felt equally long since he'd had a bath. He did not complain. If he looked like a wretch, people treated him as a wretch. One did not ask a wretch to assassinate people.

"So he'll do whatever you say?" asked one of the mine workers sitting at the table. The man's clothing was little better than Szeth's, covered with so much dirt and dust that it was difficult to tell grimy skin from grimy cloth. There were four of them, holding ceramic cups. The room smelled of mud and sweat. The ceiling was low, the windows—on the leeward side only—mere slots. The table was precariously held together with several leather straps, as the wood was cracked down the middle.

Took—Szeth's current master—set his cup down on the table's tilted side. It sagged under the weight of his arm. "Yeah, he sure will. Hey, kurp, look at me."

Szeth looked up. "Kurp" meant child in the local Bav dialect. Szeth was accustomed to such pejorative labels. Though he was in his thirty-fifth year—and his seventh year since being named Truthless—his people's large, round eyes, shorter stature, and tendency toward baldness led Easterners to claim they looked like children.

"Stand up," Took said.

Szeth did so.

"Jump up and down."

Szeth complied.

"Pour Ton's beer on your head."

Szeth reached for it.

"Hey!" Ton said, pulling the cup away. "None of that, now! Oi ain't done with this yet!"

"If you were," said Took, "he couldn't right pour it on his head, could he?"

"Get 'im to do something else, Took," Ton griped.

"All right." Took pulled out his boot knife and tossed it to Szeth. "Kurp, cut your arm up."

"Took . . ." said one of the other men, a sniffly man named Amark. "That ain't right, you know it."

Took didn't rescind the order, so Szeth complied, taking the knife and cutting at the flesh of his arm. Blood seeped out around the dirty blade.

"Cut your throat," Took said.

"Now, Took!" Amark said, standing. "Oi won't—"

"Oh hush, you," Took said. Several groups of men from other tables were watching now. "You'll see. Kurp, cut your throat."

"I am forbidden to take my own life," Szeth said softly in the Bav language. "As Truthless, it is the nature of my suffering to be forbidden the taste of death by my own hand."

Amark settled back down, looking sheepish.

"Dustmother," Ton said, "he always talks like that?"

"Like what?" Took asked, taking a gulp from his mug.

"Smooth words, so soft and proper. Like a lighteyes."

"Yeah," Took said. "He's like a slave, only better 'cuz he's a Shin. He don't run or talk back or anything. Don't have to pay him, neither. He's like a parshman, but smarter. Worth a right many spheres, Oi'd say." He eyed the other men. "Could take him to the mines with you to work, and collect his pay. He'd do things you don't wanna. Muck out the privy, whitewash the home. All kinds of useful stuff."

"Well, how'd you come by him, then?" one of the other men asked, scratching his chin. Took was a transient worker, moving from town to town. Displaying Szeth was one of the ways he made quick friends.

"Oh, now, that's a story," Took said. "Oi was traveling in the mountains down south, you know, and Oi heard this weird howling noise. It wasn't joust the wind, you know, and . . ."

The tale was a complete fabrication; Szeth's previous master—a farmer in a nearby village—had traded Szeth to Took for a sack of seeds. The farmer had gotten him from a traveling merchant, who had gotten him from a cobbler who'd won him in an illegal game of chance. There had been dozens before him.

At first, the darkeyed commoners enjoyed the novelty of owning him. Slaves were far too expensive for most, and parshmen were even more valuable. So having someone like Szeth to order around was quite the novelty. He cleaned floors, sawed wood, helped in the fields, and carried burdens. Some treated him well, some did not.

But they always got rid of him.

Perhaps they could sense the truth, that he was capable of so much more than they dared use him for. It was one thing to have a slave of your own. But when that slave talked like a lighteyes and knew more than you did? It made them uncomfortable.

Szeth tried to play the part, tried to make himself act less refined. It was very difficult for him. Perhaps impossible. What would these men say if they knew that the man who emptied their chamber pot was a Shardbearer and a Surgebinder? A Windrunner, like the Radiants of old? The moment he summoned his Blade, his eyes would turn from dark green to pale—almost glowing—sapphire, a unique effect of his particular weapon.

Best that they never discovered. Szeth gloried in being wasted; each day he was made to clean or dig instead of kill was a victory. That evening five years ago still haunted him. Before then, he had been ordered to kill—but always in secret, silently. Never before had he been given such deliberately terrible instructions.

Kill, destroy, and cut your way to the king. Be seen doing it. Leave witnesses. Wounded but alive. . . .

". . . and *that* is when he swore to serve me my entire life," Took finished. "He's been with me ever since."

The listening men turned to Szeth. "It is true," he said, as he'd been ordered earlier. "Every word of it."

Took smiled. Szeth didn't make him uncomfortable; he apparently considered it natural that Szeth obeyed him. Perhaps as a result he would remain Szeth's master longer than the others.

"Well," Took said, "Oi should be going. Need to get an early start tomorrow. More places to see, more unseen roads to dare . . ."

He liked to think of himself as a seasoned traveler, though as far as Szeth could tell, he just moved around in a wide circle. There were many small mines—and therefore small villages—in this part of Bavland. Took had probably been to this same village years back, but the mines made for a lot of transient workers. It was unlikely he'd be remembered, unless someone had noted his terribly exaggerated stories.

Terrible or not, the other miners seemed to thirst for more. They urged him on, offering him another drink, and he modestly agreed.

Szeth sat quietly, legs folded, hands in his lap, blood trickling down his arm. Had the Parshendi known what they were consigning him to by tossing his Oathstone away as they fled Kholinar that night? Szeth had been required to recover it, then stand there beside the road, wondering if he would be discovered and executed—*hoping* he'd be discovered and executed—until a passing merchant had cared enough to inquire. By then, Szeth had stood only in a loincloth. His honor had forced him to discard the white clothing, as it would have made him easier to recognize. He had to preserve himself so that he could suffer.

After a short explanation that left out incriminating details, Szeth had found himself riding in the back of the merchant's cart. The merchant—a man named Avado—had been clever enough to realize that in the wake of the king's death, foreigners might be treated poorly. He'd made his way to Jah Keved, never knowing that he harbored Gavilar's murderer as his serving man.

The Alethi didn't search for him. They assumed that he, the infamous "Assassin in White," had retreated with the Parshendi. They probably expected to discover him in the middle of the Shattered Plains.

The miners eventually tired of Took's increasingly slurred stories. They bid him farewell, ignoring his broad hints that another cup of beer would prompt him to tell his greatest tale: that of the time when he'd seen the Nightwatcher herself and stolen a sphere that glowed black at night. That tale always discomforted Szeth, as it reminded him of the strange black sphere Gavilar had given him. He'd hidden that carefully in Jah Keved. He didn't know what it was, but he didn't want to risk a master taking it from him.

When nobody offered Took another drink, he reluctantly stumbled from his chair and waved Szeth to follow him from the tavern. The street was dark outside. This town, Ironsway, had a proper town square, several hundred homes, and three different taverns. That made it practically a metropolis for Bavland—the small, mostly ignored stretch of land just north of the mountains near Silnasen. The area was technically part of Jah Keved, but even its highprince tended to stay away from it.

Szeth followed his master through the streets toward the poorer district. Took was too cheap to pay for a room in the nice, or even modest, areas of a town. Szeth looked over his shoulder, wishing that the Second Sister—known as Nomon to these Easterners—had risen to give a little more light.

Took stumbled drunkenly, then fell over in the street.

Szeth sighed. It would not be the first night he carried his master home to his bed. He knelt to lift Took.

He froze. A warm liquid was pooling beneath his master's body. Only then did he notice the knife in Took's neck.

Szeth instantly came alert as a group of footpads slipped out of the alleyway. One raised a hand, the knife in it reflecting starlight, preparing to throw at Szeth. He tensed. There were infused spheres he could draw upon in Took's pouch.

"Wait," hissed one of the footpads.

The man with the knife paused. Another man came closer, inspecting Szeth. "He's Shin. Won't hurt a cremling."

Others pulled the corpse into the alleyway. The one with the knife raised his weapon again. "He could still yell."

"Then why hasn't he? Oi'm telling you, they're harmless. Almost like parshmen. We can sell him."

"Maybe," the second said. "He's terrified. Look at 'im."

"Come 'ere," the first footpad said, waving Szeth forward.

He obeyed, walking into the alley, which was suddenly illuminated as the other footpads pulled open Took's pouch.

"Kelek," one of them said, "hardly worth the effort. A handful of chips and two marks, not a single broam in the lot."

"Oi'm telling you," the first man said. "We can sell this fellow as a slave. People like Shin servants."

"He's just a kid."

"Nah. They all look like that. Hey, whacha got there?" The man plucked a twinkling, sphere-size chunk of rock from the hand of the man counting the spheres. It was fairly ordinary, a simple piece of rock with a few quartz crystals set into it and a rusty vein of iron on one side. "What is this?"

"Worthless," one of the men said.

"I am required to tell you," Szeth said quietly, "that you are holding my Oathstone. So long as you possess it, you are my master."

"What's that?" one of the footpads said, standing.

The first one closed his hand around the stone, shooting a wary glance at the others. He looked back at Szeth. "Your master? What does that mean exactly, in precise terms and all?"

"I must obey you," Szeth said. "In all things, though I will not follow an order to kill myself." He also couldn't be ordered to give up his Blade, but there was no need to mention that at the moment.

"You'll obey me?" the footpad said. "You mean, you'll do what Oi say?"

"Yes."

"*Anything* Oi say?"

Szeth closed his eyes. "Yes."

"Well, ain't that something interestin'," the man said, musing. "Something interestin' indeed. . . ."

PART

TWO

The Illuminating Storms

DALINAR • KALADIN • ADOLIN

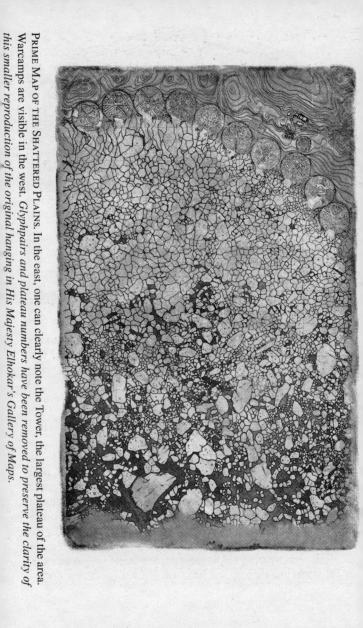

PRIME MAP OF THE SHATTERED PLAINS. In the east, one can clearly note the Tower, the largest plateau of the area. Warcamps are visible in the west. *Glyphpairs and plateau numbers have been removed to preserve the clarity of this smaller reproduction of the original hanging in His Majesty Elhokar's Gallery of Maps.*

Old friend, I hope this missive finds you well. Though, as you are now essentially immortal, I would guess that wellness on your part is something of a given.

"Today," King Elhokar announced, riding beneath the bright open sky, "is an excellent day to slay a god. Wouldn't you say?"

"Undoubtedly, Your Majesty." Sadeas's reply was smooth, quick, and said with a knowing smile. "One might say that gods, as a rule, should fear the Alethi nobility. Most of us at least."

Adolin gripped his reins a little more tightly; it put him on edge every time Highprince Sadeas spoke.

"Do we have to ride up here at the front?" Renarin whispered.

"I want to listen," Adolin replied softly.

He and his brother rode near the front of the column, near the king and his highprinces. Behind them extended a grand procession: a thousand soldiers in Kholin blue, dozens of servants, and even women in palanquins to scribe accounts of the hunt. Adolin glanced at them all as he reached for his canteen.

He was wearing his Shardplate, and so he had to be careful when grabbing it, lest he crush it. One's muscles reacted with increased speed, strength, and dexterity when wearing the armor, and it took practice to use it correctly. Adolin was still occasionally caught by surprise, though he'd held this suit—inherited from his mother's side of the family—since his sixteenth birthday. That was now seven years past.

He turned and took a long drink of lukewarm water. Sadeas rode to the king's left, and Dalinar—Adolin's father—was a solid figure riding at the king's right. The final highprince on the hunt was Vamah, who wasn't a Shardbearer.

The king was resplendent in his golden Shardplate—of course, Plate could make any man look regal. Even *Sadeas* looked impressive when wearing his red Plate, though his bulbous face and ruddy complexion weakened the effect. Sadeas and the king flaunted their Plate. And . . . well, perhaps Adolin did too. He'd had his painted blue, a few ornamentations welded onto the helm and pauldrons to give an extra look of danger. How could you *not* show off when wearing something as grand as Shardplate?

Adolin took another drink, listening to the king talk about his excitement for the hunt. Only one Shardbearer in the procession—indeed, only one Shardbearer in the entirety of the ten armies—used no paint or ornamentations on his Plate. Dalinar Kholin. Adolin's father preferred to leave his armor its natural slate-grey color.

Dalinar rode beside the king, his face somber. He rode with his helm tied to his saddle, exposing a square face topped by short black hair that had gone white at the temples. Few women had ever called Dalinar Kholin handsome; his nose was the wrong shape, his features blocky rather than delicate. It was the face of a warrior.

He rode astride a massive black Ryshadium stallion, one of the largest horses that Adolin had ever seen—and while the king and Sadeas looked regal in their armor, somehow Dalinar managed to look like a soldier. To him, the Plate was not an ornament. It was a tool. He never seemed to be surprised by the strength or speed the armor lent him. It was as if, for Dalinar Kholin, wearing his Plate was his natural state—it was the times without that were abnormal. Perhaps that was one reason he'd earned the reputation of being one of the greatest warriors and generals who ever lived.

Adolin found himself wishing, passionately, that his father would do a little more these days to live up to that reputation.

He's thinking about the visions, Adolin thought, regarding his father's distant expression and troubled eyes. "It happened again last night," Adolin said softly to Renarin. "During the highstorm."

"I know," Renarin said. His voice was measured, controlled. He always paused before he replied to a question, as if testing the words in his mind. Some women Adolin knew said Renarin's ways made them feel as if he were dissecting them with his mind. They'd shiver when they spoke of him, though Adolin had never found his younger brother the least bit discomforting.

"What do you think they mean?" Adolin asked, speaking quietly so only Renarin could hear. "Father's . . . episodes."

"I don't know."

"Renarin, we *can't* keep ignoring them. The soldiers are talking. Rumors are spreading through all ten armies!"

Dalinar Kholin was going mad. Whenever a highstorm came, he fell to the floor and began to shake. Then he began raving in gibberish. Often, he'd stand, blue eyes delusional and wild, swinging and flailing. Adolin had to restrain him lest he hurt himself or others.

"He sees things," Adolin said. "Or he thinks he does."

Adolin's grandfather had suffered from delusions. When he'd grown old, he'd thought he was back at war. Was that what happened to Dalinar? Was he reliving youthful battles, days when he'd earned his renown? Or was it that terrible night he saw over and over, the night when his brother had been murdered by the Assassin in White? And why did he so often mention the Knights Radiant soon after his episodes?

It all made Adolin feel sick. Dalinar was the Blackthorn, a genius of the battlefield and a living legend. Together, he and his brother had reunited Alethkar's warring highprinces after centuries of strife. He had defeated countless challengers in duels, had won dozens of battles. The entire kingdom looked up to him. And now this.

What did you do, as a son, when the father you loved—the greatest man alive—started to lose his wits?

Sadeas was speaking about a recent victory. He'd won another gemheart two days back, and the king—it appeared—hadn't heard of it. Adolin tensed at the boasts.

"We should move back," Renarin said.

"We are of rank enough to be here," Adolin said.

"I don't like how you get when you're around Sadeas."

We have to keep an eye on the man, Renarin, Adolin thought. *He knows Father is weakening. He'll try to strike.* Adolin forced himself to smile, however. He tried to be relaxed and confident for Renarin. Generally, that wasn't difficult. He'd happily spend his entire life dueling, lounging, and courting the occasional pretty girl. Of late, however, life didn't seem content to let him enjoy its simple pleasures.

". . . model of courage lately, Sadeas," the king was saying. "You've done very well in capturing gemhearts. You are to be commended."

"Thank you, Your Majesty. Though the competition grows unexciting, as some people don't seem interested in participating. I guess even the best weapons eventually grow dull."

Dalinar, who might once have responded to the veiled slur, said nothing. Adolin gritted his teeth. It was flat-out unconscionable for Sadeas to be taking shots at his father in his present state. Perhaps Adolin should offer the pompous bastard a challenge. You didn't duel highprinces—it just wasn't done, not unless you were ready to make a big storm of it. But maybe he was. Maybe—

"Adolin . . ." Renarin said warningly.

Adolin looked to the side. He'd held out his hand, as if to summon his Blade. He picked up his reins with the hand instead. *Storming man,* he thought. *Leave my father alone.*

"Why don't we talk about the hunt?" Renarin said. As usual, the younger Kholin rode with a straight back and perfect posture, eyes hidden behind his spectacles, a model of propriety and solemnity. "Aren't you excited?"

"Bah," Adolin said. "I never find hunts as interesting as everyone says they're going to be. I don't care how big the beast is—in the end, it's really just butchery."

Now, dueling, *that* was exciting. The feel of the Shardblade in your hand, of facing someone crafty, skilled, and careful. Man against man, strength against strength, mind against mind. Hunting some dumb beast just couldn't compare to that.

"Maybe you should have invited Janala along," Renarin said.

"She wouldn't have come," Adolin said. "Not after . . . well, you know. Rilla was very vocal yesterday. It was best to just leave."

"You really should have been wiser in your treatment of her," Renarin said, sounding disapproving.

Adolin mumbled a noncommittal reply. It wasn't *his* fault that his relationships often burned out quickly. Well, technically, this time it *was* his fault. But it wasn't usually. This was just an oddity

The king began complaining about something. Renarin and Adolin had lagged behind, and Adolin couldn't hear what was being said.

"Let's ride up closer," Adolin said, nudging his mount forward.

Renarin rolled his eyes, but followed.

⁂

Unite them.

The words whispered in Dalinar's mind. He couldn't rid himself of them. They consumed him as he trotted Gallant across a rocky, boulder-strewn plateau on the Shattered Plains.

"Shouldn't we be there by now?" the king asked.

"We're still two or three plateaus away from the hunting site, Your Majesty," Dalinar said, distracted. "It will be another hour, perhaps, observing proper protocols. If we had vantage, we could probably see the pavilion to—"

"Vantage? Would that rock formation up ahead do?"

"I suppose," Dalinar said, inspecting the towerlike length of rock. "We could send scouts to check."

"Scouts? Bah. I need a run, Uncle. I'll bet you five full broams that I can beat you to the top." And with that, the king galloped away in a thunder of hooves, leaving behind a shocked group of lighteyes, attendants, and guards.

"Storm it!" Dalinar cursed, kicking his horse into motion. "Adolin, you have command! Secure the next plateau, just in case."

His son, who had been lagging behind, nodded sharply. Dalinar galloped after the king, a figure in golden armor and a long blue cape. Hoofbeats pounded the stone, rock formations whipping past. Ahead, the steep, spikelike spire of rock rose from the lip of the plateau. Such formations were common out here on the Shattered Plains.

Curse that boy. Dalinar still thought of Elhokar as a boy, though the king was in his twenty-seventh year. But sometimes he acted like a boy. Why couldn't he give more warning before leaping into one of these stunts?

Still, as Dalinar rode, he admitted to himself that it *did* feel good to charge freely, helm off, face to the wind. His pulse picked up as he got into the race, and he forgave its impetuous beginning. For the moment, Dalinar let himself forget his troubles and the words that had been echoing in his head.

The king wanted a race? Well, Dalinar would give him one.

He charged past the king. Elhokar's stallion was a good breed, but it could never match Gallant, who was a full Ryshadium, two hands taller and much stronger than an ordinary horse. The animals chose their own riders, and only a dozen men in all of the warcamps were so fortunate. Dalinar was one, Adolin another.

In seconds, Dalinar reached the formation's base. He threw himself from the saddle while Gallant was still moving. He hit hard, but the Shardplate absorbed the impact, stone crunching beneath his metal boots as he skidded to a stop. Men who hadn't ever worn Plate—particularly those who were accustomed to its inferior cousin, simple plate and mail—could never understand. Shardplate wasn't merely armor. It was so much more.

He ran to the bottom of the rock formation as Elhokar galloped up behind. Dalinar leaped—Plate-assisted legs propelling him up some eight feet—and grabbed a handhold in the stone. With a heave, he pulled himself up, the Plate lending him the strength of many men. The Thrill of contest began to rise within him. It wasn't nearly as keen as the Thrill of battle, but it was a worthy substitute.

Rock scraped below. Elhokar had begun to climb as well. Dalinar didn't look down. He kept his eyes fixed on the small natural platform at the top of the forty-foot-high formation. He groped with steel-covered fingers, finding another handhold. The gauntlets covered his hands, but the ancient armor somehow transferred sensation to his fingers. It was as if he were wearing thin leather gloves.

A scraping sound came from the right, accompanied by a voice cursing softly. Elhokar had taken a different path, hoping to pass Dalinar, but the king had found himself at a section without handholds above. His progress was stalled.

The king's golden Shardplate glittered as he glanced at Dalinar. Elhokar set his jaw and looked upward, then launched himself in a powerful leap toward an outcropping.

Fool boy, Dalinar thought, watching the king seem to hang in the air for a moment before he snatched the projecting rock and dangled. Then the king pulled himself up and continued to climb.

Dalinar moved furiously, stone grinding beneath his metal fingertips, chips falling free. The wind ruffled his cape. He heaved, strained, and pushed himself, managing to get just ahead of the king. The top was mere feet away. The Thrill sang at him. He reached for the goal, determined to win. He couldn't lose. He had to—

Unite them.

He hesitated, not quite certain why, and let his nephew get ahead.

Elhokar hauled himself to his feet atop the rock formation, then laughed in triumph. He turned toward Dalinar, holding out a hand. "Stormwinds, Uncle, but you made a fine race of it! At the end there, I thought for sure you had me."

The triumph and joy in Elhokar's face brought a smile to

Dalinar's lips. The younger man needed victories these days. Even little ones would do him good. Gloryspren—like tiny golden translucent globes of light—began to pop into existence around him, attracted by his sense of accomplishment. Blessing himself for hesitating, Dalinar took the king's hand, letting Elhokar pull him up. There was just enough room on top of the natural tower for them both.

Breathing deeply, Dalinar slapped the king on the back with a clank of metal on metal. "That *was* a fine contest, Your Majesty. And you played it very well."

The king beamed. His golden Shardplate gleamed in the noonday sun; he had his faceplate up, revealing light yellow eyes, a strong nose, and a clean-shaven face that was almost too handsome, with its full lips, broad forehead, and firm chin. Gavilar had looked like that too, before he'd suffered a broken nose and that terrible scar on his chin.

Below them, the Cobalt Guard and some of Elhokar's attendants rode up, including Sadeas. His Plate gleamed red, though he wasn't a full Shardbearer—he had only the Plate, not the Blade.

Dalinar looked up. From this height, he could scan a large swath of the Shattered Plains, and he had an odd moment of familiarity. He felt as if he'd been atop this vantage point before, looking down at a broken landscape.

The moment was gone in a heartbeat.

"There," Elhokar said, pointing with a golden, gauntleted hand. "I can see our destination."

Dalinar shaded his eyes, picking out a large cloth pavilion three plateaus away, flying the king's flag. Wide, permanent bridges led there; they were relatively close to the Alethi side of the Shattered Plains, on plateaus Dalinar himself maintained. A fully grown chasmfiend living here was his to hunt, the wealth at its heart his privilege to claim.

"You were correct again, Uncle," Elhokar said.

"I try to make a habit of it."

"I can't blame you for that, I suppose. Though I can beat you at a race now and then."

Dalinar smiled. "I felt like a youth again, chasing after your father on some ridiculous challenge."

Elhokar's lips tightened to a thin line, and the gloryspren faded away. Mentioning Gavilar soured him; he felt others compared him unfavorably to the old king. Unfortunately, he was often right.

Dalinar moved on quickly. "We must have seemed of the ten fools, charging away like that. I do wish you'd given me more notice to prepare your honor guard. This *is* a war zone."

"Bah. You worry too much, Uncle. The Parshendi haven't attacked this close to our side of the Plains in years."

"Well, you seemed worried about your safety two nights ago."

Elhokar sighed audibly. "How many times must I explain this to you, Uncle? I can face enemy soldiers with Blade in hand. It's what they might send when we're not looking, when all is dark and quiet, that you should be trying to protect me from."

Dalinar didn't reply. Elhokar's nervousness—paranoia, even—regarding assassination was strong. But who could blame him, considering what had happened to his father?

I'm sorry, brother, he thought, as he did every time he thought of the night when Gavilar had died. Alone, without his brother to protect him.

"I looked into the matter you asked me about," Dalinar said, forcing away bad memories.

"You did? What did you discover?"

"Not much, I'm afraid. There were no traces of trespassers on your balcony, and none of the servants reported any strangers in the area."

"There *was* someone watching me in the darkness that night."

"If so, they haven't returned, Your Majesty. And they left no clues behind."

Elhokar seemed dissatisfied, and the silence between them grew stark. Below, Adolin met with scouts and prepared for the troop crossing. Elhokar had protested at how many men

Dalinar had brought. Most of them wouldn't be needed on the hunt—the Shardbearers, not the soldiers, would slay the beast. But Dalinar *would* see his nephew protected. Parshendi raids had grown less bold during the years of fighting—Alethi scribes guessed their numbers were three-quarters their prior strength, though it was difficult to judge—but the king's presence might be enough to entice them into a reckless attack.

The winds blew across Dalinar, returning with them that faint familiarity he'd felt a few minutes before. Standing atop a peak, looking out at desolation. A sense of an awful and amazing perspective.

That's it, he thought. *I did* stand atop a formation like this. It happened during—

During one of his visions. The very first one.

You must unite them, the strange, booming words had told him. *You must prepare. Build of your people a fortress of strength and peace, a wall to resist the winds. Cease squabbling and unite. The Everstorm comes.*

"Your Majesty," Dalinar found himself saying. "I . . ." He trailed off as quickly as he began. What could he say? That he'd been seeing visions? That—in defiance of all doctrine and common sense—he thought those visions might be from the Almighty? That he thought they should withdraw from the battlefield and go back to Alethkar?

Pure foolishness.

"Uncle?" the king asked. "What do you want?"

"Nothing. Come, let's get back to the others."

⁘

Adolin twisted one of his hogshide reins around his finger while he sat astride his horse, awaiting the next batch of scout reports. He'd managed to get his mind off his father and Sadeas, and was instead contemplating just how he was going to explain his falling out with Rilla in a way that would earn him some sympathy with Janala.

Janala loved ancient epic poems; could he phrase the falling out in dramatic terms? He smiled, thinking of her luxurious black hair and sly smile. She'd been daring, teasing at him while he was known to be courting someone else. He could use that too. Maybe Renarin was right, perhaps he should have invited her on the hunt. The prospect of fighting a greatshell would have been far more interesting to him if someone beautiful and long-haired were watching. . . .

"New scout reports are in, Brightlord Adolin," Tarilar said, jogging up.

Adolin turned his mind back to business. He'd taken up position with some members of the Cobalt Guard beside the base of the high rock formation where his father and the king were still conversing. Tarilar, scoutlord, was a gaunt-faced man with a thick chest and arms. From some angles, his head looked so relatively small on his body that it appeared to have been smashed.

"Proceed," Adolin said.

"Advance runners have met with the lead huntmaster and have returned. There are no sightings of Parshendi on any nearby plateaus. Companies Eighteen and Twenty-one are in position, though there are still eight companies to go."

Adolin nodded. "Have Company Twenty-one send some outriders to watch from plateaus fourteen and sixteen. And two each on plateaus six and eight."

"Six and eight? Behind us?"

"If I were going to ambush the party," Adolin said, "I'd round back this way and cut us off from fleeing. Do it."

Tarilar saluted. "Yes, Brightlord." He hurried away to pass the orders.

"You really think that's necessary?" Renarin asked, riding up beside Adolin.

"No. But Father will want it done anyway. You know he will."

There was motion up above. Adolin looked up just in time to see the king leap off the rock formation, cape streaming behind him as he fell some forty feet to the rock floor. Adolin's father stood at the lip above, and Adolin could imagine him cursing to himself at what he saw as a foolhardy move. Shardplate could withstand a fall that far, but it was high enough to be dangerous.

Elhokar landed with an audible crack, throwing up chips of stone and a large puff of Stormlight. He managed to stay upright. Adolin's father took a safer way down, descending to a lower ledge before jumping.

He seems to take the safer pathway more and more often lately, Adolin thought idly. *And he often seems to find reasons to give me command as well.* Thoughtful, Adolin trotted his horse out of the shadow of the rock formation. He needed to get a report from the rear guard—his father would want to hear it.

His path took him past a group of lighteyes from Sadeas's party. The king, Sadeas, and Vamah each had a collection of attendants, aides, and sycophants accompanying them. Looking at them riding in their comfortable silks, open-fronted jackets, and shade-covered palanquins made Adolin aware of his sweaty, bulky armor. Shardplate was wonderful and empowering, but beneath a hot sun, it could still leave a man wishing for something less confining.

But, of course, he couldn't have worn casual clothing like the others. Adolin was to be in uniform, even on a hunt. The Alethi War Codes commanded it. Never mind that nobody had followed those Codes in centuries. Or at least nobody but Dalinar Kholin—and, by extension, his sons.

Adolin passed a pair of lounging lighteyes, Vartian and Lomard, two of Sadeas's recent hangers-on. They were talking loudly enough that Adolin could hear. Probably on purpose. "Chasing after the king again," Vartian said, shaking his head. "Like pet axehounds nipping at their master's heels."

"Shameful," Lomard said. "How long has it been since Dalinar won a gemheart? The only time he can get one is when the king lets them hunt it without competition."

Adolin set his jaw and rode on. His father's interpretation of the Codes wouldn't let Adolin challenge a man to a duel while he was on duty or in command. He chafed at the needless restrictions, but Dalinar had spoken as Adolin's commanding officer. That meant there was no room for argument. He'd have to find a way to duel the two idiot sycophants in another setting, put them in their places. Unfortunately, he couldn't duel everyone who spoke out against his father.

The biggest problem was, the things they said had some real truth to them. The Alethi princedoms were like kingdoms unto themselves, still mostly autonomous despite having accepted Gavilar as king. Elhokar had inherited the throne, and Dalinar, by right, had taken the Kholin Princedom as his own.

However, most of the highprinces gave only token nods to the paramount rule of the king. That left Elhokar without land that was specifically his own. He tended to act like a highprince of the Kholin Princedom, taking great interest in its day-to-day management. So, while Dalinar should have been a ruler unto himself, he instead bent to Elhokar's whims and dedicated his resources to protecting his nephew. That made him weak in the eyes of the others—nothing more than a glorified bodyguard.

Once, when Dalinar had been feared, men had not dared whisper about these things. But now? Dalinar went on fewer and fewer plateau assaults, and his forces lagged behind in capturing precious gemhearts. While the others fought and won, Dalinar and his sons spent their time in bureaucratic administration.

Adolin wanted to be out there fighting, killing Parshendi. What was the good of following the Codes of War when he rarely got to *go* to war? *It's the fault of those delusions.* Dalinar wasn't weak, and he certainly wasn't a coward, no matter what people said. He was just troubled.

The rearguard captains weren't formed up yet, so Adolin decided to give the king a report instead. He trotted up toward the king—joining Sadeas, who was doing the same. Not unexpectedly, Sadeas frowned at him. The highprince hated that Adolin had a Blade while Sadeas had none; he had coveted one for years now.

Adolin met the highprince's eyes, smiling. *Anytime you want to duel me for my Blade, Sadeas, go ahead and try.*

What Adolin wouldn't do to get that eel of a man in the dueling ring.

When Dalinar and the king rode up, Adolin spoke quickly, before Sadeas could speak. "Your Majesty, I have scout reports."

The king sighed. "More of nothing, I expect. Honestly, Uncle, must we have a report on every little detail of the army?"

"We are at war, Your Majesty," Dalinar said.

Elhokar sighed sufferingly.

You're a strange man, cousin, Adolin thought. Elhokar saw murderers in every shadow, yet often dismissed the Parshendi threat. He'd go charging off like he had today, with no honor guard, and would leap off a forty-foot-tall rock formation. Yet he'd stay up nights, terrified of assassination.

"Give your report, son," Dalinar said.

Adolin hesitated, now feeling foolish at the lack of substance to what he had to say. "The scouts have seen no sign of the Parshendi. They've met with the huntmaster. Two companies have secured the next plateau, and the other eight will need some time to cross. We're close, though."

"Yes, we saw from above," Elhokar said. "Perhaps a few of us could ride ahead. . . ."

"Your Majesty," Dalinar said. "The point of bringing my troops along would be somewhat undermined if you left them behind."

Elhokar rolled his eyes. Dalinar did not yield, his expression as immobile as the rocks around them. Seeing him like that—firm, unyielding before a challenge—made Adolin smile with pride. Why couldn't he be like this *all* of the time? Why did he back down so often before insults or challenges?

"Very well," the king said. "We'll take a break and wait while the army crosses."

The king's attendants responded immediately, men climbing off horses, women having their palanquin bearers set them down. Adolin moved off to get that rearguard report. By the time he returned, Elhokar was practically holding court. His servants had set up a small awning to give him shade, and others served wine. Chilled, using one of the new fabrials that could make things cold.

Adolin removed his helm and wiped his brow with his saddle rag, again wishing he could join the others and enjoy a little wine. Instead, he climbed down from his horse and went looking for his father. Dalinar stood outside the awning, gauntleted hands clasped behind his back, looking eastward, toward the Origin—the distant, the unseen place where highstorms began. Renarin stood at his side, looking out as well, as if trying to see what it was that his father found so interesting.

Adolin rested a hand on his brother's shoulder, and Renarin smiled at him. Adolin knew that his brother—now nineteen years old—felt out of place. Though he wore a side sword, he barely knew how to use it. His blood weakness made it difficult for him to spend any reasonable amount of time practicing.

"Father," Adolin said. "Maybe the king was right. Perhaps we should have moved on quickly. I'd rather have this entire hunt over with."

Dalinar looked at him. "When I was your age, I looked forward to a hunt like this. Taking down a greatshell was the highlight of a young man's year."

Not this again, Adolin thought. Why was everyone so offended that he didn't find hunts exciting? "It's just an oversized chull, Father."

"These 'oversized chulls' grow to fifty feet tall and are capable of crushing even a man in Shardplate."

"Yes," Adolin said, "and so we'll bait it for hours while baking in the hot sun. If it decides to show up, we'll pelt it with arrows, only closing in once it's so weak it can barely resist as we hack it to death with Shardblades. Very honorable."

"It's not a duel," Dalinar said, "it's a hunt. A grand tradition."

Adolin raised an eyebrow at him.

"And yes," Dalinar added. "It can be tedious. But the king was insistent."

"You're just still smarting over the problems with Rilla, Adolin," Renarin said. "You were eager a week ago. You really should have invited Janala."

"Janala hates hunts. Thinks they're barbarous."

Dalinar frowned. "Janala? Who's Janala?"

"Daughter of Brightlord Lustow," Adolin said.

"And you're courting her?"

"Not yet, but I've sure been trying."

"What happened to that other girl? The short one, with the fondness for silver hair ribbons?"

"Deeli?" Adolin said. "Father, I stopped courting her over two months back!"

"You did?"

"Yes."

Dalinar rubbed his chin.

"There have been two between her and Janala, Father," Adolin noted. "You really need to pay more attention."

"Almighty help any man who tries to keep track of your tangled courtships, son."

"The most recent was Rilla," Renarin said.

Dalinar frowned. "And you two . . ."

"Had some problems yesterday," Adolin said. He coughed, determined to change the subject. "Anyway, don't you find it odd that the king would insist on coming to hunt the chasmfiend himself?"

"Not particularly. It isn't often that a full-sized one makes its way out here, and the king rarely gets to go on plateau runs. This is a way for him to fight."

"But he's so paranoid! Why does he now want to go and hunt, exposing himself on the Plains?"

Dalinar looked toward the king's awning. "I know he seems odd, son. But the king is more complex a man than many give him credit for being. He worries that his subjects see him as a coward because of how much he fears assassins, and so he finds ways to prove his courage. Foolish ways, sometimes—but he's not the first man I've known who will face battle without fear, yet cower in terror about knives in the shadows. The hallmark of insecurity is bravado.

"The king is learning to lead. He needs this hunt. He needs to prove to himself, and to others, that he's still strong and worthy to command a kingdom at war. That's why I encouraged him. A successful hunt, under controlled circumstances, could bolster his reputation and his confidence."

Adolin slowly closed his mouth, his father's words cutting down his complaints. Strange, how much the king's actions made sense when explained that way. Adolin looked up at his father. *How can the others whisper that he's a coward? Can't they see his wisdom?*

"Yes," Dalinar said, eyes growing distant. "Your cousin is a better man than many think him, and a stronger king. At least he could be. I just have to figure out how to persuade him to leave the Shattered Plains."

Adolin started. *"What?"*

"I didn't understand at first," Dalinar continued. "Unite them. I'm supposed to unite them. But aren't they already united? We fight together here on the Shattered Plains. We have a common enemy in the Parshendi. I'm beginning to see that we're united only in name. The highprinces give lip service to Elhokar, but this war—this siege—is a game to them. A competition against one another.

"We can't unite them here. We need to return to Alethkar and stabilize our homeland, learn how to work together as one nation. The Shattered Plains divide us. The others worry too much about winning wealth and prestige."

"Wealth and prestige are what being Alethi is *about*, Father!" Adolin said. Was he really hearing this? "What of the Vengeance Pact? The highprinces vowed to seek retribution upon the Parshendi!"

"And we *have* sought it." Dalinar looked to Adolin. "I realize that it sounds terrible, son, but some things are more important than vengeance. I loved Gavilar. I miss him fiercely, and I hate the Parshendi for what they did. But Gavilar's life work was to unite Alethkar, and I'll go to Damnation before I let it break apart."

"Father," Adolin said, feeling pained, "if there's something wrong here, it's that we're not trying hard enough. You think the highprinces are playing games? Well, show them the way it should be done! Instead of talking of retreat, we should be talking of advancing, striking at the Parshendi instead of besieging them."

"Perhaps."

"Either way, we cannot speak of withdrawing," Adolin said. The men *already* talked of Dalinar losing his spine. What would they say if they got hold of this? "You haven't brought this up with the king, have you?"

"Not yet. I haven't found the right way."

"Please. Don't talk to him about it."

"We shall see." Dalinar turned back toward the Shattered Plains, his eyes growing distant again.

"Father . . ."

"You've made your point, son, and I've replied to it. Do not press the issue. Have you gotten the report from the rear guard?"

"Yes."

"What of the vanguard?"

"I just checked with them and . . ." He trailed off. Blast. It had been long enough that it was probably time to move the king's party onward. The last of the army couldn't leave this plateau until the king was safely on the other side.

Adolin sighed and went off to collect the report. Before long, they were all across the chasm and riding over the next plateau. Renarin trotted up to Adolin and tried to engage him in conversation, but Adolin gave only halfhearted replies.

He was beginning to feel an odd longing. Most of the older men in the army—even those only a few years older than Adolin—had fought alongside his father during the glory days. Adolin found himself jealous of all of those men who had known his father and had seen him fight when he hadn't been so wrapped up in the Codes.

The changes in Dalinar had begun with the death of his brother. That terrible day was when everything had started to go wrong. The loss of Gavilar had nearly crushed Dalinar, and Adolin would *never* forgive the Parshendi for bringing his father such pain. Never. Men fought on the Plains for different reasons, but this was why Adolin had come. Perhaps if they beat the Parshendi, his father would go back to the man he had been. Perhaps those ghostly delusions that haunted him would vanish.

Ahead, Dalinar was speaking quietly with Sadeas. Both men wore frowns. They barely tolerated one another, though they had once been friends. That had also changed the night of Gavilar's death. What had happened between them?

The day wore on, and they eventually arrived at the hunt site—a pair of plateaus, one where the creature would be lured up to attack, and another one a safe distance away for those who would watch. Like most others, these plateaus had an uneven surface inhabited by hardy plants adapted to regular storm exposure. Rocky shelves, depressions, and uneven footing made fighting on them treacherous.

Adolin joined his father, who waited beside the final bridge as the king moved over onto the viewing plateau, followed by a company of soldiers. The attendants would be next.

"You're doing well with your command, son," Dalinar said, nodding to a group of soldiers as they passed and saluted.

"They're good men, Father. They hardly need someone to command them during a march from plateau to plateau."

"Yes," Dalinar said. "But you need experience leading, and they need to learn to see you as a commander." Renarin trotted up to them on his horse; it was probably time to cross to the viewing plateau. Dalinar nodded for his sons to go first.

Adolin turned to go, but hesitated as he noticed something on the plateau behind them. A rider, moving quickly to catch up with the hunting party, coming from the direction of the warcamps.

"Father," Adolin said, pointing.

Dalinar turned immediately, following the gesture. However, Adolin soon recognized the newcomer. Not a messenger, as he'd expected.

"Wit!" Adolin called, waving.

The newcomer trotted up to them. Tall and thin, the King's Wit rode easily on a black gelding. He wore a stiff black coat and black trousers, a color matched by his deep onyx hair. Though he wore a long, thin sword tied to his waist, as far as Adolin knew, the man had never drawn it. A dueling foil rather than a military blade, it was mostly symbolic.

Wit nodded to them as he approached, wearing one of those keen smiles of his. He had blue eyes, but he wasn't really a lighteyes. Nor was he a darkeyes. He was . . . well, he was the King's Wit. That was a category all its own.

"Ah, young Prince Adolin!" Wit exclaimed. "You actually managed to pry yourself away from the camp's young women long enough to join this hunt? I'm impressed."

Adolin chuckled uncomfortably. "Well, that's been a topic of some discussion lately. . . ."

Wit raised an eyebrow.

Adolin sighed. Wit would find out eventually anyway—it was virtually impossible to keep anything from the man. "I made a lunch appointment with one woman yesterday, but I was . . . well, I was courting another. And she's the jealous type. So now neither will speak with me."

"It's a constant source of amazement that you get yourself into such messes, Adolin. Each one is more exciting than the previous!"

"Er, yes. Exciting. That's *exactly* how it feels."

Wit laughed again, though he maintained a sense of dignity in his posture. The King's Wit was not a silly court fool such as one might find in other kingdoms. He was a sword, a tool maintained by the king. Insulting others was beneath the dignity of the king, so just as one used gloves when forced to handle something vile, the king retained a Wit so he didn't have to debase himself to the level of rudeness or offensiveness.

This new Wit had been with them for some months, and there was something . . . different about him. He seemed to know things that he shouldn't, important things. Useful things.

Wit nodded to Dalinar. "Your Lordship."

"Wit," Dalinar said stiffly.

"And young Prince Renarin!"

Renarin kept his eyes down.

"No greeting for me, Renarin?" Wit said, amused.

Renarin said nothing.

"He thinks you'll mock him if he speaks to you, Wit," Adolin said. "Earlier this morning, he told me he'd determined not to say anything around you."

"Wonderful!" Wit exclaimed. "Then I can say whatever I wish, and he'll not object?"

Renarin hesitated.

Wit leaned in to Adolin. "Have I told you about the night Prince Renarin and I had two days back, walking the streets of the warcamp? We came across these two sisters, you see, blue eyed and—"

"That's a lie!" Renarin said, blushing.

"Very well," Wit said without missing a beat, "I'll confess there were actually *three* sisters, but Prince Renarin quite unfairly ended up with two of them, and I didn't wish to diminish my reputation by—"

"Wit." Dalinar was stern as he cut in.

The black-clad man looked to him.

"Perhaps you should restrict your mockery to those who deserve it."

"Brightlord Dalinar. I believe that was what I *was* doing."

Dalinar's frown deepened. He never had liked Wit, and picking on Renarin was a sure way to raise his ire. Adolin could understand that, but Wit was almost always good-natured with Renarin.

Wit moved to leave, passing Dalinar as he did. Adolin could barely overhear what was said as Wit leaned over to whisper something. "Those who 'deserve' my mockery are those who can benefit from it, Brightlord Dalinar. That one is less fragile than you think him." He winked, then turned his horse to move on over the bridge.

"Stormwinds, but I like that man," Adolin said. "Best Wit we've had in ages!"

"I find him unnerving," Renarin said softly.

"That's half the fun!"

Dalinar said nothing. The three of them crossed the bridge, passing Wit, who had stopped to torment a group of officers—lighteyes of low enough rank that they needed to serve in the army and earn a wage. Several of them laughed while Wit poked fun at another.

The three of them joined the king, and were immediately approached by the day's huntmaster. Bashin was a short man with a sizable paunch; he wore rugged clothing with a leather overcoat and a wide-brimmed hat. He was a darkeyes of the first nahn, the highest and most prestigious rank a darkeyes could have, worthy even of marrying into a lighteyed family.

Bashin bowed to the king. "Your Majesty! Wonderful timing! We've just tossed down the bait."

"Excellent," Elhokar said, climbing from the saddle. Adolin and Dalinar did likewise, Shardplate clinking softly, Dalinar untying his helm from the saddle. "How long will it take?"

"Two or three hours is likely," Bashin said, taking the reins of the king's horse. Grooms took the two Ryshadium. "We've set up over there."

Bashin pointed toward the hunting plateau, the smaller plateau where the actual fighting would take place away from the attendants and the bulk of the soldiers. A group of hunters led a lumbering chull around its perimeter, towing a rope draped over the side of the cliff. That rope would be dragging the bait.

"We're using hog carcasses," Bashin explained. "And we poured hog's blood over the sides. The chasmfiend has been spotted by patrols here a good dozen times. He's got his nest nearby, for certain—he's not here to pupate. He's too big for that, and he's remained in the area too long. So it should be a fine hunt! Once he arrives, we'll loose a group of wild hogs as distractions, and you can begin weakening him with arrows."

They had brought grandbows: large steel bows with thick strings and such a high draw weight that only a Shardbearer could use them, to fire shafts as thick as three fingers. They were recent creations, devised by Alethi engineers through the use of fabrial science, and each required a small infused gemstone to maintain the strength of its pull without warping the metal. Adolin's aunt Navani—the widow of King Gavilar, mother of Elhokar and his sister Jasnah—had led the research to develop the bows.

It would be nice if she hadn't left, Adolin thought idly. Navani was an interesting woman. Things were never boring around her.

Some had started calling the bows Shardbows, but Adolin didn't like the term. Shardblades and Shardplate were something special. Relics from another time, a time when the Radiants had walked Roshar. No amount of fabrial science had even approached re-creating them.

Bashin led the king and his highprinces toward a pavilion at the center of the viewing plateau. Adolin joined his father, intending to give a report on the crossing. About half of the soldiers were in place, but many of the attendants were still making their way across the large, permanent bridge onto the viewing plateau. The king's banner flapped above the pavilion, and a small refreshment station had been erected. A soldier at the back was setting up the rack of four grandbows. They were sleek and dangerous-looking, with thick black shafts in four quivers beside them.

"I think you'll have a fine day for the hunt," Bashin said to Dalinar. "Judging by reports, the beast is a big one. Larger than you've ever slain before, Brightlord."

"Gavilar always wanted to slay one of these," Dalinar said wistfully. "He loved greatshell hunts, though he never got a chasmfiend. Odd that I've now killed so many."

The chull pulling the bait bleated in the distance.

"You need to go for the legs on this one, Brightlords," Bashin said. Pre-hunt advice was one of Bashin's responsibilities, and he took those seriously. "Chasmfiends, well, you're used to attacking them in their chrysalises. Don't forget how mean they are when they're not pupating. With one this big, use a distraction and come in from . . ." He trailed off, then groaned, cursing softly. "Storms take that animal. I swear, the man who trained it must have been daft."

He was looking across at the next plateau. Adolin followed

his glance. The crablike chull that had been towing the bait was lumbering away from the chasm with a slow, yet determined gait. Its handlers were yelling, running after it.

"I'm sorry, Brightlord," Bashin said. "It's been doing this all day."

The chull bleated in a gravelly voice. Something seemed wrong to Adolin.

"We can send for another one," Elhokar said. "It shouldn't take too long to—"

"Bashin?" Dalinar said, his voice suddenly alarmed. "Shouldn't there be *bait* on the end of that beast's rope?"

The huntmaster froze. The rope the chull was towing was frayed at the end.

Something dark—something mind-numbingly enormous—rose out of the chasm on thick, chitinous legs. It climbed onto the plateau—not the small plateau where the hunt was supposed to take place, but the viewing plateau where Dalinar and Adolin stood. The plateau filled with attendants, unarmed guests, female scribes, and unprepared soldiers.

"Aw, Damnation," Bashin said.

TEN HEARTBEATS

I realize that you are probably still angry. That is pleasant to know. Much as your perpetual health, I have come to rely upon your dissatisfaction with me. It is one of the cosmere's great constants, I should think.

Ten heartbeats.
One.

That was how long it took to summon a Shardblade. If Dalinar's heart was racing, the time was shorter. If he was relaxed, it took longer.
Two.

On the battlefield, the passing of those beats could stretch like an eternity. He pulled his helm on as he ran.
Three.

The chasmfiend slammed an arm down, smashing the bridge filled with attendants and soldiers. People screamed, plunging into the chasm. Dalinar dashed forward on Plate-enhanced legs, following the king.
Four.

The chasmfiend towered like a mountain of interlocking carapace the color of dark violet ink. Dalinar could see why the Parshendi called these things gods. It had a twisted, arrowhead-like face, with a mouth full of barbed mandibles. While it was vaguely crustacean, this was no bulky, placid chull. It had four wicked foreclaws set into broad shoulders, each claw the size of a horse, and a dozen smaller legs that clutched the side of the plateau.

Five.

Chitin made a grinding noise against stone as the creature finished pulling itself onto the plateau, snatching a cart-pulling chull with a swift claw.

Six.

"To arms, to arms!" Elhokar bellowed ahead of Dalinar. "Archers, fire!"

Seven.

"Distract it from the unarmed!" Dalinar bellowed at his soldiers.

The creature cracked the chull's shell—platter-size fragments clattering to the plateau—then stuffed the beast into its maw and began looking down at the fleeing scribes and attendants. The chull stopped bleating as the monster crunched down.

Eight.

Dalinar leaped a rocky shelf and sailed five yards before slamming into the ground, throwing up chips of rock.

Nine.

The chasmfiend bellowed with an awful screeching sound. It trumpeted with four voices, overlapping one another.

Archers drew. Elhokar yelled orders just in front of Dalinar, his blue cape flapping.

Dalinar's hand tingled with anticipation.

Ten!

His Shardblade—Oathbringer—formed in his hand, coalescing from mist, appearing as the tenth beat of his heart thudded in his chest. Six feet long from tip to hilt, the Blade would have been unwieldy in the hands of any man not wearing Shardplate. To Dalinar, it felt perfect. He'd carried Oathbringer since his youth, Bonding to it when he was twenty Weepings old. It was long and slightly curved, a handspan wide, with wavelike serrations near the hilt. It curved at the tip like a fisherman's hook, and was wet with cold dew.

This sword was a part of him. He could sense energy racing

along its blade, as if it were eager. A man never really knew life itself until he charged into battle with Plate and Blade.

"Make it *angry!*" Elhokar bellowed, his Shardblade—Sunraiser—springing from mist into his hand. It was long and thin with a large crossguard, and was etched up the sides with the ten fundamental glyphs. He didn't want the monster to escape; Dalinar could hear it in his voice. Dalinar was more worried about the soldiers and attendants; this hunt had already turned terribly wrong. Perhaps they should distract the monster long enough for everyone to escape, then pull back and let it dine on chulls and hogs.

The creature screamed its multivoiced wail again, slamming a claw down among the soldiers. Men screamed; bones splintered and bodies crumpled.

Archers loosed, aiming for the head. A hundred shafts zipped into the air, but only a few hit the soft muscle between plates of chitin. Behind them, Sadeas was calling for his grandbow. Dalinar couldn't wait for that—the creature was here, dangerous, killing his men. The bow would be too slow. This was a job for the Blade.

Adolin charged past, riding Sureblood. The lad had gone racing for his horse, rather than charging like Elhokar had. Dalinar himself had been forced to stay with the king. The other horses—even the warhorses—panicked, but Adolin's white Ryshadium stallion held steady. In a moment, Gallant was there, trotting beside Dalinar. Dalinar grabbed the reins and heaved himself into the air with Plate-enhanced legs, jumping up into the saddle. The force of his landing might have strained the back of an ordinary horse, but Gallant was made of stronger stone than that.

Elhokar closed his helm, the sides misting.

"Hold back, Your Majesty," Dalinar called, riding past. "Wait until Adolin and I weaken it." Dalinar reached up, slamming down his own visor. The sides misted, locking it into place, and the sides of the helm became translucent to him. You still needed the eye slit—looking through the sides was like looking through dirty glass—but the translucence was one of the most wonderful parts of Shardplate.

Dalinar rode into the monster's shadow. Soldiers scrambled about, clutching spears. They hadn't been trained to fight thirty-foot-tall beasts, and it was a testament to their valor that they formed up anyway, trying to draw attention away from the archers and the fleeing attendants.

Arrows rained down, bouncing off the carapace and becoming more deadly to the troops below than they were to the chasmfiend. Dalinar raised his free arm to shade his eye slit as an arrow clanged off his helm.

Adolin fell back as the beast swung at a batch of archers, crushing them with one of its claws. "I'll take left," Adolin yelled, voice muffled by his helm.

Dalinar nodded, cutting to the right, galloping past a group of dazed soldiers and into sunlight again as the chasmfiend raised a foreclaw for another sweep. Dalinar raced under the limb, transferring Oathbringer to his left hand and holding the sword out to the side, slashing it through one of the chasmfiend's trunklike legs.

The Blade sheared the thick chitin with barely a tug of resistance. As always, it didn't cut living flesh, though it killed the leg as surely as if it had been cut free. The large limb slipped, falling numb and useless.

The monster roared with its deep, overlapping, trumpeting voices. On the other side, Dalinar could make out Adolin slicing at a leg.

The creature shook, turning toward Dalinar. The two legs that had been cut dragged lifelessly. The monster was long and narrow like a crayfish, and had a flattened tail. It walked on fourteen legs. How many could it lose before collapsing?

Dalinar rounded Gallant, meeting up with Adolin, whose blue Shardplate was gleaming, cape streaming behind him. They switched sides as they turned in wide arcs, each heading for another leg.

"Meet your enemy, monster!" Elhokar bellowed.

Dalinar turned. The king had found his mount and had managed to get it under control. Vengeance wasn't a Ryshadium, but the animal was of the best Shin stock. Astride the animal, Elhokar charged, Blade held above his head.

Well, there was no forbidding him the fight. He should be all right in his Plate so long as he kept moving. "The legs, Elhokar!" Dalinar shouted.

Elhokar ignored him, charging directly for the beast's chest. Dalinar cursed, heeling Gallant as the monster swung. Elhokar turned at the last moment, leaning low, ducking under the blow. The chasmfiend's claw hit stone with a cracking sound. It roared in anger at missing Elhokar, the sound echoing through the chasms.

The king veered toward Dalinar, riding past him in a rush. "I'm distracting it, you fool. Keep attacking!"

"I have the Ryshadium!" Dalinar yelled back at him. "I'll distract—I'm faster!"

Elhokar ignored him again. Dalinar sighed. Elhokar, characteristically, could not be contained. Arguing would only cost more time and more lives, so Dalinar did as he'd been told. He rounded to the side for another approach, Gallant's hooves beating against the stone ground. The king drew the monster's direct attention, and Dalinar was able to ride in and slam his Blade through another leg.

The beast emitted four overlapping screams and turned toward Dalinar. But as it did, Adolin rode past on the other side, cutting at another leg with a deft strike. The leg slumped, and arrows rained down as archers continued to fire.

The creature shook, confused by the attacks coming from every side. It was getting weak, and Dalinar raised his arm, gesturing. The command ordered the rest of the foot soldiers to retreat toward the pavilion. Orders given, he slipped in and killed another leg. That meant five down. Perhaps it was time to let the beast limp away; killing it now wasn't worth risking lives.

He called to the king, who rode—Blade held out to the side—a short distance away. The king glanced at him, but obviously didn't hear. As the chasmfiend loomed in the background, Elhokar wheeled Vengeance in a sharp right turn toward Dalinar.

There was a soft *snap*, and suddenly the king—and his saddle—went tumbling through the air. The horse's quick turn had caused the saddle girth to break. A man in Shard-plate was heavy and put a great strain on both his mount and saddle.

Dalinar felt a spike of fear, and he reined in Gallant. Elhokar slammed to the ground, dropping his Shardblade. The weapon reverted to mist, vanishing. It was a protection to keep a Blade from being taken by your enemies; they vanished unless you willed them to stay when releasing them.

"Elhokar!" Dalinar bellowed. The king rolled, cape wrapping around his body, then came to rest. He lay dazed for a moment; the armor was cracked on one shoulder, leaking Stormlight. The Plate would have cushioned the fall. He'd be all right.

Unless—

A claw loomed above the king.

Dalinar felt a moment of panic, turning Gallant to charge toward the king. He was going to be too slow! The beast would—

An enormous arrow slammed into the chasmfiend's head, cracking chitin. Purple gore spurted free, causing the beast to trump in agony. Dalinar twisted in the saddle.

Sadeas stood in his red Plate, taking another massive arrow from an attendant. He drew, launching the thick bolt into the chasmfiend's shoulder with a sharp crack.

Dalinar raised Oathbringer in salute. Sadeas acknowledged, raising his bow. They were not friends, and they did not like one another.

But they *would* protect the king. That was the bond that united them.

"Get to safety!" Dalinar yelled to the king as he charged past. Elhokar stumbled to his feet and nodded.

Dalinar moved in. He *had* to distract the beast long enough for Elhokar to get away. More of Sadeas's arrows flew true, but the monster started to ignore them. Its sluggishness vanished, and its bleats became angry, wild, crazed. It was growing truly enraged.

This was the most dangerous part; there would be no

retreating now. It would follow them until it either killed them or was slain.

A claw smashed to the ground just beside Gallant, throwing chips of stone into the air. Dalinar hunkered low, careful to keep his Shardblade out, and he cut free another leg. Adolin had done the same on the other side. Seven legs down, half of them. How long before the beast dropped? Normally, at this stage, they had launched several dozen arrows into the animal. It was difficult to guess what one would do without that prior softening—besides that, he'd never fought one this large before.

He turned Gallant, trying to draw the creature's attention. Hopefully, Elhokar had—

"Are you a god!" Elhokar bellowed.

Dalinar groaned, looking over his shoulder. The king had *not* fled. He strode toward the beast, hand to the side.

"I defy you, creature!" Elhokar screamed. "I claim your life! They will see their gods crushed, just as they will see their king dead at my feet! I *defy* you!"

Damnation's own fool! Dalinar thought, rounding Gallant. Elhokar's Shardblade re-formed in his hands, and he charged toward the monster's chest, his cracked shoulder leaking Stormlight. He got close and swung at the beast's torso, cutting free a piece of chitin—like a person's hair or nails, it could be cut by a Blade. Then Elhokar slammed his weapon into the monster's breast, seeking its heart.

The beast roared and shook, knocking Elhokar free. The king barely kept hold of his Blade. The beast spun. That movement, unfortunately, brought its tail at Dalinar. He cursed, yanking Gallant in a tight turn, but the tail came too quickly. It slammed into Gallant, and in a heartbeat Dalinar found himself rolling, Oathbringer tumbling from his fingers and slicing a gash in the stone ground before puffing to mist.

"Father!" a distant voice yelled.

Dalinar came to rest on the stones, dizzy. He raised his head to see Gallant stumbling to its feet. Blessedly, the horse hadn't broken a leg, though the animal bled from scrapes and was favoring one leg.

"Away!" Dalinar said. The command word would send the horse to safety. Unlike Elhokar, *it* would obey.

Dalinar climbed to his feet, unsteady. A scraping sound came from his left, and Dalinar spun just in time for the chasmfiend's tail to take him in the chest, tossing him backward.

Again the world lurched, and metal hit stone in a cacophony as he slid.

No! he thought, getting a gauntleted hand beneath himself and heaving, using the momentum of his slide to throw himself upright. As the sky spun, something seemed to *right*, as if the Plate itself knew which way was up. He landed—still moving, feet grinding on stone.

He got his balance, then charged toward the king, beginning the process of summoning his Shardblade again. Ten heartbeats. An eternity.

The archers continued to fire, and more than a few of their shafts bristled from the chasmfiend's face. It ignored them, though Sadeas's larger arrows still seemed to distract it. Adolin had sheared through another leg, and the creature lumbered uncertainly, eight of its fourteen legs dragging uselessly.

"Father!"

Dalinar turned to see Renarin—dressed in a stiff blue Kholin uniform, with a long coat buttoning to the neck—riding across the rocky ground. "Father, are you well? Can I help?"

"Fool boy!" Dalinar said, pointing. "Go!"

"But—"

"You're unarmored and unarmed!" Dalinar bellowed. "Get back before you get yourself killed!"

Renarin pulled his roan horse to a halt.

"GO!"

Renarin galloped away. Dalinar turned and ran toward Elhokar, Oathbringer misting into existence in his waiting hand. Elhokar continued to hack at the beast's lower torso, and sections of flesh blackened and died when the Shardblade struck. If he rammed the Shardblade in just right, he could stop the heart or lungs, but that would be difficult while the beast was upright.

Adolin—stalwart as always—had dismounted beside the king. He tried to stop the claws, striking at them as they fell. Unfortunately, there were four claws and only one of Adolin. Two swung at him at once, and though Adolin sliced a chunk out of one, he didn't see the other sweeping at his back.

Dalinar called out too late. Shardplate *snapped* as the claw tossed Adolin into the air. He arced and hit in a tumble. His Plate didn't shatter, thank the Heralds, but the breastplate and side cracked widely, leaking trails of white smoke.

Adolin rolled lethargically, hands moving. He was alive.

No time to think about him now. Elhokar was alone.

The beast struck, pounding the ground beside the king, knocking him off his feet. His Blade vanished and Elhokar fell face-first on the stones.

Something changed inside of Dalinar. Reservations vanished. Other concerns became meaningless. His brother's son was in danger.

He had failed Gavilar, had lain drunk in his wine while his brother fought for his life. Dalinar should have been there to defend him. Only two things remained of his beloved brother, two things that Dalinar could protect in a hope to earn some form of redemption: Gavilar's kingdom and Gavilar's son.

Elhokar was alone and in danger.

Nothing else mattered.

⁂

Adolin shook his head, dazed. He slammed his visor up, taking a gasp of fresh air to clear his mind.

Fighting. They were fighting. He could hear men screaming, rocks shaking, an enormous bleating sound. He smelled something moldy. Greatshell blood.

The chasmfiend! he thought. Before his mind was even clear, Adolin began summoning his Blade again and forced himself to his hands and knees.

The monster loomed a short distance away, a dark shadow upon the sky. Adolin had fallen near its right side. As his vision lost its fuzziness, he saw that the king was down, and his armor was cracked from the blow he'd taken earlier.

The chasmfiend raised a massive claw, preparing to slam it down. Adolin knew—suddenly—that disaster was upon them. The king would be killed on a simple hunt. The kingdom would shatter, the highprinces divided, the one tenuous link that kept them together cut away.

No! Adolin thought, stunned, still dazed, trying to stumble forward.

And then he saw his father.

Dalinar charged toward the king, moving with a speed and grace no man—not even one wearing Shardplate—should be able to manage. He leaped over a rock shelf, then ducked and skidded beneath a claw swinging for him. Other men thought they understood Shardblades and Shardplate, but Dalinar Kholin . . . at times, he proved them all children.

Dalinar straightened and leaped—still moving forward—cresting by inches a second claw that smashed apart the rocky shelf behind him.

It was all just a moment. A breath. The third claw was falling toward the king, and Dalinar roared, leaping forward. He dropped his Blade—it hit the ground and puffed away—as he skidded beneath the falling claw. He raised his hands and—

And he caught it. He bent beneath the blow, going down on one knee, and the air rang with a resounding clang of carapace against armor.

But he *caught it.*

Stormfather! Adolin thought, watching his father stand over the king, bowed beneath the enormous weight of a monster many times his size. Shocked archers hesitated. Sadeas lowered his grandbow. Adolin's breath caught in his chest.

Dalinar held back the claw and matched its strength, a figure in dark, silvery metal that almost seemed to glow. The beast trumpeted above, and Dalinar bellowed back a powerful, defiant yell.

In that moment, Adolin knew he was seeing *him.* The Blackthorn, the very man he'd been wishing he could fight alongside. The Plate of Dalinar's gauntlets and shoulders began to crack, webs of light moving down the ancient metal. Adolin finally shook himself into motion. *I have to help!*

His Shardblade formed in his hand and he scrambled to the side and sheared through the leg nearest to him. There was a crack in the air. With so many legs down, the beast's other legs couldn't hold its weight, particularly when it was trying so hard to crush Dalinar. The remaining legs on its right side snapped with a sickening crunch, spraying out violet ichor, and the beast toppled to the side.

The ground shook, nearly knocking Adolin to his knees. Dalinar tossed aside the now-limp claw, Stormlight from the many cracks steaming above him. Nearby, the king picked himself up off the ground—it had been mere seconds since he'd fallen.

Elhokar stumbled to his feet, looking at the fallen beast. Then he turned to his uncle, the Blackthorn.

Dalinar nodded thankfully to Adolin, then gestured sharply toward what passed for the beast's neck. Elhokar nodded, then summoned his Blade and rammed it deeply into the monster's flesh. The creature's uniform green eyes blackened and shriveled, smoke twisting into the air.

Adolin walked up to join his father, watching as Elhokar plunged his Blade into the chasmfiend's chest. Now that the beast was dead, the Blade could cut its flesh. Violet ichor spurted out, and Elhokar dropped his sword and reached into the wound, questing with Plate-enhanced arms, grabbing something.

He ripped free the beast's gemheart—the enormous gemstone that grew within all chasmfiends. It was lumpy and uncut, but it was a pure emerald and as big as a man's head. It was the largest gemheart Adolin had ever seen, and even the small ones were worth a fortune.

Elhokar held aloft the grisly prize, golden gloryspren appearing around him, and the soldiers yelled in triumph.

Let me first assure you that the element is quite safe. I have found a good home for it. I protect its safety like I protect my own skin, you might say.

The morning after his decision in the highstorm, Kaladin made certain to arise before the others. He threw off his blanket and strode through the room full of blanketed lumps. He didn't feel excited, but he *did* feel resolute. Determined to fight again.

He began that fight by throwing the door open to the sunlight. Groans and curses sounded behind him as the groggy bridgemen awoke. Kaladin turned toward them, hands on hips. Bridge Four currently had thirty-four members. That number fluctuated, but at least twenty-five were needed to carry the bridge. Anything below that, and the bridge would topple for certain. Sometimes, it did even with more members.

"Up and organize!" Kaladin shouted in his best squad-leader's voice. He shocked himself with the authority in it.

The men blinked bleary eyes.

"That *means*," Kaladin bellowed, "out of the barrack and form ranks! You'll do it now, storm you, or I'll haul you out one by one myself!"

Syl fluttered down and landed on his shoulder, watching

curiously. Some of the bridgemen sat up, staring at him, baffled. Others turned over in their blankets, putting their backs to him.

Kaladin took a deep breath. "So be it." He strode into the room and chose a lean Alethi named Moash. He was a strong man; Kaladin needed an example, and one of the skinnier men like Dunny or Narm wouldn't do. Plus, Moash was one of those who'd turned over to go back to sleep.

Kaladin grabbed Moash by one arm and heaved, pulling with all his strength. Moash stumbled to his feet. He was a younger man, perhaps near Kaladin's age, and had a hawkish face.

"Storm off!" Moash snapped, pulling his arm back.

Kaladin punched Moash right in the gut, where he knew it would wind him. Moash gasped in shock, doubling over, and Kaladin stepped forward to grab him by the legs, slinging Moash over his shoulder.

Kaladin almost toppled from the weight. Luckily, carrying bridges was harsh but effective strength training. Of course, few bridgemen survived long enough to benefit from it. It didn't help that there were unpredictable lulls between runs. That was part of the problem; the bridge crews spent most of their time staring at their feet or doing menial chores, then were expected to run for miles carrying a bridge.

He carted the shocked Moash outside and set him down on the stone. The rest of the camp was awake, woodworkers arriving at the lumberyard, soldiers jogging to their breakfast or training. The other bridge crews, of course, were still asleep. They were often allowed to sleep late, unless they were on morning bridge duty.

Kaladin left Moash and walked back into the low-ceilinged barrack. "I'll do the same to each of you, if I have to."

He didn't have to. The shocked bridgemen filed out into the light, blinking. Most stood bare-backed to the sunlight, wearing only knee-length trousers. Moash climbed to his feet, rubbing his stomach and glaring at Kaladin.

"Things are going to change in Bridge Four," Kaladin said. "For one thing, there will be no more sleeping in."

"And what are we going to do instead?" Sigzil demanded. He had dark brown skin and black hair—that meant he was Makabaki, from southwestern Roshar. He was the only bridgeman without a beard, and judging by his smooth accent, he was probably Azish or Emuli. Foreigners were common in bridge crews—those who didn't fit in often made their way to the crem of an army.

"Excellent question," Kaladin said. "We are going to train. Each morning before our daily chores, we will run the bridge in practice to build up our endurance."

More than one of the men's expressions grew dark at this.

"I know what you are thinking," Kaladin said. "Aren't our lives hard enough? Shouldn't we be able to relax during the brief times we have for it?"

"Yeah," said Leyten, a tall, stout man with curly hair. "That's right."

No," Kaladin snapped. "Bridge runs exhaust us because we spend most of our days lounging. Oh, I know we have chores—foraging in the chasms, cleaning latrines, scrubbing floors. But the soldiers don't expect us to work hard; they just want us busy. The work helps them ignore us.

"As your bridgeleader, my primary duty is to keep you alive. There's not much I can do about the Parshendi arrows, so I have to do something about *you.* I have to make you stronger, so that when you charge that last leg of a bridge run—arrows flying—you can run quickly." He met the eyes of the men in the line, one at a time. "I intend to see that Bridge Four never loses another man."

The men stared at him incredulously. Finally, a hefty, thick-limbed man at the back bellowed out a laugh. He had tan skin, deep red hair, and was nearly seven feet tall, with large arms and a powerful torso. The Unkalaki—simply called Horneaters by most—were a group of people from the middle of Roshar, near Jah Keved. He'd given his name as "Rock" the previous night.

"Crazy!" said the Horneater. "Is crazy man who now thinks to lead us!" He laughed in a deep-bellied way. The others joined him, shaking their heads at Kaladin's speech. A few laughterspren—minnowlike silver spirits that darted through the air in circular patterns—began to zip about them.

"Hey Gaz," Moash called, cupping his hand around his mouth.

The short, one-eyed sergeant was chatting with some soldiers nearby. "What?" Gaz yelled back with a scowl.

"This one wants us to carry bridges about as practice," Moash called back. "Do we have to do what he says?"

"Bah," Gaz said, waving a hand. "Bridgeleaders only have authority in the field."

Moash glanced back at Kaladin. "Looks like you can storm off, friend. Unless you're going to beat us all into submission."

They broke apart, some men wandering back into the barrack, some walking toward the mess halls. Kaladin was left standing alone on the stones.

"That didn't go so well," Syl said from his shoulder.

"No. It didn't."

"You look surprised."

"No, just frustrated." He glared at Gaz. The bridge sergeant turned away from him pointedly. "In Amaram's army, I was given men who were inexperienced, but never ones who were blatantly insubordinate."

"What's the difference?" Syl asked. Such an innocent question. The answer should have been obvious, but she cocked her head in confusion.

"The men in Amaram's army knew they had worse places they could go. You could punish them. These bridgemen know they've reached the bottom." With a sigh, he let some of his tension bleed away. "I'm lucky I got them out of the barrack."

"So what do you do now?"

"I don't know." Kaladin glanced to the side, where Gaz still stood chatting with the soldiers. "Actually, yes I do."

Gaz caught sight of Kaladin approaching and displayed a look of urgent, wide-eyed horror. He broke off his conversation and hastily rushed around the side of a stack of logs.

"Syl," Kaladin said, "could you follow him for me?"

She smiled, then became a faint line of white, shooting

through the air and leaving a trail that vanished slowly. Kaladin stopped where Gaz had been standing.

Syl zipped back a short time later and reassumed her girlish form. "He's hiding between those two barracks." She pointed. "He's crouched there, watching to see if you follow."

With a smile, Kaladin took the long way around the barracks. In the alleyway, he found a figure crouching in the shadows, watching in the other direction. Kaladin crept forward, then grabbed Gaz's shoulder. Gaz let out a yelp, spinning, swinging. Kaladin caught the fist easily.

Gaz looked up at Kaladin with horror. "I wasn't going to lie! Storm you, you *don't* have authority anywhere other than on the field. If you hurt me again, I'll have you—"

"Calm yourself, Gaz," Kaladin said, releasing the man. "I'm not going to hurt you. Not yet, at least."

The shorter man backed away, rubbing his shoulder and glaring at Kaladin.

"Today's third pass," Kaladin said. "Payday."

"You get your pay in an hour like everyone else."

"No. You have it now; I saw you talking to the courier there." He held out his hand.

Gaz grumbled, but pulled out a pouch and counted spheres. Tiny, tentative white lights shone at their centers. Diamond marks, each worth five diamond chips. A single chip would buy a loaf of bread.

Gaz counted out four marks, though there were five days to a week. He handed them to Kaladin, but Kaladin left his hand open, palm forward. "The other one, Gaz."

"You said—"

"Now."

Gaz jumped, then pulled out a sphere. "You have a strange way of keeping your word, lordling. You promised me . . ."

He trailed off as Kaladin took the sphere he'd just been given and handed it back.

Gaz frowned.

"Don't forget where this comes from, Gaz. I'll keep to my word, but you aren't keeping part of my pay. I'm *giving* it to you. Understand?"

Gaz looked confused, though he did snatch the sphere from Kaladin's hand.

"The money stops coming if something happens to me," Kaladin said, tucking the other four spheres into his pocket. Then he stepped forward. Kaladin was a tall man, and he loomed over the much shorter Gaz. "Remember our bargain. Stay out of my way."

Gaz refused to be intimidated. He spat to the side, the dark spittle clinging to the rock wall, oozing slowly. "I ain't going to lie for you. If you think one cremstained mark a week will—"

"I expect only what I said. What is Bridge Four's camp duty today?"

"Evening meal. Scrubbing and cleaning."

"And bridge duty?"

"Afternoon shift."

That meant the morning would be open. The crew would like that; they could spend payday losing their spheres on gambling or whores, perhaps forgetting for a short time the miserable lives they lived. They'd have to be back for afternoon duty, waiting in the lumberyard in case there was a bridge run. After evening meal, they'd go scrub pots.

Another wasted day. Kaladin turned to walk back to the lumberyard.

"You aren't going to change anything," Gaz called after him. "Those men are bridgemen for a reason."

Kaladin kept walking, Syl zipping down from the roof to land on his shoulder.

"You don't have authority," Gaz called. "You're not some squadleader on the field. You're a storming *bridgeman*. You hear me? You can't have authority without a rank!"

Kaladin left the alleyway behind. "He's wrong."

Syl walked around to hang in front of his face, hovering there while he moved. She cocked her head at him.

"Authority doesn't come from a rank," Kaladin said, fingering the spheres in his pocket.

"Where does it come from?"

"From the men who give it to you. That's the only way to

get it." He looked back the way he'd come. Gaz hadn't left the alleyway yet. "Syl, you don't sleep, do you?"

"Sleep? A spren?" She seemed amused by the concept.

"Would you watch over me at night?" he said. "Make sure Gaz doesn't sneak in and try something while I'm sleeping? He may try to have me killed."

"You think he'd actually do that?"

Kaladin thought for a moment. "No. No, probably not. I've known a dozen men like him—petty bullies with just enough power to be annoying. Gaz is a thug, but I don't think he's a murderer. Besides, in his opinion, he doesn't *have* to hurt me; he just has to wait until I get killed on a bridge run. Still, best to be safe. Watch over me, if you would. Wake me if he tries something."

"Sure. But what if he just goes to more important men? Tells them to execute you?"

Kaladin grimaced. "Then there's nothing I can do. But I don't think he'd do that. It would make him look weak before his superiors."

Besides, beheading was reserved for bridgemen who wouldn't run at the Parshendi. So long as he ran, he wouldn't be executed. In fact, the army leaders seemed hesitant to do much to punish bridgemen at all. One man had committed murder while Kaladin had been a bridgeman, and they'd strung the fool up in a highstorm. But other than that, all Kaladin had seen was a few men get their wages garnished for brawling, and a couple get whipped for being too slow during the early part of a bridge run.

Minimal punishments. The leaders of this army understood. The lives of bridgemen were as close to hopeless as possible; shove them down too much further, and the bridgemen might just stop caring and let themselves be killed.

Unfortunately, that also meant that there wouldn't be much Kaladin could do to punish his own crew, even if he'd had that authority. He had to motivate them in another way. He crossed the lumberyard to where the carpenters were constructing new bridges. After some searching, Kaladin found what he wanted—a thick plank waiting to be fitted into a new portable bridge. A handhold for a bridgeman had been affixed to one side.

"Can I borrow this?" Kaladin asked a passing carpenter.

The man raised a hand to scratch a sawdust-powdered head. "Borrow it?"

"I'll stay right here in the lumberyard," Kaladin explained, lifting the board and putting it on his shoulder. It was heavier than he'd expected, and he was thankful for the padded leather vest.

"We'll need it eventually . . ." the carpenter said, but didn't offer enough of an objection to stop Kaladin from walking away with the plank.

He chose a level stretch of stone directly in front of the barracks. Then he began to trot from one end of the lumberyard to the other, carrying the board on his shoulder, feeling the heat of the rising sun on his skin. He went back and forth, back and forth. He practiced running, walking, and jogging. He practiced carrying the plank on his shoulder, then carrying it up high, arms stretched out.

He worked himself ragged. In fact, he felt close to collapsing several times, but every time he did, he found a reserve of strength from somewhere. So he kept moving, teeth gritted against the pain and fatigue, counting his steps to focus. The apprentice carpenter he'd spoken to brought a supervisor over. That supervisor scratched his head beneath his cap, watching Kaladin. Finally, he shrugged, and the two of them withdrew.

Before long, he drew a small crowd. Workers in the lumberyard, some soldiers, and a large number of bridgemen. Some from the other bridge crews called gibes, but the members of Bridge Four were more withdrawn. Many ignored him. Others—grizzled Teft, youthful-faced Dunny, several more—stood watching in a line, as if they couldn't believe what he was doing.

Those stares—stunned and hostile though they were—were part of what kept Kaladin going. He also ran to work out his frustration, that boiling, churning pot of anger within. Anger at himself for failing Tien. Anger at the Almighty for creating a world where some dined in luxury while others died carrying bridges.

It felt surprisingly good to wear himself down in a way he chose. He felt as he had those first few months after Tien's death, training himself on the spear to forget. When the noon bells rang—calling the soldiers to lunch—Kaladin finally stopped and set the large plank down on the ground. He rolled his shoulder. He'd been running for hours. Where had he found the strength?

He jogged over to the carpenter's station, dripping sweat to the stones, and took a long drink from the water barrel. The carpenters usually chased off bridgemen who tried that, but none said a word as Kaladin slurped down two full ladles of metallic rainwater. He shook the ladle free and nodded to a pair of apprentices, then jogged back to where he'd left the plank.

Rock—the large, tan-skinned Horneater—was hefting it, frowning.

Teft noticed Kaladin, then nodded to Rock. "He bet a few of us a chip each that you'd used a lightweight board to impress us."

If they could have felt his exhaustion, they wouldn't have been so skeptical. He forced himself to take the plank from Rock. The large man let it go with a bewildered look, watching as Kaladin ran the plank back to where he'd found it. He waved his thanks to the apprentice, then trotted back to the small cluster of bridgemen. Rock was reluctantly paying out chips on his bet.

"You're dismissed for lunch," Kaladin told them. "We have afternoon bridge duty, so be back here in an hour. Assemble at the mess hall at last bell before sundown. Our camp chore today is cleaning up after supper. Last one to arrive has to do the pots."

They gave him bemused expressions as he trotted away from the lumberyard. Two streets away, he ducked into an alleyway and leaned against the wall. Then, wheezing, he sank to the ground and stretched out.

He felt as if he'd strained every muscle in his body. His

legs burned, and when he tried to make his hand into a fist, the fingers were too weak to fully comply. He breathed in and out in deep gasps, coughing. A passing soldier peeked in, but when he saw the bridgeman's outfit, he left without a word.

Eventually, Kaladin felt a light touch on his chest. He opened his eyes and found Syl lying prone in the air, face toward his. Her feet were toward the wall, but her posture—indeed, the way her dress hung—made it seem as if she were standing upright, not face toward the ground.

"Kaladin," she said, "I have something to tell you."

He closed his eyes again.

"Kaladin, this is important!" He felt a slight *jolt* of energy on his eyelid. It was a very strange sensation. He grumbled, opening his eyes and forcing himself to sit. She walked in the air, as if circumnavigating an invisible sphere, until she was standing up in the right direction.

"I have decided," Syl declared, "that I'm glad you kept your word to Gaz, even if he is a disgusting person."

It took Kaladin a moment to realize what she was talking about. "The spheres?"

She nodded. "I thought you might break your word, but I'm glad you didn't."

"All right. Well, thank you for telling me, I guess."

"Kaladin," she said petulantly, making fists at her side. "This is *important.*"

"I . . ." He trailed off, then rested his head back against the wall. "Syl, I can barely breathe, let alone think. Please. Just tell me what's bothering you."

"I know what a lie is," she said, moving over and sitting on his knee. "A few weeks ago, I didn't even understand the *concept* of lying. But now I'm happy that you didn't lie. Don't you see?"

"No."

"I'm changing." She shivered—it must have been an intentional action, for her entire figure fuzzed for a moment. "I know things I didn't just a few days ago. It feels so strange."

"Well, I guess that's a good thing. I mean, the more you understand, the better. Right?"

She looked down. "When I found you near the chasm after the highstorm yesterday," she whispered, "you were going to kill yourself, weren't you?"

Kaladin didn't respond. Yesterday. That was an eternity ago.

"I gave you a leaf," she said. "A *poisonous* leaf. You could have used it to kill yourself or someone else. That's what you were probably planning to use it for in the first place, back in the wagons." She looked back up into his eyes, and her tiny voice seemed terrified. "Today, I know what death is. Why do I know what death is, Kaladin?"

Kaladin frowned. "You've always been odd, for a spren. Even from the start."

"From the very start?"

He hesitated, thinking back. No, the first few times she'd come, she'd acted like any other windspren. Playing pranks on him, sticking his shoe to the floor, then hiding. Even when she'd persisted with him during the months of his slavery, she'd acted mostly like any other spren. Losing interest in things quickly, flitting around.

"Yesterday, I didn't know what death was," she said. "Today I do. Months ago, I didn't know I was acting oddly for a spren, but I grew to realize that I was. How do I even know *how* a spren is supposed to act?" She shrank down, looking smaller. "What's happening to me? What am I?"

"I don't know. Does it matter?"

"Shouldn't it?"

"I don't know what I am either. A bridgeman? A surgeon? A soldier? A slave? Those are all just labels. Inside, I'm me. A very different me than I was a year ago, but I can't worry about that, so I just keep moving and hope my feet take me where I need to go."

"You aren't angry at me for bringing you that leaf?"

"Syl, if you hadn't interrupted me, I'd have stepped off into the chasm. That leaf was what I needed. It was the right thing, somehow."

She smiled, and watched as Kaladin began to stretch. Once he finished, he stood and stepped out onto the street again, mostly recovered from his exhaustion. She zipped into the air and rested on his shoulder, sitting with her arms back and her feet hanging down in front, like a girl on the side of a cliff. "I'm glad you're not angry. Though I *do* think that you're to blame for what's happening to me. Before I met you, I never had to think about death or lying."

"That's how I am," he said dryly. "Bringing death and lies wherever I go. Me and the Nightwatcher."

She frowned.

"That was—" he began.

"Yes," she said. "That was sarcasm." She cocked her head. "I know what sarcasm is." Then she smiled deviously. "I know what sarcasm is!"

Stormfather, Kaladin thought, looking into those gleeful little eyes. *That strikes me as ominous.*

"So, wait," he said. "This sort of thing has never happened to you before?"

"I don't know. I can't remember anything farther back than about a year ago, when I first saw you."

"Really?"

"That's not odd," Syl said, shrugging translucent shoulders. "Most spren don't have long memories." She hesitated. "I don't know why I know that."

"Well, maybe this is normal. You could have gone through this cycle before, but you've just forgotten it."

"That's not very comforting. I don't like the idea of forgetting."

"But don't death and lying make you uncomfortable?"

"They do. But, if I were to lose these memories . . ." She glanced into the air, and Kaladin traced her movements, noting a pair of windspren darting through the sky on a gusting breeze, uncaring and free.

"Scared to go onward," Kaladin said, "but terrified to go back to what you were."

She nodded.

"I know how you feel," he said. "Come on. I need to eat, and there are some things I want to pick up after lunch."

You do not agree with my quest. I understand that, so much as it is possible to understand someone with whom I disagree so completely.

Four hours after the chasmfiend attack, Adolin was still overseeing the cleanup. In the struggle, the monster had destroyed the bridge leading back to the warcamps. Fortunately, some soldiers had been left on the other side, and they'd gone to fetch a bridge crew.

Adolin walked amid the soldiers, gathering reports as the late afternoon sun inched toward the horizon. The air had a musty, moldy scent. The smell of greatshell blood. The beast itself lay where it had fallen, chest cut open. Some soldiers were harvesting its carapace amid cremlings that had come out to feast on the carcass. To Adolin's left, long lines of men lay in rows, using cloaks or shirts as pillows on the ragged plateau surface. Surgeons from Dalinar's army tended them. Adolin blessed his father for always bringing the surgeons, even on a routine expedition like this one.

He continued on his way, still wearing his Shardplate. The troops could have made their way back to the warcamps by another route—there was still a bridge on the other side, leading farther out onto the Plains. They could have moved eastward, then wrapped back around. Dalinar, however, had made the call—much to Sadeas's dismay—that they would wait and tend the wounded, resting the few hours it would take to get a bridge crew.

Adolin glanced toward the pavilion, which tinkled with laughter. Several large rubies glowed brightly, set atop poles, with worked golden tines holding them in place. They were fabrials that gave off heat, though there was no fire involved. He didn't understand how fabrials worked, though the more spectacular ones needed large gemstones to function.

Once again, the other lighteyes enjoyed their leisure while he worked. This time he didn't mind. He would have found it difficult to enjoy himself after such a disaster. And it *had* been a disaster. A minor lighteyed officer approached, carrying a final list of casualties. The man's wife read it, then they left him with the sheet and retreated.

There were nearly fifty men dead, twice as many wounded. Many were men Adolin had known. When the king had been given the initial estimate, he had brushed aside the deaths, indicating that they'd be rewarded for their valor with positions in the Heraldic Forces above. He seemed to have conveniently forgotten that he'd have been one of the casualties himself, if not for Dalinar.

Adolin sought out his father with his eyes; Dalinar stood at the edge of the plateau, looking eastward again. What did he search for out there? This wasn't the first time Adolin had seen such extraordinary actions from his father, but they had seemed particularly dramatic. Standing beneath the massive chasmfiend, holding it back from killing his nephew, Plate glowing. That image was fixed in Adolin's memory.

The other lighteyes stepped more lightly around Dalinar now, and during the last few hours, Adolin hadn't heard a single mention of his weakness, not even from Sadeas's men. He feared it wouldn't last. Dalinar *was* heroic, but only infrequently. In the weeks that followed, the others would begin to talk again of how he rarely went on plateau assaults, about how he'd lost his edge.

Adolin found himself thirsting for more. Today when Dalinar had leaped to protect Elhokar, he'd acted like the stories said he had during his youth. Adolin wanted that man back. The kingdom needed him.

Adolin sighed, turning away. He needed to give the final casualty report to the king. Likely he'd be mocked for it, but perhaps—in waiting to deliver it—he might be able to listen in on Sadeas. Adolin still felt he was missing something about that man. Something his father saw, but he did not.

So, steeling himself for the barbs, he made his way toward the pavilion.

※

Dalinar faced eastward with gauntleted hands clasped behind his back. Somewhere out there, at the center of the Plains, the Parshendi made their base camp.

Alethkar had been at war for nearly six years, engaging in an extended siege. The siege strategy had been suggested by Dalinar himself—striking at the Parshendi base would have required camping on the Plains, weathering highstorms, and relying on a large number of fragile bridges. One failed battle, and the Alethi could have found themselves trapped and surrounded, without any way back to fortified positions.

But the Shattered Plains could also be a trap for the Parshendi. The eastern and southern edges were impassable—the plateaus there were weathered to the point that many were little more than spires, and the Parshendi could not jump the distance between them. The Plains were edged by mountains, and packs of chasmfiends prowled the land between, enormous and dangerous.

With the Alethi army boxing them in on the west and north—and with scouts placed south and east just in case—the Parshendi could not escape. Dalinar had argued that the Parshendi would run out of supplies. They'd either have to expose themselves and try to escape the Plains, or would have to attack the Alethi in their fortified warcamps.

It had been an excellent plan. Except, Dalinar hadn't anticipated the gemhearts.

He turned from the chasm, walking across the plateau. He itched to go see to his men, but he needed to show trust in

Adolin. He was in command, and he would do well by it. In fact, it seemed he was already taking some final reports over to Elhokar.

Dalinar smiled, looking at his son. Adolin was shorter than Dalinar, and his hair was blond mixed with black. The blond was an inheritance from his mother, or so Dalinar had been told. Dalinar himself remembered nothing of the woman. She had been excised from his memory, leaving strange gaps and foggy areas. Sometimes he could remember an exact scene, with everyone else crisp and clear, but *she* was a blur. He couldn't even remember her name. When others spoke it, it slipped from his mind, like a pat of butter sliding off a too-hot knife.

He left Adolin to make his report and walked up to the chasmfiend's carcass. It lay slumped over on its side, eyes burned out, mouth lying open. There was no tongue, just the curious teeth of a greatshell, with a strange, complex network of jaws. Some flat platelike teeth for crushing and destroying shells and other, smaller mandibles for ripping off flesh or shoving it deeper into the throat. Rockbuds had opened nearby, their vines reaching out to lap up the beast's blood. There was a connection between a man and the beast he hunted, and Dalinar always felt a strange melancholy after killing a creature as majestic as a chasmfiend.

Most gemhearts were harvested quite differently than the one had been today. Sometime during the strange life cycle of the chasmfiends, they sought the western side of the Plains, where the plateaus were wider. They climbed up onto the tops and made a rocky chrysalis, waiting for the coming of a highstorm.

During that time, they were vulnerable. You just had to get to the plateau where it rested, break into its chrysalis with some mallets or a Shardblade, then cut out the gemheart. Easy work for a fortune. And the beasts came frequently, often several times a week, so long as the weather didn't get too cold.

Dalinar looked up at the hulking carcass. Tiny, near-invisible spren were floating out of the beast's body, vanishing into the air. They looked like the tongues of smoke that might come off a candle after being snuffed. Nobody knew what kind of spren they were; you only saw them around the freshly killed bodies of greatshells.

He shook his head. The gemhearts had changed everything for the war. The Parshendi wanted them too, wanted them badly enough to extend themselves. Fighting the Parshendi for the greatshells made sense, for the Parshendi could not replenish their troops from home as the Alethi could. So contests over the greatshells were both profitable and a tactically sound way of advancing the siege.

With the evening coming on, Dalinar could see lights twinkling across the Plains. Towers where men watched for chasmfiends coming up to pupate. They'd watch through the night, though chasmfiends rarely came in the evening or night. The scouts crossed chasms with jumping poles, moving very lightly from plateau to plateau without the need of bridges. Once a chasmfiend was spotted the scouts would sound warning, and it became a race—Alethi against Parshendi. Seize the plateau and hold it long enough to get out the gemheart, attack the enemy if they got there first.

Each highprince wanted those gemhearts. Paying and feeding thousands of troops was not cheap, but a single gemheart could cover a highprince's expenses for months. Beyond that, the larger a gemstone was when used by a Soulcaster, the less likely it was to shatter. Enormous gemheart stones offered near-limitless potential. And so, the highprinces raced. The first one to a chrysalis got to fight the Parshendi for the gemheart.

They could have taken turns, but that was not the Alethi way. Competition was doctrine to them. Vorinism taught that the finest warriors would have the holy privilege of joining the Heralds after death, fighting to reclaim the Tranquiline Halls from the Voidbringers. The highprinces were allies, but they were also rivals. To give up a gemheart to another . . . well, it felt wrong. Better to have a contest. And so what had been a war had become sport instead. Deadly sport—but that was the best kind.

Dalinar left the fallen chasmfiend behind. He understood each step in the process of what had happened during these six years. He'd even hastened some of them. Only now did he worry. They *were* making headway in cutting down the Parshendi numbers, but the original goal of vengeance for Gavilar's murder had nearly been forgotten. The Alethi lounged, they played, and they idled.

Even though they'd killed plenty of Parshendi—as many as a quarter of their originally estimated forces were dead—this was just taking so long. The siege had lasted six years, and could easily take another six. That troubled him. Obviously the Parshendi had expected to be besieged here. They'd prepared supply dumps and had been ready to move their entire population to the Shattered Plains, where they could use these Heralds-forsaken chasms and plateaus like hundreds of moats and fortifications.

Elhokar had sent messengers, demanding to know why the Parshendi had killed his father. They had never given an answer. They'd taken credit for his murder, but had offered no explanation. Of late, it seemed that Dalinar was the only one who still wondered about that.

Dalinar turned to the side; Elhokar's attendants had retired to the pavilion, enjoying wine and refreshments. The large open-sided tent was dyed violet and yellow, and a light breeze ruffled the canvas. There was a small chance that another highstorm might arrive tonight, the stormwardens said. Almighty send that the army was back to the camp if one did come.

Highstorms. Visions.

Unite them. . . .

Did he really believe in what he'd seen? Did he really think that the Almighty himself had spoken to him? Dalinar Kholin, the Blackthorn, a fearsome warlord?

Unite them.

At the pavilion, Sadeas walked out into the night. He had removed his helm, revealing a head of thick black hair that curled and tumbled around his shoulders. He cut an imposing figure in his Plate; he certainly looked much better in armor than he did wearing one of those ridiculous costumes of lace and silk that were popular these days.

Sadeas caught Dalinar's eyes, nodding slightly. *My part is done,* that nod said. Sadeas strolled for a moment, then reentered the pavilion.

So. Sadeas had remembered the reason for inviting Vamah on the hunt. Dalinar would have to seek out Vamah. He made his way toward the pavilion. Adolin and Renarin lurked near the king. Had the lad given his report yet? It seemed likely that Adolin was trying—yet again—to listen in on Sadeas's conversations with the king. Dalinar would have to do something about that; the boy's personal rivalry with Sadeas was understandable, perhaps, but counterproductive.

Sadeas was chatting with the king. Dalinar made to go find Vamah—the other highprince was near the back of the pavilion—but the king interrupted him.

"Dalinar," the king said. "Come here. Sadeas tells me he has won three gemhearts in the last few weeks alone!"

"He has indeed," Dalinar said, approaching.

"How many have you won?"

"Including the one today?"

"No," the king said. "Before this."

"None, Your Majesty," Dalinar admitted.

"It's Sadeas's bridges," Elhokar said. "They're more efficient than yours."

"I may not have won anything the last few weeks," Dalinar said stiffly, "but my army has won its share of skirmishes in the past." *And the gemhearts can go to Damnation, for all I care.*

"Perhaps," Elhokar said, "but what have you done lately?"

"I have been busy with other important things."

Sadeas raised an eyebrow. "More important than the war? More important than vengeance? Is that possible? Or are you just making excuses?"

Dalinar gave the other highprince a pointed look. Sadeas just shrugged. They were allies, but they were *not* friends. Not any longer.

"You should switch to bridges like his," Elhokar said.

"Your Majesty," Dalinar said. "Sadeas's bridges waste many lives."

"But they are also fast," Sadeas said smoothly. "Relying on wheeled bridges is foolish, Dalinar. Getting them over this plateau terrain is slow and plodding."

"The Codes state that a general may not ask a man to do anything he would not do himself. Tell me, Sadeas. Would *you* run at the front of those bridges you use?"

"I wouldn't eat gruel either," Sadeas said dryly, "or cut ditches."

"But you might if you had to," Dalinar said. "The bridges are different. Stormfather, you don't even let them use armor or shields! Would you enter combat without your Plate?"

"The bridgemen serve a very important function," Sadeas snapped. "They distract the Parshendi from firing at my soldiers. I tried giving them shields at first. And you know what? The Parshendi ignored the bridgemen and fired volleys onto my soldiers and horses. I found that by doubling the number of bridges on a run, then making them extremely light—no armor, no shields to slow them—the bridgemen work far better.

"You see, Dalinar? The Parshendi are too tempted by the exposed bridgemen to fire at anyone else! Yes, we lose a few bridge crews in each assault, but rarely so many that it hinders us. The Parshendi just keep firing at them—I assume that, for whatever reason, they think killing the bridgemen hurts us. As if an unarmored man carrying a bridge was worth the same to the army as a mounted knight in Plate." Sadeas shook his head in amusement at the thought.

Dalinar frowned. *Brother,* Gavilar had written. *You must find the most important words a man can say. . . .* A quote from the ancient text *The Way of Kings.* It would disagree strongly with the things Sadeas was implying.

"Regardless," Sadeas continued. "Surely you can't argue with how effective my method has been."

"Sometimes," Dalinar said, "the prize is not worth the costs. The means by which we achieve victory are as important as the victory itself."

Sadeas looked at Dalinar incredulously. Even Adolin and Renarin—who had come closer—seemed shocked by the statement. It was a very un-Alethi way of thinking.

With the visions and the words of that book spinning in his mind lately, Dalinar wasn't feeling particularly Alethi.

"The prize is worth *any* cost, Brightlord Dalinar," Sadeas said. "Winning the competition is worth any effort, any expense."

"It is a war," Dalinar said. "*Not* a contest."

"Everything is a contest," Sadeas said with a wave of his hand. "All dealings among men are a contest in which some will succeed and others fail. And some are failing quite spectacularly."

"My father is one of the most renowned warriors in Alethkar!" Adolin snapped, butting into the group. The king raised an eyebrow at him, but otherwise stayed out of the conversation. "You saw what he did earlier, Sadeas, while you were hiding back by the pavilion with your bow. My father held off the beast. You're a cowa—"

"Adolin!" Dalinar said. That was going too far. "Restrain yourself."

Adolin clenched his jaw, hand to his side, as if itching to summon his Shardblade. Renarin stepped forward and gently placed a hand on Adolin's arm. Reluctantly, Adolin backed down.

Sadeas turned to Dalinar, smirking. "One son can barely control himself, and the other is incompetent. This is your legacy, old friend?"

"I am proud of them both, Sadeas, whatever you think."

"The firebrand I can understand," Sadeas said. "You were once impetuous just like him. But the other one? You saw how he ran out onto the field today. He even forgot to draw his sword or bow! He's useless!"

Renarin flushed, looking down. Adolin snapped his head up. He thrust his hand to the side again, stepping forward toward Sadeas.

"Adolin!" Dalinar said. "I will handle this!"

Adolin looked at him, blue eyes alight with rage, but he did not summon his Blade.

Dalinar turned his attention to Sadeas, speaking very softly, very pointedly. "Sadeas. Surely I did not just hear you openly—before the king—call my son *useless*. Surely you would not say that, as such an insult would *demand* that I summon my Blade and seek your blood. Shatter the Vengeance Pact. Cause the king's two greatest allies to kill one another. Surely you would not have been that foolish. Surely I misheard."

Everything grew still. Sadeas hesitated. He didn't back down; he met Dalinar's gaze. But he did hesitate.

"Perhaps," Sadeas said slowly, "you did hear the wrong words. I would not insult your son. That would not have been . . . wise of me."

An understanding passed between them, stares locked, and Dalinar nodded. Sadeas did as well—one curt nod of the head. They would not let their hatred of one another become a danger to the king. Barbs were one thing, but dueling offenses were another. They couldn't risk that.

"Well," Elhokar said. He allowed his highprinces to jostle and contend for status and influence. He believed they were all stronger for it, and few faulted him; it was an established method of rule. More and more, Dalinar found himself disagreeing.

Unite them. . . .

"I guess we can be done with that," Elhokar said.

To the side, Adolin looked unsatisfied, as if he'd really been hoping that Dalinar would summon his Blade and confront Sadeas. Dalinar's own blood felt hot, the Thrill tempting him, but he shoved it down. No. Not here. Not now. Not while Elhokar needed them.

"Perhaps we can be done, Your Majesty," Sadeas said. "Though I doubt this particular discussion between Dalinar and me will ever be done. At least until he relearns how to act as a man should."

"I said that is quite enough, Sadeas," Elhokar said.

"Quite enough, you say?" a new voice added. "I believe that a single word from Sadeas is 'quite enough' for anyone." Wit picked his way through the groups of attendants, holding a cup of wine in one hand, silver sword belted at his side.

"Wit!" Elhokar exclaimed. "When did you get here?"

"I caught up to your party just before the battle, Your Majesty," Wit said, bowing. "I was going to speak with you, but the chasmfiend beat me to you. I hear your conversation with it was rather energizing."

"But, you arrived hours ago, then! What have you been doing? How could I have missed seeing you here?"

"I had . . . things to be about," Wit said. "But I couldn't stay away from the hunt. I wouldn't want you to lack for me."

"I've done well so far."

"And yet, you were still Witless," Wit noted.

Dalinar studied the black-clad man. What to make of Wit? He *was* clever. And yet, he was too free with his thoughts, as he'd shown with Renarin earlier. This Wit had a strange air about him that Dalinar couldn't quite place.

"Brightlord Sadeas," Wit said, taking a sip of wine. "I'm terribly sorry to see you here."

"I should think," Sadeas said dryly, "that you would be happy to see me. I seem always to provide you with such entertainment."

"That is unfortunately true," Wit said.

"Unfortunately?"

"Yes. You see, Sadeas, you make it too easy. An uneducated, half-brained serving boy with a hangover could make mock of you. I am left with no need to exert myself, and your very nature makes mockery of my mockery. And so it is that through sheer stupidity you make me look incompetent."

"Really, Elhokar," Sadeas said. "Must we put up with this . . . creature?"

"I like him," Elhokar said, smiling. "He makes me laugh."

"At the expense of those who are loyal to you."

"Expense?" Wit cut in. "Sadeas, I don't believe you've ever paid me a sphere. Though no, please, don't offer. I can't take your money, as I know how many others you *must* pay to get what you wish of them."

Sadeas flushed, but kept his temper. "A whore joke, Wit? Is that the best you can manage?"

Wit shrugged. "I point out truths when I see them, Brightlord Sadeas. Each man has his place. Mine is to make insults. Yours is to be in-sluts."

Sadeas froze, then grew red-faced. "You are a fool."

"If the Wit is a fool, then it is a sorry state for men. I shall offer you this, Sadeas. If you can speak, yet say nothing ridiculous, I will leave you alone for the rest of the week."

"Well, I think that shouldn't be too difficult."

"And yet you failed," Wit said, sighing. "For you said 'I think' and I can imagine nothing so ridiculous as the concept of *you* thinking. What of you, young Prince Renarin? Your father wishes me to leave you alone. Can you speak, yet say nothing ridiculous?"

Eyes turned toward Renarin, who stood just behind his brother. Renarin hesitated, eyes opening wide at the attention. Dalinar grew tense.

"Nothing ridiculous," Renarin said slowly.

Wit laughed. "Yes, I suppose that will satisfy me. Very clever. If Brightlord Sadeas should lose control of himself and finally kill me, perhaps you can be King's Wit in my stead. You seem to have the mind for it."

Renarin perked up, which darkened Sadeas's mood further. Dalinar eyed the highprince; Sadeas's hand had gone to his sword. Not a Shardblade, for Sadeas didn't have one. But he did carry a lighteyes's side sword. Plenty deadly; Dalinar had fought beside Sadeas on many occasions, and the man was an expert swordsman.

Wit stepped forward. "So what of it, Sadeas?" he asked softly. "You going to do Alethkar a favor and rid it of us both?"

Killing the King's Wit was legal. But by so doing, Sadeas would forfeit his title and lands. Most men found it a poor enough trade not to do it in the open. Of course, if you could assassinate a Wit without anyone knowing it was you, that was something different.

Sadeas slowly removed his hand from the hilt of his sword, then nodded curtly to the king and strode away.

"Wit," Elhokar said, "Sadeas has my favor. There's no need to torment him so."

"I disagree," Wit said. "The king's favor may be torment enough for most men, but not him."

The king sighed and looked toward Dalinar. "I should go placate Sadeas. I've been meaning to ask you, though. Have you looked into the issue I asked you about earlier?"

Dalinar shook his head. "I have been busy with the needs of the army. But I will look into it now, Your Majesty."

The king nodded, then hastened off after Sadeas.

"What was that, Father?" Adolin asked. "Is it about the people he thinks were spying on him?"

"No," Dalinar said. "This is something new. I'll show you shortly."

Dalinar looked toward Wit. The black-clad man was popping his knuckles one at a time, looking at Sadeas, seeming contemplative. He noticed Dalinar watching and winked, then walked away.

"I *like* him," Adolin repeated.

"I might be persuaded to agree," Dalinar said, rubbing his chin. "Renarin," Dalinar said, "go and get a report on the wounded. Adolin, come with me. We need to check into the matter the king spoke of."

Both young men looked confused, but they did as requested. Dalinar started across the plateau toward where the carcass of the chasmfiend lay.

Let us see what your worries have brought us this time, nephew, he thought.

∴

Adolin turned the long leather strap over in his hands. Almost a handspan wide and a finger's width thick, the strap ended in a ragged tear. It was the girth to the king's saddle, the strap that wrapped under the horse's barrel. It had broken suddenly during the fight, throwing the saddle—and the king—from horseback.

"What do you think?" Dalinar asked.

"I don't know," Adolin said. "It doesn't *look* that worn, but I guess it was, otherwise it wouldn't have snapped, right?

Dalinar took the strap back, looking contemplative. The soldiers still hadn't returned with the bridge crew, though the sky was darkening.

"Father," Adolin said. "Why would Elhokar ask us to look into this? Does he expect us to discipline the grooms for not properly caring for his saddle? Is it . . ." Adolin trailed off, and he suddenly understood his father's hesitation. "The king thinks the strap was cut, doesn't he?"

Dalinar nodded. He turned it over in his gauntleted fingers, and Adolin could see him thinking about it. A girth could get so worn that it would snap, particularly when strained by the weight of a man in Shardplate. This strap had broken off at the point where it had been affixed to the saddle, so it would have been easy for the grooms to miss it. That was the most rational explanation. But when looked at with slightly more irrational eyes, it could seem that something nefarious had happened.

"Father," Adolin said, "he's getting increasingly paranoid. You know he is."

Dalinar didn't reply.

"He sees assassins in every shadow," Adolin continued. "Straps break. That doesn't mean someone tried to kill him."

"If the king is worried," Dalinar said, "we should look into it. The break *is* smoother on one side, as if it were sliced so that it would rip when it was stressed."

Adolin frowned. "Maybe." He hadn't noticed that. "But think about it, Father. Why would someone cut his strap? A fall from horseback wouldn't harm a Shardbearer. If it was an assassination attempt, then it was an incompetent one."

"If it was an assassination attempt," Dalinar said, "even an incompetent one, then we have something to worry about. It happened on our watch, and his horse was cared for by our grooms. We will look into this."

Adolin groaned, some of his frustration slipping out. "The others already whisper that we've become bodyguards and pets of the king. What will they say if they hear that we're chasing down his every paranoid worry, no matter how irrational?"

"I have never cared what they say."

"We spend all our time on bureaucracy while others win wealth and glory. We rarely go on plateau assaults because we're busy doing things like *this*! We need to be out there, fighting, if we're ever going to catch up to Sadeas!"

Dalinar looked at him, frown deepening, and Adolin bit off his next outburst.

"I see that we're no longer talking about this broken girth," Dalinar said.

"I . . . I'm sorry. I spoke in haste."

"Perhaps you did. But then again, perhaps I needed to hear it. I noticed that you didn't particularly like how I held you back from Sadeas earlier."

"I know you hate him too, Father."

"You do not know as much as you presume you do," Dalinar said. "We'll do something about that in a moment. For now, I swear . . . this strap *does* look like it was cut. Perhaps there is something we're not seeing. This could have been part of something larger that didn't work the way it had been anticipated."

Adolin hesitated. It seemed overcomplicated, but if there was a group who liked their plots overly complicated, it was the Alethi lighteyes. "Do you think one of the highprinces may have tried something?"

"Maybe," Dalinar said. "But I doubt any of them want him dead. So long as Elhokar rules, the highprinces get to fight in this war their way and fatten their purses. He doesn't make many demands of them. They like having him as their king."

"Men can covet the throne for the distinction alone."

"True. When we return, see if anyone has been bragging too much of late. Check to see if Roion is still bitter about Wit's insult at the feast last week and have Talata go over the contracts Highprince Bethab offered to the king for the use of his chulls. In previous contracts, he's tried to slip in language that would favor his claim in a succession. He's been bold ever since your aunt Navani left."

Adolin nodded.

"See if you can backtrack the girth's history," Dalinar said. "Have a leatherworker look at it and tell you what he thinks of the rip. Ask the grooms if they noticed anything, and watch to see if any have received any suspicious windfalls of spheres lately." He hesitated. "And double the king's guard."

Adolin turned, glancing at the pavilion. Sadeas was strolling out of it. Adolin narrowed his eyes. "Do you think—"

"No," Dalinar interrupted.

"Sadeas is an eel."

"Son, you *have* to stop fixating on him. He likes Elhokar, which can't be said of most of the others. He's one of the few I'd trust the king's safety to."

"I wouldn't do the same, Father, I can tell you that."

Dalinar fell silent for a moment. "Come with me." He handed Adolin the saddle strap, then began to cross the plateau toward the pavilion. "I want to show you something about Sadeas."

Resigned, Adolin followed. They passed the lit pavilion. Inside, darkeyed men served food and drink while women sat and scribed messages or wrote accounts of the battle. The lighteyes spoke with one another in verbose, excited tones, complimenting the king's bravery. The men wore dark, masculine colors: maroon, navy, forest green, deep burnt orange.

Dalinar approached Highprince Vamah, who stood outside the pavilion with a group of his own lighteyed attendants. He was dressed in a fashionable long brown coat that had slashes cut through it to expose the bright yellow silk lining. It was a subdued fashion, not as ostentatious as wearing silks on the outside. Adolin thought it looked nice.

Vamah himself was a round-faced, balding man. The short hair that remained stuck straight up, and he had light grey eyes. He had a habit of squinting—which he did as Dalinar and Adolin approached.

What is this about? Adolin wondered.

"Brightlord," Dalinar said to Vamah. "I have come to make certain your comfort has been seen to."

"My comfort would be *best* seen to if we could be on our way back." Vamah glared over at the setting sun, as if blaming it for some misdeed. He wasn't normally so foul-mooded.

"I'm certain that my men are moving as quickly as they can," Dalinar said.

"It wouldn't be nearly as late if you hadn't slowed us so much on the way here," Vamah said.

"I like to be careful," Dalinar said. "And, speaking of care, there is something I've been meaning to talk to you about. Might my son and I speak to you alone for a moment?"

Vamah scowled, but let Dalinar lead him away from his attendants. Adolin followed, more and more baffled.

"The beast was a large one," Dalinar said to Vamah, nodding toward the fallen chasmfiend. "The biggest I've seen."

"I suppose."

"I hear you've had success on your recent plateau assaults, killing a few cocooned chasmfiends of your own. You are to be congratulated."

Vamah shrugged. "The ones we won were small. Nothing like that gemheart that Elhokar took today."

"A small gemheart is better than none," Dalinar said politely. "I hear that you have plans to augment the walls of your warcamp."

"Hum? Yes. Fill in a few of the gaps, improve the fortification."

"I'll be certain to tell His Majesty that you'll be wanting to purchase extra access to the Soulcasters."

Vamah turned to him, frowning. "Soulcasters?"

"For lumber," Dalinar said evenly. "Surely you don't intend to fill in the walls without using scaffolding? Out here, on these remote plains, it's fortunate that we have Soulcasters to provide things like wood, wouldn't you say?"

"Er, yes," Vamah said, expression darkening further. Adolin looked from him to his father. There was a subtext to the conversation. Dalinar wasn't speaking only of wood for the walls—the Soulcasters were the means by which all of the highprinces fed their armies.

"The king is quite generous in allowing access to the Soulcasters," Dalinar said. "Wouldn't you agree, Vamah?"

"I take your point, Dalinar," Vamah said dryly. "No need to keep bashing the rock into my face."

"I've never been known as a subtle man, Brightlord," Dalinar said. "Just an effective one." He walked away, waving for Adolin to follow. Adolin did so, looking over his shoulder at the other highprince.

"He's been complaining vocally about the fees that Elhokar charges to use his Soulcasters," Dalinar said softly. It was the primary form of taxation the king levied on the highprinces. Elhokar himself didn't fight for, or win, gemhearts except on the occasional hunt. He stood aloof from fighting personally in the war, as was appropriate.

"And so . . . ?" Adolin said.

"So I reminded Vamah of how much he relies on the king."

"I suppose that's important. But what does it have to do with Sadeas?"

Dalinar didn't answer. He kept walking across the plateau, stepping up to the lip of the chasm. Adolin joined him, waiting. A few seconds later, someone approached from behind in clinking Shardplate, then Sadeas stepped up beside Dalinar at the lip of the chasm. Adolin narrowed his eyes at the man, and Sadeas raised an eyebrow, but said nothing about his presence.

"Dalinar," Sadeas said, turning his eyes forward, looking out across the Plains.

"Sadeas." Dalinar's voice was controlled and curt.

"You spoke with Vamah?"

"Yes. He saw through what I was doing."

"Of course he did." There was a hint of amusement in Sadeas's voice. "I wouldn't have expected anything else."

"You told him you were increasing what you charge him for wood?"

Sadeas controlled the only large forest in the region. "Doubling it," Sadeas said.

Adolin looked over his shoulder. Vamah was watching them stand there, and his expression was as thunderous as a highstorm, angerspren boiling up from the ground around him like small pools of bubbling blood. Dalinar and Sadeas together sent him a very sound message. *Why . . . this is probably why they invited him on the hunt,* Adolin realized. *So they could maneuver him.*

"Will it work?" Dalinar asked.

"I'm certain it will," Sadeas said. "Vamah's an agreeable enough fellow, when prodded—he'll see that it's better to use the Soulcasters than spend a fortune running a supply line back to Alethkar."

"Perhaps we should tell the king about these sorts of things," Dalinar said, glancing at the king, who stood in the pavilion, oblivious of what had been done.

Sadeas sighed. "I've tried; he hasn't a mind for this sort of work. Leave the boy to his preoccupations, Dalinar. His are the grand ideals of justice, holding the sword high as he rides against his father's enemies."

"Lately, he seems less preoccupied with the Parshendi, and more worried about assassins in the night," Dalinar said. "The boy's paranoia worries me. I don't know where he gets it."

Sadeas laughed. "Dalinar, are you *serious*?"

"I'm always serious."

"I know, I know. But surely you can see where the boy comes by the paranoia!"

"From the way his father was killed?"

"From the way his uncle treats him! A thousand guards? Halts on each and every plateau to let soldiers 'secure' the next one over? Really, Dalinar?"

"I like to be careful."

"Others call that being paranoid."

"The Codes—"

"The Codes are a bunch of idealized nonsense," Sadeas

said, "devised by poets to describe the way they think things *should* have been."

"Gavilar believed in them."

"And look where it got him."

"And where were you, Sadeas, when he was fighting for his life?"

Sadeas's eyes narrowed. "So we're going to rehash that now? Like old lovers, crossing paths unexpectedly at a feast?"

Adolin's father didn't reply. Once again, Adolin found himself baffled by Dalinar's relationship with Sadeas. Their barbs were genuine; one needed only look in their eyes to see that the men could barely stand one another.

And yet, here they were, apparently planning and executing a joint manipulation of another highprince.

"I'll protect the boy my way," Sadeas said. "You do it your way. But don't complain to me about his paranoia when you insist on wearing your uniform to bed, just in case the Parshendi suddenly decide—against all reason and precedent—to attack the warcamps. 'I don't know where he gets it' indeed!"

"Let's go, Adolin," Dalinar said, turning to stride away. Adolin followed.

"Dalinar," Sadeas called from behind.

Dalinar hesitated, looking back.

"Have you found it yet?" Sadeas asked. "Why he wrote what he did?"

Dalinar shook his head.

"You're not going to find the answer," Sadeas said. "It's a foolish quest, old friend. One that's tearing you apart. I know what happens to you during storms. Your mind is unraveling because of all this stress you put upon yourself."

Dalinar returned to walking away. Adolin hurried after him. What had that last part been about? Why "he" wrote? Men didn't write. Adolin opened his mouth to ask, but he could sense his father's mood. This was not a time to prod him.

He walked with Dalinar up to a small rock hill on the plateau. They picked their way up it to the top, and from there looked out at the fallen chasmfiend. Dalinar's men continued harvesting its meat and carapace.

He and his father stood there for a time, Adolin brimming with questions, yet unable to find a way to phrase them.

Eventually, Dalinar spoke. "Have I ever told you what Gavilar's final words to me were?"

"You haven't. I've always wondered about that night."

"'Brother, follow the Codes tonight. There is something strange upon the winds.' That's what he said to me, the last thing he told me just before we began the treaty-signing celebration."

"I didn't realize that Uncle Gavilar followed the Codes."

"He's the one who first showed them to me. He found them as a relic of old Alethkar, back when we'd first been united. He began following them shortly before he died." Dalinar grew hesitant. "Those were odd days, son. Jasnah and I weren't sure what to think of the changes in Gavilar. At the time, I thought the Codes foolishness, even the one that commanded an officer to avoid strong drink during times of war. Especially that one." His voice grew even softer. "I was unconscious on the ground when Gavilar was murdered. I can remember voices, trying to wake me up, but I was too addled by my wine. I should have been there for him."

He looked to Adolin. "I cannot live in the past. It is foolishness to do so. I blame myself for Gavilar's death, but there is nothing to be done for him now."

Adolin nodded.

"Son, I keep hoping that if I make you follow the Codes long enough, you will see—as I have—their importance. Hopefully you will not need as dramatic an example of it as I did. Regardless, you need to understand. You speak of Sadeas, of beating him, of competing with him. Do you know of Sadeas's part in my brother's death?"

"He was the decoy," Adolin said. Sadeas, Gavilar, and Dalinar had been good friends up until the king's death. Everyone knew it. They had conquered Alethkar together.

"Yes," Dalinar said. "He was with the king and heard the soldiers crying that a Shardbearer was attacking. The decoy idea was Sadeas's plan—he put on one of Gavilar's robes and fled in Gavilar's place. It was suicide, what he did. Wearing no Plate, making a Shardbearer assassin chase him. I honestly think it was one of the bravest things I've ever known a man to do."

"But it failed."

"Yes. And there's a part of me that can never forgive Sadeas for that failure. I know it's irrational, but he should have *been* there, with Gavilar. Just like I should have been. We both failed our king, and we cannot forgive one another. But the two of us are still united in one thing. We made a vow on that day. We'd protect Gavilar's son. No matter what the cost, no matter what other things came between us, *we would protect Elhokar*.

"And so that's why I'm here on these Plains. It isn't wealth or glory. I care nothing for those things, not any longer. I came for the brother I loved, and for the nephew I love in his own right. And, in a way, this is what divides Sadeas and me even as it unites us. Sadeas thinks that the best way to protect Elhokar is to kill the Parshendi. He drives himself, and his men, brutally, to get to those plateaus and fight. I believe a part of him thinks I'm breaking my vow by not doing the same.

"But that's not the way to protect Elhokar. He needs a stable throne, allies that support him, not highprinces that bicker. Making a strong Alethkar will protect him better than killing our enemies will. This was Gavilar's life's work, uniting the highprinces . . ."

He trailed off. Adolin waited for more, but it did not come.

"Sadeas," Adolin finally said. "I'm . . . surprised to hear you call him brave."

"He *is* brave. And cunning. Sometimes, I make the mistake of letting his extravagant dress and mannerisms lead me to underestimate him. But there's a good man inside of him, son. He is not our enemy. We can be petty sometimes, the two of us. But he works to protect Elhokar, so I ask you to respect that."

How did one respond to that? *You hate him, but you ask*

me not to? "All right," Adolin said. "I'll watch myself around him. But, Father, I still don't trust him. Please. At least consider the possibility that he's not as committed as you are, that he's playing you."

"Very well," Dalinar said. "I'll consider it."

Adolin nodded. It was something. "What of what he said at the end? Something about writing?"

Dalinar hesitated. "It is a secret he and I share. Other than us, only Jasnah and Elhokar know of it. I've contemplated for a time whether I should tell you, as you will take my place should I fall. I spoke to you of the last words my brother said to me."

"Asking you to follow the Codes."

"Yes. But there is more. Something else he said to me, but not with spoken words. Instead, these are words that . . . he wrote."

"Gavilar could *write*?"

"When Sadeas discovered the king's body, he found words written on the fragment of a board, using Gavilar's own blood. 'Brother,' they said. 'You must find the most important words a man can say.' Sadeas hid the fragment away, and we later had Jasnah read the words. If it is true that he could write—and other possibilities seem implausible—it was a shameful secret he hid. As I said, his actions grew very odd near the end of his life."

"And what does it mean? Those words?"

"It's a quote," Dalinar said. "From an ancient book called *The Way of Kings*. Gavilar favored readings from the volume near the end of his life—he spoke to me of it often. I didn't realize the quote was from it until recently; Jasnah discovered it for me. I've now had the text of the book read to me a few times, but so far, I find nothing to explain why he wrote what he did." He paused. "The book was used by the Radiants as a kind of guidebook, a book of counsel on how to live their lives."

The Radiants? *Stormfather!* Adolin thought. The delusions his father had . . . they often seemed to have something to do with the Radiants. This was further proof that the delusions were related to Dalinar's guilt over his brother's death.

But what could Adolin do to help?

Metal footsteps ground on the rock behind. Adolin turned, then nodded in respect as the king approached, still wearing his golden Shardplate, though he'd removed the helm. He was several years Adolin's senior, and had a bold face with a prominent nose. Some said they saw in him a kingly air and a regal bearing, and women Adolin trusted had confided that they found the king quite handsome.

Not as handsome as Adolin, of course. But still handsome.

The king was married, however; his wife the queen managed his affairs back in Alethkar. "Uncle," Elhokar said. "Can we not be on our way? I'm certain that we Shardbearers could leap the chasm. You and I could be back at the warcamps shortly."

"I will not leave my men, Your Majesty," Dalinar said. "And I doubt you want to be running across the plateaus for several hours alone, exposed, without proper guards."

"I suppose," the king said. "Either way, I did want to thank you for your bravery today. It appears that I owe you my life yet again."

"Keeping you alive is something else I try very hard to make a habit, Your Majesty."

"I am glad for it. Have you looked into the item I asked you about?" He nodded to the girth, which Adolin realized he was still carrying in a gauntleted hand.

"I did," Dalinar said.

"Well?"

"We couldn't decide, Your Majesty," Dalinar said, taking the strap and handing it to the king. "It *may* have been cut. The tear is smoother along one side. Like it was weakened so that it would rip."

"I knew it!" Elhokar held the strap up and inspected it.

"We are not leatherworkers, Your Majesty," Dalinar said. "We need to give both sides of the strap to experts and get their opinions. I have instructed Adolin to look into the matter further."

"It *was* cut," Elhokar said. "I can see it clearly, right here.

I keep telling you, Uncle. Someone is trying to kill me. They want me, just like they wanted my father."

"Surely you don't think the *Parshendi* did this," Dalinar said, sounding shocked.

"I don't know *who* did it. Perhaps someone on this very hunt."

Adolin frowned. What was Elhokar implying? The majority of the people on this hunt were Dalinar's men.

"Your Majesty," Dalinar said frankly, "we *will* look into the matter. But you have to be prepared to accept that this might have just been an accident."

"You don't believe me," Elhokar said flatly. "You *never* believe me."

Dalinar took a deep breath, and Adolin could see that his father had to struggle to keep his temper. "I'm *not* saying that. Even a potential threat to your life worries me very much. But I *do* suggest that you avoid leaping to conclusions. Adolin has pointed out that this would be a terribly clumsy way to try to kill you. A fall from horseback isn't a serious threat to a man wearing Plate."

"Yes, but during a hunt?" Elhokar said. "Perhaps they wanted the chasmfiend to kill me."

"We weren't supposed to be in danger from the hunt," Dalinar said. "We were *supposed* to pelt the greatshell from a distance, then ride up and butcher it."

Elhokar narrowed his eyes, looking at Dalinar, then at Adolin. It was almost as if the king were suspicious of *them*. The look was gone in a second. Had Adolin imagined it? *Stormfather!* he thought.

From behind, Vamah began calling to the king. Elhokar glanced at him and nodded. "This isn't over, Uncle," he said to Dalinar. "Look into that strap."

"I will."

The king handed the strap back, then left, armor clinking.

"Father," Adolin said immediately, "did you see—"

"I'll speak to him about it," Dalinar said. "Sometime when he isn't so worked up."

"But—"

"I will speak to him, Adolin. You look into that strap. And go gather your men." He nodded toward something in the distant west. "I think I see that bridge crew coming."

Finally, Adolin thought, following his gaze. A small group of figures was crossing the plateau in the distance, bearing Dalinar's banner and leading a bridge crew carrying one of Sadeas's mobile bridges. They'd sent for one of those, as they were faster than Dalinar's larger, chull-pulled bridges.

Adolin hurried off to give the orders, though he found himself distracted by his father's words, Gavilar's final message, and now the king's look of distrust. It seemed he would have plenty to preoccupy his mind on the long ride back to the camps.

⁘

Dalinar watched Adolin rush away to do as ordered. The lad's breastplate still bore a web of cracks, though it had stopped leaking Stormlight. With time, the armor would repair itself. It could re-form even if it was completely shattered.

The lad liked to complain, but he was as good a son as a man could ask for. Fiercely loyal, with initiative and a strong sense of command. The soldiers liked him. Perhaps he was a little too friendly with them, but that could be forgiven. Even his hotheadedness could be forgiven, assuming he learned to channel it.

Dalinar left the young man to his work and went to check on Gallant. He found the Ryshadium with the grooms, who had set up a horse picket on the southern side of the plateau. They had bandaged the horse's scrapes, and he was no longer favoring his leg.

Dalinar patted the large stallion on the neck, looking into those deep black eyes. The horse seemed ashamed. "It wasn't your fault you threw me, Gallant," Dalinar said in a soothing voice. "I'm just glad you weren't harmed too badly." He turned to a nearby groom. "Give him extra feed this evening, and two crispmelons."

"Yes sir, Brightlord. But he won't eat extra food. He never does if we try to give it to him."

"He'll eat it tonight," Dalinar said, patting the Ryshadium's neck again. "He only eats it when he feels he deserves it, son."

The lad seemed confused. Like most of them, he thought of Ryshadium as just another breed of horse. A man couldn't really understand until he'd had one accept him as rider. It was like wearing Shardplate, an experience that was completely indescribable.

"You'll eat both of those crispmelons," Dalinar said, pointing at the horse. "You deserve them."

Gallant blustered.

"You *do*," Dalinar said. The horse nickered, seeming content. Dalinar checked the leg, then nodded to the groom. "Take good care of him, son. I'll ride another horse back."

"Yes, Brightlord."

They got him a mount—a sturdy, dust-colored mare. He was extra careful when he swung into the saddle. Ordinary horses always seemed so fragile to him.

The king rode out after the first squad of troops, Wit at his side. Sadeas, Dalinar noted, rode behind, where Wit couldn't get at him.

The bridge crew waited silently, resting as the king and his procession crossed. Like most of Sadeas's bridge crews, this one was constructed from a jumble of human refuse. Foreigners, deserters, thieves, murderers, and slaves. Many probably deserved their punishment, but the frightful way Sadeas chewed through them put Dalinar on edge. How long would it be before he could no longer fill the bridge crews with the suitably expendable? Did any man, even a murderer, deserve such a fate?

A passage from *The Way of Kings* came to Dalinar's head unbidden. He'd been listening to readings from the book more often than he'd represented to Adolin.

I once saw a spindly man carrying a stone larger than his head upon his back, the passage went. *He stumbled beneath the weight, shirtless under the sun, wearing only a loincloth.*

He tottered down a busy thoroughfare. People made way for him. Not because they sympathized with him, but because they feared the momentum of his steps. You dare not impede one such as this.

The monarch is like this man, stumbling along, the weight of a kingdom on his shoulders. Many give way before him, but so few are willing to step in and help carry the stone. They do not wish to attach themselves to the work, lest they condemn themselves to a life full of extra burdens.

I left my carriage that day and took up the stone, lifting it for the man. I believe my guards were embarrassed. One can ignore a poor shirtless wretch doing such labor, but none ignore a king sharing the load. Perhaps we should switch places more often. If a king is seen to assume the burden of the poorest of men, perhaps there will be those who will help him with his own load, so invisible, yet so daunting.

Dalinar was shocked that he could remember the story word for word, though he probably shouldn't have been. In searching for the meaning behind Gavilar's last message, he'd listened to readings from the book almost every day of the last few months.

He'd been disappointed to find that there was no clear meaning behind the quote Gavilar had left. He'd continued to listen anyway, though he tried to keep his interest quiet. The book did not have a good reputation, and not just because it was associated with the Lost Radiants. Stories of a king doing the work of a menial laborer were the least of its discomforting passages. In other places, it outright said that lighteyes were *beneath* darkeyes. That contradicted Vorin teachings.

Yes, best to keep this quiet. Dalinar had spoken truly when he'd told Adolin he didn't care what people said about him. But when the rumors impeded his ability to protect Elhokar, they could become dangerous. He had to be careful.

He turned his mount and clopped up onto the bridge, then nodded his thanks to the bridgemen. They were the lowest in the army, and yet they bore the weight of kings.

ALETHI CODES OF WAR

Readiness · The officer will be prepared at all times for battle. Never drunken on wine, never without his weapon.

Inspiration · The officer will wear his uniform when in public, to look ready for war and to give strength to his troops.

Restraint · The officer will refrain from needless duels, arguments, or squabbles with other officers in camp, to prevent injury to men who may be needed to command.

Leadership
The officer will require no action of his soldiers that he would not be willing to perform himself.

Honor
The officer will not abandon allies on the field, nor will he seek to profit from the loss of his allies.

16

COCOONS

SEVEN AND A HALF YEARS AGO

"He wants to send me to Kharbranth," Kal said, perched atop his rock. "To train to become a surgeon."

"What, *really*?" Laral asked, as she walked across the edge of the rock just in front of him. She had golden streaks in her otherwise black hair. She wore it long, and it streamed out behind her in a gust of wind as she balanced, hands out to the sides.

The hair was distinctive. But, of course, her eyes were more so. Bright, pale green. So different from the browns and blacks of the townspeople. There really *was* something different about being a lighteyes.

"Yes, really," Kal said with a grunt. "He's been talking about it for a couple of years now."

"And you didn't tell me?"

Kal shrugged. He and Laral were atop a low ridge of boulders to the east of Hearthstone. Tien, his younger brother, was picking through rocks at the base. To Kal's right, a grouping of shallow hillsides rolled to the west. They were sprinkled with lavis polyps, a planting halfway to being harvested.

He felt oddly sad as he looked over those hillsides, filled with working men. The dark brown polyps would grow like melons filled with grain. After being dried, that grain would feed the entire town and their highprince's armies. The ardents who passed through town were careful to explain that the Calling of a farmer was a noble one, one of the highest save for the Calling of a soldier. Kal's father whispered under his breath that he saw far more honor in feeding the kingdom than he did in fighting and dying in useless wars.

"Kal?" Laral said, voice insistent. "Why didn't you *tell* me?"

"Sorry," he said. "I wasn't sure if Father was serious or not. So I didn't say anything."

That was a lie. He'd known his father was serious. Kal just hadn't wanted to mention leaving to become a surgeon, particularly not to Laral.

She placed her hands on her hips. "I thought you were going to go become a soldier."

Kal shrugged.

She rolled her eyes, hopping down off her ridge onto a stone beside him. "Don't you want to become a lighteyes? Win a Shardblade?"

"Father says that doesn't happen very often."

She knelt down before him. "I'm sure *you* could do it." Those eyes, so bright and alive, shimmering green, the color of life itself.

More and more, Kal found that he liked looking at Laral. Kal knew, logically, what was happening to him. His father had explained the process of growing with the precision of a surgeon. But there was so much *feeling* involved, emotions that his father's sterile descriptions hadn't explained. Some of those emotions were about Laral and the other girls of the town. Other emotions had to do with the strange blanket of melancholy that smothered him at times when he wasn't expecting.

"I . . ." Kal said.

"Look," Laral said, standing up again and climbing atop her rock. Her fine yellow dress ruffled in the wind. One more year, and she'd start wearing a glove on her left hand, the mark that a girl had entered adolescence. "Up, come on. Look."

Kal hauled himself to his feet, looking eastward. There,

snarlbrush grew in dense thickets around the bases of stout markel trees.

"What do you see?" Laral demanded.

"Brown snarlbrush. Looks like it's probably dead."

"The Origin is out there," she said, pointing. "This is the stormlands. Father says we're here to be a windbreak for more timid lands to the west." She turned to him. "We've got a noble heritage, Kal, darkeyes and lighteyes alike. That's why the best warriors have always been from Alethkar. Highprince Sadeas, General Amaram . . . King Gavilar himself."

"I suppose."

She sighed exaggeratedly. "I *hate* talking to you when you're like this, you know."

"Like what?"

"Like you are now. You know. Moping around, sighing."

"*You're* the one who just sighed, Laral."

"You know what I mean."

She stepped down from the rock, walking over to go pout. She did that sometimes. Kal stayed where he was, looking eastward. He wasn't sure how he felt. His father really wanted him to be a surgeon, but he wavered. It wasn't just because of the stories, the excitement and wonder of them. He felt that by being a soldier, he could change things. Really change them. A part of him dreamed of going to war, of protecting Alethkar, of fighting alongside heroic lighteyes. Of doing good someplace other than a little town that nobody important ever visited.

He sat down. Sometimes he dreamed like that. Other times, he found it hard to care about anything. His dreary feelings were like a black eel, coiled inside of him. The snarlbrush out there survived the storms by growing together densely about the bases of the mighty markel trees. Their bark was coated with stone, their branches thick as a man's leg. But now the snarlbrush was dead. It hadn't survived. Pulling together hadn't been enough for it.

"Kaladin?" a voice asked from behind him.

He turned to find Tien. Tien was ten years old, two years Kal's junior, though he looked much younger. While other kids called him a runt, Lirin said that Tien just hadn't hit his height yet. But, well, with those round, flushed cheeks and that slight build, Tien *did* look like a boy half his age. "Kaladin," he said, eyes wide, hands cupped together. "What are you looking at?"

"Dead weeds," Kal said.

"Oh. Well, you *need* to see this."

"What is it?"

Tien opened his hands to reveal a small stone, weathered on all sides but with a jagged break on the bottom. Kal picked it up, looking it over. He couldn't see anything distinctive about it at all. In fact, it was dull.

"It's just a rock," Kal said.

"Not *just* a rock," Tien said, taking out his canteen. He wetted his thumb, then rubbed it on the flat side of the stone. The wetness darkened the stone, and made visible an array of white patterns in the rock. "See?" Tien asked, handing it back.

The strata of the rock alternated white, brown, black. The pattern was remarkable. Of course, it *was* still just a rock. But for some reason, Kal found himself smiling. "That's nice, Tien." He moved to hand the rock back.

Tien shook his head. "I found it for you. To make you feel better."

"I . . ." It was just a stupid rock. Yet, inexplicably, Kal *did* feel better. "Thanks. Hey, you know what? I'll bet there's a lurg or two hiding in these rocks somewhere. Want to see if we can find one?"

"Yes, yes, yes!" Tien said. He laughed and began moving down the rocks. Kal moved to follow, but paused, remembering something his father had said.

He poured some water on his hand from his own canteen and flung it at the brown snarlbrush. Wherever sprayed droplets fell, the brush grew instantly green, as if he were throwing paint. The brush wasn't dead; it just dried out, waiting for the storms to come. Kal watched the patches of green slowly fade back to tan as the water was absorbed.

"Kaladin!" Tien yelled. He often used Kal's full name, even though Kal had asked him not to. "Is this one?"

Kal moved down across the boulders, pocketing the rock he'd been given. As he did so, he passed Laral. She was looking westward, toward her family's mansion. Her father was the citylord of Hearthstone. Kal found his eyes lingering on her again. That hair of hers was beautiful, with the two stark colors.

She turned to Kal and frowned.

"We're going to hunt some lurgs," he explained, smiling and gesturing toward Tien. "Come on."

"You're cheerful suddenly."

"I don't know. I feel better."

"How does he do that? I wonder."

"Who does what?"

"Your brother," Laral said, looking toward Tien. "He changes you."

Tien's head popped up behind some stones and he waved eagerly, bouncing up and down with excitement.

"It's just hard to be gloomy when he's around," Kal said. "Come on. Do you want to watch the lurg or not?"

"I suppose," Laral said with a sigh. She held out a hand toward him.

"What's that for?" Kal asked, looking at her hand.

"To help me down."

"Laral, you're a better climber than me *or* Tien. You don't need help."

"It's polite, stupid," she said, proffering her hand more insistently. Kal sighed and took it, then she proceeded to hop down without even leaning on it or needing his help. *She,* he thought, *has been acting very strange lately.*

The two of them joined Tien, who jumped down into a hollow between some boulders. The younger boy pointed eagerly. A silky patch of white grew in a crevice on the rock. It was made of tiny threads spun together into a ball about the size of a boy's fist.

"I'm right, aren't I?" Tien asked. "That is one?"

Kal lifted the flask and poured water down the side of the stone onto the patch of white. The threads dissolved in the simulated rainwater, the cocoon melting to reveal a small creature with slick brown and green skin. The lurg had six legs that it used to grip the stone, and its eyes were in the center of its back. It hopped off the stone, searching for insects. Tien laughed, watching it bounce from rock to rock, sticking to the stones. It left behind patches of mucus wherever it landed.

Kal leaned back against the stone, watching his brother, remembering days—not so long ago—when chasing lurgs had been more exciting.

"So," Laral said, folding her arms. "What are you going to do? If your father tries to send you to Kharbranth?"

"I don't know," Kal said. "The surgeons won't take anyone before their sixteenth Weeping, so I've got time to think." The best surgeons and healers trained in Kharbranth. Everyone knew that. The city was said to have more hospitals than taverns.

"It sounds like your father is forcing you to do what he wants, not what you want," Laral said.

"That's the way everyone does it," Kal said, scratching his head. "The other boys don't mind becoming farmers because their fathers were farmers, and Ral just became the new town carpenter. He didn't mind that it was what his father did. Why should I mind being a surgeon?"

"I just—" Laral looked angry. "Kal, if you go to war and find a Shardblade, then you'd be a lighteyes. . . . I mean . . . Oh, this is useless." She settled back, folding her arms even more tightly.

Kal scratched his head. She really *was* acting oddly. "I wouldn't mind going to war, winning honor and all that. Mostly, I'd like to travel. See what other lands are like." He'd heard tales of exotic animals, like enormous crustaceans or eels that sang. Of Rall Elorim, City of Shadows, or Kurth, City of Lightning.

He'd spent a lot of time studying these last few years. Kal's mother said he should be allowed to have a childhood, rather than focusing so much on his future. Lirin argued that the tests to be admitted by the Kharbranthian surgeons were very rigorous. If Kal wanted a chance with them, he'd have to begin learning early.

And yet, to become a soldier . . . The other boys dreamed of joining the army, of fighting with King Gavilar. There was talk of going to war with Jah Keved, once and for all. What would it be like, to finally see some of the heroes from stories? To fight with Highprince Sadeas, or Dalinar the Blackthorn?

Eventually, the lurg realized that it had been tricked. It settled down on a rock to spin its cocoon again. Kal grabbed a small, weathered stone off the ground, then laid a hand on Tien's shoulder, stopping the boy from prodding the tired amphibian. Kal moved forward and nudged the lurg with two fingers, making it hop off the boulder and onto his stone. He handed this to Tien, who watched with wide eyes as the lurg spun its cocoon, spitting out the wet silk and using tiny hands to shape it. That cocoon would be watertight from the inside, sealed by dried mucus, but rainwater outside would dissolve the sack.

Kal smiled, then lifted the flask and drank. This was cool, clean water, which had already had the crem settled out. Crem—the sludgy brown material that fell with rainwater—could make a man sick. Everybody knew that, not just surgeons. You always let water sit for a day, then poured off the fresh water on top and used the crem to make pottery.

The lurg eventually finished its cocoon. Tien immediately reached for the flask.

Kal held the flask high. "It'll be tired, Tien. It won't jump around anymore."

"Oh."

Kal lowered the flask, patting his brother's shoulder. "I put it on that stone so you could carry it around. You can get it out later." He smiled. "Or you could drop it in Father's bathwater through the window."

Tien grinned at that prospect. Kal ruffled the boy's dark hair. "Go see if you can find another cocoon. If we catch two, you'll have one to play with *and* one to slip into the bath-water."

Tien carefully set the rock aside, then scampered up over the boulders. The hillside here had broken during a high-storm several months back. Shattered, as if it had been hit by the fist of some enormous creature. People said that it could have been a home that got destroyed. They burned prayers of thanks to the Almighty while at the same time whispering of dangerous things that moved in the darkness at full storm. Were the Voidbringers behind the destruction, or had it been the shades of the Lost Radiants?

Laral was looking toward the mansion again. She smoothed her dress nervously—lately she took far more care, not getting her clothes dirty as she once had.

"You still thinking about war?" Kal asked.

"Um. Yes. I am."

"Makes sense," he said. An army had come through re-cruiting just a few weeks back and had picked up a few of the older boys, though only after Citylord Wistiow had given permission. "What do you think broke the rocks here, during the highstorm?"

"I couldn't say."

Kal looked eastward. What sent the storms? His father said no ship had ever sailed for the Origin of Storms and returned safely. Few ships ever even left the coast. Being caught on the open seas during a storm meant death, so the stories said.

He took another sip from his flask, then capped it, saving the rest in case Tien found another lurg. Distant men worked the fields, wearing overalls, laced brown shirts, and sturdy boots. It was worming season. A single worm could ruin an entire polyp's worth of grain. It would incubate inside, slowly eating as the grain grew. When you finally opened up the polyp in the fall, all you'd find was a big fat slug the size of two men's hands. And so they searched in the spring, going over each polyp. Where they found a burrow, they'd stick in a reed tipped with sugar, which the worm would latch on to. You pulled it out and squished it under your heel, then patched the hole with crem.

It could take weeks to properly worm a field, and farmers usually went over their hills three or four times, fertilizing as they went. Kal had heard the process described a hundred times over. You didn't live in a town like Hearthstone without listening to men gripe about worms.

Oddly, he noticed a group of older boys gathering at the foot of one of the hills. He recognized all of them, of course. Jost and Jest, brothers. Mord, Tift, Naget, Khav, and others. They each had solid, Alethi darkeyes names. Not like Kaladin's own name. It was different.

"Why aren't they worming?" he asked.

"I don't know," Laral said, shifting her attention to the boys. She got an odd look in her eyes. "Let's go see." She started down the hillside before Kal had a chance to object.

He scratched his head, looking toward Tien. "We're going down to the hillside there."

A youthful head popped up behind a boulder. Tien nodded energetically, then turned back to his searching. Kal slipped off the boulder and walked down the slope after Laral. She reached the boys, and they regarded her with uncomfortable expressions. She'd never spent much time with them, not like she had with Kal and Tien. Her father and his were pretty good friends, for all that one was lighteyed and the other dark.

Laral took a perch on a nearby rock, waiting and saying nothing. Kal walked up. Why had she wanted to come down here, if she wasn't going to talk to the other boys?

"Ho, Jost," Kal said. Senior among the boys at fourteen, Jost was nearly a man—and he looked it too. His chest was broad beyond his years, his legs thick and stocky, like those of his father. He was holding a length of wood from a sapling that had been shaved into a rough approximation of a quarterstaff. "Why aren't you worming?"

It was the wrong thing to say, and Kal knew it immediately. Several of the boys' expressions darkened. It was a sore point to them that Kal never had to work the hills. His protests—that he spent hours upon hours memorizing muscles, bones, and cures—fell on uncaring ears. All they saw was a boy who got to spend his days in the shade while they toiled in the burning sun.

"Old Tarn found a patch of polyps that ain't growing right," Jost finally said, shooting a glance at Laral. "Let us go for the day while they talked over whether to try another planting there, or just let them grow and see what comes of it."

Kal nodded, feeling awkward as he stood before the nine boys. They were sweaty, the knees of their trousers stained with crem and patched from rubbing stone. But Kal was clean, wearing a fine pair of trousers his mother had purchased just a few weeks before. His father had sent him and Tien out for the day while he tended to something at the citylord's manor. Kal would pay for the break with late-night studying by Stormlight, but no use explaining that to the other boys.

"So, er," Kal said, "what were you all talking about?"

Rather than answering, Naget said, "Kal, you know things." Light haired and spindly, he was the tallest of the bunch. "Don't you? About the world and the like?"

"Yeah," Kal said, scratching his head. "Sometimes."

"You ever heard of a darkeyes becoming a lighteyes?" Naget asked.

"Sure," Kal said. "It can happen, Father says. Wealthy darkeyed merchants marry lowborn lighteyes and join their family. Then maybe have lighteyed children. That sort of thing."

"No, not like that," Khav said. He had low eyebrows and always seemed to have a perpetual scowl on his face. "You know. Real darkeyes. Like us."

Not like you, the tone seemed to imply. Kal's family were the only one of second nahn in the town. Everyone else was fourth or fifth, and Kal's rank made them uncomfortable around him. His father's strange profession didn't help either.

It all left Kal feeling distinctly out-of-place.

"You know how it can happen," Kal said. "Ask Laral. She was just talking about it. If a man wins a Shardblade on the battlefield, his eyes become light."

"That's right," Laral said. "Everybody knows it. Even a *slave* could become a lighteyes if he won a Shardblade."

The boys nodded; they all had brown, black, or other dark-colored eyes. Winning a Shardblade was one of the main reasons common men went to war. In Vorin kingdoms, everyone had a chance to rise. It was, as Kal's father would say, a fundamental tenet of their society.

"Yeah," Naget said impatiently. "But have you ever *heard* of it happening? Not just in stories, I mean. Does it happen for real?"

"Sure," Kal said. "It must. Otherwise, why would so many men go to war?"

"Because," Jest said, "we've gotta prepare men to fight for the Tranquiline Halls. We've gotta send soldiers to the Heralds. The ardents are always talking of it."

"In the same breaths that they tell us it's all right to be a farmer too," Khav said. "Like, farming's some lonely second place or something."

"Hey," Tift said. "My fah's a farmer, and he's right good at it. It's a noble Calling! All your fahs are farmers."

"All right, fine," Jost said. "But we ain't talking of that. We're talking of Shardbearers. You go to war, you can win a Shardblade and become a lighteyes. My fah, see, he *should* have been given that Shardblade. But the man who was with him, he took it while my fah was knocked out. Told the officer that *he'd* been the one to kill the Shardbearer, so he got the Blade, and my fah—"

He was cut off by Laral's tinkling laughter. Kal frowned. That was a different kind of laughter than he normally heard from her, much more subdued and kind of annoying. "Jost, you're claiming your father won a *Shardblade*?" she said.

"No. It was taken from him," the larger boy said.

"Didn't your father fight in the wastescum skirmishes up north?" Laral said. "Tell him, Kaladin."

"She's right, Jost. There weren't any Shardbearers there—just Reshi raiders who thought they'd take advantage of the new king. They've never had any Shardblades. If your father saw one, he must be remembering incorrectly."

"Remembering incorrectly?" Jost said.

"Er, sure," Kal said quickly. "I'm not saying he's lying, Jost. He just might have some trauma-induced hallucinations, or something like that."

The boys grew silent, looking at Kal. One scratched his head.

Jost spat to the side. He seemed to be watching Laral from the corner of his eye. She pointedly looked at Kal and smiled at him.

"You always got to make a man feel like an idiot, don't you, Kal?" Jost said.

"What? No, I—"

"You want to make my fah sound like a fool," Jost said, face red. "And you want to make me sound stupid. Well, some of us ain't lucky enough to spend our days eating fruit and laying about. We've got to work."

"I don't—"

Jost tossed the quarterstaff to Kal. He caught it awkwardly. Then Jost took the other staff from his brother. "You insult my fah, you get a fight. That's honor. You have honor, lordling?"

"I'm no lordling," Kal spat. "Stormfather, Jost, I'm only a few nahn higher than you are."

Jost's eyes grew angrier at the mention of nahn. He held up his quarterstaff. "You going to fight me or not?" Angerspren began to appear in small pools at his feet, bright red.

Kal knew what Jost was doing. It wasn't uncommon for the boys to look for a way to make themselves look better than him. Kal's father said it had to do with their insecurity. He'd have told Kal to just drop the quarterstaff and walk away.

But Laral was sitting right there, smiling at him. And men didn't become heroes by walking away. "All right. Sure." Kal held up his quarterstaff.

Jost swung immediately, more quickly than Kal had anticipated. The other boys watched with a mixture of glee, shock, and amazement. Kal barely managed to get his staff up. The lengths of wood cracked together, sending a jolt up Kal's arms.

Kal was knocked off balance. Jost moved quickly, stepping to the side and swinging his staff down and hitting Kal in the foot. Kal cried out as a flash of agony lanced up his leg, and he released the staff with one hand and reached down.

Jost swung his staff around and hit Kal's side. Kal gasped, letting the staff clatter to the stones and grabbing his side as he fell to his knees. He breathed out in huffing breaths, straining against the pain. Small, spindly painspren—glowing pale orange hand shapes, like stretching sinew or muscles—crawled from the stone around him.

Kal dropped one hand to the stones, leaning forward as he held his side. *You'd better not have broken any of my ribs, you cremling,* he thought.

To the side, Laral pursed her lips. Kal felt a sudden, overpowering shame.

Jost lowered his staff, looking abashed. "Well," he said. "You can see that my fah trained me right good. Maybe that will show you. The things he says are true, and—"

Kal growled in anger and pain, snatching his quarterstaff from the ground and leaping at Jost. The older boy cursed, stumbling backward as he raised his weapon. Kal bellowed, slamming his weapon forward.

Something changed in that moment. Kal felt an energy as he held the weapon, an excitement that washed away his pain. He spun, smashing the staff into one of Jost's hands.

Jost let go with that hand, screaming. Kal brought his weapon around and slammed it into the boy's side. Kal had never held a weapon before, never been in a fight any more dangerous than a wrestling match with Tien. But the length of wood felt *right* in his fingers. He was amazed by how wonderful the moment felt.

Jost grunted, stumbling again, and Kal brought his weapon back around, preparing to smash Jost's face. He raised his staff, but then froze. Jost was bleeding from the hand Kal had hit. Just a little, but it was blood.

He'd hurt someone.

Jost growled and lurched upright. Before Kal could protest, the larger boy swept Kal's legs from underneath him, sending him to the ground, knocking the breath from his lungs. That set afire the wound in his side, and the painspren scampered across the ground, latching on to Kal's side, looking like an orange scar as they fed on Kal's agony.

Jost stepped back. Kal lay on his back, breathing. He didn't know what to feel. Holding the staff in that moment had felt wonderful. Incredible. At the same time, he could see Laral to the side. She stood up and, instead of kneeling to help him, turned and walked away, toward her father's mansion.

Tears welled in Kal's eyes. With a shout, he rolled over and grabbed the quarterstaff again. He would *not* give in!

"None of that now," Jost said from behind. Kal felt something hard on his back, a boot shoving him down to the stone. Jest took the staff from Kal's fingers.

I failed. I . . . lost. He hated the feeling, hated it far more than the pain.

"You did well," Jost said grudgingly. "But leave off. I don't want to have to hurt you for real."

Kal bowed his head down, letting his forehead rest on the warm, sunlit rock. Jost removed his foot, and the boys withdrew, chatting, their boots scraping on rock. Kal forced himself to his hands and knees, then up onto his feet.

Jost turned back, wary, holding his quarterstaff in one hand.

"Teach me," Kal said.

Jost blinked in surprise. He glanced at his brother.

"Teach me," Kal pled, stepping forward. "I'll worm for you, Jost. My father gives me two hours off each afternoon. I'll do your work then if you'll teach me, in the evenings, what your father is teaching you with that staff."

He *had* to know. Had to feel the weapon in his hands again. Had to see if that moment he'd felt had been a fluke. Jost considered, then finally shook his head. "Can't. Your fah would kill me. Get those surgeon's hands of yours all covered with calluses? Wouldn't be right." He turned away. "You go be what you are, Kal. I'll be what I am."

Kal stood for a long while, watching them go. He sat down on the rock. Laral's figure was growing distant. There were some servants coming down the hillside to fetch her. Should he chase after her? His side still hurt, and he was annoyed at her for leading him down to the others in the first place. And, above all, he was *still* embarrassed.

He lay back down, emotions welling inside of him. He had trouble sorting through them.

"Kaladin?"

He turned, ashamed to find tears in his eyes, and saw Tien sitting on the ground behind him. "How long have you been there?" Kal snapped.

Tien smiled, then set a rock on the ground. He climbed to his feet and hurried away, not stopping when Kal called after him. Grumbling, Kal forced himself to his feet and walked over to pick up the rock.

It was another dull, ordinary stone. Tien had a habit of finding those and thinking they were incredibly precious. He had an entire collection of them back in the house. He knew where he'd found each one, and could tell you what was special about it.

With a sigh, Kal began walking back toward the town.

You go be what you are. I'll be what I am.

His side smarted. Why hadn't he hit Jost when he'd had the chance? Could he train himself out of freezing in battle like that? He could learn to hurt. Couldn't he?

Did he want to?

You go be what you are.

What did a man do if he didn't *know* what he was? Or even what he wanted to be?

Eventually, he reached Hearthstone proper. The hundred or so buildings were set in rows, each one shaped like a wedge with the low side pointing stormward. The roofs were of thick wood, tarred to seal out the rain. The northern and southern sides of the buildings rarely had windows, but the fronts—facing west away from the storms—were nearly all window. Like the plants of the stormlands, the lives of men here were dominated by the highstorms.

Kal's home was near the outskirts. It was larger than most, built wide to accommodate the surgery room, which had its own entrance. The door was ajar, so Kal peeked in. He'd expected to see his mother cleaning, but instead found that his father had returned from Brightlord Wistiow's manor. Lirin sat on the edge of the operating table, hands in his lap, bald head bowed. He held his spectacles in his hand, and he looked exhausted.

"Father?" Kal asked. "Why are you sitting in the dark?"

Lirin looked up. His face was somber, distant.

"Father?" Kal asked, growing more concerned.

"Brightlord Wistiow has been carried by the winds."

"He's *dead*?" Kal was so shocked he forgot his side. Wistiow had *always* been there. He couldn't be gone. What of Laral? "He was healthy just last week!"

"He has always been frail, Kal," Lirin said. "The Almighty calls all men back to the Spiritual Realm eventually."

"You didn't do anything?" Kal blurted out; he regretted the words immediately.

"I did all I could," his father said, rising. "Perhaps a man with more training than I . . . Well, there is no use in regrets." He walked to the side of the room, removing the black covering from the goblet lamp filled with diamond spheres. It lit the room immediately, blazing like a tiny sun.

"We have no citylord then," Kal said, raising a hand to his head. "He had no son. . . ."

"Those in Kholinar will appoint us a new citylord," Lirin said. "Almighty send them wisdom in the choice." He looked at the goblet lamp. Those were the citylord's spheres. A small fortune.

Kal's father put the covering right back on the goblet, as if he hadn't just removed it. The motion plunged the room back into darkness, and Kal blinked as his eyes adjusted.

"He left these to us," Kal's father said.

Kal started. "*What?*"

"You're to be sent to Kharbranth when you turn sixteen. These spheres will pay your way—Brightlord Wistiow requested it be done, a last act to care for his people. You will go and become a true master surgeon, then return to Hearthstone."

In that moment, Kal knew his fate had been sealed. If Brightlord Wistiow had demanded it, Kal would go to Kharbranth. He turned and walked from the surgery room, passing out into the sunlight, not saying another word to his father.

He sat down on the steps. What *did* he want? He didn't know. That was the problem. Glory, honor, the things Laral had said . . . none of those really mattered to him. But there had been *something* there when he'd held the quarterstaff. And now, suddenly, the decision had been taken from him.

The rocks Tien had given him were still in his pocket. He pulled them out, then took his canteen off his belt and washed them with water. The first one he'd been given showed the white swirls and strata. It appeared the other one had a hidden design too.

It looked like a face, smiling at him, made of white bits in the rock. Kal smiled despite himself, though it quickly faded. A rock wasn't going to solve his problems.

Unfortunately, though he sat for a long while thinking, it didn't look like anything would solve his problems. He wasn't sure he wanted to be a surgeon, and he felt suddenly constricted by what life was forcing him to become.

But that one moment holding the quarterstaff sang to him. A single moment of clarity in an otherwise confusing world.

17

A BLOODY, RED SUNSET

Might I be quite frank? Before, you asked why I was so concerned. It is for the following reason:

He's *old*," Syl said with awe, flitting around the apothecary. "Really old. I didn't know men got this old. You sure he's not decayspren wearing a man's skin?"

Kaladin smiled as the apothecary shuffled forward with his cane, oblivious of the invisible windspren. His face was as full of chasms as the Shattered Plains themselves, weaving out in a pattern from his deeply recessed eyes. He wore a pair of thick spectacles on the tip of his nose, and was dressed in dark robes.

Kaladin's father had told him of apothecaries—men who walked the line between herbalists and surgeons. Common people regarded the healing arts with enough superstition that it was easy for an apothecary to cultivate an arcane air. The wooden walls were draped with cloth glyphwards styled in cryptic patterns, and behind the counter were shelves with rows of jars. A full human skeleton hung in the far corner, held together by wires. The windowless room was lit with bundles of garnet spheres hanging from the corners.

Despite all that, the place was clean and tidy. It had the familiar scent of antiseptic Kaladin associated with his father's surgery.

"Ah, young bridgeman." The short apothecary adjusted his spectacles. He stooped forward, running his fingers through his wispy white beard. "Come for a ward against danger, perhaps? Or maybe a young washwoman in the camp has caught your eye? I have a potion which, if slipped into her drink, will make her regard you with favor."

Kaladin raised an eyebrow.

Syl, however, opened her mouth in an amazed expression. "You should give that to Gaz, Kaladin. It would be nice if he liked you more."

I doubt that's what it's intended for, Kaladin thought with a smile.

"Young bridgeman?" the apothecary asked. "Is it a charm against evil you desire?"

Kaladin's father had spoken of these things. Many apothecaries purveyed supposed love charms or potions to cure all manner of ailments. They'd contain nothing more than some sugar and a few pinches of common herbs to give a spike of alertness or drowsiness, depending on the purported effect. It was all nonsense, though Kaladin's mother *had* put great stock in glyphwards. Kaladin's father had always expressed disappointment in her stubborn way of clinging to "superstitions."

"I need some bandages," Kaladin said. "And a flask of lister's oil or knobweed sap. Also, a needle and gut, if you have any."

The apothecary's eyes opened wide in surprise.

"I'm the son of a surgeon," Kaladin admitted. "Trained by his hand. He was trained by a man who had studied in the Great Concourse of Kharbranth."

"Ah," the apothecary said. "Well." He stood up straighter, setting aside his cane and brushing his robes. "Bandages, you said? And some antiseptic? Let me see. . . ." He moved back behind the counter.

Kaladin blinked. The man's age hadn't changed, but he didn't seem nearly as frail. His step was firmer, and his voice had lost its whispering raspiness. He searched through his bottles, mumbling to himself as he read off his labels. "You could just go to the surgeon's hall. They would charge you far less."

"Not for a bridgeman," Kaladin said, grimacing. He'd been turned away. The supplies there were for real soldiers.

"I see," the apothecary said, setting a jar on the counter, then bending down to poke in some drawers.

Syl flitted over to Kaladin. "Every time he bends I think he'll snap like a twig." She *was* growing able to understand abstract thought, and at a surprisingly rapid pace.

I know what death is. . . . He still wasn't certain whether to feel sorry for her or not.

Kaladin picked up the small bottle and undid the cork, smelling what was inside. "Larmic mucus?" He grimaced at the foul smell. "That's not nearly as effective as the two I asked for."

"But it's far cheaper," the old man said, coming up with a large box. He opened the lid, revealing sterile white bandages. "And you, as has been noted, are a bridgeman."

"How much for the mucus, then?" He'd been worried about this; his father had never mentioned how much his supplies cost.

"Two bloodmarks for the bottle."

"That's what you consider *cheap*?"

"Lister's oil costs two sapphire marks."

"And knobweed sap?" Kaladin said. "I saw some reeds of it growing just outside of camp! It can't be *that* rare."

"And do you know how much sap comes from a single plant?" the apothecary asked, pointing.

Kaladin hesitated. It wasn't true sap, but a milky substance that you could squeeze from the stalks. Or so his father had said. "No," Kaladin admitted.

"A single drop," the man said. "If you're lucky. It's cheaper than lister's oil, sure, but more expensive than the mucus. Even if the mucus *does* stink like the Nightwatcher's own backside."

"I don't have that much," Kaladin said. It was five diamond marks to a garnet. Ten days' pay to buy one small jar of antiseptic. Stormfather!

The apothecary sniffed. "The needle and gut will cost two clearmarks. Can you afford that, at least?"

"Barely. How much for the bandages? Two full emeralds?"

"They're just old scraps that I bleached and boiled. Two clearchips an arm length."

"I'll give a mark for the box."

"Very well." Kaladin reached into his pocket to get the spheres as the old apothecary continued, "You surgeons, all the same. Never give a blink to consider where your supplies come from. You just use them like there will be no end."

"You can't put a price on a person's life," Kaladin said. One of his father's sayings. It was the main reason that Lirin had never charged for his services.

Kaladin brought out his four marks. He hesitated when he saw them, however. Only one was still glowing with its soft crystal light. The other three were dull, the bits of diamond barely visible at the center of the drops of glass.

"Here now," the apothecary said, squinting. "You trying to pass dun spheres off on me?" He snatched one before Kaladin could complain, then fished around under his counter. He brought up a jeweler's loupe, removing his spectacles and holding the sphere up toward the light. "Ah. No, that's a real gemstone. You should get your spheres infused, bridgeman. Not everyone is as trusting as I am."

"They were glowing this morning," Kaladin protested. "Gaz must have paid me with run-down spheres."

The apothecary removed his loupe and replaced the spectacles. He selected three marks, including the glowing one.

"Could I have that one?" Kaladin asked.

The apothecary frowned.

"Always keep a glowing sphere in your pocket," Kaladin said. "It's good luck."

"You certain you don't want a love potion?"

"If you get caught in the dark, you'll have light," Kaladin said tersely. "Besides, as you said, most people aren't as trusting as you."

Reluctantly, the apothecary traded the infused sphere for

the dead one—though he did check it with the loupe to be certain. A dun sphere was worth just as much as an infused one; all you had to do was leave it out in a highstorm, and it would recharge and give off light for a week or so.

Kaladin pocketed the infused sphere and picked up his purchase. He nodded farewell to the apothecary, and Syl joined him as he stepped out into the camp's street.

He'd spent some of the afternoon listening to soldiers at the mess hall, and he'd learned some things about the warcamps. Things he should have learned weeks ago, but had been too despondent to care about. He now understood more about the chrysalises on the plateaus, the gemhearts they contained, and the competition between the highprinces. He understood why Sadeas pushed his men so hard, and he was beginning to see why Sadeas turned around if they got to the plateau later than another army. That wasn't very common. More often, Sadeas arrived first, and the other Alethi armies that came up behind them had to turn back.

The warcamps were enormous. All told, there were over a hundred thousand troops in the various Alethi camps, many times the population of Hearthstone. And that wasn't counting the civilians. A mobile warcamp attracted a large array of camp followers; stationary warcamps like these on the Shattered Plains brought even more.

Each of the ten warcamps filled its own crater, and was filled with an incongruous mix of Soulcast buildings, shanties, and tents. Some merchants, like the apothecary, had the money to build a wooden structure. Those who lived in tents took them down for storms, then paid for shelter elsewhere. Even within the crater, the stormwinds were strong, particularly where the outer wall was low or broken. Some places— like the lumberyard—were completely exposed.

The street bustled with the usual crowd. Women in skirts and blouses—the wives, sisters, or daughters of the soldiers, merchants, or craftsmen. Workers in trousers or overalls. A large number of soldiers in leathers, carrying spear and shield. All were Sadeas's men. Soldiers of one camp didn't mix with those of another, and you stayed away from another bright-lord's crater unless you had business there.

Kaladin shook his head in dismay.

"What?" Syl asked, settling on his shoulder.

"I hadn't expected there to be so much discord among the camps here. I thought it would all be one king's army, unified."

"People are discord," Syl said.

"What does that mean?"

"You all act differently and think differently. Nothing else is like that—animals act alike, and all spren are, in a sense, virtually the same individual. There's harmony in that. But not in you—it seems that no two of you can agree on anything. All the world does as it is supposed to, except for humans. Maybe that's why you so often want to kill each other."

"But not *all* windspren act alike," Kaladin said, opening the box and tucking some of the bandages into the pocket he'd sewn into the inside of his leather vest. "You're proof of that."

"I know," she said softly. "Maybe now you can see why it bothers me so."

Kaladin didn't know how to respond to that. Eventually, he reached the lumberyard. A few members of Bridge Four lounged in the shade on the east side of their barrack. It would be interesting to see one of those barracks get made—they were Soulcast directly from air into stone. Unfortunately, Soulcastings happened at night, and under strict guard to keep the holy rite from being witnessed by anyone other than ardents or very high-ranking lighteyes.

The first afternoon bell sounded right as Kaladin reached the barrack, and he caught a glare from Gaz for nearly being late for bridge duty. Most of that "duty" would be spent sitting around, waiting for the horns to blow. Well, Kaladin didn't intend to waste time. He couldn't risk tiring himself by carrying the plank, not when a bridge run could be imminent, but perhaps he could do some stretches or—

A horn sounded in the air, crisp and clean. It was like the

mythical horn that was said to guide the souls of the brave to heaven's battlefield. Kaladin froze. As always, he waited for the second blast, an irrational part of him needing to hear confirmation. It came, sounding a pattern indicating the location of the pupating chasmfiend.

Soldiers began to scramble toward the staging area beside the lumberyard; others ran into camp to fetch their gear. "Line up!" Kaladin shouted, dashing up to the bridgemen. "Storm you! Every man in a line!"

They ignored him. Some of the men weren't wearing their vests, and they clogged the barrack doorway, all trying to get in. Those who had their vests ran for the bridge. Kaladin followed, frustrated. Once there, the men gathered around the bridge in a carefully prearranged manner. Each man got a chance to be in the best position: running in front up to the chasm, then moving to the relative safety of the back for the final approach.

There was a strict rotation, and errors were neither made nor tolerated. Bridge crews had a brutal system of self-management: If a man tried to cheat, the others forced him to run the final approach in front. That sort of thing was supposed to be forbidden, but Gaz turned a blind eye toward cheaters. He also refused bribes to let men change positions. Perhaps he knew that the only stability—the only hope—the bridgemen had was in their rotation. Life wasn't fair, being a bridgeman wasn't fair, but at least if you ran the deathline and survived, the next time you got to run at the back.

There was one exception. As bridgeleader, Kaladin got to run in the front most of the way, then move to the back for the assault. His was the safest position in the group, though no bridgeman was truly safe. Kaladin was like a moldy crust on a starving man's plate; not the first bite, but still doomed.

He got into position. Yake, Dunny, and Malop were the last stragglers. Once they'd taken their places, Kaladin commanded the men to lift. He was half surprised to be obeyed, but there was almost always a bridgeleader to give commands during a run. The voice changed, but the simple orders did not. Lift, run, lower.

Twenty bridges charged down from the lumberyard and toward the Shattered Plains. Kaladin noticed a group of bridgemen from Bridge Seven watching with relief. They'd been on duty until the first afternoon bell; they'd avoided this run by mere moments.

The bridgemen worked hard. It wasn't just because of threats of beatings—they ran so hard because they wanted to arrive at the target plateau before the Parshendi did. If they did so, there would be no arrows, no death. And so running their bridges was the one thing the bridgemen did without reservation or laziness. Though many hated their lives, they still clung to them with white-knuckled fervor.

They clomped across the first of the permanent bridges. Kaladin's muscles groaned in protest at being worked again so soon, but he tried not to dwell on his fatigue. The high-storm's rains from the night before meant that most plants were still open, rockbuds spewing out vines, flowering bran-zahs reaching clawlike branches out of crevices toward the sky. There were also occasional prickletacs: the needly, stone-limbed little shrubs Kaladin had noticed his first time through the area. Water pooled in the numerous crevices and depressions on the surface of the uneven plateau.

Gaz called out directions, telling them which pathway to take. Many of the nearby plateaus had three or four bridges, creating branching paths across the Plains. The running became rote. It was exhausting, but it was also familiar, and it was nice to be at the front, where he could see where he was going. Kaladin fell into his usual step-counting mantra, as he'd been advised to do by that nameless bridgeman whose sandals he still wore.

Eventually, they reached the last of the permanent bridges. They crossed a short plateau, passing the smoldering ruins of a bridge the Parshendi had destroyed during the night. How had the Parshendi managed that, during a highstorm? Earlier, while listening to the soldiers, he'd learned that the soldiers regarded the Parshendi with hatred, anger, and not a little awe. These Parshendi weren't like the lazy, nearly mute parshmen who worked throughout Roshar. These Parshendi were warriors of no small skill. That still struck Kaladin as incongruous. Parshmen? Fighting? It was just so strange.

Bridge Four and the other crews got their bridges down, spanning a chasm where it was narrowest. His men collapsed to the ground around their bridge, relaxing while the army crossed. Kaladin nearly joined them—in fact, his knees nearly buckled in anticipation.

No, he thought, steadying himself. *No. I stand.*

It was a foolish gesture. The other bridgemen barely paid him any heed. One man, Moash, even swore at him. But now that Kaladin had made the decision, he stubbornly stuck to it, clasping his hands behind his back and falling into parade rest while watching the army cross.

"Ho, little bridgeman!" a soldier called from among those waiting their turn. "Curious at what *real* soldiers look like?"

Kaladin turned toward the man, a solid, brown-eyed fellow with arms the size of many men's thighs. He was a squadleader, by the knots on the shoulder of his leather jerkin. Kaladin had borne those knots once.

"How do you treat your spear and shield, squadleader?" Kaladin called back.

The man frowned, but Kaladin knew what he was thinking. A soldier's gear was his life; you cared for your weapon as you'd care for your children, often seeing to its upkeep before you took food or rest.

Kaladin nodded to the bridge. "This is *my* bridge," he said in a loud voice. "It is my weapon, the only one allowed me. Treat her well."

"Or you'll do what?" called one of the other soldiers, prompting laughter among the ranks. The squadleader said nothing. He looked troubled.

Kaladin's words were bravado. In truth, he hated the bridge. Still, he remained standing.

A few moments later, Highprince Sadeas himself crossed on Kaladin's bridge. Brightlord Amaram had always seemed so heroic, so distinguished. A gentleman general. This Sadeas was a different creature entirely, with that round face, curly hair, and lofty expression. He rode as if he were in a parade, one hand lightly holding the reins before him, the other carrying his helm under his arm. His armor was painted red, and the helm bore frivolous tassels. There was so much pointless pomp that it nearly overshadowed the wonder of the ancient artifact.

Kaladin forgot his fatigue and formed his hands into fists. Here was a lighteyes he could hate even more than most, a man so callous that he threw away the lives of hundreds of bridgemen each month. A man who had expressly forbidden his bridgemen to have shields for reasons Kaladin still didn't understand.

Sadeas and his honor guard soon passed, and Kaladin realized that he probably should have bowed. Sadeas hadn't noticed, but it could have made trouble if he had. Shaking his head, Kaladin roused his bridge crew, though it took special prodding to get Rock—the large Horneater—up and moving. Once across the chasm, his men picked up their bridge and jogged toward the next chasm.

The process was repeated enough times that Kaladin lost count. At each crossing, he refused to lie down. He stood with hands behind his back, watching the army pass. More soldiers took note of him, jeering. Kaladin ignored them, and by the fifth or sixth crossing, the jeers faded. The one other time he saw Brightlord Sadeas, Kaladin gave a bow, though it made his stomach twist to do so. He did not serve this man. He did not give this man allegiance. But he *did* serve his men of Bridge Four. He would save them, and that meant he had to keep himself from being punished for insolence.

"Reverse runners!" Gaz called. "Cross and reverse!"

Kaladin turned sharply. The next crossing would be the assault. He squinted, looking into the distance, and could just barely make out a line of dark figures gathering on another plateau. The Parshendi had arrived and were forming up. Behind them, a group worked on breaking open the chrysalis.

Kaladin felt a spike of frustration. Their speed hadn't been enough. And—tired though they were—Sadeas would want to attack quickly, before the Parshendi could get the gemheart out of its shell.

The bridgemen rose from their rest, silent, haunted. They knew what was coming. They crossed the chasm and pulled the bridge over, then rearranged themselves in reverse order. The soldiers formed ranks. It was all so silent, like men preparing to carry a bier to the pyre.

The bridgemen left a space for Kaladin at the back, sheltered and protected. Syl alighted on the bridge, looking at the spot. Kaladin walked up to it, so tired, mentally and physically. He'd pushed himself too hard in the morning, then again by standing instead of resting. What had possessed him to do such a thing? He could barely walk.

He looked over the bridgemen. His men were resigned, despondent, terrified. If they refused to run, they'd be executed. If they did run, they'd face the arrows. They didn't look toward the distant line of Parshendi archers. Instead, they looked down.

They are your men, Kaladin told himself. *They need you to lead them, even if they don't know it.*

How can you lead from the rear?

He stepped out of line and rounded the bridge; two of the men—Drehy and Teft—looked up in shock as he passed. The deathpoint—the spot in the very center of the front—was being held by Rock, the beefy, tan-skinned Horneater. Kaladin tapped him on the shoulder. "You're in my spot, Rock."

The man glanced at him, surprised. "But—"

"To the back with you."

Rock frowned. Nobody ever tried to jump *ahead* in the order. "You're airsick, lowlander," he said with his thick accent. "You wish to die? Why do you not just go leap into the chasm? That would be easier."

"I'm bridgeleader. It's my privilege to run at the front. Go."

Rock shrugged, but did as ordered, taking Kaladin's position at the back. Nobody said a word. If Kaladin wanted to get himself killed, who were they to complain?

Kaladin looked over the bridgemen. "The longer we take to get this bridge down, the more arrows they can loose at us. Stay firm, stay determined, and *be quick*. Raise bridge!"

The men lifted, inner rows moving underneath and situating themselves in rows of five across. Kaladin stood at the very front with a tall, stout man named Leyten to his left, a spindly man named Murk to his right. Adis and Corl were at the edges. Five men in front. The deathline.

Once all of the crews had their bridges up, Gaz gave the command. "Assault!"

They ran, dashing alongside the standing ranks of the army, passing soldiers holding spears and shields. Some watched with curiosity, perhaps amused at the sight of the lowly bridgemen running so urgently to their deaths. Others looked away, perhaps ashamed of the lives it would cost to get them across that chasm.

Kaladin kept his eyes forward, squelching that incredulous voice in the back of his mind, one that screamed he was doing something very stupid. He barreled toward the final chasm, focused on the Parshendi line. Figures with black and crimson skin holding bows.

Syl flitted close to Kaladin's head, no longer in the form of a person, streaking like a ribbon of light. She zipped in front of him.

The bows came up. Kaladin hadn't been at the deathpoint during a charge this bad since his first day on the crew. They always put new men into rotation at the deathpoint. That way, if they died, you didn't have to worry about training them.

The Parshendi archers drew, aiming at five or six of the bridge crews. Bridge Four was obviously in their sights.

The bows loosed.

"Tien!" Kaladin screamed, nearly mad with fatigue and frustration. He bellowed the name aloud—uncertain why—as a wall of arrows zipped toward him. Kaladin felt a jolt of energy, a surge of sudden strength, unanticipated and unexplained.

The arrows landed.

Murk fell without a sound, four or five arrows striking him, spraying his blood across the stones. Leyten dropped as well, and with him both Adis and Corl. Shafts struck the ground at Kaladin's feet, shattering, and a good half dozen hit the wood around Kaladin's head and hands.

Kaladin didn't know if he'd been hit. He was too flush with energy and alarm. He continued running, screaming, holding the bridge on his shoulders. For some reason, a group of Parshendi archers ahead lowered their bows. He saw their marbled skin, strange reddish or orange helms, and simple brown clothing. They appeared confused.

Whatever the reason, it gained Bridge Four a few precious moments. By the time the Parshendi raised their bows again, Kaladin's team had reached the chasm. His men fell into line with the other bridge crews—there were only fifteen bridges now. Five had fallen. They closed the gaps as they arrived.

Kaladin screamed for the bridgemen to drop amid another spray of arrows. One sliced open the skin near his ribs, deflecting off the bone. He felt it hit, but didn't feel any pain. He scrambled around the side of the bridge, helping push. Kaladin's team slammed the bridge into place as a wave of Alethi arrows distracted the enemy archers.

A troop of cavalry charged across the bridges. The bridgemen were soon forgotten. Kaladin fell to his knees beside the bridge as the others of his crew stumbled away, bloodied and hurt, their part in the battle over.

Kaladin held his side, feeling the blood there. *Straight laceration, only about an inch long, not wide enough to be of danger.*

It was his father's voice.

Kaladin panted. He needed to get to safety. Arrows zipped over his head, fired by the Alethi archers.

Some people take lives. Other people save lives.

He wasn't done yet. Kaladin forced himself to his feet and staggered to where someone lay beside the bridge. It was a bridgeman named Hobber; he had an arrow through the leg. The man moaned, holding his thigh.

Kaladin grabbed him under the arms and pulled him away from the bridge. The man cursed at the pain, dazed, as Kaladin towed him to a cleft behind a small bulge in the rock where Rock and some of the other bridgemen had sought shelter.

After dropping off Hobber—the arrow hadn't hit any major

arteries, and he would be fine for a time yet—Kaladin turned and tried to rush back out onto the battlefield proper. He slipped, however, stumbling in his fatigue. He hit the ground hard, grunting.

Some take lives. Some save lives.

He pushed himself to his feet, sweat dripping from his brow, and scrambled back toward the bridge, his father's voice in his ears. The next bridgeman he found, a man named Koorm, was dead. Kaladin left the body.

Gadol had a deep wound in the side where an arrow had passed completely through him. His face was covered with blood from a gash on his temple, and he'd managed to crawl a short distance from the bridge. He looked up with frenzied black eyes, orange painspren waving around him. Kaladin grabbed him under the arms and towed him away just before a thundering charge of cavalry trampled the place where he'd been lying.

Kaladin dragged Gadol over to the cleft, noting two more dead. He did a quick count. That made twenty-nine bridgemen, including the dead he'd seen. Five were missing. Kaladin stumbled back out onto the battlefield.

Soldiers had bunched up around the back of the bridge, archers forming at the sides and firing into the Parshendi lines as the heavy cavalry charge—led by Highprince Sadeas himself, virtually indestructible in his Shardplate—tried to push the enemy back.

Kaladin wavered, dizzy, dismayed at the sight of so many men running, shouting, firing arrows and throwing spears. Five bridgemen, probably dead, lost in all of that—

He spotted a figure huddled just beside the chasm lip with arrows flying back and forth over his head. It was Dabbid, one of the bridgemen. He curled up, arm twisted at an awkward angle.

Kaladin charged in. He threw himself to the ground and crawled beneath the zipping arrows, hoping that the Parshendi would ignore a couple of unarmed bridgemen. Dabbid didn't even notice when Kaladin reached him. He was in shock, lips moving soundlessly, eyes dazed. Kaladin grabbed him awkwardly, afraid to stand up too high lest an arrow hit him.

He dragged Dabbid away from the edge in a clumsy half crawl. He kept slipping on blood, falling, abrading his arms on the rock, hitting his face against the stone. He persisted, towing the younger man out from underneath the flying arrows. Finally, he got far enough away that he risked standing. He tried to pick up Dabbid. But his muscles were so weak. He strained and slipped, exhausted, falling to the stones.

He lay there, gasping, the pain of his side finally washing over him. *So tired.* . . .

He stood up shakily, then tried again to grab Dabbid. He blinked away tears of frustration, too weak to even pull the man.

"Airsick lowlander," a voice growled.

Kaladin turned as Rock arrived. The massive Horneater grabbed Dabbid under the arms, pulling him. "Crazy," he grumbled to Kaladin, but easily lifted the wounded bridgeman and carried him back to the hollow.

Kaladin followed. He collapsed in the hollow, his back to the rock. The surviving bridgemen huddled around him, eyes haunted. Rock set Dabbid down.

"Four more," Kaladin said between gasps. "We have to find them. . . ."

"Murk and Leyten," Teft said. The older bridgeman had been near the back this run, and hadn't taken any wounds. "And Adis and Corl. They were in the front."

That's right, Kaladin thought, exhausted. *How could I forget.* . . . "Murk is dead," he said. "The others might live." He tried to stumble to his feet.

"Idiot," Rock said. "Stay here. Is all right. I will do this thing." He hesitated. "Guess I'm an idiot too." He scowled, but went back out onto the battlefield. Teft hesitated, then chased after him.

Kaladin breathed in and out, holding his side. He couldn't decide if the pain of the arrow impact hurt more than the cut. *Save lives.* . . .

He crawled over to the three wounded. Hobber—with an

arrow through the leg—would wait, and Dabbid had only a broken arm. Gadol was the worst off, with that hole in his side. Kaladin stared at the wound. He didn't have an operating table; he didn't even have antiseptic. How was he supposed to do anything?

He shoved despair aside. "One of you go fetch me a knife," he told the bridgemen. "Take it off the body of a soldier who has fallen. Someone else build a fire!"

The bridgemen looked at each other.

"Dunny, you get the knife," Kaladin said as he held his hand to Gadol's wound, trying to stanch the blood. "Narm, can you make a fire?"

"With what?" the man asked.

Kaladin pulled off his vest and shirt, then handed the shirt to Narm. "Use this as tinder and gather some fallen arrows for wood. Does anyone have flint and steel?"

Moash did, fortunately. You carried anything valuable you had with you on a bridge run; other bridgemen might steal it if you left it behind.

"Move quickly!" Kaladin said. "Someone else, go rip open a rockbud and get me the watergourd inside."

They stood for a few moments. Then, blessedly, they did as he demanded. Perhaps they were too stunned to object. Kaladin tore open Gadol's shirt, exposing the wound. It was bad, terribly bad. If it had cut the intestines or some of the other organs . . .

He ordered one of the bridgemen to hold a bandage to Gadol's forehead to stanch the smaller blood flow there—anything would help—and inspected the wounded side with the speed his father had taught him. Dunny returned quickly with a knife. Narm was having trouble with the fire, though. The man cursed, trying his flint and steel again.

Gadol was spasming. Kaladin pressed bandages to the wound, feeling helpless. There wasn't a place he could make a tourniquet for a wound like this. There wasn't anything he could do but—

Gadol spit up blood, coughing. "They break the land itself!" he hissed, eyes wild. "They want it, but in their rage they will destroy it. Like the jealous man burns his rich things rather than let them be taken by his enemies! They come!"

He gasped. And then he fell still, his dead eyes staring upward, bloody spittle running in a trail down his cheek. His final, haunting words hung over them. Not far away, soldiers fought and screamed, but the bridgemen were silent.

Kaladin sat back, stunned—as always—by the pain of losing someone. His father had always said that time would dull his sensitivity.

In this, Lirin had been wrong.

He felt so tired. Rock and Teft were hurrying back toward the cleft in the rock, bearing a body between them.

They wouldn't have brought anyone unless he was still alive, Kaladin told himself. *Think of the ones you can help.* "Keep that fire going!" he said, pointing at Narm. "Don't let it die! Someone heat the blade in it."

Narm jumped, noticing as if for the first time that he'd actually managed to get a small flame started. Kaladin turned away from the dead Gadol and made room for Rock and Teft. They deposited a very bloody Leyten on the ground. He was breathing shallowly and had two arrows sticking from him, one from the shoulder, the other from the opposite arm. Another had grazed his stomach, and the cut there had been widened by movement. It looked like his left leg had been trampled by a horse; it was broken, and he had a large gash where the skin had split.

"The other three are dead," Teft said. "He nearly is too. Nothing much we can do. But you said to bring him, so—"

Kaladin knelt down immediately, working with careful, efficient speed. He pressed a bandage against the side, holding it in place with his knee, then tied a quick bandage on the leg, ordering one of the bridgemen to hold it firm and elevate the limb. "Where's that knife!" Kaladin yelled, hurriedly tying a loose tourniquet around the arm. He needed to stop the blood right now; he'd worry about saving the arm later.

Youthful Dunny rushed over with the heated blade. Kaladin lifted the side bandage and quickly cauterized the wound there. Leyten was unconscious, his breathing growing more shallow.

"You will *not* die," Kaladin muttered. "You will not die!" His mind was numb, but his fingers knew the motions. For a moment, he was back in his father's surgery room, listening to careful instruction. He cut the arrow from Leyten's arm, but left the one in his shoulder, then sent the knife back to be reheated.

Peet finally returned with the watergourd. Kaladin snatched it, using it to clean the leg wound, which was the nastiest, as it had been caused by trampling. When the knife came back, Kaladin pulled the arrow free of the shoulder and cauterized the wound as best he could, then used another of his quickly disappearing bandages to tie the wound.

He splinted the leg with arrow shafts—the only thing they had. With a grimace, he cauterized the wound there too. He hated to cause so many scars, but he couldn't afford to let any more blood be lost. He was going to need antiseptic. How soon could he get some of that mucus?

"Don't you *dare* die!" Kaladin said, barely conscious that he was speaking. He quickly tied off the leg wound, then used his needle and thread to sew the arm wound. He bandaged it, then untied the tourniquet most of the way.

Finally, he settled back, looking at the wounded man, completely drained. Leyten was still breathing. How long would that last? The odds were against him.

The bridgemen stood or sat around Kaladin, looking strangely reverent. Kaladin tiredly moved over to Hobber and saw to the man's leg wound. It didn't need to be cauterized. Kaladin washed it out, cut away some splinters, then sewed it. There were painspren all around the man, tiny orange hands stretching up from the ground.

Kaladin sliced off the cleanest portion of bandage he'd used on Gadol and tied it around Hobber's wound. He hated the uncleanliness of it, but there was no other choice. Then he set Dabbid's arm with some arrows he had the other bridgemen fetch, using Dabbid's shirt to tie them in place. Then, finally, Kaladin sat back against the lip of stone, letting out a long, fatigued breath.

Bangs of metal on metal and shouts of soldiers rang from behind. He felt *so* tired. Too tired to even close his eyes. He just wanted to sit and stare at the ground forever.

Teft settled down beside him. The grizzled man had the watergourd, which still had some liquid in the bottom. "Drink, lad. You need it."

"We should clean the wounds of the other men," Kaladin said numbly. "They took scrapes—I saw some had cuts—and they should—"

"Drink," Teft said, his crackly voice insistent.

Kaladin hesitated, then drank the water. It tasted strongly bitter, like the plant from which it had been taken.

"Where'd you learn to heal men like that?" Teft asked. Several of the nearby bridgemen turned toward him at the question.

"I wasn't always a slave," Kaladin whispered.

"These things you did, they won't make a difference," Rock said, walking up. The massive Horneater squatted down. "Gaz makes us leave behind wounded who cannot walk. Is standing order from above."

"I'll deal with Gaz," Kaladin said, resting his head back against the stone. "Go return that knife to the body you took it off. I don't want to be accused of thievery. Then, when the time comes to leave, I want two men in charge of Leyten and two men in charge of Hobber. We'll tie them to the top of the bridge and carry them. At the chasms, you'll have to move quickly and untie them before the army crosses, then retie them at the end. We'll also need someone to lead Dabbid, if his shock hasn't passed."

"Gaz won't stand for this thing," Rock said.

Kaladin closed his eyes, declining further argument.

The battle was a long one. As evening approached, the Parshendi finally retreated, jumping away across the chasms with their unnaturally powerful legs. There was a chorus of shouts from the Alethi soldiers, who had won the day. Kaladin forced himself to his feet and went looking for Gaz. It would be a while yet before they could get the chrysalis open—it was like pounding on stone—but he needed to deal with the bridge sergeant.

He found Gaz watching from well behind the battle lines. He glanced at Kaladin with his one eye. "How much of that blood is yours?"

Kaladin looked down, realizing for the first time that he was crusted with dark, flaking blood, most belonging to the men he'd worked on. He didn't answer the question. "We're taking our wounded with us."

Gaz shook his head. "If they can't walk, they stay behind. Standing orders. Not my choice."

"We're taking them," Kaladin said, no more firm, no more loud.

"Brightlord Lamaril won't stand for it." Lamaril was Gaz's immediate superior.

"You'll send Bridge Four last, to lead the wounded soldiers back to camp. Lamaril won't go with that troop; he'll go on ahead with the main body, as he won't want to miss Sadeas's victory feast."

Gaz opened his mouth.

"My men will move quickly and efficiently," Kaladin said, interrupting him. "They won't slow anyone." He took the last sphere from his pocket and handed it over. "You won't say anything."

Gaz took the sphere, snorting. "One clearmark? You think that will make me take a risk this big?"

"If you don't," Kaladin said, voice calm, "I will kill you and let them execute me."

Gaz blinked in surprise. "You'd never—"

Kaladin took a single step forward. He must have looked a dreadful sight, covered in blood. Gaz paled. Then he cursed, holding up the dark sphere. "And a dun sphere at that."

Kaladin frowned. He was sure it had still glowed before the bridge run. "That's your fault. You gave it to me."

"Those spheres were newly infused last night," Gaz said. "They came straight from Brightlord Sadeas's treasurer. What did you do with them?"

Kaladin shook his head, too exhausted to think. Syl landed on his shoulder as he turned to walk back to the bridgemen.

"What are they to you?" Gaz called after him. "Why do you even care?"

"They're my men."

He left Gaz behind. "I don't trust him," Syl said, looking over her shoulder. "He could just say you threatened him and send men to arrest you."

"Maybe he will," Kaladin said. "I guess I just have to count on him wanting more of my bribes."

Kaladin continued on, listening to the shouts of the victors and the groans of their wounded. The plateaus were littered with corpses, bunched up along the edges of the chasm, where the bridges had made a focus for the battle. The Parshendi—as always—had left their dead behind. Even when they won, they reportedly left their dead. The humans sent back bridge crews and soldiers to burn their dead and send their spirits to the afterlife, where the best among them would fight in the Heralds' army.

"Spheres," Syl said, still looking at Gaz. "That doesn't seem like much to count on."

"Maybe. Maybe not. I've seen the way he looks at them. He wants the money I give him. Perhaps badly enough to keep him in line." Kaladin shook his head. "What you said earlier is right; men are unreliable in many things. But if there's one thing you *can* count on, it's their greed."

It was a bitter thought. But it had been a bitter day. A hopeful, bright beginning, and a bloody, red sunset.

Just like every day.

*Ati was once a kind and generous man, and you saw what
became of him. Rayse, on the other hand, was among the
most loathsome, crafty, and dangerous individuals I had
ever met.*

Yeah, this was cut," the portly leatherworker said, holding
up the straps as Adolin watched. "Wouldn't you agree,
Yis?"

The other leatherworker nodded. Yis was a yellow-eyed
Iriali, with stark golden hair. Not blond, golden. There was
even a metallic sheen to it. He kept it short and wore a cap.
Obviously, he didn't want to draw attention to it. Many considered a lock of Iriali hair to be a ward of good luck.

His companion, Avaran, was an Alethi darkeyes who wore
an apron over his vest. If the two men worked in the traditional
way, one would labor on the larger, more robust pieces—like
saddles—while the other specialized in fine detail. A group of
apprentices toiled in the background, cutting or sewing hogshide.

"Sliced," Yis agreed, taking the straps from Avaran. "I
concur."

"Well hie me to Damnation," Adolin muttered. "You mean
Elhokar was actually *right*?"

"Adolin," a feminine voice said from behind. "You said we'd be going on a walk."

"That's what we're doing," he said, turning to smile. Janala stood with arms folded, wearing a sleek yellow dress of impeccable fashion, buttoning up the sides, cupping around the neck with a stiff collar embroidered with crimson thread.

"I had imagined," she said, "that a walk would involve more *walking*."

"Hm," he said. "Yes. We'll be getting right to that soon. It'll be grand. Lots of prancing, sauntering, and, er . . ."

"Promenading?" Yis the leatherworker offered.

"Isn't that a type of drink?" Adolin asked.

"Er, no, Brightlord. I'm fairly certain it's another word for walking."

"Well, then," Adolin said. "We'll do plenty of it too. Promenading. I always love a good promenading." He rubbed his chin, taking the strap back. "How certain are you about this strap?"

"There's really no room for question, Brightlord," Avaran said. "That's not a simple tear. You should be more careful."

"Careful?"

"Yes," Avaran said. "Make sure that no loose buckles are scraping the leather, cutting into it. This looks like it came from a saddle. Sometimes, people let the girth straps hang down when setting the saddle for the night, and they get pinched underneath something. I'd guess that caused the slice."

"Oh," Adolin said. "You mean it wasn't cut intentionally?"

"Well, it could have been that," Avaran said. "But why would someone cut a girth like this?"

Why indeed, Adolin thought. He bid farewell to the two leatherworkers, tucked the strap into his pocket, then held out his elbow to Janala. She took it with her freehand, obviously happy to finally be free of the leatherworking shop. It had a faint odor about it, though not nearly as bad as a tannery. He'd seen her reaching for her handkerchief a few times, acting as if she wanted to hold it up to her nose.

They stepped out into the midday sunlight. Tibon and

Marks—two lighteyed members of the Cobalt Guard—waited outside with Janala's handmaiden, Falksi, who was a young Azish darkeyes. The three fell into step behind Adolin and Janala as they walked out onto the street of the warcamp, Falksi muttering under her breath in an accented voice about the lack of a proper palanquin for her mistress.

Janala didn't seem to mind. She breathed deeply of the open air and clung to his arm. She was quite beautiful, even if she did like to talk about herself. Talkativeness was normally an attribute he was fond of in a woman, but today he had trouble paying attention as Janala began telling him about the latest court gossip.

The strap had been cut, but the leatherworkers had both assumed that it was the result of an accident. That implied they'd seen cuts like this before. A loose buckle or other mishap slicing the leather.

Except this time, that cut had thrown the king in the middle of a fight. Could there be something to it?

". . . wouldn't you say, Adolin?" Janala asked.

"Undoubtedly," he said, listening with half an ear.

"So you'll talk to him?"

"Hum?"

"Your father. You'll ask him about letting the men abandon that dreadfully unfashionable uniform once in a while?"

"Well, he's rather set on the idea," Adolin said. "Besides, it's really not *that* unfashionable."

Janala gave him a flat stare.

"All right," he admitted. "It is a little drab." Like every other high-ranked lighteyed officer in Dalinar's army, Adolin wore a simple blue outfit of militaristic cut. A long coat of solid blue—no embroidery—and stiff trousers in a time when vests, silk accents, and scarves were the fashion. His father's Kholin glyphpair was emblazoned quite obtrusively on the back and breast, and the front fastened with silver buttons up both sides. It was simple, distinctly recognizable, but awfully plain.

"Your father's men love him, Adolin," Janala said. "But his requirements *are* growing tiresome."

"I know. Trust me. But I don't think I can change his mind." How to explain? Despite six years at war, Dalinar wasn't weakening in his resolve to hold to the Codes. If anything, his dedication to them was strengthening.

At least now Adolin understood somewhat. Dalinar's beloved brother had made one last request: Follow the Codes. True, that request had been in reference to a single event, but Adolin's father was known to take things to extremes.

Adolin just wished he wouldn't make the same requirement of everyone else. Individually, the Codes were only minor inconveniences—always be in uniform when in public, never be drunken, avoid dueling. In aggregate, however, they were burdensome.

His response to Janala was cut off as a set of horns blared through the camp. Adolin perked up, spinning, looking eastward toward the Shattered Plains. He counted off the next series of horns. A chrysalis had been spotted on plateau one-forty-seven. That was within striking distance!

He held his breath, waiting for a third series of horns to blare, calling Dalinar's armies to battle. That would only happen if his father ordered it.

Part of him knew those horns wouldn't come. One-forty-seven was close enough to Sadeas's warcamp that the other highprince would certainly try for it.

Come on, Father, Adolin thought. *We can race him for it!*

No horns came.

Adolin glanced at Janala. She'd chosen music as her Calling and paid little attention to the war, though her father was one of Dalinar's cavalry officers. From her expression, Adolin could tell that even she understood what the lack of a third horn meant.

Once again, Dalinar Kholin had chosen not to fight.

"Come on," Adolin said, turning and moving in another direction, practically towing Janala along by her elbow. "There's something else I want to check into."

Dalinar stood with hands clasped behind his back, looking out over the Shattered Plains. He was on one of the lower terraces outside Elhokar's elevated palace—the king didn't reside in one of the ten warcamps, but in a small compound elevated along a hillside nearby. Dalinar's climb to the palace had been interrupted by the horns.

He stood long enough see Sadeas's army gathering inside his camp. Dalinar could have sent a soldier to prepare his own men. He was close enough.

"Brightlord?" a voice asked from the side. "Do you wish to continue?"

You protect him your way, Sadeas, Dalinar thought. *I'll protect him my way.*

"Yes, Teshav," he said, turning to continue walking up the switchbacks.

Teshav joined him. She had streaks of blond in her otherwise black Alethi hair, which she wore up in an intricate crossing weave. She had violet eyes, and her pinched face bore a concerned expression. That was normal; she always seemed to need something to worry about.

Teshav and her attendant scribe were both wives of his officers. Dalinar trusted them. Mostly. It was hard to trust anyone completely. *Stop it,* he thought. *You're starting to sound as paranoid as the king.*

Regardless, he'd be very glad for Jasnah's return. If she ever decided to return. Some of his higher officers hinted to him that he should marry again, if only to have a woman who could be his primary scribe. They thought he rejected their suggestions because of love for his first wife. They didn't know that she was gone, vanished from his mind, a blank patch of fog in his memory. Though, in a way, his officers were right. He hesitated to remarry because he hated the idea of replacing her. He'd had everything of his wife taken from him. All that remained was the hole, and filling it to gain a scribe seemed callous.

Dalinar continued on his way. Other than the two women, he was attended by Renarin and three members of the Cobalt

Guard. The latter wore deep blue felt caps and cloaks over silvery breastplates and deep blue trousers. They were light-eyes of low rank, able to carry swords for close fighting.

"Well, Brightlord," Teshav said, "Brightlord Adolin asked me to report the progress of the saddle girth investigation. He's speaking with leatherworkers at this very moment, but so far, there is very little to say. Nobody witnessed anyone interfering with the saddle or His Majesty's horse. Our spies say there are no whispers of anyone in the other warcamps bragging, and nobody in our camp has suddenly received large sums of money, so far as we've discovered."

"The grooms?"

"Say they checked over the saddle," she said, "but when pressed, they admit that they can't *specifically* remember checking the girth." She shook her head. "Carrying a Shard-bearer places great strain on both horse and saddle. If there were only some way to tame more Ryshadium. . . ."

"I think you'll sooner tame the highstorms, Brightness. Well, this is good news, I suppose. Better for us all that this strap business turns out to be nothing. Now, there is another item I wish you to look into."

"It is my pleasure to serve, Brightlord."

"Highprince Aladar has begun to talk of taking a short vacation back to Alethkar. I want to know if he's serious."

"Yes, Brightlord." Teshav nodded. "Would that be a problem?"

"I'm honestly not sure." He didn't trust the highprinces, but at least with them all here, he could watch them. If one of them returned to Alethkar, the man could scheme unchecked. Of course, even brief visits might help stabilize their homeland.

Which was more important? Stability or the ability to watch over the others? *Blood of my fathers,* he thought. *I wasn't made for this politicking and scheming. I was made to wield a sword and ride down enemies.*

He'd do what needed to be done anyway. "I believe you said you had information on the king's accounts, Teshav?"

"Indeed," she said as they continued the short hike. "You

were correct to have me look into the ledgers, as it appears that three of the highprinces—Thanadal, Hatham, and Vamah—are well behind in their payments. Other than yourself, only Highprince Sadeas has actually paid ahead on what is owed, as the tenets of war require."

Dalinar nodded. "The longer this war stretches, the more comfortable the highprinces are getting. They're starting to question. Why pay high wartime rates for Soulcasting? Why not move farmers out here and start growing their own food?"

"Pardon, Brightlord," Teshav said as they turned around a switchback. Her attendant scribe walked behind, several ledgers clipped to boards carried in a satchel. "But do we really wish to discourage that? A second stream of supplies could be valuable as a redundancy."

"The merchants already provide redundancy," Dalinar said. "Which is one of the reasons I haven't chased them off. I wouldn't mind another, but the Soulcasters are the only hold we have on the highprinces. They owed Gavilar loyalty, but they feel little of that for his son." Dalinar narrowed his eyes. "This is a vital point, Teshav. Have you read the histories I suggested?"

"Yes, Brightlord."

"Then you know. The most fragile period in a kingdom's existence comes during the lifetime of its founder's heir. During the reign of a man like Gavilar, men stay loyal because of their respect for him. During subsequent generations, men begin to see themselves as part of a kingdom, a united force that holds together because of tradition.

"But the son's reign . . . that's the dangerous point. Gavilar isn't here to hold everyone together, but there isn't yet a tradition of Alethkar being a kingdom. We've *got* to carry on long enough for the highprinces to begin seeing themselves as part of a greater whole."

"Yes, Brightlord."

She didn't question. Teshav was deeply loyal to him, as were most of his officers. They didn't question why it was so important to him that the ten princedoms regard themselves as one nation. Perhaps they assumed it was because of Gavilar.

Indeed, his brother's dream of a united Alethkar was part of it. There was something else, though.

The Everstorm comes. The True Desolation. The Night of Sorrows.

He suppressed a shiver. The visions certainly didn't make it sound like he had a great deal of time to prepare.

"Draft a missive in the king's name," Dalinar said, "decreasing Soulcasting costs for those who have made their payments on time. That should wake up the others. Give it to Elhokar's scribes and have them explain it to him. Hopefully he will agree with the need."

"Yes, Brightlord," Teshav said. "If I might note, I was quite surprised that you suggested I read those histories. In the past, such things haven't been particular to your interests."

"I do a lot of things lately that aren't particular to my interests or my talents," Dalinar said with a grimace. "My lack of capacity doesn't change the kingdom's needs. Have you gathered reports of banditry in the area?"

"Yes, Brightlord." She hesitated. "The rates are quite alarming."

"Tell your husband I give him command of the Fourth Battalion," Dalinar said. "I want the two of you to work out a better pattern of patrol in the Unclaimed Hills. So long as the Alethi monarchy has a presence here, I do *not* want it to be a land of lawlessness."

"Yes, Brightlord," Teshav said, sounding hesitant. "You realize that means you've committed two entire battalions to patrolling?"

"Yes," Dalinar said. He had asked for help from the other highprinces. Their reactions had ranged from shock to mirth. None had given him any soldiers.

"That is added to the battalion you assigned to peacekeeping in the areas between warcamps and the exterior merchant markets," Teshav added. "In total, that's over a quarter of your forces here, Brightlord."

"The orders stand, Teshav." he said. "See to it. But first, I have more to discuss with you regarding the ledgers. Go on ahead to the ledger room and wait for us there."

She nodded respect. "Of course, Brightlord." She withdrew with her attendant.

Renarin stepped up to Dalinar. "She wasn't pleased about that, Father."

"She wishes her husband to be fighting," Dalinar said. "They all hope that I'll win another Shardblade out there, then give it to them." The Parshendi had Shards. Not many, but even a single one was surprising. Nobody had an explanation for where they'd gotten them. Dalinar had won a Parshendi Shardblade and Plate during his first year here. He'd given both to Elhokar to award to a warrior he felt would be the most useful to Alethkar and the war effort.

Dalinar turned and entered the palace proper. The guards at the doorway saluted him and Renarin. The young man kept his eyes forward, staring at nothing. Some people thought him emotionless, but Dalinar knew he was just preoccupied.

"I've been meaning to speak with you, son," Dalinar said. "About the hunt last week."

Renarin's eyes flickered downward in shame, the edges of his mouth pulling back in a grimace. Yes, he *did* have emotions. He just didn't show them as often as others.

"You realize that you shouldn't have rushed into battle as you did," Dalinar said sternly. "That chasmfiend could have killed you."

"What would you have done, Father, if it had been me in danger?"

"I don't fault your bravery; I fault your wisdom. What if you'd had one of your fits?"

"Then perhaps the monster would have swept me off the plateau," Renarin said bitterly, "and I would no longer be such a useless drain on everyone's time."

"Don't say such things! Not even in jest."

"Was it jest? Father, I can't fight."

"Fighting is not the only thing of value a man can do." The ardents were very specific about that. Yes, the highest Calling of men was to join the battle in the afterlife to reclaim the Tranquiline Halls, but the Almighty accepted the excellence of any man or woman, regardless of what they did.

You just did your best, picking a profession and an attribute of the Almighty to emulate. A Calling and a Glory, it was said. You worked hard at your profession, and you spent your life trying to live according to a single ideal. The Almighty would accept that, particularly if you were lighteyed—the better your blood as a lighteyes, the more innate Glory you had already.

Dalinar's Calling was to be a leader, and his chosen Glory was determination. He'd chosen both in his youth, though he now viewed them very differently than he once had.

"You are right, of course, Father," Renarin said. "I am not the first hero's son to be born without any talent for warfare. The others all got along. So shall I. Likely I will end up as citylord of a small town. Assuming I don't tuck myself away in the devotaries." The boy's eyes turned forward.

I still think of him as "the boy," Dalinar thought. *Even though he's now in his twentieth year.* Wit had been right. Dalinar underestimated Renarin. *How would I react, if I were forbidden to fight? Kept back with the women and the merchants?*

Dalinar would have been bitter, particularly against Adolin. In fact, Dalinar *had* often been envious of Gavilar during their boyhood. Renarin, however, was Adolin's greatest supporter. He all but worshipped his elder brother. And he was brave enough to dash heedless into the middle of a battlefield where a nightmare creature was smashing spearmen and tossing aside Shardbearers.

Dalinar cleared his throat. "Perhaps it is time to again try training you in the sword."

"My blood weakness—"

"Won't matter a bit if we get you into a set of Plate and give you a Blade," Dalinar said. "The armor makes any man strong, and a Shardblade is nearly as light as air itself."

"Father," Renarin said flatly, "I'll never be a Shardbearer. You yourself have said that the Blades and Plate we win from the Parshendi must go to the most skilled warriors."

"None of the other highprinces give up their spoils to the

king," Dalinar said. "And who would fault me if, for once, I made a gift to my son?"

Renarin stopped in the hallway, displaying an unusual level of emotion, eyes opening wider, face eager. "You are serious?"

"I give you my oath, son. If I can capture another Blade and Plate, they will go to you." He smiled. "To be honest, I'd do it simply for the joy of seeing Sadeas's face when you become a full Shardbearer. Beyond that, if your strength is made equal to others, I expect that your natural skill will make you shine."

Renarin smiled. Shardplate wouldn't solve everything, but Renarin would have his chance. Dalinar would see to it. *I know what it's like to be a second son,* he thought as they continued walking toward the king's chambers, *overshadowed by an older brother you love yet envy at the same time. Stormfather, but I do.*

I still feel that way.

⋅⟡⋅

"Ah, good Brightlord Adolin," the ardent said, walking forward with open arms. Kadash was a tall man in his later years, and wore the shaved head and square beard of his Calling. He also had a twisting scar that ran around the top of his head, a memento from his earlier days as an army officer.

It was uncommon to find a man such as him—a lighteyes who had once been a soldier—in the ardentia. In fact, it was odd for any man to change his Calling. But it wasn't forbidden, and Kadash had risen far in the ardentia considering his late start. Dalinar said it was a sign of either faith or perseverance. Perhaps both.

The warcamp's temple had started as a large Soulcast dome, then Dalinar had granted money and stonemasons to transform it into a more suitable house of worship. Carvings of the Heralds now lined the inside walls, and broad windows carved on the leeward side had been set with glass to let in the light. Diamond spheres blazed in bunches hung from the high ceiling, and stands had been set up for the instruction, practice, and testing of the various arts.

Many women were in at the moment, receiving instruction from the ardents. There were fewer men. Being at war, it was easy to practice the masculine arts in the field.

Janala folded her arms, scanning the temple with obvious dissatisfaction as she stood beside Adolin. "First a stinky leatherworker's shop, now the temple? I had assumed we would walk someplace at least *faintly* romantic."

"Religion's romantic," Adolin said, scratching his head. "Eternal love and all that, right?"

She eyed him. "I'm going to go wait outside." She turned and walked out with her handmaiden. "And someone get me a storming palanquin."

Adolin frowned, watching her go. "I'll have to buy her something quite expensive to make up for this, I suspect."

"I don't see what the problem is," Kadash said. "*I* think religion is romantic."

"You're an ardent," Adolin said flatly. "Besides, that scar makes you a little too unsightly for my tastes." He sighed. "It's not so much the temple that has set her off, but my lack of attention. I haven't been a very good companion today."

"You have matters pressing upon your mind, bright one?" Kadash asked. "Is this about your Calling? You haven't made much progress lately."

Adolin grimaced. His chosen Calling was dueling. By working with the ardents to make personal goals and fulfill them, he could prove himself to the Almighty. Unfortunately, during war, the Codes said Adolin was supposed to limit his duels, as frivolous dueling could wound officers who might be needed in battle.

But Adolin's father avoided battle more and more. So what was the point of not dueling? "Holy one," Adolin said, "we need to speak somewhere we can't be overheard."

Kadash raised an eyebrow and led Adolin around the central apex. Vorin temples were always circular with a gently sloping mound at the center, by custom rising ten feet high. The building was dedicated to the Almighty, maintained by

Dalinar and the ardents he owned. All devotaries were welcome to use it, though most would have their own chapter houses in one of the warcamps.

"What is it you wish to ask of me, bright one?" the ardent asked once they reached a more secluded section of the vast chamber. Kadash was deferential, though he had tutored and trained Adolin during his childhood.

"Is my father going mad?" Adolin asked. "Or could he really be seeing visions sent by the Almighty, as I think he believes?"

"That's a rather blunt question."

"You've known him longer than most, Kadash, and I know you to be loyal. I also know you to be one who keeps his ears open and notices things, so I'm sure you've heard the rumors." Adolin shrugged. "Seems like a time for bluntness if there ever was one."

"I take it, then, the rumors are not unfounded."

"Unfortunately, no. It happens during every highstorm. He raves and thrashes about, and afterward claims to have seen things."

"What sorts of things?"

"I'm not certain, precisely." Adolin grimaced. "Things about the Radiants. And perhaps . . . about what is to come."

Kadash looked disturbed. "This is dangerous territory, bright one. What you are asking me about risks tempting me to violate my oaths. I am an ardent, owned by and loyal to your father."

"But he is not your religious superior."

"No. But he *is* the Almighty's guardian of this people, set to watch me and make certain I don't rise above my station." Kadash pursed his lips. "It is a delicate balance we walk, bright one. Do you know much of the Hierocracy, the War of Loss?"

"The church tried to seize control," Adolin said, shrugging. "The priests tried to conquer the world—for its own good, they claimed."

"That was part of it," Kadash said. "The part we speak of most often. But the problem goes much deeper. The church back then, it clung to knowledge. Men were not in command of their own religious paths; the priests controlled the doctrine, and few members of the Church were allowed to know theology. They were taught to follow the priests. Not the Almighty or the Heralds, but the priests."

He began walking, leading Adolin around the back rim of the temple chamber. They passed statues of the Heralds, five male, five female. In truth, Adolin knew very little of what Kadash was saying. He'd never had much of a mind for history that didn't relate directly to the command of armies.

"The problem, bright one," Kadash said, "was mysticism. The priests claimed that common men could not understand religion or the Almighty. Where there should have been openness, there was smoke and whispers. The priests began to claim visions and prophecies, though such things had been denounced by the Heralds themselves. Voidbinding is a dark and evil thing, and the soul of it was to try to divine the future."

Adolin froze. "Wait, you're saying—"

"Don't get ahead of me please, bright one," Kadash assured, turning back toward him. "When the priests of the Hierocracy were cast down, the Sunmaker made a point of interrogating them and going through their correspondences with one another. It was discovered that there *had* been no prophecies. No mystical promises from the Almighty. That had all been an excuse, fabricated by the priests to placate and control the people."

Adolin frowned. "Where are you going with this, Kadash?"

"As close as I dare to the truth, bright one," the ardent said. "As I cannot be as blunt as you."

"You think my father's visions are fabrications, then."

"I would never accuse my highprince of lying," Kadash said. "Or even of feebleness. But neither can I condone mysticism or prophecy in any form. To do so would be to deny Vorinism. The days of the priests are gone. The days of lying to the people, of keeping them in darkness, are gone. Now, each man chooses his own path, and the ardents help him achieve closeness to the Almighty through it. Instead of shadowed prophecies and pretend powers held by a few, we have a population who understand their beliefs and their relationship with their God."

He stepped closer, speaking very softly. "Your father is not to be mocked or diminished. If his visions are true, then it is between him and the Almighty. All I can say is this: I know something of what it is to be haunted by the death and destruction of war. I see in your father's eyes much of what I have felt, but worse. My personal opinion is that the things he sees are likely more a reflection of his past than any mystical experience."

"So he is going mad," Adolin whispered.

"I did not say that."

"You implied that the Almighty probably wouldn't send visions like these."

"I did."

"And that his visions are a product of his own mind."

"*Likely* so," the ardent said, raising his finger. "A delicate balance, you see. One that is particularly difficult to keep when speaking to my highprince's own son." He reached out, taking Adolin's arm. "If any are to help him, it must be you. It would not be the place of any other, even myself."

Adolin nodded slowly. "Thank you."

"You should likely go see to that young woman now."

"Yes," Adolin said with a sigh. "I fear that even with the right gift, she and I are not long for courting. Renarin will mock me again."

Kadash smiled. "Best not to give up so easily, bright one. Go now. But do return sometime so we can speak of your goals in regard to your Calling. It has been too long since you've Elevated."

Adolin nodded and hurried from the chamber.

※

After hours going over the ledgers with Teshav, Dalinar and Renarin reached the hallway before the king's chambers. They walked in silence, the soles of their boots clapping the marble flooring, the sound echoing against stone walls.

The corridors of the king's war palace were growing richer by the week. Once, this hallway had been just another Soulcast stone tunnel. As Elhokar settled in, he had ordered improvements. Windows were cut into the leeward side. Marble tiling was set into the floor. The walls were carved with reliefs, with mosaic trim at the corners. Dalinar and Renarin passed a group of stonemasons carefully cutting a scene of Nalan'Elin, emitting sunlight, the sword of retribution held over his head.

They reached the king's antechamber, a large, open room guarded by ten members of the King's Guard, dressed in blue and gold. Dalinar recognized each face; he had personally organized the unit, handpicking its members.

Highprince Ruthar waited to see the king. He had brawny arms folded in front of him, and wore a short black beard that surrounded his mouth. His red silk coat was cut short and did not button; almost more of a sleeved vest, it was a mere token nod to traditional Alethi uniform. The shirt underneath was ruffled and white, and his blue trousers were loose, with wide cuffs.

Ruthar glanced Dalinar's way and nodded to him—a minor token of respect—then turned to chat with one of his attendants. He cut off, however, as the guards at the doorway stepped aside to let Dalinar enter. Ruthar sniffed in annoyance. Dalinar's easy access to the king galled the other highprinces.

The king wasn't in his wardroom, but the wide doors to his balcony were open. Dalinar's guardsmen waited behind as he stepped out onto the balcony, Renarin hesitantly following. The light outside was dimming as sunset neared. Setting the war palace up high like this was tactically sound, but it meant the place was mercilessly buffeted by storms. That was an old campaign conundrum. Did one choose the best position to weather storms, or did one seize the high ground?

Most would have chosen the former; their warcamps on the edge of the Shattered Plains were unlikely to be attacked, making the advantage of the high ground less important. But kings tended to prefer height. In this instance, Dalinar had encouraged Elhokar, just in case.

The balcony itself was a thick platform of rock cut onto the top of the small peak, edged with an iron railing. The king's rooms were a Soulcast dome sitting atop the natural formation, with covered ramps and stairways leading to tiers lower on the hillside. Those housed the king's various attendants: guards, stormwardens, ardents, and distant family members. Dalinar had his own bunker at his warcamp. He refused to call it a palace.

The king leaned against the railing, two guards watching from a distance. Dalinar motioned for Renarin to join them, so that he could speak with the king in private.

The air was cool—spring having come for a time—and it was sweet with the scents of evening: blooming rockbuds and wet stone. Below, the warcamps were starting to come alight, ten sparkling circles filled with watchfires, cookfires, lamps, and the steady glow of infused gems. Elhokar stared over the camps and toward the Shattered Plains. They were utterly dark, save for the occasional twinkle of a watchpost.

"Do they watch us, from out there?" Elhokar asked as Dalinar joined him.

"We know their raiding bands move at night, Your Majesty," Dalinar said, resting one hand on the iron railing. "I can't help but think they watch us."

The king's uniform had the traditional long coat with buttons up the sides, but it was loose and relaxed, and ruffled lace poked out of the collar and cuffs. His trousers were solid blue, and were cut in the same baggy fashion as Ruthar's. It all looked so informal to Dalinar. Increasingly, their soldiers were being led by a slack group who dressed in lace and spent their evenings at feasts.

This is what Gavilar foresaw, Dalinar thought. *This is why he grew so insistent that we follow the Codes.*

"You look thoughtful, Uncle," Elhokar said.

"Just considering the past, Your Majesty."

"The past is irrelevant. I only look forward."

Dalinar was not certain he agreed with either statement.

"I sometimes think I should be able to see the Parshendi," Elhokar said. "I feel that if I stare long enough, I will find them, pin them down so I can challenge them. I wish they'd just fight me, like men of honor."

"If they were men of honor," Dalinar said, clasping his hands behind his back, "then they would not have killed your father as they did."

"Why did they do it, do you suppose?"

Dalinar shook his head. "That question has churned in my head, over and over, like a boulder tumbling down a hill. Did we offend their honor? Was it some cultural misunderstanding?"

"A cultural misunderstanding would imply that they *have* a culture. Primitive brutes. Who knows why a horse kicks or an axehound bites? I shouldn't have asked."

Dalinar didn't reply. He'd felt that same disdain, that same anger, in the months following Gavilar's assassination. He could understand Elhokar's desire to dismiss these strange, wildland parshmen as little more than animals.

But he'd *seen* them during those early days. Interacted with them. They were primitive, yes, but not brutes. Not stupid. *We never really understood them,* he thought. *I guess that's the crux of the problem.*

"Elhokar," he said softly. "It may be time to ask ourselves some difficult questions."

"Such as?"

"Such as how long we will continue this war."

Elhokar started. He turned, looking at Dalinar. "We'll keep fighting until the Vengeance Pact is satisfied and my father is avenged!"

"Noble words," Dalinar said. "But we've been away from Alethkar for six years now. Maintaining two far-flung centers of government is not healthy for the kingdom."

"Kings often go to war for extended periods, Uncle."

"Rarely do they do it for so long," Dalinar said, "and rarely do they bring every Shardbearer and highprince in the kingdom with them. Our resources are strained, and word from home is that the Reshi border encroachments grow increasingly bold. We are still fragmented as a people, slow to trust one another, and the nature of this extended war—without a clear path to victory and with a focus on riches rather than capturing ground—is not helping at all."

Elhokar sniffed, wind blowing at them atop the peaked rock. "You say there's no clear path to victory? We've been winning! The Parshendi raids are coming less frequently, and aren't striking as far westward as they once did. We've killed thousands of them in battle."

"Not enough," Dalinar said. "They still come in strength. The siege is straining us as much as, or more than, it is them."

"Weren't *you* the one to suggest this tactic in the first place?"

"I was a different man, then, flush with grief and anger."

"And you no longer feel those things?" Elhokar was incredulous. "Uncle, I can't believe I'm hearing this! You aren't *seriously* suggesting that I abandon the war, are you? You'd have me slink home, like a scolded axehound?"

"I said they were difficult questions, Your Majesty," Dalinar said, keeping his anger in check. It was taxing. "But they *must* be considered."

Elhokar breathed out, annoyed. "It's true, what Sadeas and the others whisper. You're changing, Uncle. It has something to do with those episodes of yours, doesn't it?"

"They are unimportant, Elhokar. Listen to me! What are we willing to give, in order to get vengeance?"

"Anything."

"And if that means everything your father worked for? Do we honor his memory by undermining his vision for Alethkar, all to get revenge in his name?"

The king hesitated.

"You pursue the Parshendi," Dalinar said. "That is laudable. But you can't let your passion for just retribution blind you to the needs of our kingdom. The Vengeance Pact has kept the highprinces channeled, but what will happen once we win? Will we shatter? I think we need to forge them together, to unite them. We fight this war as if we were ten different nations, fighting beside one another but not *with* one another."

The king didn't respond immediately. The words, finally, seemed to be sinking in. He was a good man, and shared more with his father than others chose to admit.

He turned away from Dalinar, leaning against the railing. "You think I'm a poor king, don't you, Uncle?"

"What? Of course not!"

"You always talk about what I *should* be doing, and where I am lacking. Tell me truthfully, Uncle. When you look at me, do you wish you saw my father's face instead?"

"Of course I do," Dalinar said.

Elhokar's expression darkened.

Dalinar laid a hand on his nephew's shoulder. "I'd be a poor brother if I didn't wish that Gavilar had lived. I failed him—it was the greatest, most terrible failure of my life." Elhokar turned to him, and Dalinar held his gaze, raising a finger. "But just because I loved your father does *not* mean that I think you are a failure. Nor does it mean I do not love you in your own right. Alethkar itself could have collapsed upon Gavilar's death, but *you* organized and executed our counterattack. You are a fine king."

The king nodded slowly. "You've been listening to readings from that book again, haven't you?"

"I have."

"You sound like him, you know," Elhokar said, turning back to look eastward again. "Near the end. When he began to act . . . erratically."

"Surely I'm not so bad as that."

"Perhaps. But this is much like how he was. Talking about an end to war, fascinated by the Lost Radiants, insisting everyone follow the Codes . . ."

Dalinar remembered those days—and his own arguments with Gavilar. *What honor can we find on a battlefield while our people starve?* the king had once asked him. *Is it honor when our lighteyes plot and scheme like eels in a bucket, slithering over one another and trying to bite each other's tails?*

Dalinar had reacted poorly to his words. Just as Elhokar was reacting to his words now. *Stormfather! I* am *starting to sound like him, aren't I?*

That was troubling, yet somehow encouraging at the same time. Either way, Dalinar realized something. Adolin was right. Elhokar—and the highprinces with him—would never respond to a suggestion that they retreat. Dalinar was approaching the conversation in the wrong way. *Almighty be blessed for sending me a son willing to speak his mind.*

"Perhaps you are right, Your Majesty," Dalinar said. "End the war? Leave a battlefield with an enemy still in control? That would shame us."

Elhokar nodded in agreement. "I'm glad you see sense."

"But something *does* have to change. We need a better way to fight."

"Sadeas has a better way already. I spoke of his bridges to you. They work so well, and he's captured so many gemhearts."

"Gemhearts are meaningless," Dalinar said. "*All* of this is meaningless if we don't find a way to get the vengeance we all want. You can't tell me you enjoy watching the highprinces squabble, practically ignoring our real purpose in being here."

Elhokar fell silent, looking displeased.

Unite them. He remembered those words, booming in his head. "Elhokar," he said, an idea occurring to him. "Do you remember what Sadeas and I spoke of to you when we first came here to war? The specialization of the highprinces?"

"Yes," Elhokar said. In the distant past, each of the ten highprinces in Alethkar had been given a specific charge for the governing of the kingdom. One had been the ultimate law in regard to merchants, and his troops had patrolled the roadways of all ten princedoms. Another had administrated judges and magistrates.

Gavilar had been very taken by the idea. He claimed it was a clever device, meant to force the highprinces to work together. Once, this system had forced them to submit to one another's authority. Things hadn't been done that way in centuries, ever since the fragmenting of Alethkar into ten autonomous princedoms.

"Elhokar, what if you named me Highprince of War?" Dalinar asked.

Elhokar didn't laugh; that was a good sign. "I thought you and Sadeas decided that the others would revolt if we tried something like that."

"Perhaps I was wrong about that too."

Elhokar appeared to consider it. Finally, the king shook his head. "No. They barely accept my leadership. If I did something like this, they'd assassinate me."

"I'd protect you."

"Bah. You don't even take the *present* threats on my life seriously."

Dalinar sighed. "Your Majesty, I *do* take threats to your life seriously. My scribes and attendants are looking into the strap."

"And what have they discovered?"

"Well, so far we have nothing conclusive. Nobody has taken credit for trying to kill you, even in rumor. Nobody saw anything suspicious. But Adolin is speaking with leatherworkers. Perhaps he'll bring something more substantial."

"It *was* cut, Uncle."

"We will see."

"You don't believe me," Elhokar said, face growing red. "You should be trying to find out what the assassins' plan was, rather than pestering me with some arrogant quest to become overlord of the entire army!"

Dalinar gritted his teeth. "I do this for you, Elhokar."

Elhokar met his eyes for a moment, and his blue eyes flashed with suspicion again, as they had the week before.

Blood of my fathers! Dalinar thought. *He's getting worse.*

Elhokar's expression softened a moment later, and he seemed to relax. Whatever he'd seen in Dalinar's eyes had comforted him. "I know you try for the best, Uncle," Elhokar said. "But you have to admit that you've been erratic lately. The way you react to storms, your infatuation with my father's last words—"

"I'm trying to understand him."

"He grew weak at the end," Elhokar said. "Everyone knows it. I won't repeat his mistakes, and you should avoid them as well—rather than listening to a book that claims that lighteyes should be the slaves of the darkeyes."

"That's *not* what it says," Dalinar said. "It has been misinterpreted. It's mostly just a collection of stories which teach that a leader should serve those he leads."

"Bah. It was written by the Lost Radiants!"

"They didn't write it. It was their inspiration. Nohadon, an ordinary man, was its author."

Elhokar glanced at him, raising an eyebrow. *See,* it seemed to say. *You defend it.* "You are growing weak, Uncle. I will not exploit that weakness. But others will."

"I am *not* getting weak." Yet again, Dalinar forced himself to be calm. "This conversation has gone off the path. The highprinces need a single leader to force them to work together. I vow that if you name me Highprince of War, I *will* see you protected."

"As you saw my father protected?"

Dalinar's mouth snapped shut.

Elhokar turned away. "I should not have said that. It was uncalled for."

"No," Dalinar said. "No, it was one of the truest things you have said to me, Elhokar. Perhaps you are right to distrust my protection."

Elhokar glanced at him, curious. "Why do you react that way?"

"What way?"

"Once, if someone had said that to you, you'd have summoned your Blade and demanded a duel! Now you agree with them instead."

"I—"

"My father started refusing duels, near the end." Elhokar tapped on the railing. "I see why you feel the need for a Highprince of War, and you may have a point. But the others very much like the present arrangement."

"Because it is comfortable to them. If we are going to

win, we will *need* to upset them." Dalinar stepped forward. "Elhokar, maybe it's been long enough. Six years ago, naming a Highprince of War might well have been a mistake. But now? We know one another better, and we've been working united against the Parshendi. Perhaps it is time to take the next step."

"Perhaps," the king said. "You think they are ready? I'll let you prove it to me. If you can show me that they are willing to work with you, Uncle, then I'll consider naming you Highprince of War. Is that satisfactory?"

It was a solid compromise. "Very well."

"Good," the king said, standing up. "Then let us part for now. It is growing late, and I have yet to hear what Ruthar wishes of me."

Dalinar nodded his farewell, walking back through the king's chambers, Renarin trailing him.

The more he considered, the more he felt that this was the right thing to do. Retreating would not work with the Alethi, particularly not with their current mind-set. But if he could shock them out of their complacency, force them to adopt a more aggressive strategy . . .

He was still lost in thought considering that as they left the king's palace and made their way down the ramps to where their horses waited. He climbed astride Gallant, nodding his thanks to the groom who had cared for the Ryshadium. The horse had recovered from his fall during the hunt, his leg solid and hale.

It was a short distance back to Dalinar's warcamp, and they rode in silence. *Which of the highprinces should I approach first?* Dalinar thought. *Sadeas?*

No. No, he and Sadeas were already seen working together too often. If the other highprinces began to smell a stronger alliance, it would drive them to turn against him. Best that he approach less powerful highprinces first and see if he could get them to work with him in some way. A joint plateau assault, perhaps?

He'd have to approach Sadeas eventually. He didn't relish the thought. Things were always so much easier when the two of them could work at a safe distance from one another. He—

"Father," Renarin said. He sounded dismayed.

Dalinar sat upright, looking around, hand going for his side sword even while he prepared to summon his Shardblade. Renarin pointed. Eastward. Stormward.

The horizon was growing dark.

"Was there supposed to be a highstorm today?" Dalinar asked, alarmed.

"Elthebar said it was unlikely," Renarin said. "But he's been wrong before."

Everyone could be wrong about highstorms. They could be predicted, but it was never an exact science. Dalinar narrowed his eyes, heart thumping. Yes, he could sense the signs now. The dust picking up, the scents changing. It was evening, but there should still be more light left. Instead, it was rapidly growing darker and darker. The very air felt more frantic.

"Should we go to Aladar's camp?" Renarin said, pointing. They were nearest Highprince Aladar's warcamp, and perhaps only a quarter-hour ride from the rim of Dalinar's own.

Aladar's men would take him in. Nobody would forbid shelter to a highprince during a storm. But Dalinar shuddered, thinking of spending a highstorm trapped in an unfamiliar place, surrounded by another highprince's attendants. They would see him during an episode. Once that happened, the rumors would spread like arrows above a battlefield.

"We ride!" he called, kicking Gallant into motion. Renarin and the guardsmen fell in behind him, hooves a thunder to precurse the coming highstorm. Dalinar leaned low, tense. The grey sky grew clotted with dust and leaves blown ahead of the stormwall and the air grew dense with humid anticipation. The horizon burgeoned with thickening clouds. Dalinar and the others galloped past Aladar's perimeter guards, who bustled with activity, holding their coats or cloaks against the wind.

"Father?" Renarin called from behind. "Are you—"

"We have time!" Dalinar shouted.

They eventually reached the jagged wall of the Kholin

warcamp. Here, the remaining soldiers wore blue and white and saluted. Most had already retreated to their enclosures. He had to slow Gallant to get through the checkpoint. However, it would just be another short gallop to his quarters. He turned Gallant, preparing to go.

"Father!" Renarin said, pointing eastward.

The stormwall hung like a curtain in the air, speeding toward the camp. The massive sheet of rain was a silvery grey, the clouds above onyx black, lit from within by occasional flashes of lightning. The guards who had saluted him were hurrying to a nearby bunker.

"We can make it," Dalinar said. "We—"

"Father!" Renarin said, riding up beside him and catching his arm. "I'm sorry."

The wind whipped at them, and Dalinar gritted his teeth, looking at his son. Renarin's spectacled eyes were wide with concern.

Dalinar glanced at the stormwall again. It was only moments away.

He's right.

He handed Gallant's reins to an anxious soldier, who took the reins of Renarin's mount as well, and the two of them dismounted. The groom rushed away, towing the horses into a stone stable. Dalinar almost followed—there would be fewer people to watch him in a stable—but a nearby barrack had the door open, and those inside waved anxiously. That would be safer.

Resigned, Dalinar joined Renarin, dashing to the stone-walled barrack. The soldiers made room for them; there was a group of servants packed inside as well. In Dalinar's camp, no one was forced to weather the tempests in stormtents or flimsy wooden shacks, and nobody had to pay for protection inside stone structures.

The occupants seemed shocked to see their highprince and his son step in; several paled as the door thumped shut. Their only light was from a few garnets mounted on the walls. Someone coughed, and outside a scattering of windblown rock chips sprayed against the building. Dalinar tried to ignore the uncomfortable eyes around him. Wind howled outside. Perhaps nothing would happen. Perhaps this time—

The storm hit.

It began.

STARFALLS

He holds the most frightening and terrible of all of the Shards. Ponder on that for a time, you old reptile, and tell me if your insistence on nonintervention holds firm. Because I assure you, Rayse will not be similarly inhibited.

Dalinar blinked. The stuffy, dimly lit barrack was gone. Instead, he stood in darkness. The air was thick with the scent of dried grain, and when he reached out with his left hand, he felt a wooden wall. He was in a barn of some sort.

The cool night was still and crisp; there was no sign of a storm. He felt carefully at his side. His side sword was gone, as was his uniform. Instead, he wore a homespun belted tunic and a pair of sandals. It was the type of clothing he'd seen depicted on ancient statues.

Stormwinds, where have you sent me this time? Each of the visions was different. This would be the twelfth one he'd seen. *Only twelve?* he thought. It seemed like so many more, but this had only begun happening to him a few months ago.

Something moved in the darkness. He flinched in surprise as something living pressed against him. He nearly struck it, but froze when he heard it whimper. He carefully lowered his arm, feeling the figure's back. Slight and small—a child. She was quivering.

"Father." Her voice trembled. "Father, what is happening?" As usual, he was being seen as someone of this place and time. The girl clutched him, obviously terrified. It was too dark to see the fearspren he suspected were climbing up through the ground.

Dalinar rested his hand on her back. "Hush. It will be all right." It seemed the right thing to say.

"Mother . . ."

"She will be fine."

The girl huddled more closely against him in the black room. He remained still. Something felt wrong. The building creaked in the wind. It wasn't well built; the plank beneath Dalinar's hand was loose, and he was tempted to push it free so he could peek out. But the stillness, the terrified child . . . There was an oddly putrid scent in the air.

Something scratched, ever so softly, at the barn's far wall. Like a fingernail being drawn across a wooden tabletop.

The girl whimpered, and the scraping sound stopped. Dalinar held his breath, heart beating furiously. Instinctively, he held his hand out to summon his Shardblade, but nothing happened. It would never come during the visions.

The far wall of the building exploded inward.

Splintered wood flew through the darkness as a large shape burst in. Lit only by moonglow and starlight from outside, the black thing was bigger than an axehound. He couldn't make out details, but it seemed to have an unnatural wrongness to its form.

The girl screamed, and Dalinar cursed, grabbing her with one arm and rolling to the side as the black thing leaped for them. It nearly got the child, but Dalinar whipped her out of the creature's path. Breathless with terror, her scream cut off.

Dalinar spun, pushing the girl behind him. His side hit a stack of sacks filled with grain as he edged away. The barn fell silent. Salas's violet light shone in the sky outside, but the small moon wasn't bright enough to illuminate the barn's interior, and the creature had moved into a shadowed recess. He couldn't see much of it.

It seemed part of the shadows. Dalinar tensed, fists

forward. It made a soft wheezing noise, eerie and faintly reminiscent of rhythmic whispering.

Breathing? Dalinar thought. *No. It's sniffing for us.*

The thing darted forward. Dalinar whipped a hand to the side and grabbed one of the grain sacks, pulling it in front of himself. The beast struck the sack, its teeth ripping into it, and Dalinar pulled, tearing the coarse fabric and flinging a fragrant cloud of dusty lavis grain into the air. Then he stepped to the side and kicked the beast as hard as he could.

The creature felt too soft under his foot, as if he'd kicked a waterskin. The blow knocked it to the ground, and it made a hissing sound. Dalinar flung the bag and its remaining contents upward, filling the air with more dried lavis and dust.

The beast scrambled to its feet and twisted around, smooth skin reflecting moonlight. It seemed disoriented. Whatever it was, it hunted by smell, and the dust in the air confused it. Dalinar grabbed the girl and threw her over his shoulder, then dashed past the confused creature, barreling through the hole in the broken wall.

He burst out into violet moonlight. He was in a small lait—a wide rift in the stone with good enough drainage to avoid flooding and a high stone outcropping to break the highstorms. In this case, the eastern rock formation was shaped like an enormous wave, creating shelter for a small village.

That explained the flimsiness of the barn. Lights flickered here and there across the hollow, indicating a settlement of several dozen homes. He was on the outskirts. There was a hogpen to Dalinar's right, distant homes to his left, and just ahead—nestled against the rock hill—was a midsized farmhouse. It was built in an archaic style, with crem bricks for walls.

His decision was easy. The thing had moved quickly, like a predator. Dalinar wouldn't outrun it, so he charged toward the farmhouse. The sound of the beast breaking out through the barn wall came from behind. Dalinar reached the home, but the front door was barred. Dalinar cursed loudly, pounding on it.

Claws scraped on stone from behind as the thing bounded

toward them. Dalinar threw his shoulder against the door just as it opened.

He stumbled inside, dropping the girl to the floor as he found his balance. A middle-aged woman stood inside; violet moonlight revealed that she had thick curly hair and a wide-eyed terrified expression. She slammed the door closed behind him, then barred it.

"Praise the Heralds," she exclaimed, scooping up the girl. "You found her, Heb. Bless you."

Dalinar sidled up to the glassless window, looking out. The shutter appeared to be broken loose, making the window impossible to latch closed.

He couldn't see the creature. He glanced back over his shoulder. The building's floor was simple stone and there was no second story. A fireless brick hearth was set on one side, with a rough-cast iron pot hanging above it. It all looked so primitive. What year was this?

It's just a vision, he thought. *A waking dream.*

Why did it feel so real, then?

He looked back out the window. It was silent outside. A twin row of rockbuds grew on the right side of the yard, probably curnips or some other kind of vegetable. Moonlight reflected off the smooth ground. Where was the creature? Had it—

Something slick-skinned and black leapt up from below and crashed against the window. It shattered the frame, and Dalinar cursed, falling as the thing landed on him. Something sharp slashed his face, cutting open his cheek, spilling blood across his skin.

The girl screamed again.

"Light!" Dalinar bellowed. "Get me light!" He slammed his fist into the side of the creature's too-soft head, using his other arm to push back a clawed paw. His cheek burned with pain, and something raked his side, slashing his tunic and cutting his skin.

With a heave he threw the creature off him. It crashed against the wall, and he rolled to his feet, gasping. As the beast righted itself in the dark room, Dalinar scrambled away, old instincts kicking in, pain evaporating as the battle Thrill surged through him. He needed a weapon! A stool or a table leg. The room was so—

Light flickered on as the woman uncovered a lit pottery lamp. The primitive thing used oil, not Stormlight, but was more than enough to illuminate her terrified face and the girl clinging to her robelike dress. The room had a low table and a pair of stools, but his eyes were drawn to the small hearth.

There, gleaming like one of the Honorblades of ancient lore, was a simple iron fire poker. It leaned against the stone hearth, tip white with ash. Dalinar lunged forward, snatching it in one hand, twirling it to feel out its balance. He had been trained in classical Windstance, but he fell into Smokestance instead, as it was better with an imperfect weapon. One foot forward, one foot behind, sword—or, in this case, poker—held forward with the tip toward his opponent's heart.

Only years of training allowed him to maintain his stance as he saw what he was facing. The creature's smooth, dark-as-midnight skin reflected light like a pool of tar. It had no visible eyes and its black, knifelike teeth bristled in a head set on a sinuous, boneless neck. The six legs were slender and bent at the sides, appearing far too thin to bear the weight of the fluid, inklike body.

This isn't a vision, Dalinar thought. *It's a nightmare.*

The creature raised its head, clicking teeth together, and made a hissing sound. Tasting the air.

"Sweet wisdom of Battar," the woman breathed, holding her child close. Her hands shook as she held up the lamp, as if to use it as a weapon.

A scraping came from outside, and was followed by another set of spindly legs slinking over the lip of the broken window. This new beast climbed into the room, joining its companion, which crouched anxiously, sniffing at Dalinar. It seemed wary, as if it could sense that it faced an armed—or at least determined—opponent.

Dalinar cursed himself for a fool, raising one hand to his side to stanch the blood. He knew, logically, that he was really back in the barrack with Renarin. This was all happening in his mind; there was no need for him to fight.

But every instinct, every shred of honor he had, drove him to step to the side, placing himself between the woman and the beasts. Vision, memory, or delusion, he could *not* stand aside.

"Heb," the woman said, her voice nervous. Who did she see him as? Her husband? A farmhand? "Don't be a fool! You don't know how—"

The beasts attacked. Dalinar leapt forward—remaining in motion was the essence of Smokestance—and spun between the creatures, striking to the side with his poker. He hit the one on the left, ripping a gash in its too-smooth skin.

The wound bled smoke.

Moving behind the creatures, Dalinar swung again, sweeping low at the feet of the unwounded beast, knocking it off balance. With the follow-through, he slammed the side of the poker into the face of the wounded beast as it turned and snapped at him.

The old Thrill, the sense of battle, consumed him. It did not enrage him, as it did some men, but everything seemed to become clearer, crisper. His muscles moved easily; he breathed more deeply. He came *alive*.

He leaped backward as the creatures pressed at him. With a kick, he knocked over the table, tumbling it at one of the beasts. He drove the poker at the open maw of the other. As he had hoped, the inside of its mouth was sensitive. The creature let out a pained hiss and scrambled back.

Dalinar moved to the overturned table and kicked off one of the legs. He scooped it up, falling into Smokestance's sword-and-knife form. He used the wooden leg to fend off one creature while he thrust three times at the face of the other, ripping a gash in its cheek that bled smoke; it came out as a hiss.

There were distant screams outside. *Blood of my fathers,* he thought. *These aren't the only two.* He needed to be done, and quickly. If the fight dragged on, they'd wear him down faster than he wore them down. Who even knew if beasts like this got tired?

Bellowing, he jumped forward. Sweat streamed from his forehead, and the room seemed to grow just faintly darker. Or, no, more focused. Just him and the beasts. The only wind was that of his weapons spinning, the only sound that of his feet hitting the floor, the only vibration that of his heart thumping.

His sudden whirlwind of blows shocked the creatures. He smashed the table leg against one, forcing it back, then threw himself at the other one, earning a rake of the claws against his arm as he rammed the poker into the beast's chest. The skin resisted at first, but then broke, his poker moving through easily after that.

A powerful jet of smoke burst out around Dalinar's hand. He pulled his arm free, and the creature stumbled back, legs growing thinner, body deflating like a leaking wineskin.

He knew he'd exposed himself in attacking. There was nothing to do but throw his arm up as the other beast leapt on him, slashing his forehead and his arm, biting his shoulder. Dalinar screamed, slamming the table leg again and again at the beast's head. He tried forcing the creature back, but it was terribly strong.

So Dalinar let himself slip to the ground and kicked upward, tossing the beast over his head. The fangs ripped free of Dalinar's shoulder with a spray of blood. The beast hit the floor in a mess of black legs.

Dizzy, Dalinar forced himself to his feet and fell into his stance. *Always keep the stance.* The creature got to its feet at about the same time, and Dalinar ignored the pain, ignored the blood, letting the Thrill give him focus. He leveled the poker. The table leg had fallen from his blood-slick fingers.

The beast crouched, then charged. Dalinar let the fluid nature of Smokestance direct him, stepping to the side and smashing the poker into the beast's legs. It tripped as Dalinar turned around, wielding his poker with both hands and *slamming* it directly down into the creature's back.

The powerful blow broke the skin, passed through the creature's body, and hit the stone floor. The creature struggled, legs working ineffectively, as smoke hissed out the holes in its back and stomach. Dalinar stepped away, wiping blood from his forehead, leaving the weapon to fall to the side and clang to the ground, still impaling the beast.

"*Three Gods*, Heb," the woman whispered.

He turned to find her looking completely shocked as she stared at the deflating carcasses. "I should have helped," she mumbled, "should have grabbed something to hit them. But you were so fast. It—it was just a few heartbeats. Where— How—?" She focused on him. "I've never seen anything like it, Heb. You fought like a . . . like one of the Radiants themselves. Where did you learn that?"

Dalinar didn't answer. He pulled off his shirt, grimacing as the pain of his wounds returned. Only the shoulder was immediately dangerous, but it was bad; his left arm was growing numb. He ripped the shirt in half, tying one portion around his gashed right forearm, then wadded the rest and pressed it against his shoulder. He walked over and pulled the poker free of the deflated body, which now resembled a black silk sack. Then he moved to the window. The other homes showed signs of being attacked, fires burning, faint screams hanging on the wind.

"We need to get someplace safe," he said. "Is there a cellar nearby?"

"A what?"

"Cave in the rock, man-made or natural."

"No caves," the woman said, joining him at the window. "How would men make a hole in the *rock*?"

With a Shardblade or a Soulcaster. Or even with basic mining—though that could be difficult, as the crem would seal up caverns and highstorm rains made for an extremely potent risk of flooding. Dalinar looked out the window again. Dark shapes moved in the moonlight; some were coming in their direction.

He wavered, dizzy. Blood loss. Gritting his teeth, he

steadied himself against the frame of the window. How long was this vision going to last? "We need a river. Something to wash away the trail of our scent. Is there one nearby?"

The woman nodded, growing pale faced as she noticed the dark forms in the night.

"Get the girl, woman."

"'The girl'? Seeli, our *daughter*. And since when have you called me woman? Is Taffa so hard to say? Stormwinds, Heb, what has gotten into you?"

He shook his head, moving to the door and throwing it open, still carrying the poker. "Bring the lamp. The light won't give us away; I don't think they can see."

The woman obeyed, hurrying to collect Seeli—she looked to be about six or seven—then followed Dalinar out, the clay lamp's fragile flame quivering in the night. It looked a little like a slipper.

"The river?" Dalinar asked.

"You know where—"

"I hit my head, Taffa," Dalinar said. "I'm dizzy. It's hard to think."

The woman looked worried at that, but seemed to accept this answer. She pointed away from the village.

"Let's go," he said, moving out into the darkness. "Are attacks by these beasts common?"

"During Desolations, perhaps, but not in my life! Stormwinds, Heb. We need to get you to—"

"No," he said. "We keep moving."

They continued along a path, which ran up toward the back side of the wave formation. Dalinar kept glancing back at the village. How many people were dying below, murdered by those beasts from Damnation? Where were the landlord's soldiers?

Perhaps this village was too remote, too far from a city-lord's direct protection. Or perhaps things didn't work that way in this era, this place. *I'll see the woman and child to the river, then I'll return to organize a resistance. If anyone is left.*

The thought seemed laughable. He had to use the poker to

keep himself upright. How was *he* going to organize a resistance?

He slipped on a steep portion of the trail, and Taffa set down the lamp, grabbing his arm, concerned. The landscape was rough with boulders and rockbuds, their vines and leaves extended in the cool, wet night. Those rustled in the wind. Dalinar righted himself, then nodded to the woman, gesturing for her to continue.

A faint scraping sounded in the night; Dalinar turned, tense.

"Heb?" the woman asked, sounding afraid.

"Hold up the light."

She raised the lamp, illuminating the hillside in flickering yellow. A good dozen midnight patches, skins too smooth, were creeping over rockbuds and boulders. Even their teeth and claws were black.

Seeli whimpered, pulling close to her mother.

"Run," Dalinar said softly, raising his poker.

"Heb, they're—"

"Run!" he bellowed.

"They're in front of us too!"

He spun, picking out the dark patches ahead. He cursed, looking around. "There," he said, pointing to a nearby rock formation. It was tall and flat. He shoved Taffa forward, and she towed Seeli, their single-piece, blue dresses rippling in the wind.

They ran more quickly than he could in his state, and Taffa reached the rock wall first. She looked up, as if to climb to the top. It was too steep for that; Dalinar just wanted something solid to put at his back. He stepped onto a flat, open section of rock before the formation and raised his weapon. Black beasts crawled carefully over the stones. Could he distract them, somehow, and let the other two flee? He felt so dizzy.

What I'd give for my Shardplate . . .

Seeli whimpered. Her mother tried to comfort her, but the woman's voice was unnerved. She knew. Knew those bundles of blackness, like living night, would rip them and tear them. What was that word she'd used? Desolation. The book spoke of them. The Desolations had happened during the near-mythical shadowdays, before real history began. Before mankind had defeated the Voidbringers and taken the war to heaven.

The Voidbringers. Was that what these things were? Myths. Myths come to life to kill him.

Several of the creatures lunged forward, and he felt the Thrill surge within him again, strengthening him as he swung. They jumped back, cautious, testing for weakness. Others sniffed the air, pacing. They wanted to get at the woman and child.

Dalinar jumped at them, forcing them away, uncertain where he found the strength. One got close, and he swung at it, falling into Windstance, as it was most familiar. The sweeping strikes, the grace.

He struck at the beast, scoring it on its flank, but two others jumped at him from the side. Claws raked his back, and the weight threw him to the stones. He cursed, rolling, punching a creature and tossing it back. Another bit his wrist, causing him to drop the poker in a flash of pain. He bellowed and slammed his fist into the creature's jaw and it opened reflexively, freeing his hand.

The monsters pressed forward. Somehow he got to his feet and stumbled back against the rock wall. The woman threw the lamp at a creature that got too close, spraying oil across the stones and setting it alight. The fire didn't seem to bother the creatures.

The move exposed Seeli, as Taffa fell off balance in the throw. A monster knocked her down, and others scrambled for the child—but Dalinar leaped for her, wrapping his arms around her, huddling down and turning his back on the monsters. One leaped on his back. Claws sliced his skin.

Seeli whimpered in terror. Taffa was screaming as the monsters overwhelmed her.

"Why are you showing me this!" Dalinar bellowed into the night. "Why must I live *this* vision? Curse you!" Claws raked his back; he clutched Seeli, back arching in pain. He cast his eyes upward, toward the sky.

And there, he saw a brilliant blue light falling through the air.

It was like a star rock, dropping at an incredible speed. Dalinar cried out as the light hit the ground a short distance away, cracking the stone, spraying rock chips in the air. The ground shook. The beasts froze.

Dalinar turned numbly to the side, then he watched in amazement as the light stood up, limbs unfolding. It wasn't a star at all. It was a man—a man in glowing blue Shardplate, bearing a Shardblade, trails of Stormlight rising from his body.

The creatures hissed furiously, suddenly throwing themselves at the figure, ignoring Dalinar and the other two. The Shardbearer raised his Blade and struck forward with skill, stepping into the attacks.

Dalinar lay stunned. This was unlike any Shardbearer he had ever seen. The Plate glowed with an even blue light, and glyphs—some familiar, others not—were etched into the metal. They trailed blue vapor.

Moving fluidly, Plate clinking, the man struck at the beasts. He effortlessly sheared a monster in half, flinging pieces into the night that trailed black smoke.

Dalinar pulled himself to Taffa. She was alive, though her side was torn and flayed. Seeli tugged at her, weeping. *Need to . . . do something . . .* Dalinar thought dully.

"Be at peace," a voice said.

Dalinar lurched, turning to see a woman in delicate Shardplate kneeling beside him, holding something bright. It was a topaz entwined with a heliodor, both set into a fine metal framework, each stone as big as a man's hand. The woman had light tan eyes that almost seemed to glow in the night, and she wore no helm. Her hair was pulled back into a bun. She raised a hand and touched his forehead.

Ice washed across him. Suddenly, his pain was gone.

The woman reached out and touched Taffa. The flesh on her side regrew in an eyeblink; the torn muscle remained where it was, but other flesh just *grew* where the chunks had been torn out. The skin knitted up over it without flaw, and the female Shardbearer wiped away the blood and torn flesh with a white cloth.

Taffa looked up, awed. "You came," she whispered. "Bless the Almighty."

The female Shardbearer stood; her armor glowed with an even amber light. She smiled and turned to the side, a Shardblade forming from mist into her hand as she rushed to aid her companion.

A woman Shardbearer, Dalinar thought. He'd never seen such a thing.

He stood up, hesitant. He felt strong and healthy, as if he'd just awakened from a good night's sleep. He glanced down at his arm, pulling off his makeshift bandage. He had to wipe free blood and some torn skin, but underneath, the skin was perfectly healed. He took a few deep breaths. Then shrugged, picked up his poker, and joined the fight.

"Heb?" Taffa called from behind. "Are you insane?"

He didn't respond. He couldn't very well just sit there while two strangers fought to protect him. There were dozens of the black creatures. As he watched, one landed a scraping hit on the Shardbearer in blue, and the claw scored the Shardplate, digging into and cracking it. The danger to these Shardbearers was real.

The female Shardbearer turned to Dalinar. She had her helm on now. When had she put it on? She seemed shocked as Dalinar threw himself at one of the black beasts, slashing it with his poker. He fell into Smokestance and fended against its counterattack. The female Shardbearer turned to her companion, then the two of them fell into stances forming a triangle with Dalinar, his position closest to the rock formation.

With two Shardbearers alongside him, the fighting went remarkably better than it had back at the house. He only managed to dispatch a single beast—they were quick and strong, and he fought defensively, trying to distract and keep pressure off the Shardbearers. The creatures did not retreat. They continued to attack until the last one was sliced in two by the female Shardbearer.

Dalinar stopped, puffing, lowering his poker. Other lights had fallen—and still were falling—from the sky in the direction of the village; presumably, some of these strange Shardbearers had landed there as well.

"Well," a strong voice said, "I must say that I've never before had the pleasure of fighting alongside a comrade with such . . . unconventional means."

Dalinar turned to find the male Shardbearer regarding him. Where had the man's helm gone? The Shardbearer stood with his Blade resting on his armored shoulder, and he inspected Dalinar with eyes of such bright blue, they were almost white. Were those eyes actually *glowing*, leaking Stormlight? His skin was dark brown, like a Makabaki, and he had short black curly hair. His armor no longer glowed, though one large symbol—emblazoned across the front of the breastplate—still gave off a faint blue light.

Dalinar recognized the symbol, the particular pattern of the stylized double eye, eight spheres connected with two at the center. It had been the symbol of the Lost Radiants, back when they'd been called the Knights Radiant.

The female Shardbearer watched the village.

"Who trained you in the sword?" the male knight asked Dalinar.

Dalinar met the eyes of the knight. He had no idea how to respond.

"This is my husband Heb, good knight," Taffa said, rushing forward, leading her daughter by the hand. "He's never seen a sword, far as I know."

"Your stances are unfamiliar to me," the knight said. "But they were practiced and precise. This level of skill comes only with years of training. I have rarely seen a man—knight or soldier—fight as well as you did."

Dalinar remained silent.

"No words for me, I see," the knight said. "Very well. But should you wish to put that mysterious training of yours to use, come to Urithiru."

"Urithiru?" Dalinar said. He'd heard that name somewhere.

"Yes," the knight said. "I cannot promise you a position in one of the orders—that decision is not mine—but if your skill with the sword is similar to your skill with hearth-tending implements, then I am confident you will find a place with us." He turned eastward, toward the village. "Spread the word. Signs like this one are not without import. A Desolation is coming." He turned to his companion. "I will go. Guard these three and lead them to the village. We cannot leave them alone in the dangers of this night."

His companion nodded. The blue knight's armor began to glow faintly, then he launched into the air, as if falling straight up. Dalinar stumbled back, shocked, watching the glowing blue figure rise, then arc downward toward the village.

"Come," the woman said, voice ringing inside her helm. She began to hurry down the incline.

"Wait," Dalinar said, hastening after her, Taffa scooping up her daughter and following. Behind them, the oil was burning out.

The female knight slowed to allow Dalinar and Taffa to keep pace with her.

"I must know," Dalinar said, feeling foolish. "What year is it?"

The knight turned to him. Her helm was gone. He blinked; when had that happened? Unlike her companion, she had light skin—not pale like someone from Shinovar, but a natural light tan, like an Alethi. "It is Eighth Epoch, three thirty-seven."

Eighth Epoch? Dalinar thought. *What does that mean?* This vision had been different from the others. They had been more brief, for one thing. And the voice that spoke to him. Where was it?

"Where am I?" Dalinar asked the knight. "What kingdom?"

The knight frowned. "Are you not healed?"

"I am well. I just . . . I need to know. Which kingdom am I in?"

"This is Natanatan."

Dalinar released an inhaled breath. *Natanatan.* The Shattered Plains lay in the land that had once been Natanatan. The kingdom had fallen centuries ago.

"And you fight for Natanatan's king?" he asked.

She laughed. "The Knights Radiant fight for no king and for all of them."

"Then where do you live?"

"Urithiru is where our orders are centered, but we live in cities all across Alethela."

Dalinar froze in place. Alethela. It was the historical name for the place that had become Alethkar. "You cross kingdom borders to fight?"

"Heb," Taffa said. She seemed very concerned. "You were the one who promised me that the Radiants would come protect us, just before you went out searching for Seeli. Is your mind still muddled? Lady knight, could you heal him again?"

"I should save Regrowth for others who might be wounded," the woman said, glancing at the village. The fighting seemed to be dying down.

"I'm fine," Dalinar said. "Alethk . . . Alethela. You live there?"

"It is our duty and our privilege," the woman said, "to stay vigilant for the Desolation. One kingdom to study the arts of war so that the others might have peace. We die so that you may live. It has ever been our place."

Dalinar stood still, sorting through that.

"All who can fight are needed," the woman said. "And all who have a *desire* to fight should be compelled to come to Alethela. Fighting, even this fighting against the Ten Deaths, changes a person. We can teach you so that it will not destroy you. Come to us."

Dalinar found himself nodding.

"Every pasture needs three things," the woman said, voice changing, as if she were quoting from memory. "Flocks to grow, herdsmen to tend, and watchers at the rim. We of Alethela are those watchers—the warriors who protect and fight. We maintain the terrible arts of killing, then pass them on to others when the Desolation comes."

"The Desolation," he said. "That means the Voidbringers, right? Those are what we fought this night?"

The knight sniffed dismissively. "Voidbringers? These? No, this was Midnight Essence, though who released it is still a mystery." She looked to the side, expression growing distant. "Harkaylain says the Desolation is close, and he is not often wrong. He—"

A sudden screaming sounded in the night. The knight cursed, looking toward it. "Wait here. Call out if the Essence returns. I will hear." She dashed off into the darkness.

Dalinar raised a hand, torn between following and staying to watch over Taffa and her daughter. *Stormfather!* he thought, realizing they'd been left in darkness, now that the knight's glowing armor was gone.

He turned back to Taffa. She stood on the trail beside him, eyes looking oddly distracted.

"Taffa?" he asked.

"I miss these times," Taffa said.

Dalinar jumped. That voice wasn't hers. It was a man's voice, deep and powerful. It was the voice that spoke to him during every vision.

"Who are you?" Dalinar asked.

"They were one, once," Taffa—or whatever it was—said. "The orders. Men. Not without problems or strife, of course. But focused."

Dalinar felt a chill. Something about that voice always seemed faintly familiar to him. It had even in the first vision. "Please. You have to tell me what this is, why you are show-ing me these things. Who are you? Some servant of the Al-mighty?"

"I wish I could help you," Taffa said, looking at Dalinar but ignoring his questions. "You have to unite them."

"As you've said before! But I need help. The things the knight said about Alethkar. Are they true? Can we really be that way again?"

"To speak of what might be is forbidden," the voice said. "To speak of what was depends on perspective. But I will try to help."

"Then give me more than vague answers!"

Taffa regarded him, somber. Somehow, by starlight alone, he could make out her brown eyes. There was something deep, something daunting, hiding behind them.

"At least tell me this," Dalinar said, grasping for a specific question to ask. "I have trusted Highprince Sadeas, but my son—Adolin—thinks I am a fool to do so. Should I continue to trust Sadeas?"

"Yes," the being said. "This is important. Do not let strife consume you. Be strong. Act with honor, and honor will aid you."

Finally, Dalinar thought. *Something concrete.*

He heard voices. The dark landscape around Dalinar grew vague. "No!" He reached for the woman. "Don't send me back yet. What should I do about Elhokar, and the war?"

"I will give you what I can." The voice was growing indistinct. "I am sorry for not giving more."

"What kind of answer is that?" Dalinar bellowed. He shook himself, struggling. Hands held him. Where had they come from? He cursed, batting them away, twisting, trying to break free.

Then he froze. He was in the barrack at the Shattered Plains, soft rain rattling on the roof. The bulk of the storm had passed. A group of soldiers held Dalinar down while Renarin watched with concern.

Dalinar grew still, mouth open. He had been yelling. The soldiers looked uncomfortable, glancing at each other, not meeting his gaze. If it was like before, he'd have acted out his role in the vision, speaking in gibberish, flailing around.

"My mind is clear now," Dalinar said. "It's all right. You can all let me go."

Renarin nodded to the others, and they hesitantly released him. Renarin tried to make some stuttering excuses, telling them that his father was simply eager for combat. It didn't sound very convincing.

Dalinar retreated to the back of the barrack, sitting down on the floor between two rolled up bedrolls, just breathing in and out and thinking. He trusted the visions, yet his life in the warcamps had been difficult enough lately without people presuming him mad.

Act with honor, and honor will aid you.

The vision had told him to trust Sadeas. But he'd never be able to explain that to Adolin—who not only hated Sadeas, but thought the visions were delusions from Dalinar's mind. The only thing to do was keep going as he had.

And find a way, somehow, to get the highprinces to work together.

SEVEN YEARS AGO

I can save her," Kal said, pulling off his shirt.

The child was only five. She'd fallen far.

"I can save her." He was mumbling. A crowd had gathered. It had been two months since Brightlord Wistiow's death; they still didn't have a replacement citylord. He had barely seen Laral at all in that time.

Kal was only thirteen, but he'd been trained well. The first danger was blood loss; the child's leg had broken, a compound fracture, and it was spurting red where bone had split the skin. Kal found his hands trembling as he pressed his fingers against the wound. The broken bone was slick, even the jagged end, wetted by blood. Which arteries had been torn?

"What are you doing to my daughter?" Thick-shouldered Harl pushed through the onlookers. "You cremling, you storm's leavings! Don't touch Miasal! Don't—"

Harl broke off as several of the other men pulled him back. They knew that Kal—who had been passing by chance—was the girl's best hope. Alim had already been sent to fetch Kal's father.

"I can save her," Kal said. Her face was pale, and she didn't move. That head wound, maybe it . . .

Can't think about that. One of the lower leg arteries was

severed. He used his shirt to tie a tourniquet to stop the blood, but it kept slipping. Fingers still pressed against the cut, he called, "Fire! I need fire! Hurry! And someone give me your shirt!"

Several men rushed off as Kal elevated the leg. One of the men hurriedly handed over his shirt. Kal knew where to pinch to cut off the artery; the tourniquet slipped, but his fingers did not. He held that artery closed, pressing the shirt on the rest of the wound until Valama came back with a candle's flame.

They'd already begun heating a knife. Good. Kal took the knife, burning it into the wound, releasing the sharply pungent smell of scorched flesh. A cool wind blew across them, carrying it away.

Kal's hands stopped shaking. He *knew* what to do. He moved with skill that surprised even him, perfectly cauterizing, as his training took control. He still needed to tie off the artery—a cauterization might not hold on an artery this large—but the two together should work.

When he was done, the bleeding had stopped. He sat back, smiling. And then he noticed that Miasal's head wound wasn't bleeding either. Her chest wasn't moving.

"No!" Harl fell to his knees. "No! Do something!"

"I . . ." Kal said. He'd stopped the bleeding. He'd . . .

He'd lost her.

He didn't know what to say, how to respond. A deep, terrible, sickness washed over him. Harl shoved him aside, wailing, Kal fell backward. He found himself shaking again as Harl clutched the corpse.

Around them, the crowd was silent.

⁘

An hour later, Kal sat on the steps in front of the surgery room, crying. It was a soft thing, his grief. A shake here. A few persistent tears, slipping down his cheeks.

He sat with knees up, arms wrapped around his legs, trying to figure out how to stop hurting. Was there a salve to take away this pain? A bandage to stop the flow from his eyes? He should have been able to *save* her.

Footsteps approached, and a shadow fell on him. Lirin knelt down beside him. "I inspected your work, son. You did well. I'm proud."

"I failed," Kal whispered. His clothing was stained red. Before he'd washed the blood free of his hands, it had been scarlet. But soaked into his clothing, it was a duller reddish brown.

"I've known men who practiced for hours and hours, yet still froze when confronted by a wounded person. It's harder when it takes you by surprise. *You* didn't freeze, you went to her, administered help. And you did it well."

"I don't want to be a surgeon," Kal said. "I'm terrible at it."

Lirin sighed, rounding the steps, sitting down beside his son. "Kal, this happens. It's unfortunate, but you couldn't have done more. That little body lost blood too quickly."

Kal didn't reply.

"You have to learn when to care, son," Lirin said softly. "And when to let go. You'll see. I had similar problems when I was younger. You'll grow calluses."

And this is a good thing? Kal thought, another tear trickling down his cheek. *You have to learn when to care . . . and when to let go. . . .*

In the distance, Harl continued to wail.

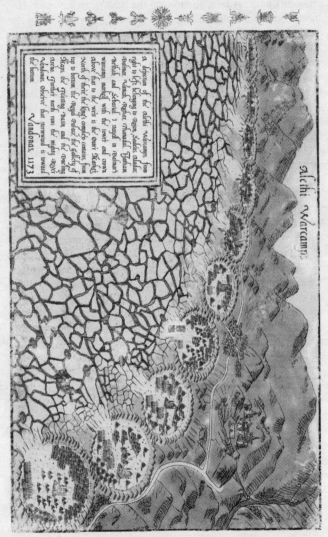

Map of Alethi warcamps by the painter Vandonas, who visited the
warcamps once and painted perhaps an idealized representation of
them.

One need only look at the aftermath of his brief visit to Sel to see proof of what I say.

Kaladin didn't want to open his eyes. If he opened his eyes, he'd be awake. And if he were awake, that pain—the burning in his side, the aching of his legs, the dull throb in his arms and shoulders—wouldn't be just a nightmare. It would be real. And it would be his.

He stifled a groan, rolling onto his side. It all ached. Every length of muscle, every inch of skin. His head pounded. It seemed that his very *bones* were sore. He wanted to lie motionless and throbbing until Gaz was forced to come and tow him out by his ankles. That would be easy. Didn't he deserve to do what was easy, for once?

But he couldn't. To stop moving, to give up, would be the same as dying, and he could not let that happen. He'd made his decision already. He would help the bridgemen.

Curse you, Hav, he thought. *You can boot me out of my bunk even now.* Kaladin threw off his blanket, forcing himself to stand. The door to the barrack was cracked open to let in fresh air.

He felt worse standing up, but the life of a bridgeman wouldn't wait for him to recover. You either kept up or you got crushed. Kaladin steadied himself, hand against the unnaturally smooth, Soulcast rock of the barrack wall. Then he took a deep breath and crossed the room. Oddly, more than a few of the men were awake and sitting up. They watched Kaladin in silence.

They were waiting, Kaladin realized. *They wanted to see if I'd get up.*

He found the three wounded where he'd left them at the front of the barrack. He held his breath as he checked on Leyten. Amazingly, he was still alive. His breathing was still shallow, his pulse weak and his wounds dire, but he was alive.

He wouldn't stay that way long without antiseptic. None of the wounds looked infected with rotspren yet, but it would only be a matter of time in these dirty confines. He needed some of the apothecary's salves. But how?

He checked the other two. Hobber was smiling openly. He was round-faced and lean, with a gap between his teeth and short, black hair. "Thank you," he said. "Thank you for saving me."

Kaladin grunted, inspecting the man's leg. "You'll be fine, but you won't be able to walk for a few weeks. I'll bring food from the mess hall for you."

"Thank you," Hobber whispered, taking Kaladin's hand, clutching it. He actually seemed to be tearing up.

That smile forced back the gloom, made the aches and soreness fade. Kaladin's father had described that kind of smile. Those smiles weren't why Lirin had become a surgeon, but they *were* why he'd remained one.

"Rest," Kaladin said, "and keep that wound clean. We don't want to attract any rotspren. Let me know if you see any. They are small and red, like tiny insects."

Hobber nodded eagerly and Kaladin moved to Dabbid. The youthful bridgeman looked just as he had the day before, staring forward, eyes unfocused.

"He was sitting like that when I fell asleep too, sir," Hobber said. "It's like he hasn't moved all night. Gives me the chills, it does."

Kaladin snapped his fingers in front of Dabbid's eyes. The

man jumped at the sound, focusing on the fingers, following them as Kaladin moved his hand.

"He's been hit in the head, I think," Hobber said.

"No," Kaladin said. "It's battle shock. It will wear off." *I hope.*

"If you say so, sir," Hobber said, scratching at the side of his head.

Kaladin stood and pushed the door open all the way, lighting the room. It was a clear day, the sun just barely over the horizon. Already, sounds drifted from the warcamp, a blacksmith working early, hammer on metal. Chulls trumpeting in the stables. The air was cool, chilly, clinging to the vestiges of night. It smelled clean and fresh. Spring weather.

You got up, Kaladin told himself. *Might as well get on with it.* He forced himself to go out and do his stretches, body complaining at each motion. Then he checked his own wound. It wasn't too bad, though infection could make it worse.

Stormwinds take that apothecary! he thought, fetching a ladle full of water from the bridgeman barrel, using it to wash his wound.

He immediately regretted the bitter thought against the elderly apothecary. What was the man to do? Give Kaladin the antiseptic for free? It was Highprince Sadeas he should be cursing. Sadeas was responsible for the wound, and was also the one who had forbidden the surgeon's hall to give supplies to bridgemen, slaves, and servants of the lesser nahns.

By the time he finished stretching, a handful of bridgemen had risen to get something to drink. They stood around the barrel, regarding Kaladin.

There was only one thing to do. Setting his jaw, Kaladin crossed the lumber grounds and located the plank he'd carried the day before. The carpenters hadn't yet added it to their bridge, so Kaladin picked it up and walked back to the barracks. Then he began practicing the same way he had yesterday.

He couldn't go as fast. In fact, much of the time, he could only walk. But as he worked, his aches soothed. His headache faded. His feet and shoulders still hurt, and he had a deep, latent exhaustion. But he didn't embarrass himself by falling over.

In his practice, he passed the other bridgeman barracks. The men in front of them were barely distinguishable from those in Bridge Four. The same dark, sweat-stained leather vests over bare chests or loosely tied shirts. There was the occasional foreigner, Thaylens or Vedens most often. But they were unified in their scraggly appearances, unshaven faces, and haunted eyes. Several groups watched Kaladin with outright hostility. Were they worried that his practice would encourage their own bridgeleaders to work them?

He had hoped that some members of Bridge Four might join his workout. They'd obeyed him during the battle, after all, even going so far as to help him with the wounded. His hope was in vain. While some bridgemen watched, others ignored him. None took part.

Eventually, Syl flitted down and landed on the end of his plank, riding like a queen on her palanquin. "They're talking about you," she said as he passed the Bridge Four barrack again.

"Not surprising," Kaladin said between puffs.

"Some think you've gone mad," she said. "Like that man who just sits and stares at the floor. They say the battle stress broke your mind."

"Maybe they're right. I didn't consider that."

"What *is* madness?" she asked, sitting with one leg up against her chest, vaporous skirt flickering around her calves and vanishing into mist.

"It's when men don't think right," Kaladin said, glad for the conversation to distract him.

"Men *never* seem to think right."

"Madness is worse than normal," Kaladin said with a smile. "It really just depends on the people around you. How different are you from them? The person that stands out is mad, I guess."

"So you all just . . . vote on it?" she asked, screwing up her face.

"Well, not so actively. But it's the right idea."

She sat thoughtfully for a time longer. "Kaladin," she finally said. "Why do men lie? I can see what lies are, but I don't know *why* people do it."

"Lots of reasons," Kaladin said, wiping the sweat from his brow with his free hand, then using it to steady the plank.

"Is it madness?"

"I don't know if I'd say that. Everyone does it."

"So maybe you're all a little mad."

He chuckled. "Yes, perhaps."

"But if everyone does it," she said, leaning her head on her knee, "then the one who *doesn't* would be the one who is mad, right? Isn't that what you said earlier?"

"Well, I guess. But I don't think there's a person out there who hasn't ever lied."

"Dalinar."

"Who?"

"The king's uncle," Syl said. "Everyone says he never lies. Your bridgemen even talk about it sometimes."

That's right. The Blackthorn. Kaladin had heard of him, even in his youth. "He's a lighteyes. That means he lies."

"But—"

"They're all the same, Syl. The more noble they look, the more corrupt they are inside. It's all an act." He fell quiet, surprised at the vehemence of his bitterness. *Storm you, Amaram. You did this to me.* He'd been burned too often to trust the flame.

"I don't think men were always this way," she said absently, getting a far-off look in her face. "I . . ."

Kaladin waited for her to continue, but she didn't. He passed Bridge Four again; many of the men relaxed, backs to the barrack wall, waiting for the afternoon shade to cover them. They rarely waited inside. Perhaps staying inside all day was too gloomy, even for bridgemen.

"Syl?" he finally prompted. "Were you going to say something?"

"It seems I've heard men talk about times when there were no lies."

"There are stories," Kaladin said, "about the times of the Heraldic Epochs, when men were bound by honor. But you'll always find people telling stories about supposedly better days. You watch. A man joins a new team of soldiers, and the first thing he'll do is talk about how wonderful his old team was. We remember the good times and the bad ones, forgetting that most times are neither good nor bad. They just are."

He broke into a jog. The sun was growing warm overhead, but he wanted to move.

"The stories," he continued between puffs, "they prove it. What happened to the Heralds? They abandoned us. What happened to the Knights Radiant? They fell and became tarnished. What happened to the Epoch Kingdoms? They crashed when the church tried to seize power. You can't trust anyone with power, Syl."

"What do you do, then? Have no leaders?"

"No. You give the power to the lighteyes and leave it to corrupt them. Then try to stay as far from them as possible." His words felt hollow. How good a job had *he* done staying away from lighteyes? He always seemed to be in the thick of them, caught in the muddy mire they created with their plots, schemes, and greed.

Syl fell silent, and after that last jog, he decided to stop his practicing. He couldn't afford to strain himself again. He returned the plank. The carpenters scratched their heads, but didn't complain. He made his way back to the bridgemen, noticing that a small group of them—including Rock and Teft—were chatting and glancing at Kaladin.

"You know," Kaladin said to Syl, "talking to you probably doesn't do anything for my reputation of being insane."

"I'll do my best to stop being so interesting," Syl said, alighting on his shoulder. She put her hands on her hips, then plopped down to a sitting position, smiling, obviously pleased with her comment.

Before Kaladin could get back to the barrack, he noticed Gaz hustling across the lumberyard toward him. "You!" Gaz said, pointing at Kaladin. "Hold a season."

Kaladin stopped, waiting with folded arms.

"I've news for you," Gaz said, squinting with his good eye. "Brightlord Lamaril heard what you did with the wounded."

"How?"

"Storms, boy!" Gaz said. "You think people wouldn't talk? What were you going to do? Hide three men in the middle of us all?"

Kaladin took a deep breath, but backed down. Gaz was right. "All right. What does it matter? We didn't slow the army."

"Yeah," Gaz said, "but Lamaril isn't too polished on the idea of paying and feeding bridgemen who can't work. He took the matter to Highprince Sadeas, intending to have you strung up."

Kaladin felt a chill. Strung up would mean hung out during a highstorm for the Stormfather to judge. It was essentially a death sentence. "And?"

"Brightlord Sadeas refused to let him do it," Gaz said.

What? Had he misjudged Sadeas? But no. This was part of the act.

"Brightlord Sadeas," Gaz said grimly, "told Lamaril to let you keep the soldiers—but to forbid them food or pay while they're unable to work. Said it would show why he's forced to leave bridgemen behind."

"That cremling," Kaladin muttered.

Gaz paled. "Hush. That's the highprince himself you're talking about, boy!" He glanced about to see if anyone had heard.

"He's trying to make an example of my men. He wants the other bridgemen to see the wounded suffer and starve. He wants it to seem like he's doing a *mercy* by leaving the wounded behind."

"Well, maybe he's right."

"It's heartless," Kaladin said. "He brings back wounded soldiers. He leaves the bridgemen because it's cheaper to find new slaves than it is to care for wounded ones."

Gaz fell silent.

"Thank you for bringing me this news."

"News?" Gaz snapped. "I was *sent* to give you orders,

lordling. Don't try to get extra food from the mess hall for your wounded; you'll be refused." With that, he rushed away, muttering to himself.

Kaladin made his way back to the barrack. *Stormfather!* Where was he going to get food enough to feed three men? He could split his own meals with them, but while bridgemen were kept fed, they weren't given an excess. Even feeding one man beyond himself would be a stretch. Trying to split the meals four ways would leave the wounded too weak to recover and Kaladin too weak to run bridges. And he *still* needed antiseptic! Rotspren and disease killed far more men in war than the enemy did.

Kaladin stepped up to the men lounging by the barrack. Most were going about the usual bridgeman activities— sprawled on the ground and despondently staring into the air, sitting and despondently staring at the ground, standing and despondently staring into the distance. Bridge Four wasn't on bridge duty at all this day, and they didn't have work detail until third afternoon bell.

"Gaz says our wounded are to be refused food or pay until they are well," Kaladin said to the collected men.

Some of them—Sigzil, Peet, Koolf—nodded, as if this was what they'd expected.

"Highprince Sadeas wants to make an example of us," Kaladin said. "He wants to *prove* that bridgemen aren't worth healing, and he's going to do it by making Hobber, Leyten, and Dabbid die slow, painful deaths." He took a deep breath. "I want to pool our resources to buy medicine and get food for the wounded. We can keep those three alive if a few of you will split your meals with them. We'll need about two dozen or so clearmarks to buy the right medicine and supplies. Who has something they can spare?"

The men stared at him, then Moash started laughing. Others joined him. They waved dismissive hands and broke up, walking away, leaving Kaladin with his hand out. "Next time it could be you!" he called. "What will you do if you're the one that needs healing?"

"I'll die," Moash said, not even bothering to look back. "Out on the field, quickly, rather than back here over a week's time."

Kaladin lowered his hand. He sighed, turning, and almost ran into Rock. The beefy, towerlike Horneater stood with arms folded, like a tan-skinned statue. Kaladin looked up at him, hopeful.

"Don't have any spheres," Rock said with a grunt. "Is all spent already."

Kaladin sighed. "It wouldn't have mattered anyway. Two of us couldn't afford to buy the medicine. Not alone."

"I will give some food," Rock grumbled.

Kaladin glanced back at him, surprised.

"But *only* for this man with arrow in his leg," Rock said, arms still folded.

"Hobber?"

"Whatever," Rock said. "He looks like he could get better. Other one, he will die. Is certain. And I have no pity for man who sits there, not doing anything. But for the other one, you may have my food. Some of it."

Kaladin smiled, raising a hand and gripping the larger man's arm. "Thank you."

Rock shrugged. "You took my place. Without this thing, I would be dead."

Kaladin smirked at that logic. "I'm not dead, Rock. You'd be fine."

Rock shook his head. "I'd be dead. Is something strange about you. All men can see it, even if they don't want to speak of this thing. I looked at bridge where you were. Arrows hit all around you—beside your head, next to your hands. But they weren't hitting you."

"Luck."

"Is no such thing." Rock glanced at Kaladin's shoulder. "Besides, there is *mafah'liki* who always follows you." The large Horneater bowed his head reverently to Syl, then made a strange gesture with his hand touching his shoulders and then his forehead.

Kaladin started. "You can *see* her?" He glanced at Syl. As a windspren, she could appear to those she wanted to—and that generally only meant Kaladin.

Syl seemed shocked. No, she hadn't appeared to Rock specifically.

"I am *alaii'iku*," Rock said, shrugging.

"Which means . . ."

Rock scowled. "Airsick lowlanders. Is there nothing proper you know? Anyway, you are special man. Bridge Four, it lost eight runners yesterday counting the three wounded."

"I know," Kaladin said. "I broke my first promise. I said I wasn't going to lose a single one."

Rock snorted. "We are bridgemen. We die. Is how this thing works. You might as well promise to make the moons catch each other!" The large man turned, pointing toward one of the other barracks. "Of the bridges that were fired upon, most lost many men. Five bridges fell. They lost over twenty men each and needed soldiers to help get bridges back. Bridge Two lost eleven men, and it wasn't even a focus of firing."

He turned back to Kaladin. "Bridge Four lost eight. Eight men, during one of the worst runs of the season. And, perhaps, you will save two of those. Bridge Four lost fewest men of any bridge that the Parshendi tried to drop. Bridge Four *never* loses fewest men. Everyone knows how it is."

"Luck—"

Rock pointed a fat finger at him, cutting him off. "Airsick lowlander."

It *was* just luck. But, well, Kaladin would take it for the small blessing it was. No use arguing when someone had finally decided to start listening to him.

But one man wasn't enough. Even if both he and Rock went on half rations, one of the sick men would starve. He needed spheres. He needed them desperately. But he was a slave; it was illegal for him to earn money in most ways. If only he had something he could sell. But he owned nothing. He . . .

A thought occurred to him.

"Come on," he said, striding away from the barrack. Rock

followed curiously. Kaladin searched through the lumber-yard until he found Gaz speaking with a bridgeleader in front of Bridge Three's barrack. As was growing more common, Gaz grew pale when Kaladin approached, and made as if to scurry away.

"Gaz, wait!" Kaladin said, holding out his hand. "I have an offer for you."

The bridge sergeant froze. Beside Gaz, Bridge Three's leader shot Kaladin a scowl. The way the other bridgemen had been treating him suddenly made sense. They were perturbed to see Bridge Four come out of a battle in such good shape. Bridge Four was supposed to be unlucky. Everyone needed someone else to look down on—and the other bridge crews could be consoled by the small mercy that they weren't in Bridge Four. Kaladin had upset that.

The dark-bearded bridgeleader retreated, leaving Kaladin and Rock alone with Gaz.

"What are you offering this time?" Gaz said. "More dun spheres?"

"No," Kaladin said, thinking quickly. This would have to be handled *very* carefully. "I'm out of spheres. But we can't continue like this, you avoiding me, the other bridge crews hating me."

"Don't see what we can do about it."

"I tell you what," Kaladin said, as if suddenly having a thought. "Is anyone on stone-gathering detail today?"

"Yeah," Gaz said, gesturing over his shoulder. "Bridge Three. Bussik there was just trying to convince me that his team is too weak to go. Storms blast me, but I believe him. Lost two-thirds of his men yesterday, and *I'll* be the one who gets chewed out when they don't gather enough stones to meet quota."

Kaladin nodded sympathetically. Stone gathering was one of the least desirable work details; it involved traveling outside of the camp and filling wagons with large rocks. Soulcasters fed the army by turning rocks into grain, and it was easier for them—for reasons only they knew—if they had distinct, separate stones. So men gathered rocks. It was menial, sweaty, tiring, mindless work. Perfect for bridge-men.

"Why don't you send a different bridge team?" Kaladin asked.

"Bah," Gaz said. "You know the kind of trouble that makes. If I'm seen playing favorites, I never hear an end of the complaining."

"Nobody will complain if you make Bridge Four do it."

Gaz glanced at him, single eye narrowed. "I didn't think you'd react well to being treated differently."

"I'll do it," Kaladin said, grimacing. "Just this once. Look, Gaz, I don't want to spend the rest of my time here fighting against you."

Gaz hesitated. "Your men are going to be angry. I won't let them think it was me who did this to them."

"I'll tell them that it was my idea."

"All right, then. Third bell, meet at the western checkpoint. Bridge Three can clean pots." He walked away quickly, as if to escape before Kaladin changed his mind.

Rock stepped up beside Kaladin, watching Gaz. "The little man is right, you know. The men will *hate* you for this thing. They were looking forward to easy day."

"They'll get over it."

"But why change for harder work? Is true—you are crazy, aren't you?"

"Maybe. But that craziness will get us outside of the warcamp."

"What good is that?"

"It means everything," Kaladin said, glancing back at the barrack. "It means life and death. But we're going to need more help."

"Another bridge crew?"

"No, I mean that we—you and I—will need help. One more man, at least." He scanned the lumberyard, and noted someone sitting in the shadow of Bridge Four's barrack. Teft. The grizzled bridgeman hadn't been among the group that had laughed at Kaladin earlier, but he *had* been quick to help yesterday, going with Rock to carry Leyten.

Kaladin took a deep breath and strode out across the grounds, Rock trailing behind. Syl left his shoulder and zipped into the air, dancing on a sudden gust of wind. Teft looked up as Kaladin and Rock approached. The older man had fetched breakfast, and he was eating alone, a piece of flatbread peeking out beneath his bowl.

His beard was stained by the curry, and he regarded Kaladin with wary eyes before wiping his mouth on his sleeve. "I like my food, son," he said. "Hardly think they feed me enough for one man. Let alone two."

Kaladin squatted in front of him. Rock leaned up against the wall and folded his arms, watching quietly.

"I need you, Teft," Kaladin said.

"I said—"

"Not your food. You. Your loyalty. Your allegiance."

The older man continued to eat. He didn't have a slave brand, and neither did Rock. Kaladin didn't know their stories. All he knew was that these two had helped when others hadn't. They weren't completely beaten down.

"Teft—" Kaladin began.

"I've given my loyalty before," the man said. "Too many times now. Always works out the same."

"Your trust gets betrayed?" Kaladin asked softly.

Teft snorted. "Storms, no. I betray *it*. You can't depend on me, son. I belong here, as a bridgeman."

"I depended on you yesterday, and you impressed me."

"Fluke."

"I'll judge that," Kaladin said. "Teft, we're *all* broken, in one way or another. Otherwise we wouldn't be bridgemen. I've failed. My own brother died because of me."

"So why keep caring?"

"It's either that or give up and die."

"And if death is better?"

It came back to this problem. This was why the bridgemen didn't care if he helped the wounded or not.

"Death isn't better," Kaladin said, looking Teft in the eyes. "Oh, it's easy to say that now. But when you stand on the ledge and look down into that dark, endless pit, you change your mind. Just like Hobber did. Just like I've done." He hesitated, seeing something in the older man's eyes. "I think you've seen it too."

"Aye," Teft said softly. "Aye, I have."

"So, are you with us in this thing?" Rock said, squatting down.

Us? Kaladin thought, smiling faintly.

Teft looked back and forth between the two of them. "I get to keep my food?"

"Yes," Kaladin said.

Teft shrugged. "All right then, I guess. Can't be any harder than sitting here and having a staring contest with mortality."

Kaladin held out a hand. Teft hesitated, then took it.

Rock held out a hand. "Rock."

Teft looked at him, finished shaking Kaladin's hand, then took Rock's. "I'm Teft."

Stormfather, Kaladin thought. *I'd forgotten that most of them don't even bother to learn each other's names.*

"What kind of name is Rock?" Teft asked, releasing the hand.

"Is a stupid one," Rock said with an even face. "But at least it has meaning. Does your name mean anything?"

"I guess not," Teft said, rubbing his bearded chin.

"Rock, this is not my real name," the Horneater admitted. "Is just what lowlanders can pronounce."

"What's your real name, then?" Teft asked.

"You won't be able to say it."

Teft raised an eyebrow.

"Numuhukumakiaki'aialunamor," Rock said.

Teft hesitated, then smiled. "Well, I guess in that case, Rock will do just fine."

Rock laughed, settling down. "Our bridgeleader has a plan. Something glorious and daring. Has something to do with spending our afternoon moving stones in the heat."

Kaladin smiled, leaning forward. "We need to gather a certain kind of plant. A reed that grows in small patches outside the camp. . . ."

*In case you have turned a blind eye to that disaster, know
that Aona and Skai are both dead, and that which they
held has been Splintered. Presumably to prevent anyone
from rising up to challenge Rayse.*

Two days after the incident with the highstorm, Dalinar
walked with his sons, crossing the rocky ground toward
the king's feasting basin.

Dalinar's stormwardens projected another few weeks of
spring, followed by a return to summer. Hopefully it wouldn't
turn to winter instead.

"I've been to three more leatherworkers," Adolin said
softly. "They have different opinions. It seems that even before the strap was cut—if it was cut—it was worn, so that's
interfering with things. The best consensus has been that the
strap *was* sliced, but not necessarily by a knife. It could have
just been natural wear-and-tear."

Dalinar nodded. "That's the only evidence that even hints
there might be something odd about the girth breaking."

"So we admit that this was just a result of the king's paranoia."

"I'll talk to Elhokar," Dalinar decided. "Let him know
we've run into a wall and see if there are any other avenues
he'd like us to pursue."

"That'll do." Adolin seemed to grow hesitant about something. "Father. Do you want to talk about what happened during the storm?"

"It was nothing that hasn't happened before."

"But—"

"Enjoy the evening, Adolin," Dalinar said firmly. "I'm all right. Perhaps it's good for the men to see what is happening. Hiding it has only inspired rumors, some of them even worse than the truth."

Adolin sighed, but nodded.

The king's feasts were always outdoors, at the foot of Elhokar's palace hill. If the stormwardens warned of a highstorm—or if more mundane weather turned bad—then the feast was canceled. Dalinar was glad for the outdoor location. Even with ornamentation, Soulcast buildings felt like caverns.

The feast basin had been flooded, turning it into a shallow artificial lake. Circular dining platforms rose like small stone islands in the water. The elaborate miniature landscape had been fabricated by the king's Soulcasters, who had diverted the water from a nearby stream. *It reminds me of Sela Tales,* Dalinar thought as he crossed the first bridge. He'd visited that western region of Roshar during his youth. *And the Purelake.*

There were five islands, and the railings of the bridges connecting them were done in scrollwork so fine that after each feast, the railings had to be stowed away lest a highstorm ruin them. Tonight, flowers floated in the slow current. Periodically, a miniature boat—only a handspan wide—sailed past, bearing an infused gemstone.

Dalinar, Renarin, and Adolin stepped onto the first dining platform. "One cup of blue," Dalinar said to his sons. "After that, keep to the orange."

Adolin sighed audibly. "Couldn't we, just this once—"

"So long as you are of my house, you follow the Codes. My will is firm, Adolin."

"Fine," Adolin said. "Come on, Renarin." The two broke off from Dalinar to remain on the first platform, where the younger lighteyes congregated.

Dalinar crossed to the next island. This middle one was for the lesser lighteyes. To its left and right lay the segregated dining islands—men's island on the right, women's island on the left. On the three central ones, however, the genders mingled.

Around him, the favored invitees took advantage of their king's hospitality. Soulcast food was inherently bland, but the king's lavish feasts always served imported spices and exotic meats. Dalinar could smell roasting pork on the air, and even chickens. It had been a long time since he'd been served meat from one of the strange Shin flying creatures.

A darkeyed servant passed, wearing a gauzy red robe and carrying a tray of orange crab legs. Dalinar continued across the island, weaving around groups of revelers. Most drank violet wine, the most intoxicating and flavorful of the colors. Almost no one was in battle attire. A few men wore tight, waist-length jackets, but many had dropped all pretense, choosing instead loose silk shirts with ruffled cuffs worn with matching slippers. The rich material glistened in the lamplight.

These creatures of fashion shot glances at Dalinar, appraising him, weighing him. He could remember a time when he would have been swarmed by friends, acquaintances—and yes, even sycophants—at a feast like this. Now, none approached him, though they gave way before him. Elhokar might think his uncle was growing weak, but his reputation quelled most lesser lighteyes.

He soon approached the bridge to the final island—the king's island. Pole-mounted gem lamps ringed it, glowing with blue Stormlight, and a firepit dominated the center of the platform. Deep red coals simmered in its bowels, radiating warmth. Elhokar sat at his table just behind the firepit, and several highprinces ate with him. Tables along the sides of the platform were occupied by male or female diners—never both at the same.

Wit sat on a raised stool at the end of the bridge leading onto the island. Wit actually dressed as a lighteyes should—he wore a stiff black uniform, silver sword at his waist. Dalinar shook his head at the irony.

Wit was insulting each person as they stepped onto the island. "Brightness Marakal! What a disaster that hairstyle is; how brave of you to show it to the world. Brightlord Marakal, I wish you'd warned us you were going to attend; I'd have forgone supper. I do so hate being sick after a full meal. Brightlord Cadilar! How good it is to see you. Your face reminds me of someone dear to me."

"Really?" wizened Cadilar said, hesitating.

"Yes," Wit said, waving him on, "my horse. Ah, Brightlord Neteb, you smell unique today—did you attack a wet whitespine, or did one just sneeze on you? Lady Alami! No, please, don't speak—it's much easier to maintain my illusions regarding your intelligence that way. And Brightlord Dalinar." Wit nodded to Dalinar as he passed. "Ah, my dear Brightlord Taselin. Still engaged in your experiment to prove a maximum threshold of human idiocy? Good for you! Very empirical of you."

Dalinar hesitated beside Wit's chair as Taselin waddled by with a huff. "Wit," Dalinar said, "do you have to?"

"Two what, Dalinar?" Wit said, eyes twinkling. "Eyes, hands, or spheres? I'd lend you one of the first, but—by definition—a man can only have one I, and if it is given away, who would be Wit then? I'd lend you one of the second, but I fear my simple hands have been digging in the muck far too often to suit one such as you. And if I gave you one of my spheres, what would I spend the remaining one on? I'm quite attached to both of my spheres, you see." He hesitated. "Or, well, you *can't* see. Would you like to?" He stood up off his chair and reached for his belt.

"Wit," Dalinar said dryly.

Wit laughed, clapping Dalinar on the arm. "I'm sorry. This lot brings out the basest humor in me. Perhaps it's that muck I spoke of earlier. I do try so hard to be elevated in my loathing of them, but they make it difficult."

"Care for yourself, Wit," Dalinar said. "This lot won't suffer you forever. I wouldn't see you dead by their knives; I see a fine man within you."

"Yes," Wit said, scanning the platform. "He tasted quite

delicious. Dalinar, I fear I'm not the one who needs that warning. Speak your fears at a mirror a few times when you get home tonight. There are rumors about."

"Rumors?"

"Yes. Terrible things. Grow on men like warts."

"Tumors?"

"Both. Look, there is talk about you."

"There is always talk about me."

"This is worse than most," Wit said, meeting his eyes. "Did you really speak of abandoning the Vengeance Pact?"

Dalinar took a deep breath. "That was between me and the king."

"Well, he must have spoken of it to others. This lot are cowards—and no doubt that makes them feel like experts on the subject, for they've certainly been calling you that a great deal lately."

"Stormfather!"

"No, I'm Wit. But I understand how easy a mistake that is to make."

"Because you blow so much air," Dalinar growled, "or because you make so much noise?"

A wide smile split Wit's face. "Why, Dalinar! I'm impressed! Maybe I should make *you* Wit! Then I could be a highprince instead." He stopped. "No, that would be bad. I'd go mad after a mere second of listening to them, then would likely slaughter the lot. Perhaps appoint cremlings in their places. The kingdom would undoubtedly fare better."

Dalinar turned to go. "Thank you for the warning."

Wit sat back down on his stool as Dalinar walked away. "You're welcome. Ah, Brightlord Habatab! How thoughtful of you to wear a red shirt with a sunburn like that! If you continue to make my job this easy, I fear my mind shall become as dull as Brightlord Tumul's! Oh, Brightlord Tumul! How unexpected it is to see you standing there! I didn't mean to insult your stupidity. Really, it's quite spectacular and worthy of much praise. Lord Yonatan and Lady Meirav, I'll forgo an insult for you this once on account of your recent wedding, though I do find your hat quite impressive, Yonatan. I trust it is convenient to wear on your head something that doubles as a tent at night. Ah, and is that Lady *Navani* behind you? How long have you been back at the Plains and how did I not notice the smell?"

Dalinar froze. *What?*

"Obviously your own stench overpowered mine, Wit," a warm feminine voice said. "Has no one done my son a service and assassinated you yet?"

"No, no assassins yet," Wit said, amused. "I guess I've already got too much ass sass of my own."

Dalinar turned with shock. Navani, the king's mother, was a stately woman with intricately woven black hair. And she was *not* supposed to be here.

"Oh really, Wit," she said. "I thought that kind of humor was beneath you."

"So are you, technically," Wit said, smiling, from atop his high-legged stool.

She rolled her eyes.

"Unfortunately, Brightness," Wit replied with a sigh, "I've taken to framing my insults in terms this lot will understand. If it will please you, I shall attempt to improve my diction to more elevated terms." He paused. "I say, do you know any words that rhyme with bescumber?"

Navani just turned her head and looked at Dalinar with a pair of light violet eyes. She wore an elegant dress, its shimmering red surface unbroken by embroidery. The gems in her hair—which was streaked with a few lines of grey—were red as well. The king's mother was known as one of the most beautiful women in Alethkar, though Dalinar had always found that description inadequate, for surely there wasn't a woman on all of Roshar to match her beauty.

Fool, he thought, tearing his eyes away from her. *Your brother's widow.* With Gavilar dead, Navani was now to be treated as Dalinar's sister. Besides, what of his own wife? Dead these ten years, wiped by his foolishness from his mind. Even if he couldn't remember her, he should honor her.

Why had Navani returned? As women called out greetings to her, Dalinar hurriedly made his way over to the king's table. He sat down; a servant arrived in moments with a plate for him—they knew his preferences.

It was steaming peppered chicken, cut in medallions and laid atop fried round slices of tenem, a soft, light orange vegetable. Dalinar grabbed a piece of flatbread and slipped his dining knife from the sheath on his right calf. So long as he was eating, it would be a breach of etiquette for Navani to approach him.

The food was good. It always was at these feasts of Elhokar's—in that, the son was like the father. Elhokar nodded to Dalinar from the end of the table, then continued his conversation with Sadeas. Highprince Roion sat a few seats down from him. Dalinar had an appointment with him in a few days, the first of the highprinces he'd approach and try to convince to work with him on a joint plateau assault.

No other highprinces came to sit near Dalinar. Only they—and people with specific invitations—could sit at the king's table. One man lucky enough to receive such an invitation sat on Elhokar's left, obviously uncertain if he should join in the conversation or not.

Water gurgled in the stream behind Dalinar. Before him, the festivities continued. It was a time for relaxation, but the Alethi were a reserved people, at least when compared with more passionate folk like the Horneaters or the Reshi. Still, his people seemed to have grown more opulent and self-indulgent since his childhood. Wine flowed freely and foods sizzled fragrantly. On the first island, several young men had stepped into a sparring ring for a friendly duel. Young men at a feast often found reason to remove their coats and show off their swordsmanship.

The women were more modest with their displays, but they engaged in them as well. On Dalinar's own island, several women had set up easels where they were sketching, painting, or doing calligraphy. As always, they kept their left hands shrouded in their sleeves, delicately creating art with the right. They sat on high stools, the kind that Wit had been using—in fact, Wit had probably stolen one for his little performance. A few of them attracted creationspren, the tiny shapes rolling across the tops of their easels or tables.

Navani had gathered a group of important lighteyed women to a table. A servant passed by in front of Dalinar, bringing the women some food. It appeared to also have been made with the exotic chicken, but had been mixed with steamed methi fruit and covered in a reddish-brown sauce. As a boy, Dalinar had secretly tried women's food out of curiosity. He'd found it distastefully sweet.

Navani placed something on her table, a device of polished brass about the size of a fist, with a large, infused ruby at its center. The red Stormlight lit the entire table, throwing shadows down the white tablecloth. Navani picked up the device, rotating it to show her dinner companions its leglike protrusions. Turned that way, it looked vaguely crustacean.

I've never seen a fabrial like that before. Dalinar looked up at her face, admiring the contours of her cheek. Navani was a renowned artifabrian. Perhaps this device was—

Navani glanced at him, and Dalinar froze. She flashed the briefest of smiles at him, covert and knowing, then turned away before he could react. *Storming woman!* he thought, pointedly turning his attention to his meal.

He was hungry, and got so involved in his food that he almost didn't notice Adolin approaching. The blond youth saluted Elhokar, then hurried to take one of the vacant seats beside Dalinar. "Father," Adolin said in a hushed tone, "have you heard what they're saying?"

"About what?"

"About you! I've fought three duels so far against men who described you—and our house—as cowards. They're saying you asked the king to abandon the Vengeance Pact!"

Dalinar gripped the table and nearly rose to his feet. But he stopped himself. "Let them speak if they wish," he said, turning back to his meal, stabbing a chunk of peppered chicken with his knife and raising it to his lips.

"Did you really do it?" Adolin asked. "Is that what you talked about at the meeting with the king two days back?"

"It is," Dalinar admitted.

That elicited a groan from Adolin. "I was worried already. When I—"

"Adolin," Dalinar interjected. "Do you trust me?"

Adolin looked at him, the youth's eyes wide, honest, but pained. "I want to. Storms, Father. I really want to."

"What I am doing is important. It *must be done*."

Adolin leaned in, speaking softly. "And what if they *are* delusions? What if you're just . . . getting old."

It was the first time someone had confronted him with it so directly. "I would be lying if I didn't admit that I'd considered it, but there was no sense in second-guessing myself. I believe they're real. I *feel* they're real."

"But—"

"This is not the place for this discussion, son," Dalinar said. "We can talk of it later, and I will listen to—and consider—your objections. I promise."

Adolin drew his lips to a line. "Very well."

"You are right to be worried for our reputation," Dalinar said, resting an elbow on the table. "I had assumed that Elhokar would have the tact to keep our conversation quiet, but I should have asked him to do so directly. You were right about his reaction, by the way. I realized during the conversation he would never retreat, so I changed to another tactic."

"Which is?"

"Winning the war," Dalinar said firmly. "No more scuffling over gemhearts. No more patient, indefinite siege. We find a way to lure a large number of Parshendi onto the Plains, then execute an ambush. If we can kill a large enough number of them, we destroy their capacity to wage war. Failing that, we find a way to strike at their center and kill or capture their leaders. Even a chasmfiend stops fighting when it's been decapitated. The Vengeance Pact would be fulfilled, and we could go home."

Adolin took a long moment considering, then he nodded sharply. "All right."

"No objections?" Dalinar asked. Normally, his elder son had plenty.

"You just asked me to trust you," Adolin said. "Besides, striking harder at the Parshendi? That's a tactic I can get behind. We'll need a good plan, though—a way to counter the very objections you yourself raised six years ago."

Dalinar nodded, tapping the table with his finger. "Back then, even I thought of us as separate princedoms. If we had attacked the center individually, each army alone, we'd have been surrounded and destroyed. But if all ten armies went together? With our Soulcasters to provide food, with the soldiers carrying portable shelters to set up for highstorms? Over a hundred and fifty thousand troops? Let the Parshendi try to surround us then. With the Soulcasters, we could even create wood for bridges if we had to."

"That would take a lot of trust," Adolin said hesitantly. He glanced down the high table, toward Sadeas. His expression darkened. "We'd be stuck out there, together and isolated, for days. If the highprinces started squabbling midmarch, it could be disastrous."

"We'll get them to work together first," Dalinar said. "We're close, closer than we've ever been. Six years, and not a single highprince has allowed his soldiers to skirmish against those of another."

Except back in Alethkar. There, they still fought meaningless battles over land rights or old offenses. It was ridiculous, but stopping the Alethi from warring was like trying to stop the winds from blowing.

Adolin was nodding. "It's a good plan, Father. Far better than talk of retreating. They won't like giving up the plateau skirmishes, though. They like the game of it."

"I know. But if I can get one or two of them to start pooling soldiers and resources for plateau assaults, it might be a step toward what we'll need for the future. I'd still rather find a way to lure a large force of Parshendi out onto the Plains and meet them on one of the larger plateaus, but I haven't yet been able to figure out how to do that. Either way, our separate armies will need to learn to work together."

"And what do we do about what people are saying about you?"

"I'll release an official refutation," Dalinar said. "I'll have to be careful not to make it sound like the king was in error, while also explaining the truth."

Adolin sighed. "An official refutation, Father?"

"Yes."

"Why not fight a duel?" Adolin asked, leaning in, sounding eager. "Some stuffy pronouncement may explain your ideas, but it won't make people *feel* them. Pick someone who is naming you coward, challenge them, and remind everyone what a mistake it is to insult the Blackthorn!"

"I cannot," Dalinar said. "The Codes forbid it for one of my stature." Adolin probably shouldn't be dueling either, but Dalinar had not forced a complete prohibition on him. Dueling was his life. Well, that and the women he courted.

"Then charge me with the honor of our house," Adolin said. "I'll duel them! I'll face them with Plate and Blade and show them what your honor means."

"That would be the same thing as me doing it, son."

Adolin shook his head, staring at Dalinar. He seemed to be searching for something.

"What?" Dalinar asked.

"I'm trying to decide," Adolin said. "Which one has changed you most. The visions, the Codes, or that book. If there's any difference between them."

"The Codes are separate from the other two," Dalinar said. "They are a tradition of old Alethkar."

"No. They're related, Father. All three. They're tied together in you, somehow."

Dalinar thought on that for a moment. Could the lad have a point? "Have I told you the story of the king carrying the boulder?"

"Yes," Adolin said.

"I have?"

"Twice. And you made me listen to the passage being read another time."

"Oh. Well, in that same section, there's a passage about the nature of *forcing* people to follow you as opposed to *letting* them follow you. We do too much forcing in Alethkar.

Dueling someone because they claim I'm a coward doesn't change their beliefs. It might stop them from making the claims, but it doesn't change hearts. I know I'm right about this. You'll just have to trust me on this as well."

Adolin sighed, standing. "Well, an official refutation is better than nothing, I guess. At least you haven't given up on defending our honor entirely."

"I never will," Dalinar said. "I just need to be careful. I cannot afford to divide us any further." He turned back to his meal, stabbing his last piece of chicken with his knife and shoving it in his mouth.

"I'll get back to the other island, then," Adolin said. "I . . . Wait, is that *Aunt Navani*?"

Dalinar looked up, surprised to see Navani walking toward them. Dalinar glanced at his plate. His food was gone; he'd eaten the last bit without realizing it.

He sighed, steeling himself, and rose to greet her. "Mathana," Dalinar said, bowing and using the formal term for an older sister. Navani was only three months his senior, but it was still applicable.

"Dalinar," she said, a faint smile on her lips. "And dear Adolin."

Adolin smiled broadly; he rounded the table and hugged his aunt. She rested her clothed safehand on his shoulder, a gesture reserved only for family.

"When did you return?" Adolin asked, releasing her.

"Just this afternoon."

"And *why* did you return?" Dalinar asked stiffly. "I was under the impression that you were going to aid the queen in protecting the king's interests in Alethkar."

"Oh, Dalinar," Navani said, voice fond. "So stiff, as always. Adolin, dear, how goes courtship?"

Dalinar snorted. "He continues to change partners like he's in a dance that involves particularly quick music."

"Father!" Adolin objected.

"Well, good for you, Adolin," Navani said. "You're too young to get tied down. The purpose of youth is to experience variety while it is still interesting." She glanced at

Dalinar. "It isn't until we get older that we should be forced to be boring."

"Thank you, Aunt," Adolin said with a grin. "Excuse me. I need to go tell Renarin that you've returned." He hurried away, leaving Dalinar standing awkwardly across the table from Navani.

"Am I that much of a threat, Dalinar?" Navani asked, raising an eyebrow at him.

Dalinar glanced down, realizing that he was still gripping his dining knife—a wide, serrated blade that could double as a weapon in a pinch. He let it clatter to the table, then winced at the noise. All of the confidence he'd felt speaking with Adolin seemed gone in a heartbeat.

Compose yourself! he thought. *She's just family.* Every time he spoke with Navani, he felt as if he were facing a predator of the most dangerous breed.

"Mathana," Dalinar said, realizing they were still standing on opposite sides of the narrow table. "Perhaps we should move to . . ."

He trailed off as Navani waved to an attending girl who was barely old enough to wear a woman's sleeve. The child rushed forward, bearing a low stool. Navani pointed to the spot beside her, a spot only a few feet from the table. The child hesitated, but Navani pointed more insistently and the child set the stool down.

Navani sat gracefully, not sitting *at* the king's table—which was a masculine dining place—but certainly sitting near enough to be challenging protocol. The serving girl withdrew. At the end of the table, Elhokar noticed his mother's actions, but said nothing. One did not reprove Navani Kholin, not even if one were king.

"Oh, sit down, Dalinar," she said, voice growing testy. "We have matters of some moment to discuss."

Dalinar sighed, but sat. The seats around them were still empty, and both the music and the hum of conversation on the island were loud enough to keep people from overhearing them. Some women had taken to playing flutes, musicspren spinning around them in the air.

"You ask why I returned," Navani said, voice soft. "Well, I have three reasons. First, I wanted to bring word that the Vedens have perfected their 'half-shards' as they call them. They're claiming the shields can stop blows from a Shard-blade."

Dalinar folded his arms before him on the table. He'd heard rumors of this, though he'd discounted them. Men were always claiming to be close to creating new Shards, yet the promises were never fulfilled. "Have you seen one?"

"No. But I have confirmation from someone I trust. She says they can only take the shape of a shield and don't lend any of Plate's other enhancements. But they *can* block a Shardblade."

It was a step—a very small step—toward Shardplate. That was disturbing. He wouldn't believe it himself until he'd seen what these "half-shards" could do. "You could have sent this news via spanreed, Navani."

"Well, I realized soon after reaching Kholinar that leaving here had been a political mistake. More and more, these warcamps are the true center of our kingdom."

"Yes," Dalinar said quietly. "Our absence from our homeland is dangerous." Hadn't that been the very argument that had convinced Navani to go home in the first place?

The stately woman waved a dismissive hand. "I have determined that the queen is sufficiently endowed with the requisite skills needed to hold Alethkar. There are schemes and plots—there will always be schemes and plots—but the truly important players inevitably make their way here."

"Your son continues to see assassins around every corner," Dalinar said softly.

"And shouldn't he? After what happened to his father . . ."

"True, but I fear he carries it to extremes. He mistrusts even his allies."

Navani folded her hands in her lap, freehand lying atop safehand. "He's not very good at this, is he?"

Dalinar blinked in shock. "What? Elhokar is a good man! He has more integrity than any other lighteyes in this army."

"But his rule is weak," Navani said. "You must admit that."

"He is king," Dalinar said firmly, "and my nephew. He has both my sword and my heart, Navani, and I will not hear ill spoken of him, even by his own mother."

She eyed him. Was she testing his loyalty? Much like her daughter, Navani was a political creature. Intrigue made her blossom like a rockbud in calm wet air. However, unlike Jasnah, Navani was hard to trust. At least with Jasnah one knew where one stood—once again, Dalinar found himself wishing she'd put aside her projects and return to the Shattered Plains.

"I'm not speaking ill of my son, Dalinar," Navani said. "We both know I am as loyal to him as you are. But I like to know what I'm working with, and that requires a definition. He is seen as weak, and I intend to see him protected. Despite himself, if necessary."

"Then we work for the same goals. But if protecting him was the second reason you returned, what was the third?"

She smiled a violet-eyed, red-lipped smile at him. A meaningful smile.

Blood of my ancestors . . . Dalinar thought. *Stormwinds, but she's beautiful. Beautiful and deadly.* It seemed a particular irony to him that his wife's face had been erased from his mind, and yet he could remember in complete and intricate detail the months this woman had spent toying with him and Gavilar. She'd played them off one another, fanning their desire before finally choosing the elder son.

They'd all known the entire time that she would choose Gavilar. It had hurt anyway.

"We need to talk sometime in private," Navani said. "I want to hear your opinion on some of the things being said in camp."

That probably meant the rumors about him. "I—I'm very busy."

She rolled her eyes. "I'm sure you are. We're meeting anyway, once I've had time to settle here and put out feelers. How about one week from today? I'll come read to you from that book of my husband's, and afterward we can chat. We'll do it in a public place. All right?"

He sighed. "Very well. But—"

"Highprinces and lighteyes," Elhokar suddenly proclaimed. Dalinar and Navani turned toward the end of the table, where the king stood wearing his uniform complete with royal cape and crown. He raised a hand toward the island. The people hushed, and soon the only sound was that of the water burbling through the streams.

"I'm sure many of you have heard the rumors regarding the attempt on my life during the hunt three days ago," Elhokar announced. "When my saddle girth was cut."

Dalinar glanced at Navani. She raised her freehand toward him and rocked it back and forth, indicating that she didn't find the rumors to be persuasive. She knew about the rumors, of course. Give Navani five minutes in a city and she'd know anything and everything of significance being gossiped about.

"I assure you, I was never in real danger," Elhokar said. "Thanks, in part, to the protection of the King's Guard and the vigilance of my uncle. However, I believe it wise to treat all threats with due prudence and seriousness. Therefore, I am appointing Brightlord Torol Sadeas to be Highprince of Information, charging him to unearth the truth regarding this attempt on my life."

Dalinar blinked in shock. Then he closed his eyes and let out a soft groan.

"Unearth the truth," Navani said skeptically. "Sadeas?"

"Blood of my . . . He thinks I'm ignoring the threats to him, so he's looking to Sadeas instead."

"Well, I suppose that's all right," she said. "I *kind of* trust Sadeas."

"Navani," Dalinar said, opening his eyes. "The incident happened on a hunt I planned, under the protection of my guard and my soldiers. The king's horse was prepared by my grooms. He publicly asked me to look into this strap business, and now he's just taken the investigation away from me."

"Oh dear." She understood. This was nearly the same thing as Elhokar proclaiming that he suspected Dalinar. Any information Sadeas unearthed regarding this "assassination attempt" could only reflect unfavorably on Dalinar.

When Sadeas's hatred of Dalinar and his love of Gavilar

conflicted, which would win? *But the vision. It said to trust him.*

Elhokar sat back down, and the buzz of conversation resumed across the island at a higher pitch. The king seemed oblivious of what he had just done. Sadeas was smiling broadly. He rose from his place, bidding farewell to the king, then began mingling.

"You still argue he isn't a bad king?" Navani whispered. "My poor, distracted, oblivious boy."

Dalinar stood up, then walked down the table to where the king continued to eat.

Elhokar looked up. "Ah, Dalinar. I suspect you'll want to give Sadeas your aid."

Dalinar sat down. Sadeas's half-eaten meal still sat on the table, brass plate scattered with chunks of meat and torn flatbread. "Elhokar," Dalinar forced out, "I just spoke to you a few days ago. I asked to be Highprince of War, and you said it was too dangerous!"

"It is," Elhokar said. "I spoke to Sadeas about it, and he agreed. The highprinces will never stand for someone being put over them in war. Sadeas mentioned that if I started with something less threatening, like appointing someone to Highprince of Information, it might prepare the others for what you want to do."

"Sadeas suggested this," Dalinar said flatly.

"Of course," Elhokar said. "It is time we had a Highprince of Information, and he specifically noted the cut girth as something he wanted to look into. He knows you've always said you aren't suited to these sorts of things."

Blood of my fathers, Dalinar thought, looking out at the center of the island, where a group of lighteyes gathered around Sadeas. *I've just been outmaneuvered. Brilliantly.*

The Highprince of Information had authority over criminal investigations, particularly those of interest to the Crown. In a way, it was nearly as threatening as a Highprince of War, but it wouldn't seem so to Elhokar. All he saw was that he would finally have someone willing to listen to his paranoid fears.

Sadeas was a clever, clever man.

"Don't look so morose, Uncle," Elhokar said. "I had no idea you'd want the position, and Sadeas just seemed so excited at the idea. Perhaps he'll find nothing at all, and the leather was simply worn out. You'll be vindicated in always telling me that I'm not in as much danger as I think I am."

"Vindicated?" Dalinar asked softly, still watching Sadeas. *Somehow, I doubt that is likely.*

MANY USES

You have accused me of arrogance in my quest. You have accused me of perpetuating my grudge against Rayse and Bavadin. Both accusations are true.

Kaladin stood up in the wagon bed, scanning the landscape outside the camp as Rock and Teft put his plan—such as it was—into action.

Back home, the air had been drier. If you went about on the day before a highstorm, everything seemed desolate. After storms, plants soon pulled back into their shells, trunks, and hiding places to conserve water. But here in the moister climate, they lingered. Many rockbuds never quite pulled into their shells completely. Patches of grass were common. The trees Sadeas harvested were concentrated in a forest to the north of the warcamps, but a few strays grew on this plain. They were enormous, broad-trunked things that grew with a westward slant, their thick, fingerlike roots clawing into the stone and—over the years—cracking and breaking the ground around them.

Kaladin hopped down from the cart. His job was to hoist up stones and place them on the bed of the vehicle. The other bridgemen brought them to him, laying them in heaps nearby.

Bridgemen worked across the broad plain, moving among rockbuds, patches of grass, and bunches of weeds that poked out from beneath boulders. Those grew most heavily on the west side, ready to pull back into their boulder's shadow if a highstorm approached. It was a curious effect, as if each boulder were the head of an aged man with tufts of green and brown hair growing out from behind his ears.

Those tufts were extremely important, for hidden among them were thin reeds known as knobweed. Their rigid stalks were topped with delicate fronds that could retract into the stem. The stems themselves were immobile, but they were fairly safe growing behind boulders. Some would be pulled free in each storm—perhaps to attach themselves in a new location once the winds abated.

Kaladin hoisted a rock, setting it on the bed of the wagon and rolling it beside some others. The rock's bottom was wet with lichen and crem.

Knobweed wasn't rare, but neither was it as common as other weeds. A quick description had been enough to send Rock and Teft searching with some success. The breakthrough, however, had happened when Syl had joined the hunt. Kaladin glanced to the side as he stepped down for another stone. She zipped around, a faint, nearly invisible form leading Rock from one stand of reeds to another. Teft didn't understand how the large Horneater could consistently find so many more than he did, but Kaladin didn't feel inclined to explain. He still didn't understand why Rock could see Syl in the first place. The Horneater said it was something he'd been born with.

A pair of bridgemen approached, youthful Dunny and Earless Jaks towing a wooden sled bearing a large stone. Sweat trickled down the sides of their faces. As they reached the wagon, Kaladin dusted off his hands and helped them lift the boulder. Earless Jaks scowled at him, muttering under his breath.

"That's a nice one," Kaladin said, nodding to the stone. "Good work."

Jaks glared at him and stalked off. Dunny gave Kaladin a shrug, then hurried after the older man. As Rock had guessed, getting the crew assigned to stone-gathering duty had not helped Kaladin's popularity. But it had to be done. It was the only way to help Leyten and the other wounded.

Once Jaks and Dunny left, Kaladin nonchalantly climbed into the wagon bed and knelt down, pushing aside a tarp and uncovering a large pile of knobweed stems. They were about as long as a man's forearm. He made as if he were moving stones around in the bed, but instead tied a large double handful of the reeds into a bundle using thin rockbud vines.

He dropped the bundle over the side of the wagon. The wagon driver had gone to chat with his counterpart on the other wagon. That left Kaladin alone, save for the chull that sat hunkered down in its rock shell, watching the sun with beady crustacean eyes.

Kaladin hopped down from the wagon and placed another rock in the bed. Then, he knelt as if to pull a large stone out from under the wagon. With deft hands, however, he tied the reeds into place underneath the bed right beside two other bundles. The wagon had a large open space to the side of the axle, and a wood dowel there provided an excellent place for mounting the bundles.

Jezerezeh send that nobody thinks to check the bottom as we roll back into camp.

The apothecary said one drop came per stem. How many reeds would Kaladin need? He felt he knew the answer to that question without even giving it much thought.

He'd need every drop he could get.

He climbed out and lifted another stone into the wagon. Rock was approaching; the large, tan-skinned Horneater carried an oblong stone that would have been too large for most of the bridgemen to handle alone. Rock shuffled forward slowly, Syl zipping around his head and occasionally landing on the rock to watch him.

Kaladin climbed down and trotted across the uneven ground to help. Rock nodded in thanks. Together they hauled the stone to the wagon and set it down on the bed. Rock wiped his brow, turning his back to Kaladin. Sprouting from his pocket was a handful of reeds. Kaladin swiped them and tucked them beneath the tarp.

"What do we do if someone notices this thing we are doing?" Rock asked casually.

"Explain that I'm a weaver," Kaladin said, "and that I thought I'd weave myself a hat to keep off the sun."

Rock snorted.

"I might do just that," Kaladin said. He wiped his brow. "It would be nice in this heat. But best nobody sees. The mere fact that we want the reeds would probably be enough to make them deny them to us."

"This thing is true," Rock said, stretching and glancing upward as Syl zipped over in front of him. "I miss the Peaks."

Syl pointed, and Rock bowed his head in reverence before following after her. Once she had him going in the right direction, however, she flitted back to Kaladin, bobbing up into the air as a ribbon, then falling down to the side of the wagon and re-forming her womanly shape, her dress fluttering around her.

"I," she declared, raising a finger, "like him very much."

"Who? Rock?"

"Yes," she said, folding her arms. "He is *respectful*. Unlike others."

"Fine," Kaladin said, lifting another stone into the wagon. "You can follow him around instead of bothering me." He tried not to show worry as he said it. He had grown accustomed to her company.

She sniffed. "I can't follow him. He's too respectful."

"You just said you *liked* that."

"I do. Also, I detest it." She said that with unaffected frankness, as if oblivious of the contradiction. She sighed, sitting down on the side of the wagon. "I led him to a patch of chull dung as a prank. He didn't even yell at me! He just looked at it, as if trying to figure out some hidden meaning." She grimaced. "That's not normal."

"I think the Horneaters must worship spren or something," Kaladin said, wiping his brow.

"That's silly."

"People believe much sillier things. In some ways, I guess

it makes sense to revere the spren. You *are* kind of odd and magical."

"I'm not odd!" she said, standing up. "I'm beautiful and articulate." She planted her hands on her hips, but he could see in her expression that she wasn't really mad. She seemed to be changing by the hour, growing more and more . . .

More and more what? Not exactly humanlike. More individual. Smarter.

Syl fell silent as another bridgeman—Natam—approached. The long-faced man was carrying a smaller stone, obviously trying not to strain himself.

"Ho, Natam," Kaladin said, reaching down to take the stone. "How goes the work?"

Natam shrugged.

"Didn't you say you were once a farmer?"

Natam rested beside the wagon, ignoring Kaladin.

Kaladin set down the rock, moving it into place. "I'm sorry to make us work like this, but we need the good will of Gaz and the other bridge crews."

Natam didn't respond.

"It will help keep us alive," Kaladin said. "Trust me."

Natam just shrugged yet again, then wandered away.

Kaladin sighed. "This would be a lot easier if I could pin the duty change on Gaz."

"That wouldn't be very honest," Syl said, affronted.

"Why do you care so much about honesty?"

"I just do."

"Oh?" Kaladin said, grunting as he moved back to his work. "And leading men to piles of dung? How honest is that?"

"That's different. It was a joke."

"I fail to see how . . ."

He trailed off as another bridgeman approached. Kaladin doubted anyone else had Rock's strange ability to see Syl, and didn't want to be seen talking to himself.

The short, wiry bridgeman had said his name was Skar, though Kaladin couldn't see any obvious scars on his face. He had short dark hair and angular features. Kaladin tried to engage him in conversation too, but got no response. The man even went so far as to give Kaladin a rude gesture before tromping back out.

"I'm doing something wrong," Kaladin said, shaking his head and hopping down from the sturdy wagon.

"Wrong?" Syl stepped up to the lip of the wagon, watching him.

"I thought that seeing me rescue those three might give them hope. But they're still indifferent."

"Some watched you run earlier," Syl said, "when you were practicing with the plank."

"They watched," Kaladin said. "But they don't care about helping the wounded. Nobody besides Rock, that is—and he's only doing it because he has a debt to me. Even Teft wasn't willing to share his food."

"They're selfish."

"No. I don't think that word can apply to them." He lifted a stone, struggling to explain how he felt. "When I was a slave . . . well, I'm still a slave. But during the worst parts, when my masters were trying to beat out of me the ability to resist, I was like these men. I didn't care enough to be selfish. I was like an animal. I just did what I did without thinking."

Syl frowned. Little wonder—Kaladin himself didn't understand what he was saying. Yet, as he spoke, he began to work out what he meant. "I've shown them that we can survive, but that doesn't mean anything. If those lives aren't *worth* living, then they aren't ever going to care. It's like I'm offering them piles of spheres, but not giving them anything to spend their wealth on."

"I guess," Syl said. "But what can you do?"

He looked back across the plain of rock, toward the warcamp. The smoke of the army's many cookfires rose from the craters. "I don't know. But I think we're going to need a *lot* more reeds."

⁂

That night, Kaladin, Teft, and Rock walked the makeshift streets of Sadeas's warcamp. Nomon—the middle moon—

shone with his pale, blue-white light. Oil lanterns hung in front of buildings, indicating taverns or brothels. Spheres could provide more consistent, renewable light, but you could buy a bundle of candles or a pouch of oil for a single sphere. In the short run, it was often cheaper to do that, particularly if you were hanging your lights in a place they could be stolen.

Sadeas didn't enforce a curfew, but Kaladin had learned that a lone bridgeman had best remain in the lumberyard at night. Half-drunken soldiers in stained uniforms sauntered past, whispering in the ears of whores or boasting to their friends. They called insults at the bridgemen, laughing riotously. The streets felt dark, even with the lanterns and the moonlight, and the haphazard nature of the camp—some stone structures, some wooden shanties, some tents—made it feel disorganized and dangerous.

Kaladin and his two companions stepped aside for a large group of soldiers. Their coats were unbuttoned, and they were only mildly drunk. A soldier eyed the bridgemen, but the three of them together—one of them being a brawny Horneater—were enough to dissuade the soldier from doing more than laughing and shoving Kaladin as he passed.

The man smelled of sweat and cheap ale. Kaladin kept his temper. Fight back, and he'd be docked pay for brawling.

"I don't like this," Teft said, glancing over his shoulder at the group of soldiers. "I'm going back to the camp."

"You will be staying," Rock growled.

Teft rolled his eyes. "You think I'm scared of a lumbering chull like you? I'll go if I want to, and—"

"Teft," Kaladin said softly. "We need you."

Need. That word had strange effects on men. Some ran when you used it. Others grew nervous. Teft seemed to long for it. He nodded, muttering to himself, but stayed with them as they went on.

They soon reached the wagonyard. The fenced-off square of rock was near the western side of the camp. It was deserted for the night, the wagons sitting in long lines. Chulls lay slumbering in the nearby pen, looking like small hills. Kaladin crept forward, wary of sentries, but apparently nobody worried about something as large as a wagon being stolen from the middle of the army.

Rock nudged him, then pointed to the shadowy chull pens. A lone boy sat upon a pen post, staring up at the moon. Chulls were valuable enough to watch over. Poor lad. How often was he required to wait up nights guarding the sluggish beasts?

Kaladin crouched down beside a wagon, the other two mimicking him. He pointed down one row, and Rock moved off. Kaladin pointed the other direction, and Teft rolled his eyes, but did as asked.

Kaladin sneaked down the middle row. There were about thirty wagons, ten per row, but checking was quick. A brush of the fingers against the back plank, looking for the mark he'd made there. After just a few minutes, a shadowed figure entered Kaladin's row. Rock. The Horneater gestured to the side and held up five fingers. Fifth wagon from the top. Kaladin nodded and moved off.

Just as he reached the indicated wagon, he heard a soft yelp from the direction Teft had gone. Kaladin flinched, then peeked up toward the sentry. The boy was still watching the moon, kicking his toes absently against the post next to him.

A moment later, Rock and a sheepish Teft scurried up to Kaladin. "Sorry," Teft whispered. "The walking mountain startled me."

"If I am being a mountain," Rock grumbled, "then why weren't you hearing me coming? Eh?"

Kaladin snorted, feeling the back of the indicated wagon, fingers brushing the X mark in the wood. He took a breath, then climbed under the wagon on his back.

The reeds were still there, tied in twenty bundles, each about as thick as a handspan. "Ishi, Herald of Luck be praised," he whispered, untying the first bundle.

"All there, eh?" Teft said, leaning down, scratching at his beard in the moonlight. "Can't believe we found so many. Must have pulled up every reed on the entire plain."

Kaladin handed him the first bundle. Without Syl, they wouldn't have found a third this many. She had the speed of an insect in flight, and she seemed to have a sense of where to find things. Kaladin untied the next bundle, handing it out. Teft tied it to the other, making a larger bundle.

As Kaladin worked, a flurry of small white leaves blew under the wagon and formed into Syl's figure. She slid to a stop beside his head. "No guards anywhere I could see. Just a boy in the chull pens." Her white-blue translucent figure was nearly invisible in the darkness.

"I hope these reeds are still good," Kaladin whispered. "If they dried out too much . . ."

"They'll be fine. You worry like a worrier. I found you some bottles."

"You did?" he asked, so eager that he nearly sat up. He caught himself before smacking his head.

Syl nodded. "I'll show you. I couldn't carry them. Too solid."

Kaladin quickly untied the rest of the bundles, handing them out to the nervous Teft. Kaladin scooted out, then took two of the larger, tied-together bundles of three. Teft took two of the others, and Rock managed three by tucking one under his arm. They'd need a place to work where they wouldn't be interrupted. Even if the knobweed seemed worthless, Gaz would find a way to ruin the work if he saw what was happening.

Bottle first, Kaladin thought. He nodded to Syl, who led them out of the wagonyard and to a tavern. It looked to have been hastily built from second-rate lumber, but that didn't stop the soldiers inside from enjoying themselves. Their rowdiness made Kaladin worry about the entire building collapsing.

Behind it, in a splintery half-crate, lay a pile of discarded liquor bottles. Glass was precious enough that whole bottles would be reused, but these had cracks or broken tops. Kaladin set down his bundles, then selected three nearly whole bottles. He washed them in a nearby water barrel before tucking them into a sack he'd brought for the purpose.

He picked up his bundles again, nodding to the others. "Try to look like you're doing something monotonous," he said. "Bow your heads." The other two nodded, and they walked out into a main road, carrying the bundles as if on some work detail. They drew far less attention than they had before.

They avoided the lumberyard proper, crossing the open field of rock used as the army's staging area before walking down the slope of rock leading to the Shattered Plains. A sentry saw them, and Kaladin held his breath, but he said nothing. He probably assumed from their postures that they had a reason to be doing what they were. If they tried to leave the warcamp, it would be a different story, but this section down near the first few chasms wasn't off limits.

Before long, they approached the place where Kaladin had nearly killed himself. What a difference a few days could make. He felt like a different person—a strange hybrid of the man he had once been, the slave he'd become, and the pitiful wretch he still had to fight off. He remembered standing on the edge of the chasm, looking down. That darkness still terrified him.

If I fail to save the bridgemen, that wretch will take control again. This time he'll get his way. . . . That gave Kaladin a shiver. He set his bundles down beside the chasm ledge, then sat. The other two followed more hesitantly.

"We're going to toss them into the chasm?" Teft asked, scratching his beard. "After all that work?"

"Of course not," Kaladin said. He hesitated; Nomon was bright, but it was still night. "You don't have any spheres, do you?"

"Why?" Teft asked, suspicious.

"For light, Teft."

Teft grumbled, pulling out a handful of garnet chips. "Was going to spend these tonight. . . ." he said. They glowed in his palm.

"All right," Kaladin said, slipping out a reed. What had his father said about these? Hesitantly, Kaladin broke off the furry top of the reed, exposing the hollow center. He took the reed by the other end and ran his fingers down its length, squeezing it tight. Two drops of milky white liquid dripped into the empty liquor bottle.

Kaladin smiled in satisfaction, then squeezed his fingers along the length again. Nothing came out this time, so he tossed the reed into the chasm. For all his talk of hats, he didn't want to leave evidence.

"I thought you said we aren't throwing them in!" Teft accused.

Kaladin held up the liquor bottle. "Only after we have this out."

"What is it?" Rock leaned closer, squinting.

"Knobweed sap. Or, rather, knobweed milk—I don't think it's really sap. Anyway, it's a powerful antiseptic."

"Anti . . . what?" Teft asked.

"It scares away rotspren," Kaladin said. "They cause infection. This milk is one of the best antiseptics there is. Spread it on a wound that's already infected, and it will still work." That was good, because Leyten's wounds had begun to turn an angry red, rotspren crawling all over.

Teft grunted, then glanced at the bundles. "There are a lot of reeds here."

"I know," Kaladin said, handing over the other two bottles. "That's why I'm glad I don't have to milk them all on my own."

Teft sighed, but sat down and untied a bundle. Rock did so without the complaining, sitting with his knees bent to the sides, feet pressed together to hold the bottle as he worked.

A faint breeze blew up, rattling some of the reeds. "Why do you care about them?" Teft finally asked.

"They're my men."

"That's not what being bridgeleader means."

"It means whatever we decide," Kaladin said, noting that Syl had come over to listen. "You, me, the others."

"You think they'll let you do that?" Teft asked. "The lighteyes and the captains?"

"You think they'll pay enough attention to even notice?"

Teft hesitated, then grunted, milking another reed.

[423]

"Perhaps they will," Rock said. There was a surprising level of delicacy to the large man's motions as he milked the reeds. Kaladin hadn't thought those thick fingers would be so careful, so precise. "Lighteyes, they are often noticing those things that you wish they would not."

Teft grunted again, agreeing.

"How did you come here, Rock?" Kaladin asked. "How does a Horneater end up leaving his mountains and coming to the lowlands?"

"You shouldn't ask those kinds of things, son," Teft said, wagging a finger at Kaladin. "We don't talk about our pasts."

"We don't talk about *anything*," Kaladin said. "You two didn't even know each other's names."

"Names are one thing," Teft grumbled. "Backgrounds, they're different. I—"

"Is all right," Rock said. "I will speak of this thing."

Teft muttered to himself, but he did lean forward to listen when Rock spoke.

"My people have no Shardblades," Rock said in his low, rumbling voice.

"That's not unusual," Kaladin said. "Other than Alethkar and Jah Keved, few kingdoms have many Blades." It was a matter of some pride among the armies.

"This thing is not true," Rock said. "Thaylenah has five Blades and three full suits of Plate, all held by the royal guards. The Selay have their share of both suits and Blades. Other kingdoms, such as Herdaz, have a single Blade and set of Plate—this is passed down through the royal line. But the Unkalaki, we have not a single Shard. Many of our *nuatoma*— this thing, it is the same as your lighteyes, only their eyes are not light—"

"How can you be a lighteyes without light eyes?" Teft said with a scowl.

"By having dark eyes," Rock said, as if it were obvious. "We do not pick our leaders this way. Is complicated. But do not interrupt story." He milked another reed, tossing the husk into a pile beside him. "The *nuatoma*, they see our lack of Shards as great shame. They want these weapons very badly.

It is believed that the *nuatoma* who first obtains a Shardblade would become king, a thing we have not had for many years. No peak would fight another peak where a man held one of the blessed Blades."

"So you came to *buy* one?" Kaladin asked. No Shard-bearer would sell his weapon. Each was a distinctive relic, taken from one of the Lost Radiants after their betrayal.

Rock laughed. "Ha! Buy? No, we are not so foolish as this. But my *nuatoma*, he knew of your tradition, eh? It says that if a man kills a Shardbearer, he may take the Blade and Plate as his own. And so my *nuatoma* and his house, we made a grand procession, coming down to find and kill one of your Shardbearers."

Kaladin almost laughed. "I assume it proved more difficult than that."

"My *nuatoma* was not a fool," Rock said, defensive. "He knew this thing would be difficult, but your tradition, it gives us hope, you see? Occasionally, a brave *nuatoma* will come down to duel a Shardbearer. Someday, one will win, and we will have Shards."

"Perhaps," Kaladin said, tossing an empty reed into the chasm. "Assuming they agree to duel you in a bout to the death."

"Oh, they always duel," Rock said, laughing. "The *nuatoma* brings many riches and promises all of his possessions to the victor. Your lighteyes, they cannot pass by a pond so warm! To kill an Unkalaki with no Shardblade, they do not see this thing as difficult. Many *nuatoma* have died. But is all right. Eventually, we will win."

"And have one set of Shards," Kaladin said. "Alethkar has dozens."

"One is a beginning," Rock said, shrugging. "But my *nuatoma* lost, so I am bridgeman."

"Wait," Teft said. "You came all of this way with your brightlord, and once he lost, you up and joined a bridge crew?"

"No, no, you do not see," Rock said. "My *nuatoma*, he challenged Highprince Sadeas. Is well known that there are many Shardbearers here on Shattered Plains. My *nuatoma* thought it easier to fight man with only Plate first, then win Blade next."

"And?" Teft said.

"Once my *nuatoma* lost to Brightlord Sadeas, all of us became his."

"So you're a slave?" Kaladin asked, reaching up and feeling the marks on his forehead.

"No, we do not have this thing," Rock said. "I was not a slave of my *nuatoma*. I was his family."

"His *family*?" Teft said. "Kelek! You're a lighteyes!"

Rock laughed again, loud and full-bellied. Kaladin smiled despite himself. It seemed like so long since he'd heard someone laugh like that. "No, no. I was only *umarti'a*—his cousin, you would say."

"Still, you were related to him."

"On the Peaks," Rock said, "the relatives of a brightlord are his servants."

"What kind of system is that?" Teft complained. "You have to be a servant to your own relatives? Storm me! I'd rather die, I think I would."

"It is not so bad," Rock said.

"You don't know my relatives," Teft said, shivering.

Rock laughed again. "You would rather serve someone you do not know? Like this Sadeas? A man who is no relation to you?" He shook his head. "Lowlanders. You have too much air here. Makes your minds sick."

"Too much air?" Kaladin asked.

"Yes," Rock said.

"How can you have too much air? It's all around."

"This thing, it is difficult to explain." Rock's Alethi was good, but he sometimes forgot to add in common words. Other times, he remembered them, speaking his sentences precisely. The faster he spoke, the more words he forgot to put in.

"You have too much air," Rock said. "Come to the Peaks. You will see."

"I guess," Kaladin said, shooting a glance at Teft, who just shrugged. "But you're wrong about one thing. You said that we serve someone we don't know. Well, I *do* know Brightlord Sadeas. I know him well."

Rock raised an eyebrow.

"Arrogant," Kaladin said, "vengeful, greedy, corrupt to the core."

Rock smiled. "Yes, I think you are right. This man is not among the finest of lighteyes."

"There are no 'finest' among them, Rock. They're all the same."

"They have done much to you, then?"

Kaladin shrugged, the question uncovering wounds that weren't yet healed. "Anyway, your master was lucky."

"Lucky to be slain by a Shardbearer?"

"Lucky he didn't win," Kaladin said, "and discover how he'd been tricked. They wouldn't have let him walk away with Sadeas's Plate."

"Nonsense," Teft broke in. "Tradition—"

"Tradition is the blind witness they use to condemn us, Teft," Kaladin said. "It's the pretty box they use to wrap up their lies. It makes us serve them."

Teft set his jaw. "I've lived a lot longer than you, son. I know things. If a common man killed an enemy Shardbearer, he'd become a lighteyes. That's the way of it."

He let the argument lapse. If Teft's illusions made him feel better about his place in this mess of a war, then who was Kaladin to dissuade him? "So you were a servant," Kaladin said to Rock. "In a brightlord's retinue? What kind of servant?" He struggled for the right word, remembering back to the times he'd interacted with Wistiow or Roshone. "A footman? A butler?"

Rock laughed. "I was cook. My *nuatoma* would not come down to the lowlands without his own cook! Your food here, it has so many spices that you cannot taste anything else. Might as well be eating stones powdered with pepper!"

"*You* should talk about food," Teft said, scowling. "A Horneater?"

Kaladin frowned. "Why do they call your people that, anyway?"

"Because they eat the horns and shells of the things they catch," Teft said. "The outsides."

Rock smiled, with a look of longing. "Ah, but the taste is so good."

"You actually eat the shells?" Kaladin asked.

"We have very strong teeth," Rock said proudly. "But there. You now know my story. Brightlord Sadeas, he wasn't certain what he should do with most of us. Some were made soldiers, others serve in his household. I fixed him one meal and he sent me to bridge crews." Rock hesitated. "I may have, uh, enhanced the soup."

"Enhanced?" Kaladin asked, raising an eyebrow.

Rock seemed to grow embarrassed. "You see, I was quite angry about my *nuatoma*'s death. And I thought, these lowlanders, their tongues are all scorched and burned by the food they eat. They have no taste, and . . ."

"And what?" Kaladin asked.

"Chull dung," Rock said. "It apparently has stronger taste than I assumed."

"Wait," Teft said. "You put *chull dung* in Highprince Sadeas's soup?"

"Er, yes," Rock said. "Actually, I put this thing in his bread too. And used it as a garnish on the pork steak. And made a chutney out of it for the buttered garams. Chull dung, it has many uses, I found."

Teft laughed, his voice echoing. He fell on his side, so amused that Kaladin was afraid he'd roll right into the chasm. "Horneater," Teft finally said, "I owe you a drink."

Rock smiled. Kaladin shook his head to himself, amazed. It suddenly made sense.

"What?" Rock said, apparently noticing his expression.

"This is what we need," Kaladin said. "*This!* It's the thing I've been missing."

Rock hesitated. "Chull dung? This is the thing you need?"

Teft burst into another round of laugher.

"No," Kaladin said. "It's . . . well, I'll show you. But first we need this knobweed sap." They'd barely made their way through one of the bundles, and already his fingers were aching from the milking.

"What of you, Kaladin?" Rock asked. "I have been telling you my story. You will tell me yours? How did you come to those marks on your forehead?"

"Yeah," Teft said, wiping his eyes. "Whose food did *you* trat in?"

"I thought you said it was taboo to ask about a bridgeman's past," Kaladin said.

"You made Rock share, son," Teft said. "It's only fair."

"So if I tell my story, that means you'll tell yours?"

Teft scowled immediately. "Now look, I ain't going to—"

"I killed a man," Kaladin said.

That quieted Teft. Rock perked up. Syl, Kaladin noticed, was still watching with interest. That was odd for her; normally, her attention wavered quickly.

"You killed a man?" Rock said. "And after this thing, they made you a slave? Is not the punishment for murder usually death?"

"It wasn't murder," Kaladin said softly, thinking of the scraggly bearded man in the slave wagon who had asked him these same questions. "In fact, I was thanked for it by someone very important."

He fell silent.

"And?" Teft finally asked.

"And . . ." Kaladin said, looking down at a reed. Nomon was setting in the west, and the small green disk of Mishim— the final moon—was rising in the east. "And it turns out that lighteyes don't react very well when you turn down their gifts."

The others waited for more, but Kaladin fell silent, working on his reeds. It shocked him, how painful it still was to remember those events back in Amaram's army.

Either the others sensed his mood, or they felt what he'd said was enough, for they each turned back to their work and prodded no further.

Neither point makes the things I have written to you here untrue.

The king's Gallery of Maps balanced beauty and function. The expansive domed structure of Soulcast stone had smooth sides that melded seamlessly with the rocky ground. It was shaped like a long loaf of Thaylen bread, and had large skylights in the ceiling, allowing the sun to shine down on handsome formations of shalebark.

Dalinar passed one of these, pinks and vibrant greens and blues growing in a gnarled pattern as high as his shoulders. The crusty, hard plants had no true stalks or leaves, just waving tendrils like colorful hair. Except for those, shalebark seemed more rock than vegetation. And yet, scholars said it must be a plant for the way it grew and reached toward the light.

Men did that too, he thought. *Once.*

Highprince Roion stood in front of one of the maps, hands clasped behind his back, his numerous attendants clogging the other side of the gallery. Roion was a tall, light-skinned man with a dark, well-trimmed beard. He was thinning on top. Like most of the others, he wore a short, open-fronted jacket, exposing the shirt underneath. Its red fabric poked out above the jacket's collar.

So sloppy, Dalinar thought, though it was very fashionable. Dalinar just wished that current fashion weren't so, well, sloppy.

"Brightlord Dalinar," Roion said. "I have difficulty seeing the point of this meeting."

"Walk with me, Brightlord Roion," Dalinar said, nodding to the side.

The other man sighed, but joined Dalinar and walked the pathway between the clusters of plants and the wall of maps. Roion's attendants followed; they included both a cupbearer and a shieldbearer.

Each map was illuminated by diamonds, their enclosures made of mirror-polished steel. The maps were inked, in detail, onto unnaturally large, seamless sheets of parchment. Such parchment was obviously Soulcast. Near the center of the chamber they came to the Prime Map, an enormous, detailed map fixed in a frame on the wall. It showed the entirety of the Shattered Plains that had been explored. Permanent bridges were drawn in red, and plateaus close to the Alethi side had blue glyphpairs on them, indicating which highprince controlled them. The eastern section of the map grew less detailed until the lines vanished.

In the middle was the contested area, the section of plateaus where the chasmfiends most often came to make their chrysalises. Few came to the near side, where the permanent bridges were. If they did come, it was to hunt, not to pupate.

Controlling the nearby plateaus was still important, as a highprince—by agreement—could not cross a plateau maintained by one of the others unless he had permission. That determined who had the best pathways to the central plateaus, and it also determined who had to maintain the watchposts and permanent bridges on that plateau. Those plateaus were bought and sold among the highprinces.

A second sheet of parchment to the side of the Prime Map listed each highprince and the number of gemhearts he had won. It was a very Alethi thing to do—maintain motivation by making it very clear who was winning and who lagged behind.

Roion's eyes immediately went to his own name on the list. Of all the highprinces, Roion had won the fewest gemhearts.

Dalinar reached his hand up to the Prime Map, brushing the parchment. The middle plateaus were named or numbered for ease of reference. Foremost of them was a large plateau that stood defiantly near the Parshendi side. The Tower, it was called. An unusually massive and oddly shaped plateau that the chasmfiends seemed particularly fond of using as a spot for pupating.

Looking at it gave him pause. The size of a contested plateau determined the number of troops you could field on it. The Parshendi usually brought a large force to the Tower, and they had rebuffed the Alethi assaults there twenty-seven times now. No Alethi had ever won a skirmish upon it. Dalinar had been turned back there twice himself.

It was just too close to the Parshendi; they could always get there first and form up, using the slope to give them excellent high ground. *But if we could corner them there,* he thought, *with a large enough force of our own . . .* It could mean trapping and killing a huge number of Parshendi troops. Maybe enough of them to break their ability to wage war on the Plains.

It was something to consider. Before that could happen, however, Dalinar would need alliances. He ran his fingers westward. "Highprince Sadeas has been doing very well lately." Dalinar tapped Sadeas's warcamp. "He's been buying plateaus from other highprinces, making it easier and easier for him to get to the battlefields first."

"Yes," Roion said, frowning. "One hardly needs to see a map to know that, Dalinar."

"Look at the scope of it," Dalinar said. "Six years of continuous fighting, and nobody has even *seen* the center of the Shattered Plains."

"That's never been the point. We hold them in, besiege them, starve them out, and force them to come to us. Wasn't that *your* plan?"

"Yes, but I never imagined it would take this long. I've been thinking that it might be time to change tactics."

"Why? This one works. Hardly a week goes by without a couple of clashes with the Parshendi. Though, might I point out that *you* have hardly been a model of inspiration in battle lately." He nodded to Dalinar's name on the smaller sheet.

There were a good number of scratches next to his name, noting gemhearts won. But very few of them were fresh.

"There are some who say the Blackthorn has lost his sting," Roion said. He was careful not to insult Dalinar outright, but he went further than he once would have. News of Dalinar's actions while trapped in the barrack had spread.

Dalinar forced himself to be calm. "Roion, we cannot continue to treat this war as a game."

"All wars are games. The greatest kind, with the pieces lost real lives, the prizes captured making for real wealth! This is the life for which men exist. To fight, to kill, to win." He was quoting the Sunmaker, the last Alethi king to unite the highprinces. Gavilar had once revered his name.

"Perhaps," Dalinar said. "Yet what is the point? We fight to get Shardblades, then use those Shardblades to fight to get more Shardblades. It's a circle, round and round we go, chasing our tails so we can be better at chasing our tails."

"We fight to prepare ourselves to reclaim heaven and take back what is ours."

"Men can train without going to war, and men can fight without it being meaningless. It wasn't always this way. There were times when our wars *meant* something."

Roion raised an eyebrow. "You're almost making me believe the rumors, Dalinar. They say you've lost your taste for combat, that you no longer have the will to fight." He eyed Dalinar again. "Some are saying that it is time to abdicate in favor of your son."

"The rumors are wrong," Dalinar snapped.

"That is—"

"They are *wrong*," Dalinar said firmly, "if they claim

that I no longer care." He rested his fingers on the surface of the map again, running them across the smooth parchment. "I care, Roion. I care deeply. About this people. About my nephew. About the future of this war. And that is why I suggest we pursue an aggressive course from now on."

"Well, that is good to hear, I suppose."

Unite them. . . .

"I want you to try a joint plateau assault with me," Dalinar said.

"What?"

"I want the two of us to try coordinating our efforts and attack at the same time, working together."

"Why would we want to do that?"

"We could increase our chances of winning gemhearts."

"If more troops increased my chances of winning," Roion said, "then I'd just bring more of my own. The plateaus are too small for fielding large armies, and mobility is more important than sheer numbers."

It was a valid point; on the Plains, more didn't necessarily mean better. Close confines and a requisite forced march to the battlefield changed warfare significantly. The exact number of troops used depended on the size of the plateau and the highprince's personal martial philosophy.

"Working together wouldn't just be about fielding more troops," Dalinar said. "Each highprince's army has different strengths. I'm known for my heavy infantry; you have the best archers. Sadeas's bridges are the fastest. Working together, we could try new tactics. We expend too much effort getting to the plateau in haste. If we weren't so rushed, competing against one another, maybe we could surround the plateau. We could try letting the Parshendi arrive first, then assault them on *our* terms, not theirs."

Roion hesitated. Dalinar had spent days deliberating with his generals about the possibility of a joint assault. It seemed that there would be distinct advantages, but they wouldn't know for certain until someone tried it with him.

He actually seemed to be considering. "Who would get the gemheart?"

"We split the wealth equally," Dalinar said.

"And if we capture a Shardblade?"

"The man who won it would get it, obviously."

"And that's most likely to be you," Roion said, frowning. "As you and your son already have Shards."

It was the great problem of Shardblades and Shardplate—winning either was highly unlikely unless you already had Shards yourself. In fact, having only one or the other often wasn't enough. Sadeas had faced Parshendi Shardbearers on the field, and had always been forced to retreat, lest he be slain himself.

"I'm certain we could arrange something more equitable," Dalinar finally said. If he won Shards, he'd been hoping to be able to give them to Renarin.

"I'm sure," Roion said skeptically.

Dalinar drew in a breath. He needed to be bolder. "What if I offer them to you?"

"Excuse me?"

"We try a joint attack. If I win a Shardblade or Plate, you get the first set. But I keep the second."

Roion's eyes narrowed. "You'd do that?"

"On my honor, Roion."

"Well, nobody would doubt that. But can you blame a man for being wary?"

"Of what?"

"I am a highprince, Dalinar," Roion said. "My princedom is the smallest, true, but I am my own man. I would not see myself subordinated to someone greater."

You've already become part of something greater, Dalinar thought with frustration. *That happened the moment you swore fealty to Gavilar.* Roion and the others refused to make good on their promises. "Our kingdom can be so much more than it is, Roion."

"Perhaps. But perhaps I'm satisfied with what I have. Either way, you make an interesting proposal. I shall have to think on it further."

"Very well," Dalinar said, but his instinct said that Roion would decline the offer. The man was too suspicious. The highprinces barely trusted one another enough to work together when there *weren't* Shardblades and gems at stake.

"Will I be seeing you at the feast this evening?" Roion asked.

"Why wouldn't you?" Dalinar asked with a sigh.

"Well, the stormwardens have been saying that there *could* be a highstorm tonight, you see—"

"I will be there," Dalinar said flatly.

"Yes, of course," Roion said, chuckling. "No reason why you wouldn't be." He smiled at Dalinar and withdrew, his attendants following.

Dalinar sighed, turning to study the Prime Map, thinking through the meeting and what it meant. He stood there for a long time. Looking down on the Plains, as if a god far above. The plateaus looked like close islands, or perhaps jagged pieces set in a massive stained-glass window. Not for the first time, he felt as if he should be able to make out a pattern to the plateaus. If he could see more of them, perhaps. What would it mean if there *was* an order to the chasms?

Everyone else was so concerned with looking strong, with proving themselves. Was he really the only one who saw how frivolous that was? Strength for strength's sake? What good was strength unless you did something with it?

Alethkar was a light, once, he thought. *That's what Gavilar's book claims, that's what the visions are showing me. Nohadon was king of Alethkar, so long ago. In the time before the Heralds left.*

Dalinar felt as if he could almost see it. The secret. The thing that had made Gavilar so excited in the months before his death. If Dalinar could just stretch a little farther, he'd make it out. See the pattern in the lives of men. And finally know.

But that was what he'd been doing for the last six years. Grasping, stretching, reaching just a little farther. The farther he reached, the more distant those answers seemed to become.

⁂

Adolin stepped into the Gallery of Maps. His father was still there, standing alone. Two members of the Cobalt Guard watched over him from a distance. Roion was nowhere to be seen.

Adolin approached slowly. His father had that look in his eyes, the absent one he got so often lately. Even when he wasn't having an episode, he wasn't entirely here. Not in the way he once had been.

"Father?" Adolin said, stepping up to him.

"Hello, Adolin."

"How was the meeting with Roion?" Adolin asked, trying to sound cheerful.

"Disappointing. I'm proving far worse at diplomacy than I once was at war-making."

"There's no profit in peace."

"That's what everyone says. But we had peace once, and seemed to do just fine. Better, even."

"There hasn't been peace since the Tranquiline Halls," Adolin said immediately. "'Man's life on Roshar is conflict.'" It was a quotation from *The Arguments*.

Dalinar turned to Adolin, looking amused. "Quoting scripture at me? You?"

Adolin shrugged, feeling foolish. "Well, you see, Malasha is rather religious, and so earlier today I was listening to—"

"Wait," Dalinar said. "Malasha? Who's that?"

"Daughter of Brightlord Seveks."

"And that other girl, Janala?"

Adolin grimaced, thinking back to the disastrous walk they'd gone on the other day. Several nice gifts had yet to repair that. She didn't seem half as excited about him now that he wasn't courting someone else. "Things are rocky. Malasha seems like a better prospect." He moved on quickly. "I take it that Roion won't soon be going on any plateau assault with us."

Dalinar shook his head. "He's too afraid that I'm trying to maneuver him into a position where I can seize his lands. Perhaps it was wrong to approach the weakest highprince first. He'd rather hunker down and try to weather what comes at him, holding what he has, as opposed to making a risky play for something greater."

Dalinar stared at the map, looking distant again. "Gavilar

dreamed of unifying Alethkar. Once I thought he'd achieved it, despite what he claimed. The longer I work with these men, the more I realize that Gavilar was right. We failed. We defeated these men, but we *never* unified them."

"So you still intend to approach the others?"

"I do. I only need one to say yes in order to start. Who do you think we should go to next?"

"I'm not sure," Adolin said. "But for now, I think you should know something. Sadeas has sent to us, asking permission to enter our warcamp. He wants to interview the grooms who cared for His Majesty's horse during the hunt."

"His new position gives him the right to make those kinds of demands."

"Father," Adolin said, stepping closer, speaking softly. "I think he's going to move against us."

Dalinar looked at him.

"I know you trust him," Adolin said quickly. "And I understand your reasons now. But *listen* to me. This move puts him in an ideal position to undermine us. The king has grown paranoid enough that he's suspicious even of you and me—I know you've seen it. All Sadeas needs to do is find imaginary 'evidence' linking us to an attempt to kill the king, and he'll be able to turn Elhokar against us."

"We may have to risk that."

Adolin frowned. "But—"

"I trust Sadeas, son," Dalinar said. "But even if I didn't, we couldn't forbid him entry or block his investigation. We'd not only look guilty in the king's eyes, but we'd be denying his authority as well." He shook his head. "If I ever want the other highprinces to accept me as their leader in war, I have to be willing to allow Sadeas his authority as Highprince of Information. I can't rely upon the old traditions for my authority yet deny Sadeas the same right."

"I suppose," Adolin admitted. "But we could still prepare. You can't tell me you're not a little worried."

Dalinar hesitated. "Perhaps. This maneuver of Sadeas's is aggressive. But I've been told what to do. 'Trust Sadeas. Be strong. Act with honor, and honor will aid you.' That is the advice I've been given."

"From where?"

Dalinar looked to him, and it became obvious to Adolin.

"So we're betting the future of our house on these visions now," Adolin said flatly.

"I wouldn't say that," Dalinar replied. "If Sadeas did move against us, I wouldn't simply let him shove us over. But I'm also not going to make the first move against him."

"Because of what you've seen," Adolin said, growing frustrated. "Father, you said you'd listen to what I had to say about the visions. Well, please listen now."

"This isn't the proper place."

"You always have an excuse," Adolin said. "I've tried to approach you about it five times now, and you always rebuff me!"

"Perhaps it's because I know what you'll say," Dalinar said. "And I know it won't do any good."

"Or perhaps it's because you don't want to be confronted by the truth."

"That's enough, Adolin."

"No, no it's not! We're mocked in every one of the warcamps, our authority and reputation diminishes by the day, and *you* refuse to do anything substantial about it!"

"Adolin. I will *not* take this from my son."

"But you'll take it from everyone else? Why is that, Father? When others say things about us, you let them. But when Renarin or I take the smallest step toward what *you* view as being inappropriate, we're immediately chastised! Everyone else can speak lies, but I can't speak the truth? Do your sons mean so little to you?"

Dalinar froze, looking as if he'd been slapped.

"You aren't *well*, Father," Adolin continued. Part of him realized that he had gone too far, that he was speaking too loudly, but it boiled out anyway. "We need to stop tiptoeing around it! *You* need to stop making up increasingly irrational explanations to reason away your lapses! I know it's hard to accept, but sometimes, people get old. Sometimes, the mind stops working right.

"I don't know what's wrong. Maybe it's your guilt over Gavilar's death. That book, the Codes, the visions—maybe they're all attempts to find escape, find redemption, something. What you see *is not* real. Your life now is a rationalization, a way of trying to pretend that what's happening isn't happening. But I'll go to *Damnation itself* before I'll let you drag the entire house down without speaking my mind on it!"

He practically shouted those last words. They echoed in the large chamber, and Adolin realized he was shaking. He had never, in all his years of life, spoken to his father in such a way.

"You think I haven't wondered these things?" Dalinar said, his voice cold, his eyes hard. "I've gone through each point you've made a dozen times over."

"Then maybe you should go over them a few more."

"I *must* trust myself. The visions are trying to show me something important. I cannot prove it or explain how I know. But it's true."

"Of course you think that," Adolin said, exasperated. "Don't you see? That's exactly what you *would* feel. Men are very good at seeing what they want to! Look at the king. He sees a killer in every shadow, and a worn strap becomes a convoluted plot to take his life."

Dalinar fell silent again.

"Sometimes, the simple answers *are* the right ones, Father!" Adolin said. "The king's strap just wore out. And you . . . you're seeing things that aren't there. I'm sorry."

They locked expressions. Adolin didn't look away. He wouldn't look away.

Dalinar finally turned from him. "Leave me, please."

"All right. Fine. But I want you to think about this. I want you to—"

"Adolin. *Go.*"

Adolin gritted his teeth, but turned and stalked away. *It needed to be said,* he told himself as he left the gallery.

That didn't make him feel any less sick about having to be the one who said it.

THE BUTCHER

SEVEN YEARS AGO

It ain't right, what they do," the woman's voice said. "You ain't supposed to cut into folks, peering in to see what the Almighty placed hidden for good reason."

Kal froze, standing in an alleyway between two houses in Hearthstone. The sky was wan overhead; winter had come for a time. The Weeping was near, and highstorms were infrequent. For now, it was too cold for plants to enjoy the respite; rockbuds spent winter weeks curled up inside their shells. Most creatures hibernated, waiting for warmth to return. Fortunately, seasons generally lasted only a few weeks. Unpredictability. That was the way of the world. Only after death was there stability. So the ardents taught, at least.

Kal wore a thick, padded coat of breachtree cotton. The material was scratchy but warm, and had been dyed a deep brown. He kept the hood up, his hands in his pockets. To his right sat the baker's place—the family slept in the triangular crawlspace in back, and the front was their store. To Kal's left was one of Hearthstone's taverns, where lavis ale and mudbeer flowed in abundance during winter weeks.

He could hear two women, unseen but chatting a short distance way.

"You know that he stole from the old citylord," one woman's

voice said, keeping her voice down. "An entire goblet full of spheres. The surgeon says they were a gift, but he was the only one there when the citylord died."

"There *is* a document, I hear," the first voice said.

"A few glyphs. Not a proper will. And whose hand wrote those glyphs? The surgeon himself. It ain't right, the citylord not having a woman there to be scribe. I'm telling you. It ain't right what they do."

Kal gritted his teeth, tempted to step out and let the women see that he'd heard them. His father wouldn't approve, though. Lirin wouldn't want to cause strife or embarrassment.

But that was his father. So Kal marched right out of the alleyway, passing Nanha Terith and Nanha Relina standing and gossiping in front of the bakery. Terith was the baker's wife, a fat woman with curly dark hair. She was in the middle of another calumny. Kal gave her a sharp look, and her brown eyes showed a satisfying moment of discomfiture.

Kal crossed the square carefully, wary of patches of ice. The door to the bakery slammed shut behind him, the two women fleeing inside.

His satisfaction didn't last long. Why did people always say such things about his father? They called him morbid and un-natural, but would scurry out to buy glyphwards and charms from a passing apothecary or luckmerch. The Almighty pity a man who actually did something *useful* to help!

Still stewing, Kal turned a few corners, walking to where his mother stood on a stepladder at the side of the town hall, carefully chipping at the eaves of the building. Hesina was a tall woman, and she usually kept her hair pulled back into a tail, then wrapped a kerchief around her head. Today, she wore a knit hat over that. She had a long brown coat that matched Kal's, and the blue hem of her skirt just barely peeked out at the bottom.

The objects of her attention were a set of icicle-like pen-dants of rock that had formed on the edges of the roof. High-storms dropped stormwater, and stormwater carried crem. If left alone, crem eventually hardened into stone. Buildings grew stalactites, formed by stormwater slowly dripping from the eaves. You had to clean them off regularly, or risk weighing down the roof so much that it collapsed.

She noticed him and smiled, her cheeks flushed from the cold. With a narrow face, a bold chin, and full lips, she was a pretty woman. At least Kal thought so. Prettier than the baker's wife, for sure.

"Your father dismissed you from your lessons already?" she asked.

"Everyone hates Father," Kal blurted out.

His mother turned back to her work. "Kaladin, you're thirteen. You're old enough to know not to say foolish things like that."

"It's true," he said stubbornly. "I heard some women talking, just now. They said that Father stole the spheres from Brightlord Wistiow. They say that Father enjoys slicing people open and doing things that ain't natural."

"*Aren't* natural."

"Why can't I speak like everyone else?"

"Because it isn't proper."

"It's proper enough for Nanha Terith."

"And what do you think of her?"

Kal hesitated. "She's ignorant. And she likes to gossip about things she doesn't know anything about."

"Well, then. If you wish to emulate her, I can obviously find no objection to the practice."

Kal grimaced. You had to watch yourself when speaking with Hesina; she liked to twist words about. He leaned back against the wall of the town hall, watching his breath puff out in front of him. Perhaps a different tactic would work. "Mother, *why* do people hate Father?"

"They don't hate him," she said. However, his calmly asked question got her to continue. "But he *does* make them uncomfortable."

"Why?"

"Because some people are frightened of knowledge. Your father is a learned man; he knows things the others can't understand. So those things must be dark and mysterious."

"They aren't afraid of luckmerches and glyphwards."

"Those you can understand," his mother said calmly. "You burn a glyphward out in front of your house, and it will turn away evil. It's easy. Your father won't give someone a ward to heal them. He'll insist that they stay in bed, drinking water, taking some foul medicine, and washing their wound each day. It's hard. They'd rather leave it all to fate."

Kal considered that. "I think they hate him because he fails too often."

"There is that. If a glyphward fails, you can blame it on the will of the Almighty. If your father fails, then it's his fault. Or such is the perception." His mother continued working, flakes of stone falling to the ground around her. "They'll never actually *hate* your father—he's too useful. But he'll never really be one of them. That's the price of being a surgeon. Having power over the lives of men is an uncomfortable responsibility."

"And if I don't want that responsibility? What if I just want to be something normal, like a baker, or a farmer, or . . ." *Or a soldier,* he added in his mind. He'd picked up a staff a few times in secret, and though he'd never been able to replicate that moment when he'd fought Jost, there *was* something invigorating about holding a weapon. Something that drew him and excited him.

"I think," his mother said, "that you'll find the lives of bakers and farmers are not so enviable."

"At least they have friends."

"And so do you. What of Tien?"

"Tien's not my friend, Mother. He's my brother."

"Oh, and he can't be both at once?"

Kal rolled his eyes. "You know what I mean."

She climbed down from the stepladder, patting his shoulder. "Yes, I do, and I'm sorry to make light of it. But you put yourself in a difficult position. You want friends, but do you really want to *act* like the other boys? Give up your studies so you can slave in the fields? Grow old before your time, weathered and furrowed by the sun?"

Kal didn't reply.

"The things that others have always seem better than what you have," his mother said. "Bring the stepladder."

Kal followed dutifully, rounding the town hall to the other side, then putting down the ladder so his mother could climb up to begin work again.

"The others think Father stole those spheres." Kal shoved his hands in his pockets. "They think he wrote out that order from Brightlord Wistiow and had the old man sign it when he didn't know what he was doing."

His mother was silent.

"I hate their lies and gossip," Kal said. "I hate them for making up things about us."

"Don't hate them, Kal. They're good people. In this case, they're just repeating what they've heard." She glanced at the citylord's manor, distant upon a hill above the town. Every time Kal saw it, he felt like he should go up and talk to Laral. But the last few times he'd tried, he hadn't been allowed to see her. Now that her father was dead, her nurse oversaw her time, and the woman didn't think mingling with boys from the town was appropriate.

The nurse's husband, Miliv, had been Brightlord Wistiow's head steward. If there was a source of bad rumors about Kal's family, it probably came from him. He never *had* liked Kal's father. Well, Miliv wouldn't matter soon. A new citylord was expected to arrive any day.

"Mother," Kal said, "those spheres are just sitting there doing nothing but glowing. Can't we spend some to keep you from having to come out here and work?"

"I like working," she said, scraping away again. "It clears the head."

"Didn't you just tell me that I wouldn't like having to labor? My face furrowed before its time, or something poetic like that?"

She hesitated, then laughed. "Clever boy."

"Cold boy," he grumbled, shivering.

"I work because I want to. We can't spend those spheres—they're for your education—and so my working is better than forcing your father to charge for his healings."

"Maybe they'd respect us more if we did charge."

"Oh, they respect us. No, I don't think that is the problem."

She looked down at Kal. "You know that we're second nahn."

"Sure," Kal said, shrugging.

"An accomplished young surgeon of the right rank could draw the attention of a poorer noble family, one who wished money and acclaim. It happens in the larger cities."

Kal glanced up at the mansion again. "That's why you encouraged me to play with Laral so much. You wanted to marry me off to her, didn't you?"

"It was a possibility," his mother said, returning to her work.

He honestly wasn't certain how he felt about that. The last few months had been strange for Kal. His father had forced him into his studies, but in secret he'd spent his time with the staff. Two possible paths. Both enticing. Kal *did* like learning, and he longed for the ability to help people, bind their wounds, make them better. He saw true nobility in what his father did.

But it seemed to Kal that if he could fight, he could do something even more noble. Protect their lands, like the great lighteyed heroes of the stories. And there was the way he felt when holding a weapon.

Two paths. Opposites, in many ways. He could only choose one.

His mother kept chipping away at the eaves, and—with a sigh—Kal fetched a second stepladder and set of tools from the workroom, then joined her. He was tall for his age, but he still had to stand high on the ladder. He caught his mother smiling as he worked, no doubt pleased at having raised such a helpful young man. In reality, Kal just wanted the chance to pound on something.

How would he feel, marrying someone like Laral? He'd never be her equal. Their children would have a chance of being lighteyed or darkeyed, so even his children might outrank him. He knew he'd feel terribly out of place. That was another aspect of becoming a surgeon. If he chose that path, he would be choosing the life of his father. Choosing to set himself apart, to be isolated.

If he went to war, however, he would have a place. Maybe he could even do the nearly unthinkable, win a Shardblade and become a true lighteyes. Then he could marry Laral and not have to be her inferior. Was that why she'd always encouraged him to become a soldier? Had she been thinking about these kinds of things, even back then? Back then, these kinds of decisions—marriage, his future—had seemed impossibly far-off to Kal.

He felt so young. Did he really have to consider these questions? It would still be another few years before the surgeons of Kharbranth would let him take their tests. But if he *were* going to become a soldier instead, he'd have to join the army before that happened. How would his father react if Kal just up and went with the recruiters? Kal wasn't certain he'd be able to face Lirin's disappointed eyes.

As if in response to his thoughts, Lirin's voice called from nearby. "Hesina!"

Kal's mother turned, smiling and tucking a stray lock of dark hair back into her kerchief. Kal's father rushed down the street, his face anxious. Kal felt a sudden jolt of worry. Who was wounded? Why hadn't Lirin sent for him?

"What is it?" Kal's mother asked, climbing down.

"He's here, Hesina," Kal's father said.

"About time."

"Who?" Kal asked, jumping down from the stepladder. "Who's here?"

"The new citylord, son," Lirin said, his breath puffing in the cold air. "His name is Brightlord Roshone. No time to change, I'm afraid. Not if we want to catch his first speech. Come on!"

The three of them hurried away, Kal's thoughts and worries banished in the face of the chance to meet a new lighteyes.

"He didn't send word ahead," Lirin said under his breath.

"That could be a good sign," Hesina replied. "Maybe he doesn't feel he needs everyone to dote on him."

"That, or he's inconsiderate. Stormfather, I hate getting a new Landed. Always makes me feel like I'm throwing a handful of stones into a game of breakneck. Will we throw the queen or the tower?"

"We shall see soon enough," Hesina said, glancing at Kal. "Don't let your father's words unnerve you. He always gets pessimistic at times like this."

"I do *not*," Lirin said.

She gave him a look.

"Name one other time."

"Meeting my parents."

Kal's father pulled up short, blinking. "Stormwinds," he muttered, "let's hope this doesn't go *half* as poorly as that."

Kal listened with curiosity. He'd never met his mother's parents; they weren't often spoken of. Soon, the three of them reached the south side of town. A crowd was gathered, and Tien was already there, waiting. He waved in his excitable way, jumping up and down.

"Wish I had half that boy's energy," Lirin said.

"I've got a place for us picked out!" Tien called eagerly, pointing. "By the rain barrels! Come on! We're going to miss it!"

Tien scurried over, climbing atop the barrels. Several of the town's other boys noticed him, and they nudged one another, one making some comment Kal couldn't hear. It set the others laughing at Tien, and that immediately made Kal furious. Tien didn't deserve mockery just because he was a little small for his age.

This wasn't a good time to confront the other boys, though, so Kal sullenly joined his parents beside the barrels. Tien smiled at him, standing atop his barrel. He'd piled a few of his favorite rocks near him, stones of different colors and shapes. There were rocks all around them, and yet Tien was the only person he knew who found wonder in them. After a moment's consideration, Kal climbed atop a barrel—careful not to disturb any of Tien's rocks—so he too could get a better view of the citylord's procession.

It was enormous. There must have been a dozen wagons in that line, following a fine black carriage pulled by four sleek black horses. Kal gawked despite himself. Wistiow had only owned one horse, and it had seemed as old as he was.

Could one man, even a lighteyes, own that much furniture?

Where would he put it all? And there were people too. Dozens of them, riding in the wagons, walking in groups. There were also a dozen soldiers in gleaming breastplates and leather skirts. This lighteyes even had his own honor guard.

Eventually the procession reached the turn-off to Hearthstone. A man riding a horse led the carriage and its soldiers forward to the town while most of the wagons continued up to the manor. Kal grew increasingly excited as the carriage rolled slowly into place. Would he finally get to see a real, lighteyed hero? The word around town claimed it was likely that the new citylord would be someone King Gavilar or Highprince Sadeas had promoted because he'd distinguished himself in the wars to unite Alethkar.

The carriage turned sideways so that the door faced the crowd. The horses snorted and stomped the ground, and the carriage driver hopped down and quickly opened the door. A middle-aged man with a short, grey-streaked beard stepped out. He wore a ruffled violet coat, tailored so that it was short at the front—reaching only to his waist—but long at the back. Beneath it, he wore a golden takama, a long, straight skirt that went down to his calves.

A takama. Few wore them anymore, but old soldiers in town spoke of the days when they'd been popular as warrior's garb. Kal hadn't expected the takama to look so much like a woman's skirt, but still, it was a good sign. Roshone himself seemed a little too old, a little too flabby, to be a true soldier. But he wore a sword.

The lighteyed man scanned the crowd, a distasteful look on his face, as if he'd swallowed something bitter. Behind the man, two people peeked out. A younger man with a narrow face and an older woman with braided hair. Roshone studied the crowd, then shook his head and turned around to climb back in the carriage.

Kal frowned. Wasn't he going to say anything? The crowd seemed to share Kal's shock; a few of them began whispering in anxiety.

"Brightlord Roshone!" Kal's father called.

The crowd hushed. The lighteyed man glanced back.

People shied away, and Kal found himself shrinking down beneath that harsh gaze. "Who spoke?" Roshone demanded, his voice a low baritone.

Lirin stepped forward, raising a hand. "Brightlord. Was your trip pleasant? Please, can we show you the town?"

"What is your name?"

"Lirin, Brightlord. Hearthstone's surgeon."

"Ah," Roshone said. "You're the one who let old Wistiow die." The brightlord's expression darkened. "In a way, it's your fault I'm in this pitiful, miserable quarter of the kingdom." He grunted, then climbed back in the carriage and slammed the door. Within seconds, the carriage driver had replaced the stairs, climbed into his place, and started turning the vehicle around.

Kal's father slowly let his arm fall to his side. The townspeople began to chatter immediately, gossiping about the soldiers, the carriage, the horses.

Kal sat down on his barrel. *Well,* he thought. *I guess we could expect a warrior to be curt, right?* The heroes from the legends weren't necessarily the polite types. Killing people and fancy talking didn't always go together, old Jarel had once told him.

Lirin walked back, his expression troubled.

"Well?" Hesina said, trying to sound cheerful. "What do you think? Did we throw the queen or the tower?"

"Neither."

"Oh? And what did we throw instead?"

"I'm not sure," he said, glancing over his shoulder. "A pair and a trio, maybe. Let's get back home."

Tien scratched his head in confusion, but the words weighed on Kal. The tower was three pairs in a game of breakneck. The queen was two trios. The first was an outright loss, the other an outright win.

But a pair and a trio, that was called the butcher. Whether you won or not would depend on the other throws you made.

And, more importantly, on the throws of everyone else.

*I am being chased. Your friends of the Seventeenth Shard,
I suspect. I believe they're still lost, following a false trail I
left for them. They'll be happier that way. I doubt they
have any inkling what to do with me should they actually
catch me.*

I stood in the darkened monastery chamber,'" Litima read,
standing at the lectern with the tome open before her, "'its
far reaches painted with pools of black where light did not
wander. I sat on the floor, thinking of that dark, that Unseen.
I could not know, for certain, what was hidden in that night.
I suspected there were walls, sturdy and thick, but could I
know without seeing? When all was hidden, what could a
man rely upon as True?'"

Litima—one of Dalinar's scribes—was tall and plump and
wore a violet silk gown with yellow trim. She read to Dalinar
as he stood, regarding the maps on the wall of his sitting
room. That room was fitted with handsome wood furnishings
and fine woven rugs imported up from Marat. A crystal ca-
rafe of afternoon wine—orange, not intoxicating—sat on a
high-legged serving table in the corner, sparkling with the
light of the diamond spheres hanging in chandeliers above.

"'Candle flames,'" Litima continued. The selection was
from *The Way of Kings*, read from the very copy that Gavilar

had once owned. "'A dozen candles burned themselves to death on the shelf before me. Each of my breaths made them tremble. To them, I was a behemoth, to frighten and destroy. And yet, if I strayed too close, *they* could destroy *me*. My invisible breath, the pulses of life that flowed in and out, could end them freely, while my fingers could not do the same without being repaid in pain.'"

Dalinar idly twisted his signet ring in thought; it was sapphire with his Kholin glyphpair on it. Renarin stood next to him, wearing a coat of blue and silver, golden knots on the shoulders marking him as a prince. Adolin wasn't there. Dalinar and he had been stepping gingerly around one another since their argument in the Gallery.

"'I understood in a moment of stillness,'" Litima read. "'Those candle flames were like the lives of men. So fragile. So deadly. Left alone, they lit and warmed. Let run rampant, they would destroy the very things they were meant to illuminate. Embryonic bonfires, each bearing a seed of destruction so potent it could tumble cities and dash kings to their knees. In later years, my mind would return to that calm, silent evening, when I had stared at rows of living lights. And I would understand. To be given loyalty is to be infused like a gemstone, to be granted the frightful license to destroy not only one's self, but all within one's care.'"

Litima fell still. It was the end of the sequence.

"Thank you, Brightness Litima," Dalinar said. "That will do."

The woman bowed her head respectfully. She gathered her youthful ward from the side of the room and they withdrew, leaving the book on the lectern.

That sequence had become one of Dalinar's favorites. Listening to it often comforted him. Someone else had known, someone else had understood, how he felt. But today, it didn't bring the solace it usually did. It only reminded him of Adolin's arguments. None had been things Dalinar hadn't considered himself, but being confronted with them by someone he trusted had shaken everything. He found himself staring at his maps, smaller copies of those that hung in the Gallery.

They had been re-created for him by the royal cartographer, Isasik Shulin.

What if Dalinar's visions really *were* just phantasms? He'd often longed for the glory days of Alethkar's past. Were the visions his mind's answer to that, a subconscious way of letting himself be a hero, of giving himself justification for doggedly seeking his goals?

A disturbing thought. Looked at another way, those phantom commands to "unify" sounded a great deal like what the Hierocracy had said when it had tried to conquer the world five centuries before.

Dalinar turned from his maps and walked across the room, his booted feet falling on a soft rug. Too nice a rug. He'd spent the better part of his life in one warcamp or another; he'd slept in wagons, stone barracks, and tents pulled tight against the leeward side of stone formations. Compared with that, his present dwelling was practically a mansion. He felt as if he should cast out all of this finery. But what would that accomplish?

He stopped at the lectern and ran his fingers along the thick pages filled with lines in violet ink. He couldn't read the words, but he could almost *feel* them, emanating from the page like Stormlight from a sphere. Were the words of this book the cause of his problems? The visions had started several months after he'd first listened to readings from it.

He rested his hand on the cold, ink-filled pages. Their homeland was stressed nearly to breaking, the war was stalled, and suddenly he found himself captivated by the very ideals and myths that had led to his brother's downfall. This was a time the Alethi needed the Blackthorn, not an old, tired soldier who fancied himself a philosopher.

Blast it all, he thought. *I thought I'd figured this out!* He closed the leather-bound volume, the spine crackling. He carried it to the bookshelf and returned it to its place.

"Father?" Renarin asked. "Is there something I can do for you?"

"I wish there were, son." Dalinar tapped the spine of the book lightly. "It's ironic. This book was once considered one of the great masterpieces of political philosophy. Did you know that? Jasnah told me that kings around the world used to study it daily. Now, it is considered borderline blasphemous."

Renarin gave no reply.

"Regardless," Dalinar said, walking back to the wall map. "Highprince Aladar refused my offer of an alliance, just as Roion did. Do you have a thought on whom should I approach next?"

"Adolin says we should be far more worried about Sadeas's ploy to destroy us than we are."

The room fell silent. Renarin had a habit of doing that, felling conversations like an enemy archer hunting officers on the battlefield.

"Your brother is right to worry," Dalinar said. "But moving against Sadeas would undermine Alethkar as a kingdom. For the same reason, Sadeas won't risk acting against us. He'll see."

I hope.

Horns suddenly sounded outside, their deep, resounding calls echoing. Dalinar and Renarin froze. Parshendi spotted on the Plains. A second set came. Twenty-third plateau of the second quadrant. Dalinar's scouts thought the contested plateau close enough for their forces to reach first.

Dalinar dashed across the room, all other thoughts discarded for the moment, his booted feet thumping on the thick rug. He threw open the door and charged down the Stormlight-illuminated hallway.

The war room door was open, and Teleb—highofficer on duty—saluted as Dalinar entered. Teleb was a straight-backed man with light green eyes. He kept his long hair in a braid and had a blue tattoo on his cheek, marking him as an Oldblood. At the side of the room, his wife, Kalami, sat behind a long-legged desk on a high stool. She wore her dark hair with only two small side braids pinned up, the rest hanging down the back of her violet dress to brush the top of the stool. She was a historian of note, and had requested permission to record meetings like this one; she planned to scribe a history of the war.

"Sir," Teleb said. "A chasmfiend crawled atop the plateau here less than a quarter hour ago." He pointed to the battle map, which had glyphs marking each plateau. Dalinar stepped up to it, a group of his officers gathering around him.

"How far would you say that is?" Dalinar asked, rubbing his chin.

"Perhaps two hours," Teleb said, indicating a route one of his men had drawn on the map. "Sir, I think we have a good chance at this one. Brightlord Aladar will have to traverse six unclaimed plateaus to reach the contested area, while we have a nearly direct line. Brightlord Sadeas would have trouble, as he'd have to work his way around several large chasms too wide to cross with bridges. I'll bet he won't even try for it."

Dalinar did, indeed, have the most direct line. He hesitated, though. It had been months since he'd last gone on a plateau run. His attention had been diverted, his troops needed for protecting roadways and patrolling the large markets that had grown up outside the warcamps. And now, Adolin's questions weighed upon him, pressing him down. It seemed like a terrible time to go out to battle.

No, he thought. *No, I need to do this.* Winning a plateau skirmish would do much for his troops' morale, and would help discredit the rumors in camp.

"We march!" Dalinar declared.

A few of the officers whooped in excitement, an extreme show of emotion for the normally reserved Alethi.

"And your son, Brightlord?" Teleb asked. He'd heard of the confrontation between them. Dalinar doubted there was a person in all ten warcamps who hadn't heard of it.

"Send for him," Dalinar said firmly. Adolin probably needed this as much as, or more than, Dalinar did.

The officers scattered. Dalinar's armor bearers entered a moment later. It had only been a few minutes since the horns had sounded, but after six years of fighting, the machine of war ran smoothly when battle called. From outside, he heard the horns' third set begin, calling his forces to battle.

The armor bearers inspected his boots—checking to be certain the laces were tight—then brought a long padded vest to throw over his uniform. Next, they set the sabatons—armor for his boots—on the floor before him. They encased his boots entirely and had a rough surface on the bottoms that seemed to cling to rock. The interiors glowed with the light of the sapphires in their indented pockets.

Dalinar was reminded of his most recent vision. The Radiant, his armor glowing with glyphs. Modern Shardplate didn't glow like that. Could his mind have fabricated that detail? Would it have?

No time to consider that now, he thought. He discarded his uncertainties and worries, something he'd learned to do during his first battles as a youth. A warrior needed to be focused. Adolin's questions would still be waiting for him when he got back. For now, he couldn't afford self-doubt or uncertainty. It was time to be the Blackthorn.

He stepped into the sabatons, and the straps tightened of their own accord, fitting around his boots. The greaves came next, going over his legs and knees, locking on to the sabatons. Shardplate wasn't like ordinary armor; there was no mesh of steel mail and no leather straps at the joints. Shardplate seams were made of smaller plates, interlocking, overlapping, incredibly intricate, leaving no vulnerable gaps. There was very little rubbing or chafing; each piece fit together perfectly, as if it had been crafted specifically for Dalinar.

One always put the armor on from the feet upward. Shardplate was extremely heavy; without the enhanced strength it provided, no man would be able to fight in it. Dalinar stood still as the armor bearers affixed the cuisses over his thighs and locked them to the culet and faulds across his waist and lower back. A skirt made of small, interlocking plates came next, reaching down to just above the knees.

"Brightlord," Teleb said, stepping up to him. "Have you given thought to my suggestion about the bridges?"

"You know how I feel about man-carried bridges, Teleb,"

Dalinar said as the armor bearers locked his breastplate into place, then worked on the rerebraces and vambraces for his arms. Already, he could feel the strength of the Plate surging through him.

"We wouldn't have to use the smaller bridges for the assault," Teleb said. "Just for getting to the contested plateau."

"We'd still have to bring the chull-pulled bridges to get across that last chasm," Dalinar said. "I'm not convinced that bridge crews would move us any more quickly. Not when we have to wait for those animals."

Teleb sighed.

Dalinar reconsidered. A good officer was one who accepted orders and fulfilled them, even when he disagreed. But the mark of a great officer was that he also tried to innovate and offer appropriate suggestions.

"You may recruit and train a single bridge crew," Dalinar said. "We shall see. In these races, even a few minutes can be meaningful."

Teleb smiled. "Thank you, sir."

Dalinar waved with his left hand as the armor bearers locked the gauntlet onto his right. He made a fist, tiny plates curving perfectly. The left gauntlet followed. Then the gorget went over his head, covering his neck, the pauldrons on his shoulders, and the helm on his head. Finally, the armor bearers affixed his cape to the pauldrons.

Dalinar took a deep breath, feeling the Thrill build for the approaching battle. He strode from the war room, footfalls firm and *solid*. Attendants and servants scattered before him, making way. Wearing Shardplate again after a long period without was like waking up after a night of feeling groggy or disoriented. The spring of the step, the impetus the armor seemed to lend him, made him want to race down the hallway and—

And why not?

He broke into a sprint. Teleb and the others cried out in surprise, rushing to keep up. Dalinar outpaced them easily, reaching the front gates of the complex and leaping through, throwing himself off the long steps leading down from his enclave. He exulted, grinning as he hung in the air, then slammed to the ground. The force cracked the stone beneath him, and he crouched into the impact.

Before him, neat rows of barracks ran through his war-camp, formed in radials with a meeting ground and mess hall at the center of each battalion. His officers reached the top of the stairs, looking down with amazement. Renarin was with them, wearing his uniform that had never seen battle, his hand raised against the sunlight.

Dalinar felt foolish. Was he a youth just given his first taste of Shardplate? *Back to work. Stop playing.*

Perethom, his infantrylord, saluted as Dalinar strode up. "Second and Third Battalions are on duty today, Brightlord. Forming ranks to march."

"First Bridge Squad is gathered, Brightlord," Havarah—the bridgelord—said, striding up. He was a short man, with some Herdazian blood in him as evidenced by his dark, crystalline fingernails, though he didn't wear a sparkflicker. "I have word from Ashelem that the archery company is ready."

"Cavalry?" Dalinar asked. "And where is my son?"

"Here, Father," called a familiar voice. Adolin—his Shardplate painted a deep Kholin blue—made his way through the gathering crowd. His visor was up, and he looked eager, though when he met Dalinar's eyes, he glanced away immediately.

Dalinar held up a hand, quieting several officers who were trying to give him reports. He strode to Adolin, and the youth looked up, meeting his gaze.

"You said what you felt you must," Dalinar said.

"And I'm not sorry I did," Adolin replied. "But I *am* sorry for how, and where, I said it. That won't happen again."

Dalinar nodded, and that was enough. Adolin seemed to relax, a weight coming off his shoulders, and Dalinar turned back to his officers. In moments, he and Adolin were leading a hurried group to the staging area. As they did, Dalinar did note Adolin waving to a young woman who stood beside the way, wearing a red dress, her hair up in a very nice braiding.

"Is that—er—"

"Malasha?" Adolin said. "Yes."

"She looks nice."

"Most of the time she is, though she's somewhat annoyed that I wouldn't let her come with me today."

"She wanted to come into *battle*?"

Adolin shrugged. "Says she's curious."

Dalinar said nothing. Battle was a masculine art. A woman wanting to come to the battlefield was like . . . well, like a man wanting to read. Unnatural.

Ahead, in the staging area, the battalions were forming ranks, and a squat lighteyed officer hurried up to Dalinar. He had patches of red hair on his otherwise dark Alethi head and a long, red mustache. Ilamar, the cavalrylord.

"Brightlord," he said, "my apologies for the delay. Cavalry is mounted and ready."

"We march, then," Dalinar said. "All ranks—"

"Brightlord!" a voice said.

Dalinar turned as one of his messengers approached. The darkeyed man wore leathers marked with blue bands on the arms. He saluted, saying, "Highprince Sadeas has demanded admittance to the warcamp!"

Dalinar glanced at Adolin. His son's expression darkened.

"He claims the king's writ of investigation grants him the right," the messenger said.

"Admit him," Dalinar said.

"Yes, Brightlord," the messenger said, turning back. One of the lesser officers, Moratel, went with him so that Sadeas could be welcomed and escorted by a lighteyes as befitted his station. Moratel was least among those in attendance; everyone understood he was the one Dalinar would send.

"What do you think Sadeas wants this time?" Dalinar said quietly to Adolin.

"Our blood. Preferably warm, perhaps sweetened with a shot of tallew brandy."

Dalinar grimaced, and the two of them hurried past the ranks of soldiers. The men had an air of anticipation, spears held high, darkeyed citizen officers standing at the sides with axes on their shoulders. At the front of the force, a group of chulls snorted and rummaged at the rocks by their feet; harnessed to them were several enormous mobile bridges.

Gallant and Adolin's white stallion Sureblood were waiting, their reins held at the ready by grooms. Ryshadium hardly needed handlers. Once, Gallant had kicked open his stall and made his way to the staging grounds on his own when a groom had been too slow. Dalinar patted the midnight destrier on the neck, then swung into the saddle.

He scanned the staging field, then raised his arm to give the command to move. However, he noticed a group of mounted men riding up to the staging field, led by a figure in dark red Shardplate. Sadeas.

Dalinar stifled a sigh and gave the command to move out, though he himself waited for the Highprince of Information. Adolin came over on Sureblood, and he gave Dalinar a glance that seemed to say, "Don't worry, I'll behave."

As always, Sadeas was a model of fashion, his armor painted, his helm ornamented with a completely different metallic pattern than he had worn last time. This one was shaped like a stylized sunburst. It looked almost like a crown.

"Brightlord Sadeas," Dalinar said. "This is an inconvenient time for your investigation."

"Unfortunately," Sadeas said, reining in. "His Majesty is very eager to have answers, and I cannot stop my investigation, even for a plateau assault. I need to interview some of your soldiers. I'll do it on the way out."

"You want to come *with* us?"

"Why not? I won't delay you." He glanced at the chulls, who lurched into motion, pulling the bulky bridges. "I doubt that even were I to decide to *crawl*, I could slow you any further."

"Our soldiers need to concentrate on the upcoming battle, Brightlord," Adolin said. "They should not be distracted."

"The king's will must be done," Sadeas said, shrugging, not even bothering to look at Adolin. "Need I present the writ? Surely you don't intend to forbid me."

Dalinar studied his former friend, looking into those eyes, trying to see into the man's soul. Sadeas lacked his characteristic smirk; he usually wore one of those when he was pleased with how a plot was going. Did he realize that Dalinar knew how to read his expressions, and so masked his emotions? "No need to present anything, Sadeas. My men are at your disposal. If you have need of anything, simply ask. Adolin, with me."

Dalinar turned Gallant and galloped down the line toward the front of the marching army. Adolin followed reluctantly, and Sadeas remained behind with his attendants.

The long ride began. The permanent bridges here were Dalinar's, maintained and guarded by his soldiers and scouts, connecting plateaus that he controlled. Sadeas spent the trip riding near the middle of the column of two thousand. He periodically sent an attendant to pull certain soldiers out of line.

Dalinar spent the ride mentally preparing himself for the battle ahead. He spoke with his officers about the layout of the plateau, got a report on where specifically the chasmfiend had chosen to make its chrysalis, and sent scouts ahead to watch for Parshendi. Those scouts carried their long poles to get them from plateau to plateau without bridges.

Dalinar's force eventually reached the end of the permanent bridges, and had to start waiting for the chull bridges to be lowered across the chasms. The big machines were built like siege towers, with enormous wheels and armored sections at the side where soldiers could push. At a chasm, they unhooked the chulls, pushed the machine forward by hand, and ratcheted a crank at the back to lower the bridge. Once the bridge was set down, the machinery was unlocked and pulled across. The bridge was built so they could lock the machine onto the other side, pull the bridge up, then turn and hook the chulls up again.

It was a slow process. Dalinar watched from horseback, fingers tapping the side of his hogshide saddle as the first chasm was spanned. Perhaps Teleb was right. Could they use lighter, more portable bridges to get across these early chasms, then resort to the siege bridges only for the final assault?

A clatter of hooves on rock announced someone riding up

the side of the column. Dalinar turned, expecting Adolin, and instead found Sadeas.

Why *had* Sadeas asked to be Highprince of Information, and why was he so dogged in pursuing this matter of the broken girth? If he did decide to create some kind of false implication of Dalinar's guilt . . .

The visions told me to trust him, Dalinar told himself firmly. But he was growing less certain about them. How much dared he risk on what they'd said?

"Your soldiers are quite loyal to you," Sadeas noted as he arrived.

"Loyalty is the first lesson of a soldier's life," Dalinar said. "I would be worried if these men *hadn't* yet mastered it."

Sadeas sighed. "Really, Dalinar. Must you always be so sanctimonious?"

Dalinar didn't reply.

"It's odd, how a leader's influence can affect his men," Sadeas said. "So many of these are like smaller versions of you. Bundles of emotion, wrapped up and tied until they become stiff from the pressure. They're so sure in some ways, yet so insecure in others."

Dalinar kept his jaw clenched. *What is your game, Sadeas?*

Sadeas smiled, leaning in, speaking softly. "You want so badly to snap at me, don't you? Even in the old days, you hated it when someone implied that you were insecure. Back then, your displeasure often ended with a head or two rolling across the stones."

"I killed many who did not deserve death," Dalinar said. "A man should not fear losing his head because he took one too many sips of wine."

"Perhaps," Sadeas said lightly. "But don't you ever want to let it out, as you used to? Doesn't it pound on you inside, like someone trapped within a large drum? Beating, banging, trying to claw free?"

"Yes," Dalinar said.

The admission seemed to surprise Sadeas. "And the Thrill, Dalinar. Do you still feel the Thrill?"

Men didn't often speak of the Thrill, the joy and lust for

battle. It was a private thing. "I feel each of the things you mention, Sadeas," Dalinar said, eyes forward. "But I don't always let them out. A man's emotions are what define him, and control is the hallmark of true strength. To lack feeling is to be dead, but to act on every feeling is to be a child."

"That has the stink of a quote about it, Dalinar. From Gavilar's little book of virtues, I assume?"

"Yes."

"Doesn't it bother you at all that the Radiants betrayed us?"

"Legends. The Recreance is an event so old, it might as well be in the shadowdays. What did the Radiants really do? Why did they do it? We don't know."

"We know enough. They used elaborate tricks to imitate great powers and pretend a holy calling. When their deceptions were discovered, they fled."

"Their powers were not lies. They were real."

"Oh?" Sadeas said, amused. "You know this? Didn't you just say the event was so old, it might as well have been in the shadowdays? If the Radiants had such marvelous powers, why can nobody reproduce them? Where did those incredible skills go?"

"I don't know," Dalinar said softly. "Perhaps we're just not worthy of them any longer."

Sadeas snorted, and Dalinar wished he'd bitten his tongue. His only evidence for what he said was his visions. And yet, if Sadeas belittled something, he instinctively wanted to stand up for it.

I can't afford this. I need to be focused on the battle ahead.

"Sadeas," he said, determined to change the topic. "We need to work harder to unify the warcamps. I want your help, now that you're Highprince of Information."

"To do what?"

"To do what needs to be done. For the good of Alethkar."

"That's exactly what I'm doing, old friend," Sadeas said. "Killing Parshendi. Winning glory and wealth for our kingdom. Seeking vengeance. It would be best for Alethkar if you'd stop wasting so much time in camp—and stop talking of fleeing like cowards. It would be *best* for Alethkar if you'd start acting like a man again."

"Enough, Sadeas!" Dalinar said, more loudly than he'd intended. "I gave you leave to come along for your investigation, not to taunt me!"

Sadeas sniffed. "That book ruined Gavilar. Now it's doing the same to you. You've listened to those stories so much they've got your head full of false ideals. Nobody ever really lived the way the Codes claim."

"Bah!" Dalinar said, waving a hand and turning Gallant. "I don't have time for your snideness today, Sadeas." He trotted his horse away, furious at Sadeas, then even more furious at himself for losing his temper.

He crossed the bridge, stewing, thinking of Sadeas's words. He found himself remembering a day when he stood with his brother beside the Impossible Falls of Kholinar.

Things are different now, Dalinar, Gavilar had said. *I see now, in ways I never did before. I wish I could show you what I mean.*

It had been three days before his death.

❖

Ten heartbeats.

Dalinar closed his eyes, breathing in and out—slowly, calmingly—as they prepared themselves behind the siege bridge. Forget Sadeas. Forget the visions. Forget his worries and fears. Just focus on the heartbeats.

Nearby, chulls scraped the rock with their hard, carapaced feet. The wind blew across his face, smelling wet. It always smelled wet out here, in these humid stormlands.

Soldiers clanked, leather creaked. Dalinar raised his head toward the sky, his heart thumping deep within him. The brilliant white sun stained his eyelids red.

Men shifted, called, cursed, loosened swords in their sheaths, tested bowstrings. He could *feel* their tension, their anxiety mixed with excitement. Among them, anticipation-spren began to spring from the ground, streamers connected by one side to the stone, the others whipping in the air. Some fearspren boiled up among them.

"Are you ready?" Dalinar asked softly. The Thrill was rising within him.

"Yes." Adolin's voice was eager.

"You never complain about the way we attack," Dalinar said, eyes still closed. "You never challenge me on this."

"This is the best way. They're my men too. What is the point of being a Shardbearer if we cannot lead the charge?"

The tenth heartbeat sounded in Dalinar's chest; he could always hear the beats when he was summoning his Blade, no matter how loud the world around him was. The faster they passed, the sooner the sword arrived. So the more urgent you felt, the sooner you were armed. Was that intentional, or just some quirk of the Shardblade's nature?

Oathbringer's familiar weight settled into his hand.

"Go," Dalinar said, snapping his eyes open. He slammed his visor down as Adolin did the same, Stormlight rising from the sides as the helms sealed shut and became translucent. The two of them burst out from behind the massive bridge— one Shardbearer on each side, a figure of blue and another of slate grey.

The energy of the armor pulsed through Dalinar as he dashed across the stone ground, arms pumping in rhythm with his steps. The wave of arrows came immediately, loosed from the Parshendi kneeling on the other side of the chasm. Dalinar flung his arm up in front of his eye slit as arrows sprayed across him, scraping metal, some shafts snapping. It felt like running against a hailstorm.

Adolin bellowed a war cry from the right, voice muffled by his helm. As they approached the chasm lip, Dalinar lowered his arm despite the arrows. He needed to be able to judge his approach. The gulf was mere feet away. His Plate gave him a surge of strength as he reached the edge of the chasm.

Then leaped.

For a moment, he soared above the inky chasm, cape flapping, arrows filling the air around him. He was reminded of the flying Radiant from his vision. But this was nothing so mystical, just a standard Shardplate-assisted jump. Dalinar cleared the chasm and crashed back to the ground on the other side, sweeping his Blade down and across to slay three Parshendi with a single blow.

Their eyes burned black and smoke rose as they collapsed. He swung again. Bits of armor and weapons sprayed into the air where arrows had once flown, sheared free by his Blade. As always, it sliced apart anything inanimate, but blurred when it touched flesh, as if turning to mist.

The way it reacted to flesh and cut steel so easily, it sometimes felt to Dalinar like he was swinging a weapon of pure smoke. As long as he kept the Blade in motion, it could not get caught in chinks or stopped by the weight of what it was cutting.

Dalinar spun, sweeping out with his Blade in a line of death. He sheared through souls themselves, leaving Parshendi to drop dead to the ground. Then he kicked, tossing a corpse into the faces of the Parshendi nearby. A few more kicks sent corpses flying—a Plate-driven kick could easily send a body tumbling thirty feet—clearing the ground around him for better footing.

Adolin hit the plateau not far away, spinning and falling into Windstance. Adolin shoved his shoulder into a group of archers, tossing them backward and throwing several into the chasm. Gripping his Shardblade with both hands, he did an initial sweep as Dalinar had, cutting down six enemies.

The Parshendi were singing, many of them wearing beards that glowed with small uncut gemstones. Parshendi always sang as they fought; that song changed as they abandoned their bows—pulling out axes, swords, or maces—and threw themselves at the two Shardbearers.

Dalinar put himself at the optimal distance from Adolin, allowing his son to protect his blind spots, but not getting too close. The two Shardbearers fought, still near the lip of the chasm, cutting down the Parshendi who tried desperately to push them backward by sheer force of numbers. This was their best chance to defeat the Shardbearers. Dalinar and

Adolin were alone, without their honor guard. A fall from this height would certainly kill even a man in Plate.

The Thrill rose within him, so sweet. Dalinar kicked away another corpse, though he didn't need the extra room. They'd noticed that the Parshendi grew enraged when you moved their dead. He kicked another body, taunting them, drawing them toward him to fight in pairs as they often did.

He cut down a group that came, singing in voices angry at what he'd done to their dead. Nearby, Adolin began to lay about him with punches as the Parshendi got too close; he was fond of the tactic, switching between using his sword in two hands or one. Parshendi corpses flew this way and that, bones and armor shattered by the blows, orange Parshendi blood spraying across the ground. Adolin moved back to his Blade a moment later, kicking away a corpse.

The Thrill consumed Dalinar, giving him strength, focus, and power. The glory of the battle grew grand. He'd stayed away from this too long. He saw with clarity now. They *did* need to push harder, assault more plateaus, win the gemhearts.

Dalinar was the Blackthorn. He was a natural force, never to be halted. He was death itself. He—

He felt a sudden stab of powerful revulsion, a sickness so strong that it made him gasp. He slipped, partially on a patch of blood, but partially because his knees grew suddenly weak.

The corpses before him suddenly seemed a horrifying sight. Eyes burned out like spent coals. Bodies limp and broken, bones shattered where Adolin had punched them. Heads cracked open, blood and brains and entrails spilled around them. Such butchery, such death. The Thrill vanished.

How could a man *enjoy* this?

The Parshendi surged toward him. Adolin was there in a heartbeat, attacking with more skill than any other man Dalinar had known. The lad was a genius with the Blade, an artist with paint of only one shade. He struck expertly, forcing the Parshendi back. Dalinar shook his head, recovering his stance.

He forced himself to resume fighting, and as the Thrill began to rise again, Dalinar hesitantly embraced it. The odd sickness faded, and his battle reflexes took control. He spun into the Parshendi advance, sweeping out with his Blade in broad, aggressive strokes.

He *needed* this victory. For himself, for Adolin, and for his men. Why had he been so horrified? The Parshendi had murdered Gavilar. It was right to kill them.

He was a soldier. Fighting was what he did. And he did it well.

The Parshendi advance unit broke before his assault, scattering back toward a larger mass of their troops, who were forming ranks in haste. Dalinar stepped back and found himself looking down at the corpses around him, with their blackened eyes. Smoke still curled from a few.

The sick feeling returned.

Life ended so quickly. The Shardbearer was destruction incarnate, the most powerful force on a battlefield. *Once these weapons meant protecting,* a voice inside of him whispered.

The three bridges crashed to the ground a few feet away, and the cavalry charged across a moment later, led by compact Ilamar. A few windspren danced past in the air, nearly invisible. Adolin called for his horse, but Dalinar just stood, looking down at the dead. Parshendi blood was orange, and it smelled like mold. Yet their faces—marbled black or white and red—looked so human. A parshman nurse had practically raised Dalinar.

Life before death.

What *was* that voice?

He glanced back across the chasm, toward where Sadeas—well outside of bow range—sat with his attendants. Dalinar could sense the disapproval in his ex-friend's posture. Dalinar and Adolin risked themselves, taking a dangerous leap across the chasm. An assault of the type Sadeas had pioneered would cost more lives. But how many lives would Dalinar's army lose if one of its Shardbearers was pushed into the chasm?

Gallant charged across the bridge alongside a line of soldiers, who cheered for the Ryshadium. He slowed near Dalinar, who grabbed the reins. Right now, he was needed. His men were fighting and dying, and this was not a time for regret or second-guessing.

A Plate-enhanced jump put him in the saddle. Then, Shardblade raised high, he charged into battle to kill for his men. That was not what the Radiants had fought for. But at least it was something.

·:·

They won the battle.

Dalinar stepped back, feeling fatigued as Adolin did the honors of harvesting the gemheart. The chrysalis itself sat like an enormous, oblong rockbud, fifteen feet tall and attached to the uneven stone ground by something that looked like crem. There were bodies all around it, some human, others Parshendi. The Parshendi had tried to get into it quickly and flee, but they'd only managed to get a few cracks into the shell.

The fighting had been most furious here, around the chrysalis. Dalinar rested back against a shelf of rock and pulled his helm off, exposing a sweaty head to the cool breeze. The sun was high overhead; the battle had lasted two hours or so.

Adolin worked efficiently, using his Shardblade with care to shave off a section of the outside of the chrysalis. Then he expertly plunged it in, killing the pupating creature but avoiding the region with the gemheart.

Just like that, the creature was dead. Now the Shardblade could cut it, and Adolin carved away sections of flesh. Purple ichor spurted out as he reached in, questing for the gemheart. The soldiers cheered as he pulled it free, gloryspren hovering above the entire army like hundreds of spheres of light.

Dalinar found himself walking away, helm held in his left hand. He crossed the battlefield, passing surgeons tending the wounded and teams who were carrying his dead back to the bridges. There were sleds behind the chull carts for them, so they could be burned properly back at camp.

There were a lot of Parshendi corpses. Looking at them now, he was neither disgusted nor excited. Just exhausted.

He'd gone to battle dozens, perhaps hundreds of times. Never before had he felt as he had this day. That revulsion had distracted him, and that could have gotten him killed. Battle was no time for reflection; you had to keep your mind on what you were doing.

The Thrill had seemed subdued the entire battle, and he hadn't fought nearly as well as he once had. This battle should have brought him clarity. Instead, his troubles seemed magnified. *Blood of my fathers,* he thought, stepping up to the top of a small rock hill. *What is happening to me?*

His weakness today seemed the latest, and most potent, argument to fuel what Adolin—and, indeed, what many others—said about him. He stood atop the hill, looking eastward, toward the Origin. His eyes went that direction so often. Why? What was—

He froze, noticing a group of Parshendi on a nearby plateau. His scouts watched them warily; it was the army that Dalinar's people had driven off. Though they'd killed a lot of Parshendi today, the vast majority had still escaped, retreating when they realized the battle was lost to them. That was one of the reasons the war was lasting so long. The Parshendi understood strategic retreat.

This army stood in ranks, grouped in warpairs. A commanding figure stood at their head, a large Parshendi in glittering armor. Shardplate. Even at a distance, it was easy to tell the difference between it and something more mundane.

That Shardbearer hadn't been here during the battle itself. Why come now? Had he arrived too late?

The armored figure and the rest of the Parshendi turned and left, leaping across the chasm behind them and fleeing back toward their unseen haven at the center of the Plains.

Reproduction of a woodblock print image that some scholars date to a few generations after Aharietiam. Described as a depiction of a Voidbringer.

27

CHASM DUTY

If anything I have said makes a glimmer of sense to you, I trust that you'll call them off. Or maybe you could astound me and ask them to do something productive for once.

Kaladin pushed his way into the apothecary's shop, the door banging shut behind him. As before, the aged man pretended to be feeble, feeling his way with a cane until he recognized Kaladin. Then he stood up straighter. "Oh. It's you."

It had been two more long days. Daytime spent working and training—Teft and Rock now practiced with him—evenings spent at the first chasm, retrieving the reeds from their hiding place in a crevice and then milking for hours. Gaz had seen them go down last night, and the bridge sergeant was undoubtedly suspicious. There was no helping that.

Bridge Four had been called out on a bridge run today. Thankfully, they'd arrived before the Parshendi, and none of the bridge crews had lost any men. Things hadn't gone so well for the regular Alethi troops. The Alethi line had eventually buckled before the Parshendi assault, and the bridge crews had been forced to lead a tired, angry, and defeated troop of soldiers back to the camp.

Kaladin was bleary-eyed with fatigue from staying up late working on the reeds. His stomach growled perpetually from being given a fraction of the food it needed, as he shared his meals with two wounded. That all ended today. The apothecary walked back behind his counter, and Kaladin stepped up to it. Syl darted into the room, her small ribbon of light turning into a woman midtwist. She flipped like an acrobat, landing on the table in a smooth motion.

"What do you need?" the apothecary asked. "More bandages? Well, I might just—"

He cut off as Kaladin slapped a medium-sized liquor bottle down on the table. It had a cracked top, but would still hold a cork. He pulled this free, revealing the milky white knobweed sap inside. He'd used the first of what they'd harvested to treat Leyten, Dabbid, and Hobber.

"What's this?" the elderly apothecary asked, adjusting his spectacles and leaning down. "Offering me a drink? I don't take the stuff these days. Unsettles the stomach, you know."

"It's not liquor. It's knobweed sap. You said it was expensive. Well, how much will you give me for this?"

The apothecary blinked, then leaned in closer, giving the contents a whiff. "Where'd you get this?"

"I harvested it from the reeds growing outside of camp."

The apothecary's expression darkened. He shrugged. "Worthless, I'm afraid."

"What?"

"The wild weeds aren't potent enough." The apothecary replaced the cork. A strong wind buffeted the building, blowing under the door, stirring the scents of the many powders and tonics he sold. "This is practically useless. I'll give you two clearmarks for it, which is being generous. I'll have to distill it, and will be lucky to get a couple of spoonfuls."

Two marks! Kaladin thought with despair. *After three days of work, three of us pushing ourselves, getting only a few hours of sleep each night? All for something worth only a couple days' wage?*

But no. The sap had *worked* on Leyten's wound, making the rotspren flee and the infection retreat. Kaladin narrowed his eyes as the apothecary fished two marks out of his money pouch, setting them on the table. Like many spheres, these were flattened slightly on one side to keep them from rolling away.

"Actually," the apothecary said, rubbing his chin. "I'll give you three." He took out one more mark. "Hate to see all of your effort go to waste."

"Kaladin," Syl said, studying the apothecary. "He's nervous about something. I think he's lying!"

"I know," Kaladin said.

"What's that?" the apothecary said. "Well, if you knew it was worthless, why did you spend so much effort on it?" He reached for the bottle.

Kaladin caught his hand. "We got two or more drops from each reed, you know."

The apothecary frowned.

"Last time," Kaladin said, "you told me I'd be lucky to get one drop per reed. You said that was why knobweed sap was so expensive. You said nothing about 'wild' plants being weaker."

"Well, I didn't think you'd go and try gathering them, and . . ." He trailed off as Kaladin locked eyes with him.

"The army doesn't know, do they?" Kaladin asked. "They aren't aware how valuable those plants outside are. You harvest them, you sell the sap, and you make a killing, since the military needs a *lot* of antiseptic."

The old apothecary cursed, pulling his hand back. "I don't know what you're talking about."

Kaladin took his jar. "And if I go to the healing tent and tell them where I got this?"

"They'd take it from you!" the man said urgently. "Don't be a fool. You've a slave brand, boy. They'll think you stole it."

Kaladin moved to walk away.

"I'll give a skymark," the apothecary said. "That's half what I'd charge the military for this much."

Kaladin turned. "You charge them *two skymarks* for something that only takes a couple of days to gather?"

"It's not just me," the apothecary said, scowling. "Each of the apothecaries charges the same. We got together, decided on a fair price."

"How is *that* a fair price?"

"We have to make a living here, in this Almighty-forsaken land! It costs us money to set up shop, to maintain ourselves, to hire guards."

He fished in his pouch, pulling out a sphere that glowed deep blue. A sapphire sphere was worth about twenty-five times a diamond one. As Kaladin made one diamond mark a day, a skymark was worth as much as Kaladin made in half a month. Of course, a common darkeyed soldier earned five clearmarks a day, which would make this a week's wages to them.

Once, this wouldn't have seemed like much money to Kaladin. Now it was a fortune. Still, he hesitated. "I should expose you. Men die because of you."

"No they don't," the apothecary said. "The highprinces have more than enough to pay this, considering what they make on the plateaus. We supply them with bottles of sap as often as they need them. All you'd do by exposing us is let monsters like Sadeas keep a few more spheres in their pockets!"

The apothecary was sweating. Kaladin was threatening to topple his entire business on the Shattered Plains. And so much money was being earned on the sap that this could grow *very* dangerous. Men killed to keep such secrets.

"Line my pocket or line the brightlords'," Kaladin said. "I guess I can't argue with that logic." He set the bottle back on the counter. "I'll take the deal, provided you throw in some more bandages."

"Very well," the apothecary said, relaxing. "But stay away from those reeds. I'm surprised you found any nearby that hadn't already been harvested. My workers are having an increasingly difficult time."

They don't have a windspren guiding them, Kaladin thought. "Then why would you want to discourage me? I could get more of this for you."

"Well, yes," the apothecary said. "But—"

"It's cheaper if you do it yourself," Kaladin said, leaning down. "But this way you have a clean trail. I provide the sap, charging one skymark. If the lighteyes ever discover what the apothecaries have been doing, you can claim ignorance—all you know is that some bridgeman was selling you sap, and you resold it to the army at a reasonable markup."

That seemed to appeal to the old man. "Well, perhaps I won't ask too many questions about how you harvested this. Your business, young man. Your business indeed. . . ." He shuffled to the back of his store, returning with a box of bandages. Kaladin accepted it and left the shop without a word.

"Aren't you worried?" Syl said, floating up beside his head as he entered the afternoon sunlight. "If Gaz discovers what you're doing, you could get into trouble."

"What more could they do to me?" Kaladin asked. "I doubt they'd consider this a crime worth stringing me up for."

Syl looked backward, forming into little more than a cloud with the faint suggestion of a female form. "I can't decide if it's dishonest or not."

"It's not dishonest; it's business." He grimaced. "Lavis grain is sold the same way. Grown by the farmers and sold at a pittance to merchants, who carry it to the cities and sell it to other merchants, who sell it to people for four or five times what it was originally bought for."

"So why did it bother you?" Syl asked, frowning as they avoided a troop of soldiers, one of whom tossed the pit of a palafruit at Kaladin's head. The soldiers laughed.

Kaladin rubbed his temple. "I've still got some strange scruples about charging for medical care because of my father."

"He sounds like he's a very generous man."

"For all the good it did him."

Of course, in a way, Kaladin was just as bad. During his early days as a slave, he'd have done almost anything for a chance to walk around unsupervised like this. The army perimeter was guarded, but if he could sneak the knobweed in, he could probably find a way to sneak himself out.

With that sapphire mark, he even had money to aid him. Yes, he had the slave brand, but some quick if painful work with a knife could turn that into a "battle scar" instead. He could talk and fight like a soldier, so it would be plausible. He'd be taken for a deserter, but he could live with that.

That had been his plan for most of the later months of his enslavement, but he'd never had the means. It took money to travel, to get far enough away from the area where his description would be in circulation. Money to buy lodging in a seedy section of town, a place where nobody asked questions, while he healed from his self-inflicted wound.

In addition, there had always been the others. So he'd stayed, trying to get as many out as he could. Failing every time. And he was doing it again.

"Kaladin?" Syl asked from his shoulder. "You look very serious. What are you thinking?"

"I'm wondering if I should run. Escape this storm-cursed camp and find myself a new life."

Syl fell silent. "Life is hard here," she finally said. "I don't know if anyone would blame you."

Rock would, he thought. *And Teft.* They'd worked for that knobweed sap. They didn't know what it was worth; they thought it was only for healing the sick. If he ran, he'd be betraying them. He'd be abandoning the bridgemen.

Shove over, you fool, Kaladin thought to himself. *You won't save these bridgemen. Just like you didn't save Tien. You should run.*

"And then what?" he whispered.

Syl turned to him. "What?"

If he ran, what good would it do? A life working for chips in the underbelly of some rotting city? No.

He couldn't leave them. Just like he'd never been able to leave anyone who he'd thought needed him. He had to protect them. He *had* to.

For Tien. And for his own sanity.

❖

"Chasm duty," Gaz said, spitting to the side. The spittle was colored black from the yamma plant he chewed.

"What?" Kaladin had returned from selling the knobweed to discover that Gaz had changed Bridge Four's work detail. They weren't scheduled to be on duty for any bridge runs—their run the day before exempted them. Instead, they were supposed to be assigned to Sadeas's smithy to help lift ingots and other supplies.

That sounded like difficult work, but it was actually among the easiest jobs bridgemen got. The blacksmiths felt they didn't need the extra hands. That, or they presumed that clumsy bridgemen would just get in the way. On smithy duty, you usually only worked a few hours of the shift and could spend the rest lounging.

Gaz stood with Kaladin in the early afternoon sunlight. "You see," Gaz said, "you got me thinking the other day. Nobody cares if Bridge Four is given unfair work details. Everyone hates chasm duty. I figured you wouldn't care."

"How much did they pay you?" Kaladin asked, stepping forward.

"Storm off," Gaz said, spitting again. "The others resent you. It'll do your crew good to be seen paying for what you did."

"Surviving?"

Gaz shrugged. "Everyone knows you broke the rules in bringing back those men. If the others do what you did, we'd have each barrack filled with the dying before the leeward side of a month was over!"

"They're *people*, Gaz. If we don't 'fill the barracks' with wounded, it's because we're leaving them out there to die."

"They'll die here anyway."

"We'll see."

Gaz watched him, eyes narrow. It seemed like he suspected that Kaladin had somehow tricked him in taking the stone-gathering duty. Earlier, Gaz had apparently gone down to the chasm, probably trying to figure out what Kaladin and the other two had been doing.

Damnation, Kaladin thought. He'd thought he had Gaz cowed enough to stay in line. "We'll go," Kaladin snapped, turning away. "But I'm not taking the blame among my men for this one. They'll know you did it."

"Fine," Gaz called after him. Then, to himself, he

continued, "Maybe I'll get lucky and a chasmfiend will eat the lot of you."

◆◇◆

Chasm duty. Most bridgemen would rather spend all day hauling stones than get assigned to the chasms.

With an unlit oil-soaked torch tied to his back, Kaladin climbed down the precarious rope ladder. The chasm was shallow here, only about fifty feet down, but that was enough to take him into a different world. A world where the only natural light came from the rift high in the sky. A world that stayed damp on even the hottest days, a drowned landscape of moss, fungus, and hardy plants that survived in even dim light.

The chasms were wider at the bottom, perhaps a result of highstorms. They caused enormous floods to crash through the chasms; to be caught in a chasm during a highstorm was death. A sediment of hardened crem smoothed the pathway on the floor of the chasms, though it rose and fell with the varying erosion of the underlying rock. In some few places, the distance from the chasm floor to the edge of the plateau above was only about forty feet. In most places, however, it was closer to a hundred or more.

Kaladin jumped off the ladder, falling a few feet and landing with a splash in a puddle of rainwater. After lighting the torch, he held it high, peering along the caliginous rift. The sides were slick with a dark green moss, and several thin vines he didn't recognize trailed down from intermediate ledges above. Bits of bone, wood, and torn cloth lay strewn about or wedged into clefts.

Someone splashed to the ground beside him. Teft cursed, looking down at his soaked legs and trousers as he stepped out of the large puddle. "Storms take that cremling Gaz," the aging bridgeman muttered. "Sending us down here when it isn't our turn. I'll have his beans for this."

"I am certain that he is very scared of you," Rock said, stepping down off the ladder onto a dry spot. "Is probably back in camp crying in fear."

"Storm off," Teft said, shaking the water from his left leg. The two of them carried unlit torches. Kaladin had lit his with a flint and steel, but the others did not. They needed to ration the torches.

The other men of Bridge Four began to gather near the bottom of the ladder, staying in a clump. Every fourth man lit his torch, but the light didn't do much to dispel the gloom; it just allowed Kaladin to see more of the unnatural landscape. Strange, tube-shaped fungi grew in cracks. They were a wan yellow, like the skin of a child with jaundice. Scuttling cremlings moved away from the light. The tiny crustaceans were a translucent reddish color; as one scrambled past on the wall, he realized that he could see its internal organs through its shell.

The light also revealed a twisted, broken figure at the base of the chasm wall a short distance away. Kaladin raised his torch and stepped up to it. It was beginning to stink already. He raised a hand, unconsciously covering his nose and mouth as he knelt down.

It was a bridgeman, or had been, from one of the other crews. He was fresh. If he'd been here longer than a few days, the highstorm would have washed him away to some distant place. Bridge Four gathered behind Kaladin, looking silently at the one who had chosen to throw himself into the chasm.

"May you someday find a place of honor in the Tranquiline Halls, fallen brother," Kaladin said, his voice echoing. "And may we find a better end than you." He stood, holding his torch high, and led the way past the dead sentry. His crew followed nervously.

Kaladin had quickly understood the basic tactics of fighting on the Shattered Plains. You wanted to advance forcefully, pressing your enemy to the plateau's edge. That was why the battles often turned bloody for the Alethi, who usually arrived after the Parshendi.

The Alethi had bridges, while these odd Eastern parshmen could leap most chasms, given a running start. But both had trouble when squeezed toward the cliffs, and that generally resulted in soldiers losing their footing and tumbling into the void. The numbers were significant enough for the Alethi to want to recover lost equipment. And so bridgemen were sent on chasm duty. It was like barrow robbing, only without the barrows.

They carried sacks, and would spend hours walking around, looking for the corpses of the fallen, searching for anything of value. Spheres, breastplates, caps, weapons. Some days, when a plateau run was recent, they could try to make their way all the way out to where it had happened and scavenge from those bodies. But highstorms generally made that futile. Wait even a few days, and the bodies would be washed someplace else.

Beyond that, the chasms were a bewildering maze, and getting to a specific contested plateau and then returning in a reasonable time was near impossible. General wisdom was to wait for a highstorm to push the bodies toward the Alethi side of the Plains—highstorms always came east to west, after all—and then send bridgemen down to search them out.

That meant a lot of random wandering. But over the years, enough bodies had fallen that it wasn't too difficult to find places to harvest. The crew was required to bring up a specific amount of salvage or face docked pay for the week, but the quota wasn't onerous. Enough to keep the bridgemen working, but not enough to force them to fully exert themselves. Like most bridgeman work, this was meant to keep them occupied as much as anything else.

As they walked down the first chasm, some of his men got out their sacks and picked up pieces of salvage they passed. A helmet here, a shield there. They kept a keen watch for spheres. Finding a valuable fallen sphere would result in a small reward for the whole crew. They weren't allowed to bring their own spheres or possessions into the chasm, of course. And on their way out, they were searched thoroughly. The humiliation of that search—which included any place a sphere might be hidden—was part of the reason chasm duty was so loathed.

But only a part. As they walked, the chasm floor widened to about fifteen feet. Here, marks scarred the walls, gashes where the moss had been scraped away, the stone itself scored. The bridgemen tried not to look at those marks. Occasionally, chasmfiends stalked these pathways, searching for either carrion or a suitable plateau to pupate upon. Encountering one of them was uncommon, but possible.

"Kelek, but I hate this place," Teft said, walking beside Kaladin. "I heard that once an entire bridge crew got eaten by a chasmfiend, one at a time, after it backed them into a dead end. It just sat there, picking them off as they tried to run past."

Rock chuckled. "If they were all eaten, then who was returning to tell this story?"

Teft rubbed his chin. "I dunno. Maybe they just never returned."

"Then perhaps they fled. Deserting."

"No," Teft said. "You can't get out of these chasms without a ladder." He glanced upward, toward the narrow rift of blue seventy feet above, following the curve of the plateau.

Kaladin glanced up as well. That blue sky seemed so distant. Unreachable. Like the light of the Halls themselves. And even if you could climb out at one of the shallower areas, you'd either be trapped on the Plains without a way to cross chasms, or you'd be close enough to the Alethi side that the scouts would spot you crossing the permanent bridges. You could try going eastward, toward where the plateaus were worn away to the point that they were just spires. But that would take weeks of walking, and would require surviving multiple highstorms.

"You ever been in a slot canyon when rains come, Rock?" Teft asked, perhaps thinking along the same lines.

"No," Rock replied. "On the Peaks, we have not these things. They only exist where foolish men choose to live."

"*You* live here, Rock," Kaladin noted.

"And I am foolish," the large Horneater said, chuckling. "Did you not notice this thing?" These last two days had changed him a great deal. He was more affable, returning in some measure to what Kaladin assumed was his normal personality.

"I was *talking*," Teft said, "about slot canyons. You want to guess what will happen if we get trapped down here in a highstorm?"

"Lots of water, I guess," Rock said.

"Lots of water, looking to go any place it can," Teft said. "It gathers into enormous waves and goes crashing through these confined spaces with enough force to toss boulders. In fact, an *ordinary* rain will feel like a highstorm down here. A highstorm . . . well, this would probably be the worst place in Roshar to be when one hits."

Rock frowned at that, glancing upward. "Best not to be caught in the storm, then."

"Yeah," Teft said.

"Though, Teft," Rock added, "it would give you bath, which you very much need."

"Hey," Teft grumbled. "Is that a comment on how I smell?"

"No," Rock said. "Is comment on what *I* have to smell. Sometimes, I am thinking that a Parshendi arrow in the eye would be better than smelling entire bridge crew enclosed in barrack at night!"

Teft chuckled. "I'd take offense at that if it weren't true." He sniffed at the damp, moldy chasm air. "This place ain't much better. It smells worse than a Horneater's boots in winter down here." He hesitated. "Er, no offense. I mean personally."

Kaladin smiled, then glanced back. The thirty or so other bridgemen followed like ghosts. A few seemed to be edging close to Kaladin's group, as if trying to listen in without being obvious.

"Teft," Kaladin said. " 'Smells worse than a Horneater's boots'? How in the Halls isn't he supposed to take offense at *that* phrase?"

"It's just an expression," Teft said, scowling. "It was out of my mouth before I realized what I was saying."

"Alas," Rock said, pulling a tuft of moss off the wall, inspecting it as they walked. "Your insult has offended me. If we were at the Peaks, we would have to duel in the traditional *alil'tiki'i* fashion."

"Which is what?" Teft asked. "With spears?"

Rock laughed. "No, no. We upon the Peaks are not barbarians like you down here."

"How then?" Kaladin asked, genuinely curious.

"Well," Rock said, dropping the moss and dusting off his hands, "is involving much mudbeer and singing."

"How's *that* a duel?"

"He who can still sing after the most drinks is winner. Plus, soon, everyone is so drunk that they probably forget what argument was about."

Teft laughed. "Beats knives at dawn, I suppose."

"I guess that depends," Kaladin said.

"Upon what?" Teft asked.

"On whether or not you're a knife merchant. Eh, Dunny?"

The other two glanced to the side, where Dunny had moved up close to listen. The spindly youth jumped and blushed. "Er—I—"

Rock chuckled at Kaladin's words. "Dunny," he said to the youth. "Is odd name. What is meaning of it?"

"Meaning?" Dunny asked. "I don't know. Names don't always have a meaning."

Rock shook his head, displeased. "Lowlanders. How are you to know who you are if your name has no meaning?"

"So your name means something?" Teft asked. "Nu . . . ma . . . nu . . ."

"Numuhukumakiaki'aialunamor," Rock said, the native Horneater sounds flowing easily from his lips. "Of course. Is description of very special rock my father discovered the day before my birth."

"So your name is a whole sentence?" Dunny asked, uncertain—as if he wasn't sure he belonged.

"Is poem," Rock said. "On the Peaks, everyone's name is poem."

"Is that so?" Teft said, scratching at his beard. "Must make calling the family at mealtime a bit of a chore."

Rock laughed. "True, true. Is also making for some interesting arguments. Usually, the best insults on the Peaks are in the form of a poem, one which is similar in composition and rhyme to the person's name."

"Kelek," Teft muttered. "Sounds like a lot of work."

"Is why most arguments end in drinking, perhaps," Rock said.

Dunny smiled hesitantly. "Hey you big buffoon, you smell like a wet hog, so go out by the moon, and jump yourself in the bog."

Rock laughed riotously, his booming voice echoing down the chasm. "Is good, is good," he said, wiping his eyes. "Simple, but good."

"That almost had the sound of a song to it, Dunny," Kaladin said.

"Well, it was the first thing that came to mind. I put it to the tune of 'Mari's Two Lovers' to get the beat right."

"You can sing?" Rock asked. "I must be hearing."

"But—" Dunny said.

"Sing!" Rock commanded, pointing.

Dunny yelped, but obeyed, breaking into a song that wasn't familiar to Kaladin. It was an amusing tale involving a woman and twin brothers who she thought were the same person. Dunny's voice was a pure tenor, and he seemed to have more confidence when he sang than when he spoke.

He was good. Once he moved to the second verse, Rock began humming in a deep voice, providing a harmony. The Horneater was obviously very practiced at song. Kaladin glanced back at the other bridgemen, hoping to pull some more into the conversation or the song. He smiled at Skar, but got only a scowl in return. Moash and Sigzil—the dark-skinned Azish man—wouldn't even look at him. Peet looked only at his feet.

When the song was finished, Teft clapped appreciatively. "That's a better performance than I've heard at many an inn."

"Is good to meet a lowlander who can sing," Rock said, stooping down to pick up a helm and stuff it in his bag. This particular chasm didn't seem to have much in the way of salvage this time. "I had begun thinking you were all as tone deaf as my father's old axehound. Ha!"

Dunny blushed, but seemed to walk more confidently.

They continued, occasionally passing turns or rifts in the stone where the waters had deposited large clusters of salvage. Here, the work turned more gruesome, and they'd often have to pull out corpses or piles of bones to get what they wanted, gagging at the scent. Kaladin told them to leave the more sickening or rotted bodies for now. Rotspren tended to cluster around the dead. If they didn't find enough salvage later, they could get those on the way back.

At every intersection or branch, Kaladin made a white mark on the wall with a piece of chalk. That was the bridge-leader's duty, and he took it seriously. He wouldn't have his crew getting lost out in these rifts.

As they walked and worked, Kaladin kept the conversation going. He laughed—forced himself to laugh—with them. If that laugher felt hollow to him, the others didn't seem to notice. Perhaps they felt as he did, that even forced laughter was preferable to going back to the self-absorbed, mournful silence that cloaked most bridgemen.

Before long, Dunny was laughing and talking with Teft and Rock, his shyness faded. A few others hovered just behind—Yake, Maps, a couple of others—like wild creatures drawn to the light and warmth of a fire. Kaladin tried to draw them into the conversation, but it didn't work, so eventually he just let them be.

Eventually, they reached a place with a significant number of fresh corpses. Kaladin wasn't sure what combination of waterflow had made this section of chasm a good place for that—it looked the same as other stretches. A little narrower perhaps. Sometimes they could go to the same nooks and find good salvage there; other times, those were empty, but other places would have dozens of corpses.

These bodies looked like they'd floated in the wash of the highstorm flood, then been deposited as the water slowly receded. There were no Parshendi among them, and they were broken and torn from either their fall or the crush of the flood. Many were missing limbs.

The stink of blood and viscera hung in the humid air. Kaladin held his torch aloft as his companions fell silent. The chill kept the bodies from rotting too quickly, though the dampness counteracted some of that. The cremlings had begun chewing the skin off hands and gnawing out the eyes. Soon the stomachs would bloat with gas. Some rotspren—tiny, red, translucent—scrambled across the corpses.

Syl floated down and landed on his shoulder, making disgusted noises. As usual, she offered no explanation for her absence.

The men knew what to do. Even with the rotspren, this was too rich a place to pass up. They went to work, pulling the corpses into a line so they could be inspected. Kaladin waved for Rock and Teft to join him as he picked up some stray bits of salvage that lay on the ground around the corpses. Dunny tagged along.

"Those bodies wear the highprince's colors," Rock noted as Kaladin picked up a dented steel cap.

"I'll bet they're from that run a few days back," Kaladin said. "It went badly for Sadeas's forces."

"*Brightlord* Sadeas," Dunny said. Then he ducked his head in embarrassment. "Sorry, I didn't mean to correct you. I used to forget to say the title. My master beat me when I did."

"Master?" Teft asked, picking up a fallen spear and pulling some moss off its shaft.

"I was an apprentice. I mean, before . . ." Dunny trailed off, then looked away.

Teft had been right; bridgemen didn't like talking about their pasts. Anyway, Dunny was probably right to correct him. Kaladin would be punished if he were heard omitting a lighteyes's honorific.

Kaladin put the cap in his sack, then rammed his torch into a gap between two moss-covered boulders and started helping the others get the bodies into a line. He didn't prod the men toward conversation. The fallen deserved some reverence—if that was possible while robbing them.

Next, the bridgemen stripped the fallen of their armor. Leather vests from the archers, steel breastplates from the foot soldiers. This group included a lighteyes in fine clothing beneath even finer armor. Sometimes the bodies of fallen lighteyes would be recovered from the chasms by special teams so the corpse could be Soulcast into a statue. Darkeyes, unless they were very wealthy, were burned. And most soldiers who fell into the chasms were ignored; the men in camp spoke of the chasms being hallowed resting places, but the truth was that the effort to get the bodies out wasn't worth the cost or the danger.

Regardless, to find a lighteyes here meant that his family hadn't been wealthy enough, or concerned enough, to send men out to recover him. His face was crushed beyond recognition, but his rank insignia identified him as seventh dahn. Landless, attached to a more powerful officer's retinue.

Once they had his armor, they pulled daggers and boots off everyone in line—boots were *always* in demand. They left the fallen their clothing, though they took off the belts and cut free many shirt buttons. As they worked, Kaladin sent Teft and Rock around the bend to see if there were any other bodies nearby.

Once the armor, weapons, and boots had been separated, the most grisly task began: searching pockets and pouches for spheres and jewelry. This pile was the smallest of the lot, but valuable. They didn't find any broams, which meant no pitiful reward for the bridgemen.

As the men performed their morbid task, Kaladin noticed the end of a spear poking out of a nearby pool. It had gone unnoticed in their initial sweep.

Lost in thought, he fetched it, shaking off the water, carrying it over to the weapons pile. He hesitated there, holding the spear over the pile with one hand, cold water dripping from it. He rubbed his finger along the smooth wood. He could tell from the heft, balance, and sanding that it was a good weapon. Sturdy, well made, well kept.

He closed his eyes, remembering days as a boy holding a quarterstaff.

Words spoken by Tukks years ago returned to him, words spoken on that bright summer day when he'd first held a weapon in Amaram's army. *The first step is to care,* Tukks's voice seemed to whisper. *Some talk about being emotionless in battle. Well, I suppose it's important to keep your head. But I hate that feeling of killing while calm and cold. I've seen that those who care fight harder, longer, and better than those who don't. It's the difference between mercenaries and real soldiers. It's the difference between fighting to defend your homeland and fighting on foreign soil.*

It's good to care when you fight, so long as you don't let it consume you. Don't try to stop yourself from feeling. You'll hate who you become.

The spear quivered in Kaladin's fingers, as if begging him to swing it, spin it, dance with it.

"What are you planning to do, lordling?" a voice called. "Going to ram that spear into your own gut?"

Kaladin glanced up at the speaker. Moash—still one of Kaladin's biggest detractors—stood near the line of corpses. How had he known to call Kaladin "lordling"? Had he been talking to Gaz?

"He claims he's a deserter," Moash said to Narm, the man working next to him. "Says he was some important soldier, a squadleader or the like. But Gaz says that's all stupid boasting. They wouldn't send a man to the bridges if he actually knew how to fight."

Kaladin lowered the spear.

Moash smirked, turning back to his work. Others, however, had now noticed Kaladin. "Look at him," Sigzil said. "Ho, bridgeleader! You think that you're grand? That you are better than us? You think pretending that we're your own personal troop of soldiers will change anything?"

"Leave him alone," Drehy said. He shoved Sigzil as he passed. "At least he tries."

Earless Jacks snorted, pulling a boot free from a dead foot.

"He cares about looking important. Even if he *was* in the army, I'll bet he spent his days cleaning out latrines."

It appeared that there was something that would pull the bridgemen out of their silent stupors: loathing for Kaladin. Others began talking, calling gibes.

". . . his fault we're down here . . ."

". . . wants to run us ragged during our only free time, just so he can feel important . . ."

". . . sent us to carry rocks to show us he could shove us around . . ."

". . . bet he's never held a spear in his life."

Kaladin closed his eyes, listening to their scorn, rubbing his fingers on the wood.

Never held a spear in his life. Maybe if he'd never picked up that first spear, none of this would have happened.

He felt the smooth wood, slick with rainwater, memories jumbling in his head. Training to forget, training to get vengeance, training to learn and make sense of what had happened.

Without thinking about it, he snapped the spear up under his arm into a guard position, point down. Water droplets from its length sprayed across his back.

Moash cut off in the middle of another gibe. The bridgemen sputtered to a stop. The chasm became quiet.

And Kaladin was in another place.

He was listening to Tukks chide him.

He was listening to Tien laugh.

He was hearing his mother tease him in her clever, witty way.

He was on the battlefield, surrounded by enemies but ringed by friends.

He was listening to his father tell him with a sneer in his voice that spears were only for killing. You could not kill to protect.

He was alone in a chasm deep beneath the earth, holding the spear of a fallen man, fingers gripping the wet wood, a faint dripping coming from somewhere distant.

Strength surged through him as he spun the spear up into an advanced kata. His body moved of its own accord, going through the forms he'd trained in so frequently. The spear danced in his fingers, comfortable, an extension of himself. He spun with it, swinging it around and around, across his neck, over his arm, in and out of jabs and swings. Though it had been months since he'd even held a weapon, his muscles knew what to do. It was as if the *spear itself* knew what to do.

Tension melted away, frustration melted away, and his body sighed in contentment even as he worked it furiously. This was familiar. This was welcome. This was what it had been created to do.

Men had always told Kaladin that he fought like nobody else. He'd felt it on the first day he'd picked up a quarterstaff, though Tukks's advice had helped him refine and channel what he could do. Kaladin had *cared* when he fought. He'd never fought empty or cold. He fought to keep his men alive.

Of all the recruits in his cohort, he had learned the quickest. How to hold the spear, how to stand to spar. He'd done it almost without instruction. That had shocked Tukks. But why should it have? You were not shocked when a child knew how to breathe. You were not shocked when a skyeel took flight for the first time. You should not be shocked when you hand Kaladin Stormblessed a spear and he knows how to use it.

Kaladin spun through the last motions of the kata, chasm forgotten, bridgemen forgotten, fatigue forgotten. For a moment, it was just him. Him and the wind. He fought with her, and she laughed.

He snapped the spear back into place, holding the haft at the one-quarter position, spearhead down, bottom of the haft tucked underneath his arm, end rising back behind his head. He breathed in deeply, shivering.

Oh, how I've missed that.

He opened his eyes. Sputtering torchlight revealed a group of stunned bridgemen standing in a damp corridor of stone, the walls wet and reflecting the light. Moash dropped a handful of spheres in stunned silence, staring at Kaladin with mouth agape. Those spheres plopped into the puddle at his feet, causing it to glow, but none of the bridgemen noticed. They just stared at Kaladin, who was still in a battle stance, half crouched, trails of sweat running down the sides of his face.

He blinked, realizing what he'd done. If word got back to Gaz that he was playing around with spears . . . Kaladin stood up straight and dropped the spear into the pile of weapons. "Sorry," he whispered to it, though he didn't know why. Then, louder, he said, "Back to work! I don't want to be caught down here when night falls."

The bridgemen jumped into motion. Down the chasm corridor, he saw Rock and Teft. Had they seen the entire kata? Flushing, Kaladin hurried up to them. Syl landed on his shoulder, silent.

"Kaladin, lad," Teft said reverently. "That was—"

"It was meaningless," Kaladin said. "Just a kata. Meant to work the muscles and make you practice the basic jabs, thrusts, and sweeps. It's a lot showier than it is useful."

"But—"

"No, really," Kaladin said. "Can you imagine a man swinging a spear around his neck like that in combat? He'd be gutted in a second."

"Lad," Teft said. "I've *seen* katas before. But never one like that. The way you moved . . . The speed, the grace . . . And there was some sort of spren zipping around you, between your sweeps, glowing with a pale light. It was beautiful."

Rock started. "You could see that?"

"Sure," Teft said. "Never seen a spren like that. Ask the other men—I saw a few of them pointing."

Kaladin glanced at his shoulder, frowning at Syl. She sat primly, legs crossed and hands folded atop her knee, pointedly not looking at him.

"It was nothing," Kaladin repeated.

"No," Rock said. "That it certainly was not. Perhaps *you* should challenge Shardbearer. You could become brightlord!"

"I *don't* want to be a brightlord," Kaladin snapped, perhaps more harshly than he should have. The other two jumped. "Besides," he added, looking away from them. "I tried that once. Where's Dunny?"

"Wait," Teft said, "you—"

"Where is Dunny?" Kaladin said firmly, punctuating each word. *Stormfather. I need to keep my mouth shut.*

Teft and Rock shared a glance, then Teft pointed. "We found some dead Parshendi around the bend. Thought you'd want to know."

"Parshendi," Kaladin said. "Let's go look. Might have something valuable." He'd never looted Parshendi bodies before; fewer of them fell into the chasms than Alethi.

"Is true," Rock said, leading the way, carrying a lit torch. "Those weapons they have, yes, very nice. And gemstones in their beards."

"Not to mention the armor," Kaladin said.

Rock shook his head. "No armor."

"Rock, I've *seen* their armor. They always wear it."

"Well, yes, but we cannot use this thing."

"I don't understand," Kaladin said.

"Come," Rock said, gesturing. "Is easier than explaining."

Kaladin shrugged, and they rounded the corner, Rock scratching at his red-bearded chin. "Stupid hairs," he muttered. "Ah, to have it right again. A man is not proper man without proper beard."

Kaladin rubbed his own beard. One of these days, he'd save up and buy a razor and be rid of the blasted thing. Or, well, probably not. His spheres would be needed elsewhere.

They rounded the corner and found Dunny pulling the Parshendi bodies into a line. There were four of them, and they looked like they'd been swept in from another direction. There were a few more Alethi bodies here too.

Kaladin strode forward, waving Rock to bring the light, and knelt to inspect one of the Parshendi dead. They were like parshmen, with skin in marbled patterns of black and crimson. Their only clothing was knee-length black skirts. Three wore beards, which was unusual for parshmen, and those were woven with uncut gemstones.

Just as Kaladin had expected, they wore armor of a pale red color. Breastplates, helms on the heads, guards on the arms and legs. Extensive armor for regular foot soldiers. Some of it was cracked from the fall or the wash. It wasn't metal, then. Painted wood?

"I thought you said they weren't armored," Kaladin said. "What are you trying to tell me? That you don't dare take it off the dead?"

"Don't dare?" Rock said. "Kaladin, Master Brightlord, brilliant bridgeleader, spinner of spear, perhaps *you* will get it off them."

Kaladin shrugged. His father had instilled in him a familiarity with the dead and dying, and though it felt bad to rob the dead, he was not squeamish. He prodded the first Parshendi, noting the man's knife. He took it and looked for the strap that held the shoulder guard in place.

There was no strap. Kaladin frowned and peered underneath the guard, trying to pry it up. The skin lifted with it. "Stormfather!" he said. He inspected the helm. It was grown into the head. Or grown *from* the head. "What *is* this?"

"Do not know," Rock said, shrugging. "It is looking like they grow their own armor, eh?"

"That's ridiculous," Kaladin said. "They're just people. People—even parshmen—don't *grow* armor."

"Parshendi do," Teft said.

Kaladin and the other two turned to him.

"Don't look at me like that," the older man said with a scowl. "I worked in the camp for a few years before I ended up as a bridgeman—no, I'm not going to tell you how, so storm off. Anyway, the soldiers talk about it. The Parshendi grow carapaces."

"I've *known* parshmen," Kaladin said. "There were a couple of them in my hometown, serving the citylord. None of them grew armor."

"Well, these are a different kind of parshman," Teft said with a scowl. "Bigger, stronger. They can jump *chasms*, for Kelek's sake. And they grow armor. That's just how it is."

There was no disputing it, so they just moved on to gathering what they could. Many Parshendi used heavy weapons—axes, hammers—and those hadn't been carried along with the bodies like many of the spears and bows Alethi soldiers had.

But they did find several knives and one ornate sword, still in a sheath at the Parshendi's side.

The skirts didn't have pockets, but the corpses did have pouches tied to their waists. These just carried flint and tinder, whetstones, or other basic supplies. So, they knelt to begin pulling the gemstones from the beards. Those gemstones had holes drilled through them to facilitate weaving, and Stormlight infused them, though they didn't glow as brightly as they would have if they'd been properly cut.

As Rock pulled the gemstones out of the final Parshendi's beard, Kaladin held one of the knives up near Dunny's torch, inspecting the detailed carving. "Those look like glyphs," he said, showing it to Teft.

"I can't read glyphs, boy."

Oh, right, Kaladin thought. Well, if they were glyphs, they weren't ones he was familiar with. Of course, you could draw most glyphs in complex ways that made it hard to read them, unless you knew exactly what to look for. There was a figure at the center of the hilt, nicely carved. It was a man in fine armor. Shardplate, certainly. A symbol was etched behind him, surrounding him, spreading out from his back like wings.

Kaladin showed it to Rock, who had walked up to see what he found so fascinating. "The Parshendi out here are supposed to be barbarians," Kaladin said. "Without culture. Where did they get knives like these? I'd swear this is a picture of one of the Heralds. Jezerezeh or Nalan."

Rock shrugged. Kaladin sighed and returned the knife to its sheath, then dropped it into his sack. Then they rounded the curve back to the others. The crew had gathered up sacks full of armor, belts, boots, and spheres. Each took up a spear to carry back to the ladder, holding them like walking sticks. They'd left one for Kaladin, but he tossed it to Rock. He didn't trust himself to hold one of them again, worried he'd be tempted to fall into another kata.

The walk back was uneventful, though with the darkening sky, the men began jumping at every sound. Kaladin engaged

Rock, Teft, and Dunny in conversation again. He was able to get Drehy and Torfin to talk a little as well.

They safely reached the first chasm, much to the relief of his men. Kaladin sent the others up the ladder first, waiting to go up last. Rock waited with him, and as Dunny finally started up—leaving Rock and Kaladin alone—the tall Horneater put a hand on Kaladin's shoulder, speaking in a soft voice.

"You do good work here," Rock said. "I am thinking that in a few weeks, these men will be yours."

Kaladin shook his head. "We're bridgemen, Rock. We don't *have* a few weeks. If I take that long winning them over, half of us will be dead."

Rock frowned. "Is not a happy thought."

"That's why we have to win over the other men *now*."

"But how?"

Kaladin looked up at the dangling ladder, shaking as the men climbed up. Only four could go at a time, lest they overload it. "Meet me after we're searched. We're going to the camp market."

"Very well," Rock said, swinging onto the ladder as Earless Jaks reached the top. "What will be our purpose in this thing?"

"We're going to try out my secret weapon."

Rock laughed as Kaladin held the ladder steady for him. "And what weapon is this?"

Kaladin smiled. "Actually, it's you."

※

Two hours later, at Salas's first violet light, Rock and Kaladin walked back into the lumberyard. It was just past sunset, and many of the bridgemen would soon be going to sleep.

Not much time, Kaladin thought, gesturing for Rock to carry his burden to a place near the front of Bridge Four's barrack. The large Horneater set his burden down next to Teft and Dunny, who had done as Kaladin had ordered, building a small ring of stones and setting up some stumps of wood from the lumberyard scrap pile. That wood was free for any-one to take. Even bridgemen were allowed; some liked to take chunks to whittle.

Kaladin got out a sphere for light. The thing Rock had been carrying was an old iron cauldron. Even though it was secondhand, it had cost Kaladin a fair chunk of the knob-weed sap money. The Horneater began to unpack supplies from inside the cauldron as Kaladin arranged some wood scraps inside the ring of stones.

"Dunny, water, if you please," Kaladin said, getting out his flint. Dunny ran off to fetch a bucket from one of the rain barrels. Rock finished emptying the cauldron, laying out small packages that had cost another substantial portion of Kala-din's spheres. He had only a handful of clearchips left.

As they worked, Hobber limped out of the barrack. He was mending quickly, though the other two wounded that Kaladin had treated were still in bad shape.

"What are you up to, Kaladin?" Hobber asked just as Ka-ladin got a flame started.

Kaladin smiled, standing. "Have a seat."

Hobber did just that. He hadn't lost the near-devotion he'd shown Kaladin for saving his life. If anything, his loyalty had grown stronger.

Dunny returned with a bucket of water, which he poured into the cauldron. Then he and Teft ran off to get more. Kaladin built up the flames and Rock began to hum to himself as he diced tubers and unwrapped some seasonings. In under a half hour, they had a roaring flame and a simmering pot of stew.

Teft sat down on one of the stumps, warming his hands. "This is your secret weapon?"

Kaladin sat down next to the older man. "Have you known many soldiers in your life, Teft?"

"A few."

"You ever known any who could turn down a warm fire and some stew at the end of a hard day?"

"Well, no. But bridgemen ain't soldiers."

That was true. Kaladin turned to the barrack doorway. Rock and Dunny started up a song together and Teft began to clap along. Some of the men from other bridge crews were up late, and they gave Kaladin and the others nothing more than scowls.

Figures shifted inside the barrack, shadows moving. The door was open, and the scents of Rock's stew grew strong. Inviting.

Come on, Kaladin thought. *Remember why we live. Remember warmth, remember good food. Remember friends, and song, and evenings spent around the hearth.*

You aren't dead yet. Storm you! If you don't come out . . .

It all suddenly seemed so contrived to Kaladin. The singing was forced, the stew an act of desperation. It was all just an attempt to briefly distract from the pathetic life he had been forced into.

A figure moved in the doorway. Skar—short, square-bearded, and keen-eyed—stepped out into the firelight. Kaladin smiled at him. A forced smile. Sometimes that was all one could offer. *Let it be enough,* he prayed, standing up, dipping a wooden bowl into Rock's stew.

Kaladin held the bowl toward Skar. Steam curled from the surface of the brownish liquid. "Will you join us?" Kaladin asked. "Please."

Skar looked at him, then back down at the stew. He laughed, taking the stew. "I'd join the Nightwatcher herself around a fire if there was stew involved!"

"Be careful," Teft said. "That's Horneater stew. Might be snail shells or crab claws floating in it."

"There is not!" Rock barked. "Is unfortunate that you have unrefined lowlander tastes, but I prepare the food such as I am ordered by our dear bridgeleader."

Kaladin smiled, letting out a deep breath as Skar sat down. Others trailed out after him, taking bowls, sitting. Some stared into the fire, not saying much, but others began to laugh and sing. At one point, Gaz walked past, eyeing them with his single eye, as if trying to decide if they were breaking any camp regulations. They weren't. Kaladin had checked.

Kaladin dipped out a bowl of stew and held it toward Gaz. The bridge sergeant snorted in derision and stalked away.

Can't expect too many miracles in one night, Kaladin

thought with a sigh, settling back down and trying the stew. It was quite good. He smiled, joining in the next verse of Dunny's song.

⁂

The next morning, when Kaladin called for the bridgemen to rise, three-quarters of them piled out of the barrack—everyone but the loudest complainers: Moash, Sigzil, Narm, and a couple of others. The ones who came to his call looked surprisingly refreshed, despite the long evening spent singing and eating. When he ordered them to join him in practice carrying the bridge, almost all of those who had risen joined him.

Not everyone, but enough.

He had a feeling that Moash and the others would give in before too long. They'd eaten his stew. Nobody had turned that down. And now that he had so many, the others would feel foolish not joining in. Bridge Four was his.

Now he had to keep them alive long enough for that to mean something.

28

DECISION

For I have never been dedicated to a more important purpose, and the very pillars of the sky will shake with the results of our war here. I ask again. Support me. Do not stand aside and let disaster consume more lives. I've never begged you for something before, old friend.
I do so now.

Adolin was frightened.

He stood beside his father on the staging ground. Dalinar looked . . . weathered. Creases running back from his eyes, furrows in his skin. Black hair going white like bleached rock along the sides. How could a man standing in full Shardplate—a man who yet retained a warrior's frame despite his age—look fragile?

In front of them, two chulls followed their handler, stepping up onto the bridge. The wooden span linked two piles of cut stones, a mock chasm only a few feet deep. The chulls' whiplike antennae twitched, mandibles clacking, fist-size black eyes glancing about. They pulled a massive siege bridge, rolling on creaking wooden wheels.

"That's much wider than the bridges Sadeas uses," Dalinar said to Teleb, who stood beside them.

"It's necessary to accommodate the siege bridge, Brightlord."

Dalinar nodded absently. Adolin suspected that he was the only one who could see that his father was distressed. Dalinar maintained his usual confident front, his head high, his voice firm when he spoke.

Yet, those eyes. They were too red, too strained. And when Adolin's father felt strained, he grew cold and businesslike. When he spoke to Teleb, his tone was too controlled.

Dalinar Kholin was suddenly a man laboring beneath great weight. And Adolin had helped put him there.

The chulls advanced. Their boulderlike shells were painted blue and yellow, the colors and pattern indicating the island of their Reshi handlers. The bridge beneath them groaned ominously as the larger siege bridge rolled onto it. All around the staging area, soldiers turned to look. Even the workmen cutting a latrine into the stony ground on the eastern side stopped to watch.

The groans from the bridge grew louder. Then they became sharp cracks. The handlers halted the chulls, glancing toward Teleb.

"It's not going to hold, is it?" Adolin asked.

Teleb sighed. "Storm it, I was hoping . . . Bah, we made the smaller bridge too thin when we widened it. But if we make it thicker, it will get too heavy to carry." He glanced at Dalinar. "I apologize for wasting your time, Brightlord. You are correct; this is akin to the ten fools."

"Adolin, what do you think?" Dalinar asked.

Adolin frowned. "Well . . . I think perhaps we should keep working with it. This is only the first attempt, Teleb. Perhaps there's still a way. Design the siege bridges to be narrower, maybe?"

"That could be very costly, Brightlord," Teleb said.

"If it helps us win one extra gemheart, the effort would be paid for several times over."

"Yes," Teleb said, nodding. "I will speak with Lady Kalana. Perhaps she can devise a new design."

"Good," Dalinar said. He stared at the bridge for an extended moment. Then, oddly, he turned to look toward the other side of the staging area, where the workers had been cutting the latrine ditch.

"Father?" Adolin asked.

"Why do you suppose," Dalinar said, "there are no Shardplate-like suits for workmen?"

"What?"

"Shardplate gives awesome strength, but we rarely use it for anything other than war and slaughter. Why did the Radiants fashion only weapons? Why didn't they make productive tools for use by ordinary men?"

"I don't know," Adolin said. "Perhaps because war was the most important thing around."

"Perhaps," Dalinar said, voice growing softer. "And perhaps that's a final condemnation of them and their ideals. For all of their lofty claims, they never gave their Plate or its secrets to the common people."

"I . . . I don't understand why that's important, Father."

Dalinar shook himself slightly. "We should get on with our inspections. Where's Ladent?"

"Here, Brightlord." A short man stepped up to Dalinar. Bald and bearded, the ardent wore thick, blue-grey layered robes from which his hands barely extended. The effect was of a crab who was too small for his shell. It looked terribly hot, but he didn't seem to mind.

"Send a messenger to the Fifth Battalion," Dalinar told him. "We'll be visiting them next."

"Yes, Brightlord."

Adolin and Dalinar began to walk. They'd chosen to wear their Shardplate for this day's inspections. That wasn't uncommon; many Shardbearers found any excuse they could to wear Plate. Plus, it was good for the men to see their highprince and his heir in their strength.

They drew attention as they left the staging area and entered the warcamp proper. Like Adolin, Dalinar went about unhelmed, though the gorget of his armor was tall and thick, rising like a metal collar up to his chin. He nodded to soldiers who saluted.

"Adolin," Dalinar said. "In combat, do you feel the Thrill?"

Adolin started. He knew immediately what his father meant, but he was shocked to hear the words. This wasn't often discussed. "I . . . Well, of course. Who doesn't?"

Dalinar didn't reply. He had been so reserved lately. Was that pain in his eyes? *The way he was before,* Adolin thought, *deluded but confident. That was actually better.*

Dalinar said nothing more, and the two of them continued through the camp. Six years had let the soldiers settle in thoroughly. Barracks were painted with company and squad symbols, and the space between them was outfitted with firepits, stools, and canvas-shaded dining areas. Adolin's father had forbidden none of this, though he had set guidelines to discourage sloppiness.

Dalinar had also approved most requests for families to be brought to the Shattered Plains. The officers already had their wives, of course—a good lighteyes officer was really a team, the man to command and fight, the woman to read, write, engineer, and manage camp. Adolin smiled, thinking of Malasha. Would she prove to be the one for him? She'd been a little cold to him lately. Of course, there was Danlan. He'd only just met her, but he was intrigued.

Regardless, Dalinar had also approved requests by dark-eyed common soldiers to bring their families. He even paid half of the cost. When Adolin had asked why, Dalinar had replied that he didn't feel right forbidding them. The warcamps were never attacked anymore, so there was no danger. Adolin suspected his father felt that since he was living in a luxurious near-palace, his men might as well have the comfort of their families.

And so it was that children played and ran through the camp. Women hung wash and painted glyphwards as men sharpened spears and polished breastplates. Barrack interiors had been partitioned to create rooms.

"I think you were right," Adolin said as they walked, trying to draw his father out of his contemplations. "To let so many bring their families here, I mean."

"Yes, but how many will leave when this is over?"

"Does it matter?"

"I'm not certain. The Shattered Plains are now a de facto Alethi province. How will this place appear in a hundred years? Will those rings of barracks become neighborhoods? The outer shops become markets? The hills to the west become fields for planting?" He shook his head. "The gemhearts will always be here, it seems. And so long as they are, there will be people here as well."

"That's a good thing, isn't it? So long as those people are Alethi." Adolin chuckled.

"Perhaps. And what will happen to the value of gemstones if we continue to capture gemhearts at the rate we have?"

"I . . ." That was a good question.

"What happens, I wonder, when the scarcest, yet most desirable, substance in the land suddenly becomes commonplace? There's much going on here, son. Much we haven't considered. The gemhearts, the Parshendi, the death of Gavilar. You will have to be ready to consider these things."

"Me?" Adolin said. "What does that mean?"

Dalinar didn't answer, instead nodding as the commander of the Fifth Battalion hastened up to them and saluted. Adolin sighed and saluted back. The Twenty-first and Twenty-second Companies were doing close order drill here—an essential exercise whose true value few outside the military ever appreciated. The Twenty-third and Twenty-fourth Companies were doing extended order—or combat—drill, practicing the formations and movements used on the battlefield.

Fighting on the Shattered Plains was very different from conventional warfare, as the Alethi had learned from some embarrassing early losses. The Parshendi were squat, muscular, and had that strange, skin-grown armor of theirs. It didn't cover as fully as plate, but it was far more efficient than what most foot soldiers had. Each Parshendi was essentially an extremely mobile heavy infantryman.

The Parshendi always attacked in pairs, eschewing a regular line of battle. That should have made it easy for a disciplined line to defeat them. But each pair of Parshendi had such momentum—and was so well armored—that they could break right through a shield wall. Alternatively, their jumping prowess could suddenly deposit entire ranks of Parshendi behind Alethi lines.

Beyond all that, there was that distinctive way they moved as a group in combat. They maneuvered with an inexplicable coordination. What had seemed at first to be mere barbarian savagery turned out to disguise something more subtle and dangerous.

They'd found only two reliable ways to defeat the Parshendi. The first was to use a Shardblade. Effective, but of limited application. The Kholin army had only two Blades, and while Shards were incredibly powerful, they needed proper support. An isolated, outnumbered Shardbearer could be tripped and toppled by his adversaries. In fact, the one time Adolin had seen a full Shardbearer fall to a regular soldier, it had happened because he had been swarmed by spearmen who broke his breastplate. Then a lighteyed archer had slain him from fifty paces, winning the Shards for himself. Not exactly a heroic end.

The other reliable way to fight Parshendi depended on quick-moving formations. Flexibility mixed with discipline: flexibility to respond to the uncanny way Parshendi fought, discipline to maintain lines and make up for individual Parshendi strength.

Havrom, Fifth Battalionlord, waited for Adolin and Dalinar with his companylords in a line. They saluted, right fists to right shoulders, knuckles outward.

Dalinar nodded to them. "Have my orders been seen to, Brightlord Havrom?"

"Yes, Highprince." Havrom was built like a tower, and wore a beard with long sides after the Horneater fashion, chin clean-shaven. He had relatives among the Peakfolk. "The men you wanted are waiting in the audience tent."

"What's this?" Adolin asked.

"I'll show you in a moment," Dalinar said. "First, review the troops."

Adolin frowned, but the soldiers were waiting. One company at a time, Havrom had the men fall in. Adolin walked before them, inspecting their lines and uniforms. They were neat and orderly, though Adolin knew that some of the soldiers in their army grumbled at the level of polish required of them. He happened to agree with them on that point.

At the end of the inspection, he questioned a few random men, asked their rank and if they had any specific concerns. None had any. Were they satisfied or just intimidated?

When he was done, Adolin returned to his father.

"You did that well," Dalinar said.

"All I did was walk down a line."

"Yes, but the presentation was good. The men know you care for their needs, and they respect you." He nodded, as if to himself. "You've learned well."

"I think you're reading too much into a simple inspection, Father."

Dalinar nodded to Havrom, and the battalionlord led the two of them to an audience tent near the side of the practice field. Adolin, puzzled, glanced at his father.

"I had Havrom gather the soldiers that Sadeas spoke to the other day," Dalinar said. "The ones he interviewed while we were on our way to the plateau assault."

"Ah," Adolin said. "We'll want to know what he asked them."

"Yes," Dalinar said. He gestured for Adolin to enter before him, and they walked in—tailed by a few of Dalinar's ardents. Inside, a group of ten soldiers waited on benches. They rose and saluted.

"At ease," Dalinar said, clasping plated hands behind his back. "Adolin?" Dalinar nodded toward the men, indicating that Adolin should take the lead in the questioning.

Adolin stifled a sigh. Again? "Men, we need to know what Sadeas asked you and how you responded."

"Don't worry, Brightlord," said one of the men, speaking with a rural northern Alethi accent. "We didn't tell him nothing."

The others nodded vigorously.

"He's an eel, and we know it," another added.

"He is a highprince," Dalinar said sternly. "You will treat him with respect."

The soldier paled, then nodded.

"What, *specifically*, did he ask you?" Adolin asked.

"He wanted to know our duties in the camp, Brightlord," the man said. "We're grooms, you see."

Each soldier was trained in one or two additional skills beyond those of combat. Having a group of soldiers who could care for horses was useful, as it kept civilians from plateau assaults.

"He asked around," said one of the men. "Or, well, his people did. Found out we were in charge of the king's horse during the chasmfiend hunt."

"But we didn't say nothing," the first soldier repeated. "Nothing to get you into trouble, sir. We're not going to give that ee—er, that highprince, Brightlord sir, the rope to hang you, sir."

Adolin closed his eyes. If they had acted this way around Sadeas, it would have been more incriminating than the cut girth itself. He couldn't fault their loyalty, but they acted as if they assumed Dalinar *had* done something wrong, and needed to defend him.

He opened his eyes. "I spoke to some of you before, I recall. But let me ask again. Did any of you see a cut strap on the king's saddle?"

The men looked at each other, shaking heads. "No, Brightlord," one of the men replied. "If we'd seen it, we'd have changed it, right we would."

"But, Brightlord," one of the men added, "there was a lot of confusion that day, and a lot of people. Wasn't a right regular plateau assault or nothing like that. And, well, to be honest, sir, who'd have thought that we'd need to protect the king's saddle, of all things under the Halls?"

Dalinar nodded to Adolin, and they stepped out of the tent. "Well?"

"They probably didn't do much to help our cause," Adolin

said with a grimace. "Despite their ardor. Or, rather, because of it."

"Agreed, unfortunately." Dalinar let out a sigh. He waved to Tadet; the short ardent was standing to the side of the tent. "Interview them separately," Dalinar told him softly. "See if you can tease specifics from them. Try to find out the exact words Sadeas used, and what their exact responses were."

"Yes, Brightlord."

"Come, Adolin," Dalinar said. "We've still got a few inspections to do."

"Father," Adolin said, taking Dalinar's arm. Their armor clinked softly.

Dalinar turned to him, frowning, and Adolin made a quick gesture toward the Cobalt Guard. A request for space to speak. The guards moved efficiently and quickly, clearing a private space around the two men.

"What is this about, Father?" Adolin demanded softly.

"What? We're doing inspections and seeing to camp business."

"And in each case, you shove me out into the lead," Adolin said. "Awkwardly, in a few cases, I might add. What's wrong? What's going on inside that head of yours?"

"I thought you had a distinct problem with the things going on inside my head."

Adolin winced. "Father, I—"

"No, it's all right, Adolin. I'm just trying to make a difficult decision. It helps me to move about while I do it." Dalinar grimaced. "Another man might find a place to sit and brood, but that never seems to help me. I've got too much to do."

"What is it you're trying to decide?" Adolin asked. "Perhaps I can help."

"You already have. I—" Dalinar cut off, frowning. A small force of soldiers was walking up to the Fifth Battalion's practice yards. They were escorting a man in red and brown. Those were Thanadal's colors.

"Don't you have a meeting with him this evening?" Adolin asked.

"Yes," Dalinar said.

Niter—head of the Cobalt Guard—ran to intercept the newcomers. He could be overly suspicious at times, but that wasn't a terrible trait for a bodyguard to have. He returned to Dalinar and Adolin shortly. Tan-faced, Niter bore a black beard, cut short. He was a lighteyes of very low rank, and had been with the guard for years. "He says that Highprince Thanadal will be unable to meet with you today as planned."

Dalinar's expression grew dark. "I will speak to the runner myself."

Reluctantly, Niter waved the spindly fellow forward. He approached and dropped to one knee before Dalinar. "Brightlord."

This time, Dalinar didn't ask for Adolin to take the lead. "Deliver your message."

"Brightlord Thanadal regrets that he is unable to attend you this day."

"And did he offer another time to meet?"

"He regrets to say that he has grown too busy. But he would be happy to speak with you at the king's feast one evening."

In public, Adolin thought, *where half the men nearby will be eavesdropping while the other half—likely including Thanadal himself—will probably be drunk.*

"I see," Dalinar said. "And did he give any indication of when he'd no longer be so busy?"

"Brightlord," the messenger said, growing uncomfortable. "He said that if you pressed, I should explain that he has spoken with several of the other highprinces, and feels he knows the nature of your inquiry. He said to tell you he does not wish to form an alliance, nor does he have any intention of going on a joint plateau assault with you."

Dalinar's expression grew darker. He dismissed the messenger with a wave, then turned to Adolin. The Cobalt Guard still kept a space open around them so they could talk.

"Thanadal was the last of them," Dalinar said. Each highprince had turned him down in his own way. Hatham with exceeding politeness, Bethab by letting his wife give the explanation, Thanadal with hostile civility. "All of them but Sadeas, at least."

"I doubt it would be wise to approach him with this, Father."

"You're probably right." Dalinar's voice was cold. He was angry. Furious, even. "They're sending me a message. They've never liked the influence I have over the king, and they're eager to see me fall. They don't want to do something I ask them to, just in case it might help me regain my footing."

"Father, I'm sorry."

"Perhaps it's for the best. The important point is that I have failed. I *can't* get them to work together. Elhokar was right." He looked to Adolin. "I would like you to continue inspections for me, son. There's something I want to do."

"What?"

"Just some work I see needs to be done."

Adolin wanted to object, but he couldn't think of the words to say. Finally, he sighed and gave a nod. "You'll tell me what this is about, though?"

"Soon," Dalinar promised. "Very soon."

※

Dalinar watched his son leave, striding purposefully away. He would make a good highprince. Dalinar's decision was a simple one.

Was it time to step aside, and let his son take his place?

If he took this step, Dalinar would be expected to stay out of politics, retiring to his lands and leaving Adolin to rule. It was a painful decision to contemplate, and he had to be careful not to make it hastily. But if he really was going mad, as everyone in the camp seemed to believe, then he *had* to step down. And soon, before his condition progressed to the point that he no longer had the presence of mind to let go.

A monarch is control, he thought, remembering a passage from *The Way of Kings. He provides stability. It is his service and his trade good. If he cannot control himself, then how can he control the lives of men? What merchant worth his Stormlight won't partake of the very fruit he sells?*

Odd, that those quotes still came to him, even as he was wondering if they had—in part—driven him to madness. "Niter," he said. "Fetch my warhammer. Have it waiting for me at the staging field."

Dalinar wanted to be moving, working, as he thought. His guards hastened to keep up as he strode down the pathway between the barracks of Battalions Six and Seven. Niter sent several men to fetch the weapon. His voice sounded strangely excited, as if he thought Dalinar was going to do something impressive.

Dalinar doubted he would think it so. He eventually strode out onto the staging field, cape fluttering behind him, plated boots clanking against the stones. He didn't have to wait long for the hammer; it came pulled by two men on a small cart. Sweating, the soldiers heaved it from the cart, the haft as thick as a man's wrist and the front of the head larger than an outspread palm. Two men together could barely lift it.

Dalinar grabbed the hammer with one gauntleted hand, swinging it up to rest on his shoulder. He ignored the soldiers performing exercises on the field, walking to where the group of dirty workers chipped at the latrine ditch. They looked up at him, horrified to see the highprince himself looming over them in full Shardplate.

"Who's in charge here?" Dalinar asked.

A scruffy civilian in brown trousers raised a nervous hand. "Brightlord, how may we serve you?"

"By relaxing for a little while," Dalinar said. "Out with you."

The worried workers scrambled out. Lighteyed officers gathered behind, confused by Dalinar's actions.

Dalinar gripped the haft of his warhammer in a gauntleted hand; the metal shaft was wrapped tightly with leather. Taking a deep breath, he leaped down into the half-finished ditch, lifted the hammer, then swung, slamming the weapon down against the rock.

A powerful *crack* rang across the practice field, and a wave of shock ran up Dalinar's arms. The Shardplate absorbed most of the recoil, and he left a large crack in the stones. He hefted and swung again, this time breaking free a large section of rock. Though it would have been difficult for two or three ordinary men to lift, Dalinar grabbed it with one hand and tossed it aside. It clattered across the stones.

Where *were* the Shards for ordinary men? Why hadn't the ancients, who were so wise, created anything to help them? As Dalinar continued to work, beats of his hammer throwing chips and dust into the air, he easily did the work of twenty men. Shardplate could be used for so many things to ease the lives of workers and darkeyes across Roshar.

It felt good to be working. To be doing something useful. Lately, he felt as if his efforts had been akin to running about in circles. The work helped him think.

He *was* losing his thirst for battle. That worried him, as the Thrill—the enjoyment and longing for war—was part of what drove the Alethi as a people. The grandest of masculine arts was to become a great warrior, and the most important Calling was to fight. The Almighty himself depended on the Alethi to train themselves in honorable battle so that when they died, they could join the Heralds' army and win back the Tranquiline Halls.

And yet, thinking about killing was starting to sicken him. It had grown worse since that last bridge assault. What would happen next time he went into battle? He could not lead this way. That was a major reason that abdicating in favor of Adolin looked right.

He continued to swing. Again and again, beating against the stones. Soldiers gathered above and—despite his orders—the workers did not leave to relax. They watched, dumbfounded, as a Shardbearer did their work. Occasionally, he summoned his Blade and used it to cut the rock, slicing out sections before returning to the hammer to break them apart.

He probably looked ridiculous. He couldn't do the work of all of the laborers in camp, and he had important tasks to fill his time. There was no reason for him to get down in a trench and toil. And yet it felt so *good*. So wonderful to pitch in directly with the needs of the camp. The results of what he did to protect Elhokar were often difficult to gauge; it was fulfilling to be able to do something where his progress was obvious.

But even in this, he was acting according to the ideals that had infected him. The book spoke of a king carrying the burdens of his people. It said that those who led were the lowest of men, for they were required to serve everyone. It all swirled around in him. The Codes, the teachings of the book, the things the visions—or delusions—showed.

Never fight other men except when forced to in war.

Bang!

Let your actions defend you, not your words.

Bang!

Expect honor from those you meet, and give them the chance to live up to it.

Bang!

Rule as you would be ruled.

Bang!

He stood waist-deep in what would eventually be a latrine, his ears filled with the groans of breaking stone. He was coming to believe those ideals. No, he'd already come to believe them. Now he was living them. What would the world be like if all men lived as the book proclaimed?

Someone had to start. Someone had to be the model. In this, he had a reason *not* to abdicate. Whether or not he was mad, the way he now did things was better than the way Sadeas or the others did them. One needed only look at the lives of his soldiers and his people to see that was true.

Bang!

Stone could not be changed without pounding. Was it the same with a man like him? Was that why everything was so hard for him suddenly? But why him? Dalinar wasn't a philosopher or idealist. He was a soldier. And—if he admitted the truth—in earlier years, he'd been a tyrant and a warmonger. Could twilight years spent pretending to follow the precepts of better men erase a lifetime of butchery?

He had begun to sweat. The swath he had cut through the ground was as wide as a man was tall, as deep as his chest, and some thirty yards long. The longer he worked, the more people gathered to watch and whisper.

Shardplate was sacred. Was the highprince really digging a *latrine* with it? Had the stress affected him that profoundly? Frightened of highstorms. Growing cowardly. Refusing to duel or defend himself from slurs. Afraid of fighting, wishing to give up the war.

Suspected of trying to kill the king.

Eventually, Teleb decided that letting all the people stare down at Dalinar wasn't respectful, and he ordered the men back to their separate duties. He cleared away the workers, taking Dalinar's order to heart and commanding them to sit in the shade and "converse in a lighthearted manner." From someone else, that command might have been said with a smile, but Teleb was as literal as the rocks themselves.

Still Dalinar worked. He knew where the latrine was supposed to end; he'd approved the work order. A long, sloping trough was to be cut, then covered with oiled and tarred boards to seal in the scent. A latrine house would be set at the high end, and the contents could be Soulcast to smoke once every few months.

The work felt even better once he was alone. One man, breaking rocks, pounding beat after beat. Like the drums the Parshendi had played on that day so long past. Dalinar could feel those beats still, could hear them in his mind, shaking him.

I'm sorry, brother.

He had spoken to the ardents about his visions. They felt that the visions were most likely a product of an overtaxed mind.

He had no reason to believe the truth of anything the visions showed him. In following them, he had done more than just ignore Sadeas's maneuvers; he'd depleted his resources precariously. His reputation was on the brink of ruin. He was in danger of dragging down the entire Kholin house.

And that was the most important point in favor of him abdicating. If he continued, his actions could very well lead to the deaths of Adolin, Renarin, and Elhokar. He would risk his own life for his ideals, but could he risk the lives of his sons?

Chips sprayed, bouncing off his Plate. He was beginning to feel worn and tired. The Plate didn't do the work for him—it enhanced his strength, so each strike of the hammer was his own. His fingers were growing numb from the repeated vibration of the hammer's haft. He was close to a decision. His mind was calm, clear.

He swung the hammer again.

"Wouldn't the Blade be more efficient?" asked a dry, feminine voice.

Dalinar froze, the hammer's head resting on broken stone. He turned to see Navani standing beside the trough, wearing a gown of blue and soft red, her grey-sprinkled hair reflecting light from a sun that was unexpectedly close to setting. She was attended by two young women—not her own wards, but ones she had "borrowed" from other lighteyed women in the camp.

Navani stood with her arms folded, the sunlight behind her like a halo. Dalinar hesitantly raised an armored forearm to block the light. "Mathana?"

"The rockwork," Navani said, nodding to the trough. "Now, I wouldn't *presume* to make judgments; hitting things is a masculine art. But are you not in the possession of a sword that can cut through stone as easily as—I once had it described to me—a highstorm blows over a Herdazian?"

Dalinar looked back at the rocks. Then he raised his hammer again and slammed it into the stones, making a satisfying crunch. "Shardblades are too good at cutting."

"Curious," she said. "I'll do my best to pretend there was sense in that. As an aside, has it ever struck you that most masculine arts deal with destroying, while feminine arts deal with creation?"

Dalinar swung again. *Bang!* Remarkable how much easier it was to have a conversation with Navani while not looking directly at her. "I do use the Blade to cut down the sides and middle. But I still have to break up the rocks. Have you ever tried to lift out a chunk of stone that has been sliced by a Shardblade?"

"I can't say that I have."

"It's not easy." *Bang!* "Blades make a very thin cut. The rocks still press against one another. It's hard to grasp or move them." *Bang!* "It's more complicated than it seems." *Bang!* "This is the best way."

Navani dusted a few chips of stone from her dress. "And more messy, I see."

Bang!

"So, are you going to apologize?" she asked.

"For?"

"For missing our appointment."

Dalinar froze in midswing. He'd completely forgotten that, at the feast when she'd first returned, he'd agreed to have Navani read for him today. He hadn't told his scribes of the appointment. He turned toward her, chagrined. He'd been angered because Thanadal had canceled their appointment, but at least *he* had thought to send a messenger.

Navani stood with arms folded, safehand tucked away, sleek dress seeming to burn with sunlight. She bore a hint of a smile on her lips. By standing her up, he'd put himself—by honor—in her power.

"I'm truly sorry," he said. "I've had some difficult things to consider lately, but that doesn't excuse forgetting you."

"I know. I'll ponder a way to let you make up for the lapse. But for now, you should know that one of your spanreeds is flashing."

"What? Which one?"

"Your scribes say it is the one bound to my daughter."

Jasnah! It had been weeks since they'd last communicated; the messages he'd sent her had prompted only the tersest of answers. When Jasnah was deeply immersed in one of her projects, she often ignored all else. If she was sending to him now, either she'd discovered something or she was taking a break to renew her contacts.

Dalinar turned to look down the latrine. He'd nearly completed it; and he realized he'd been unconsciously planning to make his final decision once he reached the end. He itched to continue working.

But if Jasnah wanted to converse . . .

He needed to talk with her. Perhaps he could persuade her to return to the Shattered Plains. He would feel a lot more secure about abdicating if he knew that she would come watch over Elhokar and Adolin.

Dalinar tossed aside his hammer—his pounding had bent the haft a good thirty degrees and the head was a misshapen lump—and jumped out of the ditch. He'd have a new weapon forged; that was not unusual for Shardbearers.

"Your pardon, Mathana," Dalinar said, "but I fear I must beg your leave so soon after begging your forgiveness. I must receive this communication."

He bowed to her and turned to hurry away.

"Actually," Navani said from behind, "I think *I'll* beg something of you. It has been months since I've spoken with my daughter. I'll join you, if you'll permit it."

He hesitated, but he couldn't deny her so soon after giving her offense. "Of course." He waited as Navani walked to her palanquin and settled herself. The bearers lifted it, and Dalinar struck out again, the bearers and Navani's borrowed wards walking close.

"You are a kind man, Dalinar Kholin," Navani said, that same sly smile on her lips as she sat back in the cushioned chair. "I'm afraid that I'm compelled to find you fascinating."

"My sense of honor makes me easy to manipulate," Dalinar said, eyes forward. Dealing with her was *not* something he needed right now. "I know it does. No need to toy with me, Navani."

She laughed softly. "I'm not trying to take advantage of you, Dalinar, I—" She paused. "Well, perhaps I am taking advantage of you just a little. But I'm not 'toying' with you. This last year in particular, you've begun to *be* the person the others all *claim* that they are. Can't you see how intriguing that makes you?"

"I don't do it to be intriguing."

"If you did, it wouldn't work!" She leaned toward him.

"Do you know why I picked Gavilar instead of you all those years ago?"

Blast. Her comments—her presence—were like a goblet of dark wine poured into the middle of his crystal thoughts. The clarity he'd sought in hard labor was quickly vanishing. Did she have to be so forward? He didn't answer the question. Instead, he picked up his pace and hoped that she'd see he didn't want to discuss the topic.

It was no use. "I didn't pick him because he would become king, Dalinar. Though that's what everyone says. I chose him because you *frightened* me. That intensity of yours . . . it scared your brother too, you know."

He said nothing.

"It's still in there," she said. "I can see it in your eyes. But you've wrapped armor around it, a glistening set of Shardplate to contain it. That is part of what I find fascinating."

He stopped, looking at her. The palanquin bearers halted. "This would not work, Navani," he said softly.

"Wouldn't it?"

He shook his head. "I will not dishonor my brother's memory." He regarded her sternly, and she eventually nodded.

When he continued walking, she said nothing, though she did eye him slyly from time to time. Eventually, they reached his personal complex, marked by fluttering blue banners with the glyphpair *khokh* and *linil*, the former drawn in the shape of a tower, the second forming a crown. Dalinar's mother had drawn the original design, the same his signet ring bore, though Elhokar used a sword and crown instead.

The soldiers at the entrance to his complex saluted, and Dalinar waited for Navani to join him before entering. The cavernous interior was lit by infused sapphires. Once they reached his sitting chamber, he was again struck by just how lavish it had gotten over the months.

Three of his clerks waited with their attending girls. All six stood up when he entered. Adolin was also there.

Dalinar frowned at the youth. "Shouldn't you be seeing to the inspections?"

Adolin started. "Father, I finished those hours ago."

"You did?" *Stormfather! How long did I spend pounding on those stones?*

"Father," Adolin said, stepping up to him. "Can we speak privately for a moment?" As usual, Adolin's black-peppered blond hair was an unruly mop. He'd changed from his Plate and bathed, and now he wore a fashionable—though battle-worthy—uniform with a long blue coat, buttoned at the sides, and straight, stiff brown trousers beneath.

"I'm not ready to discuss that as yet, son," Dalinar said softly. "I need a little more time."

Adolin studied him, eyes concerned. *He will make a fine highprince,* Dalinar thought. *He's been reared to it in a way that I never was.*

"All right then," Adolin said. "But there's something else I want to ask you." He pointed toward one of the clerks, a woman with auburn hair and only a few strands of black. She was lithe and long-necked, wearing a green dress, her hair arranged high on her head in a complex set of braids held together with four traditional steel hair-spikes.

"This is Danlan Morakotha," Adolin said softly to Dalinar. "She came into camp yesterday to spend a few months with her father, Brightlord Morakotha. She has been calling on me recently, and I took the liberty of offering her a position among your clerks while she is here."

Dalinar blinked. "What about . . ."

"Malasha?" Adolin sighed. "Didn't work out."

"And this one?" Dalinar asked, voice hushed, yet incredulous. "How long did you say she's been in camp? Since yesterday? And you've already got her *calling* on you?"

Adolin shrugged. "Well, I do have a reputation to maintain."

Dalinar sighed, eyeing Navani, who stood close enough to hear. She pretended—for propriety—that she wasn't listening in. "You know, it is customary to eventually choose just one woman to court." *You're going to need a good wife, son. Perhaps very soon.*

"When I'm old and boring, perhaps," Adolin said, smiling

at the young woman. She *was* pretty. But only in camp one day? *Blood of my ancestors,* Dalinar thought. He'd spent three years courting the woman who'd eventually become his wife. Even if he couldn't remember her face, he *did* remember how persistently he'd pursued her.

Surely he'd loved her. All emotion regarding her was gone, wiped from his mind by forces he should never have tempted. Unfortunately, he *did* remember how much he'd desired Navani, years before meeting the woman who would become his wife.

Stop that, he told himself. Moments ago, he'd been on the brink of deciding to abdicate his seat as highprince. It was no time to let Navani distract him.

"Brightness Danlan Morakotha," he said to the young woman. "You are welcome among my clerks. I understand that I've received a communication?"

"Indeed, Brightlord," the woman said, curtsying. She nodded to the line of five spanreeds sitting on his bookshelf, set upright in pen holders. The spanreeds looked like ordinary writing reeds, except that each had a small infused ruby affixed. The one on the far right pulsed slowly.

Litima was there, and though she had seniority, she nodded for Danlan to fetch the spanreed. The young woman hurried to the bookshelf and moved the still-blinking reed to the small writing desk beside the lectern. She carefully clipped a piece of paper onto the writing board and put the ink vial into its hole, twisting it snugly into place and then pulling the stopper. Lighteyed women were very proficient at working with just their freehand.

She sat down, looking up at him, seeming slightly nervous. Dalinar didn't trust her, of course—she could easily be a spy for one of the other highprinces. Unfortunately, there weren't *any* women in camp he trusted completely, not with Jasnah gone.

"I am ready, Brightlord," Danlan said. She had a breathy, husky voice. Just the type that attracted Adolin. He hoped she wasn't as vapid as those he usually picked.

"Proceed," Dalinar said, waving Navani toward one of the room's plush easy chairs. The other clerks sat back down on their bench.

Danlan turned the spanreed's gemstone one notch, indicating that the request had been acknowledged. Then she checked the levels on the sides of the writing board—small vials of oil with bubbles at the center, which allowed her to make the board perfectly flat. Finally, she inked the reed and placed it on the dot at the top left of the page. Holding it upright, she twisted the gemstone setting one more time with her thumb. Then she removed her hand.

The reed remained in place, tip against the paper, hovering as if held in a phantom hand. Then it began to write, mimicking the exact movements Jasnah made miles away, writing with a reed conjoined to this one.

Dalinar stood beside the writing table, armored arms folded. He could see that his proximity made Danlan nervous, but he was too anxious to sit.

Jasnah had elegant handwriting, of course—Jasnah rarely did anything without taking the time to perfect it. Dalinar leaned forward as the familiar—yet indecipherable—lines appeared on the page in stark violet. Faint wisps of reddish smoke floated up from the gemstone.

The pen stopped writing, freezing in place.

" 'Uncle,' " Danlan read, " 'I presume that you are well.' "

"Indeed," Dalinar replied. "I am well cared for by those around me." The words were code indicating that he didn't trust—or at least didn't know—everyone listening. Jasnah would be careful not to send anything too sensitive.

Danlan took the pen and twisted the gemstone, then wrote out the words, sending them across the ocean to Jasnah. Was she still in Tukar? After Danlan finished writing, she returned it to the dot at the top left—the spot where the pens were both to be placed so Jasnah could continue the conversation—then turned the gemstone back to the previous setting.

" 'As I expected, I have found my way to Kharbranth,' " Danlan read. " 'The secrets I seek are too obscure to be contained even in the Palanaeum, but I find hints. Tantalizing fragments. Is Elhokar well?'"

Hints? Fragments? Of what? She had a penchant for drama, Jasnah did, though she wasn't as flamboyant about it as the king.

"Your brother tried very hard to get himself killed by a chasmfiend a few weeks back," Dalinar replied. Adolin smiled at that, leaning with his shoulder against the bookcase. "But evidently the Heralds watch over him. He is well, though your presence here is sorely missed. I'm certain he could use your counsel. He is relying heavily on Brightness Lalai to act as clerk."

Perhaps that would make Jasnah return. There was little love lost between herself and Sadeas's cousin, who was the king's head scribe in the queen's absence.

Danlan scratched away, writing the words. To the side, Navani cleared her throat.

"Oh," Dalinar said, "add this: Your mother is here in the warcamps again."

A short time later, the pen wrote of its own volition. "'Send my mother my respect. Keep her at arm's length, Uncle. She bites.'"

From the side, Navani sniffed, and Dalinar realized he hadn't signaled that Navani was actually listening. He blushed as Danlan continued speaking. "'I cannot speak of my work via spanreed, but I'm growing increasingly concerned. There *is* something here, hidden by the sheer number of accrued pages in the historical record.'"

Jasnah was a Veristitalian. She'd explained it to him once; they were an order of scholars who tried to find the truth in the past. They wished to create unbiased, factual accounts of what had happened in order to extrapolate what to do in the future. He wasn't clear on why they thought themselves different from conventional historians.

"Will you be returning?" Dalinar asked.

"'I cannot say,'" Danlan read after the reply came. "'I do not dare stop my research. But a time may soon come when I dare not stay away either.'"

What? Dalinar thought.

" 'Regardless,' " Danlan continued, " 'I have some questions for you. I need you to describe for me again what happened when you met that first Parshendi patrol seven years ago.' "

Dalinar frowned. Despite the Plate's augmentation, his digging had left him feeling tired. But he didn't dare sit on one of the room's chairs while wearing his Plate. He took off one of his gauntlets, though, and ran his hand through his hair. He wasn't fond of this topic, but part of him was glad of the distraction. A reason to hold off on making a decision that would change his life forever.

Danlan looked at him, prepared to dictate his words. Why did Jasnah want this story again? Hadn't she written an account of these very events in her biography of her father?

Well, she would eventually tell him why, and—if her past revelations were any indication—her current project would be of great worth. He wished Elhokar had received a measure of his sister's wisdom.

"These are painful memories, Jasnah. I wish I'd never convinced your father to go on that expedition. If we'd never discovered the Parshendi, then they couldn't have assassinated him. The first meeting happened when we were exploring a forest that wasn't on the maps. This was south of the Shattered Plains, in a valley about two weeks' march from the Drying Sea."

During Gavilar's youth, only two things had thrilled him—conquest and hunting. When he hadn't been seeking one, it had been the other. Suggesting the hunt had seemed rational at the time. Gavilar had been acting oddly, losing his thirst for battle. Men had started to say that he was weak. Dalinar had wanted to remind his brother of the good times in their youth. Hence the hunt for a legendary chasmfiend.

"Your father wasn't with me when I ran across them," Dalinar continued, thinking back. Camping on humid, forested hills. Interrogating Natan natives via translators. Looking for scat or broken trees. "I was leading scouts up a tributary of the Deathbend River while your father scouted downstream. We found the Parshendi camped on the other side. I didn't believe it at first. Parshmen. *Camped*, free and organized. And they carried weapons. Not crude ones, either. Swords, spears with carved hafts . . ."

He trailed off. Gavilar hadn't believed either, when Dalinar told him. There was no such thing as a free parshman tribe. They were servants, and always had been servants.

"'Did they have Shardblades then?'" Danlan said. Dalinar hadn't realized that Jasnah had made a response.

"No."

A scratched reply eventually came. "'But they have them now. When did you first see a Parshendi Shardbearer?'"

"After Gavilar's death," Dalinar said.

He made the connection. They'd always wondered why Gavilar had wanted a treaty with the Parshendi. They wouldn't have needed one just to harvest the greatshells on the Shattered Plains; the Parshendi hadn't lived on the Plains then.

Dalinar felt a chill. Could his brother have *known* that these Parshendi had access to Shardblades? Had he made the treaty hoping to get out of them where they'd found the weapons?

Is it his death? Dalinar wondered. *Is that the secret Jasnah's looking for?* She'd never shown Elhokar's dedication to vengeance, but she thought differently from her brother. Revenge wouldn't drive her. But *questions*. Yes, questions would.

"'One more thing, Uncle,'" Danlan read. "'Then I can go back to digging through this labyrinth of a library. At times, I feel like a cairn robber, sifting through the bones of those long dead. Regardless. The Parshendi, you once mentioned how quickly they seemed to learn our language.'"

"Yes," Dalinar said. "In a matter of days, we were speaking and communicating quite well. Remarkable." Who would have thought that parshmen, of all people, had the wit for such a marvel? Most he'd known didn't do much speaking at all.

"'What were the first things they spoke to you about?'" Danlan said. "'The very *first* questions they asked? Can you remember?'"

Dalinar closed his eyes, remembering days with the Parshendi camped just across the river from them. Gavilar had become fascinated by them. "They wanted to see our maps."

"Did they mention the Voidbringers?"

Voidbringers? "Not that I recall. Why?"

" 'I'd rather not say right now. However, I want to show you something. Have your scribe get out a new sheet of paper.' "

Danlan affixed a new page to the writing board. She put the pen to the corner and let go. It rose and began to scratch back and forth in quick, bold strokes. It was a drawing. Dalinar stood up and stepped closer, and Adolin crowded near. Reed and ink wasn't the best medium, and drawing across spans wasn't precise. The pen leaked tiny globs of ink in places it wouldn't have on the other side, and though the inkwell was in the exact same place—allowing Jasnah to re-ink both her reed and Dalinar's at the same time—his reed sometimes ran out before the one on the other side.

Still, the picture was marvelous. *This isn't Jasnah*, Dalinar realized. Whoever was doing the drawing was far, far more talented than his niece.

The picture resolved into a depiction of a tall shadow looming over some buildings. Hints of carapace and claws showed in the thin ink lines, and shadows were made by drawing finer lines close together.

Danlan set it aside, getting out a third sheet of paper. Dalinar held the drawing up, Adolin at his side. The nightmarish beast in the lines and shadows was faintly familiar. Like . . .

"It's a chasmfiend," Adolin said, pointing. "It's distorted— far more menacing in the face and larger at the shoulders, and I don't see its second set of foreclaws—but someone was obviously trying to draw one of them."

"Yes," Dalinar said, rubbing his chin.

" 'This is a depiction from one of the books here,' " Danlan read. " 'My new ward is quite skilled at drawing, and so I had her reproduce it for you. Tell me. Does it remind you of anything?' "

A new ward? Dalinar thought. It had been years since

Jasnah had taken one. She always said she didn't have the time. "This picture's of a chasmfiend," Dalinar said.

Danlan wrote the words. A moment later, the reply came. "'The book describes this as a picture of a Voidbringer.'" Danlan frowned, cocking her head. "'The book is a copy of a text originally written in the years before the Recreance. However, the illustrations are copied from another text, even older. In fact, some think that picture was drawn only two or three generations after the Heralds departed.'"

Adolin whistled softly. That would make it very old indeed. So far as Dalinar understood, they had few pieces of art or writing dating from the shadowdays, *The Way of Kings* being one of the oldest, and the only complete text. And even it had survived only in translation; they had no copies in the original tongue.

"'Before you jump to conclusions,'" Danlan read, "'I'm not implying that the Voidbringers were the same thing as chasmfiends. I believe that the ancient artist didn't *know* what a Voidbringer looked like, and so she drew the most horrific thing she knew of.'"

But how did the original artist know what a chasmfiend looked like? Dalinar thought. *We only just discovered the Shattered Plains—*

But of course. Though the Unclaimed Hills were now empty, they had once been an inhabited kingdom. Someone in the past had known about chasmfiends, known them well enough to draw one and label it a Voidbringer.

"'I must go now,'" Jasnah said via Danlan. "'Care for my brother in my absence, Uncle.'"

"Jasnah," Dalinar sent, choosing his words very carefully. "Things are difficult here. The storm begins to blow unchecked, and the building shakes and moans. You may soon hear news that shocks you. It would be very nice if you could return and lend your aid."

He waited quietly for the reply, the spanreed scratching. "'I should like to promise a date when I will come.'" Dalinar could almost hear Jasnah's calm, cool voice. "'But I cannot estimate when my research will be completed.'"

"This is very important, Jasnah," Dalinar said. "Please reconsider."

" 'Be assured, Uncle, that I *am* coming. Eventually. I just can't say when.' "

Dalinar sighed.

" 'Note,' " Jasnah wrote, " 'that I am most eager to see a chasmfiend for myself.' "

"A dead one," Dalinar said. "I have no intention of letting you repeat your brother's experience of a few weeks ago."

" 'Ah,' " Jasnah sent back, " 'dear, overprotective Dalinar. One of these years, you will *have* to admit that your favored niece and nephew have grown up.' "

"I'll treat you as adults so long as you act the part," Dalinar said. "Come speedily, and we'll get you a *dead* chasmfiend. Take care."

They waited to see if a further response came, but the gem stopped blinking, Jasnah's transmission complete. Danlan put away the spanreed and the board, and Dalinar thanked the clerks for their aid. They withdrew; Adolin looked as if he wanted to linger, but Dalinar gestured for him to leave.

Dalinar looked down at the picture of the chasmfiend again, unsatisfied. What had he gained from the conversation? More vague hints? What could be so important about Jasnah's research that she would ignore threats to the kingdom?

He would have to compose a more forthright letter to her once he'd made his announcement, explaining why he had decided to step down. Perhaps that would bring her back.

And, in a moment of shock, Dalinar realized that he had made his decision. Sometime between leaving the trench and now, he'd stopped treating his abdication as an *if* and started thinking of it as a *when*. It was the right decision. He felt sick about it, but certain. A man sometimes needed to do things that were unpleasant.

It was the discussion with Jasnah, he realized. *The talk of her father.* He *was* acting like Gavilar at the end. That had nearly undermined the kingdom. Well, he needed to stop himself before he got that far. Perhaps whatever was happening to him was some kind of disease of the mind, inherited from their parents. It—

"You are quite fond of Jasnah," Navani said.

Dalinar started, turning away from the picture of the chasmfiend. He'd assumed she'd followed Adolin out. But she still stood there, looking at him.

"Why is it," Navani said, "that you encourage her so strongly to return?"

He turned to face Navani, and realized that she'd sent her two youthful attendants out with the clerks. They were now alone.

"Navani," he said. "This is inappropriate."

"Bah. We're family, and I have questions."

Dalinar hesitated, then walked to the center of the room. Navani stood near the door. Blessedly, her attendants had left open the door at the end of the antechamber, and beyond it were two guards in the hall outside. It wasn't an ideal situation, but so long as Dalinar could see the guards and they him, his conversation with Navani was just barely proper.

"Dalinar?" Navani asked. "Are you going to answer me? Why is it you trust my daughter so much when others almost universally revile her?"

"I consider their disdain for her to be a recommendation," he said.

"She is a heretic."

"She refused to join any of the devotaries because she did not believe in their teachings. Rather than compromise for the sake of appearances, she has been honest and has refused to make professions she does not believe. I find that a sign of honor."

Navani snorted. "You two are a pair of nails in the same doorframe. Stern, hard, and storming annoying to pull free."

"You should go now," Dalinar said, nodding toward the hallway. He suddenly felt very exhausted. "People will talk."

"Let them. We need to plan, Dalinar. You are the most important highprince in—"

"Navani," he cut in. "I'm going to abdicate in favor of Adolin."

She blinked in surprise.

"I'm stepping down as soon as I can make the necessary arrangements. It will be a few days at most." Speaking the words felt odd, as if saying them made his decision real.

Navani looked pained. "Oh, Dalinar," she whispered. "This is a terrible mistake."

"It is mine to make. And I must repeat my request. I have many things to think about, Navani, and I can't deal with you right now." He pointed at the doorway.

Navani rolled her eyes, but left as requested. She shut the door behind her.

That's it, Dalinar thought, letting out a long exhalation. *I've made the decision.*

Too weary to remove his Plate unassisted, he sank down onto the floor, resting his head back against the wall. He would tell Adolin of his decision in the morning, then announce it at a feast within the week. From there, he would return to Alethkar and his lands.

It was over.

THE END OF

Part Two

İNTERLUDES

❖

RYSN • AXIES • SZETH

Rysn hesitantly stepped down from the caravan's lead wagon. Her feet fell on soft, uneven ground that sank down a little beneath her. That made her shiver, particularly since the too-thick grass didn't move away as it should. Rysn tapped her foot a few times. The grass didn't so much as quiver.

"It's not going to move," Vstim said. "Grass here doesn't behave the way it does elsewhere. Surely you've heard that." The older man sat beneath the bright yellow canopy of the lead wagon. He rested one arm on the side rail, holding a set of ledgers with the other hand. One of his long white eyebrows was tucked behind his ear and he let the other trail down beside his face. He preferred stiffly starched robes—blue and red—and a flat-topped conical hat. It was classic Thaylen merchant's clothing: several decades out of date, yet still distinguished.

"I've heard of the grass," Rysn said to him. "But it's just so *odd*." She stepped again, walking in a circle around the lead wagon. Yes, she'd heard of the grass here in Shinovar, but she'd assumed that it would just be lethargic. That people said it didn't disappear because it moved too slowly.

But no, that wasn't it. It didn't move *at all*. How did it survive? Shouldn't it have all been eaten away by animals? She shook her head in wonder, looking up across the plain. The grass completely *covered* it. The blades were all crowded together, and you couldn't see the ground. What a mess it was.

"The ground is springy," she said, rounding back to her original side of the wagon. "Not just because of the grass."

"Hmm," Vstim said, still working on his ledgers. "Yes. It's called soil."

"It makes me feel like I'm going to sink down to my knees. How can the Shin stand living here?"

"They're an interesting people. Shouldn't you be setting up the device?"

Rysn sighed, but walked to the rear of the wagon. The other wagons in the caravan—six in all—were pulling up and forming a loose circle. She took down the tailgate of the lead wagon and heaved, pulling out a wooden tripod nearly as tall as she was. She carried it over one shoulder, marching to the center of the grassy circle.

She was more fashionable than her babsk; she wore the most modern of clothing for a young woman her age: a deep blue patterned silk vest over a light green long-sleeved shirt with stiff cuffs. Her ankle-length skirt—also green—was stiff and businesslike, utilitarian in cut but embroidered for fashion.

She wore a green glove on her left hand. Covering the safehand was a silly tradition, just a result of Vorin cultural dominance. But it was best to keep up appearances. Many of the more traditional Thaylen people—including, unfortunately, her babsk—still found it scandalous for a woman to go about with her safehand uncovered.

She set up the tripod. It had been five months since Vstim became her babsk and she his apprentice. He'd been good to her. Not all babsk were; by tradition, he was more than just her master. He was her father, legally, until he pronounced her ready to become a merchant on her own.

She did wish he wouldn't spend so much time traveling to such *odd* places. He was known as a great merchant, and she'd assumed that great merchants would be the ones visiting exotic cities and ports. Not ones who traveled to empty meadows in backward countries.

Tripod set up, she returned to the wagon to fetch the fabrial. The wagon back formed an enclosure with thick sides and top to offer protection against highstorms—even the weaker ones in the West could be dangerous, at least until one got through the passes and into Shinovar.

She hurried back to the tripod with the fabrial's box. She slid off the wooden top and removed the large heliodor inside. The pale yellow gemstone, at least two inches in diameter, was fixed inside a metal framework. It glowed gently, not as bright as one might expect of such a sizable gem.

She set it in the tripod, then spun a few of the dials underneath, setting the fabrial to the people in the caravan. Then she pulled a stool from the wagon and sat down to watch. She'd been astonished at what Vstim had paid for the device— one of the new, recently invented types that would give warning if people approached. Was it really so important?

She sat back, looking up at the gemstone, watching to see if it grew brighter. The odd grass of the Shin lands waved in the wind, stubbornly refusing to withdraw, even at the strongest of gusts. In the distance rose the white peaks of the Misted Mountains, sheltering Shinovar. Those mountains caused the highstorms to break and fade, making Shinovar one of the only places in all of Roshar where highstorms did not reign.

The plain around her was dotted with strange, straight-trunked trees with stiff, skeletal branches full of leaves that didn't withdraw in the wind. The entire landscape had an eerie feel to it, as if it were dead. Nothing moved. With a start, Rysn realized she couldn't see any spren. Not a one. No windspren, no lifespren, nothing.

It was as if the entire land were slow of wit. Like a man who was born without all his brains, one who didn't know when to protect himself, but instead just stared at the wall drooling. She dug into the ground with a finger, then brought it up to inspect the "soil," as Vstim had called it. It was dirty stuff. Why, a strong gust could uproot this entire field of grass and blow it away. Good thing the highstorms couldn't reach these lands.

Near the wagons, the servants and guards unloaded crates and set up camp. Suddenly, the heliodor began to pulse with a brighter yellow light. "Master!" she called, standing. "Someone's nearby."

Vstim—who had been going through crates—looked up sharply. He waved to Kylrm, head of the guards, and his six men got out their bows.

"There," one said, pointing.

In the distance, a group of horsemen was approaching. They didn't ride very quickly, and they led several large animals—like thick, squat horses—pulling wagons. The gemstone in the fabrial pulsed more brightly as the newcomers got closer.

"Yes," Vstim said, looking at the fabrial. "That is going to be *very* handy. Good range on it."

"But we knew they were coming," Rysn said, rising from her stool and walking over to him.

"This time," he said. "But if it warns us of bandits in the dark, it'll repay its cost a dozen times over. Kylrm, lower your bows. You know how they feel about those things."

The guards did as they were told, and the group of Thaylens waited. Rysn found herself tucking her eyebrows back nervously, though she didn't know why she bothered. The newcomers were just Shin. Of course, Vstim insisted that she shouldn't think of them as savages. He seemed to have great respect for them.

As they approached, she was surprised by the variety in their appearance. Other Shin she'd seen had worn basic brown robes or other worker's clothing. At the front of this group, however, was a man in what must be Shin finery: a bright, multicolored cloak that completely enveloped him, tied closed at the front. It trailed down on either side of his horse, drooping almost to the ground. Only his head was exposed.

Four men rode on horses around him, and they wore more subdued clothing. Still bright, just not *as* bright. They wore shirts, trousers, and colorful capes.

At least three dozen other men walked alongside them, wearing brown tunics. More drove the three large wagons.

"Wow," Rysn said. "He brought a lot of servants."

"Servants?" Vstim said.

"The fellows in brown."

Her babsk smiled. "Those are his guards, child."

"What? They look so dull."

"Shin are a curious folk," he said. "Here, warriors are the lowliest of men—kind of like slaves. Men trade and sell them between houses by way of little stones that signify ownership, and any man who picks up a weapon must join them and be treated the same. The fellow in the fancy robe? *He's* a farmer."

"A landowner, you mean?"

"No. As far as I can tell, he goes out every day—well, the days when he's not overseeing a negotiation like this—and works the fields. They treat all farmers like that, lavish them with attention and respect."

Rysn gaped. "But most villages are *filled* with farmers!"

"Indeed," Vstim said. "Holy places, here. Foreigners aren't allowed near fields or farming villages."

How strange, she thought. *Perhaps living in this place has affected their minds.*

Kylrm and his guards didn't look terribly pleased at being so heavily outnumbered, but Vstim didn't seem bothered. Once the Shin grew close, he walked out from his wagons without a hint of trepidation. Rysn hurried after him, her skirt brushing the grass below.

Bother, she thought. Another problem with its not retracting. If she had to buy a new hem because of this dull grass, it was going to make her very cross.

Vstim met up with the Shin, then bowed in a distinctive way, hands toward the ground. "*Tan balo ken tala,*" he said. She didn't know what it meant.

The man in the cloak—the *farmer*—nodded respectfully, and one of the other riders dismounted and walked forward. "Winds of Fortune guide you, my friend." He spoke Thaylen very well. "He who adds is happy for your safe arrival."

"Thank you, Thresh-son-Esan," Vstim said. "And my thanks to he who adds."

"What have you brought for us from your strange lands, friend?" Thresh said. "More metal, I hope?"

Vstim waved and some of the guards brought over a heavy crate. They set it down and pried off the top, revealing its peculiar contents. Pieces of scrap metal, mostly shaped like bits of shell, though some were formed like pieces of wood. It looked to Rysn like garbage that had—for some inexplicable reason—been Soulcast into metal.

"Ah," Thresh said, squatting down to inspect the box. "Wonderful!"

"Not a bit of it was mined," Vstim said. "No rocks were broken or smelted to get this metal, Thresh. It was Soulcast from shells, bark, or branches. I have a document sealed by five separate Thaylen notaries attesting to it."

"You needn't have done such a thing as this," Thresh said. "You have once earned our trust in this matter long ago."

"I'd rather be proper about it," Vstim said. "A merchant who is careless with contracts is one who finds himself with enemies instead of friends."

Thresh stood up, clapping three times. The men in brown with the downcast eyes lowered the back of a wagon, revealing crates.

"The others who visit us," Thresh noted, walking to the wagon. "All they seem to care about are horses. Everyone wishes to buy horses. But never you, my friend. Why is that?"

"Too hard to care for," Vstim said, walking with Thresh. "And there's too often a poor return on the investment, valuable as they are."

"But not with these?" Thresh said, picking up one of the light crates. There was something alive inside.

"Not at all," Vstim said. "Chickens fetch a good price, and they're easy to care for, assuming you have feed."

"We brought you plenty," Thresh said. "I cannot believe you buy these from us. They are not worth nearly so much as you outsiders think. And you give us metal for them! Metal that bears no stain of broken rock. A miracle."

Vstim shrugged. "Those scraps are practically worthless where I come from. They're made by ardents practicing with Soulcasters. They can't make food, because if you get it wrong, it's poisonous. So they turn garbage into metal and throw it away."

"But it can be forged!"

"Why forge the metal," Vstim said, "when you can carve an object from wood in the precise shape you want, *then* Soulcast it?"

Thresh just shook his head, bemused. Rysn watched with her own share of confusion. This was the *craziest* trade exchange she'd ever seen. Normally, Vstim argued and haggled like a crushkiller. But here, he freely revealed that his wares were worthless!

In fact, as conversation proceeded, the two both took pains to explain how worthless their goods were. Eventually, they came to an agreement—though Rysn couldn't grasp how—and shook hands on the deal. Some of Thresh's soldiers began to unload their boxes of chickens, cloth, and exotic dried meats. Others began carting away boxes of scrap metal.

"You couldn't trade me a soldier, could you?" Vstim asked as they waited.

"They cannot be sold to an outsider, I am afraid."

"But there was that one you traded me . . ."

"It's been nearly seven years!" Thresh said with a laugh. "And still you ask!"

"You don't know what I got for him," Vstim said. "And you gave him to me for practically nothing!"

"He was Truthless," Thresh said, shrugging. "He wasn't worth anything at all. You *forced* me to take something in trade, though to confess, I had to throw your payment into a river. I could not take money for a Truthless."

"Well, I suppose I can't take offense at that," Vstim said, rubbing his chin. "But if you ever have another, let me know. Best servant I ever had. I still regret that I traded him."

"I will remember, friend," Thresh said. "But I do not think it likely we will have another like him." He seemed to grow distracted. "Indeed, I should hope that we never do. . . ."

Once the goods were exchanged, they shook hands again, then Vstim bowed to the farmer. Rysn tried to mimic what he did, and earned a smile from Thresh and several of his companions, who chattered in their whispering Shin language.

Such a long, boring ride for such a short exchange. But Vstim was right; those chickens would be worth good spheres in the East.

"What did you learn?" Vstim said to her as they walked back toward the lead wagon.

"That Shin are odd."

"No," Vstim said, though he wasn't stern. He never seemed to be stern. "They are simply different, child. Odd people are those who act erratically. Thresh and his kind, they are anything but erratic. They may be a little *too* stable. The world is changing outside, but the Shin seem determined to remain the same. I've tried to offer them fabrials, but they find them worthless. Or unholy. Or too holy to use."

"Those are rather different things, master."

"Yes," he said. "But with the Shin, it's often hard to distinguish among them. Regardless, what did you *really* learn?"

"That they treat being humble like the Herdazians treat boasting," she said. "You both went out of your way to show how worthless your wares were. I found it strange, but I think it might just be how they haggle."

He smiled widely. "And already you are wiser than half the men I've brought here. Listen. Here is your lesson. *Never* try to cheat the Shin. Be forthright, tell them the truth, and—if anything—undervalue your goods. They will love you for it. And they'll pay you for it too."

She nodded. They reached the wagon, and he got out a strange little pot. "Here," he said. "Use a knife and go cut out some of that grass. Be sure to cut down far and get plenty of the soil. The plants can't live without it."

"Why am I doing this?" she asked, wrinkling her nose and taking the pot.

"Because," he said. "You're going to learn to care for that plant. I want you to keep it with you until you stop thinking of it as odd."

"But why?"

"Because it will make you a better merchant," he said.

She frowned. Must he be so strange so much of the time? Perhaps that was why he was one of the only Thaylens who could get a good deal out of the Shin. He was as odd as they were.

She walked off to do as she was told. No use complaining. She did get out a rugged pair of gloves first, though, and roll up her sleeves. She was *not* going to ruin a good dress for a pot of drooling, wall-staring, imbecile grass. And that was that.

AXIES
THE COLLECTOR

Axies the Collector groaned, lying on his back, skull pounding with a headache. He opened his eyes and looked down the length of his body. He was naked.

Blight it all, he thought.

Well, best to check and see if he was hurt too badly. His toes pointed at the sky. The nails were a deep blue color, not uncommon for an Aimian man like himself. He tried to wiggle them and, pleasingly, they actually moved.

"Well, that's something," he said, dropping his head back to the ground. It made a squishing sound as it touched something soft, likely a bit of rotting garbage.

Yes, that was what it was. He could smell it now, pungent and rank. He focused on his nose, sculpting his body so that he could no longer smell. *Ah,* he thought. *Much better.*

Now if he could only banish the pounding in his head. Really, did the sun *have* to be so garish overhead? He closed his eyes.

"You're still in my alley," a gruff voice said from behind him. That voice had awakened him in the first place.

"I shall vacate it presently," Axies promised.

"You owe me rent. One night's sleep."

"In an alleyway?"

"Finest alleyway in Kasitor."

"Ah. Is that where I am, then? Excellent."

A few heartbeats of mental focus finally banished the headache. He opened his eyes, and this time found the sunlight quite pleasant. Brick walls rose toward the sky on either side of him, overgrown with a crusty red lichen. Small heaps of rotting tubers were scattered around him.

No. Not scattered. They looked to be arranged carefully. Odd, that. They were likely the source of the scents he'd noticed earlier. Best to leave his sense of smell inhibited.

He sat up, stretching, checking his muscles. All seemed to be in working order, though he had quite a few bruises. He'd deal with those in a bit. "Now," he said, turning, "you wouldn't happen to have a spare pair of pants, would you?"

The owner of the voice turned out to be a scraggly-bearded man sitting on a box at the end of the alleyway. Axies didn't recognize him, nor did he recognize the location. That wasn't surprising, considering that he'd been beaten, robbed, and left for dead. Again.

The things I do in the name of scholarship, he thought with a sigh.

His memory was returning. Kasitor was a large Iriali city, second in size only to Rall Elorim. He'd come here by design. He'd also gotten himself drunk by design. Perhaps he should have picked his drinking companions more carefully.

"I'm going to guess that you don't have a spare pair of pants," Axies said, standing and inspecting the tattoos on his arm. "And if you did, I'd suggest that you wear them yourself. Is that a lavis sack you have on?"

"You owe me rent," the man grumbled. "And payment for destroying the temple of the northern god."

"Odd," Axies said, looking over his shoulder toward the alleyway's opening. There was a busy street beyond. The good people of Kasitor would likely not take well to his nudity. "I don't *recall* destroying any temples. Normally I'm quite cognizant of that sort of thing."

"You took out half of Hapron Street," the beggar said. "Number of homes as well. I'll let that slide."

"Mighty kind of you."

"They've been wicked lately."

Axies frowned, looking back at the beggar. He followed the man's gaze, looking down at the ground. The heaps of rotting vegetables had been placed in a very particular arrangement. Like a city.

"Ah," Axies said, moving his foot, which had been planted on a small square of vegetable.

"That was a bakery," the beggar said.

"Terribly sorry."

"The family was away."

"That's a relief."

"They were worshipping at the temple."

"The one I . . ."

"Smashed with your head? Yes."

"I'm certain you'll be kind to their souls."

The beggar narrowed his eyes at him. "I'm still trying to decide how you fit into things. Are you a Voidbringer or a Herald?"

"Voidbringer, I'm afraid," Axies said. "I mean, I *did* destroy a temple."

The beggar's eyes grew more suspicious.

"Only the sacred cloth can banish me," Axies continued. "And since you don't . . . I say, what is that you're holding?"

The beggar looked down at his hand, which was touching one of the ratty blankets draped over one of his equally ratty boxes. He perched atop them, like . . . well, like a god looking down over his people.

Poor fool, Axies thought. It was really time to be moving on. Wouldn't want to bring any bad luck down upon the addled fellow.

The beggar held up the blanket. Axies shied back, raising his hands. That made the beggar smile a grin that could have used a few more teeth. He hopped off his box, holding the blanket up wardingly. Axies shied away.

The beggar cackled and threw the blanket at him. Axies snatched it from the air and shook a fist at the beggar. Then he retreated from the alleyway while wrapping the blanket around his waist.

"And lo," the beggar said from behind, "the foul beast was banished!"

"And lo," Axies said, fixing the blanket in place, "the foul beast avoided imprisonment for public indecency." Iriali were very particular about their chastity laws. They were very particular about a lot of things. Of course, that could be said for most peoples—the only difference was the things they were particular about.

Axies the Collector drew his share of stares. Not because of his unconventional clothing—Iri was on the northwestern rim of Roshar, and its weather therefore tended to be much warmer than that of places like Alethkar or even Azir. A fair number of the golden-haired Iriali men went about wearing only waist wraps, their skin painted various colors and patterns. Even Axies's tattoos weren't that noteworthy here.

Perhaps he drew stares because of his blue nails and crystalline deep blue eyes. Aimians—even Siah Aimians—were rare. Or perhaps it was because he cast a shadow the wrong way. Toward light, instead of away from it. It was a small thing, and the shadows weren't long, with the sun so high. But those who noticed muttered or jumped out of the way. Likely they'd heard of his kind. It hadn't been *that* long since the scouring of his homeland. Just long ago enough for stories and legends to have crept into the general knowledge of most peoples.

Perhaps someone important would take exception to him and have him brought before a local magistrate. Wouldn't be the first time. He'd learned long ago not to worry. When the Curse of Kind followed you, you learned to take what happened as it happened.

He began to whistle softly to himself, inspecting his tattoos and ignoring those observant enough to gawk. *I remember writing something somewhere . . .* he thought, looking over his wrist, then twisting his arm over and trying to see if there were any new tattoos on the back. Like all Aimians, he could change the color and markings of his skin at will. That was convenient, as when you were very regularly robbed of everything you owned, it was blighted difficult to keep a proper notebook. And so, he kept his notes on his skin, at least until he could return to a safe location and transcribe them.

Hopefully, he hadn't gotten so drunk that he'd written his observations someplace inconvenient. He'd done that once, and reading the mess had required two mirrors and a very confused bathing attendant.

Ah, he thought, discovering a new entry near the inside of his left elbow. He read it awkwardly, shuffling down the incline.

Test successful. Have noted spren who appear only when one is severely intoxicated. Appear as small brown bubbles clinging to objects nearby. Further testing may be needed to prove they were more than a drunken hallucination.

"Very nice," he said out loud. "Very nice indeed. I wonder what I should call them." The stories he'd heard called them sudspren, but that seemed silly. Intoxicationspren? No, too unwieldy. Alespren? He felt a surge of excitement. He'd been hunting this particular type of spren for years. If they proved real, it would be quite a victory.

Why did they appear only in Iri? And why so infrequently? He'd gotten himself stupidly drunk a dozen times, and had only found them once. If, indeed, he had ever really found them.

Spren, however, could be very elusive. Sometimes, even the most common types—flamespren, for instance—would refuse to appear. That made it particularly frustrating for a man who had made it his life's work to observe, catalogue, and study every single type of spren in Roshar.

He continued whistling as he made his way through the town to the dockside. Around him flowed large numbers of the golden-haired Iriali. The hair bred true, like black Alethi hair—the purer your blood was, the more locks of gold you had. And it wasn't merely blond, it was truly gold, lustrous in the sun.

He had a fondness for the Iriali. They weren't *nearly* as prudish as the Vorin peoples to the east, and were rarely inclined to bickering or fighting. That made it easier to hunt spren. Of course, there were also spren you could find only during war.

A group of people had gathered at the docks. *Ah,* he thought, *excellent. I'm not too late.* Most were crowding onto a purpose-built viewing platform. Axies found himself a place to stand, adjusted his holy blanket, and leaned back against the railing to wait.

It wasn't long. At precisely seven forty-six in the morning—the locals could use it to set their timepieces—an enormous, sea-blue spren surged from the waters of the bay. It was translucent, and though it appeared to throw out waves as it rose, that was illusory. The actual surface of the bay wasn't disturbed.

It takes the shape of a large jet of water, Axies thought, creating a tattoo along an open portion of his leg, scribing the words. *The center is of the deepest blue, like the ocean depths, though the outer edges are a lighter shade. Judging by the masts of the nearby ships, I'd say that the spren has grown to a height of at least a hundred feet. One of the largest I've ever seen.*

The column sprouted four long arms that came down around the bay, forming fingers and thumbs. They landed on golden pedestals that had been placed there by the people of the city. The spren came at the same time every day, without fail.

They called it by name, Cusicesh, the Protector. Some worshipped it as a god. Most simply accepted it as part of the city. It was unique. One of the few types of spren he knew of that seemed to have only a single member.

But what kind *of spren is it?* Axies wrote, fascinated. *It has formed a face, looking eastward. Directly toward the Origin. That face is shifting, bewilderingly quick. Different human faces appear on the end of its stumplike neck, one after another in blurred succession.*

The display lasted a full ten minutes. Did any of the faces repeat? They changed so quickly, he couldn't tell. Some seemed male, others female. Once the display was finished, Cusicesh retreated down into the bay, sending up phantom waves again.

Axies felt drained, as if something had been leeched from him. That was reported to be a common reaction. Was he imagining it because it was expected? Or was it real?

As he considered, a street urchin scrambled past and grabbed his wrap, yanking it free and laughing to himself. He tossed it to some friends and they scrambled away.

Axies shook his head. "What a bother," he said as people around him began to gasp and mutter. "There are guards nearby, I assume? Ah yes. Four of them. Wonderful." The four were already stalking toward him, golden hair falling around their shoulders, expressions stern.

"Well," he said to himself, making a final notation as one of the guards grabbed him on the shoulder. "It appears I'll have another chance to search for captivityspren." Odd, how those had eluded him all these years, despite his numerous incarcerations. He was beginning to consider them mythological.

The guards towed him off toward the city dungeons, but he didn't mind. Two new spren in as many days! At this rate, it might only take a few more centuries to complete his research.

Grand indeed. He resumed whistling to himself.

A WORK OF ART

Szeth-son-son-Vallano, Truthless of Shinovar, crouched on a high stone ledge at the side of the gambling den. The ledge was meant for holding a lantern; both his legs and the shelf were hidden by his long, enveloping cloak, making him seem to be hanging from the wall.

There were few lights nearby. Makkek liked Szeth to remain cloaked in shadow. He wore a formfitting black costume beneath the cloak, the lower part of his face covered by a cloth mask; both were of Makkek's design. The cloak was too big and the clothing too tight. It was a terrible outfit for an assassin, but Makkek demanded drama, and Szeth did as his master commanded. Always.

Perhaps there was something useful to the drama. With only his eyes and bald head showing, he unnerved the people who passed by. Shin eyes, too round, slightly too large. The people here thought them similar to the eyes of a child. Why did that disturb them so?

Nearby, a group of men in brown cloaks sat chatting and rubbing their thumbs and forefingers together. Wisps of smoke rose between their fingers, accompanied by a faint crackling sound. Rubbing firemoss was said to make a man's mind more receptive to thoughts and ideas. The one time Szeth had tried it, it had given him a headache and two blistered fingers. But once you grew the calluses, it could apparently be euphoric.

The circular den had a bar at the center, serving a wide variety of drinks at a wider variety of prices. The barmaids were dressed in violet robes that had plunging necklines and were open at the sides. Their safehands were exposed, something that the Bavlanders—who were Vorin by descent—seemed to find extremely provocative. So odd. It was just a hand.

Around the perimeter of the den, various games were in progress. None of them were overt games of chance—no dice throws, no bets on card flips. There were games of breakneck, shallowcrab fights, and—oddly—guessing games. That was another oddity about Vorin peoples; they avoided overtly guessing the future. A game like breakneck would have throws and tosses, but they wouldn't bet on the outcome. Instead, they'd bet on the hand they held after the throws and the draws.

It seemed a meaningless distinction to Szeth, but it was deeply steeped in the culture. Even here, in one of the vilest pits in the city—where women walked with their hands exposed and men spoke openly of crimes—nobody risked offending the Heralds by seeking to know the future. Even predicting the highstorms made many uncomfortable. And yet they thought *nothing* of walking on stone or using Stormlight for everyday illumination. They ignored the spirits of things that lived around them, and they ate whatever they wanted on any day they wanted.

Strange. So strange. And yet this was his life. Recently, Szeth had begun to question some of the prohibitions he had once followed so strictly. How could these Easterners *not* walk on stone? There was no soil in their lands. How could they get about without treading on stone?

Dangerous thoughts. His way of life was all that remained to him. If he questioned Stone Shamanism, would he then question his nature as Truthless? Dangerous, dangerous. Though his murders and sins would damn him, at least his soul would be given to the stones upon his death. He would continue to exist. Punished, in agony, but not exiled to nothingness.

Better to exist in agony than to vanish entirely.

Makkek himself strode the floor of the gambling den, a woman on each arm. His scrawny leanness was gone, his face having slowly gained a juicy plumpness, like a fruit ripening after the drowning's waters. Also gone were his ragged footpad's garments, replaced with luxurious silks.

Makkek's companions—the ones with him when they'd killed Took—were all dead, murdered by Szeth at Makkek's orders. All to hide the secret of the Oathstone. Why were these Easterners always so ashamed of the way they controlled Szeth? Was it because they feared another would steal the Oathstone from them? Were they terrified that the weapon they employed so callously would be turned against them?

Perhaps he feared that if it were known how easily Szeth was controlled, it would spoil their reputation. Szeth had overheard more than one conversation centered around the mystery of Makkek's terribly effective bodyguard. If a creature like Szeth served Makkek, then the master himself must be even more dangerous.

Makkek passed the place where Szeth lurked, one of the women on his arms laughing with tinkling sound. Makkek glanced at Szeth, then gestured curtly. Szeth bowed his masked head in acknowledgment. He slid from his place, dropping to the ground, oversized cloak fluttering.

Games stilled. Men both drunken and sober turned to watch Szeth, and as he passed the three men with the firemoss, their fingers went limp. Most in the room knew what Szeth was about this night. A man had moved into Bornwater and opened his own gambling den to challenge Makkek. Likely this newcomer didn't believe the reputation of Makkek's phantom assassin. Well, he had reason to be skeptical. Szeth's reputation *was* inaccurate.

He was far, *far* more dangerous than it suggested.

He ducked out of the gambling den, passing up the steps, through the darkened storefront and then out into the yard. He tossed the cloak and face mask into a wagon as he passed. The cloak would only make noise, and why cover his face? He was the only Shin in town. If someone saw his eyes, they'd know who he was. He retained the tight black clothing; changing would take too much time.

Bornwater was the largest town in the area; it hadn't taken Makkek long to outgrow Staplind. Now he was talking of moving up to Kneespike, the city where the local landlord had his mansion. If that happened, Szeth would spend months wading in blood as he systematically tracked down and killed each and every thief, cutthroat, and gambling master who refused Makkek's rule.

That was months off. For now, there was Bornwater's interloper, a man named Gavashaw. Szeth prowled through the streets, eschewing Stormlight or Shardblade, counting on his natural grace and care to keep him unseen. He enjoyed his brief freedom. These moments—when he wasn't trapped in one of Makkek's smoke-filled dens—were too few lately.

Slipping between buildings—moving swiftly in the darkness, with the wet, cold air on his skin—he could almost think himself back in Shinovar. The buildings around him were not of blasphemous stone, but earthen ones, built with clay and soil. Those low sounds were not muffled cheers from within another of Makkek's gambling dens, but the thunder and whinnies of wild horses on the plains.

But no. In Shinovar he'd never smelled refuse like that—pungency compounded by weeks spent marinating. He was not home. There was no place for him in the Valley of Truth.

Szeth entered one of the richer sections of town, where buildings had more space between homes. Bornwater was in a lait, protected by a towering cliffside to the east. Gavashaw had arrogantly made his home in a large mansion on the eastern side of town. It belonged to the provincial landlord; Gavashaw had his favor. The landlord had heard of Makkek and his quick rise to prominence in the underground, and supporting a rival was a good way to create an early check on Makkek's power.

The citylord's local mansion was three stories tall, with a stone wall surrounding the compact, neatly gardened grounds. Szeth approached in a low crouch. Here on the outskirts of town, the ground was spotted with bulbous rockbuds. As he passed, the plants rustled, pulling back their vines and lethargically closing their shells.

He reached the wall and pressed himself against it. It was the time between the first two moons, the darkest period of night. The hateful hour, his people called it, for it was one of the only times when the gods did not watch men. Soldiers walked the wall above, feet scraping the stones. Gavashaw probably thought himself safe in this building, which was secure enough for a powerful lighteyes.

Szeth breathed in, infusing himself with Stormlight from the spheres in his pouch. He began to glow, luminescent vapors rising from his skin. In the darkness, it was quite noticeable. These powers had never been intended for assassination; Surgebinders had fought during the light of day, battling the night but not embracing it.

That was not Szeth's place. He would simply have to take extra care not to be seen.

Ten heartbeats after the passing of the guards, Szeth Lashed himself to the wall. That direction became down for him, and he was able to run up the side of the stone fortification. As he reached the top, he leaped forward, then briefly Lashed himself backward. He spun over the top of the wall in a tucked flip, then Lashed himself back to the wall again. He came down with feet planted on the stones, facing the ground. He ran and Lashed himself downward again, dropping the last few feet.

The grounds were laced with shalebark mounds, cultivated to form small terraces. Szeth ducked low, picking his way through the mazelike garden. There were guards at the building's doorways, watching by the light of spheres. How easy it would be to dash up, consume the Stormlight, and plunge the men into darkness before cutting them down.

But Makkek had not expressly commanded him to be so destructive. Gavashaw was to be assassinated, but the method was up to Szeth. He picked one that would not require killing the guards. That was what he always did, when given the chance. It was the only way to preserve what little humanity he had left.

He reached the western wall of the mansion and Lashed himself to it, then ran up it onto the roof. It was long and flat, sloped gently eastward—an unnecessary feature in a lait, but Easterners saw the world by the light of the highstorms. Szeth quickly crossed to the rear of the building, to where a small rock dome covered a lower portion of the mansion. He dropped down onto the dome, Stormlight streaming from his body. Translucent, luminescent, pristine. Like the ghost of a fire burning from him, consuming his soul.

He summoned his Shardblade in the stillness and dark, then used it to slice a hole in the dome, angling his Blade so that the chunk of rock did not fall down inside. He reached down with his free hand and infused the stone circle with Light, Lashing it toward the northwest section of the sky. Lashing something to a distant point like that was possible, but imprecise. It was like trying to shoot an arrow a great distance.

He stepped back as the stone circle lurched free and fell up into the air, streaming Stormlight as it soared toward the splattered paint drops of stars above. Szeth leapt into the hole, then immediately Lashed himself to the ceiling. He twisted in the air, landing with his feet planted on the underside of the dome beside the lip of the hole he'd cut. From his perspective, he was now standing at the bottom of a gigantic stone bowl, the hole cut in the very bottom, looking out on the stars beneath.

He walked up the side of the bowl, Lashing himself to the right. In seconds he was on the floor, reoriented so that the dome rose above him. Distantly, he heard a faint crashing: The chunk of stone, Stormlight exhausted, had fallen back to the ground. He had aimed it out of the town. Hopefully, it had not caused any accidental deaths.

The guards would now be distracted, searching for the source of the distant crash. Szeth breathed in deeply, draining his second pouch of gemstones. The light streaming from him became brighter, letting him see the room around him.

As he'd suspected, it was empty. This was a rarely used feasting hall, with cold firepits, tables, and benches. The air was still, silent, and musty. Like that of a tomb. Szeth hurried to the door, slid his Shardblade between it and the frame, and sliced through the deadbolt. He eased the door open. The Stormlight rising from his body illuminated the dark hallway outside.

Early during his time with Makkek, Szeth had been careful not to use the Shardblade. As his tasks had grown more difficult, however, he'd been forced to resort to it to avoid unnecessary killing. Now the rumors about him were populated with tales of holes cut through stone and dead men with burned eyes.

Makkek had begun to believe those rumors. He hadn't yet demanded that Szeth relinquish the Blade—if he did so, he would discover the second of Szeth's two forbidden actions. He was required to carry the Blade until his death, after which Shin Stone Shamans would recover it from whomever had killed him.

He moved through the hallways. He wasn't worried about Makkek taking the Blade, but he *was* worried about how bold the thief lord was growing. The more successful Szeth was, the more audacious Makkek became. How long before he stopped using Szeth to kill minor rivals, instead sending him to kill Shardbearers or powerful lighteyes? How long before someone made the connection? A Shin assassin with a Shardblade, capable of mysterious feats and extreme stealth? Could this be the now-infamous Assassin in White? Makkek could draw the Alethi king and highprinces away from their war on the Shattered Plains and bring them crashing down upon Jah Keved. Thousands would die. Blood would fall like the rain of a highstorm—thick, pervasive, destructive.

He continued down the hallway in a swift low run, Shardblade carried in a reverse grip, extending out behind him. Tonight, at least, he assassinated a man who deserved his fate. Were the hallways too quiet? Szeth hadn't seen a soul since leaving the rooftop. Could Gavashaw have been foolish enough to place all of his guards outside, leaving his bedchamber undefended?

Ahead, the doors into the master's rooms lay unwatched and dark at the end of a short hallway. Suspicious.

Szeth crept up to the doors, listening. Nothing. He hesitated, glancing to the side. A grand stairway led up to the second floor. He hustled over and used his Blade to shear free a wooden knob from the newel post. It was about the size of a small melon. A few hacks with the Blade cut a cloak-sized section of drapery free from a window. Szeth hurried back to the doors and infused the wooden sphere with Stormlight, giving it a Basic Lashing that pointed it westward, directly ahead of him.

He cut through the latch between the doors and eased one open. The room beyond was dark. Was Gavashaw gone for the evening? Where would he go? This city was not safe for him yet.

Szeth placed the wooden ball in the middle of the drape, then held it up and dropped it. It fell forward, toward the far wall. Wrapped in the fabric, the ball looked vaguely like a person in a cloak running through the room in a crouch.

No concealed guards struck at it. The decoy bounced off a latched window, then came to rest hanging against the wall. It continued to leak Stormlight.

That light illuminated a small table with an object atop it. Szeth squinted, trying to make out what it was. He edged forward, slinking into the room, closer and closer to the table.

Yes. The object on the table was a head. One with Gavashaw's features. Shadows thrown by Stormlight gave the grisly face an even more haunted cast. Someone had beaten Szeth to the assassination.

"Szeth-son-Neturo," a voice said.

Szeth turned, spinning his Shardblade around and falling into a defensive stance. A figure stood on the far side of the room, shrouded in the darkness. "Who are you?" Szeth demanded, his Stormlight aura growing brighter once he stopped holding his breath.

"Are you satisfied with this, Szeth-son-Neturo?" the voice asked. It was male and deep. What was that accent? The man wasn't Veden. Alethi, perhaps? "Are you satisfied with trivial crimes? Killing over meaningless turf in backwater mining villages?"

Szeth didn't reply. He scanned the room, looking for motion in the other shadows. None seemed to be hiding anyone.

"I've watched you," the voice said. "You've been sent to intimidate shopkeepers. You've killed footpads so unimportant even the authorities ignore them. You've been shown off to impress whores, as if they were high lighteyed ladies. What a waste."

"I do as my master demands."

"You are squandered," the voice said. "You are not meant for petty extortions and murders. Using you like this, it's like hitching a Ryshadium stallion to a run-down market wagon. It's like using a Shardblade to slice vegetables, or like using the finest parchment as kindling for a washwater fire. It is a *crime*. You are a work of art, Szeth-son-Neturo, a god. And each day Makkek throws dung at you."

"Who are you?" Szeth repeated.

"An admirer of the arts."

"Do not call me by my father's name," Szeth said. "He should not be sullied by association with me."

The sphere on the wall finally ran out of Stormlight, dropping to the floor, the drapery muffling its fall. "Very well," the figure said. "But do you not rebel against this frivolous use of your skills? Were you not meant for greatness?"

"There is no greatness in killing," Szeth said. "You speak like a *kukori*. Great men create food and clothing. He who adds is to be revered. I am he who takes away. At least in the killing of men such as these I can pretend to be doing a service."

"This from the man who nearly toppled one of the greatest kingdoms in Roshar?"

"This from the man who committed one of the most heinous slaughters in Roshar," Szeth corrected.

The figure snorted. "What you did was a mere breeze compared to the storm of slaughter Shardbearers wreak on a battlefield each day. And *those* are breezes compared to the tempests you are capable of."

Szeth began to walk away.

"Where are you going?" the figure asked.

"Gavashaw is dead. I must return to my master."

Something hit the floor. Szeth spun, Shardblade down. The figure had dropped something round and heavy. It rolled across the floor toward Szeth.

Another head. It came to rest on its side. Szeth froze as he made out the features. The pudgy cheeks were stained with blood, the dead eyes wide with shock: Makkek.

"How?" Szeth demanded.

"We took him seconds after you left the gambling den."

"We?"

"Servants of your new master."

"My Oathstone?"

The figure opened his hand, revealing a gemstone suspended in his palm by a chain wrapped around his fingers. Sitting beside it, now illuminated, was Szeth's Oathstone. The figure's face was dark; he wore a mask.

Szeth dismissed his Shardblade and went down on one knee. "What are your orders?"

"There is a list on the table," the figure said, closing his hand and hiding the Oathstone. "It details our master's wishes."

Szeth rose and walked over. Beside the head, which rested on a plate to contain the blood, was a sheet of paper. He took it, and his Stormlight illuminated some two dozen names written in the warrior's script of his homeland. Some had a note beside them with instructions on how they were to be killed.

Glories within, Szeth thought. "These are some of the most powerful people in the world! Six highprinces? A Selay gerontarch? The *king* of Jah Keved?"

"It is time you stopped wasting your talent," the figure said, walking to the far wall, resting his hand upon it.

"This will cause chaos," Szeth whispered. "Infighting. War. Confusion and pain such as the world has rarely known."

The chained gemstone on the man's palm flashed. The wall vanished, turned to smoke. A Soulcaster.

The dark figure glanced at Szeth. "Indeed. Our master directs that you are to use tactics similar to those you employed so well in Alethkar years ago. When you are done, you will receive further instructions."

He then exited through the opening, leaving Szeth horrified. This was his nightmare. To be in the hands of those who understood his capabilities and who had the ambition to use them properly. He stood for a time, silent, long past when his Stormlight ran out.

Then, reverently, he folded the list. He was surprised that his hands were so steady. He should be trembling.

For soon the world itself would shake.

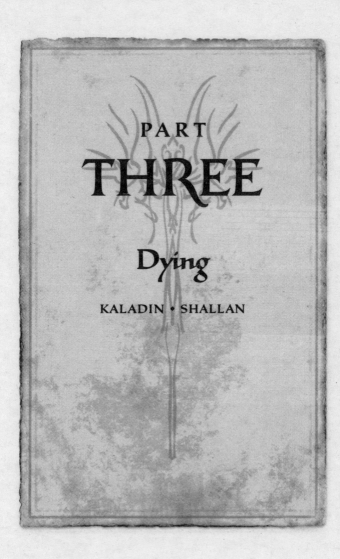

PART
THREE

Dying

KALADIN • SHALLAN

View of the City of Bells, from the Port to the Conclave, connected by the Kalihsu

Kharanuth

29

ERRORGANCE

"The ones of ash and fire, who killed like a swarm, relentless before the Heralds."

—Noted in Masly, page 337. Corroborated by Coldwin and Hasavah.

I t sounds like you're getting into Jasnah's good graces quickly, the spanreed wrote out. *How long before you can make the switch?*

Shallan grimaced, turning the gemstone on the reed. *I don't know,* she wrote back. *Jasnah keeps a close watch on the Soulcaster, as you'd expect. She wears it all day. At night, she locks it away in her safe and wears the key around her neck.*

She turned the gemstone, then waited for a reply. She was in her chamber, a small, stone-carved room inside Jasnah's quarters. Her accommodations were austere: A small bed, a nightstand, and the writing table were her only furniture. Her clothing remained in the trunk she had brought. No rug adorned the floor, and there were no windows, as the rooms were in the Kharbranthian Conclave, which was underground.

That does make it troubling, the reed wrote. Eylita—Nan Balat's betrothed—was the one doing the writing, but all three of Shallan's surviving brothers would be in the room back in Jah Keved, contributing to the conversation.

I'm guessing she takes it off while bathing, Shallan wrote. *Once she trusts me more, she may begin using me as a bathing attendant. That may present an opportunity.*

That is a good plan, the spanreed wrote. *Nan Balat wants me to point out that we are very sorry to make you do this. It must be difficult for you to be away so long.*

Difficult? Shallan picked up the spanreed and hesitated.

Yes, it was difficult. Difficult not to fall in love with the freedom, difficult not to get too absorbed in her studies. It had been only two months since she'd convinced Jasnah to take her as a ward, but already she felt half as timid and twice as confident.

The most difficult thing of all was knowing that it would soon end. Coming to study in Kharbranth was, without doubt, the most wonderful thing that had ever happened to her.

I will manage, she wrote. *You are the ones living the difficult life, maintaining our family's interests at home. How are you doing?*

It took time for them to reply. *Poorly,* Eylita finally sent. *Your father's debts are coming due, and Wikim can barely keep the creditors distracted. The highprince ails, and everyone wants to know where our house stands on the question of succession. The last of the quarries is running out. If it becomes known that we no longer have resources, it will go badly for us.*

Shallan grimaced. *How long do I have?*

A few more months, at best, Nan Balat sent back via his betrothed. *It depends on how long the highprince lasts and whether or not anyone realizes why Asha Jushu is selling our possessions.* Jushu was the youngest of the brothers, just older than Shallan. His old gambling habit was actually coming in handy. For years, he'd been stealing things from their father and selling them to cover his losses. He pretended he was still doing that, but he brought the money back to help. He was a good man, despite his habit. And, all things considered, he really couldn't be blamed for much of what he'd done. None of them could.

Wikim thinks that he can keep everyone at bay for a while

longer. But we are getting desperate. The sooner you return with the Soulcaster, the better.

Shallan hesitated, then wrote, *Are we certain this is the best way? Perhaps we should simply ask Jasnah for help.*

You think she would respond to that? they wrote back. *She would help an unknown and disliked Veden house? She would keep our secrets?*

Probably not. Though Shallan was increasingly certain that Jasnah's reputation was exaggerated, the woman did have a ruthless side to her. She would not leave her important studies to go help Shallan's family.

She reached for the reed to reply, but it started scribbling again. *Shallan,* it said. *This is Nan Balat; I have sent the others away. It is only Eylita and me writing you now. There is something you need to know. Luesh is dead.*

Shallan blinked in surprise. Luesh, her father's steward, had been the one who had known how to use the Soulcaster. He was one of the few people she and her brothers had determined they could trust.

What happened? she wrote after switching to a new sheet of paper.

He died in his sleep, and there's no reason to suspect he was killed. But Shallan, a few weeks after his passing, some men visited here claiming to be friends of our father. In private with me, they implied they knew of Father's Soulcaster and suggested strongly *that I was to return it to them.*

Shallan frowned. She still carried her father's broken Soulcaster in the safepouch of her sleeve. *Return it?* she wrote.

We never did figure out where Father got it, Nan Balat sent. *Shallan, he was involved in something. Those maps, the things Luesh said, and now this. We continue to pretend that Father is alive, and occasionally he gets letters from other lighteyes that speak of vague "plans." I think he was going to make a play to become highprince. And he was supported by some very powerful forces.*

These men who came, they were dangerous, Shallan. The type of men you do not cross. And they want their Soulcaster back. Whoever they are, I suspect they gave it to Father so he could create wealth and make a bid for the succession. They know he's dead.

I believe that if we don't return a working Soulcaster to them, we could all be in serious danger. You need to bring Jasnah's fabrial to us. We'll quickly use it to create new quarries of valuable stone, and then we can give it up to these men. Shallan, you must succeed. I was hesitant about this plan when you suggested it, but other avenues are quickly vanishing.

Shallan felt a chill. She read over the paragraphs a few times, then wrote, *If Luesh is dead, then we don't know how to use the Soulcaster. That is problematic.*

I know, Nan Balat sent. *See if you can figure that out. This is dangerous, Shallan. I know it is. I'm sorry.*

She took a deep breath. *It must be done,* she wrote.

Here, Nan Balat sent. *I wanted to show you something. Have you ever seen this symbol?* The sketch that followed was crude. Eylita wasn't much of an artist. Fortunately, it was a simple picture—three diamond shapes in a curious pattern.

I've never seen it, Shallan wrote. *Why?*

Luesh wore a pendant with this symbol on it, Nan Balat sent. *We found it on his body. And one of the men who came searching for the Soulcaster had the same pattern tattooed on his hand, just below his thumb.*

Curious, Shallan wrote. *So Luesh . . .*

Yes, Nan Balat sent. *Despite what he said, I think he must have been the one who brought the Soulcaster to Father. Luesh was involved in this, perhaps as liaison between Father and the people backing him. I tried to suggest that they could back me instead, but the men just laughed. They did not stay long or give a specific time by which the Soulcaster must be returned. I doubt they'd be satisfied to receive a broken one.*

Shallan pursed her lips. *Balat, have you thought that we might be risking a war? If it becomes known that we've stolen an Alethi Soulcaster . . .*

No, there wouldn't be a war, Nan Balat wrote back. *King Hanavanar would just turn us over to the Alethi. They'd execute us for the theft.*

Wonderfully comforting, Balat, she wrote. *Thank you so much.*

You're welcome. We're going to have to hope that Jasnah doesn't realize that you took the Soulcaster. It seems likely she'll assume that hers broke for some reason.

Shallan sighed. *Perhaps,* she wrote.

Take care, Nan Balat sent her.

You too.

And that was it. She set the spanreed aside, then read over the entire conversation, memorizing it. Then she crumpled up the sheets and walked into the sitting room of Jasnah's quarters. She wasn't there—Jasnah rarely broke from her studies—so Shallan burned the conversation in the hearth.

She stood for a long moment, watching the fire. She was worried. Nan Balat was capable, but they all bore scars from the lives they'd led. Eylita was the only scribe they could trust, and she . . . well, she was incredibly nice but not very clever.

With a sigh, Shallan left the room to return to her studies. Not only would they help get her mind off her troubles, but Jasnah would grow testy if she dallied too long.

❖

Five hours later, Shallan wondered why it was she'd been so eager.

She *did* enjoy her chances at scholarship. But recently, Jasnah had set her to study the history of the Alethi monarchy. It wasn't the most interesting subject around. Her boredom was compounded by her being forced to read a number of books that expressed opinions she found ridiculous.

She sat in Jasnah's alcove at the Veil. The enormous wall of lights, alcoves, and mysterious researchers no longer awed her. The place was becoming comfortable and familiar. She was alone at the moment.

Shallan rubbed her eyes with her freehand, then slid her book closed. "I," she muttered, "am really coming to hate the Alethi monarchy."

"Is that so?" a calm voice said from behind. Jasnah walked

past, wearing a sleek violet dress, followed by a parshman porter with a stack of books. "I'll try not to take it personally."

Shallan winced, then blushed furiously. "I didn't mean *individually*, Brightness Jasnah. I meant categorically."

Jasnah lithely took her seat in the alcove. She raised an eyebrow at Shallan, then gestured for the parshman to set down his burden.

Shallan still found Jasnah an enigma. At times, she seemed a stern scholar annoyed by Shallan's interruptions. At other times, there seemed to be a hint of wry humor hiding behind the stern facade. Either way, Shallan was finding that she felt remarkably comfortable around the woman. Jasnah encouraged her to speak her mind, something Shallan had taken to gladly.

"I assume from your outburst that this topic is wearing on you," Jasnah said, sorting through her volumes as the parshman withdrew. "You expressed interest in being a scholar. Well, you must learn that this *is* scholarship."

"Reading argument after argument from people who refuse to see any other point of view?"

"They're confident."

"I'm not an expert on confidence, Brightness," Shallan said, holding up a book and inspecting it critically. "But I'd like to think that I could recognize it if it were before me. I don't think that's the right word for books like this one from Mederia. They feel more arrogant than confident to me." She sighed, setting the book aside. "To be honest, 'arrogant' doesn't feel like quite the right word. It's not specific enough."

"And what *would* be the right word, then?"

"I don't know. 'Errorgant,' perhaps."

Jasnah raised a skeptical eyebrow.

"It means to be twice as certain as someone who is merely arrogant," Shallan said, "while possessing only one-tenth the requisite facts."

Her words drew a hint of a smile from Jasnah. "What you are reacting against is known as the Assuredness Movement, Shallan. This *errorgance* is a literary device. The scholars are intentionally overstating their case."

"The Assuredness Movement?" Shallan asked, holding up one of her books. "I guess I could get behind that."

"Oh?"

"Yes. Much easier to stab it in the back from that position."

That got only an eyebrow raise. So, more seriously, Shallan continued. "I suppose I can understand the device, Brightness, but these books you've given me on King Gavilar's death are more and more irrational in defending their points. What began as a rhetorical conceit seems to have descended into name-calling and squabbling."

"They are trying to provoke discussion. Would you rather that the scholars hide from the truth, like so many? You would have men prefer ignorance?"

"When reading these books, scholarship and ignorance feel much alike to me," Shallan said. "Ignorance may reside in a man hiding from intelligence, but scholarship can seem ignorance hidden behind intelligence."

"And what of intelligence without ignorance? Finding truth while not dismissing the possibility of being wrong?"

"A mythological treasure, Brightness, much like the Dawnshards or the Honorblades. Certainly worth seeking, but only with great caution."

"Caution?" Jasnah said, frowning.

"It would make you famous, but actually *finding* it would destroy us all. Proof that one can be both intelligent *and* accept the intelligence of those who disagree with you? Why, I should think it would undermine the scholarly world in its entirety."

Jasnah sniffed. "You go too far, child. If you took half the energy you devote to being witty and channeled it into your work, I daresay you could be one of the greatest scholars of our age."

"I'm sorry, Brightness," Shallan said. "I . . . well, I'm confused. Considering the gaps in my education, I assumed you would have me studying things deeper in the past than a few years ago."

Jasnah opened one of her books. "I have found that youths like you have a relative lack of appreciation for the distant past. Therefore, I selected an area of study that is both more recent and sensational, to ease you into true scholarship. Is the murder of a king not of interest to you?"

"Yes, Brightness," Shallan said. "We children love things that are shiny and loud."

"You have quite the mouth on you at times."

"At times? You mean it's not there at others? I'll have to . . ." Shallan trailed off, then bit her lip, realizing she'd gone too far. "Sorry."

"Never apologize for being clever, Shallan. It sets a bad precedent. However, one must apply one's wit with care. You often seem to say the first passably clever thing that enters your mind."

"I know," Shallan said. "It's long been a foible of mine, Brightness. One my nurses and tutors tried very hard to discourage."

"Likely through strict punishments."

"Yes. Making me sit in the corner holding books over my head was the preferred method."

"Which, in turn," Jasnah said with a sigh, "only trained you to make your quips *more* quickly, for you knew you had to get them out before you could reconsider and suppress them."

Shallan cocked her head.

"The punishments were incompetent," Jasnah said. "Used upon one such as yourself, they were actually encouragement. A game. How much would you have to say to earn a punishment? Could you say something so clever that your tutors missed the joke? Sitting in the corner just gave you more time to compose retorts."

"But it's unseemly for a young woman to speak as I so often do."

"The only 'unseemly' thing is to not channel your intelligence usefully. Consider. You have trained yourself to do something very similar to what annoys you in the scholars: cleverness without thought behind it—intelligence, one might say, without a foundation of proper consideration." Jasnah turned a page. "Errorgant, wouldn't you say?"

Shallan blushed.

"I prefer my wards to be clever," Jasnah said. "It gives me more to work with. I should bring you to court with me. I suspect that Wit, at least, would find you amusing—if only because your apparent natural timidity and your clever tongue make such an intriguing combination."

"Yes, Brightness."

"Please, just remember that a woman's mind is her most precious weapon. It must not be employed clumsily or prematurely. Much like the aforementioned knife to the back, a clever gibe is most effective when it is unanticipated."

"I'm sorry, Brightness."

"It wasn't an admonition," Jasnah said, turning a page. "Simply an observation. I make them on occasion: Those books are musty. The sky is blue today. My ward is a smart-lipped reprobate."

Shallan smiled.

"Now, tell me what you've discovered."

Shallan grimaced. "Not much, Brightness. Or should I say too much? Each writer has her own theories on why the Parshendi killed your father. Some claim he must have insulted them at the feast that night. Others say that the entire treaty was a ruse, intended to get the Parshendi close to him. But that makes little sense, as they had much better opportunities earlier."

"And the Assassin in White?" Jasnah asked.

"A true anomaly," Shallan said. "The undertexts are filled with commentary about him. Why would the Parshendi hire an outside assassin? Did they fear they could not accomplish the job themselves? Or perhaps they didn't hire him, and were framed. Many think that is unlikely, considering that the Parshendi took credit for the murder."

"And your thoughts?"

"I feel inadequate to draw conclusions, Brightness."

"What is the point of research if not to draw conclusions?"

"My tutors told me that supposition was only for the very experienced," Shallan explained.

Jasnah sniffed. "Your tutors were idiots. Youthful immaturity is one of the cosmere's great catalysts for change,

Shallan. Do you realize that the Sunmaker was only seventeen when he began his conquest? Gavarah hadn't reached her twentieth Weeping when she proposed the theory of the three realms."

"But for every Sunmaker or Gavarah, are there not a hundred Gregorhs?" He had been a youthful king notorious for beginning a pointless war with kingdoms that had been his father's allies.

"There was only *one* Gregorh," Jasnah said with a grimace, "thankfully. Your point is a valid one. Hence the purpose of education. To be young is about action. To be a scholar is about *informed* action."

"Or about sitting in an alcove reading about a six-year-old murder."

"I would not have you studying this if there were no point to it," Jasnah said, opening up another of her own books. "Too many scholars think of research as purely a cerebral pursuit. If we *do* nothing with the knowledge we gain, then we have wasted our study. Books can store information better than we can—what we do that books cannot is *interpret*. So if one is not going to draw conclusions, then one might as well just leave the information in the texts."

Shallan sat back, thoughtful. Presented that way, it somehow made her want to dig back into the studies. What was it that Jasnah wanted her to do with the information? Once again, she felt a stab of guilt. Jasnah was taking great pains to instruct her in scholarship, and she was going to reward the woman by stealing her most valuable possession and leaving a broken replacement. It made Shallan feel sick.

She had expected study beneath Jasnah to involve meaningless memorization and busywork, accompanied by chastisement for not being smart enough. That was how her tutors had approached her instruction. Jasnah was different. She gave Shallan a topic and the freedom to pursue it as she wished. Jasnah offered encouragement and speculation, but nearly all of their conversations turned to topics like the true nature of scholarship, the purpose of studying, the beauty of knowledge and its application.

Jasnah Kholin truly loved learning, and she wanted others to as well. Behind the stern gaze, intense eyes, and rarely smiling lips, Jasnah Kholin truly believed in what she was doing. Whatever that was.

Shallan raised one of her books, but covertly eyed the spines of Jasnah's latest stack of tomes. More histories about the Heraldic Epochs. Mythologies, commentaries, books by scholars known to be wild speculators. Jasnah's current volume was called *Shadows Remembered*. Shallan memorized the title. She would try to find a copy and look through it.

What was Jasnah pursuing? What secrets was she hoping to pry from these volumes, most of them centuries-old copies of copies? Though Shallan had discovered some secrets regarding the Soulcaster, the nature of Jasnah's quest—the reason the princess had come to Kharbranth—remained elusive. Maddeningly, yet tantalizingly, so. Jasnah liked to speak of the great women of the past, ones who had not just recorded history, but shaped it. Whatever it was she studied, she felt that it was important. World-changing.

You mustn't be drawn in, Shallan told herself, settling back with book and notes. *Your goal is not to change the world. Your goal is to protect your brothers and your house.*

Still, she needed to make a good show of her wardship. And that gave her a reason to immerse herself for two hours until footsteps in the hallway interrupted. Likely the servants bringing the midday meal. Jasnah and Shallan often ate on their balcony.

Shallan's stomach grumbled as she smelled the food, and she gleefully set aside her book. She usually sketched at lunch, an activity that Jasnah—despite her dislike of the visual arts—encouraged. She said that highborn men often thought drawing and painting to be "enticing" in a woman, and so Shallan should maintain her skills, if only for the purpose of attracting suitors.

Shallan didn't know whether to find that insulting or not. And what did it say about Jasnah's own intentions for marriage that she herself never bothered with the more becoming feminine arts like music or drawing?

"Your Majesty," Jasnah said, rising smoothly.

Shallan started and looked hastily over her shoulder. The elderly king of Kharbranth was standing in the doorway, wearing magnificent orange and white robes with detailed embroidery. Shallan scrambled to her feet.

"Brightness Jasnah," the king said. "Am I interrupting?"

"Your company is never an interruption, Your Majesty," Jasnah said. She had to be as surprised as Shallan was, yet didn't display a moment of discomfort or anxiety. "We were soon to take lunch, anyway."

"I know, Brightness," Taravangian said. "I hope you don't mind if I join you." A group of servants began bringing in food and a table.

"Not at all," Jasnah said.

The servants hurried to set things up, putting two different tablecloths on the round table to separate the genders during dining. They secured the half-moons of cloth—red for the king, blue for the women—with weights at the center. Covered plates filled with food followed: a clear, cold stew with sweet vegetables for the women, a spicy-smelling broth for the king. Kharbranthians preferred soups for their lunches.

Shallan was surprised to see them set a place for her. Her father had never eaten at the same table as his children—even she, his favorite, had been relegated to her own table. Once Jasnah sat, Shallan did likewise. Her stomach growled again, and the king waved for them to begin. His motions seemed ungainly compared with Jasnah's elegance.

Shallan was soon eating contentedly—with grace, as a woman should, safehand in her lap, using her freehand and a skewer to spear chunks of vegetable or fruit. The king slurped, but he wasn't as noisy as many men. Why had he deigned to visit? Wouldn't a formal dinner invitation have been more proper? Of course, she'd learned that Taravangian wasn't known for his mastery of protocol. He was a popular king, beloved by the darkeyes as a builder of hospitals. However, the lighteyes considered him less than bright.

He was not an idiot. In lighteyed politics, unfortunately, being only average was a disadvantage. As they ate, the silence drew out, becoming awkward. Several times, the king looked as if he wanted to say something, but then turned back to his soup. He seemed intimidated by Jasnah.

"And how is your granddaughter, Your Majesty?" Jasnah eventually asked. "She is recovering well?"

"Quite well, thank you," Taravangian said, as if relieved to begin conversing. "Though she now avoids the narrower corridors of the Conclave. I do want to thank you for your aid."

"It is always fulfilling to be of service, Your Majesty."

"If you will forgive my saying so, the ardents do not think much of your service," Taravangian said. "I realize it is likely a sensitive topic. Perhaps I shouldn't mention it, but—"

"No, feel free," Jasnah said, eating a small green lurnip from the end of her skewer. "I am not ashamed of my choices."

"Then you'll forgive an old man's curiosity?"

"I always forgive curiosity, Your Majesty," Jasnah said. "It strikes me as one of the most genuine of emotions."

"Then where did you find it?" Taravangian asked, nodding toward the Soulcaster, which Jasnah wore covered by a black glove. "How did you keep it from the devotaries?"

"One might find those questions dangerous, Your Majesty."

"I've already acquired some new enemies by welcoming you."

"You will be forgiven," Jasnah said. "Depending on the devotary you have chosen."

"Forgiven? Me?" The elderly man seemed to find that amusing, and for a moment, Shallan thought she saw deep regret in his expression. "Unlikely. But that is something else entirely. Please. I stand by my questions."

"And I stand by my evasiveness, Your Majesty. I'm sorry. I do forgive your curiosity, but I cannot reward it. These secrets are mine."

"Of course, of course." The king sat back, looking embarrassed. "Now you probably assume I brought this meal simply to ambush you about the fabrial."

"You had another purpose, then?"

"Well, you see, I've heard the most wonderful things about

your ward's artistic skill. I thought that maybe . . ." He smiled at Shallan.

"Of course, Your Majesty," Shallan said. "I'd be happy to draw your likeness."

He beamed as she stood, leaving her meal half eaten and gathering her things. She glanced at Jasnah, but the older woman's face was unreadable.

"Would you prefer a simple portrait against a white background?" Shallan asked. "Or would you prefer a broader perspective, including surroundings?"

"Perhaps," Jasnah said pointedly, "you should wait until the meal is finished, Shallan?"

Shallan blushed, feeling a fool for her enthusiasm. "Of course."

"No, no," the king said. "I'm quite finished. A wider sketch would be perfect, child. How would you like me to sit?" He slid his chair back, posing and smiling in a grandfatherly way.

She blinked, fixing the image in her mind. "That is perfect, Your Majesty. You can return to your meal."

"Don't you need me to sit still? I've posed for portraits before."

"It's all right," Shallan assured him, sitting down.

"Very well," he said, pulling back to the table. "I do apologize for making you use me, of all people, as a subject for your art. This face of mine isn't the most impressive one you've depicted, I'm sure."

"Nonsense," Shallan said. "A face like yours is just what an artist needs."

"It is?"

"Yes, the—" She cut herself off. She'd been about to quip, *Yes, the skin is enough like parchment to make an ideal canvas.* ". . . that handsome nose of yours, and wise furrowed brow. It will be quite striking in the black charcoal."

"Oh, well then. Proceed. Though I still can't see how you'll work without me holding a pose."

"Brightness Shallan has some unique talents," Jasnah said. Shallan began her sketch.

"I suppose that she must!" the king said. "I've seen the drawing she did for Varas."

"Varas?" Jasnah asked.

"The Palanaeum's assistant chief of collections," the king said. "A distant cousin of mine. He says the staff is quite taken with your young ward. How did you find her?"

"Unexpectedly," Jasnah said, "and in need of an education."

The king cocked his head.

"The artistic skill, I cannot claim," Jasnah said. "It was a preexisting condition."

"Ah, a blessing of the Almighty."

"You might say that."

"But you would not, I assume?" Taravangian chuckled awkwardly.

Shallan drew quickly, establishing the shape of his head. He shuffled uncomfortably. "Is it hard for you, Jasnah? Painful, I mean?"

"Atheism is not a disease, Your Majesty," Jasnah said dryly. "It's not as if I've caught a foot rash."

"Of course not, of course not. But . . . er, isn't it difficult, having nothing in which to believe?"

Shallan leaned forward, still sketching, but keeping her attention on the conversation. Shallan had assumed that training under a heretic would be a little more exciting. She and Kabsal—the witty ardent whom she'd met on her first day in Kharbranth—had chatted several times now about Jasnah's faith. However, around Jasnah herself, the topic almost never came up. When it did, Jasnah usually changed it.

Today, however, she did not. Perhaps she sensed the sincerity in the king's question. "I wouldn't say that I have nothing to believe in, Your Majesty. Actually, I have much to believe in. My brother and my uncle, my own abilities. The things I was taught by my parents."

"But, what is right and wrong, you've . . . Well, you've discarded that."

"Just because I do not accept the teachings of the devotaries does not mean I've discarded a belief in right and wrong."

"But the *Almighty* determines what is right!"

"Must someone, some unseen *thing*, declare what is right for it to *be* right? I believe that my own morality—which answers only to my heart—is more sure and true than the morality of those who do right only because they fear retribution."

"But that is the soul of law," the king said, sounding confused. "If there is no punishment, there can be only chaos."

"If there were no law, some men would do as they wish, yes," Jasnah said. "But isn't it remarkable that, given the chance for personal gain at the cost of others, so many people choose what is right?"

"Because they fear the Almighty."

"No," Jasnah said. "I think something innate in us understands that seeking the good of society is usually best for the individual as well. Humankind is noble, when we give it the chance to be. That nobility is something that exists independent of any god's decree."

"I just don't see how *anything* could be outside God's decrees." The king shook his head, bemused. "Brightness Jasnah, I don't mean to argue, but isn't the very definition of the Almighty that all things exist because of him?"

"If you add one and one, that makes two, does it not?"

"Well, yes."

"No god needs declare it so for it to be true," Jasnah said. "So, could we not say that mathematics exists outside the Almighty, independent of him?"

"Perhaps."

"Well," Jasnah said, "I simply claim that morality and human will are independent of him too."

"If you say that," the king said, chuckling, "then you've removed all purpose for the Almighty's existence!"

"Indeed."

The balcony fell silent. Jasnah's sphere lamps cast a cool, even white light across them. For an uncomfortable moment, the only sound was the scratching of Shallan's charcoal on her drawing pad. She worked with quick, scraping motions, disturbed by the things that Jasnah had said. They made her feel hollow inside. That was partly because the king, for all his affability, was not good at arguing. He was a dear man, but no match for Jasnah in a conversation.

"Well," Taravangian said, "I must say that you make your points quite effectively. I don't accept them, though."

"My intention is not to convert, Your Majesty," Jasnah said. "I am content keeping my beliefs to myself, something most of my colleagues in the devotaries have difficulty doing. Shallan, have you finished yet?"

"Quite nearly, Brightness."

"But it's been barely a few minutes!" the king said.

"She has remarkable skill, Your Majesty," Jasnah said. "As I believe I mentioned."

Shallan sat back, inspecting her piece. She'd been so focused on the conversation, she'd just let her hands do the drawing, trusting in her instincts. The sketch depicted the king, sitting in his chair with a wise expression, the turretlike balcony walls behind him. The doorway into the balcony was to his right. Yes, it was a good likeness. Not her best work, but—

Shallan froze, her breath catching, her heart lurching in her chest. She had drawn *something* standing in the doorway behind the king. Two tall and willowy creatures with cloaks that split down the front and hung at the sides too stiffly, as if they were made of glass. Above the stiff, high collars, where the creatures' heads should be, each had a large, floating symbol of twisted design full of impossible angles and geometries.

Shallan sat, stunned. Why had she drawn those things? What had driven her to—

She snapped her head up. The hallway was empty. The creatures hadn't been part of the Memory she'd taken. Her hands had simply drawn them of their accord.

"Shallan?" Jasnah said.

By reflex, Shallan dropped her charcoal and grabbed the sheet in her freehand, crumpling it. "I'm sorry, Brightness. I paid too much attention to the conversation. I let myself grow sloppy."

"Well, certainly we can at least *see* it, child," the king said, standing.

Shallan tightened her grip. "Please, no!"

"She has an artist's temperament at times, Your Majesty." Jasnah sighed. "There will be no getting it out of her."

"I'll do you another, Your Majesty," Shallan said. "I'm *so* sorry."

He rubbed his wispy beard. "Yes, well, it was going to be a gift for my granddaughter. . . ."

"By the end of the day," Shallan promised.

"That would be wonderful. You're certain you don't need me to pose?"

"No, no, that won't be necessary, Your Majesty," Shallan said. Her pulse was still racing and she couldn't shake the image of those two distorted figures from her mind, so she took another Memory of the king. She could use that to create a more suitable picture.

"Well then," the king said. "I suppose I should be going. I wish to visit one of the hospitals and the sick. You can send the drawing to my rooms, but take your time. Really, it is quite all right."

Shallan curtsied, crushed paper still held to her breast. The king withdrew with his attendants, several parshmen entering to remove the table.

"I've never known you to make a mistake in drawing," Jasnah said, sitting back down at the desk. "At least not one so horrible that you destroyed the paper."

Shallan blushed.

"Even the master of an art may err, I suppose. Go ahead and take the next hour to do His Majesty a proper portrait."

Shallan looked down at the ruined sketch. The creatures were simply her fancy, the product of letting her mind wander. That was all. Just imagination. Perhaps there was something in her subconscious that she'd needed to express. But what could the figures mean, then?

"I noticed that at one point when you were speaking to the king, you hesitated," Jasnah said. "What didn't you say?"

"Something inappropriate."

"But clever?"

"Cleverness never seems quite so impressive when regarded outside the moment, Brightness. It was just a silly thought."

"And you replaced it with an empty compliment. I think you misunderstood what I was trying to explain, child. I do not wish for you to remain silent. It is good to be clever."

"But if I'd spoken," Shallan said, "I'd have insulted the king, perhaps confused him as well, which would have caused him embarrassment. I am certain he knows what people say about his slowness of thought."

Jasnah sniffed. "Idle words. From foolish people. But perhaps it was wise not to speak, though keep in mind that *channeling* your capacities and *stifling* them are two separate things. I'd much prefer you to think of something both clever and appropriate."

"Yes, Brightness."

"Besides," Jasnah said, "I believe you might have made Taravangian laugh. He seems haunted by something lately."

"You don't find him dull, then?" Shallan asked, curious. She herself didn't think the king dull or a fool, but she'd thought someone as intelligent and learned as Jasnah might not have patience for a man like him.

"Taravangian is a wonderful man," Jasnah said, "and worth a hundred self-proclaimed experts on courtly ways. He reminds me of my uncle Dalinar. Earnest, sincere, concerned."

"The lighteyes here say he's weak," Shallan said. "Because he panders to so many other monarchs, because he fears war, because he doesn't have a Shardblade."

Jasnah didn't reply, though she looked disturbed.

"Brightness?" Shallan prodded, walking to her own seat and arranging her charcoals.

"In ancient days," Jasnah said, "a man who brought peace to his kingdom was considered to be of great worth. Now that same man would be derided as a coward." She shook her head. "It has been centuries coming, this change. It should terrify us. We could do with more men like Taravangian, and I shall require you to never call him dull again, not even in passing."

"Yes, Brightness," Shallan said, bowing her head. "Did you really believe the things you said? About the Almighty?"

Jasnah was quiet for a moment. "I do. Though perhaps I overstated my conviction."

"The Assuredness Movement of rhetorical theory?"

"Yes," Jasnah said. "I suppose that it was. I must be careful not to put my back toward you as I read today."

Shallan smiled.

"A true scholar must not close her mind on any topic," Jasnah said, "no matter how certain she may feel. Just because I have not yet found a convincing reason to join one of the devotaries does not mean I never will. Though each time I have a discussion like the one today, my convictions grow firmer."

Shallan bit her lip. Jasnah noticed the expression. "You will need to learn to control that, Shallan. It makes your feelings obvious."

"Yes, Brightness."

"Well, out with it."

"Just that your conversation with the king was not entirely fair."

"Oh?"

"Because of his, well, you know. His limited capacity. He did quite remarkably, but didn't make the arguments that someone more versed in Vorin theology might have."

"And what arguments might such a one have made?"

"Well, I'm not very well trained in that area myself. But I do think that you ignored, or at least minimized, one vital part of the discussion."

"Which is?"

Shallan tapped at her breast. "Our hearts, Brightness. I believe because I feel something, a closeness to the Almighty, a peace that comes when I live my faith."

"The mind is capable of projecting expected emotional responses."

"But didn't you yourself argue that the way we act—the way we feel about right and wrong—was a defining attribute of our humanity? You used our innate morality to prove your point. So how can you discard my feelings?"

"Discard them? No. Regard them with skepticism? Perhaps. Your feelings, Shallan—however powerful—are your own. Not mine. And what I feel is that spending my life trying to earn the favor of an unseen, unknown, and unknowable being who watches me from the sky is an exercise in sheer futility." She pointed at Shallan with her pen. "But your rhetorical method is improving. We'll make a scholar of you yet."

Shallan smiled, feeling a surge of pleasure. Praise from Jasnah was more precious than an emerald broam.

But . . . I'm not going to be a scholar. I'm going to steal the Soulcaster and leave.

She didn't like to think about that. That was something else she'd have to get over; she tended to avoid thinking about things that made her uncomfortable.

"Now hurry and be about the king's sketch," Jasnah said, lifting a book. "You still have a great deal of real work to do once you are done drawing."

"Yes, Brightness," Shallan said.

For once, however, she found sketching difficult, her mind too troubled to focus.

"They were suddenly dangerous. Like a calm day that became a tempest."

—This fragment is the origin of a Thaylen proverb that was eventually reworked into a more common derivation. I believe it may reference the Voidbringers. See Ixsix's *Emperor,* fourth chapter.

Kaladin walked from the cavernous barrack into the pure light of first morning. Bits of quartz in the ground sparkled before him, catching the light, as if the ground were sparking and burning, ready to burst from within.

A group of twenty-nine men followed him. Slaves. Thieves. Deserters. Foreigners. Even a few men whose only sin had been poverty. Those had joined the bridge crews out of desperation. The pay was good when compared with nothing, and they were promised that if they survived a hundred bridge runs, they would be promoted. Assignment to a watch post—which, in the mind of a poor man, sounded like a life of luxury. Being paid to stand and look at things all day? What kind of insanity was that? It was like being rich, almost.

They didn't understand. Nobody survived a hundred bridge runs. Kaladin had been on two dozen, and he was already one of the most experienced living bridgemen.

Bridge Four followed him. The last of the holdouts—a thin man named Bisig—had given in yesterday. Kaladin preferred to think that the laughter, the food, and the humanity had finally gotten to him. But it had probably been a few glares or under-the-breath threats from Rock and Teft.

Kaladin turned a blind eye to those. He'd eventually need the men's loyalty, but for now, he'd settle for obedience.

He guided them through the morning exercises he'd learned his very first day in the military. Stretches followed by jumping motions. Carpenters in brown work overalls and tan or green caps passed on their way to the lumberyard, shaking their heads in amusement. Soldiers on the short ridge above, where the camp proper began, looked down and laughed. Gaz watched from beside a nearby barrack, arms folded, single eye dissatisfied.

Kaladin wiped his brow. He met Gaz's eye for a long moment, then turned back to the men. There was still time to practice hauling the bridge before breakfast.

⁂

Gaz had never gotten used to having just one eye. *Could* a man get used to that? He'd rather have lost a hand or a leg than that eye. He couldn't stop feeling that *something* hid in that darkness he couldn't see, but others could. What lurked there? Spren that would drain his soul from his body? The way a rat could empty an entire wineskin by chewing the corner?

His companions called him lucky. "That blow could have taken your life." Well, at least then he wouldn't have had to live with that darkness. One of his eyes was always closed. Close the other, and the darkness swallowed him.

Gaz glanced left, and the darkness scuttled to the side. Lamaril stood leaning against a post, tall and slim. He was not a massive man, but he was not weak. He was all lines. Rectangular beard. Rectangular body. Sharp. Like a knife.

Lamaril waved Gaz over, so he reluctantly approached. Then he took a sphere out of his pouch and passed it over. A topaz mark. He hated losing it. He always hated losing money.

"You owe me twice as much as this," Lamaril noted, raising the sphere up to look through it as it sparkled in the sunlight.

"Well, that's all you'll get for now. Be glad you get anything."

"Be glad I've kept my mouth shut," Lamaril said lazily, leaning back against his post. It was one that marked the edge of the lumberyard.

Gaz gritted his teeth. He hated to pay, but what else could he do? *Storms take him. Raging storms take him!*

"You have a problem, it seems," Lamaril said.

At first, Gaz thought he meant the half payment. The lighteyed man nodded toward Bridge Four's barracks.

Gaz eyed the bridgemen, unsettled. The youthful bridge-leader barked an order, and the bridgemen raced the span of the lumberyard in a jog. He already had them running in time with one another. That one change meant so much. It sped them up, helped them think like a team.

Could this boy actually have military training, as he'd once claimed? Why would he be wasted as a bridgeman? Of course, there was that *shash* brand on his forehead. . . .

"I don't see a problem," Gaz said with a grunt. "They're fast. That's good."

"They're insubordinate."

"They follow orders."

"*His* orders, perhaps." Lamaril shook his head. "Bridgemen exist for one purpose, Gaz. To protect the lives of more valuable men."

"Really? And here I thought their purpose was to carry bridges."

Lamaril gave him a sharp look. He leaned forward. "Don't try me, Gaz. And don't forget your place. Would you like to join them?"

Gaz felt a spike of fear. Lamaril was a very lowly lighteyes, one of the landless. But he *was* Gaz's immediate superior, a liaison between bridge crews and the higher-ranked lighteyes who oversaw the lumberyard.

Gaz looked down at the ground. "I'm sorry, Brightlord."

"Highprince Sadeas holds an edge," Lamaril said, leaning

back against his post. "He maintains it by pushing us all. Hard. Each man in his place." He nodded toward the members of Bridge Four. "Speed is not a bad thing. Initiative is not a bad thing. But men with initiative like that boy's are not often happy in their position. The bridge crews function as they are, without need for modification. Change can be unsettling."

Gaz doubted that any of the bridgemen really understood their place in Sadeas's plans. If they knew why they were worked as pitilessly as they were—and why they were forbidden shields or armor—they likely would just cast themselves into the chasm. Bait. They were bait. Draw the Parshendi attention, let the savages think they were doing some good by felling a few bridges' worth of bridgemen every assault. So long as you took plenty of men, that didn't matter. Except to those who were slaughtered.

Stormfather, Gaz thought, *I hate myself for being a part of this.* But he'd hated himself for a long time now. It wasn't anything new to him. "I'll do something," he promised Lamaril. "A knife in the night. Poison in the food." That twisted his insides. The boy's bribes were small, but they were all that let him keep ahead of his payments to Lamaril.

"No!" Lamaril hissed. "You want it seen that he was really a threat? The real soldiers are already talking about him." Lamaril grimaced. "The last thing we need is a martyr inspiring rebellion among the bridgemen. I don't want any *hint* of it; nothing our highprince's enemies could take advantage of." Lamaril glanced at Kaladin, jogging past again with his men. "That one has to fall on the field, as he deserves. Make certain it happens. And get me the rest of the money you owe, or you'll soon find yourself carrying one of those bridges."

He swept away, forest-green cloak fluttering. In his time as a soldier, Gaz had learned to fear the minor lighteyes the most. They were galled by their closeness in rank to the darkeyes, yet those darkeyes were the only ones they had any authority over. That made them dangerous. Being around a man like Lamaril was like handling a hot coal with bare fingers. There was no way to avoid burning yourself. You just hoped to be quick enough to keep the burns to a minimum.

Bridge Four ran by. A month ago, Gaz wouldn't have believed this possible. A group of bridgemen, *practicing*? And all it seemed to have cost Kaladin was a few bribes of food and some empty promises that he would protect them.

That shouldn't have been enough. Life as a bridgeman was hopeless. Gaz *couldn't* join them. He just couldn't. Kaladin the lordling had to fall. But if Kaladin's spheres vanished, Gaz could just as easily end up as a bridgeman for failing to pay Lamaril. *Storming Damnation!* he thought. It was like trying to choose which claw of the chasmfiend would crush you.

Gaz continued to watch Kaladin's crew. And *still* that darkness waited for him. Like an itch that couldn't be scratched. Like a scream that couldn't be silenced. A tingling numbness that he could never be rid of.

It would probably follow him even into death.

❖

"Bridge up!" Kaladin bellowed, running with Bridge Four. They raised the bridge over their heads while still moving. It was harder to run this way, holding the bridge up, rather than resting it on the shoulders. He felt its enormous weight on his arms.

"Down!" he ordered.

Those at the front let go of the bridge and ran out to the sides. The others lowered the bridge in a quick motion. It hit the ground awkwardly, scraping the stone. They got into position, pretending to move it across a chasm. Kaladin helped at the side.

We'll need to practice on a real chasm, he thought as the men finished. *I wonder what kind of bribe it would take for Gaz to let me do that.*

The bridgemen, finished with their mock bridge run, looked toward Kaladin, exhausted but excited. He smiled at them. As a squadleader those months in Amaram's army, he'd learned that praise should be honest, but it should never be withheld.

"We need to work on that set-down," Kaladin said. "But overall, I'm impressed. Two weeks and you're already working together as well as some teams I trained for months. I'm pleased. And proud. Go get something to drink and take a break. We'll do one or two more runs before work detail."

It was stone-gathering duty again, but that was nothing to complain about. He'd convinced the men that lifting the stones would improve their strength, and had enlisted the few he trusted the most to help gather the knobweed, the means by which he continued to—just barely—keep the men supplied with extra food and build his stock of medical supplies.

Two weeks. An easy two weeks, as the lives of bridgemen went. Only two bridge runs, and on one they'd gotten to the plateau too late. The Parshendi had escaped with the gemheart before they'd even arrived. That was good for bridgemen.

The other assault hadn't been too bad, by bridgeman numbers. Two more dead: Amark and Koolf. Two more wounded: Narm and Peet. A fraction of what the other crews had lost, but still too many. Kaladin tried to keep his expression optimistic as he walked to the water barrel and took a ladle from one of the men, drinking it down.

Bridge Four would drown in its own wounded. They were only thirty strong, with five wounded who drew no pay and had to be fed out of the knobweed income. Counting those who'd died, they'd taken nearly thirty percent casualties in the weeks he'd begun trying to protect them. In Amaram's army, that rate of casualties would have been catastrophic.

Back then, Kaladin's life had been one of training and marching, punctuated by occasional frenzied bursts of battle. Here, the fighting was relentless. Every few days. That kind of thing could—*would*—wear an army down.

There has to be a better way, Kaladin thought, swishing the lukewarm water in his mouth, then pouring another ladle on his head. He couldn't continue to lose two men a week to death and wounds. But how could they survive when their own officers didn't care if they lived or died?

He barely kept himself from throwing the ladle into the barrel in frustration. Instead, he handed it to Skar and gave him an encouraging smile. A lie. But an important one.

Gaz watched from the shadow of one of the other bridgeman barracks. Syl's translucent figure—shaped now like

[589]

floating knobweed fluff—flitted around the bridge sergeant. Eventually, she made her way over to Kaladin, landing on his shoulder, taking her female form.

"He's planning something," she said.

"He hasn't interfered," Kaladin said. "He hasn't even tried to stop us from having the nightly stew."

"He was talking to that lighteyes."

"Lamaril?"

She nodded.

"Lamaril's his superior," Kaladin said as he walked into the shade of Bridge Four's barrack. He leaned against the wall, looking over at his men by the water barrel. They talked to one another now. Joked. Laughed. They went out drinking together in the evenings. Stormfather, but he never thought he'd be *glad* that the men under his command went drinking.

"I didn't like their expressions," Syl said, sitting down on Kaladin's shoulder. "Dark. Like thunderclouds. I didn't hear what they were saying. I noticed them too late. But I don't like it, particularly that Lamaril."

Kaladin nodded slowly.

"You don't trust him either?" Syl asked.

"He's a lighteyes." That was enough.

"So we—"

"So we do nothing," Kaladin said. "I can't respond unless they try something. And if I spend all of my energy worrying about what they *might* do, I won't be able to solve the problems we're facing right now."

What he didn't add was his real worry. If Gaz or Lamaril decided to have Kaladin killed, there was little he could to do to stop them. True, bridgemen were rarely executed for anything other than failing to run their bridge. But even in an "honest" force like Amaram's, there had been rumors of trumped-up charges and fake evidence. In Sadeas's undisciplined, barely regulated camp, nobody would blink if Kaladin—a *shash*-branded slave—were strung up on some nebulous charge. They could leave him for the highstorm, washing their hands of his death, claiming that the Stormfather had chosen his fate.

Kaladin stood up straight and walked toward the carpentry section of the lumberyard. The craftsmen and their apprentices were hard at work cutting lengths of wood for spear hafts, bridges, posts, or furniture.

The craftsmen nodded to Kaladin as he passed. They were familiar with him now, used to his odd requests, like pieces of lumber long enough for four men to hold and run with to practice keeping cadence with one another. He found a half-finished bridge. It had eventually grown out of that one plank that Kaladin had used.

Kaladin knelt down, inspecting the wood. A group of men worked with a large saw just to his right, slicing thin rounds off a log. Those would probably become chair seats.

He ran his fingers along the smooth hardwood. All mobile bridges were made of a kind of wood called makam. It had a deep brown color, the grain almost hidden, and was both strong and light. The craftsmen had sanded this length smooth, and it smelled of sawdust and musky sap.

"Kaladin?" Syl asked, walking through the air then stepping onto the wood. "You look distant."

"It's ironic how well they craft these bridges," he said. "This army's carpenters are far more professional than its soldiers."

"That makes sense," she said. "The craftsmen want to make bridges that last. The soldiers I listen to, they just want to get to the plateau, grab the gemheart, and get away. It's like a game to them."

"That's astute. You're getting better and better at observing us."

She grimaced. "I feel more like I'm remembering things I once knew."

"Soon you'll hardly be a spren at all. You'll be a little translucent philosopher. We'll have to send you off to a monastery to spend your time in deep, important thoughts."

"Yes," she said, "like how to best get the ardents there to accidentally drink a mixture that will turn their mouths blue." She smiled mischievously.

Kaladin smiled back, but kept running his finger across the wood. He still didn't understand why they wouldn't let bridgemen carry shields. Nobody would give him a straight answer on the question. "They use makam because it's strong enough for its weight to support a heavy cavalry charge," he said. "We should be able to use this. They deny us shields, but we already carry one on our shoulders."

"But how would they react if you try that?"

Kaladin stood. "I don't know, but I also don't have any other choice."

Trying this would be a risk. A huge risk. But he'd run out of nonrisky ideas days ago.

※

"We can hold it here," Kaladin said, pointing for Rock, Teft, Skar, and Moash. They stood beside a bridge turned up on its side, its underbelly exposed. The bottom was a complicated construction, with eight rows of three positions accommodating up to twenty-four men directly underneath, then sixteen sets of handles—eight on each side—for sixteen more men on the outside. Forty men, running shoulder to shoulder, if they had a full complement.

Each position underneath the bridge had an indentation for the bridgeman's head, two curved blocks of wood to rest on his shoulders, and two rods for handholds. The bridgemen wore shoulder pads, and those who were shorter wore extras to compensate. Gaz generally tried to assign new bridgemen to crews based on their height.

That didn't hold for Bridge Four, of course. Bridge Four just got the leftovers.

Kaladin pointed to several rods and struts. "We could grab here, then run straight forward, carrying the bridge on its side to our right at a slant. We put our taller men on the outside and our shorter men on the inside."

"What good would that do?" Rock asked, frowning.

Kaladin glanced at Gaz, who was watching from nearby. Uncomfortably close. Best not to speak of why he really wanted to carry the bridge on its side. Besides, he didn't want to get the men's hopes up until he knew if it would work.

"I just want to experiment," he said. "If we can shift posi-

tions occasionally, it might be easier. Work different muscles."
Syl frowned as she stood on the top of the bridge. She always
frowned when Kaladin obscured the truth.

"Gather the men," Kaladin said, waving to Rock, Teft,
Skar, and Moash. He'd named the four as his subsquad com-
manders, something that bridgemen didn't normally have.
But soldiers worked best in smaller groups of six or eight.

Soldiers, Kaladin thought. *Is that how I think of them?*

They didn't fight. But yes, they were soldiers. It was too
easy to underestimate men when you considered them to be
"just" bridgemen. Charging straight at enemy archers without
shields took courage. Even when you were compelled to do it.

He glanced to the side, noticing that Moash hadn't left
with the other three. The narrow-faced man had dark green
eyes and brown hair flecked with black.

"Something wrong, soldier?" Kaladin asked.

Moash blinked in surprise at the use of the word, but he and
the others had grown to expect all kinds of unorthodoxy from
Kaladin. "Why did you make me leader of a subsquad?"

"Because you resisted my leadership longer than almost
any of the others. And you were flat-out more vocal about it
than *any* of them."

"You made me a squad leader because I refused to obey
you?"

"I made you squad leader because you struck me as capable and intelligent. But beyond that, you weren't swayed too
easily. You're strong-willed. I can use that."

Moash scratched his chin, with its short beard. "All right
then. But unlike Teft and that Horneater, I don't think you're
a gift straight from the Almighty. I don't trust you."

"Then why obey me?"

Moash met his eyes, then shrugged. "Guess I'm curious."
He moved off to gather his squad.

⁂

What in the raging winds . . . Gaz thought, dumbfounded as
he watched Bridge Four charge past. What had possessed
them to try carrying the bridge to the *side*?

It required them to clump up in an odd way, forming three rows instead of five, awkwardly clutching the underside of the bridge and holding it off to their right. It was one of the strangest things he'd ever seen. They could barely all fit, and the handholds weren't made for carrying the bridge that way.

Gaz scratched his head as he watched them pass, then held out a hand, stopping Kaladin as he jogged by. The lordling let go of the bridge and hurried up to Gaz, wiping his brow as the others continued running. "Yes?"

"What is that?" Gaz said, pointing.

"Bridge crew. Carrying what I believe is . . . yes, it's a *bridge*."

"I didn't ask for lip," Gaz snarled. "I want an explanation."

"Carrying the bridge over our heads gets tiring," Kaladin said. He was a tall man, tall enough to tower over Gaz. *Storm it, I will* not *be intimidated!* "This is a way to use different muscles. Like shifting a pack from one shoulder to the other."

Gaz glanced to the side. Had something moved in the darkness?

"Gaz?" Kaladin asked.

"Look, lordling," Gaz said, looking back to him. "Carrying it overhead may be tiring, but carrying it like *that* is just plain stupid. You look like you're about to stumble over one another, and the handholds are terrible. You can barely fit the men."

"Yes," Kaladin said more softly. "But a lot of the time, only half of a bridge crew will survive a bridge run. We can carry it back this way when there are fewer of us. It will let us shift positions, at least."

Gaz hesitated. *Only half a bridge crew . . .*

If they carried the bridge like that on an actual assault, they'd go slowly, expose themselves. It could be a *disaster*, for Bridge Four at least.

Gaz smiled. "I like it."

Kaladin looked shocked. "*What?*"

"Initiative. Creativity. Yes, keep practicing. I'd very much like to see you make a plateau approach carrying the bridge that way."

Kaladin narrowed his eyes. "Is that so?"

"Yes," Gaz said.

"Well then. Perhaps we will."

Gaz smiled, watching Kaladin retreat. A disaster was exactly what he needed. Now he just had to find some other way to pay Lamaril's blackmail.

BENEATH THE SKIN

SIX YEARS AGO

Don't make the same mistake I did, son."

Kal looked up from his folio. His father sat on the other side of the operating room, one hand to his head, half-empty cup of wine in his other. Violet wine, among the strongest of liquors.

Lirin set the cup down, and the deep purple liquid—the color of cremling blood—shivered and trembled. It refracted Stormlight from a couple of spheres sitting on the counter.

"Father?"

"When you get to Kharbranth, stay there." His voice was slurred. "Don't get sucked back to this tiny, backward, *foolish* town. Don't force your beautiful wife to live away from everyone else she's ever known or loved."

Kal's father didn't often get drunk; this was a rare night of indulgence. Perhaps because Mother had gone to sleep early, exhausted from her work.

"You've always said I should come back," Kal said softly.

"I'm an idiot." His back to Kal, he stared at the wall splashed with white light from the spheres. "They don't want me here. They never wanted me here."

Kal looked down at his folio. It contained drawings of dissected bodies, the muscles splayed and pulled out. The drawings were so detailed. Each had glyphpairs to designate every part, and he'd committed those to memory. Now he studied the procedures, delving into the bodies of men long dead.

Once, Laral had told him that men weren't supposed to see beneath the skin. These folios, with their pictures, were part of what made everyone so mistrustful of Lirin. Seeing beneath was like seeing beneath the clothing, only worse.

Lirin poured himself more wine. How much the world could change in a short time. Kal pulled his coat close against the chill. A season of winter had come, but they couldn't afford charcoal for the brazier, for patients no longer gave offerings. Lirin hadn't stopped healing or surgery. The townspeople had simply stopped their donations, all at a word from Roshone.

"He shouldn't be able to do this," Kal whispered.

"But he can," Lirin said. He wore a white shirt and black vest atop tan trousers. The vest was unbuttoned, the front flaps hanging down by his sides, like the skin pulled back from the torsos of the men in Kal's drawings.

"We could spend the spheres," Kal said hesitantly.

"Those are for your education," Lirin snapped. "If I could send you now, I would."

Kal's father and mother had sent a letter to the surgeons in Kharbranth, asking them to let Kal take the entry tests early. They'd responded in the negative.

"He wants us to spend them," Lirin said, words slurred. "That's why he said what he did. He's trying to bully us into needing those spheres."

Roshone's words to the townspeople hadn't *exactly* been a command. He'd just implied that if Kal's father was too foolish to charge, then he shouldn't be paid. The next day, people had stopped donating.

The townsfolk regarded Roshone with a confusing mixture of adoration and fear. In Kal's opinion, he didn't deserve either. Obviously, the man had been banished to Hearthstone because he was so bitter and flawed. He clearly didn't deserve to be among the *real* lighteyes, who fought for vengeance on the Shattered Plains.

"Why do the people try so hard to please him?" Kal asked of his father's back. "They never reacted this way around Brightlord Wistiow."

"They do it because Roshone is unappeasable."

Kal frowned. Was that the wine talking?

Kal's father turned, his eyes reflecting pure Stormlight. In those eyes, Kal saw a surprising lucidity. He wasn't so drunk after all. "Brightlord Wistiow let men do as they wished. And so they ignored him. Roshone lets them know he finds them contemptible. And so they scramble to please him."

"That makes no sense," Kal said.

"It is the way of things," Lirin said, playing with one of the spheres on the table, rolling it beneath his finger. "You'll have to learn this, Kal. When men perceive the world as being right, we are content. But if we see a hole—a deficiency—we scramble to fill it."

"You make it sound noble, what they do."

"It is in a way," Lirin said. He sighed. "I shouldn't be so hard on our neighbors. They're petty, yes, but it's the pettiness of the ignorant. I'm not disgusted by them. I'm disgusted by the one who manipulates them. A man like Roshone can take what is honest and true in men and twist it into a mess of sludge to walk on." He took a sip, finishing the wine.

"We should just spend the spheres," Kal said. "Or send them somewhere, to a moneylender or something. If they were gone, he'd leave us alone."

"No," Lirin said softly. "Roshone is not the kind to spare a man once he is beaten. He's the type who keeps kicking. I don't know what political mistake landed him in this place, but he obviously can't get revenge on his rivals. So we're all he has." Lirin paused. "Poor fool."

Poor fool? Kal thought. *He's trying to destroy our lives, and that's all Father can say?*

What of the stories men sang at the hearths? Tales of clever herdsmen outwitting and overthrowing a foolish lighteyed man. There were dozens of variations, and Kal had heard them all. Shouldn't Lirin fight back somehow? Do something other than sit and wait?

But he didn't say anything; he knew exactly what Lirin would say. *Let me worry about it. Get back to your studies.*

Sighing, Kal settled back in his chair, opening his folio again. The surgery room was dim, lit by the four spheres on the table and a single one Kal used for reading. Lirin kept most of the spheres closed up in their cupboard, hidden away. Kal held up his own sphere, lighting the page. There were longer explanations of procedures in the back that his mother could read to him. She was the only woman in the town who could read, though Lirin said it wasn't uncommon among wellborn darkeyed women in the cities.

As he studied, Kal idly pulled something from his pocket. A rock that had been sitting on his chair for him when he'd come in to study. He recognized it as a favorite one that Tien had been carrying around recently. Now he'd left it for Kaladin; he often did that, hoping that his older brother would be able to see the beauty in it too, though they all just looked like ordinary rocks. He'd have to ask Tien what he found so special about this particular one. There was always something.

Tien spent his days now learning carpentry from Ral, one of the men in the town. Lirin had set him to it reluctantly; he'd been hoping for another surgery assistant, but Tien couldn't stand the sight of blood. He froze every time, and hadn't gotten used to it. That was troubling. Kal had hoped that his father would have Tien as an assistant when he left. And Kal *was* leaving, one way or another. He hadn't decided between the army or Kharbranth, though in recent months, he'd begun leaning toward becoming a spearman.

If he took that route, he'd have to do it stealthily, once he was old enough that the recruiters would take him over his parents' objections. Fifteen would probably be old enough. Five more months. For now, he figured that knowing the muscles—and vital parts of a body—would be pretty useful for either a surgeon or a spearman.

A thump came at the door. Kal jumped. It hadn't been a knock, but a *thump*. It came again. It sounded like something heavy pushing or slamming against the wood.

"What in the stormwinds?" Lirin said, rising from his

stool. He crossed the small room; his undone vest brushed the operating table, button scraping the wood.

Another thump. Kal scrambled out of his chair, closing the folio. At fourteen and a half, he was nearly as tall as his father now. A scraping came at the door, like nails or claws. Kal raised a hand toward his father, suddenly terrified. It was late at night, dark in the room, and the town was silent.

There was *something* outside. It sounded like a beast. Inhuman. A den of whitespines were said to be making trouble nearby, striking at travelers on the roadway. Kal had an image in his head of the reptilian creatures, as big as horses but with carapace across their backs. Was one of them sniffing at the door? Brushing it, trying to force its way in?

"Father!" Kal yelped.

Lirin pulled open the door. The dim light of the spheres revealed not a monster, but a man wearing black clothing. He had a long metal bar in his hands, and he wore a black wool mask with holes cut for the eyes. Kal felt his heart race in panic as the would-be intruder leapt backward.

"Didn't expect to find anyone inside, did you?" Kal's father said. "It's been years since there was a theft in the town. I'm ashamed of you."

"Give us the spheres!" a voice called out of the darkness. Another figure moved in the shadows, and then another.

Stormfather! Kal clutched the folio to his chest with trembling hands. *How many are there?* Highwaymen, come to rob the town! Such things happened. More and more frequently these days, Kal's father said.

How could Lirin be so calm?

"Those spheres ain't yours," another voice called.

"Is that so?" Kal's father said. "Does that make them yours? You think he'd let you keep them?" Kal's father spoke as if they weren't bandits from outside the town. Kal crept forward to stand just behind his father, frightened—but at the same time ashamed of that fear. The men in the darkness were shadowy, nightmarish things, moving back and forth, faces of black.

"We'll give them to him," one voice said.

"No need for this to get violent, Lirin," another added. "You ain't going to spend them anyway."

Kal's father snorted. He ducked into the room. Kal cried out, moving back as Lirin threw open the cabinet where he kept the spheres. He grabbed the large glass goblet that he stored them in; it was covered with a black cloth.

"You want them?" Lirin called, walking to the doorway, passing Kal.

"Father?" Kal said, panicked.

"You want the light for yourself?" Lirin's voice grew louder. "Here!"

He pulled the cloth free. The goblet exploded with fiery radiance, the brightness nearly blinding. Kal raised his arm. His father was a shadowed silhouette that seemed to hold the sun itself in its fingers.

The large goblet shone with a calm light. Almost a *cold* light. Kal blinked away tears, his eyes adjusting. He could see the men outside clearly now. Where dangerous shadows had once loomed, cringing men now raised hands. They didn't seem so intimidating; in fact, the cloths over their faces looked ridiculous.

Where Kal had been afraid, he now felt strangely confident. For a moment, it wasn't light his father held, but understanding itself. *That's Luten,* Kal thought, noticing a man who limped. It was easy to distinguish him, despite the mask. Kal's father had operated on that leg; it was because of him that Luten could still walk. He recognized others too. Harl was the one with the wide shoulders, Balsas the man wearing the nice new coat.

Lirin didn't say anything to them at first. He stood with that light blazing, illuminating the entire stone square outside. The men seemed to shrink down, as if they knew he recognized them.

"Well?" Lirin said. "You've threatened violence against me. Come. Hit me. Rob me. Do it knowing I've lived among you almost my entire life. Do it knowing that I've healed your children. Come in. Bleed one of your own!"

The men faded into the night without a word.

"They lived high atop a place no man could reach, but all could visit. The tower city itself, crafted by the hands of no man."

—Though *The Song of the Last Summer* is a fanciful tale of romance from the third century after the Recreance, it is likely a valid reference in this case. See page 27 of Varala's translation, and note the undertext.

They got better at carrying the bridge on its side. But not much better.

Kaladin watched Bridge Four pass, moving awkwardly, maneuvering the bridge at their sides. Fortunately, there were plenty of handles on the bridge's underside, and they'd found how to grip them in the right way. They had to carry it at less steep an angle than he'd wanted. That would expose their legs, but maybe he could train them to adjust to it as the arrows flew.

As it was, their carry was slow, and the bridgemen were so bunched up that if the Parshendi managed to drop a man, the others would stumble over him. Lose just a few men, and the balance would be upset so they'd drop it for certain.

This will have to be handled very carefully, Kaladin thought. Syl fluttered along behind the bridge crew as a flurry of nearly translucent leaves. Beyond her, something caught Kaladin's eye: a uniformed soldier leading a ragged group of men in a despondent clump. *Finally,* Kaladin thought. He'd been waiting for another group of recruits. He waved curtly to Rock. The Horneater nodded; he'd take over training. It was time for a break anyway.

Kaladin jogged up the short incline at the rim of the lumberyard, arriving just as Gaz intercepted the newcomers.

"What a sorry batch," Gaz said. "I thought we'd been sent the dregs last time, but this lot . . ."

Lamaril shrugged. "They're yours now, Gaz. Split them up how you like." He and his soldiers departed, leaving the unfortunate conscripts. Some wore decent clothing; they'd be recently caught criminals. The rest had slave brands on their foreheads. Seeing them brought back feelings that Kaladin had to force down. He still stood on the very top of a steep slope; one wrong step could send him tumbling back down into that despair.

"In a line, you cremlings," Gaz snapped at the new recruits, pulling free his cudgel and waving it. He eyed Kaladin, but said nothing.

The group of men hastily lined up.

Gaz counted down the line, picking out the taller members. "You five men, you're in Bridge Six. Remember that. Forget it, and I'll see you get a whipping." He counted off another group. "You six men, you're in Bridge Fourteen. You four at the end, Bridge Three. You, you, and you, Bridge One. Bridge Two doesn't need any . . . You four, Bridge Seven."

That was all of them.

"Gaz," Kaladin said, folding his arms. Syl landed on his shoulder, her small tempest of leaves forming into a young woman.

Gaz turned to him.

"Bridge Four is down to thirty fighting members."

"Bridge Six and Bridge Fourteen have fewer than that."

"They each had twenty-nine and you just gave them both a big helping of new members. And Bridge One is at thirty-seven, and you sent *them* three new men."

"You barely lost anyone on the last run, and—"

Kaladin caught Gaz's arm as the sergeant tried to walk away. Gaz flinched, lifting his cudgel.

Try it, Kaladin thought, meeting Gaz's eye. He almost wished that the sergeant would.

Gaz gritted his teeth. "Fine. One man."

"I pick him," Kaladin said.

"Whatever. They're all worthless anyway."

Kaladin turned to the group of new bridgemen. They'd gathered into clusters by which bridge crew Gaz had put them in. Kaladin immediately turned his attention to the taller men. By slave standards, they appeared well fed. Two of them looked like they'd—

"Hey, gancho!" a voice said from another group. "Hey! You want me, I think."

Kaladin turned. A short, spindly man was waving to him. The man had only one arm. Who would assign him to be a bridgeman?

He'd stop an arrow, Kaladin thought. *That's all some bridgemen are good for, in the eyes of the uppers.*

The man had brown hair and deep tan skin just a shade too dark to be Alethi. The fingernails on his hand were slate-colored and crystalline—he was a Herdazian, then. Most of the newcomers shared the same defeated look of apathy but this man was *smiling,* though he wore a slave's mark on his head.

That mark is old, Kaladin thought. *Either he had a kind master before this, or he has somehow resisted being beaten down.* The man obviously didn't understand what awaited him as a bridgeman. No person would smile if they understood that.

"You can use me," the man said. "We Herdazians are great fighters, gon." He pronounced that last word like "gone" and it appeared to refer to Kaladin. "You see, this one time, I was with, sure, three men and they were drunk and all but I still beat them." He spoke at a very quick pace, his thick accent slurring the words together.

He'd make a terrible bridgeman. He *might* be able to run with the bridge on his shoulders, but not maneuver it. He even looked a little flabby around the waist. Whatever bridge crew got him would put him right in the front and let him take an arrow, then be rid of him.

Gotta do what you can to stay alive, a voice from his past seemed to whisper. *Turn a liability into an advantage. . . .*

Tien.

"Very well," Kaladin said, pointing. "I'll take the Herdazian at the back."

"*What?*" Gaz said.

The short man sauntered up to Kaladin. "Thanks, gancho! You'll be glad you picked me."

Kaladin turned to walk back, passing Gaz. The bridge sergeant scratched his head. "You pushed me that hard so you could pick the one-armed runt?"

Kaladin walked on without a word for Gaz. Instead, he turned to the one-armed Herdazian. "Why did you want to come with me? You don't know anything about the different bridge crews."

"You were only picking one," the man said. "That means one man gets to be special, the others don't. I've got a good feeling about you. It's in your eyes, gancho." He paused. "What's a bridge crew?"

Kaladin found himself smiling at the man's nonchalant attitude. "You'll see. What's your name?"

"Lopen," the man said. "Some of my cousins, they call me *the* Lopen because they haven't ever heard anyone else named that. I've asked around a lot, maybe one hundred . . . or two hundred . . . lots of people, sure. And nobody has heard of that name."

Kaladin blinked at the torrent of words. Did the man ever stop to breathe?

Bridge Four was taking their break, their massive bridge resting on one side and giving shade. The five wounded had joined them and were chatting; even Leyten was up, which was encouraging. He'd been having a lot of trouble walking, what with that crushed leg. Kaladin had done what he could, but the man would always have a limp.

The only one who didn't talk to the others was Dabbid, the

man who had been so profoundly shocked by battle. He followed the others, but he didn't talk. Kaladin was starting to fear that the man would never recover from his mind fatigue.

Hobber—the round-faced, gap-toothed man who had taken an arrow to the leg—was walking without a crutch. It wouldn't be long before he could start running bridges again, and a good thing, too. They needed every pair of hands they could get.

"Head to the barrack there," Kaladin said to Lopen. "There's a blanket, sandals, and vest for you in the pile at the very back."

"Sure," Lopen said, sauntering off. He waved at a few of the men as he passed.

Rock walked up to Kaladin, folding his arms. "Is new member?"

"Yes," Kaladin said.

"The only kind Gaz would give us, I assume." Rock sighed. "This thing, we should have expected it. He will give us only the very most useless of bridgemen from now on."

Kaladin was tempted to say something in the way of agreement, but hesitated. Syl would probably see it as a lie, and that would annoy her.

"This new way of carrying the bridge," Rock said. "Is not very useful, I think. Is—"

He cut off as a horn call blared over the camp, echoing against stone buildings like the bleat of a distant greatshell. Kaladin grew tense. His men were on duty. He waited, tense, until the third set of horns blew.

"Line up!" Kaladin yelled. "Let's move!"

Unlike the other nineteen crews on duty, Kaladin's men didn't scramble about in confusion, but assembled in an orderly fashion. Lopen dashed out, wearing a vest, then hesitated, looking at the four squads, not knowing where to go. He'd be cut to ribbons if Kaladin put him in front, but he'd probably just slow them down anywhere else.

"Lopen!" Kaladin shouted.

The one-armed man saluted. *Does he think he's actually in the military?* "You see that rain barrel? Go get some waterskins from the carpenter's assistants. They told me we could borrow some. Fill as many as you can, then catch up down below."

"Sure, gancho," Lopen said.

"Bridge up!" Kaladin shouted, moving into position at the front. "Shoulder carry!"

Bridge Four moved. While some of the other bridge crews were crowded around their barracks, Kaladin's team charged across the lumberyard. They were first down the incline, and reached the first permanent bridge before the army even formed up. There, Kaladin ordered them to put their bridge down and wait.

Shortly thereafter, Lopen trotted down the hillside—and, surprisingly, Dabbid and Hobber were with him. They couldn't move fast, not with Hobber's limp, but they had constructed a sort of litter with a tarp and two lengths of wood. Piled into the middle of it were a good twenty waterskins. They trotted up to the bridge team.

"What's this?" Kaladin said.

"You told me to bring whatever I could carry, gon," Lopen said. "Well, we got this thing from the carpenters. They use it to carry pieces of wood, they said, and they weren't using it so we took it and now we're here. Ain't that right, moolie?" He said that last to Dabbid, who just nodded.

"Moolie?" Kaladin asked.

"Means mute," Lopen said, shrugging. "'Cuz he doesn't seem to talk much, you see."

"I see. Well, good job. Bridge Four, back in position. Here comes the rest of the army."

The next few hours were what they had grown to expect from bridge runs. Grueling conditions, carrying the heavy bridge across plateaus. The water proved a huge help. The army occasionally watered the bridgemen during runs, but never as often as the men needed it. Being able to take a drink after crossing each plateau was as good as having a half-dozen more men.

But the real difference came from the practice. Bridge Four's men no longer fell exhausted each time they set a bridge down. The work was still difficult, but their bodies were ready for it. Kaladin caught more than a few glances of surprise or envy from the other bridge crews as his men laughed and joked instead of collapsing. Running a bridge once a week or so—as the other men did—just wasn't enough. An extra meal each night combined with training had built up his men's muscles and prepared them to work.

The march was a long one, as long as Kaladin had ever made. They traveled eastward for hours. That was a bad sign. When they aimed for closer plateaus, they often got there before the Parshendi. But this far out they were racing just to prevent the Parshendi from escaping with the gemheart; there was no chance they'd arrive before the enemy.

That meant it would probably be a difficult approach. *We're not ready for the side carry,* Kaladin thought nervously, as they finally drew close to an enormous plateau rising in an unusual shape. He'd heard of it—the Tower, it was called. No Alethi force had ever won a gemheart here.

They set their bridge down before the penultimate chasm, positioning it, and Kaladin felt a foreboding as the scouts crossed. The Tower was wedge-shaped, uneven, with the eastern point rising far into the air, creating a steep hillside. Sadeas had brought a large number of soldiers; this plateau was enormous, allowing the deployment of a larger force. Kaladin waited, anxious. Maybe they'd be lucky, and the Parshendi would already be gone with the gemheart. It was possible, this far out.

The scouts came charging back. "Enemy lines on the opposing rim! They haven't gotten the chrysalis open yet!"

Kaladin groaned softly. The army began to cross on his bridge, and Bridge Four regarded him, solemn, expressions grim. They knew what would come next. Some of them, perhaps many of them, would not survive.

It was going to be very bad this time. On previous runs, they'd had a buffer. When they'd lost four or five men, they'd still been able to keep going. Now they were running with just thirty members. Every man they lost would slow them measurably, and the loss of just four or five more would cause them to wobble, or even topple. When that happened, the Parshendi would focus everything on them. He'd seen it happen before. If a bridge crew started to teeter, the Parshendi pounced.

Besides, when a bridge crew was visibly low on numbers, it always got targeted by the Parshendi to be taken down. Bridge Four was in trouble. This run could easily end with fifteen or twenty deaths. Something had to be done.

This was it.

"Gather close," Kaladin said.

The men frowned, stepping up to him.

"We're going to carry the bridge in side position," Kaladin said softly. "I'll go first. I'm going to steer; be ready to go in the direction I do."

"Kaladin," Teft said, "side position is slow. It was an interesting idea, but—"

"Do you trust me, Teft?" Kaladin asked.

"Well, I guess." The grizzled man glanced at the others. Kaladin could see that many of them did not, at least not fully.

"This will work," Kaladin said intently. "We're going to use the bridge as a shield to block arrows. We need to hurry out in front, faster than the other bridges. It'll be hard to outrun them with the side carry, but it's the only thing I can think of. If it doesn't work, I'll be in front, so I'll be the first to drop. If I die, move the bridge to shoulder-carry. We've practiced doing that. Then you'll be rid of me."

The bridgemen were silent.

"What if we don't want to be rid of you?" long-faced Natam asked.

Kaladin smiled. "Then run swiftly and follow my lead. I'm going to turn us unexpectedly during the run; be ready to change directions."

He went back to the bridge. The common soldiers were across, and the lighteyes—including Sadeas in his ornate Shardplate—were riding over the span. Kaladin and Bridge Four followed, then pulled the bridge behind them. They shoulder-carried it to the front of the army and put it down, waiting for the other bridges to get in place. Lopen and the other two water-carriers hung back with Gaz; it looked like they wouldn't get into trouble for not running. That was a small blessing.

Kaladin felt sweat bead on his forehead. He could just barely make out the Parshendi ranks ahead, on the other side of the chasm. Men of black and crimson, shortbows held at the ready, arrows nocked. The enormous slope of the Tower rose behind them.

Kaladin's heart beat faster. Anticipationspren sprung up around members of the army, but not his team. To their credit, there weren't any fearspren either—not that they didn't feel fear, they just weren't as panicked as the other bridge crews, so the fearspren went there instead.

Care, Tukks seemed to whisper at him from the past. *The key to fighting isn't lack of passion, it's controlled passion. Care about winning. Care about those you defend. You have to care about something.*

I care, Kaladin thought. *Storm me as a fool, but I do.*

"Bridges up!" Gaz's voice echoed across the front lines, repeating the order given him by Lamaril.

Bridge Four moved, quickly turning the bridge on its side and hoisting it up. The shorter men made a line, holding the bridge up to their right, with the taller men forming a bunched-up line behind them, reaching through and lifting or reaching high and steadying the bridge. Lamaril gave them a harsh look, and Kaladin's breath caught in his throat.

Gaz stepped up and whispered something to Lamaril. The lighteyes nodded slowly, and said nothing. The assault call sounded.

Bridge Four charged.

From behind them, arrows flew in a wave over the bridge crews' heads, arcing down toward the Parshendi. Kaladin ran, jaw clenched. He had trouble keeping himself from stumbling over the rockbuds and shalebark growths. Fortunately, though his team was slower than normal, their practice and endurance meant they were still faster than the other crews. With Kaladin at their lead, Bridge Four managed to get out ahead of the others.

That was important, because Kaladin angled his team slightly to the right, as if his crew were just a tad off-course with the heavy bridge at the side. The Parshendi knelt down and began to chant together. Alethi arrows fell among them, distracting some, but the others raised bows.

Get ready . . . Kaladin thought. He pushed harder, and felt a sudden surge of strength. His legs stopped straining, his breath stopped wheezing. Perhaps it was the anxiety of battle, perhaps it was numbness setting in, but the unexpected strength gave him a slight sense of euphoria. He felt as if something were buzzing within him, mixing with his blood.

In that moment it felt like he was *pulling* the bridge behind him all alone, like a sail towing the ship beneath it. He turned farther to the right, running at a deeper angle, putting himself and his men in full sight of the Parshendi archers.

The Parshendi continued to chant, somehow knowing—without orders—when to draw their bows. They pulled arrows to marbled cheeks, sighting on the bridgemen. As expected, many aimed at his men.

Almost close enough!

Just a few heartbeats more . . .

Now!

Kaladin turned sharply to the left just as the Parshendi loosed. The bridge moved with him, now charging with the face of the bridge pointed toward the archers. Arrows flew, snapping against the wood, digging into it. Some arrows rattled against the stone beneath their feet. The bridge resounded with the impacts.

Kaladin heard desperate screams of pain from the other bridge crews. Men fell, some of them probably on their first run. In Bridge Four, nobody cried out. Nobody fell.

Kaladin turned the bridge again, running angled in the other direction, the bridgemen exposed again. The surprised Parshendi nocked arrows. Normally, they fired in waves. That gave Kaladin an opportunity, for as soon as the Parshendi got the arrows drawn, he turned, using the bulky bridge as a shield.

Again, arrows snapped into the wood. Again, other bridge

crews screamed. Again, Kaladin's zigzagging run protected his men.

One more, Kaladin thought. This would be the tough one. The Parshendi would know what he was doing. They'd be ready to fire once he turned back.

He turned.

Nobody fired.

Amazed, he realized that the Parshendi archers had turned all of their attention to the other bridge crews, seeking easier targets. The space in front of Bridge Four was virtually empty.

The chasm was near, and—despite his angling—Kaladin brought his team in on-mark to place their bridge in the right spot. They all had to be aligned close together for the cavalry charge to work. Kaladin quickly gave the order to drop. Some of the Parshendi archers turned their attention back, but most ignored them, firing their arrows at the other crews.

A crash from behind announced a bridge falling. Kaladin and his men pushed, the Alethi archers behind pelting the Parshendi to distract them and keep them from shoving the bridge back. Still pushing, Kaladin risked a glance over his shoulder.

The next bridge in line was close. It was Bridge Seven, but they were floundering, arrow after arrow striking them, cutting them down in rows. They fell as he watched, bridge crashing to the stones. Now Bridge Twenty-seven was wavering. Two other bridges were already down. Bridge Six had reached the chasm, but just barely, over half its members down. Where were the other bridge crews? He couldn't tell from his quick glance, and had to turn back to his work.

Kaladin's men placed their bridge with a thump, and Kaladin gave the call to pull back. He and his men dashed away to let the cavalry charge across. But no cavalry came. Sweat dripping from his brow, Kaladin spun.

Five other bridge crews had set their bridges, but others were still struggling to reach the chasm. Unexpectedly, they'd tried tilting their bridges to block the arrows, emulating

Kaladin and his team. Many stumbled, some men attempting to lower the bridge for protection while others still ran forward.

It was chaos. These men hadn't practiced the side carry. As one straggling crew tried to hold their bridge up in the new position, they dropped it. Two more bridge crews were cut down completely by the Parshendi, who continued to fire.

Heavy cavalry charged, crossing the six bridges that had been set. Normally, two riders abreast on each bridge added up to a mass of a hundred horsemen, thirty to forty across and three ranks deep. That depended on many bridges aligned in a row, allowing an effective charge against the hundreds of Parshendi archers.

But the bridges had been set too erratically. Some cavalry got across, but they were scattered, and couldn't ride down the Parshendi without fear of being surrounded.

Foot soldiers had started to help push Bridge Six into place. *We should go help,* Kaladin realized. *Get those other bridges across.*

But it was too late. Though Kaladin stood near the battle-field, his men—as was their practice—had fallen back to the nearest rock outcropping for shelter. The one they'd chosen was close enough to see the battle, but was well protected from arrows. The Parshendi always ignored bridgemen after the initial assault, though the Alethi were careful to leave rear guards to protect the landing point and watch for Parshendi trying to cut off their retreat.

The soldiers finally maneuvered Bridge Six into place, and two more bridge crews got theirs down, but half of the bridges hadn't made it. The army had to reorganize on the run, dashing forward to support the cavalry, splitting to cross where the bridges had been set.

Teft left the outcropping and grabbed Kaladin by the arm, tugging him back to relative safety. Kaladin allowed himself to be pulled along, but he still looked at the battlefield, a hor-rible realization coming to him.

Rock stepped up beside Kaladin, clapping him on the shoulder. The large Horneater's hair was plastered to his head with sweat, but he was smiling broadly. "Is miracle! Not a single man wounded!"

Moash stepped up beside them. "Stormfather! I can't believe what we just did. Kaladin, you've changed bridge runs forever!"

"No," Kaladin said softly. "I've completely undermined our assault."

"I— What?"

Stormfather! Kaladin thought. The heavy cavalry had been cut off. A cavalry charge needed an unbroken line; it was the intimidation as much as anything that made it work.

But here, the Parshendi could dodge out of the way, then come at the horsemen from the flanks. And the foot soldiers hadn't gotten in quickly enough to help. Several groups of horsemen fought completely surrounded. Soldiers bunched up around the bridges that had been set, trying to get across, but the Parshendi had a solid foothold and were repelling them. Spearmen fell from the bridges, and the Parshendi then managed to topple one entire bridge into the chasm. The Alethi forces were soon on the defensive, the soldiers focused on holding the bridgeheads to secure an avenue of retreat for the cavalry.

Kaladin watched, really *watched*. He'd never studied the tactics and needs of the entire army in these assaults. He'd considered only the needs of his own crew. It was a foolish mistake, and he should have known better. He *would* have known better, if he'd still thought of himself as a real soldier. He hated Sadeas; he hated the way the man used bridge crews. But he shouldn't have changed Bridge Four's basic tactics without considering the larger scheme of the battle.

I deflected attention to the other bridge crews, Kaladin thought. *That got us to the chasm too soon, and slowed some of the others.*

And, since he'd run out in front, many other bridgemen had gotten a good view of how he'd used the bridge as a shield. That had led them to emulate Bridge Four. Each of the crews had ended up running at a different speed, and the Alethi archers hadn't known where to focus their volleys to soften the Parshendi for the bridge landings.

Stormfather! I've just cost Sadeas this battle.

There would be repercussions. The bridgemen had been forgotten while the generals and captains scrambled to revise their battle plans. But once this was over, they would come for him.

Or maybe it would happen sooner. Gaz and Lamaril, with a group of reserve spearmen, were marching toward Bridge Four.

Rock stepped up beside Kaladin on one side, a nervous Teft on the other, holding a stone in his hands. The bridgemen behind Kaladin began to mutter.

"Stand down," Kaladin said softly to Rock and Teft.

"But, Kaladin!" Teft said. "They—"

"Stand down. Gather the bridgemen. Get them back to the lumberyard safely, if you can." *If any of us escape this disaster.*

When Rock and Teft didn't back away, Kaladin stepped forward. The battle still raged on the Tower; Sadeas's group— led by the Shardbearer himself—had managed to claim a small section of ground and were holding it doggedly. Corpses piled up on both sides. It wouldn't be enough.

Rock and Teft moved up beside Kaladin again, but he stared them down, forcing them back. Then he turned to Gaz and Lamaril. *I'll point out that Gaz told me to do this,* he thought. *He suggested I use a side carry on a bridge assault.*

But no. There were no witnesses. It would be his word against Gaz's. That wouldn't work—plus, that argument would leave Gaz and Lamaril with good reason to see Kaladin dead immediately, before he could speak to their superiors.

Kaladin needed to do something else.

"Do you have any idea what you've done?" Gaz sputtered as he grew near.

"I've upended the army's strategy," Kaladin said, "throwing the entire assault force into chaos. You've come to punish me so that when your superiors come screaming to you for what happened, you can at least show that you acted quickly to deal with the one responsible."

Gaz paused, Lamaril and the spearmen stopping around him. The bridge sergeant looked surprised.

"If it's worth anything," Kaladin said grimly, "I didn't know this would happen. I was just trying to survive."

"Bridgemen aren't *supposed* to survive," Lamaril said curtly. He waved to a pair of his soldiers, then pointed at Kaladin.

"If you leave me alive," Kaladin said, "I promise I will tell your superiors that you had nothing to do with this. If you kill me, it will look like you were trying to hide something."

"Hide something?" Gaz said, glancing at the battle on the Tower. A stray arrow clattered across the rocks a short distance from him, shaft breaking. "What would we have to hide?"

"Depends. This very well *could* look like it was your idea from the start. Brightlord Lamaril, you didn't stop me. You could have, but you didn't, and soldiers saw Gaz and you speaking when you saw what I did. If I can't vouch for your ignorance of what I was going to do, then you'll look very, very bad."

Lamaril's soldiers looked to their leader. The lighteyed man scowled. "Beat him," he said, "but don't kill him." He turned and marched back toward the Alethi reserve lines.

The beefy spearmen walked up to Kaladin. They were darkeyed, but they might as well have been Parshendi for all the sympathy they would show him. Kaladin closed his eyes and steeled himself. He couldn't fight them all off. Not and remain with Bridge Four.

A spear butt to the gut knocked him to the ground, and he gasped as the soldiers began to kick. One booted foot tore open his belt pouch. His spheres—too precious to leave in the barrack—scattered across the stones. They had somehow lost their Stormlight, and were now dun, their life run out.

The soldiers kept kicking.

Analysis of four world cities and their underlying forms based on city plans found in the archives of the Palanaeum, Kharbranth.

Akinah

When one removes the current streets and main byways of Akinah, Thaylen City, Vedenar, and Kholinar and combines the street blocks into larger shapes, leaving behind the natural rock formations upon which these cities were originally built, the underlying pattern of the stone becomes more clear.

Thaylen City

The divine ten-part symmetry of Akinah is accentuated when the shape of the city is viewed from above. Amidst the lines of Thaylen City a star pattern emerges. Twisting streets of Vedenar become an organized pattern of arrows and circles.

Vedenar

In the case of Kholinar, even the city walls follow the contour of the subcartographal rock formations known as the Windblades. The walls incorporate the formations, using them to augment the defensive strength of the city.

Kholinar

I am left wondering if this is a strange coincidence. And if not, then what does it all mean?

The Scholar, Kabsal

CYMATICS

"They changed, even as we fought them. Like shadows they were, that can transform as the flame dances. Never underestimate them because of what you first see."

—Purports to be a scrap collected from Talatin, a Radiant of the Order of Stonewards. The source—Guvlow's *Incarnate*—is generally held as reliable, though this is from a copied fragment of "The Poem of the Seventh Morning," which has been lost.

Sometimes, when Shallan walked into the Palanaeum proper—the grand storehouse of books, manuscripts, and scrolls beyond the study areas of the Veil—she grew so distracted by the beauty and scope of it that she forgot everything else.

The Palanaeum was shaped like an inverted pyramid carved down into the rock. It had balcony walkways suspended around its perimeter. Slanted gently downward, they ran around all four walls to form a majestic square spiral, a giant staircase pointing toward the center of Roshar. A series of lifts provided a quicker method of descending.

Standing at the top level's railing, Shallan could see only halfway to the bottom. This place seemed too large, too grand, to have been shaped by the hands of men. How had the terraced levels been aligned so perfectly? Had Soulcasters been used to create the open spaces? How many gemstones would that have taken?

The lighting was dim; there was no general illumination, only small emerald lamps focused to illuminate the walkway floors. Ardents from the Devotary of Insight periodically moved through the levels, changing the spheres. There had to be hundreds upon hundreds of the emeralds here; apparently, they made up the Kharbranthian royal treasury. What better place for them than the extremely secure Palanaeum? Here they could both be protected and serve to illuminate the enormous library.

Shallan continued on her way. Her parshman servant carried a sphere lantern containing a trio of sapphire marks. The soft blue light reflected against the stone walls, portions of which had been Soulcast into quartz purely for ornamentation. The railings had been carved from wood, then transformed to marble. When she ran her fingers across one, she could feel the original wood's grain. At the same time, it had the cold smoothness of stone. An oddity that seemed designed to confuse the senses.

Her parshman carried a small basket of books full of drawings by famous natural scientists. Jasnah had begun allowing Shallan to spend some of her study time on topics of her own choosing. Just a single hour a day, but it was remarkable how precious that hour had become. Recently, she'd been digging through Myalmr's *Western Voyages*.

The world was a wondrous place. She hungered to learn more, wished to observe each and every one of its creatures, to have sketches of them in her books. To organize Roshar by capturing it in images. The books she read, though wonderful, all felt incomplete. Each author would be good with words or with drawings, but rarely both. And if the author *was* good with both, then her grasp of science would be poor.

There were so many holes in their understanding. Holes that Shallan could fill.

No, she told herself firmly as she walked. *That's not what I'm here to do.*

It was getting harder and harder to stay focused on the

theft, though Jasnah—as Shallan had hoped—had begun using her as a bathing attendant. That might soon present the opportunity she needed. And yet, the more she studied, the more she hungered for knowledge.

She led her parshman to one of the lifts. There, two other parshmen began lowering her. Shallan eyed the basket of books. She could spend her time on the lift reading, maybe finish that section of *Western Voyages* . . .

She turned away from the basket. *Stay focused.* On the fifth level down, she stepped out into the smaller walkway that connected the lift to the sloping ramps set into the walls. Upon reaching the wall, she turned right and continued down a little farther. The wall was lined with doorways and, finding the one she wanted, she entered a large stone chamber filled with tall bookshelves. "Wait here," she said to her parshman as she dug her drawing folio out of the basket. She tucked it under her arm, took the lantern, and hurried into the stacks.

One could disappear for hours in the Palanaeum and never see another soul. Shallan rarely saw anyone while searching out an obscure book for Jasnah. There were ardents and servants to fetch volumes, of course, but Jasnah thought it important for Shallan to practice doing it herself. Apparently the Kharbranthian filing system was now standard for many of Roshar's libraries and archives.

At the back of the room, she found a small desk of cobwood. She set her lantern on one side and sat on the stool, getting out her portfolio. The room was silent and dark, her lantern light revealing the ends of bookshelves to her right and a smooth stone wall to her left. The air smelled of old paper and dust. Not wet. It was never damp in the Palanaeum. Perhaps the dryness had something to do with the long troughs of white powder at the ends of each room.

She undid her portfolio's leather ties. Inside, the top sheets were blank, and the next few contained drawings she'd done of people in the Palanaeum. More faces for her collection. Hidden in the middle was a far more important set of drawings: sketches of Jasnah performing Soulcastings.

The princess used her Soulcaster infrequently; perhaps she

hesitated to use it when Shallan was around. But Shallan had caught a handful of occasions, mostly when Jasnah had been distracted, and had apparently forgotten she wasn't alone.

Shallan held up one picture. Jasnah, sitting in the alcove, hand to the side and touching a crumpled piece of notepaper, a gem on her Soulcaster glowing. Shallan held up the next picture. It depicted the same scene just seconds later. The paper had become a ball of flames. It hadn't burned. No, it had *become fire*. Tongues of flame coiling, a flash of heat in the air. What had been on it that Jasnah wished to hide?

Another picture showed Jasnah Soulcasting the wine in her cup into a chunk of crystal to use as a paperweight, the goblet itself holding down another stack, on one of the rare occasions when they'd dined—and studied—on a patio outside the Conclave. There was also the one of Jasnah burning words after running out of ink. When Shallan had seen her burning letters into a page, she'd been amazed at the Soulcaster's precision.

It seemed that this Soulcaster was attuned to three Essences in particular: Vapor, Spark, and Lucentia. But it should be able to create any of the Ten Essences, from Zephyr to Talus. That last one was the most important to Shallan, as Talus included stone and earth. She *could* create new mineral deposits for her family to exploit. It would work; Soulcasters were very rare in Jah Keved, and her family's marble, jade, and opal would sell at a premium. They couldn't create actual gemstones with a Soulcaster—that was said to be impossible—but they could create other deposits of near equal value.

Once those new deposits ran out, they'd have to move to less lucrative trades. That would be all right, though. By then, they'd have paid off their debts and compensated those to whom promises had been broken. House Davar would become unimportant again, but would not collapse.

Shallan studied the pictures again. The Alethi princess seemed remarkably casual about Soulcasting. She held one of the most powerful artifacts in all of Roshar, and she used it to create *paperweights*? What else did she use the Soulcaster for, when Shallan wasn't watching? Jasnah seemed to use it less frequently in her presence now than she had at first.

Shallan fished in the safepouch inside her sleeve, bringing out her father's broken Soulcaster. It had been sheared in two places: across one of the chains and through the setting that held one of the stones. She inspected it in the light, looking— not for the first time—for signs of that damage. The link in the chain had been replaced perfectly and the setting reforged equally well. Even knowing exactly where the cuts had been, she couldn't find any flaw. Unfortunately, repairing only the outward defects hadn't made it functional.

She hefted the heavy construction of metal and chains. Then she put it on, looping chains around her thumb, small finger, and middle finger. There were no gemstones in the device at present. She compared the broken Soulcaster to the drawings, inspecting it from all sides. Yes, it looked identical. She'd worried about that.

Shallan felt her heart flutter as she regarded the broken Soulcaster. Stealing from Jasnah had seemed acceptable when the princess had been a distant, unknown figure. A heretic, presumably ill-tempered and demanding. But what of the real Jasnah? A careful scholar, stern but fair, with a surprising level of wisdom and insight? Could Shallan really steal from her?

She tried to still her heart. Even as a little child, she'd been this way. She could remember her tears at fights between her parents. She was not good with confrontation.

But she'd do it. For Nan Balat, Tet Wikim, and Asha Jushu. Her brothers depended on her. She pressed her hands against her thighs to keep them from shaking, breathing in and out. After a few minutes, nerves under control, she took off the damaged Soulcaster and returned it to her safepouch. She gathered up her papers. They might be important in discovering how to use the Soulcaster. What was she going to do about that? Was there a way to ask Jasnah about using a Soulcaster without arousing suspicion?

A light flickering through nearby bookcases startled her, and she tucked away her folio. It turned out to be just an old, berobed female ardent, shuffling with a lantern and followed by a parshman servant. She didn't look in Shallan's direction as she turned between two rows of shelves, her lantern's light shining out through the spaces between the books. Lit that way—with her figure hidden but the light streaming between the shelves—it looked as if one of the Heralds themselves were walking through the stacks.

Her heart racing again, Shallan raised her safehand to her breast. *I make a terrible thief,* she thought with a grimace. She finished gathering her things and moved through the stacks, lantern held before her. The head of each row was carved with symbols, indicating the date the books had entered the Palanaeum. That was how they were organized. There were enormous cabinets filled with indexes on the top level.

Jasnah had sent Shallan to fetch—and then read—a copy of *Dialogues,* a famous historical work on political theory. However, this was also the room that contained *Shadows Remembered*—the book Jasnah was reading when the king had visited. Shallan had later looked it up in the index. It might have been reshelved by now.

Suddenly curious, Shallan counted off the rows. She stepped in and counted shelves inward. Near the middle and at the bottom, she found a thin red volume with a red hogshide cover. *Shadows Remembered.* Shallan set her lantern on the ground and slipped the book free, feeling furtive as she flipped through the pages.

She was confused by what she discovered. She hadn't realized this was a book of children's stories. There was no undertext commentary, just a collection of tales. Shallan sat down on the floor, reading through the first one. It was the story of a child who wandered away from his home at night and was chased by Voidbringers until he hid in a cavern beside a lake. He whittled a piece of wood into a roughly human shape and sent it floating across the lake, fooling the creatures into attacking and eating it instead.

Shallan didn't have much time—Jasnah would grow suspicious if she remained down here too long—but she skimmed the rest of the stories. They were all of a similar style, ghost stories about spirits or Voidbringers. The only commentary was at the back, explaining that the author had been curious about the folktales told by common darkeyes. She had spent years collecting and recording them.

Shadows Remembered, Shallan thought, *would have been better off forgotten.*

This was what Jasnah had been reading? Shallan had expected *Shadows Remembered* to be some kind of deep philosophical discussion of a hidden historical murder. Jasnah was a Veristitalian. She constructed the truth of what happened in the past. What kind of truth could she find in stories told to frighten disobedient darkeyed children?

Shallan slid the volume back in place and hurried on her way.

⁂

A short time later, Shallan returned to the alcove to discover that her haste had been unnecessary. Jasnah wasn't there. Kabsal, however, was.

The youthful ardent sat at the long desk, flipping through one of Shallan's books on art. Shallan noticed him before he saw her, and she found herself smiling despite her troubles. She folded her arms and adopted a dubious expression. "Again?" she asked.

Kabsal leaped up, slapping the book closed. "Shallan," he said, his bald head reflecting the blue light of her parshman's lantern. "I came looking for—"

"For Jasnah," Shallan said. "As always. And yet, she's never here when you come."

"An unfortunate coincidence," he said, raising a hand to his forehead. "I am a poor judge of timing, am I not?"

"And is that a basket of bread at your feet?"

"A gift for Brightness Jasnah," he said. "From the Devotary of Insight."

"I doubt a bread basket is going to persuade her to renounce her heresy," Shallan said. "Perhaps if you'd included jam."

The ardent smiled, picking up the basket and pulling out a small jar of red simberry jam.

"Of course, I've told you that Jasnah doesn't like jam,"

Shallan said. "And yet you bring it anyway, knowing jam to be among my favorite foods. And you've done this oh . . . a dozen times in the last few months?"

"I'm growing a bit transparent, aren't I?"

"Just a tad," she said, smiling. "It's about my soul, isn't it? You're worried about me because I'm apprenticed to a heretic."

"Er . . . well, yes, I'm afraid."

"I'd be insulted," Shallan said. "But you *did* bring jam." She smiled, waving for her parshman to deposit her books and then wait beside the doorway. Was it true that there were parshmen on the Shattered Plains who were *fighting*? That seemed hard to credit. She'd never known any parshman to as much as raise their voice. They didn't seem bright enough for disobedience.

Of course, some reports she'd heard—including those Jasnah had made her read when studying King Gavilar's murder—indicated that the Parshendi weren't like other parshmen. They were bigger, had odd armor that grew from their skin itself, and spoke far more frequently. Perhaps they weren't parshmen at all, but some kind of distant cousin, a different race entirely.

She sat down at the desk as Kabsal got out the bread, her parshman waiting at the doorway. A parshman wasn't much of a chaperone, but Kabsal *was* an ardent, which meant technically she didn't need one.

The bread had been purchased from a Thaylen bakery, which meant it was fluffy and brown. And, since he was an ardent, it didn't matter that jam was a feminine food—they could enjoy it together. She eyed him as he cut the bread. The ardents in her father's employ had all been crusty men or women in their later years, stern-eyed and impatient with children. She'd never even *considered* that the devotaries would attract young men like Kabsal.

During these last few weeks, she'd found herself thinking of him in ways that would better have been avoided.

"Have you considered," he noted, "what kind of person you declare yourself to be by preferring simberry jam?"

"I wasn't aware that my taste in jams could be that significant."

"There are those who have studied it," Kabsal said, slathering on the thick red jam and handing her the slice. "You run across some very odd books, working in the Palanaeum. It's not hard to conclude that perhaps *everything* has been studied at one time or another."

"Hum," Shallan said. "And simberry jam?"

"According to *Palates of Personality*—and before you object, *yes* it is a real book, and that is its title—a fondness for simberries indicates a spontaneous, impulsive personality. And also a preference for—" He cut off as a wadded-up piece of paper bounced off his forehead. He blinked.

"Sorry," Shallan said. "It just kind of happened. Must be all that impulsiveness and spontaneity I have."

He smiled. "You disagree with the conclusions?"

"I don't know," she said with a shrug. "I've had people tell me they could determine my personality based on the day I was born, or the position of Taln's Scar on my seventh birthday, or by numerological extrapolations of the tenth glyphic paradigm. But I think we're more complicated than that."

"People are more complicated than the numerological extrapolations of the tenth glyphic paradigm?" Kabsal said, spreading jam on a piece of bread for himself. "No wonder I have such difficulty understanding women."

"Very funny. I *mean* that we're more complex than mere bundles of personality traits. Am I spontaneous? Sometimes. You might describe my chasing Jasnah here to become her ward that way. But before that, I spent seventeen years being about as *un*spontaneous as someone could be. In many situations—if I'm encouraged—my tongue can be quite spontaneous, but my actions rarely are. We're *all* spontaneous sometimes, and we're *all* conservative sometimes."

"So you're saying that the book is right then. It says you're spontaneous; you're spontaneous sometimes. Ergo, it's correct."

"By that argument, it's right about *everybody*."

"One hundred percent accurate!"

"Well, not one hundred percent," Shallan said, swallowing another bite of the sweet, fluffy bread. "As has been noted, Jasnah hates jam of all kinds."

"Ah yes," Kabsal said. "She's a *jam heretic* too. Her soul is in more danger than I had realized." He grinned and took a bite of his bread.

"Indeed," Shallan said. "So what else does that book of yours say about me—and half the world's population—because of our enjoyment of foods with far too much sugar in them?"

"Well, a fondness for simberry is also supposed to indicate a love of the outdoors."

"Ah, the outdoors," Shallan said. "I visited that mythical place once. It was so very long ago, I've nearly forgotten it. Tell me, does the sun still shine, or is that just my dreamy recollection?"

"Surely your studies aren't *that* bad."

"Jasnah is inordinately fond of dust," Shallan said. "I believe she thrives on it, feeding off the particles like a chull crunching rockbuds."

"And you, Shallan? On what do *you* thrive?"

"Charcoal."

He looked confused at first, then glanced at her folio. "Ah yes. I was surprised at how quickly your name, and pictures, spread through the Conclave."

Shallan ate the last of her bread, then wiped her hand on a damp rag Kabsal had brought. "You make me sound like a disease." She ran a finger through her red hair, grimacing. "I guess I do have the coloring of a rash, don't I?"

"Nonsense," he said sternly. "You shouldn't say such things, Brightness. It's disrespectful."

"Of myself?"

"No. Of the Almighty, who made you."

"He made cremlings too. Not to mentions rashes and diseases. So being compared to one is actually an honor."

"I fail to follow that logic, Brightness. As he created all things, comparisons are meaningless."

"Like the claims of your *Palates* book, eh?"

"A point."

"There are worse things to be than a disease," she said, idly thoughtful. "When you have one, it reminds you that you're alive. Makes you fight for what you have. When the disease has run its course, normal healthy life seems wonderful by comparison."

"And would you not rather be a sense of euphoria? Bringing pleasant feelings and joy to those you infect?"

"Euphoria passes. It is usually brief, so we spend more time longing for it than enjoying it." She sighed. "Look what we've done. Now I'm depressed. At least turning back to my studies will seem exciting by comparison."

He frowned at the books. "I was under the impression that you enjoyed your studies."

"As was I. Then Jasnah Kholin stomped into my life and proved that even something pleasant could become boring."

"I see. So she's a harsh mistress?"

"Actually, no," Shallan said. "I'm just fond of hyperbole."

"I'm not," he said. "It's a real bastard to spell."

"Kabsal!"

"Sorry," he said. Then he glanced upward. "Sorry."

"I'm sure the ceiling forgives you. To get the Almighty's attention, you might want to burn a prayer instead."

"I owe him a few anyway," Kabsal said. "You were saying?"

"Well, Brightness Jasnah isn't a harsh mistress. She's actually everything she's said to be. Brilliant, beautiful, mysterious. I'm fortunate to be her ward."

Kabsal nodded. "She is said to be a sterling woman, save for one thing."

"You mean the heresy?"

He nodded.

"It's not as bad for me as you think," she said. "She's rarely vocal about her beliefs unless provoked."

"She's ashamed, then."

"I doubt that. Merely considerate."

He eyed her.

"You needn't worry about me," Shallan said. "Jasnah doesn't try to persuade me to abandon the devotaries."

Kabsal leaned forward, growing more somber. He was older than she—a man in his mid-twenties, confident, self-assured, and earnest. He was practically the only man near her age that she'd ever talked to outside of her father's careful supervision.

But he was also an ardent. So, of course, nothing could come of it. Could it?

"Shallan," Kabsal said gently, "can you not see how we—how I—would be concerned? Brightness Jasnah is a very powerful and intriguing woman. We would expect her ideas to be infectious."

"Infectious? I thought you said *I* was the disease."

"I never said that!"

"Yes, but I pretended you did. Which is virtually the same thing."

He frowned. "Brightness Shallan, the ardents *are* worried about you. The souls of the Almighty's children are our responsibility. Jasnah has a history of corrupting those with whom she comes in contact."

"Really?" Shallan asked, genuinely interested. "Other wards?"

"It is not my place to say."

"We can move to another place."

"I'm firm on this point, Brightness. I will not speak of it."

"Write it, then."

"Brightness . . ." he said, voice taking on a suffering tone.

"Oh, all right," she said, sighing. "Well, I can assure you, my soul is quite well and thoroughly *un*infected."

He sat back, then cut another piece of bread. She found herself studying him again, but grew annoyed at her own girlish foolishness. She would soon be returning to her family, and he was only visiting her for reasons relating to his Calling. But she truly *was* fond of his company. He was the only one here in Kharbranth that she felt she could really talk to. And he was handsome; the simple clothing and shaved head only highlighted his strong features. Like many young ardents, he kept his beard short and neatly trimmed. He spoke with a refined voice, and he was so well-read.

"Well, if you're certain about your soul," he said, turning back to her. "Then perhaps I could interest you in our devotary."

"I have a devotary. The Devotary of Purity."

"But the Devotary of Purity isn't the place for a scholar. The Glory it advocates has nothing to do with your studies or your art."

"A person doesn't need a devotary that focuses directly on their Calling."

"It is nice when the two coincide, though."

Shallan stifled a grimace. The Devotary of Purity focused on—as one might imagine—teaching one to emulate the Almighty's honesty and wholesomeness. The ardents at the devotary hall hadn't known what to make of her fascination with art. They'd always wanted her to do sketches of things they found "pure." Statues of the Heralds, depictions of the Double Eye.

Her father had chosen the devotary for her, of course.

"I just wonder if you made an informed choice," Kabsal said. "Switching devotaries is allowed, after all."

"Yes, but isn't recruitment frowned upon? Ardents competing for members?"

"It is indeed frowned upon. A deplorable habit."

"But you do it anyway?"

"I curse occasionally too."

"I hadn't noticed. You're a very curious ardent, Kabsal."

"You'd be surprised. We're not nearly as stuffy a bunch as we seem. Well, except Brother Habsant; he spends so much time staring at the rest of us." He hesitated. "Actually, now I think about it, he might actually *be* stuffed. I don't know that I've ever seen him move. . . ."

"We're getting distracted. Weren't you trying to recruit me to your devotary?"

"Yes. And it's not so uncommon as you think. All of the devotaries engage in it. We do a lot of frowning at one another for our profound lack of ethics." He leaned forward again, growing more serious. "My devotary has relatively few members, as we don't have as much exposure as others. So whenever someone seeking knowledge comes to the Palanaeum, we take it upon ourselves to inform them."

"Recruit them."

"Let them see what it is they are missing." He took a bite of his bread and jam. "In the Devotary of Purity, did they teach you about the nature of the Almighty? The divine prism, with the ten facets representing the Heralds?"

"They touched on it," she said. "Mostly we talked about achieving my goals of . . . well, purity. Somewhat boring, I'll admit, since there wasn't much chance for *im*purity on my part."

Kabsal shook his head. "The Almighty gives everyone talents—and when we pick a Calling that capitalizes on them, we are worshipping him in the most fundamental way. A devotary—and its ardents—should help nurture that, encouraging you to set and achieve goals of excellence." He waved to the books stacked on the desk. "This is what your devotary should be helping you with, Shallan. History, logic, science, art. Being honest and good is important, but we should be working harder to encourage the natural talents of people, rather than forcing them to adapt to the Glories and Callings we feel are most important."

"That is a reasonable argument, I guess."

Kabsal nodded, looking thoughtful. "Is it any wonder a woman like Jasnah Kholin turned away from that? Many devotaries encourage women to leave difficult studies of theology to the ardents. If only Jasnah had been able to see the true beauty of our doctrine." He smiled, digging a thick book out of his bread basket. "I really had hoped, originally, to be able to show her what I mean."

"I doubt she'd react well to that."

"Perhaps," he said idly, hefting the tome. "But to be the one who finally convinced her!"

"Brother Kabsal, that sounds almost like you're seeking distinction."

He blushed, and she realized she'd said something that genuinely embarrassed him. She winced, cursing her tongue.

"Yes," he said. "I do seek distinction. I *shouldn't* wish so badly to be the one who converts her. But I do. If she would just listen to my proof."

"Proof?"

"I have real evidence that the Almighty exists."

"I'd like to see it." Then she raised a finger, cutting him off. "Not because I doubt his existence, Kabsal. I'm just curious."

He smiled. "It will be my pleasure to explain. But first, would you like another slice of bread?"

"I should say no," she said, "and avoid excess, as my tutors trained me. But instead I'll say yes."

"Because of the jam?"

"Of course," she said, taking the bread. "How did your book of oracular preserves describe me? Impulsive and spontaneous? I can do that. If it means jam."

He slathered a piece for her, then wiped his fingers on his cloth and opened his book, flipping through the pages until he reached one that had a drawing on it. Shallan slid closer for a better look. The picture wasn't of a person; it depicted a pattern of some kind. A triangular shape, with three outlying wings and a peaked center.

"Do you recognize this?" Kabsal asked.

It seemed familiar. "I feel that I should."

"It's Kholinar," he said. "The Alethi capital, drawn as it would appear from above. See the peaks here, the ridges there? It was built around the rock formation that was already there." He flipped the page. "Here's Vedenar, capital of Jah Keved." This one was a hexagonal pattern. "Akinah." A circular pattern. "Thaylen City." A four-pointed star pattern.

"What does it mean?"

"It is proof that the Almighty is in all things. You can see him here, in these cities. Do you see how symmetrical they are?"

"The cities were built by men, Kabsal. They wanted symmetry because it is holy."

"Yes, but in each case they built around existing rock formations."

"That doesn't mean anything," Shallan said. "I do believe,

but I don't know if *this* is proof. Wind and water can create symmetry; you see it in nature all the time. The men picked areas that were roughly symmetrical, then designed their cities to make up for any flaws."

He turned to his basket again, rummaging. He came out with—of all things—a metal plate. As she opened her mouth to ask a question, he held up his finger again and set the plate down on a small wooden stand that raised it a few inches above the tabletop.

Kabsal sprinkled white, powdery sand on the sheet of metal, coating it. Then he got out a bow, the kind drawn across strings to make music.

"You came prepared for this demonstration, I see," Shallan noted. "You really *did* want to make your case to Jasnah."

He smiled, then drew the bow across the edge of the metal plate, making it vibrate. The sand hopped and bounced, like tiny insects dropped onto something hot.

"This," he said, "is called cymatics. The study of the patterns that sounds make when interacting with a physical medium."

As he drew the bow again, the plate made a sound, almost a pure note. It was actually enough to draw a single music-spren, which spun for a moment in the air above him, then vanished. Kabsal finished, then gestured to the plate with a flourish.

"So . . . ?" Shallan asked.

"Kholinar," he said, holding up his book for comparison.

Shallan cocked her head. The pattern in the sand looked *exactly* like Kholinar.

He dropped more sand on the plate and then drew the bow across it at another point and the sand rearranged itself.

"Vedenar," he said.

She compared again. It was an exact match.

"Thaylen City," he said, repeating the process at another spot. He carefully chose another point on the plate's edge and bowed it one final time. "Akinah. Shallan, proof of the Almighty's existence is in the very cities we live in. Look at the perfect symmetry!"

She had to admit, there was something compelling about the patterns. "It could be a false correlation. Both caused by the same thing."

"Yes. The Almighty," he said, sitting. "Our very language is symmetrical. Look at the glyphs—each one can be folded in half perfectly. And the alphabet too. Fold any line of text down across itself, and you'll find symmetry. Surely you know the story, that both glyphs and letters came from the Dawnsingers?"

"Yes."

"Even our names. Yours is nearly perfect. Shallan. One letter off, an ideal name for a lighteyed woman. Not *too* holy, but ever so close. The original names for the ten Silver Kingdoms. Alethela, Valhav, Shin Kak Nish. Perfect, symmetrical."

He reached forward, taking her hand. "It's here, around us. Don't forget that, Shallan, no matter what she says."

"I won't," she said, realizing how he'd guided the conversation. He'd said he believed her, but still he'd gone through his proofs. It was touching and annoying at the same time. She did not like condescension. But, then, could one really blame an ardent for preaching?

Kabsal looked up suddenly, releasing her hand. "I hear footsteps." He stood, and Shallan turned as Jasnah walked into the alcove, followed by a parshman carrying a basket of books. Jasnah showed no surprise at the presence of the ardent.

"I'm sorry, Brightness Jasnah," Shallan said, standing. "He—"

"You are not a captive, child," Jasnah interrupted brusquely. "You are allowed visitors. Just be careful to check your skin for tooth marks. These types have a habit of dragging their prey out to sea with them."

Kabsal flushed. He moved to gather up his things.

Jasnah waved for the parshman to place her books on the table. "Can that plate reproduce a cymatic pattern corresponding to Urithiru, priest? Or do you only have patterns for the standard four cities?"

Kabsal looked at her, obviously shocked to realize that

she knew exactly what the plate was for. He picked up his book. "Urithiru is just a fable."

"Odd. One would think that your type would be used to believing in fables."

His face grew redder. He finished packing his things, then nodded curtly to Shallan and walked hastily from the room.

"If I may say so, Brightness," Shallan said, "that was *exceptionally* rude of you."

"I'm prone to such bouts of incivility," Jasnah said. "I'm certain he has heard what I'm like. I simply wanted to make sure he got what he expected."

"You haven't acted that way toward other ardents in the Palanaeum."

"The other ardents in the Palanaeum haven't been working to turn my ward against me."

"He wasn't . . ." Shallan trailed off. "He was simply worried about my soul."

"Has he asked you to try to steal my Soulcaster yet?"

Shallan felt a sudden spike of shock. Her hand went to the safepouch in her sleeve. Did Jasnah know? *No,* Shallan told herself. *No, listen to the question.* "He didn't."

"Watch," Jasnah said, opening a book. "He will eventually. I've experience with his type." She looked at Shallan, and her expression softened. "He's not interested in you. Not in any of the ways you think. In particular, this isn't about your soul. It's about me."

"That is somewhat arrogant of you," Shallan said, "don't you think?"

"Only if I'm wrong, child," Jasnah said, turning back to her book. "And I rarely am."

"I walked from Abamabar to Urithiru."

—This quote from the Eighth Parable of *The Way of Kings*
seems to contradict Varala and Sinbian, who both claim the city
was inaccessible by foot. Perhaps there was a way constructed,
or perhaps Nohadon was being metaphorical.

B *ridgemen aren't supposed to survive. . . .*
Kaladin's mind felt fuzzy. He knew that he *hurt*, but
other than that, he floated. As if his head were detached from
his body and bouncing off the walls and ceilings.

"Kaladin!" a concerned voice whispered. "Kaladin, please.
Please don't be hurt anymore."

Bridgemen aren't supposed to survive. Why did those
words bother him so much? He remembered what had happened, using the bridge as a shield, throwing the army off,
dooming the assault. *Stormfather*, he thought, *I'm an idiot!*

"Kaladin?"

It was Syl's voice. He risked opening his eyes and looked
out on an upside-down world, sky extending below him, familiar lumberyard in the air above him.

No. *He* was upside down. Hanging against the side of
Bridge Four's barrack. The Soulcast building was fifteen feet
tall at its peak, with a shallowly slanted roof. Kaladin was

tied by his ankles to a rope, which would—in turn—be affixed to a ring set into the slanted roof. He'd seen it happen to other bridgemen. One who had committed a murder in camp, another who had been caught stealing for the fifth time.

His back was to the wall so that he faced eastward. His arms were free, hanging down at his sides, and they almost touched the ground. He groaned again, hurting everywhere.

As his father had trained him, he began to prod his side to check for broken ribs. He winced as he found several that were tender, at least cracked. Probably broken. He felt at his shoulder too, where he feared that his collarbone was broken. One of his eyes was swollen. Time would show if he'd sustained any serious internal damage.

He rubbed his face, and flakes of dried blood cracked free and fluttered toward the ground. Gash on his head, bloodied nose, split lip. Syl landed on his chest, feet planted on his sternum, hands clasped before her. "Kaladin?"

"I'm alive," he mumbled, words slurred by his swollen lip. "What happened?"

"You were beaten by those soldiers," she said, seeming to grow smaller. "I've gotten back at them. I made one of them trip three times today." She looked concerned.

He found himself smiling. How long could a man hang like this, blood going to his head?

"There was a lot of yelling," Syl said softly. "I think several men were demoted. The soldier, Lamaril, he . . ."

"What?"

"He was executed," Syl said, even more quietly. "Highprince Sadeas did it himself, the hour the army got back from the plateau. He said something about the ultimate responsibility falling on the lighteyes. Lamaril kept screaming that you had promised to absolve him, and that Gaz should be punished instead."

Kaladin smirked ruefully. "He shouldn't have had me beaten senseless. Gaz?"

"They left him in his position. I don't know why."

"Right of responsibility. In a disaster like this, the lighteyes are supposed to take most of the blame. They like to make a show of obeying old precepts like that, when it suits them. Why am I still alive?"

"Something about an example," Syl said, wrapping her translucent arms around herself. "Kaladin, I feel cold."

"You can feel temperature?" Kaladin said, coughing.

"Not usually. I can now. I don't understand it. I . . . I don't like it."

"It'll be all right."

"You shouldn't lie."

"Sometimes it's all right to lie, Syl."

"And this is one of those times?"

He blinked, trying to ignore his wounds, the pressure in his head, trying to clear his mind. He failed on all counts. "Yes," he whispered.

"I think I understand."

"So," Kaladin said, resting his head back, the parietal knob of his skull resting against the wall, "I'm to be judged by the highstorm. They'll let the storm kill me."

Hanging here, Kaladin would be exposed directly to the winds and everything they would throw at him. If you were prudent and took appropriate action, it *was* possible to survive outside in a highstorm, though it was a miserable experience. Kaladin had done it on several occasions, hunkered down, taking shelter in the lee of a rock formation. But hanging on a wall facing directly stormward? He'd be cut to ribbons and crushed by stones.

"I'll be right back," Syl said, dropping off his chest, taking the form of a falling stone, then changing into windblown leaves near the ground and fluttering away, curving to the right. The lumberyard was empty. Kaladin could smell the crisp, chill air, the land bracing for a highstorm. The lull, it was called, when the wind fell still, the air cold, the pressure dropping, the humidity rising right before a storm.

A few seconds later, Rock poked his head around the wall, Syl on his shoulder. He crept up to Kaladin, a nervous Teft following. They were joined by Moash; despite the latter's protests that he didn't trust Kaladin, he looked almost as concerned as the other two.

"Lordling?" Moash said. "You awake?"

"I'm conscious," Kaladin croaked. "Everyone get back from the battle all right?"

"All of our men, sure enough," Teft said, scratching at his beard. "But we lost the battle. It was a disaster. Over two hundred bridgemen dead. Those who survived were only enough to carry eleven bridges."

Two hundred men, Kaladin thought. *That's my fault. I protected my own at the cost of others. I was too hasty.*

Bridgemen aren't supposed to survive. There's something about that. He wouldn't be able to ask Lamaril. That man had gotten what he deserved, though. If Kaladin had the ability to choose, such would be the end of all lighteyes, the king included.

"We wanted to say something," Rock said. "Is from all of the men. Most wouldn't come out. Highstorm coming, and—"

"It's all right," Kaladin whispered.

Teft nudged Rock to continue.

"Well, is this. We will remember you. Bridge Four, we won't go back to how we were. Maybe all of us will die, but we'll show the new ones. Fires at night. Laughter. Living. We'll make a tradition out of it. For you." Rock and Teft knew about the knobweed. They could keep earning extra money to pay for things.

"You did this for us," Moash put in. "We'd have died on that field. Perhaps as many as died in the other bridge crews. This way, we're only going to lose one."

"I say it isn't right, what they're doing," Teft said with a scowl. "We talked about cutting you down. . . ."

"No," Kaladin said. "That would only earn you a similar punishment."

The three men shared glances. It seemed they'd come to the same conclusion.

"What did Sadeas say?" Kaladin asked. "About me."

"That he understood how a bridgeman would want to save his life," Teft said, "even at others' expense. He called you a selfish coward, but acted like that was all that could be expected."

"He says he's letting the Stormfather judge you," Moash added. "Jezerezeh, king of Heralds. He says that if you deserve to live, you will. . . ." He trailed off. He knew as well as the others that unprotected men didn't survive highstorms, not like this.

"I want you three to do something for me," Kaladin said, closing his eyes against the blood trickling down his face from his lip, which he'd cracked open by speaking.

"Anything, Kaladin," Rock said.

"I want you to go back into the barrack and tell the men to come out after the storm. Tell them to look up at me tied here. Tell them I'll open my eyes and look back at them, and they'll know that I survived."

The three bridgemen fell silent.

"Yes, of course, Kaladin," Teft said. "We'll do it."

"Tell them," Kaladin continued, voice firmer, "that it won't end here. Tell them I *chose* not to take my own life, and so there's no way in *Damnation* I'm going to give it up to Sadeas."

Rock smiled one of those broad smiles of his. "By the *uli'tekanaki*, Kaladin. I almost believe you'll do it."

"Here," Teft said, handing him something. "For luck."

Kaladin took the object in a weak, bloodstained hand. It was a sphere, a full skymark. It was dun, the Stormlight gone from it. *Carry a sphere with you into the storm,* the old saying said, *and at least you'll have light by which to see.*

"It's all we were able to save from your pouch," Teft said. "Gaz and Lamaril got the rest. We complained, but what were we to do?"

"Thank you," Kaladin said.

Moash and Rock retreated to the safety of the barrack, Syl leaving Rock's shoulder to stay with Kaladin. Teft lingered too, as if thinking to spend the storm with Kaladin. He eventually shook his head, muttering, and joined the others. Kaladin thought he heard the man calling himself a coward.

The door to the barrack shut. Kaladin fingered the smooth glass sphere. The sky was darkening, and not just because the sun was setting. Blackness gathered. The highstorm.

Syl walked up the side of the wall, then sat down on it,

looking at him, tiny face somber. "You told them you'd survive. What happens if you don't?"

Kaladin's head was pounding with his pulse. "My mother would cringe if she knew how quickly the other soldiers taught me to gamble. First night in Amaram's army, and they had me playing for spheres."

"Kaladin?" Syl said.

"Sorry," Kaladin said, rocking his head from side to side. "What you said, it reminded me of that night. There's a term in gambling, you see. 'In for all,' they say. It's when you put all of your money on one bet."

"I don't understand."

"I'm putting it all on the long bet," Kaladin whispered. "If I die, then they'll come out, shake their heads, and tell themselves they knew it would happen. But if I live, they'll remember it. And it will give them hope. They might see it as a miracle."

Syl was silent for a moment. "Do you want to be a miracle?"

"No," Kaladin whispered. "But for them, I will be."

It was a desperate, foolish hope. The eastern horizon, inverted in his sight, was growing darker. From this perspective, the storm was like the shadow of some enormous beast lumbering across the ground. He felt the disturbing fuzziness of a person who had been hit too hard on the head. Concussion. That was what it was called. He was having trouble thinking, but he didn't want to fall unconscious. He wanted to stare at the highstorm straight on, though it terrified him. He felt the same panic he'd felt looking down into the black chasm, back when he'd nearly killed himself. It was the fear of what he could not see, what he could not know.

The stormwall approached, the visible curtain of rain and wind at the advent of a highstorm. It was a massive wave of water, dirt, and rocks, hundreds of feet high, thousands upon thousands of windspren zipping before it.

In battle, he'd been able to fight his way to safety with the skill of his spear. When he'd stepped to the edge of the chasm, there had been a line of retreat. This time, there was nothing. No way to fight or avoid that black beast, that shadow spanning the entirety of the horizon, plunging the world into an early night. The eastern edge of the crater that made the warcamp had been worn away, and Bridge Four's barrack was first in its row. There was nothing between him and the Plains. Nothing between him and the storm.

Staring at that raging, blustering, churning wave of wind-pushed water and debris, Kaladin felt as if he were watching the end of the world descend upon him.

He took a deep breath, the pain of his ribs forgotten, as the stormwall crossed the lumberyard in a flash and slammed into him.

A LIGHT BY WHICH TO SEE

"Though many wished Urithiru to be built in Alethela, it was obvious that it could not be. And so it was that we asked for it to be placed westward, in the place nearest to Honor."

—Perhaps the oldest surviving original source mentioning the city, requoted in *The Vavibrar*, line 1804. What I wouldn't give for a way to translate the Dawnchant.

The force of the stormwall nearly knocked him unconscious, but the sudden chill of it shocked him lucid.

For a moment, Kaladin couldn't feel anything but that coldness. He was pressed against the side of the barrack by the extended blast of water. Rocks and bits of branch crashed against the stone around him; he was already too numb to tell how many slashed or beat against his skin.

He bore it, dazed, eyes pressed shut and breath held. Then the stormwall passed, crashing onward. The next blast of wind came in from the side—the air was swirling and gusting from all directions now. The wind flung him sideways—his back scraping against stone—and up into the air. The wind stabilized, blowing out of the east again. Kaladin hung in darkness, and his feet yanked against the rope. In a panic, he realized that he was now flapping in the wind like a kite, tied to the ring in the barrack's slanted roof.

Only that rope kept him from being blown along with the other debris to be tumbled and tossed before the storm across the entirety of Roshar. For those few heartbeats, he could not think. He could only feel the panic and the cold—one boiling out of his chest, the other trying to freeze him from the skin inward. He screamed, clutching his single sphere as if it were a lifeline. The scream was a mistake, as it let that coldness course into his mouth. Like a spirit forcing its arm down his throat.

The wind was like a maelstrom, chaotic, moving in different directions. One buffet ripped at him, then passed, and he fell to the roof of the barrack with a thud. Almost immediately, the terrible winds tried to lift him again, pounding his skin with waves of icy water. Thunder crashed, the heartbeat of the beast that had swallowed him. Lightning split the darkness like white teeth in the night. The wind was so loud it nearly drowned out the thunder; howling and moaning.

"Grab the roof, Kaladin!"

Syl's voice. So soft, so small. How could he hear it at all?

Numbly, he realized he was lying facedown on the sloped roof. It wasn't so steeply peaked that he was immediately pitched off, and the wind was generally blowing him backward. He did as Syl said, grabbing the lip of the roof with cold, slick fingers. Then he lay facedown, head tucked between his arms. He still had the sphere in his hand, pressed against the stone rooftop. His fingers started to slip. The wind was blowing so hard, trying to push him to the west. If he let go, he'd end up dangling in the air again. His rope tether was not long enough for him to get to the other side of the shallow-peaked rooftop, where he'd be sheltered.

A boulder hit the roof beside him—he couldn't hear its impact or see it in the tempest's darkness, but he could *feel* the building vibrate. The boulder rolled forward and crashed down to the ground. The entire storm didn't have such force, but occasional gusts could pick up and toss large objects, hurling them hundreds of feet.

His fingers slipped further.

"The ring," Syl whispered.

The ring. The rope tied his legs to a steel ring on the side of the roof behind him. Kaladin let go, then snatched the ring as he was blown backward. He clutched to it. The rope continued down to his ankles, about the length of his body. He thought for a moment of untying the ropes, but he didn't dare let go of the ring. He clung there, like a pennant flapping in the wind, holding the ring in both hands, sphere cupped inside one of them and pressed against the steel.

Each moment was a struggle. The wind yanked him left, then hurled him right. He couldn't know how long it lasted; time had no meaning in this place of fury and tumult. His numbed, battered mind started to think he was in a nightmare. A terrible dream inside his head, full of black, living winds. Screams in the air, bright and white, the flash of lightning revealing a terrible, twisted world of chaos and terror. The very buildings seemed blown sideways, the entire world askew, warped by the storm's terrible power.

In those brief moments of light when he dared to look, he thought he saw Syl standing in front of him, her face to the wind, tiny hands forward. As if she were trying to hold back the storm and split the winds as a stone divided the waters of a swift stream.

The cold of the rainwater numbed the scrapes and bruises. But it also numbed his fingers. He didn't feel them slipping. The next he knew, he was whipping in the air again, tossed to the side, being slammed down against the roof of the barrack.

He hit hard. His vision flashed with sparkling lights that melded together and were followed by blackness.

Not unconsciousness, blackness.

Kaladin blinked. All was still. The storm was quiet, and everything was purely dark. *I'm dead,* he thought immediately. But why could he feel the wet stone roof beneath him? He shook his head, dripping rainwater down his face. There was no lightning, no wind, no rain. The silence was unnatural.

He stumbled to his feet, managing to stand on the gently

sloped roof. The stone was slick beneath his toes. He couldn't feel his wounds. The pain just wasn't there.

He opened his mouth to call out into the darkness, but hesitated. That silence was not to be broken. The air itself seemed to weigh less, as did he. He almost felt as if he could float away.

In that darkness, an enormous face appeared just in front of his. A face of blackness, yet faintly traced in the dark. It was wide, the breadth of a massive thunderhead, and extended far to either side, yet it was somehow still visible to Kaladin. Inhuman. Smiling.

Kaladin felt a deep chill—a rolling prickle of ice—scurry down his spine and through his entire body. The sphere suddenly burst to life in his hand, flaring with a sapphire glow. It illuminated the stone roof beneath him, making his fist blaze with blue fire. His shirt was in tatters, his skin lacerated. He looked down at himself, shocked, then looked up at the face.

It was gone. There was only the darkness.

Lightning flashed, and Kaladin's pains returned. He gasped, falling to his knees before the rain and the wind. He slipped down, face hitting the rooftop.

What had that been? A vision? A delusion? His strength was fleeing him, his thoughts growing muddled again. The winds weren't as strong now, but the rain was still so cold. Lethargic, confused, nearly overwhelmed by his pain, he brought his hand up to the side and looked at the sphere. It was glowing. Smeared with his blood and glowing.

He hurt so much, and his strength had faded. Closing his eyes, he felt himself enveloped by a second blackness. The blackness of unconsciousness.

⁂

Rock was the first to the door when the highstorm subsided. Teft followed more slowly, groaning to himself. His knees hurt. His knees *always* hurt near a storm. His grandfather had complained about that in his later years, and Teft had called him daft. Now he felt it too.

Storming Damnation, he thought, wearily stepping outside. It was still raining, of course. These were the after-flurries of drizzle that trailed a highstorm, the riddens. A few rainspren sat in puddles, like blue candles, and a few windspren danced in the stormwinds. The rain was cold, and he splashed through puddles that soaked his sandaled feet, chilling them straight through the skin and muscle. He hated being wet. But, then, he hated a lot of things.

For a while, life had been looking up. Not now.

How did everything go so wrong so quickly? he thought, holding his arms close, walking slowly and watching his feet. Some soldiers had left their barracks and stood nearby, wearing raincloaks, watching. Probably to make certain nobody had snuck out to cut Kaladin down early. They didn't try to stop Rock, though. The storm had passed.

Rock charged around the side of the building. Other bridgemen left the barrack behind as Teft followed Rock. Storming Horneater. Like a big lumbering chull. He actually believed. He thought they'd find that foolish young bridgeleader alive. Probably figured they'd discover him having a nice cup of tea, relaxing in the shade with the Stormfather himself.

And you don't believe? Teft asked himself, still looking down. *If you don't, why are you following? But if you did believe, you'd look. You wouldn't stare at your feet. You'd look up and see.*

Could a man both believe, and not believe, at the same time? Teft stopped beside Rock and—steeling himself—looked up at the wall of the barrack.

There he saw what he'd expected and what he'd feared. The corpse looked like a hunk of slaughterhouse meat, skinned and bled. Was that a person? Kaladin's skin was sliced in a hundred places, dribbles of blood mixing with rainwater running down the side of the building. The lad's body still hung by the ankles. His shirt had been ripped off; his bridgeman trousers were ragged. Ironically, his face was cleaner now than when they'd left him, washed by the storm.

Teft had seen enough dead men on the battlefield to know what he was looking at. *Poor lad,* he thought, shaking his head as the rest of Bridge Four gathered around him and Rock, quiet, horrified. *You almost made me believe in you.*

Kaladin's eyes snapped open.

The gathered bridgemen gasped, several cursing and falling to the ground, splashing in the pools of rainwater. Kaladin drew in a ragged breath, wheezing, eyes staring forward, intense and unseeing. He exhaled, blowing flecks of bloody spittle out over his lips. His hand, hanging below him, slipped open.

Something dropped to the stones. The sphere Teft had given him. It splashed into a puddle and stopped there. It was dun, no Stormlight in it.

What in the name of Kelek? Teft thought, kneeling. *You left a sphere out in the storm, and it gathered Stormlight. Held in Kaladin's hand, this one should have been fully infused. What had gone wrong?*

"*Umalakai'ki!*" Rock bellowed, pointing. "*Kama mohoray namavau—*" He stopped, realizing he was speaking the wrong language. "Somebody be helping me get him down! Is still alive! We need ladder and knife! Hurry!"

The bridgemen scrambled. The soldiers approached, muttering, but they didn't stop the bridgemen. Sadeas himself had declared that the Stormfather would choose Kaladin's fate. Everyone knew that meant death.

Except . . . Teft stood up straight, holding the dun sphere. *An empty sphere after a storm,* he thought. *And a man who's still alive when he should be dead. Two impossibilities.*

Together they bespoke something that should be even *more* impossible.

"Where's that ladder!" Teft found himself yelling. "Curse you all, hurry, hurry! We need to get him bandaged. Somebody go fetch that salve he always puts on wounds!"

He glanced back at Kaladin, then spoke much more softly. "And you'd *better* survive, son. Because I want some answers."

> "Taking the Dawnshard, known to bind any creature void-
> ish or mortal, he crawled up the steps crafted for Heralds,
> ten strides tall apiece, toward the grand temple above."

—From *The Poem of Ista*. I have found no modern explanation
of what these "Dawnshards" are. They seem ignored by scholars, though talk of them was obviously prevalent among those
recording the early mythologies.

*It was not uncommon for us to meet native peoples while
traveling through the Unclaimed Hills,* Shallan read. *These
ancient lands were once one of the Silver Kingdoms, after
all. One must wonder if the great-shelled beasts lived among
them back then, or if the creatures have come to inhabit the
wilderness left by humankind's passing.*

She settled back in her chair, the humid air warm around
her. To her left, Jasnah Kholin floated quietly in the pool in-
set in the floor of the bathing chamber. Jasnah liked to soak
in the bath, and Shallan couldn't blame her. During most of
Shallan's life, bathing had been an ordeal involving dozens
of parshmen carting heated buckets of water, followed by a
quick scrub in the brass tub before the water cooled.

Kharbranth's palace offered far more luxury. The stone
pool in the ground resembled a small personal lake, luxuri-

ously warmed by clever fabrials that produced heat. Shallan didn't know much about fabrials yet, though part of her was very intrigued. This type was becoming increasingly common. Just the other day, the Conclave staff had sent Jasnah one to heat her chambers.

The water didn't have to be carried in but came out of pipes. At the turn of a lever, water flowed in. It was warm when it entered, and was kept heated by the fabrials set into the sides of the pool. Shallan had bathed in the chamber herself, and it was absolutely marvelous.

The practical decor was of rock decorated with small colorful stones set in mortar up the sides of the walls. Shallan sat beside the pool, fully dressed, reading as she waited on Jasnah's needs. The book was Gavilar's account—as spoken to Jasnah herself years ago—after his first meeting with the strange parshmen later known as the Parshendi.

Occasionally, during our explorations, we'd meet with natives, she read. *Not parshmen. Natan people, with their pale bluish skin, wide noses, and wool-like white hair. In exchange for gifts of food, they would point us to the hunting grounds of greatshells.*

Then we met the parshmen. I'd been on a half-dozen expeditions to Natanatan, but never had I seen anything like this! Parshmen, living on their own? All logic, experience, and science declared that to be an impossibility. Parshmen need the hand of civilized peoples to guide them. This has been proven time and time again. Leave one out in the wilderness, and it will just sit there, doing nothing, until someone comes along to give it orders.

Yet here was a group who could hunt, make weapons, build buildings, and—indeed—create their own civilization. We soon realized that this single discovery could expand, perhaps overthrow, all we understood about our gentle servants.

Shallan moved her eyes down to the bottom of the page where—separated by a line—the undertext was written in a small, cramped script. Most books dictated by men had an undertext, notes added by the woman or ardent who scribed the book. By unspoken agreement, the undertext was never shared out loud. Here, a wife would sometimes clarify—or even contradict—the account of her husband. The only way to preserve such honesty for future scholars was to maintain the sanctity and secrecy of the writing.

It should be noted, Jasnah had written in the undertext to this passage, *that I have adapted my father's words—by his own instruction—to make them more appropriate for recording.* That meant she made his dictation sound more scholarly and impressive. *In addition, by most accounts, King Gavilar originally ignored these strange, self-sufficient parshmen. It was only after explanation by his scholars and scribes that he understood the import of what he'd discovered. This inclusion is not meant to highlight my father's ignorance; he was, and is, a warrior. His attention was not on the anthropological import of our expedition, but upon the hunt that was to be its culmination.*

Shallan closed the cover, thoughtful. The volume was from Jasnah's own collection—the Palanaeum had several copies, but Shallan wasn't allowed to bring the Palanaeum's books into a bathing chamber.

Jasnah's clothing lay on a bench at the side of the room. Atop the folded garments, a small golden pouch held the Soulcaster. Shallan glanced at Jasnah. The princess floated face-up in the pool, black hair fanning out behind her in the water, her eyes closed. Her daily bath was the one time she seemed to relax completely. She looked much younger now, stripped of both clothing and intensity, floating like a child resting after a day of active swimming.

Thirty-four years old. That seemed ancient in some regards—some women Jasnah's age had children as old as Shallan. And yet it was also young. Young enough that Jasnah was praised for her beauty, young enough that men declared it a shame she wasn't yet married.

Shallan glanced at the pile of clothing. She carried the broken fabrial in her safepouch. She could swap them here and now. It was the opportunity she'd been waiting for. Jasnah now trusted her enough to relax, soaking in the bathing chamber without worrying about her fabrial.

Could Shallan really do it? Could she betray this woman who had taken her in?

Considering what I've done before, she thought, *this is nothing.* It wouldn't be the first time she betrayed someone who trusted her.

She stood up. To the side, Jasnah cracked an eye.

Blast, Shallan thought, tucking the book under her arm, pacing, trying to look thoughtful. Jasnah watched her. Not suspiciously. Curiously.

"Why did your father want to make a treaty with the Parshendi?" Shallan found herself asking as she walked.

"Why wouldn't he want to?"

"That's not an answer."

"Of course it is. It's just not one that tells you anything."

"It would help, Brightness, if you would give me a *useful* answer."

"Then ask a useful question."

Shallan set her jaw. "What did the Parshendi have that King Gavilar wanted?"

Jasnah smiled, closing her eyes again. "Closer. But you can probably guess the answer to that."

"Shards."

Jasnah nodded, still relaxed in the water.

"The text doesn't mention them," Shallan said.

"My father didn't speak of them," Jasnah said. "But from things he said . . . well, I now suspect that they motivated the treaty."

"Can you be sure he knew, though? Maybe he just wanted the gemhearts."

"Perhaps," Jasnah said. "The Parshendi seemed amused at our interest in the gemstones woven into their beards." She smiled. "You should have seen our shock when we discovered where they'd gotten them. When the lanceryn died off during the scouring of Aimia, we thought we'd seen the last gemhearts of large size. And yet here was another great-shelled beast with them, living in a land not too distant from Kholinar itself.

"Anyway, the Parshendi were willing to share them with us, so long as they could still hunt them too. To them, if you took the trouble to hunt the chasmfiends, their gemhearts were yours. I doubt a treaty would have been needed for that. And yet, just before leaving to return to Alethkar, my father suddenly began talking fervently of the need for an agreement."

"So what happened? What changed?"

"I can't be certain. However, he once described the strange actions of a Parshendi warrior during a chasmfiend hunt. Instead of reaching for his spear when the greatshell appeared, this man held his hand to the side in a very suspicious way. Only my father saw it; I suspected he believed the man planned to summon a Blade. The Parshendi realized what he was doing, and stopped himself. My father didn't speak of it further, and I assume he didn't want the world's eyes on the Shattered Plains any more than they already were."

Shallan tapped her book. "It seems tenuous. If he was sure about the Blades, he must have seen more."

"I suspect so as well. But I studied the treaty carefully, after his death. The clauses for favored trade status and mutual border crossing could very well have been a step toward folding the Parshendi into Alethkar as a nation. It certainly would have prevented the Parshendi from trading their Shards to other kingdoms without coming to us first. Perhaps that was all he wanted to do."

"But why kill him?" Shallan said, arms crossed, strolling in the direction of Jasnah's folded clothing. "Did the Parshendi realize that he intended to have their Shardblades, and so struck at him preemptively?"

"Uncertain," Jasnah said. She sounded skeptical. Why did *she* think the Parshendi killed Gavilar? Shallan nearly asked, but she had a feeling she wouldn't get any more out of Jasnah. The woman expected Shallan to think, discover, and draw conclusions on her own.

Shallan stopped beside the bench. The pouch holding the

Soulcaster was open, the drawstrings loose. She could see the precious artifact curled up inside. The swap would be easy. She had used a large chunk of her money to buy gemstones that matched Jasnah's, and had put them into the broken Soulcaster. The two were now exactly identical.

She still hadn't learned anything about using the fabrial; she'd tried to find a way to ask, but Jasnah avoided speaking of the Soulcaster. Pushing harder would be suspicious. Shallan would have to get information elsewhere. Perhaps from Kabsal, or maybe from a book in the Palanaeum.

Regardless, the time was upon her. Shallan found her hand going to her safepouch, and she felt inside of it, running her fingers along the chains of her broken fabrial. Her heart beat faster. She glanced at Jasnah, but the woman was just lying there, floating, eyes closed. What if she opened her eyes?

Don't think of that! Shallan told herself. *Just do it. Make the swap. It's so close. . . .*

"You are progressing more quickly than I had assumed you would," Jasnah said suddenly.

Shallan spun, but Jasnah's eyes were still closed. "I was wrong to judge you so harshly because of your prior education. I myself have often said that passion outperforms upbringing. You have the determination and the capacity to become a respected scholar, Shallan. I realize that the answers seem slow in coming, but continue your research. You will have them eventually."

Shallan stood for a moment, hand in her pouch, heart thumping uncontrollably. She felt sick. *I can't do it,* she realized. *Stormfather, but I'm a fool. I came all of this way . . . and now I can't do it!*

She pulled her hand from her pouch and stalked back across the bathing chamber to her chair. What was she going to tell her brothers? Had she just doomed her family? She sat down, setting her book aside and sighing, prompting Jasnah to open her eyes. Jasnah watched her, then righted herself in the water and gestured for the hairsoap.

Gritting her teeth, Shallan stood up and fetched the soap tray for Jasnah, bringing it over and squatting down to proffer it. Jasnah took the powdery hairsoap and mashed it in her hand, lathering it before putting it into her sleek black hair with both hands. Even naked, Jasnah Kholin was composed and in control.

"Perhaps we have spent too much time indoors of late," the princess said. "You look penned up, Shallan. Anxious."

"I'm fine," Shallan said brusquely.

"Hum, yes. As evidenced by your perfectly reasonable, relaxed tone. Perhaps we need to shift some of your training from history to something more hands-on, more visceral."

"Like natural science?" Shallan asked, perking up.

Jasnah tilted her head back. Shallan knelt down on a towel beside the pool, then reached down with her freehand, massaging the soap into her mistress's lush tresses.

"I was thinking philosophy," Jasnah said.

Shallan blinked. "Philosophy? What good is that?" *Isn't it the art of saying nothing with as many words as possible?*

"Philosophy is an important field of study," Jasnah said sternly. "Particularly if you're going to be involved in court politics. The nature of morality must be considered, and preferably before one is exposed to situations where a moral decision is required."

"Yes, Brightness. Though I fail to see how philosophy is more 'hands-on' than history."

"History, by definition, cannot be experienced directly. As it is happening, it is the present, and that is philosophy's realm."

"That's just a matter of definition."

"Yes," Jasnah said, "all words have a tendency to be subject to how they are defined."

"I suppose," Shallan said, leaning back, letting Jasnah dunk her hair to clean off the soap.

The princess began scrubbing her skin with mildly abrasive soap. "That was a particularly bland response, Shallan. What happened to your wit?"

Shallan glanced at the bench and its precious fabrial. After all this time, she had proven too weak to do what needed to be done. "My wit is on temporary hiatus, Brightness," she said. "Pending review by its colleagues, sincerity and temerity."

Jasnah raised an eyebrow at her.

Shallan sat back on her heels, still kneeling on the towel. "How *do* you know what is right, Jasnah? If you don't listen to the devotaries, how do you decide?"

"That depends upon one's philosophy. What is most important to you?"

"I don't know. Can't you tell me?"

"No," Jasnah replied. "If I gave you the answers, I'd be no better than the devotaries, prescribing beliefs."

"They aren't evil, Jasnah."

"Except when they try to rule the world."

Shallan drew her lips into a thin line. The War of Loss had destroyed the Hierocracy, shattering Vorinism into the devotaries. That was the inevitable result of a religion trying to rule. The devotaries were to teach morals, not enforce them. Enforcement was for the lighteyes.

"You say you can't give me answers," Shallan said. "But can't I ask for the advice of someone wise? Someone who's gone before? Why write our philosophies, draw our conclusions, if not to influence others? You yourself told me that information is worthless unless we use it to make judgments."

Jasnah smiled, dunking her arms and washing off the soap. Shallan caught a victorious glimmer in her eye. She wasn't necessarily advocating ideas because she believed them; she just wanted to push Shallan. It was infuriating. How was Shallan to know what Jasnah really thought if she adopted conflicting points of view like this?

"You act as if there were one answer," Jasnah said, gesturing to Shallan to fetch a towel and climbing from the pool. "A single, eternally perfect response."

Shallan hastily complied, bearing a large, fluffy towel. "Isn't that what philosophy is about? Finding the answers? Seeking the truth, the real meaning of things?"

Toweling off, Jasnah raised an eyebrow at her.

"What?" Shallan asked, suddenly self-conscious.

"I believe it is time for a field exercise," Jasnah said. "Outside of the Palanaeum."

"Now?" Shallan asked. "It's so late!"

"I told you philosophy was a hands-on art," Jasnah said, wrapping the towel around herself, then reaching down and taking the Soulcaster out of its pouch. She slipped the chains around her fingers, securing the gemstones to the back of her hand. "I'll prove it to you. Come, help me dress."

※

As a child, Shallan had relished those evenings when she'd been able to slip away into the gardens. When the blanket of darkness rested atop the grounds, they had seemed a different place entirely. In those shadows, she'd been able to imagine that the rockbuds, shalebark, and trees were some foreign fauna. The scrapings of cremlings climbing out of cracks had become the footsteps of mysterious people from far-off lands. Large-eyed traders from Shinovar, a greatshell rider from Kadrix, or a narrowboat sailor from the Purelake.

She didn't have those same imaginings when walking Kharbranth at night. Imagining dark wanderers in the night had once been an intriguing game—but here, dark wanderers were likely to be real. Instead of becoming a mysterious, intriguing place at night, Kharbranth seemed much the same to her—just more dangerous.

Jasnah ignored the calls of rickshaw pullers and palanquin porters. She walked slowly in a beautiful dress of violet and gold, Shallan following in blue silk. Jasnah hadn't taken time to have her hair done following her bath, and she wore it loose, cascading across her shoulders, almost scandalous in its freedom.

They walked the Ralinsa—the main thoroughfare that led down the hillside in switchbacks, connecting Conclave and port. Despite the late hour, the roadway was crowded, and many of the men who walked here seemed to bear the night inside of them. They were gruffer, more shadowed of face. Shouts still rang through the city, but those carried the night in them too, measured by the roughness of their words and the sharpness of their tones. The steep, slanted hillside that formed the city was no less crowded with buildings than always, yet these too seemed to draw in the night. Blackened, like stones burned by a fire. Hollow remains.

The bells still rang. In the darkness, each ring was a tiny scream. They made the wind more present, a living thing that caused a chiming cacophony each time it passed. A breeze rose, and an avalanche of sound came tumbling across the Ralinsa. Shallan nearly found herself ducking before it.

"Brightness," Shallan said. "Shouldn't we call for a palanquin?"

"A palanquin might inhibit the lesson."

"I'll be all right learning that lesson during the day, if you wouldn't mind."

Jasnah stopped, looking off the Ralinsa and toward a darker side street. "What do you think of that roadway, Shallan?"

"It doesn't look particularly appealing to me."

"And yet," Jasnah said, "it is the most direct route from the Ralinsa to the theater district."

"Is that where we're going?"

"We aren't 'going' anywhere," Jasnah said, taking off down the side street. "We are acting, pondering, and learning."

Shallan followed nervously. The night swallowed them; only the occasional light from late-night taverns and shops offered illumination. Jasnah wore her black, fingerless glove over her Soulcaster, hiding the light of its gemstones.

Shallan found herself creeping. Her slippered feet could feel every change in the ground underfoot, each pebble and crack. She looked about nervously as they passed a group of workers gathered around a tavern doorway. They were darkeyes, of course. In the night, that distinction seemed more profound.

"Brightness?" Shallan asked in a hushed tone.

"When we are young," Jasnah said, "we want simple answers. There is no greater indication of youth, perhaps, than the desire for everything to be *as it should*. As it has ever been."

Shallan frowned, still watching the men by the tavern over her shoulder.

"The older we grow," Jasnah said, "the more we question. We begin to ask why. And yet, we still want the answers to be simple. We assume that the people around us—adults, leaders—will have those answers. Whatever they give often satisfies us."

"I was never satisfied," Shallan said softly. "I wanted more."

"You were mature," Jasnah said. "What you describe happens to most of us, as we age. Indeed, it seems to me that aging, wisdom, and *wondering* are synonymous. The older we grow, the more likely we are to reject the simple answers. Unless someone gets in our way and demands they be accepted regardless." Jasnah's eyes narrowed. "You wonder why I reject the devotaries."

"I do."

"Most of them seek to stop the questions." Jasnah halted. Then she briefly pulled back her glove, using the light beneath to reveal the street around her. The gemstones on her hand—larger than broams—blazed like torches, red, white, and grey.

"Is it wise to be showing your wealth like that, Brightness?" Shallan said, speaking very softly and glancing about her.

"No," Jasnah said. "It is most certainly not. Particularly not here. You see, this street has gained a particular reputation lately. On three separate occasions during the last two months, theatergoers who chose this route to the main road were accosted by footpads. In each case, the people were murdered."

Shallan felt herself grow pale.

"The city watch," Jasnah said, "has done nothing. Taravangian has sent them several pointed reprimands, but the captain of the watch is cousin to a very influential lighteyes in the city, and Taravangian is not a terribly powerful king. Some suspect that there is more going on, that the footpads might be bribing the watch. The politics of it are irrelevant at the moment for, as you can see, no members of the watch are guarding the place, despite its reputation."

Jasnah pulled her glove back on, plunging the roadway back into darkness. Shallan blinked, her eyes adjusting.

"How foolish," Jasnah said, "would you say it is for us to come here, two undefended women wearing costly clothing and bearing riches?"

"*Very* foolish. Jasnah, can we go? Please. Whatever lesson you have in mind isn't worth this."

Jasnah drew her lips into a line, then looked toward a narrow, darker alleyway off the road they were on. It was almost completely black now that Jasnah had replaced her glove.

"You're at an interesting place in your life, Shallan," Jasnah said, flexing her hand. "You are old enough to wonder, to ask, to reject what is presented to you simply *because* it was presented to you. But you also cling to the idealism of youth. You feel there must be some single, all-defining Truth—and you think that once you find it, all that once confused you will suddenly make sense."

"I . . ." Shallan wanted to argue, but Jasnah's words were tellingly accurate. The terrible things Shallan had done, the terrible thing she had planned to do, haunted her. Was it possible to do something horrible in the name of accomplishing something wonderful?

Jasnah walked into the narrow alleyway.

"Jasnah!" Shallan said. "What are you doing?"

"This is philosophy in action, child," Jasnah said. "Come with me."

Shallan hesitated at the mouth of the alleyway, her heart thumping, her thoughts muddled. The wind blew and bells rang, like frozen raindrops shattering against the stones. In a moment of decision, she rushed after Jasnah, preferring company, even in the dark, to being alone. The shrouded glimmer of the Soulcaster was barely enough to light their way, and Shallan followed in Jasnah's shadow.

Noise from behind. Shallan turned with a start to see several dark forms crowding into the alley. "Oh, Stormfather," she whispered. Why? Why was Jasnah doing this?

Shaking, Shallan grabbed at Jasnah's dress with her

freehand. Other shadows were moving in front of them, from the far side of the alley. They grew closer, grunting, splashing through foul, stagnant puddles. Chill water had already soaked Shallan's slippers.

Jasnah stopped moving. The frail light of her cloaked Soulcaster reflected off metal in the hands of their stalkers. Swords or knives.

These men meant murder. You didn't rob women like Shallan and Jasnah, women with powerful connections, then leave them alive as witnesses. Men like these were not the gentlemen bandits of romantic stories. They lived each day knowing that if they were caught, they would be hanged.

Paralyzed by fear, Shallan couldn't even scream.

Stormfather, Stormfather, Stormfather!

"And now," Jasnah said, voice hard and grim, "the lesson." She whipped off her glove.

The sudden light was nearly blinding. Shallan raised a hand against it, stumbling back against the alley wall. There were four men around them. Not the men from the tavern entrance, but others. Men she hadn't noticed watching them. She could see the knives now, and she could also see the murder in their eyes.

Her scream finally broke free.

The men grunted at the glare, but shoved their way forward. A thick-chested man with a dark beard came up to Jasnah, weapon raised. She calmly reached her hand out—fingers splayed—and pressed it against his chest as he swung a knife. Shallan's breath caught in her throat.

Jasnah's hand sank into the man's skin, and he froze. A second later he burned.

No, he *became fire*. Transformed into flames in an eyeblink. Rising around Jasnah's hand, they formed the outline of a man with head thrown back and mouth open. For just a moment, the blaze of the man's death outshone Jasnah's gemstones.

Shallan's scream trailed off. The figure of flames was strangely beautiful. It was gone in a moment, the fire dissipating into the night air, leaving an orange afterimage in Shallan's eyes.

The other three men began to curse, scrambling away, tripping over one another in their panic. One fell. Jasnah turned casually, brushing his shoulder with her fingers as he struggled to his knees. He became crystal, a figure of pure, flawless quartz—his clothing transformed along with him. The diamond in Jasnah's Soulcaster faded, but there was still plenty of Stormlight left to send rainbow sparkles through the transformed corpse.

The other two men fled in opposite directions. Jasnah took a deep breath, closing her eyes, lifting her hand above her head. Shallan held her safehand to her breast, stunned, confused. Terrified.

Stormlight shot from Jasnah's hand like twin bolts of lightning, symmetrical. One struck each of the footpads and they popped, puffing into smoke. Their empty clothing dropped to the ground. With a sharp snap, the smokestone crystal on Jasnah's Soulcaster cracked, its light vanishing, leaving her with just the diamond and the ruby.

The remains of the two footpads rose into the air, small billows of greasy vapor. Jasnah opened her eyes, looking eerily calm. She tugged her glove back on—using her safehand to hold it against her stomach and sliding her freehand fingers in. Then she calmly walked back the way they had come. She left the crystal corpse kneeling with hand upraised. Frozen forever.

Shallan pried herself off the wall and hastened after Jasnah, sickened and amazed. Ardents were forbidden to use their Soulcasters on people. They rarely even used them in front of others. And how had Jasnah struck down two men at a distance? From everything Shallan had read—what little there was to find—Soulcasting required physical contact.

Too overwhelmed to demand answers, she stood silent—freehand held to the side of her head, trying to control her trembling and her gasping breaths—as Jasnah called for a palanquin. One came eventually, and the two women climbed in.

The bearers carried them toward the Ralinsa, their steps jostling Shallan and Jasnah, who sat across from one another in the palanquin. Jasnah idly popped the broken smokestone from her Soulcaster, then tucked it into a pocket. It could be sold to a gemsmith, who could cut smaller gemstones from the salvaged pieces.

"That was horrible," Shallan finally said, hand still held to her breast. "It was one of the most awful things I've ever experienced. You *killed* four men."

"Four men who were planning to beat, rob, kill, and possibly rape us."

"You tempted them into coming for us!"

"Did I force them to commit any crimes?"

"You showed off your gemstones."

"Can a woman not walk with her possessions down the street of a city?"

"At night?" Shallan asked. "Through a rough area? Displaying wealth? You all but asked for what happened!"

"Does that make it right?" Jasnah said, leaning forward. "Do you condone what the men were planning to do?"

"Of course not. But that doesn't make what you did right either!"

"And yet, those men are off the street. The people of this city are that much safer. The issue that Taravangian has been so worried about has been solved, and no more theatergoers will fall to those thugs. How many lives did I just save?"

"I know how many you just took," Shallan said. "And through the power of something that should be holy!"

"Philosophy in action. An important lesson for you."

"You did all this just to prove a point," Shallan said softly. "You did this to *prove* to me that you could. Damnation, Jasnah, how could you *do* something like that?"

Jasnah didn't reply. Shallan stared at the woman, searching for emotion in those expressionless eyes. *Stormfather. Did I ever really know this woman? Who is she, really?*

Jasnah leaned back, watching the city pass. "I did *not* do this just to prove a point, child. I have been feeling for some time that I took advantage of His Majesty's hospitality. He doesn't realize how much trouble he could face for allying himself with me. Besides, men like those . . ." There was something in her voice, an edge Shallan had never heard before.

What was done to you? Shallan wondered with horror. *And who did it?*

"Regardless," Jasnah continued, "tonight's actions came about because I chose this path, not because of anything I felt you needed to see. However, the opportunity also presented a chance for instruction, for questions. Am I a monster or am I a hero? Did I just slaughter four men, or did I stop four murderers from walking the streets? Does one *deserve* to have evil done to her by consequence of putting herself where evil can reach her? Did I have a right to defend myself? Or was I just looking for an excuse to end lives?"

"I don't know," Shallan whispered.

"You will spend the next week researching it and thinking on it. If you wish to be a scholar—a *true* scholar who changes the world—then you will need to face questions like this. There will be times when you must make decisions that churn your stomach, Shallan Davar. I'll have you ready to make those decisions."

Jasnah fell silent, looking out the side as the palanquin bearers marched them up to the Conclave. Too troubled to say more, Shallan suffered the rest of the trip in silence. She followed Jasnah through the hushed hallways to their rooms, passing scholars on their way to the Palanaeum for some midnight study.

Inside their rooms, Shallan helped Jasnah undress, though she hated touching the woman. She shouldn't have felt that way. The men Jasnah had killed were terrible creatures, and she had little doubt that they would have killed her. But it wasn't the act itself so much as the cold callousness of it that bothered her.

Still feeling numb, Shallan fetched Jasnah a sleeping robe as the woman removed her jewelry and set it on the dressing table. "You could have let the other three get away," Shallan said, walking back toward Jasnah, who had sat down to brush her hair. "You only needed to kill one of them."

"No, I didn't," Jasnah said.

"Why? They would have been too frightened to do something like that again."

"You don't know that. I sincerely wanted those men *gone*. A careless barmaid walking home the wrong way cannot protect herself, but I can. And I will."

"You have no authority to do so, not in someone else's city."

"True," Jasnah said. "Another point to consider, I suppose." She raised the brush to her hair, pointedly turning away from Shallan. She closed her eyes, as if to shut Shallan out.

The Soulcaster sat on the dressing table beside Jasnah's earrings. Shallan gritted her teeth, holding the soft, silken robe. Jasnah sat in her white underdress, brushing her hair.

There will be times when you must make decisions that churn your stomach, Shallan Davar. . . .

I've faced them already.

I'm facing one now.

How *dare* Jasnah do this? How *dare* she make Shallan a part of it? How *dare* she use something beautiful and holy as a device for destruction?

Jasnah didn't deserve to own the Soulcaster.

With a swift move of her hand, Shallan tucked the folded robe under her safearm, then shoved her hand into her safepouch and popped out the intact smokestone from her father's Soulcaster. She stepped up to the dressing table, and—using the motion of placing the robe onto the table as a cover—made the exchange. She slid the working Soulcaster into her safehand within its sleeve, stepping back as Jasnah opened her eyes and glanced at the robe, which now sat innocently beside the nonfunctional Soulcaster.

Shallan's breath caught in her throat.

Jasnah closed her eyes again, handing the brush toward Shallan. "Fifty strokes tonight, Shallan. It has been a fatiguing day."

Shallan moved by rote, brushing her mistress's hair while clutching the stolen Soulcaster in her hidden safehand, panicked that Jasnah would notice the swap at any moment.

She didn't. Not when she put on her robe. Not when she tucked the broken Soulcaster away in her jewelry case and locked it with a key she wore around her neck as she slept.

Shallan walked from the room stunned, in turmoil. Exhausted, sickened, confused.

But undiscovered.

Shalebark

Shale snail?

Cremlings

FIVE AND A HALF YEARS AGO

"Kaladin, look at this rock," Tien said. "It changes colors when you look at it from different sides."

Kal looked away from the window, glancing at his brother. Now thirteen years of age, Tien had turned from an eager boy into an eager adolescent. Though he'd grown, he was still small for his age, and his mop of black and brown hair still refused all attempts at order. He was squatting beside the lacquered cobwood dinner table, eyes level with the glossy surface, looking at a small, lumpish rock.

Kal sat on a stool peeling longroots with a short knife. The brown roots were dirty on the outside and sticky when he sliced into them, so working on them coated his fingers with a thick layer of crem. He finished a root and handed it up to his mother, who washed it off and sliced it into the stew pot.

"Mother, look at this," Tien said. Late-afternoon sunlight streamed through the leeside window, bathing the table. "From this side, the rock sparkles red, but from the other side, it's green."

"Perhaps it's magical," Hesina said. Chunk after chunk of longroot plunked into the water, each splash with a slightly different note.

"I think it must be," Tien said. "Or it has a spren. Do spren live in rocks?"

"Spren live in everything," Hesina replied.

"They can't live in *everything*," Kal said, dropping a peel into the pail at his feet. He glanced out the window, watching the road that led from the town to the citylord's mansion.

"They do," Hesina said. "Spren appear when something changes—when fear appears, or when it begins to rain. They are the heart of change, and therefore the heart of all things."

"This longroot," Kal said, holding it up skeptically.

"Has a spren."

"And if you slice it up?"

"Each bit has a spren. Only smaller."

Kal frowned, looking over the long tuber. They grew in cracks in the stone where water collected. They tasted faintly of minerals, but were easy to grow. His family needed food that didn't cost much, these days.

"So we eat spren," Kal said flatly.

"No," she said, "we eat the roots."

"When we *have* to," Tien added with a grimace.

"And the spren?" Kal pressed.

"They are freed. To return to wherever it is that spren live."

"Do I have a spren?" Tien said, looking down at his chest.

"You have a soul, dear. You're a person. But the pieces of your body may very well have spren living in them. Very small ones."

Tien pinched at his skin, as if trying to pry the tiny spren out.

"Dung," Kal said suddenly.

"Kal!" Hesina snapped. "That's not talk for mealtime."

"Dung," Kal said stubbornly. "It has spren?"

"I suppose it does."

"Dungspren," Tien said, then snickered.

His mother continued to chop. "Why all of these questions, suddenly?"

Kal shrugged. "I just— I don't know. Because."

He'd been thinking recently about the way the world worked, about what he was to do with his place in it. The other

[670]

boys his age, they didn't wonder about their place. Most *knew* what their future held. Working in the fields.

Kal had a choice, though. Over the last several months, he'd finally made that choice. He would become a soldier. He was fifteen now, and could volunteer when the next recruiter came through town. He planned to do just that. No more wavering. He would learn to fight. That was the end of it. Wasn't it?

"I want to understand," he said. "I just want everything to make sense."

His mother smiled at that, standing in her brown work dress, hair pulled back in a tail, the top hidden beneath her yellow kerchief.

"What?" he demanded. "Why are you smiling?"

"You *just* want everything to make sense?"

"Yes."

"Well next time the ardents come through the town to burn prayers and Elevate people's Callings, I'll pass the message along." She smiled. "Until then, keep peeling roots."

Kal sighed, but did as she told him. He checked out the window again, and nearly dropped the root in shock. The carriage. It was coming down the roadway from the mansion. He felt a flutter of nervous hesitation. He'd planned, he'd thought, but now that the time was upon him, he wanted to sit and keep peeling. There would be another opportunity, surely. . . .

No. He stood, trying to keep the anxiety from his voice. "I'm going to go rinse off." He held up crem-covered fingers.

"You should have washed the roots off first as I told you," his mother noted.

"I know," Kal said. Did his sigh of regret sound fake? "Maybe I'll just wash them all off now."

Hesina said nothing as he gathered up the remaining roots, crossed to the door, heart thumping, and stepped out into the evening light.

"See," Tien said from behind, "from this side it's green. I don't think it's a spren, Mother. It's the light. It makes the rock change. . . ."

The door swung closed. Kal set down the tubers and charged through the streets of Hearthstone, passing men chopping wood, women throwing out dishwater, and a group of grandfathers sitting on steps and looking at the sunset. He dunked his hands into a rain barrel, but didn't stop as he shook the water free. He ran around Mabrow Pigherder's house, up past the commonwater—the large hole cut into the rock at the center of the town to catch rain—and along the breakwall, the steep hillside against which the town was built to shield it from storms.

Here, he found a small stand of stumpweight trees. Knobby and about as tall as a man, they grew leaves only on their leeward sides, running down the length of the tree like rungs on a ladder, waving in the cool breeze. As Kal got close, the large, bannerlike leaves snapped up close to the trunks, making a series of whipping sounds.

Kal's father stood on the other side, hands clasped behind his back. He was waiting where the road from the manor turned past Hearthstone. Lirin turned with a start, noticing Kal. He wore his finest clothing: a blue coat, buttoning up the sides, like a lighteyes's coat. But it was over a pair of white trousers that showed wear. He studied Kal through his spectacles.

"I'm going with you," Kal blurted. "Up to the mansion."

"How did you know?"

"Everyone knows," Kal said. "You think they wouldn't talk if Brightlord Roshone invited you to dinner? You, of all people?"

Lirin looked away. "I told your mother to keep you busy."

"She tried." Kal grimaced. "I'll probably hear a storm of it when she finds those longroots sitting outside the front door."

Lirin said nothing. The carriage rolled to a stop nearby, wheels grinding against the stone.

"This will not be a pleasant, idle meal, Kal," Lirin said.

"I'm not a fool, Father." When Hesina had been told there was no more need for her to work in the town . . . Well, there was a reason they'd been reduced to eating longroots. "If you're going to confront him, then you should have someone to support you."

"And that someone is you?"

"I'm pretty much all you have."

The coachman cleared his throat. He didn't get down and open the door, the way he did for Brightlord Roshone.

Lirin eyed Kal.

"If you send me back, I'll go," Kal said.

"No. Come along if you must." Lirin walked up to the carriage and pulled open the door. It wasn't the fancy, gold-trimmed vehicle that Roshone used. This was the second carriage, the older brown one. Kal climbed in, feeling a surge of excitement at the small victory—and an equal measure of panic.

They were going to face Roshone. Finally.

The benches inside were amazing, the red cloth covering them softer than anything Kal had ever felt. He sat down, and the seat was surprisingly springy. Lirin sat across from Kal, pulling the door closed, and the coachman snapped his whip at the horses. The vehicle turned around and rattled back up the road. As soft as the seat was, the ride was terribly bumpy, and it rattled Kal's teeth against one another. It was worse than riding in a wagon, though that was probably because they were going faster.

"Why didn't you want us to know about this?" Kal asked.

"I wasn't certain I'd go."

"What else would you do?"

"Move away," Lirin said. "Take you to Kharbranth and escape this town, this kingdom, and Roshone's petty grudges."

Kal blinked in shock. He'd never thought of that. Suddenly everything seemed to expand. His future changed, wrapping upon itself, folding into a new form entirely. Father, Mother, Tien . . . *with* him. "Really?"

Lirin nodded absently. "Even if we didn't go to Kharbranth, I'm sure many Alethi towns would welcome us. Most have never had a surgeon to care for them. They do the best they can with local men who learned most of what they know from superstition or working on the occasional wounded chull. We could even move to Kholinar; I'm skilled enough to get work as a physician's assistant there."

"Why don't we go, then? Why *haven't* we gone?"

Lirin watched out the window. "I don't know. We should leave. It makes sense. We have the money. We aren't wanted here. The citylord hates us, the people mistrust us, the Stormfather himself seems inclined to knock us down." There was something in Lirin's voice. Regret?

"I tried very hard to leave once," Lirin said, more softly. "But there's a tie between a man's home and his heart. I've cared for these people, Kal. Delivered their children, set their bones, healed their scrapes. You've seen the worst of them, these last few years, but there was a time before that, a good time." He turned to Kal, clasping his hands in front of him, the carriage rattling. "They're mine, son. And I'm theirs. They're my responsibility, now that Wistiow has gone. I can't leave them to Roshone."

"Even if they *like* what he's doing?"

"Particularly because of that." Lirin raised a hand to his head. "Stormfather. It sounds more foolish now that I say it."

"No. I understand. I think." Kal shrugged. "I guess, well, they still come to us when they're hurt. They complain about how unnatural it is to cut into a person, but they still come. I used to wonder why."

"And did you come to a conclusion?"

"Kind of. I decided that in the end, they'd rather be alive to curse at you a few more days. It's what they do. Just like healing them is what you do. And they *used* to give you money. A man can say all kinds of things, but where he sets his spheres, that's where his heart is." Kal frowned. "I guess they *did* appreciate you."

Lirin smiled. "Wise words. I keep forgetting that you're nearly a man, Kal. When did you go and grow up on me?"

That night when we were nearly robbed, Kal thought immediately. *That night when you shone light on the men outside, and showed that bravery had nothing to do with a spear held in battle.*

"You're wrong about one thing, though," Lirin said. "You told me that they *did* appreciate me. But they still do. Oh, they grumble—they've always done that. But they also leave food for us."

Kal started. "They do?"

"How do you think we've been eating these last four months?"

"But—"

"They're frightened of Roshone, so they're quiet about it. They left it for your mother when she went to clean or put it in the rain barrel when it's empty."

"They tried to rob us."

"And those very men were among the ones who gave us food as well."

Kal pondered that as the carriage arrived at the manor house. It had been a long time since he'd visited the large, two-story building. It was constructed with a standard roof that sloped toward the stormward side, but was much larger. The walls were of thick white stones, and it had majestic square pillars on the leeward side.

Would he see Laral here? He was embarrassed by how infrequently he thought about her these days.

The mansion's front grounds had a low stone wall covered with all kinds of exotic plants. Rockbuds lined the top, their vines draping down the outside. Clusters of a bulbous variety of shalebark grew along the inside, bursting with a variety of bright colors. Oranges, reds, yellows, and blues. Some outcroppings looked like heaps of clothing, with folds spread like fans. Others grew out like horns. Most had tendrils like threads that waved in the wind. Brightlord Roshone paid much more attention to his grounds than Wistiow had.

They walked up past the whitewashed pillars and entered between the thick wooden stormdoors. The vestibule inside had a low ceiling and was decorated with ceramics; zircon spheres gave them a pale blue cast.

A tall servant in a long black coat and a bright purple cravat greeted them. He was Natir, the steward now that Miliv had died. He'd been brought in from Dalilak, a large coastal city to the north.

Natir led them to a dining room where Roshone sat at a long darkwood table. He'd gained weight, though not enough to be called fat. He still had that grey-flecked beard, and his hair was greased back down to his collar. He wore white trousers and a tight red vest over a white shirt.

He'd already begun his meal, and the spicy scents made Kal's stomach rumble. How long had it been since he'd had pork? There were five different dipping sauces on the table, and Roshone's wine was a deep, crystalline orange. He ate alone, no sign of Laral or his son.

The servant gestured toward a side table set up in a room next to the dining hall. Kal's father took one look at it, then walked to Roshone's table and sat down. Roshone paused, skewer halfway to his lips, spicy brown sauce dripping to the table before him.

"I'm of the second nahn," Lirin said, "and I have a personal invitation to dine with you. Surely you follow the precepts of rank closely enough to give me a place at your table."

Roshone clenched his teeth, but did not object. Taking a deep breath, Kal sat down beside his father. Before he left to join the war on the Shattered Plains, he *had* to know. Was his father a coward or a man of courage?

By the light of spheres at home, Lirin had always seemed weak. He worked in his surgery room, ignoring what the townspeople said about him. He told his son he couldn't practice with the spear and forbade him to think of going to war. Weren't those the actions of a coward? But five months ago, Kal had seen courage in him that he'd never expected.

And in the calm blue light of Roshone's palace, Lirin met the eyes of a man far above him in rank, wealth, and power. And did not flinch. How did he do it? Kal's heart thumped uncontrollably. He had to put his hands in his lap to keep them from betraying his nervousness.

Roshone waved to a serving man, and within a short time, new places had been set. The periphery of the room was dark. Roshone's table was an illuminated island amid a vast black expanse.

There were bowls of water for dipping one's fingers and stiff white cloth napkins beside them. A lighteyes's meal. Kal had rarely eaten such fine food; he tried not to make a fool of himself as he hesitantly took a skewer and imitated Roshone, using his knife to slide down the bottommost chunk of meat, then raising it and biting. The meat was savory and tender, though the spices were much hotter than he was accustomed to.

Lirin did not eat. He rested his elbows on the table, watching the Brightlord dine.

"I wished to offer you the chance to eat in peace," Roshone said eventually, "before we talked of serious matters. But you don't seem inclined to partake of my generosity."

"No."

"Very well," Roshone said, taking a piece of flatbread from the basket and wrapping it around his skewer, pulling off several vegetable chunks at once and eating them with the bread. "Then tell me. How long do you think you can defy me? Your family is destitute."

"We do just fine," Kal cut in.

Lirin glanced at him, but did not chastise him for speaking. "My son is correct. We can live. And if that doesn't work, we can leave. I will not bend to your will, Roshone."

"If you left," Roshone said, holding up a finger, "I would contact your new citylord and tell him of the spheres stolen from me."

"I would win an inquest over that. Besides, as a surgeon, I am immune to most demands you could make." It was true; men and their apprentices who served an essential function in towns were afforded special protection, even from lighteyes. The Vorin legal code of citizenship was complex enough that Kaladin still had difficulty understanding it.

"Yes, you would win an inquest," Roshone said. "You were so meticulous, preparing the exact right documents. You were the only one with Wistiow when he stamped them. Odd, that none of his clerks were there."

"Those clerks read him the documents."

"And then left the room."

"Because they were ordered to leave by Brightlord Wistiow. They have admitted this, I believe."

Roshone shrugged. "I don't need to *prove* that you stole the spheres, surgeon. I simply have to continue doing as I have been. I know that your family eats scraps. How long will you continue to make them suffer for your pride?"

"They won't be intimidated. And neither will I."

"I'm not asking if you're intimidated. I'm asking if you're *starving*."

"Not by any means," Lirin said, voice growing dry. "If we lack for something to eat, we can feast upon the attention you lavish upon us, *Brightlord*. We feel your eyes watching, hear your whispers to the townspeople. Judging from the degree of your concern with us, it would seem that *you* are the one who is intimidated."

Roshone fell still, skewer held limply in his hand, brilliant green eyes narrowed, lips pursed tight. In the dark, those eyes almost seemed to *glow*. Kal had to stop himself from cringing under the weight of that disapproving gaze. There was an air of command about lighteyes like Roshone.

He's not a real lighteyes! He's a reject. I'll see real ones eventually. Men of honor.

Lirin held the gaze evenly. "Every month we resist is a blow to your authority. You can't have me arrested, since I would win an inquest. You've tried to turn the other people against me, but they know—deep down—that they need me."

Roshone leaned forward. "I do not like your little town."

Lirin frowned at the odd response.

"I do not like being treated like an *exile*," Roshone continued. "I do not like living so far from anything—everything—important. And most of all, I do not like darkeyes who think themselves above their stations."

"I have trouble feeling sympathy for you."

Roshone sneered. He looked down at his meal, as if it had lost any flavor. "Very well. Let us make an . . . accommodation. I will take nine-tenths of the spheres. You can have the rest."

Kal stood up indignantly. "My father will never—"

"Kal," Lirin cut in. "I can speak for myself."

"Surely you won't make a deal, though."

Lirin didn't reply immediately. Finally, he said, "Go to the kitchens, Kal. Ask them if they have some food more to your tastes."

"Father, no—"

"Go, son." Lirin's voice was firm.

Was it true? After all of this, would his father simply *capitulate*? Kal felt his face grow red, and he fled the dining room. He knew the way to the kitchens. During his childhood, he'd often dined there with Laral.

He left not because he was told to, but because he didn't want his father or Roshone to see his emotions: chagrin at having stood to denounce Roshone when his father planned to make a deal, humiliation that his father would *consider* a deal, frustration at being banished. Kal was mortified to find himself crying. He passed a couple of Roshone's house soldiers standing at the doorway, lit only by a very low-trimmed oil lamp on the wall. Their rough features were highlighted in amber hues.

Kal hastened past them, turning a corner before pausing beside a plant stand, struggling with his emotions. The stand displayed an indoor vinebud, one bred to remain open; a few conelike flowers climbed up from its vestigial shell. The lamp on the wall above it burned with a tiny, strangled light. These were the back rooms of the mansion, near the servant quarters, and spheres were not used for light here.

Kal leaned back, breathing in and out. He felt like one of the ten fools—specifically Cabine, who acted like a child though he was adult. But what was he to think of Lirin's actions?

He wiped his eyes, then pushed his way through the swinging doors into the kitchens. Roshone still employed Wistiow's chef. Barm was a tall, slender man with dark hair that he wore braided. He walked down the line of his kitchen counter, giving instructions to his various subchefs as a couple of parshmen walked in and out through the mansion's back doors, carrying in crates of food. Barm carried a long metal spoon, which he banged on a pot or pan hanging from the ceiling each time he gave an order.

He barely spared Kal a brown-eyed glance, then told one

of his servants to go fetch some flatbread and fruited tallew rice. A child's meal. Kal felt even more embarrassed that Barm had known instantly why he had been sent to the kitchens.

Kal walked to the dining nook to wait for the food. It was a whitewashed alcove with a slate-topped table. He sat down, elbows on the stone, head on his hands.

Why did it make him so angry to think that his father might bargain away most of the spheres in exchange for safety? True, if that happened, there wouldn't be enough to send Kal to Kharbranth. But he'd already decided to become a soldier. So it didn't matter. Did it?

I am going to join the army, Kal thought. *I'll run away, I'll . . .*

Suddenly, that dream—that plan—seemed incredibly childish. It belonged to a boy who ought to eat fruited meals and deserved to be sent away when the men talked of important topics. For the first time, the thought of not training with the surgeons filled him with regret.

The door into the kitchens banged open. Roshone's son, Rillir, sauntered in, chatting with the person behind him. ". . . don't know *why* Father insists on keeping everything so dreary around here all the time. Oil lamps in the hallways? Could he be any more provincial? It would do him some real good if I could get him out on a hunt or two. We might as well get some use out of being in this remote place."

Rillir noticed Kal sitting there, but passed over him as one might register the presence of a stool or a shelf for wine: noting it, but otherwise ignoring it.

Kal's own eyes were on the person who followed Rillir. Laral. Wistiow's daughter.

So much had changed. It had been so long, and seeing her brought up old emotions. Shame, excitement. Did she know that his parents had been hoping to marry him to her? Merely seeing her again almost flustered him completely. But no. His father could look Roshone in the eyes. He could do the same with her.

Kal stood up and nodded to her. She glanced at him, and

blushed faintly, walking in with an old nurse in tow—a chaperone.

What had happened to the Laral he'd known, the girl with the loose yellow and black hair who liked climbing on rocks and running through fields? Now she was wrapped up in sleek yellow silk, a stylish lighteyed woman's dress, her neatly coiffed hair dyed black to hide the blond. Her left hand was hidden modestly in her sleeve. Laral *looked* like a lighteyes.

Wistiow's wealth—what was left of it—had gone to her. And when Roshone had been given authority over Hearthstone and granted the mansion and surrounding lands, Highprince Sadeas had given Laral a dowry in compensation.

"You," Rillir said, nodding to Kal and speaking in a smooth, city accent. "Be a good lad and fetch us some supper. We'll take it here in the nook."

"I'm not a kitchen servant."

"So?"

Kal flushed.

"If you're expecting some kind of tip or reward for just fetching me a meal . . ."

"I'm not— I mean—" Kal looked to Laral. "Tell him, Laral."

She looked away. "Well, go on, boy," she said. "Do as you're told. We're hungry."

Kal gaped at her, then felt his face redden even more. "I'm . . . I'm not going to fetch you anything!" he managed to say. "I wouldn't do it no matter how many spheres you offer me. I'm not an errand boy, I'm a surgeon."

"Oh, you're *that* one's son."

"I am," Kal said, surprised at how proudly he felt those words. "I'm not going to be bullied by you, Rillir Roshone. Just like my father isn't bullied by yours."

Except, they are making a deal right now. . . .

"Father didn't mention how amusing you were," Rillir said, leaning back against the wall. He seemed a decade older than Kal, not a mere two years. "So you find it shameful to fetch a man his meal? Being a surgeon makes you that much better than the kitchen staff?"

"Well, no. It's just not my Calling."

"Then what is your Calling?"

"Making sick people well."

"And if I don't eat, won't I be sick? So couldn't you call it your duty to see me fed?"

Kal frowned. "It's . . . well, it's not the same thing at all."

"I see it as being very similar."

"Look, why don't you just go get yourself some food?"

"It's not my Calling."

"Then what *is* your Calling?" Kal returned, throwing the man's own words back at him.

"I'm cityheir," Rillir said. "My duty is to lead—to see that jobs get done and that people are occupied in productive work. And as such, I give important tasks to idling darkeyes to make them useful."

Kal hesitated, growing angry.

"You see how his little mind works," Rillir said to Laral. "Like a dying fire, burning what little fuel it has, pumping out smoke. Ah, and look, his face grows red from the heat of it."

"Rillir, please," Laral said, laying her hand on his arm.

Rillir glanced at her, then rolled his eyes. "You're as provincial as my father sometimes, dear." He stood up straight and—with a look of resignation—led her past the nook and into the kitchen proper.

Kal sat back down hard, nearly bruising his legs on the bench with the force of it. A serving boy brought him his food and set it on the table, but that only reminded Kal of his childishness. So he didn't eat it; he just stared at it until, eventually, his father walked into the kitchen. Rillir and Laral were gone by then.

Lirin walked to the alcove and surveyed Kal. "You didn't eat."

Kal shook his head.

"You should have. It was free. Come on."

They walked in silence from the mansion into the dark night. The carriage awaited them, and soon Kal again sat facing his father. The driver climbed into place, making the vehicle quiver, and a snap of his whip set the horses in motion.

"I want to be a surgeon," Kal said suddenly.

His father's face—hidden in shadow—was unreadable. But when he spoke, he sounded confused. "I know that, son."

"No. I want to be a surgeon. I don't want to run away to join the war."

Silence in the darkness.

"You were *considering* that?" Lirin asked.

"Yes," Kal admitted. "It was childish. But I've decided for myself that I want to learn surgery instead."

"Why? What made you change?"

"I need to know how *they* think," Kal said, nodding back toward the mansion. "They're trained to speak their sentences in knots, and I have to be able to face them and talk back at them. Not fold like . . ." He hesitated.

"Like I did?" Lirin asked with a sigh.

Kal bit his lip, but had to ask. "How many spheres did you agree to give him? Will I still have enough to go to Kharbranth?"

"I didn't give him a thing."

"But—"

"Roshone and I talked for a time, arguing over amounts. I pretended to grow hotheaded and left."

"Pretended?" Kal asked, confused.

His father leaned forward, whispering to make certain the driver couldn't hear. With the bouncing and the noise of the wheels on the stone, there was little danger of that. "He has to think that I'm willing to bend. Today's meeting was about giving the *appearance* of desperation. A strong front at first, followed by frustration, letting him think that he'd gotten to me. Finally a retreat. He'll invite me again in a few months, after letting me 'sweat.' "

"But you won't bend then, either?" Kal whispered.

"No. Giving him any of the spheres would make him greedy for the rest. These lands don't produce as they used to, and Roshone is nearly broke from losing political battles. I still don't know which highlord was behind sending him here to torment us, though I wish I had him for a few moments in a dark room. . . ."

The ferocity with which Lirin said that shocked Kal. It was the closest he'd ever heard his father come to threatening real violence.

"But why go through this in the first place?" Kal whispered. "You said that we can keep resisting him. Mother thinks so too. We won't eat well, but we won't starve."

His father didn't reply, though he looked troubled.

"You need to make him think that we're capitulating," Kal said. "Or that we're close to doing so. So that he'll stop looking for ways to undermine us? So he'll focus his attention on making a deal and not—"

Kal froze. He saw something unfamiliar in his father's eyes. Something like guilt. Suddenly it made sense. Cold, terrible sense.

"Stormfather," Kal whispered. "You *did* steal the spheres, didn't you?"

His father remained silent, riding in the old carriage, shadowed and black.

"That's why you've been so tense since Wistiow died," Kal whispered. "The drinking, the worrying . . . You're a thief! We're a family of thieves."

The carriage turned, and the violet light of Salas illuminated Lirin's face. He didn't look half so ominous from that angle—in fact, he looked fragile. He clasped his hands before him, eyes reflecting moonlight. "Wistiow was not lucid during the final days, Kal," he whispered. "I knew that, with his death, we would lose the promise of a union. Laral had not reached her day of majority, and the new citylord wouldn't let a darkeyes take her inheritance through marriage."

"So you *robbed* him?" Kal felt himself shrinking.

"I made certain that promises were kept. I had to do something. I couldn't trust to the generosity of the new citylord. Wisely, as you can see."

All of this time, Kal had assumed that Roshone was persecuting them out of malice and spite. But it turned out he was *justified*. "I can't believe it."

"Does it change so much?" Lirin whispered. His face looked haunted in the dim light. "What is different now?"

"Everything."

"And yet nothing. Roshone still wants those spheres, and we still deserve them. Wistiow, if he'd been fully lucid, would have given us those spheres. I'm certain."

"But he didn't."

"No."

Things were the same, yet different. One step, and the world flipped upside down. The villain became the hero, the hero the villain. "I—" Kal said. "I can't decide if what you did was incredibly brave or incredibly wrong."

Lirin sighed. "I know how you feel." He sat back. "Please, don't tell Tien what we've done." What *we've* done. Hesina had helped him. "When you are older, you'll understand."

"Maybe," Kal said, shaking his head. "But one thing hasn't changed. I want to go to Kharbranth."

"Even on stolen spheres?"

"I'll find a way to pay them back. Not to Roshone. To Laral."

"She'll be a Roshone before too long," Lirin said. "We should expect an engagement between her and Rillir before the year is out. Roshone will not let her slip away, not now that he's lost political favor in Kholinar. She represents one of the few chances his son has for an alliance with a good house."

Kal felt his stomach turn at the mention of Laral. "I have to learn. Perhaps I can . . ."

Can what, he thought. *Come back and convince her to leave Rillir for me? Ridiculous.*

He looked up suddenly at his father, who had bowed his head, looking sorrowful. He *was* a hero. A villain too. But a hero to his family. "I won't tell Tien," Kal whispered. "And I'm going to use the spheres to travel to Kharbranth and study."

His father looked up.

"I want to learn to face lighteyes, like you do," Kal said. "Any of them can make a fool of me. I want to learn to talk like them, think like them."

"I want you to learn so that you can help people, son. Not so you can get back at the lighteyes."

"I think I can do both. If I can learn to be clever enough."

Lirin snorted. "You're plenty clever, son. You've got enough of your mother in you to talk circles around a lighteyes. The university will show you how, Kal."

"I want to start going by my full name," he replied, surprising himself. "Kaladin." It was a man's name. He'd always disliked how it sounded like the name of a lighteyes. Now it seemed to fit.

He wasn't a darkeyed farmer, but he wasn't a lighteyed lord either. Something in between. Kal had been a child who wanted to join the army because it was what other boys dreamed of. Kaladin would be a man who learned surgery and all the ways of the lighteyes. And someday he would return to this town and prove to Roshone, Rillir, and Laral herself that they had been wrong to dismiss him.

"Very well," Lirin said. "Kaladin."

38

ENVISAGER

"Born from the darkness, they bear its taint still, marked upon their bodies much as the fire marks their souls."

—I consider Gashash-son-Navammis a trustworthy source, though I'm not certain about this translation. Find the original quote in the fourteenth book of *Seld* and retranslate it myself, perhaps?

Kaladin floated.

Persistent fever, accompanied by cold sweats and hallucinations. Likely cause is infected wounds; clean with antiseptic to ward away rotspren. Keep the subject hydrated.

He was back in Hearthstone with his family. Only he was a grown man. The soldier he had become. And he didn't fit with them anymore. His father kept asking, How did this happen? You *said* you wanted to become a surgeon. A surgeon . . .

Broken ribs. Caused by trauma to the side, inflicted by a beating. Wrap the chest and prevent the subject from taking part in strenuous activity.

Occasionally, he'd open his eyes and see a dark room. It was cold, the walls made of stone, with a high roof. Other people lay in lines, covered in blankets. Corpses. They were corpses. This was a warehouse where they were lined up for sale. Who bought corpses?

Highprince Sadeas. He bought corpses. They still walked after he bought them, but they *were* corpses. The stupid ones refused to accept it, pretending they were alive.

Lacerations on face, arms, and chest. Outer layer of skin stripped away in several patches. Caused by prolonged exposure to highstorm winds. Bandage wounded areas, apply a denocax salve to encourage new skin growth.

Time was passing. A lot of it. He should be dead. Why wasn't he dead? He wanted to lie back and let it happen.

But no. *No.* He had failed Tien. He had failed Goshel. He had failed his parents. He had failed Dallet. Dear Dallet.

He would not fail Bridge Four. He would *not*!

Hypothermia, caused by extreme cold. Warm subject and force him to remain seated. Do not let him sleep. If he survives a few hours, there will likely be no lasting aftereffects.

If he survives a few hours . . .

Bridgemen weren't supposed to survive.

Why would Lamaril say that? What army would employ men who were supposed to die?

His perspective had been too narrow, too shortsighted. He needed to understand the army's objectives. He watched the battle's progress, horrified. What had he done?

He needed to go back and change it. But no. He was wounded, wasn't he? He was bleeding on the ground. He was one of the fallen spearmen. He was a bridgeman from Bridge Two, betrayed by those fools in Bridge Four, who diverted all of the archers.

How dare they? How *dare* they?

How dare they survive by killing me!

Strained tendons, ripped muscles, bruised and cracked bones, and pervasive soreness caused by extreme conditions. Enforce bed rest by any means necessary. Check for large and persistent bruises or pallor caused by internal hemorrhaging. That can be life-threatening. Be prepared for surgery.

He saw the deathspren. They were fist-size and black, with many legs and deep red eyes that glowed, leaving trails of burning light. They clustered around him, skittering this way and that. Their voices were whispers, scratchy sounds like paper being torn. They terrified him, but he couldn't escape them. He could barely move.

Only the dying could see deathspren. You saw them, then died. Only the very, very lucky few survived after that. Death-spren knew when the end was close.

Blistered fingers and toes, caused by frostnip. Make sure to apply antiseptic to any blisters that break. Encourage the body's natural healing. Permanent damage is unlikely.

Standing before the deathspren was a tiny figure of light. Not translucent, as she had always appeared before, but of pure white light. That soft, feminine face had a nobler, more angular cast to it now, like a warrior from a forgotten time. Not childlike at all. She stood guard on his chest, holding a sword made of light.

That glow was so pure, so sweet. It seemed to be the glow of life itself. Whenever one of the deathspren got too close, she would charge at it, wielding her radiant blade.

The light warded them off.

But there were a lot of deathspren. More and more each time he was lucid enough to look.

Severe delusions caused by trauma to the head. Maintain observation of subject. Do not allow alcohol intake. Enforce rest. Administer fathom bark to reduce cranial swelling. Firemoss can be used in extreme cases, but beware letting the subject form an addiction.

If medication fails, trepanning the skull may be needed to relieve pressure.

Usually fatal.

❖

Teft entered the barrack at midday. Ducking into the shadowy interior was like entering a cave. He glanced to the left, where the other wounded usually slept. They were all outside at the moment, getting some sun. All five were doing well, even Leyten.

Teft passed the lines of rolled-up blankets at the sides of the room, walking to the back of the chamber where Kaladin lay.

Poor man, Teft thought. *What's worse, being sick near to death, or having to stay all the way back here, away from the light?* It was necessary. Bridge Four walked a precarious line. They had been allowed to cut Kaladin down, and so far nobody had tried to stop them from caring for him. Practically the entire army had heard Sadeas give Kaladin to the Stormfather for judgment.

Gaz had come to see Kaladin, then had snorted to himself in amusement. He'd likely told his superiors that Kaladin would die. Men didn't live long with wounds like those.

Yet Kaladin hung on. Soldiers were going out of their way to try to get a peek at him. His survival was incredible. People were talking in camp. Given to the Stormfather for judgment, then spared. A miracle. Sadeas wouldn't like that. How long would it be before one of the lighteyes decided to relieve their brightlord of the problem? Sadeas couldn't take any overt action—not without losing a great deal of credibility—but a quiet poisoning or suffocation would abbreviate the embarrassment.

So Bridge Four kept Kaladin as far from outside eyes as possible. And they always left someone with him. Always.

Storming man, Teft thought, kneeling beside the feverish patient in his tousled blankets, eyes closed, face sweaty, body bound with a frightful number of bandages. Most were stained red. They didn't have the money to change them often.

Skar kept watch currently. The short, strong-faced man sat at Kaladin's feet.

"How is he?" Teft asked.

Skar spoke softly. "He seems to be getting worse, Teft. I heard him mumble about dark shapes, thrashing and telling them to keep back. He opened his eyes. He didn't seem to see me, but he saw *something.* I swear it."

Deathspren, Teft thought, feeling a chill. *Kelek preserve us.*

"I'll take a turn," Teft said, sitting. "You go get something to eat."

Skar stood, looking pale. It would crush the others' spirit for Kaladin to survive the highstorm, then die of his wounds. Skar shuffled from the room, shoulders slumped.

Teft watched Kaladin for a long while, trying to gather his thoughts, his emotions. "Why now?" he whispered. "Why here? After so many have watched and waited, you come here?"

But of course, Teft was getting ahead of himself. He didn't *know* for certain. He only had assumptions and hopes. No, not hopes—*fears*. He had rejected the Envisagers. And yet, here he was. He fished in his pocket and pulled out three small diamond spheres. It had been a long, long while since he'd saved anything of his wages, but he'd held on to these, thinking, worrying. They glowed with Stormlight in his hand.

Did he really want to know?

Gritting his teeth, Teft moved closer to Kaladin's side, looking down at the unconscious man's face. "You bastard," he whispered. "You storming bastard. You took a bunch of hanged men and lifted them up just enough to breathe. Now you're going to leave them? I won't have it, you hear. I *won't*."

He pressed the spheres into Kaladin's hand, wrapping the limp fingers around them, then laying the hand on Kaladin's abdomen. Then Teft sat back on his heels. What would happen? All the Envisagers had were stories and legends. Fool's tales, Teft had called them. Idle dreams.

He waited. Of course, nothing happened. *You're as big a fool as any, Teft,* he told himself. He reached for Kaladin's hand. Those spheres would buy a few drinks.

Kaladin gasped suddenly, drawing in a short, quick, powerful breath.

The glow in his hand faded.

Teft froze, eyes widening. Wisps of Light began to rise from Kaladin's body. It was faint, but there was no mistaking that glowing white Stormlight streaming off his frame. It was as if Kaladin had been bathed in sudden heat, and his very skin steamed.

Kaladin's eyes snapped open, and they leaked light too. He gasped again loudly, and the trailing wisps of light began to twist around the exposed cuts on his chest. A few of them pulled together and knit themselves up.

Then it was gone, the Light of those tiny chips expended. Kaladin's eyes closed and he relaxed. His wounds were still bad, his fever still raging, but some color had returned to his skin. The puffy redness around several cuts had diminished.

"My God," Teft said, realizing he was trembling. "Almighty, cast from heaven to dwell in our hearts . . . It is true." He bowed his head to the rock floor, squeezing his eyes shut, tears leaking from their corners.

Why now? he thought again. *Why here?*

And, in the name of all heaven, why me?

He knelt for a hundred heartbeats, counting, thinking, worrying. Eventually, he pulled himself to his feet and retrieved the spheres—now dun—from Kaladin's hand. He'd need to trade them for spheres with Light in them. Then he could return and let Kaladin drain those as well.

He'd have to be careful. A few spheres each day, but not too many. If the boy healed too quickly, it would draw too much attention.

And I need to tell the Envisagers, he thought. *I need to . . .*

The Envisagers were gone. Dead, because of what he had done. If there were others, he had no idea how to locate them.

Who would he tell? Who would believe him? Kaladin himself probably didn't understand what he was doing.

Best to keep it quiet, at least until he could figure out what to do about it.

39

BURNED INTO HER

"Within a heartbeat, Alezarv was there, crossing a distance that would have taken more than four months to travel by foot."

—Another folktale, this one recorded in *Among the Darkeyed*, by Calinam. Page 102. Stories of instantaneous travel and the Oathgates pervade these tales.

Shallan's hand flew across the drawing board, moving as if of its own accord, charcoal scratching, sketching, smudging. Thick lines first, like trails of blood left by a thumb drawn across rough granite. Tiny lines like scratches made by a pin.

She sat in her closetlike stone chamber in the Conclave. No windows, no ornamentation on the granite walls. Just the bed, her trunk, the nightstand, and the small desk that doubled as a drawing table.

A single ruby broam cast a bloody light on her sketch. Usually, to produce a vibrant drawing, she had to consciously memorize a scene. A blink, freezing the world, imprinting it into her mind. She hadn't done that during Jasnah's annihilation of the thieves. She'd been too frozen by horror or morbid fascination.

Despite that, she could see each of those scenes in her mind just as vividly as if she'd deliberately memorized them.

And these memories didn't vanish when she drew them. She couldn't rid her mind of them. Those deaths were burned into her.

She sat back from her drawing board, hand shaking, the picture before her an exact charcoal representation of the suffocating nightscape, squeezed between alley walls, a tortured figure of flame rising toward the sky. At that moment, its face still held its shape, shadow eyes wide and burning lips agape. Jasnah's hand was toward the figure, as if warding, or worshipping.

Shallan drew her charcoal-stained fingers to her chest, staring at her creation. It was one of dozens of drawings she'd done during the last few days. The man turned into fire, the other frozen into crystal, the two transmuted to smoke. She could only draw one of those two fully; she'd been facing down the alleyway to the east. Her drawings of the fourth man's death were of smoke rising, clothing already on the ground.

She felt guilty for being unable to record his death. And she felt stupid for that guilt.

Logic did not condemn Jasnah. Yes, the princess had gone willingly into danger, but that didn't remove responsibility from those who had chosen to hurt her. The men's actions were reprehensible. Shallan had spent the days poring through books on philosophy, and most ethical frameworks exonerated the princess.

But Shallan had been there. She'd watched those men die. She'd seen the terror in their eyes, and she *felt* terrible. Hadn't there been another way?

Kill or be killed. That was the Philosophy of Starkness. It exonerated Jasnah.

Actions are not evil. Intent is evil, and Jasnah's intent had been to stop men from harming others. That was the Philosophy of Purpose. It lauded Jasnah.

Morality is separate from the ideals of men. It exists whole somewhere, to be approached—but never truly understood—by the mortal. The Philosophy of Ideals. It claimed that removing evil was ultimately moral, and so in destroying evil men, Jasnah was justified.

Objective must be weighed against methods. If the goal is worthy, then the steps taken are worthwhile, even if some of them—on their own—are reprehensible. The Philosophy of Aspiration. It, more than any, called Jasnah's actions ethical.

Shallan pulled the sheet from her drawing board and tossed it down beside the others scattered across her bed. Her fingers moved again, clutching the charcoal pencil, beginning a new picture on the blank sheet strapped in place on the table, unable to escape.

Her theft nagged at her as much as the killings did. Ironically, Jasnah's demand that Shallan study moralistic philosophy forced her to contemplate her own, terrible actions. She'd come to Kharbranth to steal the fabrial, then use it to save her brothers and their house from massive debt and destruction. Yet in the end, this wasn't why Shallan had stolen the Soulcaster. She'd taken it because she was angry with Jasnah.

If the intentions were more important than the action, then she had to condemn herself. Perhaps the Philosophy of Aspiration—which stated that objectives were more important than the steps taken to achieve them—would agree with what she'd done, but that was the philosophy she found most reprehensible. Shallan sat here sketching, condemning Jasnah. But Shallan was the one who had betrayed a woman who had trusted her and taken her in. Now she was planning to commit heresy with the Soulcaster by using it although she was not an ardent.

The Soulcaster itself lay in the hidden part of Shallan's trunk. Three days, and Jasnah had said nothing about the disappearance. She wore the fake each day. She said nothing, acted no differently. Maybe she hadn't tried Soulcasting. Almighty send that she didn't go out and put herself into danger again, expecting to be able to use the fabrial to kill men who attacked her.

Of course, there was one other aspect of that night that Shallan had to think of. She carried a concealed weapon that she hadn't used. She felt foolish for not even thinking of getting it out that night. But she wasn't accustomed to—

Shallan froze, realizing for the first time what she'd been drawing. Not another scene from the alleyway, but a lavish room with a thick, ornamented rug and swords on the walls. A long dining table, set with a half-eaten meal.

And a dead man in fine clothing, lying face-first on the floor, blood pooling around him. She jumped back, tossing aside the charcoal, then crumpled up the paper. Shaking, she moved over and sat down on the bed among the pictures. Dropping the crumpled drawing, she raised her fingers to her forehead, feeling the cold sweat there.

Something was wrong with her, with her drawings.

She had to get out. Escape the death, the philosophy and the questions. She stood and hurriedly strode into the main room of Jasnah's quarters. The princess herself was away researching, as always. She hadn't demanded that Shallan come to the Veil today. Was that because she realized that her ward needed time to think alone? Or was it because she suspected Shallan of stealing the Soulcaster, and no longer trusted her?

Shallan hurried through the room. It was furnished only with the basics provided by King Taravangian. Shallan pulled open the door to the hallway, and nearly ran into a master-servant who had been reaching up to knock.

The woman started, and Shallan let out a yelp. "Brightness," the woman said, bowing immediately. "Apologies. But one of your spanreeds is flashing." The woman held up the reed, affixed on the side with a small blinking ruby.

Shallan breathed in and out, stilling her heart. "Thank you," she said. She, like Jasnah, left her spanreeds in the care of servants because she was often away from her rooms, and was likely to miss any attempt to contact her.

Still flustered, she was tempted to leave the thing and continue on her way. However, she did need to speak with her brothers, Nan Balat particularly, and he'd been away the last few times she'd contacted home. She took the spanreed and closed the door. She didn't dare return to her rooms, with all of those sketches accusing her, but there was a desk and a spanreed board in the main room. She sat there, then twisted the ruby.

Shallan? the reed wrote. *Are you comfortable?* It was a code phrase, meant to indicate to her that it was indeed Nan Balat—or, at least, his betrothed—on the other side.

My back hurts and my wrist itches, she wrote back, giving the other half of the code phrase.

I'm sorry I missed your other communications, Nan Balat sent. *I had to attend a feast in Father's name. It was with Sur Kamar, so it wasn't really something I could miss, despite the day of traveling each way.*

It's all right, Shallan wrote. She took a deep breath. *I have the item.* She turned the gem.

The reed was still for a long moment. Finally, a hurried hand wrote, *Praise the Heralds. Oh, Shallan. You've done it! You are on your way back to us, then? How can you use the spanreed on the ocean? Are you in port?*

I haven't left, Shallan wrote.

What? Why?

Because it would be too suspicious, she wrote. *Think about it, Nan Balat. If Jasnah tries the item and finds it broken, she might not immediately decide that she's been had. That changes if I've suddenly and suspiciously left for home.*

I have to wait until she's made the discovery, then see what she does next. If she realizes that her fabrial was replaced with a fake, then I can deflect her toward other culprits. She's already suspicious of the ardentia. If—on the other hand— she assumes that her fabrial has broken somehow, I'll know we're free.

She twisted the gem, setting the spanreed in place.

The question she'd been expecting came next. *And if she immediately assumes that you did it? Shallan, what if you can't deflect her suspicion? What if she orders a search of your chambers and they find the hidden compartment?*

She picked up the pen. *Then it is still better for me to be here,* she wrote. *Balat, I have learned much about Jasnah Kholin. She is incredibly focused and determined. She will not let me escape if she thinks I have robbed her. She will hunt me down, and will use* all *of her resources to exact retribution. We'd have our own king and highprinces on our property in days, demanding that we turn over the fabrial. Stormfather! I'll bet Jasnah has contacts in Jah Keved that she could reach before I got back. I'd find myself in custody the moment I landed.*

Our only hope is to deflect her. If that doesn't work, better for me to be here and suffer her wrath quickly. Likely she would take the Soulcaster and banish me from her sight. If we make her work and chase after me, though . . . She can be very ruthless, Balat. It would not go well for us.

The response was long in coming. *When did you get so good at logic, small one?* he finally sent. *I see that you've thought this through. Better than I have, at least. But Shallan, our time is running out.*

I know, she wrote. *You said you could hold things together for a few more months. I ask you to do that. Give me two or three weeks, at least, to see what Jasnah does. Besides, while I am here, I can look into how the thing works. I haven't found any books that give hints, but there are so many here, maybe I just haven't found the right one yet.*

Very well, he wrote. *A few weeks. Be careful, small one. The men who gave Father his fabrial visited again. They asked after you. I'm worried about them. Even more than I worry about our finances. They disturb me in a profound way. Farewell.*

Farewell, she wrote back.

So far, there had been no hint of reaction from the princess. She hadn't even mentioned the Soulcaster. That made Shallan nervous. She wished that Jasnah would just say something. The waiting was excruciating. Each day, while she sat with Jasnah, Shallan's stomach churned with anxiety until she was nauseated. At least—considering the killings a few days ago—Shallan had a very good excuse for looking disturbed.

Cold, calm logic. Jasnah herself would be proud.

A knock came at the door, and Shallan quickly gathered up the conversation she'd had with Nan Balat and burned it in the hearth. A palace maid entered a moment later, carrying a basket in the crook of her arm. She smiled at Shallan. It was time for the daily cleaning.

Shallan had a strange moment of panic at seeing the woman. She wasn't one of the maids Shallan recognized. What if Jasnah had sent her or someone else to search Shallan's room? Had she done so already? Shallan nodded to the woman and then—to assuage her worries—she walked to her room and closed the door. She rushed to the chest and checked the hidden compartment. The fabrial was there. She lifted it out, inspecting it. Would she know if Jasnah somehow reversed the exchange?

You're being foolish, she told herself. *Jasnah's subtle, but she's not that subtle.* Still, Shallan stuffed the Soulcaster in her safepouch. It just barely fit inside the envelope-like cloth container. She'd feel safer knowing she had it on her while the maid cleaned her room. Besides, the safepouch might be a better hiding place for it than her trunk.

By tradition, a woman's safepouch was where she kept items of intimate or very precious import. To search one would be like strip-searching her—considering her rank, either would be virtually unthinkable unless she were obviously implicated in a crime. Jasnah could probably force it. But if Jasnah could do that, she could order a search of Shallan's room, and her trunk would be under particular scrutiny. The truth was, if Jasnah chose to suspect her, there would be little Shallan could do to hide the fabrial. So the safepouch was as good a place as any.

She gathered up the pictures she'd drawn and put them upside-down on the desk, trying not to look at them. She didn't want those to be seen by the maid. Finally, she left, taking her portfolio. She felt that she needed to get outside and escape for a while. Draw something other than death and murder. The conversation with Nan Balat had only served to upset her more.

"Brightness?" the maid asked.

Shallan froze, but the maid held up a basket. "This was dropped off for you with the master-servants."

She hesitantly accepted it, looking inside. Bread and jam. A note, tied to one of the jars, read: *Bluebar jam. If you like it, it means you're mysterious, reserved, and thoughtful.* It was signed Kabsal.

Shallan placed the basket's handle in the crook of her safearm's elbow. Kabsal. Maybe she should go find him. She always felt better after a conversation with him.

But no. She was going to leave; she couldn't keep stringing him, or herself, along. She was afraid of where the relationship was going. Instead, she made her way to the main cavern and then to the Conclave's exit. She walked out into the sunlight and took a deep breath, looking up into the sky as servants and attendants parted around her, swarming in and out of the Conclave. She held her portfolio close, feeling the cool breeze on her cheeks and the contrasting warmth of the sunlight pressing down on her hair and forehead.

In the end, the most disturbing part was that Jasnah had been right. Shallan's world of simple answers had been a foolish, childish place. She'd clung to the hope that she could find truth, and use it to explain—perhaps justify—what she had done back in Jah Keved. But if there was such a thing as truth, it was far more complicated and murky than she'd assumed.

Some problems didn't seem to have any good answers. Just a lot of wrong ones. She could choose the source of her guilt, but she couldn't choose to be rid of that guilt entirely.

※

Two hours—and about twenty quick sketches—later, Shallan felt far more relaxed.

She sat in the palace gardens, sketchpad in her lap, drawing snails. The gardens weren't as extensive as her father's, but they were far more varied, not to mention blessedly secluded. Like many modern gardens, they were designed with walls of cultivated shalebark. This one's made a maze of living stone. They were short enough that, when standing, she could see the way back to the entrance. But if she sat down on one of the numerous benches, she could feel alone and unseen.

She'd asked a groundskeeper the name of the most prominent shalebark plant; he'd called it "plated stone." A fitting name, as it grew in thin round sections that piled atop one another, like plates in a cupboard. From the sides, it looked like weathered rock that exposed hundreds of thin strata. Tiny little tendrils grew up out of pores, waving in the wind. The stonelike casings had a bluish shade, but the tendrils were yellowish.

Her current subject was a snail with a low horizontal shell edged with little ridges. When she tapped, it would flatten itself into a rift in the shalebark, appearing to become part of the plated stone. It blended in perfectly. When she let it move, it nibbled at the shalebark—but didn't chew it away.

It's cleaning the shalebark, she realized, continuing her sketch. *Eating off the lichen and mold.* Indeed, a cleaner trail extended behind it.

Patches of a different kind of shalebark—with fingerlike protrusions growing up into the air from a central knob—grew alongside the plated stone. When she looked closely, she noted little cremlings—thin and multilegged—crawling along it, eating at it. Were they too cleaning it?

Curious, she thought, beginning a sketch of the miniature cremlings. They had carapaces shaded like the shalebark's fingers, while the snail's shell was a near duplicate of the yellow and blue colorings of the plated stone. It was as if they had been designed by the Almighty in pairs, the plant giving safety to the animal, the animal cleaning the plant.

A few lifespren—tiny, glowing green specks—floated around the shalebark mounds. Some danced amid the rifts in the bark, others in the air like dust motes zigzagging up, only to fall again.

She used a finer-tipped charcoal pencil to scribble some thoughts about the relationship between the animals and the plants. She didn't know of any books that spoke of relationships like this one. Scholars seemed to prefer studying big, dynamic animals, like greatshells or whitespines. But this seemed a beautiful, wondrous discovery to Shallan.

Snails and plants can help one another, she thought. *But I betray Jasnah.*

She glanced toward her safehand, and the pouch hidden inside. She felt more secure having the Soulcaster near. She hadn't yet dared try to use it. She'd been too nervous about the theft, and had worried about using the object near Jasnah. Now, however, she was in a nook deep within the maze, with only one curving entrance into her dead end. She stood up casually, looking around. No one else was in the gardens, and she was far enough inside that it would take minutes for anyone to get to her.

Shallan sat back down, setting aside her drawing pad and pencil. *I might as well see if I can figure out how to use it,* she thought. *Maybe there's no need to keep searching the Palanaeum for a solution.* So long as she stood up and glanced about periodically, she could be certain she wouldn't be approached or seen by accident.

She removed the forbidden device. It was heavy in her hand. Solid. Taking a deep breath, she looped the chains over her fingers and around her wrist, the gemstones set against the back of her hand. The metal was cold, the chains loose. She flexed her hand, pulling the fabrial tight.

She'd anticipated a feeling of power. Prickles on her skin, perhaps, or a sense of strength and might. But there was nothing.

She tapped the three gemstones—she'd placed her smokestone into the third setting. Some other fabrials, like spanreeds, worked when you tapped the stones. But that was foolish, as she'd never seen Jasnah do that. The woman just closed her eyes and touched something, Soulcasting it. Smoke, crystal, and fire were what this Soulcaster was best at. Only once had she seen Jasnah create anything else.

Hesitant, Shallan took a piece of broken shalebark from the base of one of the plants. She held it up in her freehand, then closed her eyes.

Become smoke! she commanded.

Nothing happened.

Become crystal! she commanded instead.

She cracked an eye. There was no change.

Fire. Burn! You're fire! You—

She paused, realizing the stupidity of that. A mysteriously burned hand? No, that wouldn't be *at all* suspicious. Instead, she focused on crystal. She closed her eyes again, holding the image of a piece of quartz in her mind. She tried to *will* the shalebark to change.

Nothing happened, so she just tried focusing, imagining the shalebark transforming. After a few minutes of failure, she tried making the pouch change instead, then tried the bench, then tried one of her hairs. Nothing worked.

Shallan checked to make certain she was still alone, then sat down, frustrated. Nan Balat had asked Luesh how the devices worked, and he'd said that it was easier to show than explain. He'd promised to give them answers if she actually managed to steal Jasnah's.

Now he was dead. Was she doomed to carry this one back to her family, only to immediately give it away to those dangerous men, never using it to gain wealth to protect her house? All because they didn't know how to activate it?

The other fabrials she'd used had been simple to activate, but those were constructed by contemporary artifabrians. Soulcasters were fabrials from ancient times. They wouldn't employ modern methods of activation. She stared at the glowing gemstones suspended on the back of her hand. How would she figure out the method of using a tool thousands of years old, one forbidden to any but ardents?

She slid the Soulcaster back into her safepouch. It seemed she was back to searching the Palanaeum. That or asking Kabsal. But would she manage that without looking suspicious? She broke out his bread and jam, eating and thinking idly. If Kabsal didn't know, and if she couldn't find the answers by the time she left Kharbranth, were there other options? If she took the artifact to the Veden king—or maybe the ardents—might they be able to protect her family in exchange for the gift? After all, she couldn't really be blamed for stealing from a heretic, and so long as Jasnah didn't know who had the Soulcaster, they would be safe.

For some reason, that made her feel even worse. Stealing the Soulcaster to save her family was one thing, but turning it over to the very ardents whom Jasnah disdained? It seemed a greater betrayal.

Yet another difficult decision. *Well then,* she thought, *it's a good thing Jasnah is so determined to train me in how to deal with those. By the time all this is done, I should be quite the expert. . . .*

40

EYES OF
RED AND BLUE

"Death upon the lips. Sound upon the air. Char upon the skin."

—From "The Last Desolation" by Ambrian, line 335.

Kaladin stumbled into the light, shading his eyes against the burning sun, his bare feet feeling the transition from cold indoor stone to sun-warmed stone outside. The air was lightly humid, not muggy as it had been in previous weeks.

He rested his hand on the wooden doorframe, his legs quivering rebelliously, his arms feeling as if he'd carried a bridge for three days straight. He breathed deeply. His side should have blazed with pain, but he felt only a residual soreness. Some of his deeper cuts were still scabbed over, but the smaller ones had vanished completely. His head was surprisingly clear. He didn't even have a headache.

He rounded the side of the barrack, feeling stronger with each step, though he kept his hand on the wall. Lopen followed behind; the Herdazian had been watching over Kaladin when he awoke.

I should be dead, Kaladin thought. *What is going on?*

On the other side of the barrack he was surprised to find the men carrying their bridge in daily practice. Rock ran at the front center, giving the marching beat as Kaladin had once done. They reached the other side of the lumberyard and turned around, charging back. Only when they were almost past the barrack did one of the men in front—Moash—notice Kaladin. He froze, nearly causing the entire bridge crew to trip.

"What is wrong with you?" Torfin yelled from behind, head enveloped by the wood of the bridge.

Moash didn't listen. He ducked out from under the bridge, looking at Kaladin with wide eyes. Rock gave a hasty shout for the men to put down the bridge. More saw him, adopting the same reverent expressions as Moash. Hobber and Peet, their wounds sufficiently healed, had started practicing with the others. That was good. They'd be drawing pay again.

The men walked up to Kaladin, silent in their leather vests. They kept their distance, hesitant, as if he were fragile. Or holy. Kaladin was bare-chested, his nearly healed wounds exposed, and wore only his knee-length bridgeman's trousers.

"You really need to practice what to do if one of you trips or stumbles, men," Kaladin said. "When Moash stopped abruptly, you all about fell over. That could be a disaster on the field."

They stared at him, incredulous, and he couldn't help but smile. In a moment, they crowded around him, laughing and thumping him on the back. It wasn't an entirely appropriate welcome for a sick man, particularly when Rock did it, but Kaladin did appreciate their enthusiasm.

Only Teft didn't join in. The aging bridgeman stood at the side, arms folded. He seemed concerned. "Teft?" Kaladin asked. "You all right?"

Teft snorted, but showed a hint of a grin. "I just figure those lads don't bathe often enough for me to want to get close enough for a hug. No offense."

Kaladin laughed. "I understand." His last "bath" had been the highstorm.

The highstorm.

The other bridgemen continued to laugh, asking how he felt, proclaiming that Rock would have to fix something *extra* special for their nightly fireside meal. Kaladin smiled and nodded, assuring them he felt well, but he was remembering the storm.

He recalled it distinctly. Holding to the ring atop the building, his head down and eyes closed against the pelting torrent. He remembered Syl, standing protectively before him, as if she could turn back the storm itself. He couldn't see her about now. Where was she?

He also remembered the face. The Stormfather himself? Surely not. A delusion. Yes . . . yes, he'd certainly been delusional. Memories of deathspren were blended with relived parts of his life—and both mixed with strange, sudden *shocks* of strength—icy cold, but refreshing. It had been like the cold air of a crisp morning after a long night in a stuffy room, or like rubbing the sap of gulket leaves on sore muscles, making them feel warm and cold at the same time.

He could remember those moments so clearly. What had caused them? The fever?

"How long?" he said, checking over the bridgemen, counting them. Thirty-three, counting Lopen and the silent Dabbid. Almost all were accounted for. Impossible. If his ribs were healed, then he must have been unconscious for four weeks, at least. How many bridge runs?

"Ten days," Moash said.

"Impossible," Kaladin said. "My wounds—"

"Is why we're so surprised to see you up and walking!" Rock said, laughing. "You must have bones like granite. Is my name you should be having!"

Kaladin leaned back against the wall. Nobody corrected Moash. An entire crew of men couldn't lose track of the weeks like that. "Idolir and Treff?" he asked.

"We lost them," Moash said, growing solemn. "We did two bridge runs while you were unconscious. Nobody badly wounded, but two dead. We . . . we didn't know how to help them."

That made the men grow subdued. But death was the way of bridgemen, and they couldn't afford to dwell for long on the lost. Kaladin did decide, however, that he'd need to train a few of the others in healing.

But how was he up and walking? Had he been less injured than he'd assumed? Hesitantly, he prodded at his side, feeling for broken ribs. Just a little sore. Other than the weakness, he felt as healthy as he ever had. Perhaps he should have paid a little more attention to his mother's religious teachings.

As the men turned back to talking and celebrating, he noticed the looks they gave him. Respectful, reverent. They remembered what he'd said before the highstorm. Looking back, Kaladin realized he'd been a little delirious. It now seemed an incredibly arrogant proclamation, not to mention that it smelled of prophecy. If the ardents discovered that . . .

Well, he couldn't undo what he'd done. He'd just have to continue. *You were already balancing over a chasm,* Kaladin thought to himself. *Did you have to scale an even* higher *cliffside?*

A sudden, mournful horn call sounded across the camp. The bridgemen fell silent. The horn sounded twice more.

"Figures," Natam said.

"We're on duty?" Kaladin asked.

"Yeah," Moash said.

"Line up!" Rock snapped. "You know what to do! Let's show Captain Kaladin that we haven't forgotten how to do this."

"'Captain' Kaladin?" Kaladin asked as the men lined up.

"Sure, gancho," Lopen said from beside him, speaking with that quick accent that seemed so at odds with his nonchalant attitude. "They tried to make Rock bridgeleader, sure, but we just started calling you 'captain' and him 'squadleader.' Made Gaz angry." Lopen grinned.

Kaladin nodded. The other men were so joyous, but he was finding it difficult to share their mood.

As they formed up around their bridge, he began to realize the source of his melancholy. His men were right back where they'd started. Or worse. He was weakened and injured, and had offended the highprince himself. Sadeas would not be pleased when he learned that Kaladin had survived his fever.

The bridgemen were still destined to be cut down one by

one. The side carry had been a failure. He hadn't saved his men, he'd just given them a short stay of execution.

Bridgemen aren't supposed to survive. . . .

He suspected why that was. Gritting his teeth, he let go of the barrack wall and crossed to where the bridgemen stood in line, leaders of the subsquads doing a quick check of their vests and sandals.

Rock eyed Kaladin. "And what is this thing you believe you are doing?"

"I'm joining you," Kaladin said.

"And what would you tell one of the men if *they* had just gotten up from a week with the fevers?"

Kaladin hesitated. *I'm not like the other men,* he thought, then regretted it. He couldn't start believing himself invincible. To run now with the crew, as weak as he was, would be sheer idiocy. "You're right."

"You can help me and the moolie carry water, gancho," Lopen said. "We're a team now. Go on every run."

Kaladin nodded. "All right."

Rock eyed him.

"If I'm feeling too weak at the end of the permanent bridges, I'll go back. I promise."

Rock nodded reluctantly. The men marched under the bridge to the staging area, and Kaladin joined Lopen and Dabbid, filling waterskins.

※

Kaladin stood at the edge of the precipice, hands clasped behind his back, sandaled toes at the very edge of the cliff. The chasm stared up at him, but he did not meet its gaze. He was focused on the battle being waged on the next plateau.

This approach had been an easy one; they'd arrived at the same time as the Parshendi. Instead of bothering to kill bridgemen, the Parshendi had taken a defensive position in the center of the plateau, around the chrysalis. Now Sadeas's men fought them.

Kaladin's brow was slick with sweat from the day's heat,

and he still felt a lingering exhaustion from his sickness. Yet it wasn't nearly as bad as it should have been. The surgeon's son was baffled.

For the moment, the soldier overruled the surgeon. He was transfixed by the battle. Alethi spearmen in leathers and breastplates pressed a curved line against the Parshendi warriors. Most Parshendi used battle-axes or hammers, though a few wielded swords or clubs. They all had that red-orange armor growing from their skin, and they fought in pairs, singing all the while.

It was the worst kind of battle, the kind that was close. Often, you'd lose far fewer men in a skirmish where your enemies quickly gained the upper hand. When that happened, your commander would order the retreat to cut his losses. But close battles . . . they were brutal, blood-soaked things. Watching the fighting—the bodies dropped to the rocks, the weapons flashing, the men pushed off the plateau—reminded him of his first fights as a spearman. His commander had been shocked at how easily Kaladin dealt with seeing blood. Kaladin's father would have been shocked at how easily Kaladin spilled it.

There was a big difference between his battles in Alethkar and the fights on the Shattered Plains. There, he'd been surrounded by the worst—or at least worst-trained—soldiers in Alethkar. Men who didn't hold their lines. And yet, for all their disorder, those fights had made sense to him. These here on the Shattered Plains still did not.

That had been his miscalculation. He'd changed battlefield tactics before understanding them. He would not make that mistake again.

Rock stepped up beside Kaladin, joined by Sigzil. The thick-limbed Horneater made for quite a contrast to the short, quiet Azish man. Sigzil's skin was a deep brown—not true black, like some parshmen's. He tended to keep to himself.

"Is bad battle," Rock said, folding his arms. "The soldiers will not be happy, whether or not they win."

Kaladin nodded absently, listening to the yells, screams, and curses. "Why do they fight, Rock?"

"For money," Rock said. "And for vengeance. You should know this thing. Is it not your king who Parshendi killed?"

"Oh, I understand why *we* fight," Kaladin said. "But the Parshendi. Why do *they* fight?"

Rock grinned. "Is because they don't very much like the idea of being beheaded for killing your king, I should think! Very unaccommodating of them."

Kaladin smiled, though he found mirth unnatural while watching men die. He had been trained too long by his father for any death to leave him unmoved. "Perhaps. But, then, why do they fight for the gemhearts? Their numbers are dwindling because of skirmishes like these."

"You know this thing?" Rock asked.

"They raid less frequently than they used to," Kaladin said. "People talk about it in camp. And they don't strike as close to the Alethi side as they once did."

Rock nodded thoughtfully. "It seems logical. Ha! Perhaps we will soon win this fight and be going home."

"No," Sigzil said softly. He had a very formal way of speaking, with barely a hint of an accent. What language did the Azish speak, anyway? Their kingdom was so distant that Kaladin had only ever met one other. "I doubt that. And I can tell you why they fight, Kaladin."

"Really?"

"They must have Soulcasters. They need the gemstones for the same reason we do. To make food."

"It sounds reasonable," Kaladin said, hands still clasped behind his back, feet in a wide stance. Parade rest still felt natural to him. "Just conjecture, but a reasonable one. Let me ask you something else, then. Why can't bridgemen have shields?"

"Because this thing makes us too slow," Rock said.

"No," Sigzil said. "They could send bridgemen with shields out in front of the bridges, running in front of us. It wouldn't slow anyone down. Yes, you would have to field more bridgemen—but you'd save enough lives with those shields to make up for the larger roster."

Kaladin nodded. "Sadeas fields more of us than he needs already. In most cases, more bridges land than he needs."

"But why?" Sigzil asked.

"Because we make good targets," Kaladin said softly, understanding. "We're put out in front to draw Parshendi attention."

"Of course we are," Rock said, shrugging. "Armies always do these things. The poorest and the least trained go first."

"I know," Kaladin said, "but usually, they're at least given some measure of protection. Don't you see? We're not just an expendable initial wave. We're *bait*. We're exposed, so the Parshendi can't help but fire at us. It allows the regular soldiers to approach without being hurt. The Parshendi archers are aiming at the bridgemen."

Rock frowned.

"Shields would make us less tempting," Kaladin said. "That's why he forbids them."

"Perhaps," Sigzil said from the side, thoughtful. "But it seems foolish to waste troops."

"Actually, it *isn't* foolish," Kaladin said. "If you have to repeatedly attack fortified positions, you can't afford to lose your trained troops. Don't you see? Sadeas has only a limited number of trained men. But untrained ones are easy to find. Each arrow that strikes down a bridgeman is one that *doesn't* hit a soldier you've spent a great deal of money outfitting and training. That's why it's better for Sadeas to field a large number of bridgemen, rather than a smaller—but protected—number."

He should have seen it earlier. He had been distracted by how important bridgemen were to the battles. If the bridges didn't arrive at the chasms, then the army couldn't cross. But each bridge crew was kept well stocked with bodies, and twice as many bridge crews were sent on an assault as were needed.

Seeing a bridge fall must give the Parshendi a great sense of satisfaction, and they usually got to drop two or three bridges on every bad chasm run. Sometimes more. So long as bridgemen were dying, and the Parshendi didn't spend their time firing on soldiers, Sadeas had reason to keep the bridgemen vulnerable. The Parshendi should have seen through it, but it was very hard to turn your arrow away from the unarmored man carrying the siege equipment. The Parshendi were said to be unsophisticated fighters. Indeed, watching the battle on the other plateau—studying it, focusing—he saw that was true.

Where the Alethi maintained a straight, disciplined line—each man protecting his partners—the Parshendi attacked in independent pairs. The Alethi had superior technique and tactics. True, each of the Parshendi was superior in strength, and their skill with those axes was remarkable. But Sadeas's Alethi troops were well trained in modern formations. Once they got a foothold—and if they could prolong the battle—their discipline often saw them to victory.

The Parshendi haven't fought in large-scale battles before this war, Kaladin decided. *They're used to smaller skirmishes, perhaps against other villages or clans.*

Several of the other bridgemen joined Kaladin, Rock, and Sigzil. Before long, the majority of them were standing there, some imitating Kaladin's stance. It took another hour before the battle was won. Sadeas proved victorious, but Rock was right. The soldiers were grim; they'd lost many friends this day.

It was a tired, battered group of spearmen that Kaladin and the others led back to camp.

⁂

A few hours later, Kaladin sat on a chunk of wood beside Bridge Four's nightly fire. Syl sat on his knee, having taken the form of a small, translucent blue and white flame. She'd come to him during the march back, spinning around gleefully to see him up and walking, but had given no explanation for her absence.

The real fire crackled and popped, Rock's large pot bubbling on top of it, some flamespren dancing on the logs. Every couple of seconds, someone asked Rock if the stew was done yet, often banging on his bowl with a good-natured smack of the spoon. Rock said nothing, stirring. They all knew that nobody ate until he declared the stew finished; he was very particular about not serving "inferior" food.

The air smelled of boiling dumplings. The men were laughing. Their bridgeleader had survived execution and today's bridge run hadn't cost a single casualty. Spirits were high.

Except for Kaladin's.

He understood now. He understood just how futile their struggle was. He understood why Sadeas hadn't bothered to acknowledge Kaladin's survival. He was already a bridgeman, and being a bridgeman was a death sentence.

Kaladin had hoped to show Sadeas that his bridge crew could be efficient and useful. He'd hoped to prove that they deserved protection—shields, armor, training. Kaladin thought that if they acted like soldiers, maybe they would be *seen* as soldiers.

None of that would work. A bridgeman who survived was, by definition, a bridgeman who had failed.

His men laughed and enjoyed the fire. They trusted him. He'd done the impossible, surviving a highstorm, wounded, tied to a wall. Surely he would perform another miracle, this time for them. They were good men, but they thought like foot soldiers. The officers and the lighteyes would worry about the long term. The men were fed and happy, and that was enough for now.

Not for Kaladin.

He found himself face-to-face with the man he'd left behind. The one he'd abandoned that night he'd decided not to throw himself into the chasm. A man with haunted eyes, a man who had given up on caring or hoping. A walking corpse.

I'm going to fail them, he thought.

He couldn't let them continue running bridges, dying off one by one. But he also couldn't think of an alternative. And so their laughter tore at him.

One of the men—Maps—stood, holding up his arms, quieting the others. It was the time between moons, and so he was lit mostly by the firelight; there was a spray of stars in the sky above. Several of those moved about, the tiny pinpricks of light chasing after one another, zipping around like distant, glowing insects. Starspren. They were rare.

Maps was a flat-faced fellow, his beard bushy, his eyebrows thick. Everyone called him Maps because of the birthmark on his chest that he swore was an exact map of Alethkar, though Kaladin hadn't been able to see the resemblance.

Maps cleared his throat. "It's a good night, a special night, and all. We've got our bridgeleader back."

Several of the men clapped. Kaladin tried not to show how sick he felt inside.

"We've got good food coming," Maps said. He eyed Rock. "It *is* coming, ain't it, Rock?"

"Is coming," Rock said, stirring.

"You're sure about that? We could go on another bridge run. Give you a little extra time, you know, five or six more hours. . . ."

Rock gave him a fierce look. The men laughed, several banging their bowls with their spoons. Maps chuckled, then he reached to the ground behind the stone he was using for a seat. He pulled out a paper-wrapped package and tossed it to Rock.

Surprised, the tall Horneater barely caught it, nearly dropping it into the stew.

"From all of us," Maps said, a little awkwardly, "for making us stew each night. Don't think we haven't noticed how hard you work on it. We relax while you cook. And you always serve everyone else first. So we bought you something to thank you." He wiped his nose on his arm, spoiling the moment slightly, and sat back down. Several of the other bridgemen thumped him on the back, complimenting his speech.

Rock unwrapped the package and stared into it for a long while. Kaladin leaned forward, trying to get a look at the contents. Rock reached in and held the item up. It was a straight razor of gleaming silvery steel; there was a length of wood covering the sharp side. Rock pulled this off, inspecting the blade. "You airsick fools," he said softly. "Is beautiful."

"There's a piece of polished steel too," said Peet. "For a

mirror. And some beard soap and a leather strop for sharpening."

Amazingly, Rock grew teary-eyed. He turned away from the pot, bearing his gifts. "Stew is ready," he said. Then he ran into the barrack building.

The men sat quietly. "Stormfather," youthful Dunny finally said, "you think we did the right thing? I mean, the way he complains and all . . ."

"I think it was perfect," Teft said. "Just give the big lout some time to recover."

"Sorry we didn't get you nothin', sir," Maps said to Kaladin. "We didn't know you'd be awake and all."

"It's all right," Kaladin said.

"Well," Skar said. "Is someone going to serve that stew, or will we all just sit here hungry until it burns?"

Dunny jumped up, grabbing the ladle. The men gathered around the pot, jostling one another as Dunny served. Without Rock there to snap at them and keep them in line, it was something of a melee. Only Sigzil did not join in. The quiet, dark-skinned man sat to the side, eyes reflecting the flames.

Kaladin rose. He was worried—terrified, really—that he might become that wretch again. The one who had given up on caring because he saw no alternative. So he sought conversation, walking over toward Sigzil. His motion disturbed Syl, who sniffed and buzzed up onto his shoulder. She still held the form of a flickering flame; having that on his shoulder was even *more* distracting. He didn't say anything; if she knew it bothered him, she'd be likely to do it more. She *was* still a windspren, after all.

Kaladin sat down next to Sigzil. "Not hungry?"

"They are more eager than I," Sigzil said. "If previous evenings are a reliable guide, there will still be enough for me once they have filled their bowls."

Kaladin nodded. "I appreciated your analysis out on the plateau today."

"I am good at that, sometimes."

"You're educated. You speak like it and you act like it."

Sigzil hesitated. "Yes," he finally said. "Among my people, it is not a sin for a male to be keen of mind."

"It isn't a sin for Alethi either."

"My experience is that you care only about wars and the art of killing."

"And what have you seen of us besides our army?"

"Not much," Sigzil admitted.

"So, a man of education," Kaladin said thoughtfully. "In a bridge crew."

"My education was never completed."

"Neither was mine."

Sigzil looked at him, curious.

"I apprenticed as a surgeon," Kaladin said.

Sigzil nodded, thick dark hair falling around his shoulders. He'd been one of the only bridgemen who bothered shaving. Now that Rock had a razor, maybe that would change. "A surgeon," he said. "I cannot say that is surprising, considering how you handled the wounded. The men say that you're secretly a lighteyes of very high rank."

"*What?* But my eyes are dark brown!"

"Pardon me," Sigzil said. "I didn't speak the right word—you don't *have* the right word in your language. To you, a lighteyes is the same as a leader. In other kingdoms, though, other things make a man a . . . curse this Alethi language. A man of high birth. A brightlord, only without the eyes. Anyway, the men think you must have been raised outside of Alethkar. As a leader."

Sigzil looked back at the others. They were beginning to sit back down, attacking their stew with vigor. "It's the way you lead so naturally, the way you make others want to listen to you. These are things they associate with lighteyes. And so they have invented a past for you. You will have a difficult time disabusing them of it now." Sigzil eyed him. "Assuming it is a fabrication. I was there in the chasm the day you used that spear."

"A spear," Kaladin said. "A darkeyed soldier's weapon, not a lighteyes's sword."

"To many bridgemen, the difference is minimal. All are so far above us."

"So what is your story?"

Sigzil smirked. "I wondered if you were going to ask. The others mentioned that you have pried into their origins."

"I like to know the men I lead."

"And if some of us are murderers?" Sigzil asked quietly.

"Then I'm in good company," Kaladin said. "If it was a lighteyes you killed, then I might buy you a drink."

"Not a lighteyes," Sigzil said. "And he is not dead."

"Then you're not a murderer," Kaladin said.

"Not for want of trying." Sigzil's eyes grew distant. "I thought for certain I had succeeded. It was not the wisest choice I made. My master . . ." He trailed off.

"Is he the one you tried to kill?"

"No."

Kaladin waited, but no more information was forthcoming. *A scholar,* he thought. *Or at least a man of learning. There has to be a way to use this.*

Find a way out of this death trap, Kaladin. Use what you have. There has *to be a way.*

"You were right about the bridgemen," Sigzil said. "We are sent to die. It is the only reasonable explanation. There is a place in the world. Marabethia. Have you heard of it?"

"No," Kaladin said.

"It is beside the sea, to the north, in the Selay lands. The people are known for their great fondness for debate. At each intersection in the city they have small pedestals on which a man can stand and proclaim his arguments. It is said that everyone in Marabethia carries a pouch with an overripe fruit just in case they pass a proclaimer with whom they disagree."

Kaladin frowned. He hadn't heard so many words from Sigzil in all the time they'd been bridgemen together.

"What you said earlier, on the plateau," Sigzil continued, eyes forward, "it made me think of the Marabethians. You see, they have a curious way of treating condemned criminals. They dangle them over the seaside cliff near the city, down near the water at high tide, with a cut sliced in each cheek.

There is a particular species of greatshell in the depths there. The creatures are known for their succulent flavor, and of course they have gemhearts. Not nearly as large as the ones in these chasmfiends, but still nice. So the criminals, they become bait. A criminal may demand execution instead, but they say if you hang there for a week and are not eaten, then you can go free."

"And does that often happen?" Kaladin asked.

Sigzil shook his head. "Never. But the prisoners almost always take the chance. The Marabethians have a saying for someone who refuses to see the truth of a situation. 'You have eyes of red and blue,' they say. Red for the blood dripping. Blue for the water. It is said that these two things are all the prisoners see. Usually they are attacked within one day. And yet, most still wish to take that chance. They prefer the false hope."

Eyes of red and blue, Kaladin thought, imagining the morbid picture.

"You do a good work," Sigzil said, rising, picking up his bowl. "At first, I hated you for lying to the men. But I have come to see that a false hope makes them happy. What you do is like giving medicine to a sick man to ease his pain until he dies. Now these men can spend their last days in laughter. You are a healer indeed, Kaladin Stormblessed."

Kaladin wanted to object, to say that it wasn't a false hope, but he couldn't. Not with his heart in his stomach. Not with what he knew.

A moment later, Rock burst from the barrack. "I feel like a true *alil'tiki'i* again!" he proclaimed, holding aloft his razor. "My friends, you cannot know what you have done! Someday, I will take you to the Peaks and show you the hospitality of kings!"

Despite all of his complaining, he hadn't shaved his beard off completely. He had left long, red-blond sideburns, which curved down to his chin. The tip of the chin itself was shaved clean, as were his lips. On the tall, oval-faced man, the look was quite distinctive. "Ha!" Rock said, striding up to the fire. He grabbed the nearest men there and hugged them both to him, causing Bisig to nearly spill his stew. "I will make you all family for this. A peak dweller's *humaka'aban* is his pride! I feel like a true man again. Here. This razor belongs not to me, but to us all. Any who wishes to use it must do so. Is my honor to share with you!"

The men laughed, and a few took him up on the offer. Kaladin wasn't one of them. It just . . . didn't seem to matter to him. He accepted the bowl of stew Dunny brought him, but didn't eat. Sigzil chose not to sit back down beside him, retreating to the other side of the campfire.

Eyes of red and blue, Kaladin thought. *I don't know if that fits us.* For him to have eyes of red and blue, Kaladin would have to believe that there was at least a small chance the bridge crew could survive. This night, Kaladin had trouble convincing himself.

He'd never been an optimist. He saw the world as it was, or he tried to. That was a problem, though, when the truth he saw was so terrible.

Oh, Stormfather, he thought, feeling the crushing weight of despair as he stared down at his bowl. *I'm falling back to the wretch I was. I'm losing my grip on this, on myself.*

He couldn't carry the hopes of all the bridgemen.

He just wasn't strong enough.

Axehound

FIVE AND A HALF YEARS AGO

Kaladin pushed past the shrieking Laral and stumbled into the surgery room. Even after years working with his father, the amount of blood in the room was shocking. It was as if someone had dumped out a bucket of bright red paint.

The scent of burned flesh hung in the air. Lirin worked frantically on Brightlord Rillir, Roshone's son. An evil-looking, tusklike thing jutted from the young man's abdomen, and his lower right leg was crushed. It hung by only a few tendons, splinters of bone poking out like reeds from the waters of a pond. Brightlord Roshone himself lay on the side table, groaning, eyes squeezed shut as he held his leg, which was pierced by another of the bony spears. Blood leaked from his improvised bandage, flowed down the side of the table, and dripped to the floor to mix with his son's.

Kaladin stood in the doorway gaping. Laral continued to scream. She clutched the doorframe as several of Roshone's guards tried to pull her away. Her wails were frantic. "Do something! Work harder! He can't! He was where it happened and I don't care and let me go!" The garbled phrases degenerated into screeches. The guards finally got her away.

"Kaladin!" his father snapped. "I need you!"

Shocked into motion, Kaladin entered the room, scrubbing

his hands then gathering bandages from the cabinet, stepping in blood. He caught a glimpse of Rillir's face; much of the skin on the right side had been scraped off. The eyelid was gone, the blue eye itself sliced open at the front, deflated like the skin of a grape pressed for wine.

Kaladin hastened to his father with the bandages. His mother appeared at the doorway a moment later, Tien behind her. She raised a hand to her mouth, then pulled Tien away. He stumbled, looking woozy. She returned in a moment without him.

"Water, Kaladin!" Lirin cried. "Hesina, fetch more. Quickly!"

His mother jumped to help, though she rarely assisted in the surgery anymore. Her hands shook as she grabbed one of the buckets and ran outside. Kaladin took the other bucket, which was full, to his father as Lirin eased the length of bone from the young lighteyes's gut. Rillir's remaining eye fluttered, head quivering.

"What *is* that?" Kaladin asked, pressing the bandage to the wound as his father tossed the strange object aside.

"Whitespine tusk," his father said. "Water."

Kaladin grabbed a sponge, dunked it in the bucket, and used it to squeeze water into Rillir's gut wound. That washed away the blood, giving Lirin a good look at the damage. He quested with his fingers as Kaladin got some needle and thread ready. There was already a tourniquet on the leg. Full amputation would come later.

Lirin hesitated, fingers inside the gaping hole in Rillir's belly. Kaladin cleaned the wound again. He looked up at his father, concerned.

Lirin pulled his fingers out and walked to Brightlord Roshone. "Bandages, Kaladin," he said curtly.

Kaladin hurried over, though he shot a look over his shoulder at Rillir. The once-handsome young lighteyes trembled again, spasming. "Father . . ."

"Bandages!" Lirin said.

"What are you doing, surgeon?" Roshone bellowed. "What of my son?" Painspren swarmed around him.

"Your son is dead," Lirin said, yanking the tusk free from Roshone's leg.

The lighteyes bellowed in agony, though Kaladin couldn't tell if that was because of the tusk or his son. Roshone clenched his jaw as Kaladin pressed the bandage down on his leg. Lirin dunked his hands in the water bucket, then quickly wiped them with knobweed sap to frighten off rotspren.

"My son *is not dead*," Roshone growled. "I can see him moving! Tend to him, surgeon."

"Kaladin, get the dazewater," Lirin ordered gathering his sewing needle.

Kaladin hurried to the back of the room, steps splashing blood, and threw open the far cupboard. He took out a small flask of clear liquid.

"What are you doing?" Roshone bellowed, trying to sit up. "Look at my son! Almighty above, *look* at him!"

Kaladin turned hesitantly, pausing as he poured dazewater on a bandage. Rillir was spasming more violently.

"I work under three guidelines, Roshone," Lirin said, forcibly pressing the lighteyes down against his table. "The guidelines every surgeon uses when choosing between two patients. If the wounds are equal, treat the youngest first."

"Then see to my son!"

"If the wounds are not equally threatening," Lirin continued, "treat the worst wound first."

"As I've been *telling you*!"

"The third guideline supersedes them both, Roshone," Lirin said, leaning down. "A surgeon must know when someone is beyond their ability to help. I'm sorry, Roshone. I would save him if I could, I promise you. But I cannot."

"No!" Roshone said, struggling again.

"Kaladin! Quickly!" Lirin said.

Kaladin dashed over. He pressed the bandage of dazewater to Roshone's chin and mouth, just below the nose, forcing the lighteyed man to breathe the fumes. Kaladin held his own breath, as he'd been trained.

Roshone bellowed and screamed, but the two of them held him down, and he was weak from blood loss. Soon, his bellows became softer. In seconds, he was speaking in gibberish and grinning to himself. Lirin turned back to the leg wound while Kaladin went to throw away the dazewater bandage.

"No. Administer it to Rillir." His father didn't look away from his work. "It's the only mercy we can give him."

Kaladin nodded and used the dazewater bandage on the wounded youth. Rillir's breathing grew less frantic, though he didn't seem conscious enough to notice the effects. Then Kaladin threw the bandage with the dazewater into the brazier; heat negated the effects. The white, puffy bandage wrinkled and browned in the fire, steam streaming off it as the edges burst into flame.

Kaladin returned with the sponge and washed out Roshone's wound as Lirin prodded at it. There were a few shards of tusk trapped inside, and Lirin muttered to himself, getting out his tongs and razor-sharp knife.

"Damnation can take them all," Lirin said, pulling out the first sliver of tusk. Behind him, Rillir fell still. "Isn't sending half of us to war enough for them? Do they have to seek death even when they're living in a quiet township? Roshone should never have gone looking for the storming whitespine."

"He was *looking* for it?"

"They went hunting it," Lirin spat. "Wistiow and I used to joke about lighteyes like them. If you can't kill men, you kill beasts. Well, this is what you found, Roshone."

"Father," Kaladin said softly. "He's not going to be pleased with you when he awakes." The brightlord was humming softly, lying back, eyes closed.

Lirin didn't respond. He yanked out another fragment of tusk, and Kaladin washed out the wound. His father pressed his fingers to the side of the large puncture, inspecting it.

There was one more sliver of tusk, jutting from a muscle inside the wound. Right beside that muscle thumped the femoral artery, the largest in the leg. Lirin reached in with his knife, carefully cutting free the sliver of tusk. Then he paused for a moment, the edge of his blade just hairs from the artery.

If that were cut . . . Kaladin thought. Roshone would be

dead in minutes. He was only alive right now because the tusk had missed the artery.

Lirin's normally steady hand quivered. Then he glanced up at Kaladin. He withdrew the knife without touching the artery, then reached in with his tongs to pull the sliver free. He tossed it aside, then calmly reached for his thread and needle.

Behind them, Rillir had stopped breathing.

❖

That evening, Kaladin sat on the steps to his house, hands in his lap.

Roshone had been returned to his estate to be cared for by his personal servants. His son's corpse was cooling in the crypt below, and a messenger had been sent to request a Soulcaster for the body.

On the horizon, the sun was red as blood. Everywhere Kaladin looked, the world was red.

The door to the surgery closed, and his father—looking as exhausted as Kaladin felt—tottered out. He eased himself down, sighing as he sat beside Kaladin, looking at the sun. Did it look like blood to him too?

They didn't speak as the sun slowly sank before them. Why was it most colorful when it was about to vanish for the night? Was it angry at being forced below the horizon? Or was it a showman, giving a performance before retiring?

Why was the most colorful part of people's bodies—the brightness of their blood—hidden beneath the skin, never to be seen unless something went wrong?

No, Kaladin thought. *The blood isn't the most colorful part of a body. The eyes can be colorful too.* The blood and the eyes. Both representations of one's heritage. And one's nobility.

"I saw inside a man today," Kaladin finally said.

"Not for the first time," Lirin said, "and certainly not for the last. I'm proud of you. I expected to find you here crying, as you usually do when we lose a patient. You're learning."

"When I said I saw inside a man," Kaladin said, "I wasn't talking about the wounds."

Lirin didn't respond for a moment. "I see."

"You would have let him die if I hadn't been there, wouldn't you?"

Silence.

"Why didn't you?" Kaladin said. "It would have solved so much!"

"It wouldn't have been letting him die. It would have been murdering him."

"You could have just let him bleed, then claimed you couldn't save him. Nobody would have questioned you. You *could* have done it."

"No," Lirin said, staring at the sunset. "No, I couldn't have."

"But why?"

"Because I'm not a killer, son."

Kaladin frowned.

Lirin had a distant look in his eyes. "Somebody has to start. Somebody has to step forward and do what is right, *because* it is right. If nobody starts, then others cannot follow. The lighteyes do their best to kill themselves, and to kill us. The others still haven't brought back Alds and Milp. Roshone just left them there."

Alds and Milp, two townsmen, had been on the hunt but hadn't returned with the party bearing the two wounded lighteyes. Roshone had been so worried about Rillir that he'd left them behind so he could travel quickly.

"The lighteyes don't care about life," Lirin said. "So I must. That's another reason why I wouldn't have let Roshone die, even if you hadn't been there. Though looking at you did strengthen me."

"I wish it hadn't," Kaladin said.

"You mustn't say such things."

"Why not?"

"Because, son. We have to be *better* than they are." He sighed, standing. "You should sleep. I may need you when the others return with Alds and Milp."

That wasn't likely; the two townsmen were probably dead

by now. Their wounds were said to be pretty bad. Plus, the whitespines were still out there.

Lirin went inside, but didn't compel Kaladin to follow.

Would I have let him die? Kaladin wondered. *Maybe even flicked that knife to hasten him on his way?* Roshone had been nothing but a blight since his arrival, but did that justify killing him?

No. Cutting that artery wouldn't have been justified. But what obligation had Kaladin to help? Withholding his aid wasn't the same thing as killing. It just *wasn't*.

Kaladin thought it through a dozen different ways, pondering his father's words. What he found shocked him. He honestly would have let Roshone die on that table. It would have been better for Kaladin's family; it would have been better for the entire town.

Kaladin's father had once laughed at his son's desire to go to war. Indeed, now that Kaladin had decided he would become a surgeon on his own terms, his thoughts and actions of earlier years felt childish to him. But Lirin thought Kaladin incapable of killing. *You can hardly step on a cremling without feeling guilty, son,* he'd said. *Ramming your spear into a man would be nowhere near as easy as you seem to think.*

But his father was wrong. It was a stunning, frightening revelation. This wasn't idle fancy or daydreaming about the glory of battle. This was real.

At that moment, Kaladin knew he *could* kill, if he needed to. Some people—like a festering finger or a leg shattered beyond repair—just needed to be removed.

"Like a highstorm, regular in their coming, yet always unexpected."

—The word Desolation is used twice in reference to their appearances. See pages 57, 59, and 64 of *Tales by Hearthlight*.

I've made my decision," Shallan declared.

Jasnah looked up from her research. In an unusual moment of deference, she put aside her books and sat with her back to the Veil, regarding Shallan. "Very well."

"What you did was both legal and right, in the strict sense of the words," Shallan said. "But it was not moral, and it *certainly* wasn't ethical."

"So morality and legality are distinct?"

"Nearly all of the philosophies agree they are."

"But what do *you* think?"

Shallan hesitated. "Yes. You can be moral without following the law, and you can be immoral while following the law."

"But you also said what I did was 'right' but not 'moral.' The distinction between those two seems less easy to define."

"An action can be right," Shallan said. "It is simply something done, viewed without considering intent. Killing four men in self-defense is right."

"But not moral?"

"Morality applies to your intent and the greater context of the situation. Seeking out men to kill is an immoral act, Jasnah, regardless of the eventual outcome."

Jasnah tapped her desktop with a fingernail. She was wearing her glove, the gemstones of the broken Soulcaster bulging beneath. It had been two weeks. Surely she'd discovered that it didn't work. How could she be so calm?

Was she trying to fix it in secret? Perhaps she feared that if she revealed it was broken, she would lose political power. Or had she realized that hers had been swapped for a different Soulcaster? Could it be, despite all odds, that Jasnah just hadn't tried to use the Soulcaster? Shallan needed to leave before too long. But if she left before Jasnah discovered the swap, she risked having the woman try her Soulcaster just after Shallan vanished, bringing suspicion directly on her. The anxious waiting was driving Shallan near to madness.

Finally, Jasnah nodded, then returned to her research.

"You have nothing to say?" Shallan said. "I just accused you of murder."

"No," Jasnah said, "murder is a legal definition. You said I killed unethically."

"You think I'm wrong, I assume?"

"You are," Jasnah said. "But I accept that you believe what you are saying and have put rational thought behind it. I have looked over your notes, and I believe you understand the various philosophies. In some cases, I think that you were quite insightful in your interpretation of them. The lesson was instructive." She opened her book.

"Then that's it?"

"Of course not," Jasnah said. "We will study philosophy further in the future; for now, I'm satisfied that you have established a solid foundation in the topic."

"But I still decided you were wrong. I still think there's an absolute Truth out there."

"Yes," Jasnah said, "and it took you two weeks of struggling to come to that conclusion." Jasnah looked up, meeting Shallan's eyes. "It wasn't easy, was it?"

"No."

"And you still wonder, don't you?"

"Yes.

"That is enough." Jasnah narrowed her eyes slightly, a consoling smile appearing on her lips. "If it helps you wrestle with your feelings, child, understand that I *was* trying to do good. I sometimes wonder if I should accomplish more with my Soulcaster." She turned back to her reading. "You are free for the rest of the day."

Shallan blinked. "What?"

"Free," Jasnah said. "You may go. Do as you please. You'll spend it drawing beggars and barmaids, I suspect, but you may choose. Be off with you."

"Yes, Brightness! Thank you."

Jasnah waved in dismissal and Shallan grabbed her portfolio and hastened from the alcove. She hadn't had any free time since the day she'd gone sketching on her own in the gardens. She'd been gently chided for that; Jasnah had left her in her rooms to rest, not go out sketching.

Shallan waited impatiently as the parshman porters lowered her lift to the Veil's ground floor, then hurried out into the cavernous central hall. A long walk later, she approached the guest quarters, nodding to the master-servants who served there. Half guards, half concierges, they monitored who entered and left.

She used her thick brass key to unlock the door to Jasnah's rooms, then slipped inside and locked the door behind her. The small sitting chamber—furnished with a rug and two chairs beside the hearth—was lit by topazes. The table still contained a half-full cup of orange wine from Jasnah's late research the night before, along with a few crumbs of bread on a plate.

Shallan hurried to her own chamber, then shut the door and took the Soulcaster out of her safepouch. The warm glow of the gemstones bathed her face in white and red light. They were large enough—and therefore bright enough—that it was hard to look at them directly. Each would be worth ten or twenty broams.

She'd been forced to hide them outside in the recent high-storm to infuse them, and that had been its own source of anxiety. She took a deep breath, then knelt and slid a small wooden stick from under the bed. A week and a half of practice, and she still hadn't managed to make the Soulcaster do . . . well, anything at all. She'd tried tapping the gems, twisting them, shaking her hand, and flexing her hand in exact mimicry of Jasnah. She'd studied picture after picture she'd drawn of the process. She tried speaking, concentrating, and even begging.

However, she'd found a book the day before that had offered what seemed like a useful tip. It claimed that humming, of all things, could make a Soulcasting more effective. It was just a passing reference, but it was more than she'd found anywhere else. She sat down on her bed and forced herself to concentrate. She closed her eyes, holding the stick, imagining it transforming into quartz. Then she began humming.

Nothing happened. She kept on humming though, trying different notes, concentrating as hard as she could. She kept her attention on the task for a good half hour, but eventually her mind began to wander. A new worry began to nibble at her. Jasnah was one of the most brilliant, insightful scholars in the world. She'd put the Soulcaster out where it could be taken. Had she intentionally duped Shallan with a fake?

It seemed an awful lot of trouble to go through. Why not just spring the trap and reveal Shallan as a thief? The fact that she couldn't get the Soulcaster to work left her straining plausibility for explanations.

She stopped humming and opened her eyes. The stick had not changed. *So much for that tip,* she thought, setting the stick aside with a sigh. She'd been so hopeful.

She lay back on the bed, resting, staring up at the brown stone ceiling, cut—like the rest of the Conclave—directly out of the mountain. Here, the stone had been left intentionally rough, evoking the roof of a cave. It was quite beautiful in a subtle way she'd never noticed before, the colors and contours of the rock rippling like a disturbed pond.

She took a sheet from her portfolio and began to sketch

the rock patterns. One sketch to calm her, and then she would get back to the Soulcaster. Perhaps she should try it on her other hand again.

She couldn't capture the colors of the strata, not in charcoal, but she could record the fascinating way the strata wove together. Like a work of art. Had some stoneworker cut this ceiling intentionally, crafting this subtle creation, or was it an accident of nature? She smiled, imagining some overworked stonecutter noticing the beautiful grain of the rock and deciding to form a wave pattern for his own personal wonder and sense of beauty.

"What are you?"

Shallan yelped, sitting up, sketchpad bouncing free of her lap. Someone had whispered those words. She'd heard them distinctly!

"Who is there?" she asked.

Silence.

"Who's there!" she said more loudly, her heart beating quickly.

Something sounded outside her door, from the sitting room. Shallan jumped, hiding the hand wearing the Soulcaster under a pillow as the door creaked open, revealing a wizened palace maid, darkeyed and dressed in a white and orange uniform.

"Oh dear!" the woman exclaimed. "I had no idea you were here, Brightness." She bowed low.

A palace maid. Here to clean the room, an everyday occurrence. Focused on her meditation, Shallan hadn't heard her enter. "Why did you speak to me?"

"Speak to you, Brightness?"

"You . . ." No, the voice had been a whisper, and it had quite distinctly come from *inside* Shallan's room. It couldn't have been the maid.

She shivered and glanced about. But that was foolish. The tiny room was easily inspected. There were no Voidbringers hiding in the corners or under her bed.

What, then, had she heard? *Noises from the woman*

cleaning, obviously. Shallan's mind had just interpreted those random sounds as words.

Forcing herself to relax, Shallan looked out past the maid into the sitting room. The woman had cleaned up the wineglass and crumbs. A broom leaned against the wall. In addition, Jasnah's door was cracked open. "Were you in Brightness Jasnah's room?" Shallan demanded.

"Yes, Brightness," the woman said. "Tidying up the desk, making the bed—"

"Brightness Jasnah does *not* like people entering her room. The maids have been told not to clean in there." The king had promised that his maids were very carefully chosen, and there had never been issues of theft, but Jasnah still insisted that none enter her bedchamber.

The woman paled. "I'm sorry, Brightness. I didn't hear! I wasn't told—"

"Hush, it's all right," Shallan said. "You'll want to go tell her what you've done. She always notices if her things were moved. It will be better for you if you go to her and explain."

"Y-Yes, Brightness." The woman bowed again.

"In fact," Shallan said, something occurring to her. "You should go now. No point putting it off."

The elderly maid sighed. "Yes, of course, Brightness." She withdrew. A few seconds later, the outside door closed and locked.

Shallan leapt up, pulling off the Soulcaster and stuffing it back in her safepouch. She hurried outside, heart thumping, the strange voice forgotten as she seized the opportunity to look into Jasnah's room. It was unlikely that Shallan would discover anything useful about the Soulcaster, but she couldn't pass up the chance—not with the maid to blame for moving things.

She felt only a glimmer of guilt for this. She'd already stolen from Jasnah. Compared with that, poking through her room was nothing.

The bedroom was larger than Shallan's, though it still felt cramped because of the unavoidable lack of windows. Jasnah's bed, a four-poster monstrosity, took up half the space. The vanity was against the far wall, and beside it the dressing table from which Shallan had originally stolen the Soulcaster. Other than a dresser, the only other thing in the room was the desk, books piled high on the left side.

Shallan never got a chance to look at Jasnah's notebooks. Might she, perhaps, have taken notes on the Soulcaster? Shallan sat at the desk, hurriedly pulling open the top drawer and poking through the brushpens, charcoal pencils, and sheets of paper. All were organized neatly, and the paper was blank. The bottom right drawer held ink and empty notebooks. The bottom left drawer had a small collection of reference books.

That left the books on the top of the table. Jasnah would have the majority of her notebooks with her as she worked. But . . . yes, there were still a few here. Heart fluttering, Shallan gathered up the three thin volumes and set them before her.

Notes on Urithiru, the first one declared inside. The notebook was full—it appeared—of quotes from and notations about various books Jasnah had found. All spoke of this place, Urithiru. Jasnah had mentioned it earlier to Kabsal.

Shallan put that book aside, looking at the next, hoping for mention of the Soulcaster. This notebook was also filled to capacity, but there was no title on it. Shallan picked through, reading some entries.

"The ones of ash and fire, who killed like a swarm, relentless before the Heralds . . ." Noted in Masly, page 337. Corroborated by Coldwin and Hasavah.

"They take away the light, wherever they lurk. Skin that is burned." Cormshen, page 104.

Innia, in her recordings of children's folktales, speaks of the Voidbringers as being "Like a highstorm, regular in their coming, yet always unexpected." The word Desolation is used twice in reference to their appearances. See pages 57, 59, and 64 of Tales by Hearthlight.

"They changed, even as we fought them. Like shadows they were, that can transform as the flame dances. Never

underestimate them because of what you first see." Purports *to be a scrap collected from Talatin, a Radiant of the Order of Stonewards. The source—Guvlow's* Incarnate—*is generally held as reliable, though this is from a copied fragment of* The Poem of the Seventh Morning, *which has been lost.*

They went on like that. Pages and pages. Jasnah had trained her in this method of note taking—once the notebook was filled, each item would be evaluated again for reliability and usefulness and copied to different, more specific notebooks.

Frowning, Shallan looked through the final notebook. It focused on Natanatan, the Unclaimed Hills, and the Shattered Plains. It collected records of discoveries by hunters, explorers, or tradesmen searching for a river passage to New Natanan. Of the three notebooks, the largest was the one that focused on the Voidbringers.

The Voidbringers again. Many people in more rural places whispered of them and other monsters of the dark. The raspings, or stormwhispers, or even the dreaded nightspren. Shallan had been taught by stern tutors that these were superstition, fabrications of the Lost Radiants, who used tales of monsters to justify their domination of mankind.

The ardents taught something else. They spoke of the Lost Radiants—called the Knights Radiant then—fighting off Voidbringers during the war to hold Roshar. According to these teachings, it was only after defeating the Voidbringers—and the departure of the Heralds—that the Radiants had fallen.

Both groups agreed that the Voidbringers were gone. Fabrications or long-defeated enemies, the result was the same. Shallan could believe that some people—some scholars, even—might believe that the Voidbringers still existed, haunting mankind. But Jasnah the skeptic? Jasnah, who denied the existence of the Almighty? Could the woman really be so twisted as to deny the existence of God, but *accept* the existence of his mythological enemies?

A knock came at the outer door. Shallan jumped, raising her hand to her breast. She hurriedly replaced the notebooks on the desk in the same order and orientation. Then, flustered, she hurried out to the door. *Jasnah wouldn't knock, you silly fool,* she told herself, unlocking and opening the door a crack.

Kabsal stood outside. The handsome, lighteyed ardent held up a basket. "I've heard reports that you have the day free." He shook the basket temptingly. "Would you like some jam?"

Shallan calmed herself, then glanced back at Jasnah's open quarters. She really should investigate more. She turned to Kabsal, meaning to tell him no, but his eyes were so inviting. That hint of a smile on his face, that good-natured and relaxed posture.

If Shallan went with Kabsal, maybe she could ask him what he knew regarding Soulcasters. That wasn't what decided it for her, however. The truth was, she *needed* to relax. She'd been so on edge lately, brain stuffed with philosophy, every spare moment spent trying to make the Soulcaster work. Was it any wonder she was hearing voices?

"I'd love some jam," she declared.

* *

"Truthberry jam," Kabsal said, holding up the small green jar. "It's Azish. Legends there say that those who consume the berries speak only the truth until the next sunset."

Shallan raised an eyebrow. They were seated on cushions atop a blanket in the Conclave gardens, not far from where she'd first experimented with the Soulcaster. "And is it true?"

"Hardly," Kabsal said, opening the jar. "The berries are harmless. But the leaves and stalks of the truthberry plant, if burned, give off a smoke that makes people intoxicated and euphoric. It appears that people often gathered the stalks for making fires. They'd eat the berries around the campfire and have a rather . . . interesting night."

"It's a wonder—" Shallan began, then bit her lip.

"What?" he prodded.

She sighed. "It's a wonder they didn't become known as birthberries, considering—" She blushed.

He laughed. "That's a good point!"

"Stormfather," she said, blushing further. "I'm terrible at being proper. Here, give me some of that jam."

He smiled, handing over a slice of bread with green jam slathered across the top. A dull-eyed parshman—appropriated from inside the Conclave—sat on the ground beside a shale-bark wall, acting as an impromptu chaperone. It felt so strange to be out with a man near her own age with only a single parshman in attendance. It felt liberating. Exhilarating. Or maybe that was just the sunlight and the open air.

"I'm *also* terrible at being scholarly," she said, closing her eyes, breathing deeply. "I like it outside far too much."

"Many of the greatest scholars spent their lives traveling."

"And for each one of them," Shallan said, "there were a hundred more stuck back in a hole of a library, buried in books."

"And they wouldn't have had it any other way. Most people with a bent for research *prefer* their holes and libraries. But you do not. That makes you intriguing."

She opened her eyes, smiling at him, then took a luscious bite of her jam and bread. This Thaylen bread was so fluffy, it was more like cake.

"So," she said as he chewed on his bite, "do you feel any more truthful, now that you've had the jam?"

"I am an ardent," he said. "It is my duty and calling to be truthful at all times."

"Of course," she said. "I'm always truthful as well. *So* full of truth, in fact, that sometimes it squeezes the lies right out my lips. There isn't a place for them inside, you see."

He laughed heartily. "Shallan Davar. I can't imagine anyone as sweet as yourself uttering a single untruth."

"Then for the sake of your sanity, I'll keep them coming in pairs." She smiled. "I'm having a terrible time, and this food is awful."

"You've just disproven an entire body of lore and mythology surrounding the eating of truthberry jam!"

"Good," Shallan said. "Jam should not have lore or mythology. It should be sweet, colorful, and delicious."

"Like young ladies, I presume."

"Brother Kabsal!" She blushed again. "That wasn't at *all* appropriate."

"And yet you smile."

"I can't help it," she said. "I'm sweet, colorful, and delicious."

"You have the colorful part right," he said, obviously amused at her deep blush. "And the sweet part. Can't speak for your deliciousness. . . ."

"Kabsal!" she exclaimed, though she wasn't entirely shocked. She'd once told herself that he was interested in her only in order to protect her soul, but that was getting more and more difficult to believe. He stopped by at least once a week.

He chuckled at her embarrassment, but that only made her blush further.

"Stop it!" She held her hand up in front of her eyes. "My face must be the color of my hair! You shouldn't say such things; you're a man of religion."

"But still a man, Shallan."

"One who said his interest in me was only academic."

"Yes, academic," he said idly. "Involving many experiments and much firsthand field research."

"Kabsal!"

He laughed deeply, taking a bite of his bread. "I'm sorry, Brightness Shallan. But it gets such a reaction!"

She grumbled, lowering her hand, but knew that he said the things—in part—because she encouraged him. She couldn't help it. Nobody had ever shown her the kind of interest that he, increasingly, did. She liked him—liked talking with him, liked listening to him. It was a wonderful way to break the monotony of study.

There was, of course, no prospect for a union. Assuming she could protect her family, she'd be needed to make a good political marriage. Dallying with an ardent owned by the king of Kharbranth wouldn't serve anyone.

I'll soon have to start hinting to him the truth, she thought. *He has to know that this won't go anywhere. Doesn't he?*

He leaned toward her. "You really are what you seem, aren't you, Shallan?"

"Capable? Intelligent? Charming?"

He smiled. "Genuine."

"I wouldn't say that," she said.

"You are. I see it in you."

"It's not that I'm genuine. I'm naive. I lived my entire childhood in my family's manor."

"You don't have the air of a recluse about you. You're so at ease at conversation."

"I had to become so. I spent most of my childhood in my own company, and I *detest* boring conversation partners."

He smiled, though his eyes held concern. "It seems a shame that one such as you would lack for attention. That's like hanging a beautiful painting facing the wall."

She leaned back on her safehand, finishing off her bread. "I wouldn't say I lacked for attention, not *quantitatively*, for certain. My father paid me plenty of attention."

"I've heard of him. A stern man, by reputation."

"He's . . ." She had to pretend he was still alive. "My father is a man of passion and virtue. Just never at the same time."

"Shallan! That might just be the wittiest thing I've heard you say."

"And perhaps the most truthful. Unfortunately."

Kabsal looked into her eyes, searching for something. What did he see? "You don't seem to care for your father much."

"Another truthful statement. The berries are working on both of us, I see."

"He's a hurtful man, I gather?"

"Yes, though never to me. I'm too precious. His ideal, perfect daughter. You see, my father is *precisely* the type of man to hang a picture facing the wrong way. That way, it can't be soiled by unworthy eyes or touched by unworthy fingers."

"That's a shame. As you look very touchable to me."

She glared. "I told you, no more of that teasing."

"That wasn't teasing," he said, regarding her with deep blue eyes. Earnest eyes. "You intrigue me, Shallan Davar."

She found her heart thumping. Oddly, a panic rose within her at the same time. "I shouldn't be intriguing."

"Why not?"

"Logic puzzles are intriguing. Mathematical computations

can be intriguing. Political maneuvers are intriguing. But women . . . they should be nothing short of baffling."

"And what if I think I'm beginning to understand you?"

"Then I'm at a severe disadvantage," she said. "As I don't understand myself."

He smiled.

"We shouldn't be talking like this, Kabsal. You're an ardent."

"A man can leave the ardentia, Shallan."

She felt a jolt. He looked steadily at her, not blinking. Handsome, soft-spoken, witty. *This could grow very dangerous very quickly,* she thought.

"Jasnah thinks you're getting close to me because you want her Soulcaster," Shallan blurted out. Then she winced. *Idiot!* That's *your response when a man hints that he might leave the service of the Almighty in order to be with you?*

"Brightness Jasnah is quite clever," Kabsal said, slicing himself another piece of bread.

Shallan blinked. "Oh, er. You mean she's *right*?"

"Right and wrong," Kabsal said. "The devotary would very, very much like to get that fabrial. I planned to ask your help eventually."

"But?"

"But my superiors thought it was a *terrible* idea." He grimaced. "They think the king of Alethkar is volatile enough that he'd march to war with Kharbranth over that. Soulcasters aren't Shardblades, but they can be equally important." He shook his head, taking a bite of bread. "Elhokar Kholin should be ashamed to let his sister use that fabrial, particularly so trivially. But if we were to steal it . . . Well, the repercussions could be felt across all of Vorin Roshar."

"Is that so?" Shallan said, feeling sick.

He nodded. "Most people don't think about it. I didn't. Kings rule and war with Shards—but their armies subsist through Soulcasters. Do you have any idea the kinds of supply lines and support personnel Soulcasters replace? Without them, warfare is virtually *impossible*. You'd need hundreds of wagons filled with food every month!"

"I guess . . . that would be a problem." She took a deep breath. "They fascinate me, these Soulcasters. I've always wondered what it would feel like to use one."

"I as well."

"So you've never used one?"

He shook his head. "There aren't any in Kharbranth."

Right, she thought. *Of course. That's why the king needed Jasnah to help his granddaughter.* "Have you ever heard anyone talk about using one?" She cringed at the bold statement. Would it make him suspicious?

He just nodded idly. "There's a secret to it, Shallan."

"Really?" she asked, heart in her throat.

He looked up at her, seeming conspiratorial. "It's really not that difficult."

"It . . . What?"

"It's true," he said. "I've heard it from several ardents. There's so much shadow and ritual surrounding Soulcasters. They're kept mysterious, aren't used where people can see. But the truth is, there's not much to them. You just put one on, press your hand against something, and tap a gemstone with your finger. It works that simply."

"That's not how Jasnah does it," she said, perhaps too defensively.

"Yes, that confused me, but supposedly if you use one long enough, you learn how to control them better." He shook his head. "I don't like the mystery that has grown up around them. It smells too much like the mysticism of the old Hierocracy. We'd better not find ourselves treading down *that* path again. What would it matter if people knew how simple the Soulcasters are to use? The principles and gifts of the Almighty are often simple."

Shallan barely listened to that last part. Unfortunately, it seemed that Kabsal was as ignorant as she. More ignorant, even. She'd tried the exact method he spoke of, and it didn't work. Perhaps the ardents he knew were lying to protect the secret.

"Anyway," Kabsal said, "I guess that's a tangent. You asked me about stealing the Soulcaster, and rest assured, I wouldn't put you in that position. I was foolish to think of it, and I was shortly forbidden to attempt it. I *was* ordered to care for your soul and see that you weren't corrupted by Jasnah's teachings, and perhaps try to reclaim Jasnah's soul as well."

"Well, that last one is going to be difficult."

"I hadn't noticed," he replied dryly.

She smiled, though she couldn't quite decide how to feel. "I kind of killed the moment, didn't I? Between us?"

"I'm glad you did," he said, dusting off his hands. "I get carried away, Shallan. At times, I wonder if I'm as bad at being an ardent as you are at being proper. I don't want to be presumptuous. It's just that the way you speak, it gets my mind churning, and my tongue starts saying whatever comes to it."

"And so . . ."

"And so we should call it a day," Kabsal said, standing. "I need time to think."

Shallan stood as well, holding out her freehand for his assistance; standing up in a sleek Vorin dress was difficult. They were in a section of the gardens where the shalebark wasn't quite so high, so once standing, Shallan could see that the king himself was passing nearby, chatting with a middle-aged ardent who had a long, narrow face.

The king often went strolling through the gardens on his midday walk. She waved to him, but the kindly man didn't see her. He was deep in conversation with the ardent. Kabsal turned, noticed the king, then ducked down.

"What?" Shallan said.

"The king keeps careful track of his ardents. He and Brother Ixil think I'm on cataloging duty today."

She found herself smiling. "You're scrapping your day's work to go on a picnic with me?"

"Yes."

"I thought you were *supposed* to spend time with me," she said, folding her arms. "To protect my soul."

"I was. But there are those among the ardents who worry that I'm a little *too* interested in you."

"They're right."

"I'll come see you tomorrow," he said, peeking up over the

top of the shalebark. "Assuming I'm not stuck in indexing all day as a punishment." He smiled at her. "If I decide to leave the ardentia, that is my choice, and they cannot forbid it— though they may try to distract me." He scrambled away as she prepared herself to tell him that he was presuming too much.

She couldn't get the words out. Perhaps because she was growing less and less certain *what* she wanted. Shouldn't she be focused on helping her family?

By now, Jasnah likely had discovered that her Soulcaster didn't work, but saw no advantage in revealing it. Shallan should leave. She could go to Jasnah and use the terrible experience in the alleyway as an excuse to quit.

And yet, she was terribly reluctant. Kabsal was part of that, but he wasn't the main reason. The truth was that, despite her occasional complaints, she *loved* learning to be a scholar. Even after Jasnah's philosophical training, even after spending days reading book after book. Even with the confusion and the stress, Shallan often felt fulfilled in a way she'd never been before. Yes, Jasnah had been wrong to kill those men, but Shallan wanted to know enough about philosophy to cite the correct reasons why. Yes, digging through historical records could be tedious, but Shallan appreciated the skills and patience she was learning; they were sure to be of value when she got to do her own deep research in the future.

Days spent learning, lunches spent laughing with Kabsal, evenings chatting and debating with Jasnah. *That* was what she wanted. And those were the parts of her life that were complete lies.

Troubled, she picked up the basket of bread and jam, then made her way back to the Conclave and Jasnah's suite. An envelope addressed to her sat in the waiting bin. Shallan frowned, breaking the seal to look inside.

Lass, it read. *We got your message. The* Wind's Pleasure *will soon be at port in Kharbranth again. Of course we'll give you passage and return to your estates. It would be my pleasure to have you aboard. We are Davar men, we are. Indebted to your family.*

We're making a quick trip over to the mainland, but will

hurry to Kharbranth next. Expect us in one week's time to pick you up.

—Captain Tozbek

The undertext, written by Tozbek's wife, read even more clearly. *We'd happily give you free passage, Brightness, if you're willing to do some scribing for us during the trip. The ledgers badly need to be rewritten.*

Shallan stared at the note for a long time. She'd wanted to know where he was and when he was planning to return, but he'd apparently taken her letter as a request to come and pick her up.

It seemed a fitting deadline. That would put her departure at three weeks after stealing the Soulcaster, as she'd told Nan Balat to expect. If Jasnah hadn't reacted to the Soulcaster switch by then, Shallan would have to take it to mean that she wasn't under suspicion.

One week. She *would* be on that ship. It made her break inside to realize it, but it had to be done. She lowered the paper and left the guest hallway, her steps taking her through the twisting corridors into the Veil.

Shortly, she stood outside Jasnah's alcove. The princess sat at her desk, reed scratching at a notebook. She glanced up. "I thought I told you that you could do whatever you want today."

"You did," Shallan said. "And I realized that what I want to do is study."

Jasnah smiled in a sly, understanding way. Almost a *self-satisfied* way. If she only knew. "Well, I'm not going to chide you for that," Jasnah said, turning back to her research.

Shallan sat, offering the bread and jam to Jasnah, who shook her head and continued researching. Shallan cut herself another slice and topped it with jam. Then she opened a book and sighed in satisfaction.

In one week, she'd have to leave. But in the meantime, she would let herself pretend a little while longer.

THE WRETCH

"They lived out in the wilds, always awaiting the Desolation—or sometimes, a foolish child who took no heed of the night's darkness."

—A child's tale, yes, but this quote from *Shadows Remembered* seems to hint at the truth I seek. See page 82, the fourth tale.

Kaladin awoke to a familiar feeling of dread.

He'd spent much of the night lying awake on the hard floor, staring up into the dark, thinking. *Why try? Why care? There is no hope for these men.*

He felt like a wanderer seeking desperately for a pathway into the city to escape wild beasts. But the city was atop a steep mountain, and no matter how he approached, the climb was always the same. Impossible. A hundred different paths. The same result.

Surviving his punishment would not save his men. Training them to run faster would not save them. They were bait. The efficiency of the bait did not change its purpose or its fate.

Kaladin forced himself to his feet. He felt ground down, like a millstone used far too long. He still didn't understand how he'd survived. *Did you preserve me, Almighty? Save me so that I could watch them die?*

You were supposed to burn prayers to send them to the

Almighty, who waited for his Heralds to recapture the Tranquiline Halls. That had never made sense to Kaladin. The Almighty was supposed to be able to see all and know all. So why did he need a prayer burned before he would do anything? Why did he need people to fight for him in the first place?

Kaladin left the barrack, stepping into the light. Then he froze.

The men were lined up, waiting. A ragged bunch of bridgemen, wearing brown leather vests and short trousers that only reached their knees. Dirty shirts, sleeves rolled to the elbows, lacing down the front. Dusty skin, mops of ragged hair. And yet now, because of Rock's gift, they all had neatly trimmed beards or clean-shaven faces. Everything else about them was worn. But their faces were clean.

Kaladin raised a hesitant hand to his face, touching his unkempt black beard. The men seemed to be waiting for something. "What?" he asked.

The men shifted uncomfortably, glancing toward the lumberyard. They were waiting for him to lead them in practice, of course. But practice was futile. He opened his mouth to tell them that, but hesitated as he saw something approaching. Four men, carrying a palanquin. A tall, thin man in a violet lighteyes's coat walked beside it.

The men turned to look. "What's this?" Hobber asked, scratching at his thick neck.

"It will be Lamaril's replacement," Kaladin said, gently pushing his way through the line of bridgemen. Syl flitted down and landed on his shoulder as the palanquin bearers stopped before Kaladin and turned to the side, revealing a dark-haired woman wearing a sleek violet dress decorated with golden glyphs. She lounged on her side, resting on a cushioned couch, her eyes a pale blue.

"I am Brightness Hashal," she said, voice lightly touched by a Kholinar accent. "My husband, Brightlord Matal, is your new captain."

Kaladin held his tongue, biting back a remark. He had some experience with lighteyes who got "promoted" to positions like this one. Matal himself said nothing, simply standing with his hand resting on the hilt of his sword. He was tall—nearly as tall as Kaladin—but spindly. Delicate hands. That sword hadn't seen much practice.

"We have been advised," Hashal said, "that this crew has been troublesome." Her eyes narrowed, focusing on Kaladin. "It seems that you have survived the Almighty's judgment. I bear a message for you from your betters. The Almighty has given you another chance to prove yourself as a bridgeman. That is all. Many are trying to read too much into what happened, so Highprince Sadeas has forbidden gawkers to come see you.

"My husband does not intend to run the bridge crews with his predecessor's laxness. My husband is a well-respected and honored associate of Highprince Sadeas himself, not some near-darkeyed mongrel like Lamaril."

"Is that so?" Kaladin said. "Then how did he end up in *this* latrine pit of a job?"

Hashal didn't display a hint of anger at the comment. She flicked her fingers to the side, and one of the soldiers stepped forward and rammed the butt of his spear toward Kaladin's stomach.

Kaladin caught it, old reflexes still too keen. Possibilities flashed through his mind, and he could see the fight before it took place.

Yank on the spear, throw the soldier off guard.

Step forward and ram an elbow into his forearm, making him drop the weapon.

Take control, spin the spear up and slam the soldier on the side of the head.

Spin into a sweep to drop the two who came to help their companion.

Raise the spear for the—

No. That would only get Kaladin killed.

Kaladin released the butt of the spear. The soldier blinked in surprise that a mere bridgeman had blocked his blow. Scowling, the soldier jerked the butt up and slammed it into the side of Kaladin's head.

Kaladin let it hit him, rolling with it, allowing it to toss him to the ground. His head rang from the shock, but his eyesight stopped spinning after a moment. He'd have a headache, but probably no concussion.

He took in a few deep breaths, lying on the ground, hands forming fists. His fingers seemed to burn where he had touched the spear. The soldier stepped back into position beside the palanquin.

"No laxness," Hashal said calmly. "If you must know, my husband *requested* this assignment. The bridge crews are essential to Brightlord Sadeas's advantage in the War of Reckoning. Their mismanagement under Lamaril was disgraceful."

Rock knelt down, helping Kaladin to his feet while scowling at the lighteyes and their soldiers. Kaladin stumbled up, holding his hand to the side of his head. His fingers felt slick and wet, and a trickle of warm blood ran down his neck to his shoulder.

"From now on," Hashal said, "aside from doing normal bridge duty, each crew will be assigned only *one* type of work duty. Gaz!"

The short bridge sergeant poked out from behind the palanquin. Kaladin hadn't noticed him there, behind the porters and the soldiers. "Yes, Brightness?" Gaz bowed several times.

"My husband wishes Bridge Four to be assigned chasm duty permanently. Whenever they are not needed for bridge duty, I want them working in those chasms. This will be far more efficient. They will know which sections have been scoured recently, and will not cover the same ground. You see? Efficiency. They will start immediately."

She rapped on the side of her palanquin, and the porters turned, bearing her away. Her husband continued to walk alongside her without saying a word, and Gaz hurried to keep up. Kaladin stared after them, holding his hand to his head. Dunny ran and fetched him a bandage.

"Chasm duty," Moash grumbled. "Great job, lordling. She'd see us dead from a chasmfiend if the Parshendi arrows don't take us."

"What are we going to do?" asked lean, balding Peet, his voice edged with worry.

"We get to work," Kaladin said, taking the bandage from Dunny.

He walked away, leaving them in a frightened clump.

�❖⋅

A short time later, Kaladin stood at the edge of the chasm, looking down. The hot light of the noon sun burned the back of his neck and cast his shadow downward into the rift, to join with those below. *I could fly,* he thought. *Step off and fall, wind blowing against me. Fly for a few moments. A few, beautiful moments.*

He knelt and grabbed the rope ladder, then climbed down into the darkness. The other bridgemen followed in a silent group. They'd been infected by his mood.

Kaladin knew what was happening to him. Step by step, he was turning back into the wretch he had been. He'd always known it was a danger. He'd clung to the bridgemen as a lifeline. But he was letting go now.

As he stepped down the rungs, a faint translucent figure of blue and white dropped beside him, sitting on a swinglike seat. Its ropes disappeared a few inches above Syl's head.

"What is wrong with you?" she asked softly.

Kaladin just kept climbing down.

"You should be happy. You survived the storms. The other bridgemen were so excited."

"I itched to fight that soldier," Kaladin whispered.

Syl cocked her head.

"I could have beaten him," Kaladin continued. "I probably could have beaten all four of them. I've always been good with the spear. No, not good. Durk called me amazing. A natural born soldier, an artist with the spear."

"Maybe you should have fought them, then."

"I thought you didn't like killing."

"I hate it," she said, growing more translucent. "But I've helped men kill before."

Kaladin froze on the ladder. *"What?"*

"It's true," she said. "I can remember it, just faintly."

"How?"

"I don't know." She grew paler. "I don't want to talk about it. But it was right to do. I feel it."

Kaladin hung for a moment longer. Teft called down, asking if something was wrong. He started to descend again.

"I didn't fight the soldiers today," Kaladin said, eyes toward the chasm wall, "because it wouldn't work. My father told me that it is impossible to protect by killing. Well, he was wrong."

"But—"

"He was wrong," Kaladin said, "because he implied that you could protect people in *other* ways. You can't. This world wants them dead, and trying to save them is pointless." He reached the bottom of the chasm, stepping into darkness. Teft reached the bottom next and lit his torch, bathing the moss-covered stone walls in flickering orange light.

"Is that why you didn't accept it?" Syl whispered, flitting over and landing on Kaladin's shoulder. "The glory. All those months ago?"

Kaladin shook his head. "No. That was something else."

"What did you say, Kaladin?" Teft raised the torch. The aging bridgeman's face looked older than usual in the flickering light, the shadows it created emphasizing the furrows in his skin.

"Nothing, Teft," Kaladin said. "Nothing important."

Syl sniffed at that. Kaladin ignored her, lighting his torch from Teft's as the other bridgemen arrived. When they were all down, Kaladin led the way out into the dark rift. The pale sky seemed distant here, like a far-off scream. This place was a tomb, with rotting wood and stagnant pools of water, good only for growing cremling larvae.

The bridgemen clustered together unconsciously as they always did in this fell place. Kaladin walked in front, and Syl fell silent. He gave Teft the chalk to mark directions, and didn't pause to pick up salvage. But neither did he walk too quickly. The other bridgemen were hushed behind them, speaking in occasional whispers too low to echo. As if their words were strangled by the gloom.

Rock eventually moved up to walk beside Kaladin. "Is difficult job, we have been given. But we are bridgemen! Life, it is difficult, eh? Is nothing new. We must have plan. How do we fight next?"

"There is no next fight, Rock."

"But we have won grand victory! Look, not days ago, you were delirious. You should have died. I know this thing. But instead, you walk, strong as any other man. Ha! Stronger. Is miracle. The *Uli'tekanaki* guide you."

"It's not a miracle, Rock," Kaladin said. "It's more of a curse."

"How is that a curse, my friend?" Rock asked, chuckling. He jumped up and into a puddle and laughed louder as it splashed Teft, who was walking just behind. The large Horneater could be remarkably childlike at times. "Living, this thing is no curse!"

"It is if it brings me back to watch you all die," Kaladin said. "Better I shouldn't have survived that storm. I'm just going to end up dead from a Parshendi arrow. We all are."

Rock looked troubled. When Kaladin offered nothing more, he withdrew. They continued, uncomfortably passing sections of scarred wall where chasmfiends had left their marks. Eventually they stumbled across a heap of bodies deposited by the highstorms. Kaladin stopped, holding up his torch, the other bridgemen peeking around him. Some fifty people had been washed into a recess in the rock, a small dead-end side passage in the stone.

The bodies were piled there, a wall of the dead, arms hanging out, reeds and flotsam stuck between them. Kaladin saw at a glance that the corpses were old enough to begin bloating and rotting. Behind him, one of the men retched, which caused a few of the others to do so as well. The scent was terrible, the corpses slashed and ripped into by cremlings and larger carrion beasts, many of which scuttled away from the light. A disembodied hand lay nearby, and a trail of blood led away. There were also fresh scrapes in the lichen as high as fifteen feet up the wall. A chasmfiend had ripped one of the bodies loose to devour. It might come back for the others.

Kaladin didn't retch. He shoved his half-burned torch between two large stones, then got to work, pulling bodies from the pile. At least they weren't rotted enough to come apart. The bridgemen slowly filled in around him, working. Kaladin let his mind grow numb, not thinking.

Once the bodies were down, the bridgemen laid them in a line. Then they began pulling off their armor, searching their pockets, taking knives from belts. Kaladin left gathering the spears to the others, working by himself off to the side.

Teft knelt beside Kaladin, rolling over a body with a head smashed by the fall. The shorter man began to undo the straps on the fallen man's breastplate. "Do you want to talk?"

Kaladin didn't say anything. He just kept working. *Don't think about the future. Don't think about what will happen. Just survive.*

Don't care, but don't despair. Just be.

"Kaladin." Teft's voice was like a knife, digging into Kaladin's shell, making him squirm.

"If I wanted to talk," Kaladin grumbled, "would I be working here by myself?"

"Fair enough," Teft said. He finally got the breastplate strap undone. "The other men are confused, son. They want to know what we're going to do next."

Kaladin sighed, then stood, turning to look at the bridgemen. "I don't know what to do! If we try to protect ourselves, Sadeas will have us punished! We're bait, and we're going to die. There's nothing I can do about it! It's hopeless."

The bridgemen regarded him with shock.

Kaladin turned from them and went back to work, kneeling beside Teft. "There," he said. "I explained it to them."

"Idiot," Teft said under his breath. "After all you've done, you're abandoning us now?"

To the side, the bridgemen turned back to work. Kaladin caught a few of them grumbling. "Bastard," Moash said. "I said this would happen."

"Abandoning you?" Kaladin hissed to Teft. *Just let me be. Let me go back to apathy. At least then there's no pain.* "Teft, I've spent hours and hours trying to find a way out, but there

[754]

isn't one! Sadeas *wants* us dead. Lighteyes get what they want; that's the way the world works."

"So?"

Kaladin ignored him, turning back to his work, pulling at the boot on a soldier whose fibula looked to have been shattered in three different places. That made it storming awkward to get the boot off.

"Well, maybe we will die," Teft said. "But maybe this isn't about surviving."

Why was *Teft*—of all people—trying to cheer him up? "If survival isn't the point, Teft, then what is?" Kaladin finally got the boot off. He turned to the next body in line, then froze.

It was a bridgeman. Kaladin didn't recognize him, but that vest and those sandals were unmistakable. He lay slumped against the wall, arms at his sides, mouth slightly open and eyelids sunken. The skin on one of the hands had slipped free and pulled away.

"I don't know what the point is," Teft grumbled. "But it seems pathetic to give up. We should keep fighting. Right until those arrows take us. You know, 'journey before destination.'"

"What does *that* mean?"

"I don't know," Teft said, looking down quickly. "Just something I heard once."

"It's something the Lost Radiants used to say," Sigzil said, walking past.

Kaladin glanced to the side. The soft-spoken Azish man set a shield on a pile. He looked up, brown skin dark in the torchlight. "It was their motto. Part of it, at least. 'Life before death. Strength before weakness. Journey before destination.'"

"Lost Radiants?" Skar said, carrying an armful of boots. "Who's bringing *them* up?"

"Teft did," Moash said.

"I did not! That was just something I heard once."

"What does it even mean?" Dunny asked.

"I said I don't know!" Teft said.

"It was supposedly one of their creeds," Sigzil said. "In

Yulay, there are groups of people who talk of the Radiants. And wish for their return."

"Who'd want them to return?" Skar said, leaning back against the wall, folding his arms. "They betrayed us to the Voidbringers."

"Ha!" Rock said. "Voidbringers! Lowlander nonsense. Is campfire tale told by children."

"They were real," Skar said defensively. "Everyone knows that."

"Everyone who listens to campfire stories!" Rock said with a laugh. "Too much air! Makes your minds soft. Is all right, though—you are still my family. Just the dumb ones!"

Teft scowled as the others continued to talk about the Lost Radiants.

"Journey before destination," Syl whispered on Kaladin's shoulder. "I like that."

"Why?" Kaladin asked, kneeling down to untie the dead bridgeman's sandals.

"Because," she replied, as if that were explanation enough. "Teft is right, Kaladin. I know you want to give up. But you can't."

"Why not?"

"Because you *can't*."

"We're assigned to chasm duty from now on," Kaladin said. "We won't be able to collect any more reeds to make money. That means no more bandages, antiseptic, or food for the nightly meals. With all of these bodies, we're bound to run into rotspren, and the men will grow sick—assuming chasmfiends don't eat us or a surprise highstorm doesn't drown us. And we'll have to keep running those bridges until Damnation ends, losing man after man. It's hopeless."

The men were still talking. "The Lost Radiants helped the other side," Skar argued. "They were tarnished all along."

Teft took offense at that. The wiry man stood up straight, pointing at Skar. "You don't know anything! It was too long ago. Nobody knows what really happened."

"Then why do all the stories say the same thing?" Skar demanded. "They abandoned us. Just like the lighteyes are abandoning us right now. Maybe Kaladin's right. Maybe there *is* no hope."

Kaladin looked down. Those words haunted him. *Maybe Kaladin is right . . . maybe there is no hope. . . .*

He'd done this before. Under his last owner, before being sold to Tvlakv and being made a bridgeman. He'd given up on a quiet night after leading Goshel and the other slaves in rebellion. They'd been slaughtered. But somehow he'd survived. Storm it all, why did *he* always survive? *I can't do it again,* he thought, squeezing his eyes shut. *I can't help them.*

Tien. Tukks. Goshel. Dallet. The nameless slave he'd tried to heal in Tvlakv's slave wagons. All had ended up the same. Kaladin had the touch of failure. Sometimes he gave them hope, but what was hope except another opportunity for failure? How many times could a man fall before he no longer stood back up?

"I just think we're ignorant," Teft grumbled. "I don't like listening to what the lighteyes say about the past. Their women write all the histories, you know."

"I can't believe you're arguing about this, Teft," Skar said, exasperated. "What next? Should we let the Voidbringers steal our hearts? Maybe they're just misunderstood. Or the Parshendi. Maybe we should just *let* them kill our king whenever they want."

"Would you two just storm off?" Moash snapped. "It doesn't matter. You heard Kaladin. Even *he* thinks we're as good as dead."

Kaladin couldn't take their voices anymore. He stumbled away, into the darkness, away from the torchlight. None of the men followed him. He entered a place of dark shadows, with only the distant ribbon of sky above for light.

Here, Kaladin escaped their eyes. In the darkness he ran into a boulder, stumbling to a stop. It was slick with moss and lichen. He stood with his hands pressed against it, then groaned and turned around to lean back against it. Syl alighted in front of him, still visible, despite the darkness. She sat down in the air, arranging her dress around her legs.

"I can't save them, Syl," Kaladin whispered, anguished.

"Are you certain?"

"I've failed every time before."

"And so you'll fail this time too?"

"Yes."

She fell silent. "Well then," she eventually said. "Let's say that you're right."

"So why fight? I told myself that I would try one last time. But I failed before I began. There's no saving them."

"Doesn't the fight itself mean anything?"

"Not if you're destined to die." He hung his head.

Sigzil's words echoed in his head. *Life before death. Strength before weakness. Journey before destination.* Kaladin looked up at the crack of sky. Like a faraway river of pure, blue water.

Life before death.

What did the saying mean? That men should seek life before seeking death? That was obvious. Or did it mean something else? That life came before death? Again, obvious. And yet the simple words spoke to him. Death comes, they whispered. Death comes to all. But life comes first. Cherish it.

Death is the destination. But the journey, that is life. That is what matters.

A cold wind blew through the corridor of stone, washing over him, bringing crisp, fresh scents and blowing away the stink of rotting corpses.

Nobody cared for the bridgemen. Nobody cared for those at the bottom, with the darkest eyes. And yet, that wind seemed to whisper to him over and over. *Life before death. Life before death. Live before you die.*

His foot hit something. He bent down and picked it up. A small rock. He could barely make it out in the darkness. He recognized what was happening to him, this melancholy, this sense of despair. It had taken him often when he'd been younger, most frequently during the weeks of the Weeping, when the sky was hidden by clouds. During those times, Tien had cheered him up, helped him pull out of his despair. Tien had always been able to do that.

Once he'd lost his brother, he'd dealt with these periods of sadness more awkwardly. He'd become the wretch, not caring—but also not despairing. It had seemed better not to feel at all, as opposed to feeling pain.

I'm going to fail them, Kaladin thought, squeezing his eyes shut. *Why try?*

Wasn't he a fool to keep grasping as he did? If only he could win once. That would be enough. As long as he could believe that he could help someone, as long as he believed that some paths led to places other than darkness, he could hope.

You promised yourself you would try one last time, he thought. *They aren't dead yet.*

Still alive. For now.

There was one thing he hadn't tried. Something he'd been too frightened of. Every time he'd tried it in the past, he'd lost everything.

The wretch seemed to be standing before him. He meant release. Apathy. Did Kaladin really want to go back to that? It was a false refuge. Being that man hadn't protected him. It had only led him deeper and deeper until taking his own life had seemed the better way.

Life before death.

Kaladin stood up, opening his eyes, dropping the small rock. He walked slowly back toward the torchlight. The bridgemen looked up from their work. So many questioning eyes. Some doubtful, some grim, others encouraging. Rock, Dunny, Hobber, Leyten. They believed in him. He had survived the storms. One miracle granted.

"There is something we could try," Kaladin said. "But it will most likely end with us all dead at the hands of our own army."

"We're bound to end up dead anyway," Maps noted. "You said so yourself." Several of the others nodded.

Kaladin took a deep breath. "We have to try to escape."

"But the warcamp is guarded!" said Earless Jaks. "Bridgemen aren't allowed out without supervision. They know we'd run."

"We'd die," Moash said, face grim. "We're miles and miles from civilization. There's nothing out here but greatshells, and no shelter from highstorms."

"I know," Kaladin said. "But it's either this or the Parshendi arrows."

The men fell silent.

"They're going to send us down here every day to rob corpses," Kaladin said. "And they don't send us with supervision, since they fear the chasmfiends. Most bridgeman work is busywork, to distract us from our fate, so we only have to bring back a small amount of salvage."

"You think we should choose one of these chasms and flee down it?" Skar asked. "They've tried to map them all. The crews never reached the other side of the Plains—they got killed by chasmfiends or highstorm floods."

Kaladin shook his head. "That's not what we're going to do." He kicked at something on the ground before him—a fallen spear. His kick sent it into the air toward Moash, who caught it, surprised.

"I can train you to use those," Kaladin said softly.

The men fell silent, looking at the weapon.

"What good would this thing do?" Rock asked, taking the spear from Moash, looking it over. "We cannot fight an army."

"No," Kaladin said. "But if I train you, then we can attack a guard post at night. We might be able to get away." Kaladin looked at them, meeting each man's eyes in turn. "Once we're free, they'll send soldiers after us. Sadeas won't let bridgemen kill his soldiers and get away with it. We'll have to hope he underestimates us and sends a small group at first. If we kill them, we might be able to get far enough away to hide. It will be dangerous. Sadeas will go to great lengths to recapture us, and we'll likely end with an entire company chasing us down. Storm it, we'll probably never escape the camp in the first place. But it's something."

He fell silent, waiting as the men exchanged uncertain glances.

"I'll do it," Teft said, straightening up.

"Me too," Moash said, stepping forward. He seemed eager.

"And I," Sigzil said. "I would rather spit in their Alethi faces and die on their swords than remain a slave."

"Ha!" Rock said. "And I shall cook you all much food to keep you full while you kill."

"You won't fight with us?" Dunny asked, surprised.

"Is beneath me," Rock said raising his chin.

"Well, I'll do it," Dunny said. "I'm your man, Captain."

Others began to chime in, each man standing, several grabbing spears from the wet ground. They didn't yell in excitement or roar like other troops Kaladin had led. They were frightened by the idea of fighting—most had been common slaves or lowly workmen. But they were willing.

Kaladin stepped forward and began to outline a plan.

The History of Man

The Expulsion
the loss of the tranquiline halls

The Desolations
War against the Voidbringers

Aharietiam
the last desolation,
defeat of the
Voidbringers

The Recreance
the fall of the Knights
Radiant

The Hierocracy
the failure of Vorinism

FIVE YEARS AGO

Kaladin hated the Weeping. It marked the end of an old year and the coming of a new one, four solid weeks of rain in a ceaseless cascade of sullen drops. Never furious, never passionate like a highstorm. Slow, steady. Like the blood of a dying year that was taking its last few shambling steps toward the cairn. While other seasons of weather came and went unpredictably, the Weeping never failed to return at the same time each year. Unfortunately.

Kaladin lay on the sloped roof of his house in Hearthstone. A small pail of pitch sat next to him, covered by a piece of wood. It was almost empty now that he'd finished patching the roof. The Weeping was a miserable time to do this work, but it was also when a persistent leak could be most irritating. They'd repatch when the Weeping ended, but at least this way they wouldn't have to suffer a steady stream of drips onto their dining table for the next weeks.

He lay on his back, staring up at the sky. Perhaps he should have climbed down and gone inside, but he was already soaked through. So he stayed. Watching, thinking.

Another army was passing through the town. One of many these days—they often came during the Weeping, resupplying and moving to new battlefields. Roshone had made a rare appearance to welcome the warlord: Highmarshal Amaram himself, apparently a distant cousin as well as head of Alethi defense in this area. He was one of the most renowned soldiers still in Alethkar; most had left for the Shattered Plains.

The small raindrops misted Kaladin. Many of the others liked these weeks—there were no highstorms, save for one right in the middle. To the townspeople, it was a cherished time to rest from farming and relax. But Kaladin longed for the sun and the wind. He actually missed the highstorms, with their rage and vitality. These days were dreary, and he found it difficult to get anything productive done. As if the lack of storms left him without strength.

Few people had seen much of Roshone since the ill-fated whitespine hunt and the death of his son. He hid in his mansion, increasingly reclusive. The people of Hearthstone trod very lightly, as if they expected that any moment he could explode and turn his rage against them. Kaladin wasn't worried about that. A storm—whether from a person or the sky—was something you could react to. But this suffocation, this slow and steady dousing of life . . . That was far, far worse.

"Kaladin?" Tien's voice called. "Are you still up there?"

"Yeah," he called back, not moving. The clouds were so *bland* during the Weeping. Could anything be more lifeless than that miserable grey?

Tien rounded to the back of the building, where the roof sloped down to touch the ground. He had his hands in the pockets of his long raincoat, a wide-brimmed hat on his head. Both looked too large for him, but clothing always seemed too large for Tien. Even when it fit him properly.

Kaladin's brother climbed onto the roof and walked up beside him, then lay down, staring skyward. Someone else might have tried to cheer Kaladin up, and they would have failed. But somehow Tien knew the right thing to do. For the moment, that was keeping silent.

"You like the rain, don't you?" Kaladin finally asked him.

"Yeah," Tien said. Of course, Tien liked pretty much everything. "Hard to stare up at like this, though. I keep blinking."

For some reason, that made Kaladin smile.

"I made you something," Tien said. "At the shop today."

Kaladin's parents were worried; Ral the carpenter had taken Tien, though he didn't really need another apprentice, and was reportedly dissatisfied with the boy's work. Tien got distracted easily, Ral complained.

Kaladin sat up as Tien fished something out of his pocket. It was a small wooden horse, intricately carved.

"Don't worry about the water," Tien said, handing it over. "I sealed it already."

"Tien," Kaladin said, amazed. "This is *beautiful*." The details were amazing—the eyes, the hooves, the lines in the tail. It looked just like the majestic animals that pulled Roshone's carriage. "Did you show this to Ral?"

"He said it was good," Tien said, smiling beneath his oversized hat. "But he told me I should have been making a chair instead. I kind of got into trouble."

"But how . . . I mean, Tien, he's got to see this is amazing!"

"Oh, I don't know about that," Tien said, still smiling. "It's just a horse. Master Ral likes things you can use. Things to sit on, things to put clothes in. But I think I can make a good chair tomorrow, something that will make him proud."

Kaladin looked at his brother, with his innocent face and affable nature. He hadn't lost either, though he was now into his teenage years. *How is it you can always smile?* Kaladin thought. *It's dreadful outside, your master treats you like crem, and your family is slowly being strangled by the citylord. And yet you smile. How, Tien?*

And why is it that you make me want to smile too?

"Father spent another of the spheres, Tien," Kaladin found himself saying. Each time their father was forced to do that, he seemed to grow a little more wan, stand a little less tall. Those spheres were dun these days, no light in them. You couldn't infuse spheres during the Weeping. They all ran out, eventually.

"There are plenty more," Tien said.

"Roshone is trying to wear us down," Kaladin said. "Bit by bit, smother us."

"It's not as bad as it seems, Kaladin," his brother said, reaching up to hold his arm. "Things are never as bad as they seem. You'll see."

So many objections rose in his mind, but Tien's smile banished them. There, in the midst of the dreariest part of the year, Kaladin felt for a moment as if he had glimpsed sunshine. He could swear he felt things grow brighter around them, the storm retreating a shade, the sky lightening.

Their mother rounded the back of the building. She looked up at them, as if amused to find them both sitting on the roof in the rain. She stepped onto the lower portion. A small group of haspers clung to the stone there; the small two-shelled creatures proliferated during the Weeping. They seemed to grow out of nowhere, much like their cousins the tiny snails, scattered all across the stone.

"What are you two talking about?" she asked, walking up and sitting down with them. Hesina rarely acted like the other mothers in town. Sometimes, that bothered Kaladin. Shouldn't she have sent them into the house or something, complaining that they'd catch a cold? No, she just sat down with them, wearing a brown leather raincoat.

"Kaladin's worried about Father spending the spheres," Tien said.

"Oh, I wouldn't worry about that," she replied. "We'll get you to Kharbranth. You'll be old enough to leave in two more months."

"You two should come with me," Kaladin said. "And Father too."

"And leave the town?" Tien said, as if he'd never considered that possibility. "But I like it here."

Hesina smiled.

"What?" Kaladin said.

"Most young men your age are trying everything they can to be *rid* of their parents."

"I can't go off and leave you here. We're a family."

"He's trying to strangle us," Kaladin said, glancing at Tien. Talking with his brother had made him feel a lot better, but his objections were still there. "Nobody pays for healing, and I know nobody will pay you for work anymore. What kind of value does Father get for those spheres he spends anyway? Vegetables at ten times the regular price, moldy grain at double?"

Hesina smiled. "Observant."

"Father taught me to notice details. The eyes of a surgeon."

"Well," she said, eyes twinkling, "did your surgeon's eyes notice the first time we spent one of the spheres?"

"Sure," Kaladin said. "It was the day after the hunting accident. Father had to buy new cloth to make bandages."

"And did we *need* new bandages?"

"Well, no. But you know how Father is. He doesn't like it when we start to run even a little low."

"And so he spent one of those spheres," Hesina said. "That he'd hoarded for months and months, butting heads with the citylord over them."

Not to mention going to such lengths to steal them in the first place, Kaladin thought. *But you know all about that.* He glanced at Tien, who was watching the sky again. So far as Kaladin knew, his brother hadn't discovered the truth yet.

"So your father resisted so long," Hesina said, "only to finally break and spend a sphere on some cloth bandages we wouldn't need for months."

She had a point. Why *had* his father suddenly decided to . . . "He's letting Roshone think he's winning," Kaladin said with surprise, looking back at her.

Hesina smiled slyly. "Roshone would have found a way to get retribution eventually. It wouldn't have been easy. Your father ranks high as a citizen, and has the right of inquest. He *did* save Roshone's life, and many could testify to the severity of Rillir's wounds. But Roshone would have found a way. Unless he felt he'd broken us."

Kaladin turned toward the mansion. Though it was hidden by the shroud of rain, he could just make out the tents of the army camped on the field below. What would it be like to live as a soldier, often exposed to storms and rain, to winds and tempests? Once Kaladin would have been intrigued, but the life of a spearman had no call for him now. His mind was filled with diagrams of muscles and memorized lists of symptoms and diseases.

"We'll keep spending the spheres," Hesina said. "One every few weeks. Partially to live, though my family has offered supplies. More to keep Roshone thinking that we're bending. And then, we send you away. Unexpectedly. You'll be gone, the spheres safely in the hands of the ardents to use as a stipend during your years of study."

Kaladin blinked in realization. They weren't losing. They were *winning*.

"Think of it, Kaladin," Tien said. "You'll live in one of the grandest cities in the world! It will be so exciting. You'll be a man of learning, like Father. You'll have clerks to read to you from any book you want."

Kaladin pushed wet hair off his forehead. Tien made it sound a lot grander than he'd been thinking. Of course, Tien could make a crem-filled puddle sound grand.

"That's true," his mother said, still staring upward. "You could learn mathematics, history, politics, tactics, the sciences . . ."

"Aren't those things women learn?" Kaladin said, frowning.

"Lighteyed women study them. But there are male scholars as well. If not as many."

"All this to become a surgeon."

"You wouldn't have to become a surgeon. Your life is your own, son. If you take the path of a surgeon, we will be proud. But don't feel that you need to live your father's life for him." She looked down at Kaladin, blinking rainwater from her eyes.

"What else would I do?" Kaladin said, stupefied.

"There are many professions open to men with a good mind and training. If you really wished to study all the arts, you could become an ardent. Or perhaps a stormwarden."

Stormwarden. He reached by reflex for the prayer sewn to his left sleeve, waiting for the day he'd need to burn it for aid. "They seek to predict the future."

"It's not the same thing. You'll see. There are so many things to explore, so many places your mind could go. The world is changing. My family's most recent letter describes amazing fabrials, like pens that can write across great distances. It might not be long before men are taught to read."

"I'd never want to learn something like that," Kaladin said, aghast, glancing at Tien. Was their own *mother* really saying these things? But then, she'd always been like this. Free, both with her mind and her tongue.

Yet, to become a stormwarden . . . They studied the high-storms, predicted them—yes—but learned about them and their mysteries. They studied the winds themselves.

"No," Kaladin said. "I want to be a surgeon. Like my father."

Hesina smiled. "If that's what you choose, then—as I said—we will be proud of you. But father and I just want you to know that you *can* choose."

They sat like that for some time, letting rainwater soak them. Kaladin kept searching those grey clouds, wondering what it was that Tien found so interesting in them. Eventually, he heard splashing below, and Lirin's face appeared at the side of the house.

"What in the . . ." he said. "All *three* of you? What are you doing up here?"

"Feasting," Kaladin's mother said nonchalantly.

"On what?"

"On irregularity, dear," she said.

Lirin sighed. "Dear, you can be very odd, you know."

"And didn't I just say that?"

"Point. Well, come on. There's a gathering in the square."

Hesina frowned. She rose and walked down the slope of the roof. Kaladin glanced at Tien, and the two of them stood. Kaladin stuffed the wooden horse in his pocket and picked his way down, careful on the slick rock, his shoes squishing. Cool water ran down Kaladin's cheeks as he stepped off onto the ground.

They followed Lirin toward the square. Kaladin's father looked worried, and he walked with the beaten-down slouch he was prone to lately. Maybe it was an affectation to fool Roshone, but Kaladin suspected there was some truth to it. His father didn't like having to give up those spheres, even if it was part of a ruse. It was too much like giving in.

Ahead, a crowd was gathering at the town square, everyone holding umbrellas or wearing cloaks.

"What is it, Lirin?" Hesina asked, sounding anxious.

"Roshone is going to put in an appearance," Lirin said. "He asked Waber to gather everyone. Full town meeting."

"In the *rain*?" Kaladin asked. "Couldn't he have waited for Lightday?"

Lirin didn't reply. The family walked in silence, even Tien growing solemn. They passed some rainspren standing in puddles, glowing with a faint blue light, shaped like ankle-high melting candles with no flame. They rarely appeared except during the Weeping. They were said to be the souls of raindrops, glowing blue rods, seeming to melt but never growing smaller, a single blue eye at their tops.

The townspeople were mostly assembled, gossiping in the rain, by the time Kaladin's family arrived. Jost and Naget were there, though neither waved to Kaladin; it had been years since they'd been anything resembling friends. Kaladin shivered. His parents called this town home, and his father refused to leave, but it felt less and less like "home" by the day.

I'll be leaving it soon, he thought, eager to walk out of Hearthstone and leave these small-minded people behind. To go to a place where lighteyes were men and women of honor and beauty, worthy of the high station given them by the Almighty.

Roshone's carriage approached. It had lost much of its luster during his years in Hearthstone, the golden paint flaking off, the dark wood chipped by road gravel. As the carriage pulled into the square, Waber and his boys finally got a small canopy erected. The rain had strengthened, and drops hit the cloth with a hollow drumming sound.

The air smelled different with all of these people around. Up on the roof, it had been fresh and clean. Now it seemed muggy and humid. The carriage door opened. Roshone had gained more weight, and his lighteyes's suit had been retailored to fit his increased girth. He wore a wooden peg on his right stump, hidden by the cuff of his trouser, and his gait was stiff as he climbed out of the carriage and ducked beneath the canopy, grumbling.

He hardly seemed the same person, with that beard and wet, stringy hair. But his eyes, they were the same. More beady now because of the fuller cheeks, but still seething as he studied the crowd. As if he had been hit with a rock when he wasn't looking, and now searched for the culprit.

Was Laral inside the carriage? Someone else moved inside, climbing out, but it turned out to be a lean man with a clean-shaven face and light tan eyes. The dignified man wore a neatly pressed, green formal military uniform and had a sword at his hip. Highmarshal Amaram? He certainly looked impressive, with that strong figure and square face. The difference between him and Roshone was striking.

Finally, Laral did appear, wearing a light yellow dress of an antique fashion, with a flaring skirt and thick bodice. She glanced up at the rain, then waited for a footman to hurry over with an umbrella. Kaladin felt his heart thumping. They hadn't spoken since the day she'd humiliated him in Roshone's mansion. And yet, she was *gorgeous*. As she had grown through her adolescence, she had gotten prettier and prettier. Some might find that dark hair sprinkled with foreigner blond to be unappealing for its indication of mixed blood, but to Kaladin it was alluring.

Beside Kaladin, his father stiffened, cursing softly.

"What?" Tien asked from beside Kaladin, craning to see.

"Laral," Kaladin's mother said. "She's wearing a bride's prayer on her sleeve."

Kaladin started, seeing the white cloth with its blue glyphpair sewn onto the sleeve of her dress. She'd burn it when the engagement was formally announced.

But . . . who? Rillir was dead!

"I'd heard rumors of this," Kaladin's father said. "It appears Roshone wasn't willing to part with the connections she offers."

"Him?" Kaladin asked, stunned. Roshone *himself* was marrying her? Others in the crowd had begun speaking as they noticed the prayer.

"Lighteyes marry much younger women all the time," Kaladin's mother said. "For them, marriages are often about securing house loyalty."

"*Him?*" Kaladin asked again, incredulous, stepping forward. "We have to stop it. We have to—"

"Kaladin," his father said sharply.

"But—"

"It is their affair, not ours."

Kaladin fell silent, feeling the larger raindrops hit his head, the smaller ones blowing by as mist. The water ran through the square and pooled in depressions. Near Kaladin, a rainspren sprang up, forming as if out of the water. It stared upward, unblinking.

Roshone leaned on his cane and nodded to Natir, his steward. The man was accompanied by his wife, a stern-looking woman named Alaxia. Natir clapped his slender hands to quiet the crowd, and soon the only sound was that of the soft rain.

"Brightlord Amaram," Roshone said, nodding to the lighteyed man in the uniform, "is absendiar highmarshal of our princedom. He is in command of defending our borders while the king and Brightlord Sadeas are away."

Kaladin nodded. Everyone knew of Amaram. He was far more important than most military men who passed through Hearthstone.

Amaram stepped forward to speak.

"You have a fine town here," Amaram said to the gathered darkeyes. He had a strong, deep voice. "Thank you for hosting me."

Kaladin frowned, glancing at the other townspeople. They seemed as confused as he by the statement.

"Normally," Amaram said, "I would leave this task to one of my subordinate officers. But as I was visiting with my cousin, I decided to come down in person. It is not so onerous a task that I need delegate it."

"Excuse me, Brightlord," said Callins, one of the farmers. "But what duty is that?"

"Why, recruitment, good farmer," Amaram said, nodding to Alaxia, who stepped forward with a sheet of paper strapped to a board. "The king took most of our armies with him on his quest to fulfill the Vengeance Pact. My forces are undermanned, and it has become necessary to recruit young men from each town or village we pass. I do this with volunteers whenever possible."

The townspeople fell still. Boys talked of running off to the army, but few of them would actually do it. Hearthstone's duty was to provide food.

"My fighting is not as glorious as the war for vengeance," Amaram said, "but it is our sacred duty to defend our lands. This tour will be for four years, and upon completing your duty, you will receive a war bonus equal to one-tenth your total wages. You may then return, or you may sign up for further duty. Distinguish yourself and rise to a high rank, and it could mean an increase of one nahn for you and your children. Are there any volunteers?"

"I'll go," Jost said, stepping forward.

"Me too," Abry added.

"Jost!" Jost's mother said, grabbing his arm. "The crops—"

"Your crops are important, darkwoman," Amaram said, "but not nearly as important as the defense of our people. The king sends back riches from the plundered Plains, and the gemstones he has captured can provide food for Alethkar in emergency. You two are both welcome. Are there any others?"

Three more boys from the town stepped forward, and one older man—Harl, who had lost his wife to the scarfever. He was the man whose daughter Kaladin hadn't been able to save after her fall.

"Excellent," Amaram said. "Are there any others?"

The townspeople were still. Oddly so. Many of the boys Kaladin had heard talk so often about joining the army looked away. Kaladin felt his heart beating, and his leg twitched, as if itching to propel him forward.

No. He was to be a surgeon. Lirin looked at him, and his

dark brown eyes displayed hints of deep concern. But when Kaladin didn't make any moves forward, he relaxed.

"Very well," Amaram said, nodding to Roshone. "We will need your list after all."

"List?" Lirin asked loudly.

Amaram glanced at him. "The need of our army is great, darkborn. I will take volunteers first, but the army *must* be replenished. As citylord, my cousin has the duty and honor of deciding which men to send."

"Read the first four names, Alaxia," Roshone said, "and the last one."

Alaxia looked down at her list, speaking with a dry voice. "Agil, son of Marf. Caull, son of Taleb."

Kaladin looked up at Lirin with apprehension.

"He can't take you," Lirin said. "We're of the second nahn and provide an essential function to the town—I as surgeon, you as my only apprentice. By the law, we are exempt from conscription. Roshone knows it."

"Habrin, son of Arafik," Alaxia continued. "Jorna, son of Loats." She hesitated, then looked up. "Tien, son of Lirin."

There was a stillness across the square. Even the rain seemed to hesitate for a moment. Then, all eyes turned toward Tien. The boy looked dumbfounded. Lirin was immune as town surgeon, Kaladin immune as his apprentice.

But not Tien. He was a carpenter's third apprentice, not vital, not immune.

Hesina gripped Tien tightly. "No!"

Lirin stepped in front of them, defensive. Kaladin stood stunned, looking at Roshone. Smiling, self-satisfied Roshone.

We took his son, Kaladin realized, meeting those beady eyes. *This is his revenge.*

"I . . ." Tien said. "The military?" For once, he seemed to lose his confidence, his optimism. His eyes opened wide, and he grew very pale. He fainted when he saw blood. He hated fighting. He was still small and spindly despite his age.

"He's too young," Lirin declared. Their neighbors sidled away, leaving Lirin's family to stand alone in the rain.

Amaram frowned. "In the cities, youths as young as eight and nine are accepted into the military."

"Lighteyed sons!" Lirin said. "To be trained as officers. They aren't sent into battle!"

Amaram frowned more deeply. He stepped out into the rain, walking up to the family. "How old are you, son?" he asked Tien.

"He's thirteen," Lirin said.

Amaram glanced at him. "The surgeon. I've heard of you." He sighed, glancing back at Roshone. "I haven't the time to engage in your petty, small-town politics, cousin. Isn't there another boy that will do?"

"It is my choice!" Roshone insisted. "Given me by the dictates of law. I send those the town can spare—well, that boy is the *first* one we can spare."

Lirin stepped forward, eyes full of anger. Highmarshal Amaram caught him by the arm. "Do not do something you would regret, darkborn. Roshone has acted according to the law."

"You hid behind the law, sneering at me, surgeon," Roshone called to Lirin. "Well, now it turns against *you*. Keep those spheres! The look on your face at this moment is worth the price of every one of them!"

"I . . ." Tien said again. Kaladin had never seen the boy so terrified.

Kaladin felt powerless. The crowd's eyes were on Lirin, standing with his arm in the grip of the lighteyed general, locking his gaze with Roshone.

"I'll make the lad a runner boy for a year or two," Amaram promised. "He won't be in combat. It is the best I can do. Every body is needed in these times."

Lirin slumped, then bowed his head. Roshone laughed, motioning Laral toward the carriage. She didn't glance at Kaladin as she climbed back in. Roshone followed, and though he was still laughing, his expression had grown hard. Lifeless. Like the dull clouds above. He had his revenge, but his son was still dead and he was still stuck in Hearthstone.

Amaram regarded the crowd. "The recruits may bring two changes of clothing and up to three stoneweights of other possessions. They *will* be weighed. Report to the army in two hours and ask for Sergeant Hav." He turned and followed Roshone.

Tien stared after him, pale as a whitewashed building. Kaladin could see his terror at leaving his family. His brother, the one who always made him smile when it rained. It was physically painful for Kaladin to see him so scared. It wasn't *right*. Tien should smile. That was who he was.

He felt the wooden horse in his pocket. Tien always brought him relief when he felt pained. Suddenly, it occurred to him that there was something he could do in turn. *It's time to stop hiding in the room when someone else holds up the globe of light,* Kaladin thought. *It's time to be a man.*

"Brightlord Amaram!" Kaladin yelled.

The general hesitated, standing on the stepstool into the carriage, one foot in the door. He glanced over his shoulder.

"I want to take Tien's place," Kaladin said.

"Not allowed!" Roshone said from inside the carriage. "The law says I may choose."

Amaram nodded grimly.

"Then what if you take me *as well*," Kaladin said. "Can I volunteer?" That way, at least, Tien wouldn't be alone.

"Kaladin!" Hesina said, grabbing him on one arm.

"It is allowed," Amaram said. "I will not turn away any soldier, son. If you want to join, you are welcome."

"Kaladin, no," Lirin said. "Don't both of you go. Don't—"

Kaladin looked at Tien, the boy's face wet beneath his wide-brimmed hat. He shook his head, but his eyes seemed hopeful.

"I volunteer," Kaladin said, turning back to Amaram. "I'll go."

"Then you have two hours," Amaram said, climbing into the carriage. "Same possession allotment as the others."

The carriage door shut, but not before Kaladin got a glimpse of an even *more* satisfied Roshone. Rattling, the vehicle splashed away, dropping a sheet of water from its roof.

"Why?" Lirin said, turning back to Kaladin, his voice ragged. "Why have you done this to me? After all of our plans!"

Kaladin turned to Tien. The boy took his arm. "Thank you," Tien whispered. "Thank you, Kaladin. *Thank you.*"

"I've lost both of you," Lirin said hoarsely, splashing away. "Storm it! Both of you." He was crying. Kaladin's mother was crying too. She clutched Tien again.

"Father!" Kaladin said, turning, amazed at how confident he felt.

Lirin paused, standing in the rain, one foot in a puddle where rainspren clustered. They inched away from him like vertical slugs.

"In four years, I will bring him home safely," Kaladin said. "I promise it by the storms and the Almighty's tenth name itself. I will *bring him back.*"

I promise. . . .

"Yelig-nar, called Blightwind, was one that could speak like a man, though often his voice was accompanied by the wails of those he consumed."

—The Unmade were obviously fabrications of folklore. Curiously, most were not considered individuals, but instead personifications of kinds of destruction. This quote is from Traxil, line 33, considered a primary source, though I doubt its authenticity.

They are an oddly welcoming group, these wild parshmen, Shallan read. It was King Gavilar's account again, recorded a year before his murder. *It has now been nearly five months since our first meeting. Dalinar continues to pressure me to return to our homeland, insisting that the expedition has stretched too long.*

The parshmen promise that they will lead me on a hunt for a great-shelled beast they call an ulo mas vara, *which my scholars say translates roughly to "Monster of the Chasms." If their descriptions are accurate, these creatures have large gemhearts, and one of their heads would make a truly impressive trophy. They also speak of their terrible gods, and we think they must be referring to several particularly large chasm greatshells.*

We are amazed to find religion among these parshmen. The mounting evidence of a complete parshman society—with civilization, culture, and a unique language—is astounding. My stormwardens have begun calling this people "the Parshendi." It is obvious this group is very different from our ordinary servant parshmen, and may not even be the same race, despite the skin patterns. Perhaps they are distant cousins, as different from ordinary parshmen as Alethi axehounds are from the Selay breed.

The Parshendi have seen our servants, and are confused by them. "Where is their music?" Klade will often ask me. I do not know what he means. But our servants do not react to the Parshendi at all, showing no interest in emulating them. This is reassuring.

The question about music may have to do with the humming and chanting the Parshendi often do. They have an uncanny ability to make music together. I swear that I have left one Parshendi singing to himself, then soon passed another out of earshot of the first, yet singing the very same song—eerily near to the other in tempo, tune, and lyric.

Their favored instrument is the drum. They are crudely made, with handprints of paint marking the sides. This matches their simple buildings, which they construct of crem and stone. They build them in the craterlike rock formations here at the edge of the Shattered Plains. I ask Klade if they worry about highstorms, but he just laughs. "Why worry? If the buildings blow down, we can build them again, can we not?"

On the other side of the alcove, Jasnah's book rustled as she turned a page. Shallan set aside her own volume, then picked through the books on the desk. Her philosophy training done for the time being, she had returned to her study of King Gavilar's murder.

She slid a small volume out from the bottom of the stack: a record dictated by Stormwarden Matain, one of the scholars who had accompanied the king. Shallan flipped through the pages, searching for a specific passage. It was a description of the very first Parshendi hunting party they encountered.

It happened after we set up beside a deep river in a heavily wooded area. It was an ideal location for a long-term camp, as the dense cobwood trees would protect against highstorm winds, and the river's gorge eliminated the risk of flooding. His Majesty wisely took my advice, sending scouting parties both upriver and down.

Highprince Dalinar's scouting party was the first to encounter the strange, untamed parshmen. When he returned to camp with his story, I—like many others—refused to believe his claims. Surely Brightlord Dalinar had simply run across the parshman servants of another expedition like our own.

Once they visited our camp the next day, their reality could no longer be denied. There were ten of them—parshmen to be sure, but bigger than the familiar ones. Some had skin marbled black and red, and others were marbled white and red, as is more common in Alethkar. They carried magnificent weapons, the bright steel etched with complex decorations, but wore simple clothing of woven narbin cloth.

Before long, His Majesty became fascinated by these strange parshmen, insisting that I begin a study of their language and society. I'll admit that my original intent was to expose them as a hoax of some kind. The more we learned, however, the more I came to realize how faulty my original assessment had been.

Shallan tapped the page, thinking. Then she pulled out a thick volume, titled *King Gavilar Kholin, a Biography*, published by Gavilar's widow, Navani, two years before. Shallan flipped through pages, scanning for a particular paragraph.

My husband was an excellent king—an inspiring leader, an unparalleled duelist, and a genius of battlefield tactics. But he didn't have a single scholarly finger on his left hand. He never showed an interest in the accounting of highstorms, was bored by talk of science, and ignored fabrials unless they had an obvious use in battle. He was a man built after the classical masculine ideal.

"Why was he so interested in them?" Shallan said out loud.

"Hmmm?" Jasnah asked.

"King Gavilar," Shallan said. "Your mother insists in her biography that he wasn't a scholar."

"True."

"But he *was* interested in the Parshendi," Shallan said. "Even before he could have known about their Shardblades. According to Matain's account, he wanted to know about their language, their society, and their music. Was that just embellishment, to make him sound more scholarly to future readers?"

"No," Jasnah said, lowering her own book. "The longer he remained in the Unclaimed Hills, the more fascinated by the Parshendi he became."

"So there's a discrepancy. Why would a man with no prior interest in scholarship suddenly become so obsessed?"

"Yes," Jasnah said. "I too have wondered about this. But sometimes, people change. When he returned, I was encouraged by his interest; we spent many evenings talking about his discoveries. It was one of the few times when I felt I really connected with my father."

Shallan bit her lip. "Jasnah," she finally asked. "Why did you assign me to research this event? You *lived* through this; you already know everything I'm 'discovering.'"

"I feel a fresh perspective may be of value." Jasnah put down her book, looking over at Shallan. "I don't intend for you to find specific answers. Instead, I hope that you will notice details I've missed. You are coming to see how my father's personality changed during those months, and that means you are digging deeply. Believe it or not, few others have caught the discrepancy you just did—though many do note his later changes, once he returned to Kholinar."

"Even so, I feel a little odd studying it. Perhaps I'm still influenced by my tutors' idea that only the classics are a proper realm of study for young ladies."

"The classics do have their place, and I will send you to classical works on occasion, as I did with your study of morality. But I intend such tangents to be adjuncts to your current projects. *Those* must be the focus, not long-lost historical conundrums."

Shallan nodded. "But Jasnah, aren't you a *historian*? Aren't those long-lost historical conundrums the meat of your field?"

"I'm a Veristitalian," Jasnah said. "We search for answers in the past, reconstructing what truly happened. To many, writing a history is not about truth, but about presenting the most flattering picture of themselves and their motives. My sisters and I choose projects that we feel were misunderstood or misrepresented, and in studying them hope to better understand the present."

Why, then, are you spending so much time studying folktales and looking for evil spirits? No, Jasnah was searching for something real. Something so important that it drew her away from the Shattered Plains and the fight to avenge her father. She intended to do something with those folktales, and Shallan's research was part of it, somehow.

That excited her. It was the sort of thing she'd wanted since she'd been a child, looking through her father's few books, frustrated that he'd chased off yet another tutor. Here, with Jasnah, Shallan was part of something—and, knowing Jasnah, it was something *big*.

And yet, she thought. *Tozbek's ship arrives tomorrow morning. I'll be leaving.*

I need to start complaining. I need to convince Jasnah that this was all so much harder than I anticipated, so that when I leave she won't be surprised. I need to cry, break down, give up. I need to—

"What is Urithiru?" Shallan found herself asking instead.

To her surprise, Jasnah answered without hesitation. "Urithiru was said to be the center of the Silver Kingdoms, a city that held ten thrones, one for each king. It was the most majestic, most amazing, most important city in all the world."

"Really? Why hadn't I heard of it before?"

"Because it was abandoned even before the Lost Radiants turned against mankind. Most scholars consider it just a myth. The ardents refuse to speak of it, due to its association with the Radiants, and therefore with the first major failure of Vorinism. Much of what we know about the city comes from fragments of lost works quoted by classical scholars. Many of those classical works have, themselves, survived only in pieces. Indeed, the single complete work we have from early years is *The Way of Kings,* and that is only because of the Vanrial's efforts."

Shallan nodded slowly. "If there were ruins of a magnificent, ancient city hidden somewhere, Natanatan—unexplored, overgrown, wild—would be the natural place to find them."

"Urithiru is *not* in Natanatan," Jasnah said, smiling. "But it is a good guess, Shallan. Return to your studies."

"The weapons," Shallan said.

Jasnah raised an eyebrow.

"The Parshendi. They carried beautiful weapons of fine, etched steel. Yet they used skin drums with crude handprints on the sides and lived in huts of stone and crem. Doesn't that strike you as incongruous?"

"Yes. I would certainly describe that as an oddity."

"Then—"

"I assure you, Shallan," Jasnah said. "The city is not there."

"But you *are* interested in the Shattered Plains. You spoke of them with Brightlord Dalinar through the spanreed."

"I did."

"What were the Voidbringers?" Now that Jasnah was actually answering, perhaps she'd say. "What were they *really*?"

Jasnah studied her with a curious expression. "Nobody knows for sure. Most scholars consider them, like Urithiru, mere myths, while theologians accept them as counterparts of the Almighty—monsters that dwelled in the hearts of men, much as the Almighty once lived there."

"But—"

"Return to your studies, child," Jasnah said, raising her book. "Perhaps we will speak of this another time."

There was an air of finality about that. Shallan bit her lip, keeping herself from saying something rude just to draw Jasnah back into conversation. *She doesn't trust me,* she thought. Perhaps with good reason. *You're leaving,* Shallan told herself again. *Tomorrow. You're sailing away from this.*

But that meant she had only one day left. One more day in the grand Palanaeum. One more day with all of these books, all of this power and knowledge.

"I need a copy of Tifandor's biography of your father," Shallan said, poking through the books. "I keep seeing it referenced."

"It's on one of the bottom floors," Jasnah said idly. "I might be able to dig out the index number."

"No need," Shallan said, standing. "I'll look it up. I need the practice."

"As you wish," Jasnah said.

Shallan smiled. She knew exactly where the book was—but the pretense of searching for it would give her time away from Jasnah. And during that time, she'd see what she could discover about the Voidbringers on her own.

⁘

Two hours later, Shallan sat at a cluttered desk at the back of one of the Palanaeum's lower-level rooms, her sphere lantern illuminating a stack of hastily gathered volumes, none of which had proven much use.

It seemed that everybody knew something about the Voidbringers. People in rural areas spoke of them as mysterious creatures that came out at night, stealing from the unlucky and punishing the foolish. Those Voidbringers seemed more mischievous than evil. But then there would be the odd story about a Voidbringer taking on the form of a wayward traveler who—after receiving kindness from a tallew farmer—would slaughter the entire family, drink their blood, then write voidish symbols across the walls in black ash.

Most people in the cities, however, saw the Voidbringers as spirits who stalked at night, a kind of evil spren that invaded the hearts of men and made them do terrible things. When a good man grew angry, it was the work of a Voidbringer.

Scholars laughed at all these ideas. Actual historical accounts—the ones she could find quickly—were contradictory. Were the Voidbringers the denizens of Damnation? If so, wouldn't Damnation now be empty, as the Voidbringers had conquered the Tranquiline Halls and cast out mankind to Roshar?

I should have known that I'd have trouble finding anything solid, Shallan thought, leaning back in her chair. *Jasnah's been researching this for months, maybe years. What did I expect to find in a few hours?*

The only thing the research had done was increase her confusion. What errant winds had brought Jasnah to this topic? It made no sense. Studying the Voidbringers was like trying to determine if deathspren were real or not. What was the point?

She shook her head, stacking her books. The ardents would reshelve them for her. She needed to fetch Tifandor's biography and return to their balcony. She rose and walked toward the room's exit, carrying her lantern in her freehand. She hadn't brought a parshman; she intended to carry back only the one book. As she reached the exit, she noticed another light approaching out on the balcony. Just before she arrived, someone stepped up to the doorway, holding aloft a garnet lantern.

"Kabsal?" Shallan asked, surprised to see his youthful face, painted violet by the light.

"Shallan?" he asked, looking up at the index inscription atop the entryway. "What are you doing here? Jasnah said you were looking for Tifandor."

"I . . . got turned around."

He raised an eyebrow at her.

"Bad lie?" she asked.

"Terrible," he said. "You're two floors up and about a thousand index numbers off. After I couldn't find you below, I asked the lift porters to take me where they brought you, and they took me here."

"Jasnah's training can be exhausting," Shallan said. "So I sometimes find a quiet corner to relax and compose myself. It's the only time I get to be alone."

Kabsal nodded thoughtfully.

"Better?" she asked.

"Still problematic. You took a break, but for *two hours*?

Besides, I remember you telling me that Jasnah's training wasn't so terrible."

"She'd believe me," Shallan said. "She thinks she's far more demanding than she is. Or . . . well, she *is* demanding. I just don't mind as much as she thinks I do."

"Very well," he said. "But what *were* you doing down here, then?"

She bit her lip, causing him to laugh.

"What?" she demanded, blushing.

"You just look so blasted *innocent* when you do that!"

"I *am* innocent."

"Didn't you just lie to me twice in a row?"

"Innocent, as in the opposite of sophisticated." She grimaced. "Otherwise, they'd have been more convincing lies. Come. Walk with me while I fetch Tifandor. If we hurry, I won't have to lie to Jasnah."

"Fair enough," he said, joining her and strolling around the perimeter of the Palanaeum. The hollow inverted pyramid rose toward the ceiling far above, the four walls expanding outward at a slant. The topmost levels were brighter and easier to make out, tiny lights bobbing along railings in the hands of ardents or scholars.

"Fifty-seven levels," Shallan said. "I can't even imagine how much work it must have been for you to create all this."

"We didn't create it," Kabsal said. "It was here. The main shaft, at least. The Kharbranthians cut out the rooms for the books."

"This formation is *natural*?"

"As natural as cities like Kholinar. Or have you forgotten my demonstration?"

"No. But why didn't you use this place as one of your examples?"

"We haven't found the right sand pattern yet," he said. "But we're sure the Almighty himself made this place, as he did the cities."

"What about the Dawnsingers?" Shallan asked.

"What about them?"

"Could they have created it?"

He chuckled as they arrived at the lift. "That isn't the kind of thing the Dawnsingers did. They were healers, kindly spren sent by the Almighty to care for humans once we were forced out of the Tranquiline Halls."

"Kind of like the opposite of the Voidbringers."

"I suppose you could say that.

"Take us down two levels," she told the parshman lift porters. They began lowering the platform, the pulleys squeaking and wood shaking beneath her feet.

"If you think to distract me with this conversation," Kabsal noted, folding his arms and leaning back against the railing, "you won't be successful. I sat up there with your disapproving mistress for well over an hour, and let me say that it was *not* a pleasant experience. I think she knows I still intend to try and convert her."

"Of course she does. She's Jasnah. She knows practically everything."

"Except whatever it is she came here to study."

"The Voidbringers," Shallan said. "That's what she's studying."

He frowned. A few moments later, the lift came to a rest on the appropriate floor. "The Voidbringers?" he said, sounding curious. She'd have expected him to be scornful or amused. *No,* she thought. *He's an ardent. He believes in them.*

"What were they?" she asked, walking out. Not far below, the massive cavern came to a point. There was a large infused diamond there, marking the nadir.

"We don't like to talk about it," Kabsal said as he joined her.

"Why not? You're an ardent. This is part of your religion."

"An unpopular part. People prefer to hear about the Ten Divine Attributes or the Ten Human Failings. We accommodate them because we, also, prefer that to the deep past."

"Because . . ." she prodded.

"Because," he said with a sigh, "of our failure. Shallan, the devotaries—at their core—are still classical Vorinism.

That means the Hierocracy and the fall of the Lost Radiants are *our* shame." He held up his deep blue lantern. Shallan strolled at his side, curious, letting him just talk.

"We believe that the Voidbringers were *real*, Shallan. A scourge and a plague. A hundred times they came upon mankind. First casting us from the Tranquiline Halls, then trying to destroy us here on Roshar. They weren't just spren that hid under rocks, then came out to steal someone's laundry. They were creatures of terrible destructive power, forged in Damnation, created from hate."

"By whom?" Shallan asked.

"What?"

"Who made them? I mean, the *Almighty* wasn't likely to have 'created something from hate.' So what made them?"

"Everything has its opposite, Shallan. The Almighty is a force of good. To balance his goodness, the cosmere needed the Voidbringers as his opposite."

"So the more good that the Almighty did, the more evil he created as a by-product? What's the point of doing any good at all if it just creates more evil?"

"I see Jasnah has continued your training in philosophy."

"That's not philosophy," Shallan said. "That's simple logic."

He sighed. "I don't think you want to get into the deep theology of this. Suffice it to say that the Almighty's pure goodness created the Voidbringers, but *men* may choose good without creating evil because as mortals they have a dual nature. Thus the only way for good to increase in the cosmere is for men to create it—in that way, good may come to outweigh evil."

"All right," she said. "But I don't buy the explanation about the Voidbringers."

"I thought you were a believer."

"I *am*. But just because I honor the Almighty doesn't mean I'm going to accept any explanation, Kabsal. It might be religion, but it still has to make sense."

"Didn't you once tell me that you didn't understand your own self?"

"Well, yes."

"And yet you expect to be able to understand the exact workings of the *Almighty*?"

She drew her lips into a line. "All right, fine. But I still want to know more about the Voidbringers."

He shrugged as she guided him into an archive room, filled with shelves of books. "I told you the basics, Shallan. The Voidbringers were an embodiment of evil. We fought them off ninety and nine times, led by the Heralds and their chosen knights, the ten orders we call the Knights Radiant. Finally, Aharietiam came, the Last Desolation. The Voidbringers were cast back into the Tranquiline Halls. The Heralds followed to force them out of heaven as well, and Roshar's Heraldic Epochs ended. Mankind entered the Era of Solitude. The modern era."

"But why is everything from before so fragmented?"

"This was thousands and thousands of years ago, Shallan," Kabsal said. "Before history, before men even knew how to forge steel. We had to be given Shardblades, otherwise we would have had to fight the Voidbringers with clubs."

"And yet we had the Silver Kingdoms and the Knights Radiant."

"Formed and led by the Heralds."

Shallan frowned, counting off rows of shelves. She stopped at the correct one, handed her lantern to Kabsal, then walked down the aisle and plucked the biography off the shelf. Kabsal followed her, holding up the lanterns.

"There's more to this," Shallan said. "Otherwise, Jasnah wouldn't be digging so hard."

"I can tell you why she's doing it," he said.

Shallan glanced at him.

"Don't you see?" he said. "She's trying to prove that the Voidbringers weren't real. She wants to demonstrate that this was all a fabrication of the Radiants." He stepped forward and turned to face her, the lanternlight rebounding from the books to either side, making his face pale. "She wants to prove once and for all that the devotaries—and Vorinism—are a gigantic fraud. *That's* what this is all about."

"Maybe," Shallan said thoughtfully. It did seem to fit. What better goal for an avowed heretic? Undermining foolish beliefs and disproving religion? It explained why Jasnah would study something as seemingly inconsequential as the Voidbringers. Find the right evidence in the historical records, and Jasnah might well be able to prove herself right.

"Haven't we been scourged enough?" Kabsal said, eyes angry. "The ardents are no threat to her. We're not a threat to anyone these days. We can't own property . . . Damnation, we're property *ourselves*. We dance to the whims of the city-lords and warlords, afraid to tell them the truths of their sins for fear of retribution. We're whitespines without tusks or claws, expected to sit at our master's feet and offer praise. Yet this is real. It's *all* real, and they ignore us and—"

He cut off suddenly, glancing at her, lips tight, jaw clenched. She'd never seen such fervor, such *fury* from the pleasant ardent. She wouldn't have thought him capable of it.

"I'm sorry," he said, turning from her, leading the way back down the aisle.

"It's all right," she said, hurrying after him, suddenly feeling depressed. Shallan had expected to find something grander, something more mysterious, behind Jasnah's secretive research. Could it all really just be about proving Vorinism false?

They walked in silence out to the balcony. And there, she realized she had to tell him. "Kabsal, I'm leaving."

He looked at her, surprised.

"I've had news from my family," she said. "I can't speak of it, but I can stay no longer."

"Something about your father?"

"Why? Have you heard something?"

"Only that he's been reclusive lately. More than normal."

She suppressed a flinch. News had gotten this far? "I'm sorry to go so suddenly."

"You'll return?"

"I don't know."

He looked into her eyes, searching. "Do you know when you'll be leaving?" he said in a suddenly cool voice.

"Tomorrow morning."

"Well then," he said. "Will you at least do me the honor of sketching me? You've never given me a likeness, though you've done many of the other ardents."

She started, realizing that was true. Despite their time together, she'd never done a sketch of Kabsal. She raised her freehand to her mouth. "I'm sorry!"

He seemed taken aback. "I didn't mean it bitterly, Shallan. It's really not that important—"

"Yes it *is*," she said, grabbing his hand, towing him along the walkway. "I left my drawing things up above. Come on." She hurried him to the lift, instructing the parshmen to carry them up. As the lift began to rise, Kabsal looked at her hand in his. She dropped it hastily.

"You're a very confusing woman," he said stiffly.

"I warned you." She held the retrieved book close to her breast. "I believe you said you had me figured out."

"I rescind that statement." He looked at her. "You're really leaving?"

She nodded. "I'm sorry. Kabsal . . . I'm not what you think I am."

"I think you're a beautiful, intelligent woman."

"Well, you have the woman part right."

"Your father is sick, isn't he?"

She didn't answer.

"I can see why you'd want to return to be with him," Kabsal said. "But surely you won't abandon your wardship forever. You'll be back with Jasnah."

"And she won't be staying in Kharbranth forever. She's been moving from place to place almost constantly for the last two years."

He looked ahead, staring out the front of the lift as they rose. Soon, they had to transfer to another lift to carry them up the next group of floors. "I shouldn't have been spending time with you," he finally said. "The senior ardents think I'm too distracted. They never like it when one of us starts looking outside the ardentia."

"Your right to court is protected."

"We're property. A man's rights can be protected at the same time that he is discouraged from exercising them. I've avoided work, I've disobeyed my superiors . . . In courting you, I've also courted trouble."

"I didn't ask you for any of that."

"You didn't discourage me."

She had no response for that, other than to feel a rising worry. A hint of panic, a desire to run away and hide. During her years of near-solitude on her father's estate, she had never dreamed of a relationship like this one. *Is that what this is?* she thought, panic swelling. *A relationship?* Her intentions in coming to Kharbranth had seemed so straightforward. How had she gotten to the point where she risked breaking a man's heart?

And, to her shame, she admitted to herself that she would miss the research more than Kabsal. Was she a horrible person for feeling that way? She *was* fond of him. He was pleasant. Interesting.

He looked at her, and there was longing in his eyes. He seemed . . . Stormfather, he seemed to really be in love with her. Shouldn't she be falling in love with him too? She didn't think she was. She was just confused.

When they reached the top of the Palanaeum's system of lifts, she practically ran out into the Veil. Kabsal followed, but they needed another lift up to Jasnah's alcove, and soon she found herself trapped with him once more.

"I could come," Kabsal said softly. "Return with you to Jah Keved."

Shallan's panic increased. She barely knew him. Yes, they had chatted frequently, but rarely about the important things. If he left the ardentia, he'd be demoted to tenth dahn, almost as low as a darkeyes. He'd be without money or house, in almost as bad a position as her family.

Her family. What would her brothers say if she brought a virtual stranger back with her? Another man to become part of their problems, privy to their secrets?

"I can see from your expression that it's not an option,"

Kabsal said. "It seems that I've misinterpreted some very important things."

"No, it's not that," Shallan said quickly. "It's just . . . Oh, Kabsal. How can you expect to make sense of my actions when even *I* can't make sense of them?" She touched his arm, turning him toward her. "I have been dishonest with you. And with Jasnah. And, most infuriatingly, with myself. I'm sorry."

He shrugged, obviously trying to feign nonchalance. "At least I'll get a sketch. Won't I?"

She nodded as the lift finally shuddered to a halt. She walked down the dark hallway, Kabsal following with the lanterns. Jasnah looked up appraisingly as Shallan entered their alcove, but did not ask why she'd taken so long. Shallan found herself blushing as she gathered her drawing tools. Kabsal hesitated in the doorway. He'd left a basket of bread and jam on the desk. The top of it was still wrapped with a cloth; Jasnah hadn't touched it, though he always offered her some as a peace offering. Without jam, since Jasnah hated it.

"Where should I sit?" Kabsal asked.

"Just stand there," Shallan said, sitting down, propping her sketchpad against her legs and holding it still with her covered safehand. She looked up at him, leaning with one hand against the doorframe. Head shaved, light grey robe draped around him, sleeves short, waist tied with a white sash. Eyes confused. She blinked, taking a Memory, then began to sketch.

It was one of the most awkward experiences of her life. She didn't tell Kabsal that he could move, and so he held the pose. He didn't speak. Perhaps he thought it would spoil the picture. Shallan found her hand shaking as she sketched, though—thankfully—she managed to hold back tears.

Tears, she thought, doing the final lines of the wall around Kabsal. *Why should I cry? I'm not the one who just got rejected. Can't my emotions make sense once in a while?*

"Here," she said, pulling the page free and holding it up. "It will smudge unless you spray it with lacquer."

Kabsal hesitated, then walked over, taking the picture in reverent fingers. "It's wonderful," he whispered. He looked up, then hurried to his lantern, opening it and pulling out the garnet broam inside. "Here," he said, proffering it. "Payment."

"I can't take that! For one thing, it's not yours." As an ardent, anything Kabsal carried would belong to the king.

"Please," Kabsal said. "I want to give you something."

"The picture is a gift," she said. "If you pay me for it, then I haven't given you anything."

"Then I'll commission another," he said, pressing the glowing sphere into her fingers. "I'll take the first likeness for free, but do another for me, please. One of the two of us together."

She paused. She rarely did sketches of herself. They felt strange to draw. "All right." She took the sphere, then furtively tucked it into her safepouch, beside her Soulcaster. It was a little odd to carry something so heavy there, but she'd gotten accustomed to the bulge and weight.

"Jasnah, do you have a mirror?" she asked.

The other woman sighed audibly, obviously annoyed by the distraction. She felt through her things, taking out a mirror. Kabsal fetched it.

"Hold it up beside your head," Shallan said, "so I can see myself."

He walked back over, doing so, looking confused.

"Angle it to the side a little," Shallan said, "all right, there." She blinked, freezing in her mind the image of her face beside his. "Have a seat. You don't need the mirror any longer. I just wanted it for reference—it helps me for some reason to place my features into the scene I want to sketch. I'll put myself sitting beside you."

He sat on the floor, and Shallan began to work, using it to distract herself from her conflicting emotions. Guilt at not feeling as strongly for Kabsal as he did for her, yet sorrow that she wouldn't be seeing him anymore. And above it all, anxiety about the Soulcaster.

Sketching herself in beside him was challenging. She worked furiously, blending the reality of Kabsal sitting and a fiction of herself, in her flower-embroidered dress, sitting with her legs to the side. The face in the mirror became her reference point, and she built her head around it. Too narrow to be beautiful, with hair too light, cheeks dotted with freckles.

The Soulcaster, she thought. *Being here in Kharbranth with it is a danger. But leaving is dangerous too. Could there be a third option? What if I sent it away?*

She hesitated, charcoal pencil hovering above the picture. Dared she send the fabrial—packaged, delivered to Tozbek in secret—back to Jah Keved without her? She wouldn't have to worry about being incriminated if her room or person were searched, though she'd want to destroy all pictures she'd drawn of Jasnah with the Soulcaster. And she wouldn't risk suspicion by vanishing when Jasnah discovered her Soulcaster didn't work.

She continued her drawing, increasingly withdrawn into her thoughts, letting her fingers work. If she sent the Soulcaster back alone, then she could stay in Kharbranth. It was a golden, tempting prospect, but one that threw her emotions further into a jumbled mess. She'd been preparing herself to leave for so long. What would she do about Kabsal? And Jasnah. Could Shallan really remain here, accepting Jasnah's freely given tutelage, after what she'd done?

Yes, Shallan thought. *Yes, I could.*

The fervency of that emotion surprised her. She would live with the guilt, day by day, if it meant continuing to learn. It was terribly selfish of her, and she was ashamed of it. But she would do it for a little longer, at least. She'd have to go back eventually, of course. She couldn't leave her brothers to face danger alone. They needed her.

Selfishness, followed by courage. She was nearly as surprised by the latter as she had been by the former. Neither was something she often associated with who she was. But she was coming to realize that she hadn't *known* who she was. Not until she left Jah Keved and everything familiar, everything she'd been expected to be.

Her sketching grew more and more fervent. She finished the figures and moved to the background. Quick, bold lines became the floor and the archway behind. A scribbled dark smudge for the side of the desk, casting a shadow. Crisp, thin lines for the lantern sitting on the floor. Sweeping, breeze-like lines to form the legs and robes of the creature standing behind—

Shallan froze, fingers drawing an unintended line of charcoal, breaking away from the figure she'd sketched directly behind Kabsal. A figure that wasn't really there, a figure with a sharp, angular symbol hovering above its collar instead of a head.

Shallan stood, throwing back her chair, sketchpad and charcoal pencil clutched in the fingers of her freehand.

"Shallan?" Kabsal said, standing.

She'd done it again. Why? The peace she'd begun to feel during the sketching evaporated in a heartbeat, and her heart started to race. The pressures returned. Kabsal. Jasnah. Her brothers. Decisions, choices, problems.

"Is everything all right?" Kabsal said, taking a step toward her.

"I'm sorry," she said. "I— I made a mistake."

He frowned. To the side, Jasnah looked up, brow wrinkled.

"It's all right," Kabsal said. "Look, let's have some bread and jam. We can calm down, then you could finish it. I don't care about a—"

"I need to go," Shallan cut in, feeling suffocated. "I'm sorry."

She brushed past the dumbfounded ardent, hurrying from the alcove, giving a wide berth to the place where the figure stood in her sketch. What was *wrong* with her?

She rushed to the lift, calling for the parshmen to lower her. She glanced over her shoulder. Kabsal stood in the hallway, looking after her. Shallan reached the lift, drawing pad clutched in her hand, her heart racing. *Calm yourself,* she thought, leaning back against the lift platform's wooden railing as the parshmen began to take her down. She looked up at the empty landing above her.

And found herself blinking, memorizing that scene. She began sketching again.

She drew with concise motions, sketchpad held against her

safearm. For illumination, she had just two very small spheres at either side, where the taut ropes quivered. She moved without thought, just *drawing*, staring upward.

She looked down at what she had drawn. Two figures stood on the landing above, wearing the too-straight robes, like cloth made from metal. They leaned down, watching her go.

She looked up again. The landing was empty. *What's happening to me?* she thought with increasing horror. When the lift hit the ground, she scrambled away, her skirt fluttering. She all but ran to the exit of the Veil, hesitating beside the doorway, ignoring the master-servants and ardents who gave her confused looks.

Where to go? Sweat trickled down the sides of her face. Where to run when you were going mad?

She cut into the main cavern's crowd. It was late afternoon, and the dinner rush had begun—servants pushing dining carts, lighteyes strolling to their rooms, scholars walking with hands behind their backs. Shallan dashed through their midst, her hair coming free of its bun, the hairspike dropping to the rock behind her with a high-pitched clink. Her loose red hair streamed behind. She reached the hallway leading to their rooms, panting, hair askew, and glanced over her shoulder. Amid the flow of traffic she'd left a trail of people looking after her in confusion.

Almost against her will, she blinked and took a Memory. She raised her pad again, gripping her charcoal pencil in slick fingers, quickly sketching the crowded cavern scene. Just faint impressions. Men of lines, women of curves, walls of sloping rock, carpeted floor, bursts of light in sphere lanterns on the walls.

And five symbol-headed figures in black, too-stiff robes and cloaks. Each had a different symbol, twisted and unfamiliar to her, hanging above a neckless torso. The creatures wove through the crowd unseen. Like predators. Focused on Shallan.

I'm just imagining it, she tried to tell herself. *I'm overtaxed, too many things weighing on me.* Did they represent her guilt? The stress of betraying Jasnah and lying to Kabsal? The things she had done before leaving Jah Keved?

She tried to stand there, waiting, but her fingers refused to remain still. She blinked, then started drawing again on a new sheet. She finished with a shaking hand. The figures were almost to her, angular not-heads hanging horrifically where faces should have been.

Logic warned that she was overreacting, but no matter what she told herself, she couldn't believe it. These were *real.* And they were coming for her.

She dashed away, surprising several servants who had been approaching her to offer assistance. She ran, slippered feet sliding on the hallway carpets, eventually reaching the door to Jasnah's rooms. Sketchpad under her arm, she unlocked it with quivering fingers, then pushed through and slammed it behind her. She locked it again and ran for her chamber. She slammed that door closed too, then turned, backing away. The only light in the room came from the three diamond marks in the large crystal goblet on her nightstand.

She got on the bed, then scrambled back as far from the door as she could, until she was against the wall, breathing through her nose with frantic breaths. She still had her sketchpad under her arm, though she'd lost the charcoal. There was more in her nightstand.

Don't do it, she thought. *Just sit and calm yourself.*

She felt a growing chill, a rising terror. She *had* to know. She scrambled to pull out the charcoal, then blinked and began to sketch her room.

Ceiling first. Four straight lines. Down the walls. Lines at the corners. Her fingers kept moving, drawing, depicting the pad itself, held before her, safehand shrouded and bracing the pad from behind. And then on. To the beings standing around her—twisted symbols unconnected to their uneven shoulders. Those not-heads had unreal angles, surfaces that melded in weird, impossible ways.

The creature at the front was reaching too-smooth fingers toward Shallan. Just inches from the right side of the sketchpad.

Oh, Stormfather . . . Shallan thought, charcoal pencil falling still. The room was empty, yet depicted right in front of her was an image of it crowded full of sleek figures. They were close enough that she should be able to feel them breathing, if they breathed.

Was there a chill in the room? Hesitantly—terrified but unable to stop herself—Shallan dropped her pencil and raised her freehand to the right.

And felt something.

She screamed then, jumping to her feet on her bed, dropping the pad, backing against the wall. Before she could consciously think of what she was doing, she was struggling with her sleeve, trying to get the Soulcaster out. It was the only thing she had resembling a weapon. No, that was stupid. She didn't know how to use it. She was helpless.

Except . . .

Storms! she thought, frantic. *I can't use that. I promised myself.*

She began the process anyway. Ten heartbeats, to bring forth the fruit of her sin, the proceeds of her most horrific act. She was interrupted midway through by a voice, uncanny yet distinct:

What are you?

She clutched her hand to her chest, losing her balance on the soft bed, falling to her knees on the rumpled blanket. She put one hand to the side, steadying herself on the nightstand, fingers brushing the large glass goblet that sat there.

"What am I?" she whispered. "I'm terrified."

This is true.

The bedroom transformed around her.

The bed, the nightstand, her sketchpad, the walls, the ceiling—everything seemed to *pop*, forming into tiny, dark glass spheres. She found herself in a place with a black sky and a strange, small white sun that hung on the horizon, too far away.

Shallan screamed as she found herself in midair, falling backward in a shower of beads. Flames hovered nearby, dozens of them, perhaps hundreds. Like the tips of candles floating in the air and moving in the wind.

She hit something. An endless dark sea, except it wasn't wet. It was made of the small beads, an entire ocean of tiny glass spheres. They surged around her, moving in an undulating swell. She gasped, flailing, trying to stay afloat.

You want me to change? a warm voice said in her mind, distinct and different from the cold whisper she had heard earlier. It was deep and hollow and conveyed a sense of great age. It seemed to come from her hand, and she realized she was grasping something there. One of the beads.

The movement of the ocean of glass threatened to tow her down; she kicked frantically, somehow managing to stay afloat.

I've been as I am for a great long time, the warm voice said. *I sleep so much. I will change. Give me what you have.*

"I don't know what you mean! Please, help me!"

I will change.

She felt suddenly cold, as if the warmth were being drawn from her. She screamed as the bead in her fingers flared to sudden warmth. She dropped it just as a shift in the ocean swell towed her under, beads rolling over one another with a soft clatter.

She fell back and hit her bed, back in her room. Beside her, the goblet on her nightstand *melted*, the glass becoming red liquid, dropping the three spheres inside to the nightstand's flooded top. The red liquid poured over the sides of the nightstand, splashing to the floor. Shallan pulled back, horrified.

The goblet had been changed into blood.

Her shocked motion thumped the nightstand, shaking it. An empty glass water pitcher had been sitting beside the goblet. Her motion knocked it over, toppling it to the ground. It shattered on the stone floor, splashing the blood.

That was a Soulcasting! she thought. She'd changed the goblet into blood, which was one of the Ten Essences. She raised her hand to her head, staring at the red liquid expanding in a pool on her floor. There seemed to be quite a lot of it.

She was so bewildered. The voice, the creatures, the sea

of glass beads and the dark, cold sky. It had all come upon her so quickly.

I Soulcast, she realized again. *I did it!*

Did it have something to do with the creatures? But she'd begun seeing them in her drawings before she'd ever stolen the Soulcaster. How . . . what . . . ? She looked down at her safehand and the Soulcaster hidden in the pouch inside her sleeve.

I didn't put it on, she thought. *Yet I used it anyway.*

"Shallan?"

It was Jasnah's voice. Just outside Shallan's room. The princess must have followed her. Shallan felt a spike of terror as she saw a line of blood leaking toward the doorway. It was almost there, and would pass underneath in a heartbeat.

Why did it have to be blood? Nauseated, she leaped to her feet, slippers soaking up the red liquid.

"Shallan?" Jasnah said, voice closer. "What was that sound?"

Shallan looked frantically at the blood, then at the sketchpad, filled with pictures of the strange creatures. What if they *did* have something to do with the Soulcasting? Jasnah would recognize them. There was a shadow under the door.

She panicked, tucking the sketchpad away in her trunk. But the blood, *it* would condemn her. There was enough that only a life-threatening wound could have created it. Jasnah would see. She'd know. Blood where there should be none? One of the Ten Essences?

Jasnah was going to know what Shallan had done!

A thought struck Shallan. It wasn't a brilliant thought, but it was a way out, and it was the only thing that occurred to her. She went to her knees and grabbed a shard of the broken glass pitcher in her safehand, through the fabric of her sleeve. She took a breath and pulled up her right sleeve, then used the glass to cut a shallow gash in her skin. In the panic of the moment, it barely even hurt. Blood welled out.

As the doorknob turned and the door opened, Shallan dropped the glass shard and lay on her side. She closed her eyes, feigning unconsciousness. The door swung open.

Jasnah gasped, immediately calling for help. She rushed to

Shallan's side, grabbing her arm and putting pressure on the wound. Shallan mumbled, as if she were barely conscious, gripping her safepouch—and the Soulcaster inside—with her safehand. They wouldn't open it, would they? She pulled her arm closer to her chest, cowering silently as more footsteps and calls sounded, servants and parshmen running into the room, Jasnah shouting for more help.

This, Shallan thought, *will not end well.*

46

CHILD OF TANAVAST

"Though I was due for dinner in Veden City that night, I insisted upon visiting Kholinar to speak with Tivbet. The tariffs through Urithiru were growing quite unreasonable. By then, the so-called Radiants had already begun to show their true nature."

—Following the firing of the original Palanaeum, only one page of Terxim's autobiography remained, and this is the only line of any use to me.

K aladin dreamed he was the storm.

He raged forward, the stormwall behind him his trailing cape, soaring above a heaving, black expanse. The ocean. His passing churned up a tempest, slamming waves into one another, lifting white caps to be caught in his wind.

He approached a dark continent and soared upward. Higher. Higher. He left the sea behind. The vastness of the continent spread out before him, seemingly endless, an ocean of rock. *So large,* he thought, awed. He hadn't understood. How could he have?

He roared past the Shattered Plains. They looked as if something very large had hit them at the center, sending rippling breaks outward. They too were larger than he'd expected; no wonder nobody had been able to find their way through the chasms.

There was a large plateau at the center, but with the darkness and the distance, he could not see much. There were lights, though. Someone lived there.

He did see that the eastern side of the plains was very different from the western side, marked by tall, spindly pillars, plateaus that had nearly been worn away. Despite that, he could see a symmetry to the Shattered Plains. From high above, the plains resembled a work of art.

In a moment, he was past them, continuing north and west to soar across the Sea of Spears, a shallow inland sea where broken fingers of rock jutted above the water. He passed over Alethkar, catching a glimpse of the great city of Kholinar, built amid formations of rock like fins rising from the stone. Then he turned southward, away from anything he knew. He crested majestic mountains, densely populated at their tips, with villages clustered near vents that emitted steam or lava. The Horneater Peaks?

He left them with rain and winds, rumbling down into foreign lands. He passed cities and open plains, villages and twisting waterways. There were many armies. Kaladin passed tents pulled flat against the leeward sides of rock formations, stakes driven into the rock to hold them taut, men hidden inside. He passed hillsides where soldiers huddled in clefts. He passed large wooden wagons, built to house lighteyes while at war. How many wars was the world fighting? Was there nowhere that was at peace?

He took a path to the southwest, blowing toward a city built in long troughs in the ground that looked like giant claw marks ripped across the landscape. He was over it in a flash, passing a hinterland where the stone itself was ribbed and rippled, like frozen waves of water. The people in this kingdom were dark-skinned, like Sigzil.

The land went on and on. Hundreds of cities. Thousands of villages. People with faint blue veins beneath their skin. A place where the pressure of the approaching highstorm blew water out of spouts in the ground. A city where people lived in gigantic, hollowed-out stalactites hanging beneath a titanic sheltered ridge.

Westward he blew. The land was so vast. So enormous. So many different people. It dazzled his mind. War seemed far less prevalent in the West than it was in the East, and that comforted him, but still he was troubled. Peace seemed a scarce commodity in the world.

Something drew his attention. Strange flashes of light. He blew toward them at the forefront of the storm. What *were* those lights? They came in bursts, forming the strangest patterns. Almost like physical things that he could reach out and touch, spherical bubbles of light that vibrated with spikes and troughs.

Kaladin crossed a strange city laid out in a triangular pattern, with tall peaks rising like sentries at the corners and center. The flashes of light were coming from a building on the central peak. Kaladin knew he would pass quickly, for as the storm, he could not retreat. Ever westward he blew.

He threw open the door with his wind, entering a long hallway with bright red tile walls, mosaic murals that he passed too quickly to make out. He rustled the skirts of tall, golden-haired serving women who carried trays of food or steaming towels. They called in a strange language, perhaps wondering who had left a window unbarred in a highstorm.

The flashes of light came from directly ahead. So transfixing. Brushing past a pretty gold- and red-haired woman who huddled frightened in a corner, Kaladin burst through a door. He had one brief glimpse of what lay beyond.

A man stood over two corpses. His pale head shaved, his clothing white, the murderer held a long, thin sword in one hand. He looked up from his victims and almost seemed to *see* Kaladin. He had large Shin eyes.

It was too late to see anything more. Kaladin blew out the window, throwing shutters wide and streaking into the night.

More cities, mountains, and forests passed in a blur. At his advent, plants curled up their leaves, rockbuds closed their shells, and shrubs withdrew their branches. Before long, he neared the western ocean.

CHILD OF TANAVAST. CHILD OF HONOR. CHILD OF ONE LONG SINCE DEPARTED. The sudden voice shook Kaladin; he floundered in the air.

THE OATHPACT WAS SHATTERED.

The booming sound made the stormwall itself vibrate. Kaladin hit the ground, separating from the storm. He skidded to a stop, feet throwing up sprays of water. Stormwinds crashed into him, but he was enough a part of them that they neither tossed nor shook him.

MEN RIDE THE STORMS NO LONGER. The voice was thunder, crashing in the air. THE OATHPACT IS BROKEN, CHILD OF HONOR.

"I don't understand!" Kaladin screamed into the tempest.

A face formed before him, the face he had seen before, the aged face as wide as the sky, its eyes full of stars.

ODIUM COMES. MOST DANGEROUS OF ALL THE SIXTEEN. YOU WILL NOW GO.

Something blew against him. "Wait!" Kaladin said. "Why is there so much war? Must we always fight?" He wasn't sure why he asked. The questions simply came out.

The storm rumbled, like a thoughtful aged father. The face vanished, shattering into droplets of water.

More softly, the voice answered, ODIUM REIGNS.

※

Kaladin gasped as he awoke. He was surrounded by dark figures, holding him down against the hard stone floor. He yelled, old reflexes taking over. Instinctively, he snapped his hands outward to the sides, each grabbing an ankle and jerking to pull two assailants off balance.

They cursed, crashing to the ground. Kaladin used the moment to twist while bringing an arm up in a sweep. He knocked free the hands pushing him down, rocked and threw himself forward, lurching into the man directly in front of him.

Kaladin rolled over him, tucking and coming up on his feet, free of his captives. He spun, flinging sweat from his brow. Where was his spear? He clutched for the knife at his belt.

No knife. No spear.

"Storm you, Kaladin!" That was Teft.

Kaladin raised a hand to his breast, breathing deliberately, dispelling the strange dream. Bridge Four. He was with Bridge Four. The king's stormwardens had predicted a highstorm in the early morning hours.

"It's all right," he said to the cursing, twisting clump of bridgemen who had been holding him down. "What were you doing?"

"You tried to go out in the storm," Moash said accusingly, extricating himself. The only light was a single diamond sphere one of the men had set in the corner.

"Ha!" Rock added, standing up and brushing himself off. "Had the door open to the rain, staring out, as if you'd been hit on the head with stone. We had to pull you back. Is not good for you to spend another two weeks sick in bed, eh?"

Kaladin calmed himself. The riddens—the quiet rainfall at the trailing end of a highstorm—continued outside, drops sprinkling the roof.

"You wouldn't wake up," Sigzil said. Kaladin glanced at the Azish man, sitting with his back to the stone wall. He hadn't tried to hold Kaladin down. "You were having some kind of fever dream."

"I feel just fine," Kaladin said. That wasn't quite true; his head ached and he was exhausted. He took a deep breath and threw back his shoulders, trying to force the fatigue away.

The sphere in the corner flickered. Then its light faded away, leaving them in darkness.

"Storm it!" Moash muttered. "That eel Gaz. He's been giving us dun spheres again."

Kaladin crossed the pitch-black barrack, stepping carefully. His headache faded away as he felt for the door. He pushed it open, letting in the faint light of an overcast morning.

The winds were weak, but the rain still fell. He stepped out, and was shortly soaked through. The other bridgemen followed him out, and Rock tossed Kaladin a small chunk of soap. Like most of the others, Kaladin wore only his loincloth, and he lathered himself up in the cold downpour. The soap smelled of oil and was gritty with the sand suspended in it. No sweet, soft soaps for bridgemen.

Kaladin tossed the bit of soap to Bisig, a thin bridgeman with an angular face. He took it gratefully—Bisig didn't say much—and began to lather up as Kaladin let the rain wash the soap from his body and hair. To the side, Rock was using a bowl of water to shave and trim his Horneater beard, long on the sides and covering the cheeks, but clean below the lips and chin. It made an odd counterpoint to his head, which he shaved up the center, from directly above the eyebrows back. He trimmed the rest of his hair short.

Rock's hand was smooth and careful, and he didn't so much as nick himself. Once finished, he stood up and waved to the men waiting behind him. One by one, he shaved any who wanted it. He occasionally paused to sharpen the razor using his whetstone and leather strop.

Kaladin raised his fingers to his own beard. He hadn't been clean-shaven since he'd been in Amaram's army, so long ago. He walked forward to join those waiting in line. When Kaladin's time came, the large Horneater laughed. "Sit, my friend, sit! Is good you have come. Your face is more like scragglebark branches than a proper beard."

"Shave it clean," Kaladin said, sitting down on the stump. "And I'd rather not have a strange pattern like yours."

"Ha!" Rock said, sharpening his razor. "You are a lowlander, my good friend. Is not right for you to wear a *humaka'aban*. I would have to thump you soundly if you tried this thing."

"I thought you said fighting was beneath you."

"Is allowed several important exceptions," Rock said. "Now stop with your talking, unless you wish to be losing a lip."

Rock began by trimming the beard down, then lathered and shaved, starting at the left cheek. Kaladin had never let another shave him before; when he'd first gone to war, he'd been young enough that he'd barely needed to shave at all. He'd grown into doing it himself as he got older.

Rock's touch was deft, and Kaladin didn't feel any nicks or

cuts. In a few minutes, Rock stood back. Kaladin raised his fingers to his chin, touching smooth, sensitive skin. His face felt cold, strange to the touch. It took him back, transformed him—just a little—into the man he had been.

Strange, how much difference a shave could make. *I should have done this weeks ago.*

The riddens had turned to drizzle, heralding the storm's last whispers. Kaladin stood up, letting the water wash bits of shorn hair from his chest. Baby-faced Dunny—the last of those waiting—sat down for his turn at being shaven. He hardly needed it at all.

"The shave suits you," a voice said. Kaladin turned to see Sigzil leaning against the wall of the barrack, just under the roof's overhang. "Your face has strong lines. Square and firm, with a proud chin. We would call it a leader's face among my people."

"I'm no lighteyes," Kaladin said, spitting to the side.

"You hate them so much."

"I hate their lies," Kaladin said. "I hate it that I used to believe they were honorable."

"And would you cast them down?" Sigzil asked, sounding curious. "Rule in their place?"

"No."

This seemed to surprise Sigzil. To the side, Syl finally appeared, having finished frolicking in the winds of the highstorm. He always worried—just a little—that she'd ride away with them and leave him.

"Have you no thirst to punish those who have treated you so?" Sigzil asked.

"Oh, I'm happy to punish them," Kaladin said. "But I have no desire to take their place, nor do I wish to join them."

"I'd join them in a heartbeat," Moash said, walking up behind. He folded his arms across his lean, well-muscled chest. "If I were in charge, things would change. The lighteyes would work the mines and the fields. They would run bridges and die by Parshendi arrows."

"Won't happen," Kaladin said. "But I won't blame you for trying."

Sigzil nodded thoughtfully. "Have either of you ever heard of the land of Babatharnam?"

"No," Kaladin said, glancing toward the camp. The soldiers were moving about now. More than a few were washing too. "That's a funny name for a country, though."

Sigzil sniffed. "Personally, I always thought Alethkar sounded like a ridiculous name. I guess it depends on where you were raised."

"So why bring up Babab . . ." Moash said.

"Babatharnam," Sigzil said. "I visited there once, with my master. They have very peculiar trees. The entire plant—trunk and all—lies down when a highstorm approaches, as if built on hinges. I was thrown in prison three times during our visit there. The Babath are quite particular about how you speak. My master was quite displeased at the amount he had to pay to free me. Of course, I think they were using any excuse to imprison a foreigner, as they knew my master had deep pockets." He smiled wistfully. "One of those imprisonments *was* my fault. The women there, you see, have these patterns of veins that sit shallowly beneath their skin. Some visitors find it unnerving, but I found the patterns beautiful. Almost irresistible . . ."

Kaladin frowned. Hadn't he seen something like that in his dream?

"I bring up Babath because they have a curious system of rule there," Sigzil continued. "You see, the elderly are given office. The older you are, the more authority you have. Everyone gets a chance to rule, if they live long enough. The king is called the Most Ancient."

"Sounds fair," Moash said, walking over to join Sigzil beneath the overhang. "Better than deciding who rules based on eye color."

"Ah yes," Sigzil said. "The Babath are very fair. Currently, the Monavakah Dynasty reigns."

"How can you have a dynasty if you choose your leaders based on their age?" Kaladin asked.

"It's actually quite easy," Sigzil said. "You just execute anyone who gets old enough to challenge you."

Kaladin felt a chill. "They *do* that?"

"Yes, unfortunately," Sigzil said. "There is a great deal of unrest in Babatharnam. It was dangerous to visit when we did. The Monavakahs make very certain that *their* family members live the longest; for fifty years, no one outside their family has become Most Ancient. All others have fallen through assassination, exile, or death on the battlefield."

"That's horrible," Kaladin said.

"I doubt many would disagree. But I mention these horrors for a purpose. You see, it has been my experience that no matter where you go, you will find some who abuse their power." He shrugged. "Eye color is not so odd a method, compared to many others I have seen. If you were to overthrow the lighteyes and place yourselves in power, Moash, I doubt that the world would be a very different place. The abuses would still happen. Simply to other people."

Kaladin nodded slowly, but Moash shook his head. "No. I'd change the world, Sigzil. And I mean to."

"And how are you going to do that?" Kaladin asked, amused.

"I came to this war to get myself a Shardblade," Moash said. "And I still mean to do it, somehow." He blushed, then turned away.

"You joined up assuming they'd make you a spearman, didn't you?" Kaladin asked.

Moash hesitated, then nodded. "Some of those who joined with me did become soldiers, but most of us got sent to the bridge crews." He glanced at Kaladin, expression growing dark. "This plan of yours had better work, lordling. Last time I ran away, I got a beating. I was told if I tried again, I'd get a slave's mark instead."

"I never promised it would work, Moash. If you've got a better idea, go ahead and share it."

Moash hesitated. "Well, if you really do teach us the spear like you promised, then I guess I don't care."

Kaladin glanced about, warily checking to see if Gaz or any bridgemen from other crews were nearby. "Keep quiet," Kaladin muttered to Moash. "Don't speak of that outside of the chasms." The rain had almost stopped; soon the clouds would break.

Moash glared at him, but remained silent.

"You don't really think they'd let you have a Shardblade, do you?" Sigzil said.

"Any man can win a Shardblade." Moash said. "Slave or free. Lighteyes or dark. It's the law."

"Assuming they follow the law," Kaladin said with a sigh.

"I'll do it somehow," Moash repeated. He glanced to the side, where Rock was closing up his razor and wiping the rainwater from his bald head.

The Horneater approached them. "I have heard of this place you spoke of, Sigzil," Rock said. "Babatharnam. My cousin cousin cousin visited there one time. They have very tasty snails."

"That is a long distance to travel for a Horneater," Sigzil noted.

"Nearly same distance as for an Azish," Rock said. "Actually, much more, since you have such little legs!"

Sigzil scowled.

"I have seen your kind before," Rock said, folding his arms.

"What?" Sigzil asked. "Azish? We are not so rare."

"No, not your race," Rock said. "Your type. What is it they are called? Visiting places around the land, telling others of what they have seen? A Worldsinger. Yes, is the right name. No?"

Sigzil froze. Then he suddenly stood up straight and stalked away from the barrack without looking back.

"Now why is he acting like this thing?" Rock asked. "I am not ashamed of being cook. Why is he ashamed of being Worldsinger?"

"Worldsinger?" Kaladin asked.

Rock shrugged. "I do not know much. Are strange people. Say they must travel to each kingdom and tell the people there of other kingdoms. Is a kind of storyteller, though they are thinking of themselves as much more."

"He's probably some kind of brightlord in his country,"

Moash said. "The way he talks. Wonder how he ended up with us cremlings."

"Hey," Dunny said, joining them. "What'd you do to Sigzil? He promised to tell me about my homeland."

"Homeland?" Moash said to the younger man. "You're from Alethkar."

"Sigzil said these violet eyes of mine aren't native to Alethkar. He thinks I must have Veden blood in me."

"Your eyes aren't violet," Moash said.

"Sure they are," Dunny said. "You can see it in bright sunlight. They're just really dark."

"Ha!" Rock said. "If you are from Vedenar, we are cousins! The Peaks are near Vedenar. Sometimes the people there have good red hair, like us!"

"Be glad that someone didn't mistake your eyes for red, Dunny," Kaladin said. "Moash, Rock, go gather your subsquads and pass the word to Teft and Skar. I want the men oiling their vests and sandals against the humidity."

The men sighed, but did as ordered. The army provided the oil. While the bridgemen were expendable, good hogshide and metal for buckles were not cheap.

As the men gathered to work, the sun broke through the clouds. The warmth of the light felt good on Kaladin's rainwet skin. There was something refreshing about the chill of a highstorm followed by the sun. Tiny rockbud polyps on the side of the building opened, drinking in the wet air. Those would have to be scraped free. Rockbuds would eat away the stone of the walls, creating pockmarks and cracks.

The buds were a deep crimson. It was Chachel, third day of the week. The slave markets would show new wares. That would mean new bridgemen. Kaladin's crew was in serious danger. Yake had caught an arrow in the arm during their last run, and Delp had caught one in the neck. There'd been nothing Kaladin could do for him, and with Yake wounded, Kaladin's team was down to twenty-eight bridge-capable members.

Sure enough, about an hour into their morning activities— caring for equipment, oiling the bridge, Lopen and Dabbid running to fetch their morning gruel pot and bring it back to the lumberyard—Kaladin caught sight of soldiers leading a line of dirty, shuffling men toward the lumberyard. Kaladin gestured to Teft, and the two of them marched up to meet Gaz.

"Afore you yell at me," Gaz said as Kaladin arrived, "understand that I can't change anything here." The slaves were bunched up, watched over by a pair of soldiers in wrinkled green coats.

"You're bridge sergeant," Kaladin said. Teft stepped up beside him. He hadn't gotten a shave, though he'd begun keeping his short, grey beard neatly trimmed.

"Yeah," Gaz said, "but I don't make assignments any more. Brightness Hashal wants to do it herself. In the name of her husband, of course."

Kaladin gritted his teeth. She'd starve Bridge Four of members. "So we get nothing."

"I didn't say *that*," Gaz said, then spat black spittle to the side. "She gave you one."

That's something, at least, Kaladin thought. There were a good hundred men in the new group. "Which one? He'd better be tall enough to carry a bridge."

"Oh, he's tall enough," Gaz said, gesturing a few slaves out of the way. "Good worker too." The men shuffled aside, revealing one man standing at the back. He was a little shorter than average, but he *was* still tall enough to carry a bridge.

But he had black and red marbled skin.

"A *parshman*?" Kaladin asked. To his side, Teft cursed under his breath.

"Why not?" Gaz said. "They're perfect slaves. Never talk back."

"But we're at *war* with them!" Teft said.

"We're at war with a tribe of oddities," Gaz said. "Those out on the Shattered Plains are right different from the fellows who work for us."

That much, at least, was true. There were a lot of parshmen in the warcamp, and—despite their skin markings—there was little similarity between them and the Parshendi warriors. None had the strange growths of armorlike carapace on their skin, for instance. Kaladin eyed the sturdy, bald man. The parshman stared at the ground; he wore only a loincloth, and he had a *thickness* about him. His fingers were thicker than those of human men, his arms stouter, his thighs wider.

"He's domesticated," Gaz said. "You don't need to worry."

"I thought parshmen were too valuable to use in bridge runs," Kaladin said.

"This is just an experiment," Gaz said. "Brightness Hashal wants to know her options. Finding enough bridgemen has been difficult lately, and parshmen could help fill in holes."

"This is foolishness, Gaz," Teft said. "I don't care if he's 'domesticated' or not. Asking him to carry a bridge against others of his kind is pure idiocy. What if he betrays us?"

Gaz shrugged. "We'll see if that happens."

"But—"

"Leave it, Teft," Kaladin said. "You, parshman, come with me." He turned to walk back down the hill. The parshman dutifully followed. Teft cursed and did so as well.

"What trick are they trying on us, do you think?" Teft asked.

"I suspect it's just what he said. A test to see if a parshman can be trusted to run bridges. Perhaps he'll do as he's told. Or perhaps he'll refuse to run, or will try to kill us. She wins regardless."

"Kelek's breath," Teft cursed. "Darker than a Horneater's stomach, our situation is. She'll see us dead, Kaladin."

"I know." He glanced over his shoulder at the parshman. He was a little taller than most, his face a little wider, but they all looked about the same to Kaladin.

The other members of Bridge Four had lined up by the time Kaladin returned. They watched the approaching parshman with surprise and disbelief. Kaladin stopped before them, Teft at his side, the parshman behind. It made him itch, to have one of them behind him. He casually stepped to the side. The parshman just stood there, eyes downward, shoulders slumped.

Kaladin glanced at the others. They had guessed, and they were growing hostile.

Stormfather, Kaladin thought. *There is something lower in this world than a bridgeman. A parshman bridgeman.* Parshmen might cost more than most slaves, but so did a chull. In fact, the comparison was a good one, because parshmen were worked like animals.

Seeing the reaction of the others made Kaladin pity the creature. And that made him mad at himself. Did he *always* have to react this way? This parshman was dangerous, a distraction for the other men, a factor they couldn't depend on.

A liability.

Turn a liability into an advantage whenever you can. Those words had been spoken by a man who cared only for his own skin.

Storm it, Kaladin thought. *I'm a fool. A downright, sodden idiot. This isn't the same. Not at all.* "Parshman," he asked. "Do you have a name?"

The man shook his head. Parshmen rarely spoke. They could, but you had to prod them into it.

"Well, we'll have to call you something," Kaladin said. "How about Shen?"

The man shrugged.

"All right then," Kaladin said to the others. "This is Shen. He's one of us now."

"A parshman?" Lopen asked, lounging beside the barrack. "I don't like him, gancho. Look how he stares at me."

"He'll kill us while we sleep," Moash added.

"No, this is *good,*" Skar said. "We can just have him run at the front. He'll take an arrow for one of us."

Syl alighted on Kaladin's shoulder, looking down at the parshman. Her eyes were sorrowful.

If you were to overthrow the lighteyes and place yourselves in power, abuses would still happen. They'd just happen to other people.

But this was a *parshman.*

Gotta do what you can to stay alive. . . .

"No," Kaladin said. "Shen is one of *us* now. I don't care

what he was before. I don't care what any of you were. We're Bridge Four. So is he."

"But—" Skar began.

"No," Kaladin said. "We're not going to treat him like the lighteyes treat us, Skar. That's all there is to it. Rock, find him a vest and sandals."

The bridgemen split up, all save Teft. "What about . . . our plans?" Teft asked quietly.

"We proceed," Kaladin said.

Teft looked uncomfortable about that.

"What's he going to do, Teft?" Kaladin asked. "Tell on us? I've never heard a parshman say more than a single word at a time. I doubt he could act as a spy."

"I don't know," Teft grumbled. "But I've never liked them. They seem to be able to talk to each other, without making any sounds. I don't like the way they look."

"Teft," Kaladin said flatly, "if we rejected bridgemen based on their looks, we'd have kicked you out weeks ago for that face of yours."

Teft grunted. Then he smiled.

"What?" Kaladin asked.

"Nothing," he said. "Just . . . for a moment, you reminded me of better days. Afore this storm came crashing down on me. You realize the odds, don't you? Fighting our way free, escaping a man like Sadeas?"

Kaladin nodded solemnly.

"Good," Teft said. "Well, since you aren't inclined to do it, I'll keep an eye on our friend 'Shen' over there. You can thank me after I stop him from sticking a knife in your back."

"I don't think we have to worry."

"You're young," Teft said. "I'm old."

"That makes you wiser, presumably?"

"Damnation no," Teft said. "The only thing it proves is that I've more experience staying alive than you. I'll watch him. You just train the rest of this sorry lot to . . ." He trailed off, looking around. "To keep from tripping over their own feet the moment someone threatens them. You understand?"

Kaladin nodded. That sounded much like something one

of Kaladin's old sergeants would say. Teft was insistent on not talking about his past, but he never *had* seemed as beaten down as most of the others.

"All right," Kaladin said, "make sure the men take care of their equipment."

"What will you be doing?"

"Walking," Kaladin said. "And thinking."

※

An hour later, Kaladin still wandered Sadeas's warcamp. He'd need to return to the lumberyard soon; his men were on chasm duty again, and had been given only a few free hours to care for equipment.

As a youth, he hadn't understood why his father had often gone walking to think. The older Kaladin grew, the more he found himself imitating his father's habits. Walking, moving, it did something to his mind. The constant passing of tents, colors cycling, men bustling—it created a sense of change, and it made his thoughts want to move as well.

Don't hedge bets with your life, Kaladin, Durk had always said. *Don't put in a chip when you have a pocket full of marks. Bet them all or leave the table.*

Syl danced before him, jumping from shoulder to shoulder in the crowded street. Occasionally she'd land on the head of someone passing in the other direction and sit there, legs crossed, as she passed Kaladin. All his spheres were on the table. He was determined to help the bridgemen. But something itched at him, a worry that he couldn't yet explain.

"You seem troubled," Syl said, landing on his shoulder. She wore a cap and jacket over her usual dress, as if imitating nearby shopkeepers. They passed the apothecary's shop. Kaladin barely bothered to glance at it. He had no knobweed sap to sell. He'd run out of supplies soon.

He'd told his men that he'd train them to fight, but that would take time. And once they were trained, how would they get spears out of the chasms to use in the escape? Sneaking them out would be tough, considering how they were searched.

They could just start fighting at the search itself, but that would only put the entire warcamp on alert.

Problems, problems. The more he thought, the more impossible his task seemed.

He made way for a couple of soldiers in forest-green coats. Their brown eyes marked them as common citizens, but the white knots on their shoulders meant they were citizen officers. Squadleaders and sergeants.

"Kaladin?" Syl asked.

"Getting the bridgemen out is as large a task as I've ever faced. Much more difficult than my other escape attempts as a slave, and I failed at each of those. I can't help wondering if I'm setting myself up for another disaster."

"It will be different this time, Kaladin," Syl said. "I can feel it."

"That sounds like something Tien would have said. His death proves that words don't change anything, Syl. Before you ask, I'm not sinking into despair again. But I *can't* ignore what has happened to me. It started with Tien. Since that moment, it seems that every time I've specifically picked people to protect, they've ended up dead. Every time. It's enough to make me wonder if the Almighty himself hates me."

She frowned. "I think you're being foolish. Besides, if anything, he'd hate the people who died, not you. *You* lived."

"I suppose it's self-centered to make it all about me. But, Syl, I survive, every time, when almost nobody else does. Over and over again. My old spearman squad, the first bridge crew I ran with, numerous slaves I tried to help escape. There's a pattern. It's getting harder and harder to ignore."

"Maybe the Almighty is preserving you," Syl said.

Kaladin hesitated on the street; a passing soldier cursed and shoved him aside. Something about this whole conversation was wrong. Kaladin moved over beside a rain barrel set between two sturdy stone-walled shops.

"Syl," he said. "You mentioned the Almighty."

"You did first."

"Ignore that for now. Do you believe in the Almighty? Do you know if he really exists?"

Syl cocked her head. "I don't know. Huh. Well, there are a lot of things I don't know. But I should know this one. I think. Maybe?" She seemed very perplexed.

"I'm not sure if I believe," Kaladin said, looking out at the street. "My mother did, and my father always spoke of the Heralds with reverence. I think he believed too, but maybe just because of the traditions of healing that are said to have come from the Heralds. The ardents ignore us bridgemen. They used to visit the soldiers, when I was in Amaram's army, but I haven't seen a single one in the lumberyard. I haven't given it much thought. Believing never seemed to help any of the soldiers."

"So if you don't believe, then there's no reason to think that the Almighty hates you."

"Except," Kaladin said, "if there *is* no Almighty, there might be something else. I don't know. A lot of the soldiers I knew were superstitious. They'd talk about things like the Old Magic and the Nightwatcher, things that could bring a man bad luck. I scoffed at them. But how long can I continue to ignore that possibility? What if all of these failures can be traced to something like that?"

Syl looked disturbed. The cap and jacket she'd been wearing dissolved to mist, and she wrapped her arms around herself as if chilled by his comments.

Odium reigns. . . .

"Syl," he said, frowning, thinking back to his strange dream. "Have you ever heard of something called Odium? I don't mean the feeling, I mean . . . a person, or something called by that name."

Syl suddenly hissed. It was a feral, disturbing sound. She zipped off his shoulder, becoming a darting streak of light, and shot up underneath the eaves of the next building.

He blinked. "Syl?" he called, drawing the attention of a couple of passing washwomen. The spren did not reappear. Kaladin folded his arms. That word had set her off. Why?

A loud series of curses interrupted his thoughts. Kaladin

spun as a man burst out of a handsome stone building across the street and shoved a half-naked woman out in front of him. The man had bright blue eyes, and his forest green coat—carried over one arm—had red knots on the shoulder. A light-eyed officer, not very high-ranking. Perhaps seventh dahn.

The half-dressed woman fell to the ground. She held the loose front of the dress to her chest, crying, her long black hair down and tied with two red ribbons. The dress was that of a lighteyed woman, except that both sleeves were short, safehand exposed. A courtesan.

The officer continued to curse as he pulled on his coat. He didn't do up the buttons. Instead, he stepped forward and kicked the whore in the belly. She gasped, painspren pulling from the ground and gathering around her. Nobody on the street paused, though most did hurry on their way, heads down.

Kaladin growled, jumping into the roadway, pushing his way past a group of soldiers. Then he stopped. Three men in blue stepped out of the crowd, moving purposefully between the fallen woman and the officer in green. Only one was light-eyed, judging by the knots on his shoulders. Golden knots. A high-ranking man indeed, second or third dahn. These obviously weren't from Sadeas's army, not with those well-pressed blue coats.

Sadeas's officer hesitated. The officer in blue rested his hand on the hilt of his sword. The other two were holding fine halberds with gleaming half-moon heads.

A group of soldiers in green moved out of the crowd and began to surround those in blue. The air grew tense, and Kaladin realized that the street—bustling just moments ago—was quickly emptying. He stood practically alone, the only one watching the three men in blue, now surrounded by seven in green. The woman was still on the ground, sniffling. She huddled next to the blue-garbed officer.

The man who had kicked her—a thick-browed brute with a mop of uncombed black hair—began to button up the right side of his coat. "You don't belong here, friends. It seems you wandered into the wrong warcamp."

"We have legitimate business," said the officer in blue. He had light golden hair, speckled with Alethi black, and a handsome face. He held his hand before him as if wishing to shake hands with Sadeas's officer. "Come now," he said affably. "Whatever your problem with this woman, I'm sure it can be resolved without anger or violence."

Kaladin moved back under the overhang where Syl had hidden.

"She's a whore," Sadeas's man said.

"I can see that," replied the man in blue. He kept his hand out.

The officer in green spat on it.

"I see," said the blond man. He pulled his hand back, and twisting lines of mist gathered in the air, coalescing in his hands as he raised them to an offensive posture. A massive sword appeared, as long as a man is tall.

It dripped with water that condensed along its cold, glimmering length. It was beautiful, long and sinuous, its single edge rippled like an eel and curved up into a point. The back bore delicate ridges, like crystal formations.

Sadeas's officer stumbled away and fell, his face pale. The soldiers in green scattered. The officer cursed at them—as vile a curse as Kaladin had ever heard—but none returned to help him. With a final glare, he scrambled up the steps back into the building.

The door slammed, leaving the roadway eerily silent. Kaladin was the only one on the street besides the soldiers in blue and the fallen courtesan. The Shardbearer gave Kaladin a glance, but obviously judged him no threat. He thrust his sword into the stones; the Blade sank in easily and stood with its hilt toward the sky.

The young Shardbearer then gave his hand to the fallen whore. "What did you do to him, out of curiosity?"

Hesitantly, she took his hand and let him pull her to her feet. "He refused to pay, claiming his reputation made it a pleasure for me." She grimaced. "He kicked me the first time after I made a comment about his 'reputation.' It apparently wasn't what he thought he was known for."

The brightlord chuckled. "I suggest you insist on being paid *first* from now on. We'll escort you to the border. I advise against returning to Sadeas's warcamp anytime soon."

The woman nodded, holding the front of her dress to her chest. Her safehand was still exposed. Sleek, with tan skin, the fingers long and delicate. Kaladin found himself staring at it and blushing. She sidled up to the brightlord while his two comrades watched the sides of the streets, halberds ready. Even with her hair disheveled and her makeup smudged, she was quite pretty. "Thank you, Brightlord. Perhaps I could interest you? There would be no charge."

The young brightlord raised an eyebrow. "Tempting," he said, "but my father would kill me. He has this thing about the old ways."

"A pity," she said, pulling away from him, awkwardly covering her chest as she slipped her arm into its sleeve. She took out a glove for her safehand. "Your father is quite prudish, then?"

"You might say that." He turned toward Kaladin. "Ho, bridgeboy."

Bridgeboy? This lordling looked to be just a few years older than Kaladin himself.

"Run and give word to Brightlord Reral Makoram," the Shardbearer said, flipping something across the street toward Kaladin. A sphere. It sparkled in the sunlight before Kaladin caught it. "He's in the Sixth Battalion. Tell him that Adolin Kholin won't make today's meeting. I'll send word to reschedule another time."

Kaladin looked down at the sphere. An emerald chip. More than he normally earned in two weeks. He looked up; the young brightlord and his two men were already retreating, the whore following.

"You rushed to help her," a voice said. He looked up as Syl floated down to rest on his shoulder. "That was very noble of you."

"Those others got there first," Kaladin said. *And one of them a lighteyes, no less. What was in it for him?*

"You still tried to help."

"Foolishly," Kaladin said. "What would I have done? Fought down a lighteyes? That would have drawn half the camp's soldiers down on me, and the whore would just have been beaten more for causing such a fracas. She could have ended up dead for my efforts." He fell silent. That sounded too much like what he'd been saying before.

He couldn't give in to assuming he was cursed, or had bad luck, or whatever it was. Superstition never got a man anywhere. But he had to admit, the pattern *was* disturbing. If he acted as he always had before, how could he expect different results? He had to try something new. Change, somehow. This was going to take more thought.

Kaladin began walking back toward the lumberyard.

"Aren't you going to do what the brightlord asked?" Syl said. She didn't show any lingering effects of her sudden fright; it was as if she wanted to pretend it hadn't happened.

"After how he treated me?" Kaladin snapped.

"It wasn't that bad."

"I'm not going to bow to them," Kaladin said. "I'm done running at their whims just because they *expect* me to do so. If he was so worried about this message, then he should have waited to make certain I was willing."

"You took his sphere."

"Earned by the sweat of the darkeyes he exploits."

Syl fell silent for a moment. "This darkness about you when you talk of them frightens me, Kaladin. You stop being yourself when you think about lighteyes."

He didn't respond, just continuing on his way. He owed that brightlord nothing, and besides, he had orders to be back in the lumberyard.

But the man *had* stepped up to protect the woman.

No, Kaladin told himself forcefully. *He was just looking for a way to embarrass one of Sadeas's officers. Everyone knows there's tension between the camps.*

And that was all he let himself think on the subject.

47

STORMBLESSINGS

ONE YEAR AGO

Kaladin turned the rock over in his fingers, letting the facets of suspended quartz catch the light. He leaned against a large boulder, one foot pressed back against the stone, his spear next to him.

The rock caught the light, spinning it in different colors, depending on the direction he turned it. Beautiful, miniature crystals shimmered, like the cities made of gemstones mentioned in lore.

Around him, Highmarshal Amaram's army prepared for battle. Six thousand men sharpened spears or strapped on leather armor. The battlefield was nearby, and, with no highstorms expected, the army had spent the night in tents.

It had been nearly four years since he'd joined Amaram's army on that rainy night. Four years. And an eternity.

Soldiers hurried this way and that. Some raised hands and called greetings to Kaladin. He nodded to them, pocketing the stone, then folded his arms to wait. In the near distance, Amaram's standard was already flying, a burgundy field blazoned with a dark green glyphpair shaped like a whitespine with tusks upraised. *Merem* and *khakh*, honor and determination. The banner fluttered before a rising sun, the morning's chill starting to give way to the heat of the day.

Kaladin turned, looking eastward. Toward a home to which he could never return. He'd decided months ago. His enlistment would be up in a few weeks, but he would sign on again. He couldn't face his parents after having broken his promise to protect Tien.

A heavyset darkeyed soldier trotted up to him, an axe strapped to his back, white knots on his shoulders. The nonstandard weapon was a privilege of being a squadleader. Gare had beefy forearms and a thick black beard, though he'd lost a large section of scalp on the right side of his head. He was followed by two of his sergeants—Nalem and Korabet.

"Kaladin," Gare said. "Stormfather, man! Why are you pestering me? On a battle day!"

"I'm well aware of what's ahead, Gare," Kaladin said, arms still folded. Several companies were already gathering, forming ranks. Dallet would see Kaladin's own squad into place. At the front, they'd decided. Their enemy—a lighteyes named Hallaw—was fond of long volleys. They'd fought his men several times before. One time in particular was burned into Kaladin's memory and soul.

He had joined Amaram's army expecting to defend the Alethi borders—and defend them he did. Against other Alethi. Lesser landlords who sought to slice off bits of Highprince Sadeas's lands. Occasionally, Amaram's armies would try to seize territory from other highprinces—lands Amaram claimed really belonged to Sadeas and had been stolen years before. Kaladin didn't know what to make of that. Of all lighteyes, Amaram was the only one he trusted. But it did seem like they were doing the same thing as the armies they fought.

"Kaladin?" Gare asked impatiently.

"You have something I want," Kaladin said. "New recruit, just joined yesterday. Galan says his name is Cenn."

Gare scowled. "I'm supposed to play this game with you *now*? Talk to me after the battle. If the boy survives, maybe I'll give him to you." He turned to leave, cronies following.

Kaladin stood up straight, picking up his spear. The motion stopped Gare in his tracks.

"It's not going to be a trouble to you," Kaladin said quietly.

"Just send the boy to my squad. Accept your payment. Stay quiet." He pulled out a pouch of spheres.

"Maybe I don't want to sell him," Gare said, turning back.

"You're not selling him. You're transferring him to me."

Gare eyed the pouch. "Well then, maybe I don't like how everyone does what *you* tell them. I don't care how good you are with a spear. My squad is my own."

"I'm not going to give you any more, Gare," Kaladin said, dropping the pouch to the ground. The spheres clinked. "We both know the boy is useless to you. Untrained, ill-equipped, too small to make a good line soldier. Send him to me."

Kaladin turned and began to walk away. Within seconds, he heard a clink as Gare recovered the pouch. "Can't blame a man for trying."

Kaladin kept walking.

"What do these recruits mean to you, anyway?" Gare called after Kaladin. "Your squad is half made up of men too small to fight properly! Almost makes a man think you *want* to get killed!"

Kaladin ignored him. He passed through the camp, waving to those who waved at him. Most everyone kept out of his way, either because they knew and respected him or they'd heard of his reputation. Youngest squadleader in the army, only four years of experience and already in command. A darkeyed man had to travel to the Shattered Plains to go any higher in rank.

The camp was a bedlam of soldiers hurrying about in last-minute preparations. More and more companies were gathering at the line, and Kaladin could see the enemy lining up on the shallow ridge across the field to the west.

The enemy. That was what they were called. Yet whenever there was an *actual* border dispute with the Vedens or the Reshi, those men would line up beside Amaram's troops and they would fight together. It was as if the Nightwatcher toyed with them, playing some forbidden game of chance, occasionally setting the men on his gameboard as allies, then setting them to kill one another the next day.

That wasn't for spearmen to think about. So he'd been told. Repeatedly. He supposed he should listen, as he figured that his duty was to keep his squad alive as best he could. Winning was secondary to that.

You can't kill to protect. . . .

He found the surgeon's station easily; he could smell the scents of antiseptics and of small fires burning. Those smells reminded him of his youth, which now seemed so far, far away. Had he ever really planned to go become a surgeon? What had happened to his parents? What of Roshone?

Meaningless, now. He'd sent word to them via Amaram's scribes, a terse note that had cost him a week's wages. They knew he'd failed, and they knew he didn't intend to return. There had been no reply.

Ven was the chief of the surgeons, a tall man with a bulbous nose and a long face. He stood watching as his apprentices folded bandages. Kaladin had once idly considered getting wounded so he could join them; all of the apprentices had some incapacitation that prevented them from fighting. Kaladin hadn't been able to do it. Wounding himself seemed cowardly. Besides, surgery was his old life. In a way, he didn't deserve it anymore.

Kaladin pulled a pouch of spheres from his belt, meaning to toss it to Ven. The pouch stuck, however, refusing to come free of the belt. Kaladin cursed, stumbling, tugging at the pouch. It came free suddenly, causing him to lose his balance again. A translucent white form zipped away, spinning with a carefree air.

"Storming windspren," he said. They were common out on these rocky plains.

He continued past the surgery pavilion, tossing the pouch of spheres to Ven. The tall man caught it deftly, making it vanish into a pocket of his voluminous white robe. The bribe would ensure that Kaladin's men were served first on the battlefield, assuming there were no lighteyes who needed the attention.

It was time to join the line. He sped up, jogging along, spear in hand. Nobody gave him grief for wearing trousers under his leather spearman's skirt—something he did so his men could recognize him from behind. In fact, nobody gave him grief about much of anything these days. That still felt odd, after so many struggles during his first years in the army.

He still didn't feel as if he belonged. His reputation set him apart, but what was he to do? It kept his men from being taunted, and after several years of dealing with disaster after disaster, he could finally pause and *think*.

He wasn't certain he liked that. Thinking had proven dangerous lately. It had been a long while since he'd taken out that rock and thought of Tien and home.

He made his way to the front ranks, spotting his men right where he'd told them to go. "Dallet," Kaladin called, as he trotted over to the mountainous spearman who was the squad's sergeant. "We're soon going to have a new recruit. I need you to . . ." He trailed off. A young man, maybe fourteen, stood beside Dallet, looking tiny in his spearman's armor.

Kaladin felt a flash of recall. Another lad, one with a familiar face, holding a spear he wasn't supposed to need. Two promises broken at once.

"He found his way here just a few minutes ago, sir," Dallet said. "I've been gettin' him ready."

Kaladin shook himself out of the moment. Tien was dead. But *Stormfather*, this new lad looked a lot like him.

"Well done," Kaladin said to Dallet, forcing himself to look away from Cenn. "I paid good money to get that boy away from Gare. That man's so incompetent he might as well be fighting for the other side."

Dallet grunted in agreement. The men would know what to do with Cenn.

All right, Kaladin thought, scanning the battlefield for a good place for his men to stand their ground, *let's get to it.*

He'd heard stories about the soldiers who fought on the Shattered Plains. The *real* soldiers. If you showed enough promise fighting in these border disputes, you were sent there. It was supposed to be safer there—far more soldiers, but fewer battles. So Kaladin wanted to get his squad there as soon as possible.

He conferred with Dallet, picking a place to hold. Eventually, the horns blew.

Kaladin's squad charged.

⋄⋄

"Where's the boy?" Kaladin said, yanking his spear out of the chest of a man in brown. The enemy soldier fell to the ground, groaning. "Dallet!"

The burly sergeant was fighting. He couldn't turn to acknowledge the yell.

Kaladin cursed, scanning the chaotic battlefield. Spears hit shields, flesh, leather; men yelled and screamed. Painspren swarmed the ground, like small orange hands or bits of sinew, reaching up from the ground amid the blood of the fallen.

Kaladin's squad was all accounted for, their wounded protected at the center. All except the new boy. Tien.

Cenn, Kaladin thought. *His name is Cenn.*

Kaladin caught sight of a flash of green in the middle of the enemy brown. A terrified voice somehow cut through the commotion. It was him.

Kaladin threw himself out of formation, prompting a call of surprise from Larn, who had been fighting at his side. Kaladin ducked past a spear thrust by an enemy, dashing over the stony ground, hopping corpses.

Cenn had been knocked to the ground, spear raised. An enemy soldier slammed his weapon down.

No.

Kaladin blocked the blow, deflecting the enemy spear and skidding to a stop in front of Cenn. There were six spearmen here, all wearing brown. Kaladin spun among them in a wild offensive rush. His spear seemed to flow of its own accord. He swept the feet out from under one man, took down another with a thrown knife.

He was like water running down a hill, flowing, always moving. Spearheads flashed in the air around him, hafts hissing with speed. Not one hit him. He could not be stopped, not when he felt like this. When he had the energy of defending the fallen, the power of standing to protect one of his men.

Kaladin snapped his spear into a resting position, crouching with one foot forward, one behind, spear held under his arm. Sweat trickled from his brow, cooled by the breeze. Odd. There hadn't been a breeze before. Now it seemed to envelop him.

All six enemy spearmen were dead or incapacitated. Kaladin breathed in and out once, then turned to see to Cenn's wound. He dropped his spear beside him, kneeling. The cut wasn't that bad, though it probably pained the lad terribly.

Getting out a bandage, Kaladin gave the battlefield one quick glance. Nearby, an enemy soldier stirred, but he was wounded badly enough that he wouldn't be trouble. Dallet and the rest of Kaladin's team were clearing the area of enemy stragglers. In the near distance, an enemy lighteyes of high rank was rallying a small group of soldiers for a counterattack. He wore full plate. Not Shardplate, of course, but silvery steel. A rich man, judging from his horse.

In a heartbeat, Kaladin was back to binding Cenn's leg—though he kept watch on the wounded enemy soldier from the corner of his eye.

"Kaladin, sir!" Cenn exclaimed, pointing at the soldier who had stirred. Stormfather! Had the boy only just noticed the man? Had Kaladin's battle senses ever been as dull as this boy's?

Dallet pushed the wounded enemy away. The rest of the squad made a ring formation around Kaladin, Dallet, and Cenn. Kaladin finished his binding, then stood, picking up his spear.

Dallet handed him back his knives. "Had me worried there, sir. Running off like that."

"I knew you'd follow," Kaladin said. "Raise the red banner. Cyn, Korater, you're going back with the boy. Dallet, hold here. Amaram's line is bulging this direction. We should be safe soon."

"And you, sir?" Dallet asked.

In the near distance, the lighteyes had failed to rally enough troops. He was exposed, like a stone left behind by a stream running dry.

"A Shardbearer," Cenn said.

Dallet snorted. "No, thank the Stormfather. Just a lighteyed officer. Shardbearers are far too valuable to waste on a minor border dispute."

Kaladin clenched his jaw, watching that lighteyed warrior. How mighty the man thought himself, sitting on his expensive horse, kept safe from the spearmen by his majestic armor and tall mount. He swung his mace, killing those around him.

These skirmishes were caused by ones like him, greedy minor lighteyes who tried to steal land while the better men were away, fighting the Parshendi. His type had far, far fewer casualties than the spearmen, and so the lives under his command became cheap things.

More and more over the last few years, each and every one of these petty lighteyes had come to represent Roshone in Kaladin's eyes. Only Amaram himself stood apart. Amaram, who had treated Kaladin's father so well, promising to keep Tien safe. Amaram, who always spoke with respect, even to lowly spearmen. He was like Dalinar and Sadeas. Not this riffraff.

Of course, Amaram had failed to protect Tien. But so had Kaladin.

"Sir?" Dallet said hesitantly.

"Subsquads Two and Three, pincer pattern," Kaladin said coldly, pointing at the enemy lighteyes. "We're taking a brightlord off his throne."

"You sure that's wise, sir?" Dallet said. "We've got wounded."

Kaladin turned toward Dallet. "That's one of Hallaw's officers. He might be the one."

"You don't know that, sir."

"Regardless, he's a battalionlord. If we kill an officer that high, we're all but guaranteed to be in the next group sent to the Shattered Plains. We're taking him. Imagine it, Dallet. Real soldiers. A warcamp with discipline and lighteyes with integrity. A place where our fighting will *mean* something."

Dallet sighed, but nodded. At Kaladin's wave, two subsquads joined him, as eager as he. Did they hate these squabbling lighteyes of their own accord, or had they picked up Kaladin's loathing?

The brightlord was surprisingly easy to take down. The problem with them—almost to a man—was that they underestimated darkeyes. Perhaps this one had a right. How many had he killed, in his years?

Subsquad three drew off the honor guard. Subsquad two distracted the lighteyes. He didn't see Kaladin approaching from a third direction. The man dropped with a knife to the eye; his face was unprotected. He screamed as he clattered to the ground, still alive. Kaladin rammed his spear down into the fallen man's face, striking three times as the horse galloped off.

The man's honor guard panicked and fled to rejoin their army. Kaladin signaled to the two subsquads by banging his spear against his shield, giving the "hold position" sign. They fanned out, and short Toorim—a man Kaladin had rescued from another squad—made as if to confirm the lighteyes was dead. He was really covertly looking for spheres.

Stealing from the dead was strictly prohibited, but Kaladin figured that if Amaram wanted the spoils, he could storming well kill the enemy himself. Kaladin respected Amaram more than most—well, more than *any*—lighteyes. But bribes weren't cheap.

Toorim walked up to him. "Nothing sir. Either he didn't bring any spheres into battle, or he has them hidden somewhere under that breastplate."

Kaladin nodded curtly, surveying the battlefield. Amaram's forces were recovering; they'd win the day before long. In fact, Amaram would probably be leading a direct surge against the enemy by now. He generally entered the battle at the end.

Kaladin wiped his brow. He'd have to send for Norby, their captainlord, to prove their kill. First he needed those healers to—

"Sir!" Toorim said suddenly.

Kaladin glanced back at the enemy lines.

"Stormfather!" Toorim exclaimed. "*Sir!*"

Toorim wasn't looking at the enemy lines. Kaladin spun, looking back at friendly ranks. There—bearing down through the soldiers on a horse the color of death itself—was an impossibility.

The man wore shining golden armor. *Perfect* golden armor, as if this were what every other suit of armor had been designed to imitate. Each piece fit perfectly; there were no holes showing straps or leather. It made the rider look enormous, powerful. Like a god carrying a majestic blade that should have been too big to use. It was engraved and stylized, shaped like flames in motion.

"Stormfather . . ." Kaladin breathed.

The Shardbearer broke out of Amaram's lines. He'd been riding through them, cutting down men as he passed. For a brief moment, Kaladin's mind refused to acknowledge that this creature—this beautiful *divinity*—could be an enemy. The fact that the Shardbearer had come through their side reinforced that illusion.

Kaladin's confusion lasted right up until the moment the Shardbearer trampled Cenn, Shardblade dropping and cutting through Dallet's head in a single, easy stroke.

"No!" Kaladin bellowed. *"No!"*

Dallet's body fell back to the ground, eyes seeming to catch alight, smoke rising from them. The Shardbearer cut down Cyn and trampled Lyndel before moving on. It was all done with nonchalance, like a woman pausing to wipe a spot on the counter.

"NO!" Kaladin screamed, charging toward the fallen men of his squad. He hadn't lost anyone this battle! He was going to protect them all!

He fell to his knees beside Dallet, dropping his spear. But there was no heartbeat, and those burned-out eyes . . . He was dead. Grief threatened to overwhelm Kaladin.

No! said the part of his mind trained by his father. *Save the ones you can!*

He turned to Cenn. The boy had taken a hoof to the chest, cracking his sternum and shattering ribs. The boy gasped, eyes upward, struggling for breath. Kaladin pulled out a bandage.

Then he paused, looking at it. A bandage? To mend a smashed chest?

Cenn stopped wheezing. He convulsed once, eyes still open. "He watches!" the boy hissed. "The black piper in the night. He holds us in his palm . . . playing a tune that no man can hear!"

Cenn's eyes glazed over. He stopped breathing.

Lyndel's face had been smashed in. Cyn's eyes smoldered, and he wasn't breathing either. Kaladin knelt in Cenn's blood, horrified, as Toorim and the two subsquads formed around him, looking as stunned as Kaladin felt.

This isn't possible. I . . . I . . .

Screaming.

Kaladin looked up. Amaram's banner of green and burgundy flew just to the south. The Shardbearer had cut through Kaladin's squad heading straight for that banner. Spearmen fled in disarray, screaming, scattering before the Shardbearer.

Anger boiled inside of Kaladin.

"Sir?" Toorim asked.

Kaladin picked up his spear and stood. His knees were covered with Cenn's blood. His men regarded him, confused, worried. They stood firm in the midst of the chaos; as far as Kaladin could tell, they were the only men who weren't fleeing. The Shardbearer had turned the ranks to mush.

Kaladin thrust his spear into the air, then began to run. His men bellowed a war cry, falling into formation behind him, charging across the flat rocky ground. Spearmen in uniforms of both colors scrambled out of the way, dropping spears and shields.

Kaladin picked up speed, legs pumping, his squad barely keeping pace. Just ahead—right before the Shardbearer—a pocket of green broke and ran. Amaram's honor guard. Faced by a Shardbearer, they abandoned their charge. Amaram himself was a solitary man on a rearing horse. He wore silvery plate armor that looked so *commonplace* when compared with the Shardplate.

Kaladin's squad charged against the flow of the army, a wedge of soldiers going the wrong way. The *only* ones going the wrong way. Some of the fleeing men paused as he charged past, but none joined.

Ahead, the Shardbearer rode past Amaram. With a sweep of the Blade, the Shardbearer slashed through the neck of Amaram's mount. Its eyes burned into two great pits, and it toppled, jerking fitfully, Amaram still in its saddle.

The Shardbearer wheeled his destrier in a tight circle, then threw himself from horseback at full speed. He hit the ground with a grinding sound, somehow remaining upright and skidding to a halt.

Kaladin redoubled his speed. Was he running to get vengeance, or was he trying to protect his highmarshal? The only lighteyes who had ever shown a modicum of humanity? Did it matter?

Amaram struggled in his bulky plate, the carcass of the horse on his leg.

The Shardbearer raised his Blade in two hands to finish him off.

Coming at the Shardbearer from behind, Kaladin screamed and swung low with the butt of his spear, putting momentum and muscle behind the blow. The spear haft shattered against the Shardbearer's back leg in a spray of wooden slivers.

The jolt of it knocked Kaladin to the ground, his arms shaking, the broken spear clutched in his hands. The Shardbearer stumbled, lowering his Blade. He turned a helmed face toward Kaladin, posture indicating utter surprise.

The twenty remaining men of Kaladin's squad arrived a heartbeat later, attacking vigorously. Kaladin scrambled to his feet and ran for the spear from a fallen soldier. He tossed his broken one away after snatching one of his knives from its sheath, snatched the new one off the ground, then turned back to see his men attacking as he had taught. They came at the foe from three directions, ramming spears between joints in the Plate. The Shardbearer glanced around, as a bemused man might regard a pack of puppies yapping around him. Not a single one of the spear thrusts appeared to pierce his armor. He shook a helmed head.

Then he struck.

The Shardblade swept out in a broad sweeping series of deadly strokes, cutting through ten of the spearmen.

Kaladin was paralyzed in horror as Toorim, Acis, Hamel, and seven others fell to the ground, eyes burning, their armor and weapons sheared completely through. The remaining spearmen stumbled back, aghast.

The Shardbearer attacked again, killing Raksha, Navar, and four others. Kaladin gaped. His men—his friends—dead, just like that. The last four scrambled away, Hab stumbling over Toorim's corpse and falling to the ground, dropping his spear.

The Shardbearer ignored them, stepping up to the pinned Amaram again.

No, Kaladin thought. *No, no, NO!* Something drove him forward, against all logic, against all sense. Sickened, agonized, *enraged.*

The hollow where they fought was empty save for them. Sensible spearmen had fled. His four remaining men achieved the ridge a short distance away, but didn't run. They called for him.

"Kaladin!" Reesh yelled. "Kaladin, no!"

Kaladin screamed instead. The Shardbearer saw him, and spun—impossibly quick—swinging. Kaladin ducked under the blow and rammed the butt of his spear against the Shardbearer's knee.

It bounced off. Kaladin cursed, throwing himself backward just as the Blade sliced the air in front of him. Kaladin rebounded and lunged forward. He made an expert thrust at his enemy's neck. The neck brace rebuffed the attack. Kaladin's spear barely scratched the Plate's paint.

The Shardbearer turned on him, holding his Blade in a two-handed grip. Kaladin dashed past, just out of range of that incredible sword. Amaram had finally pulled himself free, and he was crawling away, one leg dragging behind him—multiple fractures, from the twist of it.

Kaladin skidded to a stop, spinning, regarding the Shardbearer. This creature wasn't a god. It was everything the most petty of lighteyes represented. The ability to kill people like Kaladin with impunity.

Every suit of armor had a chink. Every man had a flaw. Kaladin thought he saw the man's eyes through the helm's slit. That slit was just big enough for a dagger, but the throw would have to be perfect. He'd have to be close. Deadly close.

Kaladin charged forward again. The Shardbearer swung his Blade out in the same wide sweep he'd used to kill so many of Kaladin's men. Kaladin threw himself downward, skidding on his knees and bending backward. The Shardblade flashed above him, shearing the top of his spear free. The tip flipped up into the air, tumbling end over end.

Kaladin strained, hurling himself back onto his feet. He whipped his hand up, flinging his knife at the eyes watching from behind impervious armor. The dagger hit the faceplate just slightly off from the right angle, bouncing against the sides of the slit and ricocheting out.

The Shardbearer cursed, swinging his huge Blade back at Kaladin.

Kaladin landed on his feet, momentum still propelling him forward. Something flashed in the air beside him, falling toward the ground.

The spearhead.

Kaladin bellowed in defiance, spinning, snatching the spearhead from the air. It had been falling tip-down, and he caught it by the four inches of haft that remained, gripping it with his thumb on the stump, the sharp point extending down beneath his hand. The Shardbearer brought his weapon around as Kaladin skidded to a stop and flung his arm to the side, *slamming* the spearhead right in the Shardbearer's visor slit.

All fell still.

Kaladin stood with his arm extended, the Shardbearer standing just to his right. Amaram had pulled himself halfway up the side of the shallow hollow. Kaladin's spearmates stood on the edge of the scene, gawking. Kaladin stood there, gasping, still gripping the haft of the spear, hand before the Shardbearer's face.

The Shardbearer creaked, then fell backward, crashing to

the ground. His Blade dropped from his fingers, hitting the ground at an angle and digging into the stone.

Kaladin stumbled away, feeling drained. Stunned. Numbed. His men rushed up, halting in a group, staring at the fallen man. They were amazed, even a little reverent.

"Is he dead?" Alabet asked softly.

"He is," a voice said from the side.

Kaladin turned. Amaram still lay on the ground, but he had pulled off his helm, dark hair and beard slicked with sweat. "If he were still alive, his Blade would have vanished. His armor is falling off of him. He is dead. Blood of my ancestors . . . you killed a Shardbearer!"

Oddly, Kaladin wasn't surprised. Just exhausted. He looked around at the bodies of men who had been his dearest friends.

"Take it, Kaladin," Coreb said.

Kaladin turned, looking at the Shardblade, which sprouted at an angle into the stone, hilt toward the sky.

"Take it," Coreb said again. "It's yours. Stormfather, Kaladin. You're a *Shardbearer*!"

Kaladin stepped forward, dazed, raising his hand toward the hilt of the Blade. He hesitated just an inch away from it.

Everything felt *wrong*.

If he took that Blade, he'd become one of them. His eyes would even change, if the stories were right. Though the Blade glistened in the light, clean of the murders it had performed, for a moment it seemed red to him. Stained with Dallet's blood. Toorim's blood. The blood of the men who had been alive just moments before.

It was a treasure. Men traded kingdoms for Shardblades. The handful of darkeyed men who had won them lived forever in song and story.

But the thought of touching that Blade sickened him. It represented everything he'd come to hate about the lighteyes, and it had just slaughtered men he loved dearly. He could not become a legend because of something like that. He looked at his reflection in the Blade's pitiless metal, then lowered his hand and turned away.

"It's yours, Coreb," Kaladin said. "I give it to you."

"*What?*" Coreb said from behind.

Ahead, Amaram's honor guard had finally returned, apprehensively appearing at the top of the small hollow, looking ashamed.

"What are you doing?" Amaram demanded as Kaladin passed him. "What— Aren't you going to take the Blade?"

"I don't want it," Kaladin said softly. "I'm giving it to my men."

Kaladin walked away, emotionally exhausted, tears on his cheeks as he climbed out of the hollow and shoved his way through the honor guard.

He walked back to the warcamp alone.

48

STRAWBERRY

"They take away the light, wherever they lurk. Skin that is burned."

—Cormshen, page 104.

Shallan sat quietly, propped up in a sterile, white-sheeted bed in one of Kharbranth's many hospitals. Her arm was wrapped in a neat, crisp bandage, and she held her drawing board in front of her. The nurses had reluctantly allowed her to sketch, so long as she did not "stress herself."

Her arm ached; she'd sliced herself more deeply than she'd intended. She'd hoped to simulate a wound from breaking the pitcher; she hadn't thought far enough ahead to realize how much like a suicide attempt it might seem. Though she'd protested that she'd simply fallen from bed, she could see that the nurses and ardents didn't accept it. She couldn't blame them.

The results were embarrassing, but at least nobody thought she might have Soulcast to make that blood. Embarrassment was worth escaping suspicion.

She continued her sketch. She was in a large, hallwaylike room in a Kharbranthian hospital, the walls lined with many beds. Other than obvious aggravations, her two days in the hospital had gone fairly well. She'd had a lot of time to think about that strangest of afternoons, when she'd seen ghosts, transformed glass to blood, and had an ardent offer to resign the ardentia to be with her.

She'd done several drawings of this hospital room. The creatures lurked in her sketches, staying at the distant edges of the room. Their presence made it difficult for her to sleep, but she was slowly growing accustomed to them.

The air smelled of soap and lister's oil; she was bathed regularly and her arm washed with antiseptic to frighten away rotspren. About half of the beds held sick women, and there were wheeled fabric dividers with wooden frames that could be rolled around a bed for privacy. Shallan wore a plain white robe that untied at the front and had a long left sleeve that tied shut to protect her safehand.

She'd transferred her safepouch to the robe, buttoning it inside the left sleeve. Nobody had looked in the pouch. When she'd been washed, they'd unbuttoned it and given it to her without a word, despite its unusual weight. One did not look in a woman's safepouch. Still, she kept hold of it whenever she could.

In the hospital, her every need was seen to, but she could not leave. It reminded her of being at home on her father's estates. More and more, that frightened her as much as the symbolheads did. She'd tasted independence, and she didn't want to go back to what she had been. Coddled, pampered, displayed.

Unfortunately, it was unlikely she'd be able to return to studying with Jasnah. Her supposed suicide attempt gave her an excellent reason to return home. She had to go. To remain, sending the Soulcaster away on its own, would be selfish considering this opportunity to leave without arousing suspicion. Besides, she'd used the Soulcaster. She could use the long trip home to figure out how she'd done it, then be ready to help her family when she arrived.

She sighed, and then with a few shadings, she finished her sketch. It was a picture of that strange place she had gone. That distant horizon with its powerful yet cold sun. Clouds running toward it above, endless ocean below, making the sun look as if it were at the end of a long tunnel. Above the ocean hovered hundreds of flames, a sea of lights above the sea of glass beads.

She lifted the picture up, looking at the sketch underneath. It depicted her, huddled on her bed, surrounded by the strange creatures. She didn't *dare* tell Jasnah what she had seen, lest it reveal that she had Soulcast, and therefore committed the theft.

The next picture was one of her, lying on the ground amid the blood. She looked up from the sketchpad. A white-clothed female ardent sat against the wall nearby, pretending to sew but really keeping watch in case Shallan decided to harm herself again. Shallan made a thin line of her lips.

It's a good cover, she told herself. *It works perfectly. Stop being so embarrassed.*

She turned to the last of her day's sketches. It depicted one of the symbolheads. No eyes, no face, just that jagged alien symbol with points like cut crystal. They *had* to have something to do with the Soulcasting. Didn't they?

I visited another place, she thought. *I think . . . I think I spoke with the spirit of the goblet.* Did a *goblet,* of all things, have a soul? Upon opening her pouch to check on the Soulcaster, she'd found that the sphere Kabsal had given her had stopped glowing. She could remember a vague feeling of light and beauty, a raging storm inside of her.

She'd taken the light from the sphere and given it to the goblet—the *spren* of the goblet—as a bribe to transform. Was that how Soulcasting worked? Or was she just struggling to make connections?

Shallan lowered the sketchpad as visitors entered the room and began moving among the patients. Most of the women sat up excitedly as they saw King Taravangian, with his orange robes and kindly, aged air. He paused at each bed to chat. She'd heard that he visited frequently, at least once a week.

Eventually he reached Shallan's bedside. He smiled at her, sitting as one of his many attendants placed a padded stool for him. "And young Shallan Davar. I was so terribly saddened to hear of your accident. I apologize for not coming earlier. Duties of state kept me."

"It is quite all right, Your Majesty."

"No, no, it is not," he said. "But it is what must be. There are many who complain that I spend too much of my time here."

Shallan smiled. Those complaints were never vociferous. The landlords and houselords who played politics in court were quite content with a king who spent so much of his time outside the palace, ignoring their schemes.

"This hospital is amazing, Your Majesty," she said. "I can't believe how well everyone is cared for."

He smiled widely. "My great triumph. Lighteyes and darkeyes alike, nobody turned away—not beggar, not whore, not sailor from afar. It's all paid for by the Palanaeum, you know. In a way, even the most obscure and useless record is helping heal the sick."

"I'm glad to be here."

"I doubt that, child. A hospital such as this one is, perhaps, the only thing a man could pour so much money into and be delighted if it were never used. It is a tragedy that you must become my guest."

"What I meant was that I'd rather be sick here than somewhere else. Though I suppose that's a little like saying it's better to choke on wine than on dishwater."

He laughed. "What a sweet thing you are," he said, rising. "Is there anything I can do to improve your stay?"

"End it?"

"I'm afraid that I can't allow that," he said, eyes softening. "I must defer to the wisdom of my surgeons and nurses. They say that you are still at risk. We must think of your health."

"Keeping me here gives me health at the expense of my wellness, Your Majesty."

He shook his head. "You mustn't be allowed to have another accident."

"I . . . I understand. But I promise that I'm feeling much better. The episode that struck me was caused by overwork. Now that I'm relaxed, I'm not in any further danger."

"That is good," he said. "But we still need to keep you for a few more days."

"Yes, Your Majesty. But could I at least have visitors?" So far, the hospital staff had insisted that she was not to be bothered.

"Yes . . . I can see how that might help you. I'll speak to the ardents and suggest that you be allowed a few visitors." He hesitated. "Once you are well again, it might be best for you to suspend your training."

She pasted a grimace on her face, trying not to feel sick at the charade. "I hate to do that, Your Majesty. But I have been missing my family greatly. Perhaps I should return to them."

"An excellent idea. I'm certain the ardents will be more likely to release you if they know you'll be going home." He smiled in a kindly way, resting a hand on her shoulder. "This world, it is a tempest sometimes. But remember, the sun always rises again."

"Thank you, Your Majesty."

The king moved away, visiting other patients, then speaking quietly with the ardents. Not five minutes passed before Jasnah walked through the doorway with her characteristic straight-backed stride. She wore a beautiful dress, deep blue with golden embroidery. Her sleek black hair was done in braids and pierced by six thin golden spikes; her cheeks glowed with blush, her lips bloodred with lip paint. She stood out in the white room like a flower upon a field of barren stone.

She glided toward Shallan on feet hidden beneath the loose folds of her silk skirt, carrying a thick book under her arm. An ardent brought her a stool, and she sat down where the king had just stood.

Jasnah regarded Shallan, face stiff, impassive. "I have been told that my tutelage is demanding, perhaps harsh. This is one reason why I often refuse to take wards."

"I apologize for my weakness, Brightness," Shallan said, looking down.

Jasnah seemed displeased. "I did not mean to suggest fault in you, child. I was attempting the opposite. Unfortunately I'm . . . unaccustomed to such behavior."

"Apologizing?"

"Yes."

"Well, you see," Shallan said, "in order to grow proficient at apologizing, you must first make mistakes. That's your problem, Jasnah. You're absolutely terrible at making them."

The woman's expression softened. "The king mentioned to me that you would be returning to your family."

"What? When?"

"When he met me in the hallway outside," she said, "and finally gave me permission to visit you."

"You make it sound as if you were waiting out there."

Jasnah didn't reply.

"But your research!"

"Can be done in the hospital waiting chamber." She hesitated. "It has been somewhat difficult for me to focus these last few days."

"Jasnah! That's quite nearly *human* of you!"

Jasnah regarded her reprovingly, and Shallan winced, immediately regretting the words. "I'm sorry. I've learned poorly, haven't I?"

"Or perhaps you are just practicing the art of the apology. So that you will not be unsettled when the need arises, as I am."

"How very clever of me."

"Indeed."

"Can I stop now, then?" Shallan asked. "I think I've had quite enough practice."

"I should think," Jasnah said, "that apology is an art of which we could use a few more masters. Do not use me as a model in this. Pride is often mistaken for faultlessness." She leaned forward. "I am sorry, Shallan Davar. In overworking you, I may have done the world a disservice and stolen from it one of the great scholars of the rising generation."

Shallan blushed, feeling more foolish and guilty. Shallan's eyes flickered to her mistress's hand. Jasnah wore the black glove that hid the fake. In the fingers of her safehand, Shallan grasped the pouch holding the Soulcaster. If Jasnah only knew.

Jasnah took the book from beneath her arm and set it on the bed beside Shallan. "This is for you."

Shallan picked it up. She opened to the front page, but it

was blank. The next one was as well, as were all inside of it. Her frown deepened, and she looked up at Jasnah.

"It's called the *Book of Endless Pages*," Jasnah said.

"Er, I'm pretty sure it's not endless, Brightness." She flipped to the last page and held it up.

Jasnah smiled. "It's a metaphor, Shallan. Many years ago, someone dear to me made a very good attempt at converting me to Vorinism. This was the method he used."

Shallan cocked her head.

"You search for truth," Jasnah said, "but you also hold to your faith. There is much to admire in that. Seek out the Devotary of Sincerity. They are one of the very smallest of the devotaries, but this book is their guide."

"One with blank pages?"

"Indeed. They worship the Almighty, but are guided by the belief that there are always more answers to be found. The book cannot be filled, as there is always something to learn. This devotary is a place where one is never penalized for questions, even those challenging Vorinism's own tenets." She shook her head. "I cannot explain their ways. You should be able to find them in Vedenar, though there are none in Kharbranth."

"I . . ." Shallan trailed off, noticing how Jasnah's hand rested fondly on the book. It was precious to her. "I hadn't thought to find ardents who were willing to question their own beliefs."

Jasnah raised an eyebrow. "You will find wise men in any religion, Shallan, and good men in every nation. Those who *truly* seek wisdom are those who will acknowledge the virtue in their adversaries and who will learn from those who disabuse them of error. All others—heretic, Vorin, Ysperist, or Maakian—are equally closed-minded." She took her hand from the book, moving as if to stand up.

"He's wrong," Shallan said suddenly, realizing something.

Jasnah turned to her.

"Kabsal," Shallan said, blushing. "He says you're researching the Voidbringers because you want to prove that Vorinism is false."

Jasnah sniffed in derision. "I would not dedicate four years of my life to such an empty pursuit. It's idiocy to try to prove a negative. Let the Vorin believe as they wish—the wise among them will find goodness and solace in their faith; the fools would be fools no matter what they believed."

Shallan frowned. So why *was* Jasnah studying the Voidbringers?

"Ah. Speak of the storm and it begins to bluster," Jasnah said, turning toward the room's entrance.

With a start, Shallan realized that Kabsal had just arrived, wearing his usual grey robes. He was arguing softly with a nurse, who pointed at the basket he carried. Finally, the nurse threw up her hands and walked away, leaving Kabsal to approach, triumphant. "Finally!" he said to Shallan. "Old Mungam can be a real tyrant."

"Mungam?" Shallan asked.

"The ardent who runs this place," Kabsal said. "I should have been allowed in immediately. After all, I know what you need to make you better!" He pulled out a jar of jam, smiling broadly.

Jasnah remained on her stool, regarding Kabsal across the bed. "I would have thought," she said dryly, "that you would allow Shallan a respite, considering how your attentions drove her to despair."

Kabsal flushed. He looked at Shallan, and she could see the pleading in his eyes.

"It wasn't you, Kabsal," Shallan said. "I just . . . I wasn't ready for life away from my family estate. I still don't know what came over me. I've never done anything like that before."

He smiled, pulling a stool over for himself. "I think," he said, "that the lack of color in these places is what keeps people sick so long. That and the lack of proper food." He winked, turning the jar toward Shallan. It was deep, dark red. "Strawberry."

"Never heard of it," Shallan said.

"It's exceedingly rare," Jasnah said, reaching for the jar. "Like most plants from Shinovar, it can't grow other places."

Kabsal looked surprised as Jasnah removed the lid and

dipped a finger into the jar. She hesitated, then raised a bit of the jam to her nose to sniff at it.

"I was under the impression that you disliked jam, Brightness Jasnah," Kabsal said.

"I do," she said. "I was simply curious about the scent. I've heard that strawberries are very distinctive." She screwed the lid back on, then wiped her finger on her cloth handkerchief.

"I brought bread as well," Kabsal said. He pulled out a small loaf of the fluffy bread. "It's nice of you not to blame me, Shallan, but I can see that my attentions were too forward. I thought, maybe, I could bring this and . . ."

"And what?" Jasnah asked. "Absolve yourself? 'I'm sorry I drove you to suicide. Here's some bread.'"

He blushed, looking down.

"Of course I'll have some," Shallan said, glaring at Jasnah. "And she will too. It was very kind of you, Kabsal." She took the bread, breaking off a chunk for Kabsal, one for herself, then one for Jasnah.

"No," Jasnah said. "Thank you."

"Jasnah," Shallan said. "Would you please at least try some?" It bothered her that the two of them got on so poorly.

The older woman sighed. "Oh, very well." She took the bread, holding it as Shallan and Kabsal ate. The bread was moist and delicious, though Jasnah grimaced as she put hers in her mouth and chewed it.

"You should really try the jam," Kabsal said to Shallan. "Strawberry is hard to find. I had to make quite a number of inquiries."

"No doubt bribing merchants with the king's money," Jasnah noted.

Kabsal sighed. "Brightness Jasnah, I realize that you are not fond of me. But I'm working very hard to be pleasant. Could you at least *pretend* to do likewise?"

Jasnah eyed Shallan, probably recalling Kabsal's guess that undermining Vorinism was the goal of her research. She didn't apologize, but also made no retort.

Good enough, Shallan thought.

"The jam, Shallan," Kabsal said, handing her a slice of bread for it.

"Oh, right." She removed the lid of the jar, holding it between her knees and using her freehand.

"You missed your ship out, I assume," Kabsal said.

"Yes."

"What's this?" Jasnah asked.

Shallan cringed. "I was planning to leave, Brightness. I'm sorry. I should have told you."

Jasnah settled back. "I suppose it was to be expected, all things considered."

"The jam?" Kabsal prodded again.

Shallan frowned. He was particularly insistent about that jam. She raised the jar and sniffed at it, then pulled back. "It smells terrible! This is jam?" It smelled like vinegar and slime.

"What?" Kabsal said, alarmed. He took the jar, sniffing at it, then pulled away, looking nauseated.

"It appears you got a bad jar," Jasnah said. "That's not how it's supposed to smell?"

"Not at all," Kabsal said. He hesitated, then stuck his finger into the jam anyway, shoving a large glob into his mouth.

"Kabsal!" Shallan said. "That's revolting!"

He coughed, but forced it down. "Not so bad, really. You should try it."

"What?"

"Really," he said, forcing it toward her. "I mean, I wanted this to be special, for you. And it turned out so horribly."

"I'm *not* tasting that, Kabsal."

He hesitated, as if considering forcing it upon her. Why was he acting so strangely? He raised a hand to his head, stood up, and stumbled away from the bed.

Then he began to rush from the room. He made it only halfway before crashing to the floor, his body sliding a little way across the spotless stone.

"Kabsal!" Shallan said, leaping out of the bed, hurrying to

his side, wearing only the white robe. He was shaking. And . . . and . . .

And so was she. The room was spinning. Suddenly she felt very, very tired. She tried to stand, but slipped, dizzy. She barely felt herself hit the floor.

Someone was kneeling above her, cursing.

Jasnah. Her voice was distant. "She's been poisoned. I need a garnet. Bring me a garnet!"

There's one in my pouch, Shallan thought. She fumbled with it, managing to undo the tie of her safehand's sleeve. *Why . . . why does she want . . .*

But no, I can't show her that. The Soulcaster!

Her mind was so fuzzy.

"Shallan," Jasnah's voice said, anxious, very soft. "I'm going to have to Soulcast your blood to purify it. It will be dangerous. *Extremely* dangerous. I'm not good with flesh or blood. It's not where my talent lies."

She needs it. To save me. Weakly, she reached in and pulled out her safepouch with her right hand. "You . . . can't . . ."

"Hush, child. Where is that garnet!"

"You can't Soulcast," Shallan said weakly, pulling the ties of her pouch open. She upended it, vaguely seeing a fuzzy golden object slip out onto the floor, alongside the garnet that Kabsal had given her.

Stormfather! Why was the room spinning so much?

Jasnah gasped. Distantly.

Fading . . .

Something happened. A flash of warmth burned through Shallan, something *inside* her skin, as if she had been dumped into a steaming hot cauldron. She screamed, arching her back, her muscles spasming.

All went black.

Rockbuds

"True" Rockbud
(or "Common Rockbud")

The term "rockbud" refers to an entire family of plants, but also to one plant in particular.

the weight is such that it always rests upright.

Lavis Polyp

The polyp grains are suspended in a gritty material not unlike sand.

They can be dried and stored in a variety of ways.

Vinebud

Really related to fingermoss?

Prickletac
(or Twisted Spine)

Actually a colony of plants, only the tips of the "branches" are alive.

Each individual bud builds upon the shell of the previous generation.

"Radiant / of birthplace / the announcer comes / to come announce / the birthplace of Radiants."

—Though I am not overly fond of the ketek poetic form as a means of conveying information, this one by Allahn is often quoted in reference to Urithiru. I believe some mistook the home of the Radiants for their birthplace.

The towering walls of the chasm rising on either side of Kaladin dripped with greenish grey moss. His torch's flames danced, light reflecting on slick, rain-wetted sections of stone. The humid air was chilly, and the highstorm had left puddles and ponds. Spindly bones—an ulna and a radius—poked from a deep puddle Kaladin passed. He didn't look to see if the rest of the skeleton was there.

Flash floods, Kaladin thought, listening to the scraping steps of the bridgemen behind him. *That water has to go somewhere, otherwise we'd have canals to cross instead of chasms.*

Kaladin didn't know if he could trust his dream or not, but he'd asked around, and it was true that the eastern edge of the Shattered Plains was more open than the western side. The plateaus had been worn away. If the bridgemen could get there, they might be able to flee to the east.

Might. Many chasmfiends lived in that area, and Alethi scouts patrolled the perimeter beyond. If Kaladin's team met them, they would have trouble explaining what a group of armed men—many with slave brands—was doing there.

Syl walked along the wall of the chasm, about level with Kaladin's head. Groundspren didn't pull her downward as they did everything else. She walked with her hands clasped behind her back, her tiny, knee-length skirt fluttering in an intangible wind.

Escape to the east. It seemed unlikely. The highprinces had tried *very* hard to explore that way, looking for a route to the center of the Plains. They'd failed. Chasmfiends had killed some groups. Others had been caught in the chasms during highstorms, despite precautions. It was impossible to predict the storms perfectly.

Other scouting parties had avoided those two fates. They'd used enormous extensible ladders to climb atop plateaus during highstorms. They'd lost many men, though, as the plateau tops provided poor cover during storms, and you couldn't bring wagons or other shelter with you into the chasms. The bigger problem, he'd heard, had been the Parshendi patrols. They'd found and killed dozens of scouting parties.

"Kaladin?" Teft asked, hustling up, splashing through a puddle where bits of empty cremling carapace floated. "You all right?"

"Fine."

"You look thoughtful."

"More breakfast-full," Kaladin said. "That gruel was particularly dense this morning."

Teft smiled. "I never took you for the glib type."

"I used to be more so. I get it from my mother. You could rarely say anything to her without getting it twisted about and tossed back to you."

Teft nodded. They walked in silence for a time, the bridgemen behind laughing as Dunny told a story about the first girl he'd ever kissed.

"Son," Teft said, "have you felt anything strange lately?"

"Strange? What kind of strange?"

"I don't know. Just . . . anything odd?" He coughed. "You know, like odd surges of strength? The . . . er, feeling that you're light?"

"The feeling that I'm *what*?"

"Light. Er, maybe, like your head is light. Light-headed. That sort of thing. Storm it, boy, I'm just checking to see if you're still sick. You were beat up pretty badly by that high-storm."

"I'm fine," Kaladin said. "Remarkably so, actually."

"Odd, eh?"

It *was* odd. It fed his nagging worry that he was subject to some kind of supernatural curse of the type that were supposed to happen to people who sought the Old Magic. There were stories of evil men made immortal, then tortured over and over again—like Extes, who had his arms torn off each day for sacrificing his son to the Voidbringers in exchange for knowledge of the day of his death. It was just a tale, but tales came from somewhere.

Kaladin lived when everyone else died. Was that the work of some spren from Damnation, toying with him like a wind-spren, but infinitely more nefarious? Letting him think that he might be able to do some good, then killing everyone he tried to help? There were supposed to be thousands of kinds of spren, many that people never saw or didn't know about. Syl followed him. Could some kind of evil spren be doing the same?

A very disturbing thought.

Superstition is useless, he told himself forcefully. *Think on it too much, and you'll end up like Durk, insisting that you need to wear your lucky boots into every battle.*

They reached a section where the chasm forked, splitting around a plateau high above. Kaladin turned to face the bridgemen. "This is as good a place as any." The bridgemen stopped, bunching up. He could see the anticipation in their eyes, the excitement.

He'd felt that once, back before he'd known the soreness and the pain of practice. Oddly, Kaladin felt he was now both more in awe of *and* more disappointed in the spear than he'd been as a youth. He loved the focus, the feeling of certainty that he felt when he fought. But that hadn't saved those who followed him.

"This is where I'm supposed to tell you what a sorry group you are," Kaladin said to the men. "It's the way I've always seen it done. The training sergeant tells the recruits that they are pathetic. He points out their weakness, perhaps spars with a few of them, tossing them on their backsides to teach them humility. I did that a few times myself when training new spearmen."

Kaladin shook his head. "Today, that's not how we'll begin. You men don't need humbling. You don't dream of glory. You dream of survival. Most of all, you *aren't* the sad, unprepared group of recruits most sergeants have to deal with. You're tough. I've seen you run for miles carrying a bridge. You're brave. I've seen you charge straight at a line of archers. You're determined. Otherwise you wouldn't be here, right now, with me."

Kaladin walked to the side of the chasm and extracted a discarded spear from some flood-strewn rubble. Once he had it, however, he realized that the spearhead had been knocked off. He almost tossed it aside, then reconsidered.

Spears were dangerous for him to hold. They made him want to fight, and might lead him to think he was who he'd once been: Kaladin Stormblessed, confident squadleader. He wasn't that man any longer.

It seemed that whenever he picked up weapons, the people around him died—friends as well as foes. So, for now, it seemed good to hold this length of wood; it was just a staff. Nothing more. A stick he could use for training.

He could face returning to the spear another time.

"It's good that you're already prepared," Kaladin said to the men. "Because we don't have the six weeks I was given to train a new batch of recruits. In six weeks, Sadeas will have half of us dead. I intend to see you all drinking mudbeer in a tavern somewhere safe by the time six weeks have passed."

Several of them gave a kind of half-cheer at that.

"We'll have to be fast," Kaladin said. "I'll have to push

you hard. That's our only option." He glanced at the spear haft. "The first thing you need to learn is that it's all right to care."

The thirty-three bridgemen stood in a double row. All had wanted to come. Even Leyten, who had been hurt so badly. They didn't have any who were wounded so badly they couldn't walk, although Dabbid continued to stare off at nothing. Rock stood with his arms folded, apparently with no intention of learning to fight. Shen, the parshman, stood at the very back. He looked at the ground. Kaladin didn't intend to put a spear in his hands.

Several of the bridgemen seemed confused by what Kaladin had said about emotions, though Teft just raised an eyebrow and Moash yawned. "What do you mean?" Drehy asked. He was a lanky blond man, long-limbed and muscled. He spoke with a faint accent; he was from somewhere far to the west, called Rianal.

"A lot of soldiers," Kaladin said, running his thumb across the pole, feeling the grain of the wood, "they think that you fight the best if you're passionless and cold. I think that's stormleavings. Yes, you need to be focused. Yes, emotions are dangerous. But if you don't care about anything, what are you? An animal, driven only to kill. Our passion is what makes us human. We *have* to fight for a reason. So I say that it's all right to care. We'll talk about controlling your fear and anger, but remember this as the first lesson I taught you."

Several of the bridgemen nodded. Most seemed confused still. Kaladin remembered being there, wondering why Tukks wasted time talking about emotions. He'd thought he understood emotion—his drive to learn the spear had come *because* of his emotions. Vengeance. Hatred. A lust for the power to exact retribution on Varth and the soldiers of his squad.

He looked up, trying to banish those memories. No, the bridgemen didn't understand his words about caring, but perhaps they would remember later, as Kaladin had.

"The second lesson," Kaladin said, slapping the decapitated spear to the rock beside him with a crack that echoed down the chasm, "is more utilitarian. Before you can learn to fight, you're going to have to learn how to stand." He dropped the spear. The bridgemen watched him with frowns of disappointment.

Kaladin fell into a basic spearman's stance, feet wide apart—but not too wide—turned sideways, knees bent in a loose crouch. "Skar, I want you to come try to push me backward."

"What?"

"Try and throw me off balance," Kaladin said. "Force me to stumble."

Skar shrugged and walked forward. He tried to shove Kaladin back, but Kaladin easily knocked his hands aside with a quick snap of the wrist. Skar cursed and came at him again, but Kaladin caught his arm and shoved him backward, causing Skar to stumble.

"Drehy, come help him," Kaladin said. "Moash, you too. Try to force me off balance."

The other two joined Skar. Kaladin stepped around the attacks, staying squarely in the middle of them, adjusting his stance to rebuff each attempt. He grabbed Drehy's arm and yanked him forward, nearly causing him to fall. He stepped into Skar's shoulder-rush, deflecting the weight of the man's body and throwing him backward. He pulled back as Moash got his arms on him, causing Moash to overbalance himself.

Kaladin remained completely unfazed, weaving between them and adjusting his center of balance by bending his knees and positioning his feet. "Combat begins with the legs," Kaladin said as he evaded the attacks. "I don't care how fast you are with a jab, how accurate you are with a thrust. If your opponent can trip you, or make you stumble, you'll lose. Losing means dying."

Several of the watching bridgemen tried to imitate Kaladin, crouching down. Skar, Drehy, and Moash had finally decided to try a coordinated rush, planning to all tackle Kaladin at once. Kaladin held up his hand. "Well done, you three." He motioned them back to stand with the others. They reluctantly broke off their attacks.

"I'm going to split you into pairs," Kaladin said. "We're going to spend all day today—and probably each day this week—working on stances. Learning to maintain one, learning to not lock your knees the moment you're threatened, learning to hold your center of balance. It will take time, but I promise you if we start here, you'll learn to be deadly far more quickly. Even if it seems that all you're doing at first is standing around."

The men nodded.

"Teft," Kaladin ordered. "Split them into pairs by size and weight, then run them through an elementary forward spear stance."

"Aye, sir!" Teft barked. Then he froze, realizing what he'd given away. The speed at which he'd responded made it obvious that Teft had been a soldier. Teft met Kaladin's eyes and saw that Kaladin knew. The older man scowled, but Kaladin returned a grin. He had a veteran under his command; that was going to make this all a lot easier.

Teft didn't feign ignorance, and easily fell into the role of the training sergeant, splitting the men into pairs, correcting their stances. *No wonder he never takes off that shirt,* Kaladin thought. *It probably hides a mess of scars.*

As Teft instructed the men, Kaladin pointed to Rock, gesturing him over.

"Yes?" Rock asked. The man was so broad of chest that his bridgeman's vest could barely fasten.

"You said something before," Kaladin said. "About fighting being beneath you?"

"Is true. I am not a fourth son."

"What does that have to do with it?"

"First son and second son are needed for making food," Rock said, raising a finger. "Is most important. Without food, nobody lives, yes? Third son is craftsman. This is me. I serve proudly. Only fourth son can be warrior. Warriors, they are not needed as much as food or crafts. You see?"

"Your profession is determined by your birth order?"

"Yes," Rock said proudly. "Is best way. On the Peaks, there is always food. Not every family has four sons. So not always is a soldier needed. I cannot fight. What man could do this thing before the *Uli'tekanaki*?"

Kaladin shot a glance at Syl. She shrugged, not seeming to care what Rock did. "All right," he said. "I've got something else I want you to do, then. Go grab Lopen, Dabbid . . ." Kaladin hesitated. "And Shen. Get him too."

Rock did so. Lopen was in the line, learning the stances, though Dabbid—as usual—stood off to the side, staring at nothing in particular. Whatever had taken him, it was far worse than ordinary battle shock. Shen stood beside him, hesitant, as if not certain of his place.

Rock pulled Lopen out of the line, then grabbed Dabbid and Shen and walked back to Kaladin.

"Gancho," Lopen said, with a lazy salute. "Guess I'll make a poor spearman, with one hand."

"That's all right," Kaladin said. "I have something else I need you to do. We'll see trouble from Gaz and our new captain—or at least his wife—if we don't bring back salvage."

"We three cannot do the work of thirty, Kaladin," Rock said, scratching at his beard. "Is not possible."

"Maybe not," Kaladin said. "But most of our time down in these chasms is spent looking for corpses that haven't been picked clean. I think we can work a lot faster. We *need* to work a lot faster, if we're going to train with the spear. Fortunately, we have an advantage."

He held out his hand, and Syl alighted on it. He'd spoken to her earlier, and she'd agreed to his plan. He didn't notice her doing anything special, but Lopen suddenly gasped. Syl had made herself visible to him.

"Ah . . ." Rock said, bowing in respect to Syl. "Like gathering reeds."

"Well flick my sparks," Lopen said. "Rock, you never said it was so pretty!"

Syl smiled broadly.

"Be respectful," Rock said. "Is not for you to speak of her in that way, little person."

The men knew about Syl, of course. Kaladin didn't speak of her, but they saw him talking to the air, and Rock had explained.

"Lopen," Kaladin said. "Syl can move far more quickly

than a bridgeman. She will search out places for you to gather, and you four can pick through things quickly."

"Dangerous," Rock said. "What if we meet chasmfiend while alone?"

"Unfortunately, we can't come back empty-handed. The *last* thing we want is Hashal deciding to send Gaz down to supervise."

Lopen snorted. "He'd never do that, gancho. Too much work down here."

"Too dangerous too," Rock added.

"Everyone says that," Kaladin said. "But I've never seen more than these scrapes on the walls."

"They're down here," Rock said. "Is not just legend. Just before you came, half a bridge crew was killed. Eaten. Most beasts come to the middle plateaus, but there are some who come this far."

"Well, I hate to put you in danger, but unless we try this, we'll have chasm duty taken from us and we'll end up cleaning latrines instead."

"All right, gancho," Lopen said. "I'll go."

"As will I," Rock said. "With *ali'i'kamura* to protect, perhaps it will be safe."

"I intend to teach you to fight eventually," Kaladin said. Then as Rock frowned, Kaladin hastily added, "You, Lopen, I mean. One arm doesn't mean you're useless. You'll be at a disadvantage, but there are things I can teach you to deal with that. Right now a scavenger is more important to us than another spear."

"Sounds swift to me." Lopen gestured to Dabbid, and the two walked over to gather sacks for the collecting. Rock moved to join them, but Kaladin took his arm.

"I haven't given up on finding an easier way out of here than fighting," Kaladin said to him. "If we never returned, Gaz and the others would probably just assume that a chasmfiend got us. If there's some way to reach the other side . . ."

Rock looked skeptical. "Many have searched for this thing."

"The eastern edge is open."

"Yes," Rock said, laughing, "and when you are able to travel that far without being eaten by chasmfiend or killed in floods, I shall name you my *kaluk'i'iki*."

Kaladin raised an eyebrow.

"Only a woman can be *kaluk'i'iki*," Rock said, as if that explained the joke.

"Wife?"

Rock laughed even louder. "No, no. Airsick lowlanders. Ha!"

"Great. Look, see if you can memorize the chasms, perhaps make a map of some kind. I suspect that most who come down here stick to the established routes. That means we're much more likely to find salvage down side passages; that's where I'll be sending Syl."

"Side passages?" Rock said, still amused. "One might begin to think you *want* me to be eaten. Ha, and by a greatshell. They are supposed to be tast*ed*, not tast*ing*."

"I—"

"No, no," Rock said. "Is a good plan. I only jest. I can be careful, and this will be good for me to do, since I do not wish to fight."

"Thank you. Maybe you'll happen upon a place we could climb out."

"I will do this thing," Rock said, nodding. "But we cannot simply climb out. The army has many scouts on the Plains. Is how they know when chasmfiends come to pupate, eh? They will see us, and we will not be able to cross chasms without bridge."

It was a good argument, unfortunately. Climb up here, and they'd be seen. Climb out in the middle, and they'd be stuck on plateaus without anywhere to go. Climb out closer to the Parshendi areas, and they'd be found by their scouts. That was assuming they *could* get out of the chasms. Though some were as shallow as forty or fifty feet, many were well over a hundred feet deep.

Syl zipped away to lead Rock and his crew, and Kaladin moved back to the main body of bridgemen to help Teft correct stances. It was difficult work; the first day always was. The bridgemen were sloppy and uncertain.

But they also showed remarkable resolve. Kaladin had never worked with a group who made fewer complaints. The bridgemen didn't ask for a break. They didn't shoot him resentful glances when he pushed them harder. The scowls they bore were at their own foibles, angry at themselves for not learning faster.

And they got it. After just a few hours, the more talented of them—Moash at the forefront—started to change into fighting men. Their stances grew firmer, more confident. When they should have been feeling exhausted and frustrated, they were more determined.

Kaladin stepped back, watching Moash fall into his stance after Teft shoved him. It was a resetting exercise—Moash would let Teft knock him backward, then would scramble back and set his feet. Time and time again. The purpose was to train oneself to revert to the stance without thinking. Kaladin normally wouldn't have started resetting exercises until the second or third day. Yet here, Moash was drinking it in after only two hours. There were two others—Drehy and Skar—who were nearly as quick to learn.

Kaladin leaned back against the stone wall. Cold water leaked down the rock beside him, and a frillbloom plant hesitantly opened its fanlike fronds beside his head: two wide, orange leaves, with spines on the tips, unfolding like opening fists.

Is it their bridgeman training? Kaladin wondered. *Or is it their passion?* He had given them a chance to fight back. That kind of opportunity changed a man.

Watching them stand resolute and capable in stances they had only just been taught, Kaladin realized something. These men—cast off by the army, forced to work themselves near to death, then fed extra food by Kaladin's careful planning—were the most fit, training-ready recruits he'd ever been given.

By seeking to beat them down, Sadeas had prepared them to excel.

*"Flame and char. Skin so terrible. Eyes like pits of black-
ness."*

—A quote from the *Iviad* probably needs no reference notation,
but this comes from line 482, should I need to locate it quickly.

S hallan awoke in a small white room.

She sat up, feeling oddly healthy. Bright sunlight illuminated the window's gossamer white shades, bursting through
the cloth and into the room. Shallan frowned, shaking her
muddled head. She felt as if she should be burned toes to ears,
her skin flaking off. But that was just a memory. She had the cut
on her arm, but otherwise she felt perfectly well.

A rustling sound. She turned to see a nurse hurrying away
down a white hallway outside; the woman had apparently seen
Shallan sit up, and was now taking the news to someone.

I'm in the hospital, Shallan thought. *Moved to a private
room.*

A soldier peeked in, inspecting Shallan. It was apparently
a guarded room.

"What happened?" she called to him. "I was poisoned,
wasn't I?" She felt a sudden shock of alarm. "Kabsal! Is he
all right?"

The guard just turned back to his post. Shallan began to

crawl out of bed, but he looked in again, glaring at her. She yelped despite herself, pulling up the sheet and settling back. She still wore one of the hospital robes, much like a soft bathing robe.

How long had she been unconscious? Why was she—

The Soulcaster! she realized. *I gave it back to Jasnah.*

The next half hour was one of the most miserable in Shallan's life. She spent it suffering the periodic glares of the guard and feeling nauseated. What had happened?

Finally, Jasnah appeared at the other end of the hallway. She was wearing a different dress, black with light grey piping. She strode toward the room like an arrow and dismissed the guard with a single word as she passed. The man hurried away, his boots louder on the stone floor than Jasnah's slippers.

Jasnah came in, and though she made no accusations, her glare was so hostile that Shallan wanted to crawl under her covers and hide. No. She wanted to crawl under the bed, dig down into the floor itself, and put stone between herself and those eyes.

She settled for looking downward in shame.

"You were wise to return the Soulcaster," Jasnah said, voice like ice. "It saved your life. *I* saved your life."

"Thank you," Shallan whispered.

"Who are you working with? Which devotary bribed you to steal the fabrial?"

"None of them, Brightness. I stole it of my own volition."

"Protecting them does you no good. Eventually you *will* tell me the truth."

"It is the truth," Shallan said, looking up, feeling a hint of defiance. "It's why I became your ward in the first place. To steal that Soulcaster."

"Yes, but for whom?"

"For *me*," Shallan said. "Is it so hard to believe that I could act for myself? Am I such a miserable failure that the only rational answer is to assume I was duped or manipulated?"

"You have no grounds to raise your voice to me, child,"

Jasnah said evenly. "And you have *every* reason to remember your place."

Shallan looked down again.

Jasnah was silent for a time. Finally, she sighed. "What were you *thinking*, child?"

"My father is dead."

"So?"

"He was not well liked, Brightness. Actually, he was *hated*, and our family is bankrupt. My brothers are trying to put up a strong front by pretending he still lives. But . . ." Dared she tell Jasnah that her father had possessed a Soulcaster? Doing so wouldn't help excuse what Shallan had done, and might get her family more deeply into trouble. "We needed something. An edge. A way to earn money quickly, or *create* money."

Jasnah was silent again. When she finally spoke, she sounded faintly amused. "You thought your salvation lay in enraging not only all the entire ardentia, but Alethkar? Do you realize what my brother would have done if he'd learned of this?"

Shallan looked away, feeling both foolish and ashamed.

Jasnah sighed. "Sometimes I forget how young you are. I can see how the theft might have looked tempting to you. It was stupid nonetheless. I've arranged passage back to Jah Keved. You will leave in the morning."

"I—" It was more than she deserved. "Thank you."

"Your friend, the ardent, is dead."

Shallan looked up, dismayed. "What happened?"

"The bread was poisoned. Backbreaker powder. Very lethal, dusted over the bread to look like flour. I suspect the bread was similarly treated every time he visited. His goal was to get me to eat a piece."

"But I ate a *lot* of that bread!"

"The jam had the antidote," Jasnah said. "We found it in several empty jars he'd used."

"It can't be!"

"I've begun investigating," Jasnah said. "I should have done so immediately. Nobody quite remembers where this 'Kabsal' came from. Though he spoke familiarly of the other ardents to you and me, they knew him only vaguely."

"Then he . . ."

"He was playing you, child. The whole time, he was using you to get to me. To spy on what I was doing, to kill me if he could." She spoke of it so evenly, so emotionlessly. "I believe he used much more of the powder during this last attempt, more than he'd ever used before, perhaps hoping to get me to breathe it in. He realized this would be his last opportunity. It turned against him, however, working more quickly than he'd anticipated."

Someone had almost killed her. Not someone, *Kabsal*. No wonder he'd been so eager to get her to taste the jam!

"I'm very disappointed in you, Shallan," Jasnah said. "I can see now why you tried to end your own life. It was the guilt."

She *hadn't* tried to kill herself. But what good would it do to admit that? Jasnah was taking pity on her; best not to give her reason not to. But what of the strange things Shallan had seen and experienced? Might Jasnah have an explanation for them?

Looking at Jasnah, seeing the cold rage hidden behind her calm exterior, frightened Shallan enough that her questions about the symbolheads and the strange place she'd visited died on her lips. How had Shallan ever thought of herself as brave? She wasn't brave. She was a fool. She remembered the times her father's rage had echoed through the house. Jasnah's quieter, more justified anger was no less daunting.

"Well, you will need to learn to live with your guilt," Jasnah said. "You might not have escaped with my fabrial, but you *have* thrown away a very promising career. This foolish scheme will stain your life for decades. No woman will take you as a ward now. You *threw it away*." She shook her head in distaste. "I hate being wrong."

With that, she turned to leave.

Shallan raised a hand. *I have to apologize. I have to say something.* "Jasnah?"

The woman did not look back, and the guard did not return.

Shallan curled up under the sheet, stomach in knots, feeling so sick that—for a moment—she wished that she'd actually dug that shard of glass in a little deeper. Or maybe that Jasnah hadn't been quick enough with the Soulcaster to save her.

She'd lost it all. No fabrial to protect her family, no wardship to continue her studies. No Kabsal. She'd never actually had him in the first place.

Her tears dampened the sheets as the sunlight outside faded, then vanished. Nobody came to check on her.

Nobody cared.

SAS NAHN

ONE YEAR AGO

Kaladin sat quietly in the waiting room of Amaram's wooden warcenter. It was constructed of a dozen sturdy sections that could be disconnected and pulled by chulls. Kaladin sat beside a window, looking out at the camp. There was a hole where Kaladin's squad had been housed. He could make it out from where he sat. Their tents had been broken down and given to other squads.

Four of his men remained. Four, out of twenty-six. And men called him lucky. Men called him Stormblessed. He'd begun to believe that.

I killed a Shardbearer today, he thought, mind numb. *Like Lanacin the Surefooted, or Evod Markmaker. Me. I killed one.*

And he didn't care.

He crossed his arms on the wooden windowsill. There was no glass in the window and he could feel the breeze. A windspren flitted from one tent to another. Behind Kaladin, the room had a thick red rug and shields on the walls. There were a number of padded wooden chairs, like the one Kaladin sat in. This was the "small" waiting chamber of the warcenter—small, yet larger than his entire house back in Hearthstone, the surgery included.

I killed a Shardbearer, he thought again. *And then I gave away the Blade and Plate.*

That single event had to be the most monumentally stupid thing anyone, in any kingdom, in any era, had ever done. As a Shardbearer, Kaladin would have been more important than Roshone—more important than Amaram. He'd have been able to go to the Shattered Plains and fight in a real war.

No more squabbling over borders. No more petty light-eyed captains belonging to unimportant families, bitter because they'd been left behind. He would never again have had to worry about blisters from boots that didn't fit, dinner slop that tasted of crem, or other soldiers who wanted to pick a fight.

He could have been rich. He'd given it all away, just like that.

And *still*, the mere thought of touching that Blade turned his stomach. He didn't want wealth, titles, armies, or even a good meal. He wanted to be able to go back and protect the men who had trusted him. Why had he chased after the Shardbearer? He should have run. But no, he'd insisted on charging at a storming *Shardbearer.*

You protected your highmarshal, he told himself. *You're a hero.*

But why was Amaram's life worth more than those of his men? Kaladin served Amaram because of the honor he had shown. He let spearmen share his comfort in the warcenter during highstorms, a different squad each storm. He insisted that his men be well fed and well paid. He didn't treat them like slime.

He did let his subordinates do so, though. And he'd broken his promise to shelter Tien.

So did I. So did I. . . .

Kaladin's insides were a twisted mess of guilt and sorrow. One thing remained clear, like a bright spot of light on the wall of a dark room. He wanted nothing to do with those Shards. He didn't even want to touch them.

The door thumped open, and Kaladin turned in his chair.

Amaram entered. Tall, lean, with a square face and long martial coat of deep green. He walked on a crutch. Kaladin eyed the wrappings and splint with a critical eye. *I could have done better.* He'd also have insisted that the patient remain in bed.

Amaram was talking to one of his stormwardens, a middle-aged man with a square beard and robes of deep black.

". . . why Thaidakar would risk this?" Amaram was saying, speaking in a soft voice. "But who else would it be? The Ghostbloods grow more bold. We'll need to find out who he was. Do we know anything about him?"

"He was Veden, Brightlord," the stormwarden said. "Nobody I recognize. But I will investigate."

Amaram nodded, falling silent. Behind the two, a group of lighteyed officers entered, one of them carrying the Shardblade, holding it on a pure white cloth. Behind this group came the four surviving members of Kaladin's squad: Hab, Reesh, Alabet, and Coreb.

Kaladin stood up, feeling exhausted. Amaram remained by the door, arms folded, as two final men entered and closed the door. These last two were also lighteyes, but lesser ones—officers in Amaram's personal guard. Had these been among those who had fled?

It was the smart thing to do, Kaladin thought. *Smarter than what I did.*

Amaram leaned on his walking staff, inspecting Kaladin with bright tan eyes. He'd been in conference with his counselors for several hours now, trying to discover who the Shardbearer had been. "You did a brave thing today, soldier," Amaram said to Kaladin.

"I . . ." What did you say to that? *I wish I'd left you to die, sir.* "Thank you."

"Everyone else fled, including my honor guard." The two men closest to the door looked down, ashamed. "But you charged in for the attack. Why?"

"I didn't really think about it, sir."

Amaram seemed displeased by the answer. "Your name is Kaladin, is it?"

"Yes, Brightlord. From Hearthstone? Remember?"

Amaram frowned, looking confused.

"Your cousin, Roshone, is citylord there. He sent my brother into the army when you came recruiting. I . . . I joined with my brother."

"Ah yes," Amaram said. "I believe I remember you." He didn't ask after Tien. "You still haven't answered my question. Why attack? It wasn't for the Shardblade. You rejected that."

"Yes, sir."

To the side, the stormwarden raised his eyebrows, as if he hadn't believed that Kaladin had turned down the Shards. The soldier holding the Shardblade kept glancing at it in awe.

"Why?" Amaram said. "Why did you reject it? I have to know."

"I don't want it, sir."

"Yes, but why?"

Because it would make me one of you. Because I can't look at that weapon and not see the faces of the men its wielder slaughtered so offhandedly.

Because . . . because . . .

"I can't really answer that, sir," Kaladin said, sighing.

The stormwarden walked over to the room's brazier, shaking his head. He began warming his hands.

"Look," Kaladin said. "Those Shards are mine. Well, I said to give them to Coreb. He's the highest ranked of my soldiers, and the best fighter among them." The other three would understand. Besides, Coreb would take care of them, once he was a lighteyes.

Amaram looked at Coreb, then nodded to his attendants. One closed the window shutters. The others pulled out swords, then began moving toward the four remaining members of Kaladin's squad.

Kaladin yelled, leaping forward, but two of the officers had positioned themselves close to him. One slammed a punch into Kaladin's gut as soon as he started moving. He was so surprised that it connected directly, and he gasped.

No.

He fought off the pain, turning to swing at the man. The man's eyes opened wide as Kaladin's fist connected, throwing him backward. Several other men piled on him. He had no weapons, and he was so tired from the battle that he could barely stay upright. They knocked him to the ground with punches to his side and back. He collapsed to the floor, pained, but still able to watch as the soldiers came at his men.

Reesh was cut down first. Kaladin gasped, stretching out a hand, struggling to his knees.

This can't happen. Please, no!

Hab and Alabet had their knives out, but fell quickly, one soldier gutting Hab as two others hacked down Alabet. Alabet's knife thumped as it hit the ground, followed by his arm, then finally his corpse.

Coreb lasted the longest, backing away, hands held forward. He didn't scream. He seemed to understand. Kaladin's eyes were watering, and soldiers grabbed him from behind, stopping him from helping.

Coreb fell to his knees and began to beg. One of Amaram's men took him at the neck, neatly severing his head. It was over in seconds.

"You bastard!" Kaladin said, gasping against his pain. "You storming bastard!" Kaladin found himself weeping, struggling uselessly at the four men holding him. The blood of the fallen spearmen soaked the boards.

They were dead. All of them were dead. Stormfather! All of them!

Amaram stepped forward, expression grim. He went down on one knee before Kaladin. "I'm sorry."

"Bastard!" Kaladin screamed as loud as he could.

"I couldn't risk them telling what they saw. This is what must be, soldier. It's for the good of the army. They're going to be told that your squad helped the Shardbearer. You see, the men must believe that *I* killed him."

"You're taking the Shards for yourself!"

"I am trained in the sword," Amaram said, "and am accustomed to plate. It will serve Alethkar best if I bear the Shards."

"You could have asked me for them! Storm you!"

"And when news got around camp?" Amaram said grimly. "That you'd killed the Shardbearer but I had the Shards? Nobody would believe that you'd given them up of your own free choice. Besides, son. You wouldn't have let me keep them." Amaram shook his head. "You'd have changed your mind. In a day or two, you'd have wanted the wealth and prestige—others would convince you of it. You'd have *demanded* that I return them to you. It took hours to decide, but Restares is right—this is what must be done. For the good of Alethkar."

"It's not about Alethkar! It's about you! Storm it, you're supposed to be better than the others!" Tears dripped from Kaladin's chin.

Amaram looked guilty suddenly, as if he knew what Kaladin had said was true. He turned away, waving to the stormwarden. The man turned from the brazier, holding something he'd been heating in the coals. A small branding iron.

"It's all an act?" Kaladin asked. "The honorable brightlord who cares about his men? Lies? All of it?"

"This *is* for my men," Amaram said. He took the Shardblade from the cloth, holding it in his hand. The gemstone at its pommel let out a flash of white light. "You can't begin to understand the weights I carry, spearman." Amaram's voice lost some of its calm tone of reason. He sounded defensive. "I can't worry about the lives of a few darkeyed spearmen when thousands of people may be saved by my decision."

The stormwarden stepped up to Kaladin, positioning the branding iron. The glyphs, reversed, read *sas nahn*. A slave's brand.

"You came for me," Amaram said, limping to the door, stepping around Reesh's body. "For saving my life, I spare yours. Five men telling the same story would have been believed, but a single slave will be ignored. The warcamp will be told that you didn't try to help your fellows—but you didn't try to stop them, either. You fled and were captured by my guard."

Amaram hesitated by the door, resting the blunt edge of the stolen Shardblade on his shoulder. The guilt was still there in his eyes, but he grew hard, covering it. "You are being discharged as a deserter and branded as a slave. But you are spared death by my mercy."

He opened the door and walked out.

The branding iron fell, searing Kaladin's fate into his skin. He let out a final, ragged scream.

THE END OF

Part Three

İNTERLUDES

◆ ◆
◆

BAXIL • GERANID • SZETH

BAXIL

Baxil hastened down the lavish palace corridor, clutching the bulky bag of tools. A sound like a footfall came from behind him and he jumped, spinning. He didn't see anything. The corridor was empty, a golden carpet lining the floor, mirrors on the walls, arched ceiling inlaid with elaborate mosaics.

"Would you *stop* that?" Av said, walking beside him. "Every time you jump I nearly cuff you one out of surprise."

"I can't help it," Baxil said. "Shouldn't we be doing this at night?"

"Mistress knows what she's doing," Av said. Like Baxil, Av was Emuli, with dark skin and hair. But the taller man was far more self-confident. He sauntered down the halls, acting as if they'd been invited, thick-bladed sword slung in a sheath over his shoulder.

If the Prime Kadasix may provide, Baxil thought, *I'd rather Av never have to draw that weapon. Thank you.*

Their mistress walked ahead of them, the only other person in the hallway. She wasn't Emuli—she didn't even seem Makabaki, though she had dark skin and long, beautiful black hair. She had eyes like a Shin, but she was tall and lean, like an Alethi. Av thought she was a mixed breed. Or so he said when they dared talk about such things. The mistress had good ears. Strangely good ears.

She stopped at the next intersection. Baxil caught himself

glancing over his shoulder again. Av elbowed him, but he couldn't help looking. Yes, the mistress claimed that the palace servants would be busy getting the new guest wing ready, but this was the home of Ashno of Sages himself. One of the richest and holiest men in all of Emul. He had hundreds of servants. What if one of them walked down this hallway?

The two men joined their mistress at the intersection. He forced his eyes forward so he wouldn't keep looking over his shoulder, but then found himself staring at the mistress. It was dangerous, being employed by a woman as beautiful as she was, with that long black hair, worn free, hanging down to her waist. She never wore a proper woman's robe, or even a dress or skirt. Always trousers, usually sleek and tight, a thin-bladed sword at her hip. Her eyes were so faintly violet they were almost white.

She was amazing. Wonderful, intoxicating, overwhelming.

Av elbowed him in the ribs again. Baxil jumped, then glared at his cousin, rubbing his belly.

"Baxil," the mistress said. "My tools."

He opened the bag, handing over a folded tool belt. It clinked as she took it, not looking at him, then she strode down the hallway to their left.

Baxil watched, uncomfortable. This was the Hallowed Hall, the place where a wealthy man placed images of his Kadasix for reverence. The mistress walked up to the first piece of art. The painting depicted Epan, Lady of Dreams. It was beautiful, a masterpiece of gold leaf on black canvas.

The mistress took a knife from her bundle and slashed the painting down the front. Baxil cringed, but said nothing. He'd almost gotten used to the casual way she destroyed art, though he was baffled by it. She did pay the two of them very well, however.

Av leaned back against the wall, picking his teeth with a fingernail. Baxil tried to imitate his relaxed pose. The large hallway was lit with topaz chips set in beautiful chandeliers, but they made no move to take them. The mistress did not approve of stealing.

"I've been thinking of seeking the Old Magic," Baxil

said, partially to keep himself from cringing as the mistress moved on to gouge out the eyes of a fine bust.

Av snorted. "Why?"

"I don't know," Baxil said. "Seems like something to do with myself. I've never sought it, you know, and they say every man gets one chance. Ask a boon of the Nightwatcher. Have you used yours?"

"Nah," Av said. "Don't fancy making the trip all the way to the Valley. Besides, my brother went. Came back with two numb hands. Never could feel anything with them again."

"What was his boon?" Baxil asked as the mistress wrapped up a vase with a cloth, then quietly shattered it on the floor and crushed the pieces.

"Don't know," Av said. "He never said. Seemed embarrassed. Probably asked for something silly, like a good haircut." Av smirked.

"I was thinking I'd make myself more useful," Baxil said. "Ask for courage, you know?"

"If you want," Av replied. "I figure there are better ways than the Old Magic. You never know what kind of curse you'll end up with."

"I could phrase my request perfectly," Baxil said.

"Doesn't work that way," Av said. "It's not a game, no matter how the stories try to put it. The Nightwatcher doesn't trick you or twist your words. You ask a boon. She gives what *she* feels you deserve, then gives you a curse to go along with it. Sometimes related, sometimes not."

"And you're an expert?" Baxil asked. The mistress was slashing another painting. "I thought you said you never went."

"I didn't," Av said. "On account of my father going, my mother going, and each of my brothers going. A few got what they wanted. Most all of them regretted the curse, save my father. He got a heap of good cloth; sold it to keep us from starving during the lurnip famine a few decades ago."

"What was his curse?" Baxil said.

"Saw the world upside down from then on."

"Really?"

"Yeah," Av said. "Twisted all about. Like people walk on

the ceilings and the sky was underneath him. Said he got used to it pretty quickly, though, and didn't really think it a curse by the time he died."

Even thinking about that curse made Baxil feel sick. He looked down at his sack of tools. If he weren't such a coward, would he—maybe—be able to convince the mistress to see him as something more than just hired muscle?

If the Prime Kadasix could provide, he thought, *it would be very nice if I could know the right thing to do. Thank you.*

The mistress returned, hair somewhat disheveled. She held out a hand. "Padded mallet, Baxil. There's a full statue back there."

He responded, pulling the mallet out of the sack and handing it to her.

"Perhaps I should get myself a Shardblade," she said absently, putting the tool up on her shoulder. "But that might make this too easy."

"I wouldn't mind if it were too easy, mistress," Baxil noted.

She sniffed, walking back down the hallway. Soon she began to pound on a statue at the far end, breaking off its arms. Baxil winced. "Someone's *going* to hear that."

"Yeah," Av said. "Probably why she waited to do it last."

At least the pounding was muffled by the padding. They had to be the only thieves who sneaked into the homes of rich men without taking anything.

"Why *does* she do this, Av?" Baxil found himself asking.

"Don't know. Maybe you should ask her."

"I thought you said I should never do that!"

"Depends," Av said. "How attached to your limbs are you?"

"Rather attached."

"Well, if you ever want that changed, start asking the mistress prying questions. Until then, shut up."

Baxil said nothing further. *The Old Magic,* he thought. *It could change me. I will go looking for it.*

Knowing his luck, though, he wouldn't be able to find it. He sighed, resting back against the wall as muted thuds continued to come from the mistress's direction.

GERANID

I'm thinking of changing my Calling," Ashir said from behind.

Geranid nodded absently as she worked on her equations. The small stone room smelled sharply of spices. Ashir was trying another new experiment. It involved some kind of curry powder and a rare Shin fruit that he'd caramelized. Something like that. She could hear it sizzling on his new fabrial hotplate.

"I'm tired of cooking," Ashir continued. He had a soft, kindly voice. She loved him for that. Partially because he liked to talk—and if you were going to have someone talk while you were attempting to think, they might as well have a soft, kindly voice.

"I don't have *passion* for it as I once did," he continued. "Besides, what good will a cook be in the Spiritual Realm?"

"Heralds need food," she said absently, scratching out a line on her writing board, then scribbling another line of numbers beneath it.

"Do they?" Ashir asked. "I've never been convinced. Oh, I've read the speculations, but it just doesn't seem rational to me. The body must be fed in the Physical Realm, but the spirit exists in a completely different state."

"A state of ideals," she replied. "So, you could create ideal foods, perhaps."

"Hmm . . . What would be the fun in that? No experimentation."

"I could do without," she said, leaning forward to inspect the room's hearth, where two flamespren danced on the logs' fire. "If it meant never again having to eat something like that green soup you made last month."

"Ah," he said, sounding wistful. "That was something, wasn't it? Completely revolting, yet made entirely from appetizing ingredients." He seemed to consider it a personal triumph. "I wonder if they eat in the Cognitive Realm. Is a food there what it sees itself as being? I'll have to read and see if anyone has ever eaten while visiting Shadesmar."

Geranid responded with a noncommittal grunt, getting out her calipers and leaning closer to the heat to measure the flamespren. She frowned, then made another notation.

"Here, love," Ashir said, walking over, then knelt beside her and offered a small bowl. "Give this a try. I think you'll like it."

She eyed the contents. Bits of bread covered with a red sauce. It was men's food, but they were both ardents, so that didn't matter.

From outside came the sounds of waves gently lapping against the rocks. They were on a tiny Reshi island, technically sent to provide for the religious needs of any Vorin visitors. Some travelers did come to them for that, occasionally even some of the Reshi. But really, this was a way of getting away and focusing on their experiments. Geranid with her spren studies. Ashir with his chemistry—through cooking, of course, as it allowed him to eat the results.

The portly man smiled affably, head shaven, grey beard neatly squared off. They both kept to the rules of their stations, despite their seclusion. One did not write the ending of a lifetime of faith with a sloppy last chapter.

"No green," she noted, taking the bowl. "That's a good sign."

"Hmmm," he said, leaning down and adjusting his spectacles to inspect her notations. "Yes. It really was fascinating the way that Shin vegetable caramelized. I'm so pleased that

Gom brought it to me. You'll have to go over my notes. I think I got the figures right, but I could be wrong." He wasn't as strong at mathematics as he was at theory. Conveniently, Geranid was just the opposite.

She took a spoon and tried the food. She didn't wear a sleeve on her safehand—another one of the advantages of being an ardent. The food was actually quite good. "Did you *try* this, Ashir?"

"Nope," he said, still looking over her figures. "You're the brave one, my dear."

She sniffed. "It's terrible."

"I can see that from how you're taking another large bite at this moment."

"Yes, but you'd hate it. No fruit. Is this fish you added?"

"A dried handful of the little minnows I caught outside this morning. Still don't know what species they are. Tasty, though." He hesitated, then looked up at the hearth and its spren. "Geranid, what *is* this?"

"I think I've had a breakthrough," she said softly.

"But the figures," he said, tapping the writing board. "You said they were erratic, and they still are."

"Yes," she said, narrowing her eyes at the flamespren. "But I can predict when they will be erratic and when they won't be."

He looked at her, frowning.

"The spren change when I measure them, Ashir," she said. "Before I measure, they dance and vary in size, luminosity, and shape. But when I make a notation, they immediately freeze in their current state. Then they remain that way permanently, so far as I can tell."

"What does it mean?" he asked.

"I'm hoping you'll be able to tell me. I have the figures. You've got the imagination, dear one."

He scratched at his beard, sitting back, and produced a bowl and spoon for himself. He'd sprinkled dried fruit over his portion; Geranid was half convinced he'd joined the ardentia because of his sweet tooth. "What happens if you erase the figures?" he asked.

"The spren go back to being variable," she said. "Length, shape, luminosity."

He took a bite of his mush. "Go into the other room."

"What?"

"Just do it. Take your writing board."

She sighed, standing up, joints popping. Was she getting *that* old? Starlight, but they'd spent a long time out on this island. She walked to the other room, where their cot was.

"What now?" she called.

"I'm going to measure the spren with your calipers," he called back. "I'll take three measurements in a row. Only write down one of the figures I give you. Don't tell me which one you're writing down."

"All right," she called back. The window was open, and she looked out over a darkening, glassy expanse of water. The Reshi Sea wasn't as shallow as the Purelake, but it was quite warm most of the time, dotted with tropical islands and the occasional monster of a greatshell.

"Three inches, seven tenths," Ashir called.

She didn't write down the figure.

"Two inches, eight tenths."

She ignored the number this time too, but got her chalk ready to write—as quietly as possible—the next numbers he called out.

"Two inches, three ten—Wow."

"What?" she called.

"It stopped changing sizes. I assume you wrote down that third number?"

She frowned, walking back into their small living chamber. Ashir's hotplate sat on a low table to her right. After the Reshi style, there were no chairs, just cushions, and all the furniture was flat and long, rather than tall.

She approached the hearth. One of the two flamespren danced about atop a log, shape changing and length flickering like the flames themselves. The other had taken on a far more stable shape. Its length no longer changed, though its form did slightly.

It seemed *locked* somehow. It almost looked like a little

person as it danced over the fire. She reached up and erased her notation. It immediately began pulsing and changing erratically like the other one.

"Wow," Ashir repeated. "It's as if it knows, somehow, that it has been measured. As if merely *defining* its form traps it somehow. Write down a number."

"What number?"

"Any number," he said. "But one that might be the size of a flamespren."

She did so. Nothing happened.

"You have to *actually* measure it," he said, tapping his spoon softly against the side of his bowl. "No pretending."

"I wonder at the precision of the instrument," she said. "If I use one that is less precise, will that give the spren more flexibility? Or is there a threshold, an accuracy beyond which it finds itself bound?" She sat down, feeling daunted. "I need to research this more. Try it for luminosity, then compare that to my general equation of flamespren luminosity as compared to the fire they're drawn to dance around."

Ashir grimaced. "That, my dear, sounds a lot like math."

"Indeed."

"Then I shall make you a snack to occupy you while you create new marvels of calculation and genius." He smiled, kissing her forehead. "You just found something wonderful," he said more softly. "I don't know what it means yet, but it might very well change everything we understand about spren. And maybe even about fabrials."

She smiled, turning back to her equations. And for once, she didn't mind at all as he began chatting about his ingredients, working out a new formula for some sugary confection he was *sure* she'd love.

DEATH WEARS WHITE

Szeth-son-son-Vallano, Truthless of Shinovar, spun between the two guards as their eyes burned out. They slumped quietly to the floor. With three quick strokes, he slashed his Shardblade through the hinges and latch of the grand door. Then he took a deep breath, absorbing the Stormlight from a pouch of gemstones at his waist. He burst alight with renewed power and kicked the door with the force of a Light-enhanced foot.

It flew backward into the room, hinges no longer holding it in place, then crashed to the floor, skidding on the stone. The large feast hall inside was filled with people, crackling hearths, and clattering plates. The heavy door slid to a halt, and the room grew quiet.

I am sorry, he thought. Then he dashed in to start the slaughter.

Chaos ensued. Screams, yells, panic. Szeth leaped atop the nearest dining table and started spinning, cutting down everyone nearby. As he did so, he made certain to listen to the sounds of the dying. He did not shut his ears to the screams. He did not ignore the wails of pain. He paid attention to each and every one.

And hated himself.

He moved forward, leaping from table to table, wielding his Shardblade, a god of burning Stormlight and death.

"Armsmen!" yelled the lighteyed man at the edge of the room. "Where are my armsmen!" Thick of waist and shoulder, the man had a square brown beard and a prominent nose. King Hanavanar of Jah Keved. Not a Shardbearer, though some rumors said that he secretly kept a Shardblade.

Near Szeth, men and women scrambled away, stumbling over one another. He dropped among them, his white clothing rippling. He cut through a man who was drawing his sword—but also sliced through three women who wanted only to escape. Eyes burned and bodies collapsed.

Szeth reached behind himself, infusing the table he'd leaped from, then Lashing it to the far wall with a Basic Lashing, the type that changed which direction was down. The large wooden table fell to the side, tumbling into people, causing more screams and more pain.

Szeth found himself crying. His orders were simple. Kill. Kill as you have never killed before. Lay the innocent screaming at your feet and make the lighteyes weep. Do so wearing white, so all know who you are. Szeth did not object. It was not his place. He was Truthless.

And he did as his masters demanded.

Three lighteyed men got up the nerve to attack him, and Szeth raised his Shardblade in salute. They screamed battle cries as they charged. He was silent. A flick of his wrist cut the blade from the first one's sword. The length of metal spun in the air as Szeth stepped between the other two, his Blade swishing through their necks. They dropped in tandem, eyes shriveling. Szeth struck the first man from behind, ramming the Blade through his back and out his chest.

The man dropped forward—a hole in his shirt, but his skin unmarred. As he hit the floor, his severed sword blade clanged to the stones beside him.

Another group came at Szeth from the side, and he drew Stormlight into his hand and flung it in a Full Lashing across the floor at their feet. This was the Lashing that bonded objects; when the men crossed it, their shoes stuck to the floor. They tripped, and found their hands and bodies Lashed to the floor as well. Szeth stepped through them mournfully, striking.

The king edged away, as if to round the chamber and escape. Szeth sprayed a table's top with a Full Lashing, then infused the entire thing with a Basic Lashing as well, pointed at the doorway. The table flipped into the air and crashed against the exit—the side bearing the Full Lashing sticking it to the wall. People tried to pry it out of the way, but that only made them bunch up as Szeth waded into them, Shardblade sweeping.

So many deaths. Why? What purpose did it fulfill?

When he'd assaulted Alethkar six years before, he'd thought that had been a massacre. He hadn't known what a true massacre was. He reached the door and found himself standing over the bodies of some thirty people, his emotions caught up in the tempest of Stormlight within him. He hated that Stormlight, suddenly, as much as he hated himself. As much as the cursed Blade he held.

And . . . and the king. Szeth spun on the man. Irrationally, his confused, broken mind blamed this man. Why had he called a feast on this night? Why couldn't he have retired early? Why had he invited so many people?

Szeth charged at the king. He passed the dead, who lay twisted on the floor, burned-out eyes staring in lifeless accusation. The king cowered behind his high table.

That high table shuddered, quivering oddly.

Something was wrong.

Instinctively, Szeth Lashed himself to the ceiling. From his viewpoint, the room flipped, and the floor was now the ceiling. Two figures burst out from beneath the king's table. Two men in Plate, carrying Shardblades, swinging.

Twisting in the air, Szeth evaded their swings, then Lashed himself back to the floor, landing on the king's table just as the king summoned a Shardblade. So the rumors were true.

The king struck, but Szeth jumped backward, landing beyond the Shardbearers. Outside, he could hear footfalls. Szeth glanced to see men pouring into the room. The newcomers carried distinctive, diamond-shaped shields. Half-shards. Szeth had heard of the new fabrials, capable of stopping a Shardblade.

"You think I didn't know you were coming?" the king yelled at him. "After you killed three of my highprinces? We're ready for you, assassin." He lifted something from beneath the table. Another of those half-shard shields. They were made of metal embedded with a gemstone hidden at the back.

"You are a fool," Szeth said, Stormlight leaking from his mouth.

"Why?" the king called. "You think I should have run?"

"No," Szeth replied, meeting his eyes. "Because you set a trap for me during a feast. And now I can blame you for their deaths."

The soldiers fanned out through the room while the two fully armored Shardbearers stepped toward him, Blades out. The king smiled.

"So let it be," Szeth said, breathing deeply, sucking in the Stormlight of the many gemstones tied in the pouches at his waist. The Light began to rage within him, like a highstorm in his chest, burning and screaming. He breathed in more than he'd ever held before, holding it until he was barely able to keep the Stormlight from ripping him apart.

Were those still tears in his eyes? Would that they could hide his crimes. He yanked the strap free at his waist, releasing his belt and the heavy spheres.

Then he dropped his Shardblade.

His opponents froze in shock as his Blade vanished to mist. Who would drop a Shardblade in the middle of a battle? It defied reason.

And so did Szeth.

You are a work of art, Szeth-son-Neturo. A god.

It was time to see.

The soldiers and Shardbearers charged. Mere heartbeats before they reached him, Szeth spun into motion, liquid tempest in his veins. He dodged between the initial sword strikes, spinning into the midst of the soldiers. Holding this much Stormlight made it easier to infuse things; the light wanted out, and it pushed against his skin. In this state, the Shardblade would only be a distraction. Szeth himself was the real weapon.

He grabbed the arm of an attacking soldier. It took only an instant to infuse and Lash him upward. The man cried out, falling into the air as Szeth ducked another sword thrust. He touched the attacker's leg, inhumanly lithe. With a look and a blink, he Lashed that man to the ceiling as well.

Soldiers cursed, slashing at him, their bulky half-shards suddenly becoming hindrances as Szeth moved among them, graceful as a skyeel, touching arms, legs, shoulders, sending a dozen, then two dozen, men flying in all directions. Most went up, but he sent a barrage of them toward the approaching Shardbearers, who cried out as squirming bodies smashed into them.

He jumped backward as a squad of soldiers came at him, Lashing himself to the far wall and spinning into the air. The room changed orientations, and he landed on the wall—which was now down for him. He ran along it toward the king, who waited behind his Shardbearers.

"Kill him!" the king said. "Storm you all! What are you doing? Kill him!"

Szeth leaped off the wall, Lashing himself downward as he flipped, landing with one knee on the dining table. Silverware and plates clinked as he grabbed a dining knife and infused once, twice, three times. He used a triple Basic Lashing, pointing it in the direction of the king, then dropped it and Lashed himself backward.

He lurched away as one of the Shardbearers struck, cutting the table in half. Szeth's released knife fell far more quickly than it should have, flashing toward the king. He barely got his shield up in time, eyes wide as the knife clanged against the metal.

Damnation, Szeth thought, Lashing himself upward with a quarter of a Basic Lashing. That didn't pull him upward, it just made him much lighter. A quarter of his weight was now pulled upward instead of downward. In essence, he became half as heavy as he had been.

He twisted, white clothing flapping gracefully as he dropped amid the common soldiers. Soldiers he'd Lashed earlier began to fall from the high ceiling, their Stormlight running out. A rain of broken bodies, crashing one by one to the floor.

Szeth came at the soldiers again. Some men fell as he sent others flying. Their expensive shields clanged to the stones, falling from dead or stunned fingers. Soldiers tried to reach him, but Szeth danced between them, using the ancient martial art of kammar, which used only the hands. It was meant as a less deadly form of fighting, focused on grabbing enemies and using their weight against them, immobilizing them.

It was also ideal when one wanted to touch and infuse someone.

He was the storm. He was destruction. At his will, men flipped into the air, fell, and died. He swept outward, touching a table and Lashing it upward with half a Basic Lashing. With half its mass pulled upward, half downward, it became weightless. Szeth sprayed it with a Full Lashing, then kicked it toward the soldiers; they stuck to it, their clothing and skin bonding to the wood.

A Shardblade hissed through the air beside him, and Szeth exhaled lightly, Stormlight rising from his lips as he ducked out of the way. The two Shardbearers attacked as bodies fell from above, but Szeth was too quick, too limber. The Shardbearers didn't work together. They were accustomed to dominating a battlefield or dueling with a single enemy. Their powerful weapons made them sloppy.

Szeth ran on light feet, held to the ground only half as much as other men. He easily leaped another swipe, Lashing himself to the ceiling to give himself just a little more lift before quarter-Lashing to make himself weighted down again. The result was an effortless leap of ten feet into the air.

The missed swing hit the ground and cut through the belt he'd dropped earlier, opening one of his large pouches. Spheres and bare gemstones sprayed across the floor. Some infused. Some dun. Szeth pulled Stormlight from those that rolled close.

Behind the Shardbearers, the king himself approached, weapon ready. He should have tried to run.

The two Shardbearers swung their oversized Blades at

Szeth. He spun away from the attacks, reaching out and snatching a shield from the air as it tumbled toward the ground. The man who had been holding it crashed to the floor a second later.

Szeth leaped at one of the Shardbearers—a man in gold armor—deflecting his weapon with the shield and pushing past him. The other man, whose Plate was red, swung too. Szeth caught the Blade on his shield, which cracked, barely holding. Still pushing it against the Blade, Szeth Lashed himself behind the Shardbearer while jumping forward.

The move flipped Szeth up and over the man. Szeth went on, falling toward the far wall as the second wave of soldiers began to drop to the floor. One crashed into the Shardbearer in red, making him stumble.

Szeth hit the wall, landing against the stones. He was so full of Stormlight. So much power, so much life, so much terrible, terrible destruction.

Stone. It was sacred. He never thought about that anymore. How could anything be sacred to him, now?

As bodies crashed into the Shardbearers, he knelt and placed his hand on a large stone in the wall before him, infusing it. He Lashed it time and time again in the direction of the Shardbearers. Once, twice, ten times, fifteen times. He kept pouring Stormlight into it. It glowed brightly. Mortar cracked. Stone ground against stone.

The red Shardbearer turned just as the massive, infused rock fell toward him, moving with twenty times the normal acceleration of a falling stone. It crashed into him, shattering his breastplate, spraying molten bits in all directions. The block hurled him across the room, crushing him against the far wall. He did not move.

Szeth was nearly out of Stormlight now. He quarter-Lashed himself to reduce his weight, then loped across the ground. Men were crushed, broken, dead around him. Spheres rolled on the floor, and he drew in their Stormlight. The Light streamed up, like the souls of those he had killed, infusing him.

He began to run. The other Shardbearer stumbled backward, holding up his Blade, stepping onto the wood of a shattered tabletop, the legs of which had broken free. The king finally realized his trap was failing. He started to flee.

Ten heartbeats, Szeth thought. *Return to me, you creation of Damnation.*

Szeth's heartbeats began to thump in his ears. He screamed—Light bursting from his mouth like radiant smoke—and threw himself to the ground as the Shardbearer swung. Szeth Lashed himself toward the far wall, skidding through the Shardbearer's legs. He immediately Lashed himself upward.

He soared into the air as the Shardbearer rounded on him again. But Szeth wasn't there. He Lashed himself back downward, dropping behind the Shardbearer to land on the broken tabletop. He stooped and infused it. A man in Shardplate might be protected from Lashings, but the things he stood upon were not.

Szeth Lashed the plank upward with a multiple Lashing. It lurched into the air, tossing aside the Shardbearer like a toy soldier. Szeth himself stayed atop the board, riding it upward in a rush of air. As it reached the lofty ceiling he threw himself off, Lashing himself downward once, twice, three times.

The tabletop crashed to the ceiling. Szeth fell with incredible speed toward the Shardbearer, who lay dazed on his back.

Szeth's Blade formed in his fingers just as he hit, driving the weapon down through Shardplate. The breastplate exploded and the Blade sank deeply through the man's chest and into the floor underneath.

Szeth stood, pulling his Shardblade free. The fleeing king looked over his shoulder with a cry of disbelieving horror. Both of his Shardbearers had fallen in a matter of seconds. The last of the soldiers nervously moved in to protect his retreat.

Szeth had stopped crying. It seemed like he couldn't cry any longer. He felt numb. His mind . . . it just couldn't think. He hated the king. Hated him so badly. And it hurt, physically hurt him, how strong that irrational hatred was.

Stormlight rising from him, he Lashed himself toward the king.

He fell, feet just above the ground, as if he were floating.

His clothing rippled. To those guards still alive, he would seem to be gliding across the ground.

He Lashed himself downward at a slight angle and began to swing his Blade as he reached the ranks of the soldiers. He ran through them as if he were moving down a steep slope. Swirling and spinning, he dropped a dozen men, graceful and terrible, drawing in more Stormlight from spheres that had been scattered on the floor.

Szeth reached the doorway, men with burning eyes falling to the ground behind him. Just outside, the king ran amid a final small group of guards. He turned and cried out as he saw Szeth, then threw up his half-shard shield.

Szeth wove through the guards, then hit the shield twice, shattering it and forcing the king backward. The man tripped, dropping his Blade. It puffed away to mist.

Szeth leaped up and Lashed himself downward with a double Basic Lashing. He hit atop the king, his increased weight breaking an arm and pinning the man to the ground. Szeth swept his Blade through the surprised soldiers, who fell as their legs died beneath them.

Finally, Szeth raised his Blade over his head, looking down at the king.

"What are you?" the man whispered, eyes watering with pain.

"Death," Szeth said, then drove his Blade point-first through the man's face and into the rock below.

PART

FOUR

Storm's Illumination

DALINAR • KALADIN • ADOLIN • NAVANI

*"I'm standing over the body of a brother. I'm weeping. Is
that his blood or mine? What have we done?"*

—Dated Vevanev, 1173, 107 seconds pre-death. Subject: an out-
of-work Veden sailor.

Father," Adolin said, pacing in Dalinar's sitting room. "This
is *insane*."

"That is appropriate," Dalinar replied dryly. "As—it appears—I am as well."

"I never claimed you were insane."

"Actually," Renarin noted, "I believe that you did."

Adolin glanced at his brother. Renarin stood beside the
hearth, inspecting the new fabrial that had been installed there
just a few days ago. The infused ruby, encased in a metal
enclosure, glowed softly and gave off a comfortable heat. It
was convenient, though it felt wrong to Adolin that no fire lay
crackling there.

The three were alone in Dalinar's sitting room, awaiting
the advent of the day's highstorm. It had been one week since
Dalinar had informed his sons of his intention to step down
as highprince.

Adolin's father sat in one of his large, high-backed chairs,
hands laced before him, stoic. The warcamps didn't know of

his decision yet—bless the Heralds—but he intended to make the announcement soon. Perhaps at tonight's feast.

"All right, fine," Adolin said. "Perhaps I said it. But I didn't mean it. Or at least I didn't mean for it to have this effect on you."

"We had this discussion a week ago, Adolin," Dalinar said softly.

"Yes, and you promised to think over your decision!"

"I have. My resolve has not wavered."

Adolin continued to pace; Renarin stood up straight, watching him as he stalked past. *I'm a fool*, Adolin thought. *Of* course *this is what Father would do. I should have seen it.*

"Look," Adolin said, "just because you might have some problems doesn't mean you have to abdicate."

"Adolin, our enemies will use my weakness against us. In fact, you believe that they are *already* doing so. If I don't give up the princedom now, matters could grow much worse than they are now."

"But I don't *want* to be highprince," Adolin complained. "Not yet, at least."

"Leadership is rarely about what we want, son. I think too few among the Alethi elite realize that fact."

"And what will happen to you?" Adolin asked, pained. He stopped and looked toward his father.

Dalinar was so *firm*, even sitting there, contemplating his own madness. Hands clasped before him, wearing a stiff blue uniform with a coat of Kholin blue, silver hair dusting his temples. Those hands of his were thick and callused, his expression determined. Dalinar made a decision and stuck to it, not wavering or debating.

Mad or not, he was what Alethkar needed. And Adolin had—in his haste—done what no warrior on the battlefield had ever been able to do: chop Dalinar Kholin's legs out from under him and send him away in defeat.

Oh, Stormfather, Adolin thought, stomach twisting in pain. *Jezerezeh, Kelek, and Ishi, Heralds above. Let me find a way to right this. Please.*

"I will return to Alethkar," Dalinar said. "Though I hate

to leave our army here down a Shardbearer. Could I . . . but no, I could not give them up."

"Of course not!" Adolin said, aghast. A Shardbearer, giving up his Shards? It almost never happened unless the Bearer was too weak and sickly to use them.

Dalinar nodded. "I have long worried that our homeland is in danger, now that every single Shardbearer fights out here on the Plains. Well, perhaps this change of winds is a blessing. I will return to Kholinar and aid the queen, make myself useful fighting against border incursions. Perhaps the Reshi and the Vedens will be less likely to strike against us if they know that they'd be facing a full Shardbearer."

"That's possible," Adolin said. "But they could also escalate and start sending a Shardbearer of their own on raids."

That seemed to worry his father. Jah Keved was the only other kingdom in Roshar that owned a substantial number of Shards, nearly as many as Alethkar. There hadn't been a direct war between them in centuries. Alethkar had been too divided, and Jah Keved was little better. But if the two kingdoms clashed in force, it would be a war the like of which hadn't been seen since the days of the Hierocracy.

Distant thunder rumbled outside, and Adolin turned sharply toward Dalinar. His father remained in his chair, staring westward, away from the storm. "We will continue this discussion afterward," Dalinar said. "For now, you two should tie my arms to the chair."

Adolin grimaced, but did as he was told without complaint.

⁘

Dalinar blinked, looking around. He was on the battlement of a single-walled fortress. Crafted from large blocks of deep red stone, the wall was sheer and straight. It was built across a rift in the leeward side of a tall rock formation overlooking an open plain of stone, like a wet leaf stuck across a crack in a boulder.

These visions feel so real, Dalinar thought, glancing at the spear he held in his hand and then down at his antiquated uniform: a cloth skirt and leather jerkin. It was hard to remember that he was really sitting in his chair, arms tied down. He couldn't feel the ropes or hear the highstorm.

He considered waiting out the vision, doing nothing. If this wasn't real, why should he participate? Yet he didn't completely believe—*couldn't* completely believe—that he was coming up with these delusions on his own. His decision to abdicate to Adolin was motivated by his doubts. Was he mad? Was he misinterpreting? At the very least, he could no longer trust himself. He didn't know what was real and what wasn't. In such a situation a man should step down from his authority and sort things through.

Either way, he felt he needed to *live* these visions, not ignore them. A desperate piece of him still hoped to come to a solution before he had to abdicate formally. He didn't let that piece gain too much control—a man had to do what was right. But Dalinar would give it this much: He would treat the vision as real while he was part of it. If there were secrets to be found here, only by playing along would he find them.

He looked about him. What was he being shown this time, and why? The spearhead on his weapon was of good steel, though his cap appeared to be bronze. One of the six men with him on the wall wore a breastplate of bronze; two others had poorly patched leather uniforms, sliced and resewn with wide stitches.

The other men lounged about, idly looking out over the wall. *Guard duty,* Dalinar thought, stepping up and scanning the landscape outside. This rock formation was at the end of an enormous plain—the perfect situation for a fortress. No army could approach without being seen long before its arrival.

The air was cold enough that clumps of ice clung to the stone in shadowed corners. The sunlight did little to dispel the cold, and the weather explained the lack of grass; the blades would be retracted into their holes, awaiting the relief of spring weather.

Dalinar pulled his cloak closer, prompting one of his companions to do the same.

"Storming weather," the man muttered. "How long's it going to last? Been eight weeks already."

Eight weeks? Forty days of winter at once? That was rare. Despite the cold, the other three soldiers looked anything but engaged by their guard duties. One was even dozing.

"Stay alert," Dalinar chided them.

They glanced at him, the one who had been dozing blinking awake. All three seemed incredulous. One—a tall, red-haired man—scowled. "This from you, Leef?"

Dalinar bit back a retort. Who did they see him as?

The chill air made his breath steam, and from behind him he could hear metal clanging as men worked at forges and anvils below. The gates to the fortress were closed, and the archer towers were manned to the left and right. They were at war, but guard duty was always boring work. It took well trained soldiers to remain alert for hours on end. Perhaps that was why there were so many soldiers here; if the quality of eyes watching could not be assured, then quantity would serve.

However, Dalinar had an advantage. The visions never showed him episodes of idle peace; they threw him into times of conflict and change. Turning points. So it was that, despite dozens of other eyes watching, he was the first to spot it.

"There!" he said, leaning out over the side of the rough-stone crenellation. "What is that?"

The redheaded man raised a hand, shading his eyes. "Nothing. A shadow."

"No, it's moving," said one of the others. "Looks like people. Marching."

Dalinar's heart began to thump in anticipation as the red-haired man called the alert. More archers rushed onto the battlement, stringing bows. Soldiers gathered in the ruddy courtyard below. Everything was made of that same red rock, and Dalinar caught one of the men referring to this place as "Feverstone Keep." He'd never heard of it.

Scouts galloped from the keep on horses. Why didn't they have outriders already?

"It has to be the rear defense force," one soldier muttered.

"They can't have gotten through our lines. Not with the Radiants fighting. . . ."

Radiants? Dalinar stepped closer to listen, but the man gave him a scowl and turned away. Whoever Dalinar was, the others didn't much care for him.

Apparently, this keep was a fallback position behind the front lines of a war. So either that approaching force was friendly, or the enemy had punched through and sent an advance element to besiege the keep. These were reserves, then, which was probably why they had been left with few horses. They still should have had outriders.

When the scouts finally did gallop back to the keep, they bore white flags. Dalinar glanced at his companions, confirming his suspicions as they relaxed. White meant friends. Yet would he have been sent here if it were that simple? If it *was* just in his mind, would it fabricate a simple, boring vision when it never had before?

"We need to be alert for a trap," Dalinar said. "Someone find out what those scouts saw. Did they identify banners only, or did they get a close look?"

The other soldiers—including some of the archers who now filled the wall top—gave him strange looks. Dalinar cursed softly, glancing back out at the shadowy oncoming force. He had a foreboding itch in the back of his skull. Ignoring the odd looks, he hefted his spear and ran down the walkway of the wall top, reaching a set of stairs. They were built in switchbacks, running in zigzags straight down the tall wall, with no railing. He'd been on such fortifications before, and knew how to keep his eyes focused on the steps to avoid vertigo.

He reached the bottom and—spear resting on his shoulder—struck out to find someone in charge. The buildings of Feverstone Keep were blocky and utilitarian, built up against one another along the rock walls of the natural rift. Most had square raincatchers on top. With good food stores—or, if lucky, a Soulcaster—such a fortification could withstand a siege for years.

He couldn't read the rank insignias, but he could recognize an officer when he saw one standing in a blood-red cloak with a group of honor guards. He had no mail, just a shiny bronze breastplate over leather, and was conferring with one of the scouts. Dalinar hurried up.

Only then did he see that the man's eyes were dark brown. That gave Dalinar a shock of incredulity. Those around him treated the man like a brightlord.

". . . the Order of the Stonewards, my lord," the still-mounted scout was saying. "And a large number of Windrunners. All on foot."

"But why?" the darkeyed officer demanded. "Why are Radiants coming here? They should be fighting the devils on the front lines!"

"My lord," the scout said, "our orders were to return as soon as we identified them."

"Well, go back and find out why they're here!" the officer bellowed, causing the scout to flinch, then turn to ride away.

The Radiants. They were usually connected to Dalinar's visions in one way or another. As the officer began to call commands to his attendants, telling them to prep empty bunkers for the knights, Dalinar followed the scout toward the wall. Men crowded near the kill slits there, peering out at the plain. Like those above, these wore motley uniforms that looked pieced together. They weren't a ragged bunch, but were obviously wearing secondhand leavings.

The scout rode through a sally port as Dalinar entered the shadow of the enormous wall, walking up to the back of a crowd of soldiers. "What is it?" he asked.

"The Radiants," one of the men said. "They've broken into a run."

"It's almost like they're going to attack," said another. He chuckled at how ridiculous that sounded, though there was an edge of uncertainty to his voice.

What? Dalinar thought, anxious. "Let me through."

Surprisingly, the men parted. As Dalinar pushed by, he could sense their confusion. He'd given the command with the authority of a highprince and a lighteyes, and they'd obeyed instinctively. Now that they saw him, they were uncertain. What was this simple guardsman doing ordering them about?

He didn't give them a chance to question him. He climbed onto the platform against the wall, where a rectangular kill slit looked through the wall and onto the plain. It was too small for a man to get through, but wide enough for archers to fire out. Through it, Dalinar saw that the approaching soldiers had formed a distinct line. Men and women in gleaming Shardplate charged forward. The scout pulled to a halt, looking at the charging Shardbearers. They ran shoulder to shoulder, not a single one out of place. Like a crystalline wave. As they drew closer, Dalinar could see that their Plate was unpainted, but it glowed either blue or amber at the joints and across glyphs at the front, as with other Radiants he'd seen in his visions.

"They don't have their Shardblades out," Dalinar said. "That's a good sign."

The scout outside backed his horse up. There looked to be a good two hundred Shardbearers out there. Alethkar owned some twenty Blades, Jah Keved a similar number. If one added up all the rest in the world, there might be enough total to equal the two powerful Vorin kingdoms. That meant, so far as he knew, there were less than a hundred Blades in all of the world. And here he saw *two hundred* Shardbearers gathered in one army. It was mind-numbing.

The Radiants slowed, falling into a trot, then a walk. The soldiers around Dalinar grew still. The leading Radiants stopped in a line, immobile. Suddenly, others began to fall from the sky. They hit with the sound of rock cracking, puffs of Stormlight blossoming from their figures. These all glowed blue.

Soon, there were some three hundred Radiants out on the field. They began summoning their Blades. The weapons appeared in their hands, like fog forming and condensing. It was done in silence. Their visors were down.

"If them charging without swords was a good sign," whispered one of the men beside Dalinar, "then what does this mean?"

A suspicion began to rise within Dalinar, the horror that he might know what this vision was about to show him. The scout, at last unnerved, turned his horse and galloped back to the keep, screaming for the door to be opened to him. As if a little wood and stone would be a protection against hundreds of Shardbearers. A single man with Plate and Blade was almost an army unto himself, and that wasn't accounting for the strange powers these people had.

The soldiers pulled the sally port open for the scout. Making a snap decision, Dalinar leaped down and charged to the opening. Behind, the officer Dalinar had seen earlier was clearing a path for himself to walk up to the kill slit.

Dalinar reached the open door, darting through it just after the scout charged back into the courtyard. Men called after Dalinar, terrified. He ignored them, running out onto the open plain. The expansive, straight wall stretched above him, like a highway up to the sun itself. The Radiants were still distant, though they'd stopped within bowshot. Transfixed by the beautiful figures, Dalinar slowed, then stopped about a hundred feet away.

One knight stepped ahead of his companions, his brilliant cape a rich blue. His Shardblade of rippling steel had intricate carvings along the center. He held it toward the keep for a moment.

Then he drove it point-first into the stone plain. Dalinar blinked. The Shardbearer removed his helm, exposing a handsome head with blond hair and pale skin, light as that of a man from Shinovar. He tossed the helm to the ground beside his Blade. It rolled slightly as the Shardbearer made fists in his gauntlets, arms at his sides. He opened his palms wide, and the gauntlets fell free to the rocky ground.

He turned, his Shardplate falling off his body—breastplate dropping free, greaves slipping off. Underneath, he wore a rumpled blue uniform. He stepped free of his bootlike sabatons and continued to walk away, Shardplate and Shardblade—the most precious treasures any man could own—tossed to the ground and abandoned like refuse.

The others began to follow suit. Hundreds of men and women, driving Shardblades into the stone and then removing their Plate. The sound of metal hitting stone came like rain. Then like thunder.

Dalinar found himself running forward. The door behind him opened and some curious soldiers left the keep. Dalinar reached the Shardblades. They sprouted from the rock like glittering silver trees, a forest of weapons. They glowed softly in a way his own Shardblade never had, but as he dashed among them, their light started to fade.

A terrible feeling struck him. A sense of immense tragedy, of pain and betrayal. Stopping where he stood, he gasped, hand to his chest. What was happening? What *was* that dreadful feeling, that screaming he swore he could almost hear?

The Radiants. They walked away from their discarded weapons. They all seemed individuals now, each walking alone despite the crowd. Dalinar charged after them, tripping over discarded breastplates and chunks of armor. He finally stumbled free of it all.

"Wait!" he called.

None of them turned.

He could now see others in the distance, far off. A crowd of soldiers, not wearing Shardplate, waiting for the Radiants to return. Who were they, and why hadn't they come forward? Dalinar caught up to the Radiants—they weren't walking very quickly—and grabbed one by the arm. The man turned; his skin was tan and his hair dark, like an Alethi. His eyes were of the palest blue. Unnaturally so, in fact—the irises were nearly white.

"Please," Dalinar said. "Tell me why you are doing this."

The former Shardbearer pulled his arm free and continued to walk away. Dalinar cursed, then ran into the midst of the Shardbearers. They were of all races and nationalities, dark skin and light, some with white Thaylen eyebrows, others with the skin ripples of the Selay. They walked with eyes forward, not speaking to one another, steps slow but resolute.

"Will someone tell me why?" Dalinar bellowed. "This is it, isn't it? The Day of Recreance, the day you betrayed mankind. But why?" None of them spoke. It was as if he didn't exist.

People spoke of betrayal, of the day the Knights Radiant turned their backs on their fellow men. What were they fighting, and why had they stopped? *Two orders of knights were mentioned,* Dalinar thought. *But there were ten orders. What of the other eight?*

Dalinar fell to his knees in the sea of solemn individuals. "Please. I must know." Nearby, some of the keep's soldiers had reached the Shardblades—but rather than chasing after the Radiants, these men were cautiously pulling the Blades free. A few officers scrambled out of the keep, calling for the Blades to be put down. They were soon outnumbered by men who began boiling out of side gates and rushing toward the weapons.

"They are the first," a voice said.

Dalinar looked up to see that one of the knights had stopped beside him. It was the man who looked Alethi. He looked over his shoulder at the crowd gathering around the Blades. Men had begun to scream at one another, everyone scrambling to get a Blade before they were all claimed.

"They are the first," the Radiant said, turning to Dalinar. Dalinar recognized the depth of that voice. It was the voice that always spoke to him in these visions. "They were the first, and they were also the last."

"Is this the Day of Recreance?" Dalinar asked.

"These events will go down in history," the Radiant said. "They will be infamous. You will have many names for what happened here."

"But why?" Dalinar asked. "Please. Why did they abandon their duty?"

The figure seemed to study him. "I have said that I cannot be of much help to you. The Night of Sorrows will come, and the True Desolation. The Everstorm."

"Then answer my questions!" Dalinar said.

"Read the book. Unite them."

"The book? *The Way of Kings*?"

The figure turned and walked from him, joining the other Radiants as they crossed the stone plain, walking toward places unknown.

Dalinar looked back at the melee of soldiers rushing for Blades. Many had already been claimed. There weren't enough Blades for everyone, and some had begun raising theirs up, using them to fend off those who got too close. As he watched, a bellowing officer with a Blade was attacked by two men behind him.

The glow from within the weapons had completely vanished.

The killing of that officer made others bold. Other skirmishes started, men scrambling to attack those who had Blades, hoping to get one. Eyes began to burn. Screams, shouts, death. Dalinar watched until he found himself in his quarters, tied to his chair. Renarin and Adolin watched nearby, looking tense.

Dalinar blinked, listening to the rain of the passing highstorm on the roof. "I've returned," he said to his sons. "You may calm yourselves." Adolin helped untie the ropes while Renarin stood up and fetched Dalinar a cup of orange wine.

Once Dalinar was free, Adolin stood back. The youth folded his arms. Renarin came back, his face pale. He looked to be having one of his episodes of weakness; indeed, his legs were trembling. As soon as Dalinar took the cup, the youth sat down in a chair and rested his head in his hands.

Dalinar sipped the sweet wine. He had seen wars in his visions before. He had seen deaths and monsters, greatshells and nightmares. And yet, for some reason, this one disturbed him more than any. He found his own hand shaking as he raised the cup for a second sip.

Adolin was still looking at him.

"Am I that bad to watch?" Dalinar asked.

"The gibberish you speak is unnerving, Father," Renarin said. "Unearthly, strange. Skewed, like a wooden building pushed to a slant by the wind."

"You thrash about," Adolin said. "You nearly tipped over the chair. I had to hold it steady until you stilled."

Dalinar stood up, sighing as he walked over to refill his cup. "And you still think I don't need to abdicate?"

"The episodes are containable," Adolin said, though he sounded disturbed. "My point was *never* to get you to abdicate. I just didn't want you relying upon the delusions to make decisions about our house's future. So long as you accept that what you see isn't real, we can move on. No reason for you to give up your seat."

Dalinar poured the wine. He looked eastward, toward the wall, away from Adolin and Renarin. "I don't accept that what I see isn't real."

"What?" Adolin said. "But I thought I convinced—"

"I accept that I'm no longer reliable," Dalinar said. "And that there's a chance I might be going mad. I accept that something is happening to me." He turned around. "When I first began seeing these visions, I believed them to be from the Almighty. You have convinced me that I may have been too hasty in my judgment. I don't know enough to trust them. I could be mad. Or they could be supernatural without being of the Almighty."

"How could that happen?" Adolin said, frowning.

"The Old Magic," Renarin said softly, still sitting.

Dalinar nodded.

"What?" Adolin said pointedly. "The Old Magic is a myth."

"Unfortunately, it is not," Dalinar said, then took another drink of the cool wine. "I know this for a fact."

"Father," Renarin said. "For the Old Magic to have affected you, you'd have had to travel to the West and seek it. Wouldn't you?"

"Yes," he said, ashamed. The empty place in his memories where his wife had once existed had never seemed as obvious to him as it did at that moment. He tended to ignore it, with good reason. She'd vanished completely, and it was sometimes difficult for him to remember that he *had* been married.

"These visions are not in line with what I've understood about the Nightwatcher," Renarin said. "Most consider her to be just some kind of powerful spren. Once you've sought her out and been given your reward and your curse, she's supposed to leave you alone. When did you seek her?"

"It's been many years now," Dalinar said.

"Then this probably isn't due to her influence," Renarin said.

"I agree," Dalinar said.

"But what did you ask for?" Adolin said, frowning.

"My curse and boon are my own, son," Dalinar said. "The specifics are not important."

"But—"

"I agree with Renarin," Dalinar said, interrupting. "This is probably not the Nightwatcher."

"All right, fine. But why bring it up?"

"Because, Adolin," Dalinar said, feeling exasperated. "I *don't know* what is happening to me. These visions seem far too detailed to be products of my mind. But your arguments made me think. I could be wrong. Or *you* could be wrong, and it could be the Almighty. Or it could be something entirely different. We don't know, and that is why it is dangerous for me to be left in command."

"Well, what I said still holds," Adolin said stubbornly. "We can contain it."

"No, we can't," Dalinar said. "Just because it has come only during highstorms in the past doesn't mean it couldn't expand to other times of stress. What if I were struck with an episode on the battlefield?" That was the very same reason they didn't let Renarin ride into battle.

"If that happens," Adolin said, "we'll deal with it. For now, we could just ignore—"

Dalinar threw a hand up into the air. "Ignore? I *cannot* ignore something like this. The visions, the book, the things I feel—they're changing every aspect of me. How can I rule if I do not follow my conscience? If I continue as highprince, I second-guess my every decision. Either I decide to trust myself, or I step down. I cannot *stomach* the thought of something in-between."

The room fell silent.

"So what do we do?" Adolin said.

"We make the choice," Dalinar said. "*I* make the choice."

"Step down or keep heeding the delusions," Adolin spat. "Either way we're letting them rule us."

"And you have a better option?" Dalinar demanded. "You've been quick to complain, Adolin, which seems a habit of yours. But I don't see you offering a legitimate alternative."

"I gave you one," Adolin said. "Ignore the visions and move on!"

"I said a *legitimate* option!"

The two stared at one another. Dalinar fought to keep his anger contained. In many ways, he and Adolin were too similar. They understood one another, and that enabled them to push in places that hurt.

"Well," Renarin said, "what if we proved whether or not the visions were true?"

Dalinar glanced at him. "What?"

"You say these dreams are detailed," Renarin said, leaning forward with hands clasped in front of him. "What, exactly, do you see?"

Dalinar hesitated, then gulped down the rest of his wine. For once he wished he had intoxicating violet instead of orange. "The visions are often of the Knights Radiant. At the end of each episode, someone—I think one of the Heralds—comes to me and commands me to unite the highprinces of Alethkar."

The room fell silent, Adolin looking disturbed, Renarin just sitting quietly.

"Today, I saw the Day of Recreance," Dalinar continued. "The Radiants abandoned their Shards and walked away. The Plate and Blades . . . faded somehow when they were abandoned. It seems such an odd detail to have seen." He looked at Adolin. "If these visions are fantasies, then I am a great deal more clever than I once thought myself."

"Do you remember any specifics we could check on?" Renarin asked. "Names? Locations? Events that might be traced in history?"

"This last one was of a place called Feverstone Keep," Dalinar said.

"I've never heard of it," Adolin said.

"Feverstone Keep," Dalinar repeated. "In my vision, there was some kind of war going on near there. The Radiants had been fighting on the front lines. They withdrew to this fortress, then abandoned their Shards there."

"Perhaps we could find something in history," Renarin said. "Proof that either this keep existed or that the Radiants didn't do what you saw there. Then we'd know, wouldn't we? If the dreams are delusions or truth?"

Dalinar found himself nodding. Proving them had never occurred to him, in part because he had assumed they were real at the start. Once he'd started questioning, he'd been more inclined to keep the nature of the visions hidden and silent. But if he knew that he was seeing real events . . . well, that would at least rule out the possibility of madness. It wouldn't solve everything, but it would help a great deal.

"I don't know," Adolin said, more skeptical. "Father, you're talking about times before the Hierocracy. Will we be able to find anything in the histories?"

"There are histories from the time when the Radiants lived," Renarin said. "That's not as far back as the shadow-days or the Heraldic Epochs. We could ask Jasnah. Isn't this what she does? As a Veristitalian?"

Dalinar looked at Adolin. "It sounds like it's worth a try, son."

"Maybe," Adolin said. "But we can't take the existence of a single place as proof. You could have heard of this Feverstone Keep, and therefore included it."

"Well," Renarin said, "that may be true. But if what Father sees are just delusions, then certainly we'll be able to prove some parts of them untrue. It seems impossible that every detail he imagines is one that he got from a story or history. *Some* aspects of the delusions would have to be pure fancy."

Adolin nodded slowly. "I . . . You're right, Renarin. Yes, it's a good plan."

"We need to get one of my scribes," Dalinar said. "So I can dictate the vision I just had while it is fresh."

"Yes," Renarin said. "The more details we have, the easier it will be to prove—or disprove—the visions."

Dalinar grimaced, setting aside his cup and walking over to the others. He sat down. "All right, but who would we use to record the dictation?"

"You have a great number of clerks, Father," Renarin said.

"And they're all either wife or daughter to one of my officers," Dalinar said. How could he explain? It was painful enough for him to expose weakness to his sons. If news of what he saw got around to his officers, it could weaken morale. There might come a time to reveal these things to his men, but he would need to do so carefully. And he'd much rather know for himself whether or not he was mad before he approached others.

"Yes," Adolin said, nodding—though Renarin still looked perplexed. "I understand. But, Father, we can't afford to wait for Jasnah to return. It could be months yet."

"Agreed." Dalinar said. He sighed. There was another option. "Renarin, send a runner for your aunt Navani."

Adolin glanced at Dalinar, raising an eyebrow. "It's a good idea. But I thought you didn't trust her."

"I trust her to keep her word," Dalinar said, resigned. "And to keep confidence. I told her of my plans to abdicate, and she didn't tell a soul." Navani was excellent at keeping secrets. Far better than the women of his court. He trusted them to an extent, but keeping a secret like this would require someone supremely exacting in their words and thoughts.

That meant Navani. She would probably find a way to manipulate him using the knowledge, but at least the secret would be safe from his men.

"Go, Renarin," Dalinar said.

Renarin nodded and stood. He had apparently recovered from his fit, and walked surefooted to the door. As he left, Adolin approached Dalinar. "Father, what will you do if we prove that I'm right, and it's just your own mind?"

"A part of me wishes for that to happen," Dalinar said, watching the door swing closed after Renarin. "I fear madness, but at least it is something familiar, something that can be dealt with. I will give you the princedom, then seek help in Kharbranth. But if these things are *not* delusions, I face another decision. Do I accept what they tell me or not? It may very well be better for Alethkar if I prove to be mad. It will be easier, at the least."

Adolin considered that, his brow furrowed, his jaw tense. "And Sadeas? He seems to be nearing the completion of his investigation. What do we do?"

It was a legitimate question. Troubles over Dalinar trusting the visions in relation to Sadeas had been what had drawn Dalinar and Adolin to argument in the first place.

Unite them. That wasn't just a command from the visions. It had been Gavilar's dream. A unified Alethkar. Had Dalinar let that dream—combined with guilt over failing his brother—drive him to construct supernatural rationalizations for seeking his brother's will?

He felt uncertain. He *hated* feeling uncertain.

"Very well," Dalinar said. "I give you leave to prepare for the worst, just in case Sadeas moves against us. Prepare our officers and call back the companies sent to patrol for bandits. If Sadeas denounces me as having tried to kill Elhokar, we will lock down our warcamp and go on alert. I don't intend to let him bring me in for execution."

Adolin looked relieved. "Thank you, Father."

"Hope it doesn't come to that, son," Dalinar said. "The moment Sadeas and I go to war in earnest, Alethkar as a nation will shatter. Ours are the two princedoms that uphold the king, and if we turn to strife, the others will either pick sides or turn to wars of their own."

Adolin nodded, but Dalinar sat back, disturbed. *I'm sorry,* he thought to whatever force was sending the visions. *But I have to be wise.*

In a way, this seemed like a second test to him. The visions had told him to trust Sadeas. Well, he would see what happened.

". . . and then it faded," Dalinar said. "After that, I found myself back here."

Navani raised her pen, looking thoughtful. It hadn't taken him long to talk through the vision. She'd scribed expertly, picking out details from him, knowing when to prod for more. She hadn't said a thing about the irregularity of the request, nor had she seemed amused by his desire to write down one of his delusions. She'd been businesslike and careful. She sat at his writing desk now, hair bound up in curls and crossed with four hairspikes. Her dress was red, matched by her lip paint, and her beautiful violet eyes were curious.

Stormfather, Dalinar thought, *but she's beautiful.*

"Well?" Adolin asked. He stood leaning against the door out of the chamber. Renarin had gone off to collect a highstorm damage report. The lad needed practice at that sort of activity.

Navani raised an eyebrow. "What was that, Adolin?"

"What do you think, Aunt?" Adolin asked.

"I have never heard of any of these places or events," Navani said. "But I believe you weren't expecting me to know of them. Didn't you say you wished me to contact Jasnah?"

"Yes," Adolin said. "But surely you have an analysis."

"I reserve judgment, dear," Navani said, standing up and folding the paper by pressing down with her safehand, holding it in place while she creased the fold tight. She smiled, walking by Adolin and patting him on the shoulder. "Let's see what Jasnah says before we do any analyzing, shall we?"

"I suppose," Adolin said. He sounded dissatisfied.

"I spent some time talking with that young lady of yours yesterday," Navani noted to him. "Danlan? I think you've made a wise choice. She's got a mind in that head of hers."

Adolin perked up. "You like her?"

"Quite a bit," Navani said. "I also discovered that she is very fond of avramelons. Did you know that?"

"I didn't, actually."

"Good. I would have hated to do all that work to find you a means of pleasing her, only to discover that you already knew it. I took the liberty of purchasing a basket of the melons on my way here. You'll find them in the antechamber, watched over by a bored soldier who didn't look like he was doing anything important. If you were to visit her with them this afternoon, I think you'd find yourself very well received."

Adolin hesitated. He probably knew that Navani was deflecting him from worrying over Dalinar. However, he relaxed, then started smiling. "Well, that might make for a pleasant change, considering events lately."

"I thought it might," Navani said. "I'd suggest going soon; those melons are perfectly ripe. Besides, I wish to speak with your father."

Adolin kissed Navani fondly on the cheek. "Thank you, Mashala." He allowed her to get away with some things that others could not; around his favored aunt, he was much like a child again. Adolin's smile widened as he made his way out the door.

Dalinar found himself smiling as well. Navani knew his son well. His smile didn't last long, however, as he realized that Adolin's departure left him alone with Navani. He stood up. "What is it you wished to ask of me?" he asked.

"I didn't say I wanted to *ask* anything of you, Dalinar," she said. "I just wanted to talk. We are family, after all. We don't spend enough time together."

"If you wish to speak, I shall fetch some soldiers to accompany us." He glanced at the antechamber outside. Adolin had shut the second door at the end, closing off his view of his guards—and their view of him.

"Dalinar," she said, walking up to him. "That *would* kind of defeat the point of sending Adolin away. I was after some privacy."

He felt himself growing stiff. "You should go now."

"Must I?"

"Yes. People will think this is inappropriate. They will talk."

"You imply that something inappropriate *could* happen, then?" Navani said, sounding almost girlishly eager.

"Navani, you are my *sister*."

"We aren't related by blood," she replied. "In some kingdoms, a union between us would be mandated by tradition, once your brother died."

"We aren't in other countries. This is Alethkar. There are rules."

"I see," she said, strolling closer to him. "And what will you do if I *don't* go? Will you call for help? Have me hauled away?"

"Navani," he said sufferingly. "Please. Don't do this again. I'm tired."

"Excellent. That might make it easier to get what I want."

He closed his eyes. *I can't take this right now.* The vision, the confrontation with Adolin, his own uncertain emotions . . . He didn't know what to make of things any longer.

Testing the visions was a good decision, but he couldn't shake the disorientation he felt from being unable to decide what to do next. He liked to make decisions and stick to them. He couldn't do that.

It grated on him.

"I thank you for your scribing and for your willingness to keep this quiet," he said, opening his eyes. "But I really must ask you to leave *now*, Navani."

"Oh, Dalinar," she said softly. She was close enough that he could smell her perfume. Stormfather, but she was beautiful. Seeing her brought to his mind thoughts of days long past, when he'd desired her so strongly that he'd nearly grown to hate Gavilar for winning her affection.

"Can't you just relax," she asked him, "just for a little while?"

"The rules—"

"Everyone else—"

"I cannot be *everyone else*!" Dalinar said, more sharply than he intended. "If I ignore our code and ethics, what am I, Navani? The other highprinces and lighteyes deserve recrimination for what they do, and I have let them know it. If *I* abandon my principles, then I become something far worse than they. A hypocrite!"

She froze.

"Please," he said, tense with emotion. "Just go. Do not taunt me today."

She hesitated, then walked away without a word.

She would never know how much he wished her to have made one more objection. In his state, he likely would have been unable to argue further. Once the door shut, he let himself sit down in his chair, exhaling. He closed his eyes.

Almighty above, he thought. *Please. Just let me know what I am to do.*

"He must pick it up, the fallen title! The tower, the crown, and the spear!"

—Dated Vevahach, 1173, 8 seconds pre-death. Subject: a prostitute. Background unknown.

A razor-edged arrow snapped into the wood next to Kaladin's face. He could feel warm blood seep from a gash on his cheek, creeping down his face, mixing with the sweat dripping from his chin.

"Stay firm!" he bellowed, charging over the uneven ground, the bridge's familiar weight on his shoulders. Nearby—just ahead and to the left—Bridge Twenty floundered, four men at the front falling to arrows, their corpses tripping up those behind.

The Parshendi archers knelt on the other side of the chasm, singing calmly despite the hail of arrows from Sadeas's side. Their black eyes were like shards of obsidian. No whites. Just that emotionless black. In those moments—listening to men scream, cry, yell, howl—Kaladin hated the Parshendi as much as he hated Sadeas and Amaram. How could they sing while they killed?

The Parshendi in front of Kaladin's crew pulled and aimed.

Kaladin screamed at them, feeling a strange surge of strength as the arrows were loosed.

The shafts zipped through the air in a focused wave. Ten shafts struck the wood near Kaladin's head, their force throwing a shudder through it, chips of wood splintering free. But not a one struck flesh.

Across the chasm, several of the Parshendi lowered their bows, breaking off their chanting. Their demonic faces bore looks of stupefaction.

"Down!" Kaladin yelled as the bridge crew reached the chasm. The ground was rough here, covered in bulbous rockbuds. Kaladin stepped on the vine from one of them, causing the plant to retract. The bridgemen heaved the bridge up and off their shoulders, then expertly stepped aside, lowering it to the ground. Sixteen other bridge crews lined up with them, setting their bridges down. Behind, Sadeas's heavy cavalry thundered across the plateau toward them.

The Parshendi drew again.

Kaladin gritted his teeth, throwing his weight against one of the wooden bars on the side, helping shove the massive construction across the chasm. He hated this part; the bridgemen were so exposed.

Sadeas's archers kept firing, moving to a focused, disruptive attack intended to force back the Parshendi. As always, the archers didn't seem to mind if they hit bridgemen, and several of those shafts flew dangerously close to Kaladin. He continued to push—sweating, bleeding—and felt a stab of pride for Bridge Four. They were already beginning to move like warriors, light on their feet, moving erratically, making it more difficult for the archers to draw a bead on them. Would Gaz or Sadeas's men notice?

The bridge thumped into place, and Kaladin bellowed the retreat. Bridgemen ducked out of the way, dodging between thick-shafted black Parshendi arrows and lighter green-fletched ones from Sadeas's archers. Moash and Rock hoisted themselves up onto the bridge and ran across it, leaping down beside Kaladin. Others scattered around the back of the bridge, ducking in front of the oncoming cavalry charge.

Kaladin lingered, waving for his men to get out of the way. Once they were all free, he glanced back at the bridge, which bristled with arrows. Not a single man down. A miracle. He turned to run—

Someone stumbled to his feet on the other side of the bridge. Dunny. The youthful bridgeman had a white and green fletched arrow sprouting from his shoulder. His eyes were wide, dazed.

Kaladin cursed, running back. Before he'd taken two steps, a black-hafted arrow took the youth in the other side. He fell to the deck of the bridge, blood spraying the dark wood.

The charging horses did not slow. Frantic, Kaladin reached the side of the bridge, but something pulled him back. Hands on his shoulder. He stumbled, spinning to find Moash there. Kaladin snarled at him, trying to shove the man aside, but Moash—using a move Kaladin himself had taught him—yanked Kaladin sideways, tripping him. Moash threw himself down, holding Kaladin to the ground as heavy cavalry thundered across the bridge, arrows cracking against their silvery armor.

Broken bits of arrow sprinkled to the ground. Kaladin struggled for a moment, but then let himself fall still.

"He's dead," Moash said, harshly. "There's nothing you could have done. I'm sorry."

There's nothing you could have done. . . .

There isn't ever anything I can do. Stormfather, why can't I save them?

The bridge stopped shaking, the cavalry smashing into the Parshendi and making space for the foot soldiers, who clanked across next. The cavalry would retreat after the foot soldiers gained purchase, the horses too valuable to risk in extended fighting.

Yes, Kaladin thought. *Think about the tactics. Think about the battle. Don't think about Dunny.*

He pushed Moash off him, rising. Dunny's corpse was mangled beyond recognition. Kaladin set his jaw and turned, striding away without looking back. He brushed past the watching bridgemen and stepped up to the lip of the chasm, clasping his hands to his forearms behind his back, feet spread. It wasn't dangerous, so long as he stood far down from the bridge. The Parshendi had put away bows and were falling back. The chrysalis was a towering, oval stone mound on the far left side of the plateau.

Kaladin wanted to watch. It helped him think like a soldier, and thinking like a soldier helped him get over the deaths of those near him. The other bridgemen tentatively approached and filled in around him, standing at parade rest. Even Shen the parshman joined them, silently imitating the others. He'd joined every bridge run so far without complaint. He didn't refuse to march against his cousins; he didn't try to sabotage the assault. Gaz was disappointed, but Kaladin wasn't surprised. That was how parshmen were.

Except the ones on the other side of the chasm. Kaladin stared at the fighting, but had difficulty focusing on the tactics. Dunny's death tore at him too much. The lad had been a friend, one of the first to support him, one of the best of the bridgemen.

Each bridgeman dead edged them closer to disaster. It would take weeks to train the men properly. They'd lose half of their number—perhaps even more—before they were anywhere near ready to fight. That wasn't good enough.

Well, you'll have to find a way to fix it, Kaladin thought. He'd made his decision, and had no room for despair. Despair was a luxury.

He broke parade rest and stalked away from the chasm. The other bridgemen turned to look after him, surprised. Kaladin had recently taken to watching entire battles standing like that. Sadeas's soldiers had noticed. Many saw it as bridgemen behaving above their station. A few, however, seemed to respect Bridge Four for the display. He knew there were rumors about him because of the storm; no doubt he was adding to them.

Bridge Four followed, and Kaladin led them across the rocky plateau. He pointedly did not look again at the broken, mangled body on the bridge. Dunny had been one of the only bridgemen to retain any hint of innocence. And now he was dead, trampled by Sadeas, struck by arrows from both sides. Ignored, forgotten, abandoned.

There was nothing Kaladin could do for him. So instead, Kaladin made his way to where the members of Bridge Eight lay, exhausted, on a patch of open stone. Kaladin remembered lying like that after his first bridge runs. Now he barely felt winded.

As usual, the other bridge crews had left their wounded behind as they retreated. One poor man from Eight was crawling toward the others, an arrow through his thigh. Kaladin walked up to him. He had dark brown skin and brown eyes, his thick black hair pulled back into a long, braided tail. Pain-spren crawled around him. He looked up as Kaladin and the members of Bridge Four loomed over him.

"Hold still," Kaladin said softly, kneeling and gently turning the man to get a good look at the wounded thigh. Kaladin prodded at it, thoughtful. "Teft, we'll need a fire. Get out your tinder. Rock, you still have my needle and thread? I'll need that. Where's Lopen with the water?"

The members of Bridge Four were silent. Kaladin looked up from the confused, wounded man.

"Kaladin," Rock said. "You know how the other bridge crews have treated us."

"I don't care," Kaladin said.

"We don't have any money left," Drehy said. "Even pooling our income, we barely have enough for bandages for our own men."

"I don't care."

"If we care for the wounded of other bridge crews," Drehy said, shaking a blond head, "we'll have to feed them, tend them. . . ."

"I will find a way," Kaladin said.

"I—" Rock began.

"Storm you!" Kaladin said, standing and sweeping his hand over the plateau. The bodies of bridgemen lay scattered, ignored. "Look at that! Who cares for them? Not Sadeas. Not their fellow bridgemen. I doubt even the Heralds themselves spare a thought for these.

"I won't stand there and watch while men die behind me. We have to be better than that! We can't look away like the lighteyes, pretending we don't see. This man is one of us. Just like Dunny was.

"The lighteyes talk about honor. They spout empty claims about their nobility. Well, I've only known *one* man in my life who was a true man of honor. He was a surgeon who would help anyone, even those who hated him. Especially those who hated him. Well, we're going to show Gaz, and Sadeas, Hashal, and any other sodden fool who cares to watch, what he taught me. Now go to work and *stop complaining!*"

Bridge Four stared at him with wide, ashamed eyes, then burst into motion. Teft organized a triage unit, sending some men to search for other wounded bridgemen and others to gather rockbud bark for a fire. Lopen and Dabbid rushed off to fetch their litter.

Kaladin knelt down and felt at the wounded man's leg, checking to see how quickly the blood leaked, and determined that he wouldn't need to cauterize. He broke the shaft and wiped the wound with some conicshell mucus for numbing. Then he pulled the wood free, eliciting a grunt, and used his personal set of bandages to wrap the wound.

"Hold this with your hands," Kaladin instructed. "And don't walk on it. I'll check on you before we march back to camp."

"How . . ." the man said. He didn't have even a hint of an accent. Kaladin had expected him to be Azish because of the dark skin. "How will I get back if I can't walk on the leg?"

"We will carry you," Kaladin said.

The man looked up, obviously shocked. "I . . ." Tears formed in his eyes. "Thank you."

Kaladin nodded curtly, turning as Rock and Moash brought over another wounded man. Teft had a fire growing; it smelled of pungent wet rockbud. The new man had hit his head and had a long gash in his arm. Kaladin held out a hand for his thread.

"Kaladin, lad," Teft said with a soft voice, handing him the thread and kneeling. "Now, don't mark this as complaining, because it ain't. But how many men can we really carry back with us?"

"We've done three before," Kaladin said. "Lashed to the top of the bridge. I'll bet we could fit three more and carry another in the water litter."

"And if we have more than seven?"

"If we bandage them right, some might be able to walk."

"And if there are still more?"

"Storm it, Teft," Kaladin said, beginning to sew. "Then we bring the ones we can and haul the bridge back out again to fetch those we left behind. We'll bring Gaz with us if the soldiers worry that we'll run away."

Teft was silent, and Kaladin steeled himself for incredulity. Instead, however, the grizzled soldier smiled. He actually seemed a little watery-eyed. "Kelek's breath. It's true. I never thought . . ."

Kaladin frowned, looking up at Teft and holding a hand to the wound to stanch the bleeding. "What was that?"

"Oh, nothing." He scowled. "Get back to work! That lad needs you."

Kaladin turned back to his sewing.

"You still carrying a full pouch of spheres with you, like I told you?" Teft asked.

"I can't very well leave them behind in the barracks. But we'll need to spend them soon."

"You'll do nothing of the sort," Teft said. "Those spheres are luck, you hear me? Keep them with you and always keep them infused."

Kaladin sighed. "I think there's something wrong with this batch. They won't hold their Stormlight. They fall dun after just a few days, every time. Perhaps it's something to do with the Shattered Plains. It has happened to the other bridgemen too."

"Odd, that," Teft said, rubbing his chin. "This was a bad approach. Three bridges down. Lots of bridgemen dead. Interesting how we didn't lose anyone."

"We lost Dunny."

"But not on the approach. You always run point, and the arrows always seem to miss us. Odd, eh?"

[927]

Kaladin looked up again, frowning. "What are you saying, Teft?"

"Nothing. Get back to that sewing! How many times do I have to tell you?"

Kaladin raised an eyebrow, but turned back to his work. Teft had been acting very strange lately. Was it the stress? A lot of people were superstitious about spheres and Stormlight.

Rock and his team brought three more wounded, then said that was all they'd found. Bridgemen who fell often ended up like Dunny, getting trampled. Well, at least Bridge Four wouldn't have to make a return trip to the plateau.

The three had bad arrow wounds, and so Kaladin left the man with the gash on his arm to them, instructing Skar to keep pressure on the unfinished sewing job. Teft heated a dagger for cauterization; these newcomers had obviously lost a lot of blood. One probably wouldn't make it.

So much of the world is at war, he thought as he worked. The dream had highlighted what others already spoke of. Kaladin hadn't known, growing up in remote Hearthstone, how fortunate his town had been to avoid battle.

The entire world warred, and he struggled to save a few impoverished bridgemen. What good did it do? And yet he continued searing flesh, sewing, saving lives as his father had taught him. He began to understand the sense of futility he'd seen in his father's eyes on those occasional darkened nights when Lirin had turned to his wine in solitude.

You're trying to make up for failing Dunny, Kaladin thought. *Helping these others won't bring him back.*

He lost the one he'd suspected would die, but saved the other four, and the one who'd taken a knock to the head was beginning to wake up. Kaladin sat back on his knees, weary, hands covered in blood. He washed them off with a stream of water from Lopen's waterskins, then reached up, finally remembering his own wound, where the arrow had sliced his cheek.

He froze. He prodded at his skin, but couldn't find the wound. He had felt blood on his cheek and chin. He'd felt the arrow slice him, hadn't he?

He stood up, feeling a chill, and raised his hand to his forehead. What was happening?

Someone stepped up beside him. Moash's now-clean-shaven face exposed a faded scar along his chin. He studied Kaladin. "About Dunny . . ."

"You were right to do what you did," Kaladin said. "You probably saved my life. Thank you."

Moash nodded slowly. He turned to look at the four wounded men; Lopen and Dabbid were giving them drinks of water, asking their names. "I was wrong about you," Moash said suddenly, holding out a hand to Kaladin.

Kaladin took the hand, hesitant. "Thank you."

"You're a fool and an instigator. But you're an honest one." Moash chuckled to himself. "If you get us killed, it won't be on purpose. Can't say that for some I've served under. Anyway, let's get these men ready for moving."

54

GIBLETISH

"The burdens of nine become mine. Why must I carry the madness of them all? Oh, Almighty, release me."

—Dated Palaheses, 1173, unknown seconds pre-death. Subject: a wealthy lighteyes. Sample collected secondhand.

The cold night air threatened that a stretch of winter might soon be coming. Dalinar wore a long, thick uniform coat over trousers and shirt. It buttoned stiffly up the chest and to the collar, and was long in the back and on the sides, coming down to his ankles, flowing at the waist like a cloak. In earlier years, it might have been worn with a takama, though Dalinar had never liked the skirtlike garments.

The purpose of the uniform was not fashion or tradition, but to distinguish him easily for those who followed him. He wouldn't have nearly the problem with the other lighteyes if they would at least wear their colors.

He stepped onto the king's feasting island. Stands had been set up at the sides where the braziers normally stood, each one bearing one of those new fabrials that gave off heat. The stream between the islands had slowed to a trickle; ice had stopped melting in the highlands.

Attendance at the feast tonight was small, though that was mostly manifest on the four islands that were not the king's.

Where there was access to Elhokar and the highprinces, people would attend even if the feast were held in the middle of a highstorm. Dalinar walked down the central pathway, and Navani—sitting at a women's dining table—caught his eyes. She turned away, perhaps still remembering his abrupt words to her at their last meeting.

Wit wasn't at his customary place insulting those who walked onto the king's island; in fact, he wasn't to be seen at all. *Not surprising,* Dalinar thought. Wit didn't like to grow predictable; he'd spent several recent feasts on his pedestal doling out insults. Likely he felt he'd played out that tactic.

All nine other highprinces were in attendance. Their treatment of Dalinar had grown stiff and cold since refusing his requests to fight together. As if they were offended by the mere offer. Lesser lighteyes made alliances, but the highprinces were like kings themselves. Other highprinces were rivals, to be kept at arm's length.

Dalinar sent a servant to fetch him food and sat down at the table. His arrival had been delayed while he took reports from the companies he'd called back, so he was one of the last to eat. Most of the others had turned to mingling. To the right, an officer's daughter was playing a serene flute melody to a group of onlookers. To the left, three women had set up sketchpads and were each drawing the same man. Women were known to challenge each other to duels in the way of men with Shardblades, though they rarely used the word. These were always "friendly competitions" or "games of talent."

His food arrived, steamed stagm—a brownish tuber that grew in deep puddles—atop a bed of boiled tallew. The grain was puffed with water, and the entire meal was drenched in a thick, peppery, brown gravy. He slid out his knife and sliced a disk off the end of the stagm. Using his knife to spread tallew over the top, he grasped the vegetable disk between two fingers and began to eat. It had been prepared both spicy and hot this night, probably because of the chill, and tasted good as he chewed, the steam from his plate fogging the air in front of him.

So far, Jasnah had not replied regarding his vision, though

Navani claimed she might be able to find something on her own. She was a renowned scholar herself, though her interests had always been more in fabrials. He glanced at her. Was he a fool to offend her as he had? Would it make her use the knowledge of his visions against him?

No, he thought. *She wouldn't be that petty.* Navani *did* seem to care for him, though her affection was inappropriate.

The chairs around him were left empty. He was becoming a pariah, first because of his talk of the Codes, then because of his attempts to get the highprinces to work with him, and finally because of Sadeas's investigation. No wonder Adolin was worried.

Suddenly, someone slid right into the seat beside Dalinar, wearing a black cloak against the chill. It wasn't one of the highprinces. Who would dare—

The figure lowered his hood, revealing Wit's hawklike face. All lines and peaks, with a sharp nose and jaw, delicate eyebrows, and keen eyes. Dalinar sighed, waiting for the inevitable stream of too-clever quips.

Wit, however, didn't speak. He inspected the crowd, his expression intense.

Yes, Dalinar thought. *Adolin is right about this one too.* Dalinar himself had judged the man too harshly in the past. He was not the fool some of his predecessors had been. Wit continued in silence, and Dalinar decided that—perhaps—the man's prank this night was to sit down beside people and unnerve them. It wasn't much of a prank, but Dalinar often missed the point of what Wit did. Perhaps it was terribly clever if one had the mind for it. Dalinar returned to his meal.

"Winds are changing," Wit whispered.

Dalinar glanced at him.

Wit's eyes narrowed, and he scanned the night sky. "It's been happening for months now. A whirlwind. Shifting and churning, blowing us round and around. Like a world spinning, but we can't see it because we're too much a part of it."

"World spinning. What foolishness is this?"

"The foolishness of men who care, Dalinar," Wit said.

"And the brilliance of those who do not. The second depend on the first—but also exploit the first—while the first misunderstand the second, hoping that the second are more like the first. And all of their games steal our time. Second by second."

"Wit," Dalinar said with a sigh. "I haven't the mind for this tonight. I'm sorry if I'm missing your intent, but I have no idea what you mean."

"I know," Wit said, then looked directly at him. "Adonalsium."

Dalinar frowned more deeply. "What?"

Wit searched his face. "Have you ever heard the term, Dalinar?"

"Ado . . . what?"

"Nothing," Wit said. He seemed preoccupied, unlike his usual self. "Nonsense. Balderdash. Figgldygrak. Isn't it odd that gibberish words are often the sounds of other words, cut up and dismembered, then stitched into something like them—yet wholly unlike them at the same time?"

Dalinar frowned.

"I wonder if you could do that to a man. Pull him apart, emotion by emotion, bit by bit, bloody chunk by bloody chunk. Then combine them back together into something else, like a Dysian Aimian. If you do put a man together like that, Dalinar, be sure to name him Gibberish, after me. Or perhaps Gibletish."

"Is that your name, then? Your real name?"

"No, my friend," Wit said, standing up. "I've abandoned my real name. But when next we meet, I'll think of a clever one for you to call me. Until then, Wit will suffice—or if you must, you may call me Hoid. Watch yourself; Sadeas is planning a revelation at the feast tonight, though I know not what it is. Farewell. I'm sorry I didn't insult you more."

"Wait, you're leaving?"

"I must. I hope to return. I'll do so if I'm not killed. Probably will anyway. Apologize to your nephew for me."

"He won't be happy," Dalinar said. "He's fond of you."

"Yes, it's one of his more admirable traits," Wit said.

"Alongside that of paying me, letting me eat his expensive food, and giving me opportunity to make sport of his friends. The cosmere, unfortunately, takes precedence over free food. Watch yourself, Dalinar. Life becomes dangerous, and you're at the center of it."

Wit nodded once, then ducked into the night. He put his hood up, and soon Dalinar couldn't separate him from the darkness.

Dalinar turned back to his meal. *Sadeas is planning a revelation at the feast tonight, though I know not what it is.* Wit was rarely wrong—though he was almost always odd. Was he really leaving, or would he still be in camp the next morning, laughing at the prank he had played on Dalinar?

No, Dalinar thought. *That wasn't a prank.* He waved over a master-servant in black and white. "Fetch my elder son for me."

The servant bowed and withdrew. Dalinar ate the rest of his food in silence, glancing occasionally at Sadeas and Elhokar. They weren't at the dining table any longer, and so Sadeas's wife had joined them. Ialai was a curvaceous woman who reportedly dyed her hair. That indicated foreign blood in her family's past—Alethi hair always bred true, proportionate to how much Alethi blood you had. Foreign blood would mean stray hairs of another color. Ironically, mixed blood was far more common in lighteyes than darkeyes. Darkeyes rarely married foreigners, but the Alethi houses often needed alliances or money from outside.

Food finished, Dalinar stepped down from the king's table onto the island proper. The woman was still playing her melancholy song. She was quite good. A few moments later, Adolin strode onto the king's island. He hurried over to Dalinar. "Father? You sent for me?"

"Stay close. Wit told me that Sadeas plans to make a storm of something tonight."

Adolin's expression darkened. "Time to go, then."

"No. We need to let this play out."

"Father—"

"But you *may* prepare," Dalinar said softly. "Just in case. You invited officers of our guard to the feast tonight?"

"Yes," Adolin said. "Six of them."

"They have my further invitation to the king's island. Pass the word. What of the King's Guard?"

"I've made sure that some of the ones guarding the island tonight are among those most loyal to you." Adolin nodded toward a space in the darkness to the side of the feasting basin. "I think we should position them over there. It'll make a good line of retreat in case the king tries to have you arrested."

"I still don't think it will come to that."

"You can't be sure. Elhokar allowed this investigation in the first place, after all. He's growing more and more paranoid."

Dalinar glanced over at the king. The younger man almost always wore his Shardplate these days, though he didn't have it on now. He seemed continually on edge, glancing over his shoulder, eyes darting from side to side.

"Let me know when the men are in position," Dalinar said.

Adolin nodded, walking away quickly.

The situation gave Dalinar little stomach for mingling. Still, standing alone and looking awkward was no better, so he made his way to where Highprince Hatham was speaking with a small group of lighteyes beside the main firepit. They nodded to Dalinar as he joined them; regardless of the way they were treating him in general, they would never turn him away at a feast like this. That simply wasn't done to one of his rank.

"Ah, Brightlord Dalinar," Hatham said in his smooth, overly polite way. The long-necked, slender man wore a ruffled green shirt underneath a robelike coat, with a darker green silk scarf around the neck. A faintly glowing ruby sat on each of his fingers; they'd each had some of their Stormlight drained away by a fabrial made for the purpose.

Of Hatham's four companions, two were lesser lighteyes and one was a short white-robed ardent Dalinar didn't know.

The last was a red-gloved Natan man with bluish skin and stark white hair, two locks dyed a deep red and braided down to hang alongside his cheeks. He was a visiting dignitary; Dalinar had seen him at the feasts. What was his name again?

"Tell me, Brightlord Dalinar," Hatham said. "Have you been paying much attention to the conflict between the Tukari and the Emuli?"

"It's a religious conflict, isn't it?" Dalinar asked. Both were Makabaki kingdoms, on the southern coast where trade was plentiful and profitable.

"Religious?" the Natan man said. "No, I wouldn't say that. All conflicts are essentially economic in nature."

Au-nak, Dalinar recalled. *That's his name.* He spoke with an airy accent, overextending all of his "ah" and "oh" sounds.

"Money is behind every war," Au-nak continued. "Religion is but an excuse. Or perhaps a justification."

"There's a difference?" the ardent said, obviously taking offense at Au-nak's tone.

"Of course," Au-nak said. "An excuse is what you make after the deed is done, while a justification is what you offer before."

"I would say an excuse is something you claim, but do not believe, Nak-ali." Hatham was using the high form of Au-nak's name. "While a justification is something you actually believe." Why such respect? The Natan must have something that Hatham wanted.

"Regardless," Au-nak said. "This particular war is over the city of Sesemalex Dar, which the Emuli have made their capital. It's an excellent trade city, and the Tukari want it."

"I've heard of Sesemalex Dar," Dalinar said, rubbing his chin. "The city is quite spectacular, filling rifts cut into the stone."

"Indeed," Au-nak said. "There's a particular composition of the stone there that lets water drain. The design is amazing. It's obviously one of the Dawncities."

"My wife would have something to say on that," Hatham said. "She makes the Dawncities her study."

"The city's pattern is central to the Emuli religion," the ardent said. "They claim it is their ancestral homeland, a gift to them from the Heralds. And the Tukari are led by that godpriest of theirs, Tezim. So the conflict *is* religious in nature."

"And if the city weren't such a fantastic port," Au-nak said, "would they be as persistent about proclaiming the city's religious significance? I think not. They're pagans, after all, so we can't presume their religion has any real importance."

Talk of the Dawncities had been popular lately among the lighteyes—the idea that certain cities could trace their origins back to the Dawnsingers. Perhaps . . .

"Have any of you heard of a place known as Feverstone Keep?" Dalinar asked.

The others shook their heads; even Au-nak had nothing to say.

"Why?" Hatham asked.

"Just curious."

The conversation continued, though Dalinar let his attention wander back toward Elhokar and his circle of attendants. When would Sadeas make his announcement? If he intended to suggest that Dalinar be arrested, he wouldn't do it at a feast, would he?

Dalinar forced his attention back to the conversation. He really should pay more heed to what was happening in the world. Once, news of which kingdoms were in conflict had fascinated him. So much had changed since the visions began.

"Perhaps it's not economic or religious in nature," Hatham said, trying to bring an end to the argument. "Everyone knows that the Makabaki tribes have odd hatreds of one another."

"Perhaps," Au-nak said.

"Does it matter?" Dalinar asked.

The others turned to him.

"It's just another war. If they weren't fighting one another, they'd find others to attack. It's what we do. Vengeance, honor, riches, religion—the reasons all just produce the same result."

The others fell still, the silence quickly growing awkward.

"Which devotary do you credit, Brightlord Dalinar?" Hatham asked, thoughtful, as if trying to remember something he'd forgotten.

"The Order of Talenelat."

"Ah," Hatham said. "Yes, it makes sense. They do hate arguing over religion. You must find this discussion terribly boring."

A safe out from the conversation. Dalinar smiled, nodding in thanks to Hatham's politeness.

"The Order of Talenelat?" Au-nak said. "I always considered that a devotary for the lesser people."

"This from a Natan," the Ardent said, stuffily.

"My family has always been devoutly Vorin."

"Yes," the ardent replied, "conveniently so, since your family has used its Vorin ties to trade favorably in Alethkar. One wonders if you are equally devout when not standing on our soil."

"I don't have to be insulted like this," Au-nak snapped.

He turned and strode away, causing Hatham to raise a hand. "Nak-ali!" Hatham called, rushing after him anxiously. "Please, ignore him!"

"Insufferable bore," the ardent said softly, taking a sip of his wine—orange, of course, as he was a man of the clergy.

Dalinar frowned at him. "You are bold, ardent," he said sternly. "Perhaps foolishly so. You insult a man Hatham wants to do business with."

"Actually, I belong to Brightlord Hatham," the ardent said. "He *asked* me to insult his guest—Brightlord Hatham wants Au-nak to think that he is shamed. Now, when Hatham agrees quickly to Au-nak's demands, the foreigner will assume it was because of this—and won't delay the contract signing out of suspicion that it is proceeding too easily."

Ah, of course. Dalinar looked after the fleeing pair. *They go to such lengths.*

Considering that, what was Dalinar to think of Hatham's politeness earlier, when he had given Dalinar a reason to explain his apparent distaste for conflict? Was Hatham preparing Dalinar for some covert manipulation?

The ardent cleared his throat. "I would appreciate it if you did not repeat to anyone what I just told you, Brightlord." Dalinar noticed Adolin returning to the king's island, accompanied by six of Dalinar's officers, in uniform and wearing their swords.

"Why did you tell me in the first place, then?" Dalinar asked, turning his attention back to the white-robed man.

"Just as Hatham wishes his partner in negotiations to know of his goodwill, I wish you to know of our goodwill toward you, Brightlord."

Dalinar frowned. He'd never had much to do with the ardents—his devotary was simple and straightforward. Dalinar got his fill of politics with the court; he had little desire to find more in religion. "Why? What should it matter if you have goodwill toward me?"

The ardent smiled. "We will speak with you again." He bowed low and withdrew.

Dalinar was about to demand more, but Adolin arrived, looking after Highprince Hatham. "What was that all about?"

Dalinar just shook his head. Ardents weren't supposed to engage in politics, whatever their devotary. They'd been officially forbidden to do so since the Hierocracy. But, as with most things in life, the ideal and the reality were two separate things. The lighteyes couldn't help but use the ardents in their schemes, and so—more and more—the devotaries found themselves a part of the court.

"Father?" Adolin asked. "The men are in place."

"Good," Dalinar said. He set his jaw and then crossed the small island. He would see this fiasco finished with, once and for all.

He passed the firepit, a wave of dense heat making the left side of his face prickle with sweat while the right side was still chilled by the autumn cold. Adolin hurried up to walk by him, hand on his side sword. "Father? What are we doing?"

"Being provocative," Dalinar said, striding right up to where Elhokar and Sadeas were chatting. Their crowd of sycophants reluctantly parted for Dalinar.

". . . and I think that—" The king cut off, glancing at Dalinar. "Yes, Uncle?"

"Sadeas," Dalinar said. "What is the status of your investigation of the cut girth strap?"

Sadeas blinked. He held a cup of violet wine in his right hand, his long, red velvet robe open at the front to expose a ruffled white shirt. "Dalinar, are you—"

"Your investigation, Sadeas," Dalinar said firmly.

Sadeas sighed, looking at Elhokar. "Your Majesty. I was actually planning to make an announcement regarding this very subject tonight. I was going to wait until later, but if Dalinar is going to be so insistent . . ."

"I am," Dalinar said.

"Oh, go ahead, Sadeas," the king said. "You have me curious now." The king waved to a servant, who rushed to quiet the flutist while another servant tapped the chimes to call for silence. In moments, the people on the island stilled.

Sadeas gave Dalinar a grimace that somehow conveyed the message, "You demanded this, old friend."

Dalinar folded his arms, keeping his gaze fixed on Sadeas. His six Cobalt Guardsmen stepped up behind him, and Dalinar noticed that a group of similar lighteyed officers from Sadeas's warcamp were listening nearby.

"Well, I wasn't planning to have such an audience," Sadeas said. "Mostly, this was planned for Your Majesty only."

Unlikely, Dalinar thought, trying to suppress his anxiety. What would he do if Adolin was right and Sadeas charged him with trying to assassinate Elhokar?

It would, indeed, be the end of Alethkar. Dalinar would not go quietly, and the warcamps would turn against one another. The nervous peace that had held them together for the last decade would come to an end. Elhokar would never be able to hold them together.

Also, if it turned to battle, Dalinar would not fare well. The others were alienated from him; he'd have enough trouble facing Sadeas—if several of the others joined against him, he would fall, horribly outnumbered. He could see how

Adolin thought it an incredible act of foolishness to have listened to the visions. And yet, in a powerfully surreal moment, Dalinar felt that he'd done the correct thing. He'd never felt it as strongly as at that moment, preparing to be condemned.

"Sadeas, don't weary me with your sense of drama," Elhokar said. "They're listening. I'm listening. Dalinar looks like he's ready to burst a vein in his forehead. Speak."

"Very well," Sadeas said, giving his wine to a servant. "My very first task as Highprince of Information was to discover the true nature of the attempt on His Majesty's life during the greatshell hunt." He waved a hand, motioning to one of his men, who hurried away. Another stepped forward, handing Sadeas the broken leather strap.

"I took this strap to three separate leatherworkers in three different warcamps. Each came to the same conclusion. It was cut. The leather is relatively new, and has been well cared for, as proven by the lack of cracking and flaking in other areas. The tear is too even. Someone slit it."

Dalinar felt a sense of dread. That was near what he had discovered, but it was presented in the worst possible light. "For what purpose—" Dalinar began.

Sadeas held up a hand. "Please, Highprince. First you demand I report, then you interrupt me?"

Dalinar fell still. Around them, more and more of the important lighteyes were gathering. He could sense their tension.

"But when was it cut?" Sadeas said, turning to address the crowd. He did have a flair for the dramatic. "That was pivotal, you see. I took leave to interview numerous men who were on that hunt. None reported seeing anything specific, though all remembered that there was one odd event. The time when Brightlord Dalinar and His Majesty raced to a rock formation. A time when Dalinar and the king were alone."

There were whispers from behind.

"There was a problem, however," Sadeas said. "One Dalinar himself raised. Why cut the strap on a Shardbearer's saddle? A foolish move. A horseback fall wouldn't be of much danger to a man wearing Shardplate." To the side, the servant Sadeas had sent away returned, leading a youth with sandy hair bearing only a few hints of black.

Sadeas fished something out of a pouch at his waist, holding it up. A large sapphire. It wasn't infused. In fact, looking closely, Dalinar could see that it was cracked—it wouldn't hold Stormlight now. "The question drove me to investigate the king's Shardplate," Sadeas said. "Eight of the ten sapphires used to infuse his Plate were cracked following the battle."

"It happens," Adolin said, stepping up beside Dalinar, hand on his side sword. "You lose a few in every battle."

"But eight?" Sadeas asked. "One or two is normal. But have you ever lost eight in one battle before, young Kholin?"

Adolin's only reply was a glare.

Sadeas tucked away the gemstone, nodding to the youth his men had brought. "This is one of the grooms in the king's employ. Fin, isn't it?"

"Y . . . Yes, brightlord," the boy stammered. He couldn't be older than twelve.

"What is it you told me earlier, Fin? Please, say it again so that all may hear."

The darkeyed youth cringed, looking sick. "Well, Brightlord sir, it was just this: Everyone spoke of the saddle being checked over in Brightlord Dalinar's camp. And I suppose it was, right as that. But I'm the one who prepared His Majesty's horse afore it was turned over to Brightlord Dalinar's men. And I did it, I promise I did. Put on his favorite saddle and everything. But . . ."

Dalinar's heart raced. He had to hold himself back from summoning his Blade.

"But what?" Sadeas said to Fin.

"But when the king's head grooms took the horse past on its way to the Highprince Dalinar's camp, it was wearing a different saddle. I swear it."

Several of those standing around them seemed confused by this admission.

"Aha!" Adolin said, pointing. "But that happened in the king's palace complex!"

"Indeed," Sadeas said, raising an eyebrow at Adolin. "How keen-minded of you, young Kholin. This discovery—mixed with the cracked gemstones—means something. I suspect that whoever attempted to kill His Majesty planted in his Shard-plate flawed gemstones that would crack when strained, losing their Stormlight. Then they weakened the saddle girth with a careful slit. The hope would be that His Majesty would fall while fighting a greatshell, allowing it to attack him. The gemstones would fail, the Plate would break, and His Majesty would fall to an 'accident' while hunting."

Sadeas raised a finger as the crowd began to whisper again. "However, it is important to realize that these events—the switching of the saddle or the planting of the gemstones—must have happened before His Majesty met up with Dalinar. I feel that Dalinar is a very unlikely suspect. In fact, my present guess is that the culprit is someone that Brightlord Dalinar has offended; that someone wanted us all to think he might be involved. It may not have actually been intended to kill His Majesty, just to cast suspicion upon Dalinar."

The island fell silent, even the whispers dying.

Dalinar stood, stunned. *I . . . I was right!*

Adolin finally broke the quiet. *"What?"*

"All evidence points to your father being innocent, Adolin," Sadeas said sufferingly. "You find this surprising?"

"No, but . . ." Adolin's brow furrowed.

Around them, the lighteyes began talking, sounding disappointed. They began to disperse. Dalinar's officers remained standing behind him, as if expecting a surprise strike.

Blood of my fathers . . . Dalinar thought. *What does it mean?*

Sadeas waved for his men to take the groom away, then nodded to Elhokar and withdrew in the direction of the evening trays, where warmed wine sat in pitchers next to toasted breads. Dalinar caught up to Sadeas as the shorter man was filling a small plate. Dalinar took him by the arm, the fabric of Sadeas's robe soft beneath his fingers.

Sadeas looked at him, raising an eyebrow.

"Thank you," Dalinar said quietly. "For not going through with it." Behind them, the flutist resumed her playing.

"For not going through with what?" Sadeas said, setting down his small plate, then prying Dalinar's fingers free. "I had hoped to make this presentation after I'd discovered more concrete proof that you weren't involved. Unfortunately, pressed as I was, the best I could do was to indicate that it was unlikely you were involved. There will still be rumors, I'm afraid."

"Wait. You *wanted* to prove me innocent?"

Sadeas scowled, picking up his plate again. "Do you know what your problem is, Dalinar? Why everyone has begun finding you so tiresome?"

Dalinar didn't reply.

"The presumption. You've grown despicably self-righteous. Yes, I asked Elhokar for this position so I could prove you innocent. Is it so storming difficult for you to believe someone else in this army might do something honest?"

"I . . ." Dalinar said.

"Of course it is," Sadeas said. "You've been looking down on us like a man standing atop a single sheet of paper, who therefore thinks himself so high as to see for miles. Well, I think that book of Gavilar's is crem, and the Codes are lies people pretended to follow so that they could justify their shriveled consciences. Damnation, I've got one of those shriveled consciences myself. But I didn't want to see you maligned for this bungled attempt to kill the king. If you'd wanted him dead, you'd have just burned out his eyes and been done with it!"

Sadeas took a drink of his steaming violet wine. "The problem is, Elhokar kept on and on about that blasted strap. And people started talking, since he was under your protection and you two rode off together like that. Stormfather only knows how they could think *you* would try to have Elhokar assassinated. You can barely bring yourself to kill Parshendi these days." Sadeas stuffed a small piece of toasted bread in his mouth, then moved to walk away.

Dalinar caught him by the arm again. "I . . . I owe you a debt. I shouldn't have treated you as I have these six years."

Sadeas rolled his eyes, chewing his bread. "This wasn't for you alone. So long as everyone thought you were behind the attempt, nobody would figure out who really tried to have Elhokar killed. And someone *did*, Dalinar. I don't accept eight gemstones cracking in one fight. The strap alone would have been a ridiculous way to attempt an assassination, but with weakened Shardplate . . . I'm half tempted to believe that the surprise arrival of the chasmfiend was orchestrated too. How someone would manage that though, I have no idea."

"And the talk of me being framed?" Dalinar asked.

"Mostly to give the others something to gossip about while I sort through what's really happening." Sadeas looked down at Dalinar's hand on his arm. "Would you let go?"

Dalinar released his grip.

Sadeas set down his plate, straightening his robe and dusting off the shoulder. "I haven't given up on you yet, Dalinar. I'm probably going to need you before this is all through. I do have to say, though, I don't know what to make of you lately. That talk of you wanting to abandon the Vengeance Pact. Is there any truth to that?"

"I mentioned it, in confidence, to Elhokar as a means of exploring options. So yes, there's truth to it, if you must know. I'm tired of this fighting. I'm tired of these Plains, of being away from civilization, of killing Parshendi a handful at a time. However, I've given up on getting us to retreat. Instead, I want to *win*. But the highprinces won't listen! They all assume that I'm trying to dominate them with some crafty trick."

Sadeas snorted. "You'd sooner punch a man in the face than stab him in the back. Blessedly straightforward."

"Ally with me," Dalinar said after him.

Sadeas froze.

"You know I'm not going to betray you, Sadeas," Dalinar said. "You trust me as the others never can. Try what I've been asking the other highprinces to agree to. Jointly assault plateaus with me."

"Won't work," Sadeas said. "There's no reason to bring more than one army on an assault. I leave half my troops behind each time as it is. There isn't room for more to maneuver."

"Yes, but think," Dalinar said. "What if we tried new tactics? Your quick bridge crews are fast, but my troops are stronger. What if you pushed quickly to a plateau with an advance force to hold off the Parshendi? You could hold until my stronger, but slower, forces arrive."

That gave Sadeas pause.

"It could mean a Shardblade, Sadeas."

Sadeas's eyes grew hungry.

"I know you've fought Parshendi Shardbearers," Dalinar said, seizing on that thread, "But you've lost. Without a Blade, you're at a disadvantage." Parshendi Shardbearers had a habit of escaping after entering battles. Regular spearmen couldn't kill one, of course. It took a Shardbearer to kill a Shardbearer. "I've slain two in the past. I don't often have the opportunity, however, because I can't get to the plateaus quickly enough. You can. Together, we can win more often, and *I* can get you a Blade. We can do this, Sadeas. Together. Like the old days."

"The old days," he said idly. "I'd like to see the Blackthorn in battle again. How would we split the gemhearts?"

"Two-thirds to you," Dalinar said. "As you've got twice as good a record at winning assaults as I have."

Sadeas looked thoughtful. "And the Shardblades?"

"If we find a Shardbearer, Adolin and I will take him. You win the Blade." He raised a finger. "But I win the Plate. To give to my son, Renarin."

"The invalid?"

"What would you care?" Dalinar said. "You already have Plate. Sadeas, this could mean *winning* the war. If we start to work together, we could bring the others in, prepare for a large-scale assault. Storms! We might not even need that. We two have the largest armies; if we could find a way to catch the Parshendi on a large enough plateau with the bulk of our troops—surrounding them so they couldn't escape—we might be able to damage their forces enough to bring an end to this all."

Sadeas mulled it over. Then he shrugged. "Very well. Send me details via messenger. But do it later. I've already missed too much of tonight's feast."

55

AN EMERALD
BROAM

*"A woman sits and scratches out her own eyes. Daughter
of kings and winds, the vandal."*

—Dated Palahevan, 1173, 73 seconds pre-death. Subject: a beggar of some renown, known for his elegant songs.

One week after losing Dunny, Kaladin stood on another
plateau, watching a battle proceed. This time, however,
he didn't have to save the wounded. They'd actually arrived
before the Parshendi. A rare but welcome event. Sadeas's army
was now holding out at the center of the plateau, protecting
the chrysalis while some of his soldiers cut into it.

The Parshendi kept leaping over the line and attacking the
men working on the chrysalis. *He's getting surrounded,* Kaladin thought. It didn't look good, which would mean a miserable return trip. Sadeas's men were bad enough when, arriving
second, they were rebuffed. Losing the gemheart after arriving first . . . would leave them even more frustrated.

"Kaladin!" a voice said. Kaladin spun to see Rock trotting
up. Was someone wounded? "Have you seen this thing?" The
Horneater pointed.

Kaladin turned, following his gesture. Another army was
approaching on an adjacent plateau. Kaladin raised eyebrows;

the banners flapped blue, and the soldiers were obviously Alethi.

"A little late, aren't they?" Moash asked, standing beside Kaladin.

"It happens," Kaladin said. Occasionally another highprince would arrive after Sadeas got to the plateau. More often, Sadeas arrived first, and the other Alethi army had to turn around. Usually they didn't get this close before doing so.

"That's the standard of Dalinar Kholin," Skar said, joining them.

"Dalinar," Moash said appreciatively. "They say he doesn't use bridgemen."

"How does he cross the chasms, then?" Kaladin asked.

The answer soon became obvious. This new army had enormous, siege-tower-like bridges pulled by chulls. They rumbled across the uneven plateaus, often having to pick their way around rifts in the stone. *They must be terribly slow,* Kaladin thought. But, in trade, the army wouldn't have to approach the chasm while being fired on. They could hide behind those bridges.

"Dalinar Kholin," Moash said. "They say he's a true lighteyes, like the men from the old days. A man of honor and of oaths."

Kaladin snorted. "I've seen plenty of lighteyes with that same reputation, and I've been disappointed by them every time. I'll tell you about Brightlord Amaram sometime."

"Amaram?" Skar asked. "The Shardbearer?"

"You've heard of that?" Kaladin asked.

"Sure," Skar said. "He's supposed to be on his way here. Everyone's talking about it in the taverns. Were you with him when he won his Shards?"

"No," Kaladin said softly. "Nobody was."

Dalinar Kholin's army approached across the plateau to the south. Amazingly, Dalinar's army came right up to the battlefield plateau.

"He's attacking?" Moash said, scratching his head. "Maybe he figures that Sadeas will lose, and wants to take a stab at it after he retreats."

"No," Kaladin said, frowning. "He's joining the battle."

The Parshendi army sent over some archers to fire on Dalinar's army, but their arrows bounced off the chulls without causing any harm. A group of soldiers unhooked the bridges and pushed them into place while Dalinar's archers set up and exchanged fire with the Parshendi.

"Does it seem Sadeas took fewer soldiers with him this run?" Sigzil asked, joining the group watching Dalinar's army. "Perhaps he planned for this. Could be why he was willing to commit like he did, letting himself get surrounded."

The bridges could be cranked to lower and extend; there was some marvelous engineering at work. As they began to work, something decidedly strange happened: Two Shardbearers, likely Dalinar and his son, leaped across the chasm and began attacking the Parshendi. The distraction let the soldiers get the large bridges into place, and some heavy cavalry charged across to help. It was a completely different method of doing a bridge assault, and Kaladin found himself considering the implications.

"He really *is* joining the battle," Moash said. "I think they're going to work together."

"It's bound to be more effective," Kaladin said. "I'm surprised they haven't tried it before."

Teft snorted. "That's because you don't understand how lighteyes think. Highprinces don't just want to win the battle, they want to win it by themselves."

"I wish I'd been recruited to his army instead," Moash said, almost reverent. The soldiers' armor gleamed, their ranks obviously well-practiced. Dalinar—the Blackthorn—had done an even better job than Amaram at cultivating a reputation for honesty. People knew of him all the way back in Hearthstone, but Kaladin understood the kinds of corruption a well-polished breastplate could hide.

Though, he thought, *that man who protected the whore on the street, he wore blue. Adolin, Dalinar's son. He seemed genuinely selfless in his defense of the woman.*

Kaladin set his jaw, casting aside those thoughts. He would not be taken in again.

He would *not*.

The fighting grew brutal for a short time, but the Parshendi were overwhelmed—smashed between two opposing forces. Soon, Kaladin's team led a victorious group of soldiers back to the camps for celebration.

※

Kaladin rolled the sphere between his fingers. The otherwise pure glass had cooled with a thin line of bubbles permanently frozen along one side. The bubbles were tiny spheres of their own, catching light.

He was on chasm scavenging duty. They'd gotten back from the plateau assault so quickly that Hashal, in defiance of logic or mercy, had sent them down into the chasm that very day. Kaladin continued to turn the sphere in his fingers. Hanging in the very center of it was a large emerald cut in a round shape, with dozens of tiny facets along the sides. A small rim of suspended bubbles clung to the side of the gemstone, as if longing to be near its brilliance.

Bright, crystalline green Stormlight shone from inside the glass, lighting Kaladin's fingers. An emerald broam, the highest denomination of sphere. Worth hundreds of lesser spheres. To bridgemen, this was a fortune. A strangely distant one, for spending it was impossible. Kaladin thought he could see some of the storm's tempest inside that rock. The light was like . . . it was like part of the storm, captured by the emerald. The light wasn't perfectly steady; it just seemed that way compared with the flickering of candles, torches, or lamps. Holding it close, Kaladin could see the light swirling, raging.

"What do we do with it?" Moash asked from Kaladin's side. Rock stood at Kaladin's other side. The sky was overcast, making it darker than usual here at the bottom. The cold weather of late had drawn back to spring, though it was uncomfortably chilly.

The men worked efficiently, quickly gathering spears, armor, boots, and spheres from the dead. Because of the short time given them—and because of the exhausting bridge run earlier—Kaladin had decided to forgo spear practice for the day. They'd load up on salvage instead and stow some of it down beneath, to be used for avoiding punishment next time.

As they'd worked, they'd found a lighteyed officer. He had been quite wealthy. This single emerald broam was worth what a bridgeman slave would make in two hundred days. In the same pouch with it, they'd found a collection of chips and marks that totaled slightly more than another emerald broam. Wealth. A fortune. Simply pocket change to a lighteyes.

"With this we could feed those wounded bridgemen for months," Moash said. "We could buy all the medical supplies we could want. Stormfather! We could probably bribe the camp's perimeter guards to let us sneak away."

"This thing will not happen," Rock said. "Is impossible to get spheres out of the chasms."

"We could swallow them," Moash said.

"You would choke. Spheres are too big, eh?"

"I'll bet I could do it," Moash said. His eyes glittered, reflecting the verdant Stormlight. "That's more money than I've ever seen. It's worth the risk."

"Swallowing won't work," Kaladin said. "You think those guards who watch us in the latrines are there to keep us from fleeing? I'll bet some sodden parshman has to go through our droppings, and I've seen them keep record of who visits and how often. We aren't the first to think of swallowing spheres."

Moash hesitated, then sighed, crestfallen. "You're probably right. Storm you, but you are. But we can't just give it to them, can we?"

"Yes, we can," Kaladin said, closing his fist around the sphere. The glow was bright enough to make his hand shine. "We'd never be able to spend it. A bridgeman with a full broam? It would give us away."

"But—" Moash began.

"We give it to them, Moash." Then he held up the pouch containing the other spheres. "But we find a way to keep these."

Rock nodded. "Yes. If we give up this expensive sphere, they will think us honest, eh? It will disguise the theft, and they will even give us small reward. But how can we do this thing, keeping the pouch?"

"I'm working on that," Kaladin said.

"Work fast, then," Moash said, glancing at Kaladin's torch, rammed between two rocks at the side of the chasm. "We'll need to head back up soon."

Kaladin opened his hand and rolled the emerald sphere between his fingers. How? "Have you ever seen anything so beautiful?" Moash asked, staring at the emerald.

"It's just a sphere," Kaladin said absently. "A tool. I once held a goblet full of a hundred diamond broams and was told they were mine. Since I never got to spend them, they were as good as worthless."

"A hundred diamonds?" Moash asked. "Where . . . how?"

Kaladin closed his mouth, cursing himself. *I shouldn't keep mentioning things like that.* "Go on," he said, tucking the emerald broam back into the black pouch. "We need to be quick."

Moash sighed, but Rock thumped him on the back good-naturedly and they joined the rest of the bridgemen. Rock and Lopen—using Syl's directions—had led them to a large mass of corpses in red-and-brown uniforms. He didn't know which highprince's men they were, but the bodies were pretty fresh. There were no Parshendi among them.

Kaladin glanced to the side, where Shen—the parshman bridgeman—worked. Quiet, obedient, stalwart. Teft still didn't trust him. A part of Kaladin was glad for that. Syl landed on the wall beside him, standing with her feet planted against the surface and looking up at the sky.

Think, Kaladin told himself. *How do we keep these spheres? There has to be a way.* But each possibility seemed too much of a risk. If they were caught stealing, they'd probably be given a different work detail. Kaladin wasn't willing to risk that.

Silent green lifespren began to fade into existence around him, bobbing around the moss and haspers. A few frillblooms opened up fronds of red and yellow beside his head. Kaladin had thought again and again about Dunny's death. Bridge Four was not safe. True, they'd lost a remarkably small number of men lately, but they were still dwindling. And each bridge run was a chance for total disaster. All it took was one time, with the Parshendi focusing on them. Lose three or four men, and they'd topple. The waves of arrows would redouble, cutting every one of them down.

It was the same old problem, the one Kaladin had beaten his head against day after day. How did you protect bridgemen when everyone wanted them exposed and endangered?

"Hey Sig," Maps said, walking by carrying an armload of spears. "You're a Worldsinger, right?" Maps had grown increasingly friendly in the last few weeks, and had proven good at getting the others talking. The balding man reminded Kaladin of an innkeeper, always quick to make his patrons feel at ease.

Sigzil—who was pulling the boots off a line of corpses—gave Rock a straight-lipped glance that seemed to say, "This is your fault." He didn't like that others had discovered he was a Worldsinger.

"Why don't you give us a tale?" Maps said, setting down his armload. "Help us pass the time."

"I am not a foolish jester or storyteller," Sigzil said, yanking off a boot. "I do not 'give tales.' I spread knowledge of cultures, peoples, thoughts, and dreams. I bring peace through understanding. It is the holy charge my order received from the Heralds themselves."

"Well why not start spreading then?" Maps said, standing and wiping his hands on his trousers.

Sigzil signed audibly. "Very well. What is it you wish to hear about?"

"I don't know. Something interesting."

"Tell us about Brightking Alazansi and the hundred-ship fleet," Leyten called.

"I am not a storyteller!" Sigzil repeated. "I speak of nations and peoples, not tavern stories. I—"

"Is there a place where people live in gouges in the ground?" Kaladin said. "A city built in an enormous complex of lines, all set into the rock as if carved there?"

"Sesemalex Dar," Sigzil said, nodding, pulling off another boot. "Yes, it is the capital of the kingdom of Emul, and is one

of the most ancient cities in the world. It is said that the city—
and, indeed, the kingdom—were named by Jezrien himself."

"Jezrien?" Malop said, standing and scratching his head.
"Who's that?" Malop was a thick-haired fellow with a bushy
black beard and a glyphward tattoo on each hand. He also
wasn't the brightest sphere in the goblet, so to speak.

"You call him the Stormfather, here in Alethkar," Sigzil
said. "Or Jezerezeh'Elin. He was king of the Heralds. Master
of the storms, bringer of water and life, known for his fury
and his temper, but also for his mercy."

"Oh," Malop said.

"Tell me more of the city," Kaladin said.

"Sesemalex Dar. It is, indeed, built in giant troughs. The
pattern is quite amazing. It protects against highstorms, as
each trough has a lip at the side, keeping water from streaming
in off the stone plain around it. That, mixed with a drainage
system of cracks, protects the city from flooding.

"The people there are known for their expert crem pottery; the city is a major waypoint in the southwest. The Emuli
are a certain tribe of the Askarki people, and they're ethni-
cally Makabaki—dark-skinned, like myself. Their kingdom
borders my own, and I visited there many times in my youth.

"It is a wondrous place, filled with exotic travelers." Sigzil
grew more relaxed as he continued to talk. "Their legal system
is very lenient toward foreigners. A man who is not of their
nationality cannot own a home or shop, but when you visit,
you are treated as a 'relative who has traveled from afar, to be
shown all kindness and leniency.' A foreigner can take dinner
at any residence he calls upon, assuming he is respectful and
offers a gift of fruit. The people are most interested in exotic
fruits. They worship Jezrien, though they don't accept him as a
figure from the Vorin religion. They name him the only god."

"The Heralds aren't gods," Teft scoffed.

"To you they aren't," Sigzil said. "Others regard them differently. The Emuli have what your scholars like to call a
splinter religion—containing some Vorin ideas. But to the
Emuli, you would be the splinter religion." Sigzil seemed to
find that amusing, though Teft just scowled.

Sigzil continued in more and more detail, talking of the flowing gowns and head-wraps of the Emuli women, the robes favored by the men. The taste of the food—salty—and the way of greeting an old friend—by holding the left forefinger to the forehead and bowing in respect. Sigzil knew an impressive amount about them. Kaladin noticed him smiling wistfully at times, probably recalling his travels.

The details were interesting, but Kaladin was more taken aback by the fact that this city—which he had flown over in his dream weeks ago—was actually real. And he could no longer ignore the strange speed at which he recovered from wounds. Something odd was happening to him. Something supernatural. What if it was related to the fact that everyone around him always seemed to die?

He knelt down to begin rifling the pockets of the dead men, a duty the other bridgemen avoided. Spheres, knives, and other useful objects were kept. Personal mementoes like unburned prayers were left with the bodies. He found a few zircon chips, which he added to the pouch.

Maybe Moash was right. If they could get this money out, could they *bribe* their way free of the camp? That would certainly be safer than fighting. So why was he so insistent on teaching the bridgemen to fight? Why hadn't he given any thought to sneaking the bridgemen out?

He had lost Dallet and the others of his original squad in Amaram's army. Did he think to compensate for that by training a new group of spearmen? Was this about saving men he'd grown to love, or was it just about proving something to himself?

His experience told him that men who could not fight were at a severe disadvantage in this world of war and storms. Perhaps sneaking out would have been the better option, but he knew little of stealth. Besides, if they sneaked away, Sadeas would still send troops after them. Trouble would track them down. Whatever their path, the bridgemen would have to kill to remain free.

He squeezed his eyes shut, remembering one of his escape attempts, when he'd kept his fellow slaves free for an entire week, hiding in the wilderness. They'd finally been caught by their master's hunters. That was when he'd lost Nalma. *None of that has to do with saving them here and now,* Kaladin told himself. *I need these spheres.*

Sigzil was still talking about the Emuli. "To them," the Worldsinger said, "the need to strike a man personally is crass. They wage war in the opposite way from you Alethi. The sword is not a weapon for a leader. A halberd is better, then a spear, and best of all a bow and arrow."

Kaladin pulled another handful of spheres—skychips—from a soldier's pocket. They were stuck to an aged hunk of sow's cheese, fragrant and moldy. He grimaced, picking the spheres out and washing them in a puddle.

"Spears, used by lighteyes?" Drehy said. "That's ridiculous."

"Why?" Sigzil said, sounding offended. "I find the Emuli way to be interesting. In some countries, it is seen as displeasing to fight at all. To the Shin, for instance, if you must fight a man, then you have already failed. Killing is, at best, a brutish way of solving problems."

"You're not going to be like Rock and refuse to fight, are you?" Skar asked, shooting a barely veiled glare at the Horneater. Rock sniffed and turned his back on the shorter man, kneeling down to shove boots into a large sack.

"No," Sigzil said. "I think we can all agree that other methods have failed. Perhaps if my master knew I still lived . . . but no. That is foolish. Yes, I will fight. And if I have to, the spear seems a favorable weapon, though I honestly would prefer to put more distance between myself and my enemies."

Kaladin frowned. "You mean with a bow?"

Sigzil nodded. "Among my people, the bow is a noble weapon."

"Do you know how to use one?"

"Alas, no," Sigzil said. "I would have mentioned it before now if I had such proficiency."

Kaladin stood up, opening the pouch and depositing the spheres in with the others. "Were there any bows among the bodies?"

The men glanced at each other, several of them shaking heads. *Storm it*, Kaladin thought. The seed of an idea had begun to sprout in his mind, but that killed it.

"Gather up some of those spears," he said. "Set them aside. We'll need them for training."

"But we have to turn them in," Malop said.

"Not if we don't take them with us up out of the chasm," Kaladin said. "Each time we come scavenging, we'll save a few spears and stash them down here. It shouldn't take long to gather enough to practice with."

"How will we get them out when it's time to escape?" Teft asked, rubbing his chin. "Spears left down here won't do these lads much good once the real fighting starts."

"I'll find a way to get them up," Kaladin said.

"You say things like that a lot," Skar noted.

"Leave off, Skar," Moash said. "He knows what he's doing."

Kaladin blinked. Had *Moash* just defended him?

Skar flushed. "I didn't mean it like that, Kaladin. I'm just asking, that's all."

"I understand. It's . . ." Kaladin trailed off as Syl flitted down into the chasm in the form of a curling ribbon.

She landed on a rock outcropping on the wall, taking on her female form. "I found another group of bodies. They're mostly Parshendi."

"Any bows?" Kaladin asked. Several of the bridgemen gawked at him until they saw him staring into the air. Then they nodded knowingly to one another.

"I think so," Syl said. "It's just down this way. Not too far."

The bridgemen had mostly finished with these bodies. "Gather up the things," Kaladin said. "I've found us another place to scavenge. We need to gather as much as we can, then stash some in a chasm where it has a good chance of not being washed away."

The bridgemen picked up their findings, slinging sacks over their shoulders and each man hefting a spear or two. Within moments, they headed down the dank chasm bottom, following Syl. They passed clefts in the ancient rock walls where old, storm-washed bones had gotten lodged, creating a mound of moss-covered femurs, tibia, skulls, and ribs. There wasn't much salvage among them.

After about a quarter-hour, they came to the place Syl had found. A scattered group of Parshendi dead lay in heaps, mixed with the occasional Alethi in blue. Kaladin knelt beside one of the human bodies. He recognized Dalinar Kholin's stylized glyphpair sewn on the coat. Why *had* Dalinar's army joined Sadeas's in battle? What had changed?

Kaladin pointed for the men to begin scavenging from the Alethi while he walked over to one of the Parshendi corpses. It was much fresher than Dalinar's man. They didn't find nearly as many Parshendi corpses as they did Alethi. Not only were there fewer of them in any given battle, but they were less likely to fall to their deaths into the chasms. Sigzil also guessed that their bodies were more dense than human ones, and didn't float or wash away as easily.

Kaladin rolled the body onto its side, and the action elicited a sudden hiss from the back of the group of bridgemen. Kaladin turned to see Shen pushing forward in an uncharacteristic display of passion.

Teft moved quickly, grabbing Shen from behind, placing him in a choke hold. The other bridgemen stood, aghast, though several fell into their stances by reflex.

Shen struggled weakly against Teft's grip. The parshman looked different from his dead cousins; close together, the differences were much more obvious. Shen—like most parshmen—was short and a little plump. Stout, strong, but not threatening. The corpse at Kaladin's feet, however, was muscled and built like a Horneater, easily as tall as Kaladin and far broader at the shoulders. While both had the marbled skin, the Parshendi had those strange red-orange growths of armor on the head, chest, arms, and legs.

"Let him go," Kaladin said, curious.

Teft glanced at him, then reluctantly did as commanded. Shen scrambled over the uneven ground and gently, but firmly, pushed Kaladin away from the corpse. Shen stood back, as if protecting it from Kaladin.

"This thing," Rock noted, stepping up beside Kaladin, "he has done it before. When Lopen and I take him scavenging."

"He's protective of the Parshendi bodies, gancho," Lopen added. "Like he'd stab you a hundred times for moving one, sure."

"They're all like that," Sigzil said from behind.

Kaladin turned, raising an eyebrow.

"Parshman workers," Sigzil explained. "They're allowed to care for their own dead; it's one of the few things they seem passionate about. They grow irate if anyone else handles the bodies. They wrap them in linen and carry them out into the wilderness and leave them on slabs of stone."

Kaladin regarded Shen. *I wonder.* . . .

"Scavenge from the Parshendi," Kaladin said to his men. "Teft, you'll probably have to hold Shen the whole time. I can't have him trying to stop us."

Teft shot Kaladin a suffering glance; he still thought they should set Shen at the front of the bridge and let him die. But he did as told, pushing Shen away and getting Moash's help to hold him.

"And men," Kaladin noted, "be respectful of the dead."

"They're Parshendi!" Leyten objected.

"I know," Kaladin said. "But it bothers Shen. He's one of us, so let's keep his irritation to a minimum."

The parshman lowered his arms reluctantly and let Teft and Moash pull him away. He seemed resigned. Parshmen were slow of thought. How much did Shen comprehend?

"Didn't you wish to find a bow?" Sigzil asked, kneeling and slipping a horned Parshendi shortbow out from underneath a body. "The bowstring is gone."

"There's another in this fellow's pouch," Maps said, pulling something out of another Parshendi corpse's belt pouch. "Might still be good."

Kaladin accepted the weapon and string. "Does anyone know how to use one of these?"

The bridgemen glanced at one another. Bows were useless for hunting most shellbeasts; slings worked far better. The bow was really only good for killing other men. Kaladin glanced at Teft, who shook his head. He hadn't been trained on a bow; neither had Kaladin.

"Is simple," Rock said, rolling over a Parshendi corpse, "put arrow on string. Point away from self. Pull very hard. Let go."

"I doubt it will be that easy," Kaladin said.

"We barely have time to train the lads in the spear, Kaladin," Teft said. "You mean to teach some of them the bow as well? And without a teacher who can use one himself?"

Kaladin didn't respond. He tucked the bow and string away in his bag, added a few arrows, then helped the others. An hour later, they marched through the chasms toward the ladder, their torches sputtering, dusk approaching. The darker it grew, the more unpleasant the chasms became. Shadows deepened, and distant sounds—water dripping, rocks falling, wind calling—took on an ominous cast. Kaladin rounded a corner, and a group of many-legged cremlings scuttled along the wall and slipped into a fissure.

Conversation was subdued, and Kaladin didn't take part. Occasionally, he glanced over his shoulder toward Shen. The silent parshman walked head down. Robbing the Parshendi corpses had seriously disturbed him.

I can use that, Kaladin thought. *But dare I?* It would be a risk. A great one. He had already been sentenced once for upsetting the balance of the chasm battles.

First the spheres, he thought. Getting the spheres out would mean he might be able to get out other items. Eventually he saw a shadow above, spanning the chasm. They had reached the first of the permanent bridges. Kaladin walked with the others a little further, until they reached a place where the chasm floor was closer to the top of the plateaus above.

He stopped here. The bridgemen gathered around him.

"Sigzil," Kaladin said, pointing. "You know something about bows. How hard do you think it would be to hit that bridge with an arrow?"

"I've occasionally held a bow, Kaladin, but I would not call myself an expert. It shouldn't be too hard, I'd imagine. The distance is what, fifty feet?"

"What's the point?" Moash asked.

Kaladin pulled out the pouch full of spheres, then raised an eyebrow at them. "We tie the bag to the arrow, then launch it up so that it sticks to the bottom of the bridge. Then when we're on a bridge run, Lopen and Dabbid can hang back to get a drink near that bridge up there. They reach under the wood and pull the arrow off. We get the spheres."

Teft whistled. "Clever."

"We could get all of the spheres," Moash said eagerly. "Even the—"

"No," Kaladin said firmly. "The lesser ones will be dangerous enough; people might begin wondering where bridgemen are getting so much money." He would have to buy his supplies from several different apothecaries to hide his influx of money.

Moash looked crestfallen, but the other bridgemen were eager. "Who wants to try?" Kaladin asked. "Maybe we should shoot a few practice shots first, then try with the bag. Sigzil?"

"I don't know if I want this on me," Sigzil said. "Maybe you should try, Teft."

Teft rubbed his chin. "Sure. I guess. How hard can it be?"

"How hard?" Rock asked suddenly.

Kaladin glanced to the side. Rock stood at the back of the group, though his height made him easy to see. He had his arms folded.

"How hard, Teft?" Rock continued. "Fifty feet is not too far, but is not easy shot. And to do it with bag of heavy spheres tied to it? Ha! You also need to get arrow close to side of bridge, so Lopen can reach. If you miss with this thing, you could lose all spheres. And what if scouts near bridges above see arrow come from chasm? Will think it suspicious, eh?"

Kaladin eyed the Horneater. *Is simple,* he'd said. *Point away from self . . . let go . . .*

"Well," Kaladin said, watching Rock from the corner of his eye. "I guess we'll just have to take that chance. Without these spheres, the wounded die."

"We could wait until the next bridge run," Teft said. "Tie

a rope to the bridge and toss it over, then tie the bag to it next time. . . ."

"Fifty feet of rope?" Kaladin said flatly. "It would draw enough attention to buy something like that."

"Nah, gancho," Lopen said. "I have a cousin who works in a place that sells rope. I could get some for you easy, with money."

"Perhaps," Kaladin said. "But you'd still have to hide it in the litter, then hang it down into the chasm without anyone seeing. And to leave it dangling there for several days? It would be noticed."

The others nodded. Rock seemed very uncomfortable. Sighing, Kaladin took out the bow and several arrows. "We'll just have to chance this. Teft, why don't you . . ."

"Oh, Kali'kalin's ghost," Rock muttered. "Here, give me bow." He shoved his way through the bridgemen, taking the bow from Kaladin. Kaladin hid a smile.

Rock glanced upward, judging the distance in the waning light. He strung the bowstring, then held out a hand. Kaladin handed him an arrow. He leveled the bow back down the chasm and launched. The arrow flew swiftly, clattering against chasm walls.

Rock nodded to himself, then pointed at Kaladin's pouch. "We take only five spheres," Rock said. "Any more would be too heavy. Is crazy to try with even five. Airsick lowlanders."

Kaladin smiled, then counted out five sapphire marks—together about two and a half months' worth of pay for a bridgeman—and placed them in a spare pouch. He handed that to Rock, who pulled out a knife and dug a notch into an arrow's shaft next to the arrowhead.

Skar folded his arms and leaned against the mossy wall. "This is stealing, you know."

"Yes," Kaladin said, watching Rock. "And I don't feel the least bit bad about it. Do you?"

"Not at all," Skar said, grinning. "I figure once someone is trying to get you killed, all expectations of your loyalty are tossed to the storm. But if someone were to go to Gaz . . ."

The other bridgemen suddenly grew nervous, and more

than a few eyes darted toward Shen, though Kaladin could see that Skar wasn't thinking of the parshman. If one of the bridgemen were to betray the rest of them, he might earn himself a reward.

"Maybe we should post a watch," Drehy said. "You know, make sure nobody sneaks off to talk to Gaz."

"We'll do no such thing," Kaladin said. "What are we going to do? Lock ourselves in the barrack, so suspicious of each other that we never get anything done?" He shook his head. "No. This is just one more danger. It's a real one, but we can't waste energy spying on each other. So we keep on going."

Skar didn't look convinced.

"We're Bridge Four," Kaladin said firmly. "We've faced death together. We have to trust each other. You can't run into battle wondering if your comrades are going to switch sides suddenly." He met the eyes of each man in turn. "I trust you. All of you. We'll make it through this, and we'll do it together."

There were several nods; Skar seemed placated. Rock finished his work cutting the arrow, then proceeded to tie the pouch tightly around the shaft.

Syl still sat on Kaladin's shoulder. "You want me to watch the others? Make sure nobody does what Skar thinks they might?"

Kaladin hesitated, then nodded. Best to be safe. He just didn't want the men to have to think that way.

Rock hefted the arrow, judging the weight. "Near impossible shot," he complained. Then, in a smooth motion, he nocked the arrow and drew to his cheek, positioning himself directly beneath the bridge. The small pouch hung down, dangling against the wood of the arrow. The bridgemen held their breath.

Rock loosed. The arrow streaked up the side of the chasm wall, almost too fast to follow. A faint click sounded as arrow met wood, and Kaladin held his breath, but the arrow did not pull free. It remained hanging there, precious spheres tied to its shaft, right next to the side of the bridge where it could be reached.

Kaladin clapped Rock on the shoulder as the bridgemen cheered him.

Rock eyed Kaladin. "I will not use bow to fight. You must know this thing."

"I promise," Kaladin said. "I'll take you if you agree, but I won't force you."

"I will not fight," Rock said. "Is not my place." He glanced up at the spheres, then smiled faintly. "But shooting bridge is all right."

"How did you learn?" Kaladin asked.

"Is secret," Rock said firmly. "Take bow. Bother me no more."

"All right," Kaladin said, accepting the bow. "But I don't know if I can promise not to bother you. I may need a few more shots in the future." He eyed Lopen. "You really think you can buy some rope without drawing attention?"

Lopen lounged back against the wall. "My cousin's never failed me."

"How many cousins do you have, anyway?" Earless Jaks asked.

"A man can never have enough cousins," Lopen said.

"Well, we need that rope," Kaladin said, the plan beginning to sprout in his mind. "Do it, Lopen. I'll make change from those spheres above to pay for it."

56

THAT STORMING BOOK

"Light grows so distant. The storm never stops. I am broken, and all around me have died. I weep for the end of all things. He has won. Oh, he has beaten us."

—Dated Palahakev, 1173, 16 seconds pre-death. Subject: a Thaylen sailor.

Dalinar fought, the Thrill pulsing within him, swinging his Shardblade from atop Gallant's back. Around him, Parshendi fell with eyes burning black.

They came at him in pairs, each team trying to hit him from a different direction, keeping him busy and—they hoped—disoriented. If a pair could rush at him while he was distracted, they might be able to shove him off his mount. Those axes and maces—swung repeatedly—could crack his Plate. It was a very costly tactic; corpses lay scattered around Dalinar. But when fighting against a Shardbearer, every tactic was costly.

Dalinar kept Gallant moving, dancing from side to side, as he swung his Blade in broad sweeps. He stayed just a little ahead of the line of his men. A Shardbearer needed space to fight; the Blades were so long that hurting one's companions was a very real danger. His honor guard would approach only if he fell or encountered trouble.

The Thrill excited him, strengthened him. He hadn't experienced the weakness again, the nausea he had on the battlefield that day weeks ago. Perhaps he'd been worried about nothing.

He turned Gallant just in time to confront two pairs of Parshendi coming at him from behind, singing softly. He directed Gallant with his knees, performing an expert sweeping side-swing, cutting through the necks of two Parshendi, then the arm of a third. Eyes burned out in the first two, and they collapsed. The third dropped his weapon from a hand that grew suddenly lifeless, flopping down, its nerves all severed.

The fourth member of that squad scrambled away, glaring at Dalinar. This was one of the Parshendi who didn't wear a beard, and it seemed that there was something odd about his face. The cheek structure was just a little off. . . .

Was that a woman? Dalinar thought with amazement. *It couldn't have been. Could it?*

Behind him, his soldiers let out cheers as a large number of Parshendi scattered away to regroup. Dalinar lowered his Shardblade, the metal gleaming, gloryspren winking into the air around him. There was another reason for him to stay out ahead of his men. A Shardbearer wasn't just a force of destruction; he was a force of morale and inspiration. The men fought more vigorously as they saw their brightlord felling foe after foe. Shardbearers changed battles.

Since the Parshendi were broken for the moment, Dalinar climbed free of Gallant and dropped to the rocks. Corpses lay unbloodied all around him, though once he approached the place where his men had been fighting, orange-red blood stained the rocks. Cremlings scuttled about on the ground, lapping up the liquid, and painspren wriggled between them. Wounded Parshendi lay staring up into the air, faces masks of pain, singing a quiet, haunting song to themselves. Often just as whispers. They never yelled as they died.

Dalinar felt the Thrill retreat as he joined his honor guard. "They're getting too close to Gallant," Dalinar said to Teleb, handing over the reins. The massive Ryshadium's coat was flecked with frothy sweat. "I don't want to risk him. Have a man run him to the back lines."

Teleb nodded, waving a soldier to obey the order. Dalinar hefted his Shardblade, scanning the battlefield. The Parshendi force was regrouping. As always, the two-person teams were the focus of their strategy. Each pair would have different weapons, and often one was clean-shaven while the other had a beard woven with gemstones. His scholars had suggested this was some kind of primitive apprenticeship.

Dalinar inspected the clean-shaven ones for signs of any stubble. There was none, and more than a few had a faintly feminine shape to their faces. Could the ones without beards all be women? They didn't appear to have much in the way of breasts, and their builds were like those of men, but the strange Parshendi armor could be masking things. The beardless ones *did* seem smaller by a few fingers, and the shapes of the faces . . . studying them, it seemed possible. Could the pairs be husbands and wives fighting together? That struck him as strangely fascinating. Was it possible that, despite six years of war, nobody had taken the time to investigate the genders of those they fought?

Yes. The contested plateaus were so far out, nobody ever brought back Parshendi bodies; they just set men to pulling the gemstones out of their beards or gathering their weapons. Since Gavilar's death, very little effort had been given to studying the Parshendi. Everyone just wanted them dead, and if there was one thing the Alethi were good at, it was killing.

And you're *supposed to be killing them now,* Dalinar told himself, *not analyzing their culture.* But he did decide to have his soldiers collect a few bodies for the scholars.

He charged toward another section of the battlefield, Shardblade before him in two hands, making certain not to outpace his soldiers. To the south, he could see Adolin's banner flying as he led his division against the Parshendi there. The lad had been uncharacteristically reserved lately. Being wrong about Sadeas seemed to have made him more contemplative.

On the west side, Sadeas's own banner flew proudly, Sadeas's forces keeping the Parshendi from the chrysalis. He'd arrived first, as before, engaging the Parshendi so Dalinar's companies could arrive. Dalinar had considered cutting out the gemheart so the Alethi could retreat, but why end the battle that quickly? He and Sadeas both felt the real point of their alliance was to crush as many Parshendi as possible.

The more they killed, the faster this war would be through. And so far, Dalinar's plan was working. The two armies complemented one another. Dalinar's assaults had been too slow, and he'd allowed the Parshendi to position themselves too well. Sadeas was fast—more so now that he could leave men behind and concentrate fully on speed—and he was frighteningly effective at getting men onto the plateaus to fight, but his men weren't trained as well as Dalinar's. So if Sadeas could arrive first, then hold out long enough for Dalinar to get his men across, the superior training—and superior Shards—of his forces worked like a hammer against the Parshendi, smashing them against Sadeas's anvil.

It was still by no means easy. The Parshendi fought like chasmfiends.

Dalinar crashed against them, swinging out with his Blade, slaying Parshendi on all sides. He couldn't help but feel a grudging respect for the Parshendi. Few men dared assault a Shardbearer directly—at least not without the entire weight of their army forcing them forward, almost against their will.

These Parshendi attacked with bravery. Dalinar spun, laying about him, the Thrill surging within. With an ordinary sword, a fighter focused on controlling his blows, striking and expecting recoil. You wanted quick, rapid strikes with small arcs. A Shardblade was different. The Blade was enormous, yet remarkably light. There was never recoil; landing a blow felt nearly like passing the sword through the air itself. The trick was to control momentum and keep the sword moving.

Four Parshendi threw themselves at him; they seemed to know that working into close quarters was one of the best ways to drop him. If they got too close, the length of his

Blade's hilt and the nature of his armor would make fighting more difficult for him. Dalinar spun in a long, waist-high attack, and noted the deaths of Parshendi by the slight tug on the Blade as it passed through their chests. He got all four of them, and felt a surge of satisfaction.

It was followed immediately by nausea.

Damnation! he thought. *Not again!* He turned toward another group of Parshendi as the eyes of the dead burned out and smoked.

He threw himself into another attack—raising his Blade in a twisting swing over his head, then bringing it down parallel to the ground. Six Parshendi died. He felt a spike of regret along with displeasure at the Thrill. Surely these Parshendi—these soldiers—deserved respect, not glee, as they were slaughtered.

He remembered the times when the Thrill had been the strongest. Subduing the highprinces with Gavilar during their youths, forcing back the Vedens, fighting the Herdazians and destroying the Akak Reshi. Once, the thirst for battle had nearly led him to attack Gavilar himself. Dalinar could remember the jealousy on that day some ten years ago, when the itch to attack Gavilar—the only worthy opponent he could see, the man who had won Navani's hand—had nearly consumed him.

His honor guard cheered as his foes dropped. He felt hollow, but he seized the Thrill and got a tight grip on his feelings and emotions. He let the Thrill pulse through him. Blessedly, the sickness went away, which was good, for another group of Parshendi charged him from the side. He executed a Windstance turn, shifting his feet, lowering his shoulder, and throwing his weight behind his Blade as he swung.

He got three in the sweep, but the fourth and final Parshendi shoved past his wounded comrades, getting inside Dalinar's reach, swinging his hammer. His eyes were wide with anger and determination, though he did not yell or bellow. He just continued his song.

His blow cracked into Dalinar's helm. It pushed his head to the side but the Plate absorbed most of the hit, a few tiny weblike lines cracking along its length. Dalinar could see them glowing faintly, releasing Stormlight at the edges of his vision.

The Parshendi was in too close. Dalinar dropped his Blade. The weapon puffed away to mist as Dalinar raised an armored arm and blocked the next hammer blow. Then he swung with his other arm, smashing his fist into the Parshendi's shoulder. The blow tossed the man to the ground. The Parshendi's song cut off. Gritting his teeth, Dalinar stepped up and kicked the man in the chest, throwing the body a good twenty feet through the air. He'd learned to be wary of Parshendi who weren't fully incapacitated.

Dalinar lowered his hands and began to resummon his Shardblade. He felt strong again, passion for battle returning to him. *I shouldn't feel bad for killing the Parshendi,* he thought. *This is right.*

He paused, noticing something. What was that on the next plateau over? It looked like . . .

Like a second Parshendi army.

Several groups of his scouts were dashing toward the main battle lines, but Dalinar could guess the news they brought. "Stormfather!" he cursed, pointing with his Shardblade. "Pass the warning! A second army approaches!"

Several men scattered in accordance to his command. *We should have expected this,* Dalinar thought. *We started bringing two armies to a plateau, so they have done the same.*

But that implied that they had limited themselves before. Did they do it because they realized that the battlefields left little room for maneuvering? Or was it for speed? But that didn't make sense—the Alethi had to worry about bridges as choke points, slowing them more and more if they brought more troops. But the Parshendi could jump the chasms. So why commit fewer troops than their all?

Curse it all, he thought with frustration. *We know so little about them!*

He shoved his Shardblade into the rock beside him, placing it intentionally so that it didn't vanish. He began calling out orders. His honor guard formed around him, ushering in scouts and sending out runners. For a short time, he became a tactical general rather than an advance warrior.

It took time to change their battlefield strategy. An army was like a massive chull at times, lumbering along, slow to react. Before his orders could be executed, the new Parshendi force began crossing over onto the north side. That was where Sadeas was fighting. Dalinar couldn't get a good view, and scout reports were taking too long.

He glanced to the side; there was a tall rock formation nearby. It had uneven sides, making it look a little like a pile of boards stacked one atop another. He grabbed his Shardblade in the middle of a report and ran across the stony ground, smashing a few Rockbuds beneath his plated boots. The Cobalt Guard and the messengers followed quickly.

At the rock formation, Dalinar tossed his Blade aside, letting it dissolve to smoke. He threw himself up and grabbed the rock, scaling the formation. Seconds later, he heaved himself up onto its flat top.

The battlefield stretched out below him. The main Parshendi army was a mass of red and black at the center of the plateau, now pressed on two sides by the Alethi. Sadeas's bridge crews waited on a western plateau, ignored, while the new force of Parshendi crossed from the north onto the battlefield.

Stormfather, but they can jump, Dalinar thought, watching the Parshendi span the gap in powerful leaps. Six years of fighting had shown Dalinar that human soldiers—particularly if lightly armored—could outrun Parshendi troops if they had to go more than a few dozen yards. But those thick, powerful Parshendi legs could send them far when they leaped.

Not a single Parshendi lost his footing as they crossed the chasm. They approached the chasm at a trot, then dashed with a burst of speed for about ten feet, launching themselves forward. The new force pushed south, directly into Sadeas's army. Raising a hand against the bright white sunlight, Dalinar found he could make out Sadeas's personal banner.

It was directly in the path of the oncoming Parshendi

force; he tended to remain at the back of his armies, in a secure position. Now, that position suddenly became the front lines, and Sadeas's other troops were too slow to disengage and react. He didn't have any support.

Sadeas! Dalinar thought, stepping right up to the lip of the stone, his cape streaming behind him in the breeze. *I need to send him my reserve spearmen—*

But no, they'd be too slow.

The spearmen couldn't get to him. But someone mounted might be able to.

"Gallant!" Dalinar bellowed, throwing himself off the rock formation. He fell to the rocks below, Plate absorbing the shock as he hit, cracking the stone. Stormlight puffed up around him, rising from his armor, and the greaves cracked slightly.

Gallant pulled away from his minders, galloping across the stones at Dalinar's call. As the horse approached, Dalinar grabbed the saddle-holds and heaved himself up and into place. "Follow if you can," he bellowed at his honor guard, "and send a runner to tell my son he now commands our army!"

Dalinar reared Gallant and galloped alongside the perimeter of the battlefield. His guard called for their horses, but they'd have difficulty keeping up with a Ryshadium.

So be it.

Fighting soldiers became a blur to Dalinar's right. He leaned low in the saddle, wind hissing as it blew over his Shardplate. He held a hand out and summoned Oathbringer. It dropped into his hand, steaming and frosted, as he turned Gallant around the western tip of the battlefield. By design, the original Parshendi army lay between his force and Sadeas's. He didn't have time to round them. So, taking a deep breath, Dalinar struck out through the middle of it. Their ranks were spread out because of how they fought.

Gallant galloped through them, and Parshendi threw themselves out of the massive stallion's way, cursing in their melodic language. Hooves beat a thunder upon the rocks; Dalinar urged Gallant on with his knees. They had to keep momentum. Some Parshendi fighting on the front against Sadeas's force turned and ran at him. They saw the opportunity. If Dalinar fell, he'd land alone, surrounded by thousands of enemies.

Dalinar's heart thumped as he held his Blade out, trying to swipe at Parshendi who came too close. Within minutes, he approached the northwestern Parshendi line. There, his enemies formed up, raising spears and setting them against the ground.

Blast! Dalinar thought. Parshendi had never set spears like that against heavy cavalry before. They were starting to learn.

Dalinar charged the formation, then wheeled Gallant at the last moment, turning parallel to the Parshendi spear wall. He swung his Shardblade out to the side, shearing the tips from their weapons and hitting a few arms. A patch of Parshendi just ahead wavered, and Dalinar took a deep breath, urging Gallant directly into them, shearing off a few spear tips. Another one bounced off his shoulder armor, and Gallant took a long gash on the left flank.

Their momentum carried them forward, trampling over the Parshendi, and with a whinny, Gallant burst free of the Parshendi line just to the side of where Sadeas's main force was engaging the enemy.

Dalinar's heart pumped. He passed Sadeas's force in a blur, galloping toward the back lines, where a churning, disorganized chaos of men tried to react to the new Parshendi force. Men screamed and died, a mess of forest green Alethi and Parshendi in black and red.

There! Dalinar saw Sadeas's banner flap for a moment before falling. He threw himself from Gallant's saddle and hit the stones. The horse turned away, understanding. His wound was bad, and Dalinar would not risk him any further.

It was time for the slaughter to begin again.

He tore into the Parshendi force from the side, and some turned, looks of surprise in their usually stoic black eyes. At times the Parshendi seemed alien, but their emotions were so human. The Thrill rose and Dalinar did not force it down. He needed it too much. An ally was in danger.

It was time to let the Blackthorn loose.

Dalinar punched through the Parshendi ranks. He felled

Parshendi like a man sweeping crumbs from the table after a meal. There was no controlled precision here, no careful engagement of a few squads with his honor guard at the back. This was a full-out attack, with all the power and deadly force of a life-long killer enhanced by Shards. He was like a tempest, slashing through legs, torsos, arms, necks, killing, killing, killing. He was a maelstrom of death and steel. Weapons bounced off his armor, leaving tiny cracks. He killed dozens, always moving, forcing his way toward where Sadeas's banner had fallen.

Eyes burned, swords flashed in the sky, and Parshendi sang. The close press of their own troops—bunching up as they hit Sadeas's line—inhibited them. But not Dalinar. He didn't have to worry about striking friends, nor did he have to worry about his weapon getting caught in flesh or stuck in armor. And if corpses got in his way, he sheared through them—dead flesh would cut like steel and wood.

Parshendi blood splashed in the air as he killed, then hacked, then shoved his way through the press. Blade from shoulder to side, back and forth, occasionally turning to sweep at those trying to kill him from behind.

He stumbled on a swath of green cloth. Sadeas's banner. Dalinar spun, searching. Behind him, he'd left a line of corpses that was quickly yet carefully being stepped past by more Parshendi focused on him. Except just to his left. None of the Parshendi there turned toward him.

Sadeas! Dalinar thought, leaping forward, cutting down Parshendi from behind. That revealed a group of them bunched in a circle, beating on something below them. Something leaking Stormlight.

Just to the side lay a large Shardbearer's hammer, fallen where Sadeas had apparently dropped it. Dalinar leaped forward, dropping his Blade and grabbing the hammer. He roared as he slammed it into the group, tossing a dozen Parshendi away from him, then turned and swung again on the other side. Bodies sprayed into the air, hurled backward.

The hammer worked better in such close quarters; the Blade would simply have killed the men, dropping their corpses to the ground, leaving him still pressed and pinned. The hammer, however, flung the bodies away. He leaped into the middle of the area he'd just cleared, positioning himself with one foot on either side of the fallen Sadeas. He began the process of summoning his Blade again and laid about him with the hammer, scattering his enemies.

At the ninth beat of his heart, he threw the hammer into the face of a Parshendi, then let Oathbringer re-form in his hands. He fell immediately into Windstance, glancing downward. Sadeas's armor leaked Stormlight from a dozen different breaks and rifts. The breastplate had been shattered completely; broken, jagged bits of metal jutted out, revealing the uniform underneath. Wisps of radiant smoke trailed from the holes.

There was no time to check if he still lived. The Parshendi now saw not one, but two Shardbearers within their grasp, and they threw themselves at Dalinar. Warrior after warrior fell as Dalinar slaughtered them in sweeps, protecting the space just around him.

He couldn't stop them all. His armor took hits, mostly on the arms and back. The armor cracked, like a crystal under too much stress.

He roared, striking down four Parshendi as two more hit him from behind, making his armor vibrate. He spun and killed one, the other barely dancing out of range. Dalinar began to pant, and when he moved quickly, he left trails of blue Stormlight in the air. He felt like a bloodied prey beast trying to fend off a thousand different snapping predators at once.

But he was no chull, whose only protection was to hide. He killed, and the Thrill rose to a crescendo within him. He sensed real danger, a chance of falling, and that made the Thrill surge. He nearly choked on it, the joy, the pleasure, the desire. The danger. More and more blows got through; more and more Parshendi were able to duck or dodge out of the way of his Blade.

He felt a breeze through the back of his breastplate. Cooling, terrible, frightening. The cracks were widening. If the breastplate burst . . .

He screamed, slamming his Blade down through a Parshendi, burning out his eyes, dropping the man without a mark on his skin. Dalinar brought his Blade up, spinning, cutting through the legs of another foe. His insides were a tempest of emotions, and his brow beneath the helm streamed with sweat. What would happen to the Alethi army if both he and Sadeas fell here? Two highprinces dead in the same battle, two sets of Plate and one Blade lost?

It couldn't happen. He wouldn't fall here. He didn't yet know if he was mad or not. He couldn't die until he knew!

Suddenly, a wave of Parshendi died that he hadn't attacked. A figure in brilliant blue Shardplate burst through them. Adolin held his massive Shardblade in a single hand, the metal gleaming.

Adolin swung again, and the Cobalt Guard rushed forward, pouring into the gap Adolin created. The Parshendi song changed tempo, becoming frantic, and they fell back as more and more troops punched through, some in green, others in blue.

Dalinar knelt down, exhausted, letting his Blade vanish. His guard surrounded him, and Adolin's army washed over them all, overrunning the Parshendi, forcing them back. In a few minutes, the area was secure.

The danger was past.

"Father," Adolin said, kneeling beside him, pulling his helm off. The youth's blond and black hair was disheveled and sweat-slick. "Storms! You gave me a fright! Are you well?"

Dalinar pulled his own helm free, sweet cooling air washing across his damp face. He took a deep breath, then nodded. "Your timing is . . . quite good, son."

Adolin helped Dalinar back to his feet. "I had to punch through the entire Parshendi army. No disrespect, Father, but what in the storms made you pull a stunt like that?"

"The knowledge that you could handle the army if I fell," Dalinar said, clapping his son on the arm, their Plate clinking.

Adolin caught sight of the back of Dalinar's Shardplate, and his eyes opened wide.

"Bad?" Dalinar asked.

"Looks like it's held together with spit and twine," Adolin said. "You're leaking Light like a wineskin used for archery practice."

Dalinar nodded, sighing. Already his Plate was feeling sluggish. He'd probably have to remove it before they returned to the camp, lest it freeze on him.

To the side, several soldiers were pulling Sadeas free of his Plate. It was so far gone that the Light had stopped save for a few tiny wisps. It could be fixed, but it would be expensive— regenerating Shardplate generally shattered the gemstones it drew Light from.

The soldiers pulled Sadeas's helm off, and Dalinar was relieved to see his former friend blinking, looking disoriented but largely uninjured. He had a cut on his thigh where one of the Parshendi had gotten him with a sword, and a few scrapes on his chest.

Sadeas looked up at Dalinar and Adolin. Dalinar stiffened, expecting recrimination—this had only happened because Dalinar had insisted on fighting with two armies on the same plateau. That had goaded the Parshendi into bringing another army. Dalinar should have set proper scouts to watch for that.

Sadeas, however, smiled a wide grin. "Stormfather, but that was close! How goes the battle?"

"The Parshendi are routed," Adolin said. "The last force resisting was the one around you. Our men are cutting the gemheart free at this moment. The day is ours."

"We win again!" Sadeas said triumphantly. "Dalinar, once in a while, it appears that senile old brain of yours can come up with a good idea or two!"

"We're the same age, Sadeas." Dalinar noted as messengers approached, bearing reports from the rest of the battlefield.

"Spread the word," Sadeas proclaimed. "Tonight, all my soldiers will feast as if they were lighteyes!" He smiled as his soldiers helped him to his feet, and Adolin moved over to take the scout reports. Sadeas waved away the help, insisting he could stand despite his wound, and began calling for his officers.

Dalinar turned to seek out Gallant and make sure the horse's wound was cared for. As he did, however, Sadeas caught his arm.

"I should be dead," Sadeas said softly.

"Perhaps."

"I didn't see much. But I thought I saw you alone. Where was your honor guard?"

"I had to leave it behind," Dalinar said. "It was the only way to get to you in time."

Sadeas frowned. "That was a terrible risk, Dalinar. Why?"

"You do not abandon your allies on the battlefield. Not unless there's no recourse. It is one of the Codes."

Sadeas shook his head. "That honor of yours is going to get you killed, Dalinar." He seemed bemused. "Not that I feel like offering a complaint about it this day!"

"If I should die," Dalinar said, "then I would do so having lived my life right. It is not the destination that matters, but how one arrives there."

"The Codes?"

"No. *The Way of Kings*."

"That storming book."

"That storming book saved your life today, Sadeas," Dalinar said. "I think I'm starting to understand what Gavilar saw in it."

Sadeas scowled at that, though he glanced at his armor, lying in pieces nearby. He shook his head. "Perhaps I shall let you tell me what you mean. I'd like to understand you again, old friend. I'm beginning to wonder if I ever really did." He let go of Dalinar's arm. "Someone bring me my storming horse! Where are my officers?"

Dalinar left, and quickly found several members of his guard seeing to Gallant. As he joined them, he was struck by the sheer number of corpses on the ground. They ran in a line where he had punched through the Parshendi ranks to get to Sadeas, a trail of death.

He looked back to where he'd made his stand. Dozens dead. Perhaps hundreds.

Blood of my fathers, Dalinar thought. *Did I do that?* He

hadn't killed in such numbers since the early days of helping Gavilar unite Alethkar. And he hadn't grown sick at the sight of death since his youth.

Yet now he found himself revolted, barely able to keep his stomach under control. He would not retch on the battlefield. His men should not see that.

He stumbled away, one hand to his head, the other carrying his helm. He should be exulting. But he couldn't. He just . . . couldn't.

You will need luck trying to understand me, Sadeas, he thought. *Because I'm having Damnation's own trouble trying to do so myself.*

Scalespray

Stumpweight

Markal

Snarlbrush

"I hold the suckling child in my hands, a knife at his throat, and know that all who live wish me to let the blade slip. Spill its blood upon the ground, over my hands, and with it gain us further breath to draw."

—Dated Shashanan, 1173, 23 seconds pre-death. Subject: a dark-eyed youth of sixteen years. Sample is of particular note.

And all the world was shattered!" Maps yelled, back arching, eyes wide, flecks of red spittle on his cheeks. "The rocks trembled with their steps, and the stones reached toward the heavens. We die! We die!"

He spasmed one last time, and the light faded from his eyes. Kaladin sat back, crimson blood slick on his hands, the dagger he'd been using as a surgical knife slipping from his fingers and clicking softly against the stone. The affable man lay dead on the stones of a plateau, arrow wound in his left breast open to the air, splitting the birthmark he'd claimed looked like Alethkar.

It's taking them, Kaladin thought. *One by one. Open them up, bleed them out. We're nothing more than pouches to carry blood. Then we die, rain it down on the stones like a highstorm's floods.*

Until only I remain. I always remain.

A layer of skin, a layer of fat, a layer of muscle, a layer of bone. That was what men were.

The battle raged across the chasm. It might as well have been another kingdom, for all the attention anyone gave the bridgemen. Die die die, then get out of our way.

The members of Bridge Four stood in a solemn ring around Kaladin. "What was that he said at the end?" Skar asked. "The rocks trembled?"

"It was nothing," said thick-armed Yake. "Just dying delirium. It happens to men, sometimes."

"More often lately, it seems," Teft said. He held his hand to his arm, where he'd hastily wrapped a bandage around an arrow wound. He wouldn't be carrying a bridge anytime soon. Maps's death and Arik's death left them with only twenty-six members now. It was barely enough to carry a bridge. The greater heaviness was very noticeable, and they had difficulty keeping up with the other bridge crews. A few more losses, and they'd be in serious trouble.

I should have been faster, Kaladin thought, looking down at Maps splayed open, his insides exposed for the sun to dry. The arrowhead had pierced his lung and lodged in his spine. Could Lirin have saved him? If Kaladin had studied in Kharbranth as his father had wished, would he have learned enough—known enough—to prevent deaths like this?

This happens sometimes, son. . . .

Kaladin raised shaking bloody hands to his face, gripping his head, as memory consumed him. A young girl, a cracked head, a broken leg, an angry father.

Despair, hate, loss, frustration, horror. How could any man live this way? To be a surgeon, to live knowing that you would be too weak to save some? When other men failed, a field of crops got worms in them. When a surgeon failed, someone died.

You have to learn when to care. . . .

As if he could choose. Banish it, like snuffing a lantern. Kaladin bowed beneath the weight. *I should have saved him, I should have saved him, I should have saved him.*

Maps, Dunny, Amark, Goshel, Dallet, Nalma. Tien.

"Kaladin." Syl's voice. "Be strong."

"If I were strong," he hissed, "they would live."

"The other bridgemen still need you. You promised them, Kaladin. You gave your oath."

Kaladin looked up. The bridgemen seemed anxious and worried. There were only eight of them; Kaladin had sent the others to look for fallen bridgemen from other crews. They'd found three initially, minor wounds that Skar could care for. No runners had come for him. Either the bridge crews had no other wounded, or those wounded were beyond help.

Maybe he should have gone to look, just in case. But— numb—he could not face yet another dying man he could not save. He stumbled to his feet and walked away from the corpse. He stepped up to the chasm and forced himself to fall into the old stance Tukks had taught him.

Feet apart, hands behind his back, clasping forearms. Straight-backed, staring forward. The familiarity brought him strength.

You were wrong, Father, he thought. *You said I'd learn to deal with the deaths. And yet here I am. Years later. Same problem.*

The bridgemen fell in around him. Lopen approached with a waterskin. Kaladin hesitated, then accepted the skin, washing off his face and hands. The warm water splashed across his skin, then brought welcome coolness as it evaporated. He let out a deep breath, nodding thanks to the short Herdazian man.

Lopen raised an eyebrow, then gestured to the pouch tied to his waist. He had recovered the newest pouch of spheres they'd stuck to the bridge with an arrow. This was the fourth time they'd done that, and had recovered them each without incident.

"Did you have any trouble?" Kaladin asked.

"No, gancho," Lopen said, smiling widely. "Easy as tripping a Horneater."

"I heard that," Rock said gruffly, standing in parade rest a short distance away.

"And the rope?" Kaladin asked.

"I dropped the whole coil right over the side," Lopen said. "But I didn't tie the end to anything. Just like you said."

"Good," Kaladin said. A rope dangling from a bridge would have just been too obvious. If Hashal or Gaz caught scent of what Kaladin was planning . . .

And where is *Gaz?* Kaladin thought. *Why didn't he come on the bridge run?*

Lopen gave Kaladin the pouch of spheres, as if eager to be rid of the responsibility. Kaladin accepted it, stuffing it into his trouser pocket.

Lopen retreated, and Kaladin fell back into parade rest. The plateau on the other side of the chasm was long and thin, with steep slopes on the sides. Just as in the last few battles, Dalinar Kholin helped Sadeas's force. He always arrived late. Perhaps he blamed his slow, chull-pulled bridges. Very convenient. His men often had the luxury of crossing without archery fire.

Sadeas and Dalinar won more battles this way. Not that it mattered to the bridgemen.

Many people were dying on the other side of the chasm, but Kaladin didn't feel a thing for them. No itch to heal them, no desire to help. Kaladin could thank Hav for that, for training him to think in terms of "us" and "them." In a way, Kaladin *had* learned what his father had talked about. In the wrong way, but it was something. Protect the "us," destroy the "them." A soldier had to think like that. So Kaladin hated the Parshendi. They were the enemy. If he hadn't learned to divide his mind like that, war would have destroyed him.

Perhaps it had done so anyway.

As he watched the battle, he focused on one thing in particular to distract himself. How *did* the Parshendi treat their dead? Their actions seemed irregular. The Parshendi soldiers rarely disturbed their dead after they fell; they'd take roundabout paths of attack to avoid dead bodies. And when the Alethi marched over the Parshendi dead, they formed points of terrible conflict.

Did the Alethi notice? Probably not. But he could see that the Parshendi revered their dead—revered them to the extent that they would endanger the living to preserve the corpses of the fallen. Kaladin could use that. He would use that. Somehow.

The Alethi eventually won the battle. Before long, Kaladin and his team were slogging back across the plateau, carrying their bridge, three wounded lashed to the top. They had found only those three, and a part of Kaladin felt sick inside as he realized another part of him was glad. He had already rescued some fifteen men from other bridge crews, and it was straining their resources—even with the money from the pouches—to feed them. Their barrack was crowded with the wounded.

Bridge Four reached a chasm, and Kaladin moved to lower his burden. The process was rote to him now. Lower the bridge, quickly untie the wounded, push the bridge across the chasm. Kaladin checked on the three wounded. Every man he rescued this way seemed bemused at what he'd done, even though he'd been doing it for weeks now. Satisfied that they were all right, he moved to stand at parade rest while the soldiers crossed.

Bridge Four fell in around him. Increasingly, they earned scowls from the soldiers—both darkeyed and lighteyed—who crossed. "Why do they do that?" Moash said quietly as a passing soldier tossed an overripe pilevine fruit at the bridgemen. Moash wiped the stringy, red fruit from his face, then sighed and fell back into his stance. Kaladin had never asked them to join him, but they did it each time.

"When I fought in Amaram's army," Kaladin said, "I dreamed about joining the troops at the Shattered Plains. Everyone knew that the soldiers left in Alethkar were the dregs. We imagined the real soldiers, off fighting in the glorious war to bring retribution to those who had killed our king. Those soldiers would treat their fellows with fairness. Their discipline would be firm. Each would be an expert with the spear, and he would not break rank on the battlefield."

To the side, Teft snorted quietly.

Kaladin turned to Moash. "Why do they treat us so, Moash?

Because they know they should be better than they are. Because they see discipline in bridgemen, and it embarrasses them. Rather than bettering themselves, they take the easier road of jeering at us."

"Dalinar Kholin's soldiers don't act like that," Skar said from just behind Kaladin. "His men march in straight ranks. There is order in their camp. If they're on duty, they don't leave their coats unbuttoned or lounge about."

Will I never stop hearing about Dalinar storming Kholin? Kaladin thought.

Men had spoken that way of Amaram. How easy it was to ignore a blackened heart if you dressed it in a pressed uniform and a reputation for honesty.

Several hours later, the sweaty and exhausted group of bridgemen tramped up the incline to the lumberyard. They dumped their bridge in its resting place. It was getting late; Kaladin would have to purchase food immediately if they were going to have supplies for the evening stew. He wiped his hands on his towel as the members of Bridge Four lined up.

"You're dismissed for evening activities," he said. "We have chasm duty early tomorrow. Morning bridge practice will have to be moved to late afternoon."

The bridgemen nodded, then Moash raised a hand. As one, the bridgemen raised their arms and crossed them, wrists together, hands in fists. It had the look of a practiced effort. After that, they trotted away.

Kaladin raised an eyebrow, tucking his towel into his belt. Teft hung back, smiling.

"What was that?" Kaladin asked.

"The men wanted a salute," Teft said. "We can't use a regular military salute—not with the spearmen already thinking we're too bigheaded. So I taught them my old squad salute."

"When?"

"This morning. While you were getting our schedule from Hashal."

Kaladin smiled. Odd, how he could still do that. Nearby, the other nineteen bridge crews on today's run dropped off their bridges, one by one. Had Bridge Four once looked like them, with those ragged beards and haunted expressions? None of them spoke to one another. Some few glanced at Kaladin as they passed, but they looked down as soon as they saw he was watching. They'd stopped treating Bridge Four with the contempt they'd once shown. Curiously, they now seemed to regard Kaladin's crew as they did everyone else in camp—as people above them. They hastened to avoid his notice.

Poor sodden fools, Kaladin thought. Could he, maybe, persuade Hashal to let him take a few into Bridge Four? He could use the extra men, and seeing those slumped figures twisted his heart.

"I know that look, lad," Teft said. "Why is it you always have to help everyone?"

"Bah," Kaladin said. "I can't even protect Bridge Four. Here, let me look at that arm of yours."

"It's not that bad."

Kaladin grabbed his arm anyway, peeling away the blood-crusted bandage. The cut was long, but shallow.

"We need antiseptic on this," Kaladin said, noting a few red rotspren crawling around on the wound. "I should probably sew it up."

"It's not that bad!"

"Still," Kaladin said, waving for Teft to follow as he approached one of the rain barrels alongside the lumberyard. The wound was shallow enough that Teft would probably be able to show the others spear thrusts and blocks tomorrow during chasm duty, but that was no excuse for leaving it alone to fester or scar.

At the rain barrel, Kaladin washed out the wound, then called for Lopen—who was standing in the shade beside the barrack—to bring his medical equipment. The Herdazian man gave that salute again, though he did it with one arm, and sauntered away to get the pack.

"So, lad," Teft said. "How do you feel? Any odd experiences lately?"

Kaladin frowned, looking up from the arm. "Storm it, Teft! That's the fifth time in two days you've asked me that. What are you getting at?"

"Nothing, nothing!"

"It *is* something," Kaladin said. "What is it you're digging for, Teft? I—"

"Gancho," Lopen said, walking up, carrying the medical supply pack over his shoulder. "Here you go."

Kaladin glanced at him, then reluctantly accepted the pack. He pulled the drawstrings open. "We'll want to—"

A quick motion came from Teft. Like a punch being thrown.

Kaladin moved by reflex, taking in a sharp breath, moving to a defensive stance, arms up, one hand a fist, the other back to block.

Something blossomed within Kaladin. Like a deep breath drawn in, like a burning liquor injected directly into his blood. A powerful wave pulsed through his body. Energy, strength, awareness. It was like the body's natural alert response to danger, only it was a hundredfold more intense.

Kaladin caught Teft's fist, moving blurringly quick. Teft froze.

"What are you doing?" Kaladin demanded.

Teft was smiling. He stepped back, pulling his fist free. "Kelek," he said, shaking his hand. "That's some grip you've got."

"Why did you try to strike me?"

"I wanted to see something," Teft said. "You're holding that pouch of spheres Lopen gave you, you see, and your own pouch with what we've gathered lately. More Stormlight than you've probably ever carried, at least recently."

"What does that have to do with anything?" Kaladin demanded. What was that heat inside of him, that burning in his veins?

"Gancho," Lopen said, his voice awed. "You're glowing."

Kaladin frowned. *What is he—*

And then he noticed it. It was very faint, but it was there, wisps of luminescent smoke curling up from his skin. Like steam coming off a bowl of hot water on a cold winter night.

Shaking, Kaladin put the medical pack on the broad rim of the water barrel. He felt a moment of coldness on his skin.

What was that? Shocked, he raised his other hand, looking at the wisps streaming off of it.

"What did you do to me?" he demanded, looking up at Teft.

The older bridgeman was still smiling.

"Answer me!" Kaladin said, stepping forward, grabbing the front of Teft's shirt. *Stormfather, but I feel strong!*

"I didn't do anything, lad," Teft said. "You've been doing this for a while now. I caught you feeding off Stormlight when you were sick."

Stormlight. Kaladin hastily released Teft, fishing at the pouch of spheres in his pocket. He yanked it free and pulled it open.

It was dark inside. All five gemstones had been drained. The white light streaming from Kaladin's skin faintly illuminated the inside of the bag.

"Now that's something," Lopen said from the side. Kaladin spun to find the Herdazian man bending down and looking at the medical pack. Why was that so important?

Then Kaladin saw it. He thought he'd set the pack on the rim of the barrel, but in his haste he'd just pressed it against the side of the barrel. The pack now clung to the wood. Stuck there, hanging as if from an invisible hook. Faintly streaming light, just like Kaladin. As Kaladin watched, the light faded, and the pack slumped free and fell to the ground.

Kaladin raised a hand to his forehead, looking from the surprised Lopen to the curious Teft. Then he glanced around the lumberyard, frantic. Nobody else was looking at them; in the sunlight, the vapors were too faint to see from a distance.

Stormfather . . . what . . . how . . .

He caught sight of a familiar shape above. Syl moved like a blown leaf, tossed this way and that, leisurely, faint.

She did it! Kaladin thought. *What has she done to me?*

He stumbled away from Lopen and Teft, running toward Syl. His footsteps propelled him forward with too much speed. "Syl!" he bellowed, stopping beneath her.

She zipped down to hover before him, changing from a leaf to a young woman standing in the air. "Yes?"

Kaladin glanced around. "Come with me," he said, hurrying to one of the alleys between barracks. He pressed himself up against a wall, standing in the shade, breathing in and out. Nobody could see him here.

Syl alighted in the air before him, hands behind her back, looking closely at him. "You're glowing."

"What have you done to me?"

She cocked her head, then shrugged.

"Syl . . ." he said threateningly, though he wasn't certain what harm he could do a spren.

"I don't know, Kaladin," she said frankly, sitting down, her legs hanging over the side of the invisible platform. "I can . . . I can only faintly remember things I used to know so well. This world, interacting with men."

"But you did do something."

"*We* have done something. It wasn't me. It wasn't you. But together . . ." She shrugged again.

"That isn't very helpful."

She grimaced. "I know. I'm sorry."

Kaladin raised a hand. In the shade, the light streaming off of him was more obvious. If someone walked by . . . "How do I get rid of it?"

"Why do you want to get rid of it?"

"Well, because . . . I . . . Because."

Syl didn't respond.

Something occurred to Kaladin. Something, perhaps, he should have asked long ago. "You're not a windspren, are you?"

She hesitated, then shook her head. "No."

"What are you, then?"

"I don't know. I bind things."

Bind things. When she played pranks, she made items stick together. Shoes stuck to the ground and made men trip. People reached for their jackets hanging on hooks and couldn't pull them free. Kaladin reached down, picking a stone up off the ground. It was as big as his palm, weathered smooth by highstorm winds and rain. He pressed it against the wall of the barrack and willed his Light into the stone.

He felt a chill. The rock began to stream with luminescent

vapors. When Kaladin pulled his hand away, the stone remained where it was, clinging to the side of the building.

Kaladin leaned close, squinting. He thought he could faintly make out tiny spren, dark blue and shaped like little splashes of ink, clustering around the place where the rock met the wall.

"Bindspren," Syl said, walking up beside his head; she was still standing in the air.

"They're holding the rock in place."

"Maybe. Or maybe they're attracted to what you've done in affixing the stone there."

"That's not how it works. Is it?"

"Do rotspren cause sickness," Syl said idly, "or are they attracted to it?"

"Everyone knows they cause it."

"And do windspren cause the wind? Rainspren cause the rain? Flamespren cause fires?"

He hesitated. No, they didn't. Did they? "This is pointless. I need to find out how to get rid of this light, not study it."

"And *why*," Syl repeated, "must you get rid of it? Kaladin, you've heard the stories. Men who walked on walls, men who bound the storms to them. Windrunners. Why would you want to be rid of something like this?"

Kaladin struggled to define it. The healing, the way he never got hit, running at the front of the bridge . . . Yes, he'd known something odd was happening. Why did it frighten him so? Was it because he feared being set apart, like his father always was as the surgeon in Hearthstone? Or was it something greater?

"I'm doing what the Radiants did," he said.

"That's what I just said."

"I've been wondering if I'm bad luck, or if I've run afoul of something like the Old Magic. Maybe this explains it! The Almighty cursed the Lost Radiants for betraying mankind. What if I'm cursed too, because of what I'm doing?"

"Kaladin," she said, "you are *not* cursed."

"You just said you don't know what's happening." He

paced in the alleyway. To the side, the rock finally plopped free and clattered to the ground. "Can you say, with all certainty, that what I'm doing might not have drawn bad luck down upon me? Do you know enough to deny it completely, Syl?"

She stood in the air, her arms folded, saying nothing.

"This . . . thing," Kaladin said, gesturing toward the stone. "It isn't natural. The Radiants betrayed mankind. Their powers left them, and they were cursed. Everyone knows the legends." He looked down at his hands, still glowing, though more faintly than before. "Whatever we've done, whatever has happened to me, I've somehow brought upon myself their same curse. That's why everyone around me dies when I try to help them."

"And you think I'm a curse?" she asked him.

"I . . . Well, you said you're part of it, and . . ."

She strode forward, pointing at him, a tiny, irate woman hanging in the air. "So you think I've caused all of this? Your failures? The deaths?"

Kaladin didn't respond. He realized almost immediately that silence might be the worst response. Syl—surprisingly human in her emotions—spun in the air with a wounded look and zipped away, forming a ribbon of light.

I'm overreacting, he told himself. He was just so unsettled. He leaned back against the wall, hand to head. Before he had time to collect his thoughts, shadows darkened the entry to the alleyway. Teft and Lopen.

"Rock talkers!" Lopen said. "You really shine in shade, gancho!"

Teft gripped Lopen's shoulder. "He's not going to tell anyone, lad. I'll make certain of it."

"Yeah, gancho," Lopen said. "I swore I'd say nothing. You can trust a Herdazian."

Kaladin looked at the two, overwhelmed. He pushed past them, running out of the alley and across the lumberyard, fleeing from watching eyes.

⋅⋅*

By the time night drew close, the light had long since stopped streaming from Kaladin's body. It had faded like a fire going out, and had only taken a few minutes to vanish.

Kaladin walked southward along the edge of the Shattered Plains, in that transitional area between the warcamps and the Plains themselves. In some areas—like at the staging area near Sadeas's lumberyard—there was a gentle slope leading down between the two. At other points, there was a short ridge, eight or so feet tall. He passed one of these now, rocks to his right, open Plains to his left.

Hollows, crevices, and nooks scored the rock. Some shadowed sections here still hid pools of water from the highstorms days ago. Creatures still scuttled around the rocks, though the cooling evening air would soon drive them to hide. He passed a place pocked with small, water-filled holes; cremlings—multilegged, bearing tiny claws, their elongated bodies plated with carapace—lapped and fed at the edges. A small tentacle snapped out, yanking one down into the hole. Probably a grasper.

Grass grew up the side of the ridge beside him, and the blades peeked from their holes. Bunches of fingermoss sprouted like flowers amid the green. The bright pink and purple fingermoss tendrils were reminiscent of tentacles themselves, waving at him in the wind. When he passed, the timid grass pulled back, but the fingermoss was bolder. The clumps would only pull into their shells if he tapped the rock near them.

Above him, on the ridge, a few scouts stood watch over the Shattered Plains. This area beneath the ridge belonged to no specific highprince, and the scouts ignored Kaladin. He would only be stopped if he tried to leave the warcamps at the southern or northern ends.

None of the bridgemen had come after him. He wasn't certain what Teft had told them. Perhaps he'd said Kaladin was distraught following Maps's death.

It felt odd to be alone. Ever since he'd been betrayed by Amaram and made a slave, he had been in the company of others. Slaves with whom he'd plotted. Bridgemen with whom he'd worked. Soldiers to guard him, slavemasters to beat him, friends to depend on him. The last time he'd been alone had been that night when he'd been tied up for the highstorm to kill him.

No, he thought. *I wasn't alone that night. Syl was there.* He lowered his head, passing small cracks in the ground to his left. Those lines eventually grew into chasms as they moved eastward.

What was happening to him? He wasn't delusional. Teft and Lopen had seen it too. Teft had actually seemed to expect it.

Kaladin *should* have died during that highstorm. And yet, he had been up and walking shortly afterward. His ribs should still be tender, but they hadn't ached in weeks. His spheres, and those of the other bridgemen near him, had consistently run out of Stormlight.

Had it been the highstorm that had changed him? But no, he'd discovered drained spheres before being hung out to die. And Syl . . . she'd as much as admitted responsibility for some of what had happened. This had been going on a long time.

He stopped beside a rock outcropping, resting against it, causing grass to shrink away. He looked eastward, over the Shattered Plains. His home. His sepulcher. This life on them was ripping him apart. The bridgemen looked up to him, thought him their leader, their savior. But he had cracks in him, like the cracks in the stone here at the edges of the Plains.

Those cracks were growing larger. He kept making promises to himself, like a man running a long distance with no energy left. Just a little farther. Run just to that next hill. Then you can give up. Tiny fractures, fissures in the stone.

It's right that I came here, he thought. *We belong together, you and I. I'm like you.* What had made the Plains break in the first place? Some kind of great weight?

A melody began playing distantly, carrying over the Plains. Kaladin jumped at the sound. It was so unexpected, so out of place, that it was startling despite its softness.

The sounds were coming from the Plains. Hesitant, yet unable to resist, he walked forward. Eastward, onto the flat, windswept rock. The sounds grew louder as he walked, but they were still haunting, elusive. A flute, though one lower in pitch than most he'd heard.

As he grew closer, Kaladin smelled smoke. A light was burning out there. A tiny campfire.

Kaladin walked out to the edge of this particular peninsula, a chasm growing from the cracks until it plunged down into darkness. At the very tip of the peninsula—surrounded on three sides by chasm—Kaladin found a man sitting on a boulder, wearing a lighteyes's black uniform. A small fire of rockbud shell burned in front of him. The man's hair was short and black, his face angular. He wore a thin, black-sheathed sword at his waist.

The man's eyes were a pale blue. Kaladin had never heard of a lighteyed man playing a flute. Didn't they consider music a feminine pursuit? Lighteyed men sang, but they didn't play instruments unless they were ardents.

This man was extremely talented. The odd melody he played was alien, almost unreal, like something from another place and time. It echoed down the chasm and came back; it almost sounded like the man was playing a duet with himself.

Kaladin stopped a short distance away, realizing that the last thing he wanted to do now was deal with a brightlord, particularly one who was eccentric enough to dress in black and wander out onto the Shattered Plains to practice his flute. Kaladin turned to go.

The music cut off. Kaladin paused.

"I always worry that I'll forget how to play her," a soft voice said from behind. "It's silly, I know, considering how long I've practiced. But these days I rarely give her the attention she deserves."

Kaladin turned toward the stranger. His flute was carved from a dark wood that was almost black. The instrument seemed too ordinary to belong to a lighteyes, yet the man held it reverently.

"What are you doing here?" Kaladin asked.

"Sitting. Occasionally playing."

"I mean, why are you here?"

"Why am I here?" the man said, lowering his flute, leaning back and relaxing. "Why are any of us here? That's a rather deep question for a first meeting, young bridgeman. I generally prefer introductions before theology. Lunch too, if it can be found. Perhaps a nice nap. Actually, practically anything should come before theology. But especially introductions."

"All right," Kaladin said. "And you are . . . ?"

"Sitting. Occasionally playing . . . with the minds of bridgemen."

Kaladin reddened, turning again to go. Let the fool lighteyes say, and do, what he wished. Kaladin had difficult decisions to think about.

"Well, off with you then," the lighteyes said from behind. "Glad you are going. Wouldn't want you too close. I'm rather attached to my Stormlight."

Kaladin froze. Then he spun. "What?"

"My spheres," the strange man said, holding up what appeared to be a fully infused emerald broam. "Everyone knows that bridgemen are thieves, or at least beggars."

Of course. He had been talking about spheres. He didn't know about Kaladin's . . . affliction. Did he? The man's eyes twinkled as if at a grand joke.

"Don't be insulted at being called a thief," the man said, raising a finger. Kaladin frowned. Where had the sphere gone? He had been holding it in that hand. "I meant it as a compliment."

"A compliment? Calling someone a thief?"

"Of course. I myself am a thief."

"You are? What do you steal?"

"Pride," the man said, leaning forward. "And occasionally boredom, if I may take the pride unto myself. I am the King's Wit. Or I was until recently. I think I shall probably lose the title soon."

"The king's what?"

"Wit. It was my job to be witty."

"Saying confusing things isn't the same as being witty."

"Ah," the man said, eyes twinkling. "Already you prove yourself more wise than most who have been my acquaintance lately. What is it to be witty, then?"

"To say clever things."

"And what is cleverness?"

"I . . ." Why was he having this conversation? "I guess it's the ability to say and do the right things at the right time."

The King's Wit cocked his head, then smiled. Finally, he held out his hand to Kaladin. "And what is your name, my thoughtful bridgeman?"

Kaladin hesitantly raised his own hand. "Kaladin. And yours?"

"I've many." The man shook Kaladin's hand. "I began life as a thought, a concept, words on a page. That was another thing I stole. Myself. Another time, I was named for a rock."

"A pretty one, I hope."

"A beautiful one," the man said. "And one that became completely worthless for my wearing it."

"Well, what do men call you now?"

"Many a thing, and only some of them polite. Almost all are true, unfortunately. You, however, you may call me Hoid."

"Your name?"

"No. The name of someone I should have loved. Once again, this is a thing I stole. It is something we thieves do." He glanced eastward, over the rapidly darkening Plains. The little fire burning beside Hoid's boulder shed a fugitive light, red from glimmering coals.

"Well, it was pleasant to meet you," Kaladin said. "I will be on my way. . . ."

"Not before I give you something." Hoid picked up his flute. "Wait, please."

Kaladin sighed. He had a feeling that this odd man was not going to let him escape until he was done.

"This is a Trailman's flute," Hoid said, inspecting the length of dark wood. "It is meant to be used by a storyteller, for him to play while he is telling a story."

"You mean to *accompany* a storyteller. Being played by someone else while he speaks."

"Actually, I meant what I said."

"How would a man tell a story while playing the flute?"

Hoid raised an eyebrow, then lifted the flute to his lips. He played it differently from flutes Kaladin had seen—instead of holding it down in front of him, Hoid held it out to the side and blew across its top. He tested a few notes. They had the same melancholy tone that Kaladin had heard before.

"This story," Hoid said, "is about Derethil and the *Wandersail*."

He began to play. The notes were quicker, sharper, than the ones he'd played earlier. They almost seemed to tumble over one another, scurrying out of the flute like children racing one another to be first. They were beautiful and crisp, rising and falling scales, intricate as a woven rug.

Kaladin found himself transfixed. The tune was powerful, almost *demanding*. As if each note were a hook, flung out to spear Kaladin's flesh and hold him near.

Hoid stopped abruptly, but the notes continued to echo in the chasm, coming back as he spoke. "Derethil is well known in some lands, though I have heard him spoken of less here in the East. He was a king during the shadowdays, the time before memory. A powerful man. Commander of thousands, leader of tens of thousands. Tall, regal, blessed with fair skin and fairer eyes. He was a man to envy."

Just as the echoes faded below, Hoid began to play again, picking up the rhythm. He actually seemed to continue just where the echoing notes grew too soft, as if there had never been a break in the music. The notes grew more smooth, suggesting a king walking through court with his attendants. As Hoid played, eyes closed, he leaned forward toward the fire. The air he blew over the flute churned the smoke, stirring it.

The music grew softer. The smoke swirled, and Kaladin thought he could make out the face of a man in the patterns of smoke, a man with a pointed chin and lofty cheekbones. It wasn't really there, of course. Just imagination. But the haunting song and the swirling smoke seemed to encourage his imagination.

"Derethil fought the Voidbringers during the days of the Heralds and Radiants," Hoid said, eyes still closed, flute just below his lips, the song echoing in the chasm and seeming to accompany his words. "When there was finally peace, he found he was not content. His eyes always turned westward, toward the great open sea. He commissioned the finest ship men had ever known, a majestic vessel intended to do what none had dared before: sail the seas during a highstorm."

The echoes tapered off, and Hoid began playing again, as if alternating with an invisible partner. The smoke swirled, rising in the air, twisting in the wind of Hoid's breath. And Kaladin almost thought he could see an enormous ship in a shipyard, with a sail as large as a building, secured to an arrowlike hull. The melody became quick and clipped, as if to imitate the sounds of mallets pounding and saws cutting.

"Derethil's goal," Hoid paused and said, "was to seek the origin of the Voidbringers, the place where they had been spawned. Many called him a fool, yet he could not hold himself back. He named the vessel the *Wandersail* and gathered a crew of the bravest of sailors. Then, on a day when a highstorm brewed, this ship cast off. Riding out into the ocean, the sail hung wide, like arms open to the stormwinds. . . ."

The flute was at Hoid's lips in a second and he stirred the fire by kicking at a piece of rockbud shell. Sparks of flame rose in the air and smoke puffed, swirling as Hoid rotated his head down and pointed the flute's holes at the smoke. The song became violent, tempestuous, notes falling unexpectedly and trilling with quick undulations. Scales rippled into high notes, where they screeched airily.

And Kaladin saw it in his mind's eye. The massive ship suddenly miniscule before the awesome power of a highstorm. Blown, carried out into the endless sea. What had this Derethil hoped or expected to find? A highstorm on land was terrible enough. But on the sea?

The sounds bounced off the echoing walls below. Kaladin

found himself sinking down to the rocks, watching the swirling smoke and rising flames. Seeing the tiny ship captured and held within a furious maelstrom.

Eventually, Hoid's music slowed, and the violent echoes faded, leaving a much gentler song. Like lapping waves.

"The *Wandersail* ran aground and was nearly destroyed, but Derethil and most of his sailors survived. They found themselves on a ring of small islands surrounding an enormous whirlpool, where, it is said, the ocean drains. Derethil and his men were greeted by a strange people with long, limber bodies who wore robes of single color and shells in their hair unlike any that grow back on Roshar.

"These people took the survivors in, fed them, and nursed them back to health. During his weeks of recovery, Derethil studied the strange people, who called themselves the Uvara, the People of the Great Abyss. They lived curious lives. Unlike the people in Roshar—who constantly argue—the Uvara always seemed to agree. From childhood, there were no questions. Each and every person went about his duty."

Hoid began the music again, letting the smoke rise unhindered. Kaladin thought he could see in it an industrious people, always working. A building rose among them with a figure at the window, Derethil, watching. The music was calming, curious.

"One day," Hoid said, "while Derethil and his men were sparring to regain strength, a young serving girl brought them refreshment. She tripped on an uneven stone, dropping the goblets to the floor and shattering them. In a flash, the other Uvara descended on the hapless child and slaughtered her in a brutal way. Derethil and his men were so stunned that by the time they regained their wits, the child was dead. Angry, Derethil demanded to know the cause of the unjustified murder. One of the other natives explained. 'Our emperor will not suffer failure.' "

The music began again, sorrowful, and Kaladin shivered. He witnessed the girl being bludgeoned to death with rocks, and the proud form of Derethil bowing above her fallen body.

Kaladin knew that sorrow. The sorrow of failure, of letting someone die when he should have been able to do something. So many people he loved had died.

He had a reason for that now. He'd drawn the ire of the Heralds and the Almighty. It had to be that, didn't it?

He knew he should be getting back to Bridge Four. But he couldn't pull himself away. He hung on the storyteller's words.

"As Derethil began to pay more attention," Hoid said, his music echoing softly to accompany him, "he saw other murders. These Uvara, these People of the Great Abyss, were prone to astonishing cruelty. If one of their members did something wrong—something the slightest bit untoward or unfavorable—the others would slaughter him or her. Each time he asked, Derethil's caretaker gave him the same answer. 'Our emperor will not suffer failure.'"

The echoing music faded, but once again Hoid lifted his flute just as it grew too soft to hear. The melody grew solemn. Soft, quiet, like a lament for one who had passed. And yet it was edged with mystery, occasional quick bursts, hinting at secrets.

Kaladin frowned as he watched the smoke spin, making what appeared to be a tower. Tall, thin, with an open structure at the top.

"The emperor, Derethil discovered, resided in the tower on the eastern coast of the largest island among the Uvara."

Kaladin felt a chill. The smoke images were just from his mind, adding to the story, weren't they? Had he really seen a tower *before* Hoid mentioned it?

"Derethil determined that he needed to confront this cruel emperor. What kind of monster would demand that such an obviously peaceful people kill so often and so terribly? Derethil gathered his sailors, a heroic group, and they armed themselves. The Uvara did not try to stop them, though they watched with fright as the strangers stormed the emperor's tower."

Hoid fell silent, and didn't turn back to his flute. Instead, he let the music echo in the chasm. It seemed to linger this time. Long, sinister notes.

"Derethil and his men came out of the tower a short time

later, carrying a desiccated corpse in fine robes and jewelry. 'This is your emperor?' Derethil demanded. 'We found him in the top room, alone.' It appeared that the man had been dead for years, but nobody had dared enter his tower. They were too frightened of him.

"When he showed the Uvara the dead body, they began to wail and weep. The entire island was cast into chaos, as the Uvara began to burn homes, riot, or fall to their knees in torment. Amazed and confused, Derethil and his men stormed the Uvara shipyards, where the *Wandersail* was being repaired. Their guide and caretaker joined them, and she begged to accompany them in their escape. So it was that Nafti joined the crew.

"Derethil and his men set sail, and though the winds were still, they rode the *Wandersail* around the whirlpool, using the momentum to spin them out and away from the islands. Long after they left, they could see the smoke rising from the ostensibly peaceful lands. They gathered on the deck, watching, and Derethil asked Nafti the reason for the terrible riots."

Hoid fell silent, letting his words rise with the strange smoke, lost to the night.

"Well?" Kaladin demanded. "What was her response?"

"Holding a blanket around herself, staring with haunted eyes at her lands, she replied, 'Do you not see, Traveling One? If the emperor is dead, and has been all these years, then the murders we committed are not his responsibility. They are our own.'"

Kaladin sat back. Gone was the taunting, playful tone Hoid had used earlier. No more mockery. No more quick tongue intended to confuse. This story had come from within his heart, and Kaladin found he could not speak. He just sat, thinking of that island and the terrible things that had been done.

"I think . . ." Kaladin finally replied, licking his dry lips, "I think that is cleverness."

Hoid raised an eyebrow, looking up from his flute.

"Being able to remember a story like that," Kaladin said, "to tell it with such care."

"Be wary of what you say," Hoid said, smiling. "If all you need for cleverness is a good story, then I'll find myself out of a job."

"Didn't you say you were already out of a job?"

"True. The king is finally without wit. I wonder what that makes him."

"Um . . . witless?" Kaladin said.

"I'll tell him you said that," Hoid noted, eyes twinkling. "But I think it's inaccurate. One can have a wit, but not a witless. What is a wit?"

"I don't know. Some kind of spren in your head, maybe, that makes you think?"

Hoid cocked his head, then laughed. "Why, I suppose that's as good an explanation as any." He stood up, dusting off his black trousers.

"Is the story true?" Kaladin asked, rising too.

"Perhaps."

"But how would we know it? Did Derethil and his men return?"

"Some stories say they did."

"But how could they? The highstorms only blow one direction."

"Then I guess the story is a lie."

"I didn't say that."

"No, I said it. Fortunately, it's the best kind of lie."

"And what kind is that?"

"Why, the kind *I* tell, of course." Hoid laughed, then kicked out the fire, grinding the last of the coals beneath his heel. It didn't really seem there had been enough fuel to make the smoke Kaladin had seen.

"What did you put in the fire?" Kaladin said. "To make that special smoke?"

"Nothing. It was just an ordinary fire."

"But, I saw—"

"What you saw belongs to you. A story doesn't live until it is imagined in someone's mind."

"What does the story mean, then?"

"It means what you want it to mean," Hoid said. "The

purpose of a storyteller is not to tell you how to think, but to give you questions to think upon. Too often, we forget that."

Kaladin frowned, looking westward, back toward the warcamps. They were alight now with spheres, lanterns, and candles. "It means taking responsibility," Kaladin said. "The Uvara, they were happy to kill and murder, so long as they could blame the emperor. It wasn't until they realized there was nobody to take the responsibility that they showed grief."

"That's one interpretation," Hoid said. "A fine one, actually. So what is it you don't want to take responsibility for?"

Kaladin started. "What?"

"People see in stories what they're looking for, my young friend." He reached behind his boulder, pulling out a pack and slinging it on his shoulder. "I have no answers for you. Most days, I feel I never have had any answers. I've come to your land to chase an old acquaintance, but I end up spending most of my time hiding from him instead."

"You said . . . about me and responsibility . . ."

"Just an idle comment, nothing more." He reached over, laying a hand on Kaladin's shoulder. "My comments are often idle. I never can get them to do any solid work. Would that I could make my words carry stones. That would be something to see." He held out the dark wood flute. "Here. I've carried her for longer than you'd believe, were I to tell you the truth. Take her for yourself."

"But I don't know how to play it!"

"Then learn," Hoid said, pressing the flute into Kaladin's hand. "When you can make the music sing back at you, then you've mastered it." He began to walk away. "And take good care of that blasted apprentice of mine. He really should have let me know he was still alive. Perhaps he feared I'd come to rescue him again."

"Apprentice?"

"Tell him I graduate him," Hoid said, still walking. "He's a full Worldsinger now. Don't let him get killed. I spent far too long trying to force some sense into that brain of his."

Sigzil, Kaladin thought. "I'll give him the flute," he called after Hoid.

"No you won't," Hoid said, turning, walking backward as he left. "It's a gift to *you*, Kaladin Stormblessed. I expect you to be able to play it when next we meet!"

And with that, the storyteller turned and broke into a jog, heading off toward the warcamps. He didn't move to go up into them, however. His shadowed figure turned to the south, as if he were intending to leave the camps. Where was he going?

Kaladin looked down at the flute in his hand. It was heavier than he had expected. What kind of wood was it? He rubbed its smooth length, thinking.

"I don't like him," Syl's voice said suddenly, coming from behind. "He's strange."

Kaladin spun to find her on the boulder, sitting where Hoid had been a moment ago.

"Syl!" Kaladin said. "How long have you been here?"

She shrugged. "You were watching the story. I didn't want to interrupt." She sat with hands in her lap, looking uncomfortable.

"Syl—"

"I'm behind what is happening to you," she said, voice soft. "I'm doing it."

Kaladin frowned, stepping forward.

"It's both of us," she said. "But without me, nothing would be changing in you. I'm . . . taking something from you. And giving something in return. It's the way it used to work, though I can't remember how or when. I just know that it was."

"I—"

"Hush," she said. "I'm talking."

"Sorry."

"I'm willing to stop it, if you want," she said. "But I would go back to being as I was before. That scares me. Floating on the wind, never remembering anything for longer than a few minutes. It's because of this tie between us that I can think again, that I can remember what and who I am. If we end it, I lose that."

She looked up at Kaladin, sorrowful.

He looked into those eyes, then took a deep breath. "Come," he said, turning, walking back down the peninsula.

She flew over, becoming a ribbon of light, floating idly in the air beside his head. Soon they reached the place beneath the ridge leading to the warcamps. Kaladin turned north, toward Sadeas's camp. The cremlings had retreated to their cracks and burrows, but many of the plants still continued to let their fronds float in the cool wind. When he passed, the grass pulled back in, looking like the fur of some black beast in the night, lit by Salas.

What responsibility are you avoiding. . . .

He wasn't avoiding responsibility. He took too much responsibility! Lirin had said it constantly, chastising Kaladin for feeling guilt over deaths he couldn't have prevented.

Though there was one thing he clung to. An excuse, perhaps, like the dead emperor. It was the soul of the wretch. Apathy. The belief that nothing was his fault, the belief that he couldn't change anything. If a man was cursed, or if he believed he didn't have to care, then he didn't need to hurt when he failed. Those failures couldn't have been prevented. Someone or something else had ordained them.

"If I'm not cursed," Kaladin said softly, "then why do I live when others die?"

"Because of us," Syl said. "This bond. It makes you stronger, Kaladin."

"Then why can't it make me strong enough to help the others?"

"I don't know," Syl said. "Maybe it can."

If I get rid of it, I'll go back to being normal. For what purpose . . . so I can die with the others?

He continued to walk in the darkness, passing lights above that made vague, faint shadows on the stones in front of him. The tendrils of fingermoss, clumped in bunches. Their shadows seemed arms.

He thought often about saving the bridgemen. And yet, as he considered, he realized that he often framed saving them in terms of saving himself. He told himself he wouldn't *let* them die, because he knew what it would do to him if they did. When he lost men, the wretch threatened to take over because of how much Kaladin hated failing.

Was that it? Was that why he searched for reasons why he might be cursed? To explain his failure away? Kaladin began to walk more quickly.

He was doing something good in helping the bridgemen—but he also was doing something selfish. The powers had unsettled him because of the responsibility they represented.

He broke into a jog. Before long, he was sprinting.

But if it wasn't about *him*—if he wasn't helping the bridgemen because he loathed failure, or because he feared the pain of watching them die—then it would be about *them*. About Rock's affable gibes, about Moash's intensity, about Teft's earnest gruffness or Peet's quiet dependability. What would he do to protect them? Give up his illusions? His excuses?

Seize whatever opportunity he could, no matter how it changed him? No matter how it unnerved him, or what burdens it represented?

He dashed up the incline to the lumberyard.

Bridge Four was making their evening stew, chatting and laughing. The nearly twenty wounded men from other crews sat eating gratefully. It was gratifying, how quickly they had lost their hollow-eyed expressions and begun laughing with the other men.

The smell of spicy Horneater stew was thick in the air. Kaladin slowed his jog, coming to a stop beside the bridgemen. Several looked concerned as they saw him, panting and sweating. Syl landed on his shoulder.

Kaladin sought out Teft. The aging bridgeman sat alone below the barrack's eaves, staring down at the rock in front of him. He hadn't noticed Kaladin yet. Kaladin gestured for the others to continue, then walked over to Teft. He squatted down before the man.

Teft looked up in surprise. "Kaladin?"

"What do you know?" Kaladin said quietly, intense. "And how do you know it?"

"I—" Teft said. "When I was a youth, my family belonged to a secret sect that awaited the return of the Radiants. I quit when I was just a youth. I thought it was nonsense."

He was holding things back; Kaladin could tell from the hesitation in his voice.

Responsibility. "How much do you know about what I can do?"

"Not much," Teft said. "Just legends and stories. Nobody really knows what the Radiants could do, lad."

Kaladin met his eyes, then smiled. "Well, we're going to find out."

*"Re-Shephir, the Midnight Mother, giving birth to abomi-
nations with her essence so dark, so terrible, so consuming.
She is here! She watches me die!"*

—Dated Shashabev, 1173, 8 seconds pre-death. Subject: a darkeyed dockworker in his forties, father of three.

I have a serious loathing of being wrong." Adolin reclined in
his chair, one hand resting leisurely on the crystal-topped
table, the other swirling wine in his cup. Yellow wine. He
wasn't on duty today, so he could indulge just a tad.

Wind ruffled his hair; he was sitting with a group of other
young lighteyes at the outdoor tables of an Outer Market wine-
shop. The Outer Market was a collection of buildings that had
grown up near the king's palace, outside the warcamps. An
eclectic mix of people passed on the street below their terraced
seating.

"I should think that everyone shares your dislike, Adolin," Jakamav said, leaning with both elbows on the table. He
was a sturdy man, a lighteyes of the third dahn from Highprince Roion's camp. "Who *likes* being wrong?"

"I've known a number of people who prefer it," Adolin said
thoughtfully. "Of course, they don't *admit* that fact. But what
else could one presume from the frequency of their error?"

Inkima—Jakamav's companion for the afternoon—gave a tinkling laugh. She was a plump thing with light yellow eyes who dyed her hair black. She wore a red dress. The color did not look good on her.

Danlan was also there, of course. She sat on a chair beside Adolin, keeping proper distance, though she'd occasionally touch his arm with her freehand. Her wine was violet. She *did* like her wine, though she seemed to match it to her outfits. A curious trait. Adolin smiled. She looked extremely fetching, with that long neck and graceful build wrapped in a sleek dress. She didn't dye her hair, though it was mostly auburn. There was nothing wrong with light hair. In fact, why was it that they all were so fond of *dark* hair, when light eyes were the ideal?

Stop it, Adolin told himself. *You'll end up brooding as much as Father.*

The other two—Toral and his companion Eshava—were both lighteyes from Highprince Aladar's camp. House Kholin was currently out of favor, but Adolin had acquaintances or friends in nearly all of the warcamps.

"Wrongness can be amusing," Toral said. "It keeps life interesting. If we were all right all the time, where would that leave us?"

"My dear," his companion said. "Didn't you once claim to me that you were nearly always right?"

"Yes," Toral said. "And so if everyone were like me, who would I make sport of? I'd dread being made so mundane by everyone else's competence."

Adolin smiled, taking a drink of his wine. He had a formal duel in the arena today, and he'd found that a cup of yellow beforehand helped him relax. "Well, you needn't worry about *me* being right too often, Toral. I was sure Sadeas would move against my father. It doesn't make sense. Why wouldn't he?"

"Positioning, perhaps?" Toral said. He was a keen fellow, known for his refined sense of taste. Adolin always wanted him along when trying wines. "He wants to look strong."

"He *was* strong," Adolin said. "He gains no more by not moving against us."

"Now," Danlan said, voice soft with a breathless quality to it, "I know that I'm quite new to the warcamps, and my assessment is bound to reflect my ignorance, but—"

"You always say that, you know," Adolin said idly. He liked her voice quite a bit.

"I always say what?"

"That you're ignorant," Adolin said. "However, you're anything but. You're among the most clever women I've met."

She hesitated, looking oddly annoyed for a moment. Then she smiled. "You shouldn't say such things—Adolin—when a woman is attempting humility."

"Oh, right. Humility. I've forgotten that existed."

"Too much time around Sadeas's lighteyes?" Jakamav said, eliciting another tinkling laugh from Inkima.

"Anyway," Adolin said. "I'm sorry. Please continue."

"I was saying," Danlan said, "that I doubt Sadeas would wish to start a war. Moving against your father in such an obvious way would have done that, wouldn't it?"

"Undoubtedly," Adolin said.

"So perhaps that is why he held himself back."

"I don't know," Toral said. "He could have cast shame on your family without attacking you—he could have implied, for instance, that you'd been negligent and foolish in not protecting the king, but that you hadn't been behind the assassination attempt."

Adolin nodded.

"That still could have started a war," Danlan said.

"Perhaps," Toral said. "But you have to admit, Adolin, that the Blackthorn's reputation is a little less than . . . impressive of late."

"And what does that mean?" Adolin snapped.

"Oh, Adolin," Toral said waving a hand and raising his cup for some more wine. "Don't be tiresome. You know what I'm saying, and you *also* know I mean no insult by it. Where *is* that serving woman?"

"One would think," Jakamav added, "that after six years out here, we could get a decent winehouse."

Inkima laughed at that too. She was *really* getting annoying.

"My father's reputation is sound," Adolin said. "Or have you not been paying attention to our victories lately?"

"Achieved with Sadeas's help," Jakamav said.

"Achieved nonetheless," Adolin said. "In the last few months, my father's saved not only Sadeas's life, but that of the king himself. He fights boldly. Surely you can see that previous rumors about him were absolutely unfounded."

"All right, all right," Toral said. "No need to get upset, Adolin. We can all agree that your father is a wonderful man. But you *were* the one who complained to us that you wanted to change him."

Adolin studied his wine. Both of the other men at the table wore the sort of outfits Adolin's father frowned upon. Short jackets over colorful silk shirts. Toral wore a thin yellow silk scarf at the neck and another around his right wrist. It was quite fashionable, and looked far more comfortable than Adolin's uniform. Dalinar would have said that the outfits looked silly, but sometimes fashion *was* silly. Bold, different. There was something invigorating about dressing in a way that interested others, moving with the waves of style. Once, before joining his father at the war, Adolin had loved being able to design a look to match a given day. Now he had only two options: summer uniform coat or winter uniform coat.

The serving maid finally arrived, bringing two carafes of wine, one yellow and one deep blue. Inkima giggled as Jakamav leaned over and whispered something in her ear.

Adolin held up a hand to forestall the maid from filling his cup. "I'm not sure I want to see my father change. Not anymore."

Toral frowned. "Last week—"

"I know," Adolin said. "That was before I saw him rescue Sadeas. Every time I start to forget how amazing my father is, he does something to prove me one of the ten fools. It happened when Elhokar was in danger too. It's like . . . my father only acts like that when he *really* cares about something."

"You imply that he doesn't really care about the war, Adolin dear," Danlan said.

"No," Adolin said. "Just that the lives of Elhokar and Sadeas might be more important than killing Parshendi."

The others took that for an explanation, moving on toward other topics. But Adolin found himself circling the thought. He felt unsettled lately. Being wrong about Sadeas was one cause; the chance that they might actually be able to prove the visions right or wrong was another.

Adolin felt trapped. He'd pushed his father to confront his own sanity, and now—by what their last conversation had established—he had all but agreed to accept his father's decision to step down if the visions proved false.

Everyone hates being wrong, Adolin thought. *Except my father said he'd* rather *be wrong, if it would be better for Alethkar.* Adolin doubted many lighteyes would rather be proven mad than right.

"Perhaps," Eshava was saying. "But that doesn't change all of his foolish restrictions. I wish he *would* step down."

Adolin started. "What? What was that?"

Eshava glanced at him. "Nothing. Just seeing if you were attending the conversation, Adolin."

"No," Adolin said. "Tell me what you were saying."

She shrugged, looking at Toral.

Toral leaned forward. "You don't think the warcamps are *ignoring* what happens to your father during highstorms, Adolin. Word is that he should abdicate because of it."

"That would be foolish," Adolin said firmly. "Considering how much success he's showing in battle."

"Stepping down would indeed be an overreaction," Danlan agreed. "Though, Adolin, I *do* wish you could get your father to relax all of these foolish restrictions our camp is under. You and the other Kholin men would be able to *truly* join society again."

"I've tried," he said, checking the position of the sun. "Trust me. And now, unfortunately, I have a duel to prepare for. If you'll excuse me."

"Another of Sadeas's sycophants?" Jakamav asked.

"No," Danlan said, smiling. "It's Brightlord Resi. There've

been some vocal provocations from Thanadal, and this might serve to shut his mouth." She looked at Adolin fondly. "I'll meet you there."

"Thanks," he said, rising, doing up the buttons on his coat. He kissed Danlan's freehand, waved to the others, and trotted out onto the street.

That was something of an abrupt departure for me, he thought. *Will they see how uncomfortable the discussion made me?* Probably not. They didn't know him as Renarin did. Adolin liked to be familiar with a large number of people, but not terribly close with any of them. He didn't even know Danlan that well yet. He *would* make his relationship with her last, though. He was tired of Renarin teasing him for jumping in and out of courtships. Danlan was very pretty; it seemed the courtship could work.

He passed through the Outer Market, Toral's words weighing on him. Adolin didn't want to become highprince. He wasn't ready. He liked dueling and chatting with his friends. Leading the army was one thing—but as highprince, he'd have to think of other things. Such as the future of the war on the Shattered Plains, or protecting and advising the king.

That shouldn't have to be our problem, he thought. But it was as his father always said. If they didn't do it, who would?

The Outer Market was far more disorganized than the markets inside Dalinar's warcamp. Here, the ramshackle buildings—mostly built of stone blocks quarried from nearby—had grown up without any specific plan. A large number of the merchants were Thaylen, with their typical caps, vests, and long, wagging eyebrows.

The busy market was one of the few places where soldiers from all ten warcamps mingled. In fact, that had become one of the main functions of the place; it was neutral ground where men and women from different warcamps could meet. It also provided a market that wasn't heavily regulated, though Dalinar had stepped in to provide some rules once the marketplace had begun to show signs of lawlessness.

Adolin nodded to a passing group of Kholin soldiers in blue, who saluted him. They were on patrol, halberds held at their shoulders, helms gleaming. Dalinar's troops kept the peace here, and his scribes watched over it. All at his own cost.

His father didn't like the layout of the Outer Market or its lack of walls. He said that a raid could be catastrophic to it, that it violated the spirit of the Codes. But it had been years since the Parshendi had raided the Alethi side of the Plains. And if they did decide to strike at the warcamps, the scouts and guards would give ample warning.

So what was the point of the Codes? Adolin's father acted as if they were vitally important. Always be in uniform, always be armed, always stay sober. Be ever vigilant while under threat of attack. But there *was* no threat of attack.

As he walked through the market, Adolin looked—really looked—for the first time and tried to see what it was his father was doing.

He could pick out Dalinar's officers easily. They wore their uniforms, as commanded. Blue coats and trousers with silver buttons, knots on the shoulders for rank. Officers who weren't from Dalinar's camp wore all kinds of clothing. It was difficult to pick them out from the merchants and other wealthy civilians.

But that doesn't matter, Adolin told himself again. *Because we're not going to be attacked.*

He frowned, passing a group of lighteyes lounging outside another winehouse. Much as he'd just been doing. Their clothing—indeed, their postures and mannerisms—made them look like they cared only about their revelry. Adolin found himself annoyed. There was a war going on. Almost every day, soldiers died. They did so while lighteyes drank and chatted.

Maybe the Codes weren't just about protecting against the Parshendi. Maybe they were about something more—about giving the men commanders they could respect and rely on. About treating war with the gravity it deserved. Maybe it was about not turning a war zone into a festival. The common men had to remain on watch, vigilant. Therefore, Adolin and Dalinar did the same.

Adolin hesitated in the street. Nobody cursed at him or

called for him to move—they could see his rank. They just went around him.

I think I see now, he thought. Why had it taken him so long?

Disturbed, he hurried on his way toward the day's match.

.⋄.

"'I walked from Abamabar to Urithiru,'" Dalinar said, quoting from memory. "'In this, the metaphor and experience are one, inseparable to me like my mind and memory. One contains the other, and though I can explain one to you, the other is only for me.'"

Sadeas—sitting beside him—raised an eyebrow. Elhokar sat on Dalinar's other side, wearing his Shardplate. He'd taken to that more and more, sure that assassins were thirsting for his life. Together, they watched the men dueling down below, at the bottom of a small crater that Elhokar had designated the warcamps' dueling arena. The rocky shelves running around the inside of the ten-foot-tall wall made excellent seating platforms.

Adolin's duel hadn't started yet, and the men who fought right now were lighteyes, but not Shardbearers. Their dull-edged dueling swords were crusted with a white, chalklike substance. When one achieved a hit on the other's padded armor, it would leave a visible mark.

"So, wait," Sadeas said to him. "This man who wrote the book . . ."

"Nohadon is his holy name. Others call him Bajerden, though we're not certain whether that was actually his real name or not."

"He decided to walk from where to where?"

"Abamabar to Urithiru," Dalinar said. "I think it must have been a great distance, from the way the story is told."

"Wasn't he a king?"

"Yes."

"But why—"

"It's confusing," Dalinar said. "But listen. You'll see." He cleared his throat and continued. "'I strode this insightful distance on my own, and forbade attendants. I had no steed beyond my well-worn sandals, no companion beside a stout staff to offer conversation with its beats against the stone. My mouth was to be my purse; I stuffed it not with gems, but with song. When singing for sustenance failed me, my arms worked well for cleaning a floor or hogpen, and often earned me a satisfactory reward.

"'Those dear to me took fright for my safety and, perhaps, my sanity. Kings, they explained, do not walk like beggars for hundreds of miles. My response was that if a beggar could manage the feat, then why not a king? Did they think me less capable than a beggar?

"'Sometimes I think that I am. The beggar knows much that the king can only guess. And yet who draws up the codes for begging ordinances? Often I wonder what my experience in life—my easy life following the Desolation, and my current level of comfort—has given me of any true experience to use in making laws. If we had to rely on what we knew, kings would only be of use in creating laws regarding the proper heating of tea and cushioning of thrones.'"

Sadeas frowned at this. In front of them, the two swordsmen continued their duel; Elhokar watched keenly. He loved duels. Bringing in sand to coat the floor of this arena had been one of his first acts at the Shattered Plains.

"'Regardless,'" Dalinar said, still quoting from *The Way of Kings*, "'I made the trip and—as the astute reader has already concluded—survived it. The stories of its excitements will stain a different page in this narrative, for first I must explain my purpose in walking this strange path. Though I was quite willing to let my family think me insane, I would not leave the same as my cognomen upon the winds of history.

"'My family traveled to Urithiru via the direct method, and had been awaiting me for weeks when I arrived. I was not recognized at the gate, for my mane had grown quite robust without a razor to tame it. Once I revealed myself, I was carried away, primped, fed, worried over, and scolded in precisely that order. Only after all of this was through was I finally asked the purpose of my excursion. Couldn't I have just taken the simple, easy, and common route to the holy city?'"

"Exactly," Sadeas interjected. "He could at the very least have ridden a horse!"

"'For my answer,'" Dalinar quoted, "'I removed my sandals and proffered my callused feet. They were comfortable upon the table beside my half-consumed tray of grapes. At this point, the expressions of my companions proclaimed that they thought me daft, and so I explained by relating the stories of my trip. One after another, like stacked sacks of tallew, stored for the winter season. I would make flatbread of them soon, then stuff it between these pages.

"'Yes, I could have traveled quickly. But all men have the same ultimate destination. Whether we find our end in a hallowed sepulcher or a pauper's ditch, all save the Heralds themselves must dine with the Nightwatcher.

"'And so, does the destination matter? Or is it the path we take? I declare that no accomplishment has substance nearly as great as the road used to achieve it. We are not creatures of destinations. It is the journey that shapes us. Our callused feet, our backs strong from carrying the weight of our travels, our eyes open with the fresh delight of experiences lived.

"'In the end, I must proclaim that no good can be achieved of false means. For the substance of our existence is not in the achievement, but in the method. The Monarch must understand this; he must not become so focused on what he wishes to accomplish that he diverts his gaze from the path he must take to arrive there.'"

Dalinar sat back. The rock beneath them had been cushioned and augmented with wooden armrests and back supports. The duel ended with one of the lighteyes—wearing green, as he was subject to Sadeas—scoring a hit on the breastplate of the other, leaving a long white mark. Elhokar clapped his approval, gauntleted hands clanking, and both duelists bowed. The winner's victory would be recorded by the women sitting in the judging seats. They also held the books of dueling code, and would adjudicate disputes or infractions.

"That is the end of your story, I presume," Sadeas said, as the next two duelists walked out onto the sand.

"It is," Dalinar said.

"And you have that entire passage memorized?"

"I likely got a few of the words wrong."

"Knowing you, that means you might have forgotten a single 'an' or 'the.'"

Dalinar frowned.

"Oh, don't be so stiff, old friend," Sadeas said. "That was a compliment. Of sorts."

"What did you think of the story?" Dalinar asked as the dueling resumed.

"It was ridiculous," Sadeas said frankly, waving for a servant to bring him some wine. Yellow, as it was yet morning. "He walked all that distance just to make the point that kings should consider the consequences of their commands?"

"It wasn't just to prove the point," Dalinar said. "I thought that myself, but I've begun to see. He walked because he wanted to experience the things his people did. He used it as a metaphor, but I think he really wanted to know what it was like to walk that far."

Sadeas took a sip of his wine, then squinted up at the sun. "Couldn't we get an awning or something set up out here?"

"I like the sun," Elhokar said. "I spend too much time locked away in those caves we call buildings."

Sadeas glanced at Dalinar, rolling his eyes.

"Much of *The Way of Kings* is organized like that passage I quoted you," Dalinar said. "A metaphor from Nohadon's life—a real event turned into an example. He calls them the forty parables."

"Are they all so ridiculous?"

"I think this one is beautiful," Dalinar said softly.

"I don't doubt that you do. You always have loved sentimental stories." He raised a hand. "That was also intended to be a compliment."

"Of sorts?"

"Exactly. Dalinar, my friend, you always have been emotional. It makes you genuine. It can also get in the way of levelheaded thinking—but so long as it continues to prompt you to save my life, I think I can live with it." He scratched his chin. "I suppose, by definition, I would have to, wouldn't I?"

"I guess."

"The other highprinces think you are self-righteous. Surely you can see why."

"I . . ." What could he say? "I don't mean to be."

"Well, you do provoke them. Take, for example, the way you refuse to rise to their arguments or insults."

"Protesting simply draws attention to the issue," Dalinar said. "The finest defense of character is correct action. Acquaint yourself with virtue, and you can expect proper treatment from those around you."

"You see, there," Sadeas said. "Who talks like that?"

"Dalinar does," Elhokar said, though he was still watching the dueling. "My father used to."

"Precisely," Sadeas said. "Dalinar, friend, the others simply cannot accept that the things you say are serious. They assume it must be an act."

"And you? What do you think of me?"

"I can see the truth."

"Which is?"

"That you are a self-righteous prude," Sadeas said lightly. "But you come by it honestly."

"I'm certain you mean that to be a compliment too."

"Actually, this time I'm just trying to annoy you." Sadeas raised his cup of wine to Dalinar.

To the side, Elhokar grinned. "Sadeas. That was quite nearly clever. Shall I have to name you the new Wit?"

"What happened to the old one?" Sadeas's voice was curious, even eager, as if hoping to hear that tragedy had befallen Wit.

Elhokar's grin became a scowl. "He vanished."

"Is that so? How disappointing."

"Bah." Elhokar waved a gauntleted hand. "He does this on occasion. He'll return eventually. Unreliable as Damnation itself, that one. If he didn't make me laugh so, I'd have replaced him seasons ago."

They fell silent, and the dueling continued. A few other lighteyes—both women and men—watched, seated on the benchlike ridges. Dalinar noted with discomfort that Navani had arrived, and was chatting with a group of women, including Adolin's latest infatuation, the auburn-haired scribe.

Dalinar's eyes lingered on Navani, drinking in her violet dress, her mature beauty. She'd recorded his most recent visions without complaint, and seemed to have forgiven him for throwing her out of his rooms so sharply. She never mocked him, never acted skeptical. He appreciated that. Should he thank her, or would she see that as an invitation?

He averted his gaze from her, but found that he couldn't watch the dueling swordsmen without catching sight of her in the corner of his eye. So, instead, he glanced up into the sky, squinting against the afternoon sun. The sounds of metal hitting metal came from below. Behind him, several large snails clung to the rock, waiting for highstorm water.

He had so many questions, so many uncertainties. He listened to *The Way of Kings* and worked to discover what Gavilar's last words had meant. As if, somehow, they held the key to both his madness and the nature of the visions. But the truth was that he didn't know anything, and he couldn't rely on his own decisions. That was unhinging him, bit by bit, point by point.

Clouds seemed less frequent here, in these windswept plains. Just the blazing sun broken by the furious highstorms. The rest of Roshar was influenced by the storms—but here in the East, the feral, untamed highstorms ruled supreme. Could any mortal king hope to claim these lands? There were legends of them being inhabited, of there being more than just unclaimed hills, desolate plains, and overgrown forests. Natanatan, the Granite Kingdom.

"Ah," Sadeas said, sounding as if he'd tasted something bitter. "Did he have to come?"

Dalinar lowered his head and followed Sadeas's gaze. Highprince Vamah had arrived to watch the dueling, retinue in tow. Though most of them wore his traditional brown and grey colorings, the highprince himself wore a long grey coat that had slashes cut across it to reveal the bright red and orange silk underneath, matched by the ruffles peeking out of the cuffs and collar.

"I thought you had a fondness for Vamah," Elhokar said.

"I tolerate him," Sadeas replied. "But his fashion sense is absolutely repulsive. Red and orange? Not even a burnt orange, but a blatant, eye-breaking orange. And the rent style hasn't been fashionable for ages. Ah, wonderful, he's sitting directly across from us. I shall be forced to stare at him for the rest of the session."

"You shouldn't judge people so harshly based on how they look," Dalinar said.

"Dalinar," Sadeas said flatly, "we are highprinces. We *represent* Alethkar. Many around the world view us as a center of culture and influence. Should I not, therefore, have the right to encourage a proper presentation to the world?"

"A proper presentation, yes," Dalinar said. "It is right for us to be fit and neat." *It would be nice if your soldiers, for instance, kept their uniforms clean.*

"Fit, neat, and fashionable," Sadeas corrected.

"And me?" Dalinar asked, looking down at his simple uniform. "Would you have me dress in those ruffles and bright colors?"

"You?" Sadeas asked. "You're completely hopeless." He raised a hand to forestall objection. "No, I am unfair. That uniform has a certain . . . timeless quality to it. The military suit, by virtue of its utility, will never be completely out of fashion. It's a safe choice—steady. In a way, you avoid the issue of fashion by not playing the game." He nodded to Vamah. "Vamah tries to play, but does so very poorly. And that is unforgivable."

"I still say you place too much importance on those silks and scarves," Dalinar said. "We are soldiers at war, not courtiers at a ball."

"The Shattered Plains are quickly becoming a destination for foreign dignitaries. It is important to present ourselves properly." He raised a finger to Dalinar. "If I am to accept your moral superiority, my friend, then perhaps it is time for you to accept my sense of fashion. One might note that *you* judge people by their clothing even more than I do."

Dalinar fell silent. That comment stung in its truthfulness. Still, if dignitaries were going to meet with the highprinces on the Shattered Plains, was it too much to ask for them to find an efficient group of warcamps led by men who at least looked like generals?

Dalinar settled back to watch the match end. By his count, it was time for Adolin's bout. The two lighteyes who had been fighting bowed to the king, then withdrew into a tent on the side of the dueling grounds. A moment later, Adolin stepped out onto the sand, wearing his deep blue Shardplate. He carried his helm under his arm, his blond-and-black hair a stylish mess. He raised a gauntleted hand to Dalinar and bowed his head to the king, then put on his helm.

The man who walked out behind him wore Shardplate painted yellow. Brightlord Resi was the only full Shardbearer in Highprince Thanadal's army—though their warcamp had three men who carried only the Blade or the Plate. Thanadal himself had neither. It wasn't uncommon for a highprince to rely on his finest warriors as Shardbearers; it made sound sense, particularly if you were the sort of general who preferred to stay behind the lines and direct tactics. In Thanadal's own princedom, the tradition for centuries had been to appoint the holder of Resi's Shards as something known as the Royal Defender.

Thanadal had recently been vocal about Dalinar's faults, and so Adolin—in a moderately subtle move—had challenged the highprince's star Shardbearer to a friendly bout. Few duels were for Shards; in this case, losing wouldn't cost either man anything other than statistics in the rankings. The match drew an unusual amount of attention, and the small arena filled over the next quarter hour while the duelists stretched and prepared. More than one woman set up a board to sketch or write impressions of the bout. Thanadal himself didn't attend.

The bout began as the highjudge in attendance, Lady Istow, called for the combatants to summon their Blades. Elhokar leaned forward again, intent, as Resi and Adolin circled one another on the sand, Shardblades materializing. Dalinar found himself leaning forward as well, though he did feel a stab of shame. According to the Codes, most duels should be avoided when Alethkar was at war. There was a fine line between sparring for practice and dueling another man for an insult, potentially leaving important officers wounded.

Resi stood in Stonestance, his Shardblade held before him in two hands, point toward the sky, arms all the way extended. Adolin used Windstance, turned sideways slightly, hands before him and elbows bent, Shardblade pointing back over his head. They circled. The winner would be the first one who completely shattered a section of the other's Plate. That wasn't too dangerous; weakened Plate could usually still rebuff a blow, even if it shattered in the process.

Resi attacked first, taking a hopping leap forward and striking by whipping his Shardblade back over his head, then down to his right in a powerful blow. Stonestance focused on that type of attack, delivering the most possible momentum and strength behind each strike. Dalinar found it unwieldy— you didn't need that much power behind a Shardblade on the battlefield, though it was helpful against other Shardbearers.

Adolin jumped back out of the way, Shardplate-enhanced legs giving him a nimbleness that defied the fact that he was wearing over a hundred stoneweights of thick armor. Resi's attack—though well-executed—left him open, and Adolin made a careful strike at his opponent's left vambrace, cracking the forearm plate. Resi attacked again, and Adolin again danced out of the way, then scored a hit on his opponent's left thigh.

Some poets described combat as a dance. Dalinar rarely felt that way about regular combat. Two men fighting with sword and shield would go at one another in a furious rush, slamming their weapons down again and again, trying to get around their opponent's shield. Less a dance, and more like wrestling with weapons.

Fighting with Shardblades, though, *that* could be like a dance. The large weapons took a great deal of skill to swing properly, and Plate was resilient, so exchanges were generally drawn out. The fights were filled with grand motions, wide sweeps. There was a fluidity to fighting with a Shardblade. A grace.

"He's quite good, you know," Elhokar said. Adolin made a hit on Resi's helm, prompting a round of applause from those watching. "Better than my father was. Better than even you, Uncle."

"He works very hard," Dalinar said. "He truly loves it. Not the war, not the fighting. The dueling."

"He could be champion, if he wished it."

Adolin did wish it, Dalinar knew. But he had refused bouts that would put him within reach of the title. Dalinar suspected that Adolin did it to hold, somewhat, to the Codes. Dueling championships and tournaments were things for those rare times between wars. It could be argued that protecting one's family honor, however, was for all times.

Either way, Adolin didn't duel for ranking, and that made other Shardbearers underestimate him. They were quick to accept duels with him, and some non-Shardbearers challenged him. By tradition, the king's own Shardplate and Blade were available for a large fee to those who both had his favor and the wish to duel a Shardbearer.

Dalinar shivered at the thought of someone else wearing his Plate or holding Oathbringer. It was unnatural. And yet, the lending of the king's Blade and Plate—or before the monarchy had been restored, the lending of a highprince's Blade and Plate—was a strong tradition. Even Gavilar had not broken it, though he had complained about it in private.

Adolin dodged another blow, but he had begun to move into Windstance's offensive forms. Resi wasn't ready for this— though he managed to hit Adolin once on the right pauldron, the blow was a glancing one. Adolin advanced, Blade sweeping in a fluid pattern. Resi backed away, falling into a parrying posture—Stonestance was one of the few to rely on those.

Adolin batted his opponent's Blade away, knocking it out of stance. Resi reset, but Adolin knocked it away again. Resi grew sloppier and sloppier getting back into stance and Adolin began to strike, hitting him on one side, then on the other. Small, quick blows, meant to unnerve.

They worked. Resi bellowed and threw himself into one of Stonestance's characteristic overhand blows. Adolin handled it perfectly, dropping his Blade to one hand, raising his left arm and taking the blow on his unharmed vambrace. It cracked badly, but the move allowed Adolin to bring his own Blade to the side and strike Resi's cracked left cuisse.

The thigh plate shattered with the sound of ripping metal, pieces blasting away, trailing smoke, glowing like molten steel. Resi stumbled back; his left leg could no longer bear the weight of the Shardplate. The match was over. More important duels might go for two or three broken plates, but that grew dangerous.

The highjudge stood, calling an end. Resi stumbled away, ripping off his helm. His curses were audible. Adolin saluted his enemy, tapping the blunt edge of his Blade to his forehead, then dismissing the Blade. He bowed to the king. Other men sometimes went into the crowd to brag or accept accolades, but Adolin retreated to the preparation tent.

"Talented indeed," Elhokar said.

"And such a . . . proper lad," Sadeas said, sipping his drink.

"Yes," Dalinar said. "At times, I wish there were peace, simply so that Adolin could dedicate himself to his dueling."

Sadeas sighed. "More talk of abandoning the war, Dalinar?"

"That's not what I meant."

"You keep complaining that you've given up that argument, Uncle," Elhokar said, turning to regard him. "Yet you continue to dance around it, speaking longingly of peace. People in the camps call you coward."

Sadeas snorted. "He's no coward, Your Majesty. I can attest to that."

"Why, then?" Elhokar asked.

"These rumors have grown far beyond what is reasonable," Dalinar said.

"And yet, you do not answer my questions," Elhokar said.

"If you could make the decision, Uncle, would you have us leave the Shattered Plains? Are you a coward?"

Dalinar hesitated.

Unite them, that voice had told him. *It is your task, and I give it to you.*

Am I a coward? he wondered. Nohadon challenged him, in the book, to examine himself. To never become so certain or high that he wasn't willing to seek truth.

Elhokar's question hadn't been about his visions. And yet, Dalinar had the distinct impression that he *was* being a coward, at least in relation to his desire to abdicate. If he left because of what was happening to him, that would be taking the easy path.

I can't leave, he realized. *No matter what happens. I have to see this through.* Even if he was mad. Or, an increasingly worrisome thought, even if the visions were real, but their origins suspect. *I have to stay. But I also have to plan, to make sure I don't tow my house down.*

Such a careful line to walk. Nothing clear, everything clouded. He'd been ready to run because he liked to make clear decisions. Well, nothing was clear about what was happening to him. It seemed that in making the decision to remain highprince, he placed one important cornerstone into rebuilding the foundation of who he was.

He would not abdicate. And that was that.

"Dalinar?" Elhokar asked. "Are you . . . well?"

Dalinar blinked, realizing that he had stopped paying attention to the king and Sadeas. Staring off into space like that wouldn't help his reputation. He turned to the king. "You want to know the truth," he said. "Yes, if I could make the order, I would take all ten armies and return to Alethkar."

Despite what others said, that was not cowardly. No, he'd just confronted cowardice inside of him, and he knew what it was. This was something different.

The king looked shocked.

"I *would* leave," Dalinar said firmly. "But not because I wish to flee or because I fear battle. It would be because I fear for Alethkar's stability; leaving this war would help secure our homeland and the loyalty of the highprinces. I would send more envoys and scholars to find out why the Parshendi killed Gavilar. We gave up on that too easily. I still wonder if the assassination was initiated by miscreants or rebels among their own people.

"I'd discover what their culture is—and yes, they do have one. If rebels weren't the cause of the assassination, I'd keep asking until I learned *why* they did it. I'd demand restitution— perhaps their own king, delivered to us for execution in turn— in exchange for granting them peace. As for the gemhearts, I'd speak with my scientists and discover a better method of holding this territory. Perhaps with mass homesteading of the area, securing all of the Unclaimed Hills, we could truly expand our borders and claim the Shattered Plains. I wouldn't *abandon* vengeance, Your Majesty, but I would approach it— and our war here—more thoughtfully. Right now, we know too little to be effective."

Elhokar looked surprised. He nodded. "I . . . Uncle, that actually makes sense. Why didn't you explain it before?"

Dalinar blinked. Just several weeks ago, Elhokar had been indignant when Dalinar had merely mentioned the idea of turning back. What had changed?

I don't give the boy enough credit, he realized. "I have had trouble explaining my own thoughts recently, Your Majesty."

"Your Majesty!" Sadeas said. "Surely you wouldn't actually consider—"

"This latest attempt on my life has me unsettled, Sadeas. Tell me. Have you made any progress in determining who put the weakened gems in my Plate?"

"Not yet, Your Majesty."

"They're trying to kill me," Elhokar said softly, huddling down in his armor. "They'll see me dead, like my father. Sometimes I do wonder if we're chasing after the ten fools here. The assassin in white—he was Shin."

"The Parshendi took responsibility for sending him," Sadeas said.

"Yes," Elhokar replied. "And yet they are savages, and

easily manipulated. It would be a perfect distraction, pinning the blame on a group of parshmen. We go to war for years and years, never noticing the real villains, working quietly in my own camp. They watch me. Always. Waiting. I see their faces in mirrors. Symbols, twisted, inhuman . . ."

Dalinar glanced at Sadeas, and the two shared a disturbed look. Was Elhokar's paranoia growing worse, or just more visible? He saw phantom cabals in every shadow, and now—with the attempt on his life—he had proof to feed those worries.

"Retreating from the Shattered Plains could be a good idea," Dalinar said carefully. "But not if it is to begin another war with someone else. We must stabilize and unify our people."

Elhokar sighed. "Chasing the assassin is only an idle thought right now. Perhaps we won't need it. I hear that your efforts with Sadeas have been fruitful."

"They have indeed, Your Majesty," Sadeas said, sounding proud—perhaps a little smug. "Though Dalinar still insists on using his own slow bridges. Sometimes, my forces are nearly wiped out before he arrives. This would work better if Dalinar would use modern bridge tactics."

"The waste of life . . ." Dalinar said.

"Is acceptable," Sadeas said. "They're mostly slaves, Dalinar. It's an honor for them to have a chance to participate in some small way."

I doubt they see it in that light.

"I wish you'd at least *try* my way," Sadeas continued. "What we've been doing so far has worked, but I worry that the Parshendi will continue to send two armies against us. I don't relish the idea of fighting both on my own before you arrive."

Dalinar hesitated. That would be a problem. But to give up the siege bridges?

"Well, why not a compromise?" Elhokar said. "Next plateau assault, Uncle, you let Sadeas's bridgemen help you for the initial march to the contested plateau. Sadeas has plenty of extra bridge crews he could lend you. He could still rush on ahead with a smaller army, but you'd follow more quickly than you have been, using his bridge crews."

"That would be the same as using my own bridge crews," Dalinar said.

"Not necessarily," Elhokar said. "You've said that the Parshendi can rarely set up and fire on you once Sadeas engages them. Sadeas's men can start the assault as usual, and you can join once he's secured a foothold for you."

"Yes . . ." Sadeas said, thoughtful. "The bridgemen *you* use will be safe, and you won't be costing any additional lives. But you'll arrive at the plateau to help me twice as quickly."

"What if you can't distract the Parshendi well enough?" Dalinar asked. "What if they still set up archers to fire on my bridgemen when I cross?"

"Then we'll retreat," Sadeas said with a sigh. "And we'll call it a failed experiment. But at least we'll have tried. This is how you get ahead, old friend. You try new things."

Dalinar scratched his chin in thought.

"Oh, go on, Dalinar," Elhokar said. "He took your suggestion to attack together. Try it once his way."

"Very well," Dalinar said. "We will see how it works."

"Excellent," Elhokar said, standing. "And now, I believe I'll go congratulate your son. That bout was exciting!"

Dalinar hadn't found it particularly exciting—Adolin's opponent hadn't ever held the upper hand. But that was the best kind of battle. Dalinar didn't buy the arguments about a 'good' fight being a close one. When you won, it was always better to win quickly and with extreme advantage.

Dalinar and Sadeas stood in respect as the king descended the stairlike stone outcroppings toward the sandy floor below. Dalinar then turned to Sadeas. "I should be leaving. Send me a clerk to detail the plateaus you feel we could try this maneuver on. Next time one of them is up for assault, I'll march my army to your staging area and we'll leave together. You and the smaller, quicker group can go on ahead, and we'll catch up once you're in position."

Sadeas nodded.

Dalinar turned to climb up the steps toward the ramp out.

"Dalinar," Sadeas called after him.

Dalinar looked back at the other highprince. Sadeas's scarf fluttered in a gust of wind, his arms folded, the metallic golden embroidery glistening. "Send me one of your clerks as well. With a copy of that book of Gavilar's. It may amuse me to hear its other stories."

Dalinar smiled. "I will do so, Sadeas."

"Above the final void I hang, friends behind, friends before. The feast I must drink clings to their faces, and the words I must speak spark in my mind. The old oaths will be spoken anew."

—Dated Betabanan, 1173, 45 seconds pre-death. Subject: a light-eyed child of five years. Diction improved remarkably when giving sample.

Kaladin glared at the three glowing topaz spheres on the ground in front of him. The barrack was dark, empty save for Teft and himself. Lopen leaned in the sunlit doorway, watching with a casual air. Outside, Rock called out commands to the other bridgemen. Kaladin had them working on battle formations. Nothing overt. It would be construed as practice for bridge carrying, but he was actually training them to obey orders and rearrange themselves efficiently.

The three little spheres—only chips—lit the stone ground around themselves in little tan rings. Kaladin focused on them, holding his breath, willing the light into him.

Nothing happened.

He tried harder, staring into their depths.

Nothing happened.

He picked one up, cupping it in his palm, raising it so that he could see the light and nothing else. He could pick out the details of the storm, the shifting, spinning vortex of light. He commanded it, willed it, begged it.

Nothing happened.

He groaned, lying back on the rock, staring at the ceiling.

"Maybe you don't want it badly enough," Teft said.

"I want it as badly as I know how. It won't budge, Teft."

Teft grunted and picked up one of the spheres.

"Maybe we're wrong about me," Kaladin said. It seemed poetically appropriate that the moment he accepted this strange, frightening part of himself, he couldn't make it work. "It could have been a trick of the sunlight."

"A trick of the sunlight," Teft said flatly. "Sticking a bag to the barrel was a trick of the light."

"All right. Then maybe it was some odd fluke, something that happened just that once."

"*And* when you were wounded," Teft said, "*and* whenever on a bridge run you needed an extra burst of strength or endurance."

Kaladin let out a frustrated sigh and tapped his head back lightly against the rock floor a few times. "Well, if I'm one of these Radiants you keep talking about, why can't I do anything?"

"I figure," the grizzled bridgeman said, rolling the sphere in his fingers, "that you're like a baby, making his legs work. At first it just kind of happens. Slowly, he figures how to make them move on purpose. You just need practice."

"I've spent a week staring at spheres, Teft. How much practice can it take?"

"Well, more than you've had, obviously."

Kaladin rolled his eyes and sat back up. "Why am I listening to you? You've admitted that you don't know any more than I do."

"I don't know anything about using the Stormlight," Teft said, scowling. "But I know what *should* happen."

"According to stories that contradict one another. You've told me that the Radiants could fly and walk on walls."

Teft nodded. "They sure could. And make stone melt by

looking at it. And move great distances in a single heartbeat. And command the sunlight. And—"

"And why," Kaladin said, "would they need to both walk on walls *and* fly? If they can fly, why would they bother running up walls?"

Teft said nothing.

"And why bother with either one," Kaladin added, "if they can just 'move great distances in a heartbeat'?"

"I'm not sure," Teft admitted.

"We can't trust the stories or legends," Kaladin said. He glanced at Syl, who had landed beside one of the spheres, staring at it with childlike interest. "Who knows what is true and what has been fabricated? The only thing we know for certain is this." He plucked up one of the spheres and held it up in two fingers. "The Radiant sitting in this room is very, very tired of the color brown."

Teft grunted. "You're not a Radiant, lad."

"Weren't we just talking about—"

"Oh, you can infuse," Teft said. "You can drink in the Stormlight and command it. But being a Radiant was more than that. It was their way of life, the things they did. The Immortal Words."

"The what?"

Teft rolled his sphere between his fingers again, holding it up and staring into its depths. "Life before death. Strength before weakness. Journey before destination. That was their motto, and was the First Ideal of the Immortal Words. There were four others."

Kaladin raised an eyebrow. "Which were?"

"I don't actually know," Teft said. "But the Immortal Words—these Ideals—guided everything they did. The four later Ideals were said to be different for every order of Radiants. But the First Ideal was the same for each of the ten: Life before death, strength before weakness, journey before destination." He hesitated. "Or so I was told."

"Yes, well, that seems a little obvious to me," Kaladin said. "Life comes before death. Just like day comes before night, or one comes before two. Obvious."

"You're not taking this seriously. Maybe that's why the Stormlight refuses you."

Kaladin stood and stretched. "I'm sorry, Teft. I'm just tired."

"Life before death," Teft said, wagging a finger at Kaladin. "The Radiant seeks to defend life, always. He never kills unnecessarily, and never risks his own life for frivolous reasons. Living is harder than dying. The Radiant's duty is to live.

"Strength before weakness. All men are weak at some time in their lives. The Radiant protects those who are weak, and uses his strength for others. Strength does not make one capable of rule; it makes one capable of service."

Teft picked up spheres, putting them in his pouch. He held the last one for a second, then tucked it away too. "Journey before destination. There are always several ways to achieve a goal. Failure is preferable to winning through unjust means. Protecting ten innocents is not worth killing one. In the end, all men die. How you lived will be far more important to the Almighty than what you accomplished."

"The Almighty? So the knights were tied to religion?"

"Isn't everything? There was some old king who came up with all this. Had his wife write it in a book or something. My mother read it. The Radiants based the Ideals on what was written there."

Kaladin shrugged, moving over to begin sorting through the pile of bridgemen's leather vests. Ostensibly, he and Teft were here checking those over for tears or broken straps. After a few moments, Teft joined him.

"Do you actually believe that?" Kaladin asked, lifting up a vest, tugging on its straps. "That anyone would follow those vows, particularly a bunch of lighteyes?"

"They weren't just lighteyes. They were Radiants."

"They were people," Kaladin said. "Men in power always pretend to virtue, or divine guidance, some kind of mandate to 'protect' the rest of us. If we believe that the Almighty put them where they are, it's easier for us to swallow what they do to us."

Teft turned a vest over. It was beginning to tear beneath

the left shoulder pad. "I never used to believe. And then . . . then I saw you infusing Light, and I began to wonder."

"Stories and legends, Teft," Kaladin said. "We want to believe that there were better men once. That makes us think it could be that way again. But people don't change. They are corrupt now. They were corrupt then."

"Maybe," Teft said. "My parents believed in all of it. The Immortal Words, the Ideals, the Knights Radiant, the Almighty. Even old Vorinism. In fact, especially old Vorinism."

"That led to the Hierocracy. The devotaries and the ardents shouldn't hold land or property. It's too dangerous."

Teft snorted. "Why? You think they'd be worse at being in charge than the lighteyes?"

"Well, you've probably got a point there." Kaladin frowned. He'd spent so long assuming the Almighty had abandoned him, or even cursed him, that it was difficult to accept that maybe—as Syl had said—he'd instead been blessed. Yes, he'd been preserved, and he supposed he should be grateful for that. But what could be worse than being granted great power, yet still being too weak to save those he loved?

Further speculation was interrupted as Lopen stood up straight in the doorway, gesturing covertly to Kaladin and Teft. Fortunately, there wasn't anything to hide anymore. In fact, there hadn't ever been anything to hide, other than Kaladin sitting on the floor and staring at the spheres like an idiot. He set aside the vest and walked to the entrance.

Hashal's palanquin was being carried directly toward Kaladin's barrack, her tall, oft-silent husband walking alongside. The sash at his neck was violet, as was the embroidery on the cuffs of his short, vestlike jacket. Gaz still hadn't reappeared. It had been a week now, and no sign of him. Hashal and her husband—along with their lighteyed attendants—did what he'd once done, and they rebuffed any questions about the bridge sergeant.

"Storm it," Teft said, stepping up beside Kaladin. "Those two make my skin itch, same way it does when I know someone's got a knife and is standing behind me."

Rock had the bridgemen lined up and waiting quietly, as if

for inspection. Kaladin walked out to join them, Teft and Lopen following behind. The bearers set the palanquin down in front of Kaladin. Open-sided with only a small canopy on the top, it was little more than an armchair on a platform. Many of the lighteyed women used them in the warcamps.

Kaladin reluctantly gave Hashal a proper bow, prompting the other bridgemen to do so as well. Now was not the time to be beaten for insubordination.

"You have such a well-trained band, bridgeleader," she said, idly scratching her cheek with a ruby-red nail, her elbow on her armrest. "So . . . efficient at bridge runs."

"Thank you, Brightness Hashal," Kaladin said, trying—but failing—to keep the stiffness and hostility from his voice. "May I ask? Gaz hasn't been seen for some days now. Is he well?"

"No." Kaladin waited for further reply, but she didn't give one. "My husband has made a decision. Your men are so good at bridge runs that you are a model to the other crews. As such, you will be on bridge duty every day from now on."

Kaladin felt a chill. "And scavenging duty?"

"Oh, there will still be time for that. You need to take torches down anyway, and plateau runs never happen at night. So your men will sleep during the day—always on call—and will work the chasms at night. A much better use of your time."

"Every bridge run," Kaladin said. "You're going to make us go on *every one*."

"Yes," she said idly, tapping for her bearers to raise her. "Your team is just too good. It must be used. You'll start full-time bridge duty tomorrow. Consider it an . . . honor."

Kaladin inhaled sharply to keep himself from saying what he thought of her "honor." He couldn't bring himself to bow as she retreated, but she didn't seem to care. Rock and the men started muttering.

Every bridge run. She'd just doubled the rate at which they'd be killed. Kaladin's team wouldn't last another few weeks. They were already so low on members that losing one or two men on an assault would cause them to flounder. The Parshendi would focus on them then, cutting them down.

"Kelek's breath!" Teft said. "She'll see us dead!"

"It's not fair," Lopen added.

"We're bridgemen," Kaladin said, looking at them. "What made you think that any kind of 'fairness' applied to us?"

"She hasn't killed us fast enough for Sadeas," Moash said. "You know that soldiers have been beaten for coming to look for you, to see the man who survived the highstorm? He hasn't forgotten about you, Kaladin."

Teft was still swearing. He pulled Kaladin aside, Lopen following, but the others remained talking among themselves. "Damnation!" Teft said softly. "They like to pretend to be evenhanded with the bridge crews. Makes 'em seem fair. Looks like they gave up on that. Bastards."

"What do we do, gancho?" Lopen asked.

"We go to the chasms," Kaladin said. "Just like we're scheduled to. Then make sure we get some extra sleep tonight, as we're apparently going to be staying up all night tomorrow."

"The men will hate going into the chasms at night, lad," Teft said.

"I know."

"But we're not ready for . . . what we need to do," Teft said, looking to make sure nobody could hear. It was only him, Kaladin, and Lopen. "It will be another few weeks at least."

"I know."

"We won't last another few weeks!" Teft said. "With Sadeas and Kholin working together, runs happen nearly every day. Just one bad run—one time with the Parshendi drawing a bead on us—and it will all be over. We'll be wiped out."

"I know!" Kaladin said, frustrated, taking a deep breath and forming fists to keep himself from exploding.

"Gancho!" Lopen said.

"What?" Kaladin snapped.

"It's happening again."

Kaladin froze, then looked down at his arms. Sure enough, he caught a hint of luminescent smoke rising from his skin. It was extremely faint—he didn't have many gemstones near him—but it was there. The wisps faded quickly. Hopefully the other bridgemen hadn't seen.

"Damnation. What did I do?"

"I don't know," Teft said. "Is it because you were angry at Hashal?"

"I was angry before."

"You breathed it in," Syl said eagerly, whipping around him in the air, a ribbon of light.

"What?"

"I saw it." She twisted herself around. "You were mad, you drew in a breath, and the Light . . . it came too."

Kaladin glanced at Teft, but of course the older bridgeman hadn't heard. "Gather the men," Kaladin said. "We're going down to our chasm duty."

"And what about what has happened?" Teft said. "Kaladin, we can't go on that many bridge runs. We'll be cut to pieces."

"I'm doing something about it today. Gather the men. Syl, I need something from you."

"What?" She landed in front of him and formed into a young woman.

"Go find us a place where some Parshendi corpses have fallen."

"I thought you were going to do spear practice today."

"That's what the men will be doing," Kaladin said. "I'll get them organized first. After that, I have a different task."

※

Kaladin clapped a quick signal, and the bridgemen made a decent arrowhead formation. They carried the spears they'd stashed in the chasm, secured in a large sack filled with stones and stuck in a crevice. He clapped his hands again, and they rearranged into a double-line wall formation. He clapped again, and they formed into a ring with one man standing behind every two as a quick step-in reserve.

The walls of the chasm dripped with water, and the bridgemen splashed through puddles. They were good. Better than they had any right to be, better—for their level of training—than any team he'd worked with.

But Teft was right. They still wouldn't last long in a fight. A few more weeks and he'd have them practiced enough with thrusts and shielding one another that they'd begin to be dangerous. Until then, they were just bridgemen who could move in fancy patterns. They needed more time.

Kaladin had to buy them some.

"Teft," Kaladin said. "Take over."

The older bridgeman gave one of those cross-armed salutes.

"Syl," Kaladin said to the spren, "let's go see these bodies."

"They're close. Come on." She zipped off down the chasm, a glowing ribbon. Kaladin started after her.

"Sir," Teft called.

Kaladin hesitated. When had Teft started calling him "sir"? Odd, how right that felt. "Yes?"

"You want an escort?" Teft stood at the head of the gathered bridgemen, who were looking more and more like soldiers, with their leather vests and spears held in practiced grips.

Kaladin shook his head. "I'll be fine."

"Chasmfiends . . ."

"The lighteyes have killed any who prowl this close to our side. Besides, if I did run into one, what difference would two or three extra men make?"

Teft grimaced behind his short, greying beard, but offered no further objection. Kaladin continued to follow Syl. In his pouch, he carried the rest of the spheres they'd discovered on bodies while scavenging. They made a habit of keeping some of each discovery and sticking them to bridges, and with Syl helping at scavenging, they now found more than they used to. He had a small fortune in his pouch. That Stormlight—he hoped—would serve him well today.

He got out a sapphire mark for light, avoiding pools of water strewn with bones. A skull protruded from one, wavy green moss growing across the scalp like hair, lifespren bobbing above. Perhaps it should have felt eerie to walk through these darkened slots alone, but they didn't bother Kaladin. This was a sacred place, the sepulcher of the lowly, the burial cavern of bridgemen and spearmen who died by lighteyed edict, spilling blood down the sides of these ragged walls. This place wasn't eerie; it was holy.

He was actually glad to be alone with his silence and the remains of those who had died. These men hadn't cared about the squabbles of those born with lighter eyes than they. These men had cared about their families or—at the very least—their sphere pouches. How many of them were trapped in this foreign land, these endless plateaus, too poor to escape back to Alethkar? Hundreds died each week, winning gems for men who were already rich, winning vengeance for a king long dead.

Kaladin passed another skull, missing its lower jaw, the crown split by an axe's blow. The bones seemed to watch him, curious, the blue Stormlight in his hand giving a haunted cast to the uneven ground and walls.

The devotaries taught that when men died, the most valiant among them—the ones who fulfilled their Callings best—would rise to help reclaim heaven. Each man would do as he had done in life. Spearmen to fight, farmers to work spiritual farms, lighteyes to lead. The ardents were careful to point out that excellence in any Calling would bring power. A farmer would be able to wave his hand and create great fields of spiritual crops. A spearman would be a great warrior, able to cause thunder with his shield and lightning with his spear.

But what of the bridgemen? Would the Almighty demand that all of these fallen rise and continue their drudgery? Would Dunny and the others run bridges in the afterlife? No ardents came to them to test their abilities or grant them Elevations. Perhaps the bridgemen wouldn't be needed in the War for Heaven. Only the very most skilled went there anyway. Others would simply slumber until the Tranquiline Halls were reclaimed.

So do I believe again now? He climbed over a boulder wedged in the chasm. *Just like that?* He wasn't sure. But it didn't matter. He would do the best he could for his bridgemen. If there was a Calling in that, so be it.

Of course, if he did escape with his team, Sadeas would replace them with others who would die in their stead.

I have to worry about what I can do, he told himself. *Those other bridgemen aren't my responsibility.*

Teft talked about the Radiants, about ideals and stories. Why couldn't men actually be like that? Why did they have to rely on dreams and fabrications for inspiration?

If you flee . . . you leave all the other bridgemen to be slaughtered, a voice whispered within him. *There has to be something you can do for them.*

No! he fought back. *If I worry about that, I won't be able to save Bridge Four. If I find a way out, we're going.*

If you leave, the voice seemed to say, *then who will fight for them? Nobody cares. Nobody. . . .*

What was it his father had said all those years ago? He did what he felt was right because someone had to start. Someone had to take the first step.

Kaladin's hand felt warm. He stopped in the chasm, closing his eyes. You couldn't feel any heat from a sphere, usually, but the one in his hand seemed warm. And then—feeling completely natural about it—Kaladin breathed in deeply. The sphere grew cold and a wave of heat shot up his arm.

He opened his eyes. The sphere in his hand was dun and his fingers were crispy with frost. Light rose from him like smoke from a fire, white, pure.

He felt alive with energy. He had no need to breathe—in fact, he held the breath in, trapping the Stormlight. Syl zipped back down the corridor toward him. She twisted around him, then came to rest in the air, taking the form of a woman. "You did it. What happened?"

Kaladin shook his head, holding his breath. Something was surging within him, like . . .

Like a storm. Raging inside his veins, a tempest sweeping about inside his chest cavity. It made him want to run, jump, yell. It almost made him want to burst. He felt as if he could walk on air. Or walls.

Yes! he thought. He broke into a run, leaping at the side of the chasm. He hit feet-first.

Then bounced off and slammed back into the ground. He was so stunned that he cried out, and he felt the storm within dampen as breath escaped.

He lay on his back as Stormlight rose from him more quickly now that he was breathing. He lay there as the last of it burned away.

Syl landed on his chest. "Kaladin? What was that?"

"Me being an idiot," he replied, sitting up and feeling an ache in his back and a sharp pain in his elbow where he'd hit the ground. "Teft said that the Radiants were able to walk on walls, and I felt so alive. . . ."

Syl walked on air, stepping as if down a set of stairs. "I don't think you're ready for that yet. Don't be so risky. If you die, I go stupid again, you know."

"I'll try to keep that in mind," Kaladin said, climbing to his feet. "Maybe I'll remove dying from my list of tasks to do this week."

She snorted, zipping into the air, becoming a ribbon again. "Come on, hurry up." She shot off down the chasm. Kaladin collected the dun sphere, then dug into the pouch for another one to provide light. Had he drained them all? No. The others still glowed strongly. He selected a ruby mark, then hurried after Syl.

She led him to a narrow chasm that contained a small group of fresh Parshendi corpses. "This is morbid, Kaladin," Syl noted, standing above the bodies.

"I know. Do you know where Lopen went?"

"I sent him scavenging nearby, fetching the things you asked him for."

"Bring him, please."

Syl sighed, but zipped away. She always got testy when he made her appear to someone other than him. Kaladin knelt down. Parshendi all looked so similar. That same square face, those blocky—almost rocklike—features. Some had the beards with bits of gemstone tied in them. Those glowed, but not brightly. Cut gemstones held Stormlight better. Why was that?

Rumors in camp claimed that the Parshendi took the wounded humans away and ate them. Rumors also said they left their dead, not caring for the fallen, never building them proper pyres. But that was false. They did care about their dead. They all seemed to have the same sensibility that Shen did; he threw a fit every time one of the bridgemen so much as touched a Parshendi corpse.

I'd better be right about this, Kaladin thought grimly, slipping a knife off one of the Parshendi bodies. It was beautifully ornamented and forged, the steel lined with glyphs Kaladin didn't recognize. He began to cut at the strange breastplate armor that grew from the corpse's chest.

Kaladin quickly determined that Parshendi physiology was very different from human physiology. Small blue ligaments held the breastplate to the skin underneath. It was attached all the way across. He continued working. There wasn't much blood; it had pooled at the corpse's back or leaked away. His knife wasn't a surgeon's tool, but it did the job just fine. By the time Syl returned with Lopen, Kaladin had gotten the breastplate free and had moved on to the carapace helm. It was harder to remove; it had grown into the skull in places, and he had to saw with the serrated section of the blade.

"Ho, gancho," Lopen said, a sack slung over his shoulder. "You don't like them at all, do you?"

Kaladin stood, wiping his hands on the Parshendi man's skirt. "Did you find what I asked for?"

"Sure did," Lopen said, letting down the sack and digging into it. He pulled out an armored leather vest and cap, the type that spearmen used. Then he took out some thin leather straps and a medium-sized wooden spearman's shield. Finally came a series of deep red bones. Parshendi bones. At the very bottom of the sack was the rope, the one Lopen had bought and tossed into the chasm, then stashed down below.

"You haven't lost your wits, have you?" Lopen asked, eyeing the bones. "Because if you have, I've got a cousin who makes this drink for people who've lost their wits, and it might make you better, sure."

"If I'd lost my wits," Kaladin said, walking over to a pool of still water to wash off the carapace helm, "would I say that I had?"

"I don't know," Lopen said, leaning back. "Maybe. Guess it doesn't matter if you're crazy or not."

"You'd follow a crazy man into battle?"

"Sure," Lopen said. "If you're crazy, you're a good type, and I like you. Not a killing-people-in-their-sleep type of crazy." He smiled. "Besides. We all follow crazies all the time. Do it every day with lighteyes."

Kaladin chuckled.

"So what's this all for?"

Kaladin didn't answer. He brought the breastplate over to the leather vest, then tied it onto the front with some of the leather straps. He did the same with the cap and the helm, though he eventually had to saw some grooves into the helm with his knife to make it stay.

Once done, Kaladin used the last straps to tie the bones together and attach them to the front of the round wooden shield. The bones rattled as he lifted the shield, but he decided it was good enough.

He took shield, cap, and breastplate and put them all into Lopen's sack. They barely fit. "All right," he said, standing up. "Syl, lead us to the short chasm." They'd spent some time investigating, finding the best place to launch arrows into the bottom of permanent bridges. One bridge in particular was close to Sadeas's warcamp—so they often traversed it on the way out on a bridge run—and spanned a particularly shallow chasm. Only about forty feet deep, rather than the usual hundred or more.

She nodded, then zipped away, leading them there. Kaladin and Lopen followed. Teft had orders to lead the others back and meet Kaladin at the base of the ladder, but Kaladin and Lopen should be far ahead of them. He spent the hike listening with half an ear as Lopen talked about his extended family.

The more Kaladin thought about what he was planning, the more brazen it seemed. Perhaps Lopen was right to question his sanity. But Kaladin had tried being rational. He'd tried being careful. That had failed; now there wasn't any more time for logic or care. Hashal obviously intended Bridge Four to be exterminated.

When clever, careful plans failed, it was time to try something desperate.

Lopen cut off suddenly. Kaladin hesitated. The Herdazian man had grown pale-faced and frozen in place. What was . . .

Scraping. Kaladin froze as well, a panic rising in him. One of the side corridors echoed with a deep grinding sound. Kaladin turned slowly, just in time to catch sight of something large—no, something *enormous*—moving down the distant chasm. Shadows in the dim light, the sound of chitinous legs scratching on rock. Kaladin held his breath, sweating, but the beast didn't come in their direction.

The scraping grew softer, then eventually faded. He and Lopen stood immobile for a long time after the last sound had vanished.

Finally, Lopen spoke. "Guess the nearby ones aren't all dead, eh, gancho?"

"Yeah," Kaladin said. He jumped suddenly as Syl zipped back to find them. He unconsciously sucked in Stormlight as he did so, and when she alighted in the air, she found him sheepishly glowing.

"What is going on?" she demanded, hands on hips.

"Chasmfiend," Kaladin said.

"Really?" She sounded excited. "We should chase after it!"

"What?"

"Sure," she said. "You could fight it, I'll bet."

"Syl . . ."

Her eyes were twinkling with amusement. Just a joke. "Come on." She zipped away.

He and Lopen stepped more softly now. Eventually Syl landed on the side of the chasm, standing there as if in mockery of when Kaladin had tried to walk up the wall.

Kaladin looked up at the shadow of a wooden bridge forty feet above. This was the shallowest chasm they'd been able to find; they tended to get deeper and deeper the farther eastward you went. More and more, he was certain that trying to escape to the east was impossible. It was too far, and surviving the highstorm floods was too difficult a challenge. The

[1048]

original plan—fighting or bribing the guards, then running—was the best one.

But they needed to live long enough to try that. The bridge above offered an opportunity, if Kaladin could reach it. He hefted his small bag of spheres and his sack full of armor and bones slung over his shoulder. He'd originally intended to have Rock shoot an arrow with a rope tied to it over the bridge, then back down into the chasm. With some men holding one end, another could have climbed up and tied the sack to the bridge's underside.

But that would risk letting an arrow shoot out of the chasm where scouts could see. They were said to be very keen-eyed, as the armies depended on them to spot chasmfiends making chrysalises.

Kaladin thought he had a better way than the arrow. Maybe. "We need rocks," he said. "Fist-size ones. A lot of them."

Lopen shrugged and began searching about. Kaladin joined him, fishing them out of puddles and pulling them from crevices. There was no shortage of stones in the chasms. In a short time, he had a large pile of rocks in a sack.

He took the pouch of spheres in his hand and tried to think the same way he had earlier, when he'd drawn in the Stormlight. *This is our last chance.*

"Life before death," he whispered. "Strength before weakness. Journey before destination."

The First Ideal of the Knights Radiant. He breathed in deeply, and a thick jolt of power shot up his arm. His muscles burned with energy, with the desire to move. The tempest spread within, pushing at his skin, causing his blood to pump in a powerful rhythm. He opened his eyes. Glowing smoke rose around him. He was able to contain much of the Light, holding it in by holding his breath.

It's like a storm inside me. It felt as if it would rip him apart.

He set the sack with the armor on the ground, but wound the rope around his arm and tied the sack of rocks to his belt. He took out a single fist-size stone and hefted it, feeling its storm-smoothed sides. *This had better work. . . .*

He infused the stone with Stormlight, frost crystallizing on his arm. He wasn't sure how he did it, but it felt natural, like pouring liquid into a cup. Light seemed to pool underneath the skin of his hand, then transfer to the rock—as if he were painting it with a vibrant, glowing liquid.

He pressed the stone to the rock wall. It fixed in place, leaking Stormlight, clinging so strongly that he couldn't pry it free. He tested his weight on it, and it held. He placed another one a little lower, then another a little higher. Then, wishing he had someone to burn him a prayer for success, he started climbing.

He tried not to think about what he was doing. Climbing on rocks stuck to the wall by . . . what? Light? Spren? He kept on going. It was a lot like climbing the stone formations back near Hearthstone with Tien, except that he could make handholds exactly where he wanted.

Should have found some rock dust to cover my hands, he thought, pulling himself up, then taking another stone from his sack and sticking it into place.

Syl walked along beside him, her casual stroll seeming to mock the difficulty of his climb. As he shifted his weight to another rock, he heard an ominous click from below. He risked a glance downward. The first of his rocks had fallen free. The ones near it were leaking Stormlight only faintly now.

The rocks led up toward him like a set of burning footprints. The storm inside him had quieted, though it still blew and raged inside his veins, thrilling and distracting at the same time. What would happen if he ran out of Light before he reached the top?

The next rock fell free. The one beside it followed a few seconds later. Lopen stood on the other side of the chasm bottom, leaning against the wall, interested but relaxed.

Keep moving! Kaladin thought, annoyed at himself for getting distracted. He turned back to his work.

Just as his arms were beginning to burn from the climb, he reached the underside of the bridge. He reached out as two more of his stones fell free. The clatter of each one was louder now, as they fell a much larger distance.

Steadying himself on the bottom of the bridge with one hand, feet still pushing against the highest rocks, he looped the end of the rope around a wooden bridge support. He pulled it around and threaded it through again to make a makeshift knot. He left plenty of extra rope on the short end.

He let the rest of the rope slide free of his shoulder and drop to the floor below. "Lopen," he called. Light steamed from his mouth as he spoke. "Pull it tight."

The Herdazian did so, and Kaladin held to his end, making the knot firm. Then he took hold of the long section of rope and let himself swing free, dangling from the bottom of the bridge. The knot held.

Kaladin relaxed. He was still steaming light, and—save for the call to Lopen—he'd been holding his breath for a good quarter hour. *That could be handy,* he thought, though his lungs were starting to burn, so he started to breathe normally. The Light didn't leave him altogether, though it escaped faster.

"All right," Kaladin said to Lopen. "Tie the other sack to the bottom of the rope."

The rope wiggled, and a few moments later Lopen called up that it was done. Kaladin gripped the rope with his legs to hold himself in place, then used his hands to pull up the length underneath, hoisting the sack full of armor. Using the rope on the short end of the knot, he slipped his pouch of dun spheres into the sack with the armor, then tied it into place underneath the bridge where—he hoped—Lopen and Dabbid would be able to get to it from above.

He looked down. The ground looked so much more distant than it would have from the bridge above. From this slightly different perspective, everything changed.

He didn't get vertigo from the height. Instead, he felt a little surge of excitement. Something about him had always liked being up high. It felt natural. It was being below—trapped in holes and unable to see the world—that was depressing.

He considered his next move.

"What?" Syl asked, stepping up to him, standing on air.

"If I leave the rope here, someone might spot it while crossing the bridge."

"So cut it free."

He looked at her, raising an eyebrow. "While dangling from it?"

"You'll be fine."

"That's a forty-foot drop! I'd break bones at the very least."

"No," Syl said. "I feel *right* about this, Kaladin. You'll be fine. Trust me."

"Trust you? Syl, you've said yourself that your memory is fractured!"

"You insulted me the other week," she said, folding her arms. "I think you owe me an apology."

"I'm supposed to apologize by cutting a rope and dropping forty feet?"

"No, you apologize by trusting me. I told you. I feel right about this."

He sighed, looking down again. His Stormlight was running out. What else could he do? Leaving the rope would be foolish. Could he tie it in another knot, one he could shake free once at the bottom?

If that type of knot existed, he didn't know how to tie it. He clenched his teeth. Then, as the last of his rocks fell off and clattered to the ground, he took a deep breath and pulled out the Parshendi knife he'd taken earlier. He moved swiftly, before he had a chance to reconsider, and sliced the rope free.

He dropped in a rush, one hand still holding the sliced rope, stomach lurching with the jarring distress of falling. The bridge shot away as if rising, and Kaladin's panicked mind immediately sent his eyes downward. This wasn't beautiful. This was terrifying. It was horrible. He was going to die! He—

It's all right.

His emotions calmed in a heartbeat. Somehow, he knew what to do. He twisted in the air, dropping the rope and hitting the ground with both feet down. He came to a crouch, resting one hand on the stone, a jolt of coldness shooting through him. His remaining Stormlight came out in a single burst, flung from his body in a luminescent smoke ring that crashed against the ground before spreading out, vanishing.

He stood up straight. Lopen gaped. Kaladin felt an ache in his legs from hitting, but it was like that of having leaped four or five feet.

"Like ten crashes of thunder on the mounts, gancho!" Lopen exclaimed. "That was incredible!"

"Thank you," Kaladin said. He raised a hand to his head, glancing at the rocks scattered about the base of the wall, then looking up at the armor tied securely up above.

"I told you," Syl said, landing on his shoulder. She sounded triumphant.

"Lopen," Kaladin said. "You think you can get that bundle of armor during the next bridge run?"

"Sure," Lopen said. "Nobody will see. They ignore us Herdies, they ignore bridgemen, and they especially ignore cripples. To them, I'm so invisible I should be walking through walls."

Kaladin nodded. "Get it. Hide it. Give it to me right before the final plateau assault."

"They aren't going to like you going into a bridge run armored, gancho," Lopen said. "I don't think this will be any different from what you tried before."

"We'll see," Kaladin said. "Just do it."

THAT WHICH WE CANNOT HAVE

"The death is my life, the strength becomes my weakness, the journey has ended."

—Dated Betabanes, 1173, 95 seconds pre-death. Subject: a scholar of some minor renown. Sample collected secondhand. Considered questionable.

T hat is why, Father," Adolin said, "you absolutely *cannot* abdicate to me, no matter *what* we discover with the visions."

"Is that so?" Dalinar asked, smiling to himself.

"Yes."

"Very well, you've convinced me."

Adolin stopped dead in the hallway. The two of them were on their way to Dalinar's chambers. Dalinar turned and looked back at the younger man.

"Really?" Adolin asked. "I mean, I actually *won* an argument with you?"

"Yes," Dalinar said. "Your points are valid." He didn't add that he'd come to the decision on his own. "No matter what, I will stay. I can't leave this fight now."

Adolin smiled broadly.

"But," Dalinar said, raising a finger. "I have a requirement. I will draft an order—notarized by the highest of my scribes and witnessed by Elhokar—that gives you the right to depose me, should I grow too mentally unstable. We won't let the other camps know of it, but I will not risk letting myself grow so crazy that it's impossible to remove me."

"All right," Adolin said, walking up to Dalinar. They were alone in the hallway. "I can accept that. Assuming you don't tell Sadeas about it. I still don't trust him."

"I'm not asking you to trust him," Dalinar said pushing the door open to his chambers. "You just need to believe that he is capable of changing. Sadeas was once a friend, and I think he can be again."

The cool stones of the Soulcast chamber seemed to hold the chill of the spring weather. It continued to refuse to slip into summer, but at least it hadn't slid into winter either. Elthebar promised that it would not do so—but, then, the stormwarden's promises were always filled with caveats. The Almighty's will was mysterious, and the signs couldn't always be trusted.

He accepted stormwardens now, though when they'd first grown popular, he'd rejected their aid. No man should try to know the future, nor lay claim to it, for it belonged only to the Almighty himself. And Dalinar wondered how stormwardens could do their research without reading. They claimed they didn't, but he'd seen their books filled with glyphs. Glyphs. They weren't meant to be used in books; they were pictures. A man who had never seen one before could still understand what it meant, based on its shape. That made interpreting glyphs different from reading.

Stormwardens did a lot of things that made people uncomfortable. Unfortunately, they were just so *useful*. Knowing when a highstorm might strike, well, that was just too tempting an advantage. Even though stormwardens were frequently wrong, they were more often right.

Renarin knelt beside the hearth, inspecting the fabrial that had been installed there to warm the room. Navani had already arrived. She sat at Dalinar's elevated writing desk, scribbling a letter; she waved a distracted greeting with her reed as Dalinar entered. She wore the fabrial he had seen her displaying at the feast a few weeks back; the multilegged contraption was attached to her shoulder, gripping the cloth of her violet dress.

"I don't know, Father," Adolin said, closing the door. Apparently he was still thinking about Sadeas. "I don't care if he's listening to *The Way of Kings*. He's just doing it to make you look less closely at the plateau assaults so that his clerks can arrange his cut of the gemhearts more favorably. He's manipulating you."

Dalinar shrugged. "Gemhearts are secondary, son. If I can reforge an alliance with him, then it's worth nearly any cost. In a way, I'm the one manipulating him."

Adolin sighed. "Very well. But I'm still going to keep a hand on my money pouch when he's near."

"Just try not to insult him," Dalinar said. "Oh, and something else. I would like you to take extra care with the King's Guard. If there are soldiers we know for certain are loyal to me, put those in charge of guarding Elhokar's rooms. His words about a conspiracy have me worried."

"Surely you don't give them credence," Adolin said.

"Something odd did happen with his armor. This whole mess stinks like cremslime. Perhaps it will turn out to be nothing. For now, humor me."

"I have to note," Navani said, "that I didn't much care for Sadeas back when you, he, and Gavilar were friends." She finished her letter with a flourish.

"He's not behind the attacks on the king," Dalinar said.

"How can you be certain?" Navani asked.

"Because it's not his way," Dalinar said. "Sadeas never wanted the title of king. Being highprince gives him plenty of power, but leaves him with someone to take the blame for large-scale mistakes." Dalinar shook his head. "He never tried to seize the throne from Gavilar, and he's even better positioned with Elhokar."

"Because my son's a weakling," Navani said. It wasn't an accusation.

"He's *not* weak," Dalinar said, "He's inexperienced. But yes, that does make the situation ideal for Sadeas. He's telling the truth—he asked to be Highprince of Information because he wants very badly to find out who is trying to kill Elhokar."

"Mashala," Renarin said, using the formal term for aunt. "That fabrial on your shoulder, what does it do?"

Navani looked down at the device with a sly smile. Dalinar could see she'd been hoping one of them would ask. Dalinar sat down; the highstorm would be coming soon.

"Oh, this? It's a type of painrial. Here, let me show you." She reached up with her safehand, pushing a clip that released the clawlike legs. She held it up. "Do you have any aches, dear? A stubbed toe, perhaps, or a scrape?"

Renarin shook his head.

"I pulled a muscle in my hand during dueling practice earlier," Adolin said. "It's not bad, but it does ache."

"Come over here," Navani said. Dalinar smiled fondly— Navani was always at her most genuine when playing with new fabrials. It was one of the few times when one got to see her without any pretense. This wasn't Navani the king's mother or Navani the political schemer. This was Navani the excited engineer.

"The artifabrian community is doing some amazing things," Navani said as Adolin proffered his hand. "I'm particularly proud of this little device, as I had a hand in its construction." She clipped it onto Adolin's hand, wrapping the clawlike legs around the palm and locking them into place.

Adolin raised his hand, turning it around. "The pain is gone."

"But you can still feel, correct?" Navani said in a self-satisfied way.

Adolin prodded his palm with the fingers of his other hand. "The hand isn't numb at all."

Renarin watched with keen interest, bespectacled eyes curious, intense. If only the lad could be persuaded to become an ardent. He could be an engineer then, if he wanted. And yet he refused. His reasons always seemed like poor excuses to Dalinar.

"It's kind of bulky," Dalinar noted.

"Well, it's just an early model," Navani said defensively. "I was working backward from one of those dreadful creations of Longshadow's, and I didn't have the luxury of refining the shape. I think it has a lot of potential. Imagine a few of these on a battlefield to dull the pain of wounded soldiers. Imagine it in the hands of a surgeon, who wouldn't have to worry about his patients' pain while working on them."

Adolin nodded. Dalinar had to admit, it did sound like a useful device.

Navani smiled. "This is a special time to be alive; we're learning all kinds of things about fabrials. This, for instance, is a diminishing fabrial—it decreases something, in this case pain. It doesn't actually make the wound any better, but it might be a step in that direction. Either way, it's a completely different type from paired fabrials like the spanreeds. If you could see the plans we have for the future . . ."

"Like what?" Adolin asked.

"You'll find out eventually," Navani said, smiling mysteriously. She removed the fabrial from Adolin's hand.

"Shardblades?" Adolin sounded excited.

"Well, no," Navani said. "The design and workings of Shardblades and Plate are completely different from everything we've discovered. The closest anyone has are those shields in Jah Keved. But as far as I can tell, they use a completely different design principle from true Shardplate. The ancients must have had a wondrous grasp of engineering."

"No," Dalinar said. "I've seen them, Navani. They're . . . well, they're ancient. Their technology is primitive."

"And the Dawncities?" Navani asked skeptically. "The fabrials?"

Dalinar shook his head. "I've seen neither. There are Shardblades in the visions, but they seem so out of place. Perhaps they were given directly by the Heralds, as the legends say."

"Perhaps," Navani said. "Why don't—"

She vanished.

Dalinar blinked. He hadn't heard the highstorm approaching.

He was now in a large, open room with pillars running

along the sides. The enormous pillars looked sculpted of soft sandstone, with unornamented, granular sides. The ceiling was far above, carved from the rock in geometric patterns that looked faintly familiar. Circles connected by lines, spreading outward from one another . . .

"I don't know what to do, old friend," a voice said from the side. Dalinar turned to see a youthful man in regal white and gold robes, walking with his hands clasped before him, hidden by voluminous sleeves. He had dark hair pulled back in a braid and a short beard that came to a point. Gold threads were woven into his hair and came together on his forehead to form a golden symbol. The symbol of the Knights Radiant.

"They say that each time it is the same," the man said. "We are never ready for the Desolations. We should be getting better at resisting, but each time we step closer to destruction instead." He turned to Dalinar, as if expecting a response.

Dalinar glanced down. He too wore ornamental robes, though not as lavish. Where was he? What time? He needed to find clues for Navani to record and for Jasnah to use in proving—or disproving—these dreams.

"I don't know what to say either," Dalinar responded. If he wanted information, he needed to act more natural than he had in previous visions.

The regal man sighed. "I had hoped you would have wisdom to share with me, Karm." They continued walking toward the side of the room, approaching a place where the wall split into a massive balcony with a stone railing. It looked out upon an evening sky; the setting sun stained the air a dirty, sultry red.

"Our own natures destroy us," the regal man said, voice soft, though his face was angry. "Alakavish was a Surgebinder. He should have known better. And yet, the Nahel bond gave him no more wisdom than an ordinary man. Alas, not all spren are as discerning as honorspren."

"I agree," Dalinar said.

The other man looked relieved. "I worried that you would find my claims too forward. Your own Surgebinders were . . . But, no, we should not look backward."

What's a Surgebinder? Dalinar wanted to scream the question out, but there was no way. Not without sounding completely out of place.

Perhaps . . .

"What do you think should be done with these Surgebinders?" Dalinar asked carefully.

"I don't know if we can force them to do anything." Their footsteps echoed in the empty room. Were there no guards, no attendants? "Their power . . . well, Alakavish proves the allure that Surgebinders have for the common people. If only there were a way to encourage them. . . ." The man stopped, turning to Dalinar. "They need to be better, old friend. We all do. The responsibility of what we've been given—whether it be the crown or the Nahel bond—needs to make *us* better."

He seemed to expect something from Dalinar. But what?

"I can read your disagreement in your face," the regal man said. "It's all right, Karm. I realize that my thoughts on this subject are unconventional. Perhaps the rest of you are right, perhaps our abilities are proof of a divine election. But if this is true, should we not be more wary of how we act?"

Dalinar frowned. That sounded familiar to him. The regal man sighed, walking to the balcony lip. Dalinar joined him, stepping outside. The perspective finally allowed him to look down on the landscape below.

Thousands of corpses confronted him.

Dalinar gasped. Dead filled the streets of the city outside, a city that Dalinar vaguely recognized. *Kholinar,* he thought. *My homeland.* He stood with the regal man at the top of a low tower, three stories high—a keep of some sort, constructed of stone. It seemed to sit where the palace would someday be.

The city was unmistakable, with its peaked stone formations rising like enormous fins into the air. The windblades, they were called. But they were less weathered than he was accustomed to, and the city around them was very different. Built of blocky stone structures, many of which had been knocked down. The destruction spread far, lining the sides of primitive streets. Had the city been hit by an earthquake?

No, those corpses had fallen in battle. Dalinar could smell

the stench of blood, viscera, smoke. The bodies lay strewn about, many near the low wall that surrounded the keep. The wall was broken in places, smashed. And there were rocks of strange shape scattered among the corpses. Stones cut like . . .

Blood of my fathers, Dalinar thought, gripping the stone railing, leaning forward. *Those aren't stones. They're creatures.* Massive creatures, easily five or six times the size of a person, their skin dull and grey like granite. They had long limbs and skeletal bodies, the forelegs—or were they arms?—set into wide shoulders. The faces were lean, narrow. Arrow-like.

"What happened here?" Dalinar asked despite himself. "It's terrible!"

"I ask myself this same thing. How could we let this occur? The Desolations are well named. I've heard initial counts. Eleven years of war, and nine out of ten people I once ruled are dead. Do we even have kingdoms to lead any longer? Sur is gone, I'm sure of it. Tarma, Eiliz, they won't likely survive. Too many of their people have fallen."

Dalinar had never heard of those places.

The man made a fist, pounding it softly against the railing. Burning stations had been set up in the distance; they had begun cremating the corpses. "The others want to blame Alakavish. And true, if he hadn't brought us to war before the Desolation, we might not have been broken this badly. But Alakavish was a symptom of a greater disease. When the Heralds next return, what will they find? A people who have forgotten them yet again? A world torn by war and squabbling? If we continue as we have, then perhaps we *deserve* to lose."

Dalinar felt a chill. He had thought that this vision must come after his previous one, but prior visions hadn't been chronological. He hadn't seen any Knights Radiant yet, but that might not be because they had disbanded. Perhaps they didn't *exist* yet. And perhaps there was a reason this man's words sounded so familiar.

Could it be? Could he really be standing beside the very man whose words Dalinar had listened to time and time again?

"There is honor in loss," Dalinar said carefully, using words repeated several times in *The Way of Kings*.

"If that loss brings learning." The man smiled. "Using my own sayings against me again, Karm?"

Dalinar felt himself grow short of breath. The man himself. Nohadon. The great king. He was real. Or he had been real. This man was younger than Dalinar had imagined him, but that humble, yet regal bearing . . . yes, it was right.

"I'm thinking of giving up my throne," Nohadon said softly.

"No!" Dalinar stepped toward him. "You mustn't."

"I cannot lead them," the man said. "Not if this is what my leadership brings them to."

"Nohadon."

The man turned to him, frowning. "What?"

Dalinar paused. Could he be wrong about this man's identity? But no. The name Nohadon was more of a title. Many famous people in history had been given holy names by the Church, before it was disbanded. Even Bajerden wasn't likely to be his real name; that was lost in time.

"It is nothing," Dalinar said. "You cannot give up your throne. The people need a leader."

"They *have* leaders," Nohadon said. "There are princes, kings, Soulcasters, Surgebinders. We never lack men and women who wish to lead."

"True," Dalinar said, "but we do lack ones who are good at it."

Nohadon leaned over the railing. He stared at the fallen, an expression of deep grief—and trouble—on his face. It was so strange to see the man like this. He was so young. Dalinar had never imagined such insecurity, such torment, in him.

"I know that feeling," Dalinar said softly. "The uncertainty, the shame, the confusion."

"You can read me too well, old friend."

"I know those emotions because I've felt them. I . . . I never assumed that you would feel them too."

"Then I correct myself. Perhaps you don't know me well enough."

Dalinar fell silent.

"So what do I do?" Nohadon asked.

"You're asking *me*?"

"You're my advisor, aren't you? Well, I should like some advice."

"I . . . You can't give up your throne."

"And what should I do with it?" Nohadon turned and walked along the long balcony. It seemed to run around this entire level. Dalinar joined him, passing places where the stone was ripped, the railing broken away.

"I haven't faith in people any longer, old friend," Nohadon said. "Put two men together, and they will find something to argue about. Gather them into groups, and one group will find reason to oppress or attack another. Now this. How do I protect them? How do I stop this from happening again?"

"You dictate a book," Dalinar said eagerly. "A grand book to give people hope, to explain your philosophy on leadership and how lives should be lived!"

"A book? Me. Write a book?"

"Why not?"

"Because it's a fantastically *stupid* idea."

Dalinar's jaw dropped.

"The world as we know it has quite nearly been destroyed," Nohadon said. "Barely a family exists that hasn't lost half its members! Our best men are corpses on that field, and we haven't food to last more than two or three months at best. And I'm to spend my time writing a book? Who would scribe it for me? All of my wordsmen were slaughtered when Yelignar broke into the chancery. You're the only man of letters I know of who's still alive."

A *man* of letters? This *was* an odd time. "I could write it, then."

"With one arm? Have you learned to write left-handed, then?"

Dalinar looked down. He had both of his arms, though apparently the man Nohadon saw was missing his right.

"No, we need to rebuild," Nohadon said. "I just wish there were a way to convince the kings—the ones still alive—not to seek advantage over one another." Nohadon tapped the balcony. "So this is my decision. Step down, or do what is needed. This isn't a time for writing. It's a time for action. And then, unfortunately, a time for the sword."

The sword? Dalinar thought. *From you, Nohadon?*

It wouldn't happen. This man would become a great philosopher; he would teach peace and reverence for others, and would not force men to do as he wished. He would *guide* them to acting with honor.

Nohadon turned to Dalinar. "I apologize, Karm. I should not dismiss your suggestions right after asking for them. I'm on edge, as I imagine that we all are. At times, it seems to me that to be human is to want that which we cannot have. For some, this is power. For me, it is peace."

Nohadon turned, walking back down the balcony. Though his pace was slow, his posture indicated that he wished to be alone. Dalinar let him go.

"He goes on to become one of the most influential writers Roshar has ever known," Dalinar said.

There was silence, save for the calls of the people working below, gathering the corpses.

"I know you're there," Dalinar said.

Silence.

"What does he decide?" Dalinar asked. "Did he unite them, as he wanted?"

The voice that often spoke in his visions did not come. Dalinar received no answer to his questions. He sighed, turning to look out over the fields of dead.

"You are right about one thing, at least, Nohadon. To be human is to want that which we cannot have."

The landscape darkened, the sun setting. That darkness enveloped him, and he closed his eyes. When he opened them, he was back in his rooms, standing with his hands on the back of a chair. He turned to Adolin and Renarin, who stood nearby, anxious, prepared to grab him if he got violent.

"Well," Dalinar said, "that was meaningless. I learned nothing. Blast! I'm doing a poor job of—"

"Dalinar," Navani said curtly, still scribbling with a reed

at her paper. "The last thing you said before the vision ended. What was it?"

Dalinar frowned. "The last . . ."

"Yes," Navani said, urgent. "The very last words you spoke."

"I was quoting the man I'd been speaking with. 'To be human is to want that which we cannot have.' Why?"

She ignored him, writing furiously. Once done, she slid off the high-legged chair, hurrying to his bookshelf. "Do you have a copy of . . . Yes, I thought you might. These are Jasnah's books, aren't they?"

"Yes," Dalinar said. "She wanted them cared for until she returned."

Navani pulled a volume off the shelf. "Corvana's *Analectics*." She set the volume on the writing desk and leafed through the pages.

Dalinar joined her, though—of course—he couldn't make sense of the page. "What does it matter?"

"Here," Navani said. She looked up at Dalinar. "When you go into these visions of yours, you know that you speak."

"Gibberish. Yes, my sons have told me."

"Anak malah kaf, del makian habin yah," Navani said. "Sound familiar?"

Dalinar shook his head, baffled.

"It sounds a lot like what father was saying," Renarin said. "When he was in the vision."

"Not 'a lot like,' Renarin," Navani said, looking smug. "It's exactly the same phrase. That is the last thing you said before coming out of your trance. I wrote down everything—as best I could—that you babbled today."

"For what purpose?" Dalinar asked.

"Because," Navani said, "I thought it might be helpful. And it was. The same phrase is in the *Analectics*, almost exactly."

"What?" Dalinar asked, incredulous. "How?"

"It's a line from a song," Navani said. "A chant by the Vanrial, an order of artists who live on the slopes of the Silent Mount in Jah Keved. Year after year, century after century, they've sung these same words—songs they claim were written in the Dawnchant by the Heralds themselves. They have the words of those songs, written in an ancient script. But the *meanings* have been lost. They're just sounds, now. Some scholars believe that the script—and the songs themselves—may indeed be in the Dawnchant."

"And I . . ." Dalinar said.

"You just spoke a line from one of them," Navani said. "Beyond that, if the phrase you just gave me is correct, you *translated* it. This could prove the Vanrial Hypothesis! One sentence isn't much, but it could give us the key to translating the entire script. It has been itching at me for a while, listening to these visions. I *thought* the things you were saying had too much order to be gibberish." She looked at Dalinar, smiling deeply. "Dalinar, you might just have cracked one of the most perplexing—and ancient—mysteries of all time."

"Wait," Adolin said. "What are you saying?"

"What I'm saying, nephew," Navani said, looking directly at him, "is that we have your proof."

"But," Adolin said. "I mean, he could have heard that one phrase . . ."

"And extrapolated an entire language from it?" Navani said, holding up a sheet full of writings. "This *is not* gibberish, but it's no language that people now speak. I suspect it is what it seems, the Dawnchant. So unless you can think of another way your father learned to speak a dead language, Adolin, the visions are most certainly real."

The room fell silent. Navani herself looked stunned by what she had said. She shook it off quickly. "Now, Dalinar," she said, "I want you to describe this vision as accurately as possible. I need the exact words you spoke, if you can recall them. Every bit we gather will help my scholars sort through this. . . ."

"In the storm I awaken, falling, spinning, grieving."

—Dated Kakanev, 1173, 13 seconds pre-death. Subject was a city guardsman.

How can you be so sure it was him, Dalinar?" Navani asked softly.

Dalinar shook his head. "I just am. That was Nohadon."

It had been several hours since the end of the vision. Navani had left her writing table to sit in a more comfortable chair near Dalinar. Renarin sat across from him, accompanying them for propriety's sake. Adolin had left to get the highstorm damage report. The lad had seemed very disturbed by the discovery that the visions were real.

"But the man you saw never spoke his name," Navani said.

"It was him, Navani." Dalinar stared toward the wall over Renarin's head, looking at the smooth brown Soulcast rock. "There was an aura of command about him, the weight of great responsibilities. A regality."

"It could have been some other king," she said. "After all, he discarded your suggestion that he write a book."

"It just wasn't the time for him to write it yet. So much death . . . He was cast down by great loss. Stormfather!

Nine out of ten people dead in war. Can you imagine such a thing?"

"The Desolations," Navani said.

Unite the people. . . . The True Desolation comes. . . .

"Do you know of any references to the Desolations?" Dalinar asked. "Not the tales ardents tell. Historical references?"

Navani held a cup of warmed violet wine in her hand, beads of condensation on the rim of the glass. "Yes, but I am the wrong one to ask. Jasnah is the historian."

"I think I saw the aftermath of one. I . . . I may have seen corpses of Voidbringers. Could that give us more proof?"

"Nothing nearly as good as the linguistics." Navani took a sip of her wine. "The Desolations are matters of ancient lore. It could be argued that you imagined what you expected to see. But those words—if we can translate them, nobody will be able to dispute that you are seeing something real." Her writing board lay on the low table between them, reed and ink set carefully across the paper.

"You intend to tell others?" Dalinar asked. "Of my visions?"

"How else will we explain what is happening to you?"

Dalinar hesitated. How could he explain? On one hand, it was a relief to know that he was not mad. But what if some force were trying to mislead him with these visions, using images of Nohadon and the Radiants because he would find them trustworthy?

The Knights Radiant fell, Dalinar reminded himself. *They abandoned us. Some of the other orders may have turned against us, as the legends say.* There was an unsettling edge to all of that. He had another stone in rebuilding the foundation of who he was, but the most important point still remained undecided. Did he trust his visions or not? He couldn't go back to believing them unquestioningly, not now that Adolin's challenges had raised real worries in his head.

Until he knew their source, he felt he shouldn't spread knowledge of them.

"Dalinar," Navani said, leaning forward. "The warcamps

speak of your episodes. Even the wives of your officers are uncomfortable. They think you fear the storms, or that you have some disease of the mind. This will vindicate you."

"How? By making me into some kind of mystic? Many will think that the breeze of these visions blows too close to prophecy."

"You see the past, Father," Renarin said. "That is not forbidden. And if the Almighty sends them, then how could men question?"

"Adolin and I both spoke with ardents," Dalinar replied. "They said it was very unlikely that this would come from the Almighty. If we do decide the visions are to be trusted, many will disagree with me."

Navani settled back, sipping her wine, safehand lying across her lap. "Dalinar, your sons told me that you once sought the Old Magic. Why? What did you ask of the Nightwatcher, and what curse did she give you in return?"

"I told them that shame is my own," Dalinar said. "And I will not share it."

The room fell silent. The flurries of rain following the highstorm had ceased falling on the roof. "It might be important," Navani finally said.

"It was long ago. Long before the visions began. I don't think it's related."

"But it could be."

"Yes," he admitted. Would that day never stop haunting him? Was not losing all memory of his wife enough?

What did Renarin think? Would he condemn his father for such an egregious sin? Dalinar forced himself to look up and meet his son's bespectacled eyes.

Curiously, Renarin didn't seem bothered. Just thoughtful.

"I'm sorry you had to discover my shame," Dalinar said, looking to Navani.

She waved indifferently. "Soliciting the Old Magic is offensive to the devotaries, but their punishments for the act are never severe. I assume that you didn't have to do much to be cleansed."

"The ardents asked for spheres to give the poor," Dalinar said. "And I had to commission a series of prayers. None of that removed the effects or my sense of guilt."

"I think you'd be surprised at how many devout lighteyes turn to the Old Magic at one point in their lives or another. The ones who can make their way to the Valley, at least. But I *do* wonder if this is related."

"Aunt," Renarin said, turning to her. "I have recently asked for a number of readings about the Old Magic. I agree with his assessment. This does not feel like the work of the Night-watcher. She gives curses in exchange for granting small desires. Always one curse and one desire. Father, I assume you know what both of those things are?"

"Yes," he said. "I know exactly what my curse was, and it does not relate to this."

"Then it is unlikely that the Old Magic is to blame."

"Yes," Dalinar said. "But your aunt is right to question. The truth is, we don't have any proof that this came from the Almighty either. Something wants me to know of the Desolations and the Knights Radiant. Perhaps we should start asking ourselves why that is."

"What *were* the Desolations, Aunt?" Renarin asked. "The ardents talk of the Voidbringers. Of mankind, and the Radiants, and of fighting. But what were they really? Do we know anything specific?"

"There are folklorists among your father's clerks who would serve you better in this matter."

"Perhaps," Dalinar added, "but I'm not sure which of them I can trust."

Navani paused. "Fair enough. Well, from what I understand, there are no primary accounts remaining. This was long, long ago. I do recall that the myth of Parasaphi and Nadris mentions the Desolations."

"Parasaphi," Renarin said. "She's the one who searched out the seedstones."

"Yes," Navani replied. "In order to repopulate her fallen people, she climbed the peaks of Dara—the myth changes, listing different modern mountain ranges as the true peaks of

Dara—to find stones touched by the Heralds themselves. She brought them to Nadris on his deathbed and harvested his seed to bring life to the stones. They hatched forth ten children, which she used to found a new nation. Marnah, I believe it was called."

"Origin of the Makabaki," Renarin said. "Mother told me that story when I was a child."

Dalinar shook his head. "Born from rocks?" The old stories rarely made much sense to him, although the devotaries had canonized many of them.

"The story mentions the Desolations at the beginning," Navani said. "Giving them credit for having wiped out Parasaphi's people."

"But what *were* they?"

"Wars." Navani took a sip of wine. "The Voidbringers came again and again, trying to force mankind off Roshar and into Damnation. Just as they once forced mankind—and the Heralds—out of the Tranquiline Halls."

"When were the Knights Radiant founded?" Dalinar asked.

Navani shrugged. "I don't know. Perhaps they were some military group from a specific kingdom, or perhaps they were originally a mercenary band. That would make it easy to see how they could eventually become tyrants."

"My visions don't imply that they were tyrants," he said. "Perhaps that is the true purpose of the visions. To make me believe lies about the Radiants. Making me trust them, perhaps trying to lead me to mimic their downfall and betrayal."

"I don't know," Navani said, sounding skeptical. "I don't think you've seen anything untrue about the Radiants. The legends tend to agree that the Radiants weren't always so bad. As much as the legends agree on anything, at least."

Dalinar stood and took her nearly empty cup, then walked over to the serving table and refilled it. Discovering that he was not mad should have helped clear things up, but instead left him more disturbed. What if the Voidbringers were behind the visions? Some stories he heard said that they could possess the bodies of men and make them do evil. Or, if they *were* from the Almighty, what was their purpose?

"I need to think on all of this," he said. "It has been a long day. Please, if I could be left to my own thoughts now."

Renarin rose and bowed his head in respect before heading to the door. Navani rose more slowly, sleek dress rustling as she set her cup on the table, then walked over to fetch her pain-drinking fabrial. Renarin left, and Dalinar walked to the doorway, waiting as Navani approached. He didn't intend to let her trap him alone again. He looked out the doorway. His soldiers were there, and he could see them. Good.

"Aren't you pleased at all?" Navani asked, lingering beside the doorway near him, one hand on the frame.

"Pleased?"

"You aren't going mad."

"And we don't know if I'm being manipulated or not," he said. "In a way, we have more questions now than we had before."

"The visions are a blessing," Navani said, laying her free hand on his arm. "I feel it, Dalinar. Don't you see how wonderful this is?"

Dalinar met her eyes, light violet, beautiful. She was so thoughtful, so clever. How he wished he could trust her completely.

She has shown me nothing but honor, he thought. *Never speaking a word to anyone else of my intention to abdicate. She hasn't so much as tried to use my visions against me.* He felt ashamed that he'd once worried that she might.

She was a wonderful woman, Navani Kholin. A wonderful, amazing, *dangerous* woman.

"I see more worries," he said. "And more danger."

"But Dalinar, you're having experiences scholars, historians, and folklorists could only dream about! I envy you, although you claim to have seen no fabrials of note."

"The ancients didn't have fabrials, Navani. I'm certain of it."

"And that changes everything we thought we understood about them."

"I suppose."

"Stonefalls, Dalinar," she said, sighing. "Does nothing bring you to passion any longer?"

Dalinar took a deep breath. "Too many things, Navani. My insides feel like a mass of eels, emotions squirming over one another. The truth of these visions is unsettling."

"It's exciting," she corrected. "Did you mean what you said earlier? About trusting me?"

"I said that?"

"You said you didn't trust your clerks, and you asked me to record the visions. There's an implication in that."

Her hand was still on his arm. She reached out with her safehand and closed the door to the hallway. He almost stopped her, but he hesitated. Why?

The door clicked closed. They were alone. And she was so beautiful. Those clever, excitable eyes, alight with passion.

"Navani," Dalinar said, forcing down his desire. "You're doing it again." Why did he let her?

"Yes, I am," she said. "I'm a stubborn woman, Dalinar." There didn't seem to be any playfulness in her tone.

"This is not proper. My brother . . ." He reached for the door to open it again.

"Your brother," Navani spat, expression flashing with anger. "Why must everyone always focus on him? Everyone always worries so much about the man who died! He's not here, Dalinar. He's gone. I miss him. But not half as much as you do, it appears."

"I honor his memory," Dalinar said stiffly, hesitating, hand on the door's latch.

"That's fine! I'm happy you do. But it's been *six years*, and all anyone can see me as is the wife of a dead man. The other women, they humor me with idle gossip, but they won't let me into their political circles. They think I'm a relic. You wanted to know why I came back so quickly?"

"I—"

"I *returned*," she said, "because I have no home. I'm expected to sit out of important events because my husband is dead! Lounge around, pampered but ignored. I make them uncomfortable. The queen, the other women at court."

"I'm sorry," Dalinar said. "But I don't—"

She raised her freehand, tapping him on the chest. "I

won't take it from you, Dalinar. We were friends before I even *met* Gavilar! You still know me as me, not some shadow of a reign that crumbled years ago. Don't you?" She looked at him, pleading.

Blood of my fathers, Dalinar thought with shock. *She's crying.* Two small tears.

He had rarely seen her so sincere.

And so he kissed her.

It was a mistake. He knew it was. He grabbed her anyway, pulling her into a rough, tight embrace and pressing his mouth to hers, unable to contain himself. She melted against him. He tasted the salt of her tears as they ran down to her lips and met his.

It lasted long. Too long. Wonderfully long. His mind screamed at him, like a prisoner chained in a cell and forced to watch something horrible. But a part of him had wanted this for decades—decades spent watching his brother court, marry, and then hold the only woman that the young Dalinar had ever wanted.

He'd told himself he would never allow this. He had denied himself feelings for Navani the moment Gavilar had won her hand. Dalinar had stepped aside.

But the taste of her—the smell of her, the warmth of her pressed against him—was too sweet. Like a blossoming perfume, it washed away the guilt. For a moment, that touch banished everything. He couldn't remember his fear at the visions, his worry about Sadeas, his shame at past mistakes.

He could only think of her. Beautiful, insightful, delicate yet strong at once. He clung to her, something he could hold on to as the rest of the world churned around him.

Eventually, he broke the kiss. She looked up at him, dazed. Passionspren, like tiny flakes of crystalline snow, floated down in the air around them. Guilt flooded him again. He tried gently to push her away, but she clung to him, holding on tight.

"Navani," he said.

"Hush." She pressed her head against his chest.

"We can't—"

"Hush," she said, more insistently.

He sighed, but let himself hold her.

"Something is going wrong in this world, Dalinar," Navani said softly. "The king of Jah Keved was assassinated. I heard it just today. He was killed by a Shin Shardbearer in white clothing."

"Stormfather!" Dalinar said.

"Something's going on," she said. "Something bigger than our war here, something bigger than Gavilar. Have you heard of the twisted things men say when they die? Most ignore it, but surgeons are talking. And stormwardens whisper that the highstorms are growing more powerful."

"I have heard," he said, finding it difficult to get the words out, intoxicated by her as he was.

"My daughter seeks something," Navani said. "She frightens me sometimes. She's so intense. I honestly believe she's the most intelligent person I've ever known. And the things she searches for . . . Dalinar, she believes that something very dangerous is near."

The sun approaches the horizon. The Everstorm comes. The True Desolation. The Night of Sorrows. . . .

"I need you," Navani said. "I've known it for years, though I feared it would destroy you with guilt, so I fled. But I couldn't stay away. Not with the way they treat me. Not with what is happening to the world. I'm terrified, Dalinar, and I need you. Gavilar was not the man everyone thought him to be. I was fond of him, but he—"

"Please," Dalinar said, "don't speak ill of him."

"Very well."

Blood of my fathers! He couldn't get her scent out of his head. He felt paralyzed, holding to her like a man clinging to a stone in the stormwinds.

She looked up at him. "Well, let it be said—then—that I was fond of Gavilar. But I'm more than fond of you. And I'm tired of waiting."

He closed his eyes. "How can this work?"

"We'll find a way."

"We'll be denounced."

"The warcamps already ignore me," Navani said, "and

they spread rumors and lies about you. What more can they do to us?"

"They'll find something. As of yet, the devotaries do not condemn me."

"Gavilar is dead," Navani said, resting her head back against his chest. "I was never unfaithful while he lived, though the Stormfather knows I had ample reason. The devotaries can say what they wish, but *The Arguments* do not forbid our union. Tradition is not the same as doctrine, and I will not hold myself back for fear of offending."

Dalinar took a deep breath, then forced himself to open his arms and pull back. "If you had hoped to soothe my worries for the day, then this didn't help."

She folded her arms. He could still feel where her safehand had touched him on the back. A tender touch, reserved for a family member. "I'm not here to soothe you, Dalinar. Quite the opposite."

"Please. I *do* need time to think."

"I won't let you put me away. I won't ignore that this happened. I won't—"

"Navani," he gently cut her off, "I will not abandon you. I promise."

She eyed him, then a wry smile crept onto her face. "Very well. But you began something today."

"*I* began it?" he asked, amused, elated, confused, worried, and ashamed at the same time.

"The kiss was yours, Dalinar," she said idly, pulling open the door and entering his antechamber.

"You seduced me to it."

"What? Seduced?" She glanced back at him. "Dalinar, I've never been more open and honest in my life."

"I know," Dalinar said, smiling. "That was the seductive part." He closed the door softly, then let out a sigh.

Blood of my fathers, he thought, *why can't these things ever be simple?*

And yet, in direct contrast with his thoughts, he felt as if the entire world had somehow become more right for having gone wrong.

"The darkness becomes a palace. Let it rule! Let it rule!"

—Kakevah 1173, 22 seconds pre-death. A darkeyed Selay man
of unknown profession.

Y ou think one of those will save us?" Moash asked,
scowling as he looked at the prayer tied about Kaladin's
upper right arm.

Kaladin glanced to the side. He stood at parade rest as
Sadeas's soldiers crossed their bridge. The chilly spring air
felt good, now that he'd started working. The sky was bright,
cloudless, and the stormwardens promised that no highstorm
was near.

The prayer tied on his arm was simple. Three glyphs: wind,
protection, beloved. A prayer to Jezerezeh—the Stormfather—to protect loved ones and friends. It was the straightforward type his mother had preferred. For all her subtlety and
wryness, whenever she'd knitted or written a prayer, it had
been simple and heartfelt. Wearing it reminded him of her.

"I can't believe you paid good money for that," Moash
said. "If there are Heralds watching, they don't pay any mind
to bridgemen."

"I've been feeling nostalgic lately, I guess." The prayer was
probably meaningless, but he'd had reason to start thinking

more about religion lately. The life of a slave made it difficult for many to believe that anyone, or anything, was watching. Yet many bridgemen had grown more religious during their captivity. Two groups, opposite reactions. Did that mean some were stupid and others were callous, or something else entirely?

"They're going to see us dead, you know," Drehy said from behind. "This is it." The bridgemen were exhausted. Kaladin and his team had been forced to work the chasms all night. Hashal had put strict requirements on them, demanding an increased amount of salvage. In order to meet the quota, they'd forgone training to scavenge.

And then today they'd been awakened for a morning chasm assault after only three hours of sleep. They were drooping as they stood in line, and they hadn't even reached the contested plateau yet.

"Let it come," Skar said quietly from the other side of the line. "They want us dead? Well, I'm not going to back down. We'll show them what courage is. They can hide behind our bridges while we charge."

"That's no victory," Moash said. "I say we attack the soldiers. Right now."

"Our own troops?" Sigzil said, turning his dark-skinned head and looking down the line of men.

"Sure," Moash said, eyes still forward. "They're going to kill us anyway. Let's take a few of them with us. Damnation, why not charge Sadeas? His guard won't expect it. I'll bet we could knock down a few and grab their spears, then be on to killing lighteyes before they cut us down."

A couple of bridgemen murmured their assent as the soldiers continued to cross.

"No," Kaladin said. "It wouldn't accomplish anything. They'd have us dead before we could so much as inconvenience Sadeas."

Moash spat. "And this will accomplish something? Damnation, Kaladin, I feel like I'm already dangling from the noose!"

"I have a plan," Kaladin said.

He waited for the objections. His other plans hadn't worked.

No one offered a complaint.

"Well then," Moash said. "What is it?"

"You'll see today," Kaladin said. "If it works, it will buy us time. If it fails, I'll be dead." He turned to look down the line of faces. "In that case, Teft has orders to lead you on an escape attempt tonight. You're not ready, but at least you'll have a chance." That was far better than attacking Sadeas as he crossed.

Kaladin's men nodded, and Moash seemed content. As contrary as he'd been originally, he had grown equally loyal. He was hotheaded, but he was also the best with the spear.

Sadeas approached, riding his roan stallion, wearing his red Shardplate, helm on but visor up. By chance, he crossed on Kaladin's bridge, though—as always—he had twenty to choose from. Sadeas didn't give Bridge Four so much as a glance.

"Break and cross," Kaladin ordered after Sadeas was over. The bridgemen crossed their bridge, and Kaladin gave the orders for them to pull it behind them, then lift.

It felt heavier than it ever had before. The bridgemen broke into a trot, rounding the army column and hustling to reach the next chasm. In the distance behind, a second army—one in blue—was following them, crossing using some of Sadeas's other bridge crews. It looked like Dalinar Kholin had given up his bulky mechanical bridges, and was now using Sadeas's own bridge crews to cross. So much for his "honor" and not sacrificing bridgeman lives.

In his pouch, Kaladin carried a large number of infused spheres, obtained from the moneychangers in exchange for a greater quantity of dun spheres. He hated taking that loss, but he needed the Stormlight.

They reached the next chasm quickly. It would be the next-to-last one, according to the word he'd gotten from Matal, Hashal's husband. The soldiers began checking their armor, stretching, anticipationspren rising in the air like small streamers.

The bridgemen set their bridge and stepped back. Kaladin noted Lopen and silent Dabbid approaching with their stretcher, waterskins and bandages inside. Lopen had hitched the stretcher to a hook at his waist, making up for his missing arm. The two moved among the members of Bridge Four, giving them water.

As he passed Kaladin, Lopen nodded toward the large bulge at the stretcher's center. The armor. "When do you want it?" Lopen asked softly, lowering the litter, then handing Kaladin a waterskin.

"Right before we run the assault," Kaladin replied. "You did well, Lopen."

Lopen winked. "A one-armed Herdazian is still twice as useful as a no-brained Alethi. Plus, so long as I've got one hand, I can still do this." He covertly made a rude gesture toward the marching soldiers.

Kaladin smiled, but was growing too nervous to feel mirth. It had been a long time since he'd gotten jitters going into a battle. He thought Tukks had beaten that out of him years ago.

"Hey," a sudden voice called, "I need some of that."

Kaladin spun to see a soldier walking over. He was exactly the type of man Kaladin had known to avoid back in Amaram's army. Darkeyed but of modest rank, he was naturally large, and had probably gotten promoted by sheer virtue of size. His armor was well maintained but the uniform beneath was stained and wrinkled, and he kept the sleeves rolled up, exposing hairy arms.

At first, Kaladin assumed that the man had seen Lopen's gesture. But the man didn't seem mad. He shoved Kaladin aside, then pulled the waterskin away from Lopen. Nearby, the soldiers waiting to cross had noticed. Their own water crews were much slower, and more than a few of the waiting men eyed Lopen and his waterskins.

It would set a terrible precedent to let the soldiers take their water—but that was a tiny problem compared with the greater one. If those soldiers swarmed around the litter to get water, they'd discover the sack full of armor.

Kaladin moved quickly, snatching the waterskin from the soldier's hand. "You have your own water crews."

The soldier looked at Kaladin, as if completely unable to

believe that a bridgeman was standing up to him. He scowled darkly, lowering his spear to his side, its butt against the ground. "I don't want to wait."

"How unfortunate," Kaladin said, stepping right up to the man, meeting him eye to eye. Silently, he cursed the idiot. If it turned into a scuffle . . .

The soldier hesitated, even more astonished to see such an aggressive threat from a bridgeman. Kaladin wasn't as thick-armed as this man, but he was a finger or two taller. The soldier's uncertainty showed in his face.

Just back down, Kaladin thought.

But no. Backing down from a bridgeman while his squad was watching? The man made a fist, knuckles cracking.

Within seconds, the entire bridge crew was there. The soldier blinked as Bridge Four formed around Kaladin in an aggressive inverted wedge pattern, moving naturally—smoothly—as Kaladin had trained them. Each one made fists, giving the soldier ample chance to see that the heavy lifting had trained these men to a physical level beyond that of the average soldier.

The man glanced back at his squad, as if looking for support.

"Do you want to spark a fight now, friend?" Kaladin asked softly. "If you hurt the bridgemen, I wonder who Sadeas will make run this bridge."

The man glanced back at Kaladin, was silent for a moment, then scowled, cursed, and stalked away. "Probably full of crem anyway," he muttered, rejoining his team.

The members of Bridge Four relaxed, though they received more than a few appreciative looks from the other soldiers in line. For once, there was something other than scowls. Hopefully they wouldn't realize that a squad of bridgemen had quickly and accurately made a battle formation commonly used in spear fighting.

Kaladin waved for his men to stand down, nodding his thanks. They fell back, and Kaladin tossed the recovered waterskin back to Lopen.

The shorter man smirked wryly. "I'll keep a tighter grip

on these things from now on, gancho." He eyed the soldier who had tried to take the water.

"What?" Kaladin asked.

"Well, I've got a cousin in the water crews, you see," Lopen said. "And I'm thinking that he might owe me a favor on account of this one time I helped his sister's friend escape a guy looking for her. . . ."

"You *do* have a lot of cousins."

"Never enough. You bother one of us, you bother us all. That's something you strawheads never seem to get. No offense or anything, gancho."

Kaladin raised an eyebrow. "Don't make trouble for the soldier. Not today." *I'll make enough of that myself here soon.*

Lopen sighed, but nodded. "All right. For you." He held up a waterskin. "You sure you don't want any?"

Kaladin didn't; his stomach was too unsettled. But he made himself take the waterskin back and drink a few mouthfuls.

Before long, the time came to cross and pull the bridge up for the last run. The assault. Sadeas's soldiers were forming ranks, lighteyes riding back and forth, calling orders. Matal waved Kaladin's crew forward. Dalinar Kholin's army had fallen behind, coming more slowly because of his larger numbers.

Kaladin took his place at the very front of his bridge. Ahead, the Parshendi were lined up with bows on the edge of their plateau, staring down the oncoming assault. Were they singing already? Kaladin thought he could hear their voices.

Moash was on Kaladin's right, Rock on his left. Only three on the deathline, because of how shorthanded they were. He'd put Shen in the very back, so he wouldn't see what Kaladin was about to do.

"I'm going to duck out from underneath once we start moving," Kaladin told them. "Rock, you take over. Keep them running."

"Very well," Rock said. "It will be hard to carry without you. We have so few men, and we are very weak."

"You'll manage. You'll have to."

Kaladin couldn't see Rock's face, not positioned under the bridge as they were, but his voice sounded troubled. "This thing you will try, is dangerous?"

"Perhaps."

"Can I help?"

"I'm afraid not, my friend. But it strengthens me to hear you ask."

Rock didn't get a chance to reply. Matal yelled for the bridge crews to go. Arrows shot overhead to distract the Parshendi. Bridge Four broke into a run.

And Kaladin ducked down and dashed out in front of them. Lopen was waiting to the side, and he tossed Kaladin the sack of armor.

Matal screamed at Kaladin in a panic, but the bridge crews were already in motion. Kaladin focused on his goal, protecting Bridge Four, and sucked in sharply. Stormlight flooded him from the pouch at his waist, but he didn't draw too much. Just enough to give him a jolt of energy.

Syl zipped in front of him, a ripple in the air, nearly invisible. Kaladin whipped the tie off the sack, pulling out the vest and throwing it awkwardly over his head. He ignored the ties at the side, getting on the helm as he leaped over a small rock formation. The shield came last, clattering with red Parshendi bones in a crisscross pattern on the front.

Even while donning the armor, Kaladin easily stayed far ahead of the heavily laden bridge crews. His Stormlight-infused legs were quick and sure.

The Parshendi archers directly ahead of him abruptly stopped singing. Several of them lowered their bows, and though it was too distant to make out their faces, he could sense their outrage. Kaladin had expected this. He'd hoped for it.

The Parshendi left their dead. Not because they were uncaring, but because they found it a terrible offense to move them. Merely touching the dead seemed a sin. If that was the case, a man desecrating corpses and wearing them into battle would be far, far worse.

As Kaladin grew closer, a different song started among

the Parshendi archers. A quick, violent song, more chant than melody. Those who had lowered their bows raised them.

And they tried with everything they had to kill him.

Arrows flew at him. Dozens of them. They weren't fired in careful waves. They flew individually, rapidly, wildly, each archer loosing at Kaladin as quickly as he could. A swarm of death bore down on him.

Pulse racing, Kaladin ducked to the left, leaping off a small outcropping. Arrows sliced the air around him, dangerously close. But while infused with the Stormlight, his muscles reacted quickly. He dodged between arrows, then turned in the other direction, moving erratically.

Behind, Bridge Four came into range, and not a single arrow was fired at them. Other bridge crews were ignored as well, many of the archers focusing on Kaladin. The arrows came more swiftly, spraying around him, bouncing off his shield. One sliced open his arm as it shot past; another snapped against his helm, nearly knocking it free.

The arm wound leaked Light, not blood, and to Kaladin's amazement it slowly began to seal up, frost crystallizing on his skin and Stormlight draining from him. He drew in more, infusing himself to the cusp of glowing visibly. He ducked, he dodged, he jumped, he ran.

His battle-trained reflexes delighted in the newfound speed, and he used the shield to knock arrows out of the air. It was as if his body had longed for this ability, as if it had been born to take advantage of the Stormlight. During the earlier part of his life, he had lived sluggish and impotent. Now he was healed. Not acting beyond his capacities—no, finally *reaching* them.

A flock of arrows sought his blood, but Kaladin spun between them, taking another slice on the arm but deflecting the others with shield or breastplate. Another flight came, and he brought his shield up, worried that he was going to be too slow. However, the arrows changed course, arcing toward his shield, slamming into it. Drawn to it.

I'm pulling them to it! He remembered dozens of bridge runs, with arrows slamming into the wood near where his hands had clung to the support bars. Always just missing him.

How long have I been doing this? Kaladin thought. *How many arrows did I draw to the bridge, pulling them away from me?*

He didn't have time to think about that. He kept moving, dodging. He felt arrows whish through the air, heard them zip, felt the splinters as they hit stone or shield and broke. He'd hoped that he would distract some of the Parshendi from firing on his men, but he'd had no idea how strong a reaction he'd get.

Part of him exulted in the thrill of ducking, dodging, and blocking the hail of arrows. He started to slow, however. He tried to suck in Stormlight, but none came. His spheres were drained. He panicked, still dodging, but then the arrowfalls began to slacken.

With a start, Kaladin realized that the bridge crews had parted around him, leaving a space for him to keep dodging while they passed him and set their burdens. Bridge Four was in place, cavalry charging across to attack the archers. Despite that, some of the Parshendi continued to fire on Kaladin, enraged. The soldiers cut these Parshendi down easily, sweeping the ground of them and making room for Sadeas's foot soldiers.

Kaladin lowered his shield. It bristled with arrows. He barely had time to take a fresh breath of air as the bridgemen reached him, calling out with joy, nearly tackling him in their excitement.

"You fool!" Moash said. "You storming fool! What was that? What were you thinking?"

"Was incredible," Rock said.

"You should be dead!" Sigzil said, though his normally stern face was split by a smile.

"Stormfather," Moash added, pulling an arrow from Kaladin's vest at the shoulder. "Look at these."

Kaladin looked down, shocked to find a dozen arrow holes in the sides of his vest and shirt where he'd narrowly avoided being hit. Three arrows stuck from the leather.

"Stormblessed," Skar said. "That's all there is to it."

Kaladin shrugged off their praise, his heart still pounding. He was numb. Amazed that he'd survived, cold from the Stormlight he'd consumed, exhausted as if he'd run a rigorous obstacle course. He looked to Teft, raising an eyebrow, nodding toward the pouch at his waist.

Teft shook his head. He'd watched; the Stormlight rising from Kaladin hadn't been visible to those observing, not in the light of day. Still, the way Kaladin had dodged would have looked incredible, even without the obvious light. If there had been stories about him before, they would grow greatly following this.

He turned to look at the passing troops. As he did, he realized something. He still had to deal with Matal. "Fall into line, men," he said.

They obeyed reluctantly, falling into place around him in a double rank. Ahead, Matal stood beside their bridge. He looked concerned, as well he should. Sadeas was riding up. Kaladin steeled himself, remembering how his previous victory—when they'd run with the bridge on its side—had been turned on its head. He hesitated, then hurried over toward the bridge where Sadeas was going to ride past Matal. Kaladin's men followed.

Kaladin arrived as Matal bowed to Sadeas, who wore his glorious red Shardplate. Kaladin and the bridgemen bowed as well.

"Avarak Matal," Sadeas said. He nodded toward Kaladin. "This man looks familiar."

"He is the one from before, Brightlord," Matal said, nervous. "The one who . . ."

"Ah yes," Sadeas said. "The 'miracle.' And you sent him forward as a decoy like that? One would think that you would be hesitant to dare such measures."

"I take full responsibility, Brightlord," Matal said, putting the best face on it.

Sadeas regarded the battlefield. "Well, luckily for you, it worked. I suppose I'll have to promote you now." He shook his head. "Those savages practically ignored the assault force.

All twenty bridges set, most with nary a casualty. It seems like a waste, somehow. Consider yourself commended. Most remarkable, the way that boy dodged . . ." He kicked his horse into motion, leaving Matal and the bridgemen behind.

It was the most backhanded promotion Kaladin had ever heard, but that would do. Kaladin smiled broadly as Matal turned to him, eyes enraged.

"You—" Matal sputtered. "You could have gotten me executed!"

"Instead I got you promoted," Kaladin said, Bridge Four forming up around him.

"I should see you strung up anyway."

"It's been tried," Kaladin said. "Didn't work. Besides, you know that from now on Sadeas is going to expect me to be out there distracting the archers. Good luck getting any other bridgeman to try that."

Matal's face grew red. He turned and stalked away to check on the other bridge crews. The two nearest—Bridge Seven and Bridge Eighteen—stood looking toward Kaladin and his team. All twenty bridges had been set? Hardly any casualties?

Stormfather, Kaladin thought. *How many archers were firing at me?*

"You did it, Kaladin!" Moash exclaimed. "You found the secret. We need to make this work. Expand it."

"I'll bet I could dodge those arrows, if that were all I was doing," Skar said. "With enough armor . . ."

"We should have more than one," Moash agreed. "Five or so, running around drawing the Parshendi attacks."

"The bones," Rock said, folding his arms. "This is what made it work. The Parshendi were so mad that they ignored bridge crew. If all five wear the bones of Parshendi . . ."

That made Kaladin consider something. He looked back, searching through the bridgemen. Where was Shen?

There. He was sitting on the rocks, distant, staring forward. Kaladin approached with the others. The parshman looked up at him, face a mask of pain, tears streaking his cheeks. He looked at Kaladin and shuddered visibly, turning away, closing his eyes.

"He sat down like that the moment he saw what you'd done, lad," Teft said, rubbing his chin. "Might not be good for bridge runs anymore."

Kaladin pulled the carapace-tied helm off his head, then ran his fingers through his hair. The carapace stuck to his clothing stank faintly, even though he'd washed it off down below. "We'll see," Kaladin said, feeling a twist of guilt. Not nearly enough to overshadow the victory of protecting his men, but enough to dampen it, at least. "For now, there are still many bridge crews that got fired upon. You know what to do."

The men nodded, trotting off to search for the wounded. Kaladin set one man to watch over Shen—he wasn't sure what else to do with the parshman—and tried not to show his exhaustion as he put his sweaty, carapace-covered cap and vest in Lopen's litter. He knelt down to go through his medical equipment, in case it was needed, and found that his hand was shaking and quivering. He pressed it down against the ground to still it, breathing in and out.

Cold, clammy skin, he thought. *Nausea. Weakness.* He was in shock.

"You all right, lad?" Teft asked, kneeling down beside Kaladin. He still wore a bandage on his arm from the wound he'd taken a few bridge runs back, but it wasn't enough to stop him from carrying. Not when there were too few as it was.

"I'll be fine," Kaladin said, taking out a waterskin, holding it in a quivering hand. He could barely get the top off.

"You don't look—"

"I'll be fine," Kaladin said again, drinking, then lowering the water. "What's important is that the men are safe."

"You going to do this every time. Whenever we go to battle?"

"Whatever keeps them safe."

"You're not immortal, Kaladin," Teft said softly. "The Radiants, they could be killed, just like any man. Sooner or later, one of those arrows will find your neck instead of your shoulder."

"The Stormlight heals."

"The Stormlight helps your body heal. That's different,

I'm thinking." Teft laid a hand on Kaladin's shoulder. "We can't lose you, lad. The men need you."

"I'm not going to avoid putting myself in danger, Teft. And I'm not going to leave the men to face a storm of arrows if I can do something about it."

"Well," Teft said, "you are going to let a few of us go out there with you. The bridge can manage with twenty-five, if it has to. That leaves us a few extra, just like Rock said. And I'll bet some of those wounded from the other crews we saved are well enough to begin helping carry. They won't dare send them back to their own crews, not so long as Bridge Four is doing what you did today, and helping the whole assault work."

"I . . ." Kaladin trailed off. He could imagine Dallet doing something like this. He'd always said that as sergeant, part of his job was to keep Kaladin alive. "All right."

Teft nodded, rising.

"You were a spearman, Teft," Kaladin said. "Don't try to deny it. How did you end up here, in these bridge crews?"

"It's where I belong." Teft turned away to supervise the search for wounded.

Kaladin sat down, then lay back, waiting for the shock to wear off. To the south, the other army—flying the blue of Dalinar Kholin—had arrived. They crossed to an adjacent plateau.

Kaladin closed his eyes to recover. Eventually, he heard something and opened his eyes. Syl sat cross-legged on his chest. Behind her, Dalinar Kholin's army had begun an assault onto the battlefield, and they managed to do so without getting fired on. Sadeas had the Parshendi cut off.

"That was amazing," Kaladin said to Syl. "What I did with the arrows."

"Still think you're cursed?"

"No. I know I'm not." He looked up at the overcast sky. "But that means the failures were all just me. I let Tien die, I failed my spearmen, the slaves I tried to rescue, Tarah . . ." He hadn't thought of her in some time. His failure with her had been different from the others, but a failure it was nonetheless. "If there's no curse or bad luck, no god above being angry at me—I have to live with knowing that with a little more effort—a little more practice or skill—I could have saved them."

Syl frowned more deeply. "Kaladin, you need to get over this. Those things aren't your fault."

"That's what my father always used to say." He smiled faintly. " 'Overcome your guilt, Kaladin. Care, but not too much. Take responsibility, but don't blame yourself.' Protect, save, help—but know when to give up. They're such precarious ledges to walk. How do I do it?"

"I don't know. I don't know any of this, Kaladin. But you're ripping yourself apart. Inside and out."

Kaladin stared at the sky above. "It was wondrous. I was a storm, Syl. The Parshendi couldn't touch me. The arrows were nothing."

"You're too new to this. You pushed yourself too hard."

" 'Save them,' " Kaladin whispered. " 'Do the impossible, Kaladin. But don't push yourself too hard. But also don't feel guilty if you fail.' Precarious ledges, Syl. So narrow . . ."

Some of his men returned with a wounded man, a square-faced Thaylen fellow with an arrow in the shoulder. Kaladin went to work. His hands were still shaking slightly, but not nearly as badly as they had been.

The bridgemen clustered around, watching. He'd started training Rock, Drehy, and Skar already, but with all of them watching, Kaladin found himself explaining. "If you put pressure here, you can slow the blood flow. This isn't too dangerous a wound, though it probably doesn't feel too good . . ."—the patient grimaced his agreement—". . . and the real problem will come from infection. Wash the wound to make sure there aren't any slivers of wood or bits of metal left, then sew it. The muscles and skin of the shoulder here are going to get worked, so you need a strong thread to hold the wound together. Now . . ."

"Kaladin," Lopen said, sounding worried.

"Wha?" Kaladin said, distracted, still working.

"Kaladin!"

Lopen had called him by his name, rather than saying *gancho*. Kaladin stood up, turning to see the short Herdazian man standing at the back of the crowd, pointing at the chasm. The battle had moved farther north, but a group of Parshendi had punched through Sadeas's line. They had bows.

Kaladin watched, stunned, as the group of Parshendi fell into formation and nocked. Fifty arrows, all pointed at Kaladin's crew. The Parshendi didn't seem to care that they were exposing themselves to attack from behind. They seemed focused on only one thing.

Destroying Kaladin and his men.

Kaladin screamed the alarm, but he felt so sluggish, so tired. The bridgemen around him turned as the archers drew. Sadeas's men normally defended the chasm to keep Parshendi from pushing over the bridges and cutting off their escape. But this time, noticing that the archers weren't trying to drop the bridges, the soldiers didn't hasten to stop them. They left the bridgemen to die, instead cutting off the Parshendi route to the bridges themselves.

Kaladin's men were exposed. Perfect targets. *No,* Kaladin thought. *No! It can't happen like this. Not after—*

A force crashed into the Parshendi line. A single figure in slate-grey armor, wielding a sword as long as many men were tall. The Shardbearer swept through the distracted archers with urgency, slicing into their ranks. Arrows flew toward Kaladin's team, but they were loosed too early, aimed poorly. A few came close as the bridgemen ducked for cover, but nobody was hit.

Parshendi fell before the sweeping Blade of the Shardbearer, some toppling into the chasm, others scrambling back. The rest died with burned-out eyes. In seconds, the squad of fifty archers had been reduced to corpses.

The Shardbearer's honor guard caught up with him. He turned, armor seeming to glow as he raised his Blade in a salute of respect toward the bridgemen. Then he charged off in another direction.

"That was him," Drehy said, standing up. "Dalinar Kholin. The king's uncle!"

"He saved us!" Lopen said.

"Bah." Moash dusted himself off. "He just saw a group of

undefended archers and took the chance to strike. Lighteyes don't care about us. Right, Kaladin?"

Kaladin stared at the place where the archers had stood. In one moment, he could have lost it all.

"Kaladin?" Moash said.

"You're right," Kaladin found himself saying. "Just an opportunity taken."

Except, why raise the Blade toward Kaladin?

"From now on," Kaladin said, "we pull back farther after the soldiers cross. They used to ignore us after the battle began, but they won't any longer. What I did today—what we're all going to be doing soon—will make them mighty angry. Angry enough to be stupid, but also angry enough to see us dead. For now, Leyten, Narm, find good scouting points and watch the field. I want to know if any Parshendi make moves toward that chasm. I'll get this man bandaged and we'll pull back."

The two scouts ran off, and Kaladin turned back to the man with the wounded shoulder.

Moash knelt beside him. "An assault against a prepared foe without any bridges lost, a Shardbearer coincidentally coming to our rescue, Sadeas himself complimenting us. You almost make me think I should get one of those armbands."

Kaladin glanced down at the prayer. It was stained with blood from a slice on his arm that the vanishing Stormlight hadn't quite been able to heal.

"Wait to see if we escape." Kaladin finished his stitching. "That's the real test."

FEAR

"I wish to sleep. I know now why you do what you do, and I hate you for it. I will not speak of the truths I see."

—Kakashah 1173, 142 seconds pre-death. A Shin sailor, left behind by his crew, reportedly for bringing them ill luck. Sample largely useless.

Y ou see?" Leyten turned the piece of carapace over in his hands. "If we carve it up at the edge, it encourages a blade—or in this case an arrow—to deflect away from the face. Wouldn't want to spoil that pretty grin of yours."

Kaladin smiled, taking back the piece of armor. Leyten had carved it expertly, putting in holes for leather straps to affix it to the jerkin. The chasm was cold and dark at night. With the sky hidden, it felt like a cavern. Only the occasional sparkle of a star high above revealed otherwise.

"How soon can you have them done?" he asked Leyten.

"All five? By the end of the night, likely. The real trick was discovering how to work it." He knocked on the carapace with the back of his knuckles. "Amazing stuff. Nearly as hard as steel, but half the weight. Hard to cut or break. But if you drill, it shapes easily."

"Good," Kaladin said. "Because I don't want five sets. I want one for each man in the crew."

Leyten raised an eyebrow.

"If they're going to start letting us wear armor," Kaladin said, "everyone gets a suit. Except Shen, of course." Matal had agreed to let them leave him behind on the bridge runs; he wouldn't even look at Kaladin now.

Leyten nodded. "All right, then. Better get me some help, though."

"You can use the wounded men. We'll cart out as much carapace as we can find."

His success had translated to an easier time for Bridge Four. Kaladin had pled that his men needed time to find carapace, and Hashal—not knowing any better—had reduced the scavenging quota. She was already pretending—quite smoothly—that the armor had been her idea the entire time, and was ignoring the question of where it had come from in the first place. When she met Kaladin's eyes, however, he saw worry. What else would he try? So far, she hadn't dared remove him. Not while he brought her so much praise from Sadeas.

"How did an apprentice armorer end up as a bridgeman anyway?" Kaladin asked as Leyten settled back down to work. He was a thick-armed man, stout and oval-faced with light hair. "Craftsmen don't usually get thrown away."

Leyten shrugged. "When a piece of armor breaks and a lighteyes takes an arrow in the shoulder, someone has to take the blame. I'm convinced my master keeps an extra apprentice especially for those kinds of situations."

"Well, his loss is our good fortune. You're going to keep us alive."

"I'll do my best, sir." He smiled. "Can't do much worse on the armor than you did yourself, though. It's amazing that breastplate didn't fall off halfway through!"

Kaladin patted the bridgeman on the shoulder, then left him to his work, surrounded by a small ring of topaz chips; Kaladin had gotten permission to bring them, explaining his men needed light to work on the armor. Nearby, Lopen, Rock, and Dabbid were returning with another load of salvage. Syl zipped ahead, leading them.

Kaladin walked down the chasm, a garnet sphere looped in a small leather carrier at his belt for light. The chasm branched here, making a large triangular intersection—a perfect place for spear training. Wide enough to give the men room to practice, yet far enough from any permanent bridges that scouts weren't likely to hear echoes.

Kaladin gave the initial instructions each day, then let Teft lead the practice. The men worked by sphere light, small piles of diamond chips at the corners of the intersection, barely enough to see by. *Never thought I'd envy those days practicing beneath the hot sun back in Amaram's army,* he thought.

He walked up to gap-toothed Hobber and corrected his stance, then showed him how to put his weight behind his spear thrusts. The bridgemen were progressing quickly, and the fundamentals were proving their merit. Some were training with the spear and the shield, practicing stances where they held lighter spears up beside the head with the shield raised.

The most skilled were Skar and Moash. In fact, Moash was surprisingly good. Kaladin walked to the side, watching the hawk-faced man. He was focused, eyes intense, jaw set. He moved in attack after attack, the dozen spheres giving him an equal number of shadows.

Kaladin remembered feeling such dedication. He'd spent a year like that, after Tien's death, driving himself to exhaustion each day. Determined to get better. Determined never to let another person die because of his lack of skill. He'd become the best in his squad, then the best in his company. Some said he'd been the best spearmen in Amaram's army.

What would have happened to him, if Tarah hadn't coaxed him out of his single-minded dedication? Would he have burned himself out, as she'd claimed?

"Moash," Kaladin called.

Moash paused, turning toward Kaladin. He didn't fall out of stance.

Kaladin waved him to approach, and Moash reluctantly trotted over. Lopen had left a few waterskins for them, hanging by their cords from a cluster of haspers. Kaladin pulled a skin free, tossing it to Moash. The other man took a drink, then wiped his mouth.

"You're getting good," Kaladin said. "You're probably the best we have."

"Thanks," Moash said.

"I've noticed you keep training when Teft lets the other men take breaks. Dedication is good, but don't work yourself ragged. I want you to be one of the decoys."

Moash smiled broadly. Each of the men had volunteered to be one of the four who would join Kaladin distracting the Parshendi. It was amazing. Months ago, Moash—along with the others—had eagerly placed the new or the weak at the front of the bridge to catch arrows. Now, to a man, they volunteered for the most dangerous jobs.

Do you realize what you could have in these men, Sadeas? Kaladin thought. *If you weren't so busy thinking of how to get them killed?*

"So what is it for you?" Kaladin said, nodding toward the dim practice ground. "Why do you work so hard? What is it you hunt?"

"Vengeance," the other man said, face somber.

Kaladin nodded. "I lost someone once. Because I wasn't good enough with the spear. I nearly killed myself practicing."

"Who was it?"

"My brother."

Moash nodded. The other bridgemen, Moash included, seemed to regard Kaladin's "mysterious" past with reverence.

"I'm glad I trained," Kaladin said. "And I'm glad you're dedicated. But you have to be careful. If I'd gotten myself killed by working so hard, it wouldn't have meant anything."

"Sure. But there's a difference between us, Kaladin."

Kaladin raised an eyebrow.

"You wanted to be able to save someone. Me, I want to kill somebody."

"Who?"

Moash hesitated, then shook his head. "Maybe I'll say, someday." He reached out, grabbing Kaladin on the shoulder. "I'd surrendered my plans, but you've returned them to me. I'll guard you with my life, Kaladin. I swear it to you, by the blood of my fathers."

Kaladin met Moash's intense eyes and nodded. "All right, then. Go help Hobber and Yake. They're still off on their thrusts."

Moash jogged off to do as told. He didn't call Kaladin "sir," and didn't seem to regard him with the same unspoken reverence as the others. That made Kaladin more comfortable with him.

Kaladin spent the next hour helping the men, one by one. Most of them were overeager, throwing themselves into their attacks. Kaladin explained the importance of control and precision, which won more fights than chaotic enthusiasm. They took it in, listening. More and more, they reminded him of his old spear squad.

That set him thinking. He remembered how he had felt when originally proposing the escape plan to the men. He'd been looking for something to do—a way to fight, no matter how risky. A chance. Things had changed. He now had a team he was proud of, friends he had come to love, and a possibility—perhaps—for stability.

If they could get the dodging and armor right, they might be reasonably safe. Maybe even as safe as his old spear squad had been. Was running still the best option?

"That is a worried face," a rumbling voice noted. Kaladin turned as Rock walked up and leaned against the wall near him, folding powerful forearms. "Is the face of a leader, say I. Always troubled." Rock raised a bushy red eyebrow.

"Sadeas will never let us go, particularly not now that we're so prominent." Alethi lighteyes considered it reprehensible for a man to let slaves escape; it made him seem impotent. Capturing those who ran away was essential to save face.

"You said this thing before," Rock said. "We will fight the men he sends after us, will seek Kharbranth, where there are no slaves. From there, the Peaks, to my people who will welcome us as heroes!"

"We might beat the first group, if he's foolish and sends

only a few dozen men. But after that he'll send more. And what of our wounded? Do we leave them here to die? Or do we take them with us and go that much more slowly?"

Rock nodded slowly. "You are saying that we need a plan."

"Yes," Kaladin said. "I guess that's what I'm saying. Either that, or we stay here . . . as bridgemen."

"Ha!" Rock seemed to take it as a joke. "Despite new armor, we would die soon. We make ourselves targets!"

Kaladin hesitated. Rock was right. The bridgemen would be used, day in and day out. Even if Kaladin slowed the death toll to two or three men a month—once, he would have considered that impossible, but now it seemed within reach—Bridge Four as it was currently composed would be gone within a year.

"I will talk with Sigzil about this thing," Rock said, rubbing his chin between the sides of his beard. "We will think. There must be a way to escape this trap, a way to disappear. A false trail? A distraction? Perhaps we can convince Sadeas that we have died during bridge run."

"How would we do that?"

"Don't know," Rock said. "But we will think." He nodded to Kaladin and sauntered off toward Sigzil. The Azish man was practicing with the others. Kaladin had tried speaking to him about Hoid, but Sigzil—typically closemouthed—hadn't wanted to discuss it.

"Hey, Kaladin!" Skar called. He was part of an advanced group that was going through Teft's very carefully supervised sparring. "Come spar with us. Show these rock-brained fools how it's really done." The others began calling for him as well.

Kaladin waved them down, shaking his head.

Teft trotted over, a heavy spear on one shoulder. "Lad," he said quietly, "I think it would be good for their morale if you showed them a thing or two yourself."

"I've already given them instruction."

"With a spear you knocked the head off of. Going very slowly, with lots of talk. They need to see it, lad. See you."

"We've been through this, Teft."

"Well, so we have."

Kaladin smiled. Teft was careful not to look angry or belligerent—he looked as if he were having a normal conversation with Kaladin. "You've been a sergeant before, haven't you?"

"Never mind that. Come on, just show them a few simple routines."

"No, Teft," Kaladin said, more seriously.

Teft eyed him. "You going to refuse to fight on the battle-field, just like that Horneater?"

"It's not like that."

"Well what is it like?"

Kaladin reached for an explanation. "I'll fight when the time comes. But if I let myself get back into it now, I'll be too eager. I'll push to attack now. I'll have trouble waiting until the men are ready. Trust me, Teft."

Teft studied him. "You're scared of it, lad."

"What? No. I—"

"I can see it," Teft said. "And I've seen it before. Last time you fought for someone, you failed, eh? So now you hesitate to take it up again."

Kaladin paused. "Yes," he admitted. But it was more than that. When he fought again, he would have to become that man from long ago, the man who had been called Stormblessed. The man with confidence and strength. He wasn't certain he could be that man any longer. That was what scared him.

Once he held that spear again, there would be no turning back.

"Well." Teft rubbed his chin. "When the time comes, I hope you're ready. Because this lot will need you."

Kaladin nodded and Teft hurried back to the others, giving some kind of explanation to mollify them.

*"They come from the pit, two dead men, a heart in their
hands, and I know that I have seen true glory."*

—Kakashah 1173, 13 seconds pre-death. A rickshaw puller.

I couldn't decide if you were interested or not," Navani said
softly to Dalinar as they slowly walked around the grounds
of Elhokar's raised field palace. "Half the time, you seemed
like a flirt—offering hints at courtship, then backing away.
The other half of the time, I was certain I had misread you.
And Gavilar was so direct. He always did prefer to seize
what he wished."

Dalinar nodded thoughtfully. He wore his blue uniform,
while Navani was in a subdued maroon dress with a thick
hem. Elhokar's gardeners had begun to cultivate the plant life
here. To their right, a twisting length of yellow shalebark rose
to waist height, like a railing. The stonelike plant was overgrown by small bunches of haspers with pearly shells slowly
opening and closing as they breathed. They looked like tiny
mouths, silently speaking in rhythm with one another.

Dalinar and Navani's pathway took a leisurely course up
the hillside. Dalinar strolled with hands clasped behind his
back. His honor guard and Navani's clerks followed behind.

A few of them looked perplexed at the amount of time Dalinar and Navani were spending with one another. How many of them suspected the truth? All? Part? None? Did it matter?

"I didn't mean to confuse you, all those years ago," he said, voice soft to keep it from prying ears. "I had intended to court you, but Gavilar expressed a preference for you. So I eventually felt I had to step aside."

"Just like that?" Navani asked. She sounded offended.

"He didn't realize that I was interested. He thought that by introducing you to him, I was indicating that he should court you. That was often how our relationship worked; I would discover people Gavilar should know, then bring them to him. I didn't realize until too late what I had done in giving you to him."

" 'Giving' me? Is there a slave's brand on my forehead of which I've been unaware?"

"I did not mean—"

"Oh hush," Navani said, her voice suddenly fond. Dalinar stifled a sigh; though Navani had matured since their youth, her moods always *had* changed as quickly as the seasons. In truth, that was part of her allure.

"Did you often step aside for him?" Navani asked.

"Always."

"Didn't that grow tiresome?"

"I didn't think about it much," Dalinar said. "When I did . . . yes, I was frustrated. But it was Gavilar. You know how he was. That force of will, that air of natural entitlement. It always seemed to surprise him when someone denied him or when the world itself didn't do as he wished. He didn't force me to defer—it was simply how life was."

Navani nodded in understanding.

"Regardless," Dalinar said, "I apologize for confusing you. I . . . well, I had difficulty letting go. I fear that—on occasion—I let too much of my true feelings slip out."

"Well, I suppose I can forgive that," she said. "Though you did spend the next two decades making certain I thought you hated me."

"I did nothing of the sort!"

"Oh? And how else was I to interpret your coldness? The way you would often leave the room when I arrived?"

"Containing myself," Dalinar said. "I had made my decision."

"Well, it looked a lot like hatred," Navani said. "Though I did wonder several times what you were hiding behind those stony eyes of yours. Of course, then *Shshshsh* came along."

As always, when the name of his wife was spoken, it came to him as the sound of softly rushing air, then slipped from his mind immediately. He could not hear, or remember, the name.

"She changed everything," Navani said. "You truly seemed to love her."

"I did," Dalinar said. Surely he had loved her. Hadn't he? He could remember nothing. "What was she like?" He quickly added, "I mean, in your opinion. How did you see her?"

"Everyone loved *Shshshsh*," Navani said. "I tried hard to hate her, but in the end, I could only be mildly jealous."

"You? Jealous of her? Whatever for?"

"Because," Navani said. "She fit you so well, never making inappropriate comments, never bullying those around her, always so calm." Navani smiled. "Thinking back, I really should have been able to hate her. But she was just so nice. Though she wasn't very . . . well . . ."

"What?" Dalinar asked.

"Clever," Navani said. She blushed, which was rare for her. "I'm sorry, Dalinar, but she just wasn't. She wasn't a fool, but . . . well . . . not everyone can be cunning. Perhaps that was part of her charm."

She seemed to think that Dalinar would be offended. "It's all right," he said. "Were you surprised that I married her?"

"Who could be surprised? As I said, she was perfect for you."

"Because we were matched intellectually?" Dalinar said dryly.

"Hardly. But you *were* matched in temperament. For a time, after I got over trying to hate her, I thought that the four of us could be quite close. But you were so stiff toward me."

"I could not allow any further . . . lapses to make you think that I was still interested." He said the last part awkwardly. After all, wasn't that what he was doing now? Lapsing?

Navani eyed him. "There you go again."

"What?"

"Feeling guilty. Dalinar, you are a wonderful, honorable man—but you really are quite prone to self-indulgence."

Guilt? As self-indulgence? "I never considered it that way before."

She smiled deeply.

"What?" he asked.

"You really are genuine, aren't you, Dalinar?"

"I try to be," he said. He glanced over his shoulder. "Though the nature of our relationship continues to perpetuate a kind of lie."

"We've lied to nobody. Let them think, or guess, what they wish."

"I suppose you are right."

"I usually am." She fell silent for a moment. "Do you regret what we have—"

"No," Dalinar said sharply, the strength of his objection surprising him. Navani just smiled. "No," Dalinar continued, more gently. "I do not regret this, Navani. I don't know how to proceed, but I am *not* going to let go."

Navani hesitated beside a growth of small, fist-size rockbuds with their vines out like long green tongues. They were grouped almost like a bouquet, growing on a large oval stone placed beside the pathway.

"I suppose it's too much to ask for you to not feel guilty," Navani said. "Can't you let yourself bend, just a little?"

"I'm not certain if I can. Particularly not now. Explaining why would be difficult."

"Could you try to? For me?"

"I . . . Well, I'm a man of extremes, Navani. I discovered that when I was a youth. I've learned, repeatedly, that the only way to control those extremes is to dedicate my life to something. First it was Gavilar. Now it's the Codes and the teachings of Nohadon. They're the means by which I bind myself. Like the enclosure of a fire, meant to contain and control it."

He took a deep breath. "I'm a weak man, Navani. I really am. If I give myself a few feet of leeway, I burst through all of my prohibitions. The momentum of following the Codes these years after Gavilar's death is what keeps me strong. If I let a few cracks into that armor, I might return to the man I once was. A man I never want to be again."

A man who had contemplated murdering his own brother for the throne—and for the woman who had married that brother. But he couldn't explain that, didn't dare let Navani know what his desire for her had once almost driven him to do.

On that day, Dalinar had sworn that he would never hold the throne himself. That was one of his restraints. Could he explain how she, without trying, pried at those restraints? How it was difficult to reconcile his long-fermenting love for her with his guilt at finally taking for himself what he'd long ago given up for his brother?

"You are not a weak man, Dalinar," Navani said.

"I am. But weakness can imitate strength if bound properly, just as cowardice can imitate heroism if given nowhere to flee."

"But there's nothing in Gavilar's book that prohibits us. It's just tradition that—"

"It feels wrong," Dalinar said. "But please, don't worry; I do enough worrying for both of us. I will find a way to make this work; I just ask your understanding. It will take time. When I display frustration, it is not with you, but with the situation."

"I suppose I can accept that. Assuming you can live with the rumors. They're starting already."

"They won't be the first rumors to plague me," he said. "I'm starting to worry less about them and more about Elhokar. How will we explain to him?"

"I doubt he'll notice," Navani said, snorting softly, resuming her walk. He followed. "He's so fixated on the Parshendi and, occasionally, the idea that someone in camp is trying to kill him."

"This might feed into that," Dalinar said. "He could read a number of conspiracies out of the two of us entering a relationship."

"Well, he—"

Horns began sounding loudly from below. Dalinar and Navani stopped to listen and identify the call.

"Stormfather," Dalinar said. "That's the *Tower itself* where a chasmfiend has been seen. It's one of the plateaus Sadeas has been watching." Dalinar felt a surge of excitement. "Highprinces have failed every time to win a gemheart there. It will be a major victory if he and I can do it together."

Navani looked troubled. "You're right about him, Dalinar. We *do* need him for our cause. But keep him at arm's length."

"Wish me the wind's favor." He reached toward her, but then stopped himself. What was he going to do? Embrace her here, in public? That would set off the rumors like fire across a pool of oil. He wasn't ready for that yet. Instead, he bowed to her, then hastened off to answer the call and collect his Shardplate.

It wasn't until he was halfway down the path that he paused to consider Navani's choice of words. She had said "We need him" for "our cause."

What was their cause? He doubted that Navani knew either. But she had already started to think of them as together in their efforts.

And, he realized, so did he.

* * *

The horns called, such a pure and beautiful sound to signify the imminence of battle. It caused a frenzy in the lumberyard. The orders had come down. The Tower was to be assaulted again—the very place where Bridge Four had failed, the place where Kaladin had caused a disaster.

Largest of the plateaus. Most coveted.

Bridgemen ran this way and that for their vests. Carpenters

and apprentices rushed out of the way. Matal shouted orders; an actual run was the only time he did that without Hashal. Bridgeleaders, showing a modicum of leadership, bellowed for their teams to line up.

A wind whipped the air, blowing wood chips and bits of dried grass into the sky. Men yelled, bells rang. And into this chaos strode Bridge Four, Kaladin at their head. Despite the urgency, soldiers stopped, bridgemen gaped, carpenters and apprentices stilled.

Thirty-five men marched in rusty orange carapace armor, expertly crafted by Leyten to fit onto leather jerkins and caps. They'd cut off arm guards and shin guards to complement the breastplates. The helms were built from several different headpieces, and had been ornamented—at Leyten's insistence—with ridges and cuts, like tiny horns or the edges of a crab's shell. The breastplates and guards were ornamented as well, cut into toothlike patterns, each one reminiscent of a saw blade. Earless Jaks had bought blue and white paint and drawn designs across the orange armor.

Each member of Bridge Four carried a large wooden shield strapped—tightly now—with red Parshendi bones. Ribs, for the most part, shaped in spiral patterns. Some of the men had tied finger bones to the centers so they would rattle, and others had attached sharp protruding ribs to the sides of their helms, giving them the look of fangs or mandibles.

The onlookers watched with amazement. It wasn't the first time they'd seen this armor, but this would be the first run where every man of Bridge Four had it. All together, it made an impressive sight.

Ten days, with six bridge runs, had allowed Kaladin and his team to perfect their method. Five men to be decoys with five more in the front holding shields and using only one arm to support the bridge. Their numbers were augmented by the wounded they'd saved from other crews, now strong enough to help carry.

So far—despite six bridge runs—there hadn't been a single fatality. The other bridgemen were whispering about a miracle. Kaladin didn't know about that. He just made certain to keep a full pouch of infused spheres with him at all times. Most of the Parshendi archers seemed to focus on him. Somehow, they could tell that he was the center of all this.

They reached their bridge and formed up, shields strapped to rods on the sides to await use. As they hefted their bridge, a spontaneous round of cheering rose up from the other crews.

"That's new," Teft said from Kaladin's left.

"Guess they finally realized what we are," Kaladin said.

"And what's that?"

Kaladin settled the bridge onto his shoulders. "We're their champions. Bridge forward!"

They broke into a trot, leading the way down from the staging yard, ushered by cheers.

◆◆◆

My father is not insane, Adolin thought, alive with energy and excitement as his armorers strapped on his Shardplate.

Adolin had stewed over Navani's revelation for days. He'd been wrong in such a horrible way. Dalinar Kholin *wasn't* growing weak. He *wasn't* getting senile. He *wasn't* a coward. Dalinar had been right, and Adolin had been wrong. After much soul searching, Adolin had come to a decision.

He was *glad* that he'd been wrong.

He grinned, flexing the fingers of his Plated hand as the armorers moved to his other side. He didn't know what the visions meant, or what the implications of those visions would be. His father was some kind of prophet, and that was daunting to consider.

But for now, it was enough that Dalinar was not insane. It was time to trust him. Stormfather knew, Dalinar had earned that right from his sons.

The armorers finished with Adolin's Shardplate. As they stepped away, Adolin hurried out of the armoring room into the sunlight, adjusting to the combined strength, speed, and weight of the Shardplate. Niter and five other members of the Cobalt Guard hastened up, one bringing Sureblood to him. Adolin took the reins, but led the Ryshadium at first, wanting more time to adapt to his Plate.

They soon entered the staging area. Dalinar, in his Shardplate, was conferring with Teleb and Ilamar. He seemed to tower over them as he pointed eastward. Already, companies of soldiers were moving out onto the lip of the Plains.

Adolin strode up to his father, eager. In the near distance, he noticed a figure riding down along the eastern rim of the warcamps. The figure wore gleaming red Shardplate.

"Father?" Adolin said, pointing. "What's he doing here? Shouldn't he be waiting for us to ride to his camp?"

Dalinar looked up. He waved for a groom to bring Gallant, and the two of them mounted. They rode down to intercept Sadeas, trailed by a dozen members of the Cobalt Guard. Did Sadeas want to call off the assault? Was he worried about failing against the Tower again?

Once they drew close, Dalinar pulled up. "You should be moving, Sadeas. Speed will be important, if we're to get to the plateau before the Parshendi take the gemheart and go."

The highprince nodded. "Agreed, in part. But we need to confer first. Dalinar, this is the Tower we're assaulting!" He seemed eager.

"Yes, and?"

"Damnation, man!" Sadeas said. "You're the one who told me we needed to find a way to trap a large force of Parshendi on a plateau. The Tower is *perfect*. They always bring a large force there, and two sides are inaccessible."

Adolin found himself nodding. "Yes," he said. "Father, he's right. If we can box them in and hit them hard . . ." The Parshendi normally fled when they took large losses. That was one of the things extending the war so long.

"It could mean a turning point in the war," Sadeas said, eyes alight. "My scribes estimate that they have no more than twenty or thirty thousand troops left. The Parshendi will commit ten thousand here—they always do. But if we can corner and kill all of them, we could nearly *destroy* their ability to wage war on these Plains."

"It'll work, Father," Adolin said eagerly. "This could be what we've been waiting for—what *you've* been waiting for.

A way to turn the war, a way to deal enough damage to the Parshendi that they can't afford to keep fighting!"

"We need troops, Dalinar," Sadeas said. "Lots of them. How many men could you field, at maximum?"

"On short notice?" Dalinar said. "Eight thousand, perhaps."

"It will have to do," Sadeas said. "I've managed to mobilize about seven thousand. We'll bring them all. Get your eight thousand to my camp, and we'll take every one of my bridge crews and march together. The Parshendi will get there first—it's inevitable with a plateau that close to their side—but if we can be fast enough, we can corner them on the plateau. Then we'll show them what a *real* Alethi army is capable of!"

"I won't risk lives on your bridges, Sadeas," Dalinar said. "I don't know that I can agree to a completely joint assault."

"Bah," Sadeas said. "I've got a new way of using bridgemen, one that doesn't cost nearly as many lives. Their casualties have dropped to almost nothing."

"Really?" Dalinar said. "Is it because of those bridgemen with armor? What made you change?"

Sadeas shrugged. "Perhaps you're getting through to me. Regardless, we need to go now. Together. With as many troops as they'll have, I can't risk engaging them and waiting for you to catch up. I want to go together and assault as closely together as we can manage. If you're still worried about the bridgemen, I can attack first and gain a foothold, then let you cross without risking bridgeman lives."

Dalinar looked thoughtful.

Come on, Father, Adolin thought. *You've been waiting for a chance to hit the Parshendi hard. This is it!*

"Very well," Dalinar said. "Adolin, send messengers to mobilize the Fourth through Eighth Divisions. Prepare the men to march. Let's end this war."

Map of the Battle of the Tower, drawn and labeled by Navani Kholin, circa 1173.

THE TOWER

"I see them. They are the rocks. They are the vengeful spirits. Eyes of red."

—Kakakes 1173, 8 seconds pre-death. A darkeyed young woman of fifteen. Subject was reportedly mentally unstable since childhood.

Several hours later, Dalinar stood with Sadeas on a rock formation overlooking the Tower itself. It had been a hard, long march. This was a distant plateau, as far eastward as they had ever struck. Plateaus beyond this point were impossible to take. The Parshendi could arrive so quickly that they had the gemheart out before the Alethi arrived. Sometimes that happened with the Tower as well.

Dalinar searched. "I see it," he said, pointing. "They don't have the gemheart out yet!" A ring of Parshendi were pounding on the chrysalis. Its shell was like thick stone, however. It was still holding.

"You should be glad you're using my bridges, old friend." Sadeas shaded his face with a gauntleted hand. "Those chasms might be too wide for a Shardbearer to jump."

Dalinar nodded. The Tower was enormous; even its huge size on the maps didn't do it justice. Unlike other plateaus, it wasn't level—instead, it was shaped like an enormous wedge that dipped toward the west, pointing a large cliff face in the stormward direction. It was too steep—and the chasms too wide—to approach from the east or south. Only three adjacent plateaus could provide staging areas for assaults, all along the western or southwestern side.

The chasms between these plateaus were unusually large, almost too wide for the bridges to span. On the nearby staging plateaus, thousands upon thousands of soldiers in blue or green were gathered, one color per plateau. Combined, they made for a larger force than Dalinar had ever seen brought against the Parshendi.

The Parshendi numbers were as large as anticipated. There were at least ten thousand of them lining up. This would be a full-scale battle, the kind Dalinar had been hoping for, the kind that would let them pit a huge number of Alethi against a large Parshendi force.

This *could* be it. The turning point in the war. Win this day, and everything would change.

Dalinar shaded his eyes as well, helm under his arm. He noted with satisfaction that Sadeas's scouting crews were crossing to adjacent plateaus where they could watch for Parshendi reinforcements. Just because the Parshendi had brought so many at first didn't mean that there were no other Parshendi forces waiting to flank them. Dalinar and Sadeas wouldn't be taken by surprise again.

"Come with me," Sadeas said. "Let us assault them together! A single grand wave of attack, across forty bridges!"

Dalinar looked down at the bridge crews; many of their members were lying exhausted on the plateau. Awaiting—likely dreading—their next task. Very few of them wore the armor Sadeas had spoken of. Hundreds of them would be slaughtered in the assault if they attacked together. But was that any different from what Dalinar did, asking his men to charge into battle to seize the plateau? Weren't they all part of the same army?

The cracks. He couldn't let them get wider. If he was going to be with Navani, he had to prove to himself he could remain firm in the other areas. "No," he said. "I will attack, but only after you've made a landing point for my bridge crews. Even that is more than I should allow. Never force your men to do as you yourself would not."

"You do charge the Parshendi!"

"I'd never do it carrying one of those bridges," Dalinar said. "I'm sorry, old friend. It's not a judgment of you. It is what I must do."

Sadeas shook his head, pulling on his helmet. "Well, it will have to do. We still planning on dining together tonight to discuss strategy?"

"I assume so. Unless Elhokar has a fit for both of us missing his feast."

Sadeas snorted. "He's going to have to grow accustomed to it. Six years of feasting every night is growing tedious. Besides, I doubt he'll feel anything but elation after we win this day and leave the Parshendi down a full third of their soldiers. See you on the battlefield."

Dalinar nodded and Sadeas jumped off the rock formation, dropping down to the surface below and joining his officers. Dalinar lingered, looking over at the Tower. It was not only larger than most plateaus, it was rougher, covered with lumpish rock formations of hardened crem. The patterns were rolling and smooth, yet very uneven—like a field full of short walls covered by a blanket of snow.

The eastern tip of the plateau rose to a point overlooking the Plains. The two plateaus they'd use were on the middle of the west side; Sadeas would take the northern one and Dalinar would assault from one just below it, once Sadeas had cleared a landing for him.

We need to push the Parshendi to the southeast, Dalinar thought, rubbing his chin, *corner them there.* Everything hinged on that. The chrysalis was up near the top, so the Parshendi were already situated in a good position for Dalinar and Sadeas to push them back against the cliff edge. The Parshendi would probably allow this, as it would give them the high ground.

If a second Parshendi army came, it would be separated from the others. The Alethi could focus on the Parshendi trapped atop the Tower while holding a defensive formation against the new arrivals. It *would* work.

He felt himself growing excited. He hopped down to a shorter outcropping, then walked down a few steplike clefts to reach the plateau floor, where his officers waited. He then rounded the rock formation, investigating Adolin's progress. The young man stood in his Shardplate, directing the companies as they crossed Sadeas's mobile bridges onto the southern staging plateau. In the near distance, Sadeas's men were forming up for the assault.

That group of armored bridgemen stood out, preparing at the front center of the formation of bridge crews. Why *were* they allowed armor? Why not the others as well? It looked like Parshendi carapace. Dalinar shook his head. The assault began, bridge crews running out ahead of Sadeas's army, approaching the Tower first.

"Where would you like to make our assault, Father?" Adolin asked, summoning his Shardblade and resting it on his pauldron, sharp side up.

"There," Dalinar said, pointing to a spot on their staging plateau. "Get the men ready."

Adolin nodded, shouting the orders.

In the distance, bridgemen began to die. *Heralds guide your paths, you poor men,* Dalinar thought. *As well as my own.*

※

Kaladin danced with the wind.

Arrows streamed around him, passing close, nearly kissing him with their painted scragglebark fletching. He had to let them get close, had to make the Parshendi feel they were near to killing him.

Despite four other bridgemen drawing their attention, despite the other men of Bridge Four behind armored with the skeletons of fallen Parshendi, most of the archers focused on Kaladin. He was a symbol. A living banner to destroy.

Kaladin spun between arrows, slapping them away with his shield. A storm raged inside him, as if his blood had been sucked away and replaced with stormwinds. It made his fingertips tingle with energy. Ahead, the Parshendi sang their angry, chanting song. The song for one who blasphemed against their dead.

Kaladin stayed at the front of the decoys, letting the arrows fall close. Daring them. Taunting them. Demanding they kill him until the arrows stopped falling and the wind stilled.

Kaladin came to rest, breath held to contain the storm within. The Parshendi reluctantly fell back before Sadeas's force. An enormous force, as far as plateau assaults went. Thousands of men and thirty-two bridges. Despite Kaladin's distraction, five bridges had been dropped, the men carrying them slaughtered.

None of the soldiers rushing across the chasm had made any specific effort to attack the archers firing on Kaladin, but the weight of numbers had forced them away. A few gave Kaladin loathing gazes, making an odd gesture by cupping a hand to the right ear and pointing at him before finally retreating.

Kaladin released his breath, Stormlight pulsing away from him. He had to walk a very fine line, drawing in enough Stormlight to stay alive, but not so much that it was visible to the watching soldiers.

The Tower rose ahead of him, a slab of stone that dipped toward the west. The chasm was so wide that he'd worried the men would drop the bridge into the chasm as they tried to place it. On the other side, Sadeas had arrayed his forces in a cupping shape, pushing the Parshendi back away, trying to give Dalinar an opening.

Perhaps attacking this way served to protect Dalinar's pristine image. He wouldn't make bridgemen die. Not directly, at least. Never mind that he stood on the backs of the men who had fallen to get Sadeas across. Their corpses were his true bridge.

"Kaladin!" a voice called from behind.

Kaladin spun. One of his men was wounded. *Storm it!* he thought, dashing up to Bridge Four. There was enough Stormlight still pulsing in his veins to stave off exhaustion. He'd grown complacent. Six bridge runs without a casualty. He should have realized it couldn't last. He pushed through the collected bridgemen to find Skar on the ground, holding his foot, red blood seeping between his fingers.

"Arrow in the foot," Skar said through gritted teeth. "In the storming foot! Who gets hit in the foot?"

"Kaladin!" Moash called urgently. The bridgemen split as Moash brought Teft in, an arrow sprouting from his shoulder between carapace breastplate and arm.

"Storm it!" Kaladin said, helping Moash set Teft down. The older bridgeman looked dazed. The arrow had dug deep into the muscle. "Somebody get pressure on Skar's foot and wrap it until I can look at it. Teft, can you hear me?"

"I'm sorry, lad," Teft mumbled, eyes glassy. "I'm . . ."

"You're all right," Kaladin said, hurriedly taking some bandages from Lopen, then nodding grimly. Lopen would heat a knife for cauterizing. "Who else?"

"Everyone else is accounted for," Drehy said. "Teft was trying to hide his wound. He must have taken it when we were shoving the bridge across."

Kaladin pressed gauze against the wound, then gestured for Lopen to hurry with the heated knife. "I want our scouts watching. Make sure the Parshendi don't try a stunt like they did a few weeks back! If they jump across that plateau to get at Bridge Four, we're dead."

"Is all right," Rock said, shading his eyes. "Sadeas is keeping his men in this area. No Parshendi will get through."

The knife came, and Kaladin held it hesitantly, a curl of smoke rising from its length. Teft had lost too much blood; there was no risking a sewing. But with the twist of the knife, Kaladin risked some bad scarring. That could leave the aging bridgeman with a stiffness that would hurt his ability to wield a spear.

Reluctantly, Kaladin pressed the knife into the wound, the flesh hissing and blood drying to black crisps. Painspren wiggled out of the ground, sinewy and orange. In a surgery, you could sew. But on the field, this was often the only way.

"I'm sorry, Teft." He shook his head as he continued to work.

Men began to scream. Arrows hit wood and flesh, sounding like distant woodsmen swinging axes.

Dalinar waited beside his men, watching Sadeas's soldiers fight. *He had better give us an opening,* he thought. *I'm starting to hunger for this plateau.*

Fortunately, Sadeas quickly gained his footing on the Tower and sent a flanking force over to carve out a section of land for Dalinar. They didn't get entirely into place before Dalinar started moving.

"One of you bridges, come with me!" he bellowed, barreling to the forefront. He was followed by one of the eight bridge teams Sadeas had lent him.

Dalinar needed to get onto that plateau. The Parshendi had noticed what was happening and had begun to put pressure on the small company in green and white that Sadeas had sent to defend his entry area. "Bridge crew, there!" Dalinar said, pointing.

The bridgemen hustled into place, looking relieved that they wouldn't be asked to place their bridge under fire of arrows. As soon as they got it into position, Dalinar charged across, the Cobalt Guard following. Just ahead, Sadeas's men broke.

Dalinar bellowed, closing his gauntleted hands around Oathbringer's hilt as the sword formed from mist. He crashed into the surging Parshendi line with a wide, two-handed sweep that dropped four men. The Parshendi began to chant in their strange language, singing their war song. Dalinar kicked a corpse aside and began to attack in earnest, frantically defending the foothold Sadeas's men had gained him. Within minutes, his soldiers surged around him.

With the Cobalt Guard watching his back, Dalinar waded into the battle, breaking enemy ranks as only a Shardbearer could. He tore pockets through the Parshendi front lines, like a fish leaping from a stream, cutting back and forth, keeping his enemies disorganized. Corpses with burned eyes and slashed clothing made a trail behind him. More and more

Alethi troops filled in the holes. Adolin crashed through a group of Parshendi nearby, his own squad of Cobalt Guardsmen a safe distance behind. He brought his whole army across—he needed to ascend quickly, pinning the Parshendi back so they couldn't escape. Sadeas was to watch the northern and western edges of the Tower.

The rhythm of the battle sang to Dalinar. The Parshendi chanting, the soldiers grunting and yelling, the Shardblade in his hands and the surging power of the Plate. The Thrill rose within him. Since the nausea didn't strike him, he carefully let the Blackthorn free, and felt the joy of dominating a battlefield and the disappointment at lacking a worthy foe.

Where were the Parshendi Shardbearers? He had seen that one in battle weeks ago. Why had he not reappeared? Would they commit so many men to the Tower without sending a Shardbearer?

Something heavy hit his armor, banging off it, causing a small puff of Stormlight to escape between the joints along his upper arm. Dalinar cursed, raising an arm to protect his face while scanning the near distance. *There,* he thought, picking out a nearby rock formation where a group of Parshendi stood swinging enormous rock slings with two hands. The head-size stones crashed into Parshendi and Alethi alike, though Dalinar was obviously the target.

He growled as another one hit, smashing against his forearm, sending a soft jolt through the Shardplate. The blow was strong enough to send a small array of cracks through his right vambrace.

Dalinar growled and threw himself into a Plate-enhanced run. The Thrill surged more strongly through him, and he rammed his shoulder into a group of Parshendi, scattering them, then spun with his Blade and cut down those too slow to get out of his way. He dodged to the side as a hail of stones fell where he'd been standing, then leaped onto a low boulder. He took two steps and jumped for the ledge where the rock-throwers were standing.

He grabbed its edge with one hand, holding his Blade with the other. The men atop the small ridge stumbled back, but Dalinar heaved himself up just high enough to swing. Oathbringer cut at their legs, and four men tumbled to the ground, feet dead. Dalinar dropped the Blade—it vanished—and used both hands to heave himself onto the ridge.

He landed in a crouch, Plate clanking. Several of the remaining Parshendi tried to swing their slings, but Dalinar grabbed a pair of head-size stones from a pile—easily palming them in his gauntleted hands—and flung them at the Parshendi. The stones hit with enough force to toss the slingmen off the formation, crushing their chests.

Dalinar smiled, then began throwing more stones. As the last Parshendi fell off the ledge, Dalinar spun, summoning Oathbringer and looking over the battlefield. A spear wall of blue and reflective steel struggled against black and red Parshendi. Dalinar's men did well, pressing the Parshendi up to the southeast, where they would be trapped. Adolin led this effort, Shardplate gleaming.

Breathing deeply from the Thrill now, Dalinar held his Shardblade up above his head, reflecting sunlight. Below, his men cheered, sending up calls that rose above the Parshendi war chant. Gloryspren sprouted around him.

Stormfather, but it felt good to be winning again. He threw himself off the rock formation, for once not taking the slow and careful way down. He fell amid a group of Parshendi, crashing to the stones, blue Stormlight rising from his armor. He spun, slaying, remembering years spent fighting alongside Gavilar. Winning, conquering.

He and Gavilar had created something during those years. A solidified, cohesive nation out of something fractured. Like master potters reconstructing a fine ceramic that had been dropped. With a roar, Dalinar cut through the line of Parshendi, to where the Cobalt Guard was fighting to catch up to him. "We press them!" he bellowed. "Pass the word! All companies up the side of the Tower!"

Soldiers raised spears and runners went to deliver his orders. Dalinar spun and charged into the Parshendi, pushing himself—and his army—forward. To the north, Sadeas's forces were stalled. Well, Dalinar's force would do the work for him. If Dalinar could spear forward here, he could slice the Parshendi in half, then crush the northern side against Sadeas and the southern side against the cliff edge.

His army surged forward behind him, and the Thrill bubbled within. It was power. Strength greater than Shardplate. Vitality greater than youth. Skill greater than a lifetime of practice. A fever of power. Parshendi after Parshendi fell before his Blade. He couldn't cut their flesh, yet he sheared through their ranks. The momentum of their attacks often carried their corpses stumbling past him even as their eyes burned. The Parshendi started to break, running away or falling back. He grinned behind his near-translucent visor.

This was life. This was control. Gavilar had been the leader, the momentum, and the essence of their conquest. But Dalinar had been the warrior. Their opponents had surrendered to Gavilar's rule, but the Blackthorn—he was the man who had scattered them, the one who had dueled their leaders and slain their best Shardbearers.

Dalinar screamed at the Parshendi, and their entire line bent, then shattered. The Alethi surged forward, cheering. Dalinar joined his men, charging at their forefront to run down the Parshendi warpairs fleeing to the north or south, trying to join larger groups who held there.

He reached a pair. One turned to hold him off with a hammer, but Dalinar cut him down in passing, then grabbed the other Parshendi and threw him down with a twist of the arm. Grinning, Dalinar raised his Blade high over his head, looming over the soldier.

The Parshendi rolled awkwardly, holding his arm, no doubt shattered as he was thrown down. He looked up at Dalinar, terrified, fearspren appearing around him.

He was only a youth.

Dalinar froze, Blade held above his head, muscles taut. Those eyes . . . that face . . . Parshendi might not be human, but their features—their expressions—were the same. Save for the marbled skin and the strange growths of carapace armor, this boy could have been a groom in Dalinar's stable. What did he see above him? A faceless monster in impervious armor? What was this youth's story? He would only have been a boy when Gavilar was assassinated.

Dalinar stumbled backward, the Thrill vanishing. One of the Cobalt Guardsmen passed by, casually ramming a sword into the Parshendi boy's neck. Dalinar raised a hand, but it was over too quickly for him to stop. The soldier didn't notice Dalinar's gesture.

Dalinar lowered his hand. His men were rushing around him, rolling over the fleeing Parshendi. The majority of the Parshendi still fought, resisting Sadeas on one side and Dalinar's force on the other. The eastern plateau edge was just a short distance to Dalinar's right—he had come up against the Parshendi force like a spear, slicing it through the center, splitting it off to the north and south.

Around him lay the dead. Many of them had fallen facedown, taken in the back by spears or arrows from Dalinar's forces. Some Parshendi were still alive, though dying. They hummed or whispered to themselves a strange, haunting song. The one they sang as they waited to die.

Their whispered songs rose like the curses of spirits on Soul's March. Dalinar had always found the death song the most beautiful of all he had heard from the Parshendi. It seemed to cut through the grunts, clangs, and screams of the nearby battle. As always, each Parshendi's song was in perfect time with that of his fellows. It was as if they could all hear the same melody somewhere far away, and sang along through sputtering, bloodied lips, with rasping breath.

The Codes, Dalinar thought, turning toward his fighting men. *Never ask of your men a sacrifice you wouldn't make yourself. Never make them fight in conditions you would refuse to fight in yourself. Never ask a man to perform an act you wouldn't soil your own hands doing.*

He felt sick. This wasn't beautiful. This wasn't glorious. This wasn't strength, power, or life. This was revolting, repellent, and ghastly.

But they killed Gavilar! he thought, searching for a way to overcome the sickness he suddenly felt.

Unite them. . . .

Roshar had been united, once. Had that included the Parshendi?

You don't know if you can trust the visions or not, he told himself, his honor guard forming up behind him. *They could be from the Nightwatcher or the Voidbringers. Or something else entirely.*

In that moment, the objections felt weak. What had the visions wanted him to do? Bring peace to Alethkar, unite his people, act with justice and honor. Could he not judge the visions based on that?

He raised his Shardblade to his shoulder, walking solemnly among the fallen toward the northern line, where the Parshendi were trapped between his men and Sadeas's. His sickness grew stronger.

What was *happening* to him?

"Father!" Adolin's shout was frantic.

Dalinar turned toward his son, who was running to him. The young man's Plate was sprayed with Parshendi blood, but as always his Blade gleamed.

"What do we do?" Adolin asked, panting.

"About what?" Dalinar asked.

Adolin turned, pointing to the southwest—toward the plateau south of the one from which Dalinar's army had begun their assault over an hour ago. There, leaping across the wide chasm, was an enormous second army of Parshendi.

Dalinar slammed his visor up, fresh air washing across his sweaty face. He stepped forward. He'd anticipated this possibility, but someone should have given warning. Where were the scouts? What was—

He felt a chill.

Shaking, he scrambled toward one of the smooth, bulging formations of rock that were plentiful on the Tower.

"Father?" Adolin said, running after him.

Dalinar climbed, seeking the top of the formation, dropping his Shardblade. He crested the rise and stood looking northward over his troops and the Parshendi. Northward, toward Sadeas. Adolin climbed up beside him, gauntleted hand slapping up his visor.

"Oh no . . ." he whispered.

Sadeas's army was retreating across the chasm to the northern staging plateau. Half of it was across already. The eight groups of bridgemen he'd lent Dalinar had pulled back and were gone.

Sadeas was abandoning Dalinar and his troops, leaving them surrounded on three sides by Parshendi, alone on the Shattered Plains. And he was taking all of his bridges with him.

"That chanting, that singing, those rasping voices."

—Kaktach 1173, 16 seconds pre-death. A middle-aged potter. Reported seeing strange dreams during highstorms during the last two years.

Kaladin wearily unwrapped Skar's wound to inspect his stitches and change the bandage. The arrow had hit on the right side of the ankle, deflecting off the knob of the fibula and scraping down through the muscles on the side of the foot.

"You were very lucky, Skar," Kaladin said, putting on the new bandage. "You'll walk on this again, assuming you do *not* put weight on it until it's healed. We'll have some of the men carry you back to camp."

Behind them, the screaming, pounding, pulsing battle raged on. The fighting was distant now, focused on the eastern edge of the plateau. To Kaladin's right, Teft drank as Lopen poured water into his mouth. The older man scowled, taking the waterskin from Lopen with his good hand. "I'm not an invalid," he snapped. He'd gotten over his initial dizziness, though he was weak.

Kaladin sat back, feeling drained. When Stormlight faded away, it left him exhausted. That should pass soon; it had been over an hour since the initial assault. He carried a few more infused spheres in his pouch; he forced himself to resist the urge to suck in their Light.

He stood up, meaning to gather some men to carry Skar and Teft toward the far side of the plateau, just in case the battle went poorly and they had to retreat. That wasn't likely; the Alethi soldiers had been doing well the last time he'd checked.

He scanned the battlefield again. What he saw made him freeze.

Sadeas was retreating.

At first, it seemed so impossible that Kaladin couldn't accept it. Was Sadeas bringing his men around to attack in another direction? But no, the rear guard was already across the bridges, and Sadeas's banner was approaching. Was the highprince wounded?

"Drehy, Leyten, grab Skar. Rock and Peet, you take Teft. Hustle to the western side of the plateau in preparation to flee. The rest of you, get into bridge positions."

The men, only now noticing what was going on, responded with anxiety.

"Moash, you're with me," Kaladin said, hastening toward their bridge.

Moash hurried up beside Kaladin. "What's going on?"

"Sadeas is pulling out," Kaladin said, watching the tide of Sadeas's men in green slide away from the Parshendi lines like wax melting. "There's no reason to. The battle's barely begun, and his forces were winning. I can only think that Sadeas must have been wounded."

"Why would they withdraw the entire army for that?" Moash said. "You don't think he is . . ."

"His banner still flies," Kaladin said. "So he's probably not dead. Unless they left it up to keep the men from panicking."

He and Moash reached the side of the bridge. Behind, the rest of the crew hastened to form a line. Matal was on the other side of the chasm, speaking with the commander of the rear guard. After a quick exchange, Matal crossed and began to run down the line of bridge crews, calling for them to prepare to carry. He glanced at Kaladin's team, but saw they were already ready, and so hurried on.

To Kaladin's right, on the adjacent plateau—the one where Dalinar had launched his assault—the eight lent bridge crews pulled away from the battlefield, crossing over to Kaladin's plateau. A lighteyed officer Kaladin didn't recognize was giving them orders. Beyond them, farther to the south, a new Parshendi force had arrived, and was pouring onto the Tower.

Sadeas rode up to the chasm. The paint on his Shardplate gleamed in the sun; it didn't bear a single scratch. In fact, his entire honor guard was unharmed. Though they had gone over to the Tower, they had disengaged the enemy and come back. Why?

And then Kaladin saw it. Dalinar Kholin's force, fighting on the upper middle slope of the wedge, was now surrounded. This new Parshendi force was flooding into sections that Sadeas had held, supposedly protecting Dalinar's retreat.

"They're abandoning him!" Kaladin said. "This was a trap. A setup. Sadeas is leaving Highprince Kholin—and all of his soldiers—to die." Kaladin scrambled around the end of the bridge, pushing through the soldiers who were coming off it. Moash cursed and followed.

Kaladin wasn't certain why he elbowed his way up to the next bridge—bridge ten—where Sadeas was crossing. Perhaps he needed to see for certain that Sadeas wasn't wounded. Perhaps he was still stunned. This was treachery on a grand scale, terrible enough that it made Amaram's betrayal of Kaladin seem almost trivial.

Sadeas trotted his horse across the bridge, the wood clattering. He was accompanied by two lighteyed men in regular armor, and all three had their helms under their arms, as if they were on parade.

The honor guard stopped Kaladin, looking hostile. He was still close enough to see that Sadeas was, indeed, completely unharmed. He was also close enough to study Sadeas's proud face as he turned his horse and looked back at the Tower. The second Parshendi force swarmed Kholin's army, trapping them. Even without that, Kholin had no bridges. He could not retreat.

"I told you, old friend," Sadeas said, voice soft but distinct, overlapping the distant screams. "I said that honor of yours would get you killed someday." He shook his head.

Then he turned his horse, trotting it away from the battlefield.

※

Dalinar cut down a Parshendi warpair. There was always another to replace it. He set his jaw, falling into Windstance and taking the defensive, holding his little rise in the hillside and acting as a rock over which the oncoming Parshendi wave would have to break.

Sadeas had planned this retreat well. His men hadn't been having trouble; they'd been ordered to fight in a way that they could easily disengage. And he had a full forty bridges to retreat across. Together, that made his abandonment of Dalinar happen quickly, by the scale of battles. Though Dalinar had immediately ordered his men to push forward, hoping to catch Sadeas while the bridges were still set, he hadn't been nearly quick enough. Sadeas's bridges were pulling away, the entirety of his army now across.

Adolin fought nearby. They were two tired men in Plate facing an entire army. Their armor had accumulated a frightening number of cracks. None were critical yet, but they did leak precious Stormlight. Wisps of it rose like the songs of dying Parshendi.

"I warned you not to trust him!" Adolin bellowed as he fought, cutting down a pair of Parshendi, then taking a wave of arrows from a team of archers who had set up nearby. The arrows sprayed against Adolin's armor, scratching the paint. One caught in a crack, widening it.

"I told you," Adolin continued to yell, lowering his arm from his face and slicing into the next pair of Parshendi just before they landed their hammers on him. "I said he was an eel!"

"I know!" Dalinar yelled back.

"We walked right into this," Adolin continued, shouting as if he hadn't heard Dalinar. "We let him take away our bridges. We let him get us onto the plateau before the second wave of Parshendi arrived. We let him control the scouts. We even *suggested* the attack pattern that would leave us surrounded if he didn't support us!"

"I know." Dalinar's heart twisted inside of him.

Sadeas was carrying out a premeditated, carefully planned, and very thorough betrayal. Sadeas hadn't been overwhelmed, hadn't retreated for safety—though that was undoubtedly what he would claim when he got back to camp. A disaster, he'd say. Parshendi everywhere. Attacking together had upset the balance, and—unfortunately—he'd been forced to pull out and leave his friend. Oh, perhaps some of Sadeas's men would talk, tell the truth, and other highprinces would undoubtedly know what really happened. But nobody would challenge Sadeas openly. Not after such a decisive and powerful maneuver.

The people in the warcamps would go along with it. The other highprinces were too displeased with Dalinar to raise a fuss. The only one who might speak up was Elhokar, and Sadeas had his ear. It wrenched Dalinar's heart. Had it all been an act? Could he really have misjudged Sadeas so completely? What of the investigation clearing Dalinar? What of their plans and reminiscences? All lies?

I saved your life, Sadeas. Dalinar watched Sadeas's banner retreat across the staging plateau. Among that distant group, a rider who wore crimson Shardplate turned and looked back. Sadeas, watching Dalinar fighting for his life. That figure paused for a moment, then turned around and rode on.

The Parshendi were surrounding the forward position where Dalinar and Adolin fought just ahead of the army. They were overwhelming his guard. He jumped down and slew another pair of enemies, but earned another blow to his forearm in the process. The Parshendi swarmed around him, and Dalinar's guard began to buckle.

"Pull away!" he yelled at Adolin, then began to back toward the army proper.

The youth cursed, but did as ordered. Dalinar and Adolin retreated back behind the front line of defense. Dalinar pulled off his cracked helm, panting. He'd been fighting nonstop long enough to get winded, despite his Shardplate. He let one of the guardsmen hand him a waterskin, and Adolin did the same. Dalinar squirted the warm water into his mouth and across his face. It had the metallic taste of stormwater.

Adolin lowered his waterskin, swishing the water in his mouth. He met Dalinar's eyes, his face haunted and grim. He knew. Just as Dalinar did. Just as the men likely did. There would be no surviving this battle. The Parshendi left no survivors. Dalinar braced himself, waiting for further accusations from Adolin. The boy had been right all along. And whatever the visions were, they had misled Dalinar in at least one respect. Trusting Sadeas had brought them to doom.

Men died just a short distance away, screaming and cursing. Dalinar longed to fight, but he needed to rest himself. Losing a Shardbearer because of fatigue would not serve his men.

"Well?" Dalinar demanded of Adolin. "Say it. I have led us to destruction."

"I—"

"This is *my* fault," Dalinar said. "I should never have risked our house for those foolish dreams."

"No," Adolin said. He sounded surprised at himself for saying it. "No, Father. It's not your fault."

Dalinar stared at his son. That was not what he'd expected to hear.

"What would you have done differently?" Adolin asked. "Would you stop trying to make something better of Alethkar? Would you become like Sadeas and the others? No. I wouldn't have you become that man, Father, regardless of what it would gain us. I wish to the Heralds that we hadn't let Sadeas trick us into this, but I will not blame you for his deceit."

Adolin reached over, gripping Dalinar's Plate-covered arm.

"You are right to follow the Codes. You were right to try to unite Alethkar. And I was a fool for fighting you on it every step along the path. Perhaps if I hadn't spent so much time distracting you, we would have seen this day coming."

Dalinar blinked, dumbfounded. This was *Adolin* speaking those words? What had changed in the boy? And why did he say this now, at the dawn of Dalinar's greatest failure?

And yet, as the words hung in the air, Dalinar felt his guilt evaporating, blown away by the screams of the dying. It *was* a selfish emotion.

Would he have had himself change? Yes, he could have been more cautious. He could have been warier of Sadeas. But would he have given up on the Codes? Would he have become the same pitiless killer he'd been as a youth?

No.

Did it matter that the visions had been wrong about Sadeas? Was he ashamed of the man that they, and the readings from the book, had made him become? The final piece fell into place inside of him, the final cornerstone, and he found that he was no longer worried. The confusion was gone. He knew what to do, at long last. No more questions. No more uncertainty.

He reached up, gripping Adolin's arm. "Thank you."

Adolin nodded curtly. He was still angry, Dalinar could see, but he chose to follow Dalinar—and part of following a leader was supporting him even when the battle turned against him.

Then they released one another and Dalinar turned to the soldiers around them. "It is time for us to fight," he said, voice growing louder. "And we do so not because we seek the glory of men, but because the other options are worse. We follow the Codes not because they bring gain, but because we loathe the people we would otherwise become. We stand here on this battlefield alone because of who we are."

The members of the Cobalt Guard standing in a ring began to turn, one at a time, looking toward him. Beyond them, reserve soldiers—lighteyed and dark—gathered closer, eyes terrified, but faces resolute.

"Death is the end of all men!" Dalinar bellowed. "What is the measure of him once he is gone? The wealth he accumulated and left for his heirs to squabble over? The glory he obtained, only to be passed on to those who slew him? The lofty positions he held through happenstance?

"No. We fight here because we understand. The end is the same. It is the *path* that separates men. When we taste that end, we will do so with our heads held high, eyes to the sun."

He held out a hand, summoning Oathbringer. "I am not ashamed of what I have become," he shouted, and found it to be true. It felt so strange to be free of guilt. "Other men may debase themselves to destroy me. Let them have their glory. For I will retain mine!"

The Shardblade formed, dropping into his hand.

The men did not cheer, but they *did* stand taller, straight-backed. A little of the terror retreated. Adolin shoved his helm on, his own Blade appearing in his hand, coated in condensation. He nodded.

Together they charged back into the battle.

And so I die, Dalinar thought, crashing into the Parshendi ranks. There he found peace. An unexpected emotion on the field of battle, but all the more welcome for that.

He did, however, discover one regret: He was leaving poor Renarin as Kholin highprince, in over his head and surrounded by enemies grown fat on the flesh of his father and brother.

I never did deliver that Shardplate I promised him, Dalinar thought. *He will have to make his way without it. Honor of our ancestors protect you, son.*

Stay strong—and learn wisdom more quickly than your father did.

Farewell.

"Let me no longer hurt! Let me no longer weep! Dai-Gonarthis! The Black Fisher holds my sorrow and consumes it!"

—Tanatesach 1173, 28 seconds pre-death. A darkeyed female street juggler. Note similarity to sample 1172-89.

Bridge Four lagged behind the rest of the army. With two wounded and four men needed to carry them, the bridge weighed them down. Fortunately, Sadeas had brought nearly every bridge crew on this run, including eight to lend to Dalinar. That meant the army didn't need to wait for Kaladin's team in order to cross.

Exhaustion saturated Kaladin, and the bridge on his shoulders seemed made of stone. He hadn't felt so tired since his first days as a bridgeman. Syl hovered in front of him, watching with concern as he marched at the head of his men, sweat drenching his face, struggling over the uneven ground of the plateau.

Ahead, the last of Sadeas's army was bunched along the chasm, crossing. The staging plateau was nearly empty. The sheer awful audacity of what Sadeas had done twisted at Kaladin's insides. He thought what had been done to him had been horrible. But here, Sadeas callously condemned thousands of men, lighteyed and dark. Supposed allies. That betrayal seemed to weigh as heavily on Kaladin as the bridge itself. It pressed on him, made him gasp for breath.

Was there no hope for men? They killed those they should have loved. What good was it to fight, what good was it to win, if there was no difference between ally and enemy? What was victory? Meaningless. What did the deaths of Kaladin's friends and colleagues mean? Nothing. The entire world was a pustule, sickeningly green and infested with corruption.

Numb, Kaladin and the others reached the chasm, though they were too late to help with the transfer. The men he'd sent ahead were there, Teft looking grim, Skar leaning on a spear to support his wounded leg. A small group of dead spearmen lay nearby. Sadeas's soldiers retrieved their wounded, when possible, but some died as they were helped along. They'd abandoned some of those here; Sadeas was obviously in a hurry to leave the scene.

The dead had been left with their equipment. Skar had probably gotten his crutch there. Some poor bridge crew would have to cross all the way back here at a later date to salvage from these, and from Dalinar's fallen.

They set their bridge down, and Kaladin wiped his brow. "Don't place the bridge across the chasm," he told the men. "We'll wait until the last of the soldiers have crossed, then carry it over on one of the other bridges." Matal eyed Kaladin and his team, but didn't order them to set their bridge. He realized that by the time they got it into position, they'd have to pull it up again.

"Isn't that a sight?" Moash said, stepping up beside Kaladin, looking back.

Kaladin turned. The Tower rose behind them, sloped in their direction. Kholin's army was a circle of blue, trapped in the middle of the slope after trying to push down and get to Sadeas before he left. The Parshendi were a dark swarm with specks of red from their marbled skins. They pressed at the Alethi ring, compressing it.

"Such a shame," Drehy said from beside their bridge, sitting on its lip. "Makes me sick."

Other bridgemen nodded, and Kaladin was surprised to see the concern in their faces. Rock and Teft joined Kaladin and Moash, all wearing their Parshendi-carapace armor. He was glad they'd left Shen back in the camp. He'd have been catatonic at the sight of it all.

Teft cradled his wounded arm. Rock raised a hand to shade his eyes and shook his head, looking eastward. "Is a shame. A shame to Sadeas. A shame to us."

"Bridge Four," Matal called. "Come on!"

Matal was waving for them to cross Bridge Six's bridge and leave the staging plateau. An idea came to Kaladin suddenly. A fantastic idea, like a blooming rockbud in his mind.

"We'll follow with our own bridge, Matal," Kaladin called. "We only just got to the chasm. We need to sit for a few minutes."

"Cross now!" Matal yelled.

"We'll just fall further behind!" Kaladin retorted. "You want to explain to Sadeas why he has to hold the entire army for one miserable bridge crew? We've got our bridge. Let my men rest. We'll catch up to you later."

"And if those savages come after you?" Matal demanded.

Kaladin shrugged.

Matal blinked, then seemed to realize how badly he wanted that to happen. "Suit yourself," he called, rushing across bridge six as the other bridges were pulled up. In seconds, Kaladin's team was alone beside the chasm, the army retreating westward.

Kaladin smiled broadly. "I can't believe it, after all that worrying . . . Men, we're free!"

The others turned to him, confused.

"We'll follow in a short while," Kaladin said eagerly, "and Matal will assume we're coming. We fall farther and farther behind the army, until we're out of sight. Then we'll turn north, use the bridge to cross the Plains. We can escape northward, and everyone will just assume the Parshendi caught us and slaughtered us!"

The other bridgemen regarded him with wide eyes.

"Supplies," Teft said.

"We have these spheres," Kaladin said, pulling out his pouch. "A wealth of them, right here. We can take the armor and weapons from the dead over there and use those to defend ourselves from bandits. It will be hard, but we *won't be chased*!"

The men were starting to grow excited. However, something gave Kaladin pause. *What of the wounded bridgemen back in the camp?*

"I'll have to stay behind," Kaladin said.

"*What?*" Moash demanded.

"Someone will need to," Kaladin said. "For the good of our wounded in camp. We can't abandon them. And if I stay behind, I can support the story. Wound me and leave me on one of the plateaus. Sadeas is *sure* to send scavengers back. I'll tell them my crew was hunted down in retribution for desecrating the Parshendi corpses, our bridge tossed into the chasm. They'll believe it; they've seen how the Parshendi hate us."

The crew was all standing now, shooting glances at one another. Uncomfortable glances.

"We're not leaving without you," Sigzil said. Many of the others nodded.

"I'll follow," Kaladin said. "We can't leave those men behind."

"Kaladin, lad—" Teft began.

"We can talk about me later," Kaladin interrupted. "Maybe I'll go with you, then sneak back into camp later to rescue the wounded. For now, go salvage from those bodies."

They hesitated.

"It's an order, men!"

They moved, offering no further complaint, rushing to pilfer from the corpses Sadeas had abandoned. That left Kaladin alone beside the bridge.

He was still unsettled. It wasn't just the wounded back in camp. What was it, then? This was a fantastic opportunity. The type he'd have practically killed to get during his years as a slave. The chance to vanish, presumed dead? The bridge-men wouldn't have to fight. They were free. Why, then, was he so anxious?

Kaladin turned to survey his men, and was shocked to see someone standing beside him. A woman of translucent white light.

It was Syl, as he'd never seen her before, the size of an ordinary person, hands clasped in front of her, hair and dress streaming to the side in the wind. He'd had no idea she could make herself so large. She stared eastward, her expression horrified, eyes wide and sorrowful. It was the face of a child watching a brutal murder that stole her innocence.

Kaladin turned and slowly looked in the direction she was staring. Toward the Tower.

Toward Dalinar Kholin's desperate army.

The sight of them twisted his heart. They fought so hope-lessly. Surrounded. Abandoned. Left alone to die.

We have a bridge, Kaladin realized. *If we could get it set . . .* Most of the Parshendi were focused on the Alethi army, with only a token reserve force down at the base near the chasm. It was a small enough group that perhaps the bridge-men could contain them.

But no. That was idiocy. There were thousands of Parsh-endi soldiers blocking Kholin's path to the chasm. And how would the bridgemen set their bridge, with no archers to support them?

Several of the bridgemen returned from their quick scav-enge. Rock joined Kaladin, staring eastward, expression be-coming grim. "This thing is terrible," he said. "Can we not do something to help?"

Kaladin shook his head. "It would be suicide, Rock. We'd have to run a full assault without an army to support us."

"Couldn't we just go back a little of the way?" Skar asked. "Wait to see if Kholin can cut his way down to us? If he does, then we could set our bridge."

"No," Kaladin said. "If we stayed out of range, Kholin would assume us to be scouts left by Sadeas. We'll have to charge the chasm. Otherwise he'd never come down to meet us."

That made the bridgemen pale.

"Besides," Kaladin added. "If we did somehow save some of those men, they'd talk, and Sadeas would know we still live. He'd hunt us down and kill us. By going back, we'd throw away our chance at freedom."

The other bridgemen nodded at that. The rest had gathered, carrying weapons. It was time to go. Kaladin tried to squelch the feeling of despair inside him. This Dalinar Kholin was probably just like the others. Like Roshone, like Sadeas, like any number of other lighteyes. Pretending virtue but corrupted inside.

But he has thousands of darkeyed soldiers with him, a part of him thought. *Men who don't deserve this terrible fate. Men like my old spear crew.*

"We owe them nothing," Kaladin whispered. He thought he could see Dalinar Kholin's banner, flying blue at the front of his army. "You got them into this, Kholin. I won't let my men die for you." He turned his back on the Tower.

Syl still stood beside him, facing eastward. It made his very soul twist in knots to see that look of despair on her face. "Are windspren attracted to wind," she asked softly, "or do they make it?"

"I don't know," Kaladin said. "Does it matter?"

"Perhaps not. You see, I've remembered what kind of spren I am."

"Is this the time for it, Syl?"

"I bind things, Kaladin," she said, turning and meeting his eyes. "I am honorspren. Spirit of oaths. Of promises. And of nobility."

Kaladin could faintly hear the sounds of the battle. Or was that just his mind, searching for something he knew to be there?

Could he hear the men dying?

Could he see the soldiers running away, scattering, leaving their warlord alone?

Everyone else fleeing. Kaladin kneeling over Dallet's body.

A green-and-burgundy banner, flying alone on the field.

"I've been here before!" Kaladin bellowed, turning back toward that blue banner.

Dalinar always fought at the front.

"What happened last time?" Kaladin yelled. "I've learned! I won't be a fool again!"

It seemed to crush him. Sadeas's betrayal, his exhaustion, the deaths of so many. He was there again for a moment, kneeling in Amaram's mobile headquarters, watching the last of his friends being slaughtered, too weak and hurt to save them.

He raised a trembling hand to his head, feeling the brand there, wet with his sweat. "I owe you nothing, Kholin."

And his father's voice seemed to whisper a reply. *Somebody has to start, son. Somebody has to step forward and do what is right,* because *it is right. If nobody starts, then others cannot follow.*

Dalinar had come to help Kaladin's men, attacking those archers and saving Bridge Four.

The lighteyes don't care about life, Lirin had said. *So I must. So we must.*

So you must. . . .

Life before death.

I've failed so often. I've been knocked to the ground and trod upon.

Strength before weakness.

This would be death I'd lead my friends to . . .

Journey before destination.

. . . death, and what is right.

"We have to go back," Kaladin said softly. "Storm it, we *have* to go back."

He turned to the members of Bridge Four. One by one, they nodded. Men who had been the dregs of the army just months before—men who had once cared for nothing but their own skins—took deep breaths, tossed away thoughts for their own safety, and nodded. They would follow him.

Kaladin looked up and sucked in a deep breath. Storm-light rushed into him like a wave, as if he'd put his lips up to a highstorm and drawn it into himself.

"Bridge up!" he commanded.

The members of Bridge Four cheered their agreement, grabbing their bridge and hoisting it high. Kaladin pulled on a shield, grabbing the straps in his hand.

Then he turned, raising it high. With a shout, he led his men in a charge back toward that abandoned blue banner.

⁂

Dalinar's Plate leaked Stormlight from dozens of small breaks; no major piece had escaped damage. Light rose above him like steam from a cauldron, lingering as Stormlight did, slowly diffusing.

The sun beat down upon him, baking him as he fought. He was so tired. It hadn't been long since Sadeas's betrayal, not as time was counted in battles. But Dalinar had pushed himself hard, staying at the very front, fighting side by side with Adolin. His Plate had lost much Stormlight. It was growing heavier, and lent him less power with each swing. Soon it would weigh him down, slowing him so the Parsh-endi could swarm over him.

He'd killed many of them. So many. A frightening num-ber, and he did it without the Thrill. He was hollow inside. Better that than pleasure.

He hadn't killed nearly enough of them. They focused on Dalinar and Adolin; with Shardbearers on the front line, any breach would soon be patched by a man in gleaming armor and a deadly Blade. The Parshendi had to bring him and Adolin down first. They knew it. Dalinar knew it. Adolin knew it.

Stories spoke of battlefields where the Shardbearers were the last ones standing, pulled down by their enemies after long, heroic fights. Completely unrealistic. If you killed the Shardbearers first, you could take their Blades and turn them against the enemy.

He swung again, muscles lagging with fatigue. Dying

first. It was a good place to be. *Ask nothing of them you wouldn't do yourself. . . .* Dalinar stumbled on the rocks, his Shardplate feeling as heavy as regular armor.

He could be satisfied with the way he'd handled his own life. But his men . . . he had failed them. Thinking of the way he had stupidly led them into a trap, that sickened him.

And then there was Navani.

Of all the times to finally begin courting her, Dalinar thought. *Six years wasted. A lifetime wasted. And now she'll have to grieve again.*

That thought made him raise his arms and steady his feet on the stone. He fought off the Parshendi. Struggling on. For her. He would not let himself fall while he still had strength.

Nearby, Adolin's armor leaked as well. The youth was extending himself more and more to protect his father. There had been no discussion of trying, perhaps, to leap the chasms and flee. With chasms so wide, the chances were slim—but beyond that, they would not abandon their men to die. He and Adolin had lived by the Codes. They would die by the Codes.

Dalinar swung again, staying at Adolin's side, fighting in that just-out-of-reach tandem way of two Shardbearers. Sweat streamed down his face inside his helm, and he shot a final glance toward the disappearing army. It was just barely visible on the horizon. Dalinar's current position gave him a good view down to the west.

Let that man be cursed for . . .

For . . .

Blood of my fathers, what is that*?*

A small force was moving across the western plateau, running toward the Tower. A solitary bridge crew, carrying their bridge.

"It can't be," Dalinar said, stepping back from the fighting, letting the Cobalt Guard—what was left of them—rush in to defend him. Distrusting his eyes, he pushed his visor up. The rest of Sadeas's army was gone, but this single bridge crew remained. Why?

"Adolin!" he bellowed, pointing with his Shardblade, a surge of hope flooding his limbs.

The young man turned, tracing Dalinar's gesture. Adolin froze. "Impossible!" he yelled. "What kind of trap is that?"

"A foolish one, if it is a trap. We are already dead."

"But why would he send one back? What purpose?"

"Does it matter?"

They hesitated for a moment amid the battle. Both knew the answer.

"Assault formations!" Dalinar yelled, turning back to his troops. Stormfather, there were so few of them left. Less than half of his original eight thousand.

"Form up," Adolin called. "Get ready to move! We're going to punch through them, men. Gather everything you've got. We've got one chance!"

A slim one, Dalinar thought, pulling his visor down. *We'll have to cut through the rest of the Parshendi army.* Even if they reached the bottom, they'd probably find the crew dead, their bridge cast into the chasm. The Parshendi archers were already forming up; there were more than a hundred of them. It would be a slaughter.

But it was a hope. A tiny, precious hope. If his army was going to fall, it would do so while trying to seize that hope.

Raising his Shardblade high, feeling a surge of strength and determination, Dalinar charged forward at the head of his men.

⁙

For the second time in one day, Kaladin ran toward an armed Parshendi position, shield before him, wearing armor cut from the corpse of a fallen enemy. Perhaps he should have felt revolted at what he'd done in creating his armor. But it was no worse than what the Parshendi had done in killing Dunny, Maps, and that nameless man who had shown Kaladin kindness on his first day as a bridgemen. Kaladin still wore that man's sandals.

Us and them, he thought. That was the only way a soldier could think of it. For today, Dalinar Kholin and his men were part of the "us."

A group of Parshendi had seen the bridgemen approaching

and was setting up with bows. Fortunately, it appeared that Dalinar had seen Kaladin's band as well, for the army in blue was beginning to cut its way toward rescue.

It wasn't going to work. There were too many Parshendi, and Dalinar's men would be tired. It was another disaster. But for once, Kaladin charged into it with eyes wide open.

This is my choice, he thought as the Parshendi archers formed up. *It's not some angry god watching me, not some spren playing tricks, not some twist of fate.*

It's me. I chose to follow Tien. I chose to charge the Shardbearer and save Amaram. I chose to escape the slave pits. And now, I choose to try to rescue these men, though I know I will probably fail.

The Parshendi loosed their arrows, and Kaladin felt an exaltation. Tiredness evaporated, fatigue fled. He wasn't fighting for Sadeas. He wasn't working to line someone's pockets. He was fighting to protect.

The arrows zipped at him and he swung his shield in an arc, spraying them away. Others came, shooting this way and that, seeking his flesh. He stayed just ahead of them, leaping as they shot for his thighs, turning as they shot for his shoulders, raising his shield when they shot for his face. It wasn't easy, and more than a few arrows got close to him, scoring his breastplate or shin guards. But none hit. He was doing it. He was—

Something was wrong.

He spun between two arrows, confused.

"Kaladin!" Syl said, hovering nearby, back to her smaller form. "There!"

She pointed toward the other staging plateau, the one nearby that Dalinar had used for his assault. A large contingent of Parshendi had jumped across to that plateau and were kneeling down, raising bows. Pointed not at him, but right at Bridge Four's unshielded flank.

"No!" Kaladin screamed, Stormlight escaping from his mouth in a cloud. He turned and ran back across the rocky plateau toward the bridge crew. Arrows launched at him from behind. One took his backplate square on, but skidded aside. Another hit his helm. He leaped over a rocky rift, dashing with all the speed his Stormlight could lend him.

The Parshendi at the side were drawing. There were at least fifty of them. He was going to be too late. He was going to—

"Bridge Four!" he bellowed. "Side carry right!"

They hadn't practiced that maneuver in weeks, but their training was manifest as they obeyed without question, dropping the bridge to their side just as the archers loosed. The flight of arrows hit the bridge's deck, bristling across the wood. Kaladin let out a relieved breath, reaching the bridge team, who had slowed to carry the bridge on the side.

"Kaladin!" Rock said, pointing.

Kaladin spun. The archers behind, on the Tower, were drawing for a large volley.

The bridge crew was exposed. The archers loosed.

He yelled again, screaming out, Stormlight infusing the air around him as he threw every bit of it he had into his shield. The scream echoed in his ears; the Stormlight burst from him, his clothing freezing and cracking.

Arrows darkened the sky. Something *hit* him, an extended impact that tossed him backward into the bridgemen. He struck hard, grunting as the force continued to push upon him.

The bridge ground to a halt, the men stopping.

All fell still.

Kaladin blinked, feeling completely drained. His body hurt, his arms tingled, his back ached. There was a sharp pain in his wrist. He groaned, opening his eyes, stumbling as Rock's hands caught him from behind.

A muted thump. The bridge being set down. *Idiots!* Kaladin thought. *Don't set it down. . . . Retreat. . . .*

The bridgemen crowded around him as he slipped to the ground, overwhelmed by having expended too much Stormlight. He blinked at what he held before him, attached to his bleeding arm.

His shield was *covered* in arrows, dozens of them, some

splitting the others. The bones crossing the shield's front had shattered; the wood was in splinters. Some of the arrows had gone through and hit his forearm. That was the pain.

Over a hundred arrows. An entire volley. Pulled into a single shield.

"By the Brightcaller's rays," Drehy said softly. "What . . . what was . . ."

"It was like a fountain of light," Moash said, kneeling beside Kaladin. "Like the sun itself burst from you, Kaladin."

"The Parshendi . . ." Kaladin croaked, and let go of the shield. The straps were broken, and as he struggled to stand, the shield all but disintegrated, falling to pieces, scattering dozens of broken arrows at his feet. A few remained stuck in his arm, but he ignored the pain, looking across at the Parshendi.

The groups of archers on both plateaus froze in stunned postures. The ones in front began to call to one another in a language Kaladin didn't understand. "Neshua Kadal!" They stood up.

And then they fled.

"What?" Kaladin said.

"I don't know," Teft said, cradling his own wounded arm. "But we're getting you to safety. Blast this arm. Lopen!"

The shorter man brought Dabbid, and they ushered Kaladin away to a more secure location toward the center of the plateau. He held his arm, numb, his exhaustion so deep that he could barely think.

"Bridge up!" Moash called. "We've still got a job to do!"

The rest of the bridgemen grimly ran back to their bridge, hoisting it up. On the Tower, Dalinar's force was fighting its way through the Parshendi toward the possible safety of the bridge crew. *They must be taking such heavy losses . . .* Kaladin thought numbly.

He stumbled and fell to the ground; Teft and Lopen pulled Kaladin into a sheltered hollow, joining Skar and Dabbid. Skar's foot bandage reddened with seeping blood, the spear he'd been using as a staff resting beside him. *Thought I told him . . . to stay off that foot. . . .*

"We need spheres," Teft said. "Skar?"

"He asked for them this morning," the lean man said. "Gave him everything I had. I think most of the men did the same."

Teft cursed softly, pulling the remaining arrows from Kaladin's arm, then wrapping it with bandages.

"Is he going to be all right?" Skar asked.

"I don't know," Teft said. "I don't know anything. Kelek! I'm an idiot. Kaladin. Lad, can you hear me?"

"It's . . . just shock . . ." Kaladin said.

"You're looking strange, gancho," Lopen said nervously. "White."

"Your skin is ashen, lad," Teft said. "It looks like you did something to yourself back there. I don't know . . . I . . ." He cursed again, smacking his hand against the stone. "I should have listened. Idiot!"

They'd laid him on his side, and he could barely see the Tower. New groups of Parshendi—ones who hadn't seen Kaladin's display—were making for the chasm, bearing weapons. Bridge Four arrived and set down their bridge. They unstrapped their shields and hurriedly retrieved spears from the sacks of salvage tied at the bridge's side. Then the men went to their positions pushing at the sides, preparing to slide the bridge across the gap.

The Parshendi teams didn't have bows. They formed up to wait, weapons out. There were easily three times as many as there were bridgemen, and more were coming.

"We've got to go help," Skar said to Lopen and Teft.

The other two nodded, and all three—two wounded and one missing an arm—climbed to their feet. Kaladin tried to do likewise, but he fell back down, legs too weak to hold him.

"Stay, lad," Teft said, smiling. "We'll handle it just fine." They gathered some spears from a stock Lopen had put in his litter, then hobbled out to join the bridge crew. Even Dabbid joined them. He hadn't spoken since being wounded on that first bridge run, so long ago.

Kaladin crawled up to the lip of the depression, watching

[1147]

them. Syl landed on the stone beside him. "Storming fools," Kaladin muttered. "Shouldn't have followed me. Proud of them anyway."

"Kaladin . . ." Syl said.

"Is there anything you can do?" He was so *storming* tired. "Something to make me stronger?"

She shook her head.

A short distance ahead, the bridgemen began to push. The bridge's wood scraped loudly as it crossed the rocks, moving out over the chasm toward the waiting Parshendi. They began singing that harsh battle song, the one they did whenever they saw Kaladin in his armor.

The Parshendi looked eager, angry, deadly. They wanted blood. They would cut into the bridgemen and rip them apart, then drop the bridge—and their corpses—into the void beneath.

It's happening again, Kaladin thought, dazed and overwhelmed. He found himself curling up, drained and shaken. *I can't get to them. They'll die. Right in front of me. Tukks. Dead. Nelda. Dead. Goshel. Dead. Dallet. Cenn. Maps. Dunny. Dead. Dead. Dead . . .*

Tien.

Dead.

Lying huddled in a hollow in the rock. The sounds of battle ringing in the distance. Death surrounding him.

In a moment, he was there again, on that most horrible of days.

⁘

Kaladin stumbled through the cursing, screaming, fighting chaos of war, clinging to his spear. He'd dropped his shield. He needed to find a shield somewhere. Shouldn't he have a shield?

It was his third real battle. He'd been in Amaram's army only a few months, but already Hearthstone seemed a world away. He reached a hollow of rock and crouched down, pushing his back to it, breathing in and out, fingers slick on the spear's shaft. He was shaking.

He'd never realized how idyllic his life had been. Away from war. Away from death. Away from those screams, the cacophony of metal on metal, metal on wood, metal on flesh. He squeezed his eyes shut, trying to block it out.

No, he thought. *Open your eyes. Don't let them find you and kill you that easily.*

He forced his eyes open, then turned and peeked out over the battlefield. It was a complete mess. They fought on a large hillside, thousands of men on either side, intermixing and killing. How could anyone keep track of anything in this insanity?

Amaram's army—Kaladin's army—was trying to hold the hilltop. Another army, also Alethi, was trying to take it from them. That was all Kaladin knew. The enemy seemed more numerous than his own army.

He'll be safe, Kaladin thought. *He will be!*

But he had trouble convincing himself. Tien's stint as a messenger boy hadn't lasted long. Recruitment was down, he'd been told, and every hand that could hold a spear was needed. Tien and the other older messenger boys had been organized into several squads of deep reserves.

Dalar said those wouldn't ever be used. Probably. Unless the army was in serious danger. Did being surrounded atop a steep hill, their lines in chaos, constitute serious danger?

Get to the top, he thought, looking up the incline. Amaram's banner still flew up there. Their soldiers must be holding. All Kaladin could see was a churning mess of men in orange and the occasional bit of forest green.

Kaladin took off at a run up the side of the hill. He didn't turn as men shouted at him, didn't check to see which side they were from. Patches of grass pulled down in front of him. He stumbled over a few corpses, dashed around a couple of scraggly stumpweight trees, and avoided places where men were fighting.

There, he thought, noting a group of spearmen ahead, standing in a line, watching warily. Green. Amaram's colors. Kaladin scrambled up to them, and the soldiers let him pass.

"Which squad are you from, soldier?" said a stocky light-eyed man with the knots of a low captain.

"Dead, sir," Kaladin forced out. "All dead. We were in Brightlord Tashlin's company, and—"

"Bah," the man said, turning to a runner. "Third report we've had that Tashlin is down. Somebody warn Amaram. East side is weakening by degrees." He looked to Kaladin. "You, off to the reserves for reassignment."

"Yes, sir," Kaladin said, numb. He glanced down the way he'd come. The incline was littered with corpses, many of them in green. Even as he watched, a group of three stragglers rushing for the top was intercepted and slaughtered.

None of the men at the top moved to help them. Kaladin could have fallen just as easily, within yards of safety. He knew that it was probably important, strategically, that these soldiers in the line maintain their positions. But it seemed so heartless.

Find Tien, he thought, trotting off toward the reserves field on the north side of the wide hilltop. Here, however, he found only more chaos. Groups of dazed men, bloodied, getting sorted into new squads and sent back out onto the field. Kaladin moved through them, searching for the squad that had been created out of the messenger boys.

He found Dalar first. The lanky, three-fingered sergeant of the reserves stood beside a tall post bearing a pair of flapping triangular banners. He was assigning newly made squads to fill out losses in the companies fighting below. Kaladin could still hear the yells.

"You," Dalar said, pointing at Kaladin. "Squad reassignment is in that direction. Get moving!"

"I need to find the squad made from messenger boys," Kaladin said.

"Why in Damnation do you want to do that?"

"How should I know?" Kaladin said, shrugging, trying to remain calm. "I just follow orders."

Dalar grunted. "Brightlord Sheler's company. Southeast side. You can—"

Kaladin was already running. This wasn't supposed to happen. Tien was supposed to stay safe. Stormfather. It hadn't even been *four months* yet!

He made his way to the southeast side of the hill and

searched out a banner flapping a quarter of the way down the incline. The stark black glyphpair read *shesh lerel*—Sheler's company. Surprised at his own determination, Kaladin brushed past the soldiers guarding the hilltop and found himself on the battlefield again.

Things looked better over here. Sheler's company was holding its ground, although assaulted by a wave of enemies. Kaladin dashed down the incline, skidding in places, sliding on blood. His fear had vanished. It had been replaced by worry for his brother.

He arrived at the company line just as enemy squads were assaulting. He tried to scramble farther behind the lines to search for Tien, but he was caught in the wave of attacks. He stumbled to the side, joining a squad of spearmen.

The enemy was on them in a second. Kaladin held his spear in two hands, standing at the edge of the other spearmen and trying not to get in their way. He didn't really know what he was doing. He barely knew enough to use his shieldmate for protection. The exchange happened quickly, and Kaladin made only a single thrust. The enemy was rebuffed, and he managed to avoid taking a wound.

He stood, panting, gripping his spear.

"You," an authoritative voice said. A man was pointing at Kaladin, knots at his shoulders. The squadleader. "About time my team got some of those reinforcements. For a time there, I thought Varth was going to get every man. Where's your shield?"

Kaladin scrambled to grab one off a fallen soldier nearby. As he was working, the squadleader swore behind him. "Damnation. They're coming again. Two prongs this time. We can't hold like this."

A man in a green messenger's vest scrambled over a nearby rock formation. "Hold against the east assault, Mesh!"

"What about that wave to the south?" the squadleader—Mesh—bellowed.

"It's handled for now. Hold east! Those are your orders!" The messenger scrambled on, delivering a similar message to the next squad in line. "Varth. Your squad is to hold east!"

Kaladin got up with his shield. He needed to go find Tien. He couldn't—

He stumbled to a stop. There, in the next squad down the line, stood three figures. Younger boys, looking small in their armor and holding their spears uncertainly. One was Tien. His team of reserves had obviously been split apart to fill holes in other squads.

"Tien!" Kaladin screamed, falling out of line as the enemy troops came upon them. Why were Tien and the other two positioned in the *middle front* of the squad formation? They barely knew how to hold a spear!

Mesh yelled after Kaladin, but Kaladin ignored him. The enemy was upon them in a moment, and Mesh's squad broke, losing their discipline and turning to a more frenzied, unorganized resistance.

Kaladin felt something like a thump against his leg. He stumbled, hitting the ground, and realized with shock that he'd been stabbed with a spear. He felt no pain. Odd.

Tien! he thought, forcing himself up. Someone loomed above him, and Kaladin reacted immediately, rolling as a spear came down for his heart. His own spear was back in his hands before he realized he'd grabbed it, and he whipped it upward.

Then he froze. He'd just driven his spear through the enemy soldier's neck. It had happened so quickly. *I just killed a man.*

He rolled over, letting the enemy drop to his knees as Kaladin yanked his spear free. Varth's squad was back a little farther. The enemy hit it a little while after attacking where Kaladin had been. Tien and the other two were still in the front.

"Tien!" Kaladin yelled.

The boy looked toward him, eyes opening wide. He actually smiled. Behind him, the rest of the squad pulled back. Leaving the three untrained boys exposed.

And, sensing weakness, the enemy soldiers descended on Tien and the others. There was an armored lighteyes at their front, in gleaming steel. He swung a sword.

Kaladin's brother fell just like that. One eyeblink and he was standing there, looking terrified. The next he was on the ground.

"No!" Kaladin screamed. He tried to get to his feet, but slipped to his knees. His leg didn't work right.

Varth's squad hurried forward, attacking the enemies—who had been distracted with Tien and the other two. They'd placed the untrained at the front to stop the momentum of the enemy attack.

"No, no, no!" Kaladin screamed. He used his spear to hoist himself to his feet, then stumbled forward. It couldn't be what he thought. It couldn't be over that quickly.

It was a miracle that nobody struck Kaladin down as he stumbled the rest of the distance. He barely thought about it. He just watched where Tien had fallen. There was thunder. No. Hooves. Amaram had arrived with his cavalry, and they were sweeping through the enemy lines.

Kaladin didn't care. He finally reached the spot. There, he found three corpses: young, small, lying in a hollow in the stone. Horrified, numb, Kaladin reached out his hand and rolled over the one that was facedown.

Tien's dead eyes stared upward.

Kaladin continued to kneel beside the body. He should have bound his wound, should have moved back to safety, but he was too numb. He just knelt.

"About time he rode down here," a voice said.

Kaladin looked up, noting a group of spearmen gathering nearby, watching the cavalry.

"He wanted them to bunch up against us," one of the spearmen said. He had knots on the shoulders. Varth, their squadleader. Such keen eyes the man had. Not a brutish lout. Lean, thoughtful.

I should feel anger, Kaladin thought. *I should feel . . . something.*

Varth looked down at him, then at the bodies of the three dead messenger boys.

"You bastard," Kaladin hissed. "You put them in front."

"You work with what you have," Varth said, nodding to

his team, then pointing at a fortified position. "If they give me men who can't fight, I'll find another use for them." He hesitated as his team marched away. He seemed regretful. "Gotta do what you can to stay alive, son. Turn a liability into an advantage whenever you can. Remember that, if you live."

With that, he jogged off.

Kaladin looked down. *Why couldn't I protect him?* he thought, looking at Tien, remembering his brother's laugh. His innocence, his smile, his excitement at exploring the hills outside Hearthstone.

Please. Please let me protect him. Make me strong enough.

He felt so weak. Blood loss. He found himself slumping to the side, and with tired hands, he tied off his wound. And then, feeling terribly vacant inside, he lay down beside Tien and pulled the body close.

"Don't worry," Kaladin whispered. When had he started to cry? "I'll bring you home. I'll protect you, Tien. I'll bring you back. . . ."

He held the body into the evening, long past the end of the battle, clinging to it as it slowly grew cold.

⁂

Kaladin blinked. He wasn't in that hollow with Tien. He was on the plateau.

He could hear men dying in the distance.

He hated thinking of that day. He almost wished he'd never gone looking for Tien. Then he wouldn't have had to watch. Wouldn't have had to kneel there, powerless, as his brother was slaughtered.

It was happening again. Rock, Moash, Teft. They were all going to die. And here he lay, powerless again. He could barely move. He felt so *drained.*

"Kaladin," a voice whispered. He blinked. Syl was hovering in front of him. "Do you know the Words?"

"All I wanted to do was protect them," he whispered.

"That's why I've come. The Words, Kaladin."

"They're going to die. I can't save them. I—"

Amaram slaughtered his men in front of him.

A nameless Shardbearer killed Dallet.

A lighteyes killed Tien.

No.

Kaladin rolled over and forced himself to his feet, wavering on weak legs.

No!

Bridge Four hadn't set its bridge yet. That surprised him. They were still pushing it across the chasm, the Parshendi crowding up on the other side, eager, their song becoming more frantic. His delusions had seemed like hours, but had passed in just a few heartbeats.

NO!

Lopen's litter was in front of Kaladin. A spear rested amid the drained water bottles and ragged bandages, steel head reflecting sunlight. It whispered to him. It terrified him, and he loved it.

When the time comes, I hope you're ready. Because this lot will need you.

He seized the spear, the first real weapon he had held since his display in the chasm so many weeks ago. Then he started to run. Slowly at first. Picking up speed. Reckless, his body exhausted. But he did not stop. He pushed forward, harder, charging toward the bridge. It was only halfway across the chasm.

Syl shot out in front of him, looking back, worried. "The *Words*, Kaladin!"

Rock cried out as Kaladin ran onto the bridge as it was moving. The wood wobbled beneath him. It was out over the chasm, but hadn't reached the other side.

"Kaladin!" Teft yelled. "What are you doing?"

Kaladin screamed, reaching the end of the bridge. Finding a tiny surge of strength somewhere, he raised his spear and threw himself off the end of the wooden platform, launching into the air above the cavernous void.

Bridgemen cried out in dismay. Syl zipped about him with worry. Parshendi looked up with amazement as a lone bridgeman sailed through the air toward them.

His drained, worn-out body barely had any strength left.

In that moment of crystallized time, he looked down on his enemies. Parshendi with their marbled red and black skin. Soldiers raising finely crafted weapons, as if to cut him from the sky. Strangers, oddities in carapace breastplates and skullcaps. Many of them wearing beards.

Beards woven with glowing gemstones.

Kaladin breathed in.

Like the power of salvation itself—like rays of sunlight from the eyes of the Almighty—Stormlight exploded from those gemstones. It surged through the air, pulled in visible streams, like glowing columns of luminescent smoke. Twisting and turning and spiraling like tiny funnel clouds until they slammed into him.

And the storm came to life again.

Kaladin hit the rocky ledge, legs suddenly strong, mind, body, and blood *alive* with energy. He fell into a crouch, spear under his arm, a small ring of Stormlight expanding from him in a wave, pushed down to the stones by his fall. Stunned, the Parshendi shied away, eyes widening, song faltering.

A trickle of Stormlight closed the wounds on his arm. He smiled, spear held before him. It was as familiar as the body of a lover long lost.

THE WORDS, a voice said, urgent, as if directly into his mind. In that moment, Kaladin was amazed to realize that he knew them, though they'd never been told to him.

"I will protect those who cannot protect themselves," he whispered.

The Second Ideal of the Knights Radiant.

⁂

A *crack* shook the air, like an enormous clap of thunder, though the sky was completely clear. Teft stumbled back— having just set the bridge in place—and found himself gaping with the rest of Bridge Four. Kaladin *exploded* with energy.

A burst of whiteness washed out from him, a wave of white smoke. Stormlight. The force of it slammed into the first rank of Parshendi, tossing them backward, and Teft had to hold his hand up against the vibrancy of the light.

"Something just changed," Moash whispered, hand up. "Something important."

Kaladin raised his spear. The powerful light began to subside, retreating. A more subdued glow began to steam off his body. Radiant, like smoke from an ethereal fire.

Nearby, some of the Parshendi fled, though others stepped up, raising weapons in challenge. Kaladin spun into them, a living storm of steel, wood, and determination.

68

ESHONAI

"They named it the Final Desolation, but they lied. Our gods lied. Oh, how they lied. The Everstorm comes. I hear its whispers, see its stormwall, know its heart."

—Tanatanes 1173, 8 seconds pre-death. An Azish itinerant worker. Sample of particular note.

Soldiers in blue yelled, screaming war cries to encourage themselves. The sounds were like a roaring avalanche behind Adolin as he swung his Blade in wild swings. There was no room for a proper stance. He had to keep moving, punching through the Parshendi, leading his men toward the western chasm.

His father's horse and his own were still safe, carrying some wounded through the back ranks. The Shardbearers didn't dare mount, though. In these close quarters, the Ryshadium would be chopped down and their riders dropped.

This was the type of battlefield maneuver that would have been impossible without Shardbearers. A rush against superior numbers? Made by wounded, exhausted men? They should have been stopped cold and crushed.

But Shardbearers could not be stopped so easily. Their armor leaking Stormlight, their six-foot Blades flashing in wide swaths, Adolin and Dalinar shattered the Parshendi defenses, creating an opening, a rift. Their men—the best-trained in the Alethi warcamps—knew how to use it. They formed a wedge behind their Shardbearers, prying the Parshendi armies open, using spearman formations to cut through and keep going forward.

Adolin moved at almost a jog. The incline of the hill worked in their favor, giving them better footing, letting them rumble down the slope like charging chulls. The chance to survive when all had been thought lost gave the men a surge of energy for one last dash toward freedom.

They took enormous casualties. Already, Dalinar's force had lost another thousand of his four, probably more. But it didn't matter. The Parshendi fought to kill, but the Alethi—this time—fought to live.

❖

Living Heralds above, Teft thought, watching Kaladin fight. Just moments ago, the lad had looked near death, skin a dull grey, hands shaking. Now he was a shining whirlwind, a storm wielding a spear. Teft had known many a battlefield, but he had never seen anything remotely like this. Kaladin held the ground before the bridge by himself. White Stormlight streamed from him like a blazing fire. His speed was incredible, nearly inhuman, and his precision—each thrust of the spear hit a neck, side, or other unarmored target of Parshendi flesh.

It was more than the Stormlight. Teft had only a fragmentary recollection of the things his family had tried to teach him, but those memories all agreed. Stormlight did not grant skill. It could not make a man into something he was not. It enhanced, it strengthened, it invigorated.

It perfected.

Kaladin ducked low, slamming the butt against the leg of a Parshendi, dropping him to the ground, and came up to block an axe swing by catching the haft with that of his spear. He let go with one hand, sweeping the tip of the spear up under the arm of the Parshendi and ramming it into his armpit. As that Parshendi fell, Kaladin pulled his spear free and slammed the end into a Parshendi head that had gotten too close. The butt of the spear shattered with a spray of wood, and the Parshendi's carapace helm exploded.

No, this wasn't just Stormlight. This was a master of the spear with his capacity enhanced to astonishing levels.

The bridgemen gathered around Teft, amazed. His wounded arm didn't seem to hurt as much as it should. "He's like a part of the wind itself," Drehy said. "Pulled down and given life. Not a man at all. A spren."

"Sigzil?" Skar asked, eyes wide. "You ever seen anything like this?"

The dark-skinned man shook his head.

"Stormfather," Peet whispered. "What . . . what *is* he?"

"He's our bridgeleader," Teft said, snapping out of his reverie. On the other side of the chasm, Kaladin barely dodged a blow from a Parshendi mace. "And he needs our help! First and second teams, you take the left side. Don't let the Parshendi get around him. Third and fourth teams, you're with me on the right! Rock and Lopen, you be ready to pull back any wounded. The rest of you, wrinkled wall formation. Don't attack, just stay alive and keep them back. And Lopen, toss him a spear that isn't broken!"

⟡

Dalinar roared, striking down a group of Parshendi swordsmen. He charged over their bodies, running up a short incline and throwing himself in a leap, dropping several feet into the Parshendi below, sweeping out with his Blade. His armor was an enormous weight upon his back, but the energy of his struggle kept him going. The Cobalt Guard—the straggling members who were left—roared and leaped off the incline behind him.

They were doomed. Those bridgemen would be dead by now. But Dalinar blessed them for their sacrifice. It might have been meaningless as an end, but it had changed the journey. *This* was how his soldiers should fall—not cornered and frightened, but fighting with passion.

He would not slide quietly into the dark. No indeed. He

shouted his defiance again as he smashed into a group of Parshendi, whirling and hauling his Shardblade in a circling sweep. He stumbled through the patch of dead Parshendi, their eyes burning as they fell.

And Dalinar burst out onto open stone.

He blinked, stunned. *We did it,* he thought in disbelief. *We cut all the way through.* Behind him, soldiers roared, their tired voices sounding nearly as amazed as he felt. Just ahead of him, a final group of Parshendi lay between Dalinar and the chasm. But their backs were turned to him. Why were they—

The bridgemen.

The *bridgemen* were fighting. Dalinar gaped, lowering Oathbringer with numb arms. That little force of bridgemen held the bridgehead, fighting desperately against the Parshendi who were trying to force them back.

It was the most amazing, most *glorious* thing Dalinar had ever seen.

Adolin let out a whoop, breaking through the Parshendi to Dalinar's left. The younger man's armor was scratched, cracked, and scored, and his helm had shattered, leaving his head dangerously exposed. But his face was exultant.

"Go, go," Dalinar bellowed, pointing. "Give them support, storm it! If those bridgemen fall, we're all dead!"

Adolin and the Cobalt Guard dashed forward. Gallant and Sureblood, Adolin's Ryshadium, galloped past, carrying three wounded each. Dalinar hated to have left so many wounded on the slopes, but the Codes were clear. In this case, protecting the men he could save was more important.

Dalinar turned to strike at the main body of Parshendi to his left, making certain the corridor remained open for his troops. Many of the soldiers scrambled toward safety, though several squads proved their mettle by forming up at the sides to keep fighting, opening the gap wider. Sweat had soaked through the brow rag attached to Dalinar's helm, and drops of it fell, overwhelming his eyebrows and falling into his left eye. He cursed, reaching to open his visor—then froze.

The enemy troops were parting. There, standing among

them, was a seven-foot-tall giant of a Parshendi in gleaming silver Shardplate. It fit as only Plate could, having molded to his large stature. His Shardblade was wicked and barbed, like flames frozen into metal. He raised it to Dalinar in a salute.

"Now?" Dalinar bellowed incredulously. "*Now* you come?"

The Shardbearer stepped forward, steel boots clanking on stone. The other Parshendi backed away.

"Why not earlier?" Dalinar demanded, hurriedly setting himself into Windstance, blinking his left eye against the sweat. He stood near the shadow of a large, oblong rock formation shaped like a book on its side. "Why wait out the entire battle only to attack now? When . . ."

When Dalinar was about to get away. Apparently the Parshendi Shardbearer had been willing to let his fellows throw themselves at Dalinar when it seemed obvious he would fall. Perhaps they let the regular soldiers try to win Shards, as was done in human armies. Now that Dalinar might escape, the potential loss of a Plate and Blade was too great, and so the Shardbearer had been sent to fight him.

The Shardbearer stepped up, speaking in the thick Parshendi language. Dalinar didn't understand a word of it. He raised his Blade and fell into stance. The Parshendi said something further, then grunted and stepped forward, swinging.

Dalinar cursed to himself, still blinded in his left eye. He dodged back, swinging his Blade and slapping the enemy's weapon. The parry shook Dalinar inside his armor. His muscles responded sluggishly. Stormlight still leaked from cracks in his armor, but it was abating. It wouldn't be much longer before the Plate stopped responding.

The Parshendi Shardbearer attacked again. His stance was unfamiliar to Dalinar, but there was something practiced about it. This wasn't a savage playing with a powerful weapon. He was a trained Shardbearer. Dalinar was once again forced to parry, something Windstance wasn't intended to do. His weight-laden muscles were too sluggish to dodge, and his Plate was too cracked to risk letting himself get hit.

The blow nearly threw him out of stance. He clenched his

teeth, throwing weight behind his weapon and intentionally overcorrecting as the Parshendi's next blow came. The Blades met with a furious clang, throwing off a shower of sparks like a bucket of molten metal dashed into the air.

Dalinar recovered quickly and threw himself forward, trying to slam his shoulder into his enemy's chest. The Parshendi was still full of power, however, his Plate uncracked. He got out of the way and quite nearly hit Dalinar on the back.

Dalinar twisted just in time. Then he turned and leaped onto a small rock formation, then stepped to a higher ledge and managed to reach the top. The Parshendi followed, as Dalinar had hoped. The precarious footing raised the stakes—which was just fine with him. A single blow could ruin Dalinar. That meant taking risks.

As the Parshendi neared the top of the formation, Dalinar attacked, using the advantage of surer footing and high ground. The Parshendi didn't bother dodging. He took a hit to the helm, which cracked, but gained a chance to swing at Dalinar's legs.

Dalinar leaped backward, feeling painfully sluggish. He barely got out of the way, and wasn't able to get in a second strike as the Parshendi climbed atop the formation.

The Parshendi man made an aggressive thrust. Setting his jaw, Dalinar raised his forearm to block and stepped into the attack, praying to the Heralds that his forearm plate would deflect the blow. The Parshendi sword connected, shattering the Plate, sending a shock up Dalinar's arm. The gauntlet on his fist suddenly felt like a lead weight, but Dalinar kept moving, swinging his sword for his own attack.

Not at the Parshendi's armor, but at the stone beneath him.

Even as the molten shards of Dalinar's forearm plate sprayed in the air, he sheared through the rock shelf under his opponent's feet. The entire section broke free, sending the Shardbearer tumbling backward toward the ground. He hit with a crash.

Dalinar slammed his fist—the one with the broken armguard—into the ground and released the gauntlet. It unlatched and he pulled his hand free into the air, sweat making it feel cold. He left the gauntlet—it wouldn't work properly now that the forearm piece was gone—and roared as he swung his Blade single-handed. He sliced through another chunk of the rock and sent it falling down toward the Shardbearer.

The Parshendi stumbled to his feet, but the rock smashed down on top of him, sending out a splash of Stormlight and a deep cracking sound. Dalinar climbed down, trying to get to the Parshendi while he was still. Unfortunately, Dalinar's right leg was dragging, and when he reached the ground, he walked in a limp. If he took the boot off, he wouldn't be able to hold up the rest of the Shardplate.

He gritted his teeth, stopping as the Parshendi stood up. He'd been too slow. The Parshendi's armor, though cracked in several places, was nowhere near as strained as Dalinar's. Impressively, he'd managed to retain his Shardblade. He leveled his armored head at Dalinar, eyes hidden behind the slit in the helm. Around them, the other Parshendi watched silently, forming a ring, but not interfering.

Dalinar raised his Blade, holding it in one gauntleted hand and one bare one. The breeze was cold on his clammy, exposed hand.

There was no use running. He fought here.

◆◆◆

For the first time in many, many months, Kaladin felt fully awake and alive.

The beauty of the spear, whistling in the air. The unity of body and mind, hands and feet reacting instantly, faster than thoughts could be formed. The clarity and familiarity of the old spear forms, learned during the most terrible time in his life.

His weapon was an extension of himself; he moved it as easily and instinctively as he did his fingers. Spinning, he cut through the Parshendi, bringing retribution to those who had slaughtered so many of his friends. Repayment for each and every arrow loosed at his flesh.

With Stormlight making an ecstatic pulse within him, he

felt a rhythm to the battle. Almost like the beat of the Parsh-endi song.

And they did sing. They'd recovered from seeing him drink in the Stormlight and speak the Words of the Second Ideal. They now attacked in waves, fervently trying to get to the bridge and knock it free. Some had leaped to the other side to attack from that direction, but Moash had led bridgemen to respond there. Amazingly, they held.

Syl twirled around Kaladin in a blur, riding the waves of Stormlight that rose from his skin, moving like a leaf on the winds of a storm. Enraptured. He'd never seen her like this before.

He didn't break his attacks—in a way, there was only *one* attack, as each strike flowed directly into the next. His spear never stopped, and together with his men, he pushed the Parsh-endi back, accepting each challenge as they stepped forward in pairs.

Killing. Slaughtering. Blood flew in the air and the dying groaned at his feet. He tried not to pay too much attention to that. They were the enemy. Yet the sheer glory of what he did seemed at odds with the desolation he caused.

He was protecting. He was saving. Yet he was killing. How could something so terrible be so beautiful at the same time?

He ducked the swing of a fine silvery sword, then brought his spear around to the side, crushing ribs. He spun the spear, shattering its already fractured length against the side of the Parshendi's comrade. He threw the remains at a third man, then caught a new spear as Lopen tossed it to him. The Herda-zian was collecting them from the fallen Alethi nearby to give to Kaladin when needed.

When you engaged a man, you learned something about him. Were your enemies careful and precise? Did they bully their way forward, aggressive and domineering? Did they spout curses to make you enraged? Were they ruthless, or did they leave an obviously incapacitated man to live?

He was impressed by the Parshendi. He fought dozens of

them, each with a slightly different style of combat. It seemed they were sending only two or four at him at a time. Their attacks were careful and controlled, and each pair fought as a team. They seemed to respect him for his skill.

Most telling, they seemed to back away from fighting Skar or Teft, who were wounded, instead focusing on Kaladin, Moash, and the other spearmen who showed the most skill. These were not the wild, uncultured savages he had been led to expect. These were professional soldiers who held to an honorable battlefield ethic he had found absent in most of the Alethi. In them, he found what he'd always hoped he would find in the soldiers of the Shattered Plains.

That realization rocked him. He found himself *respecting* the Parshendi as he killed them.

In the end, the storm within drove him forward. He had chosen a course, and these Parshendi would slaughter Dalinar Kholin's army without a moment's regret. Kaladin had committed himself. He would see himself and his men through it.

He wasn't certain how long he fought. Bridge Four held out remarkably well. Surely they didn't fight for very long, otherwise they would have been overwhelmed. Yet the multitude of wounded and dying Parshendi around Kaladin seemed to indicate hours.

He was both relieved and oddly disappointed when a figure in Plate broke through the Parshendi ranks, releasing a flood of soldiers in blue. Kaladin reluctantly stepped back, heart thumping, the storm within dampened. The light had stopped streaming off his skin noticeably. The continual supply of Parshendi with gems in their braids had kept him fueled during the early part of the fight, but the later ones had come to him without gemstones. Another indication that they weren't the simpleminded subhumans the lighteyes claimed they were. They'd seen what he was doing, and even if they hadn't understood it, they'd countered it.

He had enough Light to keep him from collapsing. But as the Alethi pushed back the Parshendi, Kaladin realized how timely their arrival had been.

I need to be very careful with this, he thought. The storm within made him thirst for motion and attack, but using it drained his body. The more of it he used, and the faster he used it, the worse it was when he ran out.

Alethi soldiers took up perimeter defense on both sides of the bridge, and the exhausted bridgemen fell back, many sitting down and holding wounds. Kaladin hurried over to them. "Report!"

"Three dead," Rock said grimly, kneeling beside bodies he'd laid out. Malop, Earless Jaks, and Narm.

Kaladin frowned in sorrow. *Be glad the rest live,* he told himself. It was easy to think. Hard to accept. "How are the rest of you?"

Five more had serious wounds, but Rock and Lopen had seen to them. Those two were learning quite well from Kaladin's instruction. There was little more Kaladin could do for the wounded. He glanced at Malop's body. The man had taken an axe cut to the arm, severing it and splintering the bone. He'd died from blood loss. If Kaladin hadn't been fighting, he might have been able to—

No. No regrets for the moment.

"Pull back across," he said to the bridgemen, pointing. "Teft, you're in command. Moash, you strong enough to stay with me?"

"Sure am," Moash said, a grin on his bloody face. He looked excited, not exhausted. All three of the dead had been on his side, but he and the others had fought remarkably well.

The other bridgemen retreated. Kaladin turned to inspect the Alethi soldiers. It was like looking into a triage tent. Every man had a wound of some sort. The ones at the center stumbled and limped. Those at the outsides still fought, their uniforms bloodied and torn. The retreat had dissolved into chaos.

He made his way through the wounded, waving for them to cross the bridge. Some did as he said. Others stood about, looking dazed. Kaladin rushed up to one group that seemed better off than most. "Who's in command here?"

"It . . ." The soldier's face had been cut across the cheek. "Brightlord Dalinar."

"Immediate command. Who's your captain?"

"Dead," the man said. "And my companylord. And his second."

Stormfather, Kaladin thought. "Across the bridge with you," he said, then moved on. "I need an officer! Who's in command of the retreat?"

Ahead, he could make out a figure in scratched blue Shardplate, fighting at the front of the group. That would be Dalinar's son Adolin. He was busy holding the Parshendi off; bothering him would not be wise.

"Over here," a man called. "I've found Brightlord Havar! He's commander of the rear guard!"

Finally, Kaladin thought, rushing through the chaos to find a bearded lighteyed man lying on the ground, coughing blood. Kaladin looked him over, noting the enormous gut wound. "Who's his second?"

"Dead," said the man beside the commander. He was lighteyed.

"And you are?" Kaladin asked.

"Nacomb Gaval." He looked young, younger than Kaladin.

"You're promoted," Kaladin said. "Get these men across the bridge as quickly as possible. If anyone asks, you've been given a field commission as commander of the rear guard. If anyone claims to outrank you, send them to me."

The man started. "Promoted . . . Who are you? Can you *do* that?"

"Someone needs to," Kaladin snapped. "Go. Get to work."

"I—"

"*Go!*" Kaladin bellowed.

Remarkably, the lighteyed man saluted him and began yelling for his squad. Kholin's men were wounded, battered, and dazed, but they were well trained. Once someone took command, orders passed quickly. Squads crossed the bridge, falling into marching formations. Likely, in the confusion, they clung to these familiar patterns.

Within minutes, the central mass of Kholin's army was flowing across the bridge like sand in an hourglass. The ring of fighting contracted. Still, men screamed and died in the anarchic tumult of sword against shield and spear against metal.

Kaladin hurriedly pulled the carapace off his armor—enraging the Parshendi didn't feel wise at the moment—then moved among the wounded, looking for more officers. He found a couple, though they were dazed, wounded, and out of breath. Apparently, those who were still battle-worthy were leading the two flanks who held back the Parshendi.

Trailed by Moash, Kaladin hurried to the central front line, where the Alethi seemed to be holding the best. Here, finally, he found someone in command: a tall, stately light-eyes with a steel breastplate and matching helm, his uniform a darker shade of blue than the others. He directed the fighting from just behind the front lines.

The man nodded to Kaladin, yelling to be heard over the sounds of battle. "You command the bridgemen?"

"I do," Kaladin said. "Why aren't your men moving across the bridge?"

"We are the Cobalt Guard," the man said. "Our duty is to protect Brightlord Adolin." The man pointed toward Adolin in his blue Shardplate just ahead. The Shardbearer seemed to be pushing toward something.

"Where's the highprince?" Kaladin yelled.

"We're not sure." The man grimaced. "His guardsmen have vanished."

"You *have* to pull back. The bulk of the army is across. If you remain here, you'll be surrounded!"

"We will not leave Brightlord Adolin. I'm sorry."

Kaladin looked around. The groups of Alethi fighting at the flanks were barely holding their ground, but they wouldn't fall back until ordered.

"Fine," Kaladin said, raising his spear and pushing his way through to the front line. Here, the Parshendi fought with vigor. Kaladin cut down one by the neck, spinning into the middle of a group, flashing out with his spear. His Stormlight was nearly gone, but these Parshendi had gemstones in their beards. Kaladin breathed in—just a little, so as to not reveal himself to the Alethi soldiers—and launched into a full attack.

The Parshendi fell back before his furious assault, and the

few members of the Cobalt Guard around him stumbled away, looking stunned. In seconds, Kaladin had a dozen Parshendi on the ground around him, wounded or dead. That opened a gap, and he tore through, Moash on his heels.

A lot of the Parshendi were focused on Adolin, whose blue Shardplate was scraped and cracked. Kaladin had never seen a suit of Shardplate in such a terrible state. Stormlight rose from those cracks in much the way it steamed from Kaladin's skin when he held—or used—a lot of it.

The fury of a Shardbearer at war gave Kaladin pause. He and Moash stopped just outside of the man's fighting range, and the Parshendi ignored the bridgemen, trying with obvious desperation to take down the Shardbearer. Adolin cut down multiple men at once—but, as Kaladin had seen only once before, his Blade did not slice flesh. Parshendi eyes burned and blackened, and dozens fell dead, Adolin collecting corpses around him like ripened fruit falling from a tree.

And yet, Adolin was obviously struggling. His Shardplate was more than just cracked—there were holes in parts. His helm was gone, though he'd replaced it with a regular spearman's cap. His left leg limped, nearly dragging. That Blade of his was deadly, but the Parshendi drew closer and closer.

Kaladin didn't dare step into range. "Adolin Kholin!" he bellowed.

The man kept fighting.

"Adolin Kholin!" Kaladin yelled again, feeling a little puff of Stormlight leave him, his voice booming.

The Shardbearer paused, then looked back at Kaladin. Reluctantly, the Shardbearer pulled back, letting the Cobalt Guard—using the path opened by Kaladin—rush forward and hold back the Parshendi.

"Who are you?" Adolin demanded, reaching Kaladin. His proud, youthful face was slick with sweat, his hair a matted mess of blond mixed with black.

"I'm the man who saved your life," Kaladin said. "I need you to order the retreat. Your troops can't fight any longer."

"My father is out there, bridgeman," Adolin said, pointing with his overly large Blade. "I saw him just moments ago.

His Ryshadium went for him, but neither horse nor man has returned. I'm going to lead a squad to—"

"You are going to *retreat*!" Kaladin said, exasperated. "Look at your men, Kholin! They can barely keep their feet, let alone fight. You're losing dozens by the minute. You need to get them out."

"I won't abandon my father," Adolin said stubbornly.

"For the peace of . . . If you fall, Adolin Kholin, these men have *nothing*. Their commanders are wounded or dead. You can't go to your father; you can barely walk! I repeat, *get your men to safety*!"

The young Shardbearer stepped back, blinking at Kaladin's tone. He looked northeastward, toward where a figure in slate grey suddenly appeared on a rock outcropping, fighting against another figure in Shardplate. "He's so close. . . ."

Kaladin took a deep breath. "I'll go for him. You lead the retreat. Hold the bridge, but only the bridge."

Adolin glared at Kaladin. He took a step, but something in his armor gave out, and he stumbled, going to one knee. Teeth gritted, he managed to rise. "Captainlord Malan," Adolin bellowed. "Take your soldiers, go with this man. Get my father out!"

The man Kaladin had spoken to earlier saluted crisply. Adolin glared at Kaladin again, then hefted his Shardblade and stalked with difficulty toward the bridge.

"Moash, go with him," Kaladin said.

"But—"

"Do it, Moash," Kaladin said grimly, glancing toward the outcropping where Dalinar fought. Kaladin took a deep breath, tucked his spear under his arm, and dashed off at a dead run.

The Cobalt Guard yelled at him, trying to keep up, but he didn't look back. He hit the line of Parshendi attackers, turned and tripped two with his spear, then leaped over the bodies and kept going. Most Parshendi in this patch were distracted by Dalinar's fight or the battle to get to the bridge; the ranks were thin here between the two fronts.

Kaladin moved quickly, drawing in more Light as he

ran, dodging and scrambling around Parshendi who tried to engage him. Within moments, he'd reached the place where Dalinar had been fighting. Though the rock shelf was now empty, a large group of Parshendi were gathered around its base.

There, he thought, leaping forward.

⋄⋆⋄

A horse whinnied. Dalinar looked up in shock as Gallant charged into the open ring of ground the watching Parshendi had made. The Ryshadium had come to him. How . . . where . . . ? The horse should have been free and safe on the staging plateau.

It was too late. Dalinar was on one knee, beaten down by the enemy Shardbearer. The Parshendi kicked, smashing his foot into Dalinar's chest, throwing him backward.

A blow to the helm followed. Another. Another. The helm exploded, and the force of the blows left Dalinar dazed. Where was he? What was happening? Why was he pinned by something so heavy?

Shardplate, he thought, struggling to rise. *I'm wearing . . . my Shardplate. . . .*

A breeze blew across his face. Head blows; you had to be careful of head blows, even when wearing Plate. His enemy stood over him, looming, and seemed to inspect him. As if searching for something.

Dalinar had dropped his Blade. The common Parshendi soldiers surrounded the duel. They forced Gallant back, making the horse whinny. He reared. Dalinar watched him, vision swimming.

Why didn't the Shardbearer just finish him? The Parshendi giant leaned down, then spoke. The words were thickly accented, and Dalinar's mind nearly dismissed them. But here, up close, Dalinar realized something. He understood what was being said. The accent was nearly impenetrable, but the words were in *Alethi.*

"It *is* you," the Parshendi Shardbearer said. "I have found you at last."

Dalinar blinked in surprise.

Something disturbed the back ranks of the watching Parshendi soldiers. There was something familiar about this scene, Parshendi all around, Shardbearer in danger. Dalinar had lived it before, but from the other side.

That Shardbearer couldn't be talking to him. Dalinar had been hit too hard on the head. He must be delusional. What was that disturbance in the ring of Parshendi watchers?

Sadeas, Dalinar found himself thinking, his mind confused. *He's come to rescue me, as I rescued him.*

Unite them. . . .

He'll come, Dalinar thought. *I know he will. I will gather them. . . .*

The Parshendi were yelling, moving, twisting. Suddenly, a figure exploded through them. Not Sadeas at all. A young man with a strong face and long, curling black hair. He carried a spear.

And he was glowing.

What? Dalinar thought, dazed.

⁂

Kaladin landed in the open circle. The two Shardbearers were at the center, one on the ground, Stormlight trailing faintly from his body. Too faintly. Considering the number of cracks, his gemstones must be almost spent. The other—a Parshendi, judging by the size and shape of the limbs—was standing over the fallen one.

Great, Kaladin thought, dashing forward before the Parshendi soldiers could collect their wits and attack him. The Parshendi Shardbearer was bent down, focused on Dalinar. The Parshendi's Plate was leaking Stormlight through a large fissure in the leg.

So—memory flashing back to the time he rescued Amaram—Kaladin got in close and slammed his spear into the crack.

The Shardbearer screamed and dropped his Blade in surprise. It puffed to mist. Kaladin whipped his spear free and dodged backward. The Shardbearer swung toward him with a

[1173]

gauntleted fist, but missed. Kaladin jumped in and—throwing his full strength behind the blow—rammed his spear into the cracked leg armor again.

The Shardbearer screamed even louder, stumbling, then fell to his knees. Kaladin tried to pull his spear free, but the man crumpled on top of it, snapping the shaft. Kaladin dodged back, now facing a ring of Parshendi, empty-handed, Storm-light streaming from his body.

Silence. And then, they began speaking again, the words they'd said before. "Neshua Kadal!" They passed it among themselves, whispering, looking confused. Then they began to chant a song he'd never heard before.

Good enough, Kaladin thought. So long as they weren't attacking him. Dalinar Kholin was moving, sitting up. Kaladin knelt down, commanding most of his Stormlight into the stony ground, retaining just enough to keep him going, but not enough to make him glow. Then he hurried over to the armored horse at the side of the ring of Parshendi.

The Parshendi shied away from him, looking terrified. He took the reins and quickly returned to the highprince.

⁖

Dalinar shook his head, trying to clear his mind. His vision still swam, but his thoughts were re-forming. What had happened? He'd been hit on the head, and . . . and now the Shard-bearer was down.

Down? What had caused the Shardbearer to fall? Had the creature really talked to him? No, he must have imagined that. That, and the young spearman glowing. He wasn't doing so now. Holding Gallant's reins, the young man waved at Dalinar urgently. Dalinar forced himself to his feet. Around them, the Parshendi were muttering something unintelligible.

That Shardplate, Dalinar thought, looking at the kneeling Parshendi. *A Shardblade . . . I could fulfill my promise to Renarin. I could . . .*

The Shardbearer groaned, holding his leg with a gauntleted hand. Dalinar itched to finish the kill. He took a step forward, dragging his unresponsive foot. Around them, the Parshendi troops watched silently. Why didn't they attack?

The tall spearman ran up to Dalinar, pulling Gallant's reins. "On your horse, lighteyes."

"We should finish him. We could—"

"On your horse!" the youth commanded, tossing the reins at him as the Parshendi troops turned to engage a contingent of approaching Alethi soldiers.

"You're supposed to be an honorable one," the spearman snarled. Dalinar had rarely been spoken to in such a way, particularly by a darkeyed man. "Well, your men won't leave without *you*, and *my* men won't leave without *them*. So you *will* get on your horse and we *will* escape this deathtrap. Do you understand?"

Dalinar met the young man's eyes. Then nodded. Of course. He was right; they had to leave the enemy Shardbearer. How would they get the armor out, anyway? Tow the corpse all the way?

"Retreat!" Dalinar bellowed to his soldiers, pulling himself into Gallant's saddle. He barely made it, his armor had so little Stormlight left.

Steady, loyal Gallant sprang into a gallop down the corridor of escape his men had bought for him with their blood. The nameless spearman dashed behind him, and the Cobalt Guard fell in around them. A larger force of his troops was ahead, on the escape plateau. The bridge still stood, Adolin waiting anxiously at its head, holding it for Dalinar's retreat.

With a rush of relief, Dalinar galloped across the wooden deck, reaching the adjoining plateau. Adolin and the last of his troops filed along behind him.

He turned Gallant, looking eastward. The Parshendi crowded up to the chasm, but did not give chase. A group of them worked on the chrysalis atop the plateau. It had been forgotten by all sides in the furor. They had never followed before, but if they changed their mind now, they could harry Dalinar's force all the way back to the permanent bridges.

But they didn't. They formed ranks and began to chant

another of their songs, the same one they sang every time the Alethi forces retreated. As Dalinar watched, a figure in cracked, silvery Shardplate and a red cape stumbled to their forefront. The helm had been removed, but it was too distant to make out any features on the black and red marbled skin. Dalinar's erstwhile foe raised his Shardblade in a motion that was unmistakable. A salute, a gesture of respect. Instinctively, Dalinar summoned his Blade, and ten heartbeats later raised it to salute in return.

The bridgemen pulled the bridge across the chasm, separating the armies.

"Set up triage," Dalinar bellowed. "We don't leave anyone behind who has a chance at living. The Parshendi will not attack us here!"

His men let out a shout. Somehow, escaping felt like more of a victory than any gemheart they'd won. The tired Alethi troops divided into battalions. Eight had marched to battle, and they became eight again—though several had only a few hundred members remaining. Those men trained for field surgery looked through the ranks while the remaining officers got survivor counts. The men began to sit down among the painspren and exhaustionspren, bloodied, some weaponless, many with torn uniforms.

On the other plateau, the Parshendi continued their odd song.

Dalinar found himself focusing on the bridge crew. The youth who had saved him was apparently their leader. Had he fought down a *Shardbearer*? Dalinar hazily remembered a quick, sharp encounter, a spear to the leg. Clearly the young man was both skilled and lucky.

The bridgeman's team acted with far more coordination and discipline than Dalinar would have expected of such lowly men. He could wait no longer. Dalinar nudged Gallant forward, crossing the stones and passing wounded, exhausted soldiers. That reminded him of his own fatigue, but now that he had a chance to sit, he was recovering, his head no longer ringing.

The leader of the bridge crew was seeing to a man's

wound, and his fingers worked with expertise. A man trained in field medicine, among *bridgemen*?

Well, why not? Dalinar thought. *It's no odder than their being able to fight so well.* Sadeas had been holding out on him.

The young man looked up. And, for the first time, Dalinar noticed the slave brands on his forehead, hidden by the long hair. The youth stood, posture hostile, folding his arms.

"You are to be commended," Dalinar said. "All of you. Why did your highprince retreat, only to send you back for us?"

Several of the bridgemen chuckled.

"He didn't send us back," their leader said. "We came on our own. Against his wishes."

Dalinar found himself nodding, and he realized that this was the only answer that made sense. "Why?" Dalinar asked. "Why come for us?"

The youth shrugged. "You allowed yourself to get trapped in there quite spectacularly."

Dalinar nodded tiredly. Perhaps he should have been annoyed at the young man's tone, but it was only the truth. "Yes, but *why* did you come? And how did you learn to fight so well?"

"By accident," the young man said. He turned back to his wounded.

"What can I do to repay you?" Dalinar asked.

The bridgeman looked back at him. "I don't know. We were going to flee from Sadeas, disappear in the confusion. We might still, but he'll certainly hunt us down and kill us."

"I could take your men to my camp, make Sadeas free you from your bondage."

"I worry that he wouldn't let us go," the bridgeman said, eyes haunted. "And I worry that your camp would offer no safety at all. This move today by Sadeas. It will mean war between you two, will it not?"

Would it? Dalinar had avoided thinking of Sadeas—survival had taken his focus—but his anger at the man was a seething pit deep within. He *would* exact revenge on Sadeas for this. But could he allow war between the princedoms? It would shatter Alethkar. More than that, it would destroy the Kholin house. Dalinar didn't have the troops or the allies to stand against Sadeas, not after this disaster.

How would Sadeas respond when Dalinar returned? Would he try to finish the job, attacking? *No,* Dalinar thought. *No, he did it this way for a reason.* Sadeas had not engaged him personally. He had abandoned Dalinar, but by Alethi standards, that was another thing entirely. He didn't want to risk the kingdom either.

Sadeas wouldn't want outright war, and Dalinar couldn't *afford* outright war, despite his seething anger. He formed a fist, turning to look at the spearman. "It will not turn to war," Dalinar said. "Not yet, at least."

"Well, if that's the case," the spearman said, "then by taking us into your camp, you commit robbery. The king's law, the Codes my men always claim you uphold, would demand that you return us to Sadeas. He *won't* let us go easily."

"I will take care of Sadeas," Dalinar said. "Return with me. I vow that you will be safe. I promise it with every shred of honor I have."

The young bridgeman met his eyes, searching for something. Such a hard man he was for one so young.

"All right," the spearman said. "We'll return. I can't leave my men back at camp and—with so many men now wounded—we don't have the proper supplies to run."

The young man turned back to his work, and Dalinar rode Gallant in search of a casualty report. He forced himself to contain his rage at Sadeas. It was difficult. No, Dalinar could not let this turn to war—but neither could he let things go back to the way they had been.

Sadeas had upset the balance, and it could never be regained. Not in the same way.

Charcoal rubbing of a relief of Nalan'Elin carved on the wall of His Majesty Elhokar Kholin's palace at the Shattered Plains, circa 1173.

69

JUSTICE

"All is withdrawn for me. I stand against the one who saved my life. I protect the one who killed my promises. I raise my hand. The storm responds."

—Tanatanev 1173, 18 seconds pre-death. A darkeyed mother of four in her sixty-second year.

Navani pushed her way past the guards, ignoring their protests and the calls of her attending ladies. She forced herself to remain calm. She *would* remain calm! What she had heard was just rumor. It *had* to be.

Unfortunately, the older she grew, the worse she became at maintaining a brightlady's proper tranquility. She hastened her step through Sadeas's warcamp. Soldiers raised hands toward her as she passed, either to offer her aid or to demand she halt. She ignored both; they'd never dare lay a finger on her. Being the king's mother gained one a few privileges.

The camp was messy and poorly laid out. Pockets of merchants, whores, and workers made their homes in shanties built on the leeward sides of barracks. Drippings of hardened crem hung from most leeward eaves, like trails of wax left to pour over the side of a table. It was a distinct contrast to the neat lines and scrubbed buildings of Dalinar's warcamp.

He will be fine, she told herself. *He'd* better *be fine!*

It was a testament to her disordered state that she barely considered constructing a new street pattern for Sadeas in her head. She made her way directly to the staging area, and arrived to find an army that hardly looked as if it had been to battle. Soldiers without any blood on their uniforms, men chatting and laughing, officers walking down lines and dismissing the men squad by squad.

That should have relieved her. This didn't *look* like a force that had just suffered a disaster. Instead, it made her even more anxious.

Sadeas, in unmarred red Shardplate, was speaking with a group of officers in the shade of a nearby canopy. She stalked up to the canopy, but here a group of guards managed to bar her way, forming up shoulder to shoulder while one went to inform Sadeas of her arrival.

Navani folded her arms impatiently. Perhaps she should have taken a palanquin, as her attending ladies had suggested. Several of them, looking beleaguered, were just arriving at the staging area. A palanquin would be faster in the long run, they had explained, as it would leave time for messengers to be sent so Sadeas could receive her.

Once, she had obeyed such proprieties. She could remember being a young woman, playing the games expertly, delighting in ways to manipulate the system. What had that gotten her? A dead husband whom she'd never loved and a "privileged" position in court that amounted to being put out to pasture.

What would Sadeas do if she just started screaming? The king's own mother, bellowing like an axehound whose antenna had been twisted? She considered it as the soldier waited for a chance to announce her to Sadeas.

From the corner of her eye, she noticed a youth in a blue uniform arriving in the staging area, accompanied by a small honor guard of three men. It was Renarin, for once bearing an expression other than calm curiosity. Wide-eyed and frantic, he hurried up to Navani.

"Mashala," he pled in his quiet voice. "Please. What have you heard?"

"Sadeas's army returned without your father's army," Navani said. "There is talk of a rout, though it doesn't look as if these men have been through one." She glared at Sadeas, giving serious contemplation to throwing a fit. Fortunately, he finally spoke with the soldier and then sent him back.

"You may approach, Brightness," the man said, bowing to her.

"About time," she growled, shoving past and passing underneath the canopy. Renarin joined her, walking more hesitantly.

"Brightness Navani," Sadeas said, clasping his hands behind his back, imposing in his crimson Plate. "I had hoped to bring you the news at your son's palace. I suppose that a disaster like this is too large to contain. I express my condolences at the loss of your brother."

Renarin gasped softly.

Navani steeled herself, folding her arms, trying to quiet the screams of denial and pain that came from the back of her mind. This was a pattern. She often saw patterns in things. In this case, the pattern was that she could never possess anything of value for long. It was always snatched from her just when it began to look promising.

Quiet, she scolded herself. "You will explain," she said to Sadeas, meeting his gaze. She'd practiced that look over the decades, and was pleased to see that it discomfited him.

"I'm sorry, Brightness," Sadeas repeated, stammering. "The Parshendi overwhelmed your brother's army. It was folly to work together. Our change in tactics was so threatening to the savages that they brought every soldier they could to this battle, surrounding us."

"And so you *left* Dalinar?"

"We fought hard to reach him, but the numbers were simply overpowering. We had to retreat lest we lose ourselves as well! I would have continued fighting, save for the fact that I saw your brother fall with my own eyes, swarmed by Parshendi with hammers." He grimaced. "They began carrying away chunks of bloodied Shardplate as prizes. Barbaric monsters."

Navani felt cold. Cold, numb. How could this happen? After finally—*finally*—making that stone-headed man see her as a woman, rather than as a sister. And now . . .

And now . . .

She set her jaw against the tears. "I don't believe it."

"I understand that the news is difficult." Sadeas waved for an attendant to fetch her a chair. "I wish I had not been forced to bring it to you. Dalinar and I . . . well, I have known him for many years, and while we did not always see the same sunrise, I considered him an ally. And a friend." He cursed softly, looking eastward. "They will pay for this. I will *see* that they pay."

He seemed so earnest that Navani found herself wavering. Poor Renarin, pale-faced and wide-eyed, seemed stunned beyond the means to speak. When the chair arrived, Navani refused it, so Renarin sat, earning a glance of disapproval from Sadeas. Renarin grasped his head in his hands, staring at the ground. He was trembling.

He's highprince now, Navani realized.

No. *No.* He was only highprince if she accepted the idea that Dalinar was dead. And he wasn't. He couldn't be.

Sadeas had all of the bridges, she thought, looking down at the lumberyard.

Navani stepped out into the late-afternoon sunlight, feeling its heat on her skin. She walked up to her attendants. "Brushpen," she said to Makal, who carried a satchel with Navani's possessions. "The thickest one. And my burn ink."

The short, plump woman opened the satchel, taking out a long brushpen with a knob of hog bristles on the end as wide as a man's thumb. Navani took it. The ink followed.

Around her, the guards stared as Navani took the pen and dipped it into the blood-colored ink. She knelt, and began to paint on the stone ground.

Art was about creation. That was its soul, its essence. Creation and order. You took something disorganized—a splash of ink, an empty page—and you built something from it. Something from nothing. The *soul* of creation.

She felt the tears on her cheeks as she painted. Dalinar

had no wife and no daughters; he had nobody to pray for him. And so, Navani painted a prayer onto the stones themselves, sending her attendants for more ink. She paced off the size of the glyph as she continued its border, making it enormous, spreading her ink onto the tan rocks.

Soldiers gathered around, Sadeas stepping from his canopy, watching her paint, her back to the sun as she crawled on the ground and furiously dipped her brushpen into the ink jars. What was a prayer, if not creation? Making something where nothing existed. Creating a wish out of despair, a plea out of anguish. Bowing one's back before the Almighty, and forming humility from the empty pride of a human life.

Something from nothing. True creation.

Her tears mixed with the ink. She went through four jars. She crawled, holding her safehand to the ground, brushing the stones and smearing ink on her cheeks when she wiped the tears. When she finally finished, she knelt back before a glyph twenty paces long, emblazoned as if in blood. The wet ink reflected sunlight, and she fired it with a candle; the ink was made to burn whether wet or dry. The flames burned across the length of the prayer, killing it and sending its soul to the Almighty.

She bowed her head before the prayer. It was only a single character, but a complex one. *Thath.* Justice.

Men watched quietly, as if afraid of spoiling her solemn wish. A cold breeze began blowing, whipping at pennants and cloaks. The prayer went out, but that was fine. It wasn't meant to burn long.

"Brightlord Sadeas!" an anxious voice called.

Navani looked up. Soldiers parted, making way for a runner in green. He hurried up to Sadeas, beginning to speak, but the highprince grabbed the man by the shoulder in a Shardplate grip and pointed, gesturing for his guards to make a perimeter. He pulled the messenger beneath the canopy.

Navani continued to kneel beside her prayer. The flames left a black scar in the shape of the glyph on the ground. Someone stepped up beside her—Renarin. He went to one knee, resting a hand on her shoulder. "Thank you, Mashala."

She nodded, standing, her freehand sprinkled with drops of red pigment. Her cheeks were still wet with tears, but she narrowed her eyes, looking through the press of soldiers toward Sadeas. His expression was thunderous, face growing red, eyes wide with anger.

She turned and pushed her way through the press of soldiers, scrambling up to the rim of the staging field. Renarin and some of Sadeas's officers joined her in staring out over the Shattered Plains.

And there they saw a creeping line of men limping back toward the warcamps, led by a mounted man in slate-grey armor.

※

Dalinar rode Gallant at the head of two thousand six hundred and fifty-three men. That was all that remained of his assault force of eight thousand.

The long trek back across the plateaus had given him time to think. His insides were still a tempest of emotions. He flexed his left hand as he rode; it was now encased by a blue-painted Shardplate gauntlet borrowed from Adolin. It would take days to regrow Dalinar's own gauntlet. Longer, if the Parshendi tried to grow a full suit from the one he had left. They would fail, so long as Dalinar's armorers fed Stormlight to his suit. The abandoned gauntlet would degrade and crumble to dust, a new one growing for Dalinar.

For now, he wore Adolin's. They had collected all of the infused gemstones among his twenty-six hundred men and used that Stormlight to recharge and reinforce his armor. It was still scarred with cracks. Healing as much damage as it had sustained would take days, but the Plate was in fighting shape again, if it came to that.

He needed to make certain it didn't. He intended to confront Sadeas, and he wanted to be armored when he did. In fact, he *wanted* to storm up the incline to Sadeas's warcamp and declare formal war on his "old friend." Perhaps summon his Blade and see Sadeas dead.

But he wouldn't. His soldiers were too weak, his position too tenuous. Formal war would destroy him and the kingdom.

He had to do something else. Something that protected the kingdom. Revenge would come. Eventually. Alethkar came first.

He lowered his blue-gauntleted fist, gripping Gallant's reins. Adolin rode a short distance away. They'd repaired his armor as well, though he now lacked a gauntlet. Dalinar had refused the gift of his son's gauntlet at first, but had given in to Adolin's logic. If one of them was going to go without, it should be the younger man. Inside Shardplate, their differences in age didn't matter—but outside of it, Adolin was a young man in his twenties and Dalinar an aging man in his fifties.

He still didn't know what to think of the visions, and their apparent failure in telling him to trust Sadeas. He'd confront that later. One step at a time.

"Elthal," Dalinar called. The highest-ranked officer who had survived the disaster, Elthal was a limber man with a distinguished face and a thin mustache. His arm was in a sling. He'd been one of those to hold the gap alongside Dalinar during the last part of the fight.

"Yes, Brightlord?" Elthal asked, jogging over to Dalinar. All of the horses save the two Ryshadium were carrying wounded.

"Take the wounded to my warcamp," Dalinar said. "Then tell Teleb to bring the entire camp to alert. Mobilize the remaining companies."

"Yes, Brightlord," the man said, saluting. "Brightlord, what should I tell them to prepare for?"

"Anything. But hopefully nothing."

"I understand, Brightlord," Elthal said, leaving to follow the orders.

Dalinar turned Gallant to march over to the group of bridgemen, still following their somber leader, a man named Kaladin. They'd left their bridge as soon as they'd reached the permanent bridges; Sadeas could send for it eventually.

The bridgemen stopped as he approached, looking as tired as he felt, then arranged themselves in a subtly hostile formation. They clung to their spears, as if certain he'd try to take them away. They had saved him, yet they obviously didn't trust him.

"I'm sending my wounded back to my camp," Dalinar said. "You should go with them."

"You're confronting Sadeas?" Kaladin asked.

"I must." *I have to know why he did what he did.* "I will buy your freedom when I do."

"Then I'm staying with you," Kaladin said.

"Me too," said a hawk-faced man at the side. Soon all of the bridgemen were demanding to stay.

Kaladin turned to them. "I should send you back."

"What?" asked an older bridgeman with a short grey beard. "You can risk yourself, but we can't? We have men back in Sadeas's camp. We need to get them out. At the very least, we need to stay together. See this through."

The others nodded. Again, Dalinar was struck by their discipline. More and more, he was certain Sadeas had nothing to do with that. It was this man at their head. Though his eyes were dark brown, he held himself like a brightlord.

Well, if they wouldn't go, Dalinar wouldn't force them. He continued to ride, and soon close to a thousand of Dalinar's soldiers broke off and marched south, toward his warcamp. The rest of them continued toward Sadeas's camp. As they drew closer, Dalinar noticed a small crowd gathering at the final chasm. Two figures in particular stood at their forefront. Renarin and Navani.

"What are *they* doing in Sadeas's warcamp?" Adolin asked, smiling through his fatigue, edging Sureblood up beside Dalinar.

"I don't know," Dalinar said. "But the Stormfather bless them for coming." Seeing their welcome faces, he began to feel it sink in—finally—that he had survived the day.

Gallant crossed the last bridge. Renarin was there waiting, and Dalinar rejoiced.

For once, the boy was displaying outright joy. Dalinar swung free from the saddle and embraced his son.

"Father," Renarin said, "you live!"

Adolin laughed, swinging out of his own saddle, armor

clanking. Renarin pulled out of the embrace and grabbed Adolin on the shoulder, pounding the Shardplate lightly with his other hand, grinning widely. Dalinar smiled as well, turning from the brothers to look at Navani. She stood with hands clasped before her, one eyebrow raised. Her face, oddly, bore a few small smears of red paint.

"You weren't even worried, were you?" he said to her.

"Worried?" she asked. Her eyes met his, and for the first time, he noticed their redness. "I was terrified."

And then Dalinar found himself grabbing her in an embrace. He had to be careful as he was in Shardplate, but the gauntlets let him feel the silk of her dress, and his missing helm let him smell the sweet floral scent of her perfumed soap. He held her as tightly as he dared, bowing his head and pressing his nose into her hair.

"Hmm," she noted warmly, "it appears that I was missed. The others are watching. They'll talk."

"I don't care."

"Hmm . . . It appears I was *very much* missed."

"On the battlefield," he said gruffly, "I thought I would die. And I realized it was all right."

She pulled her head back, looking confused.

"I have spent too much of my time worrying about what people think, Navani. When I thought my time had arrived, I realized that all my worrying had been wasted. In the end, I was pleased with how I had lived my life." He looked down at her, then mentally unlatched his right gauntlet, letting it drop to the ground with a clank. He reached up with that callused hand, cupping her chin. "I had only two regrets. One for you, and one for Renarin."

"So, you're saying you can just die, and it would be all right?"

"No," he said. "What I'm saying is that I faced eternity, and I saw peace there. That will change how I live."

"Without all of the guilt?"

He hesitated. "Being me, I doubt I'll banish it entirely. The end was peace, but living . . . that is a tempest. Still, I see things differently now. It is time to stop letting myself be shoved around by lying men." He looked up, toward the ridge above, where more soldiers in green were gathering. "I keep thinking of one of the visions," he said softly, "the latest one, where I met Nohadon. He rejected my suggestion that he write down his wisdom. There's something there. Something I need to learn."

"What?" Navani asked.

"I don't know yet. But I'm close to figuring it out." He held her close again, hand on the back of her head, feeling her hair. He wished for the Plate to be gone, to not be separated from her by the metal.

But the time for that had not yet come. Reluctantly, he released her, turning to the side, where Renarin and Adolin were watching them uncomfortably. His soldiers were looking up at Sadeas's army, gathering on the ridge.

I can't let this come to bloodshed, Dalinar thought, reaching down and putting his hand into the fallen gauntlet. The straps tightened, connecting to the rest of the armor. *But I'm also not going to slink back to my camp without confronting him.* He at least had to know the purpose of the betrayal. All had been going so well.

Besides, there was the matter of his promise to the bridgemen. Dalinar walked up the slope, bloodstained blue cloak flapping behind him. Adolin clanked up next to him on one side, Navani keeping pace on the other. Renarin followed, Dalinar's remaining sixteen hundred troops marching up as well.

"Father . . ." Adolin said, looking at the hostile troops.

"Don't summon your Blade. This will not come to blows."

"Sadeas abandoned you, didn't he?" Navani asked quietly, eyes alight with anger.

"He didn't just abandon us," Adolin spat. "He set us up, then betrayed us."

"We survived," Dalinar said firmly. The way ahead was becoming clearer. He knew what he needed to do. "He won't attack us here, but he might try to provoke us. Keep your sword as mist, Adolin, and don't let our troops make any mistakes."

The soldiers in green parted reluctantly, holding spears.

Hostile. To the side, Kaladin and his bridgemen walked near the front of Dalinar's force.

Adolin didn't summon his Blade, though he regarded Sadeas's troops around them with contempt. Dalinar's soldiers couldn't have felt easy about being surrounded by enemies once again, but they followed him onto the staging field. Sadeas stood ahead. The treacherous highprince waited with arms folded, still wearing his Shardplate, curly black hair blowing in the breeze. Someone had burned an enormous *thath* glyph on the stones here, and Sadeas stood at its center.

Justice. There was something magnificently appropriate about Sadeas standing there, treading upon justice.

"Dalinar," Sadeas exclaimed, "old friend! It appears that I overestimated the odds against you. I apologize for retreating when you were still in danger, but the safety of my men came first. I'm certain you understand."

Dalinar stopped a short distance from Sadeas. The two faced each other, collected armies tense. A cold breeze whipped at a canopy behind Sadeas.

"Of course," Dalinar said, his voice even. "You did what you had to do."

Sadeas relaxed visibly, though several of Dalinar's soldiers muttered at that. Adolin silenced them with pointed glances.

Dalinar turned, waving Adolin and his men backward. Navani gave him a raised eyebrow, but retreated with the others when he urged her. Dalinar looked back at Sadeas, and the man—looking curious—waved his own attendants back.

Dalinar walked up to the edge of the *thath* glyph, and Sadeas stepped forward until only inches separated them. They were matched in height. Standing this close, Dalinar thought he could see tension—and anger—in Sadeas's eyes. Dalinar's survival had ruined months of planning.

"I need to know why," Dalinar asked, too quietly for any but Sadeas to hear.

"Because of my oath, old friend."

"*What?*" Dalinar asked, hands forming fists.

"We swore something together, years ago." Sadeas sighed,

losing his flippancy and speaking openly. "Protect Elhokar. Protect this kingdom."

"That's what I was doing! We had the same purpose. And we were fighting together, Sadeas. It was *working*."

"Yes," Sadeas said. "But I'm confident I can beat the Parshendi on my own now. Everything we've done together, I can manage by splitting my army into two—one to race on ahead, a larger force to follow. I had to take this chance to remove you. Dalinar, can't you see? Gavilar died because of his weakness. *I* wanted to attack the Parshendi from the start, conquer them. He insisted on a treaty, which led to his death. Now you're starting to act just like him. Those same ideas, the same ways of speaking. Through you they begin to infect Elhokar. He dresses like you. He talks of the Codes to me, and of how perhaps we should enforce them through all the warcamps. He's beginning to think of *retreating*."

"And so you'd have me think this an act of honor?" Dalinar growled.

"Not at all," Sadeas said, chuckling. "I have struggled for years to become Elhokar's most trusted advisor—but there was always you, distracting him, holding his ear despite my every effort. I won't pretend this was only about honor, though there was an element of that to it. In the end, I just wanted you gone."

Sadeas's voice grew cold. "But you *are* going insane, old friend. You may name me a liar, but I did what I did today as a mercy. A way of letting you die in glory, rather than watching you descend further and further. By letting the Parshendi kill you, I could protect Elhokar from you and turn you into a symbol to remind the others what we're really doing here. Your death might have become what finally united us. Ironic, if you consider it."

Dalinar breathed in and out. It was hard not to let his anger, his indignation, consume him. "Then tell me one thing. Why not pin the assassination attempt on me? Why clear me, if you were only looking to betray me later on?"

Sadeas snorted softly. "Bah. Nobody would *really* believe that you tried to kill the king. They'd gossip, but they wouldn't believe it. Blaming you too quickly would have risked implicating myself." He shook his head. "I think Elhokar knows who tried to kill him. He's admitted as much to me, though he won't give me the name."

What? Dalinar thought. *He knows? But . . . how? Why not tell us who?* Dalinar adjusted his plans. He wasn't certain if Sadeas was telling the truth, but if he was, he could use this.

"He knows it wasn't you," Sadeas continued. "I can read that much in him, though he doesn't realize how transparent he is. Blaming you would have been pointless. Elhokar would have defended you, and I might very well have lost the position of Highprince of Information. But it *did* give me a wonderful opportunity to make you trust me again."

Unite them. . . . The visions. But the man who spoke to Dalinar in them had been dead wrong. Acting with honor *hadn't* won Sadeas's loyalty. It had just opened Dalinar up to betrayal.

"If it means anything," Sadeas said idly, "I'm fond of you. I really am. But you are a boulder in my path, and a force working—without realizing it—to destroy Gavilar's kingdom. When the chance came along, I took it."

"It wasn't simply a convenient opportunity," Dalinar said. "You set this up, Sadeas."

"I planned, but I'm often planning. I don't always act on my options. Today I did."

Dalinar snorted. "Well, you've shown me something today, Sadeas—shown it to me by the very act of trying to remove me."

"And what was that?" Sadeas asked, amused.

"You've shown me that I'm still a threat."

❖

The highprinces continued their low-pitched conversation. Kaladin stood to the side of Dalinar's soldiers, exhausted, with the members of Bridge Four.

Sadeas spared a glance for them. Matal stood in the crowd, and had been watching Kaladin's team the entire time, red-faced. Matal probably knew that he would be punished as

Lamaril had been. They should have learned. They should have killed Kaladin at the start.

They tried, he thought. *They failed.*

He didn't know what had happened to him, what had gone on with Syl and the words in his head. It seemed that Stormlight worked better for him now. It had been more potent, more powerful. But now it was gone, and he was *so* tired. Drained. He'd pushed himself, and Bridge Four, too far. Too hard.

Perhaps he and the others should have gone to Kholin's camp. But Teft was right; they needed to see this through.

He promised, Kaladin thought. *He promised he would free us from Sadeas.*

And yet, where had the promises of lighteyes gotten him in the past?

The highprinces broke off their conference, separating, stepping back from one another.

"Well," Sadeas said loudly, "your men are obviously tired, Dalinar. We can speak later about what went wrong, though I think it is safe to assume that our alliance has proven unfeasible."

"Unfeasible," Dalinar said. "A kind way of putting it." He nodded toward the bridgemen. "I will take these bridgemen with me to my camp."

"I'm afraid I cannot part with them."

Kaladin's heart sank.

"Surely they aren't worth much to you," Dalinar said. "Name your price."

"I'm not looking to sell."

"I will pay sixty emerald broams per man," Dalinar said. That drew gasps from the watching soldiers on both sides. It was easily twenty times the price of a good slave.

"Not for a thousand each, Dalinar," Sadeas said. Kaladin could see the deaths of his bridgemen in those eyes. "Take your soldiers and go. Leave my property here."

"Do not press me on this, Sadeas," Dalinar said.

Suddenly, the tension was back. Dalinar's officers lowered hands to swords, and his spearmen perked up, gripping the hafts of their weapons.

"Do not press you?" Sadeas asked. "What kind of threat is that? *Leave* my camp. It's obvious that there is nothing more between us. If you try to steal my property, I will have every justification in attacking you."

Dalinar stood in place. He looked confident, though Kaladin saw no reason why. *And another promise dies,* Kaladin thought, turning away. In the end, for all his good intentions, this Dalinar Kholin was the same as the others.

Behind Kaladin, men gasped in surprise.

Kaladin froze, then spun around. Dalinar Kholin was holding his massive Shardblade; it dripped beads of water from having just been summoned. His armor steamed faintly, Stormlight rising from the cracks.

Sadeas stumbled back, eyes wide. His honor guard drew their swords. Adolin Kholin reached his hand to the side, apparently beginning to summon his own weapon.

Dalinar took one step forward, then drove his Blade point-first into the middle of the blackened glyph on the stone. He took a step back. "For the bridgemen," he said.

Sadeas blinked. Muttering voices fell silent, and the people on the field seemed too stunned, even, to breathe.

"What?" Sadeas asked.

"The Blade," Dalinar said, firm voice carrying in the air. "In exchange for your bridgemen. All of them. Every one you have in camp. They become mine, to do with as I please, never to be touched by you again. In exchange, you get the sword."

Sadeas looked down at the Blade, incredulous. "This weapon is worth fortunes. Cities, palaces, *kingdoms.*"

"Do we have a deal?" Dalinar asked.

"Father, no!" Adolin Kholin said, his own Blade appearing in his hand. "You—"

Dalinar raised a hand, silencing the younger man. He kept his eyes on Sadeas. *"Do we have a deal?"* he asked, each word sharp.

Kaladin stared, unable to move, unable to think.

Sadeas looked at the Shardblade, eyes full of lust. He glanced at Kaladin, hesitated just briefly, then reached and grabbed the Blade by the hilt. *"Take* the storming creatures."

Dalinar nodded curtly, turning away from Sadeas. "Let's go," he said to his entourage.

"They're worthless, you know," Sadeas said. "You're of the ten fools, Dalinar Kholin! Don't you see how mad you are? This will be remembered as the most ridiculous decision ever made by an Alethi highprince!"

Dalinar didn't look back. He walked up to Kaladin and the other members of Bridge Four. "Go," Dalinar said to them, voice kindly. "Gather your things and the men you left behind. I will send troops with you to act as guards. Leave the bridges and come swiftly to my camp. You will be safe there. You have my word of honor on it."

He began to walk away.

Kaladin shook off his numbness. He scrambled after the highprince, grabbing his armored arm. "Wait. You— That— *What just happened?*"

Dalinar turned to him. Then, the highprince laid a hand on Kaladin's shoulder, the gauntlet gleaming blue, mismatched with the rest of his slate-grey armor. "I don't know what has been done to you. I can only guess what your life has been like. But know this. You will not be bridgemen in my camp, nor will you be slaves."

"But . . ."

"What is a man's life worth?" Dalinar asked softly.

"The slavemasters say one is worth about two emerald broams," Kaladin said, frowning.

"And what do you say?"

"A life is priceless," he said immediately, quoting his father.

Dalinar smiled, wrinkle lines extending from the corners of his eyes. "Coincidentally, that is the exact value of a Shardblade. So today, you and your men sacrificed to buy me twenty-six hundred priceless lives. And all I had to repay you with was a single priceless sword. I call that a bargain."

"You really think it was a good trade, don't you?" Kaladin said, amazed.

Dalinar smiled in a way that seemed strikingly paternal. "For my honor? Unquestionably. Go and lead your men to safety, soldier. Later tonight, I will have some questions for you."

Kaladin glanced at Sadeas, who held his new Blade with awe. "You said you'd take care of Sadeas. This was what you intended?"

"This wasn't taking care of Sadeas," Dalinar said. "This was taking care of you and your men. I still have work to do today."

※

Dalinar found King Elhokar in his palace sitting room.

Dalinar nodded once more to the guards outside, then closed the door. They seemed troubled. As well they should; his orders had been irregular. But they would do as told. They wore the king's colors, blue and gold, but they were Dalinar's men, chosen specifically for their loyalty.

The door shut with a snap. The king was staring at one of his maps, wearing his Shardplate. "Ah, Uncle," he said, turning to Dalinar. "Good. I had wanted to speak with you. Do you know of these rumors about you and my mother? I realize that nothing untoward could be happening, but I *do* worry about what people think."

Dalinar crossed the room, booted feet thumping on the rich rug. Infused diamonds hung in the corners of the room, and the carved walls had been set with tiny chips of quartz to sparkle and reflect the light.

"Honestly, Uncle," Elhokar said, shaking his head. "I'm growing very intolerant of your reputation in camp. What they are saying reflects poorly on me, you see, and . . ." He trailed off as Dalinar stopped about a pace from him. "Uncle? Is everything all right? My door guards reported some kind of mishap with your plateau assault today, but my mind was full of thoughts. Did I miss anything vital?"

"Yes," Dalinar said. Then he raised his leg and kicked the king in the chest.

The strength of the blow tossed the king backward against his desk. The fine wood shattered as the heavy Shardbearer crashed through it. Elhokar hit the floor, his breastplate slightly cracked. Dalinar stepped up to him, then delivered another kick to the king's side, cracking the breastplate again.

Elhokar began shouting in panic. "Guards! To me! Guards!"

Nobody came. Dalinar kicked again, and Elhokar cursed, catching his boot. Dalinar grunted, but bent down and grabbed Elhokar by the arm, then yanked him to his feet, tossing him toward the side of the room. The king stumbled on the rug, crashing through a chair. Round lengths of wood scattered, splinters spraying out.

Wide-eyed, Elhokar scrambled to his feet. Dalinar advanced on him.

"What has gone wrong with you, Uncle?" Elhokar yelled. "You're mad! Guards! Assassin in the king's chamber! Guards!" Elhokar tried to run for the door, but Dalinar threw his shoulder against the king, tossing the younger man to the ground again.

Elhokar rolled, but got a hand under himself and climbed to his knees, the other hand to the side. A puff of mist appeared in it as he summoned his Blade.

Dalinar kicked the king's hand just as the Shardblade dropped into it. The blow knocked the Blade free, and it dissolved back to mist immediately.

Elhokar frantically swung a fist at Dalinar, but Dalinar caught it, then reached down and hauled the king to his feet. He pulled Elhokar forward and slammed his fist into the king's breastplate. Elhokar struggled, but Dalinar repeated the move, smashing his gauntlet against the Plate, cracking the steel casings around his fingers, making the king grunt.

The next blow shattered Elhokar's breastplate in an explosion of molten shards.

Dalinar dropped the king to the floor. Elhokar struggled to rise again, but the breastplate was a focus for the Shardplate's power. Losing it left arms and legs heavy. He went to one knee beside the squirming king. Elhokar's Shardblade formed again, but Dalinar grabbed the king's wrist and smashed it against the stone floor, knocking the Blade free yet again. It vanished into mist.

"Guards!" Elhokar squealed. "Guards, guards, *guards*!"

"They won't come, Elhokar," Dalinar said softly. "They're my men, and I left them with orders not to enter—or let anyone else enter—no matter what they heard. Even if that included pleas for help from you."

Elhokar fell silent.

"They are my men, Elhokar," Dalinar repeated. "I trained them. I placed them there. They've always been loyal to me."

"Why, Uncle? What are you doing? Please, tell me." He was nearly weeping.

Dalinar leaned down, getting close enough to smell the king's breath. "The girth on your horse during the hunt," Dalinar said quietly. "You cut it yourself, didn't you?"

Elhokar's eyes grew wider.

"The saddles were switched before you came to my camp," Dalinar said. "You did that because you didn't want to ruin your favorite saddle when it flew free of the horse. You were planning for it to happen; you *made* it happen. That's why you've been so certain that the girth was cut."

Cringing, Elhokar nodded. "Someone was trying to kill me, but you wouldn't believe! I . . . I worried it might be you! So I decided . . . I . . ."

"You cut your own strap," Dalinar said, "to create a visible, obvious-seeming attempt on your life. Something that would get me or Sadeas to investigate."

Elhokar hesitated, then nodded again.

Dalinar closed his eyes, breathing out slowly. "Don't you realize what you did, Elhokar? You brought suspicion on me from across the camps! You gave Sadeas an opportunity to destroy me." He opened his eyes, looking down at the king.

"I had to know," Elhokar whispered. "I couldn't trust anyone." He groaned beneath Dalinar's weight.

"What of the cracked gemstones in your Shardplate? Did you place those too?"

"No."

"Then maybe you did uncover something," Dalinar said with a grunt. "I guess you can't be completely blamed."

"Then you'll let me up?"

"No." Dalinar leaned down farther. He laid a hand against

the king's chest. Elhokar stopped struggling, looking up in terror. "If I push," Dalinar said, "you die. Your ribs crack like twigs, your heart is smashed like a grape. Nobody would blame me. They all whisper that the Blackthorn should have taken the throne for himself years ago. Your guard is loyal to me. There would be nobody to avenge you. Nobody would care."

Elhokar breathed out as Dalinar pressed his hand down just slightly.

"Do you understand?" Dalinar asked quietly.

"No!"

Dalinar sighed, then released the younger man and stood up. Elhokar inhaled with a gasp.

"Your paranoia may be unfounded," Dalinar said, "or it may be well founded. Either way, you need to understand something. I am not your enemy."

Elhokar frowned. "So you're not going to kill me?"

"Storms, no! I love you like a son, boy."

Elhokar rubbed his chest. "You . . . have very odd paternal instincts."

"I spent years following you," Dalinar said. "I gave you my loyalty, my devotion, and my counsel. I swore myself to you—promising myself, *vowing* to myself, that I would never covet Gavilar's throne. All to keep my heart loyal. Despite this, you don't trust me. You pull a stunt like that one with the girth, implicating me, giving your own enemies position against you without knowing it."

Dalinar stepped toward the king. Elhokar cringed.

"Well, now you know," Dalinar said, voice hard. "If I'd wanted to kill you, Elhokar, I could have done it a dozen times over. A *hundred* times over. It appears you won't accept loyalty and devotion as proof of my honesty. Well, if you act like a child, you get treated like one. You know now, for a fact, that I don't want you dead. For if I did, I would have crushed your chest and been done with it!"

He locked eyes with the king. "Now," Dalinar said, "*do you understand*?"

Slowly, Elhokar nodded.

"Good," Dalinar said. "Tomorrow, you're going to name me Highprince of War."

"*What?*"

"Sadeas betrayed me today," Dalinar said. He walked over to the broken desk, kicking at the pieces. The king's seal rolled out of its customary drawer. He picked it up. "Nearly six thousand of my men were slaughtered. Adolin and I barely survived."

"What?" Elhokar said, forcing himself up to a sitting position. "That's impossible!"

"Far from it," Dalinar said, looking at his nephew. "He saw a chance to pull out, letting the Parshendi destroy us. So he did it. A very Alethi thing to do. Ruthless, yet still allowing him to feign a sense of honor or morality."

"So . . . you expect me to bring him to trial?"

"No. Sadeas is no worse, and no better, than the others. Any of the highprinces would betray their fellows, if they saw a chance to do it without risking themselves. I intend to find a way to unite them in more than just name. Somehow. Tomorrow, once you name me Highprince of War, I will give my Plate to Renarin to fulfill a promise. I've already given away my Blade to fulfill a different one."

He walked closer, meeting Elhokar's eyes again, then gripped the king's seal in his hand. "As Highprince of War, I will enforce the Codes in all ten camps. Then I'll coordinate the war effort directly, determining which armies get to go on which plateau assaults. All gemhearts will be won by the Throne, then distributed as spoils by you. We'll change this from a competition to a real war, and I'll use it to turn these ten armies of ours—and their leaders—into real soldiers."

"Stormfather! They'll kill us! The highprinces will revolt! I won't last a week!"

"They won't be pleased, that's for certain," Dalinar said. "And yes, this will involve a great deal of danger. We'll have to be much more careful with our guard. If you're right, someone is already trying to kill you, so we should be doing that anyway."

Elhokar stared at him, then looked at the broken furniture, rubbing his chest. "You're *serious*, aren't you?"

"Yes." He tossed the seal to Elhokar. "You're going to have your scribes draw up my appointment right after I leave."

"But I thought you said it was wrong to force men to follow the Codes," Elhokar said. "You said that the best way to change people was to live right, and then let them be influenced by your example!"

"That was before the Almighty lied to me," Dalinar said. He still didn't know what to think of that. "Much of what I told you, I learned from *The Way of Kings*. But I didn't understand something. Nohadon wrote the book at the end of his life, *after* creating order—after forcing the kingdoms to unite, after rebuilding lands that had fallen in the Desolation.

"The book was written to embody an ideal. It was given to people who already had momentum in doing what was right. That was my mistake. Before any of this can work, our people need to have a minimum level of honor and dignity. Adolin said something to me a few weeks back, something profound. He asked me why I forced my sons to live up to such high expectations, but let others go about their errant ways without condemnation.

"I have been treating the other highprinces and their lighteyes like adults. An adult can take a principle and adapt it to his needs. But we're not ready for that yet. We're children. And when you're teaching a child, you *require* him to do what is right until he grows old enough to make his own choices. The Silver Kingdoms didn't *begin* as unified, glorious bastions of honor. They were trained that way, raised up, like youths nurtured to maturity."

He strode forward, kneeling down beside Elhokar. The king continued to rub his chest, his Shardplate looking strange with the central piece missing.

"We're going to make something of Alethkar, nephew," Dalinar said softly. "The highprinces gave their oaths to Gavilar, but now ignore those oaths. Well, it's time to stop letting them. We're going to win this war, and we're going to turn

Alethkar into a place that men will envy again. Not because of our military prowess, but because people here are safe and because justice reigns. We're going to do it—or you and I are going to die in the attempt."

"You say that with eagerness."

"Because I finally know exactly what to do," Dalinar said, standing up straight. "I was trying to be Nohadon the peacemaker. But I'm not. I'm the Blackthorn, a general and a warlord. I have no talent for backroom politicking, but I am very good at training troops. Starting tomorrow, every man in each of these camps will be mine. As far as I'm concerned, they're all raw recruits. Even the highprinces."

"Assuming I make the proclamation."

"You will," Dalinar said. "And in return, I promise to find out who is trying to kill you."

Elhokar snorted, beginning to remove his Shardplate piece by piece. "After that announcement goes out, discovering who's trying to kill me will become easy. You can put every name in the warcamps on the list!"

Dalinar's smile widened. "At least we won't have to guess, then. Don't be so glum, nephew. You learned something today. Your uncle doesn't want to kill you."

"He just wants to make me a target."

"For your own good, son," Dalinar said, walking to the door. "Don't fret too much. I've got some plans on how, exactly, to keep you alive." He opened the door, revealing a nervous group of guards keeping at bay a nervous group of servants and attendants.

"He's just fine," Dalinar said to them. "See?" He stepped aside, letting the guards and servants in to attend their king.

Dalinar turned to go. Then he hesitated. "Oh, and Elhokar? Your mother and I are now courting. You'll want to start growing accustomed to that."

Despite everything else that had happened in the last few minutes, this got a look of pure astonishment from the king. Dalinar smiled and pulled the door closed, walking away with a firm step.

Most everything was still wrong. He was still furious at Sadeas, pained by the loss of so many of his men, confused at what to do with Navani, dumbfounded by his visions, and daunted by the idea of bringing the warcamps to unity.

But at least now he had something to work with.

PART

FIVE

The Silence Above

SHALLAN • DALINAR • KALADIN •
SZETH • WIT

70

Shallan lay quietly in the bed of her little hospital room. She'd cried herself dry, then had actually retched into the bedpan, over what she had done. She felt miserable.

She'd betrayed Jasnah. And Jasnah knew. Somehow, disappointing the princess felt worse than the theft itself. This entire plan had been foolish from the start.

Beyond that, Kabsal was dead. Why did she feel so sick about *that*? He'd been an assassin, trying to kill Jasnah, willing to risk Shallan's life to achieve his goals. And yet, she missed him. Jasnah hadn't seemed surprised that someone would want to kill her; perhaps assassins were a common part of her life. She likely thought Kabsal a hardened killer, but he'd been sweet with Shallan. Could that all really have been a lie?

He had to be somewhat sincere, she told herself, curled up on her bed. *If he didn't care for me, why did he try so hard to get me to eat the jam?*

He had handed Shallan the antidote first, rather than taking it himself.

And yet, he did *take it eventually,* she thought. *He put that fingerful of jam into his mouth. Why didn't the antidote save him?*

This question began to haunt her. As it did, something

else struck her, something she would have noticed earlier, had she not been distracted by her own guilt.

Jasnah had eaten the bread.

Arms wrapped around herself, Shallan sat up, pulling back to the bed's headboard. *She ate it, but she wasn't poisoned,* she thought. *My life makes no sense lately. The creatures with the twisted heads, the place with the dark sky, the Soulcasting . . . and now this.*

How had Jasnah survived? How?

With trembling fingers, Shallan reached to the pouch on the stand beside her bed. Inside, she found the garnet sphere that Jasnah had used to save her. It gave off weak light; most had been used in the Soulcasting. It was enough light to illuminate her sketchpad sitting beside the bed. Jasnah probably hadn't even bothered to look through it. She was so dismissive of the visual arts. Next to the sketchpad was the book Jasnah had given her. The *Book of Endless Pages.* Why had she left that?

Shallan picked up the charcoal pencil and flipped through to a blank page in her sketchbook. She passed several pictures of the symbol-headed creatures, some set in this very room. They lurked around her, always. At some times, she thought she saw them out of the corners of her eyes. At others, she could hear them whispering. She hadn't dared speak back to them again.

She began to draw, fingers unsteady, sketching Jasnah on that day in the hospital. Sitting beside Shallan's bed, holding the jam. Shallan hadn't taken a distinct Memory, and wasn't as accurate as if she had, but she remembered well enough to draw Jasnah with her finger stuck into the jam. She had raised that finger to smell the strawberries. Why? Why put her finger into the jam? Wouldn't raising the jar to her nose have been enough?

Jasnah hadn't made any faces at the scent. In fact, Jasnah hadn't mentioned that the jam had spoiled. She'd just replaced the lid and handed back the jar.

Shallan flipped to another blank page and drew Jasnah

with a piece of bread raised to her lips. After eating it, she'd grimaced. Odd.

Shallan lowered her pen, looking at that sketch of Jasnah, piece of bread pinched between her fingers. It wasn't a perfect reproduction, but it was close enough. In the sketch, it looked like the piece of bread was *melting*. As if it were squished unnaturally between Jasnah's fingers as she put it into her mouth.

Could it . . . could it be?

Shallan slid out of the bed, gathering the sphere and carrying it in her hand, sketchpad tucked under her arm. The guard was gone. Nobody seemed to care what happened to her; she was being shipped off in the morning anyway.

The stone floor was cold beneath her bare feet. She wore only the white robe, and felt almost naked. At least her safehand was covered. There was a door to the city outside at the end of the hallway, and she stepped through it.

She crossed quietly through the city, making her way to the Ralinsa, avoiding dark alleyways. She walked up toward the Conclave, long red hair blowing free behind her, drawing more than a few strange looks and stares. It was so late at night that nobody on the roadway cared enough to ask if she wanted help.

The master-servants at the entrance to the Conclave let her pass. They recognized her, and more than a few asked if she needed help. She declined, walking alone down to the Veil. She passed inside, then looked up at the walls full of balconies, some of them lit with spheres.

Jasnah's alcove was occupied. Of course it was. Always working, Jasnah was. She'd be particularly bothered by having lost so much time over Shallan's presumed suicide attempt.

The lift felt rickety beneath Shallan's feet as the parshmen lifted her up to Jasnah's level. She rode in silence, feeling disconnected from the world around her. Walking around through the palace—through the *city*—in only a robe? Confronting Jasnah Kholin *again*? Hadn't she learned?

But what did she have to lose?

She walked down the familiar stone hallway to the alcove,

weak violet sphere held before her. Jasnah sat at her desk. Her eyes looked uncharacteristically fatigued, dark circles underneath, her face stressed. She looked up and stiffened as she saw Shallan. "You are not welcome here."

Shallan walked in anyway, surprised by how calm she felt. Her hands should be shaking.

"Don't make me call the soldiers to get rid of you," Jasnah said. "I could have you thrown in prison for a hundred years for what you did. Do you have any idea what—"

"The Soulcaster you wear is a fake," Shallan said quietly. "It was a fake the whole time, even before I made the swap."

Jasnah froze.

"I wondered why you didn't notice the switch," Shallan said, sitting in the room's other chair. "I spent weeks confused. Had you noticed, but decided to keep quiet in order to catch the thief? Hadn't you Soulcast in all that time? It didn't make any sense. Unless the Soulcaster I stole was a decoy."

Jasnah relaxed. "Yes. Very clever of you to realize that. I keep several decoys. You're not the first to try to steal the fabrial, you see. I keep the real one carefully hidden, of course."

Shallan took out her sketchpad and searched through for a specific picture. It was the image she'd drawn of the strange place with the sea of beads, the floating flames, the distant sun in a black, black sky. Shallan regarded it for a moment. Then she turned it and held it up for Jasnah.

The look of utter shock Jasnah displayed was nearly worth the night spent feeling sick and guilty. Jasnah's eyes bulged and she sputtered for a moment, trying to find words. Shallan blinked, taking a Memory of that. She couldn't help herself.

"Where did you find that?" Jasnah demanded. "What book described that scene to you?"

"No book, Jasnah," Shallan said, lowering the picture. "I visited that place. The night when I accidentally Soulcast the goblet in my room to blood, then covered it up by faking a suicide attempt."

"Impossible. You think I'd believe—"

"There *is* no fabrial, is there, Jasnah? There's no Soulcaster.

There never has been. You use the fake 'fabrial' to distract people from the fact that you have the power to Soulcast on your own."

Jasnah fell silent.

"I did it too," Shallan said. "The Soulcaster was tucked away in my safepouch. I wasn't touching it—but that didn't matter. It was a fake. What I did, I did without it. Perhaps being near you has changed me, somehow. It has something to do with that place and those creatures."

Again, no reply.

"You suspected Kabsal of being an assassin," Shallan said. "You knew immediately what had happened when I fell; you were expecting poison, or at least were aware that it was possible. But *you* thought the poison was in the jam. You Soulcast it when you opened the lid and pretended to smell it. You didn't know how to re-create strawberry jam, and when you tried, you made that vile concoction. You thought to get rid of poison. But you inadvertently Soulcast away the *antidote*.

"You didn't want to eat the bread either, just in case there was something in it. You always refused it. When I convinced you to take a bite, you Soulcast it into something else as you put it in your mouth. You said you're terrible at making organic things, and what you created was revolting. But you got rid of the poison, which is why you didn't succumb to it."

Shallan met her former mistress's eyes. Was it the fatigue that made her so indifferent to the consequences of confronting this woman? Or was it her knowledge of the truth? "You did all that, Jasnah," Shallan finished, "with a *fake* Soulcaster. You hadn't spotted my swap yet. Don't try to tell me otherwise. I took it on the night when you killed those four thugs."

Jasnah's violet eyes showed a glimmer of surprise.

"Yes," Shallan said, "that long ago. You didn't replace it with a decoy. You didn't know you'd been tricked until I got out the fabrial and let you save me with it. It's all a lie, Jasnah."

"No," Jasnah said. "You're just delusional from your fatigue and the stress."

"Very well," Shallan said. She stood up, clutching the dim sphere. "I guess I'll have to show you. If I can."

Creatures, she said in her head. *Can you hear me?*

Yes, always, a whisper came in response. Though she'd hoped to hear it, she still jumped.

Can you return me to that place? she asked.

You need to tell me something true, it replied. *The more true, the stronger our bond.*

Jasnah is using a fake Soulcaster, Shallan thought. *I'm sure that's a truth.*

That's not enough, the voice whispered. *I must know something true about you. Tell me. The stronger the truth, the more hidden it is, the more powerful the bond. Tell me. Tell me. What are you?*

"What am I?" Shallan whispered. "Truthfully?" It was a day for confrontation. She felt strangely strong, steady. Time to speak it. "I'm a murderer. I killed my father."

Ah, the voice whispered. *A powerful truth indeed. . . .*

And the alcove vanished.

Shallan fell, dropping into that sea of dark glass beads. She struggled, trying to stay at the surface. She managed it for a moment. Then something tugged on her leg, pulling her down. She screamed, slipping beneath the surface, tiny beads of glass filling her mouth. She panicked. She was going to—

The beads above her parted. Those beneath her surged, bearing her upward, out to where someone stood, hand outstretched. Jasnah, back to the black sky, face lit by nearby hovering flames. Jasnah grasped Shallan's hand, pulling her upward, onto something. A raft. *Made* from the beads of glass. They seemed to obey Jasnah's will.

"Idiot girl," Jasnah said, waving. The sea of beads to the left split, and the raft lurched, bearing them sideways toward a few flames of light. Jasnah shoved Shallan into one of the small flames, and she fell backward off the raft.

And hit the floor of the alcove. Jasnah sat where she had been, eyes closed. A moment later, she opened them, giving Shallan an angry look.

"Idiot girl!" Jasnah repeated. "You have no *idea* how dangerous that was. Visiting Shadesmar with only a single dim sphere? Idiot!"

Shallan coughed, feeling as if she still had beads in her throat. She stumbled to her feet, meeting Jasnah's gaze. The other woman still looked angry, but said nothing. *She knows that I have her,* Shallan realized. *If I spread the truth . . .*

What would it mean? She had strange powers. Did that make Jasnah some kind of Voidbringer? What would people say? No wonder she'd created the decoy.

"I want to be part of it," Shallan found herself saying.

"Excuse me?"

"Whatever you're doing. Whatever it is you're researching. I want to be part of it."

"You have no idea what you're saying."

"I know," Shallan said. "I'm ignorant. There's a simple cure for that." She stepped forward. "I want to *know*, Jasnah. I want to be your ward in truth. Whatever the source of this thing you do, I can do it too. I want you to train me and let me be part of your work."

"You stole from me."

"I know," Shallan said. "And I'm sorry."

Jasnah raised an eyebrow.

"I won't excuse myself," Shallan said. "But Jasnah, I came here intending to steal from you. I was planning it from the beginning."

"That's supposed to make me feel better?"

"I planned to steal from Jasnah the bitter heretic," Shallan said. "I didn't realize I'd come to regret the need for that theft. Not just because of you, but because it meant leaving *this*. What I've come to love. Please. I made a mistake."

"A large one. Insurmountable."

"Don't make a larger one by sending me away. I can be someone you don't have to lie to. Someone who knows."

Jasnah sat back.

"I stole the fabrial on the night you killed those men, Jasnah," Shallan said. "I'd decided I couldn't do it, but you convinced me that truth was not as simple as I thought it. You've opened a box full of storms in me. I made a mistake. I'll make more. I need you."

Jasnah took a deep breath. "Sit down."

Shallan sat.

"You will never lie to me again," Jasnah said, raising a finger. "And you will never steal from me, or anyone, again."

"I promise."

Jasnah sat for a moment, then sighed. "Scoot over here," she said, pulling open a book.

Shallan obeyed as Jasnah took out several sheets filled with notes. "What is this?" Shallan asked.

"You wanted to be part of what I'm doing? Well, you'll need to read this." Jasnah looked down at the notes. "It's about the Voidbringers."

71

RECORDED IN BLOOD

Szeth-son-son-Vallano, Truthless of Shinovar, walked with bowed back, carrying a sack of grain down off the ship and onto the docks of Kharbranth. The City of Bells smelled of a fresh ocean morning, peaceful yet excited, fishermen calling to friends as they prepared their nets.

Szeth joined the other porters, carrying his sack through the twisting streets. Perhaps another merchant might have used a chull cart, but Kharbranth was infamous for its crowds and its steep walkways. A line of porters was an efficient option.

Szeth kept his eyes down. Partially to imitate the look of a worker. Partially to lower his gaze from the blazing sun above, the god of gods, who watched him and saw his shame. Szeth should not have been out during the day. He should have hidden his terrible face.

He felt his every step should leave a bloody footprint. The massacres he'd committed these months, working for his hidden master . . . He could hear the dead scream every time he closed his eyes. They grated against his soul, wearing it to nothing, haunting him, consuming him.

So many dead. So very many dead.

Was he losing his mind? Each time he carried out an assassination, he found himself blaming the victims. He cursed them for not being strong enough to fight back and kill him.

During each of his slaughters, he wore white, just as he had been commanded.

One foot in front of the other. Don't think. Don't focus on what you've done. On what you're . . . going to do.

He had reached the last name on the list: Taravangian, the king of Kharbranth. A beloved monarch, known for building and maintaining hospitals in his city. It was known as far away as Azir that if you were sick, Taravangian would take you in. Come to Kharbranth and be healed. The king loved all.

And Szeth was going to kill him.

At the top of the steep city, Szeth lugged his sack with the other porters around to the back of the palace structure, entering a dim stone corridor. Taravangian was a simpleminded man. That should have made Szeth feel more guilty, but he found himself consumed by loathing. Taravangian would not be smart enough to prepare for Szeth. Fool. Idiot. Would Szeth never face a foe strong enough to kill him?

Szeth had come to the city early and taken the job as a porter. He had needed to research and study, for the instructions commanded him—for once—not to kill anyone else in performing this assassination. Taravangian's murder was to be done quietly.

Why the difference? The instructions stated that he was to deliver a message. "The others are dead. I've come to finish the job." The instructions were explicit: Make certain Taravangian heard and acknowledged the words before harming him.

This was looking like a work of vengeance. Someone had sent Szeth to hunt down and destroy the men who had wronged him. Szeth laid his sack down in the palace larder. He turned automatically, following the shuffling line of porters back down the hallway. He nodded toward the servants' privy, and the portermaster waved for him to go ahead. Szeth had made this same haul on several occasions, and could be trusted—presumably—to do his business and catch up.

The privy didn't smell half as foul as he had anticipated. It was a dark room, cut into the underground cavern, but a candle burned beside a man standing at the pissing trough. He nodded to Szeth, tying up the front of his trousers and wiping his fingers on the sides as he walked to the door. He took his candle, but kindly lit a leftover stub before withdrawing.

As soon as he was gone, Szeth infused himself with Stormlight from his pouch and laid his hand on the door, performing a Full Lashing between it and the frame, locking it closed. His Shardblade came out next. In the palace, everything was built downward. Trusting the maps he'd purchased, he knelt and carved a square of rock from the floor, wider at the bottom. As it began to slide down, Szeth infused it with Stormlight, performing half a Basic Lashing upward, making the rock weightless.

Next, he Lashed himself upward with a subtle Lashing that left him weighing only a tenth his normal weight. He leapt onto the rock, and his lessened weight pushed the rock down slowly. He rode it down into the room below. Three couches with plush violet cushions lined the walls, sitting beneath fine silver mirrors. The lighteyes' privy. A lamp burned with a small flame in the sconce, but Szeth was alone.

The stone thumped softly to the floor, and Szeth leaped off. He shed his clothing, revealing a black and white masterservant's outfit underneath. He took a matching cap from the pocket and slipped it on, reluctantly dismissed his Blade, then slipped into the hallway and quickly Lashed the door shut.

These days, he rarely gave a thought to the fact that he walked on stone. Once, he would have revered a corridor of rock like this. Had that man once been him? Had he ever revered anything?

Szeth hurried onward. His time was short. Fortunately, King Taravangian kept a strict schedule. Seventh bell: private reflection in his study. Szeth could see the doorway into the study ahead, guarded by two soldiers.

Szeth bowed his head, hiding his Shin eyes and hurrying up to them. One of the men held out his hand wardingly, so Szeth grabbed it, twisting, shattering the wrist. He smashed his elbow into the man's face, throwing him back against the wall.

The man's stunned companion opened his mouth to yell, but Szeth kicked him in the stomach. Even without a Shardblade, he was dangerous, infused with Stormlight and trained in kammar. He grabbed the second guard by the hair and slammed his forehead against the rock floor. Then he rose and kicked open the door.

He walked into a room well illuminated by a double row of lamps on the left. Crammed bookcases covered the right wall from floor to ceiling. A man sat cross-legged on a small rug directly ahead of Szeth. The man looked out an enormous window cut through the rock, staring at the ocean beyond.

Szeth strode forward. "I have been instructed to tell you that the others are dead. I've come to finish the job." He raised his hands, Shardblade forming.

The king did not turn.

Szeth hesitated. He had to make certain the man acknowledged what had been said. "Did you hear me?" Szeth demanded, striding forward.

"Did you kill my guards, Szeth-son-son-Vallano?" the king asked quietly.

Szeth froze. He cursed and stepped backward, raising his Blade in a defensive stance. Another trap?

"You have done your work well," the king said, still not facing him. "Leaders dead, lives lost. Panic and chaos. Was this your destiny? Do you wonder? Given that monstrosity of a Shardblade by your people, cast out and absolved of any sin your masters might require of you?"

"I am not absolved," Szeth said, still wary. "It is a common mistake stonewalkers make. Each life I take weighs me down, eating away at my soul."

The voices . . . the screams . . . spirits below, I can hear them howling. . . .

"Yet you kill."

"It is my punishment," Szeth said. "To kill, to have no choice, but to bear the sins nonetheless. I am Truthless."

"Truthless," the king mused. "I would say that you know much truth. More than your countrymen, now." He finally turned to face Szeth, and Szeth saw that he had been wrong about this man. King Taravangian was no simpleton. He had keen eyes and a wise, knowing face, rimmed with a full white beard, the mustaches drooping like arrow points. "You have seen what death and murder do to a man. You could say, Szeth-son-son-Vallano, that you bear great sins for your people. You understand what they cannot. And so you have truth."

Szeth frowned. And then it began to make sense. He knew what would happen next, even as the king reached into his voluminous sleeve and withdrew a small rock that glittered in the light of two dozen lamps. "You were always him," Szeth said. "My unseen master."

The king set the rock on the ground between them. Szeth's Oathstone.

"You put your own name on the list," Szeth said.

"In case you were captured," Taravangian said. "The best defense against suspicion is to be grouped with the victims."

"And if I'd killed you?"

"The instructions were explicit," Taravangian said. "And, as we have determined, you are *quite* good at following them. I probably needn't say it, but I order you *not* to harm me. Now, did you kill my guards?"

"I do not know," Szeth said, forcing himself to drop to one knee and dismissing his Blade. He spoke loudly, trying to drown out the screams that he thought—for certain—must be coming from the upper eaves of the room. "I knocked them both unconscious. I believe I cracked one man's skull."

Taravangian breathed out, sighing. He rose, stepping to the doorway. Szeth glanced over his shoulder to note the aged king inspecting the guards and checking their wounds. Taravangian called for help, and other guards arrived to see to the men.

Szeth was left with a terrible storm of emotions. This kindly, contemplative man had sent him to kill and murder? He had caused the screams?

Taravangian returned.

"Why?" Szeth asked, voice hoarse. "Vengeance?"

"No." Taravangian sounded very tired. "Some of those men you killed were my dear friends, Szeth-son-son-Vallano."

"More insurance?" Szeth spat. "To keep yourself from suspicion?"

"In part. And in part because their deaths were necessary."

"Why?" Szeth asked. "What could it possibly have served?"

"Stability. Those you killed were among the most powerful and influential men in Roshar."

"How does that help stability?"

"Sometimes," Taravangian said, "you must tear down a structure to build a new one with stronger walls." He turned around, looking out over the ocean. "And we are going to need strong walls in the coming years. Very, very strong walls."

"Your words are like the hundred doves."

"Easy to release, difficult to keep," Taravangian said, speaking the words in Shin.

Szeth looked up sharply. This man spoke the Shin language and knew his people's proverbs? Odd to find in a stone-walker. Odder to find in a murderer.

"Yes, I speak your language. Sometimes I wonder if the Lifebrother himself sent you to me."

"To bloody myself so that you wouldn't have to," Szeth said. "Yes, that sounds like something one of your Vorin gods would do."

Taravangian fell silent. "Get up," he finally said.

Szeth obeyed. He would always obey his master. Taravangian led him to a door set into the side of the study. The aged man pulled a sphere lamp off the wall, lighting a winding stairwell of deep, narrow steps. They followed it down and eventually came to a landing. Taravangian pushed open another door and entered a large room that wasn't on any of the palace maps that Szeth had purchased or bribed a look at. It was long, with wide railings on the sides, giving it a terraced look. Everything was painted white.

It was filled with beds. Hundreds and hundreds of them. Many were occupied.

Szeth followed the king, frowning. An enormous hidden room, cut into the stone of the Conclave? People bustled about wearing white coats. "A hospital?" Szeth said. "You expect me to find your humanitarian efforts a redemption for what you have commanded of me?"

"This is not humanitarian work," Taravangian said, walking forward slowly, white-and-orange robes rustling. Those they passed bowed to him with reverence. Taravangian led

Szeth to an alcove of beds, each with a sickly person in it. There were healers working on them. Doing something to their arms.

Draining their blood.

A woman with a writing clipboard stood near the beds, pen held, waiting for something. What?

"I don't understand," Szeth said, watching in horror as the four patients grew pale. "You're killing them, aren't you?"

"Yes. We don't need the blood; it is merely a way to kill slowly and easily."

"Every one of them? The people in this room?"

"We try to select only the worst cases to move here, for once they are brought to this place, we cannot let them leave if they begin to recover." He turned to Szeth, eyes sorrowful. "Sometimes we need more bodies than the terminally sick can provide. And so we must bring the forgotten and the lowly. Those who will not be missed."

Szeth couldn't speak. He couldn't voice his horror and revulsion. In front of him, one of the victims—a man in his younger years—expired. Two of those remaining were children. Szeth stepped forward. He had to stop this. He had to—

"You will still yourself," Taravangian said. "And you will return to my side."

Szeth did as his master commanded. What were a few more deaths? Just another set of screams to haunt him. He could hear them now, coming from beneath beds, behind furniture.

Or I could kill him, Szeth thought. *I could stop this.*

He nearly did it. But honor prevailed, for the moment.

"You see, Szeth-son-son-Vallano," Taravangian said. "I did not send you to do my bloody work for me. I do it here, myself. I have personally held the knife and released the blood from the veins of many. Much like you, I know I cannot escape my sins. We are two men of one heart. This is one reason why I sought you out."

"But *why*?" Szeth said.

On the beds, a dying youth started speaking. One of the women with the clipboards stepped forward quickly, recording the words.

"The day was ours, but they took it," the boy cried. "Stormfather! You cannot have it. The day is ours. They come, rasping, and the lights fail. Oh, Stormfather!" The boy arched his back, then fell still suddenly, eyes dead.

The king turned to Szeth. "It is better for one man to sin than for a people to be destroyed, wouldn't you say, Szeth-son-son-Vallano?"

"I . . ."

"We do not know why some speak when others do not," Taravangian said. "But the dying see something. It began seven years ago, about the time when King Gavilar was investigating the Shattered Plains for the first time." His eyes grew distant. "It is coming, and these people see it. On that bridge between life and the endless ocean of death, they view something. Their words might save us."

"You are a monster."

"Yes," Taravangian said. "But I am the monster who will save this world." He looked at Szeth. "I have a name to add to your list. I had hoped to avoid doing this, but recent events have made it inevitable. I cannot let him seize control. It will undermine everything."

"Who?" Szeth asked, wondering if anything at all could horrify him further.

"Dalinar Kholin," Taravangian said. "I'm afraid it must be done quickly, before he can unite the Alethi highprinces. You will go to the Shattered Plains and end him." He hesitated. "It must be done brutally, I'm afraid."

"I have rarely had the luxury of working otherwise," Szeth said, closing his eyes.

The screams greeted him.

72

VERISTITALIAN

"Before I read," Shallan said, "I need to understand something. You Soulcast my blood, didn't you?"

"To remove the poison," Jasnah said. "Yes. It acted extremely quickly; as I said, it must have been a very concentrated form of the powder. I had to Soulcast your blood several times as we got you to vomit. Your body continued to absorb the poison."

"But you said you aren't good with organics," Shallan said. "You turned the strawberry jam into something inedible."

"Blood isn't the same," Jasnah said, waving her hand. "It's one of the Essences. You'll learn this, should I actually decide to teach you Soulcasting. For now, know that the pure form of an Essence is quite easy to make; the eight kinds of blood are easier to create than water, for instance. Creating something as complex as strawberry jam, however—a mush made from a fruit I'd never before tasted or smelled—was well beyond my abilities."

"And the ardents," Shallan said. "Those who Soulcast? Do they actually use fabrials, or is it all a hoax?"

"No, Soulcasting fabrials are real. Quite real. So far as I know, everyone else who does what I—what *we*—can do uses a fabrial to accomplish it."

"What of the creatures with the symbol heads?" Shallan

asked. She flipped through her sketches, then held up an image of them. "Do you see them too? How are they related?"

Jasnah frowned, taking the image. "You see beings like this? In Shadesmar?"

"They appear in my drawings," Shallan said. "They're around me, Jasnah. You don't see them? Am I—"

Jasnah held up a hand. "These are a type of spren, Shallan. They *are* related to what you do." She tapped the desk softly. "Two orders of the Knights Radiant possessed inherent Soulcasting ability; it was based on their powers that the original fabrials were designed, I believe. I had assumed that you . . . But no, that obviously wouldn't make sense. I see now."

"What?"

"I will explain as I train you," Jasnah said, handing back the sheet. "You will need a greater foundation before you can grasp it. Suffice it to say that each Radiant's abilities were tied to the spren."

"Wait, *Radiants*? But—"

"I will explain," Jasnah said. "But first, we must speak of the Voidbringers."

Shallan nodded. "You think they'll return, don't you?"

Jasnah studied her. "What makes you say that?"

"The legends say the Voidbringers came a hundred times to try to destroy mankind," Shallan continued. "I . . . read some of your notes."

"You *what*?"

"I was looking for information on Soulcasting," Shallan confessed.

Jasnah sighed. "Well, I suppose it is the least of your crimes."

"I can't understand," Shallan said. "Why are you bothering with these stories of myths and shadows? Other scholars—scholars I know you respect—consider the Voidbringers to be a fabrication. Yet you chase stories from rural farmers and write them down in your notebook. Why, Jasnah? Why do you have faith in this when you reject things that are so much more plausible?"

Jasnah looked over her sheets of paper. "Do you know the real difference between me and a believer, Shallan?"

Shallan shook her head.

"It strikes me that religion—in its essence—seeks to take natural events and ascribe supernatural causes to them. I, however, seek to take supernatural events and find the *natural* meanings behind them. Perhaps that is the final dividing line between science and religion. Opposite sides of a card."

"So . . . you think . . ."

"The Voidbringers had a natural, real-world correlate," Jasnah said firmly. "I'm certain of it. Something *caused* the legends."

"What was it?"

Jasnah handed Shallan a page of notes. "These are the best I've been able to find. Read them. Tell me what you think."

Shallan scanned the page. Some of the quotes—or at least the concepts—were familiar to her from what she'd read already.

Suddenly dangerous. Like a calm day that became a tempest.

"They were real," Jasnah repeated.

Beings of ash and fire.

"We fought with them," Jasnah said. "We fought so often that men began to speak of the creatures in metaphor. A hundred battles—ten tenfolds . . ."

Flame and char. Skin so terrible. Eyes like pits of blackness. Music when they kill.

"We defeated them . . ." Jasnah said.

Shallan felt a chill.

". . . but the legends lie about one thing," Jasnah continued. "They claim we chased the Voidbringers off the face of Roshar or destroyed them. But that's not how humans work. We don't throw away something we can use."

Shallan rose, walking to the edge of the balcony, looking out at the lift, which was slowly being lowered by its two porters.

Parshmen. With skin of black and red.

Ash and fire.

"Stormfather . . ." Shallan whispered, horrified.

"We didn't destroy the Voidbringers," Jasnah said from behind, her voice haunted. "We *enslaved* them."

The chill spring weather might finally have slipped back into summer. It was still cool at night, but not uncomfortably so. Kaladin stood on Dalinar Kholin's staging ground, looking eastward over the Shattered Plains.

Ever since the betrayal, the rescue, and the fulfilling of Kholin's oath, Kaladin had found himself nervous. Freedom. Bought with a Shardblade. It seemed impossible. His every life experience taught him to expect a trap.

He clasped his hands behind him; Syl sat on his shoulder.

"Dare I trust him?" he asked softly.

"He's a good man," Syl said. "I've watched him. Despite that *thing* he carried."

"That thing?"

"The Shardblade."

"What do you care about it?"

"I don't know," she said, wrapping her arms around herself. "It just feels *wrong* to me. I hate it. I'm glad he got rid of it. Makes him a better man."

Nomon, the middle moon, began to rise. Bright and pale blue, bathing the horizon in light. Somewhere, out across the Plains, was the Parshendi Shardbearer that Kaladin had fought. He'd stabbed the man in the leg from behind. The watching Parshendi had not interfered with the duel and had avoided attacking Kaladin's wounded bridgemen, but Kaladin had attacked one of their champions from the most cowardly position possible, interfering with a fight.

He was bothered by what he'd done, and that frustrated him. A warrior couldn't worry about who he attacked or how. Survival was the only rule of the battlefield.

Well, survival and loyalty. And he sometimes let wounded enemies live if they weren't a threat. And he saved young soldiers who needed protection. And . . .

And he'd never been good at doing what a warrior should.

Today, he'd saved a highprince—another lighteyes—and along with him thousands of soldiers. Saved them by killing Parshendi.

"Can you kill to protect?" Kaladin asked out loud. "Is that a self-contradiction?"

"I . . . I don't know."

"You acted strangely in the battle," Kaladin said. "Swirling around me. After that, you left. I didn't see much of you."

"The killing," she said softly. "It hurt me. I had to go."

"Yet you're the one who prompted me to go and save Dalinar. You wanted me to return and kill."

"I know."

"Teft said that the Radiants held to a standard," Kaladin said. "He said that by their rules, you shouldn't do terrible things to accomplish great ones. Yet what did I do today? Slaughter Parshendi in order to save Alethi. What of that? They aren't innocent, but neither are we. Not by a faint breeze or a stormwind."

Syl didn't reply.

"If I hadn't gone to save Dalinar's men," Kaladin said, "I would have allowed Sadeas to succeed in a terrible betrayal. I'd have let men die who I could have saved. I'd have been sick and disgusted with myself. I also lost three good men, bridgemen who were mere breaths away from freedom. Are the lives of the others worth that?"

"I don't have the answers, Kaladin."

"Does anyone?"

Footsteps came from behind. Syl turned. "It's him."

The moon had just risen. Dalinar Kholin, it appeared, was a punctual man.

He stepped up beside Kaladin. He carried a bundle under his arm, and he had a military air about him, even without his Shardplate on. In fact, he was more impressive without it. His muscular build indicated that he did not rely on his Plate to give him strength, and the neatly pressed uniform indicated a man who understood that others were inspired when their leader looked the part.

Others have looked just as noble, Kaladin thought. But would any man trade a *Shardblade* just to keep up appearances? And if they would, at what point did the appearance become reality?

"I'm sorry to make you meet me so late," Dalinar said. "I know it has been a long day."

"I doubt I could have slept anyway."

Dalinar grunted softly, as if he understood. "Your men are seen to?"

"Yes," Kaladin said. "Quite well, actually. Thank you." Kaladin had been given empty barracks for the bridgemen and they had received medical attention from Dalinar's best surgeons—they'd gotten it *before* the wounded lighteyed officers had. The other bridgemen, the ones who weren't from Bridge Four, had accepted Kaladin immediately, without any deliberation on the matter, as their leader.

Dalinar nodded. "How many, do you suspect, will take my offer of a purse and freedom?"

"A fair number of the men from other crews will. But I'll wager an even larger number won't. Bridgemen don't think of escape or freedom. They wouldn't know what to do with themselves. As for my own crew . . . Well, I have a feeling that they'll insist on doing whatever I do. If I stay, they'll stay. If I go, they'll go."

Dalinar nodded. "And what will you do?"

"I haven't decided yet."

"I spoke to my officers." Dalinar grimaced. "The ones who survived. They said that you gave orders to them, took charge like a lighteyes. My son still feels bitter about the way your . . . conversation with him went."

"Even a fool could see he wasn't going to be able to get to you. As for the officers, most were in shock or run ragged. I merely nudged them."

"I owe you my life twice over," Dalinar said. "And that of my son and my men."

"You paid that debt."

"No," Dalinar said. "But I've done what I can." He eyed Kaladin, as if sizing him up, judging him. "Why did your bridge crew come for us? Why, really?"

"Why did you give up your Shardblade?"

Dalinar held his eyes, then nodded. "Fair enough. I have an offer for you. The king and I are about to do something very, very dangerous. Something that will upset all the war-camps."

"Congratulations."

Dalinar smiled faintly. "My honor guard has nearly been wiped out, and the men I do have are needed to augment the King's Guard. My trust is stretched thin these days. I need someone to protect me and my family. I want you and your men for that job."

"You want a bunch of bridgemen as bodyguards?"

"The elite ones as bodyguards," Dalinar said. "Those in your crew, the ones you trained. I want the rest as soldiers for my army. I have heard how well your men fought. You trained them without Sadeas's knowing, all while running bridges. I'm curious to see what you could do with the right resources." Dalinar turned away, glancing northward. Toward Sadeas's camp. "My army is depleted. I'm going to need every man I can get, but everyone I recruit is going to be suspect. Sadeas will try to send spies into our camp. And traitors. And assassins. Elhokar thinks we won't last a week."

"Stormfather," Kaladin said. "What are you planning?"

"I'm going to take away their games, fully expecting them to react like children losing their favored toy."

"These children have armies and Shardblades."

"Unfortunately."

"And *this* is what you want me to protect you from?"

"Yes."

No quibbling. Straightforward. There was much to respect about that.

"I'll augment Bridge Four to become the honor guard," Kaladin said. "And train the rest as a spearman company. Those in the honor guard get paid like it." Generally, a lighteyes's personal guard got triple a standard spearman's wage.

"Of course."

"And I want space to train," Kaladin said. "Full right of requisition from the quartermasters. I get to set my men's schedule, and we appoint our own sergeants and squadleaders. We don't answer to any lighteyes but yourself, your sons, and the king."

Dalinar raised an eyebrow. "That last one is a little . . . irregular."

"You want me to guard you and your family?" Kaladin said. "Against the other highprinces and their assassins, who might infiltrate your army and your officers? Well, I can't be in a position where any lighteyes in the camp can order me around, now can I?"

"You have a point," Dalinar said. "You realize, however, that in doing this I would essentially be giving you the same authority as a lighteyes of fourth dahn. You'd be in charge of a thousand former bridgemen. A full battalion."

"Yes."

Dalinar thought for a moment. "Very well. Consider yourself appointed to the rank of captain—that's as high as I dare appoint a darkeyes. If I named you battalionlord, it would cause a whole mess of problems. I'll let it be known, however, that you're outside the chain of command. You don't order around lighteyes of lesser rank than you, and lighteyes of higher rank have no authority over you."

"All right," Kaladin said. "But these soldiers I train, I want them assigned to patrolling, not plateau runs. I hear you've had several full battalions hunting bandits, keeping the peace in the Outer Market, that sort of thing. That's where my men go for one year, at least."

"Easy enough," Dalinar said. "You want time to train them before throwing them into battle, I assume."

"That, and I killed a lot of Parshendi today. I found myself regretting their deaths. They showed me more honor than most members of my own army have. I didn't like the feeling, and I want some time to think about it. The bodyguards I train for you, we'll go out onto the field, but our primary purpose will be protecting you, not killing Parshendi."

Dalinar looked bemused. "All right. Though you shouldn't have to worry. I don't plan to be on the front lines much in the future. My role is changing. Regardless, we have a deal."

Kaladin held out a hand. "This is contingent on my men agreeing."

"I thought you said that they'd do what you did."

"Probably," Kaladin said. "I command them, but I don't own them."

Dalinar reached out, taking his hand, shaking it by the light of the rising sapphire moon. Then he took the bundle out from underneath his arm. "Here."

"What is this?" Kaladin said, taking the bundle.

"My cloak. The one I wore to battle today, washed and patched."

Kaladin unfurled it. It was of a deep blue, with the glyph-pair of *khokh* and *linil* sewn into the back in white embroidery.

"Each man who wears my colors," Dalinar said, "is of my family, in a way. The cloak is a simple gift, but it is one of the few things I can offer that has any meaning. Accept it with my gratitude, Kaladin Stormblessed."

Kaladin slowly refolded the cloak. "Where did you hear that name?"

"Your men," Dalinar said. "They think very highly of you. And that makes *me* think very highly of you. I need men like you, like all of you." He narrowed his eyes, looking thoughtful. "The whole kingdom needs you. Perhaps all of Roshar. The True Desolation comes. . . ."

"What was that last part?"

"Nothing," Dalinar said. "Please, go get some rest, Captain. I hope to hear good news from you soon."

Kaladin nodded and withdrew, passing the two men who acted as Dalinar's guard for the night. The hike back to his new barracks was a short one. Dalinar had given him one building for each of the bridge crews. Over a thousand men. What was he going to do with so many? He'd never commanded a group larger than twenty-five before.

Bridge Four's barrack was empty. Kaladin hesitated outside the doorway, looking in. The barrack was furnished with a bunk and locking chest for each man. It seemed a palace.

He smelled smoke. Frowning, he rounded the barrack to find the men sitting around a firepit in the back, relaxing on stumps or stones, waiting as Rock cooked them a pot of stew. They were listening to Teft, who sat with his arm bandaged, speaking quietly. Shen was there; the quiet parshman sat at the very edge of the group. They'd recovered him, along with their wounded, from Sadeas's camp.

Teft cut off as soon as he saw Kaladin, and the men turned, most of them bearing bandages of some sort. *Dalinar wants these for his bodyguards?* Kaladin thought. They were a ragged bunch indeed.

As it happened, however, he seconded Dalinar's choice. If he were going to put his life in someone's hands, he'd choose this group.

"What are you doing?" Kaladin asked sternly. "You should all be resting."

The bridgemen glanced at each other.

"It just . . ." Moash said. "It didn't feel right to go to sleep until we'd had a chance to . . . well, do this."

"Hard to sleep on a day like this, gancho," Lopen added.

"Speak for yourself," Skar said, yawning, wounded leg resting up on a stump. "But the stew is worth staying up for. Even if he does put rocks in it."

"I do not!" Rock snapped. "Airsick lowlanders."

They'd left a place for Kaladin. He sat down, using Dalinar's cloak as a cushion for his back and head. He gratefully took a bowl of stew that Drehy handed him.

"We've been talking about what the men saw today," Teft said. "The things you did."

Kaladin hesitated, spoon to his mouth. He'd nearly forgotten—or maybe he'd intentionally forgotten—that he'd shown his men what he could do with Stormlight. Hopefully Dalinar's soldiers hadn't seen. His Stormlight had been faint by then, the day bright.

"I see," Kaladin said, his appetite fleeing. Did they see him as different? Frightening? Something to be ostracized, as his father had been back in Hearthstone? Worse yet, something to be worshipped? He looked into their wide eyes and braced himself.

"It was *amazing*!" Drehy said, leaning forward.

"You're one of the Radiants," Skar said, pointing. "I believe it, even if Teft says you aren't."

"He isn't *yet*," Teft snapped. "Don't you listen?"

"Can you teach me to do what you did?" Moash cut in.

"I'll learn too, gancho," Lopen said. "You know, if you're teaching and all."

Kaladin blinked, overwhelmed, as the others chimed in.

"What can you do?"

"How does it feel?"

"Can you fly?"

He held up a hand, stanching the questions. "Aren't you alarmed by what you saw?"

Several of the men shrugged.

"It kept you alive, gancho," Lopen said. "The only thing I'd be alarmed about is how irresistible the women would find it. 'Lopen,' they'd say, 'you only have one arm, but I see that you can glow. I think that you should kiss me now.'"

"But it's strange and frightening," Kaladin protested. "This is what the Radiants did! Everyone knows they were traitors."

"Yeah," Moash said, snorting. "Just like everyone knows that the lighteyes are chosen by the Almighty to rule, and how they're always noble and just."

"We're Bridge Four," Skar added. "We've been around. We've lived in the crem and been used as bait. If it helps you survive, it's good. That's all that needs to be said about it."

"So can you teach it?" Moash asked. "Can you show us how to do what you do?"

"I . . . I don't know if it *can* be taught," Kaladin said, glancing at Syl, who bore a curious expression as she sat on a nearby rock. "I'm not certain what *it* is."

They looked crestfallen.

"But," Kaladin added, "that doesn't mean that we shouldn't try."

Moash smiled.

"Can you do it?" Drehy asked, fishing out a sphere, a small glowing diamond chip. "Right now? I want to see it when I'm expecting it."

"It's not a feastday sport, Drehy," Kaladin said.

"Don't you think we deserve it?" Sigzil leaned forward on his stone.

Kaladin paused. Then, hesitantly, he reached out a finger and touched the sphere. He inhaled sharply; drawing in the Light was becoming more and more natural. The sphere faded. Stormlight began to trickle from Kaladin's skin, and he breathed normally to make it leak faster, making it more visible. Rock pulled out a ragged old blanket—used for kindling— and tossed it over the fire, disturbing the flamespren and making a few moments of darkness before the flames chewed through.

In that darkness, Kaladin glowed, pure white Light rising from his skin.

"Storms . . ." Drehy breathed.

"So, what *can* you do with it?" Skar asked, eager. "You didn't answer."

"I'm not entirely certain what I can do," Kaladin said, holding his hand up in front of him. It faded in a moment, and the fire burned through the blanket, lighting them all again. "I've only known about it for sure for a few weeks. I can draw arrows toward me and can make rocks stick together. The Light makes me stronger and faster, and it heals my wounds."

"How *much* stronger does it make you?" Sigzil said. "How much weight can the rocks bear after you stick them together, and how long do they remain bonded? How much faster do you get? Twice as fast? A quarter again as fast? How far away can an arrow be when you draw it toward you, and can you draw other things as well?"

Kaladin blinked. "I . . . I don't know."

"Well, it seems pretty important to know that kind of stuff," Skar said, rubbing his chin.

"We can do tests," Rock folded his arms, smiling. "Is good idea."

"Maybe it will help us figure out how we can do it too," Moash noted.

"Is not thing to learn." Rock shook his head. "Is of the *holetental*. For him only."

"You don't know that for certain," Teft said.

"You don't know for certain I don't know for certain." Rock wagged a spoon at him. "Eat your stew."

Kaladin held up his hands. "You can't tell anyone about this, men. They'll be frightened of me, maybe think I'm related to the Voidbringers or the Radiants. I need your oaths on this."

He looked at them, and they nodded, one by one.

"But we want to help," Skar said. "Even if we can't learn it. This thing is part of you, and you're one of us. Bridge Four. Right?"

Kaladin looked at their eager faces and couldn't stop himself from nodding. "Yes. Yes, you can help."

"Excellent," Sigzil said. "I'll prepare a list of tests to gauge speed, accuracy, and the strength of these bonds you can create. We'll have to find a way to determine if there's anything else you can do."

"Throw him off cliff," Rock said.

"What good will that do?" Peet asked.

Rock shrugged. "If he has other abilities, this thing will make them come out, eh? Nothing like falling from cliff to make a man out of a boy!"

Kaladin regarded him with a sour expression, and Rock laughed. "It will be small cliff." He held up his thumb and forefinger to indicate a tiny amount. "I like you too much for large one."

"I think you're joking," Kaladin said, taking a bite of his stew. "But just to be safe, I'm sticking you to the ceiling tonight to keep you from trying any experiments while I'm asleep."

The bridgemen chuckled.

"Just don't glow too brightly while we're trying to sleep, eh, gancho?" Lopen said.

"I'll do my best." He took another spoonful of stew. It tasted better than usual. Had Rock changed the recipe?

Or was it something else? As he settled back to eat, the other bridgemen began chatting, speaking of home and their pasts, things that had once been taboo. Several of the men from other crews—wounded whom Kaladin had helped, even just a few lonely souls who were still awake—wandered over. The men of Bridge Four welcomed them, handing over stew and making room.

Everyone looked as exhausted as Kaladin felt, but nobody spoke of turning in. He could see why, now. Being together, eating Rock's stew, listening to the quiet chatter while the fire crackled and popped, sending dancing flakes of yellow light into the air . . .

This was more relaxing than sleep could be. Kaladin smiled, leaning back, looking upward toward the dark sky and the large sapphire moon. Then he closed his eyes, listening.

Three more men were dead. Malop, Earless Jaks, and Narm. Kaladin had failed them. But he and Bridge Four had protected hundreds of others. Hundreds who would never have to run a bridge again, would never have to face Parshendi arrows, would never have to fight again if they didn't want to. More personally, twenty-seven of his friends lived. Partially because of what he'd done, partially because of their own heroism.

Twenty-seven men lived. He'd finally managed to save someone.

For now, that was enough.

Shallan rubbed her eyes. She'd read through Jasnah's notes—at least the most important ones. Those alone had made a large stack. She still sat in the alcove, though they'd sent a parshman to get her a blanket to wrap around herself, covering up the hospital robe.

Her eyes burned from the night spent crying, then reading. She was exhausted. And yet she also felt alive.

"It's true," she said. "You're right. The Voidbringers are the parshmen. I can see no other conclusion."

Jasnah smiled, looking oddly pleased with herself, considering that she'd only convinced one person.

"So what next?" Shallan asked.

"That has to do with your previous studies."

"My studies? You mean your father's death?"

"Indeed."

"The Parshendi attacked him," Shallan said. "Killed him suddenly, without warning." She focused on the other woman. "That's what made you begin studying all of this, isn't it?"

Jasnah nodded. "Those wild parshmen—the Parshendi of the Shattered Plains—are the key." She leaned forward. "Shallan. The disaster awaiting us is all too real, all too terrible. I don't need mystical warnings or theological sermons to frighten me. I'm downright terrified in my own right."

"But we have the parshmen tamed."

"Do we? Shallan, think of what they do, how they're regarded, how often they're used."

Shallan hesitated. The parshmen were pervasive.

"They serve our food," Jasnah continued. "They work our storehouses. They tend our *children*. There isn't a village in Roshar that doesn't have some parshmen. We ignore them; we just expect them to be there, doing as they do. Working without complaint.

"Yet one group turned suddenly from peaceful friends to ferocious warriors. Something set them off. Just as it did hundreds of years ago, during the days known as the Heraldic Epochs. There would be a period of peace, followed by an invasion of parshmen who—for reasons nobody understood—had suddenly gone mad with rage. *This* was what was behind mankind's fight to keep from being 'banished to Damnation.' This was what nearly ended our civilization. These were the terrible, repeated cataclysms that were so frightening men began to speak of them as Desolations.

"We've nurtured the parshmen. We've integrated them into every part of our society. We depend on them, never realizing that we've harnessed a highstorm waiting to explode. The accounts from the Shattered Plains speak of these Parshendi's ability to communicate among themselves, allowing them to sing their songs in unison when far apart. Their minds are connected, like spanreeds. Do you realize what that means?"

Shallan nodded. What would happen if every parshman on Roshar suddenly turned against his masters? Seeking freedom, or worse—vengeance? "We'd be devastated. Civilization as we know it could collapse. We have to *do* something!"

"We are," Jasnah said. "We're gathering facts, making certain we know what we think we know."

"And how many facts do we need?"

"More. Many more." Jasnah glanced at the books. "There are some things about the histories I don't yet understand. Tales of creatures fighting alongside the parshmen, beasts of stone that might be some kind of greatshell, and other oddities that I think may have truth to them. But we've exhausted what Kharbranth can offer. Are you still certain you want to delve into this? It is a heavy burden we will bear. You won't be returning to your estates for some time."

Shallan bit her lip, thinking of her brothers. "You'd let me go now, after what I know?"

"I won't have you serving me while thinking of ways to escape." Jasnah sounded exhausted.

"I can't just abandon my brothers." Shallan's insides twisted again. "But this is bigger than them. Damnation— it's bigger than *me* or *you* or any of us. I have to help, Jasnah. I can't walk out on this. I'll find some other way to help my family."

"Good. Then go pack our things. We're leaving tomorrow on that ship I chartered for you."

"We're going to Jah Keved?"

"No. We need to get to the center of it all." She looked at Shallan. "We're going to the Shattered Plains. We need to find out if the Parshendi were ever ordinary parshmen, and if so, what set them off. Perhaps I am wrong about this, but if I am right, then the Parshendi could hold the key to turning ordinary parshmen into soldiers." Then, grimly, she continued. "And we need to do it before someone else does, then uses it against us."

"Someone else?" Shallan asked, feeling a sharp stab of panic. "There are others looking for this?"

"Of course there are. Who do you think went to so much trouble trying to have me assassinated?" She reached into a stack of papers on her desk. "I don't know much about them. For all I know, there are many groups searching for these secrets. I know of one for certain, however. They call themselves the Ghostbloods." She pulled out a sheet. "Your friend Kabsal was one. We found their symbol tattooed on the inside of his arm."

She set the sheet down. On it was a symbol of three diamonds in a pattern, overlapping one another.

It was the same symbol that Nan Balat had shown her weeks ago. The symbol worn by Luesh, her father's steward, the man who had known how to use the Soulcaster. The symbol worn by the men who had come, pressuring her family to return it. The men who had been financing Shallan's father in his bid to become highprince.

"Almighty above," Shallan whispered. She looked up. "Jasnah, I think . . . I think my *father* might have been a member of this group."

The highstorm winds began to blow against Dalinar's complex, powerful enough to make rocks groan. Navani huddled close to Dalinar, holding to him. She smelled wonderful. It felt . . . humbling to know how terrified she'd been for him.

Her joy at having him back was enough to dampen, for now, her fury at him for how he'd treated Elhokar. She would come around. It had needed to be done.

As the highstorm hit in force, Dalinar felt the vision coming on. He closed his eyes, letting it take him. He had a decision to make, a responsibility. What to do? These visions had lied to him, or had at least misled him. It seemed that he couldn't trust them, at least not as explicitly as he once had.

He took a deep breath, opened his eyes, and found himself in a place of smoke.

He turned about, wary. The sky was dark and he stood on a field of dull, bone-white rock, jagged and rough, extending in all directions. Off into eternity. Amorphous shapes made of curling grey smoke rose from the ground. Like smoke rings, only in other shapes. Here a chair. There a rockbud, with vines extended, curling to the sides and vanishing. Beside him appeared the figure of a man in uniform, silent and vaporous, rising lethargically toward the sky, mouth open. The shapes melted and distorted as they climbed higher, though they seemed to hold their forms longer than they should. It was unnerving, standing on the boundless plain, pure darkness above, smoke figures rising all around.

It wasn't like any vision he'd seen before. It was . . .

No, wait. He frowned, stepping back as the figure of a tree burst from the ground close to him. *I have seen this place before. In the first of my visions, so many months ago.* It was fuzzy in his mind. He'd been disoriented, the vision vague, as if his mind hadn't learned to accept what it was seeing. In fact, the only thing he remembered distinctly was—

"You must unite them," a powerful voice boomed.

—was the voice. Speaking to him from all around, causing the smoke figures to fuzz and distort.

"Why did you lie to me?" Dalinar demanded of the open darkness. "I did what you said, and I was betrayed!"

"Unite them. The sun approaches the horizon. The Everstorm comes. The True Desolation. The Night of Sorrows. You must prepare. Build of your people a fortress of strength and peace, a wall to resist the winds. Cease squabbling and unite."

"I need answers!" Dalinar said. "I don't trust you any longer. If you want me to listen to you, you'll need to—"

The vision changed. He spun about, finding that he was still on an open plain of rock, but the normal sun was in the sky. The stone field looked like an ordinary one on Roshar.

It was very odd for one of the visions to set him in a place without others to talk to and interact with. Though, for once, he wore his own clothing. The sharp blue Kholin uniform.

Had this happened before, the other time he'd been in that place of smoke? Yes . . . it had. This was the first time he'd been taken to somewhere he'd been before. Why?

He carefully scanned the scenery. Since the voice didn't speak to him again, he began to walk, passing cracked boulders and broken bits of shale, pebbles and rocks. There were no plants, not even rockbuds. Just an empty landscape filled with broken stones.

Eventually, he spotted a ridge. Getting to high ground felt like a good idea, though the hike seemed to take hours. The vision did not end. Time was often odd in these visions. He continued to hike up the side of the rock formation, wishing he had his Shardplate to strengthen him. Finally at the top, he walked over to the edge to look down below.

And there he saw Kholinar, his home, the capital city of Alethkar.

It had been destroyed.

The beautiful buildings had been shattered. The windblades were cast down. There were no bodies, just broken stone. This wasn't like the vision he had seen before, with Nohadon. That wasn't the Kholinar of the distant past; he could see the rubble of his own palace. But there was no rock formation like the one he stood on near Kholinar in the real world. Always before, these visions had shown him the past. Was this now a vision of the future?

"I cannot fight him any longer," the voice said.

Dalinar jumped, glancing to the side. A man stood there. He had dark skin and pure white hair. Tall, thick of chest but not massive, he wore exotic clothing of a strange cut: loose, billowing trousers and a coat that came down only to his waist. Both seemed made of gold.

Yes . . . this very thing had happened before, in his very first vision. Dalinar could remember it now. "Who are you?" Dalinar demanded. "Why are you showing me these visions?"

"You can see it there," the figure said, pointing. "If you look closely. It begins in the distance."

Dalinar glanced in that direction, annoyed. He couldn't make out anything specific. "Storm it," Dalinar said. "Won't you answer my questions for once? What is the good of all of this if you just speak in riddles?"

The man didn't answer. He just kept pointing. And . . . yes, something *was* happening. There was a shadow in the air, approaching. A wall of darkness. Like a highstorm, only *wrong*.

"At least tell me this," Dalinar said. "What time are we seeing? Is this the past, the future, or something else entirely?"

The figure didn't answer immediately. Then he said, "You're probably wondering if this is a vision of the future."

Dalinar started. "I just . . . I just asked . . ."

This was familiar. Too familiar.

He said that exact thing last time, Dalinar realized, feeling a chill. *This all happened. I'm seeing the same vision again.*

The figure squinted at the horizon. "I cannot see the future completely. Cultivation, she is better at it than I. It's as if the future is a shattering window. The further you look, the more pieces that window breaks into. The near future can be anticipated, but the distant future . . . I can only guess."

"You can't hear me, can you?" Dalinar asked, feeling a horror as he finally began to understand. "You never could."

Blood of my fathers . . . he's not ignoring me. He can't see me! He doesn't speak in riddles. It just seems that way because I took his responses as cryptic answers to my questions.

He didn't tell me to trust Sadeas. I . . . I just assumed . . .

Everything seemed to shake around Dalinar. His preconceptions, what he'd thought he'd known. The ground itself.

"That is what could happen," the figure said, nodding into the distance. "It's what I fear will happen. It's what he wants. The True Desolation."

No, that wall in the air wasn't a highstorm. It wasn't rain making that enormous shadow, but blowing dust. He remembered this vision in full, now. It had ended here, with him confused, staring out at that oncoming wall of dust. This time, however, the vision continued.

The figure turned to him. "I am sorry to do this to you. By now I hope that what you've seen has given you a foundation to understand. But I can't know for certain. I don't know who you are, or how you have found your way here."

"I . . ." What to say? Did it matter?

"Most of what I show you are scenes I have seen directly," the figure said. "But some, such as this one, are born out of my fears. If I fear it, then you should too."

The land was trembling. The wall of dust was being caused by something. Something approaching.

The ground was falling away.

Dalinar gasped. The very rocks ahead were shattering, breaking apart, becoming dust. He backed away as everything began to shake, a massive earthquake accompanied by a terrible roar of dying rocks. He fell to the ground.

There was an awful, grinding, terrifying moment of nightmare. The shaking, the destruction, the sounds of the land itself seeming to die.

Then it was past. Dalinar breathed in and out before rising on unsteady legs. He and the figure stood on a solitary pinnacle of rock. A little section that—for some reason—had been protected. It was like a stone pillar a few paces wide, rising high into the air.

Around it, the land was *gone*. Kholinar was gone. It had all fallen away into unplumbed darkness below. He felt vertigo, standing on the tiny bit of rock that—impossibly—remained.

"What is this?" Dalinar demanded, though he knew that the being couldn't hear him.

The figure looked about, sorrowful. "I can't leave much. Just these few images, given to you. Whoever you are."

"These visions . . . they're like a journal, aren't they? A history you wrote, a book you left behind, except I don't read it, I see it."

The figure looked into the sky. "I don't even know if anyone will ever see this. I am gone, you see."

Dalinar didn't respond. He looked over the pinnacle's sheer edge, down at a void, horrified.

"This isn't just about you either," the figure said, raising his hand into the air. A light winked out in the sky, one that Dalinar hadn't realized was there. Then another winked out as well. The sun seemed to be growing dimmer.

"It's about all of them," the figure said. "I should have realized he'd come for me."

"Who are you?" Dalinar asked, voicing the words to himself.

The figure still stared into the sky. "I leave this, because there must be something. A hope to discover. A chance that someone will find what to do. Do you wish to fight him?"

"Yes," Dalinar found himself saying, despite knowing that it didn't matter. "I don't know who he is, but if he wants to do *this*, then I will fight him."

"Someone must lead them."

"I will do it," Dalinar said. The words just came out.

"Someone must unite them."

"I will do it."

"Someone must protect them."

"I will do it!"

The figure was silent for a moment. Then he spoke in a clear, crisp voice. "Life before death. Strength before weakness. Journey before destination. Speak again the ancient oaths and return to men the Shards they once bore." He turned to Dalinar, meeting his eyes. "The Knights Radiant must stand again."

"I cannot comprehend how that can be done," Dalinar said softly. "But I will try."

"Men must face them together," the figure said, stepping up to Dalinar, placing a hand on his shoulder. "You cannot squabble as in times past. He's realized that you, given time, will become your own enemies. That he doesn't *need* to fight you. Not if he can make you forget, make you turn against one another. Your legends say that you won. But the truth is that we lost. And we are losing."

"Who are you?" Dalinar asked again, voice softer.

"I wish I could do more," repeated the figure in gold. "You might be able to get him to choose a champion. He is bound by some rules. All of us are. A champion could work well for you, but it is not certain. And . . . without the Dawnshards . . . Well, I have done what I can. It is a terrible, terrible thing to leave you alone."

"Who are you?" Dalinar asked again. And yet, he thought he knew.

"I am . . . *I was* . . . God. The one you call the Almighty, the creator of mankind." The figure closed his eyes. "And now I am dead. Odium has killed me. I am sorry."

"Can you feel it?" Wit asked of the open night. "Something just changed. I believe that's the sound the world makes when it pisses itself."

Three guards stood just inside the thick wooden city gates of Kholinar. The men regarded Wit with worry.

The gates were closed, and these men were of the night watch, a somewhat inappropriate title. They didn't spend time "watching" so much as chatting, yawning, gambling, or—in tonight's case—standing uncomfortably and listening to a crazy man.

That crazy man happened to have blue eyes, which let him get away with all kinds of trouble. Perhaps Wit should have been bemused by the stock these people put in something as simple as eye color, but he had been many places and seen many methods of rule. This didn't seem any more ridiculous than most others.

And, of course, there was a reason the people did what they did. Well, there was usually a reason. In this case, it just happened to be a good one.

"Brightlord?" one of the guards asked, looking at where Wit sat on his boxes. They'd been piled there and left by a merchant who had tipped the night watchmen to make certain nothing was stolen. To Wit, they simply made a convenient perch. His pack sat beside him, and on his knees he was tuning his enthir, a square, stringed instrument. You played it from above, plucking its strings while it sat on your lap.

"Brightlord?" the guard repeated. "What are you doing up there?"

"Waiting," Wit said. He looked up, glancing eastward. "Waiting for the storm to arrive."

That made the guards more uncomfortable. A highstorm was not predicted this night.

Wit began playing the enthir. "Let us have a conversation to pass the time. Tell me. What is it that men value in others?"

The music played toward an audience of silent buildings, alleys, and worn cobblestones. The guards didn't respond to him. They didn't seem to know what to make of a black-clad, lighteyed man who entered the city just before evening fell, then sat on boxes beside the gates playing music.

"Well?" Wit asked, pausing the music. "What do you think? If a man or woman were to have a talent, which would be the most revered, best regarded, considered of the most worth?"

"Er . . . music?" one of the men finally said.

"Yes, a common answer," Wit said, plucking at a few low notes. "I once asked this question of some very wise scholars. What do men consider the most valuable of talents? One mentioned artistic ability, as you so keenly guessed. Another chose great intellect. The final chose the talent to invent, the ability to design and create marvelous devices."

He didn't play a specific tune on the enthir, just plucks here and there, an occasional scale or fifth. Like chitchat in string form.

"Aesthetic genius," Wit said, "invention, acumen, creativity. Noble ideals indeed. Most men would pick one of those, if given the choice, and name them the greatest of talents." He plucked a string. "What beautiful liars we are."

The guards glanced at each other; the torches burning in brackets on the wall painted them with orange light.

"You think I'm a cynic," Wit said. "You think I'm going to tell you that men claim to value these ideals, but secretly prefer base talents. The ability to gather coin or to charm women. Well, I *am* a cynic, but in this case, I actually think those scholars were honest. Their answers speak for the souls of men. In our hearts, we want to believe in—and would choose—great accomplishment and virtue. That's why our lies, particularly to ourselves, are so beautiful."

He began to play a real song. A simple melody at first, soft, subdued. A song for a silent night when the entire world changed.

One of the soldiers cleared his throat. "So what *is* the most valuable talent a man can have?" He sounded genuinely curious.

"I haven't the faintest idea," Wit said. "Fortunately, that wasn't the question. I didn't ask what was most valuable, I asked what *men value most*. The difference between those questions is at once both tiny and as vast as the world itself."

He kept plucking his song. One did not strum an enthir. It just wasn't done, at least not by people with any sense of propriety.

"In this," Wit said, "as in all things, our actions give us away. If an artist creates a work of powerful beauty—using new and innovative techniques—she will be lauded as a master, and will launch a new movement in aesthetics. Yet what if another, working independently with that exact level of skill, were to make the same accomplishments the very next month? Would she find similar acclaim? No. She'd be called derivative.

"Intellect. If a great thinker develops a new theory of mathematics, science, or philosophy, we will name him wise. We will sit at his feet and learn, and will record his name in history for thousands upon thousands to revere. But what if another man determines the same theory on his own, then delays in publishing his results by a mere week? Will he be remembered for his greatness? No. He will be forgotten.

"Invention. A woman builds a new design of great worth—some fabrial or feat of engineering. She will be known as an innovator. But if someone with the same talent creates the same design a year later—not realizing it has already been crafted—will *she* be rewarded for her creativity? No. She'll be called a copier and a forger."

He plucked at his strings, letting the melody continue, twisting, haunting, yet with a faint edge of mockery. "And so," he said, "in the end, what must we determine? Is it the *intellect* of a genius that we revere? If it were their artistry, the beauty of their mind, would we not laud it regardless of whether we'd seen their product before?

"But we don't. Given two works of artistic majesty, otherwise weighted equally, we will give greater acclaim to the one who did it *first*. It doesn't matter what you create. It matters what you create *before anyone else*.

"So it's not the beauty itself we admire. It's not the force of intellect. It's not invention, aesthetics, or capacity itself. The greatest talent that we think a man can have?" He plucked one final string. "Seems to me that it must be nothing more than novelty."

The guards looked confused.

The gates shook. Something pounded on them from outside.

"The storm has come," Wit said, standing up.

The guards scrambled for spears left leaning beside the wall. They had a guardhouse, but it was empty; they preferred the night air.

The gate shook again, as if something enormous were outside. The guards yelled, calling to the men atop the wall. All was chaos and confusion as the gate boomed yet a third time, powerful, shaking, vibrating as if hit with a boulder.

And then a bright, silvery blade rammed between the massive doors, slicing upward, cutting the bar that held them closed. A Shardblade.

The gates swung open. The guards scrambled back. Wit waited on his boxes, enthir held in one hand, pack over his shoulder.

Outside the gates, standing on the dark stone roadway, was a solitary man with dark skin. His hair was long and matted, his clothing nothing more than a ragged, sacklike length of cloth wrapping his waist. He stood with head bowed, wet, ratty hair hanging down over his face and mixing with a beard that had bits of wood and leaves stuck in it.

His muscles glistened, wet as if he'd just swum a great distance. To his side, he carried a massive Shardblade, point down, sticking about a finger's width into the stone, his hand on the hilt. The Blade reflected torchlight; it was long, narrow, and straight, shaped like an enormous spike.

"Welcome, lost one," Wit whispered.

"Who are you!" one of the guards called, nervous, as one of the other two ran to give the alert. A Shardbearer had come to Kholinar.

The figure ignored the question. He stepped forward, dragging his Shardblade, as if it weighed a great deal. It cut the rock behind him, leaving a tiny groove in the stone. The figure walked unsteadily, and nearly tripped. He steadied himself against the gate door, and a lock of hair moved from the side of his face, exposing his eyes. Dark brown eyes, like a man of the lower class. Those eyes were wild, dazed.

The man finally noticed the two guards, who stood, terrified, with spears leveled at him. He raised his empty hand toward them. "Go," he said raggedly, speaking perfect Alethi, no hint of an accent. "Run! Raise the call! Give the warning!"

"Who are you?" one of the guards forced out. "What warning? Who attacks?"

The man paused. He raised a hand to his head, wavering. "Who am I? I . . . I am Talenel'Elin, Stonesinew, Herald of the Almighty. The Desolation has come. Oh, God . . . it has come. And I have failed."

He slumped forward, hitting the rocky ground, Shardblade clattering down behind him. It did not vanish. The guards inched forward. One prodded the man with the butt of his spear.

The man who had named himself a Herald did not move.

"What is it we value?" Wit whispered. "Innovation. Originality. Novelty. But most importantly . . . timeliness. I fear you may be too late, my confused, unfortunate friend."

THE END OF

Book One of
THE STORMLIGHT ARCHIVE

ENDNOTE

*"Above silence, the illuminating storms—dying storms—
illuminate the silence above."*

The above sample is noteworthy as it is a ketek, a complex form of holy Vorin poem. The ketek not only reads the same forward and backward (allowing for alteration of verb forms) but is also divisible into five distinct smaller sections, each of which makes a complete thought.

The complete poem must form a sentence that is grammatically correct and (theoretically) poignant in meaning. Because of the difficulty in constructing a ketek, the structure was once considered the highest and most impressive form of all Vorin poetry.

The fact that this one was uttered by an illiterate, dying Herdazian in a language he barely spoke should be of particular note. There is no record of this particular ketek in any repository of Vorin poetry, so it is very unlikely that the subject was merely repeating something he once heard. None of the ardents we showed it to had any knowledge of it, though three did praise its structure and ask to meet the poet.

We leave it to His Majesty's mind, on a strong day, to puzzle out the meaning of why the storms might be important, and what the poem may mean by indicating that there is silence both above and below said storms.

—Joshor, Head of His Majesty's Silent Gatherers,
Tanatanev 1173

ARS ARCANUM

THE TEN ESSENCES AND THEIR HISTORICAL ASSOCIATIONS

NUMBER	Gemstone	Essence	Body Focus	Soulcasting Properties	Primary / Secondary Divine Attributes
1 Jes	Sapphire	Zephyr	Inhalation	Translucent gas, air	Protecting / Leading
2 Nan	Smoke-stone	Vapor	Exhalation	Opaque gas, smoke, fog	Just / Confident
3 Chach	Ruby	Spark	The Soul	Fire	Brave / Obedient
4 Vev	Diamond	Lucentia	The Eyes	Quartz, glass, crystal	Loving / Healing
5 Palah	Emerald	Pulp	The Hair	Wood, plants, moss	Learned / Giving
6 Shash	Garnet	Blood	The Blood	Blood, all non-oil liquid	Creative / Honest
7 Betab	Zircon	Tallow	Oil	All kinds of oil	Wise / Careful
8 Kak	Amethyst	Foil	The Nails	Metal	Resolute / Builder
9 Tanat	Topaz	Talus	The Bone	Rock and stone	Dependable / Resourceful
10 Ishi	Heliodor	Sinew	Flesh	Meat, flesh	Pious / Guiding

The preceding list is an imperfect gathering of traditional Vorin symbolism associated with the Ten Essences. Bound together, these form the Double Eye of the Almighty, an eye with two pupils representing the creation of plants and creatures. This is also the basis for the hourglass shape that was often associated with the Knights Radiant.

Ancient scholars also placed the ten orders of Knights Radiant on this list, alongside the Heralds themselves, who each had a classical association with one of the numbers and Essences.

I'm not certain yet how the ten levels of Voidbinding or its cousin the Old Magic fit into this paradigm, if indeed they can. My research suggests that, indeed, there should be another series of abilities that is even more esoteric than the Voidbindings. Perhaps the Old Magic fits into those, though I am beginning to suspect that it is something entirely different.

ON THE CREATION OF FABRIALS

Five groupings of fabrial have been discovered so far. The methods of their creation are carefully guarded by the artifabrian community, but they appear to be the work of dedicated scientists, as opposed to the more mystical Surgebindings once performed by the Knights Radiant.

ALTERING FABRIALS

Augmenters: These fabrials are crafted to enhance something. They can create heat, pain, or even a calm wind, for instance. They are powered—like all fabrials—by Stormlight. They seem to work best with forces, emotions, or sensations.

The so-called half-shards of Jah Keved are created with this type of fabrial attached to a sheet of metal, enhancing its durability. I have seen fabrials of this type crafted using many different kinds of gemstone; I am guessing that any one of the ten Polestones will work.

Diminishers: These fabrials do the opposite of what augmenters do, and generally seem to fall under the same restrictions as their cousins. Those artifabrians who have taken me into confidence seem to believe that even greater fabrials are possible than what have been created so far, particularly in regard to augmenters and diminishers.

PAIRING FABRIALS

Conjoiners: By infusing a ruby and using methodology that has not been revealed to me (though I have my suspicions), you can create a conjoined pair of gemstones. The process requires splitting the original ruby. The two halves will then create parallel reactions across a distance. Spanreeds are one of the most common forms of this type of fabrial.

Conservation of force is maintained; for instance, if one is attached to a heavy stone, you will need the same strength to lift the conjoined fabrial that you would need to lift the stone itself. There appears to be some sort of process used during the creation of the fabrial that influences how far apart the two halves can go and still produce an effect.

Reversers: Using an amethyst instead of a ruby also creates conjoined halves of a gemstone, but these two work in creating *opposite* reactions. Raise one, and the other will be pressed downward, for instance.

These fabrials have only just been discovered, and already the possibilities for exploitation are being conjectured. There appear to be some unexpected limitations to this form of fabrial, though I have not been able to discover what they are.

WARNING FABRIALS

There is only one type of fabrial in this set, informally known as the Alerter. An Alerter can warn one of a nearby object, feeling, sensation, or phenomenon. These fabrials use a heliodor stone as their focus. I do not know whether this is the only type of gemstone that will work, or if there is another reason heliodor is used.

In the case of this kind of fabrial, the amount of Stormlight you can infuse into it affects its range. Hence the size of gemstone used is very important.

WINDRUNNING AND LASHINGS

Reports of the Assassin in White's odd abilities have led me to some sources of information that, I believe, are generally unknown. The Windrunners were an order of the Knights Radiant, and they made use of two primary types of Surgebinding. The effects of these Surgebindings were known—colloquially among the members of the order—as the Three Lashings.

BASIC LASHING:
GRAVITATIONAL CHANGE

This type of Lashing was one of the most commonly used Lashings among the order, though it was not the easiest to use. (That distinction belongs to the Full Lashing below.) A Basic Lashing involved revoking a being's or object's spiritual gravitational bond to the planet below, instead temporarily linking that being or object to a different object or direction.

Effectively, this creates a change in gravitational pull, twisting the energies of the planet itself. A Basic Lashing allowed a Windrunner to run up walls, to send objects or people flying off into the air, or to create similar effects. Advanced uses of this type of Lashing would allow a Windrunner to make himself or herself lighter by binding part of his or her mass upward. (Mathematically, binding a quarter of one's mass upward would halve a person's effective weight. Binding half of one's mass upward would create weightlessness.)

Multiple Basic Lashings could also pull an object or a person's body downward at double, triple, or other multiples of its weight.

FULL LASHING:
BINDING OBJECTS TOGETHER

A Full Lashing might seem very similar to a Basic Lashing, but they worked on very different principles. While one had to do with gravitation, the other had to do with the force (or Surge, as the Radiants called them) of adhesion—binding objects together as if they were one. I believe this Surge may have had something to do with atmospheric pressure.

To create a Full Lashing, a Windrunner would infuse an object with Stormlight, then press another object to it. The two objects would become bound together with an extremely powerful bond, nearly impossible to break. In fact, most materials would themselves break before the bond holding them together would.

REVERSE LASHING: GIVING AN OBJECT
A GRAVITATIONAL PULL

I believe this may actually be a specialized version of the Basic Lashing. This type of Lashing required the least amount of Stormlight of any of the three Lashings. The Windrunner would infuse something, give a mental command, and create a *pull* to the object that yanked other objects toward it.

At its heart, this Lashing created a bubble around the object that imitated its spiritual link to the ground beneath it. As such, it was much harder for the Lashing to affect objects touching the ground, where their link to the planet was strongest. Objects falling or in flight were the easiest to influence. Other objects could be affected, but the Stormlight and skill required were much more substantial.

TOR BOOKS *by*

THE STORMLIGHT ARCHIVE

The Way of Kings, Words of Radiance, Oathbringer

With more than ten years spent in research, world-building, and writing, The Stormlight Archive is a true epic in the making, a multi-volume masterpiece in the grand tradition of The Wheel of Time®.

THE MISTBORN SERIES

Mistborn, The Well of Ascension, The Hero of Ages

This modern fantasy classic dares to ask a simple question: What if the hero of prophecy fails, and the Dark Lord takes over? What follows is a story full of surprises and political intrigue, driven by a memorable heist crew.

The Alloy of Law, Shadows of Self, The Bands of Mourning

Three hundred years after the events of the Mistborn trilogy, the world is on the verge of modernity, but one scion returning from the Roughs discovers that the civilized world isn't as civilized as he'd thought.

BRANDON SANDERSON

OTHER WORKS

Elantris

Fleet, fun, and full of surprises, this is a rare epic fantasy
debut that doesn't recycle the classics. A city and people
go from blessed to bewitched, but when the latest
outcast arrives, he brings something new—hope.

Warbreaker

By using Breath and the color in everyday objects, miracles
and mischief can be accomplished—and are. But it will
take considerable quantities of each for two sisters and
a Returned God as they face the challenges ahead.

The Rithmatist

While Joel's mind for figures would make him a genius with the
magic of Rithmatics, he doesn't have the spark. But he could be
the only one able to protect the other students when they start
disappearing. A new favorite of YA readers, this fantasy has lively and
feisty characters as well as an inventive and detailed magic system.

FOLLOW TOR BOOKS 🅕🐦📷 t **TOR-FORGE.COM**
Sign up for author updates at: tor-forge.com/author/brandonsanderson
Note: Within series, books are best read in listed order.